LEGACY OF DEZROTHIA

THE COMPLETE TRILOGY

MJ COLGAN
AC LAWOR

For information contact:

dreamindiepublishing@gmail.com

Cover artwork by Angelika @colouranomaly

Cover design and Interior Formatting by MJ Colgan, MJColgan.com

Content Warning

This story contains content that might be troubling to some readers including, but not limited to attempted murder, blood, emotional abuse, murder, physical abuse, threat of rape, profanity, PTSD depictions, violence and war. Please be mindful of these, and other, possible triggers.

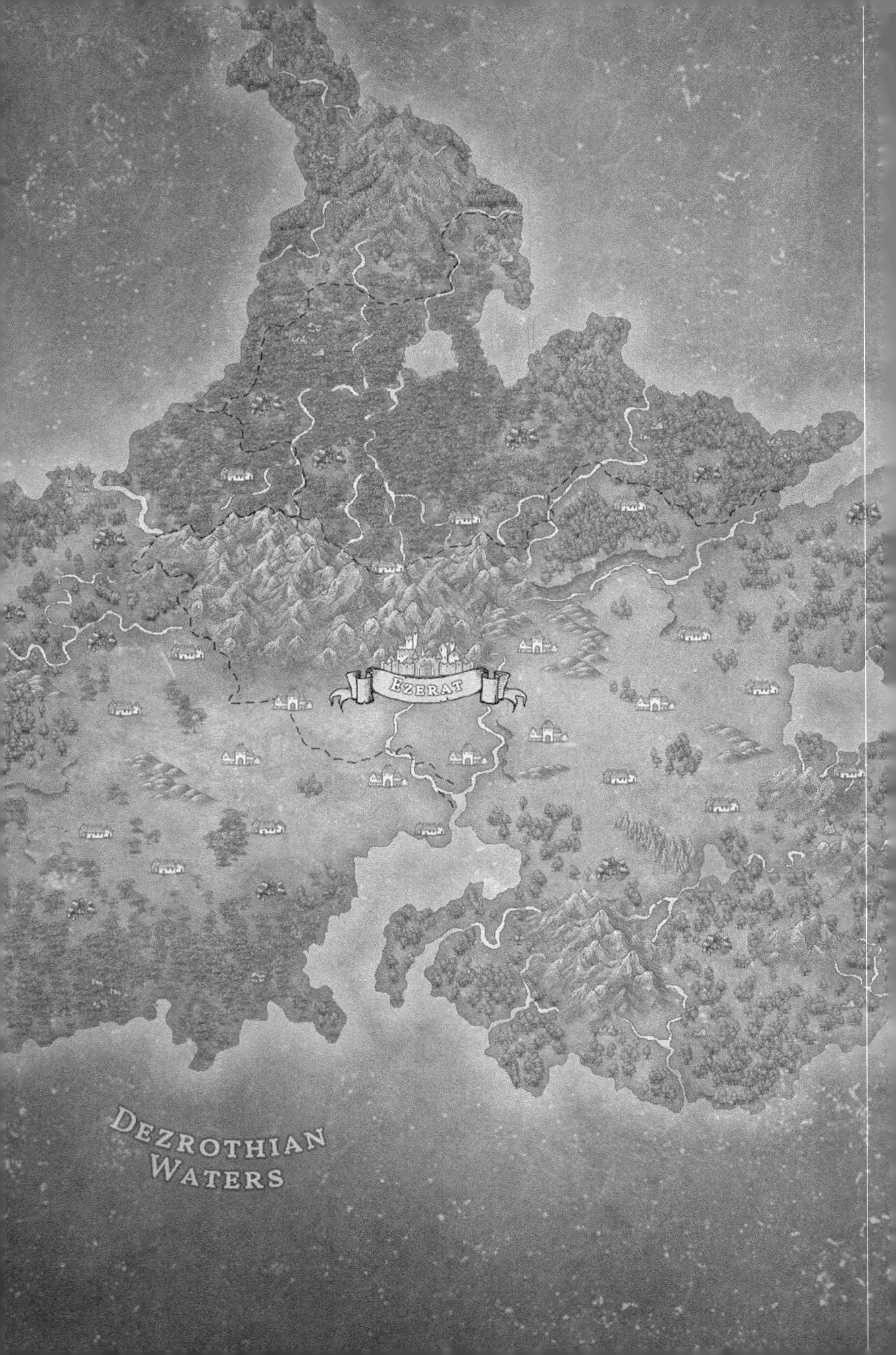

Ezerat
Dezrothian Waters

LEGACY OF DEZROTHIA

Royal Decree

The mixing of species is hereby forbidden within the Kingdom of Dezrothia, in order to preserve only the purest of bloodlines. Those with dirtied blood shall be exterminated and any who seek to break the Lore shall be punished by execution.

His Royal Majesty, King Regis

PART ONE

Lores of Ruin

CHAPTER 1

Evangelia

Reaching into my bag, I pulled out the almost empty canteen, lifting my chin to swallow a large gulp, relishing the cooling sweat trickling down my spine. I only needed a minute, just long enough to catch my breath.

Nix turned, ready to tease me for falling behind again, but the fates had other ideas. Before he got a chance to open his mouth, he stumbled. Straight over a damp tree root, concealed by the dewy leaves blanketing the forest floor.

I rolled my eyes. "For someone who grew up here, you should know better than to take your eyes off the track," I said, shaking my head.

His brows quirked. "If you kept up, I wouldn't need to keep looking back to see where you are," he taunted.

"It's not my fault your legs are so long. I have to damn near run to keep pace with you." I looked through the thick leafy canopy to the sky. The small gaps sparkled bright. "We are making good time. At this rate, we will have hours to spare."

We'd left before sunrise to collect supplies as part of the preparation for relocating camp tomorrow. Having lived in our current patch of the Fading Vale for a while now, it was well past time for us to move on. Staying in one place for any real length of time increased the risk of being found by the king's horde.

Nix sighed, running a hand through his curly hair. "It's been so long since we've had a chance to venture out to one of the villages, though. I just want to get there," he grumbled. "Besides, I hear Dorgoil has a tavern!"

Dorgoil, home of the gnomes, was the closest village to our current Camp. A six-hour hike, mostly uphill, and we were running on very little sleep.

While I panted, Nix bounced from foot to foot, impatient for us to start moving again. "I get it, I'm excited too," I said. "But if you fall over and break something, it will only take us longer, waiting for you to heal." I held the canteen out to him for a swig, then swung my pack back on.

Tightening the straps, I trundled forward. Eyes dead ahead, avoiding the moss-covered trees rising out of the earth around us.

Nix walked at my side. "Fair point. But you're hardly one to talk," he said. "Your parents told me what happened when you went to Pinefall, remember? Someone got a bit too excited to meet the pixies and–"

"*Stop,*" I whined, only half joking. "If I never have to visit that place again, it will be too soon."

A grin pulled at his lips, but he covered it, running a thumb down his bearded jawline. His facial hair was as unkempt as the waves on his head. He didn't like to use the few blades we had on preening himself. Understandably so. Besides, the scruff covering his cheeks matured the baby face he sported without it. Being older than Nix by a few years, I'd been able to join my parents on these trips on occasion before he could. Still, this was only my seventh village trip.

Whenever we packed up and moved to another area of the unforgiving forest, we usually found somewhere we had never stayed before. It helped to better evade detection. We only did this every few months, which meant opportunities to step out of the Fading Vale were rare. For me to say I never wanted to return to Pinefall again told him how serious I was about my trauma over the whole ordeal.

Nix was like an annoying little brother, but it only made me love him more. I had been the only child in our little community until Nixen came along when I was four. A happy accident. We became inseparable from that point forward. Thank the fates accidents still happened, even with a resident witch to deal with contraceptive potions.

A playful shove brushed my side, and I followed Nix's gaze up from the dense undergrowth. Larger patches of blue sky and sunlight peeked through the trees now. *Almost there.* The moment we made it to the path that led to the village of Dorgoil, Nix called, "My eyes! My eyes!" As he always did when we broke out of the canopy covered forest we called home.

The smile spread across my lips was a genuine one. The scents of flowers and fresh harvested crops were such a welcome change. Much nicer than the tree sap and earthy fungus we were used to. Nix did the same, nose high in the fresh air. The excited energy radiating from him was infectious, causing me to feel elated to be out of the Fading Vale for the first time in what seemed like forever.

Whenever the Rebel Alliance leaders determined it was time to move camp again, we begged our parents to let us be the ones to go on the supply runs. Desperate for a change of scenery from the threadbare tents and dimly lit campfires. They refused at first, but eventually agreed. Promising once we came of age, and therefore entered immortality at twenty-five, we could.

Their hesitation was understandable. They wanted to shelter us from those who wished us dead, or worse, extinct. Though immortal, we were still vulnerable and could be killed. It was just a lot harder now with our bodies' natural healing abilities. I was sure the only reason they allowed it, even now, is because they are riddled with guilt for bringing us into a world where we will spend our lifetimes in hiding, simply for existing.

As we approached the center of Dorgoil, I took in the sights of the village. Lush rolling fields and well-tended farmland flooded with sunlight created a tranquil feeling that I couldn't wait to make the most of.

Though as we crept closer, it became apparent the individual homes and community buildings were made up of sticks and twigs. Barely clinging together. The only materials available since the king exiled them so far from the city?

When King Regis took the throne almost four hundred years ago, he separated the races with his new Lore. He'd banished the gnomes to the edge of the kingdom, along with many other species he'd deemed unsavory or ranked poorly in combat skills. Like the elves and pixies. He wanted to be surrounded by the strongest beings, though not so strong he couldn't control them.

Coward.

What gnomes lacked in strength, they made up for with their incredible farming abilities; enhanced by their affinity for earth magic. The king was aware, of course, and exploited this. He took ninety percent of their harvest as a tax for living in his realm. Leaving them with not even enough to feed their own.

He and his court had so much more than they needed. It would rot and go to waste before coming close to being consumed.

Looking to Nix, I sighed. "Regardless of the poverty and segregation here, I'd still trade our life of fear in the Fading Vale for this relative peace," I mused.

"Or better yet, a life in the capital where we would have wealth and freedom," he said. "One day, Eva, we will have that." He spoke as if it wasn't a pipedream. "One day, when the king is no more and we are free to be ourselves, we will find a nice place to settle, have families and give them a life filled with making only happy memories."

He had such conviction in his voice, I almost believed him.

The royal family were high fae. Though I had only ever heard rumors and read about them, it was enough to have decided they were an entitled and conceited race. They wouldn't survive a day fending for themselves in the outer villages of the kingdom, let alone the Vale.

The little knowledge I had of Ezerat itself, the capital of Dezrothia, came from the books I'd collected over the years on trips like this. It couldn't be further from what we were used to. Its residents were made up of strong beings: shifters, witches, warlocks and high fae. All with riches and luxuries beyond our imaginings.

"If ending the king was a possibility, the rebels would have tried to by now, don't you think?" I said. "But nope, we hide and wait, and for what? For the fates to grant us a miracle?" I couldn't hide the sour tone seeping into my voice.

Nix was a dreamer, and I loved that about him. How he managed to be such an optimist, even when his very existence was everything the king despised, I'd never know.

Not only was he a *half-breed*, but half *thrakos*, making him extremely *powerful*. Where most would see these as desired qualities, King Regis saw them as threats to his rule. He spent his reign trying to eradicate those with one, let alone three, of these threats. Nix's mother was a seer witch and a leader in the Rebel Alliance. She was wise, old and formidable, but a year ago she disappeared without a note or trace.

I feared the worst.

Nix was convinced she was out there somewhere. On a greater mission, forced to leave him because of a vision or prophecy. He had many fanciful theories on her whereabouts and the possible reasons she'd have left without saying goodbye to him. Her only child and the apple of her eye. I humored him, not wanting to voice my own theories. Well more, concerns. I had never been as optimistic as him.

Like Nix, his mother was as loyal as they came. I just couldn't imagine, not even for a second, she would have gone this long without so much as sending a message via raven. Not unless something terrible had happened.

Nix inherited a touch of her magic, but his more dominant traits came from his father. A full-blooded thrakos, killed when Nix was only a boy.

Ironically, the thrakos were the only race ever created, not born. Engineered by the king himself—with the aid of a gifted warlock—they were made to be stronger than most fae. Superior senses, speed and strength. Add to that being able to wield fire and fly short distances; they were lethal.

The thrakos I knew were all decent fae, but their vast power came at a price. They had inner demons to battle.

The king made the thrakos all male; preventing families that could distract them from their duty and ensuring they were loyal to him alone. Only, it didn't quite work out like he planned.

When the thrakos were created, mating with races outside your own had been illegal for decades. In his arrogance, King Regis hadn't considered they might mate regardless of his precious Lores.

It didn't take long for a thrakos to fall in love with an injured shifter female he'd encountered on a reconnaissance operation. Apparently, he'd felt a pull toward her scent. Like one would a true mate. He'd nursed her back to health; one thing led to another, and a child was conceived.

The child was believed to be the first half thrakos in existence, but the Rebel Alliance found many more in the centuries since. Of course, when the king discovered the thrakos were able to create hybrids, they became enemy number one. He cleansed his horde with a mass extermination of any who didn't flee in time. Then refilled his ranks with shifters, witches, warlocks and high fae.

"Let's go, Eva!" Nix called, snapping me out of my reverie.

We wandered into what seemed to be the heart of the village, seeking out traders. Smiling at my best friend, I met his warm, almond eyes. We'd make this a day to remember. We had to get the boring stuff out of the way first, but then we'd have time to explore. We needed various supplies for moving camp, but also food rations. The gnomes didn't have an abundance of food to spare, but they would be happy to accept coin from any who had it.

"Ok, you sort out food," I said. "I'll find those selling anything we can use as camp equipment and clothing during the winter."

With a mock bow in my direction, off he went.

I rushed along the stretch of vendors, all with wondrous textiles displayed on their carts. Once the shopping list was dealt with, we could start enjoying ourselves. Pretending we were 'normal' for an afternoon.

An elderly female gnome, sat by her wares of beautifully woven blankets, grabbed my attention. They would be perfect for when the Fading Vale moved from cold and damp to bitter and icy, and the winter months settled in.

"How much for the blankets?" I asked, eyeing them none too keenly. I had limited coin, and it had to cover everything we needed to replenish and then some. I couldn't give my eagerness away if I had any chance of bartering. It didn't matter, I'd already set my heart on the bottle-green one that matched my eyes.

The blankets were necessary, but I needed some coin left over. I'd wanted to surprise Nix with a sword sharpening kit for a while now. Since one of the rebel leaders—a full-blooded thrakos—visited our camp not so long ago with one. Upon seeing how blunt Nix's blade was, he'd taught him how to sharpen it properly. I'd seen Nix's eyes light up when using the handy gadget.

It might not seem like a great gift to most, but when you lived with the monotony we endured, having something to help fill your days and keep your mind busy was a huge win. The fact it would also be useful was a bonus.

Nix would love one. The problem was, you couldn't even buy basics like bread and milk in the Vale, let alone tools. None of the Vale's residents would want to risk drawing attention to their whereabouts by opening a stall. Besides, they would have to keep moving and nobody would know where to find them again. Restocking would be impossible, too. Then there was the sheer size of the Vale.

"Not seen you 'round these parts before," the gnome female said, pulling my attention back from my musings. She narrowed her eyes on my fae form, distrust evident on her features. Then glimpsed the leather pouch on my hip. "Twenty silver a blanket."

My eyes widened. It was too much. Did she want to haggle? Maybe. But could I get her down to a price that would ensure we had enough for what we needed? Was the poverty in this village so bad they had to charge so much? Of course, I knew the answer already, but it still stunned me.

"I can give you ten per blanket, and I will take ten of them," I replied, maintaining eye contact. My father taught me the art of haggling, and this wasn't the first time I'd had to.

The old gnome laughed, the sound bitter. "Do I look like I was born last cycle? These are worth at least eighteen silver each," she snorted.

I sighed. This wasn't going well. And by the looks of it, Nix was having his own battle with the hunter across the path. No doubt trying to work the price down for our food too.

Lacing my words with flattery, I tried a different approach. "Of course not. I meant no disrespect, ma'am. Only, I don't have much coin, and I would love your fine blankets for the winter. How about fourteen silver each and we shake hands?" I asked, holding out my coin-laden palm.

She narrowed her beady eyes on me. "Make it fifteen and we have a deal," she said. "Better you than that horde of King Regis' getting their bloody hands on my wares and wrecking them."

Her eyes danced across the horizon, like she was looking for something.

"King Regis' horde? Here? So far from the castle?" I asked. My chest tightened at the possibility they might be so close.

Her bushy brows dropped into a deep frown. "Aye, lass, we are expecting them to come through to collect their taxes any day now. They sent word they would come early, something about a special guest joining in on a hunt nearby. Our farmers are exhausted trying to ready the goods in time." Her resentment toward the king was evident in her voice.

Tucking a strand of silver hair behind my ear, my eyes glanced around, searching for Nix. He was heading for the tavern, his bags filled with goods. "Right, well thank you for the blankets," I said, shoving the coins into her gloved palm.

Grabbing my purchases, I made a beeline for my friend.

"We need to leave," I whispered as I reached him. My senses were open, listening to every little sound as paranoia set in.

He frowned. "Calm down, Eva. We have time before they expect us back. Let's have a drink in the tavern. I already bought all the food we need, with coin to spare."

The joy in his voice at the prospect made a part of me wish the old dear hadn't said anything. We could have relaxed in blissful ignorance with an ale. But this was our reality. We would be fools not to return to camp and warn the others that we had to move now. Tomorrow might be too late.

Pulling him close, I repeated what the gnome had said. His eyes went wide in alarm. Without a second's hesitation, he grabbed half of the stack of blankets from my arms and we were moving.

Without so much as a final glance at the village we had been so desperate to explore, we raced back in the direction we came. We twisted and danced our way past the perturbed residents of Dorgoil, crossed the border and ran into the Fading Vale.

With adrenaline fueling us, we didn't stop for at least two hours straight. Hurdling the fallen trees and ducking to avoid hanging branches. Ignoring the scratches from thorny bushes and pine needles embedding into our skin.

Nix remained in his fae form, running at the same speed as me to conserve his energy. Probably in case he needed to shift when we made it back. Nix stopped dead in his tracks, slamming an arm out in front of me. "Eva, do you hear that?" His voice was low, but urgent.

Blood pounded in my ears as I listened for whatever had him spooked. My heart raced. The sounds of agonized screams coming from our camp were unmistakable. My entire body trembled as it dawned on me: we were too late. We hadn't made it in time. The horde had already found them.

Nix's throat bobbed as he wrung his hands. Dread grew in my chest. Then the distinct metallic smell of blood drifted to me on the wind and I had to clamp my jaw to stop the bile rising in my throat.

"We have to help them," I said. I didn't know where to begin. Instead, I focused on trying to calm thoughts of anguish for our friends and family. Our bags discarded, Nix took my arm. We crept closer to the thicket of trees surrounding the camp.

The thundering clashes of steel striking steel was deafening. Guttural snarls of wolves and thrakos were the only things helping to mask the pained cries of the injured.

The breath left my chest, and I struggled to draw air as I took in the fighting before us. Where were my parents? Oh fates, were they already fighting? Were they hurt?

A familiar male voice carried across the battlefield to me. "Evangelia. It's the Regis horde. You can't be here!"

My eyes darted over the fighting bodies. It was Ambrose, struggling against another wolf shifter. Only the horde's soldier was much larger as they battled in a partially shifted form. Using their claws and fangs while remaining on two feet.

Scanning the camp, my eyes landed on an unfamiliar male in the distance. High fae. Apparent by the ethereal beauty I'd read about. He stood in the middle of the carnage, his head thrown back in laughter. Enjoying the slaughter far more than any sane soldier should.

Raven black hair blew in a wild mess around his head. His leather armor, which those of us in the Vale could never hope to own, was splattered with blood. At his feet, broken bodies lay so mangled I couldn't make out who they were.

I couldn't leave our fae to be butchered like this. "But..."

Nix cut me off. "He's right, Eva," he said. "Remember your training. Don't shift. Okay? I will find you as soon as I can."

Before I could so much as blink, Nix shifted into his thrakos form.

His height remained unchanged, around six foot two. Only now there were lethal reptilian wings, blacker than the night sky, sprouting from his back. His shirt ripped open to accommodate them. Teeth sharpened into fangs, while his big chocolate eyes and mass of mousy brown hair remained unaltered.

While he disappeared in a blur of speed to join the battle, I worried at the rings adorning my fingers, searching the carnage in front of me. Where were my parents? Fates dammit, they had to be here somewhere.

Shit, shit, shit.

My heart slammed against my ribs as I pressed closer to the battlefield. My hands itched to grab the dual daggers sitting at my hips.

"Mayhem and Chaos, just like you, my sweetling," my mother had said the day she gave them to me. They were beautiful blades. With an obsidian center which bled to the sharpened gleaming metal edges. Matching the onyx streak running through my long silver hair.

My parents and I were more vulnerable than the others in the camp. The beasts inside us lay dormant thanks to the effects of the enchanted rings we wore, and they insisted I never remove.

It might be suicide for us to shift in front of anyone who wasn't a member of the Rebel Alliance, but I could still help. Having to conceal what I was my entire life meant I'd needed to hone my combat skills. I trained every day of my damned existence to be ready for if, or more realistically when, this day inevitably came.

The king had been terrorizing the fae of the Fading Vale unrepentantly for centuries. His unwavering hatred of hybrids and thrakos forced innocents into hiding. Never staying in one place for long. Knowing that being found meant being slaughtered for merely existing.

The tyrant couldn't have let them leave when he'd ascended. No, he paid off sea creatures—like the selkies and kelpies—to guard the coast, making an escape by sea to another kingdom impossible.

He even closed the portal in Ezerat, shutting off any communication with the mortal realm. The sick bastard wanted to hunt us for his own sadistic pleasure.

Slowly, I made my way deeper into camp. The fog was low, melding with the plumes of smoke coming from the fires destroying everything we had in this world.

With my vision impaired, I paused, concentrating on controlling my breathing enough to listen for any immediate threats. My toes curled as someone behind me said, "Well, well. What do we have here?" A blade of ice slid down my spine at the sound of the velvety male voice.

I whipped around, daggers drawn and ready to slice anyone who tried to threaten me.

Staring back was the black-haired male who'd been laughing maniacally, surrounded by death and despair. Now he stood mere feet away, coated in blood and smirking the most wicked smile.

He made no effort to conceal the way he looked me up and down with piercing blue eyes. Licking his perfectly symmetrical lips like he was hungry for more bloodshed.

Before the panic seized me entirely, my father's labored voice called out, "Evangelia!"

I leapt backward, blades still raised, putting some distance between me and the enemy. Frantic, my eyes darted to find where my father's voice had come from.

The battle spread wide across camp, making it near impossible to focus as the tent fires burned furiously. Bright sparks of lethal spells lit the smoke in colorful sporadic flashes. Those with witch blood dueling hard, fighting for their lives and the lives of their loved ones.

Then I saw them. *My parents.*

Held at sword point by two high fae males. One significantly taller than the other, but neither as looming as the blue-eyed demon closest to me.

Blood drained from my face, rendering me disoriented and cold, frozen in place and unblinking. As I met my parent's stares, a heart-breaking blend of love and fear shone back at me. They forced a small smile in my direction.

"Mum, Dad," I whispered.

A leather clad hand landed on my armored waist, and a shiver ran down my spine as it hit me I'd messed up. So worried for my parents, I'd taken my attention from the threat.

Who was now at my back.

"Tell me, why are fae like you hiding all the way out here, with dirty abominations no less, pretty girl?" His voice was smooth as he murmured against the shell of my ear. "A beauty like you has no business associating with the filth of the Fading Vale."

In a sudden move, I was forced to the male's side. His grip tightened on my waist and he dragged me forward, closer to my parents.

"Any last words for your future king, traitors?" he sneered. "A heartfelt speech? An appeal to my soft side to spare you? A thank you, perhaps, for ending your miserable existence? You know, that kind of thing." His sing-song lilt was mocking.

He gave them no time to respond before he gestured a sharp nod to his accomplices. Their swords raised to my parents' throats. I wanted to scream at them to transform, to defend themselves. They could end these high fae in an instant. Maybe save the whole fate's damned camp. Whatever was left of it at least.

But I knew they wouldn't.

Their shift would be felt across the Vale and someone would tell. The price on our heads would far surpass anything we could offer the villagers for their silence. Not only the ones we traded with for our survival, but the nomads we passed in the Fading Vale, too.

No, shifting wasn't an option. It was never an option. Not for us. They would never stop hunting us.

Suddenly, my pair of silver rings that matched theirs were too tight. The one I wore on the middle finger of my left hand burned. Suppressing my shift while my emotions were so out of control.

My enemy's hand grasped my chin, forcing me to face my parents.

My mother's eyes filled with tears, and my lip began to tremble.

Glassy eyes steadfastly held mine as she swallowed hard. "Turn away, don't see us like this," she whispered. "Remember what we taught you, sweetling."

She was accepting her fate, and the knowledge killed me.

The fae holding my parents swung back their swords in unison.

I tried to turn away, but the grip on me was unyielding.

Instead, I scrunched my eyes shut. It was cowardly, but I couldn't bring myself to look; I couldn't watch the fae I loved more than life itself be murdered in front of me.

The vice-like grip around my heart was too much.

Then my world came crashing down with the whistle of swords cutting through the air.

Two heavy thuds met with the cold ground.

My eyes squeezed tighter still, my legs weak. The only thing stopping me from crumbling to the ground was the strong hand on my jaw.

The pain in my chest was surely going to kill me. Part of me wanted it to.

Before my mind was able to comprehend what had happened, hands grabbed at me roughly, dragging me away. My parents' murderers were talking, not a care in their world as they bantered, but I didn't catch their cruel words.

I didn't dare open my eyes again. Not until I was certain I wouldn't see the lifeless eyes of the two fae I loved most in this world looking back at me. If I didn't see it, maybe I could convince myself none of it had really happened? Because if it were true, then all of my worst nightmares, what I feared most my entire life, had become reality.

CHAPTER 2

Nekane

ONE WEEK PRIOR

Walking in the shadow of my silent companion's hulking form, I was glad to have the castle at my back and the Crooked Claw creeping into sight.

The cobblestone streets were familiar underfoot, like a second skin. We'd done this walk so many times with one destination in mind. The tavern.

The stores we passed on the way were closing for the night, and an expensive-looking flower shop drew my eye. Not that I needed to buy anyone flowers. The sign above the entrance proclaimed it 'Florist of Fortune.' I wasn't sure whether it referred to selling overpriced bouquets, or if perhaps you received a free palm reading with every purchase.

Owned by a witch who claimed to be a seer, the place was like most shops adorning this prime stretch of Ezerat city, over the top and extravagant. Not my thing. Still, I couldn't help but be a little impressed by the signage above the door. Woven with exotic leaves and blooms of the darkest blues and palest shades of gray. Twisted and warped to spell out the shop's name.

A chill caressed me as I looked up at the cloud-covered sky. I'd overheard patrons in the Crooked Claw say the sign had been spelled to change color depending on the day's weather. Judging by the current climate, I'd say the rumors were true.

As the sun met the horizon and shopkeepers locked their doors, there was a definite crispness in the air that hadn't been there last night. Like the balmy autumn was ready to step aside for a particularly bitter winter.

I cringed as my gaze landed on a new gift shop next. 'Royal Regis Regalia.' I rolled my eyes. Its window display was brimming with royalist 'collectibles' and other cheap items. The faces of my brother and I stared back at me on tea towels and tankards.

Looking down, I considered the male at my side and our somewhat odd friendship. I'd often wondered if we spent so much time together because he enjoyed my company, or if it was out of duty. To ensure one of the kingdom's princes didn't meet an untimely end. Not that my father would care.

Alaric was the highest ranking general in my father's horde since working his way up the ranks over the last three hundred years or so. He was also the fae I considered to be my closest friend.

Despite his age, he didn't look much older than my nearly twenty-five years. My own impending immortality couldn't come soon enough. It wasn't that I was desperate to stop aging and live forever, far from it. Moreso, it was the faster healing that would come in handy.

I rubbed the ache in my jaw where my father, King of Dezrothia, struck me earlier. He lashed out whenever he was reminded of his late wife, my mother. Which was virtually every time he looked at me. Always sure to remind me it was my fault she'd died, while I tried to remind myself it was my birth that killed her, not me personally.

The king had been mad for as long as I could remember, but his insanity had only gotten worse as the years progressed. Once I finally came of age, and my body could take more hits, it would only get worse.

Since I was a boy, he always made sure the injuries I sustained could be explained away as combat training related. As soon as they healed, he would tarnish my skin with fresh marks and the cycle would continue.

Not many knew of the abuse flung upon me. After all, cuts and bruises were in no shortage for me. It was no secret that when I wasn't at the Crooked Claw, drinking myself into oblivion, I was in the castle's training halls.

Alaric was with me more often than not. Training me unyieldingly to ensure I could fight off the attacks that came all too frequently. It would prove invaluable once I came of age and the king would brutalize me all the more harshly—without much risk of going too far.

For now, he always managed to pull the final blow. Not wanting the headache of explaining to his kingdom that he'd beaten one of their princes to death.

As the easy laughter from the tavern met my ears, I snuck a glance in Alaric's direction. His grim expression gave me pause, not for the first time tonight. The entire walk had been mostly silent. While he was never chatty, he normally bantered with me at least a little.

Done with the silence, I cleared my throat. Time to break him from his brooding or tonight would prove as boring as today had been. "You know, you can talk to me," I said, keeping a teasing edge to my tone.

The sharpening of his silver eyes made it obvious his head had been elsewhere. "Yeh wouldnae like what I have to say. Probably for the best yeh keep yer nose out."

Pulling open the heavy tavern door, Alaric pushed his way inside. The sign above, boasting the words 'Crooked Claw' framing a picture of an overfull tankard, swung wide in the wake of his entry.

I loved this place. A crackling open fire sat in the center of the room. Circled by tables to ensure plenty could benefit from its heat. On the back wall was the bar. Bill, the owner, was behind it and his wife, Melina, flittered from table to table, speaking to patrons. Making sure they were all behaving, no doubt.

Bill and Melina were lion shifters and had run this tavern for close to a century. The cozy atmosphere made it a popular spot. It didn't hurt that the ale was cheap and the food never failed to warm your bones on a cold day.

I followed Alaric as he squeezed his mountainous frame through the crowded space. He led us to our usual spot at the back, lifting a hand in greeting to a few other warriors we passed. Unsurprisingly, Axel was one of them. The shifter was often with Alaric, the horde general acting as a kind of mentor to him since he'd joined the ranks. I'd been a boy at the time, but remember how quickly they seemed to hit it off. It was unusual for Alaric because he'd never been one for making friends with his soldiers, or anyone, really.

We slumped down in our darkened corner, away from the rowdy patrons. Alaric signaled for Melina to bring us some drinks and she nodded, knowing we weren't picky about what we were drinking. Despite the luxuries in the castle, where only the best would do for the king, I couldn't care less so long as the alcohol was strong.

The female was far from sweet, but when Melina arrived at our table, drinks in hand, her smile was just that. Gray peppered her rich brown mane and the fine lines around her amber eyes creased, betraying her ancient age.

"There we are, Highness." She placed our drinks down with a wink. "Alaric," she said, giving him a nod.

A large gulp and the tart ale flooded my tongue. Replacing the bitterness from my run-in with a certain bastard today with something far more palatable. Relaxing back into my seat, I looked at my friend, not meaning to admire his broad shoulders or the scar running down his face. From under his right eye all the way down to his jaw. Only partially covered by his rugged, dirty blonde hair.

He'd never told me the story of his scar, but it had to have happened a few centuries ago. Before he reached immortality. If it wasn't for his ability to heal, he would be riddled with them by now—given his long career fighting for my father.

After all, the general was a key leader in the regular hunts to find thrakos and half-breeds in the Fading Vale.

Looking up from his drained tankard, his stare met mine as he licked some frothy foam from his upper lip. He huffed. "Like I said, yer not gonnae like what I got to tell yeh," he said. "But I cannae leave yeh in the dark." *Was that a grimace?*

Alaric's accent was unusual in the capital, though where it was from exactly, I had no idea. It had this way of sending a shudder of heat through me. Especially the thicker it got. Like when he had more than a few drinks, or on the rare occasion his anger flared.

Alaric's steely gaze was unwavering. Whatever was troubling him had to do with my father. "Go on," I said. "What has my dear old dad done this time?" I blew out a sigh of frustration as he remained stoic. "Do I need to ply you with more booze to get your lips loose?"

His deep rumble of a laugh filled the space between us. "That's no' a bad idea."

I signaled Melina again, who nodded in turn. Bill was at the bar, already pouring two more drinks. I leaned forward, dropping my voice, "Want some whores too while I'm spoiling you?" I asked, giving him a wink.

Mirth danced in the air at my words. "Yeh ken I dinnae need whores. I've been fuckin' since long before yeh were even a wee twinkle in yer ma's eye." He wasn't lying. Despite being every inch an intimidating bastard, he had the shifters drooling. Fates near pawing at him.

The sharp stab of guilt at the mention of my mother sat uncomfortably in my chest. Luckily, Alaric ignored it and went on. "Now quiet down or I'll not tell yeh what yer da' told me today."

Snatching the fresh drink in front of me, I took a sip and waited.

"Yer da' is sendin' Elikai to the Fadin' Vale on a hunt. His comin' of age present," he said. "But yer not comin' with us."

The knowledge my brother was, once again, getting something handed to him by our father stung. Doing nothing to ease the weight of guilt in my chest. Ironic that the king only held disdain for me when Kai and I were nearly identical.

"Let me guess. *You're* going to lead the hunt?" Of course he was. Our father wouldn't let my brother go without the best back up.

Despite the twat looking down on Alaric for being a shifter, the wolf's ruthlessness on a battlefield was legendary. Few enemies fought him and lived to tell the tale.

"Aye, gotta make sure no ill comes to King Regis' golden boy."

The hurt turned to jealousy. "How long will you be gone?" I asked.

"Well, he wants me to collect the taxes while we're at it. By my reckonin', a few weeks? I've to take them pair of brats Elikai always has following him too."

"Graves and Sloane?"

"Fuck if I ken their names."

"I'll be sure to thank Kai for the fucking invite then." *Would it kill him to invite his own brother?*

It was my birthday too. He was well aware our father wouldn't have thought about me. I swear, sometimes it felt like Kai actually enjoyed me being left out.

Ugh. The more I thought about it, the more wound up I became. "I thought he was having a party in the ballroom?" I asked. "Whenever I've seen him around lately, it's all he's spoken about."

"Aye, you dinnae have to tell me–"

I slammed my tankard down harder than I meant to. "And collecting the taxes, too? What's that about? Training him up to take over as king one day?"

"Look, I knew yeh'd be pissed, but why're yeh so put out by it? I thought you didnae want to be king?"

He was right, but it didn't make it any easier.

"I don't. It's just... shit." I trailed off. I was going to be alone again, for weeks. There would be nothing to distract the king from my actions.

I was acting like a brat, but the shit sandwich Alaric delivered was a hard one to swallow.

"Kane–"

"Forget about it," I said, putting my mask of indifference back in place. "Let's make tonight one to remember during the weeks you are gone, yeah?"

Raising my drink to him in a mock celebration, I plastered on my widest grin, making sure it reached my dimples. It worked for everyone else, so why not try it on him?

His head was shaking, but he raised his tankard to meet mine anyway. His gaze began to wander the room. Hunting his prey for the evening.

I followed his lead, noticing one of my regular bedmates talking to a high fae couple. *Crystal.* Her name suited her. Beautiful on the outside, but if you dug a bit deeper, it was obvious she was a cheap, fake imitation of what she pretended to be.

I wasn't a fool. I knew her type well enough. She'd come to me the first time looking to lift her own status. But we ended up with an unspoken agreement of sorts. To reap the benefits of warming each other's beds, no strings, no ties. *Sometimes ties...*

It certainly didn't hurt that she enjoyed taking others to bed with us as much as I did.

Alaric stood, making his way to the bar. Thanks to the stupid Lores, he had to stick with his own race. As did I. Which narrowed his potentials down to the available shifters.

Knowing his type, I'd put good coin on the shifter female—spilling out of a red, low-cut dress—being where he was heading.

My attention moved back to Crystal. Her long, strawberry blonde hair took on a more reddish hue in the firelight. She happened to look up at that moment, a smile spreading across her attractive features as she met my eyes. All it took was a tilt of my head and she was closing the space between us. I didn't make a habit of fucking the same female more than once, but she had a way of drawing me back in.

Biting my lip, I watched the sway of her hips as she sauntered over from behind my tankard. The arch of her spine was so obviously exaggerated to entice me. She didn't need to. I was a sure thing tonight, regardless.

"Hey, handsome," she said, running her long nails through my black hair. "I was just thinking about you."

Glancing back at the high fae couple she'd been speaking to, Crystal sent them a little wave. The interest in their eyes was obvious. Crystal always was so accommodating to my desires; finding extra bodies to fill the bed. High fae we could both enjoy.

"Looking for some fun tonight?" Crystal whispered.

Why choose one when you could have all three? "Always," I murmured, brushing my lips across the hand she held out. As I took it in mine, she dipped into a curtsy.

Alaric returned with the busty brunette giggling behind him. The clatter of a key on the table had me biting my lip once more in anticipation of what was to come. *In every sense of the word.* I couldn't very well take commoners back to the castle, so the key was to the room upstairs that Alaric and I often rented.

It started as a security measure. Given my station, he couldn't relax while I was naked and in a room of strangers, fuck knows where in the city. And I didn't want to be an asshole by cockblocking him while he stood guard. Then, over the years, the heated looks thrown between everyone in that room became addictive. The dangerous thrill of skirting the Lores making it that much hotter.

Melina was happy to accommodate us. We paid her a lot of coin in return for her 'generosity.' Plus, she was old enough to not be a purist. Having lived in a time when it was normal to mate with other races. Sharing a room didn't even make her blink.

I was so fucking ready to pretend I wasn't about to face weeks alone in the castle. Evading my father at all costs.

The high fae couple joined us, eager after whatever Crystal had told them. We ordered a round of drinks, an icebreaker, but it wasn't long before Crystal's palm was brushing my leg beneath the table.

Her fingers trailed up my inner thigh until her palm settled on my cock, making it twitch. "Naughty, naughty," I murmured, dragging her into my lap. "Are you so eager to take my cock?" I asked. "To show me how good you take it in front of our new friends?" I reveled in the feeling of her pressing her thighs together, trapping my hand there.

As we headed for the stairs, I signaled Melina to send the drinks up to our room.

This was going to be fun.

CHAPTER 3
Alaric

A deep groan rose from my throat as I rode my horse along the uneven path. This was going to be a long, painful trip if Elikai and his cronies didn't shut the fuck up.

It didn't help that last night in the tavern had been wild. Not a single part of me wanted to leave the warm pile of bodies at the Crooked Claw. Not before the sun had even risen, and definitely not for *this*.

Flexing my shoulders, cuts pulled my skin. Fucking hellcat must have sunk her claws deep for them not to have healed yet. *Worth it.* My ability to heal wasn't as potent as the high fae's, but I chose not to wake Kane just to ask him to use his gifts on me. It'd speed up the process, but I'd heal soon enough without it.

My eyes rolled as the insufferable duet of spoiled gits encouraged Elikai. Endless mind-numbing, fanciful bragging about his epic achievements. He didn't need any egging on, despite having achieved fuck all to boast about.

There was no denying the prince had lucked out in the gene pool. As had his identical twin. Even among the high fae, they stood out with their alluringly good looks. Other than that, he was plain fucking average.

What had Kane said those wee shites names were again? Fuck if I remembered. I'd seen them around the castle plenty, but didn't pay them any mind. This trip would change that. We hadn't even mounted our horses yet when I decided I would likely wind up killing them. While we'd been loading up the steeds, Axel had recommended 'surprise jousting' them. I wasn't sure what that was, but it sounded like something I might enjoy.

I am a monster, after all. What was a little more blood on my hands? *Or down my throat.* The only thing stopping me was knowing who their fathers were. Two of the king's closest advisors.

The lanky one laughed, elbowing a guard who'd joined us on the hunt. "I'll slay those dirty thrakos!" he said. "They will be pissing themselves when we come riding up!"

If the thrakos were pissing themselves, it was more likely from laughing at this fucking idiot. The chorus of eye rolls from my soldiers confirmed they were thinking the same. We were warriors, not babysitters. Still, the ruler's word was final.

"I'll run the first one through before it knows what's hit it!" the fool continued.

Pursing my lips together, my jaw ticked. "A thrakos will have yeh on yer arse quicker than yeh can blink." The words left my mouth before I had a chance to regret them. "Yeh need to sneak up on them if yer gonnae have any chance of survivin'. That means learning to shut yer trap for five fuckin' min–"

The dramatic clearing of a throat cut me off. *Here we go.* Elikai putting on a fucking performance, as usual.

"Graves," he said, chest puffed out. "We both know that *I*, Prince Elikai Regis, *heir* to the Dezrothian throne, am the *best* fighter that has been seen in decades! No, centuries! No, millennia!" I took a deep breath in and held it. "It will be *I* who will have those dirty thrakos cowering at my feet! Begging for a mercy they do not deserve!"

How the fuck were identical twins so bloody different? Kane was at least a halfway decent fae. Considering where he came from. I released my breath slowly, Elikai was nothing more than a stuck-up, self–

"Alaric," he snapped, turning his attention on me. "How much *farther*?" The whine irritated my ears.

Grassy mounds rolling away in every direction were all that could be seen. Not much else surrounded us, aside from a few clusters of trees and the worn road we were trotting down.

The journey had barely begun, yet he was already complaining. If this was how the entire hunt would be, I didn't hold much hope for my already slipping sanity.

The less I said, the better. "Twice what we jus' rode, Highness."

Elikai didn't mind my bluntness, preferring the sound of his own voice. "I can't *wait* to get to the first village," he said. "The audacity of the common peasants not paying their fealty to the crown. We shall reclaim the coin we are owed, plus further tax for our trouble."

He didn't care about fealty to the crown. Only for what he thought he was owed. His eagerness betrayed him.

It was one of the many reasons I found the princeling insufferable.

Apparently, I wasn't the only one here who was struggling with him.

A brown braid of hair whipped around as Krista looked at the prince. "All due respect, Highness," she said. "But we must keep our voices down to listen for any potential trouble." I didn't need to see the look the entitled Prince gave her to know it was unpleasant. Filled with irritation, her bright, honey-colored eyes betrayed the nature of her shifter side as she fought to keep her anger concealed.

I'd heard a lot in the training hall about the new female grizzly to join our ranks. She was surprisingly nimble, handled a longsword better than most of the males, and in bear form, was known for savaging her enemies.

Savage, I could deal with. I liked savage. We needed all the savage we could get going up against the thrakos.

Elikai tsked. "Nobody would *dare* attack me. Not unless they were seeking death. Don't you see, shifter? You have the easiest job in the world hunting with me." My eyes rolled so hard I faced the inside of my skull. "Ask Alaric, he trained me once."

He was right about one thing. I *had* trained him. For several years alongside his brother, once upon the fates.

One day in particular, stood out. I'd instructed them to fight each other, to see how their training was coming along and what areas I needed to focus on for them to improve. Elikai had disarmed Kane with a dirty move and declared himself the victor—despite his underhanded tactics. The way he'd thrust his sword in the air, chin high and chest out, told me all I needed to know about the male.

"Aye Highness, I did train yeh once." I didn't bother expanding. What was the point? His version of events would likely differ.

"And wasn't I the best student you ever had," he stated. "It's why you no longer train me, isn't it?" *This wee shite is going to be the end of me.* I told enough lies as it was. I didn't like to add to the list if I could help it.

After he'd bested Kane that day, he decided that was it. He was done with his lessons at the tender age of seventeen. Then started making his way through the barracks instead, picking fights with anyone willing to draw their sword.

Never came to me for a fight, though. Which I always thought was an interesting decision on his part. Albeit a sensible one. Once it was clear he had no intention of returning to our sessions, I'd thanked the fates and didn't push the matter.

"Somethin' like that, Highness," I mumbled.

This was going to be a long fucking trip.

IT HAD BEEN another shite night's sleep camping between villages. Despite being several days into our trek, Elikai still kept everyone awake with his dramatic sighs and groans of discomfort. His ego wasn't used to sleeping on the hard ground.

We all had our roles to play, apart from the princeling and his two stooges—who'd been doing their own thing the entire trip.

I was happy to let them. Better than them being in my hair. Whenever they stuck their noses up, or the pompous prince argued his 'accommodations' weren't adequate for a royal, I'd feign a bout of deafness.

Thank the fates, we only needed to visit the pixies now before we would reach the Fading Vale at long last.

The first village in debt we'd visited had been Bouldercliff. The place seemed picturesque upon entering. Not dissimilar from some of the earlier villages we'd passed. Then you looked closer.

Everything would benefit from some sort of repair work. Missing thatch on roofs, doors off their hinges. Clothes so threadbare, you saw through them as they hung on the line.

The disparity only a few hours' ride from the castle was shocking, and it got worse the farther out we rode. The inhabitants of Ezerat city wouldn't be seen dead in clothes so worn they sagged with gaping holes.

Was the increase in poverty from the city to the towns and villages so obvious in other kingdoms? I'd never left Dezrothia to compare. Very few had after Regis took power and control of everyone's comings and goings.

The information found in the few books available in Ezerat was vague when it came to our neighboring realms. Such a source should never be taken for fact anyway, they were all fantasy and fairy-tales.

Despite Jarid's warnings, Bouldercliff had been a total fucking disaster.

The bald-headed warlock had been with the king's horde for quite some time. His job for this trip was to ensure no one got left behind. *If only he wasn't so good at his job.*

Having the princeling with us meant Jarid was on higher alert than usual. Ready to throw up a ward to shield him at the slightest hint of a threat.

When we'd approached the hills, the warlock told the brats to be cautious around the trolls who resided there. Unsurprisingly, they hadn't listened.

Trolls were big, ugly fuckers and weren't known for their friendliness or patience. They had no loyalty to the crown. They were happy living in the mountains, but King Regis hadn't liked them being so close to the city.

He'd *allowed* the spider shifters to inhabit the mountains instead and sent the trolls to these hills.

Their leader must have bribed them with something very fucking tempting, because they'd refrained from putting the prince on the dinner menu. Despite how much he deserved it.

We'd left there early, just in case. Our next stop had been the quaint village of Ulana Hill, home to the elves. They were willowy beings; though they looked similar to the high fae, their pointed ears gave them away. Their physical appearance, combined with their weakness, made them undesirable in the eyes of the king. Hence them living so far from the capital.

The elves hadn't attempted a coup either. They hadn't even offered resistance when Elikai had openly mocked their poverty. Kicking off at how light the bag of coin they'd handed over was.

The last thing they needed would be the king catching wind of them acting out. He'd set the horde on their village. It wouldn't be the first time a village was rendered to ash by the king's orders of violence.

I'd spotted the elven elder shooting daggers at some of the village folk, making some choice hand gestures behind Elikai's back. I hadn't bothered to question it. The prince's pride would not deal well with mockery. Besides, he and his pair of followers deserved it. For being complete fucking cunts.

Thank the fates, afternoon was only just upon us by the time we left Ulana Hill. Which meant we didn't have to stay the night. Instead, we rode until the sky was painted in pinks and violets.

When I'd seen the pair of fools pretending to joust with branches, I'd decided it was time to stop for the night. Rest the horses before someone lost an eye. Or I forgot why I couldn't kill them and be done with their bullshit.

Of course, Elikai had a tantrum over having to sleep in a tent again. Krista explained as patiently as she could that it had been too early to stop riding for the night. Pointing out it was Elikai's own schedule that dictated we reach the Vale on the day of his birthday. Not to mention how dangerous it was to travel in the pitch of night this far from the castle.

The stumpier of the brats hadn't liked Krista's words at all. "Who the fuck do you think you are talking to, whore?" he'd said.

While I'd been busy trying to remember his stupid fucking name, a squeal pierced the air.

Krista had decked the asshole. She didn't need to fear word getting back to the castle, only the hunt party would ever hear of it. His ego wouldn't allow him to admit to being put on his arse by a female. A shifter at that.

I'd abso-fucking-lutely be telling Kane over a pint. Just as soon as I got back, though.

He'd need a good laugh.

With every village we approached, Elikai's dark eyebrows lowered. Pinching together as he wrinkled his nose. Our final stop was Pinefall, home of the pixies, and his distaste was no less apparent.

The tax purse would be light and the harvests thin. The difficult times the pixies faced weren't limited to a few families, they'd all suffered.

Unlike me, who was a regular on these hunting trips, they wouldn't recognize the prince. Not this far out of Ezerat. The armor we wore made it clear who we were.

Krista was away, taking care of our business with Jarid, while I remained to tend the horses. Once again on babysitting duty.

"How long until the Fading Vale now?" Elikai asked for the thousandth time. Sat bone idle while I brushed down a chestnut mare.

"Couple hours' ride, I reckon. We'll be there by early afternoon," I told him.

He'd never understand the concept of looking after those around you and they will look after you in return. Soldiers and steeds included.

"Finally," he huffed, leaving to find his little friends.

He'd been particularly intolerable so far today. I'd expected as much, given it was his twenty-fifth birthday. The day he gained his immortality.

Taking a moment to wonder, I hoped Kane was well. That his father stayed away from him. Highly unlikely, given that today also marked twenty-five years since the king lost his wife to childbirth.

I fucking hated not being there to pick up the pieces.

Shaking myself out of my worry for him, I moved to my own dappled stallion. Krista returned with a few bundles under her arms and Jarid followed. A weighty sack on his back. Conserving his magic by carrying the goods manually.

We worked together, getting the horses loaded up again. Jarid was a well-seasoned rider, moving without question. It was my first time working with the female, but it was clear Krista knew what she was doing.

"Alaric," Krista said, worrying her lip. "Are you sure having those three in the Fading Vale is wise?"

I shook my head. "We've no choice, lass. If King Regis found out we didnae let his lad get his moment, he'd string me up by my bollocks'." I didn't miss the way her eyes dropped to my crotch at the mention of balls.

Husky but feminine laughter filled the air. "Rather yours than mine," she said with a suggestive wink. "But if they end up on my sword, don't say I didn't warn you." She paused, and when she spoke again, her tone was much more earnest. "I don't think I'll volunteer for a hunt again before checking the guest list."

I nodded. Lucky her. She was able to ditch out of rides such as these without much of a consequence or drawing the king's attention.

I didn't have that luxury.

WE CROSSED the border into the Vale around midday. Thick fog surrounded us, white clouds pressing in on all sides. Despite my improved shifter eyesight, it was almost impossible to make out the difference between friend and foe.

Before entering, I warned the three fuckwits to keep quiet and follow my lead. So far, they'd heeded my warnings, navigating their steeds silently through the trees. The possibility of coming across traps was high. It would be foolish to assume our prey wouldn't be forever ready for an attack.

Following the subtle scarring in the underbrush, we made in the direction we believed the rebel camp to be. A lack of any discernible sounds put the entire party on edge. There was likely a witch in residence. Creating the unnatural quiet.

After careful navigation, the shadows of a camp loomed from the thick fog and we dismounted. Tying up the horses and drawing closer to the settlement on foot.

Jarid cast a silencing spell around us as we huddled together. It wouldn't hurt to go over the plan of attack one last time.

Now we were closer, I had a better lay of the land. We could make any last-minute changes to ensure this was as successful as possible. It would be an ambush. We would slip in, slaughter everyone, and slip out again.

Brutal, barbaric, and unprovoked.

In position, Jarid dropped his spell. I thanked the fates we were all in agreement for once on the plan and inched closer.

A male loomed in front of me. Hybrid by the scent of him. I looked around to ensure everyone was in place–

A war cry wrenched the still air. Suddenly off my guard, I searched for the culprit. *Elikai.* He charged forward, his lackeys close behind, swords raised. My own target watched them too. Panicked, he whirled around to find me crouching behind him, poised to attack. I struck first. Willing my nails to shift into lethal claws as I swiped at his throat.

One down.

One kill was all I needed for the bloodlust to take me.

With the rebels in disarray and splitting up across the camp, I found my next prey. A wolf. He yelled to someone behind me, but I couldn't understand what he said as I grappled with him. His distraction was my opportunity. A red haze settled over my vision and the desire for blood became overwhelming.

My teeth sank into his throat, ripping away the flesh. The savory flavor of blood raced over my tongue. Quenching a mere fraction of my thirst.

Two down.

A thrakos shifted. Huge dark wings protruding from his spine. Flexing them, he took to the air, soaring across the battlefield. More thrakos joined him. Some smelt like half-breeds, but they still chose their winged beast. A wise decision. Their best chance of survival.

Thrakos speed was hard to match, but still, I sprinted to my next target. Catching him by surprise with my own agility.

Claws gutted the rebel, and I felt the spray of blood. Sinking deeper into my frenzied state, my only hope was that I wouldn't remember any of it once we finished savaging them all. And if I did, that my remorse wouldn't finally kill me.

CHAPTER 4

Elikai

Entering the camp of abominable half-breeds and thrakos leeches, I already knew the General's plan wasn't going to work. In theory, it would. It just didn't work for me. It was crying out for something more… extravagant.

For Father to see that I was ready for him to step aside, the hunt needed to be memorable. Epic in its retellings. The only thing that had been holding me back was waiting for my immortality. I'd wanted it to manifest early, but apparently the fates were set on it being twenty-five, down to the second, regardless of race, power or superiority.

Today, the fates were working in my favor, and just as I'd wanted, we reached the Fading Vale on the day of my coming of age. The aging process had at last slowed to a virtual stop—keeping me in my absolute prime.

Tall, dark, strong, intelligent, devilishly handsome. Master of the sword. Destined to be King of Dezrothia. Everyone I'd ever met either wanted me or wanted to be me. Usually both. I'd say it grew tiresome, but that would be a lie. What could I say? It was brilliant to be me. But it would be even better to be king.

The picture of heroism, I charged into battle. Making my first kill almost immediately. A quick stab into the stupid witch mongrel's back and through her heart was all it took. Slumping over, death descended with my blade. I slid it back out, watching the blood spread rapidly, and a smile tugged at my lips. By happy coincidence, the noise blocking spell fell with her, so I tuned my superior hearing in to my surroundings. Searching for prey.

The thrakos came from nowhere. But with a powerful shove into Graves' chest, he fell just as I intended. Directly in the foul beast's path. It hadn't expected such a move. As it paused, like it was preparing to take flight, I swung my blade in a beautiful arc, relieving it of its head.

Elation flooded my veins despite the dirty blood spraying my clothes. My first ever thrakos kill. Throwing my head back, a laugh burst from deep inside me. Mere moments into our hunt and the bodies were already piling up around me.

Glancing around the carnage, I looked for more thrakos to slay. Instead, I found two high fae traitors. Nodding toward my comrades, Graves got to his feet and Sloane appeared out from behind a tree. Looking suspiciously like he'd been using it to hide behind since the appearance of the now dead thrakos.

Ignoring the hoarse screams and weapons clanging, a sound much more interesting carried over on the wind.

"We must leave her a note. There is so much we didn't get to tell her," a female voice whispered, tripping over the words as she spoke too fast. Zeroing in on the sound, my eyes fell upon the high fae renegades.

There were two of them, and I watched as the female's gaze darted around, as though a pen and parchment would appear out of the sky. The male next to her began rummaging through bags piled high on a wagon.

It seemed we'd arrived just in time. Had they planned to leave the area? If only they'd known, the fates were always on my side. Following my lead, Graves and Sloane circled around and stepped in behind them. Then pointed their gleaming swords directly at their hearts.

As I made myself known, they froze. Taking in my remarkable form. Six and a half feet of perfection. I watched what little color they had in their faces drain away as it dawned on them—their precious note would never be written. I smirked in satisfaction. If not for me stopping them, the disgusting rebels could have passed on who knows what dangerous knowledge, or more likely drivel.

"Planning on going somewhere?" I asked.

As they moved to flee, they were confronted by their little predicament of being held at sword point. Rapid thuds of a third thundering heartbeat filled my ears. Someone was close. Glancing around the burning camp, I searched the immediate vicinity. My search stopped dead as my eyes landed on the edge of the battlefield. Another high fae female, and she was looking for something. Or someone.

Interesting.

With a burst of speed, I was upon her before she had time to flinch. I barely had to goad her before she was spinning around to face me. My blue eyes traveled up and down her lithe body. Taking her in.

My mouth tugged up at the corners. She had to be the most beautiful fae I had ever seen. *Aside from my own reflection.* The male being held by Sloane called out to the pretty young female. Did she just call them her parents? *This is going to be so much fun!*

Always the gentlemale, I allowed the traitors plenty of time to explain themselves, but when they didn't, they left me no choice. I gave the signal that would end in their demise.

It was swift. Despite me allowing for some pathetic last words from the mother. It would mean my new, pretty little pet should thank me later for being so honorable in the handling of her parents' deaths. And I enjoyed the thought of how she might thank me.

"She's coming with us!" I declared to Graves and Sloane. They stepped over the heads, which had annoyingly rolled in the way of their path to me. "We tell the others she was a prisoner of this camp, taken from the city to sell for her beauty."

They didn't need to be told twice. They knew if they breathed a word to anyone else, I would end them. Excitement to get my new toy back to my castle so I could play with her overshadowed my desire to stain my armor with any more filthy blood. For today, at least.

She was stunning. Her silver hair would gleam in the sunlight outside this dank, canopy covered swamp. Her curves would look divine in a properly fitted dress. Poor thing must feel so uncomfortable in the ridiculous clothes she was wearing. It was time to return home, where I could enjoy her properly.

"You hear that, female? The gracious Prince Elikai wants to save you. You better show him some respect and look at him," Graves spat, wiping the blood from his blade.

She kept her eyes sealed shut, ignoring Graves' order. "She's probably squeamish," Sloane added in a snicker.

"Graves, take her to the horses, she rides back with me," I said. "Sloane, clean your blade. You're as bad as the vermin we hunt. We must find the others, tell them we are leaving. Now."

The quiet bubbling of a stream nearby was welcome. Following it, I neared the edge and crouched down. Washing the tainted blood from my hands and face. It wasn't the luxury I was used to bathing in, but it was better than the alternative.

After cleaning my sword, I pulled out my spare canteen and filled it up. I couldn't very well contaminate my own. It contained only the best purified water for me to drink. Feeling a little more like myself, I rushed back to see my birthday gift. Not bothering to waste time on tightening the lid.

Thank the fates, Graves and Sloane weren't completely incompetent and had followed my orders. The guards were readying the horses, and Alaric was making his way over to the group from the opposite direction. Blood coating his mouth of all places.

Strange male.

I'd have to think about that another time when I could be bothered to give the brute a moment of my precious thoughts. Right now, there was something much more pressing to deal with.

Striding up to my pretty little pet, I poured the contents of the canteen over her silver hair. Washing away the grime coating her face. Of course, I needed to be sure she wasn't hiding any nasties. Like a huge mole. No, the fates wouldn't be so cruel.

My heart rate calmed as her, thankfully, mole-free face glared up at me. Large green eyes filled with an emotion I couldn't quite place. Adoration? Apprehension? Appreciation... Yes, that was it. Had to be. She was overcome with gratitude that I was here to rescue her. I would, of course, allow her to show that gratitude later—once she'd had several long, hot baths.

"What's your name, pretty girl?" I asked, lacing my words with charm.

"Fuck you!" she spat.

My eyes widened, nostrils flaring. That attitude simply wouldn't do; it would need to be broken out of her. Raising my hand, I fisted it in her knotted hair, pulling her forward.

My lips grazed her ear as I whispered so quietly that not even the shifters would hear. "That's no way to talk to a prince. Now is it, pretty girl?" I asked. "One who is *saving* you from this squalor and can offer you everything." She was rigid under my grip. "Now, I am going to ask you again for your name, and you are going to tell me. If you know what's good for you, you will pretend those weren't your traitorous parents I had killed back there, and stick to the story. Like a good little pet."

A sigh of defeat left her lips. The sound was intoxicating.

"Now." Pulling back, I released my hold. "What's your name, pretty pet?" I had no doubt she'd comply this time.

"E-Evangelia," she rasped.

Best. Birthday. Ever.

CHAPTER 5

Evangelia

My body was numb as they manhandled me onto a black horse, forcing me to straddle behind *him*. The evil bastard who killed my parents for sport, and my entire camp, then left them for carrion. I leaned back in an attempt to put what little space the horse's back could afford between us. But it was no use.

Reaching behind, he took my shaking hands in his and wrapped them around his waist. Pulling me closer to his back and locking my cold fingers in place.

"It's fine pretty girl. You can hold on tight to me," he said.

My thumb slid through the thick, liquid substance coating his leathers, making me flinch. The thought of what it could be had my stomach churning.

"Righ', we've a long trek home and a few stops to make on the way," a scarred male announced. A warrior. Even sat atop his horse, he was huge. His familiar accent surprised me, but not as much as the crimson smudged across his face and neck.

As the convoy of my enemies began to ride, it was clear we were leaving the Fading Vale. If I weren't so numb, perhaps I'd be relieved. Knowing the other rebel camps would be left alone to live and fight another day.

The moment we were moving, the vile individual between my thighs began to talk. "What the oaf meant to say is that we will be riding back to *my* castle. You will, of course, know who I am. Prince Elikai Regis, heir to the Dezrothian throne and your knight in shining armor."

Not a single muscle in my body reacted. Perhaps because I didn't want him to know what he said was a surprise to me. Or I'd given up already. Not caring to learn about my captor. *What's the point?*

"It's understandable you are a little shocked right now at your luck for catching such a fine male's eye," he boasted. "If it were up to me, I would get you straight back to my tub and have you cleaned up. Not bothering to collect the remainder of the pitiful coin and crops the shameful beings this far from Ezerat offer up to us. But alas, they feel the need to give back to my father, the king, for his generosity. So we must sacrifice our time."

He paused, as though expecting a pat on the back. If I had my knives filling my palms, perhaps I'd oblige.

His lies allowed my anger to break through some of the numbness. I was no fool; the villagers were forced to give what little they had over to the greedy king. To make out like it was an offering of gratitude was bullshit. A falsehood no one in the realm would buy. Not even the most loyal royalists and purists.

"For all of your beauty, I doubt there is much brain. But I can assure you, so long as you're a good little pet, you will want for nothing," he continued. "You see, pretty girl, I came of age today and plan to take the throne at my earliest opportunity. I have immense plans which I am very much looking forward to starting. I've been searching for a high fae as beautiful as you, and–"

Long minutes blurred into hours as he spoke about himself—*his* plans, *his* throne, *his* castle, *his* need for a queen.

I tuned him out, tracking my surroundings instead. Searching for an opportunity to escape. I doubted the prince would notice my absence, but the horde soldiers were a problem. I didn't need to see them to know their eyes bore into me from every direction.

As dusk gave way to the moon, my still damp hair didn't help keep the bitter cold at bay. Closing my eyes, I tried to escape into the delusion of how today was supposed to go. I hadn't seen Nix since he disappeared into the battle. The possibility he met the same fate as my parents left me paralyzed with grief.

We drew to a stop, and I banished the intrusive thoughts, opening my eyes to see where we were.

The prince dismounted and my gaze followed as he and the scarred male—the one I now knew to be the horde's general—strode toward a couple of fae in the shadows of a building. I recognized one of them.

The old female from whom I'd bought blankets only this afternoon.

Fates be cursed. Was this their idea of a sick joke? This couldn't be happening, right?

Did I not have enough pain to battle, without needing such a blatant reminder of how everything had fallen apart today?

She stood with, who I assumed to be, the village elder. Squinting her beady eyes in my direction. Just as she looked as though she was about to speak, I cut her off with a glare and a sharp shake of my head.

Any sign of her knowing me would only bring questions. I'd overheard Elikai telling the guards riding with us his bullshit version of events. The one that included 'saving' me from being a prisoner of the Fading Vale rebels.

The prince was scowling. Demanding coin on top of the harvest I knew they'd slaved to prepare in time for these gluttonous assholes.

Then he demanded a bed.

The look he gave me had me sending a silent prayer to the fates. To give me the strength to survive this sick predator.

We entered the boarding house's accommodations, and my stomach rolled.

Tutting, he shook his head. Pointing to a space on the floor, he said. "You sleep there, pretty pet."

Relief washed over me as he deemed me too unclean to share his bed. Without argument, I laid down to sleep on the floor, not caring as I watched a roach scuttle out from under the bed.

As I lay awake, my mind was plagued by the images and sounds of the ambush. So much death, and all so needless and unjust.

The king himself may not have been present for the slaughter, but he was ultimately to blame.

As much as I tried to shut it all out, I couldn't think of anything else. Despite knowing I needed to use the journey to the castle to make a plan of my own.

I needed to focus. If I didn't, my parents' sacrifice would be for naught.

MORNING CAME TOO SOON and before long, I was leaving the boarding house, still in yesterday's clothes.

The hulking, scarred male was staring at me from over by the horses. As I neared, his nose wrinkled, and I was suddenly self-conscious.

Shaking it off, I asked. "Can I help you?" Though I knew we'd never met before yesterday, he seemed familiar. Not only his accent, but his scent, too.

Familiar, yet not really, at the same time.

Leather and cedarwood filled my nostrils. I could admit it was much more pleasant than the iron-soaked scent that had been coating him the previous day.

Fates help me, I couldn't think straight. My mind was tormented with images of my parent's faces. The look in their eyes when they realized they were about to die.

And chose to accept it.

Taking a deep breath, I counted back from ten. Focusing my mind back on the male before me. He definitely reminded me of someone, but I couldn't put my finger on who.

"Nah. Yer Prince will be right out and we will be makin' our way," he said. "Long, hard ride ahead of us." His tone was dismissive as he focused on saddling his horse.

"Alaric, do leave the princess-to-be alone," Elikai's smarmy voice called as he approached me from behind.

His palm settled possessively on my waist. My heart began to thunder at his words and proximity. Panic set in and my hands reached for my daggers on instinct. Only to be reminded they were missing.

When they'd disarmed me, I had been too trapped in my turmoil to heed what was happening.

The words 'princess-to-be' circled around my mind, and memories of his ramblings on yesterday's ride assaulted me. About his queen, and the things he was looking forward to doing to her. It became sharper all of a sudden.

An alarm began to blare in my mind as I pieced it together.

My mouth clamped shut to hold back the nausea. My fight-or-flight instincts kicked in at last. He'd been talking about me…

With another deep breath, I swallowed the cold, hard facts. It was becoming clear there was no chance I would be able to escape, not with Prince Dickwad and several members of the horde watching over me.

If by some miracle I did get away, where would I go?

If there were any survivors at camp, they would have long since left the area by now. Where would I even begin looking for them?

It was inevitable, I was going to end up in the castle. But if what Elikai had been saying was true, then it didn't sound like I would be a prisoner…

It dawned that I was heading straight for the place King Regis calls home.

The place where the bastard who is to blame for the miserable existence my family and friends have had to endure lives.

The place where he would be the most vulnerable.

As Elikai's guest, or whatever I was to him, I might very well have access to the person responsible for causing a lifetime of nothing but pain and grief, fear and anguish to everyone in my life.

To me.

If I could play the part well enough, gain some trust, I might actually have a shot at the king.

It wouldn't be easy and would end in my execution, but what did I have to lose? If there was any possibility I could kill the king, and end the evil that has plagued Dezrothia for centuries, then I had to take it.

I'd have to be cautious. Couldn't charge in with no weapons and no knowledge of the castle. I would be in unfamiliar territory, relying only on the training I'd been given.

It wasn't much, not against the king. Especially after what I witnessed yesterday. But I'd managed to survive this long.

With that, the heavy weight in my chest lifted slightly. Though the cloud of grief was still present, it felt a little easier to breathe again. To properly think things through.

I had a purpose. Now just to come up with a tactic and play the long game.

CHAPTER 6

Alaric

"General, hello? Alaric?" One of my soldiers said. Which one, I had no fucking clue.

Elikai's female was proving to be an unwelcome distraction. I should be focused on the training drill, not the way her unusual silver hair billowed in the wind.

Yet here I was, watching her from the battle yard, throwing out commands that were half-hearted at best.

"What?" I snapped, whirling on the group.

"We finished the drill," the same voice said. "Are we ok to sleep now?" *Tyran*. Sweat glistened on his brow as he fought the impulse to cower. "Get rested, so we are ready for the last stretch tomorrow?" His tone was both cautious and desperate.

Elikai had demanded we make it back an entire day earlier than scheduled. Said he needed the extra time to *'prepare'* Evangelia for his party set to take place on the night of our return.

Being so heavily loaded, carrying food and coin, it would be impossible to gain a full day.

We'd be lucky to arrive a few hours earlier than expected. Of course, he wouldn't hear it. We rode from dawn until dusk every day.

The entire hunting party was exhausted from spending so many hours on horseback. But they needed these work out sessions each night to stretch out their muscles. Not that they appreciated them.

Well, aside from Krista, it seemed.

A glance around the yard of the inn we were staying at tonight showed half the group slumped on the floor. While the others were slouched against one thing or another.

Crossing my arms, I nodded. Dismissing them. They wasted no time scrambling to their rooms.

Apart from Krista. She sauntered over to me as she had every night during the relentless ride home. Preparing to make small talk again, no doubt.

I fucking hated small talk.

Resting a hand on my bicep, she fluttered her lashes. Was she at long last getting ready to make her move? Fates I hoped not. I didn't mix business with pleasure. It didn't matter how fucking badly I needed to bend a female over right now.

A shrug of my shoulders forced her to drop her hand. "Go and get some rest," I said. "We've an early start tomorrow."

Giving her my back, I strode over to the campfire. Elikai was notably absent this evening, meaning Evangelia sat alone. Not bothering to turn and check that the bear shifter had gotten the message, I perched on one of the logs circling the fire across from the female who didn't need to do anything to pull my undivided attention.

She didn't have the look of a fae rescued by her Prince Charming. More of someone heading to their execution. Which didn't make a shred of fucking sense.

I could navigate a female body with no complaints, but their minds... They were a whole other complex puzzle. One I wasn't versed in.

All I knew for certain was that every time the wind floated her scent in my direction, it did something to me. Gave me an overwhelming need to sink into a female in the most carnal way. Soon.

Just not Krista.

And ideally with Kane across from me, in a room filled with screams of pleasure. Pure lust, no messy bullshit—like feelings.

That first morning in the gnome village, after Elikai strolled over and damn near claimed her as his bride, I could have sworn I saw a flash of panic in her eyes. As though she hadn't liked his declaration. Or at least hadn't expected it.

In the days that followed, she'd remained mostly quiet. Only speaking when someone directed a question or comment her way.

The female's answers were monosyllabic and to the point. Even when Krista tried to engage her. She seemed to indulge Elikai a bit more than anyone else, but he barely spoke to her directly. More to the rest of us *about* her.

Over the past week, he'd endlessly bragged about his prowess on the battlefield to his minions. All for Evangelia's benefit. I'd lost count of how many times I'd rolled my eyes.

In reality, he'd blown the whole fuckin' ambush. He was lucky to be alive with the stupid stunt he pulled.

When he told her every villager that he'd gifted with his presence either fainted or stumbled over themselves in awe of him, I'd snorted. The truth of it was, they couldn't stand him and wanted to string him up.

It shouldn't shock me anymore how delusional he could be. Annoyingly, now that we were in the towns surrounding the city, he wasn't wrong.

He often boasted he had the most beautiful bride in the land. That, at least, I could agree with. She was one of the most beautiful females I had ever seen, and I was no young pup.

During the prince's constant spurts of bullshit, I didn't miss the way Evangelia leaned her body away from him. Almost like she was cringing. Yes, he was self-absorbed and pretentious, but even with his faults—and there were too many to count—fae never reacted to his affections that way. I'd spent enough time with his twin to know.

Not my fucking business. I was looking too far into it. Perhaps she was playing hard to get? What did I know about females? I spent no more time around them than was necessary to fuck them until we were both sated. Aside from the female soldiers I trained daily, but I kept my cock well away from the training hall.

Still, Evangelia's strange behavior had me on edge. What female in her situation didn't dream about being saved by a prince? Living out her immortal life no longer in the Fading Vale as a prisoner, but as a princess residing in a castle.

A couple of days ago, she'd *really* surprised me. We'd stopped for the night, deciding to pitch up between villages. Rather than sitting around, lost in her own head again, she'd started to help us.

She worked in silence, not needing any instruction, like she knew her way around setting up a camp. Then Elikai stopped her from doing *'peasant's work'*. Her face had dropped, like she hadn't wanted him to excuse her from the task.

Drawing in a lungful of her intoxicating scent, I found I was staring again. Why was I so drawn to her?

"Are you waiting for someone?" she asked. With her arms already wrapped around her legs, she hugged her knees tighter. Of course she would wonder why the fuck I'd sat down opposite her and stared in silence for fates knew how long. I was wondering the same fucking thing.

Clearing my too-dry throat, I said, "Where were yeh from before yeh were taken by the rebels?" I was genuinely curious. If she was going to be coming to the castle with us, I should at least try to speak to her. Learn more about her than just her name. As general, I had a duty to the king to make sure there were no threats.

Ignoring me, she gazed into the fire. "How long were yeh with the thrakos and rebel camp?" I asked, trying a different approach.

The bitter air blew through the yard with a howl. "Years," she whispered, not looking at me. Her green eyes remained dead set on the flames as she began rubbing her forearms. Winter was moving in on the land fast.

Her strange scent was similar to the campfire crackling away between us. Though more feminine with a hint of creamy vanilla. Despite the fact she'd not properly washed all week, it wasn't awful. Krista had offered to lend her some clean clothes, but Elikai had immediately refused.

It didn't matter how enticing it was to me. I would forever ignore it. Thanks to the Lores in place. Her being claimed by the heir to the throne only cemented that fact.

She hadn't looked too happy when he'd dropped the princess-to-be bombshell. Sure, it was quick, they'd just met, but maybe they were true mates?

It was rare, but not unheard of. The prince was a spoiled, jammy bastard. If anyone was going to find the other half of their soul the day they became old enough for the fates to grant one, it was him. *Entitled prick.*

Still, the last thing I needed was the king taking my head for treason.

"Well, we'll be back at the capital tomorrow with yer prince, so nothin' to worry 'bout anymore," I said.

The ungrateful brat scoffed at me.

I should leave her out here on her own, instead I asked, "What do yeh think of the villages?" I *never* made fucking small talk.

Taking a deep breath, she pushed off the log to stand. Shoulders back, she turned, looking down at me. "That the king doesn't care about his citizens," she stated. "That he sits on his pompous ass, lording over fae rather than actually caring about them."

Her tone left no room for questioning what she thought. And fuck, I was glad Elikai wasn't here. Did she have a death wish?

Maybe she'd been brainwashed while being the rebels' prisoner?

"Better watch yer tongue, lass. Words like that will get yeh killed," I said to no one. She'd already moved, heading inside, not finding the conversation worth continuing after saying her peace.

"Ah, there you are. Come Evelynn," Elikai's voice chimed as he appeared in the doorway.

Did he know her name was Evangelia? Fuck if I was going to correct him.

"Our room is this way. Pay no mind to the brute." Nudging her into the inn, his voice trailed away.

I headed to my room, thanking the fates that we would be back home tomorrow. We wouldn't make the prince's demands on timing, but he would have a good twelve hours to pretty himself for his big party.

Despite being bone tired, my mind raced as I stripped off for bed. Sleep wouldn't come to me for a long while yet.

An idea formed in my mind, and I acted on impulse. Something I never did.

Opening the window of my first-floor room, I shifted into my wolf. Then leaped out into the night.

My giant black paws hit the ground running, moving toward the capitol. It had to be a quick trip, and I had to be back at the inn before sunrise for us to set out for the day, but it was necessary.

The air rushed past me; it was always so freeing to run in my wolf form. There were no cares. Only running, hunting, eating and sleeping.

Politics and duties never came into it. It was so simple. I hated that I couldn't shift in the castle because of the wards. The king placed them there centuries ago to stop shifters from getting any ideas.

Like shifting and eating him.

He wouldn't taste nice—too bitter.

My paws slowed as I hit the cobblestone road. Turning and weaving down the narrow side streets, the darkness worked in my favor. Helping to conceal me as I reached my destination.

Creeping toward an old wooden door, I pawed and scratched at it. I couldn't shift back, not yet. It wasn't safe from prying eyes.

When the door opened, the female on the other side took one look at me before gesturing for me to get inside. Peering up and down the street first, she swiftly shut the door tight. Bolting it.

I shifted back into my fae form, not bothering to cover up or ask for clothes. Time was of the essence. Besides, she wouldn't care, having seen it all before many times.

"Ma', I've got news for yeh. I dinnae have long before I need to leave again, jus' hear me out–"

CHAPTER 7
Evangelia

The week-long ride had been arduous. Not only was it physically tiring, but mentally I was drained.

Every time I thought Elikai couldn't be any more insane, he would prove me wrong.

I'd always known the world was a dangerous place filled with evil. But the prince… He was something no amount of training or wise words from my parents could have prepared me for.

I tried not to think about them. It only led to my heart tearing in two all over again, and it wouldn't change anything. My parents were gone forever. Ripped away from me by this self-absorbed, pretentious, spoiled prick in front of me.

Then there was Nix. Whenever he entered my thoughts, I was overcome with a tidal wave of anxiety. It was the not knowing where he was or what happened to him that kept me up at night. *Nothing you can do to change that here, Eva.*

At least I had a plan. It was stupid and reckless, but having a purpose was better than feeling helpless. It helped me compartmentalize my grief too. To lock away the worry for my friends whose fates were unknown.

Now was not a time for tears. It was time to focus on how best to get close enough to the king to strike. As we approached the castle, fae lined the streets, cheering Elikai's name as though he were a saint.

At the gate, darkness descended. It took a moment to realize Elikai had thrown his cloak over me. I frowned. He hadn't worried about me being cold for the entire journey to this point, so why now?

When he righted it to cover my face and body, I realized it wasn't to keep me warm at all, but to hide me. He didn't want his admirers seeing my unkempt hair and torn commoner clothes. *Ugh, I hate him.*

He hadn't let me bathe for the entire journey, only allowing me to use a washcloth to clean the essentials. I'd asked why, and he claimed it was because he wanted my transformation from *'pauper to princess'* to be a surprise for him. That we needed to be in Ezerat for him to arrange suitable attire and makeup for me.

Utter bullshit. It was a control thing. He wanted to make me feel like I owed him for offering me the life he assumed a female like me would wish for.

Fates, it had been hard to bite my tongue, but deciding to pick my battles, I hadn't argued. It kept his advances at bay, and for that, I would bathe in pig shit if I had to.

Pushing the cloak away from my eyes, I looked up and gasped. The few books I'd found about the capital city, Ezerat, I'd read until the pages began to fall out. They hadn't prepared me in the least for what it would be like seeing it in the flesh.

Awe rushed through me as I took in the looming building. Perched atop a mountain, the natural stone blended seamlessly with that of the walls. A cobblestone road led to a pointed archway flanked with statues. The crest of the king sat above with a pride I couldn't fathom.

We passed through the gates and the royal household was revealed. Towering walls cast shadows across the courtyard. Curved towers, topped with flying flags at their peaks, protruded from the long parapets. While the body of the castle rose behind them.

Never having seen a building so imposing I couldn't look at it all at once, I gaped at the beauty of it. It pained me to admit, but I couldn't wait to get inside. To explore and find all the secrets it held.

A chuckle tugged me away from my admiration. Elikai had stopped performing for his admirers, catching me staring up at his home.

"To your liking is it, pretty girl?" he asked. I cringed at the closeness of him. He dismounted, then held out his hand to help me. Ignoring it, I climbed down.

Despite my show of disrespect, his face was full of glee. "Now," he cleared his throat. "It's time to show you my quarters. I have been looking forward to this the whole journey home."

As I shied away, he took my arm. Dragging me through the courtyard toward the castle entrance. My eyes widened as they fell upon the entryway. The grand hall was decorated with intricate, high-arching ceilings. Painted with obvious care and adoration. With huge stained-glass windows reflecting their colors across a flagstone floor.

Portraits along the walls told tales of the ruler's history in their captured images. I wanted to spend hours taking it all in. *Alone.*

There was a staircase off to the left of the room, sweeping up and out of sight. A doorway beyond opened to another bright room I couldn't quite see inside. I had never seen a place so beautiful. My brain couldn't register the details fast enough before I was pulled up the stairs.

Elikai was talking to me, but I couldn't focus on what he was saying with everything new around me. As I brushed my gaze around a room or hallway, I'd find something else to appreciate. From the staggering craftsmanship of the side tables to the sconces lining the walls. Even the doors were stunning, the wainscotting something I had only ever seen pictures of.

Without warning, I was pushed into a room. It was bright, airy, and approximately the size of an entire village inn. There was a large four-poster bed along one wall. So excessive I would get lost in it.

The most I got to sleep in a bed was on my rare village visits, and only on the occasion that our camp was more than a day's walk away. The rest of the time, I had a sleep sack.

The room was so vast, even the extravagant furniture looked lost. A chest of drawers stood beside the wardrobe, which was ajar with colorful fabric spilling out. There was a dining table with four chairs, hand carved with intricate details in a corner away from the bed.

Plush armchairs and a couch were placed in a semi-circle around the open fireplace. Burning bright as it overpowered any chill that threatened to seep in.

Off to the side was an open door. I had no idea what the room held, but at the trickling sound of running water, I tried not to get excited by the prospect of plumbing. And a proper bath.

"–having you look like you do. Once you've been cleaned up, I will come back for you." Elikai said. "Witch!" he yelled into the room. "She looks anything less than perfect, and it will be your head."

"Yes, Your Highness," a small female said, appearing from the mystery doorway. She bowed low, her gaze fixed on the floor. She wore a simple dress of blue and gray, with caramel hair pulled back from her face.

The prince turned and placed a firm hand on my shoulder, making me face him. "It won't be a quick fix. I will busy myself for the day," he said. "I ensured we made it back early today to give you adequate time to rectify the..." he paused, trying to find the words to describe my current appearance and falling short.

He waved his hand toward my face, as if that would explain everything, then looked to the other female. "Just do what you need to do, peasant," he spat. "And be sure to hide those unsightly bags under her eyes."

He squeezed my shoulder tighter. "Any problems with the handmaiden, you will tell me. I can get you a replacement easily, Evangelica."

I hated how he said it, like she wasn't standing right there. His incapability to remember my name was frustrating, but easy enough to ignore.

"I am planning a surprise for you this evening, pretty pet. You'll present every part the princess when I fetch you," he finished. Turning on his heel, he left the way we had come in.

Looking over to the handmaiden—still stooped in a bow—I said, "Oh, um... hey. I'm Evangelia."

Crossing the distance between us, I held out my hand. After a moment's hesitation, she glanced up and took it, straightening her spine.

"Thalia," she said. "My family has been serving the Regis royal family for hundreds of years. I assure you, I come with the highest training to best be able to see to your every need, milady." Her tone was gentle, but her gaze stayed on the pair of rings adorning my fingers for longer than I was comfortable with.

Could she sense the magic? My parents had said it wasn't possible.

Awkwardness hung in the air between us. "Thanks, I guess." Having never had anyone to wait on me in my life, I didn't know what to say. How to act. "But you really don't have to..." Her face dropped and I hesitated, trailing off.

"Your bath is ready," she said, beckoning me to follow. "Wouldn't want it getting cold, milady."

Standing at the edge of the tub, I inhaled the beautiful scent of rose petals. Thalia dipped her fingers into the water, muttered a spell, and steam slowly started to rise.

Happy with the temperature, she reached toward me. Insistent hands pulled at the buckles on Elikai's cloak as she tried to undress me. Stepping out of her grasp, I raised my palms. "Oh, that won't be necessary," I said. "If I can bathe in a babbling brook, I'm sure I can manage in a warm tub. Thank you all the same."

Her brows knit in confusion, then panic flared in her eyes. "How about you grab me a towel, and I can let you know when I'm done?" I suggested.

For my plan to have any chance of succeeding, I needed some allies in the castle, and there was no one better to learn the layout of the place from than a handmaiden. Her family's history with the Regis' meant her loyalties would run deep, but that was okay. I just needed to play it smart. Think about every word before speaking it.

The witch hesitated for a moment, looking from me to the door, and back again. I sighed my relief when she left, pushing the door closed to offer a modicum of privacy. *Is this how royals live?* It was a wonder they knew how to put one foot in front of the other all by themselves.

Though I wanted to dive straight in, I familiarized myself with my new surroundings first. Looking for exits. The tub was enormous, taking up an entire side. With room to fit several fae of all shapes and species at once. On the opposite side were two sinks, side by side, sat next to a toilet that flushed.

The bitter laugh that escaped me caught me by surprise as I imagined asking Prince Elikai for a bucket to relieve myself in. Just to see his reaction.

Making quick work of my clothes, I dipped my toes in to test the water. It was just on this side of scorching and felt wonderful. Stepping into the tub, I groaned at the feel of my coiled muscles relaxing.

I sat cross-legged in the water and tried not to let in the dark thoughts banging at my brain. Instead, I found myself thinking about how Thalia heated the water so perfectly and in mere seconds. Wishing I had such a gift for when I made it back to the Fading Vale alone.

I hadn't met many witches, only those who lived with us at the camp. Of them, one was full-blooded. Well, she had been, until she'd disappeared. The others were all hybrids. Still, I took their magic for granted.

A witch's power varied greatly from witch to witch. Family lines played a considerable role in their strength. Though they mostly lived in the capital and Crystal Towers, my parents taught me as a small child how to recognize one. Even if Elikai hadn't called her a witch at the top of his lungs, Thalia would have given herself away soon enough with the whisper of the spell that heated the water.

The best way to stop a witch from casting was to gag her. Or him. Stop them voicing their spells.

Closing my eyes, I remembered the day Nix and I read his mother's grimoire. The memory stung. Needing a distraction, I pulled my hair over my shoulder and started loosening the braids woven in.

The faintest of knocks sounded at the door. "Milady?" Thalia called. "Do you need any help? I am at your disposal."

A pang of guilt pinched me. Elikai made it clear her position was on the line if she didn't tend to me adequately. I highly doubted he would care whether she couldn't do her job because I refused her help.

Releasing a sigh, I said, "I suppose I could use some help detangling these braids?"

She all but threw the door open, hurrying inside, blue eyes bright. "Of course. Please allow me!" she said.

My heart raced at the prospect of someone helping me with something so intimate, but her hands were already making quick work of my hair before I could change my mind. Pulling my knees to my chest, I let her run her fingers through the knots and tangles. She paused to grab a comb, and I relaxed a little as she began brushing through.

Foam fell on my skin as she lathered up a sweet-smelling shampoo. Then, reaching for a pitcher, she filled it with fresh water. Flattening a palm against my forehead, I tilted back, closed my eyes and tried to enjoy the sensation of the soothing warm liquid trickling over my scalp.

"Thank you," I murmured, my voice a little hoarse.

Wiping the suds from my eyes with the back of my palm, I was mortified to look down and see the color of the water I now sat in. She didn't comment though, just held out a bar of soap and washcloth. Thank the fates she was leaving me to do this part myself.

After scrubbing thoroughly, I went to stand and step out, but Thalia shook her head to stop me. Without a word, she pulled out the plug, and I watched with a furrowed brow as the grimy water drained away.

While I covered myself as best as I could with my arms, she reinserted the plug and water gushed from the facet. Heat pricked my cheeks as she ran me another bath, warming it to the perfect temperature with her magic as it filled.

Three baths later, with the water rinsing clear, Thalia was at last satisfied. She handed me a thin chemise and beckoned me to follow her out of the bathing chambers.

Pulling out a measuring tape, she gestured for me to stand, arms out. Took my measurements with haste, then passed me a white fluffy dressing gown.

"Kindly wait here please milady, I won't be long."

SEEKING COMFORT IN THE FLAMES, I sat in front of a blazing fireplace. The only thing in the lavish bedchamber that reminded me of home. Of my parents.

Before long, my thoughts turned to the prince. What sort of surprise could he have in store? I dreaded to think. He was so unpredictable, making it impossible to guess what he was planning. The only thing I was certain of—it wouldn't be anything good.

Watching the flickers of red and yellow dance, guilt plagued me as my mind turned to Nix again. To my friends in the Rebel Alliance who were more like extended family. I fiddled the rings on my fingers, considering where the survivors might be hiding now.

The Fading Vale was boundless. It took weeks to walk through the forest's depths to reach the coast. Months to walk around the perimeter.

Its sheer size made it the best place for fae like me to hide. The trouble was, you could wind up lost in there for years without seeing another soul.

Shit. Nix could need me while I'm sitting here idle. In a castle, being waited on for no reason other than a prince deeming me pretty enough to be his new plaything. Fates only knew how long it would last until the novelty wore off and he grew bored.

Still, it was crucial I remained looking like a high fae and did not shift. If they found out what I was, it would be my execution, or worse...

It was best to stick to Elikai's story. So long as the king thought I was some damsel, rescued by his son from my captors in the Fading Vale, I had time. He'd be less likely to pay too close attention or start asking real questions. Like, who was I really? And what did I want?

That didn't help my little psychotic prince problem, though.

Much of what he said during our journey had made me sick to my stomach. Particularly the comments he mumbled, too hushed for anyone else's ears. I hadn't said much of anything in response, just ran my options over in my head for days.

In the end, I figured my best one was to play the part of his perfect, pretty little pet. For now, at least. Until I could kill the king.

Elikai was completely self-obsessed, with an ego big enough to fill the Vale, but the story he had woven was likely going to give me my best chance to succeed.

If I survived the role of assassin I assigned myself, I would escape, head back to the Fading Vale and look for the lost.

Until then, I couldn't break.

A knock sounded at the door, and the most delicious scent of apple and cinnamon assaulted my nostrils.

CHAPTER 8
Nekane

My body absorbed the warmth of the heated tub like a sponge, chasing away the chill seeping through the cracks in the castle walls.

I was very aware I should get out more, speak to fae, make 'friends'. Only, I didn't fancy being used. Life was fine as it was. I didn't need to welcome the potential for any drama.

Fae flocked to me for no reason other than my status. What if I wasn't a prince? What if I was just another commoner?

Once the water cooled to an uncomfortable degree, I pulled myself from it with a sigh. Time to get ready and head for the tavern. Again.

Another day, the same routine.

Crossing my wing of the castle, I passed the guest suites and communal rooms without giving much thought to anything until a bustle of commotion from Kai's wing snagged my attention. Was he back? Deciding the tavern could wait a few minutes, I followed the sound.

My brother's maid, Thalia, was red faced behind a pile of pressed sheets as she entered his chambers with haste. She hadn't been expecting him back yet, either. I opened my mouth to ask if Kai and Alaric had returned, but several more fae, all huddled together, came into view.

Castle staff and residents gathered in the stairway, climbing over each other to get a peek through the narrow windows at the end of the long hall.

The squealing and cheers coming from the courtyard below met my ears, growing louder with every step I took. Upon seeing me, the staff stepped aside, making room at the window.

Peering out, I found Kai without much effort. Sat upon his horse, with a cloaked figure behind him. Though I couldn't make out who through the thick crowd surrounding him.

I couldn't hear his words, but I had no doubt he'd be touting himself as a hero. Winning the hearts of the fae and showing them why he was much better suited for the crown than I would ever be.

Not that I cared.

He and our father were of a shared opinion about the kingdom, and I kept my opinions to myself. Self-preservation and all that.

With Kai busy, and Alaric likely needing to debrief the king before I could see him, I decided to wait in the library. My favorite room sat centrally on our floor of the castle, between mine and Kai's chambers. Near the guest suites that were never used, and the breakfast room that was always well stocked and never disappointed.

Our father had no love for books, having destroyed thousands when his reign began. Anything that so much as mentioned half-breeds had been eviscerated. Along with every text that referenced any kingdom outside Dezrothia and anything else he deemed offensive.

Once, shortly after a king and queen of a neighboring realm had visited the castle, I'd searched for books about true mates. I was young and found myself fascinated with the way the two fae looked at each other. I'd never seen that kind of affection in my short life. Though I knew better now, my naïve little mind had started to wonder if my parents had such a bond too.

Thinking back, I probably wanted to know if that was why my dad had always been such a prick to me. If the blame he put on me for his wife's death was justified. If he had loved her more deeply than even himself, and I had been the thing that had taken her from him.

With the official castle library neglected and thousands of books collecting dust, Kai and I decided to build our own library on our floor, using the room we were homeschooled in. It had been a bare, but expansive, space. With little more than two desks and a blackboard placed in its center.

We were bored and often left to our own devices while growing up. So, to fill the time between meals and classes, we planned out our vision for the library, and had the castle's carpenter build new shelves to our specifications. Gradually, we lugged every last book up the three flights of stairs to their new home.

It took years to get it to what it is now. I wasn't even sure if the king knew what we'd achieved all those years ago, but it was my sanctuary.

Well, if you didn't include the training hall and the Crooked Claw.

Kai used to spend a lot of time here too, but over the past several years, he'd lost interest and barely stepped foot inside it anymore.

AFTER I'D SPENT some time getting lost in the shelves and the pages they held, I figured I'd waited long enough. The cheering had died down outside a while ago, so I headed for Kai's chambers first. I'd given him plenty of time to settle back in and freshen up.

It would be the first time seeing each other since our coming of age. I wasn't expecting him to look any different. It was rare for anything to change from a physical point of view when you came into your immortality. I just needed to reassure myself that he was whole.

Despite having grown apart, he was still my twin, and I loved him no less. We had been so close as children, and I resented my father for treating us so differently. Not because I was the one he treated badly, but because it had driven a wedge between us. I didn't show it, but I missed the boy I used to create havoc with. We'd shared a bond that others couldn't understand.

Kai seemed pretty focused on the crown now. While I was more focused on...

What am I focused on?

Training? Females? Day drinking? All of the above?

The hunts had never appealed to me, but it would have been nice to celebrate together. While he got to go on an adventure for his coming of age, I'd spent it drunk and avoiding my father.

He was in a foul mood when he saw me on a normal day, but my coming of age was also the twenty-fifth anniversary of his wife's death, and he'd been out of control.

Despite my best efforts to avoid him, he found me as I returned to the castle, wasted, as usual. Then reminded me I was worth nothing to him. Like I needed the reminder. As expected, he'd not bothered to pull his punches either. Not now that my body healed so much faster.

As I neared Kai's door, my thoughts soured thinking of the asshole who'd sired me. Forcing a mask of indifference to blanket my features, I knocked twice before opening it to greet him.

With a fresh, winning smile in place, I stepped inside.

Coming face to face with a silver-haired beauty.

My senses swam with campfires, vanilla and rose petals. "Fuck, you smell good enough to eat," I said, licking my lips. Fates I could feast on her like a starved male for days on end, if only to be close to that scent.

A large robe hid her curves, and I cursed the castle for being so ancient and cold. My eyes traced over what little of her body was on display, zeroing in on legs that were beautiful and toned. I was willing to bet the rest of her was too.

She was ethereal. Hair that shone like polished silver, with the most unusual onyx streak framing her face. The flash of dark making her emerald green eyes glow.

While the glow from the fire, burning away in the hearth, gave her a warrior's aura. Or perhaps that was thanks to the glare she'd turned on me.

Whatever I'd planned to say next died as my mouth filled with moisture. Enraptured with thoughts of all the ways I could have this female screaming within minutes begging for my cock. Teetering on the edge of ecstasy.

Who was she?

What was she doing in here?

No way she was from the city. I'd spent years fucking my way through it, and I'd have remembered that face.

The female scowled. "I thought you were giving me the day to be ready for you?"

What the fuck was she talking about? Had we met before? Perhaps when I was drunk?

With that thought, I switched on the charm, moving to lean against the back of a nearby armchair. "As much as that sounds like a wet dream, princess, I can hardly expect I'd be lucky enough for a beauty such as yourself to be getting ready for me–"

I winked and immediately regretted it. But then her cheeks went from pink to scarlet, and a smirk tugged at my lips.

"–especially before we've even been formally introduced." I finished, giving her a dimpled smile.

The frown that creased her brow in return gave me pause. The dimples worked every time. What the fuck?

"Did I miss something?" she snapped.

Did I?

No, I hadn't met this female before.

"What I mean to say is," I paused, rubbing the back of my neck as her brows rose. "I said no such thing about giving you the day to be ready for me."

"Yes. You did." She retorted, moving to stand so she was facing me directly. "You told Thalia that I was to look like a princess for your big surprise tonight!" She said, wrapping air quotes around 'big surprise' before crossing her arms over her chest.

I swallowed the laugh creeping up my throat as it dawned on me—she had me confused for Kai. I couldn't blame her, only those closest to us could tell us apart.

"Ah, of course he did," I replied with a smirk. Pushing up from my perch, I crossed my arms, mimicking her position as I met her gaze.

How to play this? I would have to come clean soon, but fuck it was fun watching her get all worked up. The fire in her eyes made the green pop.

"He?" she seethed. "You're referring to yourself in third person now?" She unfolded her arms in exasperation. "Of course you are. Did anyone ever tell you your split personality is exhausting, Elikai?"

Her face reddened and nostrils flared as she got more frustrated.

"I agreed to play the part of your damsel in distress, but I'm drawing the line at whatever this weird role play game is you're trying. Don't think for a second that every time I look at you, I don't see the monster hiding underneath your annoyingly perfect skin," she vented.

She took a step toward me, pointing at my chest, but halted. Drawing a deep breath into her lungs. Her lips moved ever so subtly, and I could have sworn she was counting.

Perhaps I'd caught her at a bad time? Or maybe she was always this feisty? Either way, I liked it. Made a nice change. Not having a female fall at my feet and start sucking my cock, with the hope of a tiara landing on her head on the way back up.

Though it was tempting to see how long I could keep up the ruse, I was curious about something she'd said.

"I believe you have me confused for someone else, beautiful," I started, watching her eyes widen in realization as she connected the dots. "I am Nekane, identical twin of Elikai. Pleasure to meet you..." I purred, dipping slightly in a bow.

Time stood still as I waited for her to introduce herself, because who in the actual fuck was this female in Kai's room? Half-naked, no less.

Someone with a death wish, if those angry words had been intended for my brother.

Being identical twins, we had the same black hair. Mine was a little longer and swept back off my face, whereas Kai kept his shorter and neat.

We were both tall, over six feet, but I had slightly broader shoulders, likely down to the fact I trained every day with Alaric.

The way we spoke was different, too. I always thought our voices gave us away, but apparently, she'd missed all the signs.

Even the dimples didn't appear like mine did when Kai smiled.

Unless she really doesn't know him well at all...

"That sort of explains the scent," she muttered, low enough I almost didn't catch it.

I wanted to ask her what she meant, about the scent, but she started back peddling before I had a chance. "Ah, I... um, I apologize, Prince Nekane. I knew you were twins, I just. I-I didn't think about what that meant." Her gaze dropped, cheeks blazing red.

"Not to worry, beautiful. Mind telling me who you are, though?" I asked. "And what you did with my brother?" I feigned looking around the room, but I knew he wasn't here. He wasn't one to stay quiet.

"I... ah..." She took a deep breath, centering herself in a way that reminded me of Alaric. "My name is Evangelia. Prince Elikai rescued me from the Fading Vale and brought me back here," she said, as if reciting a royal report and not describing some grand rescue.

Holding her stare, I took a moment to ponder the information, and piece it together with what she'd said about him being a monster. The puzzle wasn't fitting together.

Trying to work out why Kai did the things he did was enough to give someone a brain aneurysm, but this was odd, even for him.

"So, let me get this straight. He saved your life, pampered you," I gestured to her fluffy robe, "and yet you call him a monster?"

Anger prickled beneath my skin on behalf of my brother. She may be stunning, but my loyalty was to Kai. Always.

"I-I meant it as a joke–" she stammered, but I cut her off, not wanting her excuses.

"Well, humor is clearly not a talent of yours. If you value your life, I suggest you don't attempt it again," I said.

Turning to leave, the door opened before I could reach it, and Thalia entered.

She struggled with no less than four garment bags. The kind that held those heavy, lavish ball gowns. I reached over to help take some of the weight of the load, but she pulled away from my offer.

"Your Highness!" she exclaimed, not expecting to see me. "What are you doing here? Your brother went to see the king. He could be back at any second!"

Her eyes darted to the half dressed, silver-haired enchantress, then back to me. "Please Nekane," she pleaded. "Leave Evangelia to me. Elikai is not in such a forgiving mood today," she whispered.

Huffing a sigh, I nodded to Kai's housekeeper. She was my butler's niece and had enough on her plate without me being an asshole.

"I guess I'll be seeing you around, Evangelia." I left, not bothering to close the door behind me.

MY HEAD SWAM from the delicious scent that had engulfed Kai's room, and I tried to make sense of the intriguing female certain to be its source.

While her scent might be alluring, who in their right mind called their savior a fucking monster? An ungrateful, entitled female, that's who.

The Crooked Claw was calling to me, but I didn't want to go without Alaric. He'd still be speaking with my father if Kai had joined the debrief. Decided, I made my way down to the training floor. Alaric would find me as soon as he could, and the training halls were the first place he'd check.

Stepping into the vast open space, I noted the elevated ring in the corner was free of soldiers. *Good.* The area was roped off, empty aside from the deceitfully hard tan mats within. Beyond stood the targets for archery, dummies for melee training and well-stocked weapon racks which held blunted practice weapons of every shape and size.

To the left, stretching the length of the hall, were red mats. Significantly softer than the tan ones and great for hand-to-hand combat practice. Hand-to-hand would have to wait until my sparring partner showed up.

Making my way to the practice dummies, I grabbed a short sword. The feel of it was familiar in my hand, the sheath a comforting weight at my side. Letting my muscle memory take over, I worked the dummy in front of me.

It wasn't long before my mind wandered to the female, Evangelia. What in the fates was my brother thinking?!

The mistrust and anger in her eyes plagued me. Why would she turn that on someone who'd saved her?

Even if she had been a prisoner, that didn't explain why he would bring her all the way back to the castle.

Unless he was quite taken by her?

It was unheard of for Kai to bring a female home. As was typical of him, he would soon grow bored of her, or I hoped he would. I needed to speak to Alaric about it. He would have spent time with them during the ride here. And that male made it his business to watch for potential threats. He would have a read on her.

All I knew was that she was enchanting, and that scent... I groaned thinking of it.

My muscles burned as I kept moving through the steps. It was taking longer than expected for Alaric to find me.

When I was about to give up waiting, his gruff voice came from behind me. "Nekane?"

He never called me Nekane. Not since I'd asked him to call me Kane.

"Alaric. You're back." I sheathed the sword and placed it back on the racks.

He still hadn't moved from the doorway. *Strange.* He never passed up a chance to criticize my practice form.

"How was the hunt?"

No answer.

"What's up? Everything alright?"

"Nothin' to worry about," he said, shaking his head. "Come on, let's get to the tavern for a drink. I need to be away from yer brother for a while before the ball tonight."

I nodded, letting him lead the way and forgoing a shower, knowing full well what our usual activities were at the tavern.

The tense lines of his shoulders told me there was something wrong. Or at least something he wasn't telling me. He seemed different somehow than before he had left.

As we walked, I thought about Evangelia. Again. We hadn't left things on good terms after our brief introduction. And I was no closer to understanding why she'd been more angry at Kai than grateful.

Most females would fall over themselves to be in her shoes right now. I would know, having had many try to needle their way into that position. I needed to know more about this mysterious female.

Just like I also needed to not give a shit and stop thinking about her way more than I did any other attractive fae.

Clearing my throat, I said, "I assume you spent some time with the female my brother has hidden away in his room?" My tone was neutral, but he wasn't an easy male to fool.

"Aye."

"Did Kai actually rescue her from the Fading Vale?"

"Aye."

"Well, what do you think?"

When he didn't answer, I continued pushing.

"She isn't his true mate or anything serious, right?"

He released a long, drawn out breath. "I'm not gonnae pretend to ken what goes on in Elikai's head, but he was keen to get her back here."

"She's beautiful, and her scent..." I mused, half to myself.

He shook his head, but said, "Aye..."

Did he smell it too? Or maybe he was just agreeing that she was a beauty?

"I don't trust her," I announced.

He raised a brow. "Why not?"

"Something in my gut..." but it hadn't been enough to stop me from imagining how it would be to bend her over and fuck her on the nearest surface.

To have a feisty female like that on her knees, begging me to give her what she wanted–

Shaking off that dangerous trail of thought, I spent the rest of our stroll recounting the interesting conversation I'd had with her. While Alaric remained mostly silent. Distracted.

Melina spotted us the moment our boots crossed the threshold and followed us to our usual seats. "What'll it be tonight then, boys?" She asked, a cheeky grin spreading across her face.

"Whisky." Alaric said. "Bring the bottle an' a few tumblers, Mel." I frowned, but the silence stretched between us until Melina returned with our drinks.

We didn't often hit the whisky until later into the night. After a few ales, or when we were celebrating.

"Was the hunt that bad?" I asked, trying to breaking the odd tension.

He grunted, but didn't make any effort to elaborate.

"Come on. What happened out there? You're not your usual self."

He gave me a wide-eyed stare, and for a second, I swore he stopped breathing. His eyes darted away, back to the amber liquid.

What was with that reaction? And what the fuck was that pang in my chest when he looked away?

"Dinnae look at me like I jus' booted yer arse," he grumbled, still looking anywhere but at me. "It was jus' a long trip and yer brother was the biggest pain in my arse."

Kai wasn't the easiest to get along with these days, and Alaric already had a strained relationship with him at best. Since Kai quit his lessons thinking he had already mastered the sword and no longer needed training. Foolish, but there was no changing his mind.

It was obvious Alaric wanted nothing more than to drink the night away, but we needed to get back to the castle later for Kai's belated birthday feast.

Letting my eyes wander briefly, I found there was no shortage of beautiful potential females to lie with tonight.

None of them had piercing green eyes and silver hair, though.

None of them held that look of distrust I wanted to unravel.

We sat in awkward silence for the next two drinks before leaving. I could have sworn his stare was burning into me, and I tried to meet his gaze several times. But he would glance away before I could catch him.

What was going on with him?

And why did I care so much that he wouldn't look at me?

CHAPTER 9
Elikai

After leaving my pretty little pet to her makeover, I raced to tell Father the good news. The months-long search for a bride was over at last. Not that he was aware of the search.

Sloane and Graves had rounded up the most physically attractive high fae females in Ezerat for me to browse, but they had all been… lacking.

The most accurate word I could use to describe them was 'plain'. Though that was likely too high of a compliment.

It wasn't entirely their fault. It was always going to be a difficult, if not impossible, task. Finding a female who could stand in my presence and not fade into the background was never going to be easy, but I'd expected better.

The moment I laid eyes on Angelica, though, I saw her potential. With the right amount of coin thrown at her to enhance her natural beauty, I would not only be a feared King of Dezrothia, but an envied one too.

Reaching the war room in record time—on account of my long, powerful legs—I listened at the door.

Alaric was debriefing Father in a monotone manner. Not coming close to doing my efforts in the hunt any justice. Had we been on the same trip? He really ought to be more vigilant, given his position.

The male couldn't be more boring if he tried. What my brother saw in him, and why he would constantly want to spend time with him, I had no idea. Personally, I couldn't see past the unsightly scar running down his face.

At times, I'd pondered how he'd gotten such a wound; then reminded myself I didn't care. There was something off with that male, but now was not the time to think about it.

Swinging the door wide, I entered the war room. The king and Alaric's eyes were drawn to me, but it couldn't be helped. I had this way of entering a room and stopping fae in their tracks.

Of course, all high fae had the gift of allure. Just one of many things that made us superior to all other races. But I also happened to be the most attractive of all high fae, in addition to my many other exceptional attributes. It was common for my disciples to fall over themselves to please me. Females, and some males, drooled and panted after me.

"This will have to wait Father, I have news," I announced.

"The general here was telling me you think you've found a worthy suitor, my boy?" Father inquired. His condescending tone told me he too must have been worried there would never be a female beautiful enough for his favorite son.

"Yes Father, Angelvinia is–"

"Evangelia," Alaric interrupted.

My nostrils flared. "That's what I said."

Waving my hand dismissively toward him, I focused my attention back to Father.

"She is beautiful beyond your wildest imagination. A high fae of impeccable breeding, who will birth strong heirs and be loved by all in the realm."

It wasn't a lie, exactly. She was high fae. She didn't smell like anything else. No scent of dog or witch or troll. Her ears weren't pointy like the elves, and her beauty alone marked her as high fae. I didn't know much about her lineage, but it didn't matter. I knew all I needed to.

Anticipation filled me as I waited for my father's response. I couldn't wait for him to begin planning my coronation.

"There is no need to rush, Elikai, you have plenty of time before you need to find yourself a queen," he said, completely unmoved, then turned back to the oaf.

No rush? But if I found a queen then he could retire. Step aside for my reign to begin. I'd waited until coming of age as the law required...

"Well, the fates were on my side, and I found her already, Father. I intend to announce our engagement this evening, in fact. At my coming-of-age ball."

He had to see how serious I was. Surely, he was testing me?

"Very well. I will be interested to meet her," he said. "Is that all?"

With a huff, I turned on my heel to leave. Slamming the door in my wake.

That had not gone as I had expected. It almost sounded as though Father intended to remain king for the foreseeable future.

But that couldn't be. I had plans. Plans that were only achievable as king. I ran over them in my head as I set out to find Graves and Sloane, a smirk pulling at my lips. Tonight had to go off without a hitch. I needed the elite of Dezrothia to see that the fates were on my side. That they'd gifted me with my mate, their future queen, the exact day I came of age.

We weren't true mates, but they didn't need to know that. My pretty pet already looked at me like she was sick with love. The city folk would assume for themselves, and I could act the part of a love-struck fiancée perfectly.

By the time this evening was through, I'd have the most influential fae of Ezerat coming to the same realization I had years ago. I was by far the better male for the job as king. They would be ready to bow at my feet the moment my father stepped aside.

Of course, my main priority was to prove to my father that I was ready to take over as reigning king. That would be the easiest route leading to a crown being placed on my head. It was obvious he wasn't confident in my abilities to rule right now, and that had to change, fast.

Always predictable, I heard Graves and Sloane as soon as I made it to the floor below mine. Where they lived with their parents, my father's closest advisors.

Pausing just out of sight, I listened in on their private conversation. They weren't being particularly quiet about it, but still, you never knew when you might overhear something worth banking for future blackmailing material.

"So, you got back to your room from the hunt and she was just lying there? Ready and willing?" Graves asked Sloane.

"Oh, more than ready! The dirty whore was butt ass naked and spread eagle across my bed. Instant boner, bro. Instant. Boner." His use of commoner slang made me shudder.

You would think he was some virgin with the animated way in which he was speaking.

"No fair! You should have come for me!"

"Woah, why would I come for you when I had a dirty bitch flicking her bean, gagging for some Sloaneasaurus schlong, ready to go at it?"

"We could have spit roasted her and had her squealing like a pig, letting her know why everyone calls us the Groane!"

Enough was enough. It was time to make my presence known.

Stepping into their communal living room, I made sure the look of utter disgust was painted across my fine features.

"First, no one calls you the Groane," I said. "You made it up yourselves. Your desperate attempts to make it a thing aren't working. It's rather embarrassing. And second, what in the fates are you two doing sitting around here when there is much to be done!?"

My tone left no question to how unimpressed I was with their behavior. Acting like slobs and gossiping about whores, while the event of the century was happening in mere hours!

They jumped to their feet, falling over themselves with apologies. I wasted no time dishing out my orders and detailing my clothing requirements.

Graves made extensive notes before leaving for the tailors' boutique. I would need to go there myself to ensure that it was done to my specifications, but he would be a good messenger to reiterate to the tailor the urgency. He'd also make sure the tailor dropped whatever rubbish he was making for the peasants. Creating my outfit instead.

The tailor wouldn't argue, it was an honor after all, but Graves would keep an eye and crack the whip. The clock was ticking, and it needed to be perfect.

That left Sloane with starting the preparations for tonight as quickly as possible. There was already a celebration planned for my coming of age, so the guest list and feast were in hand. Though now that it was also to be my engagement party, the decorations needed to be even more extravagant.

Pacing the room, I brainstormed aloud, deciding upon last-minute additions to my gold, white and black themed ball.

There would be will-o'-the-wisps collected in tiny decorative jars and hung, connected by string, curtaining the walls with their atmospheric ghost light. Devas fairies would be the perfect complement, dancing tirelessly around the ceiling of the expansive ballroom into the small hours of the morning. Blanketing it with the glow of fairy light.

The idea came to me on the second day of the journey back from the hunt. Of course, I'd sent some village peasants away with orders immediately. They were to collect the fairies from the woods, and deliver them to the castle in time for tonight. I'd left them with a friendly threat to their entire settlement, should they not pull it off.

Having the lights radiating from the walls and ceiling would reflect against my pretty pet's silver hair, making her glow and dazzle the eyes of the guests.

"Sloane, find the event coordinating witch," I said. "Make sure that the decorations have arrived along with the note I sent, advising that the ball is to be an engagement and coming of age event combined. I will be at the tailor waiting."

I STOOD proud while the warlock tailor took measurements of my broad chest, proportional waist and muscular thighs. Along with my substantial rise and inseam.

He listened intently as I properly briefed him on what I wanted. I knew I should never have entrusted that task to Graves. He had done poorly and we had to start over when I arrived.

The rather annoying bell above the door rattled, announcing Sloane's arrival with the event coordinating witch in tow.

She thrust mood boards in front of me, blocking my view of the mirror. Why did these fae think I cared what they thought? The only opinion I cared about was my own. And Father's if it involved me becoming king. I already told this witch what I wanted in my note, so why must she insist on giving me options for things I didn't care about?

Perhaps I should have brought Evaline to do this. It would be her job once we were wed anyway.

Would she even have the taste to pull this sort of event off? She'd been living in the Fading Vale when I found her... How long had she been there? *Oh no, no no no, does she even know how to use silverware?* Had she ever been taught in the first place? My mind spun with the millions of ways she could ruin this evening for me.

"Just stick to the brief, and do as I told you," I ordered the dithering witch. I didn't have time for this. Her voice stuttered to a halt and I decided to leave Graves here. To ensure the witch and warlock did their jobs adequately. Then sent Sloane to find an emergency etiquette teacher for a last-minute lesson for my pretty little pet.

Her transformation should be a surprise for me, but I could not risk her potentially embarrassing me in front of my father and the most influential individuals in the city.

With that thought, I bolted back into the carriage. "To the castle!"

UPON ARRIVAL, I sped to my chambers like a whippet, not wanting any of our residents to see my trepidation.

Throwing open the door to my chambers, I cupped my hands around my mouth and yelled, "Angelavine! Come!" Looking around frantically, I found her already in front of me, next to the fireplace and scrambling to her feet.

"What's happened?" she asked, panic in her voice.

"It's an emergency!" I grabbed her by the arm and dragged her to my breakfast table. "Sit."

"Prince Elikai, tell me what is going on!"

Ignoring her, I shot over to the dumbwaiter. I'd seen the maid take cutlery from it before, so slid the drawer open and grabbed one of each utensil.

Returning to the table, I laid them out in front of my little ruffian. This wasn't a job for a prince, but there was no time and it was imperative she learned from the best.

Sure to speak slowly, I began. "This is a fork. To hold it, your index fingers should point down the back, toward the prongs like this." I held each of the utensils up as I spoke of them, in turn. "We eat our food with this one that has four prongs. Three-pronged forks are for dessert, and two pronged are for holding the meat steady while it is being carved. Not that you will need to worry about that. A pretty little thing like you will never need to handle meat again."

This had better be sinking in. I really didn't have much time.

"Elikai–" Her hand rested on my forearm, giving it a tender stroke. Or maybe a push. Either way her gratitude was as clear as the fates.

"Next, we have our knives. These are not for wielding as a weapon. Like the fork, your index finger should point down the spine, toward the blade. They are for cutting your food into bite-sized pieces. This blunt one is for softer things, like butter for your bread. You wield this in a spreading motion. For slightly harder items, such as vegetables, you use it in a chopping motion. This sharp one is especially good for your meat and is wielded in a cutting action, back and forth, back and forth. Remember, you should never bite your food. It should always be small enough to fit the entire piece in your mouth. And chew delicately! No open-mouthed chewing, thank you very much," I told her.

The way she stared at me, I could just tell she was trying to please me and take it all in. "Please, Elikai–"

"Sh, sh, sh, there is no time. On to the spoons!" I cried. "We have a few of these as well, to be held lightly between thumb and forefinger. Balance it lightly on your middle finger, like this. This one here that is circular and has a deeper bevel is for your soup, and for the love of the fates, do not slurp! You gently and silently sip your dish. This is your dessert spoon. You see how it is more oval in shape and not as deep? You may use this to take a small amount of your dessert. No need to act like a pig! Then these smaller ones are your tea, coffee and sugar spoons. Remember, my pet, to never mix them up. It is essential to remember which is which, lest you be the talk of the night for all the wrong reasons."

"STOP!" She reached under the table and flipped it one hundred and eighty degrees.

Cutlery flew across the room as the table fell face down.

Ugh. I should have specified this at the start. She likely had never sat at one to eat.

"Finally. We do not. Under any circumstance. Upturn the table."

Wow, this was going to be a disaster.

"Thalia! Clean up this mess!" I had a lot of work ahead of me.

CHAPTER 10

Evangelia

After my impromptu and totally unnecessary lesson in silverware from a psychopath, a ruckus sounded outside the room, soon followed by a knock at the door.

"Finally! That will be Sloane with your next lesson," Elikai exclaimed, and I froze at the name before he hollered for him to come in.

Sloane entered, dragging a petrified fae female behind him. The pair of small spiral horns protruding from her forehead gave away that she was not high fae, but one of the other castes. Rage and sadness flooded my entire being simultaneously when I recognized Sloane as one of the males Elikai had ordered to kill–

I stopped my trail of thought before the grief consumed me and swallowed roughly. I couldn't let my emotions get the better of me, not yet anyway. I would get my revenge against every single one of them in time. But right now, I needed to focus on biting my tongue and gaining Elikai's trust in order to get closer to King Regis. He was my primary target and all I could afford to focus on right now.

"Prince Elikai," Sloane announced. "I am assured this female is the most renowned etiquette teacher in Dezrothia, and she is very hap–"

"What took so long?" Elikai spat, as if he hadn't only just finished waving cutlery in front of my face like a lunatic. He succeeded in drawing a high-pitched squeak of fear from the fae female.

"The bitch put up a fight at first. It seemed she didn't want to leave her mother's funeral early to be here. It's not like the host would have noticed her absence. She eventually came around when I explained that if she didn't come now, then she would have fun planning her father's funeral next."

No. Surely he wasn't serious? Though his tone held no sign of sarcasm or wit, telling me what he was saying was exactly what happened to the poor fae.

Elikai rolled his eyes and made a show of looking exasperated. "As captivating as

I'm sure that little story was, you are wasting my time. We have work to do before this evening's big surprise." He turned toward me, "I will be back to collect you at nightfall, pretty girl." I realized he was leaning in for a kiss too late to stop it. I just about ducked my head in time, so his lips brushed my forehead instead of landing on my mouth as intended. I had to fight every bone in my body not to cringe away or shudder. It didn't matter that he looked like a god on the outside. He'd already shown me how ugly he was too many times to count in the brief period since we first met.

He left the room, thankfully taking Sloane with him, but leaving me alone with Thalia and the new arrival. I turned my attention to the fae and took her hand on impulse. "I am so sorry for your loss," I said earnestly, the loss of my own parents still keenly felt in my chest.

Tears pooled in her eyes as she acknowledged my words with a subtle nod, but didn't say anything in response.

"They had no right to pull you away from such a moment. I wish I could send you back or undo it entirely…" I said, not that it would make up for what had happened.

What I wouldn't give to have been able to provide my parents with the honorable burial they deserved. This day had been a lot, to say the least, and I was exhausted. *Was it really only this morning we arrived at the castle?*

I walked over to the armchairs surrounding the fireplace and welcomed the two females over to join me with a wave. I slumped down and took a deep breath, counting slowly in my head as I exhaled, working up a plan to get this poor female out of the castle and back to her family.

They both followed, confusion painted across their faces. I leaned forward as they joined me, and I dropped my voice so as not to be overheard. "Thalia, you said you have family who also work for the Regis family. Could any of them kindly escort–" I looked to the fae, realizing they hadn't even introduced her by name.

"W-Willow," she said in a barely audible whisper.

I wanted to help her, comfort her and tell her that I knew how she was feeling. How I could sympathize with being ripped away from loved ones and brought here against my will, suffocating in grief. But I couldn't. All I could do was help in this small way by not keeping her from where she needed to be any longer than she'd already been gone.

"Would any of your relatives be happy to discreetly escort Willow back to her family please?"

"Yes milady, if you are sure that will be ok?" Her eyes darted around the room as if to make certain the pretentious prince wasn't about to jump out and scold her for it. "My Uncle, Westly, will be more than able to assist," she added, nervous about Elikai's reaction. I understood her hesitation, he could be terrifying when he was in a good mood. I dreaded to think what he would be like in a foul one.

"It will be fine, Thalia. The prince is very busy, as you heard. We will tell him that the lesson went well," I assured her, proud of how confident and together I sounded.

Thankfully, Thalia didn't waste any time waiting for more encouragement as she left to find her uncle. She returned shortly with a stout, but friendly looking male with sooty hair, who went straight over to Willow and held out a hand to help her to her feet.

"Milady, might I suggest we start getting you ready for this evening's celebrations?" Thalia asked as her uncle headed toward the door with a sobbing Willow. I stopped them to assure her that none of this would come back on her, and she looked a little relieved as they left.

I couldn't help but wonder whether Prince Nekane would be so quick to defend his brother if he knew of his antics and total disregard of anyone but himself. Surely, he wouldn't have taken such offense at me calling Elikai a monster if he knew the truth? My gut told me Nekane was different based only on our very brief encounter, but maybe he just hid his monster better than his twin.

"Let's do this," I said through a long sigh. Whatever Elikai had planned, I had a feeling it was going to take all the strength and patience I had left in me to get through it, and then some.

AFTER HOURS OF BEING POKED, prodded and pampered, I looked in the mirror and didn't recognize the female looking back at me. She was stunning. *I* was stunning. My hair was pulled back from my face, the black streak I inherited from my father was intricately braided with beads and rings intertwined, highlighting its contrast to the silver strands it was woven into. The half updo had been expertly shaped while the hair left down had been curled loosely to frame my face. When I moved my head, the light caught on the silver, making it shine almost iridescently, like an opal.

The dress was like nothing I'd seen before. It was floor length and made up of lightweight swaths of fabric which swayed with every move, gently layered to create a skirt that looked like it belonged on a princess from my childhood storybooks. It had a fitted bodice covered in intricate golden beading that complimented those in my hair. The beads connected the flowing sleeves and led up to my neck where they joined together with a golden crescent moon at my throat. My shoulders were bare, but where the beads connected to the sleeves they were draped in crystals.

Thalia held out a hand to balance me as I turned to look at the back of the gown, admiring where the bead work continued around and joined with another crescent moon in the center of my lower spine. The dress was all white and gold and the contrast with the silver and black of my hair should have clashed, yet it worked perfectly.

My eyes were lined with kohl, making the green even brighter than normal. I blinked several times, trying to get used to the foreign feeling of mascara. A light brush of a nude lipstick on my lips completed the look, a natural blush coating my cheeks.

I was unrecognizable, but I found it was helping me to stay calm and deal with this terrifying situation, as if I were wearing a mask.

"Milady, you are a vision," Thalia said as she continued holding my hand. I noticed too late it was the one I wore my spelled rings on. Closing my fist, I snatched my hand away, but didn't miss the way her brow furrowed as she tried to take a closer look.

"Your jewelry is lovely, milady, but I am afraid it does not match your new attire,"

Thalia said, concern in her voice as she walked over to a side table where a box lay unopened.

She returned to my side and lifted the lid to reveal a beautiful pair of earrings, complete with a matching ring. The stones looked obsidian in color until she reached inside and carefully plucked out the ring. She held it to the last of the sun's rays peeking through the window, and I realized the stone was in fact a black pearl when the light reflected, making it glisten with a green hue. The huge stone was set on a delicate silver band and exuded wealth and prosperity.

They were breath-taking pieces. I sent a silent thank you to the fates that my beast lay dormant right now, otherwise, turning them away may have been impossible. "Thank you, Thalia, but my ears are not pierced, and I intend to keep them that way. My rings may not be lavish or match my dress perfectly, but they are the last memento my parents gifted me with and are all I have left of them." The sentiment clouding my voice didn't need to be faked, but I choked back the tears, not willing to show that much emotion to anyone else. Especially within these walls.

She eyed the simple silver rings adorning my fingers again. The one masking the scent of my species was a thick plain band. The other, which suppressed my shift when I lost control of my emotions and risked shifting involuntarily, looked like wings hugging my finger, only not quite meeting in the middle.

"I didn't mean to offend milady." She paused, and I could tell that she wasn't sure whether to put words to whatever was on the tip of her tongue. She took a deep breath before meeting my eyes with a strength I hadn't seen from her until now. "Perhaps you would benefit from me concealing them for you, lest they draw Prince Elikai's notice and he demands their removal." She said it in a neutral tone, albeit dropping her voice to almost a whisper, as if the walls would be listening. But her words made me uneasy, nonetheless. *Does she know?* Or maybe she just suspected what they did? Had she sensed the spells as she held onto my hand, while I was stupidly distracted by my reflection?

More importantly, why was she offering to help me keep them hidden from the prince's attention? She didn't owe me anything. I wouldn't blame her if she told him of her suspicions.

I nodded once, and she proceeded to weave a thread of golden beads through my fingers, completely concealing the rings where they sat and creating loops of chains around my hand that eventually lead up to my wrist where she finished and tied off the link.

I stared in awe at how seamlessly she blended my precious rings into the outfit, creating this beautiful bracelet of beaded chains. "Thank you," I muttered, unable to express the depth of my gratitude. Hopefully, one day, I could. When I didn't need to hide who I was anymore, if that day ever came. I would likely be dead the moment I attempted to assassinate the king, but keeping these rings firmly in place was a matter of life or death in itself. Whether she realized it yet or not, she'd helped me immeasurably.

"Well, well, well, don't you look delectable, pretty girl?" Elikai purred, his sickly smooth voice snapping me out of my thoughts and making me jump. He moved to my side, looking over my shoulder at our reflections, and I fought my cringe as my skin crawled. He dropped his voice to a whisper and leaned in close to my ear so only I would hear his next words. "If only your parents could see you now. Perhaps they would realize, as I did, that you were wasted in that swamp. A female like you should be admired, not left to roll around in filth and eat off the floor."

His vicious words stung and reminded me of everything I had been trying so hard to compartmentalize. I sucked in a deep breath and swallowed the lump in my throat, remembering my plan to play the role of his 'pretty pet' and gain his trust. I could stab him in the back when the time came, but for now, it was time to dig deep and act the part.

I stepped away from him, needing to put some distance between us, but making out like I was just taking in his outfit. "You look rather handsome yourself, Prince Elikai," I said, hoping I sounded convincing. But if I was honest with myself, it wasn't even a lie. I hated that he looked so good. It would have been so much easier if he looked like a troll in a suit.

His fitted suit accentuated his broad shoulders and trim waist. He was wearing white as well. The tailcoat was beautiful, with golden floral beading that swirled down from his left shoulder and ended at his right thigh. Its high collar cut into the narrow lapels, the black of his shirt contrasting perfectly. The same wispy material that made the skirt of my dress adorned the pattern on his jacket, so they complemented each other seamlessly.

If our personalities aren't going to match, at least we look like a set.

The thought helped pull the mask I planned to wear into place. We didn't need to be a match made by the fates to at least look like one.

The coat fell to his mid thighs, emphasizing the powerful muscles there. His trousers were beautifully tailored to fall with the shape. Despite his hideous personality, he was one of the most beautiful males I'd ever seen. With his raven black hair and piercing blue eyes, he genuinely did take your breath away.

I was half tempted to tell him his appearance was wasted on him too, only for entirely different reasons than those he gave me. The thought that there were two of these handsome males sent a strange sensation through my stomach. Why did they have to be such pigs?

I had found my mind wandering to Prince Nekane more times than I cared to admit since our meeting earlier and the awkward way we'd left things. He intrigued me, and for some reason, I hoped I would get the opportunity to talk to him this evening. Not that I could explain the lie I told, leaving him to assume I was some ungrateful wench.

"–for your surprise, pretty girl?" *Shit*. I had no idea what he'd said before that, but I imagined it was something about how no one would be looking at me when he looked so fabulous.

He held out his arm, and as I took it, he led the way through the castle and eventually brought us to a set of grand double doors. I was desperately trying to remain calm, even though dread had its claws firmly sunk into me. I hated surprises. Where I came from, a surprise came in the form of King Regis' army, showing up to massacre you and everyone you loved.

Two guards, dressed in fancier uniforms than the ones worn when they found me in the Vale, opened the doors in unison, gesturing us through. A staircase descended ahead of us, and I went to take a shaky step forward, praying to the fates I didn't fall down them.

Before we had made it a step, the herald proclaimed, "Now presenting Prince Elikai Regis, escorting his bride-to-be, Lady Evangelia."

My eyes flew wide. *Bride-to-be?*

This was an *engagement* party? *Our* engagement party?!

I froze. The insane male had talked endlessly about finding or needing a bride on the journey here. And yes, he'd hinted at me being suitable, but we hadn't even been at the castle for half a day, and he'd arranged an engagement party?! *Fuck no*. Surely, I misheard. It hadn't even crossed my mind that I would still be in the castle, or even breathing for that matter, by the time I needed to worry about any of his twisted ramblings actually happening.

Elikai steered us to take a few steps forward, heading toward the wide staircase. Red carpet rolled down its center, held in place by golden rods. The crimson led to a ballroom so magical it took my breath away.

The insane prince paused before we reached the top step to begin our descent and pulled me close, leaning into my ear as he had done before. "Surprise, pretty pet. Welcome to my engagement party. You have three jobs; smile, look stunning, and *do not* embarrass me. It would be a shame for society's new princess-to-be to disappoint their future king and turn up dead, wouldn't you agree? Now smile, throw your head back and laugh like I just said something hilarious."

His grip was punishing, but I forced my lips into a smile, then laughed like he'd instructed. Fear filled me, willing me to run away as fast and far from this castle as possible as I continued the facade.

But I couldn't run. Running would mean failing everyone in the Vale and villages who struggled every day to survive the king's reign of terror. I just had to turn this crisis into an opportunity.

The silence lasted a millennia. Desperate for a distraction, I looked down to search out the king, and found hundreds of pairs of eyes staring up at me. Awed like I was something I really wasn't, and I sent another silent prayer to the fates that I could pull this off.

Suddenly, cheers and applause echoed off the walls, and we began our descent into what was going to be a nightmare come to life.

CHAPTER 11

Nekane

I straightened my tie as I rushed into the ballroom and found Alaric hiding in a shadowed corner, nursing a drink and scowling at everyone who dared to come near. This type of party was the opposite of what he would call fun. The fact he was here at all was a miracle. He was still acting strange. Even after drinking the afternoon away at the tavern, I figured it would be best to just act like I hadn't noticed, but that dull ache in my chest persisted.

"Alaric," I called as I pushed my way through the throng of guests trying to stop me for a conversation I had no interest in having. No doubt small talk about the weather, or worse, trying to butter me up to put in a good word with the king about one issue or another.

If only they knew that me fighting in their corner would end in the issue being immediately dismissed on the basis that every time the king looked at me, he was reminded of his hatred of me and that my birth killed his wife.

"So, you came," I said, stating the obvious as I leaned against the column next to where the general stood. I looked around the room and had to admit that the event coordinator had outdone herself.

The ballroom was already stunning in its architecture alone, but the decorations were unique and beautiful. Lights covered the walls and ceiling, and for a moment, I thought I saw real fairies dancing around. *Probably just the alcohol you consumed over lunch playing tricks on you.*

Alaric tipped his head my way, more interested in his drink than talking with me. Before I had a chance to ask what was wrong, the doors upstairs beyond the mezzanine opened, and the herald spoke.

"Now presenting Prince Elikai Regis, escorting his bride-to-be, Lady Evangelia."

The breath left my lungs as my jaw damn near hit the floor. You could hear a pin drop as the guests all raised their gaze to the couple at the top of the staircase. *Did he just say bride-to-be?!*

Evangelia looked stunning. Divine. *Edible.* Kai whispered something in her ear, and she laughed loudly, the sound ringing through the room. He was probably promising to serve her a platter of the kingdom's rarest jewels for breakfast. Or better yet, bring dragons back from extinction so she could keep one as a personal guard dog and never fear being taken again.

It took a moment for the announcement to sink in. Even when it did, every muscle in my body still wanted to claim her any chance I could get. This changed everything, taking her very much off the table and engaged to my brother. Could she be his true mate? Wouldn't that just be his fucking luck.

The party guests eventually picked their jaws up from the floor and cheered. The sound was deafening, even in such a vast space. Like a queen, Evangelia gracefully glided her way into the ballroom, and that scent of hers, campfires and warm, creamy vanilla, flooded the space. I couldn't peel my eyes away from her. She was perfect.

As Elikai showed off his prize to the most opulent fae in Ezerat, I tracked their every movement. Alaric was doing something similar next to me. The only thing going through my head was the burning desire to remove her from Kai and keep her for myself.

Eventually, Kai spotted us, and with a smirk, made his way over. "Little brother. General Alaric," he said, his voice raised enough for those around us to direct their attention our way. "I see you have found a corner to darken. Nekane, meet your future sister-in-law," he said as he stood Evangelia before me. Her smile seemed strained as she dipped into a short curtsey. So, she hadn't told him we'd already met? *Interesting.*

"Pleased to meet you, Prince Nekane," she said, and there was something almost devious in her tone. "Alaric, nice to see you again. I hope you managed to get some rest after your *successful* hunt," she continued. Was that... disdain in her voice? But why? What was she up to? Now wasn't the time for such musings. Elikai was waiting for my response.

I grinned at her, deciding I wasn't going to make this easy. I didn't owe her anything and certainly didn't think she could be trusted after the way she'd spoken of my brother. I needed to show Kai that, too. Especially now, knowing she'd accepted a proposal for marriage from him.

"Oh Evangelia, the pleasure is *always* mine," I said, sweeping up her hand to place a chaste kiss on it. Kai didn't like it one bit. He'd always preferred fae to look at, but never touch, his things. "Pleased to see you again, and looking much calmer than after our last chat," I baited, and her cheeks flushed darker, a frown forming before she smoothed it with a look of indifference.

"Last chat?" my brother asked, his brows furrowed in confusion, looking between Evangelia and I.

"Yes brother, I went to speak with yo–"

"Yes!" Evangelia's high-pitched squeak cut over me. "Prince Nekane came looking for you in the room you left me in. Thalia answered the door, of course, and I got a little flustered due to a male being at the chambers. It must have slipped my mind on account of him not being that memorable."

Did she really think that sort of insult would offend me? I wasn't now and never would be that kind of male. Though, how could the identical male to her true mate *not* be memorable? She definitely didn't want him to know what had happened between us, and I wondered again how far I could push her. *Why do I enjoy getting under her skin so damn much?*

"Ah brother, I am sorry I wasn't there to greet you with my presence. It has been some time since we spoke. I imagine you missed me terribly. Come, let's be seated and you can ask me all of your burning questions." Kai gestured to the long tables surrounding the dance floor that lay in the center of the room. "Of course, I will tell you the story of my hunt over dinner. I am sure Alaric will have done it no justice at all," he finished dramatically, before turning and leading Evangelia to the table that had a throne placed at its head.

Kai sat in the chair to the right of where our father would be seated, placing Evangelia to his own right, and then pointed to the seat to the left of the king, opposite him, for me to take.

I grimaced at the thought of being so close to my father and looking directly at the happy couple, who would, no doubt, be pawing at each other, putting me off my food and reminding me she wasn't *mine*. Couldn't be. Hopefully, Kai and his bride would at least distract my father enough that I would get through tonight mostly unscathed. Though I would still need the help of a stiff drink, or six.

The bastard who'd sired me hadn't bothered to arrive yet, but the wait staff wasted no time bringing out the first course anyway, used to him only being punctual to events directly celebrating himself. I wrinkled my nose as the putrid smell of fish soup assaulted me. But at least it masked *her*.

"So, little brother, what did Alaric tell you of the hunt?" Kai asked as he pointedly ignored the male in question, who had seated himself a bit further down the table from us. *Lucky bastard*. Despite Alaric being one of the king's most trusted generals, the asshole wouldn't want a shifter sitting with us to dine. Father had a pecking order and although shifters were pretty high up on his list, they weren't high fae.

"He told me you rescued this beauty from the imprisonment of thrakos, and that overall, it was a relatively boring trip," I said, shrugging. "Tell me brother, what more happened while you were away?"

The conversation didn't feel natural at all, but it had been getting more and more that way for some time now with Kai. It felt like the distance between us was becoming unbridgeable, and it saddened me that we were growing apart.

"Of course he didn't tell you the best part," Kai boasted, and I mentally prepared for the dramatic tale that was about to be spun. "The Fading Vale was a dreadful place and gave off the worst stench imaginable. I was leading the way, being the keen tracker that I am, when I came across the encampment that Angelicia-"

He froze dead in his tracks, blinking rapidly, as if he couldn't quite believe what he was seeing. He frantically looked around the room, before turning back and rubbing his eyes.

Following his stare, I had to smother a laugh as I took in the beautiful female at his side. She was looking up at him wide eyed over the bowl of soup she'd lifted to her puckered lips. I'd never seen my brother so utterly still until his chest finally rose as he took a deep breath in through his nose.

"What?" she asked around the succulent prawn half curled around her lip, before letting it drop into the bowl with a splash. "You said to sip from my bowl silently... Was I not quiet enough, my prince?" Her tone was saccharinely innocent, but there was a glint in her eyes that told another story.

Kai glanced around the table again before carefully guiding her hands to place the bowl back down. I didn't miss the way her mouth twitched into a half smile as he turned his attention back to me.

"And my name is *Evangelia...*" she said, before picking up her spoon and eating with the grace of a queen.

"That's what I said," he snapped. "Fates help me, you really need to work on your listening skills. Now where was I? Ah, yes, I discovered the encampment where she was imprisoned. I was overcome with rage at the injustice of such a beauty being in chains, and launched an impromptu attack to free her. By the time I had fought my way to her, the battle was over and all that was left was to set her free. I gathered her up on my horse and insisted we return to the castle so she could feel safe at last, secure in the knowledge she had the fiercest warrior in Dezrothia to watch over her." He finished, sat back and nodded to the open-mouthed onlookers, like he was silently telling them that they could now applaud.

"Well, brother, that is quite the tale," I said before we were interrupted by his fans. "To be so angered at your true mate's predicament you charged in without a care for your own life. Impressive."

I'd chosen my words carefully to get more information out of him, but I was unsure why it was so important to me to know if they were true mates or not.

"True mates?" she squeaked, her eyes wide, and I couldn't tell if it was shock or fear. "What do you mean true mates?"

"Well, isn't that what you are?" I pressed. She fidgeted, looking extremely uncomfortable under my scrutinizing gaze, but I didn't care. I would get her to confess her intentions for my brother. I couldn't allow him to be hurt by her.

"Oh, little brother, we are not true mates. We are *chosen* mates, and who wouldn't choose this stunning specimen?" he asked, turning the attention back to himself while I fought to hide my relief.

"I didn't know you were in the market to be wed?" I questioned, leaning back with my wine, suddenly feeling much more relaxed, taking in the vision that the pair made. A vision that could have easily been myself and shockingly felt right to me. Yet, it was somehow still incomplete.

"I didn't expect to find the perfect female at twenty-five either, Nekane," he said. "She was a birthday gift to me from the fates for my efforts against our enemies. Perhaps if you weren't so intent on doing nothing with your life, aside from associating with common brutes like the General down there, you would find the fates would be kinder to you too," he finished, waving his hand in Alaric's direction.

The room fell silent and I saw our father had finally decided to grace us with his presence. I bit back any reply I might have had and became very interested in the steaming bowl in front of me. I planned on keeping myself out of the direct line of fire from that particular asshole.

"Father, as I was telling you earlier, this is my new bride-to-be, Evandeling," he announced, standing from his chair and taking a nervous-looking Evangelia's hand to encourage her to stand too. My brow creased at his inability to remember her name. Was that not a sign that maybe he was rushing into this?

"Excellent. Let's eat," he said, uninterested. As I looked at Kai, his face was set in a scowl, his jaw grinding his teeth, and eyes narrowed to slits as if he were biting his tongue with some effort.

Seriously, what else had he expected from that prick, anyway?

THE REST of the meal was much the same. Awkward, fake and filled with small talk and digs at my expense. I had to fight to keep my stare from Evangelia, though seeing Kai get more and more frustrated with her was almost worth it. I could have sworn she was trying to get under his skin on purpose. It was small things, like using the wrong fork or spoon, or even just picking food up with her fingers.

Why was I still so drawn to her? Every time I saw Kai touch or correct her, I wanted to jump across the table and feed him his teeth. *She's not mine.* I didn't even like the female for fuck's sake. Well, not really. She was clearly with my brother for his status, not for the male he is. That alone would normally be enough to turn me off. I understood better than most that he could be difficult, but she had gone from being a prisoner to a princess in a week. Yet still, every smile she gave him looked forced or fake.

I couldn't sit here with these pretentious idiots much longer, and decided it would be best to leave the moment my absence would go unnoticed. Alaric and I could hit the tavern before last orders, and if there happened to be a silver-haired, green-eyed beauty there that I could sink myself into, it would be a bonus.

Most of the guests made their way to the dance floor as the music slowed down, and I thanked the fates that it seemed like the night was finally drawing to an end.

I knocked back another whisky and looked down the table to get Alaric's attention so we could leave. Unfortunately, he was too busy to notice my attempts at signaling him. Or he was purposely ignoring me. I wouldn't be surprised after the strange way he'd been acting around me all afternoon.

I hadn't met the shifter he was currently talking with before, but I couldn't miss the way she was leaning forward, putting her spilling cleavage on full display for anyone who cared to look. And Alaric was looking, if the half smirk he gave her as she stroked his arm was anything to go by.

Great, he's going to bail on me. The last thing I needed was to listen to him pleasuring a female all night while I had balls as blue as the sky in summer, and intrusive thoughts about my brother's fiancée.

As I moved to make a swift exit, I saw Kai talking to our father with his back turned away from his betrothed as she sat staring at her fish knife. She looked about as happy to be here as I was.

Fuck it. I got up and walked over to her side. What possessed me I don't know, but I did it anyway. Probably the bottle of whisky I'd made my way through.

"Dance with me, princess?" I asked, plastering on one of my most charming, dimpled smiles as the alcohol slightly slurred my words.

She looked up and rolled her eyes. "Oh, it's *you*. I'd rather not. Thanks all the same though," she said, dismissing me.

"Just one dance," I insisted, holding out my hand. To my surprise, she took it, albeit with a huff.

Throwing her napkin on the table, she allowed me to pull her from the chair, and lead her to the dance floor. "Be warned, I don't dance," she said. "So, if you are particularly fond of your expensive footwear, I would advise we go back to our seats now."

"I couldn't care less about my shoes, princess, but if that's your way of trying to get me to take my clothes off, then I would have to remind you which brother you're talking to. Again," I said, a smoldering smile tugging at my lips. *Fuck, what am I doing?* This was a bad idea, but it wasn't my first and it wouldn't be my last, so I tugged on her hand and twirled her into my arms.

Her sea glass green eyes looked up at me as I drew her close to my chest. She hesitated for a second, but then slowly drew her arms around my neck, raising to her tiptoes as she struggled to reach my height despite her heeled shoes. My hands tightened around her waist as I pulled her body flush against mine, and her scent overwhelmed me. A guttural sound escaped my throat, and she chewed her bottom lip. *Shit.* Any moment now it was going to be impossible to hide how fucking turned on I was at the feel of her perfect body molded against mine. *Oh, to feel this without fucking clothes between us.*

I began to move to the slow rhythm of the song and felt her body relax slightly, allowing me to guide us. We didn't follow any steps, just swayed together turning in slow circles.

Glancing around, I was relieved to find the only fae in the room watching us was Alaric. Kai hadn't noticed his fiancée's disappearance from the table yet, and everyone else was consumed with themselves, most likely making deals to get a foot up in society.

"So, we're dancing. What now?" she asked, tension stiffening her shoulders.

Not wanting any eavesdroppers listening in on our conversation, I brought her close, my lips to her ear. "Now you start talking, and I get to know my fiery future sister-in-law."

"Or, we accept that we don't like each other and just get on with our lives?" she countered, looking up to lock eyes with me.

"No. I prefer my idea," I said, before breaking eye contact so I could lean down into the groove of her neck, closer this time so my lips could brush against her skin as I dropped my voice to a whisper. "You see, since we first met, I've wanted to get to know you inside and out, princess. And the way I see it, you owe me, being as you well and truly ruined the first half of my plan when you accepted a marriage proposal from my twin."

She pulled back, making some distance between us as she gaped. "*That* was your plan? I don't even like you. What makes you think I would–"

I spun her out across the dance floor in a twirl, cutting her off mid-sentence. Keeping our fingers entwined, I pulled her back in, completely flush with my body, as my stubble grazed her lobe. "I don't like you either, but I don't need to like you to fuck you, princess."

She gasped as my breath caressed her flesh. With how close we were, I felt her heart rate soar between the fabric of our clothes. She was flustered, but I hadn't planned on being so affected myself too.

Changing the subject back to a topic less treasonous, before she felt something hard prodding her stomach, I asked, "Tell me, what is *your* plan here? Gain status? Riches? Why my brother and not wait to see if you find your true mate? You *are* immortal."

"Contrary to *your* belief, not everyone gets to find their true mate," she said. "Especially since *your* father declared the separation of races. Perhaps I don't have the patience to wait." Her voice was soft and low as she spoke, almost seductive, though I suspected that wasn't her intention.

"While it's true they are rare, don't you have hope? You're still young, can't be much older than me." Why couldn't I seem to hold on to the resentment I had for this female? While she was in my arms, everything else faded away. It felt *right*.

"Hope, Nekane, is for children. I used to have it…" she said, trailing off like she was suddenly remembering something.

"Oh? Tell me about it?" I blurted. "When you last had hope, I mean." Why did I want to know so badly? She was engaged to my brother for fates' sake. *She is not and never will be mine.*

"I had a happy childhood, all things considered, even if it was sheltered. My family would travel a lot, but I always had fun. Life seemed like a big adventure back then. When the attacks became more frequent, it all began to change for us. I went from a carefree child to someone who feared every little sound. I had a friend though, and he would always hold me through the hard times. I would look up at him and there was always hope in his eyes. I clung to his hope for a long time. He was at the camp when Elikai found me. I don't know if he got out, or if he was one of the ones who…" She stopped; I could feel her shift as she took a large gulping breath. As she tapered off, I spun her out again so I could process what she'd just said.

No one is that good of an actress. The emotion rolling off her was true grief, even if she held it back. What really happened on that hunt? And what attacks? Was there something happening in the kingdom that had evaded my father's notice?

Pulling her back into me felt right. Having her in my arms, pressed against me…

No. I couldn't be having these feelings, she was utterly unavailable, even if she would be the most delicious meal I'd ever taste. My errant thoughts swiftly cleared as she stiffened yet again.

"Why did I tell you that?" she gasped. Her wide eyes narrowed into daggers. "Are you using your allure on me?" she snapped, angered I would do that to her. She was high fae, so it likely wouldn't work on her anyway unless she was weak willed, but I didn't have her pegged as weak. No, she was all fire and temper.

"No," I snapped back. "I would never. I find it deplorable to use allure to force someone to tell you anything. Yes, I find it hard to read you, Evangelia, but I would never force you to tell me anything you didn't want to," I said, then shook my head. "Anyway, why push for an engagement when you just met each other? Is it just because he is a prince?" I asked. It still didn't add up. She lost someone in that hunt when she was rescued, and I could tell something traumatic had happened. But why did she want to marry Kai? For his protection?

Her eyes went distant, focused on an empty space in the air around us as she took a slow, deep breath. "Would you believe me if I said tonight's announcement was a bigger surprise for me than anyone else in this room?" she asked, so quietly it was barely audible.

My nostrils flared. I bet it was a big surprise, it must have been the best. Security beyond her wildest dreams after such a nomadic lifestyle.

"An amazing surprise for you I'm sure," I said. "So now you have the safety you always dreamed about?" I wanted to know this female. Needed to know what made her tick. I wanted her to tell me anything she was willing to share. Her voice was angelic, and it soothed me.

She barked a humorless laugh. "Would you believe me if I told you my dreams were nothing like this?" She glanced around the room, then met my eyes. "That I dreamed I would grow up to be the fiercest warrior?" She stepped back and a smile crept onto her face, as though the thought of being the 'fiercest warrior' was somehow funny now. Regardless of what was responsible for pulling up the corners of her mouth, the look was devastatingly beautiful on her. She should always be smiling. But it vanished as she said, "Nix was always my sidekick..."

"And this Nix was your friend at the camp?" I asked gently. She nodded, but didn't expand. I just stared at her, trying to fit all the pieces together and still coming up blank.

After a few moments of silent dancing, she murmured, "I'm sorry to steal your thunder tonight with the whole engagement announcement." An obvious attempt at changing the subject, but no less surprising. Our feet were still moving to the music floating around the room. "It was supposed to be your coming-of-age ball, wasn't it?"

Pulling her close again, I shook my head. She didn't need to know about my situation. Evading her question, I asked, "Tell me Evangelia, what's the real reason you didn't tell Kai that we had already met?"

"Like I said before, Nekane, it slipped my mind. In case you haven't heard, I have had a tough week despite the way my *fiancé* tells the story," she whispered, a quiet anger lacing her words.

I scoffed. "I imagine it to be very difficult being saved by your knight in shining armor and a week later living in a castle, engaged to a prince. One likely destined to be king, no less." Jealousy poured out of me and she froze in my arms. I could feel her heart racing before she pulled herself away from me. I wanted nothing more than to pull her close again and close the gap so I could feel her heat against me.

Her eyes blazed with fury as she pulled back to meet my own. "Perhaps I'm not the villain you want to think I am in this story, Nekane," she growled. Before I got chance to ask her what that meant, she turned on her heel and left, disappearing into the crowd of dancers.

Her touch had been a blazing fire and I was instantly cold without it. With her glowing silver hair and heart-stopping smile, she reminded me of a lightning storm. The epitome of dangerously beautiful. Regardless of how alluring she appeared, it didn't mean she wasn't a threat when you got too close. And fuck if she wasn't so far under my skin already that it took everything I had to stop myself from going after her.

She was absolutely not mine, and I would be smart to remember that. No matter how much my cock ached to sink into her.

CHAPTER 12

Evangelia

I lay in the tub of scorching water and tried to will my tense muscles to relax. Thankfully, Elikai was off having breakfast with the king again, as he had been every morning at this time.

It had been six days since the surprise engagement and subsequent party. Six long days of being locked away in Elikai's chambers, not even allowed to leave for mealtimes or exercise.

He kept me under lock and key, ensuring Thalia brought me what I needed to 'maintain my good looks', commenting that he didn't want to marry a malnourished waif. I was more trapped here under the ruse of a soon-to-be princess than I ever was living the restrictive life of hiding from the king's horde.

Upon leaving the extravagant celebration, we'd returned to these chambers and I realized the bastard planned for me to sleep here with him in his giant-sized bed. Like a real couple. No, thank you. I'd rather put a campfire out with my face than sleep in a bed with him. But when he had started pawing at my dress, panic had filled me.

"What's the matter, pretty girl? Feeling shy?" he'd laughed, as his hands had traveled to cup my breasts over my dress. I'd flinched away, trying to put as much distance as possible between us without running from the room. It wasn't like I could have gotten through the locked door anyway.

I'd never been with a male. Not for any particular reason. I had certainly thought about it a lot in my short thirty-four years. I just hadn't had the opportunity to meet many males who weren't either family or like family as we'd moved through the Fading Vale like ghosts.

Nix and I had tried once in our later teenage years, our hormones affecting our impulses and our bodies' needs, making us curious. Needless to say, it didn't work out, neither of us could do it. It was about as sexy as I imagined kissing a sibling would be, not that I had any. Nix was an attractive male, there just wasn't a spark, and I was pretty sure you weren't supposed to cringe while making out with someone. Or wonder how soon you could stop.

Predictably, Elikai hadn't liked my reaction to his touch one bit, and I'd scrambled for an excuse good enough to stop his advances. I'd needed him to think I was interested in him for my plan to work, but I'd die before sleeping with him to achieve it.

"P-Prince Elikai..." I'd stuttered. "As much as I really want to do this, truly I do. I... swore a vow of celibacy when I came of age, and I think it would be so much more... special if we waited until our wedding night. I will ensure I look my best then as well and... wear the finest lingerie for you." He'd taken some time to consider my words, and I had panicked it wouldn't work.

His expression gave nothing away before he'd responded. "I hadn't thought you were a virgin, pretty girl, and I won't lie, the idea of you being ruined by countless other males has turned my stomach more than once." A victorious smile had tugged at the sides of his mouth. "As a reward for pleasing me with this news, I will agree to wait until we are wed. I'll speak to the staff tomorrow about bringing our wedding forward to the soonest possible date. I wouldn't want to keep you from showcasing whatever lingerie you have in mind. Just make sure it is purple."

I'd sighed in relief while internally vowing to never wear purple underwear. With our engagement intended to be a short one, I needed to act faster with my plans to go after the king. I had mostly kept a low profile during the feast at the party, not wanting to draw attention to myself, but I had been listening in to his conversation intently, finding out his routine and movements around the castle. It seemed he spent most of his time in his suite on the top floor, which was likely heavily guarded.

Regardless of how difficult it would be to get my shot at the king, I wouldn't be able to even try while locked up in Elikai's room. So, I had been working hard to gain his trust these past six days. Plenty of stroking his ego, learning what makes him tick. Yes sir, no sir, three bags full, sir, kind of thing. So very not me, but I was desperate and would say whatever it took to gain some trust.

I'd decided that today I would ask Elikai for some freedom, no matter how small it may be. As I waited for him to return to his chambers, I found my mind wandering to another royal pain in my ass, *Prince Nekane.*

Since leaving him standing on the dance floor, I'd struggled to think of anything else. The sensation of our bodies pressed together had sent my head spinning. I remembered the way his strong hands held my waist tightly. The feeling of his breath as he'd murmured in my ear sent tingles across my flesh and heat to places I'd longed to be touched.

In that moment, I had wanted nothing more than to press into him and drown in the earthy cinnamon and sweetest apples that filled my senses in his presence. I should hate him. *I do hate him.* He blatantly hated me too. Yet as I lay about the chambers all day with nothing but my thoughts for company, all I could think about was how it would feel with nothing between us.

I loved Nix, but the time we had tried to experiment had felt nothing like this. Nix's touches had been all familiar and safe and... brotherly. On the dance floor, Nekane had been hot, possessive, and assertive. Why was I having this reaction to him? He was the identical twin of my certifiable captor, and *fiancé,* no less. An over privileged prince who was no doubt brainwashed by his father's views and would kill me the second he found out what I was. I should be sickened by him, as I was by his brother, but they just seemed so... different.

It was hard to put my finger on exactly why I knew that, but my gut told me he was a better male. *But could he be trusted?* If I set straight his assumptions about my situation with Elikai and told him the truth, would he even believe me? Or would he balk at the idea before hearing me out?

Fates help me, even thinking about him now was making me feel all kinds of hot and confused at the same time. It was bizarre that twins could look so similar, yet I reacted to them like they were opposite ends of a magnet.

"Evangely! I have news you will want to be sitting down for," Elikai announced, bursting into his chambers. "You aren't going to like it one bit I'm afraid, pretty girl." I dove out of the bath and quickly wrapped a towel around myself, knowing he wouldn't consider my privacy before barging in here.

"One moment, Elikai." I called through the door as I rushed to dry off and dress in the clothes I'd brought in to save Thalia the hassle.

Leaving the bathroom, I found Elikai tapping his foot with impatience. Raising a brow, he gestured to the couch—which was doubling up as my bed—for me to sit.

"As I have told you, I am due to become king, ideally very soon, but my father is... difficult." He sighed heavily. "He has received word from a reliable source that there was a kraken sighting off Kelpie Cove. They are notoriously powerful creatures and my father has been trying to rid Dezrothia of the foul beasts for centuries. Naturally, since my debut hunt was so epic, he needs me to attend in order for the mission to be a success, and so they don't all wind up as fish food. I'd initially dismissed it, knowing there is still much work to be done in ridding you of your roguish ways. But I have since decided it is the perfect opportunity to convince my father he should hang up his crown." He paused for effect, but when he didn't continue, I realized he was actually waiting for a response.

I took a deep breath, praying the fates wouldn't judge me for the drivel I was about to spout. "They would be nothing without you, Prince Elikai. It would be a fantastic opportunity to show your father you are more than ready to wear the crown, but does this mean you will be leaving me at the castle all alone?" I asked, trying to hide the anticipation in my voice and instead sounding upset by his news.

"Yes, pretty girl. I will be leaving at sunrise tomorrow and will be gone for hopefully no more than a week, two at the absolute most. I will, of course, ensure that Thalia puts out food for you while I am away."

He treated me like a real pet, not his fiancée and certainly not like his future queen. Thankfully, I didn't care enough, or plan on hanging around until a wedding date was set, to give a shit.

"Whatever will I do without you? I will surely lose my mind with boredom," I lied, sucking in another breath as I prepared myself to drop the big question. Would he allow me some freedom? What if he didn't? Would I be locked in this room for who knew how many more weeks? If the king was leaving with him, I could use the time to familiarize myself with the castle and the places I knew he could usually be found. Perhaps I could even find my daggers.

"My prince," I started, dropping my gaze to the floor in apparent submission. Not that he deserved it, it was the last thing I wanted to hand him. "Do you think maybe I could not be locked inside during your leave?" I reached out and took his hands, looking up at him with what I hoped looked like worried eyes. "It's just, I wouldn't want to be a nuisance asking you where everything is constantly once I am your wife. I want to be able to serve you well, be the perfect dutiful mate." I laid it on as thickly as possible, it was going to be my only shot.

He stood and began to pace, puzzling out what option would serve him better. Finally, he stopped in front of me. "Why, that is the most sense I have heard you speak! You should know about this castle. I can't be expected to hold your hand every single moment, and there will be tasks that I need you to fulfil as my wife," he mused to himself. "You shall be granted access to the castle and its grounds, but no further," he exclaimed as if it was his idea in the first place, and my heart swelled. "I shall have the guards briefed on the terms of your freedom right away."

Of course he would. *Asshole.* Why did my freedom sound like a dog on a leash, restricted to where I could go? "Thank you, Prince Elikai. I will be sure to spend my time without you wisely."

Once I was sure he had walked far enough from the chambers, my shoulders dropped and I sighed my relief. I hadn't had many wins these past couple of weeks.

"Milady," Thalia greeted as she appeared through the door Elikai had not long exited, the usual breakfast platter she bought me was notably missing. Instead, she handed me a folder with the royal crest stamped on its cover. "I just saw Prince Elikai. He said you would be needing a brief on castle life for his absence. This is the welcome pack we give to visitors," she explained. "It includes the mealtimes and where they are to be held, along with the approved map. There is a breakfast room just down the corridor and on your left which serves both princes and their guests." She paused to take a breath, and I found my stomach involuntarily tightened at the idea of a certain prince bringing his 'guests' to breakfast. "Dinner is served in the great hall on the ground floor with the rest of the castle's residents, you will find it on the map. Prince Elikai feels it is important for you to have hobbies, such as quilting or painting. I would be obliged to make any arrangements to ensure your chosen activities can take place on castle grounds, as per the prince's request. I will, of course, advise you of any events you will be required to attend on behalf of Prince Elikai during his absence, and ensure you have the best attire to wear. The prince will be back shortly once he has briefed the guards."

Was this really happening? A map of the castle? It was perfect. Sure, it would have been nice to see the city before he returned with the king and my assassination plan would need to happen. So, the little issue of having guards posted to ensure I couldn't leave the grounds was annoying, but it was still a huge win.

"This is fantastic, Thalia. Thank you so much." I said, and a small smile found her lips as she curtsied and left. More than likely busy making arrangements for Elikai's hunt.

I SAT in front of the fire studying the map as Elikai returned, and fought a cringe as he sat next to me and leaned over to see what had me so captivated. Just as I began to carefully fold the map away, he reached out, taking my ring adorned hand, and the blood left my face as I wrestled internally to keep the panic from showing.

"You seem rather fond of this cheap jewelry, pretty girl. Perhaps I should take one with me to remind me of you while I am away."

My breath caught in my chest. "Y-You wouldn't want these old things, Elikai. Besides, they wouldn't fit you." I tried to sound casual, but my refusal only spurred him on as he reached to take the solid band which blocked the scent of my race.

My mind raced, trying to decide which would be the lesser of two evils if he insisted. If he took that one, my guise would be immediately foiled. It would be impossible to try to explain away why a high fae suddenly started to give off the scents of a shifter. If he took the winged ring, I would risk shifting into my beast, especially in emotional times, which I hadn't been short of since being here. I had relied on the ring's magic for so long I could hardly remember what it was like controlling my emotions and shift by myself. But at least I'd have *some* control over it, unlike with the ring he was currently eyeing all too keenly.

"Okay," I agreed, trying to work out how best to play him. "The other one is my favorite though, so you can't have that one." I held my breath as his gaze flitted between the two rings.

Thank the fates, he played right into my hands and his attention landed on the other ring. "Well, if it is your favorite, then it is only right that I take that one instead," he said. "Then every time you see your bare finger you will think of your brave Prince, battling to clean the realm of its filth."

I let out a sigh of relief, but Elikai took it for defeat as he held out his palm. I reluctantly began slipping the ring from my finger. My hands trembling as I practiced breathing deeply, counting in my head to calm myself as I carefully removed it and dropped it into his hand. Seconds felt like an eternity as I waited to see if he noticed any change.

He scoffed. "Wow, that's lighter than I expected," he said as he weighed the ring in his hand. He briefly inspected it before placing it into his breast pocket. "Graves and Sloane have insisted on throwing me a going away party this evening in the games room across the hall."

"What kind of games will you be playing?" I asked, feigning interest, but just relieved I hadn't shifted on the spot.

"What games will *we* be playing should be the question, pretty pet. You will attend too if I am to let you have more room to explore while I am gone. It will be the perfect opportunity to practice being the perfect princess I have been tirelessly instructing you to be. If you don't embarrass me, I will reward you by playing a game of your choice, like charades."

"Forgive me Elikai, but what is charades?"

"Fates be damned!" he gasped. "You really know absolutely nothing do you? We must rectify that this evening!"

CHAPTER 13

Nekane

"Did I miss my brother at breakfast?" I asked Alaric as I let another arrow fly toward its target in the training hall. It had been days since the engagement ball, and I had neither seen my brother nor his fiancée during that time.

As the days had passed, I'd spent way more time than I should have considering their absence. I had come to the conclusion that they were locked away in his rooms together, learning her every curve and what made her scream for more. I had also been busy convincing myself of all the reasons I didn't care. Not at all.

I mean, I couldn't blame him. The things I would do to that female given a week with her in my bed. Oh, how I'd imagined her lithe body beneath mine, her face in place of Crystal's, and I suspected my imagination fell far short of what the real thing would be.

"Nah, yer brother wasnae there, but the wee lass was."

"What, really?" I lowered the bow in my hand, relaxing the string I had begun to draw taut. "What did she say? Was she ok?" *Way to play it cool, Kane.* Could it be more obvious that I had a slight infatuation with the female?

"No Kane, she wasnae, jus' like she wasnae yesterday or the day before. I'm fuckin' with yeh, but yeh proved my point anyway. Yeh need to get her out of yer head. This isnae *you,* and she isnae yours." Alaric chastised as he began to nock his next arrow. The fucker knew me too well, but I knew he wasn't totally clear headed when it came to her either. Maybe she was a witch and had us under a spell, because this just wasn't how we were with females. Ever.

"You're hardly one to talk. I saw you staring at her during the ball. You couldn't take your eyes off her–"

"Fuck off, it's my job to look out for danger. She's an unknown."

"Okay, if that's what you want to tell yourself..."

"I've shit to do and yer aim is embarrassing. Seriously Kane, as yer tutor in archery, it hurts me to watch," he sighed, but I knew he was only half joking, because there was a lot of truth in his words. I rarely missed the bullseye, and my shit aim today was just adding to his argument that I needed to rid this sorceress from my thoughts. I didn't even like her. I didn't even know her, for fuck's sake. Yes, she was hotter than the sun, but so were plenty of other high fae females.

Maybe it was the mystery of her that was throwing me off my usual vibe. The whole not giving a shit about anything and just drinking and fucking my way through life. But the draw to her was similar to the drive I had to stay around Alaric, something that had only increased since his return and her showing up.

Perhaps spending time with her would put me off. Yes, that would do it. Alaric started hanging his bow up, and I joined him. "So, what are your plans for the rest of the day if you're so busy?"

He arched a brow. "If yeh really want to ken. First, I need to check in with Axel, see how he is getting on with the new task I gave him. Jarid ran a drill with the guard an' they royally fucked up, so I plan on getting them sharpenin' every sword an' polishin' every shield an' helmet in the armory to teach them some discipline."

"What happened?" I asked.

He shook his head. "He's a good male, but they dinnae fear him enough, and they've been slackin' since I handed out more responsibility to him. He wants to be a lieutenant, but until he demands their respect, it's just not happening. An' to add on to everythin' the king has heard there was a kraken sighted off Kelpie Cove, so naturally he wants to go an' murder it."

"What's his issue with krakens?" I asked, not really knowing enough about his duties as general to comment on the rest of his to-do list.

He shook his head again. "Long story. Anyway, I'll see yeh tomorrow. Let's go for a run before breakfast."

"Okay, sure. I think I'm going to find Kai; it's been a while since we hung out."

He rolled his eyes. "Good luck with tha'," he said, and left in the direction of the soldiers' quarters.

I headed across to Kai's wing, done with him ghosting me. "Kai?" I called through his door. The last thing I wanted was to just barge in and see the lovers wrapped up in each other, but only silence rang out from the other side. Either they were ignoring me or weren't there. I let my senses out wider and found there wasn't so much as a heartbeat coming from inside. *Where the fuck are they?*

As I turned to go, I spotted Graves and Sloane leaving the breakfast room and stumbling down the corridor, armed with enough alcohol to sink a ship. If anyone knew where Kai would be, it was those two. They were obsessed with him.

I turned to follow them, raising my voice and calling out. "Graves! Sloane! Where's my brother?" The assholes just snickered and kept walking, so I sped up, not in the mood for their shit, and slung my arms around their shoulders, forcing my way between them. "You should go to see a witch if your hearing is that bad, boys. Now tell me, where is Elikai?"

Their shoulders tensed as I invaded their space, but they kept their silent treatment up all the way to the games room, located in the shared space between mine and Kai's wings.

I heard my brother's voice immediately and noticed Graves and Sloane sharing a look that said, *'Kai's not going to be happy with his party being crashed,'* but I couldn't care less. He was my twin, and I was done being ignored.

We entered the cozy space, a fire roaring already as Kai lounged on an armchair and held a very straight-backed Evangelia on his lap. She looked uncomfortable, but as she saw us enter, she smoothed her features with a mask of indifference that I had mastered myself and could recognize all the way from the Fading Vale. Weird.

"Brother!" Kai called, his arms stretched wide as if in greeting, and I didn't miss the way Eva flinched. The daggers he shot to his friends told me my intrusion was most definitely unwelcome, but fuck if I knew why. "To what do I owe the pleasure of your company, Nekane?"

"I have barely seen you since you returned," I said. "I thought we could hang out and catch up. Or are you too busy for your brother these days?" I hedged and saw Evangelia had swiftly moved to the loveseat next to the fire.

Crossing the room, I moved to take my place next to her before my brain caught up with my instincts. Although the look on Kai's face wasn't unpleasant, I knew he wouldn't be happy that his bride was no longer on his lap. Worse, sat next to me instead.

I'd already forgotten Sloane and Graves were in the room with us until one of them piped up. "Well, we are busy. We were just stocking up on refreshments to start playing a game before you tagged along."

I tore my gaze from Evangelia just as Sloane opened his trap, "Yes, you wouldn't be interested. You didn't want to play charades last time, too busy drinking with that mutt of yours." He nudged Graves, and they started to laugh at their blatant disrespect for Alaric. My instinct was to jump to his defense, but I fought it. They weren't worth the argument, and Alaric could stand up for himself. Not that they would ever have the balls to say that shit to his face.

"I've not played charades before," Evangelia murmured next to me. "Prince Elikai said that it had to be rectified tonight before he goes away with the king tomorrow. Apparently, as with everything else, he is particularly good at it. So here we are," she shrugged, gesturing to the room.

He's going away again? So soon after the last hunt? More importantly, did that mean Evangelia would be left here in the castle, without him?

Graves placed a bowl on the table in the center of the room with a thud. It was filled with scraps of parchment, and I knew the game well enough. It was the one where everyone would draw the slip instructing what they would need to act out. With the way Sloane and Graves were snickering like children, I dreaded what stupid shit they'd included.

The game started off well, simple things like reading a book, dancing and even jousting. After a few rounds, Evangelia sat forward, smiling. It was the first full smile I had seen since I arrived tonight. But she *had* been sinking whisky like it was water, so maybe she was just feeling its effects?

"Do you want to go next?" I asked her.

She nodded. "Turns out I do know this game, only Nix and I called it '*Guess It*'." Kai, Sloane, and Graves burst out laughing.

"Oh, how simple," Kai mocked. "You didn't even know the proper name for such a childish game." My blood boiled to see him act so callous toward his bride-to-be.

"Oh, poor little bumpkin," Sloane said, his tone condescending as he reached out to pat her head. My hands clenched into fists so tight, several knuckles cracked.

"*She* is to be *your* wife?" Graves laughed, before Kai glared at them both and they shut up. I set my jaw, trying to swallow my frustration.

Evangelia stood with confidence, choosing not to rise to the blatant mockery being thrown her way. I couldn't help but respect her for it. As she picked a slip out of the bowl her cheeks pinkened, but she turned to us all and began to mime it out. I had no clue what she was trying to illustrate, but it certainly wasn't innocent, and I swallowed a laugh of my own. Her hands were double-fisted, moving up and down vigorously.

The leering looks being sent her way, however, had me wanting to put my tightly clenched fists to work. I kind of expected it from Kai, he was her fiancé after all, but the other two were ogling her as well. I wanted nothing more than to gouge out their eyes so they couldn't see Evangelia's body moving up and down seductively, her perfect breasts bouncing as she made the movements more pronounced. As much as I enjoyed the view, I had to help her out, if for no other reason than to stop the others from looking at her.

"Churning butter?" I guessed, and the relief on her face was palpable as she nodded to me and quickly took a seat once more, scarlet highlighting her cheeks again.

Sloane was next to take the floor, not bothering to take a slip from the bowl, and acting out some inside joke I didn't get. I glanced at Evangelia to see if she was in on it too, but the red of her face had faded to white. Her breathing shallowed as she watched the performance being put on before us. Graves got up and started joining in and I could have sworn I saw smoke coming from–

"Enough," Kai said, bringing the game to an end without the last guess being completed. "I am bored," he whined. I wanted to ask what the fuck they had been acting out, but I didn't want to piss her off further. Even more confusing was the blatant smirk on Kai's face. He sent his fiancée a look that was anything but comforting. Not even friendly. More of a threat. I had no clue what had just happened, but the tension in the room and the anger radiating off Eva told me it was nothing good.

"What other games do you know?" I asked no one in particular. I didn't want to be here anymore, but I wanted to leave her alone with these three even less. The feeling was instinctual, clawing its way into my gut and refusing to let go.

"*Fine*," Kai drew out like a whining child. Was he always this much of an asshole, or was it because his lackeys were with him? Maybe it was Evangelia he thought he was showing off to? Though she didn't seem at all impressed by his display.

"Why not something like *Pictionary*? We have everything that we need to play…" I trailed off at the eyerolls I received from the opposite side of the room.

"I like *Pictionary*," Evangelia said. "I've never been any good at it, but it's always fun." Her face was brighter now with a small smile, and I smirked back at her, glad to have someone on my side for once.

I got up to grab the pens and wheeled the easel over. As I sat back down, they were discussing splitting teams. Having an odd number meant that there would be a team at a disadvantage, but that didn't concern me much.

Kai was demanding Evangelia come to his side. Something about it being only right that she be on his team, as he was the best artist and she could barely hold a pen the right way up.

He reached out to pull her toward him, and she flinched away from his hand. Again, for the second time tonight. It sent fire through my veins and a desire to launch my fists into his face repeatedly burned through me. I couldn't explain why I had such a strong reaction where she was concerned, but it took all of my self-control to stop from leaping across the room.

I rejoined the group, placing a hand on her shoulder. "Shall we team up?" I asked, trying to keep my voice gentle, but the way her eyes darted between my brother and I betrayed her worry. I couldn't shake the feeling that I was missing something untoward in their relationship. Fates help me, if her flinches were because he had laid his hands on her, I would personally hurt him in every way he had done to her tenfold. "Actually, don't worry about it. These fools could use my help. And it seems you have the almighty Elikai on your team." I winked and gestured to Graves and Sloane who looked like I had just kicked them in the balls. As I sat myself between her and Kai again and felt her relax against me, I suddenly felt like I'd just grown another few inches in height.

With the teams in place, we agreed to come up with the objects or scenarios we would draw on the spot, not bothering with picking from a bowl. I went first. I tried to concentrate, but the way Eva worried at her bottom lip as she watched me sent my mind to other places. I went with drawing the easiest thing I could think of, an apple.

"Ass cheeks," Graves called, pulling a laugh from Sloane.

"Apple?" Eva guessed. Kai rolled his eyes and gave her an exasperated look as he explained, like she was a child, that she could only call out the answers when *he* was drawing.

Eva nodded her understanding and said that she would go next. As she stood at the easel, she hesitated before drawing a small shape, then paused again, chewing the end of the pen.

Sloane and Graves started pointing, laughing and heckling her with cruel words about how she should just put the pen down and give up.

I stepped up behind her and cupped her hand with mine. "What are you planning to draw, princess?" I whispered in her ear and she told me.

"Here, add this," I murmured, guiding her hand across the paper. It wasn't a perfect drawing, but I was all for Kai taking a while to guess correctly, having no desire to move from where we stood. Her scent surrounded me, her back flush to my chest. She was so close I could see goosebumps raising up her neck, and I wanted to do so much more than just show her how to draw a damned training dummy.

I could feel Kai's eyes penetrating my back like daggers, and though it fates near killed me, I reluctantly pulled myself away. *He's right to be pissed.* I had no right to be standing this close to his fiancée and worse, getting hard at the thought of gripping her neck and bending her over so I could–

She is not and will not ever be mine.

Fuck, I needed to stay away from her.

Elikai guessed correctly, and we sat back down, only I leaned forward this time so we were barely touching. I busied my hands holding onto my tumbler of whisky with a vice-like grip.

Graves was up next. He started drawing a battlefield, or maybe it was a forest, pools of blood scribbled around badly drawn body parts sprawled across the paper. He drew two prisoners on their knees next, tears down their faces. Then two figures holding what looked like swords, but he didn't get a chance to finish as Evangelia jumped to her feet. Without a word, she fled the room, a hand on her stomach like she was going to be sick.

I looked around to see my brother and his idiot friends bent over, laughing at whatever had triggered her to leave so suddenly.

No one made any effort to go after her, and my mind whirled with possibilities. Was it the alcohol? Perhaps she was squeamish? Shit, maybe she was pregnant already?

CHAPTER 14
Evangelia

"Can I assist you in getting ready for the day, milady?" Thalia asked from beside my makeshift bed.

To my relief, Elikai had continued drinking in the games room long after I'd left last night. This morning, I had pretended to sleep through him getting ready to leave for his hunt, despite him making as much noise as possible. I just couldn't risk a confrontation with him when I was barely keeping my beast contained without the aid of my ring. It was like he knew and was trying to test me.

As I'd left that room and the evil monsters lurking within, I'd needed a distraction from my rage. So I'd dug my nails into my palms and bitten down on my tongue so hard I tasted blood.

I'd raced straight to the bathroom and began splashing ice cold water over my face, desperately trying to divert my beast's attention from turning back and ripping those bastards' throats out.

Thank the fates it had worked, but I hadn't risked going back to suffer their company for any longer after that. Deciding that the consequence of incurring Elikai's wrath was the lesser of two evils.

I had drunk copious amounts of whisky, thinking it would help me relax and ignore anything that the high fae pricks threw at me, but in the end it hadn't worked. I couldn't have guessed they would go so far as to act out my parents' death in charades, and then sketch out the bloody scene before my eyes in *Pictionary*.

In fact, all that the whisky had succeeded in doing was making me think it was a damn good idea to press myself up against Nekane like some horny nymph. I had no idea what game he was playing, but if his plan was to fill my head with thoughts of him and how much I'd wished we were the only two in the room, then it was working.

Thalia cleared her throat, drawing my attention back to her question still hanging in the air. "Thank you for the offer, but I can manage," I said. "You're welcome to join me for breakfast though, if you like?" It would have been nice to just talk to her outside this room and without Elikai breathing down our necks.

She shook her head. "That is very kind of you, milady, but I am afraid that is not how things are done. I am here to serve. It would be very unprofessional on my part, and it wouldn't look good on you either, welcoming a servant to your table."

I wasn't surprised by her refusal, but the way she sounded hurt that she couldn't join me was unexpected. Perhaps she needed a friend inside this castle as much as I did.

Once Thalia had left, I dressed for the day in the clothes laid out for me, another conservative, mid-length, pretty cotton dress. Perhaps I could request some leather trousers and a blouse or two?

It's not that the clothes Thalia bought me weren't lovely, they were just... restrictive. I was used to fighting leathers and comfort so I could move while training with my daggers.

What I wouldn't give to be in the Fading Vale with Mayhem and Chaos right now, training with Nix under the tutelage of my parents. I never thought I would miss it, but I did.

In the fortnight since being ripped from there, I could already feel my muscles had weakened slightly from lack of use. Since I could walk, I had trained hard almost daily with whatever we had at camp to practice with. My body wasn't used to being so inactive. Perhaps after breakfast I could go for a jog around the castle grounds and scout for potential escape routes for when the time came that I needed to make a swift exit.

If you're not already dead, that is.

I looked over the map Thalia had brought me. It was brief, but would definitely save me from getting too lost in the gargantuan castle. The top floor was marked as *'King's Quarters'* and off limits. Then there was the floor I was on. The larger wing was labeled *'Prince Elikai'* and the other *'Prince Nekane'*. The floor below this was the king's advisors' chambers, and also off limits.

Dividing the princes' chambers were numerous guest suites and communal areas. With the directions Thalia had given me, I could work out which room would be serving breakfast, and my stomach growled at the thought.

The entire floor below the advisors' suites was labeled *'horde'*, then it was the main floor we had entered upon arriving. The larger rooms were individually labeled this time; drawing room, great hall, billiard room, throne room, and the upper mezzanine of the ballroom. That must have been where we'd entered to descend the stairs at our farce of an engagement party.

Finally, the lower ground floor was labeled *'Servants' Quarters and Kitchens'*. The castle's kitchen had doors with direct access into the lower level of the ballroom where I'd danced with Nekane. Before my mind began to wander where it had no business going, again, I pocketed the map and headed for the breakfast room.

I don't know what I'd expected when I entered, but it wasn't the sound of laughter and Nekane throwing a croissant at Alaric. "Kane, I swear I'm gonnae kick yer arse!" Alaric warned, grabbing the pastry out of the air and proceeding to bite off half.

Nekane laughed, and it was a beautiful sound, but what got my attention was the delicious scent in the air. Leather and cedarwood, apple and cinnamon, mixed with freshly baked pastry.

"I'd like to see you try, big boy," Nekane replied, but there was fire in his eyes.

Neither noticed my entrance until the door clicked shut behind me. My stomach chose that moment to grumble, making blood heat my cheeks as both pairs of eyes landed on me.

"Uh… Morning," I said, tucking a few wayward strands of hair behind my ear. I walked in, avoiding eye contact, and took a chair at the far end, away from the two males who seemed to fill the room with their presence alone.

I loaded my bowl with fruit that had been beautifully prepared. I'd never even seen, let alone tasted many of the exotic-looking fruits on display, so took a little of everything, including some of my favorites that Thalia had brought me over the past week.

"My brother let you out of your cage, huh?" Nekane asked, oblivious to how accurate his choice of words was.

"So it seems," I said. I could do this, I just had to not think about how formidable his body had felt against mine, or how close his lips had been to the sensitive flesh on my neck as he helped me draw.

Nope.

I wasn't thinking about any of that.

High fae were gifted with breath-taking beauty and allure, it was just one of the reasons they thought they were the superior race, and I was just a victim of that.

It wasn't personal. Was it? No, he probably just had some strange sibling rivalry going on with Elikai, and I was caught in the middle, mistaking it for something else.

Alaric remained quiet, his gaze flicking between me and Nekane. Could he feel the tension too? I risked a glance at the scar down his face. There was something seriously attractive about rugged males with stubble, strong jaw lines and scars. Fates, what was wrong with me? I was reacting like a she-wolf in heat!

I dropped my gaze, and it settled on the plate before him. No less than twelve eggs sat waiting for him to devour. Four poached, four fried, four hard-boiled. Beside his plate was an almost empty bowl, and from here I could have sworn it looked to have the remnants of scrambled eggs inside. *So, the guy likes eggs? No wonder he's roughly the size of a barge.*

"I'm surprised my brother didn't take you with him. The way he's been keeping you hidden away and all to himself, I didn't think he would let you out of his sight," Nekane said casually. I couldn't tell if he was happy or pissed off about that.

"Elikai doesnae see the worth of takin' females to battle. Doesnae realize how savage they can be," Alaric said, his gruff voice startling me. He was an intimidating male. I fought to hold his stare as his eyes settled on me, but I got the impression that he was studying me rather than looking to murder me.

I couldn't trust myself to say anything that wouldn't give away my hatred toward the male, so I stayed quiet, making a start on the delicious fruit.

The general was right, though. Elikai would never think to find out whether I might be useful fighting at his side. Not that I would be. He would end up dead at my hand with a dagger through his back at my first opportunity.

"How are you, Eva?" Nekane asked. "You left in a hurry last night." His use of the nickname only Nix called me sent a cold shiver down my spine. I wasn't sure how I felt about the Regis prince using it.

"Fine, Nekane," I replied, trying to keep our interaction to a minimum. I didn't need any more reasons to be thinking about him.

"Kane," he corrected. "Call me Kane."

"Okay. Fine, *Kane*."

Alaric grunted. "Leave the lass alone. Clearly, she doesnae want to talk with yeh." It was the nicest thing I'd heard him say. Though maybe he just couldn't be bothered with hearing me talk. He'd been so angry and brooding for most of our time traveling together from the Fading Vale. And then he'd been sitting too far down the table at the engagement party for me to get a read on what kind of male he really was. "Ignore him lass, he's an arse."

"Glad I'm not the only one who noticed," I said with a wink. *Fates! Did I really just wink at the big, scary wolf?* What was wrong with me?!

"Well, if you two are done talking about my ass, then I am going to head down to the training hall. Alaric, you coming?" Kane asked, standing. "Evangelia," he said, tilting his head my way before moving to leave the room.

Alaric stood silently like a lethal predator, an amazing feat for a male of his stature. When the door closed behind them, it occurred to me I hadn't actually wanted them to leave.

By the time I'd eaten my fill—making sure to taste the array of egg offerings to see what all the fuss was about—I pulled out my map and decided to start exploring. I had a lot of work ahead of me. It would take a while to memorize the layout of a castle this size, and it didn't help not knowing exactly how long I had before the king would return.

I held the map out in front of me as I walked down the long corridor toward the stairs, remembering that Kane had said he was going to the training hall, but I couldn't see it marked anywhere. A quick glance over the notes Thalia had given me of potential hobbies didn't give me any indication of its whereabouts, either.

Of course, Elikai wouldn't think to tell a female where she could go to train. He just wanted a female to make him look good by being pretty and playing the dutiful wife. I shuddered.

Studying the map more closely, I spotted the floor two levels below this one labeled 'horde,' and the blueprint plan looked like it was made up of a large room that would provide ample space for training and equipment.

Then there were long corridors off it, giving access to lots of smaller rooms too. *Accommodation for the horde army?* They were small rooms by comparison to those on the plans for the king's advisors, but bigger than the servants' quarters. I glanced over the other floors too, but figured that 'horde' was most likely to house the training room and headed in that direction.

As I descended the two flights of stairs, making it to a landing, several large sweaty males walked toward a door at the end of the corridor. I hid in an alcove until hearing the door swing shut behind them and waited a few moments longer for good measure. Then chanced a glance to make sure I was alone once again.

I crept silently, keeping close to the wall before I came across a door on my left. There was the symbol of an ax carved into the wall above the frame. I reached for the handle, twisting it as I pushed. It didn't budge. *Damnit.* It must need a key, or maybe it's spelled. I wasn't really high fae, but I wasn't a witch either, so I didn't have the magic of their spells to even attempt breaking it.

I took out the map to find a blank space where this room should be. *Odd.* I made a mental note to come back some other time to satisfy my curiosity about its contents, and continued along the corridor.

The next door opened into a washroom with a row of benches running down its center, sinks lining one side while urinals and cubicles lined the other. There was an archway beyond the benches, where several shallow steps led down to a huge pool of steaming water sunk into the ground. It stretched as far as I could see without physically stepping into the room.

I moved toward the door where the males had been heading next, figuring it must be the training hall. The clanging of metal on metal grew louder as I neared and a smirk pulled at my lips that I was on the right track. On tiptoes, I peered through the square grill and found a crowd of males and females dressed in various training gear.

They circled an elevated platform which was cordoned off like an arena. From what I could see, they were mostly shifters and high fae.

Inside the arena, Alaric stood shirtless. I gave myself a second to appreciate his warrior's body before reminding myself he was off limits. Everyone here was. But his shoulders were massive, his abs well defined, and I followed that line of muscles down to the Adonis belt that created an arrow to what I assumed was something impressive, given his size. His thighs were thick, and the training trousers he wore clung to his legs.

His opponent, also shirtless and tall, although probably a few inches shorter than the general, was holding his own. His back was to me, but I could see his muscles were bunched as he held a two-handed sword and swung it with ease, as though it weighed nothing.

His body was slightly more lithe than Alaric's muscle-bound form, but still well defined. His dark hair was messy and his bronzed skin glistened with sweat from what had already been a hard session.

I'd watched the rebel camp's warriors train before, of course, but they were all like family. I was only ever interested in watching how their bodies moved from a strictly educational point of view. But maybe being so isolated from the city, towns and villages of the realm had affected me in more ways than I had thought, because apparently, I was fast becoming obsessed with the beauty of the male form and couldn't seem to look away.

I shook myself and put it down to never having been surrounded by the allure of the high fae, but that didn't explain my attraction to the shifters. I should be petrified by them, but instead I was staring open-mouthed and fates near salivating.

I had to get out of here before my mind wandered to other ways in which they could move those powerful bodies. *Who am I kidding?* It was already too late to stop it. My imagination ran wild as my body filled with the need I had never had the chance to satisfy. Not fully, anyway.

I stayed put, listening to the chatter coming from those inside. They must be guards from the king's horde. I gasped as I caught a name. *Kane*. Of course, that was who Alaric was fighting.

"Will they ever tire?"

"They have been at it since they arrived..."

"I wish I could last two minutes against the General..."

"Fates, the prince has some skills..."

"He could plunge his sword into my sheath anytime he likes."

A low growl escaped me before I could stop it, but the crowd was watching the intense duel with such awe that nobody noticed, even with their sharp hearing. I couldn't let myself be distracted by physical attraction. Kane was the twin brother of my captor, and Alaric was one of those responsible for hunting and killing my friends.

Do not let yourself forget that.

I left the training area and descended the stairs to the ground floor, heading straight for the postern gate and out into the castle grounds. Kicking off my shoes, I broke into a jog across the lush lawns, adjusting to the feel of feathery grass under foot. So different to the twigs and leaves of the forest floor.

I just needed to blow off some steam. Clear my head of the images of Kane and Alaric fighting and focus solely on the bigger picture. Killing the king and making Dezrothia a better place so my parents' sacrifice wouldn't have been in vain.

Although, I couldn't shake the nagging worry that life under his successor could prove to be just as bad.

I'D BEEN NAVIGATING my way around the castle for three days now and barely needed my map anymore.

I would wake up early to visit the breakfast room. Stocking up on food for the day, like bread and cheese, before Kane and Alaric had even risen. Then, for the most part, I avoided them for the rest of the day.

Stashing food in my room also meant I didn't need to venture to the great hall to eat with those who lived in the castle, such as the king's advisors and their families. I didn't plan on staying long once the king returned, so I had no interest in getting to know anyone, despite what I might have told Elikai.

I had been making an effort to try to get to know Thalia a little better, though. It wasn't easy trying to coax her guard down and get her to just talk to me like a normal person, instead of constantly asking what she could do for me. But I still tried and felt like we were making some progress.

She was the closest thing I had to a friend here, and my fear of getting to know Alaric and Kane better and finding that they might not actually be monsters meant my loneliness was weighing heavily.

I missed Nix so much. I just needed someone to talk to, to distract myself from the grief and worry plaguing me. I attempted to strike up conversation with Thalia whenever she was around during the day, figuring if I could find some common ground, we would at least have something to talk about.

The evenings were the hardest. At night, I curled up in front of the fire, the warmth of the flames making me feel close to my parents, while I dug deeply to hold on to the hope that Nix usually gave me.

Hope that my parents' deaths would be avenged.

Hope that I was strong enough to kill the king.

Hope that I could get out of here alive afterwards.

Hope that I would one day be reunited with my best friend.

Yeah, the evenings sucked.

Still, I was trying to be productive during the king and Elikai's absence, while remaining stealthy to not draw any attention to myself. I'd returned to the training hall several times to observe the horde, then I would practice the moves I'd seen once I was in the privacy of Elikai's chambers.

I had tried the locked door I'd discovered marked with an ax several times, returning multiple times a day with the hope that someone would accidentally leave it open. Even though there were many other rooms I had found unmarked on my map, I'd become a little obsessed with finding out what lay inside that particular one. I'd even attempted to pick the lock with some hair pins I'd requested from Thalia, to no avail.

When I finished descending the stairs, I made my way along the corridor, intending to have a quick try of the handle before secretly watching yet another training session, and saw that the door was already ajar…

My heart sped up with excitement at the prospect I would finally have my curiosity quashed. I glanced around to be sure I was alone, before pushing it open and stepping inside.

My eyes widened and my skin tingled as the castle's weapons room was revealed around me.

No wonder it wasn't on the map. The royals wouldn't want visitors finding this place, and Elikai sure as shit wouldn't want someone who he'd wronged in so many ways around sharp, pointy things that could run him through.

I hadn't seen my twin daggers since I'd been disarmed at the camp, and I missed their reassuring presence. *Could they be here?* It seemed like an obvious place to keep them. There were various weapons on display around the room, but it was probably too much to ask for my daggers to be here.

I was surprised to see that most of the weapons adorning the walls looked plain, albeit sharp and well looked after. Then again, why would King Regis outfit his soldiers with fancy blades? He wouldn't care to spread the wealth any further than it suited him. One look at some of the starving villages surrounding the Fading Vale would tell you of his greed.

Stepping further into the room, I spotted a wooden chest toward the back corner, partially hidden below a rack of spears. *It would make a great hiding place.*

Moving swiftly toward it, I worked the latch open, holding my breath as my heart thundered at the thought that I might find Mayhem and Chaos inside. I gently opened the lid to find some linen rolls that had been discarded haphazardly in the otherwise empty chest and let out a deflated sigh.

Standing, I surveyed the room again, determined not to be defeated. They had to be here, right?

I started looking in every cupboard, drawer and chest I could find, coming up short every time. Deciding I might just have to take another weapon and hide it somewhere on the castle grounds to reclaim later, I was crouched, looking under a table, when I heard the door creak open behind me, and I froze.

Shit, shit, shit.

There was no way I wouldn't be seen. My mind raced, scrambling for excuses good enough to explain away my being here, but everything I came up with was totally implausible and would likely leave me next in line for execution.

"What the fuck are yeh doin' in here?" A deep masculine voice said from behind me as the scent of leather and cedarwood fogged my senses. My heart pounded against my chest as I thought desperately on what the actual fuck I was going to say for myself.

I stood slowly, but in a blind panic found myself launching my right fist in the air and throwing a punch at the silhouette of the male behind me.

He caught my fist dead in the air, and with a quick pull, dragged me close. "Next time yeh throw a punch, Angel, it had better be a proper one," Alaric's low voice growled into my ear. Suddenly, the room felt very small, and the temperature in the small space became oppressive.

Excuses failed me, so I opted to go on the defensive. "I *can* throw a punch, asshole. I'm just out of practice, and it's dark. Next time maybe turn the light on before sneaking up on someone if you want them to punch you perfectly."

"Yer brave for someone who jus' got caught with her hands in my cookie jar. Now tell me, Angel, what the fuck were yeh doin' in my weapons room?" he snarled, so close to me now that I could feel his body heat through my thin dress.

"Uhh... nothing?"

He just stared at me, one eyebrow raised, unsurprisingly not buying my lame excuse. Desperate to avoid planning my own funeral, I went with the truth. Sort of.

"Fine, I was looking for my daggers. They are a family heirloom, and I miss having them close." He eyed me with suspicion, not saying anything as the silence stretched on, the only sounds were our breaths.

"Fine. I'll pretend I didnae see yeh, but if yeh want to learn how to punch properly, then find me in the trainin' area, and I'll show yeh," he said, and before I could answer, he turned to leave.

"Wait. Really?" I grabbed his arm, but he didn't budge. Instead, he tried to tug it out of my grasp, but when I didn't let go, I found myself flying forward with momentum and face planting straight into his chest.

I craned my neck to look at him. He was shirtless, and fates, he was one heck of a male. He'd been working out. I could taste the saltiness of his sweat-covered pecs on my lips and fought the weirdest urge to lick them.

He growled low in his chest as if he could read my mind, and I could feel the vibrations shooting straight to my core. Before I got the chance to do anything stupid, he placed his hands on my shoulders and pushed me away from him, breaking the contact completely.

"Seriously?" I asked. "You would train me? No strings attached?" Over two weeks of being virtually idle and surrounded by pricks had made me itch for a fight.

"Aye, that's what I said, lass. I saw yeh with weapons at the camp and I assume they weren't for knittin' with," he growled, assessing me in my cotton slip. "Now, fuck off before I change my mind."

I released the breath I'd been holding and muttered a quick, "Thank you," before racing back to Elikai's chambers, grinning at the prospect of training with such a warrior.

Even if he was a bit of an asshole.

CHAPTER 15
Alaric

What the fuck was I thinking?

"If yeh want to learn how to punch properly, then find me in the trainin' area, an' I'll show yeh."

My own stupid fucking words tormented me as I stood in the weapons room, trying to calm the fuck down, but the smoky sweet aroma she left everywhere she went was filling my nostrils and apparently going straight to my cock.

It hadn't helped that she had been pressed up against me mere moments ago. Then, when I'd forced myself to push her off me, I was faced with her pert nipples clearly visible beneath the too thin slip of material they called a dress around here.

I had half a mind to go and take Krista up on her blatant advances, but I didn't mix work with pleasure and wasn't about to start. It could get very fucking messy.

The little temptress had thought she was being smart, sneaking around the castle undetected these past few days. But I was part wolf and a damn good general, so not a lot happened in this castle I didn't know about.

I had felt her eyes on Kane and I fighting in the training halls, but she hadn't done anything serious enough to warrant my attention or punishment… yet. Still, I'd needed to know why she was hanging around the training floor. I'd smelled traces of her around the weapons room in particular more times than I was comfortable with, so I figured I'd lay a trap.

As soon as the door to the weapons room closed, it locked automatically with magic, thanks to the spell of one of the resident witches. None of my soldiers would be stupid enough to leave it open, ever, but she didn't know that, so I had left it ajar myself and waited. Unsurprisingly, it hadn't taken long for her to show up.

I stayed far enough away to evade detection and listened, expecting to catch her running out with a handful of weapons, but it sounded like she was searching for something specific. But what?

If she were an enemy looking for a blade for some assassination scheme, she would have been in and out. Figuring she really was looking for something important, I'd made my presence known, but instead of scrambling over her words with excuses, the little minx had thrown a punch. A fucking punch. At. My. Face. Seriously, did she have a fucking death wish?

Then she had started gobbing off like some brat, and instead of throwing her out by her ridiculously stunning hair, I had stupidly blurted out that I would train her.

Truth be told, her punch wasn't half bad. She at least knew how to form a fist without breaking a thumb, unlike most of the recruits when I started out training them, but she was still woefully underprepared to survive this castle.

Still, why had I made her that offer? It wasn't my business. Even now, I was making a mental note to ask Elikai's lackeys what the fuck they'd done with those daggers of hers. They must be important to her to risk breaking into the hordes' weapons room to find them. I understood the sentimentality, regardless of the monstrous shite I did on a daily basis. Family was still everything.

I needed to get out of this fucking room and have some of the new recruits deep clean it to rid the place of her fates cursed scent. There was something not entirely right with it, but not wrong at the same time. Just different. And confusing. Like Kane's scent was recently. Not that I would let on to being affected at all. But it was another reason not to trust the ballsy little vixen. Everything had been normal before she showed up. Boring even. Just the way I liked it.

When Regis told me he and Elikai were leaving the castle on a hunt that didn't require my presence, my life became infinitely better, but it was short-lived when I realized Evangelia would be left roaming the castle alone.

She was an unknown, a potential threat, and I still didn't know what to make of her. The fact she had both the princes practically panting after her was concerning, whether either of them could admit it or not.

She could have them under her allure. I didn't feel any major power coming from her, she wasn't on the same level as Nekane, but that didn't mean I could rule it out. Especially with the looks they had both been throwing her way, which were far from fucking innocent. I was right to stay on high alert. Subtle magic was certainly the most dangerous stuff out there.

My gut told me Elikai had machinations for her, aside from just wanting an attractive wife, but I had no idea what they could be. He didn't speak to me about these things and I certainly had no desire to talk to him to find out. Would be more likely to deck him than I would have a civil chat.

Kane, however, had been a little more covert about it. *Thank the fates*. If I didn't know him so well, it would have been easy to miss. During the week she'd spent hidden in Elikai's chambers, he'd been in a foul fucking mood. Had asked me several times if I'd seen her or tried to make out that he was looking for his brother, but I wasn't born yesterday, far fucking from it, and I could see through him.

Since she'd turned up at breakfast on the first day of Elikai's absence, I'd seen the anticipation on his face every morning since—Hope that she would grace us with her presence again. He was a fucking good-looking male without having to put in any effort. He never needed to tap into his allure, but I could have sworn he looked like he'd been making more effort in his appearance than usual the last few days.

I didn't know what she had said or done to change his impression of her, but it set me on edge. One minute he was telling me he didn't trust her, then he spent a night playing childish games with her and seemed to have forgotten she was hiding something.

He knew she was off limits, but that was probably just making him want her more. The fool was going to get himself into more trouble than she was worth. Neither of us had gone to the Crooked Claw since the engagement party, and I didn't really know why, but the draw wasn't the same. All I knew was that whenever I thought about leaving the castle and taking a female, I hadn't been able to get *her* scent out of my head.

And that just made me more suspicious of her.

I needed to kill something, but annoyingly, that was frowned upon anywhere except a battlefield, so fighting the horde soldiers would have to do. I saw Axel first and sent him to pass a message on to Thalia for me, explaining that I would be training Evangelia in basic self-defense and that she needed something suitable to wear.

First, it was time to vent some of this frustration.

IT WAS BUSIER than usual in the training halls today, and though I did my rounds, sparring against several large shifters, it felt like I was just going through the motions. What I wouldn't give for a new recruit to show up who could actually give me a run for my money. The only two I enjoyed sparring with these days were Kane and Axel, but I had to put the time in with the others, too. It was the only way they would improve.

Plus, it ensured they remain petrified of me, which helped keep them in line with minimal effort.

Just as everyone headed out of the training hall for lunch, I started toward the stairwell, planning on leaving the castle's wards to shift into my wolf and run for the afternoon.

It wasn't natural for a shifter to not be able to change at will, but the king had the witches put the wards in place all the same. Likely couldn't sleep as soundly at night with the threat of my kind being able to transform into our beasts.

The wards didn't completely stop the shift. If I tried to shift before clearing the wards, I would feel a strong resistance, like pushing against a wall. I could eventually fight through it, but doing so would fates near exhaust me in the process. Plus, the alarms would be triggered and I would have some explaining to do, which would be a big step backward in my relationship with the king, so I just went with it instead.

As I opened the door to leave, I slammed straight into Evangelia.

She wore tight fitted leather trousers with a cotton tank top, and I'd be a fucking liar if I said it wasn't a good look on her. Her hair was pulled back in a ponytail with those war braids she'd had when I first saw her in the Vale and she looked every bit like a warrior princess on the warpath. *Maybe shifting can wait.*

Fuck, I had been staring for too long. "First lesson, watch where yer fuckin' walkin', Angel," I chastised, knowing full well I had walked into her, not the other way around.

"Jerk," she muttered, but quickly raised her hand in greeting and smiled. So she didn't want to risk me changing my mind? "Is now a good time to train?" she asked, trying to sound casual, but the anticipation practically vibrated from her.

I huffed a laugh, and nodded, turning back to the mats I had just left, and waited for her to join me. She kicked off her shoes and ran to meet me without hesitation. Not many females enjoyed fighting, but she wasn't normal. She was engaged to Elikai, for fuck's sake.

"Righ', warm up. I ain't havin' yeh hurt yourself," I said, and she nodded, dropping to the mats and stretching.

As she bent, her top hung low, giving me the perfect view of her tits. Fuck, they were nice, each the perfect handful, and I needed to stop staring. *She's a fucking high fae.*

Rubbing a hand down my hideously scarred face, I found her eyes trained on me intently. "Are you okay, Alaric?" she asked. Like she cared. She was probably doing it on purpose to distract me.

I just grunted a non-committal response to her and moved to the center of the mats. "What do yeh wanna do first, then?" I asked, and she chewed her lip.

"Hand to hand combat?" She suggested, though I had a feeling that wasn't what she truly wanted and my mind drifted back to those daggers she clearly missed.

I fell into a fighting stance. The best way to learn was to do, plus it would give me an idea of what she already knew and how much of a threat she was. At my movement, she shook out her shoulders and stood in front of me, falling into a fighting stance of her own.

I didn't wait to let her know we started, but she fell into the rhythm of fighting like it was second nature. I launched myself at her, intending on grabbing her around the waist to take her down easily, but she danced out of the way and landed a solid kick to my ribs. I slid to a stop, redirecting my momentum to where my target was again. She had her hands up and tightly fisted, bouncing lightly on the balls of her feet, ready for me.

Well, isn't she just a big fucking surprise.

She knew how to fight, and at the very least she'd had some basic training. I relaxed, dropping my guard and slowly circled her, she followed, keeping her guard facing me.

She was getting tense as she anticipated my next attack, a rookie mistake. When I noticed her guard dropping, I launched forward again, grabbing her across her chest and sweeping her foot from under her as she crashed onto her back on the mats. She looked up at me and grinned, lifting her hand for me to grab it, and I pulled her to her feet.

"Okay, so you can move for a big guy," she teased, dusting herself off and turning back to me, falling into a casual guard, one fist loose in front of her chest and her other hanging low, guarding her hips.

It was a clever move, making your opponent think you weren't as skilled as you actually were. I moved again, to see if she would fall for the same move twice, but she danced inside of my guard, one hand grabbing my wrist and pulling while the other slammed into my shoulder with the aim of dislocating it.

If I wasn't a shifter with centuries of conditioning work behind me, then she likely would have succeeded. She was surprisingly strong and knew how to use her opponent's strength and momentum against them, likely meaning she was used to fighting with beings much bigger than her. *Clever girl.* No wonder she wielded twin daggers. I spun away from her, her back facing me now.

"Yeh ken how to fight," I said. I wasn't going to beat around the bush, she was trained and knew what she was doing. I had trained enough of the guards to know the signs. What was she doing here? Did the thrakos plan this? Was she undercover? A spy? Fuck, this wasn't supposed to happen.

"A little," she said, shrugging one shoulder and facing me again. It was clear she enjoyed fighting, that much was obvious from the joy shining in her eyes. I'd watched her more than I cared to admit since meeting her, and this was the first time I'd seen real joy in them.

Fine. If she wanted a fight, she would get one, and I wouldn't stop until she tapped out. I ran, and her eyes widened as she saw me barreling toward her. She tried to move, but was half a second too slow, and my shoulder rammed into her stomach.

She grabbed me, her elbow coming to slam into my back. *Cute, she thinks that will stop me.* I slammed her back into the wall, hearing the air leave her, then threw her back onto the mats to the side.

She rolled a few times, but was back on her feet quick enough, breathing heavily as her eyes narrowed. I could see the gears turning in her pretty little head. I smiled at her, but it was all teeth as I waited for her to attack.

We circled each other, predator and prey, waiting for the other to make the first move. She leapt at me, feigning a kick to my knee and landing one in my ribs on the opposite side.

As she swung her leg back up to try to reach my head, I grabbed her ankle, holding it and setting her off balance, but that didn't stop her. Using my grip as leverage, she jumped and pushed her other foot into my stomach. I let go of her and she fell to the mats, though soon managed to right herself again.

We fought and fought and fought, clashing time and time again, though neither of us really winning. Eventually, I had her in a grip, one arm banded across her waist, locking her arms by her side, my other arm across her chest.

"Give up, lass. Yeh cannae win," I whispered in her ear as she wriggled and fought against my grip.

She let out a defeated sigh. "You're right, Alaric," she conceded, giving me a seductive smile and fluttering her eyelashes. My grip barely loosened on her, but just as I thought she was about to tap out, she slammed her heel down on my instep, forcing me to let her go.

Fucking bitch, that actually hurt.

It was time to end this. She was getting cocky. I charged at her, my shoulder hitting her stomach again, but this time I took her to the floor. Pinned under me, I grabbed her hands and held them above her head as I straddled her thighs, trapping them in place and stopping her from hitting me where it would *really* fucking hurt.

She breathed heavily below me, fighting to release herself from the grip I had on her, her green eyes glaring up at me. "Fine, you win this time," she growled, trying to get her breathing under control as she yanked her hands a couple more times to try to get free of my hold. But fuck that. Being so close to her... fates, she was a looker, alright. Males would sell their souls to the deities to swap places with me right now. And that little trick she'd pulled, feigning defeat, it was fucking hot.

Maybe she wasn't all soft curves and fancy dresses. For someone so young, she had some bite to her and could fight. That was not something I had expected. But still, I needed to find out why she was really here. I needed to get my head right. *What type of female wants fighting lessons?* Definitely not the sort who is engaged to a prince.

"This time? Does that mean you'll be comin' back for me to beat yer arse again?" I teased, remaining where I was, straddling her hips. She nibbled her lower lip and wiggled under me.

"I'm just out of practice after being locked up in Elika–" she stopped herself.

"What do yeh mean locked up?" I growled.

"Um, you know, locked up at that camp... In the Fading Vale," she corrected, avoiding eye contact. She was lying, but I didn't know why. I knew she wouldn't tell me what she was hiding. She didn't trust me and she obviously wasn't stupid.

I got off her, releasing my grip on her wrists.

"Meet me tomorrow at sunrise by the castle entrance. We can work on yer stamina before breakfast."

CHAPTER 16
Evangelia

I fates near fell through the door into Elikai's chamber. Sweat clung to my braided hair, trickling into my eyes as I fought to get my breath back from, what felt like, a thousand-mile run.

Every time I tried to drop into a normal jogging pace, Alaric growled some nasty comment or command in my ear, or worse, threaten to end our sessions if I 'wasnae gonnae try.' *Asshole*. It's not that I wasn't pushing myself or taking our training together seriously, more that he was a foot taller, so his idea of jogging was basically a run for me.

Although I stayed in shape, I'd never had the freedom to run long distances, having had to stick to the confines of a small camp rather than to the expansive grounds surrounding a castle. If he knew the reality of my situation here with Elikai, he would understand I was more than motivated. Though if he knew the truth, he would put a stop to training me.

Then again, he didn't seem to be a fan of my psychotic 'fiancé'. So maybe I could tell him a bit about it? I'd just skip over the whole assassination plot I'd hatched on my way here. He was definitely suspicious of me, and rightly so. I did plan to kill his precious king at my earliest opportunity, and the training he was giving me would only aid my success. But Alaric couldn't know any of that.

Why would a pampered princess want to kill a king, after all? As I pulled off my leathers, I couldn't help the smirk tugging at my lips, knowing Elikai would have a fit if he could see me right now.

If Alaric knew who the bad guy really was in this twisted relationship between Elikai and I, who the more obvious threat to the king was, would he start to trust me? He would be one heck of an ally as long as he never caught wind of my true plans. Perhaps I could even convince him to help me get my daggers back. As far as I knew, he hadn't told anyone he'd found me ransacking the weapons room. That had to mean something.

There was no love lost between Elikai and the General. Kane, however, was a different story. He and Alaric shared a bond. It wasn't something I could or even wanted to get in between, but it intrigued me.

All the more reason I had evaded the confusing prince as much as possible. I couldn't afford to lose focus. Though on the occasions I had seen him wandering the castle, I got the feeling he was lonely. Kane was all charm and charisma, but I had started to wonder if he wore it as a mask.

My gut still told me he wasn't the same male as his identical twin, regardless of how similar they looked. Though that didn't mean he was my ally either.

"I've drawn you a bath, milady," Thalia said, stepping out of the bathroom, making me jump and fumble to cover myself as I had been pulling my sweat-soaked tank over my head. I was so caught up in my own musings I hadn't even heard her in there. *Some vigilante assassin I am going to make.*

I had only begun training with the General a couple of days ago, but Thalia was nothing if not the perfect handmaiden and had caught onto my new routine already. Alaric and I would run in the morning, then I would head straight back here to freshen up, where Thalia seemed to know to have a bath prepared, before eating the food I'd stashed away. Then I'd continue my search of the castle for a few hours until my afternoon training session with the big bad wolf.

Alaric had been an excellent distraction from my grief and the worry over controlling my shift, which had been surprisingly easy since Elikai had left. He also had the whole sexy-brooding-alpha-male thing going for him, making our sessions on the mats even more intense than they should have been.

Still, I figured it was better I drool over him than my fiancé's brother. Who I absolutely wasn't thinking about every night when left to my own thoughts. Though, in recent days, it hadn't just been him alone.

"Milady?" Thalia said, drawing me back from my sinful thoughts.

"Oh, thank you, but really, you didn't need to. And please call me Evangelia, or Eve even, just not milady. It's so... formal, and well, you just don't need to be like that with me. My friends in the Vale would tell you I am not the fancy title kind of female," I said, realizing I wasn't ready for her to call me Eva as only Nix did.

And Kane that one time, which I was still conflicted over.

I would never admit it, but I kind of liked Alaric's nickname for me. The way he growled 'Angel' in his accent reminded me of someone I knew in the Vale and gave me weird butterflies in my–

Shit. My eyes went wide, shooting to Thalia as it dawned on me what I had just said. *My friends in the Vale...* Suddenly, I was claustrophobic, like the walls of this huge room were closing in around me and I was going to suffocate as they squeezed.

I stared at the witch across from me in horror, waiting to see if she had noticed. *How could she not?* It felt like she was staring at me so hard that she could see into my soul and unravel all of my secrets.

"Okay, Eve," she said, like she was testing the name on her lips. I smiled at her, ready to pretend that my name was the only thing hanging between us if she was willing to do the same.

She cleared her throat. "My ancestors were in a witch coven with other families of witches, some of whom headed to the Fading Vale while my family moved here to work for the royals," she said. "Perhaps you know them?"

"I doubt it. The Vale is a big place," I said, trying to keep the nerves from my voice. Could she really know some of the fae hiding out there? Might she understand we weren't the monsters the king painted us to be.

As much as I wanted to continue our conversation—intrigued why she was opening up and not running for a guard—I was very conscious of being half naked, which only added to how exposed I felt.

"I haven't visited, but I've heard," she said, then dropped her gaze to the ground and mumbled, "I believe *you* may know these witches."

"A lot of folk had to go to the Vale when King Regis took the throne," I said. "What makes you think I would know these witches specifically?"

"It's one witch in particular, actually. She was the last full-blooded witch in a line of strong seers," she said, and I frowned. "My family is known for producing children with strong warding magic, which is why we ended up here, but I can also feel magical imprints. I inherited the gift from my father's side, and well, I didn't mean to, but when I touched your jewelry… I could sense her family's magic."

I stood staring at her in shock, completely dumbfounded, as I tried to piece together what she was telling me. Nix's mother was the only full-blooded witch I knew. She was a powerful seer too, some say the most powerful in existence. Could Thalia truly be talking about her?

Edelin had been missing for a while, and feared dead by all but Nix himself. She *had* been the witch to spell mine and my parents' rings, though. Which couldn't be a coincidence, could it? Could I trust Thalia enough to talk about something so personal?

It must have taken a lot for her to tell me what she had; maybe I owed her some truth. "Does the name Edelin mean anything to you?" I asked cautiously, not wanting to give too much away, but her relief was palpable. So she knew Nix's family? But what had happened? Had they left things on good terms? Could she be trusted?

Thalia passed me a robe and ushered me into the bathroom, where she sealed the door with her magic, muttering a spell so quietly the only word I caught was *silentium*.

"Yes, the Sybilline witches were always great friends of my family, the Hexenwalls. Together, with a few other families, they had a coven, but everything changed… When I saw your rings, I… I told my uncle, Westly–"

"You did what!?" I'd only met him briefly when he'd helped the etiquette teacher, Willow, but I had seen him coming and going from Nekane's wing. What if he'd told him?

Shit.

Was I a fool to be having this conversation? Was I so desperate for a friend within these walls that I would fall for some scheme they might be pulling?

"It's okay, Eve, he can be trusted. He would never risk anything happening to any of his former coven members, despite them being estranged for centuries. Besides, I can only feel the imprint of the family's magic, not exactly what your rings are spelled to do. Your secrets are your own," she explained, reassuring me somewhat.

"So what happened? What changed?" I asked.

"Edelin Sybilline was a powerful seer and a good friend of my uncle. When King Regis came into power, she didn't trust that he would leave her be as his predecessor had. She feared her gifts could be abused and went to the Vale where we now believe she allied herself with rebels."

"And what of *your* family?"

"They thought they'd be able to carry on their lives as they had with the former king. None of my family had mated outside our race, so we didn't have any half-breeds to hide. Ward magic had never been used by the royal family in the past, so when the horde came to our door, we weren't prepared." She paused, glancing up to meet my eyes. When she found me hanging on every word, she continued. "My mother was pregnant with me at the time, and to save our line from slaughter by refusing, the Hexenwall's made a deal to work for the castle. We could live and work here in peace, as long as we cast and held the wards that prevent the shifters from being able to turn easily at will–"

"Shifters can't turn within the castle?" I blurted.

"A weak shifter certainly couldn't, but strong shifters could fight through the magic, eventually. Either way, alarms would sound and alert the king."

Well, that explains a lot. But why was she telling me any of this? How did she know I could be trusted? "So, what did your uncle say? When you told him you had detected Sybilline magic on me?"

Her gaze found a spot on the floor to stare at. "To be honest, he was concerned. For you. For the Prince. For our family. But more than that, he just really wanted to make sure that Edelin was okay. He said she was the only full-blooded witch left of that bloodline, so he knew it had to be her who had spelled your rings." She peeled her eyes up to meet mine again "I couldn't say anything to you until now. I needed to be sure you were, in fact, from the Fading Vale and hadn't just been a high fae prisoner like the story the prince has told."

Her words made me unsteady on my feet. Thalia reached out to support me, holding me upright at my elbow, her eyes gentle and kind.

I had never felt any ill will from the witch, but to know that she knew of Edelin, my best friend's mother, was huge. The rebels had potential allies in the castle, and we hadn't even known.

"Perhaps it would be a good idea for us to talk about this all in more depth sometime soon? With your uncle here, too," I suggested. "I know Edelin well. Her son is my best friend, and we grew up together. I am sure we would have a lot to discuss."

Thalia's mouth dropped open at the mention of a son, but quickly recovered. "Yes, milady."

"I think we are past that now," I said.

"Sorry. *Eve.* It's somewhat of a habit," she admitted. "But yes, I will talk to Westly and let you know," she said before reaching into the bath to reheat the water just how I liked it. She left, closing the door behind her, but thankfully without a magical seal this time.

Despite the revelations, I bathed quickly and got dressed, ready to continue my exploration of the castle.

I LOVED FINDING new undiscovered places that my map purposely concealed. Everything was just so beautiful. I wanted to feel the history behind it, as well as memorize its blueprints.

I walked along an antechamber off the main hallway on the ground floor of the castle, familiar enough with this part to pocket the map. I kept close to the wall, running my fingertips along the stunning hand painted paper covering the top half above the rich wood of the wainscotting below.

Velvet drapes framed a paneled window while the space around the roaring open fireplace was host to a snug armchair and table that I thought would make the perfect cozy hideaway to unwind in. If I'd been here under different circumstances that was.

I stopped when I felt an unusual ridge along the otherwise smooth wall. Turning, I tried to see what my fingers could feel, but it didn't look any different.

Slowly, I dragged the tips of my fingers across again, feeling the groove. I dug my nails in to pry it open, but it was fruitless. Leaning back against the wall in defeat, I debated where to go next, when a faint click sounded behind me. *Inside* the panel.

I turned to find a small gap had appeared where the dip had been. I briefly scanned the area to make sure I was alone, before carefully pulling it open, revealing a tiny cubby just big enough for one fae.

Excitement drummed through my veins as I squeezed inside to see what the secret space held. It had been carved into the rough stone of the castle's wall and wasn't decorated in any way.

There was a slight step, almost like a seat, so I sat down, imagining who might have been here before me. As I began looking around the gloomy space, my eyes slowly adjusted to the darkness.

Why would a room like this even exist? Punishment for servants? Prisoners? Spies? A chilled breeze blew its way down my spine, and I glanced back to find the source.

A draft drifted in from the hewn stone. I twisted, moving to kneel on the step instead, and ran my hands across the wall in front of me. It was much smoother here, like hundreds of hands had followed the same path mine were tracing.

Toward the center, I grazed an odd, small protruding stone and pulled it free. A narrow beam of light shot through, illuminating the cubby. Panic and adrenaline laced my veins as I listened, but couldn't hear anything.

Craning my neck, I squinted one eye and peered through the hole. A gasp escaped me, unable to believe what I was seeing. The tiny peep hole lined up perfectly with a view of what could only be the castle's throne room. The perfect vantage point for someone to spy on the king and any meetings he might hold inside.

A gilded throne was carved from beautiful mahogany with dragons etched into the hand rests, the back decorated with gold studs in a rich red velvet panel. Surrounded by more carvings of images I couldn't make out from this angle.

It was gorgeous, extravagant, and absolutely not what I expected the purist king would choose to seat himself upon. It had to have been inherited from his, allegedly, less cruel predecessor.

The rest of the room was just as beautiful. The walls were lined with paintings depicting various battles and scenes of victory. The floors were a matching mahogany to the throne, though part was covered in a stretch of red carpet to create an aisle up the center, rolling up several steps which led to the throne itself.

The dais on which the throne sat was covered in more of the crimson carpet, only it spread out like a sea of blood across the entire area.

During my exploration of the castle, I'd had no desire to visit the throne room, given everything the king had decreed within those four walls. And the devastating effect his stupid Lores had on so many innocents.

As I watched the eerily empty room, I was hit by the foreboding feeling a lot of death had happened in there too. It was the perfect place to ensure a public spectacle of any apparent traitors to the throne. Guilty or otherwise.

When my thoughts took a dark turn toward what the room represented, I shook myself and stood to leave. I couldn't stay here any longer. I needed fresh air or a cold bath or to just punch something or someone.

What gave one male the right to commit atrocious crimes while playing judge, jury and executioner over an entire realm of fae? Just because they sat in that chair?

WITH THE SECRET cubby concealed once more, I made my way up to the training floor. It was a little earlier than I usually met up with Alaric, but I needed to take out some of the anger now coursing through me. Thalia may have said that the wards could suppress the shift, but they weren't used to *my* kind testing them.

As I walked, I took a deep breath and slowly counted back from ten. By the time I reached the training hall, I'd calmed down somewhat. Still absolutely in the mood for a fight, but at least I had control over my beast again.

The moment I stepped inside, I scanned the room for Alaric, but only unfamiliar faces stared back at me. I spotted the shifter female who had made up part of the guard that slaughtered my camp, and racked my brain for her name as she began to head my way. She'd tried to talk to me a few times at stopovers on the way to the castle, but I hadn't been in the mood to talk. *Understandably*. Crystal? No, Krista.

"Are you lost?" she asked, none too friendly.

"No. I'm here to train with Alaric," I said. "Have you seen him?"

She raised her brows. "He isn't here." Looking me up and down, she continued, "I heard rumors he's been spending a lot of time in here with the soon-to-be princess, I just hadn't thought there was any truth to them."

My fists clenched. "Maybe you can train with me in his absence? What better way to find out exactly how true the rumors are?" I offered.

She tsked. "What about your nails? Or worse, your perfect, pretty face?" She was smiling as she spoke, but it was all teeth and challenge. "Besides, we wouldn't want your fiancé coming back to see you all beat up… My head would be on the block if I so much as sneezed in your direction," she scoffed, and I let out a growl as I heard the muffled laughs of several other soldiers around us, listening in.

Before I could snap my comeback, a youthful male with long wavy hair approached. His thick mane was a stunning shade of brunette and he stood about as tall as Kane, though his shoulders were wider. A shifter. He gave off the same gritty vibes Alaric did, but was somehow much more approachable looking. Perhaps thanks to the spring in his easy gait. Bright green eyes crinkled in a friendly smile as he reached for my hand.

Bringing it to his lips with a chaste kiss, he said, "You must be Lady Evangelia. I'm Axel. Alaric has told me you have been quite the surprise in training." There was a lilt to his voice, though definitely not as strong as Alaric's.

"Um, thanks," I said, feeling a blush pinken my cheeks. Despite being a little flustered, his presence was calming.

I wasn't used to male attention, not like this anyway. Certainly no one in the Vale had ever spoken to me in a flirtatious manner. Elikai was a pompous asshole and just talked down to me. Graves and Sloane turned my stomach without even needing to open their mouths. Alaric was, well, Alaric. Then I guess there was Kane, he certainly had a charm to him.

"I would offer to step in for him, but as Krista was poorly explaining, it would be our heads if anything were to happen to you. Best to wait for the boss, love," Axel said. Unlike Krista, who I only just noticed had left, his tone was nothing but friendly. I instantly liked him. He reminded me a little of Nix, which made my heart sting.

"Thank you, Axel. I'll come back later, but if you see him, please could you let him know I was looking for him?"

"Sure will, love. It was good to finally meet you," he said, and it sounded genuine.

I gave him a warm smile of my own before turning to leave the room, heading back to my sofa bed in front of the fire to try to digest all that had happened in the last few hours.

CHAPTER 17

Alaric

I studied the ledgers in front of me, assessing the training and capabilities of my best soldiers. Not one name jumped out at me. I needed to find someone to step up when I was gone from the castle and none had proven they were capable.

Jarid wanted to move up the ranks, but he just didn't command the respect of his peers. Axel was strong enough, but too young and new for me to put into a position of power. I needed him to work his way through for a few more years. Besides, he was busy doing something else for me. Something only he could be trusted with. Krista was a promising recruit, and the males were starting to fall under her command. Maybe she was the candidate I was looking for? She was new, but age was on her side and she'd certainly proven her worth on the hunt a few weeks back.

I made a note of the shortlist before pushing the papers away across my desk. With the king away from the castle, the atmosphere amongst the horde who remained was much more relaxed. It was nice to see, though I would never let on. Couldn't let them think I was going soft.

Usually, I took advantage of times like this to relax at the Crooked Claw, but Kane had little interest in joining me. I'd been busy training Angel in my spare time anyway, which meant that the time I spent with Kane was limited.

Although I was just training Angel, every time I had her lithe body pinned under mine, my mind turned savage. Carnal. Fates, I needed to find someone to fuck. Someone to take my mind off her. Maybe it was time I dragged Kane's ass out.

Making my way from my office in the horde barracks, I climbed the stairs hoping to find Kane. I was definitely concerned. He had never acted this way over a female, not even that Crystal lass he liked to fuck. But little-miss-suspicious comes along and he completely changes. It just didn't sit well with me and had the potential to ruin everything.

I found him in the library, alone, and felt a wash of relief that she wasn't somehow here too. Sinking her claws deeper into him and getting him to do whatever she wanted. Maybe I was being paranoid, but I'd rather not leave it to chance.

Being older and wiser, I could ignore the temptress's allure while she got all hot and sweaty under me on the mats. No problem. Totally unaffected. But with how enamored Kane seemed to be, I didn't think it would take much effort on her part to manipulate him and set whatever her plans were in motion.

One thing I'd learned so far during our training sessions was that she hadn't asked or worried over Elikai once. That in itself spoke volumes. I had expected endless longing and fear he wouldn't come back in one piece, but she seemed to have forgotten all about him as soon as he rode out of the castle gates.

"Kane, yeh comin' to the tavern?" I asked from the doorway.

He glanced up from the book he was reading, but didn't make any attempts at moving. Ordinarily, he would be on his feet, ready to go for a night of debauchery. Especially considering we hadn't gone out in what felt like forever.

"Oi, yeh entitled brat, I'm speakin' to yeh," I said, slamming my palm into the wall beside me. Well, that got his attention.

He glared at me. "Maybe I'm not in the mood," he grumbled, closing the book in his hands, but holding the page with a finger.

"Yer always in the mood. Come on, the king is away, let's go out an' enjoy ourselves."

"And what about Eva?"

"What about her? She's Elikai's bride, not yours, and she shouldnae be any concern to yeh."

"He's left her here, alone."

A growl rumbled from my chest. "And that is for them pair to worry about, not you." She must have cast a spell over him. It was the only thing that made sense. I sighed, knowing I wasn't going to win this battle. "Yeh can stay here then. I'll jus' go on my own. Keep all the fun to myself. Yeh ken–"

"Yeah, yeah, you hate the castle..." he interrupted, having clearly not listened to a word. So I left, pulling the door closed behind me.

I headed for the castle entrance, ready to unwind for the night in the Crooked Claw and not think about a certain silver-haired temptress. Or what the fuck I was going to do to get Kane back on the right path. I'd been too easy on him over the years, become too much like a friend.

Maybe Kane did just need to fuck her to get her out of his system. He was no use to me in his current head space, so perhaps that was an option. Other than Crystal, I'd never known him to be with the same female twice, losing interest and keeping them at arm's length once he'd taken them for the ride of their lives. He was honest with them at least, told them straight that he wouldn't likely talk to them or even remember their names by morning, and even though they all agreed, the majority would come back wanting more from him. He just wasn't the kind of male who saw himself settling down.

Crystal had been different, willing to take pleasure from him with no strings attached, which suited him perfectly. She was the only female he allowed back to the castle too, which I thought maybe meant he quite liked her, but he wasn't even tempted at the moment. I'd seen her sulking around his quarters a few times the last week or so, reeking of desperation.

The king had done a number on him emotionally growing up. It was a wonder he wasn't *more* damaged. Our upbringings couldn't have been more different. Mine too was far from ideal, but I'd at least had no doubt my parents loved me. Something I had clung onto during the dark path my long life had taken.

As much as I made out like Angel was just another pain in my arse, and I certainly still didn't trust her, I had to admit that our training sessions were becoming the highlight of my day. If I was being really honest with myself, which I wasn't, I'd say it was more like the highlight of the century. I didn't need to like her to admit that she was breaking the cycle of never ending boredom immortality could bring.

In just a few days, she'd come on leaps and bounds with her hand to hand combat and grappling. We had gotten into a routine of meeting before breakfast to run, working on her stamina, and then training hard for hours in the afternoons.

She didn't trust me yet, that was still a long way off. After we'd run miles around the castle, she would slink off to Elikai's rooms to freshen up, and I wouldn't see her again until she showed up at the training halls to fight.

I needed to find out more about her past. She definitely wasn't what I had expected when we'd first brought her back to the castle, but right now, I just had a lot of questions and no answers. I had to work on gaining her trust to learn her true motivations so I could protect the future of the realm, and I had an idea how I could do just that.

Despite what I'd said to Kane, by the time I made it across the courtyard to the gates, I hesitated. *Maybe the Crooked Claw can wait another night*. With the sudden change of heart, I turned back, deciding to call it a night and spend some time with my hand instead. Fates, I needed to take the edge off before spending any more time with *her*.

I'D WOKEN EARLY, needing to get some work done before meeting Angel for our run, but as I approached my office, I found Axel had beaten me to it. Propped against the wall with arms crossed over his chest and a smirk on his face, he said, "I met Lady Evangelia."

"What's she wantin' now?" I grumbled as I pushed the door open. Once we were both inside, I triggered the ward Westly had set up long ago, ensuring no one could eavesdrop.

"Looking for you, actually. Asked me and Krista to train her in your absence. We both refused, but she was itching for a fight."

"Course she was..."

"She's really under your skin, isn't she?" Axel teased, not realizing how close he was to the truth. I just couldn't figure her out, and it bothered me to no end.

"It's just the caged beast. Yeh ken how it is, skin crawls with the need to let them out."

"Think we can go to the forest again?" he asked. The hope in his voice reminded me of myself a couple hundred years ago.

"Aye. With the king away, it's probably the best time to go," I said, settling into the chair behind my desk and nodding for Axel to take a seat himself. "Yeh manage to speak with those eejits 'bout those daggers yet?"

"Aye, spoke with them yesterday after talking to Evangelia. Can't say I enjoyed their company. You know how they are. I am just a lowly shifter compared to their superior selves. They didn't much like that I was asking things of them. Soon changed their tune when I told them it was a direct order from you via the king though."

He hated those two high fae pricks as much as me, and would happily gut them. I'd have let him if I didn't need him to be on his best behavior. It was a smart move to say it was an order from the king, though. Nobody would question it. Then again, who would they run to tell, anyway? Their daddies? I scoffed at the thought of those ancient, pompous brown noses.

"Good, so yeh have the daggers?" I didn't see them on him, but he wasn't stupid enough to just carry them about the place. I had taught him the ways of the castle personally before he'd stepped foot inside.

"Already stashed away for you. Just give me the word and I'll retrieve them." He was a good lad, one of the very few I could trust in this city. He had been working in the castle for a few decades now, though his great aunt had asked us to take him in when he was just a babe. I couldn't say no, she was practically family, which made Axel family too. He'd been under my guardianship since. Not that anyone knew that.

"Thanks lad, yeh did good. I'll arrange for us to get a run with the beast tomorrow. If I'm itchin', yeh gotta be too." I scrubbed a hand over my face, weariness settling in with the thought that the king could return any day, and who knew who was watching in his absence.

"Sounds good, boss. If you need me, you know where I'll be," he said. "Oh, and have fun with Lady Evangelia!" he finished with a wink as he released the sound-proofing ward stone and left my office.

A GLANCE at the sun told me it was time to find Angel for our morning run. I left and headed for our meeting spot at the rear entrance to the castle, which led straight out onto the grounds.

When I arrived, she was already waiting. I nodded a quick greeting before breaking into a jog. We managed several laps, but it wasn't long before she started lagging behind. She was getting better, though. In the days since we had started her cardio regime, I could see a dramatic improvement, but still not good enough by my standards.

"Come on," I said, but it came out as more of a growl. "Yeh cannae dawdle if yeh want to have the stamina to keep up with me."

She cursed, muttering something about me being a bastard. Good. She wasn't supposed to like me. "Alaric... please... two minutes..." Her breaths were coming short and fast as she panted behind me, a nice sound coming from her lips. Giving me all sorts of ideas that I definitely was not going to entertain.

I slowed my pace, coming to a stop by the entrance to the kitchens. When Angel stopped before me, fighting to catch her breath, an idea struck.

“Come on. Yer havin’ breakfast with me. If yer gonnae be trainin’, then I need to make sure yer eatin’ well so yeh dinnae keel over. No excuses, I do it with all my trainees so move yer arse,” I said, arms folded across my chest. The fire in the glare she shot me as she straightened was worth it.

For Kane to get her out of his system, they needed to actually interact, and to do that, she needed to come to breakfast. Regularly.

Surely he was smart enough to do the rest. Either they clashed, and he realized he couldn’t stand her company, or he’d fuck her senseless and dump her before his brother got back.

Then everything could get back on track. Win-win. It may seem heartless, but I’d never claimed to be a good male.

CHAPTER 18
Nekane

I stood over my bed looking at the three outfits I'd laid out for today. One week ago, I'd have rolled out of bed, put on some loose pants and not thought twice before leaving to get food, train, freshen up, then hit the tavern, and repeat.

Yet here I was, worrying about which outfit to wear so that maybe Eva wouldn't think I was a total lost cause when I accidentally, on purpose, bumped into her around the castle today. I had barely seen her since the shit show games night, and I still hadn't gotten to the bottom of what had made her leave so abruptly.

I quickly dressed and headed to breakfast, knocking on Alaric's door on the way. He wasn't there. Again. No doubt busy training with *her*. Or he'd gotten tired of waiting for me. I kept running behind my normal schedule thanks to my totally pathetic outfit interludes and pissing around with my hair.

I entered the breakfast room to find it empty, confirming my suspicions that they were together. After piling my plate high with pastries and fruit, I sat in my usual spot and dug in.

Today, I wasn't going to let Eva avoid me again. At first, I thought she was avoiding everyone, not turning up for breakfast or dinner and not hanging out in any of the communal rooms. But since she'd started training with Alaric a few days ago, I had barely seen either of them.

The door suddenly flung wide. "You've tired me out!" Eva sighed as she walked in looking over her shoulder, closely followed by Alaric. Though she was trying to sound pissed off, I didn't miss the smirk pulling at her plump lips.

"That was nothin'. Yer stamina's shite, Angel. You're to start eatin' well today, and tomorrow we're doin' an extra two laps," he replied. What the fuck had I missed? Surely Alaric didn't just call her Angel? I thought he couldn't stand her? He'd spent plenty of time telling me to stay away from her. Now he's calling her by a cutesy nickname?!

"Where have you two been?" I asked, trying to sound casual.

"Oh. Good morning, Kane," Eva said like she'd only just noticed I was in the room. She probably had, but she'd just called me Kane without sounding like she wanted to rip my balls off so that was progress.

"Morning, Eva. Care to explain what's got you all hot and panting this morning?" I asked with a smirk.

"Elikai said I should take up some hobbies, only the ones he suggested were dull, so I picked training with Alaric instead," she said, gesturing to her sweat covered clothes and then the male in question.

"Aye, she isnae half bad either, Kane. She'd give yeh a run for yer money," Alaric chimed in. Was that a compliment? From professor tough love?

"Is that so? Well, aren't you just full of surprises," I turned to Alaric, not letting his dig slide. "You know more than anyone that I don't struggle with stamina," I said with a wink, then looked back to Eva. "Maybe I'll come next time." She might have blushed, or it could have just been from her recent work out. She leaned over me, adding fruit to her breakfast bowl, and I had to swallow a moan as her scent enveloped me.

"Hmmm, maybe you should. Join us, I mean. Alaric would no doubt appreciate the backup on the mats too," she teased as she sat down across from me.

Alaric walked over, passing her a plate of eggs and murmuring something to her before he sat to consume his own mound. She rolled her eyes, but as I'd had many lectures in the past about them being a complete source of protein, I stayed quiet. Already knowing how *eggs-hilarating* his diet plans were. I had no idea why he cared so much that I ate right when he knew I spent my evenings drowning in booze.

"Maybe I will..." I answered cryptically, not wanting to say more and give away the fact that I was practically jumping inside at the idea. *Fuck, this is embarrassing.*

I'd hoped to discuss my plans for today with Alaric before finding her, but I wasn't going to miss the opportunity while I had her attention. I cleared my throat. "Have you visited Ezerat city before, princess? Has Elikai taken you yet?" I asked, trying to play it cool and act indifferent.

"No, why?" she asked suspiciously. She definitely didn't trust me, but that was fine. I didn't trust her either. You didn't need to trust someone to want to fuck, right? She was just hot and mysterious. Of course, I wanted to know more.

"I thought you might want to get out of the castle and visit the city. Today maybe?" I asked.

"Oh. I mean, I would love to, but I can't–"

"Why? Would you rather see it for the first time with Elikai?"

She snorted, quickly dabbing the orange juice running from her nose with a napkin. "It's not that. Your brother has posted guards to make sure I don't leave the grounds."

"I meant with me. Alaric can come too. The guards won't stop you if you're with us. Come on, it will be fun," I pushed, really hoping she'd agree.

Her eyes swam with distrust as they narrowed on me. "Yeah, sure. That would be great, if you mean it."

"Perfect. How long do you need to freshen up?" I asked.

"Um, give me twenty minutes?" she asked around spooning her breakfast down her throat so fast, it was a surprise she didn't choke.

"Okay. It's a date." Fuck, no, it most definitely was not. *Ground, swallow me now.* Maybe if I just kept talking, she would forget I ever said it. "We can pick you up some more training gear if Alaric hasn't scared you off yet? He's a firm teacher, but the best there is. Even now, whenever I fail one of his drills, I have to endure some war story or lecture. He knows I have no interest in the throne, never have, so he decided it was the perfect torture for my punishment to make me work harder next time or something," I said. Then turning my attention to the male in question, "Alaric, you are joining us, right?"

"Aye."

"Okay, it's a date." *Really Kane?* For fuck's sake, what's wrong with me?! Still. Not. A. Date. "Well, I will go and let Thalia know while you two finish here. Wouldn't want her thinking you had been kidnapped now would we, princess." I stood with a wink and nodded goodbye to them before getting out of the room as swiftly as possible.

ALARIC and I waited by the gates. The guards shot us weary glances every few seconds, probably getting nervous as to why we were just standing around instead of leaving quickly as we normally did.

Finally, Eva appeared. She'd swapped her training clothes for a stunning blood red dress with matching cape lined with black fur and was beaming at us across the courtyard as she hurried down the steps to our side.

"Ready, beautiful?" I asked her, holding out my elbow like I was some sort of gentlemale. "Would you like to walk or take a carriage?"

"Walking is good," she replied and took my arm as we wandered through the courtyard, down the cobblestones toward the gates and the city that surrounded the castle. The trip was silent, but it wasn't uncomfortable.

As we reached the towering gates, two guards suddenly shifted in our way and Alaric rolled his eyes. *Here we go.*

"She cannot leave," one of the guards screeched, his annoying voice making my ears ring as he pointed to Eva. "Prince Elikai said–"

"Dinnae teach yer granny to suck eggs, bud," Alaric snarled to the guards like it was some kind of threat to stop them from continuing whatever they had been about to say.

He was intimidating at the best of times and fucking terrifying when stood looming ominously over you like he was the guard right now. Still, I had no clue what he was talking about. "What do eggs have to do with anything?" I asked in confusion.

"I mean, he does like eggs..." Eva murmured quietly beside me, and I grinned down at her.

"It's a sayin' yeh fuckin' eejits," he growled.

"Sure, well, I think you just scrambled everyone's brains with that one," Eva said, glancing up at me with a smirk.

"Stop poaching my best yolks, Eva," I laughed, before seeing the guards staring at us in confusion, their body language saying they didn't plan on letting us pass.

"No disrespect, General, but Prince Elikai's instructions were clear. She is not, under any circumstances, to leave the castle–"

"Are you seriously telling me I cannot take my dearest sister-in-law-to-be for a stroll to meet her own citizens?" I cut in.

"I-I–"

"Do you really think my brother meant she could *never* leave the castle, even supervised?" I challenged them.

"But–"

"Surely you aren't insinuating that you don't trust me, *also* your Prince, along with the best damn General in the realm, to keep her safe?"

"N-No, your highness…" he stuttered, shooting a desperate look to the other guard on duty who was wisely staying out of this.

"Good. Now, I will be leaving with Lady Evangelia and General Alaric, and you will be a good guard and look after the castle, yes?" I stated, knowing my tone was condescending, but at that moment, I didn't really care. I'd never been particularly friendly with any of the guards and just wanted to get out and start showing Eva around Ezerat.

The day was pleasant, despite winter's bite, and for the first time in a while I felt at peace with Alaric at my back and Eva on my arm. Though I think we all knew that wouldn't last. This would never be possible with Elikai around.

As we entered the city center, I pointed out the academy where most of the children of Ezerat were educated, as well as various shops we passed, such as the bakery, butchers, tailors and blacksmiths.

Eva's eyes were wide with wonder, like she had never seen a place like this before. Were the towns and villages really so different?

"Ah, and here is Alaric's favorite shop…" I said, stopping by a window that had various weapons on display, along with pieces of armor.

Eva lifted her hand to touch the glass, but stopped just short of pressing her hand to it, turning to me instead. "Can we go in?" she asked, her excitement palpable. I gestured to the door and followed her lead.

She moved around the shop, flitting from piece to piece, admiring everything on display. I waved to the warlock behind the counter, who nodded and subtly flipped the sign on the door to closed, to allow us some time to browse. There were a lot of perks to being royal, I just didn't usually use them. But for some reason, I really wanted to impress her.

"See anything you like, princess?" I asked as she paused at a cabinet full of daggers.

"These are beautifully made…" she said wistfully. I moved to peer over her shoulder just as she turned to look at something else and barreled into my chest. "Oh, sorry," she gasped, flustered.

"It's fine. Do any take your fancy?" I asked, gesturing back to the cabinet. "A beautiful female deserves a beautiful blade to match." She just shook her head and moved past me toward Alaric, who was standing by the training gear. He began pointing out what she would need if their sessions were to continue.

He told her to pick out what she wanted, and I made mental notes as they discussed the correct sizing for maximum movement and comfort. A smile tugged at my lips, seeing Alaric in full tutor mode. It wasn't something I saw too often, not since I had moved from being his student in our lessons to training with him.

My brother and I weren't the only ones under her thrall. At least Elikai could do something about it, though. Was already doing a whole lot about it. Word around the castle was that the engagement would be short and the wedding extravagant.

Of course, even if I'd met her first, he would still be the better suitor. He could offer her a crown one day. All I could offer her was a few good nights in the sheets before she worked out I was pretty much emotionally unavailable and broken thanks to my father.

After we were finished, I paid the bill, ignoring the protests coming from Eva. She was to be family, after all. Besides, it didn't seem that Elikai had left her with any coin, no doubt because he had no intentions of her going out shopping for herself. Thalia had likely been charged with fetching whatever she desired.

We strolled further into the town and came upon a shop that sent a beautiful blush over her cheeks. She was staring open-mouthed at a sexy window display of the finest lingerie in the city. I felt a little awkward about going inside as it was Crystal's shop, Ezeratify, and I had been a bit of a dick to her lately.

"Um… does it… I mean… is it… always so… small?" she asked, embarrassment lacing her tone, and my fists clenched at the thought of her planning to surprise my brother with any of the garments before us.

"Aye lass, yeh never seen lingerie before?" Alaric asked, his eyes skating over the lacy pieces with interest.

"I mean… I have, but never any that look like… this," she replied, her cheeks flushing a darker red, and I couldn't help the laugh that burst from me. She was just so cute and innocent. Endearing.

"Are you trying to tell me my brother hasn't already spoiled you with sexy underwear? I figured you'd have enough to never need to wear the same set twice after you were locked away in his chamber for a week…" I trailed off, before my jealousy that he had seen every inch of that beautiful skin threatened to overwhelm me.

"HA!" Eva barked, so loudly that fae started looking to see what the commotion was before she slapped a hand over her own mouth.

I was almost worried to hear why she would have such a response. Did my brother just keep her without clothes? I could see the appeal if what I imagined she looked like was even a fraction of the truth. "Like I would wear anything like this for him," she spat, and I looked at her sharply.

What did she mean by that? Before I had a chance to ask, Alaric beat me to it, looking just as curious as I was. "What do yeh mean, lass?" His rough voice carried, and the blood drained from her face.

"Oh… um… nothing, just not something that I would wear. He, um, likes purple," she said, waving it off and squashing the hope that flared as I'd thought for a second there could be trouble in paradise.

When we were in Heirloom Couture, the most popular everyday clothing store in the city, Eva's stomach growled. I told them both to make their way to the Crooked Claw whilst I had a quick chat with the shop owner. As soon as I was done, I caught up just as they reached the tavern doors and Alaric led the way in. I gestured to Eva to follow his lead as I took the rear, taking in the mindless babble of the patrons.

It was soon broken by a loud, obnoxious voice booming around the tavern. One that was all too familiar around the castle. "And that is when I took charge behind our prince to slay those thrakos scum!" Graves yelled, one foot up on an empty chair and his hand in the air.

There were a group of high fae females around him, and I knew that wherever Graves was, Sloane was never far away. Great. They were the biggest pair of ass kissers I had ever known, and their petulant personalities had no appeal to me.

We skirted their table in favor of our usual one at the back, Alaric sliding in one side as I moved to sit beside Eva. I heard Sloane chanting something like *'The Groan'* repeatedly whilst trying to get the now confused looking females to join in. As Melina approached the table, I blocked the ridiculous chant and zeroed in on the murmurs that had already started up around us.

"Prince Nekane just walked in, do I look okay?"

"I swear General Alaric growled at me once…"

"Who's the female?"

"Do you think the trio of desserts includes those three…"

"Isn't that Elikai and his fiancée?"

"Melina," I called to her over the racket, as Alaric raised a hand to give a short wave.

"Highness, Alaric, pleasure as always. Who's this wee thing you've hidden in the corner?" she asked, looking hard at Eva.

"Ah, surely yeh've heard the news of the beauty that stole the heart of the prince, Mel?" Alaric asked.

"Melina meet Eva. Eva, this is Melina. She runs the Crooked Claw," I said, bridging the gap between the two females. Melina eyed her suspiciously, but just nodded in acknowledgement and said nothing more on the matter.

"Right then, what'll it be?" she asked, straight back to business.

"Two ales and…." Alaric turned to Eva to add what she wanted.

"Make it three," she said, talking directly to Melina, making eye contact as she held three fingers up. Melina nodded, more friendly this time, perhaps respecting Eva a little more for speaking for herself, and went to get our drinks.

"Ale? A female after my own heart," Alaric joked dryly, a smile tugging at his mouth.

"You could have had something else, you know," I told her.

She shook her head in refusal. "I like ale. I'm happy to drink it. Why else would I have ordered it?" she stated simply, a small smile on her face.

Just as Melina delivered our drinks, several females approached our table, not caring that we already had a beautiful female sitting with us.

The first boldly suggested we go to a room, the next tried to sit on my lap, the third came straight out with what she planned to do with Alaric upstairs, and the last reached out to pull me up and invited Eva to join in.

I tried to laugh it off and told them now wasn't a good time, before I turned to Eva and realized I had never seen someone look more mortified. Her eyes darted from Alaric to me, to the backs of the females, as they finally left us alone. Her face was beet red.

"So who's hungry?" I asked, changing the subject and passing a menu to them both, before pretending to be engrossed in reading the list of food offerings. When Alaric ordered a side of eggs three ways with his rare steak, the awkwardness clinging in the air dissolved as me and Eva made eye contact and burst out laughing.

Just as we were finishing up our plates, Sloane and Graves decided to burden us with their presence. "Well, who do we have here?" Graves slurred, placing his hands on the table and forcing himself into our space. I heard a low, guttural sound that I realized was coming from Alaric.

"Why, it's the whore who won't put out like a good little wench sitting with the spare and his babysitter?" Sloane scoffed, leaning his arm over his friend's shoulders.

The noise coming from Alaric grew louder and louder until he opened his mouth to growl, "Fuck. Off. Cunts." The words vibrated from his throat.

This was going to get really bad, really fast if I didn't step in. "I'm sure Kai would love to hear you talking about his female like that, asshole," I interjected before Alaric could rip their throats out. "Imagine what he would do if I told him you called his fiancée a whore..." I asked, sliding out of my seat to stand in front of them, arms folded across my chest. Alaric took that as his cue to stand to his full height beside me. *Scary bastard.*

The smile that spread across his face was all teeth and not in the least bit friendly, but pretty fucking hot all the same. Not that Sloane and Graves would have agreed as they took a small step back, holding onto each other for support, showing the tavern they couldn't handle their ale.

"There a problem here, Your Highness?" a sweet voice asked from behind the two assholes. The twats turned to see Melina standing behind them with a wicked grin on her face. "Not causing trouble now, are we boys?"

They wisely shook their heads and left, managing to remain upright for a few steps before Graves went flying over a stool, pulling Sloane down with him. Eva looked furious. If we hadn't been blocking her path to them, I had no doubt she would have launched herself at the pair of fools.

"I'll speak to–" I started, but she put her finger to my lips to quiet me.

"No. I don't need you to fight my battles. What I need is to skin those pricks alive and wear their guts for garters," she hissed, and fuck, I believed her.

As terrifying as that imagery was, I couldn't deny that such a ruthless remark coming from her mouth had my balls aching and blood rushing to my cock.

The way she leaned into me as she watched them leave, the brush of her breasts against my arm and chest, her scent enveloping me. I wanted to let her do exactly as she'd threatened just so I could fucking ravage her on their mutilated corpses afterwards.

I was so fucked for this female. This had to stop. It's not like Elikai was just fucking her, she was his fiancée for fuck's sake. I had no right to be flirting with her, let alone having thoughts about throwing her over the table we'd just left and railing her into oblivion.

And maybe it was in my head, but I could have sworn she'd been flirting back today as we'd joked and wound Alaric up. But what did my brother's friends mean when they said she didn't put out? Hadn't she spent six days in his bed? Then there was the reaction to the lingerie that just made her seem so innocent and the fact she hadn't actually brought Kai up once all day.

Something wasn't adding up. As much as I wanted to get to the bottom of it, I had to stay away from her before I lost the fight with the soul-crushing instincts, telling me to just take what I wanted and claim her.

Thankfully, Alaric appeared at our side and suggested we head back to the castle. The fact that I so desperately didn't want today to end just confirmed how right he was about calling it a day.

FOR THE WALK HOME, I took a different route from what we had taken to get here so I could show Eva more of the capital and use it as a distraction from my too confusing thoughts.

Her jovial spirit soon returned, and we bantered back and forth, Alaric even joining in occasionally, but I tried to keep it friendly this time. Platonic.

Eva stopped abruptly, her arm slipping out of the crook of my elbow. I'd been too much of a selfish asshole to shrug it off when she'd placed it there in the first place. It had just felt so right. I turned back to see what had halted her and saw her walking toward the towering windows of the Ezerat Library in a trancelike state.

"You like to read?" I asked quietly, moving closer than I should have, but still not willing to step back. It was like battling a magnetic pull.

She nodded mutely, her hand curled to her chest as she took in book after book displayed in front of her.

"I would say we could go in, but we really need to get back to the castle," I said, and she looked genuinely gutted. "I could show you my library back there though if you'd like, princess?"

"Could you? That would be amazing!" she said, turning those big beautiful emerald eyes on me as a heart-stopping smile lit up her face. "Looking at the books in this window is making me realize how much I miss reading, and how much I need to escape into a book right now more than ever," she said, turning wistful eyes back on the books.

Much as I tried, I couldn't seem to deny her. Besides, what trouble could I get myself into with her in a library?

"Come to dinner this evening in the main dining hall, and I promise to show you the library afterwards," I told her, turning to catch up with Alaric as she followed.

I had to return her before I did something stupid, like kissing my brother's betrothed, in public, no less. *Would we have the library to ourselves?* I stopped that trail of thought abruptly, forcing myself to think of something else, anything else, as the vision of pleasuring her between and against the shelves swam through my mind.

"Yeh alright, Kane?" Alaric asked quietly, sensing my inner turmoil.

"I will be," I told him as I realized that even though I couldn't have Eva, I still had him, and I knew he would be more than happy to keep me distracted.

And if that failed, I could always send for Crystal.

CHAPTER 19

Evangelia

I hate them. I hate them. I hate them.

Okay, fine. I don't hate them.

I sighed dejectedly, thinking about all the ways in which my day out with Kane and Alaric hadn't been totally awful. Truth be told, if I put aside who I was and who they were, and well, everything that had happened leading up to today, I'd say it might have been the best day I'd ever had.

I leaned back against the door to Elikai's quarters, tipping my head skyward and closing my eyes as my mind swarmed with confusing thoughts and memories of our time exploring the city of Ezerat.

What I really needed to be doing was remembering all of the reasons why it should have been miserable to spend any time with them at all. Instead, all I could think about were the times I'd laughed and joked with Kane, or the many comforting, albeit surprising, smiles I'd shared with Alaric.

Alaric had explained the various benefits of the different styles of training gear, and his usual grumpy demeanor had disappeared almost entirely when he'd spoken with genuine passion.

It had felt so natural that I'd found myself on more than one occasion wishing things were different, so days like this could be my normal, and not a one off that shouldn't have happened to begin with.

Still, I should hate them. It would make everything easier.

I dragged myself over to the couch I'd been sleeping on, but stopped short as I noticed the new addition to the room. *Is that wardrobe mine?*

I raced over to see if my suspicions were true. I'd never had a wardrobe in my life, the closest my clothes got to being displayed was hanging on a line between trees to dry, which took days with the dank conditions of the Vale, before being stuffed into the bottom of my sleep sack.

I reached for the bronze handles with both hands before opening the mahogany paneled doors wide, revealing the multitude of purchases Kane had made today. *For me.*

All of my new training clothes had already been hung inside. I couldn't help but wonder whether Kane had maybe suggested installing the wardrobe to Thalia when he went to speak with her after breakfast. He must have, it was the only explanation. I made a mental note to thank him when I saw him at dinner later as I looked over all the exquisitely crafted garments. I'd told the lovely warlock as much while Kane had been settling the bill. He'd bought everything I had so much as pointed at, and the ass had refused to listen to me when I'd said it was too much, unnecessary even.

I'd stopped showing interest in anything as soon as I'd realized how closely he was watching my reactions, but I couldn't deny how my cheeks warmed at being spoiled like this for the first time in my life.

As I continued sifting through the rail, I saw that the wardrobe wasn't only filled with training gear, but with several items I could have sworn I recognized from our brief stop in Heirloom Couture. Fitted turtlenecks, long-sleeved blouses and palazzo trousers that were all so much more me than the pretty dresses Elikai liked me to wear. They were all in bold colors like emerald green and shades of blue from royal and navy to cobalt, no pastels that would wash out my pale complexion, but deep colors that would complement my hair and eyes.

I sighed as I realized why Kane had stayed back briefly whilst Alaric and I had made our way to grab food at their favorite tavern. It would be so much easier if they were evil males like Elikai. At least with him, I could keep my guard firmly in place with no worry of cracks developing.

I wasn't the only one to feel the charms of my companions today, if the reactions from the tavern patrons was anything to go by. Neither male had seemed keen to take the beautiful fae or shifters up on their countless offers as they had fates near pawed at them, trying to drag them away to some room upstairs. But maybe they planned to return later once they didn't have me cramping their style?

They hadn't elaborated on what exactly the females were talking about, but some of what I'd overheard had sent heat directly south while I'd felt a strange bitterness toward them that had me digging my nails into my palms.

I shut the doors on my countless new outfits, contemplating what to wear to training later with Alaric as I headed for the couch, but the internal debate was foreign to me. I thought instead about how I'd promised Kane I'd meet him for dinner in the dining hall this evening, and how, in exchange, he would show me the castle's library.

I had no interest in spending time dining with the numerous other castle residents, but I figured I could bear it if it meant getting my hands on some books. Strangely, I hadn't seen a library on the map, otherwise it would have been the first place I went.

Before any of that, I had an impromptu training session with Alaric to get through. As we'd walked the steep incline toward the castle gate, he'd scolded me for how out of breath I'd been and ordered me to meet him at the training halls in an hour.

I still had some time before I needed to get ready to meet him, so I decided to relax back into one of the comfy seats near my makeshift bed, letting my slack muscles have a moment to rest as my weightless gaze found the glow of the fire. My breaths came slow and easy for the first time in what felt like a lifetime as drowsiness seeped in, and I stared into the flames in a trance, feeling my eyelids begin to droop.

"Sweetling, it's bedtime, we have an early start in the morning moving camps so no tantrums tonight please," Mummy called to me as she ducked into our tent, taking off her soaking wet windbreaker.

"Mummy, do we have to move again? Can't we live in a proper house, or a castle like in my story book? And where lots of other children live, so I can make friends with them?" I asked, closing my favorite fairy-tale about a girl who makes friends with a candle, a clock and a teapot. My favorite character was the big angry beast though because he turned out to be a goodie, but everyone thought he was scary at first.

"I'm afraid we cannot, my sweet. It is not safe for those like us, yet."

"But why? When will it be safe?"

"Get into bed and I will tell you a story," she said, tucking me in before placing a soft kiss on my forehead. "Once upon a time, several centuries ago, the kingdom was a magical place filled with laughter and love, but a new king ascended who didn't like how the kingdom had been run for the last millennia. So he made a new Lore. One that would change everything for the realm. He banned fae having children and marrying outside their race, and the punishment was terrible for those who didn't fit into his new Lores," she sighed, as though remembering better days past.

"But what if they were true mates? Like you and Daddy."

"True mates are rare, sweet girl. But yes, even they were not allowed happiness together. The king wanted to create a strong kingdom, but he was sorely misguided."

"Why?" I asked, my green eyes wide in wonder as she smiled down at me warmly.

"Because, the king is a coward and fears what he doesn't understand or can't control. It's why we hide away from him, to protect ourselves," she said in a sad sigh, brushing a strand of onyx, which streaked my otherwise silver hair, from my face. "The king does not like anyone who is stronger than he is."

"Can't we just get a new king?" I asked, and she chuckled, but it didn't reach her eyes.

"I'm afraid it is not so easy. But some decades ago, Daddy and I, along with a group of our closest friends, some of whom live with us here in the Vale, were gifted a prophecy from the fates. Now, prophecies are not easy to understand, my sweet, but it brings us hope that things will change."

"When?" I asked.

"Well, we don't know when exactly, but we have a good idea of what event will trigger it, so we made plans to be close when it happens. You remember Braxton? The thrakos who visits us occasionally and helps us to train the hybrids we find lost in the Fading Vale?" I nodded, and she continued. "Well, he, his mate, and their son, like many others, made huge sacrifices many years ago to help our cause."

"Like what, Mummy?"

"It's late, my sweet, and we have a busy day ahead of us, but I will tell you all about it one day when you are older."

"Yes, please! I hope I can help when I'm a big girl too."

"I'm sure you will, my brave little warrior, but that's enough for tonight. It's time to sleep," she said, her sad eyes glazed.

"Can you sing to me please, Mummy?" I asked, and she held my hand gently as she quietly sang her favorite lullaby until my tired eyes could no longer fight sleep–

A knock hammered at the door, and I snapped out of the memory. I was unsure of exactly how long I'd been dozing, but I guessed it must be Alaric at the door, wondering where I had gotten to.

"One moment!" I called, quickly getting dressed. I hadn't let myself think about my mother for so long that I waited for the grief to consume me, but all I felt was fondness and love. I slipped into some of my new gear and tried to remember the words of the lullaby I'd long since forgotten.

She would sing the same tune to me every night until I was around five and Nix had been born. Apparently, I'd told her I was a big girl now and didn't need to be lulled to sleep like Nix was by his mom.

I headed into the bathroom, splashed some water over my face, tied my hair back and moved for the door. I'd been out all day and the evening ahead was a busy one compared to my usual sitting around doing nothing, and I'd hoped to check in with Thalia before meeting Alaric, but she was likely busy elsewhere.

"Sorry I was late!" I said, finding Alaric's hulking form taking up the entire doorway, not wanting this to have affected his willingness to train me.

"Come on," was all he said, as he turned to start making his way along the corridor toward the stairs, assuming I would follow. Which, of course, I did, having to basically jog to keep up until we reached the training hall.

He might not be the most approachable male, but Alaric was an amazing sparring partner and teacher. I'd thought I was a pretty damn good fighter before, but he had already taught me a lot and claimed I still had plenty to learn.

I didn't think he was the type of male to say such a thing to degrade a female. I could hear the honesty and genuine desire to help me reach my potential in his voice. *Why* he wanted to help me I wasn't sure, but I wasn't one to look a gift horse in the mouth.

The realization that my family, friends and I had never stood a chance against the horde with the skills and weapons they had at their disposal was eye opening and alarming to say the least. I could only hope that Nix's thrakos form had been enough to save him. With the right training, he could best Alaric.

I needed to use Alaric's lessons to learn as much and as quickly as possible to ensure I made the most out of my shot at the king. The hardest part was remembering to hate him in the process.

We entered, moved to the mats and warmed up with some light stretches. I followed his lead, copying as he lay face down, then brought his hands close to his shoulders before straightening his arms while his hips remained on the mat. He bent one arm and began rotating his shoulder toward the floor before he must have felt my gaze on him, because he looked directly at me and we locked eyes.

We remained like that, just staring at each other's forms as I probably screwed up whatever this stretch was even called. Just as I thought he was about to break the silence and say something, he jumped to his feet weightlessly and nodded. Just like that, the army-style workout began.

Good. That was definitely a good thing. Wasn't it? Yes. Totally. I absolutely wasn't desperate to hear his accent that strangely reminded me of home, or perhaps find out if there were any stretches that required a partner.

He had me running laps around the hall, barking orders at me to change up speed, direction, keep my knees up. He scolded me for not being light enough on my feet and gave encouragement by way of growls when my stamina was slacking.

By the end of the cardio, I was breathing hard, and Alaric had a wicked look in his eyes that I couldn't decipher. As we began sparring, I got the impression he enjoyed these sessions as much as I.

I certainly never held back on him when we trained, and I liked that he was rough with me. I was learning to read his movements now, anticipating what he was going to do next, so I was better able to counter it before he could land a blow. It was exhilarating and made me feel alive.

"Righ', lass, yer doin' well, but that was jus' foreplay. Now let's get down to it. I'm gonnae come at yeh and you're goin' to try to defend yourself for a full three minutes," he told me, glancing up at the clock that was ever present on the wall, obviously making note of the time.

"Alright, Grandmaster Wolf. Bring it," I taunted back to him gleefully. He looked surprised, raising a single eyebrow at my nickname, but what else would I say to tease him?

Without warning, he grabbed me in an armlock, and I knew it was game on. He'd already taught me this move, so I knew to free my arm by spinning under his, coming up to his back, ready to kick out his knee.

He blocked me by manipulating my arm, throwing me off course, before ragdolling me across the mats as I rolled over and over. Using the momentum, I pushed myself up and stood, but he was already coming for me again.

I let him get close before I aimed an elbow into his solar plexus to wind him, but it didn't do the damage I'd hoped, so I fell back to keep him out of grabbing distance of my feet. I was breathing so hard my chest felt like it was on fire. There was no way that I was going to win here, but I had to try all the same. This wasn't an exercise in winning, it was to outlast my opponent. And he was relentless.

I ran at him, sidestepping past and around to his back, where I leapt on. I wrapped my arms around his shoulders and my legs around his right arm and waist, desperately trying to maneuver myself to get him into a headlock, but he was already pulling me off to throw me back down to the mats. Next thing I knew, I was pinned underneath his large body again.

Holy fates, this was not a terrible place to be, but dammit, I needed to win against him.

"Got yeh," Alaric purred as he looked back over his shoulder to the clock, turning back with a grin spread across his imperfectly perfect scarred face. "Gettin' better, Angel," he praised, his sinfully sexy accent thick as he gifted me with another of his rusty smiles. "I think I might actually trust yeh to fight at my back one day. Keep it up, yer doin' good."

Before I could stop myself, I pushed my hands into his hair before wrapping my arms around his neck. I pulled his strong body close and slammed his lips to mine.

I couldn't understand fully what had come over me, but at that moment, when I saw him smile down, I knew I needed to taste his lips as much as I needed air in my lungs to breathe. I arched up into him, kissing him passionately while trying to push my body closer to his so there was no space left between us, my hands tightened in his hair, and a moan escaped my throat as the sensation overwhelmed me.

Time stood still as a low growl left his chest, meeting my own and he was kissing me back with a savage vigor, propping himself up with one elbow as his other hand explored my curves before landing on my breast.

Too soon, he was pulling away, eyes wide in horror, as if my lips were coated in poison that he needed to purge from his skin. He stood swiftly and silently before casting me a hate-filled look and stalked off across the vast space, leaving me cold and alone on the mats, still panting from the kiss that had been all consuming.

I struggled to regain control of my breathing as the realization hit me that I had just crossed a line and fucked up. Big time. Why had I kissed him? Oh shit, he didn't want me like that, and I had just thrown myself at him.

Fuck. Fuck. FUCK.

I started to count to ten slowly in my head, and when I sat up, he was long gone. How the fuck was I going to face him now? What had I been thinking? I wasn't thinking, that was the problem. The whole day had just been so confusing. I'd acted on the impulse as it hit me before I had a chance to think better of it, and now I might have totally fucked everything up.

I scrambled from the room, cursing my stupidity as I raced downstairs and out into the castle grounds for some much needed air that wasn't fogged with his scent. I couldn't risk being inside and running into Alaric. What would I say? I couldn't go back to training with him now! *Fuck, I'm an idiot.* Would he tell Kane? Shit, what if he told Elikai when he returned?

I'd lost control, only not at all in the way I'd feared I'd ever lose it. I hadn't felt even the slightest need to shift, my beast surprisingly calm the entire time. But outside in the fresh air and away from Alaric, I was wrestling with myself and pushing my beast back down. The last thing I needed was to let it out, and yet she was pushing me hard to find him again and finish what we started.

"So you didn't want to see the library after all, princess?" I shot around as Kane's voice drifted to my ears and he stepped into my line of vision from behind a tree.

I had completely forgotten I was supposed to meet him straight from training. My head was a mess from the stupidly mind-blowing kiss. "Sorry, Kane," I said, unable to make eye contact. "I just came out here for some fresh air and lost track of time, I guess," I explained, trying to sound calm as I quickly looked around to make sure Alaric wasn't with him. I noticed the sun had long since disappeared and the night air was turning bitter.

"Are you ok, beautiful? You seem jittery. Did Alaric work you too hard in training?" he asked, sounding genuinely concerned.

"Alaric? No, why? Have you seen him? What did he say?"

He chuckled. "No, I haven't seen him since we got back from the city, but you are scaring me now. You sure you're ok, Eva?" He was too close, peering into my eyes as if they held the answers he was searching for.

"Yes, sorry. It's just been a busy day, and I feel bad that I stood you up for dinner. Maybe tomorrow?" I asked, trying to change the subject from Alaric and back onto how I'd also now messed up with the male in front of me.

He took my wrist and pulled me to follow him as he headed for the rear entrance to the castle. "Come on!" he called back to me, a teasing smile on his face. He rushed us through the entrance hall, up the several flights of stairs to the floor he and Elikai shared, and to a door I had yet to explore behind, assuming it was one of their guest suites.

He took my shoulders and positioned me in front of him, looking directly at the closed door, while his fingers trailed down my arms, taking my hands and slowly placing them to cover my eyes.

"No peeking, princess," he whispered seductively against my ear, so close his breath tickled the sensitive flesh on my neck and I sucked in a shaky breath. I could feel every hard line of his body pressed against my back and fought the urge to press into him again like I had in the games room. It was too much. I was still feeling the effects of the encounter earlier, and now Kane was here, flush against me.

"What's going on, Kane?" I asked, barely managing a whisper.

"Well, long story short, there once was a prince who had plans to meet a beautiful girl for dinner, only she stood him up and left him to eat in a room full of pompous pricks–"

"Kane, I'm sor–"

"But the silly prince had promised her a tour of his castle's library, and being a male of his word, he couldn't let the beautiful girl down," he rumbled against my ear, the sound was pure seduction, and I could barely hold it together as my heart thundered against my ribs.

I felt him shift toward the door, followed by the sound of the handle being turned. He carefully ushered me into the room, his hands on my waist as he positioned me just so.

He stood behind me again and gently reached up to my hands and uncovered my eyes. "What do you think, beautiful?"

I opened my eyes and gasped as the library opened up before me. It was more than I could have ever imagined. I swallowed hard as I took in the rich dark wood covering the walls, shelves inset and stacked to the heavens with books.

I looked up higher to see a second level, accessible from a curving spiral staircase in the corner. On the wall behind me was a grate for a fire to be kindled, and in front of it were lounges and armchairs. The perfect place to curl up once the perfect book had been selected to escape into.

There were several hardwood tables dotted around the room with chairs for fae to sit at, lamps at each. By the door to my left was a stand with a single book sat open upon it. I rushed over to find it was a catalog of the contents of the library, the writing a childish scrawl, but perfectly legible. To the side of it sat a bust of King Regis, only it wasn't facing the center of the room, but the wall instead.

The room was minimalistic, albeit filled to the brim with hundreds, maybe thousands, of books, making them the main focus. I couldn't take my eyes off the colorful tomes as I walked along row after row trailing my fingers over their spines, excited to discover their contents.

I could feel Kane's eyes tracking me as I took it all in greedily. I had never seen anything so magical, and he had made it even more special the way he had made sure I was facing the room at the perfect angle to see its beauty all at once.

"Kane, I… I don't have any words," I said, my distracted gaze memorizing every inch of the stunning library instead, knowing any time I got to enjoy its beauty and contents would be short-lived.

"It's my favorite room in the castle, and after I saw your reaction to the Ezerat library window this morning… Well, I couldn't wait to share it with you," he explained honestly, and we stood in comfortable silence before he continued. "I'll just leave you to get lost in the shelves, and I'll ask Thalia to send some dinner to you."

"Thank you," I said, but it came out as more of a moan.

He chuckled. "Good night, beautiful." And with that, he left.

As I looked for some romance novels to take up to Elikai's chambers, I couldn't help but wonder what would have happened if it were Kane who had been on that hunt that had found my camp instead. Would it have been a slaughter? Would I harbor the same hatred I felt toward Elikai toward him instead?

I wasn't sure, but he had unknowingly gifted me with the perfect distraction from my turmoil over what had happened with Alaric. But now that he was gone, even the library couldn't help with the panic over what had happened. *Or perhaps it could.*

I couldn't go to training, but I could hide away here while I waited for the king's return. Perhaps Thalia could help me with my daggers instead of Alaric?

I needed to talk to her and Westly soon so I could find out how far their loyalty to Edelin Sybilline went.

CHAPTER 20

Alaric

I waited for Angel by the usual doors to start our morning run, rolling my neck from side to side to loosen the kinks and stifling a yawn. I'd laid awake all night, my mind on a constant loop, wandering back to that insane kiss we'd shared yesterday.

Try as I did, I couldn't stop thinking about the way she'd felt against me. It was indescribable. And so wrong. For so many reasons. Yet all I wanted was to find her and pin her down again to finish what we'd started.

It had taken everything in me to pull away from her and leave. Every bone in my body wanted to carry on and see how far it would go, experience how good I knew it would feel.

I wasn't even sure how it had happened. Could it have been some part of her plan? A plan I was no further forward in deciphering. Could it have been a setup? Had she meant for us to get caught? Would she tell Elikai?

The female is a mind fuck.

She was never late when we met in the mornings. Normally, she would be waiting for me. Maybe she had no intention of showing up? Why should I even be surprised? I wouldn't put it past someone like *her* to just avoid the situation now that she had made things awkward as fuck.

I couldn't shake the gut-wrenching feeling of dread that had been weaving its web through my mind. These incessant thoughts of how perfect she had felt pinned beneath me. But anyone could have seen what had happened. Me, a shifter, a high-ranking official, overpowering and kissing a high fucking fae. One engaged to a fucking prince, no less! *Fuck.*

Abandoning my wait for the emerald-eyed temptress, I tried to shake myself out of my own head so I could just move on with my day. If she was going to avoid it, so could I.

As I rounded the corner to my office, I rolled my eyes when I saw Krista waiting for me. For fuck's sake. Really. Not. The. Time. As predicted, she was on me instantly, non-stop talking about training regimes, hunt structures and fuck knew what else.

I sidestepped past her to the door, yanking the handle and barely feeling the pulse of magical energy as it unlocked at my touch. She pushed in behind me, unperturbed by my blatantly ignoring her as she made sure I didn't miss the feel of her breasts brushing my arm as she squeezed by, despite the abundance of space. Though she was quiet now, at least. *Thank the fates for small mercies.*

After yesterday with Angel, I'd initially thought I'd just needed to get laid and my hand certainly hadn't helped much. But as I took in the sight of Krista, all fair skinned and toned muscles, she was without a doubt attractive, but still did absolutely nothing for me.

I swear it was like my cock was actually shying away from her the closer she got. Trying to fates near hide inside me, or turn me around to go finish what had started in the training hall.

Maybe now that I'd had a taste of the forbidden fruit, Krista throwing herself at me so unashamedly was what was turning me off. Maybe I needed to find a female who I couldn't have. Married females were always coming onto me in the Crooked Claw, but I just didn't think I was into that shit.

I slumped down in my desk chair and Krista followed like a shadow, zero fucks given as she reached down to push my knees further apart without a word.

She locked gazes with me to ensure she had my attention, pushing between my thighs. She muttered some bullshit about how I needed to loosen up and shared all the ways she could make me come just from sucking my dick. In vivid detail.

Fates, this female knew what she wanted, and usually I would be a willing participant. While I kept business and pleasure very separate, for a very good reason, if any of what she was saying rang true, I should have been seconds away from having her bent over my desk. But instead, I was seconds away from her realizing all I had was a flaccid cock and zero fucking patience for her.

"Boss…" Axel called, bursting into my office as his eyes narrowed on the sight before him. Krista was slowly sinking down to her knees, her hands trailing up my thighs as she bit down on her bottom lip, and I sat back in my chair secretly wishing it was another female. Not that he could have possibly known that part. Unless he had seen something?

I shot up, realizing this could be the perfect escape from the grizzly, who was about to be pawing at my cock any second. "Axel, right, yer here," I grunted out as I eyeballed him. "Jus' the fae I was waitin' for."

Krista stood too, shooting furious daggers at the intruder for muzzling her muffin, and with a bratty sigh she finally stepped away from me, though she didn't leave the room.

"Can't you see we were in the middle of something?" she huffed, crossing her arms across her chest and pouting.

"Didn't realize you were double booked, boss…" Axel said, and I could have kissed him for catching on and improvising. I'd trained him well. I wouldn't even be in my office right now if it wasn't for Angel bailing on her training because she couldn't handle a bit of tension.

"Nothin' like that Axel, Krista was just leavin'. Sit down and we'll talk."

Krista stiffened, her eyes darting between us as she realized she had been dismissed. Throwing her hands up dramatically, she stomped across the room, pausing in the doorway to glance back in case I had a sudden change of heart. Not likely. You had to have a heart for that.

"This is about the portal, isn't it?" she whined when she realized I wasn't going to call her back and demand she get on her knees.

"That's not for yeh to worry about. Don't yeh have somewhere to be?" Nodding stiffly, she left us alone, and I expelled a sigh as I perched on the corner of my oak desk.

"Boss, is there somethin' you wanna tell me?" Axel asked, leaning back in the chair he was now occupying. His legs stretched in front of him, crossing at the ankles, a grin on his face.

I contemplated telling him about Angel, but the fewer fae that knew, the better. It wasn't that I didn't trust him, fuck he was the only male in this city I could truly trust with everything. But when it came to Angel, my lips were better off sealed.

"Nothin' to worry about, why are yeh here anyway?"

"Coincidentally, the portal. Got something to show yeh," he said, the look on his face spelling trouble. I stood again, apparently not fated to be left the fuck alone this morning, and gestured for him to lead the way down to where the portal was hidden.

As we breached the concealed entrance, we took a torch each from the sconces lining the stone walls and lit them easily. Well-practiced in this routine. It was a maze down here in the catacombs, and if you didn't know where you were going, you could easily be lost, with no hope of being found. I had spent an entire year making sure Axel knew the way as well as I did before letting him venture down here alone.

We were heading deep inside the mountain on which the castle was built atop. Everything around us was carved out of natural stone, including the portal itself. The cavern in which it resided was as large as the castle's ballroom, only deep underground, and never failed to take my breath away.

The portal was imposing, its five pillars carved intricately with runes. Its base was pentagonal in shape, not that I had ever gotten inside. It stood taller than three males, one on top of the other, and just as wide if they were to stretch their arms and make a circle. The whole thing was capped by a slab of stone so big it would crush you to dust should the pillars ever give way.

We entered the cavern and it took a moment for my eyes to adjust. The blinding purple haze of the dome engulfing the portal—preventing anyone from approaching—lit the entire space which would be otherwise pitch black. "Right, what's the problem?" I asked, the area looking no different. The portal was still dormant, the magical dome preventing it from activating as it had been for the past fifty years since I'd discovered it.

"I have been doing as you said. Watching. Learning. And I think we need a witch. Someone who is really powerful, pure-blooded and adept at taking down barriers. This one only prevents living organisms from passing through," he explained, cutting straight to the point as he knew I preferred. He proceeded to demonstrate by throwing a rock, which sailed straight through the barrier to land in one piece on the other side.

I pressed my hand cautiously toward the barrier as Axel darted forward to stop me, but it was too late. The previously purple hue glowed flaming red at the contact and electricity sizzled against my skin as the smell of burning flesh assaulted my nostrils.

"I'll talk to some of the witches I ken we can trust," I said on a hiss as I ripped my hand back and began assessing the surroundings.

I caught a glimpse of a rat scurrying around on the floor. Before long, it ran toward the barrier, which glowed a brighter and brighter crimson as it neared. It didn't even reach the dome before it literally fucking disintegrated, and I shared a quick glance with Axel to make sure he had seen it too. He just nodded, as though this wasn't news to him.

Curious, I brought my hand up again, hovering it several inches from the barrier this time, and felt the static humming before I got a minor shock.

"You alright, boss?" Axel asked, pulling me out of my observations.

"Aye, let's get outta here. I've got what I need for this. Yeh done good." I clapped him on his back, ignoring the sting of my rapidly healing palm. The male didn't get nearly enough recognition for what he did. Not that he could. This wasn't official horde duty. "Let's go for a run outta the castle soon. I need a proper shift, an' to let the beast out."

"You know I am always up for that, boss. Don't need to ask me twice." I nodded and we discussed Axel's findings further on the walk back, but until I could get a witch's take on it, it was all just guesswork and a waste of breath.

"So you and Krista, huh?" Axel enquired.

"No."

"No as in–"

"No as in, there's no me an' Krista. She must've got sick of me pretendin' not to notice her shameless flirtin' so decided I couldnae ignore her if my cock was in her mouth."

"She sucked–"

"No. But if yer so interested, have at it. Apparently she gives the best head yeh've ever had or some shite like that."

He brought his hand to his jaw as if he was giving it some serious thought. "She's hot. It wouldn't be a chore, but I heard you haven't been getting laid all that much lately, so–"

"Axel, do me a favor an' shut the fuck up." He just grinned wolfishly, and we finished our hike in silence.

As we finally emerged from the catacombs, I told him we would meet after dinner and wasted no time starting work on tracking down a trustworthy witch.

Only problem was, being trustworthy was a rarity around here.

UNSURPRISINGLY, Angel didn't show up to practice in the afternoon. So after dinner, Axel and I regrouped and left the castle grounds.

Anticipation drummed through me at the thought of releasing the beast within. It had been too long, and my skin itched with the need. Bloodlust haunting me.

"I can see why you go to the tavern so much, boss..." Axel mused, drawing my attention to him. His head was on a swivel as he looked around at the nightlife that was booming already as the sun set, and the scantily clad females on their way out for a night of debauchery.

"Yeh ken I dinnae like to mix business an' pleasure, gettin' outta the castle gives me that much," I told him, but then noticed his eye wandering, not just to shifters, but witches and high fae too.

"Oh, come on! Lighten up," he teased with a childlike glee. "You should let me leave that damned portal more. My skills would be much better appreciated out here–"

"Get that thought outta yer head right now. Yeh dinnae move outta the Lores. Keep yer eyes to the shifters only," I scolded. He knew better. Though there was likely no harm in looking, I couldn't let him entertain the thought that he could ever do more. Not with King Regis on the throne. Not that I was one to talk. I was a walking, talking hypocrite at this point.

I rolled my shoulders. We were nearing the forested area, and my beast was clawing to get out. The anticipation killed me as I quickened my pace.

"You alright, boss? You're more wound up than usual," he asked, his concerned face appearing before me.

"Aye fine, jus' stuck in my head. This'll help though."

"Wanna talk about it?" he pressed. I shook my head, but he didn't let it go. "Come on, what is it? You're scaring me and your beast hasn't even burst free yet."

What would it hurt to tell the male? We shared plenty of secrets, what's one more? He was one of the few I could actually trust, and this particular issue was threatening to consume me. *Fuck it.*

"Somethin' happened when trainin' Angel yesterday. Somethin' that shouldnae have happened," I grumbled out, hoping that he would leave it there.

"Oh, please tell me it was scandalous," he said with a laugh. It was scandalous alright. "So what did the Lore-abiding General do? Glance at her in the most inappropriate way? Throw her down too firmly? Oh, I know, I know, you let her kick your arse?" he joked, forgetting where we were as he flung an arm over my shoulders. Not many males were tall enough. Just another thing Axel and I had in common.

"Worse, much worse," I said, shrugging him off, "The king would have my head if he ken."

"Oh, my. Are you telling me the General broke the Lores?" he mock-whispered, surprise evident on his face, but he was fates near jumping up and down wanting to know more.

Here goes nothing. "I kissed Angel. Well, she kissed me, but I didnae push her away. The opposite, really." At the ringing silence that followed, I realized he was no longer walking at my side. I turned to see him standing stock still, his mouth agape and eyes bulging.

Fuck, if Axel was reacting like this, then it was a whole fuckload worse than I had even thought. My own view on it likely tainted by how good it had felt to overpower her lithe body and taste her delicious lips.

I turned to keep walking, giving him a minute to take in the magnitude of just how many Lores we'd broken with just that ki–

Rambunctious laughter boomed from Axel's direction, and I wheeled around to see him doubled over, laughing himself hoarse. "What the–"

"And you…" he started, struggling to talk through his hysterics. "You tell *me* off for looking at witches and high fae. Someone's got a severe case of double standards, eh boss?" he joked, calming down enough to catch up. He might be finding this hilarious, but he wasn't wrong.

How could I be sure he would take my word seriously when I told him he had to be on his best behavior and stick to the Lores when I hadn't? "Come on, boss, you know I won't tell anyone, except maybe Aunt Rose. No, definitely Aunt Rose," he teased, and I scowled at him, knowing full well it didn't matter what I said. He would be sneaking off to tell the female who'd raised him at his first chance, not that she was actually his aunt by blood. "Let's just go and let our beasts out of their cages and forget about it for a little while."

"Aye, let's go," I agreed.

We stopped when we made it far enough from prying eyes, inside the copse of trees hidden at the edge of the city. I stripped off, not wanting my clothes shredded, and hid them behind a tree before shifting. *Let the hunt begin.*

"Fair play though boss, she is one fine female!" Axel rushed out, knowing I wouldn't bite when I was focused on other things. It wasn't long before he followed suit and we were finally able to let our beasts run wild for a few hours to hunt, feed and satisfy the bloodlust.

CHAPTER 21
Evangelia

As I crept my way along the corridor toward the library, being careful to avoid Alaric, I noticed a very flustered Westly racing toward Kane's chambers with a scroll in his hand. Intrigued, I followed him, being sure to keep my distance. He was so preoccupied with whatever he was doing, he wouldn't have noticed me if I'd jumped out and shouted boo.

The door click shut on Kane's room, and I moved closer, listening intently through the solid oak, drawing on my shifter hearing.

"Your presence is needed in the throne room urgently," Westly's voice said.

"Me?" Kane replied, sounding confused.

I heard Westly clearing his throat and the shuffling of paper, which must have been the scroll as it was unraveled. "There is a case of missed taxes, my Prince. The mayor of the village has been brought back to the castle by the horde for punishment, and with your father and Prince Elikai away, it falls to you to rule on his sentencing."

From what I knew about Kane, he kept well away from royal affairs. My betrothed, however, would have been in his element.

When I'd seen Westly rushing here, I'd assumed it was news of the king and Elikai's return. I was surprised that I felt strangely relieved to learn that they were still gone.

I should be counting down to take my shot at the king's life. But the thought of Elikai being back sent a pang of regret through my chest for wasting so much of his absence avoiding Kane and Alaric. Knowing I'd never get the chance again.

"Where's Alaric?" Kane asked, drawing me back to the now and reminding me I needed to disappear as they would be leaving the room at any moment. If they found me with my ear pressed against the door, it would take a lot of explaining I didn't have time for.

I needed to see for myself how Kane would handle a hearing. What better way to find out what kind of male he was, and I just so happened to know the perfect place to spy directly into the throne room.

"I didn't see Alaric on my way here, but we don't have much time. They are waiting for you to begin."

"Okay, lead the way," Kane sighed. I sprinted up the corridor, down the stairs, and paused for a quick look to check that the grand hallway was empty. Once I was satisfied that it was, I made my way to the antechamber. I trailed my fingers along the wall until I felt the ridge, throwing a look over each shoulder to ensure I was alone, and pressed the ridge until I heard a subtle click and the concealed door opened.

I crept into the cubby, pulling the door closed behind me, and knelt down as I had done before. My eyes adjusted to the dark as I began lightly running my hands against the cold stone until I plucked the pebble free to reveal the peephole. I lined my right eye up with the small hole and squinted my left to take in the throne room.

An audience had gathered in the room, looking bloodthirsty in their excitement. Did those idiots have nothing better to do?

"Presenting Prince Nekane, second Prince of Dezrothia," the herald called, and I saw Kane enter, his head high and shoulders back, giving an outward appearance of supreme confidence.

He moved to the solitary throne on the dais that loomed over everything and everyone in the room. My stomach churned as he approached his father's seat, but I wasn't exactly sure why. Perhaps it was the worry that he would turn into the male I feared he really was the moment he sat upon it. That he would be consumed by the feeling of power.

Time seemed to slow until Kane eventually sat. One of the king's advisors leaned in close, speaking directly to him as he angled his mouth away from the crowd to avoid any of us being able to lipread. A lot of good that would do with the sharp ears in the room, or out of it in my case.

"We have an elder from one of the villages who has failed to pay this season's tax. He is here for sentencing. I recommend making it hard and swift," the advisor whispered, and a frown tugged at Kane's brow.

"Which village?" he asked, neither agreeing nor disagreeing with the advice. "And what do they owe?"

"It is the village of the spider folk," the ancient male confirmed, thrusting a scroll into Kane's hands.

He took a moment to read before looking back to the advisor. "So they normally pay in silks and other textiles, and until recently, they had never missed a payment. Is that correct?" The advisor nodded. So what if they had missed a couple of payments? I had no doubt in my mind that there was an abundance in the capital already. They didn't need it. It wasn't life or death, like running out of food or a plague hitting the realm. It was luxury silk, for fates' sake. "Is there anything else I need to know?" he asked, a frown still furrowed deep in his brow.

"This is the second time they have failed to deliver, my Prince."

"Okay, well, bring him in…"

I frowned as the room waited on tenterhooks. Kane appeared to be deep in thought, and I could only hope that was because he didn't plan on dismissing them before trying to understand their struggle to pay.

I was surprised by how desperate I was for him to do the right thing, not just for the sake of the spider folk, but to prove that he was different to his twin. A better male in every way.

As I silently willed him to not take the easy route and do as his father and brother doubtlessly would, his eyes shot in my direction, as though he could see through the thick wall between us. As panic froze me in place, a male was dragged in and Kane's attention darted to him instead.

CHAPTER 22
Nekane

I couldn't shake the feeling of being watched as my mind raced with how exactly I was going to deal with the male being ushered into the room, his feet dragging across the floor and wrists shackled together.

He was thrown to the ground at the base of the steps, bruised and bloodied. I had no doubt it was the handiwork of the horde on their journey back here. I schooled my expression and leaned forward in my father's throne to get a better look at the male before me. Spider shifters were blessed with being able to produce their own silk when in spider form, it didn't make sense that they had missed their last two payments. Especially when they had a history of honoring their dues to the kingdom, at least until recently. One of many lessons from Alaric drifted through my mind.

There's always a reason for everythin'. Yeh jus' need to find it…

What was the reason for it? Well, I guess it was time to find out. I looked down at the broken male on the floor as more of Alaric's words sprung to mind.

Dinnae judge 'til yeh ken what situation yer facing…

Who knew his seemingly torturous war stories would come in handy? What would he say if he knew my only prompts of how to deal with this were coming from his random musings?

"What is your name?" I asked as the male struggled to his feet, desperately trying to swallow the pain from his injuries.

"K-Kumo, M-My Lord, M-M-Mayor of R-Rangaran," he stuttered, unable to make eye contact as he dipped his head and winced.

He was absolutely terrified. I didn't need a shifter's sense of smell to know that much. I could see it in the way he trembled and as I looked around the room, I got the sense the onlookers were basking in his fear.

I channeled my barely used high fae abilities and gently let out an invisible wave of allure directly toward him. It was only a tiny amount, but would be enough for him to start to relax a little. Him shitting himself would only give the gawkers more pleasure at his expense. Besides, I needed answers, and for that, he needed to talk.

I kept my voice neutral. "Tell me, what is going on in your village that has caused you to fail in delivering the past two seasons' taxes? Prior to that, your record was impeccable. Your village is extremely reputable for producing the best fabrics in the realm. Which has me curious, why are you not able to deliver now?"

He finally looked up at me. "W-W-Well–"

Before he could even finish his sentence, Elmer, one of my father's long-standing advisors, cut across him.

"Get on with it already! We don't have time for your pathetic stuttering!"

My head darted to the side once more to where I had felt eyes on me earlier. I could have sworn Eva's scent drifted into the room with the distant sound of a growl, but I shook it off. Now was not the time for getting distracted. Standing at my full height and nearly giving poor Kumo a heart attack, I locked Elmer's gaze with mine, glowering at him until his cheeks flamed crimson and he took a couple of involuntary steps backwards.

Did Elmer pull this shit with my father? Absolutely fucking not. Happy that he was reminded of his place, I took a seat again on the throne that made my skin crawl and turned back to the male below us.

"Ignore him, Kumo. Tell me, in your own time, what has changed," I stated as I pushed a smidge more allure his way.

"W-Well, my p-prince, y-you see, it isn't th-that we don't want to. W-W-we j-just can't."

"And why is that?"

Dinnae rush in Kane. Take a minute to assess the situation, an' let yer opponent set the pace.

"Our l-l-looms have broken."

"Okay. So why don't you have them repaired? Surely that would fix your problems?" I asked, Alaric's words and Eva's scent grounding me, even if it was all in my head.

"I-I-I p-petitioned the king, but was r-rejected, my p-prince. Our l-loom numbers have b-been diminishing for years. W-Without the aid of being able to t-trade with others a-and g-get supplies for p-parts, our h-hands are tied," he said, at last able to keep his beady black eyes in my direction.

I leaned into the advisor now closest to me, Desmond. "Is what he says true? Has the crown been petitioned before to help Rangaran?"

"Well, yes but–"

"And nothing was done?"

"Well, no, but–" he started again, frustration clear in his tone, but I wasn't about to listen to his feeble excuses.

"Right. Well then, with this in mind, what would you recommend his sentence be?" I already knew what I was going to do, Alaric's voice still rattling around my mind as if he were in the room with me, but I wanted to see what the so-called advisors had to say.

"The sentence for their insubordination should of course be death, my prince, as it was when this male's predecessor appeared before the king last season."

My heart stuttered, but I remained composed as I feigned to consider it. Kumo, however, began to whimper and beg at my feet. My father wouldn't think twice about killing this male then. But would Kai? It was so obviously us at fault here. Our lack of support to the fae meant the Rangarians were no longer able to produce enough to pay their taxes. We already had so much of their fabrics we could use it to wipe our asses and not even notice it depleting.

Punishment should fit the crime, Kane. Dinnae let tradition sway what yeh think is right.

Fuck, Alaric and his stories. Who knew they would actually be useful? The sentiment was right, though. I couldn't send this male to his death, but I couldn't imprison him either. It would just delay his death until my father's return.

There was only one way to resolve this. "What do you need to get your looms running again?" I asked the spider, pushing a little allure into my breath, and I could have sworn the walls sighed in relief. I needed honesty from him, not a lap dance, so it was important I released it slowly and only in nominal amounts.

Kumo stared, open-mouthed, for a moment. Clearly, he'd resigned himself to execution and, at the unexpected turn of events, he was now unsure if he could trust me. I didn't blame him at all. Why would he after what had happened to the mayor before him last season?

"Wood for the looms and some technicians to help with repairs," he clarified, and it was the first time he'd completed a sentence without stuttering.

"Then it is done. Speak with *my* advisor, Westly," I said, gesturing to my butler, not trusting the official advisors as far as I could throw them. "*He* will see to it you return to your village unharmed and with everything you need to restart production. Next tax season, it will be expected that your village makes up for what has been missed. Is that understood?"

I didn't know where to look as Kumo started crying, thanking me and praising my generosity. He reached out toward me and winced again as one of his many injuries hurt from his jerky movements.

I closed the gap, descending a few stairs to take his hands in mine and, without a word, pushed healing magic into him. I saw his discomfort disappear rapidly as the marks and scratches knitted themselves back together before my eyes. I couldn't help but feel that even if I'd fucked up the entire ruling, I had at least gotten this right.

"What are you doing?" Desmond hissed as I returned to the throne and we faced away from the crowd below. "Send him to his death!"

"No."

"Your father will kill us all for this!"

"Why? How do we expect villages to pay when they don't have the means? Has it escaped your notice that unless we provide them this small amount of support we will never recuperate the losses from previous seasons? It will just keep happening every season, and more and more Rangarians will die in this very room!"

"No– It's– We– It isn't done!" he spluttered, and I fought a laugh.

Leaning back in the throne, I took in the ancient males at my sides. "Do you have Regis blood in your veins? Either of you?" I challenged them. Their eyes darted from me to each other, and their silence was answer enough. "I didn't think so. Now, listen to me. You will help Westly in sorting out the materials and labor to help the mayor. If the king questions it, you are welcome to send him to me." I stood from my seat, finished with this conversation and ready to leave this cursed room. "Now, is there anything else, or is that it?"

The room was silent for a beat. Wide eyes and open mouths met my perusal as I glanced around, then muttering broke out.

"Did he just help him?"

"King Regis would never..."

"What would the king say?"

"Isn't this a good thing?"

"He is sooo sexy when he's angry."

"Shh, he might hear you. I can feel his power from here..."

I gave a quick wink in the direction of the high fae who'd called me sexy, and could have sworn the walls growled as I left the room. But it was quickly interrupted by the sound of a thud and someone's cry for help with a female who'd just fainted. I might be a mess when it came to Eva, but it was good to know I still had it.

With that insanity dealt with, I could finally breathe. How could anyone enjoy that? I was still shocked they were going to just sentence him to death instead of helping solve the problem. His village had even asked for help for fates' sake. Did the so-called king actually care about his citizens at all? Or was his treatment of me reminiscent of that of the fae he thought below him too?

As I neared the library, hope flared in my chest at the prospect that I might see Eva there. Hope that I needed to quash as I was still avoiding her, even if it did feel like a wasted use of this time while Kai was gone.

I needed to stop letting my mood hinge on that female. She should be nothing more than my brother's betrothed. She will never be more than my sister-in-law. I didn't even know her intentions. Something still didn't make sense about her, and yet I still hadn't succeeded in convincing myself she was bad news. Nor had I removed myself from the notion that she might be mine.

But Alaric seemed to like her, at least enough to train her, and he didn't usually seem to trust anyone. So why was I so conflicted?

I headed back to my chambers instead to continue the book I'd been reading before having to do kingly shit. It was a fantasy romance set in the mortal realm written by my guilty pleasure author, who wasn't even old enough to have visited the strange place.

The naughty little lynx would write some pretty taboo stuff, but then just say *'the mortals did it'*, and everyone would be like *'take my coin'*. This one was about a mortal female who couldn't choose between four males and was entertaining, to say the least.

HOURS LATER, after reading the mushy happily ever after that included an unconventional wedding and a whole bunch of kids with a whole lot of dads, I decided to find Alaric.

As I left my wing, my ears were assaulted by familiar obnoxious snickers coming from Kai's wing. *Fucking Sloane and Graves*. Why couldn't they have gone with Kai?

"Hello gentlemales," I said, sneaking up behind them as the pair startled and whipped around to face me.

"Ugh, what are you doing here, Nekane?" Sloane spat.

"Yeah, aren't you supposed to be in the throne room?" Graves added.

"That was finished hours ago. More importantly, what are *you* doing here? Last I knew, you didn't have any business being on this floor. You know, with your bestie Kai not being here and all," I said, eyeballing the pair suspiciously. They were always up to no good, making pests of themselves and acting like complete twats. Why did their fathers have to be advisors? It made them pretty much untouchable and they knew it.

"We were…erm–" Sloane began, trying to think up some bullshit reason.

"Checking on Kai's bride!" Graves exclaimed proudly, not reading Sloane's reservations about coming clean.

"We haven't seen her for a while, and Kai wanted us to make sure she's behaving while he's gone! You know what females are like. So high maintenance!" Sloane explained.

"Yeah, and so needy!" Graves added.

"You're going to her chambers to look for her?" I asked, not trusting these pigs. I'd watched her storm out of the games room that night after *Pictionary*, and though I hadn't gotten to the bottom of what had upset her, I had a feeling these fuckwits had everything to do with it.

Okay, fine, she wasn't mine to protect, but I would be damned if the fates would stop me looking out for her. As a friend. As her brother-in-law-to-be. Not a mate.

"Well, we haven't seen her around the games room, and she probably can't read, so that means the library is out. Which leaves the chambers to check next." Sloane chimed in.

"She could be training with Alaric," I suggested with a shrug.

"She… What? No, Kai would never…" Sloane said, aghast.

"You're being ridiculous, that brute would never…" Graves added, equally horrified by the idea. Why did my brother keep them around? They were utterly clueless. Didn't they just say they had been ordered to keep an eye on her? Yet this was news to them?

"Well, why don't we go have a look, hmm?" I suggested, danger lacing my tone, daring them to argue. "You want to find Eva, and I need to find Alaric anyway, so let's just walk down together?" I said as I realized I desperately didn't want to leave them alone here to find my female. Not. My. Female.

The three of us made it to the large training hall in awkward silence. It was packed. At the front was Krista. She was a ballbreaker from what I'd heard, and she definitely had everyone's attention as she pushed them through drills.

I cast my gaze around, looking for a flash of silver hair with an onyx streak. Instead, I found Alaric talking to another shifter, Axel. The only male I'd ever known to be nearly as big as Alaric himself.

Sloane and Graves scampered off to continue their search when Alaric waved me over. As I really didn't have the energy to deal with them anymore, I didn't go after them.

"Alaric," I said, giving Axel a nod. "Where's Eva? No training with her today?" I asked, trying to sound casual instead of disappointed that she wasn't here.

"Nah, it's too late for that liaison," Axel answered instead, sniggering. The male had balls to speak so freely, I'd give him that.

"Axel…" Alaric growled, chastising him as expected. I didn't mind him speaking out of turn to *me*, I just hoped he had enough sense to not do so around my brother or father. Alaric was fond of him, almost treated him like a brother, so it would be shit if he pissed off the wrong fae. "He's right though, I train with Angel here earlier in the afternoons, when it's quieter, before everyone shows up for the late afternoon drills. Not that she showed."

"She didn't turn up?" I asked. That didn't sound like her.

"Nah, she's not been down for a few days. Anyway, what's this I hear yeh've been dealin' with shite in the throne room?" Alaric deflected.

I rolled my eyes, making a show of being really put out by it. "Someone had to deal with a ruling. The king and Kai aren't here, so I had no choice. Won't be making a habit of it, mind you." I shrugged. It wasn't a big deal, more of an inconvenience. It was the first time I'd been the only one here to deal with kingly bullshit, and I don't think I fucked it up too royally.

"Well, how'd it go?" Alaric asked. Axel was practically in my face ready to hear more. That male was like a coiled spring. Hard to believe he was older than me. Must be a wolf thing. Maybe Alaric had been an excitable pup once too. I fought back a grin at the thought, and instead rolled my eyes again, letting out an exasperated sigh, not wanting anyone to think for a second I'd enjoyed being judge and jury. Very nearly an executioner too, if the idiot advisors would have had their way.

I explained the situation, keeping it brief. All the while, Alaric looked at me with an expression usually reserved for the rare occasion I handed him his ass in training. Pride. At least that's what I'd always thought it was. It was a strange thing to me, him being the only fae I had felt it from. Before he'd become my tutor in all things combat related, I'd never done anything to make anyone else proud.

As a boy, I remembered being desperate to make our father proud, the way Elikai could. But after my efforts with the library didn't get so much as a glance from him, I'd given up trying. "Turns out your boring lectures about your many war strategies didn't go in one ear and out the other," I teased, and his brows rose at that. "They actually kinda helped. A lot."

I expected him to look smug, but that gleam in his eye wasn't smug at all, and his smirk was a lot gentler than I expected it to be. Maybe I'd made the right decision? At least in Alaric's mind, but what did that say? The male was famous for his savageness.

The thought that I might have just brought my father's wrath down on an entire village instead of just the mayor flashed across my mind. I swallowed deeply at the prospect, trying to shake off the dread.

I had no doubt my father wouldn't approve of my decision to not just mindlessly kill the mayor. That in itself could definitely be enough to make him go after the village, to prove a point and right my wrongs. The male was unhinged. Best case, he'd only take his ire out on me.

"Well, maybe we aren't as fucked as I thought," Alaric grinned, snapping me out of my own head. He shared a look with Axel, who just nodded knowingly before being called away. An inside joke or something I wasn't privy to.

The room was starting to clear, so I figured now was probably as good of a time as any to ask about Eva. Again. "So what do you mean Eva hasn't been coming to train? I thought she was enjoying it? You two seemed to be getting on…" The look of pride I had been savoring soured instantly as Alaric glowered at me. So Eva was a touchy subject now? Since when? Maybe I should keep my mouth shut? Then again, no. "Do you still want to train her?" I pushed.

"She has potential, but if she doesnae–"

"Have you spoken to her about why she's bailed?"

"Nah but–"

"Then wait here. I'll go find her and you can ask her yourself. I want to, at long last, see this potential you keep talking about her having," I said, grinning at the stoic male who looked like I'd just kicked him in the balls.

The only thing I hated more than the fact that she could never be mine, was the idea of Eva not being able to defend herself adequately for whatever castle life may throw at her over the next millennia.

"I'll be back soon," I called before closing the door on the noise of the training room behind me, and making my way to Eva's chambers. I'd been keeping my distance from her since our day together in Ezerat, or at least trying. It was so fucking hard when my attraction to her was nothing short of magnetic.

As I arrived at the door, a muffled groan came from inside and I started hammering my fist against the wood. She was obviously there.

"Just leave me alone. You can tell Elikai whatever you like when he returns, right after you get your heads from up his ass!" her hot-tempered voice called from the other side. So Sloane and Graves hadn't given up trying to find her after I'd lost them in the training hall?

I tested the door, finding it was locked. "It's me, Kane. Open up."

I heard a small gasp, and then the click of a lock sounded. I waited before realizing she had no intention of opening the door. The female was infuriating. "I'll just let myself in then, shall I?" I muttered. Entering the room, my gaze fell on the massive bed first, finding it perfectly made. That wasn't right. I glanced around the space to find a lamp on the sofa by the fire, and blankets and pillows strewn around the figure cocooned inside.

"What in fate's name are you doing?" I asked, my voice louder than I'd intended. She ran her fingers through the tangled mess that was her hair, looking like she hadn't long woken up. Fuck, I wanted to see that every morning.

She stared at me oddly for a second, almost like she was seeing me for the first time, before stifling a yawn and rubbing the dark circles under her eyes. Something was troubling her and keeping her up at night. I stared hard at the pillow and blankets on the couch and the untouched bed across the room. Why wasn't she in the bed? Did she fall asleep on the couch by accident last night? But that didn't explain the bedding being there.

Maybe it was because she wasn't used to a bed? Alaric told me he struggled to sleep in one again after long campaigns of war. He would be so used to sleeping in a sleep sack that a bed was too soft.

"Nothing. I have just been having a lazy day here with a book," she said, pushing the covers away from her legs and shaking out her tight muscles before heading to the washroom.

"Alaric said you missed training. Again," I called through the wall over the sound of running water. *Fuck,* I needed my thoughts to move away from the idea of her undressing mere meters away. It took everything I had to keep my feet planted here, when all I wanted was to be in there, with her pinned against the tiled walls.

"I was actually thinking of taking up reading instead. As my Elikai-approved hobby," her muffled voice shot back. Had something happen to change her mind? Was it Graves and Sloane? They had gotten here before me. Or perhaps Alaric said something that upset her during their last training session. The male could be blunt, but his heart was in the right place, no matter how much he claimed not to have one. Perhaps she missed Kai? He had been gone for a little while now. My stomach tightened at the thought.

I let out a slow breath. This female was going to be the death of me. "You can do both. You've already had a few days off from what I've heard. Don't make me regret showing you the library," I said, reaching into the new wardrobe I'd had sent up for her, and grabbing a set of lightweight training clothes. I opened the door to the washroom an inch, forcing my gaze to fix on the floor, and threw the clothes inside.

I had been far too fucking long since I'd gotten laid, and she was far too fucking tempting. *Maybe I should hunt down Crystal?*

"No," she said, leaving the bathing chamber in just a robe. "I'm too tired to train. This is an *'Eva day'* today." she told me before making a beeline back to the blankets in front of the fire, but I wasn't going to let her laze around here, feeling sorry for herself all day for whatever reason.

In a flash of speed, I grabbed her wrist and pulled her to a stop in front of me. Our noses were practically touching as I pulled her back. Stubborn as a mule, she locked gazes with me and we stood in a battle of wills, neither willing to look away first. This close, her scent was too much, too intoxicating, too everywhere. I wanted nothing more than to taste her. I tried to remind myself of all the reasons we were destined to only ever be friends as I herded her against the nearest wall, pinning her there. Fighting to break eye contact before I gave in and tasted her lips on mine, I shifted to place my weight on my hands, caging her in, to force a fraction of distance between us.

"No," I demanded, but it came out as a growl. "This is a *'get your fine ass in gear and get to training'* day. Kai could be home at any time, and if you don't have enough of a footing in your training, then he will stop you and you know it. We both know he won't be happy with your choice in hobbies, and Alaric seems to think you have potential. It's obvious you enjoy it and have a talent for it too, despite whatever shit you're pulling not showing up for days," I ranted, moving to the wardrobe to give more space between us as my restraint dwindled. I thrust more clothes at her to distract us. She had to know I was right, and she'd never struck me as the type of female who would back down from a challenge. "Look, if you don't want to continue your sessions, then so be it, but let me see you kick his ass once before you quit," I finished, with a more playful edge to my demands.

She let out an exasperated sigh. "Will you leave me alone if I say yes?" Not the answer I was looking for, but I would take it. I gave her a firm nod and she snatched the gear from my arms before gesturing for me to wait outside.

Fuck, I really liked it when she was sassy. It was so unlike the females in the city who would say or do anything to please me. I shuddered at the thought.

Now just to get through watching her going at it with Alaric without throwing her down on the mats and showing her why she'd chosen the wrong prince.

CHAPTER 23

Evangelia

I deliberately took my time getting dressed before following Kane down to the training arena. I couldn't let him know I had spied on him during the hearing this morning, so instead I made out like I hadn't left the couch, let alone Elikai's chambers, all day.

Thankfully, my mind had been in such a spin after witnessing him show the spider folk's mayor mercy that I'd just wanted to snuggle up in front of the fire to be left alone with my thoughts. Witnessing him on that throne, however brief, had given me the kind of hope I'd only ever felt from Nix. If I hadn't seen the way he'd dealt with poor Kumo and subsequently those asshole advisors with my own eyes, I probably wouldn't have believed it.

The way he'd backed me against the wall just now, demanding I do as he said, hadn't helped my conflicting thoughts on the male one bit. It sent a rush through me, a desire to both bend to his will, yet at the same time challenge him. He raised such foreign feelings in me I just couldn't place.

A heavy sigh left me as I closed the door to Elikai's lavish room. What I wouldn't give to see my best friend now and tell him that all may not be lost. I sent a silent prayer to the fates that I would be reunited with him one day, and we could maybe even start planning for a brighter future. But until then, I needed to suck up the hit to my pride at being rejected by Alaric and continue my training sessions to strengthen my mind and body. If I had any hope of changing the lives of those who lived in constant fear of the cruel male who wore the crown, I had to.

At this point in my procrastination to get to the training halls, I imagined Kane was close to just dragging me there by my hair. At least he seemed to have bought my ruse, assuming I hadn't moved all day. Though I didn't like the idea of him thinking I was 'bone idle', it suited my purpose in this instance. I'd been so nervous he had somehow sensed my presence in the throne room that I thought he'd come to call me out on it.

I wasn't a coward, but I really, truly was not looking forward to seeing Alaric again. Fates, it was going to be so awkward. I couldn't help the huff that left my lips as we walked, and Kane glanced back, not missing a beat.

"Eva, don't make me throw you over my shoulder," he called to me, now walking backward, watching as I dawdled along.

"You wouldn't dare," I growled back, narrowing my eyes, but he definitely looked like he was contemplating it the way his eyes skated over me, as if assessing the easiest way to scoop me up. *Asshole.*

"You know the answer to that one," he smirked, throwing a wink my way before turning back around, just in time to miss the epic eye roll I sent back.

We finally found ourselves at the door to the training hall, and my stomach was in knots. Alaric was just through that door. Fates, how was I going to face him? This was a bad idea.

Just as I paused, needing a minute to pull myself together, Kane planted a hand around my waist and ushered me through the door, sensing my retreat as the mix of panic and embarrassment tugged at me to run. It wasn't just that, though. It was the confusing feelings and all-consuming need that had led me to kissing Alaric in the first place that gripped me.

The same feelings that I somehow seemed to have toward the male at my back, too. Even more so now I knew he wasn't like the male who had raised him. My head was so messed up. As much as I fought these feelings and knew they weren't right, it made it no less true.

"Alaric. Look who I found," Kane called, and the urge to hit him across the head had me clenching my fists. The wolf grunted as he turned around, but his silver eyes widened as he saw me.

"Alaric..." I tried, swallowing past the lump that had formed in my throat. What the heck did you say to someone who had rejected your advances so blatantly? That kiss had been mind blowing, even if it had been brief. It's just a shame the feeling wasn't mutual, because I don't think I'd have stopped at just kissing him.

"Angel..." he replied with a stiff nod. Well, at least he still called me that cute nickname. Maybe all wasn't completely ruined? Or perhaps it was for Kane's benefit?

"Great, now can we get to training? I need to see our little fighter here in action." Kane said, and something dark, possessive and altogether too excitable coated the words as he remained seemingly oblivious to the tension between Alaric and I. I half expected him to clap his hands with excitement, but his unrelenting grip was too busy dragging my ass to the mats.

At least Alaric had been clear about his feelings toward me. They were strictly professional. Kane, on the other hand, was giving me whiplash. One minute he was flirty, the next standoffish, another domineering, and then he was acting like my best friend. He was impossible to read, but that was probably for the best. Even if I did secretly prefer his charm to him being overly friendly. When we'd been in the city together, he'd been far too tempting. He was friendly, but also something else; something I didn't have a name for, but it had made my beast purr in contentment.

He'd also not been to visit me in the library once, even though he knew that's where I'd be. I hadn't hidden my love for books, and that room became an extension of that feeling. Of course, it was for the best. But, fates! I'd been almost desperate for him —both of them—to walk through the door. Especially after reading spicy romance scenes. Scenes that had me wishing I had someone to soothe the burning in my veins. These two irresistible males seemed to always star in those thoughts.

With a sigh, I shook off Kane's grip and moved to warm up on the mats, pointedly ignoring both males as I stretched out. Those two days off had not been good for my sorely tight muscles.

You can do this. Just pretend it never happened. I chanted to myself. *It's just any other day. Like when you had to train with Nix once you came of age after that really awkward night of seeing if there was any romantic connection.* I still cringed when I thought about him naked, only now it came with a pang of terror over where he might be. Or if he even was–

I shook myself, refusing to go down that dark, painful path. In reality, this situation was nothing like that. I could feel the impending disaster when I looked up and saw Alaric towering above me.

"C'mon then, lass, let's show him what we've been workin' on," he challenged, holding out a hand to pull me to my feet. I ignored it. I could stand just fine on my own. Besides, if he was going to pretend nothing had happened between us, then I could too.

"Fine," I said, my tone light. "Let's show Kane how I kick your ass," I teased, making sure to meet his eyes. I wasn't going to let him intimidate me.

"Yeh wish yeh kicked my arse, but if I recall last time..." He trailed off as his mind went back to that session.

"Yeah, yeah, let's not think about that and just get to the fighting." I really didn't want more reminders of how he had me pinned. It already haunted me.

Instead of checking the clock, he nodded to Kane who held a timer in his hand. We fought hard. I didn't have time to think about my next moves before Alaric was already swinging or charging at me again. He was as relentless as he was focused, and I didn't know if that was because we had an audience, or if he was just desperately trying not to think about what had happened too.

I fought my best, but once again, found myself pinned under his large body, our breaths coming hard. Alaric raised himself enough to look at Kane, who immediately stopped the timer.

"Wow! Impressive, princess. You lasted almost two minutes. Most of the horde can't even do that!" Kane said, genuinely impressed.

Alaric spat, anger in his tone. "Yer heads not in it, lass, pull it together," he growled in my face. *My* head wasn't in it? What the heck?

"Fuck you, Alaric," I growled right back at him, praying to the fates that my beast remained calm and in her cage. Surprisingly, she seemed to be enjoying whatever this was and didn't want to fight me to break free. "I have a couple of days off and don't hit my personal best, and you are trying to embarrass me about it? Don't you think I'm embarrassed enough?!" I snapped, pushing against his chest to get him off me, but he didn't budge.

"*Yer* embarrassed? Are you fuckin' kiddin' me?"

"Of fucking course I am emb–"

"Calm. Down. Both of you. What the fuck am I missing here?" Kane instructed, and we both froze at the command in his tone. I broke eye contact with Alaric to stare up at the other male now growling at me, but he wasn't finished. "Training looked like it was going great, and now you're at each other's throats? What the fuck happened?" Kane demanded.

"Ask her. She's the one havin' a fit and missin' sessions," Alaric snapped, his eyes narrowing on me, but he didn't move an inch.

It was clear Kane wasn't going to drop it, and Alaric's comment was basically permission to fess up. Taking a deep breath, I spat it out. "I kissed him, okay? It wasn't his fault. I just got caught up in the moment, and he shot me down instantly. Please don't tell your brother. Please, Kane. He will kill Alaric if he knows."

"You... He... What?" Kane said, struggling to find the words. I'd not seen the charismatic prince lost for words before. Not at all like his usual silver-tongued self. "So, she kissed you and you managed to walk away?" The question was pointed at Alaric, but when he only grunted, Kane turned his attention to me. "Eva, tell me, what *exactly* happened?"

"It just happened. It was a mistake," I said, not wanting to get into it.

"Not good enough. Tell. Me. What. Happened," Kane pressed, enunciating every word.

It wasn't a question. It was a demand, and I'd be a liar if I claimed I didn't heat up a hundred degrees at his dominance. My beast purred again, as torn as I was between these males.

"W-We had been sparring for hours. I was all hot and flustered, and when he pinned me like this, I... I just–"

"Are you hot now, princess?" Kane growled, surprising me with the question. His gaze was all fire as he stared at my compromising position, pinned under Alaric almost exactly as we'd been before.

"It doesn't matter. Alaric isn't interested. Just please don't tell–"

"Her attitude is a whole lot fuckin' colder too..." Alaric cut over my pleas, his face angled away from me, glaring at Kane. Whatever they were silently communicating, I wasn't going to be clued in on.

"Is she right? Are you not interested in her, or are you not interested in the shit that would come your way if you hadn't forced yourself to walk away?" Kane asked, his voice gravelly and eyes hooded with an emotion I couldn't be sure of, but I would guess it was desire. No. That couldn't be right, could it?

Alaric looked as surprised as me. "Yeh ken the answer to that," He eventually gritted out, still not moving his body an inch, keeping me tightly locked between him and the mats.

I might be a virgin who didn't have the first clue about stuff like this, but I could have sworn there was lust in his tone, and the hardness beginning to press against me wasn't imaginary. What the fuck was happening here? And why was it so fucking hot in this room?

"How much did you want him, beautiful? Were you disappointed when he pulled away?" Kane pried, and the sinfully seductive tone he was using made me shiver as I realized he was nowhere near done with his questioning.

I was so caught up in the moment that I couldn't even lie. "So much," I whispered, worrying my bottom lip, concerned I might be reading this all wrong, but not enough to want to risk stopping it.

"Tell me, were you wet for him?" Kane asked, and I couldn't stop my head from giving a subtle nod in answer. He turned to Alaric next, who smirked wolfishly. "Roll over so she is sitting between your thighs, facing me," he instructed, moving to lock the door on the otherwise empty room so we wouldn't be interrupted. The next thing I knew Alaric lifted me like I weighed nothing and held me as instructed.

"What are you–" I started, but Kane spoke over me to Alaric, dismissing my complaint as he approached us.

"Tell me, Alaric, is your little Angel wet? Is our chat about your dirty little secret making her burn up with desire?" Kane purred, pure sex dripping from his voice now. I'd never seen him like this. So dominant. It made me flush even hotter, his bold words sending heat straight to my core.

"Hmm. Perhaps let's start with an easier question. Are you hard Alaric?" When neither of us answered, he continued again, looking at me this time. "Is he hard at your back, princess? Tell me, do you feel him behind you?" he demanded, the heat in his eyes unmistakable as Alaric's arms gripped my waist and pulled me backwards, his hard cock indisputable as it strained against his training leathers and into my lower back.

The gasp that escaped my lungs must have been a good enough answer for Kane, who smirked at us wickedly. "Alaric..." I moaned, as I fought my body's instinct to rock against him. He tightened his grip, tilting his head so the rough feel of his stubble grazed my cheek, and the quickness of our breathing was heady.

My eyes met Kane's, and fates, the look he was giving me, giving us both, made me want nothing more than for him to come and join us. The thought alone sent a rush of heat through me again. To have them both on their knees for me...

"Tell me, Eva, what were you thinking when you kissed him?"

I licked my lips at the memory. "That I needed to taste him..." Kane closed the distance between us in a burst of speed and dropped to his knees, gripping my chin to look him directly in the eyes.

He pulled me away from Alaric to rest on my knees before him. "Do you still want a taste of him?" Kane asked, close enough that our lips were almost brushing. Fates help me, I wanted to. I wanted to taste both of them.

Kane leaned in like he was going to take my mouth with his, but instead spun me roughly to face Alaric, pressing his own hard length to my spine as he spoke right into my ear, causing goosebumps to rise along my neck. One hand pressed against my stomach, holding me back, so I was forced to feel his daunting size as it strained against his pants.

He took my hand gently and guided it up Alaric's thigh with his own, higher and higher until he smoothed our hands flat to the hard length of Alaric's cock.

The rumbling groans coming from both the males I was sandwiched between were feral, and it was intoxicating. I opened my lips to say something, anything, but all that slipped out was a breathy moan.

"I didn't hear you, beautiful... Do you still want a taste?"

As if I needed any more temptation, Kane dipped our joined hands into Alaric's leathers and pulled his cock free. "*Yes,*" I whispered, my breaths coming in short pants.

With no encouragement needed from Kane, I tried to close my hand around Alaric's thick cock, wrapping it as far as I could. I slowly began dragging my hand from base to tip, instinct taking over and driving my actions.

Kane's hand, still wrapped around mine, tightened our grip as I continued the slow movements. Alaric moaned, his hips bucking up into our fist, and I could feel myself growing wetter.

"Taste him for me..." Kane whispered in my ear, as he took his hand away and gently pushed down between my shoulder blades.

My tongue darted out, licking the glistening bead of moisture on the tip. The salty taste and smooth feel across my tongue made me eager to explore more. As I dropped my free arm to its elbow to give myself a better angle, my back arched, making my ass press more firmly into Kane. The feeling of him so close to where I wanted both of these males was making me dizzy.

Fates, is this how it's meant to feel!? If so, I never wanted it to stop. I sucked the head into my mouth and bobbed down Alaric's length, taking as much as I could. "*Fuck,* Angel..." Alaric groaned, his large hand landing on my head, fingers knotted in my hair as he guided me along his length, and I wanted him to make more of those noises.

Kane's hand trailed down my spine, causing me to arch further into his touch until he reached down and grabbed my ass roughly. "How does he taste?" he asked, his voice sending a shiver down my spine, and I moaned in pleasure. The feeling of Alaric throbbing in my mouth was addictive, and I was greedy for more.

"Enough Kane, I'm not gonnae last," Alaric warned through gritted teeth, his brogue rougher now. I wanted to push him over that edge more than anything. I needed to know what that looked like. A male as fierce and feared as him, trembling at my mercy.

Anticipation quickened my inexperienced movements as I tried to bring him to orgasm despite his words. Alaric's hand tightened in my hair, and his hips thrust with urgency as he chased his end.

I tasted his cum on my tongue and greedily lapped it up, swallowing every last drop as he threw his head back in bliss. His groans were something I would remember for the rest of my days.

"Good girl," Kane praised, his voice full of sin as he watched me finish his friend. His hand gripped my ass so tightly now it would leave a mark for days if I weren't immortal.

"Alaric, didn't she do a glorious job sucking your cock? Don't you think you should thank her?" he challenged, already pulling me to kneel. He moved to hold the base of my throat and used it to tilt my chin to look into his piercing blue eyes. Fates, he was gorgeous. "Would you like that, princess?" Kane asked, and suddenly my mouth was dry. *Fuck, yes, I wanted that.* My head nodded emphatically before I could think of the words.

"Come here, Angel," Alaric purred, and as I slid over to him, he reached the waistband of my pants and slowly began to slide them down my legs, taking my panties with them. He paused, looking at me as if for my approval, but I definitely wanted this.

I nodded, and he continued his slow removal of my pants. As I shimmied out of them, Kane growled low behind me as he got a view of my bare ass, his hands sliding up my legs to grasp it again.

"Sit between my legs like yeh were before, facin' Kane." I did as instructed, settling into the gap between his thighs and he swiftly hooked his hands under my knees to spread my legs wide before Kane, exposing me.

I watched the flames of desire turn molten in Kane's eyes as he growled low in his chest. The way he stared at me, perusing my naked flesh, was empowering. I wanted him to look. I wanted him to desire me. Even if this was the first time someone had looked at me so intimately. It felt too good to shy away.

Alaric smoothed his hands down my tank top, shaping my waist, before pulling it up and over my head, leaving me completely naked between the two powerful males.

Alaric's calloused hands cupped my breasts, his surprisingly deft fingers finding my nipples and teasing them. The moans that tumbled from my mouth were filthy, and I found I enjoyed it. While one hand remained teasing me, the other traveled down between my thighs, testing the wetness that he found there.

He circled my clit, and pleasure sparked through my veins, consuming my thoughts. It was like being struck by lightning. My eyes closed from the onslaught of new sensations I was experiencing, my head tilted back against his broad chest.

When I opened them again, swimming in the heady pleasure, the sight before me made me want to combust. Kane knelt before us while one hand leisurely stroked his now freed cock as he watched Alaric tease me. The heat that was burning between the three of us was too much. I could feel myself reaching that peak, and I didn't want this to end. It felt so good. Too good.

I needed both of them to be touching me. "Alaric, Kane… I… Oh, fates…" I moaned. I needed more. My arm reached up behind me to grasp a handful of dirty blonde hair. My other reached for Kane, needing him closer, to feel his lips on me.

Alaric's fingers dipped further down to my entrance. He pushed two inside of me as Kane kissed my outstretched palm, trailing kisses up my arm.

The general hissed. "Yer cunt's so fuckin' tight, Angel," he said, stubble grazing my face as he looked down over my shoulder and pushed further, stretching me.

A sharp pain tore through me, pulling a gasp from my lungs, and Alaric was instantly pulling his hands away, leaving me shivering without them. "Yer untouched?" he said, studying the bloodied tips of his fingers. Kane's eyes widened at the sight before him, and I suddenly desperately wanted to cover up. It felt like a bucket of ice had been thrown over us.

"I– Well… Yes. What does that matter?" I asked, embarrassment rushing through me. They were obviously used to experienced females.

"Fuck, Kane, I jus' took yer brother's betrothed's virginity with my fuckin' fingers–"

"I can fucking see that!" Kane snapped, tugging at his hair as he got to his feet and righted his pants. Alaric stood too, following suit with his own clothes, leaving me cold on the floor. Was it really so bad? I mean, this entire situation was completely messed up.

But as I waited for someone to fill the silence, the number of Lores we had broken came crashing down on me as reality set in. I wanted to curl in on myself, disappear. Why had I left my room in the first place? I knew my shield was cracking around these males, and I couldn't trust myself not to do something stupid. Reckless. Unforgivable.

"Look, this wasn't on you. I should have said something..." I rushed out, my mind a whirlwind of thoughts. "You didn't know, I didn't say. We just... Shit..." I swallowed roughly, hugging myself as I drew my knees to my chest.

I couldn't keep a single thought in my head to figure out what we were going to do. I spotted my tank and scrambled to grab it, throwing it over my head. It wasn't much, but being naked in this situation was suddenly a horrifying prospect. Kane gathered the rest of my discarded clothes while Alaric strode off to the washroom.

By the time he returned, I was dressed and stood in awkward silence while Kane was back to his relentless pacing. "I'm sorry, Angel, I didnae ken yeh were untouched or I would have been more gentle. Fuck, what am I sayin', I wouldnae've done it at all. I shouldnae've done it," Alaric apologized, breaking the silence, which I appreciated, but he didn't need to be sorry. I had wanted it as much as he had. Maybe more.

"We were all just caught up in the moment," Kane reasoned. "I don't need to explain to you both why this," he gestured between the three of us, "can't leave this room." His frustration was obvious and he tried to come up with a plausible way we could all make it out of this alive if the king or, fates forbid, Elikai ever found out.

We all nodded our agreement and started toward the training room door. Kane unlocked it with his touch and we walked in silence all the way back to our individual rooms.

Fuck. We fucked up. *I* fucked up.

But I was struggling to muster up any regret.

It all just felt so... right.

CHAPTER 24

Alaric

Fates help me. With Kane just next door and Angel only down the hall in the other wing, sleep was impossible. I tossed and turned, fighting the overwhelming desire to finish what we'd started.

Were they as wound up as me, or were they already regretting it?

I needed to get out of the castle. Now. Before I lost my internal battle and made this whole situation even worse. If that was even possible.

I could still smell her maiden's blood on my fingers. Vigorously washing my hands repeatedly did little to mask her delicious scent, and fuck if it wasn't driving my beast insane. I'd wanted nothing more than to suck it from my fingers then lick her cunt clean, but that wouldn't have ended well for any of us.

Diving out of bed and pulling my sweatpants over my perpetually rigid cock, I crept out of my room and made my way off the castle grounds. I was losing control and couldn't trust myself not to act on my instincts.

The biggest surprise tonight wasn't even how much I desired Angel, but the fact that I didn't care whether it was her or Kane who I sunk my cock into. It was just an all-encompassing need and overwhelming knowledge that it had to be one of them.

I moved swiftly out of the capital and into the neighboring woods before letting my wolf take over. I gave no care to my shredded clothes left behind. My black paws landed on the hard ground, and I ran at full speed into the copse of trees. The hunt was on, and I had a lot of pent up energy to shed.

While hunting the deer and rabbits in the forest wasn't much, it did keep my wolf happy. It wasn't what I wanted to be doing right now, but it would keep me distracted long enough that I wouldn't be a feral beast when I returned.

I slowed my gallop as I got into the thicket of trees, controlling my breathing so that I didn't startle my prey. I listened carefully for the slightest sounds and prowled silently through the undergrowth, waiting for anything to make a wrong move.

Finally, the rustling of leaves found my ears, likely a rabbit about to meet its doom. I stalked in the direction the noise came from, well-practiced moves keeping my approach silent even with my mind so thoroughly scrambled.

There it was, my small brown and gray prey snuffling around, drawing my attention. I gave myself over entirely to my wolf, who leapt on its victim and devoured it whole.

I spent hours in the forest, the need to hunt riding me hard. It felt insatiable. It had been a long time since I'd felt so completely out of control. I wasn't the pup I used to be, I was nearly three hundred and fifty years old. But every time my mind went back to that training hall and the scent of her blood, her lust... Kane stroking himself with flames dancing in his striking blue eyes, I was back into the frenzied need to hunt *them* down instead. To finish what we'd started. To do what I desired, but had never admitted to myself until now.

Kane's scent had changed since I went hunting with Elikai. I'd tried to ignore it, had put it down solely to Angel's arrival even, but now I couldn't shake the feeling that his coming of age while I'd been gone had everything to do with it.

After pushing my wolf to the point of exhaustion, I headed back toward the castle. My black fur camouflaged a lot of the blood, but the white speckling across my back, that usually made my haunches appear gray, was now completely crimson.

Blood dripped from my muzzle, coating my fur as it slid down my throat. I felt alive when I got to be the wild creature that I am. But right now, it only served to remind me of how far out of my reach those two high fae were, and how I couldn't afford the distraction. There was a much bigger game at play here, with much higher stakes, and my gut told me it would all start to unravel really fucking soon.

I needed to be ready.

But more importantly, so did Kane.

He just didn't know it yet.

CHAPTER 25
Elikai

By the time we arrived at Kelpie Cove, the kraken had already been caught in a giant net. "Drag it to shore," my father hollered, and the horde's warlocks quickly began using a levitation spell to lift the behemoth thing, while the horde's shifters speared at its flesh, making hundreds of cuts and lacerations across its slimy disgusting skin.

As the hideous thing flailed around on the black sand beach, it slowly began to bleed out as Father and I stood debating how best to kill the monstrosity without having to touch it.

Its large eyes looked at us pleadingly from its bulbous head, while it tried to beg for mercy using its telepathy, the only useful skill the krakens had been gifted with. It wasn't as useful as other abilities, like witches who had the sight, so it wasn't worth keeping them around. Besides, where would you keep it?

Each of its grotesque tentacles was the thickness of a tree trunk and covered in lethal poison-laced spiked suckers. Its skin was a hideous shade of purple, and I made a mental note to tell my pretty pet to burn all the purple underwear she would have been spending my absence tirelessly debating over.

"The kelpies believe this to be the last of their kind burdening our shores," my father said, a look of triumph crossing his face.

Of course if *I* was king, I would have succeeded in making them extinct centuries ago. Father was so lazy in his obsession with creating a pure-blooded kingdom, he'd spent way too long using the horde to only go after thrakos, half-breeds and other powerful creatures of *this* kingdom, never looking beyond Dezrothia and planning bigger. It was pathetic.

What about the surrounding kingdoms, or even the mortal realm?! His lack of ambition made me as sick as the creature before me. Something I'd always despised about Nekane, too. *I*, however, didn't have that shortcoming.

The only reason I'd come to this fates' forsaken place was to schmooze Father, so I decided now would be the perfect time to start. "I want to savor its death after what its kind had the audacity to do to you all those years ago, Father! Let it be an example of what happens when you try to assassinate the king, and with a sneak attack while at sea, no less. Cowards!" I said, feigning outrage.

"They are cowards, my boy. Or should I say... *Were* cowards," he smirked before throwing his head back and laughing maniacally in his deep timbre.

"Let's make it slow and painful!" I said, knowing what made him tick, but when I looked at the giant squid, a shiver of repulsion ran down my spine at the thought of getting any nearer. "Actually, it's hurting my eyes to look at, so perhaps not too slow, but definitely painful." Father nodded his agreement, of course, as I knew he would, and I steered him away from the foul beast.

We continued brainstorming new and inventive ways to kill the last kraken, and had almost come to a decision—one of my ideas obviously—when we were rudely interrupted by a soldier of the horde.

"Your Majesty, so sorry to interrupt–"

"Spit it out, we have a kraken to slay!" Father cut across him, and I glowered at the peasant for interrupting our father-son bonding session.

"That's what I came to tell you. The kraken is already deceased, Your Majesty. They cannot survive for long on dry land, and I believe perhaps the bleeding aided in its faster demise."

Father shot daggers toward the dead thing, bloodying the sand, and I let out a sigh as I realized my new luxurious armor and eyes were saved. The fates worked in my favor, as usual.

Although, that of course meant this trip would be for naught if I didn't manage to work my magic on Father to convince him in some other way that I was more than ready to take his crown.

Cocking my head to the side, I could tell from his flared nostrils and bared teeth that he was now in a murderous mood, having been denied his kill. Without Nekane around to take it out on, he would be insufferable.

His arm snapped out, grabbing the guard around the throat before channeling his rage into squeezing as tightly as he could, his knuckles turning white. I noted that I was definitely faster and stronger. The superior male.

Leaving him to it, I stormed back to the accommodations to wait for him to cool off so we could discuss my ascension.

As I ENTERED Father's room later that day, elegantly dressed in all black to further add to the power and authority that naturally oozed out of me, I found his harem waiting. Another perk I looked forward to inheriting.

I had no loyalties to my pretty pet. She owed everything she was and would ever be to me, but it wouldn't look good if I openly fornicated with others while I worked on convincing Father I was ready to be king. Marrying a pretty high fae to produce heirs with was par for the course. But it wasn't fair that I now had pent up energy I hadn't been able to use on slaying the kraken, so perhaps I should use it having my marvelous weapon pleasured while I waited.

I clicked my fingers at the red-headed one, gesturing for her to get on her knees, but just as the whore got into position, Father stormed in.

I improvised, swiftly backhanding her across the face, and she flew across the room with a cry of pain. "How many times do I need to tell you that I am soon to be wed to a thoroughbred high fae, you dirty whore!" I spat, turning to my father next to explain how she had tried to come onto me and ignored my outright refusal on account of my upcoming nuptials.

Father, sword in hand and already in a maddened state after the kraken debacle, strode over to the whore sprawled across the floor. He reached down to grab a fistful of her hair in his large hands and swiftly ran his blade across her neck, slitting her throat and covering me in a fountain of blood. I thanked the fates my manhood hadn't been in her mouth already. It was still a pity. I'd been looking forward to using her.

She convulsed on the floor while the rest of the whores huddled against the wall in fear, and I shot my father a disgusted look before remembering I needed something from him. I quickly smothered it with something more pleasant. "Father, I need to speak with you. It is about our hunt and my future," I said, pushing authority into my voice and feigning indifference to his outburst, though it wasn't easy. I tried to ignore the blood that coated my clothes and couldn't decide what was worse, the idea of kraken blood or that of a whore. The finery I wore would, of course, need to be burned now. A prince couldn't wear clothes stained with a peasant's blood. Father obviously wouldn't have the courtesy or presence of mind to end her life in a less messy fashion. He cared for no one but himself. I could have thought of at least a hundred different ways to have ended her without even putting a crease in my outfit, or hers.

"Fates, Elikai, get changed. I don't need to see you covered in a whore's blood," Father sneered, ignoring my statement and dismissing me entirely.

"But Father–" I tried again. I had to make him listen to me. I had to make him see sense. He needed to step aside, and let me take my rightful place.

"But nothing, boy. Get out of my sight. We will discuss this again in a few decades. Make that a few centuries if you don't leave my room right now!" He was red-faced and shaking, using the tone of voice he reserved for staff and Nekane.

How dare he. I'm his favored heir. I've been of age for weeks now! Why wasn't he seeing this? I'd found the most beautiful bride. I have everything to make me the perfect candidate to be king. His madness must be clouding his vision.

He must not be convinced of my commitment to my pretty pet yet. We weren't even married. Anyone could get engaged! I need to show him that I'm committed to seeing this through. I gasped as it dawned on me. *I need an heir.* That had to be it. I needed to secure an heir in her womb!

With that stroke of genius, I knew I needed to get back to the castle and start work right away. So, without another word, I left my father and his whores and made my way to the stables, stopping by my accommodations to pick up my bag.

Mounting my horse, which was already saddled and packed for me in readiness to leave at sunrise tomorrow, I headed straight back for Ezerat alone, taking an alternate route that was much faster than the one we'd taken to get to Kelpie Cove. The others would have only slowed me down, wasting time collecting puny taxes.

I rode and rode until darkness fell, and I made it to a small inn in a mining village. I wasn't in the least bit tired, my mind racing with excitement, but I needed to wash the unsightly whore's blood off me, and the horse needed rest. Useless thing.

I dismounted, handing the reins over to the teeny tiny ostler male before striding inside. "Prince Elikai Regis. I need your best roo–" I started, but something hit my shin mid stride and I nearly went toppling to the floor.

A shrill squeak rang out and I looked around frantically to see who or what had nearly killed me! There was a small desk, built for a child, halfway across the entryway on its side.

I moved toward it and saw a short stocky female cowering behind what I now assumed had to have been a tiny reception desk. Her hideously full chest threatened to spill out of the brown leather corset she wore as she looked up at me trembling. "You nearly killed me!" I bellowed to the dwarf.

"I'm so sorry, my prince. Please accept my most sincere apologies. I am somewhat petite for a dwarf, and you mustn't have seen me. My fault, of course! I vow I shall never get in the way of your path again!"

My eyes widened as the reality of what had happened hit me, and a roar of laughter escaped my mouth. As I pictured it in detail, imagining her flying across the entrance hall, I damn near doubled over. I'd never kicked one of the dwarven fae before, but it was definitely something I planned to make a sport out of. Just another reason I needed to become king.

"Very well. I need your finest room for tonight," I ordered, regaining my composure. "Now!"

"Of course, my prince," she said, pulling a key from a box and handing it over. "Please follow me."

I took the key and handed her my luggage, before slowly trailing behind her as she ran as fast as she could, huffing and puffing for breath as she struggled with the size and weight of my bag. It was all rather hilarious. I couldn't wait to tell Sloane and Graves.

She finally reached a door marked with a number that coincided with the tag on my key. "Here we are, my prince. I assure you, the furniture is all hand carved and sized for high fae in this suite. The kitchens are due to close shortly, but we would be obliged to serve you dinner in our dining room."

"Expect me at some point tonight," I replied, and took my bag from her easily before entering the hovel she had assigned for me. It wasn't luxury by any stretch, but it would do.

After scrubbing the blood from my skin and dressing in fresh finery, I made my way to the restaurant. I would need a full stomach if I was to ride hard again tomorrow. Before making my presence known, I stood in the doorway listening to the rowdy creatures gossiping frantically.

"What's wrong with her?"

"I heard she came from the Fading Vale..."

"I heard she came from a coven in the city..."

"Is that why the prince is here?"

"The prince is here?! Which one?"

"What's wrong with her eyes?"

"What's she saying?"

"She's been at it for hours..."

"Has anyone tried to snap her out of it?"

Intrigued, I subtly peered around the door, searching the room for the female they spoke of. Sitting at a table in the shadows toward the back of the restaurant, which was definitely more of a tavern if the drunken rabble and decor were anything to go by, was an unmoving cloaked figure.

I stepped into the room, making little effort to avoid treading on the little creatures gawking up at me as I strode up to the only other normal-sized being in the room.

As I neared, I saw that she looked like your bog standard old witch, her eyes were milky white and glowing from beneath her hood like orbs. A seer witch?! Locked in a vision, no less!

I fought to hide my grin as she babbled almost incoherently, but the words I caught got my attention... Throne lay bare... Rightful heir... Horror... Bloodshed... Deceit.

I swiftly sat in the chair opposite, snapping my fingers in her face, trying to get her attention, but she didn't even flinch. She was truly having a vision. I needed to know more. I needed to know everything about what she was seeing right now.

I clicked my fingers again in front of her disturbing, swirling eyes. Still nothing. I leaned over the table and slapped her across the cheek. Nothing.

I huffed in annoyance, bored with being ignored. "Someone bring me a bucket of cold water. Now!" I called to no one in particular. A dwarven male approached with a bucket no bigger than a dessert bowl, but it would have to do. Thank the fates my pretty pet wasn't here, or she would be terribly confused.

I snatched it from him and threw its contents at the witch's face. The prophetess sucked in a huge gulp of air, her eyes rolled forward, no longer clouded, immediately snapped into focus and met my stare dead on, like she could see directly into my soul.

"Dwarven folk aren't that small. You really should tread carefully, *King* Elikai."

CHAPTER 26
Alaric

I stared out of the window in my office, contemplating visiting my ma'. She was the wisest fae I knew, and despite my being three hundred and forty-nine years old, she was the one I needed right now.

She would likely already know some of my worries thanks to Axel, and probably already had wise words or advice she could offer me. It really had been a while since the last time I'd seen her. I should make more of an effort, but when the king was around, it was always risky. And while he'd been gone this time, I'd dedicated almost every spare minute to training Angel. Even when I wasn't training her, I was thinking about training her, making plans for our next session, or just picturing how fucking sexy it was when she got angry and didn't pull her punches.

Then there was Kane who'd had my attention for his entire life, a work in progress I should keep strictly professional. It was far too important that I steer him on the right path. I'd been so fucking proud when I'd heard the way he'd chosen to sentence the spider folk that I knew I'd chosen the right prince.

Even so, I'd been a member of the horde for over three hundred years, and never had I fucked up as badly as I had with Kane and Angel in that training hall. I could almost hear my ma's warm voice laughing at my dilemma already. She'd always thought the Lores were nonsense.

She would likely tell me I was overthinking it and to just follow my heart, but I'd avoided listening to that cold dead thing in my chest for centuries. The moment I did, all the terrible things I'd done would come flooding in, and I didn't know if I would survive it.

I took a deep breath, letting it out slowly and counting back from ten, reminding myself of my father's many lessons before my mind calmed and I decided it was time to find Kane.

He would be in his chambers after what went down yesterday, no doubt, pacing a hole in the floor as he did when stressed, and his mind needed to thrash things out. But as I approached his door, I saw Angel lingering, as if she was debating whether to knock or not. How long had she been standing here?

I nodded to her in silent acknowledgement, and she swallowed audibly before her cheeks pinked furiously. I wasn't sure if she was embarrassed I'd found her here, or if her gulp had reminded her, as it had me, of the way she'd swallowed every last drop of my cum as I'd found the most intense release of my life.

I swung Kane's door open before I had second thoughts, or worse, gave in to the impulse to slam Angel against the wall and carry on where we'd left off. My cock hardened as I pictured in perfect detail how her legs would wrap around my waist, her hands on my shoulders for leverage as she rode my fingers while my thumb circled her clit, her–

"Hello? Hey! Wolf? Eva? Mind explaining why you two just barged in my room, and why Alaric looks about ready to either fight me or fuck me?" Kane asked, snapping his fingers as if to break me out of a trance.

"Fuck. Yeah. No. I mean, nah, none of that bollocks. Elmer caught me when I came back early this mornin'," I explained, as his eyes darted between me and Angel.

"Elmer?" Kane asked, his brows knitted.

"Aye, told me to tell you pair we are needed for a dinner tonight. Also, that Regis an' Elikai are expected back in a few days." Both their eyes widened as Kane ushered us in and closed the heavy door, snapping the magical seal into place to give us some privacy from any nosey passers-by.

"Fuck..." Kane grimaced, glancing at Angel, who had turned a shade paler, as she busied herself taking in the decor of Kane's room. There wasn't much to look at. It was far smaller than Elikai's and the furniture was sparse. He just wasn't a showy male.

"So what do we do?" Angel eventually whispered, her eyes darting around quicker now, as if the walls had ears. And in this place, she was probably right to be cautious.

"We pretend like it never happened," I told them simply. It was the easiest option. "We trained together an' that was that."

"But wait. How are you even a virgin, Eva? I thought you had spent six days locked in those fucking rooms fulfilling my brother's every fantasy, and then we find you untouched. How are you engaged to Kai and untouched?"

"You counted the days?" she muttered, then shook her head. "I told him I was saving myself for marriage, and he agreed to wait..." she muttered, more to herself than anyone else. Was that embarrassment in her voice? Shame?

"You... Fuck... Is that the truth? Fuck it, it doesn't even matter..." Kane said, as his pacing quickened and he began to run his hands through his hair. His frustration was palpable. "What do you plan to do on your wedding night, Eva? I can guarantee you, if Kai even plans on keeping his word until then, he won't wait a second longer than he has to."

"I... I don't know. I just know that I really, really can't stomach the thought of being with him like that," she whispered so quietly, it was barely audible. I saw the hurt flash across Kane's face as though wondering whether that meant she couldn't stomach the thought of him either, given their identical looks, but it quickly turned to anger.

"The thought of being with him like what? Marrying him? Fucking him?" Kane asked, as his hands flew up to knot in his raven hair. "Then why did you agree to marry him in the first place? Is it to be a princess? To be fucking queen? Wealth, status, protection? What's your motivation, because I'm really fucking struggling here to understand what's going on in that head of yours!" Kane yelled, and although his questions were no different to the ones running through my head too, I felt the urge to defend her.

But how did you defend someone when all the evidence pointed to them being a prince-digging whore? I felt sick with myself for even thinking those words where she was concerned, but it didn't make it less true. Angel just stared, stunned silent by Kane's outburst.

He closed his eyes for a moment and took in a deep breath before carrying on, much calmer this time. "Look, I'm sorry. I just don't understand. Regardless of what happened yesterday between the three of us, help me understand why one minute you're celebrating your engagement and then the next you're repulsed by your fiancé? Is it cold feet?"

"I... I can't... It's more than that," she said, and her lip trembled like she was about to break down in tears. She fanned her face with her hands vigorously as if to blow them back inside before they could escape, while her breaths came in sharp, frustrated bursts.

Angel was on the verge of hyperventilating at Kane's questioning, and I couldn't help but feel sympathetic toward her. I wanted to wrap my arms around her and tell her it would be ok, that she would never have to experience the touch of a male unless she wanted it.

I hung my head back, leaning against the wall as it dawned on me that it was no use lying to myself about how under her spell I was.

On an exhale, I looked at the female in question. The expression she wore reminded me of a rabbit the moment it realized it was caught in my wolf's eye line with nowhere to turn, no chance to run and no hope of escape. "If that's how yeh feel Angel, we need to get yeh outta this castle. Yeh cannae just tell Elikai yeh changed yer mind. A male like him wouldnae take the rejection well. It'd be a death sentence," I explained to her truthfully. "I'll get yer daggers for yeh an', if Kane agrees, we'll get yeh outta here before they return. I can find someone to help yeh get back to yer village an' family. They'll be relieved to have yeh back after yer imprisonment in the Vale. But 'til then, we have to act normal. We cannae draw suspicion an' risk havin' eyes on our every move if we are to pull this off."

"No," she said, cutting the silence that started to settle in the room. Her green eyes lit with determination. "This is my mess to deal with. I will see it through."

Ignoring her protest, Kane looked up at me. "She needs to be out of the castle. I don't see we have any other option, unless Eva wants to start talking and filling in some gaps for us?"

He eyed her for a second, but she didn't offer any explanations. "No. I am staying here," was all she said, arms crossed and digging her heels in.

I could see the gears turning in Kane's head, trying to formulate a plan. I couldn't blame him for wanting answers from Angel. I had a long list of questions I wanted answers to as well. The difference was, I already knew Elikai was a prick and couldn't blame her for having second thoughts, but Kane had always fought to see the best in him.

If it came down to his brother and twin, or a beautiful female he'd just met a few weeks ago, his loyalty would be to his brother, regardless of how deep she sunk her claws into him.

"She's expected at the dinner tonight. Even if she wanted outta here, if she's not there, fae will talk an' come lookin' for her. We need to give her as much time as we can to escape," I said.

"Okay, we will attend the dinner tonight and straight afterwards we all go for a late night stroll. We can both take Eva to the Crooked Claw and get her out of the city from there. Melina and Bill could probably help. She can leave in the middle of the night. No one will even know she is gone until morning," Kane mused, lost in his own thoughts and worry. It was a good plan to be fair, one that might actually work.

Angel released a feral sound as she rounded on us. "What part of *'I am staying here'* do you two *not* understand?!" she seethed.

"Do you think I like the idea of never seeing you again?" Kane asked. "Well, I don't. I fucking hate it. But I also know that my brother wouldn't take your rejection well, and fates help you if he finds out you're not the virgin you claim you are. It would put you in danger, and I hate the idea of you in danger more than the thought of you having to leave this place and never looking back. More than the idea of you marrying Elikai–"

"He would be furious if I snuck out of here. The moment he realized I was gone, he would hunt me down and anyone he thinks could have helped me leave, and drag us all to the dungeons. I won't put you in that position. Either of you. And I certainly won't put Thalia through that either. It's not fair."

We both just stared at her, but it was Kane who spoke first. "So what? You are just going to marry him?" Kane asked, incredulous.

"If I have to, yes," Angel whispered.

I sent a silent vow to the fates I would discover her secrets and untangle the web of lies this engagement was built on.

I COULD TELL this dinner was going to drag. These stuffy old gits were all trying to butter the affluent up to give up more coin than they were already paying in taxes, all in the name of the kingdom. The only thing I was glad for was that there was plenty of alcohol. I would probably drink the night into oblivion if I wasn't so worried for Angel.

She was currently surrounded by Elmer, Charles, and Desmond, three of the king's ancient advisors, who were all talking her ear off. She couldn't look more uncomfortable if she tried.

Kane was stuck talking to Horace, who seemed to be rather keen on finding out who was going to take the throne next. Regardless of position or rank, there wasn't a single resident or staff member within these walls who didn't know full well that Kane had never shown interest in the throne or politics. But with rumors of the sentencing running rampant through the halls, Horace was clearly digging to find out whether that was about to change. If only it were that easy.

Horace was father to one of Elikai's lackeys, so that definitely had something to do with his interest in who would be the crown prince. The king had still not announced who would take the throne should he retire. His arsehole was probably twitching at the thought of his son having put all his eggs in one basket, sucking up to the wrong prince. The advisors were nothing if not desperate to cozy up to those in power.

"We will need to get you fitted for your wedding dress," I heard Desmond say. "We have your measurements, but you never know if things need to be... readjusted," he continued, casting an eye over her figure, and I found my fists clenching involuntarily.

He was a balding male who was a good few inches shorter than Angel. I hadn't liked him before I'd heard him accusing Angel of marrying Elikai because she was already carrying his spawn. Now, I wanted to rip his tongue out and watch him choke on it.

"Of course, you never know what surprises may pop up," Charles agreed, gesturing to her stomach. He was the youngest of the trio and the most recent addition to the king's advisors. Unsurprisingly, he was keen to get on Regis' good side by any means necessary. Unbeknownst to him, he'd also just secured a spot on my list of advisors who were cunts and needed to be dealt with.

"Excuse me?" she asked with a scowl, looking like she was about to punch the males herself.

I'd had centuries of experience in keeping my cool around these arseholes, so before there was an incident, I stepped in. "Lady Evangelia," I called to gain her attention as I approached the group. It felt foreign to call her by her title, but we had to keep up appearances. She looked at me like she could kiss me for coming to her aid, and fuck if I didn't wish she would.

"If you will excuse me," she told the males, as she moved my way, her relief palpable.

Despite only seeing her earlier after we left Kane's chambers for our usual training session, doing our best to act normal, I'd been looking forward to seeing her again tonight. I'd grown used to her presence in my otherwise boring and brutal existence. I was male enough to admit that I would miss her if she agreed to leaving.

"Thank you, Alaric. I don't know how much longer I could put up with them and their thinly veiled insults. They obviously don't agree with a *princess-to-be* learning some self-defense. And can you believe their biggest worry is whether I need to have my measurements retaken?" she ranted, but I could barely hold back my laugh. She was so pissed off with the pompous pricks, it was kind of adorable. Then again, their line of questioning would have come as a shock to her, considering where we'd found her.

The Fading Vale was no easy place to have lived, prisoner or not. It would have been an odd concept that folk worried over such insignificant things here in the city. With that in mind, I decided not to tell her that they thought she might be with child already. It would only infuriate her further. Not many knew she'd made Elikai promise to wait until their wedding night, and such a quick engagement was not particularly normal these days now that true mates were hard to come by, thanks to the Lores.

"Aye, I can. Only because they dinnae have anythin' else better to do than to drag others down to their level. They've lived so long that they dinnae ken what it's like to live, doesnae help yer in trousers tonight rather than a dress." I told her, using it as an excuse to give her curves a once over. "They've probably never seen a lass as beautiful as yeh out of a dress before," I explained, but the gravel in my voice betrayed my thoughts. The loose pants she wore were cinched at her waist, and the tightness of her top made me want to strip her out of it and trace those curves all over again.

Until recently, everything had started to become very monotonous for me, the days beginning to blend together. I was only half of the age of even the youngest of the advisors, so I could only imagine what their lives were like.

"They should find another hobby," she grumbled into her wine glass, and I nodded my agreement.

Her eyes trailed toward Kane, who was talking to yet another pretentious arsehole. Not one of the king's advisors this time, but one of the beneficiaries who usually made a generous donation.

We stood in surprisingly comfortable silence while we nursed our drinks, until Kane finally untangled himself from the beneficiary and marched over to us, his brow low as he took in her casual ensemble. Clearly our talk earlier over Angel wanting to stay at the castle and marry his brother, even though it seemed he repulsed her, was still plaguing his mind. Either that, or someone just said something to piss him off. Probably both.

"Please tell me you are dressed like this because you changed your mind about what we spoke of earlier?" he growled low enough for only us to hear.

Angel's smile at Kane's approach soon vanished, replaced by a scowl. "The notion that females should wear pretty dresses every time they have places to be is less of a reflection on me, and more on your sexist upbringing," she hissed, mistaking his concern for judgment. "Where I'm from, everyone dresses however they want, and as long as it's practical, nobody cares. I suggest you never visit if you have those stuck up chauvinistic views."

Before he got a chance to reply, she turned to leave, but I subtly reached out to stop her, clasping hold of her small wrist. "Wait, Angel, it's not what yeh thought. Anyway, we have a surprise for yeh," I told her. Reaching into my jacket pocket, I pulled out her daggers. She blinked several times, frozen to the spot like she couldn't believe we were giving her back her family heirloom.

"Thank you," she eventually breathed, not wasting another second before taking them and strapping them to her hips, like she had done it a thousand times. Despite her anger toward Kane, a huge weight lifted from her at having them returned to her sides. Even if they did look so obviously out of place and had immediately sparked chatter around the room, her shoulders were infinitely more relaxed.

She'd barely gotten the straps secure when dinner was announced and everyone was invited to sit. The two of them breathed a sigh in unison, relieved to escape that awkward conversation. The tension thrumming between them made me want to have them fight it out on the mats. Or bend them both over and fuck them until they stopped arguing.

Her words only led me to have more questions, though. Like what had she meant by *'where I am from'*? No one in Dezrothia viewed casual attire as acceptable at these functions. Which begged the question, where *was* she from? I was determined to find out before long.

She moved to take Elikai's place at the table, placing her directly across from Kane. Just as I took my seat further down, the doors were thrown open and the herald stepped forward.

"Announcing His Royal Highness, Prince Elikai Regis, returning from a successful hunt at Kelpie Cove!" As the room filled with applause, my stomach sank. My eyes darted up the table and landed on the deep scowl on Kane's face and the mortified look on Angel's. She paled as she slowly turned to take in her fiancé, whose eyes blazed with fury.

CHAPTER 27

Evangelia

The hair rose on the nape of my neck as I clenched my instantly clammy fists under the table, fighting back the desire to run, or worse, shift.

Tears of frustration that he had returned so soon pricked my eyes as Elikai's own darted around the room before landing on me, sitting in his chair. If Kane's reaction to my choice of clothing was bad, Elikai's would be apocalyptic.

As expected, his eyes widened and his face blazed an angry red before he stomped across the room, snapping at anyone who tried to talk to him as he made his way to my side.

"What in the ever loving fates is this!?" he snarled, not bothering to hide his fury from every set of ears in the room. Or perhaps unable to contain it to keep up appearances. Yeah, he was definitely pissed. "Why are you dressed so… so… common? Fates help me, are those blades attached to you?" he spat in horror.

"Elikai, I–"

"I was away for what, a week? What happened to you?" he asked, gesturing to my comfortable attire. I seriously didn't understand what everyone's issue was. The outfit was brand new. Most of what I'd worn my entire life prior to these last several weeks had been handed down. I met his eyes, refusing to cower under his scrutiny. He dropped his voice, low enough that only I, and possibly Kane opposite me, could hear. "I spent my precious time having you tutored to act like royalty. I leave you for little more than a week and you've gone feral again," he seethed.

"Elikai…" I muttered, not really knowing what to say, but trying desperately to think of a way out of this, a good excuse to avoid drawing more attention. Who was I kidding? I could feel every pair of eyes in the room burning into me. My beast stirred, furious that he dared speak to us like this. Reacting to Elikai's presence in a completely different way than how she responded to Kane and Alaric.

I counted back from ten in my head, calming her and reminding us both that all was not lost. I'd told Kane and Alaric in no uncertain terms of my desire to stay, much to their obvious confusion, but as tempting as their help to escape this place was, I had a job to do. Elikai was back, which meant his father probably was too, and now I had my daggers. The thought brought a smile to my lips and calmed my beast somewhat as I looked beyond Elikai to the doors, wondering where the king could be, but Elikai stepped back into my line of vision.

"Thalia better have died or something while I was gone, because she knows better than to allow this," he seethed, waving a hand at me frantically.

Kane cleared his throat from across the table. "Brother, you're back early. We were told you would be returning in another day or so with our father."

"Maybe I missed my bride dearly and decided to hurry home to her. She's as desperate as I to take our vows. Absence makes the heart grow fonder and all that," Elikai lied, looking back at me with a false smile plastered across his lips before averting his attention down the table. "You there," he shouted, clicking his fingers at the General. "Take these daggers. They have no business being strapped to a female of importance."

Alaric shot from his chair and was at my side in a blink, disarming me. I just prayed he would give them back when the time came that I needed them, but at least I knew where my daggers would be.

"Now come, pretty pe...girl, we have much work to do before we can be wed," Elikai said, now loud enough for the entire room to hear.

Before I had a chance to even stand, he grabbed my upper arm roughly and damn near dragged me out of his seat and across the dining hall. He didn't say much as he marched me back to his chambers, but his grip grew progressively tighter, despite the fact that I wasn't even putting up a fight.

He was beyond furious. The punishing grip on my arm, his fast pace and the obvious grinding of his teeth told me I was about to get a taste of what making him angry was actually like.

I could almost hear the slamming of my jail cell gate as he slammed the door behind him and confined us both inside his chambers. I should be petrified, but for some insane reason, I wasn't. Whether that was down to Alaric's skilled help training me to defend myself, or just because I'd given up caring what happened to me, I wasn't sure. Maybe both.

"Evalia, come here," he commanded. Instead, I shot him the dirtiest look I could muster and stayed put. Could he really not be bothered to remember my name, or did he do it on purpose to belittle me? "I told you to come here, so you will do it with haste!" he barked, snapping his fingers this time, before pointing to the floor next to him like he was summoning his pet hound.

"No, Elikai. How about you stay over there, and I will stay here? I will not respond to you treating me like a dog!" I said.

I was done pretending to be the meek female he thought I was. I wouldn't let myself fall under his thumb. I would play his game in public for the short time I intended to remain here, but I was done letting him think he could treat fae like possessions. He was going to be king one day for fate's sake, and the kingdom would be even more doomed than it already was if he didn't change.

Regardless of the fact that Kane had pissed me off tonight, since seeing him in that throne room, I had begun wondering whether maybe Elikai held some of the same values hidden deep down. But seeing him now, I knew without doubt there wasn't an ounce of goodness in him.

"Maybe if you didn't act like one and just did as you were told, then I wouldn't treat you as such. How dare you embarrass me out there? In front of *my* fae. You were instructed to act as my representative, and yet you present yourself like this?" he seethed, gesturing to my outfit choice of wide-legged palazzo trousers and a long-sleeved turtleneck. "Are you trying to ruin me? Are you trying to project the wrong message to the fae on purpose, or are you too dim-witted to even notice?"

I could practically taste his rage in the harsh timbre of his voice and the way he stood so rigidly. Violence was in the air, coiled like a trapped animal about to strike.

He suddenly moved in a flash of speed, getting in my face, done with my disobedience. "You have displeased me greatly, pretty girl, and your insolence ends here," he threatened, the tone of his voice chilling as he took my arms in his hands and tightened his grip.

I clamped my jaw tight, biting down on my teeth, determined not to show that he was hurting me all while remaining in control of my other half. "Get your hands off me," I ground out. "Now." But he only squeezed tighter, his manicured nails digging in, and I felt the warm trickle of blood spread over my sleeves and down my arms as he broke the skin.

"No. You're going to listen to me. Listen to me very carefully," he enunciated. "I am giving you everything, and yet you would still disappoint me so thoroughly?" Panic threatened to grip me in its clutches. His entire personality and superiority complex made him so very dangerous. More dangerous than I ever realized.

Too dangerous to ever be in control of a kingdom.

I could feel the violence radiating off him, but his voice grew eerily calm even as he continued his assault on my arms. "It ends here. If you so much as breathe the wrong way from now on, you will not live to tell the tale. Do you understand?" He paused for a few heartbeats, "Do. You. Understand?"

"I understand," I growled, desperately fighting the tears that welled in my eyes as I realized just how fucked Dezrothia really was.

Until this moment, my plan had been one thing. Kill the king. But it was clear that if by some miracle I succeeded, I would only be aiding in replacing one monster with another. Only this one could prove to be frightfully worse.

If I had any hope of helping make this realm a better place, I needed to not only kill the king, but remove Elikai from the line of succession. Unless… perhaps I didn't need to *remove* him, I could just throw some competition in his way?

Kane's performance in the throne room proved he was capable of choosing to do the right thing, but that didn't mean the power wouldn't go to his head. Even if he was a good male and his upbringing hadn't made him into a prejudiced ass, it was clear he had no interest in wearing the crown. An uninterested king wouldn't help the society either.

I couldn't blame him. Why would anyone in their right mind want that kind of responsibility? *Sometimes we just don't have the luxury of choice.* I didn't exactly want to take on the suicide mission of killing the king single handedly and likely bring upon my own death in the process, but it was the right thing to do given the position I'd found myself in. Plus, revenge would be sweet. However, Kane was in a position where he could make significant changes, but would he be willing to try? I needed to get to know him better. Open his eyes to his family's cruelty. I could maybe even speak to Alaric? See if he agreed with my line of thinking. I'd have to be clever about it–

"Sit," Elikai snapped, pulling me from my musing, and I did so without any argument this time, deciding to pick my battles as I massaged my now freed arms, which throbbed in agony, the blood beginning to dry. "Now, I imagine if I had returned home on schedule, you would have been sitting here waiting for me. And after I walked in unscathed and you got past your relief of my safe return, you would have asked me how my trip went…" He trailed off, waiting for something. "SO ASK ME WENCH!" he bellowed, a fist slamming on the table and making me jump.

"H-How did your trip go?" I stumbled out, my heart hammering.

"Oh, pretty girl, thank you for asking," he said with a smile. Even more terrifying than his anger was how rapidly it seemed to fade.

He took a deep breath before launching wholeheartedly into the tale of his trip.

And I mean *Every. Last. Detail.* Acting out conversations he'd had with the king, every last thought he'd had about the kraken, how I should burn all the purple underwear I'd *'painstakingly picked out'* as it was now his *least* favorite color.

Fates, he was beyond angry with his father. Furious at Kane too for not being there to take a beating when their father got angry on the trip. I prayed to the fates that hadn't meant what it sounded like, and it was just Elikai being dramatic.

He was even enraged at the dwarven folk, but suddenly burst out laughing. His anger at them quashed in an instant as he started talking about organizing a *'Dwarven Derby'*. I truly didn't even know where to begin with trying to puzzle that one out.

The male was beyond insane. The more I listened, the more convinced I became that if I went ahead with my plan to kill the king, without doing something to stop Elikai's succession first, I would be unleashing a complete lunatic upon the realm–

"So after the kraken selfishly died prematurely, I went to speak with Father about my future as king, and as he was in such an awful mood, he dismissed me! Said he would talk about it in a few decades! The audacity. Then it dawned on me that he mustn't be convinced of my commitment to you, pretty pet, so I realized we must right this by getting married as soon as possible, to show him that I am ready. Then the genius part of my plan can begin." He paused for a few minutes, or perhaps it was mere seconds, but I hoped never to hear whatever he was thinking in those moments as a sickening grin spread across his face. "You see, I need an heir. I need to secure an heir in your womb, and soon."

My blood pressure soared and nausea threatened to knock me off my feet at his words. He wanted to... My stomach churned as I struggled to even finish the thought. *An heir.* He wanted me to have his child...

The triumphant look across his face told me he didn't care for my opinion on such a huge proclamation, but of course he wouldn't. He was a narcissistic sociopath to the bone.

"Now, back to this," he said, pointing his finger and gesturing to my form like one might an inanimate object. I frowned in response, still dumbfounded. "We will spend tomorrow setting a wedding date and having a much needed recap on your lessons from before I left for Kelpie Cove. I see you have a wardrobe now, so we must ensure it is filled with only finery befitting a queen. That I have approved, of course." His eyes fell to the set of training leathers laid out on the arm of my sofa bed and his nostrils flared. "You will not, under any circumstances, set foot on the training floor. It is off limits to you. Permanently. Assuming you can read," he moved to the pile of books by my sleeping area and picked one up from beside the fire, "You may use the library, but only to research the kingdom, what your role will be as queen, how to serve your husband in marital duties and any other areas in which you are lacking." He tossed the book I'd been halfway through reading into the flames, and my hands flew to cover my mouth involuntarily as I gasped. "You will absolutely not be reading romantic nonsense. Your life is already a fairy-tale. Why you would feel the need to read about them is beyond me and a total waste of time. Is that clear, pretty girl?"

And just like that, I felt the guillotine hanging above my head and the invisible chains locked tightly around my wrists, but I couldn't run. I had to see this through. I had to. Even if it killed me.

"Yes, my prince," I confirmed, just as there was a gentle knock at the door.

"Come in," Elikai called, and Thalia entered, looking nervous. I couldn't blame her. I'd brought Elikai's wrath to her door too, and she didn't deserve it. "If it isn't the useless handmaiden," he sneered. "Give me one good reason why I shouldn't kill you right now for your insolen–"

"It wasn't her fault, my prince," I quickly interjected. "Thalia was very clear about wanting me to take up other hobbies, much more befitting my role. She laid out beautiful dresses every day, but I told her no. I used my position as your betrothed to shut her down, much to her distress, I assure you."

"You really were a naughty pet while I was away, weren't you?" he sniggered as he strode over and painfully grasped my chin, the psychotic edge to his voice unmissable.

I nodded as much as I could, given his tight grip, before he finally let go. I sent a silent prayer to the fates that he would buy it and Thalia would stick to my story.

"Very well," he said, turning to the female in question. "Thalia, deal with this," he said, pointing at me with disgust on his face. "I have important dwarven matters to discuss with Graves and Sloane. By the time I return, I expect you to be every bit the female I'd left before I went to risk life and limb for this realm."

At the sound of the door slamming shut, I slumped down onto the couch, and after a few seconds, Thalia rushed to my side to join me.

"Are you ok, Eve? I heard the Prince had arrived back early without the king and I came to tell you, but it was too late. He was already dragging you up the stairs and back here when I found you." I just nodded silently, my mind too full with trying to figure out which of tonight's revelations to focus on first. "You didn't need to stand up for me like that, he could have killed you."

"I'll be fine," I said. "What kind of friend would I be if I'd thrown you to the wolves for something that was my mess to sort out? We don't do that in the Vale."

"You are a good female, Eve. Don't let that prince make you feel otherwise."

"Thank you. I didn't realize how much I needed to hear that," I said, giving her a small smile. "Is Westly free for us to all meet sometime? It would be so wonderful to talk openly and share stories of mutual friends. Of course, it can't be here, now that Elikai is back, but perhaps somewhere else quiet?"

"He has been a little tied up since Prince Nekane's sentencing. Did you hear? He was called to the throne room and–"

I listened intently as Thalia told me all about the ruling and the subsequent whispers and rumors making their way through the castle. A small smile lifted my lips as it became clear that she held a lot of respect for Kane. Despite knowing the details of what happened in the throne room first hand, no one else knew I'd been watching, so I let her tell me as if I was hearing it for the first time.

"What he did was unheard of, Eve." Thalia finished.

I let out the air I'd been holding on a sigh. How could I get *him* on the throne instead? Surely Alaric had thought about it too?

With my mind made up about how disastrous it would be for Elikai to be the ruler of Dezrothia, I needed to rethink my strategy and come up with a new plan. In order to do that, I needed to stay strong and survive this place a little longer.

CHAPTER 28

Nekane

My ears rang in the silence of the breakfast room as I tried to entertain myself by building a replica of the castle, using several variations of eggs for Alaric. It was ridiculous, but I desperately needed a distraction. Besides, I didn't really have anything else to do.

I hadn't seen Eva since dinner two nights ago when Kai had returned and whisked her away. I'd never seen him so furious as he was when he saw her sitting there in her lounge clothing. I was worried for her. For them both.

Although we'd had that misunderstanding earlier in the evening about her clothing choice, I hoped she'd realized my anger wasn't about the clothes at all, she'd looked stunning, it was because I actually gave a shit about her wellbeing. In a place like this, fitting in was part of survival. Something as simple as dressing differently from how society expected you to was viewed as rebellious.

I didn't know what to think any more about her presence here, her baffling relationship with Kai, or whatever had happened between her, Alaric, and I.

I'd been willing to help her escape because I didn't want to see her miserable in a loveless marriage, or for her to suffer any repercussions for calling the wedding off. But deep down, I didn't want to see Kai hurt, either. Sure I'd flirted with her, but we'd crossed a line in the gym, and the guilt I felt for my brother was almost as crippling as my anger toward him at the way he'd spoken to Eva in the dining hall when he'd returned.

When we spoke yesterday, Alaric mentioned she hadn't been to the training hall since Kai had been back, and I wasn't surprised. She was a ghost again, like she had been before my brother left.

My gut twisted at the thought of what her absence could mean. The only other fae in this castle who could understand what I was feeling was Alaric, and we've been spending a lot of time together since she'd vanished away with Kai.

I'd expected it to be awkward between me and my tutor. I mean, the incident in the gym hadn't just been about Eva, but about all three of us. It had felt so right, and I'd been so caught up in it. The sight of them, the scent of them, the feel of them. Everything about them had just called to me, and *fuck*, I hated the knowledge that it would never happen again.

And I hated myself for royally fucking over my twin, even if he didn't know it yet. There was no doubt in my mind the anguish that had consumed Eva while I'd been questioning her motives for being here was real. She had panicked at the idea of sleeping with her husband-to-be. But why? Perhaps I would finally see her today and this heavy weight in my stomach would disappear, and I could go back to my life before her arrival.

But then, where would that leave things with me and Alaric? He's a shifter, I'm high fae. It was more than forbidden; it was a death sentence. Perhaps when Kai became king, he would make changes for the better. I couldn't be the only one that thought the Lores were stupid.

Bored of waiting for Alaric, I picked up my *egg-cellent* masterpiece and made my way to the training halls with the hope that the silver-haired siren would maybe be there with him too.

If she wasn't, then hopefully I could get him to crack a smile with my *Sculpt-à-la-Egg*. He'd been fighting an inner battle with himself since what had happened, too.

Though we pushed the boundaries of the Lore with our shenanigans in the room at the Crooked Claw more times than I could remember, he had never allowed it to go any further. It likely hadn't even crossed his mind.

I, on the other hand, thought about it. More than once. I'd found my eyes wandering, watching him as he fucked some female senseless, and imagined what it would be like if it were just me and him in the room. Not that I'd ever told him that, but he had caught me staring several times, and we'd locked eyes as we'd found our release.

As I shouldered the doors to the training hall open, I realized the stairs had done nothing for the scrambled mess on the plate. Oh, well. It hadn't looked much better to begin with.

The space was empty, apart from Alaric, who was training on his own, his face set in a scowl. I instantly started to second guess whether he would appreciate my *eggs-traordinary* gift, or slap me around the face with it.

Nah, he wouldn't waste *'perfectly good protein'*.

"She's not here," he called to me, pausing in his routine. His brows furrowed when he saw the plate in my hands.

I obviously hadn't missed the fact that Eva was missing yet again, but I wasn't surprised. I could only hope there was a good reason for it, and Kai hadn't stopped her from training completely.

"I can see that," I said, "but I actually came to see you, anyway."

"What yeh got there?" he asked, sniffing the air.

"Can't you tell?" I teased, feigning offense. "We *eggs-panded* our breakfast offerings on account of a certain grumpy general and his unhealthy obsession with–"

A noise from behind me gave me pause, and I turned to see Axel striding into the room, waving a hand in greeting. "Oh hey, Kane. Don't mind me, I just came to see... Ooo eggs, Alaric's favorite! I'm sure the boss is clucking like a proud mother hen at your *egg-cellent* choice of protein," he beamed, reminding me why I quite liked the huge male. He was like a younger, friendlier version of Alaric.

"They aren't all they're cracked up to be," I said in response, as we both turned to grin at the angry wolf in the room.

"Aren't you two fuckin' hilarious," he deadpanned.

"Some might say we are *comedi-hens*, boss," Axel chimed in.

"Omelet you in on a secret, he can't take a yolk," I shot back, trying to hold it together, swallowing down a laugh as a smirk pulled at my lips.

"Oooo, I'm *terri-fried*!" Axel said as he tried to keep his face straight, but a glance at the furious expression on Alaric's face had us both doubling over.

"Are yeh fuckin' done, yeh eedjits?" Alaric barked.

"I think so," I said, composing myself. "For now."

"For fuck's sake, I can't remember what I was here for now," Axel said, tilting his head to the side before shaking it. "It must not have been too important, boss. I'll come back later," he laughed, scratching the back of his neck.

He glanced down at the plate before he made his way toward the door to leave. "Cool castle, bro!" he called over his shoulder, and I decided right then that we should definitely start a bromance or some shit. Anyone with the balls to call a prince a bro in a realm like this was someone you wanted at your back.

Alaric shook his head and I fought another laugh at the thought. "Go warm up, an' give me those eggs before I beat yer arse!"

"Oh, so *now* you join in!"

"What the fuck are yeh talkin' about?" he growled.

"You just said 'beat your ass' as in... You know what, forget it. I'll just warm up," I said, passing him the mountain of eggs with a wink. He grunted what could have been a thanks, or a fuck you.

"So, I saw Thalia this mornin'. She said that yer brother's ordered her to take away all of Angel's trainin' gear an' burn it," Alaric explained with a grimace between mouthfuls of the rapidly cooling breakfast, as I kicked off my shoes.

"He did what?"

"He wasnae happy with her disobeying him by decidin' to do combat trainin' instead of the hobbies he'd picked out. Thalia is away now buyin' new clothes that are befittin' a female of her station."

I sighed. "Seriously, what's going on with them?" Between my brother coming home with a bride days after his twenty-fifth birthday, and now her appearing to hate him... What was the truth?

"I'm not sure to be honest with yeh, but I dinnae think Elikai is tellin' the whole truth. The day they met, when I got back to the clearin' before we started the ride home, he asked Angel her name, an' she told him to fuck off."

He paused, finished with his meal, set the plate aside and ripped off his shirt. He then proceeded to use it to wipe the runny yolk dripping down his chin before discarding it across the floor. Before I knew it, I was off the mats and closing the distance. "You missed a bit," I said, trailing my thumb down the side of his lips to the scarred stubble of his jawline. "There."

"Kane," he growled, but it wasn't anger heating his tone.

My thumb lingered where I had wiped the excess away, caught in the moment. Alaric was grasping my wrist, sucking the remnants from the digit. Fighting the groan building in my chest, I slowly pulled away. Now was not the time for this.

"So, she told him to fuck off..." I cleared my throat, getting us back on track before things were derailed any further.

"Righ', aye. There was a lot of venom in the way she said it, though. He grabbed her an' whispered somethin'. I couldnae catch everythin' he said, but whatever it was, it mustnae have been pleasant. She quickly told him her name after tha'," he recounted for me as we made our way back to the mats.

"Do you think he offered her something? Threatened her even?" None of this made any damned sense, I ran my hands through my hair and paced the mats.

"I dinnae ken what to tell yeh, jus' tellin' yeh how I ken it. Yeh ken I never really saw eye to eye with Elikai, but I wouldnae lie to yeh about him," he grumbled, and he was right. He never lied to me and that was why I could trust him. Maybe the same couldn't be said for my brother? Did he lie to me? Or did he just pick and choose what he said around me?

"Come on, let's get some trainin' done. Maybe next time yeh see her alone, jus' ask her?" he suggested, coming to join me.

"Yeah, I think we are past keeping secrets at this point."

THOUGH TRAINING HAD BEEN relentless earlier, Alaric and I had made the mistake of practicing hand to hand. As much as I'd wanted to keep my head in it, it had kept drifting to places it really shouldn't.

I'd found myself admiring the way sweat glistened on his abs, or the way his muscles flexed, and fates help me, I'd even found my mind wondering what it would be like to suck his cock more than once.

Needless to say, Alaric hadn't been doing much better. As we'd been grappling, I'd felt his incredible length hardening against my thigh, and though neither of us mentioned it, he'd decided to call it quits not long after that. I couldn't trust myself not to get caught up in it all and do something even more stupid, and I had a feeling he was probably thinking the same, so we had both headed back to our individual rooms.

Eva hadn't been at breakfast, dinner or training today, so as I entered the library this late in the evening, I wasn't clinging to much hope that she'd be here either.

I needed to speak to her about Kai. It was driving me mad, wondering if someone who I thought I knew and had always been on my side might be keeping secrets far worse than I had thought him capable of.

"Kane?" Her angelic voice carried to me, and I spun to see her on one of the armchairs by the fire, a book open in her lap.

"Eva? Is this where you have been hiding, then?" I couldn't hold back my worry for her, but she looked no worse for wear from what I could see. Actually, in the firelight, she looked stunning. The amber glow making her look like a war goddess.

"This is the only place I can go, though only since today, yesterday…" She trailed off, her eyes looking back to the fire as she hugged herself, rubbing her arms. "Elikai's not happy. He doesn't want me to train anymore," she sighed, shifting slightly to face me, and winced.

Unable to stop myself, the words spilled from my lips. "Has he hurt you, princess?" I asked, accusation lacing my tone.

"He's set the wedding in a week's time, you know?" I wasn't a fool. Alaric had taught me more than just how to fight. His lessons covered other skills, like how to read fae. She was deflecting answering my question by asking one of her own, but her words stunned me, nonetheless. A week until the wedding.

She huffed out a sad laugh that didn't meet her eyes. "He said I can keep my innocence until then, at least, but he plans on putting a babe in my belly as soon as he can…"

"What? Why? We're immortal, so there's no rush," It just didn't make sense. None of this made sense. Did I know my brother at all? Why was he so keen for a wife and children now? He'd never told me he wanted a family.

"Well because he is desperate for the throne, of course. He believes he needs to marry and make heirs for his father to realize he's ready for him to hand it over. Elikai is practically salivating for it," she explained, the fear in her voice palpable. "And I don't think anything is going to stop him from getting what he wants."

"That's ridiculous!" I snapped. She had to be lying. "Kai knows I have no desire for that fucking throne, and even if I did, there is no way our father would ever hand it to me. Why the fuck would it matter if he was married or had any fucking heirs? Are you trying to turn me against him or something? Because the way you talk about him is nothing like the male I've spent twenty-five years knowing!"

Anger heated my blood as I paced tight circles. There was no way what she was saying was true. Why would it matter if he was crowned now or in one hundred years? The throne was going to be his.

She jumped to her feet, the book in her lap discarded across the floor as she stormed over to me, fury blazing in her eyes.

"If that's what you think, then tell me, Kane," she paused, moving to get right into my personal space. "Why the fuck did he give me these after dragging me out of that dining hall?" she growled, tugging the sleeves of her silk robe down from her shoulders to reveal faded marks on her arms that curled around her biceps like handprints.

I gawped, shuffling back a step as my mouth hung wide, and I took in the obvious abuse to her arms. Marks that I knew weren't there before the dinner only a couple of days ago. My breath caught as I realized there was only one fae who could have done it. This was why she'd avoided my question, and my stomach rolled with the truth.

"Tell me he didn't give you those bruises," I demanded, my jaw clenching before I said something I would regret. For marks to be still visible days later on an immortal was a testament to how hard someone had gripped her. How hard *he* gripped her.

"Okay, Prince Nekane," she said with no emotion. "He didn't give me these bruises," she parroted back to me before storming from the room. Her actions held more emotion than her dead words.

Time slowed down, and the next thing I knew, I was hammering on Alaric's door.

When he finally opened up, I barged my way in. "If she won't let us help her leave this damned castle, we need to find a way to keep training Eva..." I rushed out, disgust welling in my throat. "She needs to keep training. She needs to be able to defend herself."

"What are yeh... Kane, slow down. What's goin' on?" Alaric leapt from his bed, grabbing my shoulders to stop my frantic pacing.

"I'll fucking kill him. He fucking hurt her, Alaric. I saw the marks myself!" I yelled, trying to shake off his vice-like grip. "The wedding is in a week! And he plans on putting a fucking babe in her as soon as he can once the wedding is done! Probably by any means too!"

"Why?" he asked, always straight to the point. Wanting the facts, not the emotions clouding my judgments.

I took a calming breath, looking him in the eye. "She said he wants the throne, but it's already going to be his one day, anyway. I don't know what the fuck is going through his head anymore. He knows I have no plans to stand in his way, yet apparently he wants to marry Eva and have heirs as soon as possible for the king to hand it over now! Does he not know our father at all?! But that's besides the point, he is fucking immortal. What's the rush?" I pushed away from him and threw my hands to my head, massaging my temples before running my fingers into my hair, savoring the pain that came when I gripped it tight. "Fuck Alaric, I don't think she was lying... She wasn't... And right now, I want nothing more than to find him and wrap my hands around his throat. He fucking hurt *our* female."

The conflict happening inside me was a war between my head and heart. I loved my brother with everything I had. My brain couldn't fathom that these were the words and actions of my twin, but my instincts were telling me to believe her, to help her, protect her.

"She isnae ours Kane. Take a breath. Count back from ten. Remember what I've taught yeh an' calm the fuck down," he said. "Where was she? When yeh spoke with her, where was she?" The male was a strategic mastermind. I'd never been able to switch off my emotions the way he could, but I trusted he cared for her enough that his sharp mind would already have started planning how best to help her.

"The library. She said it was the only place she could go..." I said, and he was silent for a few minutes.

"I'll pass a message to Thalia for Angel. She can be trusted. We can train in the library. If Angel can convince Elikai that she'll spend her days there, then he winnae suspect a thing." He paused, and we met eyes. "We need to stop that weddin', Nekane." I nodded. My heart was still pounding at the prospect that everything I'd thought I knew. Everything I'd believed three, maybe four, weeks ago, was wrong. Fuck. Was it really only weeks?

I had a sinking feeling I didn't even know half of it yet, and when I did, things were likely going to get very bad very fast between my brother and I.

One thing *was* clear to me, in the midst of the chaos inside my brain. I remembered a time when I was just a boy. My father had locked me in my room for three days without food because I'd asked him to tell me what my mother was like. Alaric had secretly delivered meals to me personally, while Kai, oddly, hadn't even noticed I had been missing.

Of the *many* times my father would visit my room in the middle of the night to use me as his personal punching bag, and how Alaric would encourage me to get back in the training gym the moment I'd healed enough to get back on my feet. How those midnight beatings had stopped the night Alaric had left the horde's sleeping quarters and moved into the former guest suite, right next door to me.

Scenes flashed in my mind of all the times this male had been there for me, and not just because of my father's actions, either. Even so recently as dealing with the spider shifters' hearing. He wasn't even there physically and still helped me immeasurably. He was the closest thing I had to family.

"Thank you. For everything," I said earnestly. "Without your voice inside my head, I'd be useless. Without your tireless training, I'd be so royally fucked. Without you picking up the pieces and putting me back together all of those times, I'd still be broken. So thank you, Alaric, for being the other part of my soul. I'd always assumed it was Kai who kept me going when my dad beat me black and blue. But he wasn't there when I felt alone, or like the whole world was against me because of what happened to my mother. I realize that now… It was you. It was always you."

CHAPTER 29
Evangelia

I woke bleary eyed to the winter sun high in the sky, streaming in through the narrow window. I'd laid awake for half the night thinking about my most recent interaction with Kane, so I'd likely slept in later than usual.

Though I'd barely scratched the surface on the list of wrongs Elikai had done to me since I'd had the misfortune of ever meeting him, I still worried the few things I'd said to Kane in the library had been too much. I'd lost my temper last night and showed him evidence of how his brother had put his hands on me, yet he hadn't wanted to believe it, cementing the fact I had no idea if I could place *any* trust in him at all when it came to his twin.

But no matter how mad I tried to stay at him, or how much I tried to convince myself to keep my walls up around him, or Alaric, for that matter, the more they crumbled. I tried to remind myself that despite the pull I felt toward them, I barely knew them.

We were on opposing sides of a war that Alaric was front and center of, for fates knew how many centuries given his rank, and that Kane didn't even seem to realize was being waged. Despite this, it was slowly killing me not to just come clean to them about everything. Lay it all on the table and see if they would step up to take on the evil plaguing the realm with me.

I'd stupidly started to care for the males, and though they were both so different, one was no less alluring to me than the other. I didn't care for the Lores forbidding species mixing, but even I realized that a female didn't get to choose two males just because they both made her feel all sorts of sinful ways. No matter how tempting they were, or how accepting of the whole situation they'd seemed to be.

I'd given them no reason to trust me, and had been lying to them or avoiding them so that I didn't need to lie to them further for weeks. It may only be a short amount of time in the grand scheme of things, particularly for an immortal, but it felt like forever.

I rolled over in my temporary sofa bed, rubbing the sleep out of my eyes, and let out a sigh as I saw that the fates had granted me one small mercy, at least. Elikai had already left for the day. He'd mentioned that he, Sloane, and Graves were going to be unavailable for most of today. I hadn't bothered asking where they were going or why. I'd just been relieved that I would get a break from listening to his outlandish plans for a time.

As I turned to my side to face the fire and flipped over my pillow, as I did several times a night since discovering that the cool side of the pillow held a soothing magic I couldn't get enough of, a scrunched up piece of paper fell to the floor.

Sitting up to reach it, I quickly uncrumpled the note and stifled a gasp as I saw a tiny silver ring tucked up inside. *My* ring.

Before even glancing at the note's contents or even who had left it, I slipped the ring onto my finger where it belonged. With the cool metal now safely pressed against my skin again, I felt calmer than I had for the past week or so.

Smoothing out the note, I recognized Thalia's handwriting instantly.

Eve,

Elikai has granted my request that we attend your wedding dress fitting today. Westly, my uncle and Nekane's butler, will be escorting us. We must prepare the carriage for the three of us to venture from the castle together today, so please kindly meet us in the courtyard at noon,

~~Thalia~~ Lia.

P.S. I found something that belonged to you discarded at the bottom of Elikai's dirty laundry from his recent travels and thought you may want it back.

My heart warmed as I noticed that, in her own way, she had given me permission to call her by a nickname. It wasn't about the name as much as it was her way of telling me she trusted me, that we were allies, and maybe even friends. Add to that the fact she'd arranged the meeting I had been so anticipating and returned my ring, I could kiss her!

I glanced at the time and realized it was almost noon! With my excitement for my meeting with Thalia and her uncle fueling me, I darted into the bathroom, quickly washed with a flannel, re-tied my hair in a messy pony and slipped into a warm navy blue, woolen dress. I raced down to the courtyard while still shrugging on a heavily lined cape which Thalia must have picked out and matched my outfit perfectly.

The courtyard was surprisingly busy this time of day. There were townsfolk milling about with their livestock; mostly lower powered shifters, who had clearly only been invited here for the purpose of paying their land tax in person. I couldn't blame them for wanting to keep the horde from their doors.

A retinue of the horde's soldiers were shuffling between them, taking note of each town's efforts and ensuring they were paid in full before sending them on their way.

Winter was certainly starting to make itself known. The ground held evidence in its shadows that there had been a frost during the night. It wouldn't be long until the snow set in. Where the sun had cast its rays over the walls, the sad, heavily trodden, green grass was revealed. Thankfully, the gravel path was thawed already as I made my way down the steps. I didn't stop until I found my companions for the day.

The carriage was at a halt, and the horses fussed as they were made to wait for me. The driver waved me over as he stood before them, soothing their agitation. I dove into the carriage to find Thalia—*Lia*—with Westly. Even though we'd only really had one real encounter, and it had been brief, I'd seen him coming and going from Kane's wing of the castle and had even practically stalked him to Kane's room that one time, so his face was familiar by now.

"I am so sorry!" I gasped as I got myself situated. "I slept in and only just found your note." Westly just smiled at me warmly, his eyes glassy with unspoken emotion. Perhaps he had been looking forward to talking about his old friends as much as I had.

"You are such a heavy sleeper lately. I did try to wake you to help you get ready, but I needed to use the time to check the carriage," she explained in a hushed voice. It was worrying how deeply I had been sleeping these days. Back in the Vale I would be on high alert at the slightest snap of a branch or rustle of leaves. Always ready for an attack. Here I was under the same roof as my worst nightmares, yet I'd grown too comfortable. "I'm glad you found my message in time," she continued, "I was about to come find you if you hadn't appeared when you did," she explained, but her tone held mirth so at least she wasn't angry at me for making them wait.

"What do you mean, check the carriage?" I asked, puzzled. Surely that wasn't a part of her job as my handmaiden?

She dropped her voice further, to a barely audible murmur. "We had to ensure there were no listening stones. I don't know if they were something you came across in the Fading Vale, but they are highly desirable here. They are spelled to enable the owner to hear everything that happens in its vicinity. We also wanted to place wards so that we may talk freely, and two witches are better than one to ensure that they aren't broken easily."

The driver closed the carriage door, and I saw the faintest shimmer of magic as the ward was sealed around us. So subtle, that if I hadn't been looking for it, I would have missed it completely. Westly knocked on the top of the box, and I jolted as we started to move.

Peering out of the curtained window, I saw we were moving toward the gates, past the track Alaric and I had run on several occasions. I realized then that I missed the giant shifter yelling at me in the early hours of the mornings.

"We have some time before the fitting, giving us a chance to talk properly," Thalia began. "The driver is a friend of our family and has said he will take the longest route to delay the ride, no questions asked. Thankfully, Elikai didn't ask for specifics on today's trip, so we have some breathing space."

I smiled, suddenly nervous about opening up to these fae who had been strangers only a handful of weeks ago. I busied myself looking at the beautiful wood of the carriage instead. It was exposed and polished lovingly except for the cushions we sat upon. It was a lot simpler than I thought it would be for one of the royal carriages, no doubt Elikai's doing, but I was glad all the same. We didn't need any extra attention than we were already getting as we exited the gates.

Once we had pulled out of the castle grounds, Thalia advised we could speak freely now, and looked between myself and Westly to see who would go first.

Not great with awkward silences, I broke first. "So, Lia tells me you knew Edelin? That the Sybilline witches were friends of your family, the Hexenwalls?" I asked tentatively.

He smiled warmly, and his eyes glazed, as if his mind was swimming with memories of happier times. "Yes, not just friends, but the closest allies. We treated each other like family. A very long time ago, we formed a coven together. When Edelin's sister, Thaelias, died she left Edelin and her niece, Alita, the last in their line. We felt the loss as deeply as one would if they'd lost a limb. Hundreds of years later, Thalia's mother named her in her memory. Our family's own small way of remembering our bond with the Sybilline's. Thaelias had been gifted a true mate from the fates, Gale, and they had a daughter together. He was a shifter warrior in the old king's, Dyvrad's, army, and was slain in the very same ambush from the usurper's horde of purists that took the king down."

There was no denying that Westly's grief was genuine. It was evident in the way he retold the story as if it had happened just last week. I'd heard awe-inspiring stories of King Dyvrad from my parents. He'd fought hard to achieve peace with the neighboring realms and ensured we were hidden from the mortal world, too. Something that King Regis had continued, but only because he was so focused on destroying his own.

Thalia passed her uncle a tissue, and he gently patted the stray tear that trickled down his cheek before he continued. "As much as the true mate bond is a blessing, it is known that when one dies, the other is surely soon to follow. For Thaelias and Gale, it was instant. She had been scrying and got trapped in a vision, her sight taking her to that battlefield. When she eventually pulled free, she let out a shriek of pure, agonized heartbreak before collapsing to the floor and never rising again, leaving their child, Alita, an orphan. We would always ward them while they scried, but there is no ward powerful enough to protect someone from having their heart torn from their chest," his voice shook, but he managed to carry on.

"We had already discovered that the king's death was in the cards, and with it would come a change that was dark and ugly. We knew we needed to try to change the course of that particular future, but we just didn't anticipate it would be so soon. When the former king was murdered, we tried to lay low, but Edelin must have had a vision that prompted her to flee with Alita to the Fading Vale. With how her visions worked, she could see hundreds of possible outcomes, so we knew that her leaving must have been the best option she could see. Of course, when King Regis changed everything with the new Lores, we understood immediately why she'd left us. Not only did she have a hybrid to protect, but she had always feared word getting out of how strong of a seer she was and her talent would be used for ill will."

"I... I don't know anyone called Alita, but Edelin has a child of her own now, a hybrid too. Nixen is his name... Or was..." My voice wobbled as I spoke my worst fear aloud for the first time.

"What do you mean, was?" Thalia asked gently, as if she was afraid to spook me.

I took a deep breath, knowing it was now or never. "I wasn't saved from the Fading Vale by Prince Elikai... I was taken." As soon as it was out, a huge weight lifted that had been bearing down on my shoulders. A quick glance at Thalia and Westly told me they weren't at all surprised, but Thalia reached out to place a reassuring hand on my knee all the same.

"My friends were murdered for sport. I was forced to watch my parents die at the hands of my now fiancé and his disgusting cronies. Then I was made to leave with them before I could find out if there were any survivors. One of which being Nix," I confessed. "I am only alive and here because Elikai took a twisted fancy to me and wanted to make me his shiny new toy. Worse still, his wife." I breathed in another lungful of air before pushing on. "He is delusional and believes I should feel indebted to him for sparing me. He thinks it will make me more malleable, to be the attractive silent wife he wants on his arm, to give him heirs even, all so that the king will hand over the crown."

I paused to lean in closer to the witch and warlock, then dropped my voice to barely a whisper. "He is desperate for power, drooling over the thought of the crown resting on his head instead of his father's. He is so insane that I fear what he would do with the power that comes with being king. Mark my words, if you think King Regis is bad, Elikai is a whole different kind of monster. He just hides it better behind his false charm and good looks."

"We know all too well that Elikai is not the male he projects to society. Thalia has come back to our quarters in need of healing potions more times than we can count for displeasing him. He is volatile, to say the least. But why does he want to be king so badly?" Westly asked.

"Honestly? I have no idea. But he scares me more than King Regis. He told me he has big plans, bigger than Dezrothia..." I trailed off, letting them absorb my words.

Westly and Thalia thought it over before falling deep into thought. As much at a loss as I at what to do about the king and his evil son.

Finally Westly spoke. "You said your friend, Edelin's son, was at the camp with you when you were attacked... What of Edelin herself?" he asked, his fear of what I might tell him of her fate broke his voice.

"She's been missing for a year. We just woke up one morning to find her gone. No signs of foul play, just gone..."

"Her husband? Or mate? What of him?"

"He was a thrakos and killed when Nix was little more than a babe."

"And you never met Alita?"

"No."

"So Edelin left her only family at the camp? With no explanation at all?" I nodded my confirmation, and he continued. "She must have known something, seen something. If she'd loved her son, even half as fiercely as she loved her sister and niece, there is no way she would have left him alone..." Westly pressed.

"She adored him. Nix was... *is* an incredible male. Smart, respectful, strong, funny, caring. She was like an aunt to me, and I have no doubt Nix was her entire reason for living. He is adamant she is alive. Like you, he believes she left for some greater reason. But what?"

We all contemplated the question in silence as my worry for Nix and his mother's fates resurfaced and suffocated me. I looked out of the window, willing air into my lungs as I caught sight of the dressmaker's shop coming into view.

It was Thalia's voice that broke the silence this time. "What can we do to help?"

Her words brought a sad smile to my lips. Joy at knowing I had allies here, but sorrow that I had no idea where to even begin making a plan that had any hope of success.

And if I was going to bring other lives in on my revenge against the crown, it needed to be a solid plan.

CHAPTER 30
Nekane

I was heading for the library to find Eva to clear the air and ask if Thalia had passed on Alaric's message about training in the library, when a messenger brought me the shit news that my father and abuser had returned to the castle.

Unsurprisingly, there was to be a feast in celebration. My father was never one to miss an opportunity to flaunt the wealth of the crown, and even though Kai had already been back from the hunt for a few days now and told anyone who would listen every minute detail, apparently a victory party was still needed.

I groaned at the thought of it and turned back toward my chambers. With my previously positive mood plummeting, it definitely was not the best time to have the conversation I'd been planning with Eva.

Why the king insisted on me being present at these functions was beyond me. I'd tried skipping them all together a long time ago, but that had only resulted in making the beatings worse. Damned if I did, damned if I didn't.

I relaxed on my bed with a book for a while before I realized it was probably time to scrub up. The better I presented, the less likely my sire was to notice me. I'd lost track of time and was probably going to end up late. I was too used to relying on Westly turning up to draw me a bath and lay out my clothes whenever there were places I needed to be. Only I hadn't seen him all day, which was strange, but I knew he'd been busy with the extra work I'd inadvertently put on him after my ruling at the sentencing a few days ago, so I could only assume he was tied up with that.

As I washed, my mind unsurprisingly wandered to Eva. Was she going to be there tonight? I hadn't seen her since our encounter in the library, and I regretted the way we'd left things. Especially the way I'd reacted to her bruises.

Part of me wished she would be, but at the same time, I didn't want her there at all. She aroused confusing emotions in me. I didn't trust her, not fully, how could I? I barely even knew her. But fuck, I wanted to. I wanted to know everything about her, inside and out.

My cock twitched at the thought and the memory of her perfect body laid bare to us that day. Had it really only been a handful of days ago? It felt like a lifetime.

I craved her even when I thought I hated her. The last thing she needed was another male fantasizing about her, but it didn't stop the memories that assaulted me. Like the sounds she'd made with Alaric and I. *Fuck*. My cock hardened despite my best efforts to dispel the erotic thoughts playing in my head on a constant loop.

Needing to take the edge off before tonight's event, I gripped my length and gently started teasing myself, imagining what it would be like to get her under me as I had a thousand times before in the short weeks since first seeing her.

I imagined the sounds of pleasure she'd make as I drove my cock into her. Would she trail her nails over me gently or dig them in? Would she be the type to take the pleasure she wanted and leave me desperate for more? Just the thought had me panting already.

This female... No, this entire fucked up situation was going to be the end of me. I couldn't get my cock hard unless I was thinking of *them*. I'd even officially revoked Crystal's invitation to the castle so the guards would no longer let her come calling at my door.

Despite the presence of everyone else in that room above the Crooked Claw, it was the look on Alaric's face when he came that I'd always been drawn to. I could admit that now, but *fuck*, when those memories flashed through my mind nowadays, it was Eva who Alaric was wringing cries of pleasure from.

I remembered the feel of his cock under mine and Eva's joined hands, the way I was pressed to her back. The moans Alaric was making as Eva had sucked him down her throat so perfectly... The memories were too much as the hand stroking my cock sped up.

Images of Eva's mouth stretched around Alaric's length, his face as he came, her swallowing every last drop–

I came hard, my breaths coming in short, sharp gasps as I rode it out, gradually slowing my strokes. Hopefully, that would be enough to sate the stray thoughts, but who was I kidding? I never felt fully sated these days.

Still breathless, I cleaned up, dressed, and hurried down to the feast. Maybe Eva wouldn't be there after all, and I wouldn't be forced to smell that sweet vanilla and campfire scent that trailed wherever she went, but Alaric definitely would be.

Tonight I planned on getting drunk. I would keep to myself, avoid everyone, and hope the night went by quickly. I was mostly worried I couldn't stomach seeing my brother after what Eva had told me, not without confronting him. After seeing the marks he'd left on her otherwise flawless skin, I didn't know if I had the self-control it would take not to challenge him for her there and then. For her safety, as much as my own sanity.

I knew this wasn't the place to do it. But I *would* talk to him. And soon. I had to. I needed the truth, and it had to come from his own lips.

I surveyed the room, my lip curling as I was met with the grotesque sight waiting on the long tables laid out for the meal. A huge tentacle stretched the length of each table, including the head table where I would have to sit. Its purplish skin charred and the poisonous spikes and suckers had been removed. Amid the lavishly decorated grand dining hall, the severed limbs stood out like a scene from a nightmare. As I looked closer, I saw that my father's sick trophies were decorated with a circle of roasted potatoes and the vibrant pop of bright vegetables in every shape and size. Spoils of war were what they would call it. Barbaric was what it truly was.

Downing the whisky in my hand, I signaled for the wait staff to refill my glass. As long as they kept it coming, I could hold it together.

"King Regis, Sovereign of Dezrothia, Eliminator of the Krakens," the herald's voice rang out from the huge double doors. Cringing, I looked at my father as he entered the hall, his dark hair gleaming under the light of the chandelier. His waist now rotund from sitting on his ass the majority of the time instead of leading from the front lines.

He was ornately dressed, as one would expect from the king. We caught eyes briefly, and he scowled before looking away and smoothing his features back to something more pleasant, as the applauding fae in the room stood and celebrated him.

I didn't get it. Why did they cheer for him? What had he done that was so great? He was an asshole, but apparently I was the only one who could see it. Even Alaric seemed to have a good relationship with him, something I'd never understood, given how much he knew.

I moved to sit at the king's table in my usual spot as Eva entered. I froze as I took her in and stifled a growl when I saw how my brother's arm was wrapped around her waist, holding her flush to his hip. She was stunning, even with the expression of pure horror painted across her face as she approached, staring at the table centerpieces. She wore a long-sleeved blush colored gown. Her hair pinned up to reveal her nape that I so desperately wanted to trail kisses down. She looked every part the princess. Right down to the delicate tiara nestled in her hair and the two elegant rings on her fingers.

As we took our seats, Kai whispered something in her ear. A week ago, I would have been jealous. I would have assumed it was sweet nothings, but now, I wasn't so sure, and my heart hurt with the loss of the bond between us as twins.

"Brother, nice to see you away from your usual duties of propping up the bar. I sincerely hope you didn't drink them dry again?" Kai admonished me like I was a naughty child, and I clenched my fists. This was going to be a long night.

"Kai, Eva..." I said with a nod at them both in turn.

I didn't have the energy to pretend to play happy fucking family. How could I pretend I didn't know Eva had marks on her arms. Arms that were coincidentally covered up tonight. Had he hurt her again?

Our father stood, leaning on the table with his fists and staring down at everyone in attendance. "Tonight, we celebrate the extinction of a pest that has long plagued our seas!" he bellowed, slapping the table hard as spit escaped his mouth with every other word. Fates help us all, he was going to do a speech, and I wasn't wearing waterproof clothes or earplugs.

He rose to his full height. "The last kraken has been slain!" He gestured to the sickening display adorning our table. "Like the hydra, they no longer pose a threat to us and our society. Kelpie Cove is once more at peace, and our lands and portals remain secure from invaders, mortal or otherwise. Let us celebrate tonight that one more enemy to the crown is no more!"

Chants erupted around the room. "Long live the king!" They were truly happy we had driven yet another species to extinction.

I chanced a glance at Kai and his face was turning deep red, eyes narrowed on the king, as his knuckles turned white around his cutlery. He looked ready to murder, and I cast my mind back to Eva's words about his intentions for the crown.

"Father–" Kai started, but he waved him off for all to see.

"Not now, child. I will deal with your little stunt another time," he said dismissively, and I watched as my brother's jaw hung open, stunned speechless.

As the evening droned on, the allure of alcohol wasn't as strong as it had been at the beginning of the night. I found I wanted to stay alert, so I focused on eavesdropping on conversations around the table instead.

They all had the same theme, excitement that the purist views of the king were being executed. Kai's voice broke through to me, and what he was spouting was nothing short of repulsive.

"Well, soon we won't need to worry about those filthy half breeds. I have a plan, you see. One that ensures their total annihilation. They are abominations that shouldn't exist, and I can't wait until we rid ourselves of them. Then there is the thrakos, my father's own magically made mistakes, to deal with. There cannot be many of them or their disgusting progeny left..." He held the attention of everyone in earshot. So many were enraptured with his nonchalance as he spoke about murdering other races.

I tuned into my father again. He was having an almost identical conversation, but it was clear that Elikai had drawn the attention of more folk to listen to his drivel than the king himself.

"They asked for this fate. If the krakens had the sense to listen to me when I offered them a deal one hundred and fifty years ago, like the selkies and kelpies did, I would have let them live. The smarter ones knew which side would win and grabbed it. They were the ones who have hunted the krakens for me all these years. Krakens were much sneakier than those hydras, though. Stupid creatures mounted a full scale attack, and we were able to completely wipe them out in one fell swoop," he boasted.

It wasn't as if they could have ran for safety or had any chance of making it out of that attack alive. The sea creatures of this realm were tied to Dezrothian Waters. To stray too far was to remove their magic, and to remove their magic meant certain death. It was only now that I realized just how wrong it was to bind their magic to the waters, unlike the other denizens of Kelpie Cove.

I turned back to listen to Kai again. "If I were king, I'd be planning to increase the horde's presence in the Fading Vale to eradicate them swiftly, at long last. Their creation was a fool's mistake in the first place, but they have been allowed to breathe Dezrothian air for far too long. They can't escape to other realms, with the portals warded and lying obsolete, so they would be trapped." He was as bad as the king. Like

Father, like son? *What does that say about me?* Eva's hands were curled around her napkin, knuckles bone white and jaw set as she ground her teeth.

I felt the urgent and overwhelming need to reach out to her, get her attention, calm whatever war was waging in her head, distract her with a game of footsie under the table. Do something. Anything–

"And what did these species ever do to you?" Her sharp tongue cut through the chatter before I'd managed to act, and the crowd was immediately silent. *Fuck.*

Cords of muscle were instantly visible in Kai's neck as his jaw clenched and eyes blazed. He looked murderous, but it was the king's attention that had my stomach knotted.

"Did you become sympathetic to the creatures while you were held captive, girl?" he sneered. "They shouldn't exist, their entire existence is unnatural," he went on, unsurprisingly, leaving out the part where it was he who had fucked up by creating them in the first place. I'd never seen a thrakos, but from what I'd heard they were savage beings. Intimidating without even trying.

My father's voice was calm, but I knew that was when he was the most dangerous. His full attention was on Eva as his gaze fell to her chest, lingering long enough for me to want to gouge out his eyes, and dropped to her hands where she continued gripping the napkin.

"Interesting jewelry you wear, girl. Elikai, haven't I taught you not to buy such cheap–"

"*I* didn't buy that," Kai rushed out, grabbing her left hand and trying to pry them from her fingers with force as she fought to pull out of his hold.

"They're a family heirloom," Eva squeaked out, the scrutiny of the jewelry bringing everyone's attention even more firmly to her. "They have been in my family for generations, they are the last reminder I have of my family, Your Majesty…"

I glanced at Alaric. It wasn't the first time we had heard such a line from her. He whipped his head around to eye the rings in question, and his own hand shot to the necklace he always wore, his eyebrows furrowed.

Regardless of my ever growing list of reasons to be suspicious of her, I couldn't let her keep vomiting words to cover up whatever secrets she was so desperately trying to hide from my father. He was an asshole, but he wasn't a complete idiot. He would notice.

"It's my only reminder–"

"What happened to the ring you got for our dearest mother?" I cut over her on a slur, feigning being more affected by the alcohol than I actually was. "Maybe she should have that ring, seeing as she will be queen herself, one day." To emphasize the thought, I drained the glass of wine on the table.

I knew my words were stupid and would be like a red rag to a bull, but that was the point. "Come with me," was all my father said, pushing to stand. Ice ran in my veins even though I'd known what would happen when I'd stupidly jumped in to take the attention from Eva. I was no fucking hero, but it's like I couldn't help making seriously bad decisions wherever she was concerned.

He was already up and out of his seat, no doubt walking to his favorite private chamber across the hallway and a few doors down from here.

Without a word, I moved to follow, knowing what was to come would only be worse if I delayed it. I refused to look back at Eva as I left. I'd not told her about this, and suspected Elikai wouldn't have either. It was better that she assumed my father just wanted to catch up, or possibly take me with him to get the ring I had mentioned.

As soon as I entered the chamber, something was thrown, and I ducked as it narrowly missed my head by millimeters, smashing against the wall. The bastard didn't normally need a reason to flip on me, he just did it to sate some twisted need he had, but this time I had basically asked for it.

"You think I wouldn't hear?" he growled at me from across the room as we began to circle each other. "You think I wouldn't find out you undermined my fucking authority?"

What the fuck was he talking about? My confusion must have been plain as day on my face as he threw something else at me. I dodged and saw it was a chair this time. *Thanks Dad.*

"You had one job while I was gone. One easy fucking job that fell to you to deal with. All you had to do was sentence that cretin mayor to death. What did you do instead? You fucking helped it!?" he seethed, kicking over more furniture and pacing closer and closer to me. Closing the gap.

Well, fuck. I had said to send him to me if he didn't like it. "I just thought–" I ducked again as a bronze bust came sailing at my head.

"You don't get to think!" he roared as he jolted forward and grabbed me by the scruff of my neck. "You are good for nothing. A total fucking waste of space! Why don't you just die already?!"

Usually, I'd take his words to heart, and this would be around the time that the flashbacks of being a defenseless child at his mercy would overwhelm me. Only this time, the cold hatred I harbored for him was welling up from deep inside, fueling me, feeding my power instead of crippling it.

I was done with him. "Because you made me this way, because I'm the fucking cockroach that won't qu–" I was cut off with a backhand to the jaw. The sharp sting of his gaudy ring caught me across the cheek before a ping of metal hit the hard stone floor.

A laugh bubbled from my chest. *This is what the great King Regis could do?* Maybe it was my still new immortality dulling his blows, or maybe now I just wasn't letting the memories cripple me anymore. I was finally clear headed enough to fight back. I would show him exactly how fucking powerful of a high fae I'd grown to be. I blocked a fist aimed at my jaw, sick of him taking his pound of flesh, and his eyes widened in surprise.

He was relentless in his pursuit. The problem with fighting someone who was this angry was that their movements were unpredictable. There was no pattern. Making it more difficult to remain two steps ahead because they hadn't been thought of yet. Still, he was nothing compared to fighting Alaric. Now *he* was a savage bastard when he wanted to be.

We both managed to land some hard blows, but he was definitely tiring quicker than I was. The countless hours spent in the training hall put me at an advantage. He pulled back slightly, and we began circling again.

"Imagine the shame to hear your own flesh and blood helped a pathetic failure because he didn't have the balls to just kill it. You are just as bad as that stupid little sympathizer bitch out there your brother has hanging off him! Luckily, I know your brother isn't as pitiful as you and will do what needs to be done to put her right!"

Whatever was holding me back snapped. He didn't get to call Eva a bitch. She was everything. She was the sun. She was a queen. She was *mine*.

He swung his arm wide and threw all of his power into his next punch. But instead of ducking out of the way, I caught it dead in the air with my palm. Fury scorched my veins as my grip grew tighter and tighter around my father's hand as I ground my jaw.

"What did you just call her?" I dared him, dropping my voice to a growl. My grip crushed every bone in his hand as something like a pin pierced one of my fingers. I ignored the sharp pain and dug a little deeper instead, drawing more power into my hold on him.

He didn't answer, but his eyes bugged. It was the first time I hadn't been too damaged or too drunk to fight him back. It was the first time he'd ever seen me as the threat I was.

He lifted a leg in a kick, but I blocked it, landing a blow in his sternum with my free fist instead. Panicking, he tried to grab my throat with his free hand, but I grabbed him at the wrist and began to squeeze, pushing him backwards toward the stone wall while keeping hold of the punishing grip I had.

I didn't recognize him as I saw true fear shining back at me in his eyes as they filled with... were those tears? Interesting. I was still enraged and yet felt entirely disconnected as I watched this male break. He had held such power before. Yet now, he was reacting to the pain I was inflicting on him.

"Insolent brat," he spat, clearly not fully ready to submit. Yet.

"This insolent brat is about to crush every bone in your fucking hands to dust. When I let go, I can promise you will never be able to lay these pathetic hands on another innocent again. Do you understand me?"

The last word came out as more of a slur, and he paused for a second before throwing his head back and laughing in my face. "I was wondering when it would reach your bloodstream. You might want to let go of my fist before you overdose... or don't," he said with a sickening tooth-filled smile, and nothing but confidence.

"Wh-at..." I tried, but my tongue wasn't working right. My grip began to loosen involuntarily. My arms started to feel weak. My legs felt like they were going numb beneath my own weight.

Something was wrong. Very fucking wrong.

"For a second there I thought you'd actually managed to fight its effects," he sneered, his disgust at my show of strength evident. "You see this," he tilted his head to the ring on his middle finger, part covered by my own hand which I only now noticed was tingling. "A lesser being would have been paralyzed in seconds. If it wasn't for my powerful blood running in your veins, you would have succumbed far quicker."

Panic was wrapping itself around my heart as I started piecing his words together and took in the details of the ring in question. It was damaged now, the cap I never knew could be opened was missing and revealed a small, thin and very fucking sharp polished piece of metal. A mixture of a needle and a thorn that had been lodged in my skin for who knew how long.

He shook free from my now feeble grip easily and landed a hard blow to my stomach which had me doubling over before my legs completely gave out. I fell on the floor in a heap, taking the impact with my face as I lay there, rapidly losing the ability to move entirely. My father barked a laugh.

He rolled me onto my back with his foot as he towered over me, looking down at my defenseless form. I was completely trapped in my own body as whatever poison that spike had been laced with flooded its way through my system.

"Now that I have your full attention, I shall tell you the story of how this ring came to be," he said smugly, before stamping down so hard on my ribcage that I heard multiple cracks.

Though I couldn't move a single muscle now, the poison hadn't made me numb to pain. I felt every inch of the agony without being able to make my mouth work enough to even release a groan at the anguish from my severely broken ribs, desperately fighting the poison to heal.

"It was long before your time that I eradicated the hydra, as you should know. Those grotesque snakes were vermin to our waters and had no right to be as powerful as they were. But I am not a wasteful king, and the blood of a hydra is one of the most venomous toxins in the realm. Just before my reign began, I met a powerful warlock who had an obsession with experimenting on powerful creatures. He and I worked together on many wonderfully terrible things. Until he messed up." He let out an exaggerated sigh. "It was a shame he got it so wrong with the thrakos and I was left with no choice but to kill him, silencing the only other being in existence who held the secret to how they were made. I couldn't have those foul beasts learning there had been a way to fix their little bloodlust issue now could I? How else could I ensure the kingdom turned against the filthy beasts than through complete fear of them. Anyway, this ring I wear, as you recently discovered, is one of my ingenious secret weapons. Well, it was before your face broke it!" he hissed, like it was my fault he'd backhanded me so hard the cap had snapped. In his anger, he landed another savage kick to my gut before continuing with his disturbing story.

"It only takes the smallest drop. Too much and hydra blood goes from temporarily paralyzing to fatal. We had many failed attempts before we discovered the perfect dosage, and the warlock set to work on magically creating the blade which just sunk into your finger," he tsked, reaching for me and pulling me to my still useless feet, holding my dead weight off the ground. "Watching you battle the effect of the hydra's blood might be the closest I've ever come to being impressed by you," he admitted with a fist in my shirt, and our gazes locked. It was the nicest thing he'd ever said to me.

"So disappointing you should finally show some semblance of my bloodline and waste it on fighting poison instead of fighting the worthless creatures infecting my lands," he sneered before slamming me against the wall and pummeling his rapidly healing fist into my gut over and over.

My breathing was becoming difficult as he attacked me with blow after blow. The pain was getting overwhelming, and I could taste blood bubbling up in the back of my throat.

If he didn't stop soon, I was either going to pass out or drown in my own blood. He'd said the paralysis was temporary, and I clung on to the hope, as my body took the worst beating of my life, that soon I'd be able to move enough to defend myself.

The problem was, he'd also made it clear that the length of time in which the needle had pierced my skin had far surpassed the dose that they had tested. What if I never regained the use of my limbs? What if my immortality couldn't heal me before I succumbed? I'd never get the chance to patch things up with Eva, and that regret seared through my chest. But at least I'd already had the chance to thank Alaric for his role in my life.

After what felt like an age, the evil monster who had sired me dropped me in a heap on the floor, apparently tired of pulverizing my lifeless form. He bent to pick something up from beside me and spat in my direction before he left the room without another word.

Breathing was too painful and the gurgling in my throat didn't sound too good either. He had definitely broken several ribs and probably damaged who knew how many organs. My head pounded sharp and heavy as I closed my eyes to fight off the growing nausea. I was overcome with exhaustion as my body tried to simultaneously heal me and fight the poison.

After fates knew how long, I managed to regain some feeling. It started with my toes and worked slowly throughout my body as my healing abilities began to remove the poison.

It was an agonizing process, but as the paralysis freed me from its cruel grasp, I sighed in relief and managed to drag myself over to the wall to sit up. Not wanting anyone to come in here and find me face down on the cold floor.

I rested my head against the wall, my arm clutching my ribs as I tried to steady my breathing. The gurgling finally stopped, and I did my best to ignore the pain.

As I sat there, I could feel the painful bruises lose some of their bite as they began to heal. Hopefully, they would fade and the headache would become less blinding.

The door opened and I prayed to the fates that it wasn't my father coming back for more. I just needed a little bit more time to sit here alone. Maybe a nap, or at least a rest to combat the exhaustion.

I looked up to see Alaric rushing toward me, as much as I didn't want him to see me like this, it was the figure behind him that had my stomach twisting.

Eva was hurrying in behind him, closing the door and rushing to my side, worry etched on her features.

This was going to be a fun conversation.

CHAPTER 31

Evangelia

After what felt like hours, the king finally reentered the dining hall. His bloodied knuckles were visible as he was swiftly handed a napkin to wipe the sweat from his brow before proceeding to clean the evidence of whatever he'd just done with Kane from his fists, which looked almost disfigured. *Shit.* Had they always looked like that?

From the moment they had left the room, the king leading as Kane had trailed behind him looking pale, but still holding his head high, I had been driving myself insane trying to work out what the fuck was going on.

Now, after seeing the king, all of my darker theories behind them having left became the most likely reality, and I needed to get out of this room and find him.

Kane had only stepped in and said what he had to his father to distract him from questioning me, to protect me. There was no doubt in my mind that was his intention. But why would he do that? I had given him no reason to trust me, let alone protect me.

I'd been an idiot. I should have kept my cool and not said anything while they were laughing and joking about their disgusting treatment of the thrakos and hybrids.

I just couldn't bite my tongue any longer. The atrocities decorating the tables had thrown me completely. As I'd heard the conversations around me, distant memories of my parents and friends had flooded my brain, as vivid flashbacks to the last day I had been in the Fading Vale came rushing to the forefront.

The smell of blood and screams of fear consumed my senses until I was ready to burst. Before I could stop myself, the words had left my lips, but all I had achieved was drawing the king's attention, which happened to be the absolute last thing I needed.

There had been no point in saying anything. What had I hoped to achieve? To change the minds of the high fae around the table? Explain that maybe they shouldn't be so quick to judge? The only thing the gathered crowd seemed capable of or interested in doing was judging others. Whether it be looking down at them because they assumed they were somehow better, or bitching about the 'garish' dress someone else was wearing. They were constantly judging.

I looked down to Alaric's end of the table, hoping to make eye contact, but he wasn't there. I looked around the room subtly, hoping he'd already left to find Kane.

Was he ok? Was he even alive? He may be immortal, but they had been gone for a long time and there was only so much even a high fae's body could take. I needed to see him. It wasn't a choice. It was an instinct driving me toward him. To care for him. Take away his pain, mentally and physically.

My eyes stopped dead as they found Alaric. He was near the doorway, as if he had tried to leave, but that shifter bitch, Krista, had his arm. From where I sat, I could see her face clearly. Her eyes were hooded as she made a show of biting her bottom lip suggestively before she raised on her tiptoes, pulled him toward her and whispered something in his ear.

I slammed my palm down on the table as anger consumed me, drawing a few eyes, but it didn't matter. The fucking jezebel was trying to stake a claim. Again. On *my* male.

I was blindsided by where that thought had come from. All I knew was that it was strong and drove a growl from my chest of its own accord. I had to battle with the impulse to rip her away from him and stake a claim of my own.

I'd felt possessive like this before toward Kane, but had assumed it was my beast. Now that I had the ring back, she lay dormant, so that meant this was all me. I'd have to think on that another time though. Right now, Alaric had his hands full, and I had another male who might be in much more urgent need of my attention.

I looked at the fae in my immediate vicinity. Thank the fates, Elikai was sitting with his father again, so he hadn't heard the rumble that came from my throat. He was, no doubt, giving the king his full attention if it meant he could continue with his game of trying to convince him to hand over the crown at the earliest opportunity.

It was now or never. I had to know he was alright, had to see him with my own eyes and hear from his mouth that his own father had taken him somewhere and beaten him.

I stood to excuse myself, and with Elikai's attention elsewhere, everyone around me would assume I was going to powder my nose or some shit. I schooled my expression, trying to hide the frown that had been heavy on my brow since Kane had disappeared.

Outwardly, I appeared like any other fae going to the restroom, but inside, dread churned in my stomach as I neared the door. What condition would he be in? Perhaps he had already healed himself and just didn't want to return to the dinner. I couldn't blame him for not wanting to celebrate his father's return if this was his treatment.

Ignoring Alaric and Krista, I made it out of the room and let out the breath I had been holding. Elikai hadn't noticed, or if he had, he hadn't said anything.

My hands began to shake as I started checking doors along the hallway before a large hand grabbed my wrist firmly and another wrapped itself around my mouth. I swallowed my scream as I smelled leather and cedarwood coming from my assailant. He turned me to face him, his hand now gripping my shoulder as the other raised to his lips and gestured for me to be quiet.

Alaric locked eyes with me, making sure he had my undivided attention, then nodded toward a door across the corridor and started pulling me along behind him. I let out a shaky breath, realizing the minutes were ticking on. How long had it been since the king returned to the hall already? What would we see beyond that door?

He wasted no time opening it, confident that this was where Kane would be. Had it happened before then? I quickly entered behind Alaric's hulking form, closing the door silently behind me.

My gaze followed the trail of blood drops leading to the back wall, where I finally saw him.

He was in a bad way. One arm was being used to prop himself up, while the other hugged his chest. His pained breaths came in sharp, ragged bursts as he looked up, seeing Alaric first before noticing my presence.

We locked eyes for a second. The pain swimming in them nearly knocked me off my feet, but I needed to be strong for him, so I rushed over.

"Eva... leave," he croaked.

"Kane, are you okay? What happened? Did he do this to you? How badly are you hurt?" The questions just kept spilling out as I dropped to his side. I tried desperately to calm my emotions from the panic at seeing someone, *him*, in such a state.

I tried to take in all of his injuries to determine what needed more urgent attention, but there were so many of them I couldn't just pick one to focus on. Had his body already started the healing process, the blood and bruising making it look worse than his condition currently was, or was there something else going on inside that could be fatal to even an immortal?

"I'll be healed up and good as new in no time. Now please, leave," he pleaded through gritted teeth. Clearly, talking was a struggle. He shifted his upper body and winced. I shifted closer, ready to help him.

"Why are yeh healin' so slowly?" Alaric asked Kane as he crouched down next to him, checking him over with concern in his expression.

"Poison..." Kane croaked.

"What kind?" Alaric asked, as if he wasn't at all surprised that the king would do such a thing. Or perhaps he wanted the information so he knew how to best help.

"Blood of the hydra," Kane confirmed, but Alaric shook his head in denial.

"Not possible."

"Very possible. I'll explain later. Right now, I just need to sleep. You should both just go–"

"Angel, heal him," Alaric ordered, cutting Kane off from finishing his sentence. Like we would leave him, anyway.

I scoffed. "How do you expect me to do that?" I shot back, realizing my mistake the moment the words had finished leaving my lips. I froze in the darkened room, but I didn't miss Alaric's narrowed eyes. Kane hadn't seemed to notice, not that I could blame him. *He must be exhausted.* Healing these injuries as well as fighting the effects of poison, he shouldn't even be conscious right now. A sign of how powerful this male was. He just didn't seem to feel the need to show his power to the realm and have them worship him for it like his twin did.

"The same way I expect every fuckin' high fae to heal someone, with their natural gift."

"I, uh, I can't. I mean, well, I can but, you know, not right now, because..." *Shit shit shit. Words Eva!* "The king would be angry if I healed him, and he saw me leaving the dining hall so he would know it was me or at least suspect and–"

"She's right," Kane cut in, saving me from digging myself an even deeper hole. "Even if he hadn't seen her leave, it wouldn't be worth the risk." He was already sounding better than he had been just a few short minutes ago, and I relaxed a little, knowing this wasn't fatal.

"What were you thinking? Talking to your father like that? It doesn't take a genius to know he is a violent male who doesn't take kindly to being backed into a corner or challenged! Just how drunk are you?" My temper flaring, anger taking the place of my anxiety.

"Will you leave me alone if I say I was totally wasted and didn't know what I was saying?" He tried to smirk, slamming up his walls and hiding behind humor as I'd realized he did often. Though the wince that tugged at his face showed just how much pain he was still in.

"No, but–"

"Eva, you can't be here. Just go. Please," he begged.

"Just tell me one thing... Did you do that for me? To stop your father's questions?" I asked, fiddling with the solid band of the two rings, eager for his answer, but nervous at the same time. I didn't even know what it would mean if my suspicions were true, but I didn't want to lie to him anymore. I needed to know he cared for me in the same way I cared for him. Seeing him so broken made it clear as a summer's day that I wasn't indifferent to this male. Even though he shared a face with my tormentor, to me, they looked nothing alike. They were nothing alike in any way. Polar opposites. Where Elikai was cruel, Kane was merciful. Where Elikai was egomaniacal, Kane was an altruist. I knew that now as surely as I knew I was no high fae.

"It wouldn't have taken a genius to work out you were hiding something when he brought up your choice in jewelry," he said simply, avoiding my question and grimacing slightly as he reached for my hand to take a closer look. "But honestly, I am done trying to figure out what your motives are for being here. You have secrets you have no intention of sharing with me, or Alaric. We will help you leave this castle at the first chance we get, if you ever want to. We are already working on how to save you from this marriage, but honestly, I'm done trying to figure you out, princess..." He had given up on me, and a glance at Alaric told me he was feeling much the same as Kane.

My throat closed up as tears filled my eyes. If only things had been different...

Despite his words, he remained holding onto my hand, absently stroking it with his thumb. He shared a confusing look with Alaric, who offered him a small smile. One of his reassuring ones that shouldn't be as rare as they were, because they made you feel like, regardless of what was going on in the realm around you, he had your back, and it would all be okay.

"Eva, go. I couldn't live with myself if something happened to you because you were caught in here." He looked at me with a desperation I could feel deep in my soul.

He doesn't want you here. I looked to Alaric for help, but he just shook his head and nodded toward the door.

"Go on, Angel, yeh'll be missed more than either of us."

I gently pulled my hand out of Kane's grasp and crossed the room to the door, where I listened against the wood until I was sure no one else was there before reaching for the handle.

I looked back at the two males. I could only imagine how much pain Kane was in. Not just physically, but the mental anguish that he must feel. For the only parent he had to poison and then beat him to the point of severe injury, leaving marks that even immortals would take time to heal from... it made my heart hurt. I knew he wanted to think the best of his awful twin brother, and it had been obvious from our heated conversation in the library, he didn't want to believe what I was telling him about his brother's plans, or about where the marks he'd seen on my arms with his own eyes had come from.

But where was his brother now? I thought back to things Elikai had said about the King's treatment of Kane. How he'd said Kane wasn't on the Kraken hunt for their father to take out his anger on... The evidence that this was a regular occurrence was undeniable.

"Look after him..." I said to Alaric.

"Always, Angel."

I opened the door a crack, but remained looking back at them. "If things had been different... If I had any choice... I would tell you everything," I admitted. "I'd put everything out there on the table and you could decide for yourselves whether I was worthy of your help and your time. And if by some miracle you didn't hate me, and the Lores were different, and this–" I turned fully to gesture between the three of us, "–weren't impossible, and you wanted it, wanted me... Well, I just wanted you to know that I would choose you. Both of you."

Before they could reply, I dashed out the door. My heart thundered against my ribs, trying to push away the hope that either of them felt the same way.

CHAPTER 32

Elikai

"He could have chosen somewhere less steep and wet and slippery to meet, and not in the frost of winter… but nooo, he chose a gloomy cave halfway down a mountain. It's bloody treacherous out here. These shoes are brand new, and I've already scuffed them twice. My father won't be happy!" Sloane moaned to Graves as I waited, just out of sight.

I'd watched in a mixture of amusement and frustration as the fools had painstakingly clambered down the rough terrain of the rocky mountain on which the castle was built.

I had met them yesterday in the courtyard between wedding preparations to point out the cave entrance in the distance, telling them to meet me here before first light and not to let anyone see them under any circumstances.

I had been clear that it was of utmost importance that nobody knew about this place and came looking. I had something to show them, or someone should I say. A secret weapon. *My* secret weapon. And I absolutely was not going to share it with my father.

I stepped out of the shadows, making Graves nearly keel over in fright, jumping backwards and stepping on Sloane's foot–

"My shoes!" he cried to Graves before pushing him off.

I tsked. "You will forget all about your ugly, new shoes when you see why I have brought you here," I cut in before Graves could shove Sloane back and they ended up fighting like prepubescent boys. "I have a job for you, one that will include you both making that trek multiple times a day for the foreseeable future, so you better stop whining before I change my mind about bestowing you this honor."

"No problem, Kai!" Sloane rushed out.

"Yeah, it was so easy to get here, Kai. I can't wait to do it more often," Graves added.

I rolled my eyes and waved for them to follow me. The sun was just starting to rise, casting light into the cave entrance where we now stood, but it would be useless against the pitch darkness we would meet just around the corner.

"Did you bring the torches like I told you?"

"Yes, here." Graves said as he took the torches out of his bag and handed them to each of us. Sloane used his initiative, for once, and reached into his pocket, taking out some matches and lighting them up.

I turned, and they followed as we entered the catacombs deep beneath the castle. I'd memorized every entrance in and out of this place since I'd stumbled across its blueprints.

Back when I was a boy and hadn't realized yet how repulsive Nekane's lack of ambition was, we had spent a lot of time together. At some point, we had decided to clear out the former castle library as our father had no interest in books, and we moved it up to the floor we shared.

I'd quickly grown bored with carting books up the staircase like some mule. My interest, however, had been reinvigorated after I uncovered the blueprints to the castle along with detailed maps no one seemed to know existed, leading to the discovery of many hidden nooks.

The catacombs were tricky in their design and sheer scale. If you took a wrong turn, even with my outstanding tracking and navigating abilities, you could be lost forever to their depths.

With that in mind, I had left my new weapon just a few passages in. First left, follow it straight until you reach the rat skeleton, then second right and through the opening into a cavern.

I'd already hired a peasant to add some basics to the place, a bed, chair and table, then swiftly rung his neck and had him thrown off the side of the mountain. I'd even brought some things of my own with the idea that it would better aid the weapon's ability to trust me, and therefore, its usefulness to me.

The problem with a weapon of this nature was you had to feed it, and well, I had grown tired of being the only one able to bring food and water here multiple times a day. So I'd decided it was time to delegate, enabling me to visit less often so I could use my precious time on other matters, like becoming king and impregnating my pretty pet.

I stopped just short of our destination, needing to be very clear about what would happen should this secret get out.

I locked them both in my most kingly and intimidating stare until Sloane let out a squeak. "What I am about to show you doesn't go any further than this cave. If you so much as breathe a word about it outside these catacombs, or if a single soul grows suspicious of you venturing down here, I can promise you a very long, painful death at my hand. Do. You. Understand?"

They nodded frantically in agreement, as I'd known they would. They were nothing if not obsessed with me, and I couldn't really blame them.

My second favorite portrait of myself looked back at me as we entered, and I turned, arms wide with a huge victorious smirk, to see Sloane and Graves tilting their heads in confusion at the cloaked female sitting at the table in front of them.

I was so excited I could burst.

"Graves, Sloane. Meet Edelin Sybilline."

CHAPTER 33
Evangelia

I awoke early to the sound of an eerie silence ringing in my ears. A quick glance around confirmed my suspicion that Elikai wasn't here. Again. I wasn't complaining. I didn't want to spend any more time alone in a room with him than I had to. I was more curious as to where he'd needed to be so early.

Not wanting to risk him returning while I was still here, I threw on a robe and headed for my only sanctuary in this cursed castle before he could stop me.

Since meeting with Thalia and Westly, I had been racking my brain for a new plan. Much to my frustration, I'd come to the conclusion that I couldn't make an attempt on the king's life until I had spoken to Alaric. I had to at least gauge what the likelihood was of Kane staking his claim to the throne. Would he claim his birthright? Would he even want it? Of course, this was if I could even remove the first obstacle.

Between desperately missing being able to talk to Nix, knowing he would have so much to say about this, and feeling like I was failing my parents by delaying the plan I'd been so set on for weeks, I had also thought a lot about what the realm might be like under Kane's leadership.

He was a good male. Damaged, but no less powerful, fair and just, from what I'd seen, anyway. He clearly cared for the fae of Dezrothia, even if he pretended not to notice them. He was always polite to staff both inside and out of the castle, and I'd never heard him join in at the dinner table when the topic turned to hybrids and thrakos, so I could only hope that meant maybe he didn't have the same prejudiced views.

If he did, then he would be as bad for the throne as his father and brother, but I was trying not to think about that. Even with who he was, it would have likely been drilled into him from the moment he was born.

I let out a groan of frustration, tired of going round in circles. I was as delusional as

Elikai if I thought I had any hope of helping to orchestrate getting that crown on Kane's beautiful head, but I had to try.

While I was stuck here, puzzling over things I was completely unqualified to deal with, I figured I may as well devour as many books as possible. Maybe I could even find one that would help me plan an escape, for whenever the day came that I finally got to drive a blade through the rat who called himself our ruler. Kane and Alaric certainly wouldn't be offering assistance any longer. If only there was a book titled *'Secret Passageways out of Regis' Castle'*, but the fates were never that kind to me.

I made my way through the hall and down to the library. As I entered the empty room, I headed straight for the catalog of books to see if there were any more detailed blueprints to the map I had been given by Lia. I searched under 'B' for blueprints, 'M' for maps, even 'S' on the off chance of finding that secret passageway book I fantasized about, but nothing was standing out as obvious.

Instead, I stuck to my newfound favorite—romance.

I moved to the towering shelves and ran my fingers along the dust covered spines, hoping one would leap out at me. Eventually, I just grabbed one at random. The choice was just too overwhelming, and I wasn't used to dealing with an out-of-control list of books to read.

I settled into my favorite spot, the deep red armchair that felt like a cushiony hug from a friendly giant and stood perfectly angled before the fire's light. I was ready to get lost in the pages while the crackling fireplace calmed my irrepressible thoughts.

I didn't know how long I spent immersed in its pages, but my heart had begun to beat wildly at the words. This definitely wasn't a sunshine and roses romance. This was much raunchier, and the more I read, the more I couldn't help wondering what would have happened if things hadn't come to such a rapid halt in that training hall–

"Fancy seeing you here..." a low voice behind me murmured quietly as the scent of apple and cinnamon gave away exactly who it was without me needing to look. A shiver fell down my spine as his breath ghosted my nape.

"Kane," I gasped, snapping the book closed. I hadn't expected anyone to join me here, especially this early in the day. "What are you doing here?"

He didn't look like a prince today, wearing loose gray cotton pants that bunched at the bottom of his muscular calves and a black fitted training top. I could see some faint marks and bruising still, courtesy of his pig of a father, but otherwise, he'd healed well. Physically, at least.

"Alaric won't let me train. He said I need to take today off. I told him it was bullshit, and I was fine, but he just got all growly and told me to fuck off, so I came to find a book instead. You know how growly he gets," he shrugged before casually folding his arms across his chest, making his biceps bulge. He circled to come to stand in front of me, giving me a full view of him.

I couldn't resist letting my eyes trail across his ripped muscles, my lips parting slightly. The book I'd been reading had filled my mind with desires I hadn't had a chance to shake off, and while our last conversation left me a bit shaken, the book's effects seemed to be stronger.

I trailed my gaze back up to his eyes. There was darkness in them, his stare predatory as he assessed me. I tugged the bottom of my nightie down, only then remembering I had come straight to the library without getting properly dressed for the day.

I began stretching it down over my knees, willing it to appear longer than it was, less revealing, but it did little to help cover me up.

He obviously had no intention of bringing up our chat last night if the silence filling the room was anything to go by, so I figured I'd just go with it and not push the subject. Who was I to demand anything from him when I couldn't offer up any answers of my own?

"Well, I'm glad you are almost as good as new," I said honestly. "I guess now you don't have all that hideous swelling on your face, you can share the library with me if you'd like," I joked, trying to lighten the mood. I didn't want there to be any tension today. I didn't have the energy for it, and suspected he wouldn't either, despite his claims of being 'fine'.

"Did you find something to tickle your fancy, princess?" he asked, his gaze traveling over my bare legs.

The explicit scene I'd been in the middle of devouring when he'd entered, chose that moment to dance around in my mind. I bit down on my bottom lip at the memory of how I'd imagined a certain charming prince taking the hero's place... Before a huge growly shifter joined us... I mean, them... the characters.

I shivered all the way down to my core at the thought as I fidgeted in my chair. "Oh, you know..." I said, waving the book casually. "Just some mushy romance." I stood to escape, planning to hide the book back in the shelves, but as I moved away, he grabbed it from my hand before I'd even seen him move.

I whirled on him, my body heat rocketing. "Hey! Give that back!" I whisper yelled as he lifted it above his head, using his height to keep it out of reach as he briefly inspected the cover.

I lifted up onto my tiptoes, desperately trying to snatch it back from him, but all I achieved was making my nightdress ride up, revealing my underwear. I could not let him see what I'd been reading. The thought alone was mortifying.

Fates, what if he already knew the book? I couldn't take the embarrassment and teasing that would come.

I placed my hand on his chest for more leverage, reaching for it as his natural scent filled my senses even more so now that we were so close. He winced fractionally, but shook it off. "Oh, I didn't realize you were into *these* kinds of books, princess," he taunted, his mouth so close to mine now. "Tell me, how far did you get, little minx? Has he taken her against the wall yet?" he whispered, low and seductive. "It's one of my favorite scenes... But perhaps you would have preferred him to have been a little less rough with her?"

The tingling sensation in my chest was rapidly moving south as my entire body heated. I knew exactly what chapter he was referring to and fates damn me, but I'd loved that he hadn't treated her like fragile glass.

I looked up at the prince before me, meeting his stunning blue eyes. He knew I wasn't experienced, far from it, so maybe he was just trying to embarrass me. *Two can play that game.*

"Mmm," I said, like I'd just taken a bite of the juiciest apple. I might not have allure, but it'd still had the desired effect if his hooded gaze was anything to go by. I laced my next words with pure seduction, tugging him down closer to me so I could whisper directly into his ear. "I think I preferred the part where he devoured her like his last meal..."

My breaths were coming heavier now, my plan to just tease him back completely backfiring. My hand was still pressed to his chest, where I'd used him to keep my balance. His face was so close I could feel the electricity sparking between us.

It was too much. He was off limits. I knew I shouldn't let him get under my skin, yet that is exactly where I wanted him. The fact that it was impermissible only spurring me on.

I startled as a thud sounded against the floor near my feet, ripping my attention from him for the briefest moment while I looked down to see what it was.

He'd dropped the book.

I smirked inwardly as I realized he was as affected as I was by our little game and lifted my green eyes back up to meet the blue of his–

Without a second's warning, he captured my lips with his own. His arm encircled my waist as he pulled me close, gripping the back of my head firmly with his free hand as he began slowly devouring my mouth.

Completely forgetting what I'd been about to say, my hands slipped around his neck. I tightened my hold, kissing him back with vigor, and he smiled his approval against my lips.

I knew I shouldn't, knew it could get us killed, but I couldn't resist the taste of him as his mouth explored mine, like he wanted to learn every curve and crevice.

After what'd happened between us during my training session with Alaric, it was like my body had been awoken, and I needed this as much as I needed air in my lungs. Needed him. Needed *them*.

I let go of his neck just long enough to tug his top off over his head, and he released me to help. Discarding it across the polished floor before slamming his mouth back against mine, even more frantically this time. A moan slipped from my throat as our tongues collided.

We remained locked in the passion of the kiss while he moved me backwards until I was sandwiched between his firm, toned flesh and the cold, hard shelves.

Capturing my wrists in his hand, he held them above my head, none too gently. He pulled away briefly, looking me over greedily with his lust filled eyes, and my gaze traveled, taking in every inch of this magnificent male until it landed on his bare chest. *Shit*. His ribs! They were still black and blue from last night. Reality hit hard and fast. This was getting really intense, really quickly. I was due to marry his brother in less than a week, for fates' sake!

"Kane, wait," I said, meeting his eyes as I tried to gather my thoughts again. Instead, his lips trailed down my throat, his teeth grazing my pulse, sending a shiver through me. Oh fates, why did that feel so good? *"Kane–"* I tried again, but it slipped out as more of a whimper. Did I really sound like that?

The hand on my waist began to trail around and down my spine, cupping my ass, and I swallowed reflexively as he pressed himself even tighter against me. He was solid, and by the fates I wanted him, throbbed at the mere thought.

"Tell me you don't want this. Tell me now so I can walk away from you..." he groaned into my ear, his breathing heavy. I couldn't say no, didn't want to say no. My body burned to be touched, touched by him.

"If we are going to do this, I want to be honest with you about one thing at least," I told him, and he met my eyes, waiting. "If we do this, I need you to know that, for me, Alaric is as much a part of whatever this is as you are..."

The most sinful smile spread across his lips, and he nodded his response before capturing my lips in a rough kiss. That, along with the blue flames of desire blazing in his eyes, were all I needed to confirm he felt the same way. That I didn't need to feel too much guilt that I had these feelings for both of them. That he wanted it all too, with both of us. I sent a silent prayer to the fates that Alaric would feel the same way.

"Fates, I want you..." I whispered, breaking the last of his restraint. He freed my hands to lift me off the floor and wrap my legs around his waist. I ground down on his erection straining between us, provoking a feral sound from his chest as he moved us to my favorite chesterfield.

He straddled me across his lap as he pulled me in for a desperate kiss, and I pressed firmer on his solid cock, seeking more friction.

"You are *mine* princess, I can't give you to Kai..." Kane growled, pulling the thin straps of my nightdress down to reveal my chest. His lips followed the material, and he took one of the dusky hardened tips in his mouth, grazing it with his teeth, sending tremors through my body.

Fuck, it felt so good. I was drowning in the pleasure he was giving me, and I never wanted it to end. I rolled my hips again, wanting more, needing everything he could give me. When he let out a moan, letting my nipple go, more heat filled me. I was on fire, and I wanted more.

"You undo me," he murmured against my tingling flesh. "No matter how hard I try to stay away, the fates find a way of pulling me toward you, my beautiful princess."

Before I had a chance to think about exactly what his words meant, he was grabbing my nightdress and ripping it up over my head. His hands trailed back to my ass as he leaned back to admire me on his lap with a look that said he had just unwrapped his favorite gift.

His hand grabbed me roughly, as the fingers of his other dipped down to my core and ran back and forth across me, feeling the wetness that pooled there. "So wet for me already..." He smirked, rolling his hips in sinful motions as he continued to stroke me.

"Then do something about it," I groaned, the heat suffusing through me was too much and not enough. I could feel myself wanting to reach that crest, but the asshole below me held all the power and refused to give me what I wanted.

I leaned forward, placing my hands on his chest and changing up the angle to where his fingers could reach me. I dipped my lips close enough to his, though how I managed not to give in to the desire to kiss him was surprising.

He growled low under his breath at the movement, then his fingers were touching me directly as he pushed my underwear to the side, and I almost exploded right there. It was incredible and yet not enough.

I moaned in desperation, resting my forehead against his as I let myself just feel. I needed him to push me off that cliff, or better yet dive with me. My thighs quaked with need, and I bit my lip before I said something I'd regret later.

He dipped a finger inside of me, and I clenched around it. "*More,*" I growled. Despite the ring suppressing my beast, she raised her head with interest.

"So fucking greedy, princess. Tell me, how much do you want me to make you come? Do you want me to fucking wreck you?" he snarled throatily and, damn it all, those words...

I moaned above him, nodding as I bit my lip. "Words, beautiful. I want you to tell me what you want," he said, emphasizing his point by thrusting a second finger inside of me. There was no sharp pain like there had been with Alaric, only pleasure.

I kissed him hard and desperate, my hips rolling and grinding on his fingers. The sensation of his hard cock straining through his cotton pants was overwhelming. Building me to my crescendo, I was almost at that glorious peak, when he withdrew his fingers.

"Fucking asshole," I panted, but he just smirked.

"I still want the words, princess. Tell me exactly what you want me to do to you," he whispered against my skin, his voice full of lust as he kissed and nibbled his way along my collarbone.

I moaned, my hips rocking over him. I dragged my hands over his chest to the waistband of his bottoms, teasing his skin.

"I want you to take these off, and I want you to take my panties off. I need you inside me, Kane. I want you to fuck me until neither of us can move or think straight," I told him truthfully, surprised by the confidence in my own voice. My nails gently scratched the sensitive flesh they trailed, and he groaned.

"Your wish is my pleasure, my queen," he rumbled, bringing our chests flush together, our lips hovering just a fraction apart.

Holy shit.

He nipped my lips before tossing me onto the large sofa as if I weighed nothing, his hands pulling my underwear off, slowly revealing my most private area to his eyes. I should have been embarrassed, but like last time, I wanted him to see all of me.

He stood to drop those light gray pants that succeeded in hiding nothing of his size, and my eyes devoured the sight of him, my tongue darting out to lick my lips.

Despite the bruises that still marred his body, I wanted him desperately. He sank to his knees between my spread thighs, as he placed a gentle kiss on my lips, and proceeded to work his way down my body as I writhed beneath him.

He kissed every inch of skin he could reach, one hand on my sternum encouraging me to lean back while his other traced my flesh to my breast, his rough hand massaging the globe as his mouth reached my hips. I bucked up into him. My throat was dry, and every pant and moan was meant as encouragement to keep him going.

When he finally got to where I needed him, he pushed my thighs wide and licked through the wetness soaking my pussy.

He groaned as he freely devoured me, hooking arms around my thighs and tugging me closer to his mouth. I gasped, his name the only coherent word to leave me as I grasped his hair to pull his mouth closer to devour it. The growl of approval from him only served to send me further into a frenzy.

This was how I died. Death by Nekane Regis' mouth, and what a glorious end to my immortality it would be.

"Fuck, more!" I moaned. "Kane, I need more, I need… I need you..." I panted. As if that was the sign from the fates he'd been waiting for, he pulled a hand back, and plunged two fingers deep inside of me as he set a fast and delicious pace.

I moaned, the waves of pleasure as he sucked my clit and curled his fingers inside my sheath, finding the perfect spot that would undo me. My back arched off the cushions as I was forced over the cliff I had been desperate to fall from.

I opened my bleary eyes to see him licking the mess I made on his face like it was the sweetest treat, and shit, if that wasn't the most erotic thing I had ever seen.

His eyes were lidded, enrapturing me in his stare. He kissed his way up my body, and I felt his impressive cock nudge at my entrance.

I brought my heavy legs around his waist to pull him flush against my body, groaning at the feel of him sliding through my wetness and grinding against my overly sensitive clit. He dropped a kiss to my neck and rocked his hips as my breath stuttered out of me.

"You ready, beautiful?" he whispered in my ear, sending shivers through my entire being. He lined himself up, and before I could answer him, he pushed inside. He was clearly trying to be gentle, his lips feather light on my neck, but the breathy moan that left me was all the encouragement he needed.

He straightened between my thighs, smoothing his hands down my waist as he slowly dragged his length in and out.

He was stunning, a messenger sent from the fates to ruin me.

Concentration furrowed his brow as he moved with controlled thrusts. It was everything I had hoped it would be, but it also wasn't enough. I needed more, craved more.

Planting my heels on his firm ass, I pulled him to me, forcing him to slam inside. Fuck me. That was what I needed. Hard, rough, primal. I could have sworn my beast purred as my back arched and a hand shot out to grasp him.

"Harder," I growled at him, my other half begging to be let out to play with him. He braced his hand on the cushion behind me, his other reaching around to my ass and tilting my hips into a new angle. It was divine, and as he thrust into me harder, I swore I could see stars. My hand curled, nails digging into his flesh to hold on as he followed my command.

His harsh breaths came in time with his thrusts, sending sparks through my body and setting me alight. "*Yes...*" I moaned. The sensation was addictive. As I found purchase on an elbow, the sight before me of Kane plowing in and out was sinful.

"*Fuck,*" he groaned. "You're so fucking tight, so fucking perfect. So. Fucking. *Mine.*"

The way his muscles flexed as he thrust, his raven hair falling into his eyes and the half lidded look he kept trained on my face was heady. I feared I would never get enough of it.

"Are you ready to show me what you want?" he asked, slowing down and leaning across me to nip at my lips. I was up for trying anything with this male.

"Yes," I purred, smirking.

I yelped as I was suddenly lifted from the cushions and he rolled to sit with me in his lap once again, his cock remaining firmly seated within me.

"Ride me. Show me what you want and take it," he commanded roughly. His hand smoothed down my back to hold my hips.

The new angle was incredible. I rolled my hips and moaned at the sensation of him sliding deeper than before. Placing one hand on his shoulder and the other beside his head, I leaned forward to kiss him, meeting his lips in a desperate moment, and lifted my hips, testing the movement.

Did it always feel this amazing? I could only hope, because I didn't want it to ever stop.

I sped up, riding him and chasing the crescendo again. I wanted, no, needed, to reach it. I tried to keep tasting his sinful lips, but the moans and pants falling from my own meant I had to give them up.

I sat up in his lap, my hands falling to his spread thighs behind me. Fates, it was so good, the angle hitting all the right places deep inside of me.

My inexperienced hips found their own rhythm, the tightening of Kane's hands spurring me on. The sinful sounds that were spilling from his lips made me bite down on my own. Fuck, his noises were made to arouse, to make you want to force more from him.

He started cursing under his breath and my thighs were beginning to burn from exertion. Disappointment seared through my chest, worried I was doing something wrong as he started guiding my hips faster.

"*Fuck!*" he gritted out, "Come for me. I can feel you are so close, riding my cock like the queen you are. Use me, take your reward," he ordered, and oh fates, the filthy words brought me closer to the precipice, moans spilling freely.

He brought a hand around the front of my hips and his thumb pressed on my clit, working in slow circles. I could feel my stomach quivering with every little rotation. I was so close. Fates, I needed it so badly.

"Yes, fuck yes, come on my cock," he ground out, thrusting in time with my desperate hips. I fell over the edge again, my orgasm consuming me. I arched, a scream tearing from my lips.

The fluttering from my core sent waves of pleasure out to the rest of my body, heating me up until I thought I might combust.

"*Fuck*, Evangelia..." he groaned as his hands tightened to bruising. His hips jerked erratically before he stilled.

Our breathing heavy, I opened my eyes to look at him, and the smile he gave me should have been illegal. Shit, this male was going to break me, and I was going to beg him to do it.

"You are amazing," he said, his hands cupping my face and bringing us together in a delicious kiss.

Why did it have to be Elikai who claimed me as his bride?

We stayed there, basking in the feeling of bliss as we caught our breath.

Kane broke the silence. "I was meant to tell you earlier, but you can be very... distracting," he started. "I have a surprise for you. Well, another surprise, only this time it's not my cock," he said with a wink. Gently, he rolled me onto the cushions and started to dress, before gathering my nighty up off the floor and handing it to me so I could do the same. It only occurred to me then how foolish we'd been. Anyone could have walked in on us.

I hurried to cover up before turning my attention back to what he'd been saying. "Two surprises in one day? I'd say aren't I lucky, but I'm not really a fan of surprises. If you'd ever lived in the Fading Vale, you'd understand," I mumbled, half joking as contentment thrummed through my veins, and I realized how natural it felt to play with him.

"Well, I hope I didn't tire you out too much because I'm going to get Alaric to come here, and he is going to start training you again. Starting today."

"But–"

"Look, if you won't let us help you get out of the castle and back to wherever your family is from, then please just let us help you with this. You'll have to be careful of course, but it would make us feel a little better knowing you could protect yourself," he told me, and the concern in his voice made me want to start kissing him again.

"Alaric is really going to train me again? How? I mean, Thalia mentioned something, but..." I trailed off. Since I'd been banned from the training floor completely, I was unsure just how they thought they could get around that.

His face lit up with a devilish smirk. "He is going to train you right here. In the library. I just hope you don't find the memories of what we just did to be too distracting." He winked. "I know they will be for me."

CHAPTER 34
Alaric

I let the scalding water pour over me as I lost myself to the memories of last night and how much of a fucking disaster it had been.

As soon as I'd seen the king stalking to the far corner of the hall and Kane silently following him, I'd known what that cunt was about to do to him.

It wasn't the first time, far fucking from it. The need to protect him, to race in there and rip out the king's entrails to wrap them around his neck, had nearly consumed me this time.

I'd had an internal battle with my body to stay seated. I'd anxiously waited for the right time to go to him as I pretended to give a fuck what the prick sitting next to me was saying. The only thing that stopped me was wanting to keep an eye on Angel.

When the king had eventually returned, I made a blunt non-apology to end the conversation I'd been having about who the fuck knew what, and strode straight for the doors.

But fucking Krista had chosen that moment to stop me. I'd cursed the fates that the female still hadn't gotten the fucking memo that she made me about as hard as a wet noodle. I'd shrugged her off quickly enough when I caught sight of Angel disappearing out of the dining hall.

I'd needed to get to Kane desperately; they'd been in that room for too long, and I could smell the blood in the air. As I'd gotten to the hallway, I saw her listening at various doors and knew immediately she was searching for Kane too. I didn't know why, but I knew I'd needed to let her see him, not to pity him, but to understand him, so I'd pulled her behind me as I'd followed the smell of blood.

He'd been a fucking mess. Worse than I'd ever seen him. My only hope had been that he could see how much Angel cared for him from the anguish in her eyes at seeing him hurt.

Then she'd refused to heal him, which had really pissed me off. I was damned near furious when Kane had actually fucking agreed with her. Seeing him in that bloody heap had sent my beast rattling in its cage, my wolf howling for the king's blood. Retaliation needed for harming what was ours.

As I pulled myself from the heated water of the shower and back to the now, a bang sounded on the door to my room. Usually folk waited at my office if they needed to speak with me, or left a message. Very few actually came to my personal space.

I wrapped a towel around my waist and headed for the door. "Alaric," Kane said, pushing past me to stand in the middle of the room, and the most divine scent hit me like a hammer.

"Someone better be dyin' or dead," I glared at him, wondering what could be so important that it couldn't wait. I'd already dismissed him from training for today, couldn't he just rest up like his body needed?

"Nothing like that," he said, waving me off. "Eva's agreed."

"Agreed? To what?"

"She's in the library waiting for you, to train her, you know… In secret?" Kane drawled.

I finally took in his appearance. He had that freshly fucked look about him. I had seen it enough times to recognize it. I could feel the rumblings of a growl building from the pits of my gut at the mere thought he had been fucking someone else.

I somehow managed to swallow it down. It didn't matter. He was high fae, and the Lores meant fuck all could happen between us. He could screw anyone he damn well wanted to, and I couldn't say a fates' damned thing about it.

I didn't breathe too deeply, not wanting to know exactly who his partner had been. Jealousy was a bitch, and I was a bastard who had killed for less.

"Good. Righ' then, I'll get down to see her. Thalia brought me some stuff to give to her jus' in case she was up for it. Turns out she didnae burn them. Said she knew they meant a lot to Angel, sneaky witch."

I gripped the towel at my waist, about to strip off, when I noticed Kane still standing like a fool.

"Is there anythin' else or yeh wantin' a gawk at my cock?" That seemed to jolt him out of whatever stupor he was in, and his cheeky grin and wink as he left had me shaking my head. That wasn't a no, even if he *had* left the room.

I dressed, grabbed the training clothes that Thalia had given me, along with Angel's daggers that I'd kept after disarming her, and headed for the library. Thalia was a good egg. She knew what it took to survive this castle and its tyrants.

I sent a message with one of the servants to find Axel and get him to bring equipment up to my room, where I'd left another note telling him to bring everything to the library instead. There were too many eyes and ears in this place to know who could be trusted.

I opened the door to the library, and the smell hit me again, there was no avoiding it. There was no denying what I had suspected Kane had been up to was true either. He *had* fucked someone.

Only, for some reason, I hadn't expected it to have been Angel, but she was fucking glowing.

His scent of apples and cinnamon coated her and mixed with her campfire and vanilla, and it made me salivate at the thought of tasting them together. Something I knew couldn't happen, but I would be lying if I said I didn't think about it all too fucking often lately.

When Angel saw me, her face brightened briefly, before setting into a scowl. Maybe I wasn't who she had been expecting after all? The pang in my chest at the thought was sharper than I was willing to admit.

"You've seen Kane?" she asked.

"Aye. He sent me here to–"

Her hand darted out fast, angled just right to slap me square across the jaw, but she wasn't good enough. Not yet anyway. I caught it millimeters away from my marred face. "You knew, didn't you?" she spat, not ready to back down on whatever had pissed her off, accusation lacing her tone. Knew what? That she'd been fucking Kane in here not long ago when she was meant to be marrying his brother in a few days? But why the fuck would she be trying to hit me for that?

The fact she was wearing such a short fucking nightdress that was barely covering her ass wasn't helping me focus. "You're gonnae have to be more specific, Angel," I managed over my dry as fuck mouth, using the wrist I still held to draw her closer.

"Last night, what happened with Kane…"

Oh, of course. She was going to berate me after Kane's beating last night. Like I had any sway whatsoever in talking the king down. It hadn't stopped me trying at the beginning, but I needed to keep him on my side for reasons that were my own and had nothing to do with her. So as much as it had fucking killed me, I'd had to let it happen.

"Aye, I ken what the king does to him," I admitted.

"And you don't stop it from happening?" The hurt in her voice was palpable, further cementing that she truly did feel something for him. Though it still didn't make it any easier to tell her that my hands were tied on this.

"Yeh think I could barge in an' stop the king from doin' anythin'? My head would be on a pike before I could blink! Yeh think I dinnae want to help him? Trust me, I've been watchin' the king brutalize his son for the past twenty years, an' it might shock yeh to ken that's nothin' on what he sends his horde to do, me in-fuckin'-cluded. There is nothin' I could've done. No more than yeh could've," I told her, dropping her arm and folding my own against my chest.

I liked Angel, more than I cared to admit. She had bigger balls than half the kingdom, but she just didn't know the ways around here. If I had my way, I would have rid the king of his head and served it on a silver platter the first time I discovered that he had beaten Kane. No, the first time I'd set foot in this castle, but it wasn't that easy.

"You could have–"

"I've done what I could for him," I sighed, cutting off whatever she was going to say. I understood her frustration, probably more than she even realized. I ached knowing what Kane had to suffer through.

I turned my attention to why I was even here in the first place and threw the bag in my hands at her. "Now, get changed an' use what yer feelin' to come at me. While we're waitin' on Axel to come with more weapons, we can do some hand to hand."

Thankfully, she did as I asked her without argument, though it didn't alleviate the furrow in her brows much.

As we began, it was clear that what had happened between Kane and his father was weighing heavily on her mind, or maybe it was what came later in this very room. She was being sloppy, but not from being unable to train for a few days. It clearly came from distraction. I couldn't help but wonder if she was reminded of her time with him with every movement she made, and I wanted to know everything.

I realized I wasn't jealous. Oh no, I was disappointed I hadn't been here to join them.

I dove forward as if to tackle her to the ground, but shifted my weight at the last second and pinned her against the wall next to a small table before her mind had time to keep up. "What yeh thinkin' about, Angel? Yer head is somewhere else, fancy sharin' the why with me?"

"I'm fine, just pre-wedding jitters–"

"I can smell him on yeh, yeh ken? I ken he fucked yeh, an' with the way yer blushin' right now, I ken he fucked yeh good an' hard."

Her cheeks were scarlet when she finally met my eyes, craning her head as she licked her lips nervously.

"Yeh ken, it's got me wonderin' what yeh would smell like with my scent all over yer tight body too..." She shuddered, and I noted she became softer and more pliable with every word I hissed in her ear.

I spun her around, forcing her cheek against the cold stone wall roughly and pressed into her back, my hardening cock showing her exactly what I thought about it.

"Alaric..." she moaned. Fuck, that sound was so sinful. It made me want to forget everything I'd spent over three hundred years working toward and give in to the temptation to claim her completely.

"Yeh like the sound of that, don't yeh? Naughty girl... Yeh want both me an' Kane to absolutely destroy you... So fuckin' greedy."

Her back arched and her arse pressed into me. My hand moved to her hip and I pulled her tight against my straining cock. Her arousal was thick in the air, and I wanted nothing more than to taste it, taste what Kane had left behind, and I had every intention of doing so the moment I could.

"Kane fucked this cunt, what? Hours ago? Minutes?" I growled, my hand dipping to cup her over the training leathers she wore. "And yer already thinkin' of someone else fuckin' yeh. Is his cum still drippin' from yeh? An' yer wantin' me to add mine to it as well?" I intended on embarrassing her, but I really hoped it was fucking true.

She let out a strangled moan, and I was half a second away from ripping her clothes off and making good on my words–

"Uh, Alaric..." A male voice came from the entrance of the library. Fates give me a fucking break! With difficulty, I pulled away from Angel to glare at Axel over my shoulder.

"Axel..." I growled. I'd asked him here, but right now wanted to kill him for interrupting us.

"So uh... your weapons, boss," he said, placing the bag on the nearest table to him.

"M'lady," he nodded to Angel, whose face was still flushed, but her eyes were now filled with alarm.

She didn't need to fear Axel going to Elikai or the king. He was loyal to only me, but she didn't know that. No one did.

I stalked over to grab the weapons bag, but his eyes stayed firmly glued to my Angel. Oh no, that wouldn't do. My beast was prowling. It couldn't get out, but that didn't stop it egging me on to rip him apart.

No one got to look at her like that. Well, except Kane. "See anythin' that yeh like boy?" I growled at him, getting in his face. "I raise yeh, give yeh a job, keep yeh outta trouble an' yeh come an' gawk at *her*," I bristled.

I'd told him before that he was to keep his eyes to himself and other shifters only. After I told him about kissing her, he dared to even look at *my* female? Some part of me knew my reaction was a bit much, but fuck if I could remember why that mattered.

"I, ah.. S-Sorry, boss... I'll leave you alone..." he stuttered, one hand raised in surrender while the other clasped his chain around his neck that matched mine, as if soothing a charging bull, before hurrying back out the door again.

The second he'd left, I calmed. He must have sensed how close I was to losing my shit. And now that he wasn't here and I could think again, I really shouldn't have reacted like that to Axel, of all fae.

I was so fucked for this female, and she was to be married in four days. To fucking Elikai Regis.

Thanks to Axel's interruption, I managed to pull myself back from the brink of ravaging Angel, who was leaning her back against the shelves now. Desire still lit up her eyes as they roamed over me.

I let myself stare at her a moment longer, taking in the curves of her willing body. *Fuck*. What had I been about to do to her? Anything and everything she'd have fucking let me.

I let out a breath and turned my back to her. It was a good thing Axel had come in when he had. I couldn't let myself get distracted by her again. This was training only. Work, not pleasure.

Somehow, I managed to keep my head out of the gutter for the remainder of the training session, but that blush remained on her face the entire time. I really hoped she was thinking about what I'd said, and not just about Kane.

Fuck, the female was under my skin, and I needed to know where she stood. I couldn't let my feelings for Angel, or Kane for that matter, come between them. Come between the bond we shared.

I'D BEEN CALLED to dinner in the king's solar room, one of my least favorite things to endure as a general.

I shuddered as I remembered the last time we'd met here, when he'd told me he was sending me on a hunt with Elikai for his coming of age. Had that really only been a month ago?

I could hear Elikai before I'd even had the displeasure of entering the room.

"–then you wouldn't believe the sheer audacity of these peasants, Father–"

I rolled my eyes. What was he bletherin' on about now? It was unusual for me to be called to dine with the king and for anyone else to be present. So, why Elikai? Unless he was actually considering giving him the crown? Surely not. The male enjoyed the power too much himself.

"I didn't see any suggestion of that..." Angel's soft voice carried to me just as I reached the door. Why was she here, too?

The solar room was located on the topmost floor of the castle, in a tower off the grand chambers, where the king himself resided. Though I hated coming here because it usually meant the king had some task or operation he wanted me to run, it was still one of my favorite rooms in the castle.

It was beautiful in its simplicity. The curved walls were plain, but broken up by the rich purple drapes that dropped all the way to the flagstone floor and framed the stunning windows. There were no arrow slits like most in the castle, but imposing works of art, made up of three panes of stained glass, and on clear days, they enjoyed the best view of Dezrothia the capital had to offer.

A chunky solid wood table sat in the center of the circular room, where I found not only the king sat at its head, but Elikai, Angel, and Kane sat with him too. "Alaric, you finally joined us," the king's voice boomed as I entered, and suddenly all eyes were on me.

I could see the confusion on Elikai's face, a smirk on Kane's as his eyes trailed over me, and Angel gave me the biggest doe eyes, panic filling her expression. "Yer Majesty..." I half bowed as I walked to sit on the solitary couch near the flickering fireplace set into the wall, purposely separating myself from the high fae as the king preferred.

"I have matters to discuss with you. Are you trying to be difficult? You'd have me shout to be heard? Sit there," he commanded, waving his hand at the empty chair next to Kane.

I swallowed down what I wanted to say in reply and gently lowered myself into the chair, waiting with trepidation for what was to come next. You could cut the tension in the room with a knife. My gut feeling didn't often lead me wrong, and it was telling me whatever this was about, it wouldn't be good.

"General Alaric, I'd wanted to discuss security for the upcoming wedding, but my boy here," he gestured to Elikai, "has brought to light some interesting information. So I'm interested to know, what are your thoughts on the villages?" he asked, likely not considering that I might have heard Elikai before I'd entered and already began to consider the options of what his line of questioning may be about.

"To be honest with yeh, majesty, I think it depends where yeh look. The further out from the capital yeh get, the less loyalty yeh'll find," I told him, speaking honestly, though I did choose my words carefully. It was important to always include some fact in whatever I told him to keep his trust and to not draw his ire.

Angel's face was a mask as she looked at me, cold indifference settling there. *Good girl.* If I wasn't getting to know her so well, I too would have assumed she had no opinion on the matter. So she was a fast learner, and speaking out at the dinner table the other night had taught her a thing or two about dealing with King Regis. Good.

"That settles it," he announced, slamming his fist down on the table. "I need to remind these villagers who they are dealing with, and more importantly, who owns them," he proclaimed. "Especially after what this fool," he gestured to Kane this time, "did at the last hearing in my absence."

Kane wisely ignored him, probably unsure why he'd even been invited here in the first place. But knowing the king, it was purely so he could remind him of how disappointed he was with him.

"We will leave the day after the wedding. It's an annoying delay, but it wouldn't look good for me to not be present." Elikai scowled, but managed to keep his mouth shut for once. "I will need you to put together the best you have for my security detail, and I want enough time to really remind these ungrateful weaklings who their king is. We will spend nearly a week in every village–"

He rambled on. And as he spoke, I was working out everything in my head, trying to stay a few thoughts ahead, as I always did. "Yer Majesty, that's at least a three to four month trip. Six or more if yeh want to travel in comfort," I hedged, not missing the gleam of excitement in Elikai's expression.

"Fine, fine. I can leave my advisors in charge for the time I am gone," he dismissed, and in the space of a heartbeat Elikai's face had gone from glee to something really fucking murderous.

Maybe Angel was onto something about him wanting the throne desperately? Leaving the advisors in control would mean that neither of the twins would have any power during the king's absence, and that would chafe on a power hungry asshole like Elikai.

Not to mention the hit to his ego. It would make him look weak, and to outsiders it would look as though the king didn't trust him to step up and rule in his stead, which would then result in the fae of Dezrothia questioning whether he would be fit to rule at all. *Much like they already do with Kane.*

I watched Elikai carefully as the dinner crawled on torturous and slow. The topic mostly involved discussing the finer details of the upcoming dreaded trip. The size of the party he wanted versus how many were needed to be left to defend the castle, who would escort each member of his harem he decided to take with him, and the route we should take were all considered.

All in all, there was a lot to organize in just four days. The parts that interested the king barely scratched the surface of the logistics involved in a six month long slog. But to refuse him would be a death sentence.

And as much as I didn't want to go, I needed to be there. It was the only way to have at least a semblance of influence over how badly he was going to terrorize the villagers.

By the time Regis had retired for the evening, Kane had already long escaped, and I knew he wouldn't be happy that I would be leaving for so long. Though I could only hope he would understand why one day. That I would get a chance to explain it to him. All of it.

Elikai had gone sulking off after his father. No doubt to try and convince him of some scheme, or have a tantrum about the advisors being put in charge instead of him.

I sat with Angel across from me, her head resting on her fist as she met my gaze, her brow furrowed. "You remind me of someone..." she said thoughtfully, her head tilting as if looking at me from another angle would help solve the mystery. "Your eyes and lips are wrong, but the coloring is right, the shape of your nose and jawline too..."

My heart thumped painfully in my chest as I registered the description she was giving. "What're yeh talkin' about Angel?"

"Call me crazy but... you remind me of someone from the Fading Vale. He was huge like you, brave, and kind, and like an uncle to me once," she murmured wistfully as she sat up.

We remained in comfortable silence for a while, as she must have gotten lost in her memories of that place, perhaps the other prisoners she had left behind.

"Can I trust you with a secret, Alaric?"

"Always, Angel..." I told her, and I meant it. I would take her secrets to the grave.

"I grew up there..." she blurted.

"The Fadin' Vale? They had yeh from a babe? Or yeh wasnae a prisoner?"

"Both really..." she confirmed cautiously.

I cast my mind back to that first day we'd met. The way she'd been armed, no obvious marks to say she'd been tied up or chained, the look she'd given Elikai after we'd finished our attack on the camp... Her camp.

Fuck.

How had I missed this in the first place?

She'd been a member of that fucking camp of rebels, not a prisoner, and we'd fates near killed every being there.

Those who lived in the Fading Vale didn't do it by choice. They were driven there into hiding, always running, never safe. Why had she been raised there, though? Could she be part thrakos? She didn't smell like a half-breed, but come to think of it, I had never been able to get past her natural scent of campfires and vanilla.

I drew in a deep breath, and other than her usual alluring scent, I couldn't actually smell much of anything that would indicate her race. I knew some concealed parts of their nature or other halves, so there were means of masking it, but how was she doing it?

I glanced across the two rings she always wore for a brief second before she circled the table and claimed Kane's seat next to me. "Given what I just told you, can I still trust you?" I nodded. "Is it safe to talk here?" she asked tentatively. I nodded again, and she sucked in a deep breath before surprising the shit out of me by launching into her story. "The day you, Elikai and the horde attacked, I'd been out to gather supplies with my best friend, Nix. We raced back when we heard Regis' army was close by, but it was too late." Her shoulders sagged. "We'd been due to relocate. Had you come any sooner we might have been more prepared to fight, less distracted with packing the camp for our next destination. Had you come later, you would have missed us entirely. The thought keeps me up at night. It's like the fates wanted us to be slaughtered." She let out a long sigh.

This had been eating her up, and she'd had no one she could trust enough to tell. Fae she loved had been killed, and she had no one to mourn with. The only fae around her were those responsible for their deaths, whether they'd been there or not. But I'd been there. I'd allowed the bloodlust to consume me, not that it was any excuse.

Why would she now feel like she could trust me with this? Because I bore a vague resemblance to someone she'd known? Someone she'd trusted? Was she so desperate to find a connection to where she'd grown up–

"He slaughtered them, you know? My parents, I mean… Elikai slaughtered them r-right in f-front of me." The break in her voice broke something in me, too.

I reached out, grabbing her hand in mine. I needed to give her comfort. Make it better. But it was too late for that.

"He th-threatened me, t-told me that he would kill me too if I didn't go along with his story–"

"Fuck off, he didnae?" The words rushed out before I could stop them, as I slammed my chair out from under me and stood over her, wanting to kill something, needing to kill something… To kill *him*.

She placed her hand on my wrist as if to stop me and guided me to retake my seat. The only thing that kept me from going after that cunt right now was the worry in her eyes over finally opening up.

"Every night he would remind me of what he'd done and why he'd done it. The ride home was awful, but I preferred the days to the nights. At least during the day I could ignore everything, pretend that none of it was real and that I was just riding out to get supplies from another village. At night though… At night I couldn't escape him. He wouldn't touch me, thank the fates, but he would tell me what he wanted to do to me like some paid whore." A shudder ran through her, and she trailed off.

Fire was running through my veins, but I pulled her close and held on tight. I didn't like Elikai at the best of times, had never seen what Kane did in him, but he was sounding more and more like his father with every word of Angel's truth finally coming out.

I wanted to give her some truth of my own, knowing it was probably just what she needed to hear. But I couldn't. "I'm sorry, Angel," I murmured into her hair, placing a kiss there, and she just nodded.

I knew I needed to say more, but I couldn't trust myself. Not until I'd had time to think about what she'd just confessed and decide what the fuck I was going to do about it.

CHAPTER 35
Nekane

I stood on the stool getting measured for my suit to wear tomorrow while Burton, the warlock tailor kneeling before me, took my measurements at a painstakingly slow pace.

Why he didn't just use a spell or something to hurry things along I'd never know, but the male clearly loved his profession, which was probably what made him the best in the city.

My mind had decided to get stuck on a loop for the last few days, only able to think about two things, both of which could get me killed, or worse, get her killed.

The first, how to stop this fucking wedding, and the second, claiming Eva in the castle library.

The moans of pleasure that came from her mouth should have been illegal. The smell of her bare flesh and her delicious pert breasts that were so perfect they had to have been made for my hands. The feel of her heat as she'd rocked against my straining cock, begging for more, and fuck, I had given it to her.

There was something so fucking sexy about making her ask for what she'd wanted. I'd never expected those words to actually leave her lips. I'd intended to tease her, but she'd risen to it. And fuck if it wasn't the hottest thing I'd ever experienced. I was definitely not innocent when it came to sex, far from it, but I'd be lying if I said it hadn't felt like I was getting my dick wet for the first time with her.

When I'd entered her glistening wet pussy, I didn't think I'd last for two thrusts, like some horny teenager. But the fates had been on my side for once, and I'd held out to enjoy every second of her tight pussy as she'd clenched around my cock and convulsed in ecstasy–

Oh, fuck. No.

I drew my attention back to the room, realizing too late that this was a dangerous road to go down when not in the privacy of my chambers, where I'd been having to calm my dick down several times a day since.

In fact, this was probably the worst possible time and place for this to happen. *Please, fucking no.*

Burton was measuring up my inner thigh, desperately trying to look anywhere else as my hard-on strained against my undergarments. Fuck, it was pretty much pointing at his fucking face with the angle he knelt on the floor. *Why me?*

Think of something else. Anything else. *Alaric.* His hulking form as we fought in the ring together, the way his powerful muscles flexed and sweat rolled down his sculpted abs, his perfectly imperfect scar, Eva's mouth stretching around his thick shaft–

Nope, that didn't help one bit, made it so much fucking worse. Think of something else, Kane. *My brother*, pawing at my female at the dinner table. Forcing her close, to whisper who knew fucking what, in her ear. Him dragging her out of the room none too gently when he'd returned from the kraken hunt. The king, kicking me relentlessly while I lay paralyzed, Eva's face as she'd walked into that room and looked at me with pity in her eyes as I'd had to grit my teeth through the pain of just trying to do something as simple as breathe…

Yep, that did it. Not that it would stop old Burty down there thinking I just stood to attention because he touched me with his measuring tape. I hadn't even wanted to come here in the first fucking place when Westly had found me at breakfast. Kai had sent him to tell me I needed to make an effort for once in my life, and not embarrass him on his 'big day'.

When wasn't it his big fucking day? There was always something he was showing off. This time, it just happened to be *my* queen. No, *his* queen. No, she's definitely *mine*.

"Are we done here?" I questioned, avoiding eye contact at all costs after my impromptu boner in his face situation.

"Yes, Your Highness. You can go down– I mean get down now. Please step down. Everything is down here. I mean to say, I took your measurements down here," he waved his black leatherbound notebook around frantically as if that would help distract from his awkward babbling. "I will be sure to follow your briefs closely, the wedding planner's briefs, on the color scheme and what not. The suit will be sent to the castle this evening." *Poor guy.*

"Thank you, Burton," I replied, stepping off the stool, roughly pulling my clothes back on and managing to escape the shop with three strides.

Thank fuck Alaric hadn't come with me and witnessed that shit show. I would never live it down. *Down…* Burton's new favorite word, if his rambling was anything to go by. At least now I had a third thing to plague my mind relentlessly.

As I walked through the main cobbled street of Ezerat, blowing on my hands to warm them as the thin ice cracked under my feet, there was a real buzz in the air despite the bitter day. The businesses booming as the red-cheeked passersby readied themselves excitedly for the upcoming royal wedding.

Only the most elite would be invited to the wedding itself at the castle, but Ezerat wasn't short on elite. There would be hundreds gathered in the castle and thousands piling onto the grounds to try to steal a glimpse of the new princess in her stunning dress.

She could wear a hessian sack and still look every bit a royal. There was a fire in her eyes that just had a way of drawing you in. High fae were all beautiful in their own right, but she was like something else.

Those who weren't invited to the reception, such as shop owners, street vendors and tradesfolk, would be hosting parties in their homes and in the streets to celebrate and toast the happy couple, too. If only they knew the half of it. The darkness that lurked behind the closed castle doors.

I wondered if the surrounding towns and villages would share in the excitement too, or if word wouldn't spread that far. I'd really have to visit them at some point. Experience things through their eyes.

I'd never had the chance to leave the capital. Never had any reason to. But, perhaps I could finally do something productive with my lifetime of training and join the ranks in the horde? Then I would get to see the entire realm, as Alaric probably had on his countless missions and hunts. Maybe find others experiencing problems like they had been in Rangaran, but were understandably hiding it from the so-called king.

I entered the Crooked Claw, contemplating whether I'd been a fool to bury my head in the sand and turn a blind eye for all these years while my brother had been planning all sorts of who knew what for the realm's future. Or perhaps I'd been a coward, not wanting to know because to do anything about it was to receive another beating. But I was immortal now, and few knew the power that thrummed within me.

I shook the wayward thoughts aside, there was nothing I could do, anyway. I was here to check in with Melina, so I looked around until my gaze landed on the elderly lioness. She was over by the fireplace, her brow furrowed as she stirred a cauldron of hot soup or stew. The smell had me salivating. She certainly wouldn't get an invite to the nuptials being a shifter and all, but she would be in for a booming night with those toasting to the prince and princess.

But with that came trouble. It would be worse than usual given the king's Lores and subsequent favoritism toward certain races over the 'weaker' ones. It still caused friction between some fae, according to Alaric, but I'd never really seen it. Apparently, it was mostly the older folk who'd lived in a time before my father came into power. They usually sucked it up, but add alcohol to the mix and it was asking for drama with a capital D.

"Melina, how's it going pretty lady?" I asked, painting on my usual charming smile.

"Highness, long time no see," she said, pulling me in for a hug. "Not so bad. Would be better if those fools would behave though," she said, gesturing over to a booth in the center of the room. I followed her hand and saw Kai, Sloane, Graves and several other high fae acting like a bunch of dicks, females hanging off their every limb. "Are you here for my famous mutton stew? You must be freez–"

A growl rose in my throat when I saw that Kai was getting a lap dance from none other than Crystal. "What the fuck are you doing?" I roared from where I stood, even making Melina startle at the loud outburst.

I could feel his allure from here as everyone stopped and turned their head in my direction. Well, everyone except for the male in question.

I briefly registered Melina's hand, trying to stop me, but it was too late. I stalked toward him, pushing any fucker aside who was unfortunate enough to be in my way. "What. The. Fuck. Are. You. Doing?" I seethed.

"Kane, it's not what it looks–" Crystal started.

"Not you," I snapped. "I'm talking to my fucking brother," I told her, not taking my eyes off Kai. I swear, I didn't recognize him anymore. I barely recognized myself these days. I knew that my protectiveness toward his fiancée was unreasonable, but it had me moving toward my brother with anger in my veins, no less. Since sleeping with Eva, I knew I was becoming unreasonably attached to her. No other female seemed to do it for me anymore.

"Oh, it's you," he drawled, rolling his eyes like I was some kind of inconvenience. "Have you come to join us? We all know you enjoy the company of good looking fae..." he taunted, gesturing to the others who were with him.

"What the fuck are you doing?" I demanded, my tone deep and getting in his face so he knew I wasn't fucking around. Alaric's words entered my head, warning me to keep my cool and never to act on emotion, but it was easier said than done.

I desperately tried to calm myself down enough not to snatch him by the scruff, drag him outside and vent my frustration that had been building. I was so close to tipping over the precipice that my nails were biting into my palms as my muscles quivered, desperate for the fight.

The entire room was silent, minus my brother and his idiot friends who thought themselves immune to my wrath, or maybe they were just too caught up in themselves to notice the danger lurking at their doorstep.

"I am doing this thing that mortals do. It's called a bachelor party. Some call it a stag, but that just wouldn't do. I'm no animal or mutt like the shifters. Anyway, it is to celebrate my final night as a single male. I plan on making it a spectacular celebration, going out with a *bang*, you could say."

He turned away from me, laughing wildly at his own joke, before he proceeded to slap Crystal's ass so hard the cry of pain that left her lips held not even an ounce of pleasure.

"And what about Evangelia?" I asked. But as I looked at Crystal sitting in his lap, it dawned on me. I didn't have a leg to stand on, and Eva hadn't been innocent either. It wasn't long ago that the two of us had been in a similar position. The way she rode–

Nope, not going there again. Not right now, at least.

"What about the frigid whore?" Kai sneered, before turning to his moronic friends as they all laughed at his insult toward his betrothed.

"Can't expect the future king to suffer blue balls, can you?" Graves added, my ire now pointed toward him.

"Yeah, she's not put out even once for him! Can you believe that? Saving herself for marriage, the stupid bitch!" Sloane chimed in with a look of repulsion across his face.

"Though he finally gets to defile her tomorrow, train her in the way he wants her. I'm kind of jealous... she's gonna be so tight," Graves groaned.

"Fuck yeah, maybe when your done with her Kai, we can introduce her to The Groane..." Sloane added, and though I had no fucking clue what that was, it was likely for the best because I probably wouldn't fucking like it.

My anger hit boiling point as I waited for my brother to introduce those cunts' faces to his fist. Put them in their fucking place. Cut out their tongues and feed them to the lions so they couldn't so much as utter a single word of disrespect like that toward his fiancée ever again.

But he didn't. He fucking laughed with them. And I was so fucking shocked I just stood there dumbfounded.

"Aw, what's the matter, Nekane?" my brother asked patronizingly, his eyes never leaving Crystal's ass as he moved her hips to grind on his crotch. "You've got that same look you get every year when you wake up on All Fates Day with no presents," he said mockingly, for the entire tavern to hear.

Alaric was right. He was a cunt, and I was so fucking done with him. Done with being plagued by guilt for my feelings toward his fiancée, done with looking for the good in him, done with letting him think he was the superior twin.

Just. Fucking. Done.

"Fuck you, Elikai, you don't deserve her," I seethed, turning on my heel and leaving as quickly as I could before I said or did anything implicating, putting Eva's safety in any more jeopardy than it already was.

As I began the walk back to the castle, someone behind me called my name. "Kane! Hold on! Wait up! Just wait a minute, you whippersnapper!"

I stopped at that last one, a choked laugh threatening to slip out and break me from the hold of my anger. "What did you call me?" I turned to look at him, confirming what I already knew. It was Bill, Melina's husband, chasing after me.

"What do you want, Bill? Just tell Melina thanks for the offer, but I'm really not in the mood for stew now. Besides, if I go back there, I might actually murder my brother, and then what will you all do for a future king, eh?"

"I could answer that, but I know I'd be wasting my breath right now with the mood you're in," he said, coming to a stop in front of me. "Anyway, I wanted to ask you what that was all about. You are a good patron of ours, and I don't think I have ever seen you so furious. I'm surprised the windows didn't blow with the power radiating from you back there. Female troubles?"

His prideful and wizened face was in a wide smile as he looked up to me, my larger frame towering over the millennia old male, but he would probably have given me a run for my money in his prime.

"I remember when I mated with Melina. I couldn't stand another male so much as looking in her direction. Took fates near half a century for me to calm down," he laughed, scratching the back of his neck. His adoration for his mate was obvious.

"Oh, no, I don't have a mate. She's Elikai's–" I started.

"Nonsense, I know the look of a male who is defending his mate–"

"I promise you, Bill, she isn't my mate."

"How can you be so sure?" he asked, and I considered for a second how I reacted to Eva so oddly. Her scent was so unique to me and enticing, but Alaric's was the same...

It had to be something to do with not long coming of age. She couldn't be my mate. Right?

Clearly not expecting a reply or having given up waiting for me to respond, Bill turned and headed back into the tavern, leaving me stunned in the street.

No, it wasn't possible. The fates wouldn't be so cruel. Would they? My mind whirled the entire walk home with Bill's words and Elikai's actions. I tried to ignore the hypocrisy that dashed across my mind with what I had been doing with Eva, but still I needed to punch something.

I MARCHED STRAIGHT to the training room as soon as I arrived home, in the hope that Alaric would be there. I couldn't understand how Elikai's head could be turned when he had the greatest treasure in the realm marrying him tomorrow. Or maybe it was just me who found her so alluring, and Alaric too, I guess. Which made no sense at all with Bill's theory about her being my mate.

Elikai certainly didn't seem to be trying to win her heart, and it baffled me. If things were different, if I'd met her first, I'd have no reason to ever look at another female again.

Much to my disappointment, the training hall was empty. I contemplated going to Alaric's office or chambers to find him, but settled on going for a run instead, needing to work off this energy.

I jogged through the courtyard to the edge of the castle grounds and started making my way around the outskirts of the forest. By the time I reached the other side, I was barely breaking a sweat and still no less furious on Eva's behalf. Even though I knew full well she'd not been loyal to him either. I stopped by a tree on the forest edge, running my fingers through my hair, it was such a fucking headache.

"There he is!" A deep baritone I didn't recognize hushed from my right. I turned, looking in the direction the voice had come from to find three shifters ambling toward me. I didn't need to smell the alcohol to see they were drunk, the tallest male in the middle cracking his neck from side to side.

I stilled, wondering why they were hanging around so close to the castle grounds, while I sized them up. I didn't know all the horde soldiers personally, but I spent enough time in the training hall to be able to recognize them, and these glowering faces were definitely new to me. So what did they want?

"Oi, Highn-ass!" the one in the middle yelled. He was a similar height to me, with a hardened face and shaggy, dark hair. He had a stocky build with shoulders for days and carrying some timber. A bear shifter. Well, fuck, this was going to be fun. Bears were pretty rare in the capital, preferring to live in the mountains further north.

So these jackasses knew I was a royal, and they were clearly pissed off at me. But why? I'd never met these males before. Maybe it was just a general hatred for high fae? The crown?

"You think you are better than us?" the slightly shorter male with a thick neck on the left called out as they neared. I instinctively reached for my sword, ready for them to charge at any moment, only to remember I'd not bothered carrying a weapon to my suit fitting. Well, unless you counted the one I'd nearly taken Burty's eye out with. So awkward.

I sniffed the air, and through the reek of stale ale and whisky I deciphered what the other halves of the two shifters flanking the grizzly fucker were. *Hyenas.*

I'd never fought a hyena before. They tended to be too excitable and untrustworthy to follow orders, and therefore weren't suitable for the discipline needed to be in the horde. But my father found other uses for them. Though I didn't know exactly what, I imagined he kept them around to carry out other dirty work when he didn't want to get his own hands dirty or send an entire army.

"Where are your lackeys this time, Prince Eli-cunt?" the bigger of the two hyenas taunted, his hand reaching for something concealed inside his jacket while I planted my feet wide, ready for anything.

But shit, that was actually kinda funny. Just a shame I had no idea what the fuck my brother had done to piss these bastards off so thoroughly. Why did I have to share a face with him?

"Look, I don't know what the fuck your talking abou–" I was cut off as a bottle sailed through the air, aimed at my head. I ducked to avoid it, hearing it smash against the tree behind me as I straightened. "You've got the wrong pr–"

"Shut up! Just 'cause you're royalty doesn't make you better than us!" the bear growled, only a few meters between us now, and I clenched my fists.

We were far enough from the castle walls for the wards to not have any effect on their shift here, right on the outer edge of the forested area where the hordes' shifters came to run free. But it was only the four of us out here right now.

I'd need to be careful to stay out of reach of the bear's claws, they were particularly deadly. I couldn't decide whether I'd rather fight him when he was partially shifted or full bruin. As for the hyenas, they would be nearly impossible to predict, but I was looking forward to it.

It was times like these when I was glad I'd trained regularly with a shifter most of my life. Not just any shifter, but a true savage with a sharp brain made for strategy and war. I knew all about their weight distribution, how to fight against one partially shifted, their strengths and weaknesses, and most importantly, how to keep myself alive.

"You should leave now, while you have the chance," I gritted, righting my stance.

Unfortunately, my warning fell on deaf ears as the leader of the group just laughed, nodded to his friends, and launched their attack.

CHAPTER 36

Evangelia

I was curled up in my usual spot in the library, clutching my knees tightly to my chest, but the flames failed to warm the ice in my bones. My original plan to escape into another world was proving impossible, as the pages weren't enough to calm the rolling of my stomach. Not even the memories of this room seemed to be able to chase the dread away tonight.

Claustrophobia held me tightly in its clutches as thoughts of self-doubt assaulted me more than usual, but I couldn't let the idea of my impending wedding scare me from my course. Only, all my life, it had been drilled into me to run from danger and not look back. Remaining cooped up in the castle, biding my time when I probably knew it well enough now to break free, was completely unnatural.

Dragging myself to my feet, I moved to the window for some fresh air, figuring it might help ease the feeling of suffocating. I took a few rasping breaths and tried to center myself, but was distracted by muffled voices off in the distance.

The expansive grounds were always quiet at this time of night, but over toward the trees lining the forest, three dark figures headed toward a lone male. Their silhouettes highlighted by the moonlight in the clear sky.

Listening intently, not even my shifter hearing was sharp enough to make out the exact words, but I would know that voice anywhere. Kane.

Frowning, I watched the hulking figures stalk closer toward him, their words also fuzzy, but the tone aggressive as I noticed Kane's stance change. Was he readying for a fight?

The group stilled for a moment, and unease prickled over my skin. Without warning, they launched as one, barreling into the shadow of the forest, and I lost sight of my prince. *Shit.*

I needed to help him, but from what I could tell, they were big males, far bigger than me, and I didn't have any weapons.

Nodding to myself as I settled on a plan, I sprinted for Alaric's chambers. I'd never been inside his rooms before, but I knew it was the door next to Kane's.

I reached for the handle, not wasting time with knocking, but the door didn't budge. I slammed my palm against the hardwood repeatedly, my breaths coming quicker as panic crept up my spine. "Alaric! Alaric are you in there? Come quick, Kane needs us!"

The door swung wide, as the huge male filled the doorway looking like he'd just been in the middle of a bath. One look at my ashen face, he quickly pulled me inside so he could start drying off. I tried to keep my eyes from his brawn and focus on why I was here. No matter how much I wanted to see below that tiny towel.

"Start fuckin' talkin', Angel," he growled, skipping underwear and pulling on some leathers.

I tried to keep it short as I was drowning in worry that Kane could be fighting for his life. Every second counted so I couldn't mince my words. "I was in the library and went to the window for some air. There were three figures approaching a lone fae on the edge of the forest. I didn't recognize them, but I heard Kane's voice. Then they attacked, and I lost sight of him as they disappeared into the trees. We need to go, quick!"

"Were they armed?"

"Not that I could see but–"

"Alright."

"Did you not hear me? Kane is being attacked! Right now! I would recognize his voice anywhere, it was him! We have to help him! Why aren't you more worried? Did you have something to do with this?"

He'd finished dressing and stalked toward me, driving me backwards until my back hit the wood of the door. His scent was intoxicating, and there was barely an inch between us. He towered over me, his arm reached up and leaned on the door, caging me in. "Calm the fuck down, Angel. Firstly, if yeh think I had anythin' to do with Kane bein' attacked, then yeh dinnae fuckin' ken me at all," he growled in my face, holding up a single finger, then a second joined it. "Secondly, he can look after himself, three males are a lot to handle, especially if he's not armed, but dinnae fuckin' underestimate that male. I trained him myself. Lastly, an' most importantly, if yeh're comin' with me, then yeh better promise me yeh will do exactly as I say an' not race in there."

"But what if he needs help?"

He growled. "Promise me or I'm lockin' yer fine arse in here, an' I'm goin' on my own."

"Fine," I begrudgingly agreed, and he nodded, pulling the door I was pressed against open and sweeping past. I followed in silence as he led the way with his long strides until we reached the rear entrance to the castle. I pointed out where I'd last seen Kane, and we took off across the frozen lawn in a sprint. I silently thanked the fates for the running we'd done together.

As we approached the tree line, Alaric held out an arm to stop me and held a finger to his lips. Concentrating intently. I held my breath, listening for sounds that told me where Kane might be.

Grunts were coming from further inside the thicket of trees, and Alaric waved me forward as we crept in, crouching low and treading carefully over the frost coated leaves. We were silent on our approach, the shadows ahead of us moving around.

I moved to get a closer look, but before I could get far, I was pulled tight to his chest as he ducked behind a wide tree. I looked up at him, his warmth surrounding me in a protective blanket despite Kane being in danger.

The sounds of fighting reached my ears, heavy breathing and even heavier hits. The crisp winter air crystallized around me as my breaths grew more panicked. I tried to crawl away, Kane needed help–

Alaric placed a surprisingly gentle hand on my arm and shook his head. I sighed, but turned my attention back to the scuffle, just in time to find the largest of the three had shifted into a massive fucking bear.

Terror overwhelmed me, heightened further as his two companions shifted into hyenas. Surely Alaric wasn't going to let him fight them alone in their shifted forms? Just as I opened my mouth, the bear charged, and Kane, the cheeky and fun loving prince I had come to know, grappled with the massive beast, lifting him off the forest floor to throw him across the clearing.

A strangled sound escaped my throat. There were shifters out there who wouldn't have managed such a feat. It was terrifying, and yet also incredibly sexy. Kane's head swiveled to where I was being held by Alaric behind the tree, his large hand smothering my mouth.

The wolf had scooped me up and pulled me into his embrace the moment the sound left me. His scent calmed me somewhat, though my heart still pounded erratically against my ribs. Kane had to know we were here. I peeked out to see his stare still fixed on our tree. His eyes narrowed in suspicion as his nostrils flared as if he were scenting us.

Finally, he returned his focus to the fight at hand as one of the hyenas leapt at him. Its deadly jaws snapping in his face as he wrestled it. I wanted to yell out when I saw him stumble over something on the ground and lose his balance, throwing him onto his back. What was that littering the undergrowth Kane was trying to navigate?

Alaric tugged me back again, sensing I was a distraction for our fighter. I glared at him, which he returned tenfold. I didn't know for sure if he understood the silent challenge and *fuck you* in my eyes, but if his eye roll was anything to go by, he got it loud and clear.

I shifted a little, unable to see the fighting anymore, but my focus landed on whatever had caused Kane to lose his balance. My eyes narrowed on it, it was a mutilated corpse. I had seen something similar in the Fading Vale. Thrakos kills were unmistakable. What the fates were thrakos doing this close to the capital?

My mind was abuzz with thoughts of finding them. Maybe I could form a plan with them to take out the king? An alliance. I already had a witch and warlock who'd offered their aid, but thrakos would be a game changer.

"Hah!" I was broken out of my musing by an unknown voice. "Look boys, it isn't even Eli-cunt. It's the fucking waste-of-space spare that sleeps his way through everyone's wives," the bear shifter accused. The hyenas, still in their shifted forms, barked and snorted in what I assumed was supposed to be laughter. "Your brother humiliated us at the tavern tonight, and you will pay for his wrongs in blood!"

Alaric's grip tightened on me, holding my back to his chest, and stopped me from spinning around to see the asshole who dared taunt my male. As the minutes ticked on, there were more grunts of fighting, more scuffling, some whimpers, sickening crunches of fists meeting flesh and breaking of bones.

Not knowing what was happening was killing me, especially as Alaric was free to look over his shoulder and wouldn't be missing a thing. I sighed. I had to trust him that Kane didn't need our help.

Just as I started wiggling again to get out of Alaric's arms, a strong voice sounded, "I told you already!"

My breath stuttered to a halt as I realized the voice belonged to Kane. Only, he sounded fine, no, more than fine. His voice was powerful, with a cruel edge to it I'd never heard before. Fates only knew how, but he must have gotten the upper hand. Now that he did, what would he do about it? He couldn't... he wouldn't... *would* he? I renewed my efforts to free myself. I had to stop him–

"Angel, stop," Alaric growled in my ear as his grip tightened around me further. Was he really going to let this happen? My heart pounded as I heard shuffling across the frozen ground.

"Get out of here," Kane thundered. "Be thankful I am not my brother or the king. Keep your lives and call it a mercy that I let you leave! Now GO!"

Alaric finally freed me as I peeked out again from behind the tree. Kane stood in the clearing, the moonlight outlining his silhouette. His back was to us, fists clenched at his sides as he looked down to his right at the pile of huge beasts on the ground. I couldn't make out much, but the highlighted lines of his face were contorted in fury.

As they desperately crawled and clambered over each other to escape, Kane looked every inch an avenger sent by the fates themselves. He had never looked more terrifying to me than in that moment, nor more beautiful. He was breathtaking, and he was fighting everything that had to have been drilled into him from the moment he was born to show these wastes of space mercy.

Something cemented in my mind at that moment. He was mine. And I could only hope Alaric agreed to be mine too.

But first I had to marry Elikai. If nothing else, it would at least buy me more time with these incredible males.

"I know you're there," Kane's voice rang out. When Alaric finally let go of me and we faced him in his victory, I realized that Alaric had been testing him.

As the General, he should have gone in and saved the prince from getting his hands dirty, torn those shifters limb from limb in retaliation for lifting a hand against a prince of the realm. But he hadn't. In those moments while I waited to see what Kane was going to do with his upper hand, Alaric had been waiting with bated breath, too.

But why?

CHAPTER 37

Alaric

I leaned against the frame of the castle entryway, staring down the steps to the courtyard as the crisp wind howled, dread weighing heavy in my gut for the day ahead.

Witches and warlocks were milling around below, their arms dancing through the air as they hung bunting with their spells. Onyx flags strung together with the finest silver silk webs, caringly weaved by the spider folk, draped from one side of the courtyard to the other in zigzags. The effect was breathtaking and succeeded in making the castle look like a much happier place than it really was.

"The package arrived late last night from Rangaran as a thank you for helping with getting their production back up and running, or so Westly tells me. I was kind of busy..." Kane's voice said from my side as he joined me. No shit, he'd been busy. "But as far as Elikai and my father are concerned, it was a wedding gift, nothing more."

I nodded, crossing my arms across my chest as I saw four shifters struggling with the weight of a giant clothed tower, which I could only assume was the cake.

I was so fucking proud of how he'd dealt with the spider and then those thugs last night, but I couldn't tell him why. Not yet. It was so fucking important, but it wasn't urgent. I needed a clearer sign from the fates first, but what that would be I had no fucking clue. *Elusive cunts.*

He wasn't quite ready to hear what I had to tell him, though. I knew that much. But he would be. Just as soon as I got this six-month trip terrorizing the villages of Dezrothia out of the way. I grimaced at the thought that I would be leaving the very next day to do just that.

Regardless, I'd spent the last few nights debating whether I should break my word to Angel and tell Kane what I'd learned that evening in the solar room. I had decided I needed to tell him before this sham of a wedding could happen.

How I felt personally about the female getting married today didn't hold any weight. But Kane. Prince Nekane. He was a worthy male for her, and I could tell they would make each other happy.

She would help him grow, sharing her experiences from her upbringing in the Vale to keep him grounded, while he would treat her like his queen. I had no doubt, even if it would kill me to not be a part of it. I was already dead inside, and the flicker in my chest would soon be stunted with the atrocities I'd commit on this next trip.

If only Kane wasn't still racked with guilt over his feelings for Angel—with his brother having claimed her as his bride and having no idea of what had been going on —I wondered whether he would do something more drastic to end this wedding. Claim her himself.

I knew what Angel had told me would give him that push. Sating his lust was one thing, but I knew from the day in the library that he had already succumbed and only fallen harder. My theory of him fucking her out of his system was long forgotten.

The problem was, if I told him and he acted on his emotions, then they could both end up on the execution block.

Fuck, what was the answer to the fucking dilemma?

"Breakfast?" Kane asked, giving me a smile so small his dimples didn't even appear. Defeat seemed to hang heavy, and it didn't suit him.

I lost the little appetite I had when I saw who greeted us in the small room. "Angel?" My steps halted in the doorway as I took in her complexion. She was the palest shade of green.

"Are you okay, princess?" Kane asked, but he had to know it was a stupid question. An idiot could see she really didn't look well.

"Morning... Yeah, I'm fine... I think," she answered, staring at her fruit as she pushed it around the bowl, her fork visibly shaking in her hand, but I didn't miss her giving Kane a once over after last night's fight.

"I'm so sorry." Kane said earnestly, sitting down next to her and grabbing her free hand while I went to find a bottle of something strong and a few shot glasses. "You are miserable, and I'm to blame for not knowing how to talk to my own brother without making things worse. We should have gotten you out of here..."

"Why would you even think that, Kane? This isn't your fault. You have to know that. And getting out of here would be impossible. The horde are out in force, security is tight and fae are already arriving at the castle. Besides, I chose to stay."

I was the one who had failed her. She had opened up to me, and I'd been so fucking stuck between saving her and what I'd been working toward for over three centuries that I hadn't been able to choose her.

She looked up at me, making eye contact before she continued. Addressing both of us this time. "I'm marrying Elikai... And as much as I don't want to, there are worse fates." She gulped and forced a smile, though it didn't meet her eyes. "Trust me when I tell you the fates can be far crueler than this. Honestly, I feel like I'm here and all of this is happening for a reason. I just have to trust that this is my path..." She swallowed hard, her eyes back to the bowl of fruit as she continued prodding at it.

I let out a sigh. Kane looked lost. Angel was putting on a brave face, but it was bullshit, and I could tell she had no intention of coming clean to Kane as she had to me. *Today would surely kill me.*

I could feel their pain and despair clearer than I'd ever felt my own. Every time I tried to picture my Angel walking down the aisle, or Kane's face as he watched it, something primal inside me screamed how wrong it was, but it was too late.

"If he tries anything, tonight I mean, if he puts his hands on you and you still don't want it, come to me and I swear I will protect you," Kane told her earnestly, and I knew he meant every word. He would take on Elikai's wrath if he tried to touch her like that, but only if he was sure she didn't want it. And so far, she'd only told him that she had cold feet.

"What else were yeh plannin' to tell him?" I asked. "It's a miracle he's waited this long..."

Silence enveloped the room while she pondered, and I knocked back a shot. "I could tell him it's my time, that I'm bleeding."

A growl suddenly cut through the room, and I realized it was coming from me. I quickly tried to cover it with a cough, making out like the whisky had been too strong or gone down the wrong way, but Kane would see through it.

"Yer gonnae tell him yer goin' into heat?" I ground out, pouring a shot for all of us this time and handing them out. We didn't waste a second knocking them back, and I saw Angel shudder as she swallowed hers, probably not as used to drinking spirits as me and Kane were, or maybe it was nerves.

The idea that she was going to tell him she was going into heat would be the worst possible idea. Especially after Elikai told her that he wanted to put a babe in her. It would only make him relentless in his pursuit.

"Eve– Umm, I mean, milady?" Thalia's sweet voice interrupted from the doorway. "It's time to get you ready for the ceremony."

We all knew what today was, but it suddenly felt all the more real. "Well, let's get one last shot in. Come here Thalia, yer doin' one too," I said, grabbing a fourth glass and pouring us all a drink.

"Here's to makin' it through the day," I said, as they all raised their glasses and chorused the words.

The females eventually left, and it was just me and Kane. The powerful male looked broken, reminding me of the boy he'd been all those years ago. I had to tell him her secrets. It was the only way. I just needed to make sure he didn't bolt off after Elikai and ruin everything. Fates, I'd wanted to.

"Kane, let's go for a walk," I told him, and he nodded, following me out of the room.

"I'm the worst person," he started, and I recognized the spiral he was about to go down. "My brother met her first, and she agreed to marry him. Though he can be a total asshole, and I'm done looking at him with rose-tinted glasses, I shouldn't have let things get this far. I think I lo–"

"General Alaric," Westly's voice called from ahead of us, cutting off whatever Kane was about to tell me. "The king wants you guarding his quarters–"

"Boss," Axel called from behind us a beat later, sweating like he'd just run all over the castle looking for me. "The king has summoned you to guard his chambers, said you should know to be there personally on a day like today. He's pissed," he told me warily, rubbing the back of his neck and eyeing me apologetically. *Fuck.*

I pulled Kane into a hug and dropped my voice. "Listen. There's somethin' I need to tell yeh. About her. But it'll have to wait for now. It's important that yeh keep a straight head today though, an' I'll speak to yeh in a bit. Alrigh'?" I said, pulling away and taking hold of his arms. He just nodded, still looking dejected.

I turned to go and guard the king whose arsehole was clearly twitching, knowing he was a royal cunt and there were lots of fae in the castle today who agreed and would see it as an opportunity to strike.

CHAPTER 38
Nekane

I was stood in front of the floor-length mirror when Westly came in to check on me, ensuring I was wearing my attire properly as he immediately busied himself by smoothing my shirt down under the waistcoat. Not that it fucking mattered.

The black shirt, white tie, and golden waistcoat combo actually looked amazing. The tie had a delicate fleur-de-lis stitched into it, and when it caught the sunlight, it gleamed with what I was sure was real golden thread.

Burton had done an amazing job, despite the faux pas I refused to think about ever again. It fit me like a glove, and I hoped it would help cement the mask I needed to wear to get through today, protecting my heart that had finally started to beat with purpose.

I couldn't help but think that if this was what I was wearing, then what in the fates would Elikai show up in? He was nothing if not extravagant, and why would his wedding be any different? My bet was a full golden suit or some shit.

Westly stood behind me, holding the matching black jacket open for me to allow him to pull it up so that it sat properly. He moved away for a moment before returning with the ceremonial sword I was to wear. It was a symbol of my royalty, and a surprising addition to the outfit considering my father's hatred of me, but I supposed keeping up appearances was required even for that mad old asshole.

Once Westly had decided that I looked the part, he finally let me escape my rooms and get to where I wanted to be. With Eva. Alaric had said he had something to tell me about her, but he was tied up watching my father's back, so maybe she'd just tell me herself.

I knocked on the door once, knowing Kai wouldn't be around, and entered. It reminded me of the day she'd arrived just weeks ago, and it was a pretty similar scenario.

My gaze was drawn to her immediately. Everything else disappeared, and at the sight I forgot how to breathe, let alone why I was here.

She was a vision.

The white dress was off the shoulders, exposing her collarbones, and beautifully fitted to her curves all the way down to her knees where it flared.

It was when she turned to look at me that I noticed it was intricately beaded with golden accents, sparkling in the ray of sun that lit her up even more like a spotlight. The train was being pulled out behind her by Thalia, as I stood gawking. It had to be twice as long as Eva was tall.

Her hair was pulled into an updo with small tendrils curling down, exposing her neck. A delicate tiara glistened in the light.

She'd been beautiful before, didn't need any makeup, dresses or jewels to hold your attention, but now she was a goddess, absolutely ethereal, her beauty enrapturing.

Never had I wanted to claim her more than at this moment. "You... you're... Wow... just wow." In my life, I had not once been unable to find words when talking to a female, but I couldn't form a single sentence to even attempt telling her how I felt about her.

"You look pretty good yourself," she smiled sadly, and Thalia gave a short bow before leaving us alone. "Where's Alaric?"

"He got called away to guard duties, but I doubt he'd do any better finding the words right now." I closed the space between us, tucking a loose curl behind her ear. "How I want to just steal you away..." I told her truthfully, capturing her face gently in my hands.

"You know, that doesn't sound so bad. Think you can cover my tracks in this dress?" She managed a grin as her hands came up to rest on my chest.

"Fuck, if only I could. You are the most captivating being I've ever met, you know that?" I told her, watching as a blush spread across her cheeks.

"Kane... I... I have been meaning to tell you something for some time now, and I guess now could well be my last chance."

"Tell me what?"

"I wish... I wish it had been you that found me that day in the Vale," she whispered, and I dropped my forehead to hers. The comfort I felt doing so was incredible. It was just as warming as when Alaric had done it to me not so long ago.

"I need to talk to Kai. I have to convince him to call off the wedding without repercussions. I don't know how, but I know I can't let you marry him. I want you so fucking much, I can't bear it." I locked my eyes with hers, letting her see into my soul so there wouldn't be any doubt in her mind that my next words were the truth. "You are mine, princess. You know that, right? It doesn't matter what happens, or if you leave this place and I never see you again. You will always be mine," I murmured against her lips, it was taking everything in me not to kiss her. I didn't think I could stop if I did.

But she took the extra step for me, pressing her lips to mine in a short, sweet kiss. The smile she gave me when she pulled back was blinding. I closed the gap again, kissing her slowly, savoring every moment, and she melted into me.

Even if it was filled with anxiety and a future so unknown, she owned my heart.

There was only one other being I allowed this close to me, and he had been my confidant for years, closer now than ever thanks to this female, kissing me back with longing.

If only this was our day… That I was breaking tradition because I couldn't resist her siren's call for one last kiss before I met her down that aisle.

She was every bit the enchantress, but I couldn't find it in me to be mad about it anymore. I forced myself to step away from her before I got carried away and showed her exactly how much she meant to me. It was time to confront my brother.

"I'll be back for you, princess," I'd told her before making my way to the top floor of the castle. The king's quarters, where I knew Elikai would be. This chat was long overdue.

"KANE, yeh ken yeh shouldnae be here," Alaric growled as I approached the door he guarded. I'd known he would be here, but would he really stop me?

"I have to talk to him. You, of all fae, should understand. Whatever it is we have with that female down there, it's deeper than anything I can describe with words." When he still didn't move an inch, I carried on. "You feel it too, Alaric, I can see it. You just have centuries more experience than I at masking your emotions. Would it kill you to let your guard down for once in your life to feel something that is real? We can't let her go through with this when we know it will make her miserable!" I saw Krista approaching and used the opportunity to brush past him, knowing he wouldn't say anything on the matter with others around to listen.

"Kane…" Alaric warned, but he didn't stop me as I stepped into the room.

The first thing I saw was that I'd been right about my brother's golden suit. I had to resist shielding my eyes as he turned to face me and the sun caught the gleaming strands. He wore his suit with a black waistcoat, completely opposite to me, apart from his tie. His own ceremonial sword lay discarded on the ottoman.

"Brother," I started, making my presence known. "I need to talk with you." A weird sense of foreboding sent a chill prickling down my spine, but I shook it off.

Once upon a time, I would have known how he would react to what I was about to say, or at least had an idea. But now? I had no fucking clue, but it wouldn't be good.

"What is it, Nekane? I don't have time for casual conversation," he said, dismissing me, and I knew that this was going to go down like a sack of potatoes.

"Elikai. It's the wedding I'm here to talk to you about. You can't marry–" I started, but our father chose that moment to storm into the room.

He pulled a face like he'd just eaten something sour when his eyes landed on me. "Nekane, shut up and get out. Nobody invited you here. Nobody wants you here, and nobody cares about what you have to say." He spat venom with every word. "If you're bored, perhaps you could think about how you ruined our lives when you killed my wife. Your own mother!" he snapped viciously. I knew that he was itching for a fight, but this was important, and I refused to let the memories of being a boy at his mercy suffocate me.

"No! You fucking get out! I am here to talk to my brother. If my presence offends you, then be my guest and remove yourself from it!" I growled back, only for him to strike me across the face. Predictable, but no less painful. I noticed Elikai watching with fascination, making no effort to diffuse the situation.

"Insolent boy. You're not a very fast learner. Do I need to teach you another lesson?" he threatened, but I'd had enough.

"Just try it, Father," I spat at him. "Just fucking try–"

He lunged for me, and I sidestepped it. Elikai stood in place, assessing his appearance as my father and I began to brawl. Despite what he believed, I was, in fact, a quick study and knew to be cautious of any jewelry he wore, not willing to fall for that awful, paralyzing trick twice.

My eyes widened when he reached for my brother's sword from the ottoman. He'd never turned such a weapon on me before. Hadn't been able to trust himself not to kill me in his rage.

He wouldn't have cared, but it would have brought questions he didn't care to deal with to his gates. I pulled my own sword from its dark sheath to parry the swing, and my gut told me today was the day I had to fight my own father for my life.

These swords weren't just for show. They were just as sharp and well-forged as any other sword. Possibly more so as nothing but the best would do for the King of Dezrothia, and they'd never seen a day's battle to have blunted.

Their beautiful detailing was just a mask to deter your attention from their deadliness. My twin and I had swords that were complete opposites, and the irony again wasn't lost on me, knowing what I did now about him; mine was black with onyx and rubies adorning the hilt, where his was silver with sapphires and opals.

I risked a glance back at Elikai, who still made no attempt to help, even with the clangs of our swords clattering together. I was certain to never go on the offensive, knowing I just needed to tire the king, make him sloppy and disarm him at the first chance.

I sent another desperate glance to my brother, who was now watching us with interest. When did he become such an asshole? Probably while I was drowning my sorrows and burying my head in random pussy, or cock, at the Crooked Claw.

I knew he'd known about the beatings I'd regularly suffered through the years, but I always assumed that... what? He kept his mouth shut to save himself? That sounded like the sly, arrogant male my brother was turning out to be.

I risked another glance in his direction, and the way he was watching us sent a tremor down my spine.

It was a mistake to allow myself to be distracted. Father knocked my guard open and moved to lunge with the hope of spearing me on the end of the sword. I moved out of the way just in time, jumping around to his back. I didn't know how long I could keep up just defending myself when the king looked to have murder on his mind.

He wasn't tiring quickly enough. I had to change my tactics if I was going to walk away from here alive, and now I had someone to live for, multiple fae waiting for me, so I did what I had to.

I went on the offensive for the first time in this battle of bastards, attacking him over and over, breaking his resolve and strength blow by blow, as he continued to block my strikes with flashes of silver.

Finally, he was tiring, his defensive blocks losing their strength, and I knew he was likely about to submit. I was going to win, and I could almost taste the victory in the air.

He moved in a last-ditch attempt to lunge at me, sweat beading on his brow, face reddened in exhaustion as I retreated a few paces to dodge his sloppy swordsmanship.

A foreign grip tugged my arm, firm and fast, distracting my attention for a split second as it met resistance, and everything slowed.

All oxygen was vanquished from the room as I looked up to see my sword sinking through the king's flesh, inch by inch. My fingers and toes went completely numb as it kept going, slicing straight through his chest. I felt physically sick as I realized there was no way the blade would have missed his heart. Not from this angle. Not at such close proximity. It was a deadly wound intended to kill, even an immortal.

His mouth widened in a silent scream, the silver sword he'd held clattering to the ground as I struggled to find air to fill my lungs. His eyes trailed my arm to the hand which had manipulated me into driving my own sword through him.

I followed the same line as his dying eyes and saw the golden sleeve of my twin's suit.

He was gripping my forearm, his knuckles white as his other hand was wrapped around my own. I didn't need to see his face to know it would be showing the opposite reaction to mine.

I squeezed my eyes shut in disbelief, unable to fathom what was happening, but the thud of our father's body hitting the floor pulled me back into razor sharp focus. The world around me sped up again the moment I looked my identical twin in the eyes, the same eyes that looked back at me in the mirror. I shook my head, my mouth gaping wide. I didn't recognize him.

His eyes were crazed and filled with a traitorously triumphant gleam. He looked down at our father's body convulsing on the floor, blood gurgling in his throat, before he let out a low rattle, took his last breath and stopped moving entirely.

"No, no, no, no, no. Kai? Dad? What… What? I… he… he was tiring, he was going to submit…"

I'd killed my own father.

Alaric rushed in, his eyes darting frantically from me, my bloodied sword, Elikai who was now standing several paces back from the gruesome scene, not a hair out of place, and the king dead on the floor.

"What the fuck have yeh done…" Alaric breathed, before sinking to his knees, his head hanging low in defeat.

The king was dead.

Long live the king.

PART TWO
Princes of Prophecy

CHAPTER 1

Alaric

Act first and ask the fates for forgiveness later.

The concept wasn't new to me. Fuck, it'd been my modus operandi for as long as I could recall. Far too long for me to consider wasting time with prayers to save my soul, anyway.

Could there be another way to deal with this? Possibly. Was it worth the risk of wasting time to figure it out? Absolutely fucking not.

Crouched over my former puppeteers' not yet cooled corpse, I was more than ready; I was willing and looking forward to channeling the rage coursing through me into doing what needed to be done.

Some might argue with themselves, might need time to convince their head, their heart, and their soul that it was for the greater good first. But not me.

I knew full well I wouldn't be able to wash the blood from my hands anytime soon. Just like how I knew it would likely haunt me. But there was no self doubt. No hope for another way. No internal debate about whether it's right or wrong. Whether I should or shouldn't. It just was. I would deal with it.

For the crown.

For the realm.

For *him*.

I tore my eyes away from Kane and surveyed the room from my position.

Kneeling beside the dead king, the metallic scent of blood was almost overwhelming as I eyed the windows the thrakos had most likely come through.

His wide wings shattered the panes of glass into a thousand glittering fragments as he forcefully plunged himself to where the king had slept soundly for so many years.

I could almost hear the smash, followed by the thud of heavy boots as they slammed down on the shard-littered floor with a crunch.

I could see the body of his majesty, his chest mutilated where the thrakos had thrust its clawed hand through his flesh and ripped out his heart.

I could smell the crimson pool where the innocent bystander lay, having only made it a few steps into the room before their fate was also sealed.

Then me.

Deep, red liquid dripped down my already savaged face while defensive cuts down my arm caused blood to drip at my side.

This would become our new reality. Soon.

"Tell him. Admit to Alaric what you did!" Kane hissed, cutting through my thoughts and bringing me back to *this* reality.

The one where it looked like Kane had just slain his father. His black ceremonial sword–the one that so many castle folk would have witnessed him carrying on the way here–was discarded next to the body and coated in the King's lifeblood.

"No can do, I'm afraid, little brother," Elikai's smarmy voice followed in reply, completely unaffected by the death of his father. "We can't have you two spinning tales of how I played any part in the unfortunate demise of the King, now can we? No matter how *small* that part may have been."

I glared up just in time to see him pressing his forefinger and thumb together patronizingly.

That fucking cunt.

My fists clenched and my teeth gritted, as he cemented what I already suspected to be true the second I'd entered the massacre that was the king's chambers. Well, former king. He'd orchestrated this mess and was now pinning it on Kane.

Anger heated my veins like molten lava as my blood boiled, the pressure rising to the surface, threatening to erupt and spill over with Elikai in the volcano's path. I'd get the full story later. There was no time now. But there was no doubt in my mind that was what was happening.

It was true that Kane hated his father, but he was only here right now for *her*.

He had planned on talking Elikai out of marrying our Angel, not slaughtering the King. Cold-blooded murder wasn't his style. He fought hard, but fair and honorably. I, however, didn't have an ounce of that innocence left in me.

"Elikai–" Kane started, his own anger bubbling below the surface, but it mixed with a tone of astonishment and disbelief as the truth of the evilness that dwelled beneath his twin's charming facade sunk in once and for all. As though he was surprised that someone so like him could be so different.

"Nekane, might I offer some big brotherly advice? Perhaps, and this is just a suggestion, you should spend more time working out how to make father's death look like an attack from someone who *isn't* his own traitorous flesh and blood, and less time here reminding me of how it's all your fault that I am now but a grieving orphan. First mother, now–"

My lips pulled back in a snarl that I couldn't fight. Fates how I wished I could murder him right here and now. Instead I growled, "Dont yeh fuckin' dare finish that sentence, it's fuckin' bullshit and yeh ken it!"

If there was any way in which I could fashion this to implicate that prick, I would.

Unfortunately, I'd already determined that there was no way to twist this scene to stop him from worming his way out of it. It pained me to admit it, but whatever he'd done and however he'd done it, he had played it smart and kept his hands squeaky clean.

The scenario I had conjured in my mind would at least help Kane though, which would do for now. Even if it meant costing me my reputation. And I would.

For *him*.

I ignored the two high fae arguing with each other in favor of visualizing the steps I would take the moment Elikai fled.

I'd watched the princeling for long enough to know that as soon as he was through with torturing his brother, he would leave us with the cleanup. He'd said as much already.

I glanced toward the three windows lining the wall to my left, noting that I would need to sacrifice the one furthest from the body to make it believable.

If it had been the window closest to where the King now lay, someone would notice the lack of glass present beneath him. It made no sense for him to fall before the intruder had entered, after all.

With that decided, it left the other guard, Krista, who I had ordered to remain outside when I'd heard the commotion.

She was a good warrior with a lot of potential, and she unwaveringly listened to my command. But there was only so long before she would charge in here, concerned that I hadn't returned to my place beside her on guard yet.

I pulled out of my musings once more when I saw Elikai take a gold hued handkerchief from his suit pocket and methodically use it to pick up Kane's sword, which lay on the opposite side of the body to where I was.

What he said next was something I'd been a fuckin' fool for not foreseeing, but he was already backing away, his free hand on the door handle, ready to leave at a second's notice.

"I think I will keep a hold of this for the foreseeable future," he told Kane, carefully moving the arm holding the sword so it was concealed just under the cover of his open suit jacket.

What little color remained in Kane's face disappeared as he gaped in shock. I practically saw the cogs working in his brain as he realized, too late, that his sick brother wasn't done with his twisted games.

"I am a busy male, and something tells me I am about to become even busier. So, whatever you are planning to do to cover up this mess, get on with it quickly." His hand on the door handle turned the knob, but he wasn't finished, "Oh, by the way, don't worry about me. I will be sure to look the epitome of shock and grief when news breaks of our father's tragic passing, as is proper for the next in line."

With a smile sickly enough to reintroduce you to the eggs you ate for breakfast, he disappeared through the door.

"What the fuck..." Kane breathed, dragging a hand through his raven black hair while his eyes darted between the door, his late father and me. "I swear, I didn't–"

I cut him off. "I already ken yeh didn't." Now wasn't the time or place to discuss it.

"Listen to me, Kane. Yeh need to get outtae here." I ordered. "I'll sort this mess out so it'll no' come back to yeh–"

Knock, knock, knock.

"Sir, is everything okay?" Krista called. *Fuck.* We were out of time.

"Aye." I called back to her, then looked up at Kane again, my expression leaving no question over how serious I was. "Yeh need to get that sword back from yer brother, so fuckin' move."

He was breaking, but I couldn't offer him the comfort he needed. Not yet.

Time wasn't on our side and if I was diverted from my plan in order to be the shoulder he needed, it could be the difference between us succeeding to get out of the corner his sick brother had backed us into, and losing our heads.

So, I had to be his childhood tutor instead right now, barking instructions with every expectation that he followed them.

If Kane had questions, which I'm sure he did, he didn't voice them as he stared hard at me through his glassy, but no less piercing, blue eyes and nodded. *Good.*

Soon he would know what I had planned to save his arse. And one day he would realize that this was for the best. I couldn't afford for him to be implicated in this. Too much was at stake. I couldn't let him take the fall.

I moved so that my back was facing Kane and rolled up the sleeve of my uniform, covering my right arm. "Oh, an' send Krista in." I called after him as an afterthought, steadying myself to do what needed to be done.

The moment Kane's footsteps left the room and the door slammed in his wake, I shifted. Only partially. Just enough to grow claws, but still it was plenty for the ward alarms to be triggered to blare.

I didn't waste a moment as I plunged the claws of my beast straight into the King's chest. Gripping the cold, blackened heart, I yanked it out easily.

"Alaric–" Krista gasped over the racket, her honey eyes wide as she processed what she was seeing. Her King's heart. In *my* hand.

I could have left it at that. Taken the fall. But I'd worked too damned long and hard to give it all up just like that. And Kane needed me more than ever.

For *him.*

Wearing a mask of coldness, I dropped the heart with a squelch, then stood and began moving, calmly but swiftly, toward her, using her shock to my advantage.

Leaning in close to her frozen form, I purred in her ear. "I wish I could say I'm sorry for this."

"For wha-" But I cut her question short.

Where words were supposed to come out, it was blood filling her throat instead as her mouth flapped open and closed around the pooling blood.

Her eyes widened in horror. My fist was inside her chest and I could feel the pulsing of her life in my hand for the briefest moment before I snuffed it out and she crumpled on the floor.

Without so much as a glance at her lifeless body, I moved to the windows across from the gruesome scene. I was running out of time.

The wards were still blaring, and I knew that a herd of horde soldiers would already be running up the stairs by now, making their way to this very room.

I took a decorative marble bust with me as I stepped onto the balcony; accessed through the oak and glass doors between two of the windows.

With my clean, albeit slightly weaker arm, I adjusted my grip on the heavy rock. I had one shot to throw this just right and then I could get the fuck out of here.

I took aim and held my breath, launching it at my target.

It felt like an age as it soared through the air, but in reality, it was only a blink before it found its mark and crashed through the window, back into the King's suite.

Exactly as I'd envisioned in my plan.

I released my breath and moved back inside, sliding the lock on the doors into place and was relieved to see that I was still the only breathing being in here. I replaced the surprisingly undamaged bust to its rightful place, ensuring that no one realized I used it in this fabrication.

Closing my eyes, I dragged the claws of my right hand down my scarred face, ignoring the sting. Then slashed randomly at my opposite arm and my chest several times for good measure, before letting go of the transformation.

I grimaced as my blood joined the pools already staining the floor.

The wounds were already knitting themselves back together as I looked down at my blood coated hand and forearm. I hadn't done what I did only to get caught red-handed. I grimaced at how literal that was, considering I had just plunged my fist into two chests already.

I rolled my sleeve back down to cover most of the King and Krista's blood, then gripped my self-inflicted scrapes to give the appearance that it was from my own injuries.

With the stage set, it was time to play the role of defeated general. I wouldn't lie; it grated at my pride, but, more important than that, it was the only way I could protect Kane.

The wards were still wailing in my ears as a group of the horde came barging into the room. Adrenaline fueled me to act the part, but my fucking emotions were putting up a fight as I tried to squash any feelings I might have over Krista's death deep down in the pit that I always stored such memories.

Now isn't the time to feel guilt.

"General Alaric, Sir wha–" the tall high fae soldier cut himself off as he took in the nightmare worthy, gory room. His breath caught in his throat as his eyes landed on one of the bodies. "The King!" He exclaimed, before quickly slamming a hand over his mouth when I held my bloodied hand up to quiet him.

I allowed the genuine anger and frustration at the whole fucking mess to seep into my voice as I launched into the tale that implicated an unknown thrakos for being single-handedly responsible for what they were seeing.

Blood everywhere.

Their King, dead.

Their colleague, dead.

Their general, beaten and bloodied.

I didn't mince my words, just recited the lies as if they were facts not to be argued with or questioned.

The thrakos were already villains in the Kingdom's eyes and so they were the perfect scapegoat to lay blame on. The King, or more accurately the late King, Augustus Regis, was notorious in his hunting of them. No one would be surprised that one came for revenge, and by the looks on the faces of the surrounding soldiers, they had completely fallen for it.

Then again, they had no reason to question my word.

I finished by barking my orders to them and the moment I heard their chorus of 'Yes, Sir's' over the roaring noise, I left; desperate for just a minute to myself before having to get the full story out of Kane of what had really happened. Then deal with how to turn today's fucking disaster around to benefit me.

Unsurprisingly, the ear-splitting sound of the ward alarms had already sparked utter chaos in the corridors, although word would not have reached their ears yet of their King's death.

It wasn't the fear of *knowing* that something had happened that set the civilians into a frenzy like this after all, but the *not knowing* what they were to fear yet that scared them so greatly. That an unknown threat could be lurking around any corner.

Every set of panicked eyes tried to meet mine as I pushed my way through the crowded halls towards my room, fear heightening when they noticed the blood and healing injuries.

I ignored every pleading look for answers as I passed. It wasn't my job to tell them about fucking anything. They'd find out soon enough, and when they did, the dark cloud of failure would follow my every move like a shadow as they fell for the lie that *I'd* woven.

Of the general who'd been unable to stop his monarch's demise from happening right under his nose, yet still breathed to tell the tale. Incapable. Weak. A failure. Lies I would gladly live with if it meant saving Kane from the beheading his brother had nearly caused, and now so easily hung over his head.

My jaw twitched as the headache throbbing across my temples gathered strength with my every step, my skull pounded vigorously and my control teetered on the edge.

It was getting harder to push down the beast's desire to fight, kill, maim... something.

I needed an outlet. I needed to get this blood off my skin and the events of what I'd just done suppressed like I did every time I had to do unforgivable things.

I could barely feel the pain of my self-inflicted injuries as the skin worked rapidly to knit itself together again. They'd leave my skin unblemished soon enough–aside from the permanent scar marring my face–as if they were never there.

But I'd know, I'd remember.

Plenty of witnesses had seen me wearing the forged wounds, so they'd served their purpose. Now I needed them gone; to stop the flashbacks, both centuries old and fresh ones.

I felt a pang in my chest and winced. *Krista.*

Her death had served a purpose too, my purpose. It had been little more than a means to an end, so why did it hurt? Why did I still see the horror and betrayal on her face as if it had imprinted onto my mind?

The alarms likely wouldn't be silenced by one of the warlocks responsible until they had completed a thorough search of the castle and grounds, a search they believed me to be a part of.

The hunt for an intruder that didn't exist could take a long fucking time, but I needed it to think straight again.

I had to rein in my out-of-control emotions, clean myself up, and find Kane.

Not necessarily in that order.

CHAPTER 2
Evangelia

Thalia's mouth was still moving, but whatever she was saying was muted as an almighty wail boomed throughout the room.

My palms flew to my ears like a shield, trying to protect me from the overwhelming noise. It didn't work. The shrill sound was so loud they would likely hear it in the Fading Vale.

Wincing, I looked back to Thalia and saw she was doing much of the same in spite of her not quite so sensitive witch hearing; clearly she felt like her ears were on the verge of bleeding, too.

What in fates name is making that noise?

Worry gripped me in place momentarily as my brain tried to function around the ear-splitting racket that held it hostage. The ward alarms. It had to be. But what had triggered them?

It was concern that fueled me back into action the moment one particular name came to mind.

Kane.

He'd left me here with a promise to speak to his brother. What had happened? Had something gone really wrong? *Shit shit shit.*

Of course it had gone wrong. He'd gone to speak to Elikai. About me! What had I been thinking, letting him go?!

My stomach churned as my imagination spewed out scenario after scenario of how the two things could be related. Realistically, there were probably a million other reasons that the alarms were howling, but I couldn't think past my panic for the male I'd selfishly sent on a suicide mission without proper thought first.

I should never have let him go. I should have talked him out of it. But I was selfish. I wanted out of this farce of a wedding as much as he'd wanted to get me out of it.

If our kiss had sparked the same fire in him as it had in me, there was no way he was thinking straight when he'd come up with the ludicrous plan to tell Elikai to call the wedding off.

I should never have encouraged him. What if something had happened? What if they got into a fight… or worse, what if–

I couldn't finish the thought as my nausea flooded to the surface, making my mouth fill with saliva. I needed to do something. Anything.

Holding up a finger and mouthing to Thalia that I'd be back in a minute, I raced toward the door before she had time to argue, bunching up the skirt of my wedding dress in my fists as I went.

In the corridor, fae were appearing from every direction, behind closed doors and the stairwells, chaos began to reign.

Like me, they were all clamoring to understand what in fates name was going on, but every face was knit with fear and confusion. Clearly, no one had any more answers than I did.

I needed to find Kane, make sure he was okay. Best case scenario, he had thought better of speaking to his brother en route and had nothing to do with whatever was causing this. But I couldn't risk waiting around to find out when my gut was telling me otherwise.

Elikai would be on the top floor, in the king's quarters, so if Kane hadn't had a sudden epiphany of sense, that would be where he was too.

And then there was Alaric, he'd be standing guard. Perhaps he'd talked Kane down? Fates, I hoped so.

Or Alaric could have somehow gotten involved, wolfed out and triggered the wards…

With my sights set on the stairwell at the opposite end of the corridor, I forced my way through the rapidly growing crowds, pretending I couldn't see the multitude of staff members calling out to me and trying to stop my pursuit.

I kept pushing forward, shrugging them off. I didn't want to be rude or hurt them, but I was growing increasingly frustrated as they got in my way one by one.

Sure, they were only looking out for me, trying to stop me from running head first toward whatever unknown threat might have triggered the alarms, but they didn't know what I knew.

That war could be waging between their princes.

The castle staff weren't warriors, their fight-or-flight instincts ran on flight every time. But knowing that there was every likelihood that Kane was in danger, that he'd poked a monster and had felt its wrath, meant my own instincts were very much on fight. Protect. Save. Whatever it took.

I needed to see that he was okay. That my gut was wrong about him being caught up in this pandemonium somehow. I needed some kind of assurance that this was entirely unrelated to the princes, but I couldn't shake the feeling that I was lying to myself with those delusions.

The acrid smell of blood stopped me in my tracks, causing memories to crash into my mind of the last time my nose had been filled with the blood of several fae all at once; my last day in the Fading Vale.

I looked around frantically, searching for the source, and realized that amongst the metallic stench was something more, the intoxicatingly masculine allure of someone familiar.

Alaric.

His huge form appeared from the stairwell, shadowed in the light. His intimidating presence causing fae to fall over themselves to get out of his way.

As the path cleared, I saw what drove them away; he was covered in blood and the scent of death was undoubtedly coming from *him*. Fuck.

The look in his eyes as they met mine for the briefest moment almost had my knees buckling from underneath me. His look, so sharp and so cold, I was sure I would keel over on the spot from the pressure of it. Like daggers piercing my skin.

He looked crazed. Furious. Like he would crush my bones to dust if I took one step closer.

The danger pouring from him should have had me running scared but, for some reason, it didn't.

The fire in him called to me, drawing me in. I needed to know what in this fate's cursed realm could possibly have triggered that kind of intense fury in someone usually so clearheaded, but I couldn't get my feet to start working quickly enough to catch up to him. *Shit*.

My stomach sank as I wondered if he was so fired up because something truly awful had happened to Kane, and Alaric knew it was all my fault? No. There was no way that Alaric would have left Kane if he was in trouble.

Even if my worst fear were true and he was debilitated or dead, Alaric would be at his side, right? Surely that meant Kane was okay? And if there was a threat inside the castle, he wouldn't be heading for his room now.

Screw this! The male couldn't worm his way into my heart and then look at me like something he'd trodden in. I needed answers, and he was the best place to start.

"Alaric!" I yelled, unable to hear myself, so there was no chance he would hear me either from this distance.

He didn't so much as glance my way again before he turned down Kane's wing and toward his own guest suite.

Perhaps it was the unabating shriek of the alarm making me more easily irritated than I would normally be, or maybe the stress of the wedding, but whatever it was had my legs finally moving again, and I darted down the corridor after him.

As soon as I was within reaching distance of his door, I hammered my fist against it, but it was to no avail. He was in there, but ignoring me.

Not today, Alaric, not today.

Rattling the handle, I was surprised to find it was unlocked when the door swung open. Gathering both the skirt and train of my dress together this time, I shoved it over my arm and stepped inside his room for the very first time, determined to find out exactly what was going on.

Leather and cedar almost masked the vile scent of blood, but not entirely. A neatly made, and very much empty, four-poster bed took up most of the space, leaving room for little more than the walkway needed to get around it.

As with most rooms here, a fire heated the space. There was a single wardrobe on one side and a solitary dresser on the other. Weapons and shields hung from the stone walls, spaced out perfectly, like they were Alaric's chosen form of art. Which, knowing the male, didn't surprise me at all.

Though they had been polished to within an inch of their lives, some were clearly very old. You could tell by the way he looked after them that they each held a story very dear to him.

Walking around the bed, I reached the door to what could only be his en-suite bathing chamber.

It was ajar, but not wide enough for me to slip through the gap in this huge dress.

It opened almost fully as I pushed my way in.

He was there; head down as he leaned over the sink. Clear water gushed from the tap, hitting his skin and draining away with a red hue. He was giving his exposed skin the same treatment he'd been giving the precious metal in his bed chamber. I'd be surprised if he didn't lose a layer or two of skin with the way he was scrubbing so furiously.

The intense energy coming off him was like a force field, warning me back, but I stepped up behind him anyway.

Is he purposely ignoring me? Even with the alarm filling his ears and his eyes scrunched shut, Alaric would have noticed someone before they got this close.

His eyes were down, entirely focused on his task, as I watched him in the mirror's reflection. A sense of dread settled over me as I tried to understand what could have driven him to… to *this*.

Steam began to fog the edges of the mirror, making me wonder just how hot the water was that he was subjecting his wounds with.

They couldn't have been too severe, though, based on the way the water wasn't coming away with fresh blood. It was virtually clear now. I'd guess that the pain was more mental than physical anyway.

It was hidden in the crease of his brow and the tightness of his muscles. Whatever he was carrying clearly weighed heavily.

"What are you doing, Alaric?" I asked. I tried to keep my voice soft, despite the volume needed to be heard over the racket.

He wasn't the type to startle, but it was unmistakable the moment he finally realized he wasn't alone. His hands slammed down on the sinks rim so tightly, it cracked under his palms. At the same time, his silver eyes shot up to meet mine in the mirror.

I had to fight to hide my own shock at the emotion I found in them. They weren't glassy like someone who'd been crying. They held rage and chaos; the kind of eyes you'd expect to find looking back at you from a wanted poster nailed to a tree, leaving no question over the insanity of the criminal should you be misfortunate enough to stumble upon him.

I was suddenly very self-conscious when they briefly moved to the bodice of my wedding dress and he visibly cringed. He said something that I couldn't fully hear, though reading his lips I'd guess it was, "Get out."

His eyes closed as his nostrils sucked in a deep breath, holding it for several long seconds. I wondered if he was questioning why he hadn't picked up on my scent sooner. I knew that for me personally, I could tell exactly where he or Kane were sitting in a room, even if I were blindfolded.

"Alaric, what's wrong?" I asked loudly.

He met my eyes briefly before looking back down. I listened closely to his reply, "Nothin' yeh need to worry 'bout, Angel." His gaze remained fixated on the tap. He was dismissing me, that much was obvious, but there was no fucking way I'd be leaving him alone like this. He wasn't himself.

I reached out, placing my hand on his tightly coiled shoulder. "If you won't tell me what's wrong with you, then at least tell me what's happening in the castle. What triggered the alarms?" I asked, more stern this time.

He ignored me.

"Perhaps it's to do with the blood you were frantically washing off when I walked in here?"

He winced. "Yeh'd be better just leavin'. Yeh'll find out with the rest of them. Just. *Leave*."

My hand jolted away from his skin without conscious volition, as though his coldness physically burned.

His words reignited my annoyance at the way he'd looked at me in the corridor. Like a stranger. "Fuck you, Alaric. Just tell me and I'll go."

His eyes finally met mine again, though it seemed to pain him to do so. They truly were crazed.

A smarter female would back away slowly, then run for the Vale to put as much distance between herself and the dangerous male she was fleeing as possible.

I wasn't that female, and he knew fates damn well I wasn't.

I stood my ground, my feet rooted to the spot. He'd never hurt me, no matter how out of his mind and teetering on the edge of control he was right now. I knew that much.

He was shutting off the tap, but at my words he slammed his palms down on the vanity, making me jump back several inches. "Just. Fuckin'. Go!"

"Why?" I asked.

"Why the fuck do yeh think?" he snapped. Finally, turning around to face me. His eyes flashed down to my dress again, before he scrunched them shut.

When he opened them again a beat later, he was looking me dead in the eyes.

"I cannae trust myself around yeh righ' now. Is that what yeh wanted to hear?" he asked, slowly moving toward me, so I was forced to step back until I was barricaded in between him and the wall.

I gulped. He was practically vibrating with caged in emotion, threatening to force its way out while his guards were down. Or in the least, compromised.

He won't hurt you, Eva. I reminded myself. "Where's Kane?" I asked.

He shrugged.

He might be having a shitty fucking day, but guess what, mine was about to be a damn sight worse than whatever castle drama had gotten him so disconcerted.

The moment whatever had triggered the wards was settled, I'd be walking down an aisle. To marry a male who I hated with every ounce of my being. A male who'd ordered my parents to be murdered in front of my eyes and thought I'd thank him for it afterwards.

I realized my chest was heaving as I seethed. "Like you don't know *exactly* where that male is while something serious enough to sound the wards is going down. But fine, be an asshole. Just tell me, is he okay?"

"He's no' injured." Alaric confirmed, and I released my worry for Kane's safety in all of this on a heavy breath.

"Good." I moved to leave, but his hand snapped out, grabbing my wrist to stop me. I tried to pull away, but he was too strong. "You want me to leave, so get the fuck off of me and I will," I spat. "I have a wedding to get to, remember? In case the dress didn't give it away."

His hand dropped immediately, he looked surprised, as though he hadn't even noticed he was holding onto me until I'd told him.

It was at that moment, more than any other in these last few minutes, that I realized he wasn't just angry, or being purposely rude; he was breaking.

He was a male who was the master of self-control, of hiding any emotions, and something had happened that had made him decide to come to his room, to be alone, so he could force the shattered pieces back together in private.

As much as he was trying to hide it, this wasn't the level-headed horde general in the driver's seat right now. No, this was a male on the edge, and I couldn't find it in me to be mad at him for that.

I was debating what to do next when he said, "There will be no weddin' today." Almost too quietly to hear.

"W-what?" I stuttered, sure my ears had deceived me with all the other noise they were contending with.

"Yeh heard. The weddin' is postponed."

"Why?" I asked.

It seemed to be a push too far. He turned his back on me, his palms flat on the marble, his strong arms acting as two pillars, holding him up.

For some reason, he couldn't bring himself to answer me. Why couldn't he just spit it out? What was so bad that he couldn't bring himself to tell me?

My hand slammed against my mouth as it dawned on me. "Fates, he knows, doesn't he? He knows about the three of us?"

He shook his head sharply.

Thank the fates. But why? I needed to know, but I didn't want to watch him break, least of all under my questioning.

I looked at the door. He seemed so torn as to whether or not he wanted me to walk out of it. Whatever had happened, it had bought me time. Whether that be a day, or a week, it was time I hadn't had before to get out of this wedding.

I walked to the door, but I didn't leave. Instead, I closed it, turned the lock and returned to the male that thought he'd needed to deal with his troubles alone.

As the space between us decreased, I placed my hands on his chest. I could feel the thundering of his heart as my fingers curled around the fabric of his shirt.

Before I could pull him down, he'd closed the rest of the space between us himself as his head dipped.

His lips closed over mine, swallowing any words I might have been about to say as he pressed me backwards, tightly against the wall.

I opened for him, welcoming his taste as his tongue began to search my mouth with a desperation so intense it was as though he sought to find the answers to the problems scrambling his mind in there.

I groaned against his lips as I returned his kiss. His sweet taste was a stark contrast to the sharp stubble grazing my skin. It alighted my senses and made me want more.

My fingers dug deeper into the material, a desperate attempt to pull him completely flush to my body in spite of the large skirt in our way.

"Enough." He said suddenly, breaking the kiss and backing right up into the vanity, his breaths fast and heavy. His silver eyes hadn't lost the madness I'd found in them as he'd first met my gaze in the mirror. If anything, he'd descended further into it.

"*You* kissed *me*." I snapped, but it came out as more of a question.

"I wasnae expectin' yeh to kiss me back."

Then why kiss me at all if you weren't prepared for me to return it? I wanted to ask. But I knew the answer. It was like when he'd grabbed my hand. He hadn't meant to do it, he'd just acted on impulse and the horde general hadn't been present enough to stop it.

"Well, I did," I said instead, moving toward him. "My only regret is that you broke it so soon."

"*Angel,*" he growled.

I ignored his warning.

Even leaned back on the vanity top he was so much taller than me. I tentatively reached out to trace the faint line of a scratch on his face. It cut through his scar, but unlike that wound which must have been inflicted before he'd come of age, this one was almost healed.

Before I made contact, he'd spun us around, switching our positions, so he was behind me now. His forearm pressed against my shoulder blades, forcing me forward.

We were both facing the mirror, but I had to lift my chin to see him in its reflection with the position he held me in. The thick skirt of my dress was crushed between our bodies, but his arousal was apparent against my lower back, even through the corset as he crowded my body.

"Unless yeh want me to fuck yeh for the first time in yer wedding dress to the wrong male, dinnae fuckin' touch me righ' now."

His forced words were meant to scare me away, that much was obvious. But he'd given away more than he'd meant to.

...first time.

...wrong male.

...right now.

Unintentional words I knew he'd normally have skipped out, aware they would give away too much of how he actually felt.

The knowledge gave me confidence to be more brazen about how I felt too when I said, "And if I want you to?"

"Then I dinnae think I'd have the control it takes to refuse yeh."

I couldn't move much from this position and he knew it, but I could wiggle my hips a little, causing friction to spark against his erection.

I felt the low growl reverberating from his throat before I heard it. *"Careful,"* he warned, releasing me to take a small step back. He was still right behind me though, like he couldn't convince himself to walk away entirely.

I stayed exactly where he'd put me, leaning over the sink, looking at him in the mirror over the vanity, a challenge in my stare.

"The silver-haired temptress," he scoffed to himself, as though it was meant to have been a thought and not voiced aloud.

"And the silver-eyed soldier," I said back, biting down on my lip.

I wasn't sure what exactly caused the last tether he had on the horde general to break, but before I knew what was happening, he'd grabbed the top of my corset just below my shoulder blades and tore it open straight down the middle.

Cool air hit my exposed flesh, making me gasp as the material came apart like it had been held together by a single strand of spider silk.

It wouldn't take much for Thalia to fix it, or at least that's what I told myself as desire for the male behind me consumed me. The skirt that clung to my hips was still very much intact, though. Suddenly feeling like it dug in too tightly. Alaric clearly had the same thought as I felt his fingers slide into the waistband.

Ripped lace would be a much harder fix than the ribbons of the corset.

My head whipped around over my shoulder as the annoying thought entered my mind. "Don't you dare," I told him.

"Yeh gotta be louder than that if yeh want to be heard over the alarms," he purred into my ear.

Fates, I wanted him to do it. There was still far too much material between us. But this would be the first and last time we got to do this if the dress was damaged beyond repair. There would be no hiding it from Elikai, and he wasn't stupid enough to not connect the dots. We'd be dead by morning.

Alaric knew it too. His hands were frozen in place, a mental war no doubt waging in his mind over whether death would be worth it or not.

"Stop." I made myself say not a moment too soon.

He released the material immediately. "Fuck, Angel," he said, his palms pressed to his temples. "Just go. I told yeh I cannae trust myself around yeh righ' now."

"I'm not going anywhere, Alaric." I said, shimmying the skirt and broken–barely clinging on by a thread–corset to the floor.

His eyes were wide as he watched me step out of it slowly, and I truly felt like the temptress he'd called me under their scrutiny.

I walked toward him, naked aside from my purple lace lingerie, heels, and the jewels at my throat and wrist. With every step I took forward, he took one of his own back, until he was the one now flush against the wall.

I reached up to put my arms around his neck. He lifted me up, wrapping my legs around his waist, and I crossed them tightly behind him.

We had never been closer than we were when he started kissing his way down my throat, his teeth grazing the sensitive flesh there. My groans fought with his growls, desperate to be heard over the still ringing alarms.

"I'll never get enough of that fuckin' sound," he murmured against my skin.

I wasn't sure when he turned, but I gasped as the cold wall met my back.

"Or that one," he growled.

I needed to taste him again, but the sensations his kisses sparked against my skin were addictive. Eventually, I laced my fingers in his hair, tugging back so his mouth met mine in an intoxicating kiss.

His tongue dominated my mouth, and I was utterly lost to him, the heat between us increasing into a frenzy. My thighs tightened around his waist, my hips moving against his solid body in a desperate search for friction.

"I need to be inside you," he said against my mouth and fuck, he'd get no arguments from me about that.

We were both panting when he carried me over to the sink, not breaking the kiss until he dropped me down on the marble top.

"This is yer last chance to go, 'cause the second my cock touches yer cunt, I won't be able to stop until yer screamin' my name over these fuckin' alarms."

I planted my hands firmly against his pecs and pushed him backwards. Then slid off the vanity.

His expression was unreadable as I remained silent, just staring up at him, appreciating this hulking male before me, so completely undone.

My fingers found the buttons of his trousers, unfastening them one by one. Tugging them down to his thighs, I tucked my nails into the waistband of his underwear and moved them to release his throbbing cock.

Fates help me. He was so very ready to follow through on his promise to fuck me until I screamed. I licked my lips, wanting to know if the bead of arousal tasted as sweet as his lips. But I didn't touch his hard length, no matter how much I wanted to.

The wail of the alarms was a constant reminder that this could end before it had even properly begun. And I wasn't going to leave this room until I'd felt what it was like to be dominated by this male.

Whether that was the horde general or this slightly unhinged version of himself, I needed to feel his cock between my thighs as much as he said he needed to be inside me.

I turned my back to him, then bent forward as I dragged my panties down until they could fall on their own to my ankles. Lifting one heeled foot, I stepped out of my underwear so I could stand with my legs apart, then gripped the edges of the sink where Alaric had cracked it several long minutes ago to stare back at him.

I was offering myself to him. My actions were an invitation as much as they were a challenge.

I felt his hand brush away the several wayward strands of silver off my back and moaned at his surprisingly gentle touch. I waited like a coiled spring of desire, yearning to feel him at my entrance. But he just stood there, staring at me, waiting.

He needs to hear you say it.

Fine. "Fuck me until I scream your name over these alarms, wolf."

I'd barely finished the last word when his imposing cock was pressing against me, his hands curling firmly around my hips and holding on roughly. I held onto the sink's rim tighter; the apprehension killing me.

"Yer pussy's so fuckin' wet. So fuckin' ready for me," he said, and I wanted to burst. "I can feel every clench of yer walls on my tip and I'm not even inside yeh yet. I like yeh needy."

I pushed back onto him and he surprised me as he allowed it, inch by glorious inch stretching me, but I couldn't lean back the whole way from my position.

"Fuck," I moaned. "I need more."

"You're so tight," he said. "So fucking perfect."

"Don't hold back," I challenged, and fuck, he didn't.

His palm came down on my ass, hard and fast, making me jolt as he drove the rest of his thick length inside. I cried out at the pleasure and pain of it, and he let out a savage groan of his own.

I remembered the look on his face when he'd realized he'd taken my innocence with his fingers in the training hall. It felt like an age ago. We'd waited far too long to do this.

Our eyes connected in the mirror as he moved at an unrelenting pace. I was finally being fucked by the male who'd taken my virginity, and it was everything. Thrust after thrust, deeper and deeper, as my pussy slid along his length.

I was panting hard, every other breath a moan as the pleasure built. A hand slid between my thighs, circling my clit with just the right amount of pressure to make me putty to his touch, but not enough to push me over the edge and let me orgasm.

"Fuck, that feels so good." He was teasing me relentlessly, but fates, I was so so close. "Don't tease me, Alaric, let me come," I begged. My hand met his in my wet folds in an attempt to make him give me what I needed.

"Not yet," he growled.

Grabbing my wrist, he shoved my fingers inside my mouth, making me taste my own wetness.

"So fuckin wet for me, Angel," he purred, not dropping my hand until I'd thoroughly licked and sucked my fingers clean.

With both palms on the marble to leverage once more, my hips moved in a frantic rhythm as I tried to chase my high. Nonsensical words falling from my mouth as the pleasure built to a crescendo.

"Until yeh give me what *I* want, consider *coming* to be off the table," he uttered in my ear, biting my lobe.

"Please, Alaric."

My hips met his in desperate thrusts as my mouth opened and I let out a cry that echoed off the walls like a banshee warning of the most wicked death to come.

He changed the pressure on my clit as he circled it, faster and faster. "Alaric!" I cried out, completely at his mercy.

In the mirror, he was grinning, his scar scrunched up in a way it rarely did, as I rode his cock through my orgasm.

My pussy clenched around him, and I felt him speed up, chasing his own end. His fingers left my clit, and he brought his palm down on my ass again, harder this time, and my muscles tightened around him as I cried out.

"Fuck, Angel!" he roared as he came. "*Fuck.*"

I was fighting for breath when he pulled out of me, my arms shaking as I held onto the vanity.

As though the walls were watching, the alarms ceased to ring, leaving us in a sudden stark silence. One minute before and the whole castle would have heard me screaming Alaric's name on my wedding day to another fae.

"My stunning angel, utterly ruined with my cum dripping down her cunt. Yeh've never looked more beautiful," he murmured quietly. "I always knew once would never be enough with yeh."

I didn't know what to say, I was rendered lost for words by his own.

I cleared my throat as I stood, suddenly feeling very, very naked. He was buttoning up his trousers, and I took the opportunity to step into my panties, looking at the white pile of lace bunched on the floor.

When I looked back up at him, I could see more signs of the general I knew. His walls were rebuilding around whatever had happened today.

"That was… everything I imagined it would be," I told him, tiptoeing up to kiss him on his scarred cheek.

The severity of what he'd done to my dress was banging at the door of my brain, desperate for attention I didn't want to give it, but had no choice but to face and deal with.

"I-I need to get this thing back on and find Thalia to fix the back," I said.

He nodded, gripped my chin for a last deep kiss, and then helped me into the dress. His face made it clear exactly how much he didn't want to be dressing me up for a male we both despised, but we also were both fully aware it had to be done.

I held the bodice to my chest. The hook and eye had somehow survived Alaric, and from the front, you couldn't really see much damage; it just hung looser around my chest and waist.

"Yeh cannae take that to Thalia. She'll ask questions yeh cannae give her plausible answers to." Alaric eventually said, as he unlocked the door of the bathing chamber. "Just get back to yer chambers unnoticed and I'll have Ax–"

"Hey, boss," a voice said as Alaric swung open the door.

Axel was smiling back at us from his position on the four-poster bed. I would have screamed if Alaric hadn't spotted him a moment before me and quickly covered my mouth with his palm to silence it.

He lay back against the headboard. His legs crossed at the ankles as he used a whetstone to sharpen his blade. How long had he been there? Oh fates, what had he heard? Hopefully, just a whole load of alarms ringing in his ears.

"Nice to see you, Lady Evangelia. Having a nice wedding day?" he asked me.

My mouth opened and closed around words that I couldn't find to answer his question, but thankfully Alaric didn't seem too phased by the male as he asked. "How long have yeh been here, Axel?"

"Long enough to know I needed to sneak into the blushing bride's chambers to grab her this." He pointed to the end of Alaric's bed where a silk robe lay. Definitely not his. "With time to spare to get back here and give my sword a good polishing, too," he joked with a wink to my mortified self. *What was happening?*

Alaric cracked his knuckles, and just like that, Axel changed, becoming more serious somehow. "Luckily, I haven't been here long enough for them to have sent another guard looking for you yet. You're needed elsewhere, boss. I was about to come–"

"Alrigh' Axel. Enough," Alaric snapped, apparently having all the information he needed. Snatching the robe from the bed, he held it up for me to shrug into.

"Erm. What about her wedding dress, boss?" Axel asked. Clearly, he'd noticed it wasn't exactly intact. "I could get it to a tailor, but it likely won't be today, what with all the–"

"Tomorrow's fine." Alaric said, cutting him off, again. "Elikai will be... busy with other stuff today," Axel's brows raised, but he eventually nodded, like there was some kind of unspoken understanding between the two of them.

What other stuff could Elikai be so busy with? He'd been very set on this wedding when I'd last seen him.

"Thank you, Axel, for offering to take it to a tailor, but it's OK, honestly. The robe is great, I'll get back to Elikai's room now and Thalia can help me fix it. She won't ask questions about how it got, umm... damaged."

I was suddenly very desperate to leave, practically squirming on the spot under Axel and Alaric's scrutiny over the dress.

"I assume Elikai, uhh... wasn't there when you were?" I asked.

"No, m'lady. Last I saw, he was heading to the advisor's floor with that Charles fella and, well, I've been basically blind ever since." He rubbed his eyes dramatically. "Did your fiancé tell you he intended to cover himself from head to toe in gold today, by the way? Was the plan for the suit to act as a beacon at the end of the aisle, maybe? You know, to make sure you knew which prince the groom wa–"

"No' funny, Axel," Alaric warned. I wasn't sure whether to laugh, cry, or be offended. So I stuck with being mortified. How much did Axel actually know? Did Alaric tell this male everything? Apparently, yes.

"Just trying to lighten the mood is all, boss. Anyway, Charles spotted me and told me to find you. And thank the fates it *was* me."

Alaric and I exhaled our relief simultaneously. I wrapped the robe tightly around myself, thankful that the back would be covered, so none of the ruined dress would be on show for the short walk back.

"I have to go," I said. "But first, what aren't you telling me? You are both obviously fully aware that the wedding isn't happening today, but why? Surely someone would tell the bride," I asked accusingly.

The male's eyes met across the room. A silent conversation must have passed between them because Axel shrugged, then Alaric nodded.

Clearing his throat, the horde general said, "There'll be no wedding today, Angel, 'cause the King is dead."

My mouth fell open.

I wasn't sure how much time passed as I stood there like that, gaping. Surely Axel was about to start laughing or something, telling me Alaric was just joking.

But why would he joke about that?

The. King. Is. Dead.

I could have sworn that was what he'd said. I glanced between the two of them a few times, without really registering their presence.

"Angel," a voice called, but I didn't answer. There was no way this was real, so what was the point? It was just a figment of my imagination. The stress of my capture had finally caught up to me, and I'd imagined every moment since crossing the threshold into Alaric's room.

It was more believable than what I thought I'd heard come out of Alaric's mouth.

"Fuck, boss, I think you broke her," another voice said. Though it sounded very similar to Axel. Did I know the male well enough to be able to imagine his voice so accurately? Or perhaps it was only to the version of Axel in this weird dream realm?

My brain completely stopped working as it tried to process the mere idea that the king was gone, never to plague Dezrothia again. But most of my thoughts about it came back blank.

"Angel," a voice snapped again, pulling me back to the here and now this time.

It *was* Alaric. This was very much real. And I had questions. Lots of questions. Had there been an accident? Had he been killed? Was that why the alarms went off? How had Kane taken the news?

"I dinnae have long enough to explain this twice, so if yeh want to hear wha' happened, yeh can stay while I tell Axel."

I nodded.

"Sit down, if yeh need to."

I did.

CHAPTER 3

Nekane

"Prince Nekane," a voice called from behind me, causing the hair on my nape to lift as I stiffened.

This was it.

They thought I'd killed him.

Alaric had given me one job. Find my brother and get my sword back.

I'd failed.

I turned slowly to face him. My legs had been jelly as I'd roamed the crowded corridors, desperately trying to find my brother; now it felt like they were going to crumble to dust as Desmond, a loyal advisor of my father, looked back at me.

There was a guard with him, too. A bald-headed male who I'd faced in the training ring several times over the years. Even wearing his finest armor, he was heavily armed: a sword at his hip, a bow at his back and a dagger in his hand. Braced and ready to strike, a model of his training as a member of the King's guard.

"Come with us," Desmond said, his tone void of emotion.

It was done. *I* was done.

They'd come to arrest me for treason. My life was over, and just when I'd finally decided to stop fucking wasting it.

I'd be charged with killing a King, for committing patricide and murdering my own father. I would lose my head before the sun had set tonight.

I sent a silent prayer to the fates that Eva and Alaric wouldn't have to witness it. That they were safe and that they'd find a way to be together when I was gone.

Everything had happened so quickly in that room, it had been a complete and utter blur. But now, as it played back in my mind, it was in painfully slow motion and as vividly sharp as the blade that had sunk into my father's chest, ending his life.

My fingers wrapped around my arm, where Elikai's hand had grabbed me. I could feel the ghost of its outline, like it was still there, haunting me. Or perhaps it was just a bruise from how much force he'd used. Would my body heal it before I died, or would it forever remain on my skin? I guess it didn't really matter.

I think I'd been in shock when Alaric had burst in. My mind had been both too full and completely blank at once. The look in my father's eyes as all signs of life had drained away from him, replayed over and over in my mind. Every time I closed my eyes, all I could see was the reflection of the fool in his glassy eyes. Me. I was the fucking fool, and now it was time to face my fate.

I swallowed, then nodded to Desmond and the guard. There was no point in arguing my case. Elikai had known exactly what he was doing, using me to do his dirty work. And I had played into his hands perfectly.

I WASN'T EVEN ENTIRELY sure what part of the castle I'd ended up in, let alone where we were heading, as they walked soundlessly and I followed, knowing any one of my steps could be my last.

Eventually, we reached a door, and they nodded for me to go inside.

I'd made it three more steps when a body slammed into mine, forcing the breath I'd been holding to leave my chest, winding me.

Arms came around me in a tight lock as I stumbled back against the stone wall.

"Nekane! Brother mine, thank the fates you are safe!" Elikai's shrill voice cried close to my ear, blindsiding me. "What's happening? Why have they brought us here?"

I shoved out of his grip, the taste of repulsion on my tongue at his nearness.

Not wanting to look so much in his direction, my eyes searched the room. I didn't recognize it. There were no windows, only the fire to light the small space that held little more than a small table with a chessboard on its top and a few dark green wing-back chairs dotted around the room.

This wasn't an arrest. That much was becoming clear. What *was* happening?

Desmond and Charles were huddled close together by the door, talking to the guard; their proximity was most likely so they could communicate over the alarms I'd barely registered until now.

I tried to listen and heard mention of an announcement, something about the wards, and then Alaric's name, but didn't catch much of anything else in between to put together the pieces.

Fates, I hoped Alaric was okay. He said he'd deal with it, and I'd known he meant covering it up so it wouldn't come back on me.

Why would he even get involved in something so much bigger than whatever loyalty or feelings he held for me personally? I hadn't even managed to ask him how he planned to do it. This wasn't just some fight I'd got into at the Crooked Claw. His King had died and everything had pointed at me being the murderer.

Judging by the fact I was still breathing now, whatever he'd done, it had worked.

With a nod, the guard opened the door to leave, and I realized the sirens were even louder out in the hallways. The door closed behind him, leaving just Elikai, the two advisors and I.

I retraced the steps we had taken to get here in my head. We were on the advisor's floor, and this must be where they congregated when they wanted some privacy from the rest of the castle.

Desmond cleared his throat and Charles tightened his grip on the handkerchief he was clutching to his chest. "Prince Elikai." He bowed to my brother next to me. "Prince Nekane," he said, tilting his head a little in my direction. "Sorry to drag you both away here, but we felt some privacy would be necessary for what we must divulge. I am afraid that we must be the bearers of the most tragic news."

"Tragic news?" Elikai gasped. "On the day I am to be wed to my beautiful Evangeline? Well, that doesn't sound good. What is it?"

My brother was still wearing his golden wedding suit and ceremonial sword, but if I was reading this situation right and he hadn't told the advisors I'd killed our father, then I'd say he'd hidden my sword before Charles had brought him here. But where?

"It's your father," Desmond said, dropping his gaze to the floor. "He was attacked in his chambers. By a thrakos."

I froze. A thrakos? *Is that what Alaric had told them?*

Elikai gasped. "Is he okay? Did he kill the foul creature? Is he injured?"

My mouth was dry as my mind reeled at the implications. Pinning it on the thrakos was clever, albeit unfair, but how did Alaric plan to convince them if they wanted proof?

Then again, why would they question Alaric's word or judgment? They wouldn't.

"I-I'm afraid your father didn't m-make it, your highness."

"I beg your pardon?! You mean to tell me the King is dead?! That's not possible!" Elikai yelled. His voice was so loud the alarms sounded little more than a background hum. The way he could lie so convincingly was disturbing, but not at all surprising.

Nothing he does will surprise me ever again, I vowed.

"I am sorry, my prince. But I have been to see his body myself to confirm it," Charles said.

"Where did this happen? How did this happen? Where were the guards who were supposed to watch him? I want to hear from them this instant!" he demanded.

The sick bastard was enjoying this.

"He was in his chambers, your highness. It came in through the window and tore out the King's heart before General Alaric or the female guard could reach him. You could see they'd put up a fight. They tried desperately to kill the beast. The female lost her life, and the general barely made it away with his."

Wait. The female did what? What female?

"This thrakos, you said he managed to kill two fae?" I asked, finally finding my voice, because there was no way that was possible. I had been there. Alaric and Elikai were the only other two present. Unless...

Alaric, what have you done?

"Ignore Nekane, he is clearly in shock. You know his brain takes longer to digest the most mundane of information at the best of times. This is a lot for him to process. His silly questions must be forgiven," Elikai said, forgetting to feign tears, too eager to take more stabs at me. "The King, *our father,* was murdered!"

"I heard what they said, Elikai," I gritted through my clenched jaw.

"Oh fates, Nekane!" he sobbed. "I refuse to believe our father is gone!"

Charles wiped an invisible tear from his eye. I didn't fall for it. The advisors' hearts were as unfeeling as my brothers, and as dead as my fathers.

I struggled to beat back the nausea as I realized everyone in this fucking room was just acting. They didn't care that lives had been lost. Elikai felt no remorse. He felt no responsibility for these deaths. The advisors probably welcomed the excitement of something new in their unending, dull lives.

"Rest assured, your highnesses. The guards will turn the castle upside down and search every inch of the grounds until the thrakos is found."

"You mean to tell me *it got away?!*" Elikai seethed.

"Another guard was sent to find General Alaric for an update. We'd hoped he would be here to answer any of your questions about what happened by now. Hopefully, he is killing the creature responsible as we speak."

He wasn't.

And I'd heard enough.

"Thank you for telling us," I said. "My brother and I would appreciate a moment alone."

"Of course. You understand we will need to make an announcement soon? The alarms have triggered panic and we need to give the many fae who gathered here today for the wedding some answers as to what set them off?"

"I understand," I said. "Have the alarms turned off, too. We will meet you in the ballroom shortly."

Desmond and Charles bowed, muttered their condolences, and the second they left, I moved.

Elikai was still dabbing his eyes with the golden handkerchief when my hand closed around his throat and I slammed him against the wall.

If I'd taken him by surprise, he hid it well. "Now, now, Nekane," he gasped out around the increasingly tight grip I had on his neck. "Calm down."

"Where's my sword?" I demanded.

"Somewhere… safe."

"Not good enough. *Tell. Me. Where. It. Is.*" I said, forcing allure into my words. I hated the gift, but I hated my brother more.

He laughed. Fucking laughed. "That won't… work on me… brother."

"Just fucking tell me!" I squeezed tighter still.

"N-o," he croaked.

"What do you want for it? What will it take?" He didn't answer.

I released my grip a fraction, only enough so he could answer me. "There is nothing you have that I want."

It was true. There was nothing I could do to talk him around. There was nothing I could offer him that he wanted. The only way for me to get the sword back was by finding it myself.

Having come to this conclusion, I let him drop to the floor and didn't bother wasting another word or second glance on him as I turned and quickly left the room.

THE ADVISORS COULD WAIT to make their announcement, I thought, as I pushed open the door to Alaric's chambers.

I wasn't sure what I had planned to say to him, but the moment I saw him standing at the foot of his bed, my lips were moving. "You killed that female guard to cover up for me!?" I accused.

"Ugh. He hadn't got to that bit yet," a disgruntled voice said, as though I'd just given him the spoiler to end all spoilers in his current read.

My eyes shot to the source of the voice, the area of the bed that was concealed behind the door. It was one of Alaric's guards who'd spoken, the one who he seemed most friendly with, Axel. But what held my attention was the female perched on the opposite side of the four-poster bed.

Eva.

"Kane," she gasped, getting to her feet.

She wore a robe which covered most of her wedding dress but didn't look quite as put together as she had earlier. I quickly turned to close the door behind me, locking the four of us in.

By the time I turned back, her arms were around my neck. "Alaric just told us what happened to your father. About what Elikai somehow made you do–"

"He did?"

She nodded. "Whatever happened, it wasn't your fault. You know that right?" she asked, but I was currently more concerned over what Alaric was thinking when he'd decided to call whatever the fuck this meeting was and start telling others the truth of what had happened in my father's chambers. Or at least to the best of his knowledge.

I wouldn't have lied to Eva–I'd have told her at some point–I just didn't think it would be before Elikai had given her the bullshit version. As for Axel...

"It'll go no further than these four walls," Alaric said, and I was immediately reminded of why I'd been so desperate to find him in the first place.

"So you told them everything? What about the part of what you did to that poor female?"

Alaric winced.

"What female?" Eva asked.

My eyes remained focused on Alaric. "It was the other guard, wasn't it? The one you told me to send in as I left!"

"Aye," he admitted, his eyes on the floor. "Her name was Krista."

"Why?"

"Because I had no fuckin' choice, Kane."

"Of course you had a fucking choice! Her blood is on my hands now, too. She had nothing to do with it! She wasn't even in the room."

"Your highness," Axel interjected. "If you don't keep your voice down, there will be a whole lot more blood on your hands."

I hated that he was right. I just couldn't understand why Alaric would do this to save *me.*

Alaric's tone was flat when he said matter-of-factly, "It was yer life or hers. I couldnae risk her livin' to tell the tale as she'd seen it. It wouldnae add up with the one I needed them to believe. She knew yeh were in the room. Like me, she'd have heard enough to connect the dots. Letting her live wasnae a risk I was willin' to take."

"Sometimes good fae have to do really fuckin' bad things for the greater good, Prince Nekane," Axel said, like it made complete fucking sense to him. "Don't think for a second that decision was one Alaric would have taken lightly."

"I didn't say that," I snapped, more hostile than he deserved.

Eva reached out and took my hand. She looked from Alaric to me and back to Alaric again.

Her eyes didn't leave his when she said, "What he did in that room fates near broke him." Then she looked at me when she said, "In this realm, there are plenty of fae willing to kill to save themselves, but it's rare to find someone willing to kill to save another. It's awful that an innocent was mixed up in this, but I can't say I'm not glad he did what he did."

"Sorry, Kane," Alaric said. "But I'd do it again. It really wasnae a choice."

I put myself in his position, and I knew I would have done exactly the same thing if it was him whose life was in jeopardy. It certainly wouldn't have been easy, but I'd have done it no less.

My anger at him faded, replaced by worry for him. The last thing he needed after everything he'd done for me in that room was my misplaced rage.

I would drop it, for now. But I wouldn't easily forget it.

I sighed. "I didn't manage to get the sword, or convince Elikai to hand it over," I admitted.

"We'll find it," Alaric said with more confidence than I had about it.

But that would have to wait. We were all due to be at an announcement soon, and showing up together would be suspicious, to say the least.

"What are you doing here anyway, Princess? My brother will be looking for you."

"Shit, I need to go and find Thalia before he finds me," she said.

"Elikai's maid?"

"Yes, it's a long story and now really isn't the time for it, I promise."

"Ok, well, I just left him on the advisor's floor, but I imagine he'll be coming to break the news soon. The false version."

"Which is?" she asked.

Alaric shook his head. "Angel, yeh need to go, *now*."

"Right. I'll see you at the announcement, I imagine," she said, and I unlocked the door for her. "Thank you. And I really am sorry, Kane. For your loss."

I nodded, unsure how to respond to that yet. It hadn't sunk in. It still felt like I might wake up at some point and realize this had just been a warning about my brother in the form of a nightmare.

CHAPTER 4

Elikai

Fates, I can't wait for everyone to see me wearing my crown, I thought as I left Graves and Sloane on the advisor's floor, finally able to hear myself think again now that a warlock had reset the wards.

This day had been a series of the most fortunate events, and it couldn't have gone any more perfectly if I'd actually planned it.

Everything from the moment the opportunity to murder my father had presented itself to watching my brother's face drop when he realized his tantrum over the sword was getting him exactly nowhere, not to mention every stroke of genius I had in between.

My only regret was having to keep my inspiring role in it all a secret. My dream, my goal, my greatest desire was suddenly so close I could taste it.

Delaying my wedding day to Eveline was a sacrifice I was willing to make, regardless of how bothersome it was to have to wait. I wouldn't risk my wedding being overshadowed by the death of a king, our nuptials could take place shortly after my ascent to the throne. My coronation was the priority now.

A pretty, obedient queen birthing my heirs remained a necessity, though I had no intention of ever stepping down. My sons would be strong and savage, raised to be both my most loyal subjects and my personal guards. My daughters would be the most beautiful in all of Dezrothia, fine bargaining chips to forge alliances when I needed them.

I had plans for this realm. Big plans. Not just this realm, but many others, and being undefeatable would secure my place to rule forever.

I would surround myself with a shield of my very own high fae warrior descendants. An added flare to the power I already exuded. I would be triumphant in my reign.

I'd sent Sloane to tell his father, Desmond, that I would meet them in the ballroom for the announcement, but first I needed to collect my blushing bride.

Nothing was more heartrending than a tragedy taking place on a day that was supposed to have been a joyous occasion, and my pretty pet in white would be the perfect reminder to all that my father's death had come at the worst possible time for me.

They'd see their future king putting the realm before his own happiness and be compelled to bow to me as their new ruler with haste. Then they'd say that I was ready to step up and lead where a weaker fae would crumble.

Swinging the door to my chambers wide, I found my pretty pet. She was having the final finishing touches made to her gown by the servant witch. *Poor thing wants to look perfect for me.* It would break her heart when she realized that no aisle awaited her today.

"Prince Elikai, you're here," she gasped, clearly relieved to see me. She must have been so worried about me when the alarms were triggered.

"I am here, pretty girl. But we must leave now. Something awful has happened, and we need to get to the ballroom immediately."

"Really? Is it to do with the alarms that were going off?" she asked.

"Yes, but there's no time to explain. We cannot be late," I told her as the maid stepped back and looked at a job well done. The dress was exactly as I'd pictured it, and my future queen was a vision for all to behold.

I'd decided to let her hear the news for the first time publicly at the announcement. It would be to my benefit that all could see the look on her face as she realized our marriage would have to be postponed. Then I could console her and the crowd would melt at my feet. It was all just so perfect.

"What about Thalia?" she asked, as though she thought the maid might be invited to the ballroom where Dezrothia's most elite had gathered for my special day. I almost laughed.

"Exactly," I said. "What about her? Now, we must hurry."

Grabbing her arm, I dragged her after me, down the stairs leading to the entrance hall in which the ballroom was off of.

It was Charles who met us at the large door. He bowed and gestured for us to follow him in.

I spied Nekane almost immediately. His suit jacket and waistcoat were missing, and he stood slumped over the mezzanine rail, running his hands through his hair as he looked down at the fae below.

Make the most of it, little brother, it is not your job to look down on my subjects. It is mine.

I tucked Evangelie under my arm as we approached Desmond. He stood at the top of the stairs, ready to tell Dezrothia's finest their king's fate.

We glided in to stand to his left, then Nekane and the general dragged their feet as they took their position to his right.

"Make this quick," I told Desmond. The male liked the sound of his own voice and I had places to be, plans to make and a seer to meet with. "It's just too painful," I added, taking my handkerchief out.

"Good fae of Ezerat," he began. "Today, you were all invited to the castle to celebrate the love of Prince Elikai and Lady Evangelia. But as you gather here now, it is instead to share news that is most heartbreaking."

While Desmond paused for effect, I hugged my pretty pet closely with one arm and held the handkerchief tightly to my upper lip with the other. I could feel my brother's penetrating stare. Blinking slowly at him, I gave a slight nod and the saddest of smiles.

The advisor cleared his throat. "On this day, our much loved and brave ruler, King Augustus Regis, has been slain!"

A chorus of sharp gasps echoed around the entire ballroom.

"His life was cut short by one of the foul beasts he vowed to rid us of, and dedicated centuries to tirelessly pursuing. A thrakos!"

Another round of sharp gasps. I hid my smirk with my handkerchief as the irony hit me.

If the stupid male hadn't created the thrakos so poorly in the first place, he needn't have wasted centuries trying to fix his mistake by hunting them. He could have dreamed bigger.

"Our most trusted General, Alaric, and another guard, tried to save him, but alas, it was too late. While the general saw to the king, the intruder fled."

More sharp gasps.

"Do not fear, the horde have already uncovered evidence of the thrakos's presence in a wooded area nearby, and I assure you that our soldiers will not sleep until the loathsome creature is exterminated–"

"Publicly!" I cut in, deciding it was my time to take over. "Fae of Ezerat, fear not! I will not rest until I find the murderer of my dear father and king, Augustus Regis! The creature cannot have gone far. He could even be among us right now!" Nekane flinched in my peripheral vision.

My pretty pet was frozen in my arms. I cupped her face in my hand, placed a chaste kiss on her lips, and gently wiped a nonexistent tear from her cheek.

As I knew there would be, there was a song of coos as the fae below remembered why they had been invited to the castle today, and sadness filled the room as they realized that the King was not the only victim of today's calamity.

Trying to regain control of his announcement, Desmond said, "Funeral arrangements will be made with haste and Dezrothia will begin its month of mourning before the new king is crowned, as is tradition." Then he yelled, "The king is dead!"

"LONG LIVE THE KING!" my voice rang out, and everyone echoed my words.

I walked over to Nekane, embraced him in a show of grief-stricken siblings, then murmured in his ear, "Now, brother, you had better start learning to do *exactly* as I say or that bloodied sword of yours might just make its way somewhere it can be found. And I'm sure I don't need to tell you why that would be very problematic for you, now do I?"

CHAPTER 5
Evangelia

I crept along the somber castle corridor, grateful that everyone was too busy preparing for Augustus Regis' funeral to notice me.

We were just hours away from his entombment, but in the several long days that had passed since his death, or more accurately, murder, I'd felt like I had been cut adrift. The lack of a plan sending me into a tailspin.

I'd been so sure that the fates had put me here to kill the late king myself that now I was just filled with an uncomfortable purposelessness. I'd be lying if I said it hadn't crossed my mind that perhaps the traumatic events that had brought me here might have made it a little easier to convince myself there had to be a bigger reason.

Every day of this last week I'd thought about what to do, whether it was time to escape, but every day something or other had convinced me it wasn't time. Not yet.

When Elikai had left his chambers, fates near beaming a few short moments ago, I'd decided to follow silently.

Ensuring I kept a good distance behind him, I was determined to find out what was putting such a big smile on his face the same day he was to bury his father. Of course, I knew he wasn't upset about the funeral, quite the opposite, but usually he was a master of at least acting the part.

This morning, though, he hadn't been able to keep up appearances to contain his excitement, and I needed to know why.

I didn't think I could detest the male more than I already did, but then he'd turned from narcissism to murder and blackmail, and I realized I absolutely could.

I reached the stairs just in time to see him enter the throne room below, just off the grand hallway. Could this be where he'd hidden Kane's sword?

What are you up to, Elikai?

I smiled to myself as I remembered that I just happened to know the perfect place that would allow me to see straight into that room unnoticed, and carefully made my way to the antechamber corridor that ran parallel with the throne room.

Elikai insisted it wasn't safe for 'someone like me' to roam the castle with a thrakos on the loose, and I could hardly tell him I knew the thrakos story was bullshit. I'd take the company of a thrakos over an unhinged prince any day of the week, but I wasn't about to tell him that either.

In the days since the King's death, he'd resumed locking me in his chambers while he was busy doing fates knew what from sunrise until long after sunset. Or so he believed.

With Thalia's help, I'd managed to sneak out a few times to help Kane with his search for the sword, but there were only so many places I could look on this floor of the castle, and it was risky to stray too far in case he came looking for me.

I hadn't told Thalia what I was searching for. It was safer for her to not know, but she was very good at not asking questions, which I loved her for. She and I had bonded so much in such a relatively short space of time since choosing to trust each other. She truly felt like a friend.

Alaric and Axel had left the castle to 'hunt down the thrakos responsible' shortly after the announcement. Returning two days later with the news the entire kingdom had been waiting for–the perpetrator had been found and dealt with.

I wasn't entirely sure where they'd spent those days, or what they'd actually been doing, but it had worked. They'd managed to successfully cover up that neither of the princes had been present during their father's murder.

Kane had been stronger and more resilient than I'd expected, given everything he was dealing with. He was searching for that sword with absolute steely determination. Any love he might have still had for his brother seemed to have been utterly vanquished now. Understandably.

I'd tried to help him search whenever I could, and I was confident I hadn't left a single stone unturned when it came to places Elikai could have hidden it in and around his chambers. But it was a big castle, with expansive grounds. The castle itself was lined with hidden passages, secret doors and clever hiding spots; he could have hidden it anywhere, with any luck it would be in the one I was heading toward.

I worried whether we'd ever find it, not that I'd admit that to Kane. When the only light he brought to his searches came from hope, I couldn't be the darkness to snuff it out.

With the king's murder allegedly avenged and the funeral taking place later this morning, the realm could officially begin its mourning period.

Of course, it had not impressed Elikai that he would not be crowned for another four weeks following the burial of his father. But as the master of keeping up appearances, he seemed to be sucking it up. For now.

Everything was to be on hold for the duration of the mourning period; collecting taxes, sending the horde on hunts, waging war... It was a millennia old tradition. A time for peace, meant to be used to reflect on the monarch's service to his realm.

Though my mother hadn't often spoken in much detail about the past, I recalled her telling me of how the realm had been so devastated by the death of the last king that even the trees and flowers appeared to weep during his mourning period.

In my opinion, Augustus deserved nothing but tears of joy to be shed upon his demise, having done nothing to make a positive impact during his reign. Even tears of joy were more than the male deserved.

I reached the section of wall that concealed the secret room I'd once accidentally stumbled upon and traced my fingers across the surface to find the ridge I needed to press down on.

It opened with a *click*, and I blinked rapidly as I entered, hoping it might help my eyes adjust quicker to the darkness that assaulted them. I lined my right eye up with the small hole and squinted to focus on the scene beyond.

Elikai was alone. He sat on the gilded throne that had been carved eons ago by a predecessor. Shaped from dark mahogany, it gleamed in the light, the rich wood and gold reflecting in the sunlight.

No expense had been spared, the seat was decorated with rich, red velvet and golden studs–it was the centerpiece of the room. His hands resting on the dragons engraved on the arm rests, an ankle perched on his knee, looking very confident and casual. Like he belonged there. *Asshole*.

The sight of him in the royal seat filled me with dread as a shudder trickled down the length of my spine, making me squirm uncomfortably. I had seen what happened in this throne room from this same secret place before. Though it was a more merciful time I witnessed, I had no doubts about how Elikai clearly looked forward to committing his own atrocities.

He looked far too comfortable there, and the thought of him on the throne as king was too dreadful to think too hard about.

I waited with bated breath for something to happen, and a few moments later, movement to the left of the vast room grabbed my attention.

Even squinting through my tiny peephole, I could see how royally pissed off Kane was as he entered the room, followed by a stone-faced Alaric. My heart skipped a few beats, as it did every time I saw them. It was strange how much I missed them even when we were all living under the same roof, but it didn't stop the flutters in my stomach as they crossed the room as I watched on from my hiding place in the wall.

"Well, it's about time you showed up, Nekane," Elikai sneered, standing from the throne and walking toward the space where a table and chairs had obviously been set up for whatever this meeting was.

I bit my tongue as I fought the urge to call through the thick, damp wall that Elikai had barely arrived a few minutes before they had, but they already knew he was a prick, so I thought better of it. The male just made me so angry.

"This meeting wasn't supposed to take place for another few weeks yet, but I see you managed to convince the advisors it needed to happen now," Kane said.

"I simply told Desmond that there was no harm in preparing for the realm's future *while* we mourn. I see you brought the useless general. Tell me, Alaric, how are you enjoying the whispers and the looks of shame everywhere you tread?"

"You have no fucking right to be dragging Alaric's name through the dirt like you are. You know damn well he had nothing to do with it. You should be thanking him for everything he h–"

"Pha," Elikai laughed, cutting Kane off. "He should be thankful he still has a job. Besides, I am still waiting for some gratitude from you, *King killer*. If it wasn't for me, it would be *your* funeral we were to attend today, not father's."

"You want me to thank you?" Kane said incredulously. "I can barely bring myself to look at you. But if it's a thank you you're wanting, then give me my fucking sword back!" he demanded, slamming his hands down on the table so hard I was surprised it didn't splinter under his palms.

I didn't miss the quick flicker of fear in Elikai's eyes, but he swiftly covered it with a smirk. "Now, little brother, why would I want to do that? My way is so much more interesting," he mocked.

Fates, his narcissism is boundless.

Kane ran a hand through his unkempt raven hair. "Elikai…" he tried again, his voice more exasperated now, but not exactly pleading.

"Nekane, listen and listen well because this is the last time I will say this. That sword is in *my* safekeeping, somewhere you will never think to look. So unless you are so bored with your sorry existence that you have a death wish, I suggest you drop it and just learn to live with doing what I tell you, when I tell you, and how I tell you. I can guarantee that is the best way to ensure it remains hidden."

The way Elikai spoke was so calm, so matter of fact, not at all like he was blackmailing his own brother. I suddenly felt claustrophobic as I thought about the severity of the situation, the power and control Elikai had over not just Kane, but Alaric as well.

The latter mentioned male had been disturbingly still and silent throughout the exchange, glowering like he might explode at any moment, and a large part of me wanted him to.

When I'd found out that Alaric had covered up the murder by blaming the thrakos, I'd been both frustrated and saddened by what it would mean for the innocent race. They were already villainized and hiding in the Fading Vale, and it only added to the realms' already unfair and unwarranted hatred of them.

I understood that they were the perfect ones to blame. It would be easy enough to convince everyone not to look any further or deeper for the guilty party, but it pained me no less.

Fates, they'd already had cold, hard proof that thrakos had been in the city recently; the blood drained carcasses we had found in the woods when Kane had fought the bear shifter and his idiot hyena friends would have been unmistakable evidence.

"He's already coverin' for yer arse, boy. Somethin' he wouldnae need to do if yeh hadnae manipulated everythin'," Alaric seethed. His tone and the look on his face left no question over exactly how furious he was with Elikai and his games.

"Nekane, does *he* really need to be here? His accent is just so… off putting," Elikai whined, purposely not looking in Alaric's direction as he spoke, and I couldn't help but roll my eyes at his pettiness.

Thankfully, Desmond and Charles, two of the royal advisors, entered just then, looking even paler than their usual ancient selves normally did. *This can't be good.*

"What's wrong?" Kane asked, not missing a beat as he took in their appearance.

Charles looked at Desmond, who then cleared his throat. "It seems there has been a slight issue with the late King's Last Will and Testament," he said as they made their way to stand beside the table.

So that's what this meeting's about. This was why Elikai had such a spring in his step on his way here; the advisors were here to read the will.

Charles gestured for the Princes to take the chairs at either end. "You may want to take a seat, your highnesses."

Alaric moved into position to stand behind Kane. It was subtle, but it made it clear to everyone he was declaring his loyalty to one brother over the other.

"What 'slight issue'? If it's the fact that as the crowned Prince, I have yet to see a crown placed on my head, I would agree. Yes, that is an issue," Elikai said, before he remembered himself. "For the kingdom, of course. To leave them without a ruler for the duration of the mourning period is a risk I am incredibly uncomfortable with."

The two advisors shared a worried glance. "My Prince, when Desmond and I visited your father's safe to retrieve his Last Will and Testament, we found a stack of journals, s-some dating back hundreds of years, along with some sort of r-research file, but no will."

Elikai pushed his chair out quickly to stand, towering over them in a gesture meant to intimidate. "Then find where it is being kept and bring it here already!" he ordered.

"Just sit down an' shut up for a minute," Alaric growled.

Gobsmacked, Elikai did an excellent impression of a fish as he looked around for someone to punish Alaric for what he'd just said, but no one came forward.

"I assure you, my prince, we have looked everywhere we can think of," Charles said.

"I'm sure you have," Kane said, in an attempt to calm the room. "What kind of research file was it, Charles?" he asked. He looked sincerely curious when he looked at the old advisor, imploring him to continue.

Charles looked to Desmond, who eventually said, "Perhaps it would be easier to first go back to the beginning. When your grandfather, Firion Regis, was alive and chief counsel to King Dyvrad."

What? Augustus' father was chief counsel to the previous King?

His eyes narrowed off into the distance as he cast his mind back through his centuries old memories. "You may be aware that your father was raised here in the castle. From what I remember of Augustus, he was pleasant and quite the outspoken and ambitious boy. It seemed that his close friendship with the Dyvrad princess was what kept him in check though, because it was when their friendship came to an abrupt end that he started to change. As the years went by, he spoke out against the way King Dyvrad ruled and whispers spread of how the high fae were the superior race and should therefore be in charge. Of course, some agreed with his way of thinking, but most were happy with the way things were–"

"What does this have to do with anything?" Elikai interrupted. "Just get to the point."

Alaric shot him a warning glare that spoke to it being his one and only.

"When we couldn't locate the will, we began to look through the various journals.

And, well, it appears he had some help in overthrowing King Dyvrad. From what we have read, he made a deal with King Vandenburg of the Mount Mortum Kingdom, and it is the bargain he made that has everything to do with the news we must now bring."

"Spit it out!" Elikai snapped.

"I-it was common knowledge within the castle that King Dyvrad did not see eye to eye with King Vandenburg. Dyvrad had never liked the way Vandenburg ruled over the fae of his realm so cruelly, and tensions were at an all-time high between Dezrothia and Mount Mortum. Augustus shared many similar beliefs to the Vandenburgs, and his ambitious nature eventually led him to desire the throne for himself. The problem was, he was not an heir, so in order to get it, he would need to usurp King Dyvrad. And for that, he needed substantial backing, both financially and with soldiers on the ground. With a war on the horizon between the two realms, King Vandenburg knew he would not win."

You could hear a pin drop as he checked to be sure everyone was following, and at Kane's nod of encouragement, he continued.

"It seems your father entered an alliance when marrying your mother, Kahina. If the information we found in the safe is true, which we believe it is, then she was actually the niece of King Vandenburg. The deal was that your father was to marry her and produce an heir with Vandenburg blood, thus ensuring the kingdoms would become allied in the strongest way should war ever visit. In return, King Vandenburg would help Augustus in his plight for the throne."

The silence was heavy as tension grew within the room.

I was surprised when it was Alaric who spoke next. "There were rumors for centuries that he must've gotten support from somewhere, so it makes sense, but I'm no' seein' what this has to do with the Princes? It doesnae matter how he got the crown, jus' that he succeeded."

Desmond nodded. "Yes, Augustus' plan worked, thanks to the aid of King Vandenburg, and therefore he was oath bound to marry Kahina and produce an heir. However, years into his reign, after implementing the Lores and the creation of the thrakos, he received information from a warlock who claimed to have infiltrated a rebel camp within the Fading Vale."

My nails dug into the wall I was leaning against in irritation, and I bit my lip to keep myself from betraying my hiding place by letting a vexed huff escape. The way he said the last two words in a shuddered whisper, like saying the name of the place I'd grown up aloud was akin to bringing a curse to your door.

"The warlock had allegedly been rejected when applying for a position within the horde. So, he had taken it upon himself to become an unofficial spy for the crown, hoping to gain knowledge great enough to prove his worth to the King. However, he hadn't accounted for the fact that the knowledge he brought back with him would be a threat to the alliance between King Regis and King Vandenburg. It was the end of him, and he was permanently silenced."

"What knowledge?" Kane asked, and I found my toes were curling in anticipation.

"The warlock claimed to have placed listening stones in the rebel camp leader's tent. One day, he'd heard them talking of an ancient and powerful seer that had prophesied the coming of twin heirs. The research file we found holds this prophecy and what appears to be centuries of notes and scribbles trying to decode it."

Kane leaned forward on his elbows, his brow furrowed as he tried to make it make sense. "Why would a prophecy about twins threaten his alliance?"

"This is ridiculous and a waste of my time," Elikai sneered. "Stop talking in riddles and just tell us what the prophecy says so we can get on with discussing what to do about the will."

Charles opened the file he had been holding with visibly shaking hands. He cleared his throat, shared a quick nervous glance with Desmond again, then began to read from the paper.

When twin heirs are born, the raven shall mourn.

From the coming of age, the brave can change.

Those impure shall grow, to rise with the low.

The throne will lay bare, for the true rightful heir.

One will bring horror, one will bring honor.

The chance to transcend, before one will ascend.

To bring forth this feat, much bloodshed and deceit.

With the blood of the last, restore what has passed.

Awareness and recognition trickled down my spine the more he read. I knew those words, but from where? I'd never received a prophecy from the fates, and no one had ever told me of one they'd received, so why was it so familiar?

"Based on the contents of this file, your father spent centuries analyzing it, and it seems he thought he'd found a loophole that would ensure his throne would not '*lay bare*'."

Kane took the file from Charles and started scanning its contents, while Elikai looked bored, not even making an attempt to work out whatever Charles was obviously too scared to say.

I replayed the prophecy in my mind, desperately trying to commit it to memory before the words slipped away from me.

Alaric was already several strides ahead, not worrying about the words but what it meant. "There isnae a will 'cause he didnae name a crown prince..." he muttered as though to himself.

As the words left his lips, the brothers met eyes across the table, clashing together like two waves on a bluff amid a hurricane.

What am I missing?

Shit, I seriously needed to write the damned prophecy down while it was still fresh in my head.

"Exactly," Charles said, clasping his hands together, like the answer was all of a sudden blindingly clear for everyone. Then again, I seemed to be the only one struggling to keep up, and they weren't aware I was even listening, so they were hardly about to share with the class.

"Though he never appears to have managed to work out the whole thing, the late King Regis believed that part of the prophecy meant his heirs would be his undoing. But he couldn't refuse to have children as it would bring King Vandenburg's wrath to his door by breaking his oath. When parts of the prophecy began to unfold, he thought the best chance he had at changing the course of Fate, and remaining firmly in power himself, was to simply not officially *choose* an heir, thus meaning neither prince could be the *'true, rightful heir'*."

I gasped, pulling back from the peephole to slam a hand over my mouth, hoping that I had not been heard and my hiding place revealed.

This is huge. It meant Kane could try for the crown, but then… no, no, no–

I flattened myself up against the wall again so as not to miss anything, but by the time I lined my eye up once more, Elikai had shot to his feet and snatched the file from Kane's hands.

"You *will* support my claim, Nekane," he said, his voice laced with allure he didn't even try to hide. Then he stormed out of the room, leaving everyone else behind with their shock.

I had a sickening feeling I knew *exactly* what he intended to do if Kane dared stand in his way. *Fates, where is that fucking sword?*

I waited for everyone to leave the throne room, completely dumbfounded as I tried to digest everything that had just come to light before me.

This wasn't just huge, it had the potential to alter the realm as we knew it. Kane had the chance to change so many lives for the better across Dezrothia.

Suddenly, light infiltrated the tight space, causing me to jump back and shield my eyes from the onslaught of it.

Something seized my arm. A large hand with thick fingers. It tightened firmly and before I could even blink, let alone defend myself, I was being dragged out and into the antechamber like I weighed nothing.

Shit, shit, shit!

CHAPTER 6

Nekane

Like I didn't have enough to deal with right now. Between the unintentional murder of my father, and my brother playing hide and seek with the murder weapon; the fates have decided to throw a prophecy at us.

Fucking great. Just perfect. This is exactly what I'd wanted when I woke up this morning. The day was already filled with 'fun'. Why not add a prophecy to the will reading and the funeral?

I don't know what I'd done to piss the fates off so thoroughly, but I was pretty convinced at this point that they wouldn't stop until I broke. I was already paddling desperately to keep my head above the water, but it was like being terrorized by a Kraken who was dead set on pulling me down into the darkness and refusing to let me go.

The sensation of Alaric's skin brushing against mine pulled me out of my head, and I realized he was subtly steering me off my original path from the throne room, heading for the staircase and toward the corridor on our left instead.

I'd assumed we'd be heading up to the library, but he had somewhere else in mind to discuss that shitshow and information overload that had just been shared with us.

Tilting my chin, I gave him a questioning look, noticing the muscles in his bare arms were tense as he balled his fists at his side.

"This way," he said through a clenched jaw, and I followed.

I rarely bothered with this part of the castle near the throne room. *Perhaps it would be a good place to look for the sword next?*

Fates, I'd tried all the places I could think of that Elikai was likely to have hidden it and had no luck. With the razor's edge of a guillotine hanging over my neck, capable of falling free and without warning at any moment, anything was worth trying. If Alaric knew of somewhere I didn't, I had no problem giving it a try at this point.

We entered a small room that looked barely used. The thick curtains were drawn, blocking out the day. Flames in the fireplace softly crackled, giving off a soft light in the room and the plush oversized chair in the corner tempted me to return here with a good book and just escape from it all.

I went to stand beside the comfort of the blaze, leaning my forearm on the mantel and trying to give off the appearance of being calmer than I actually was. I needn't have bothered though, because apparently Alaric had lost his ever loving mind.

He was caressing an oddly specific patch of wall at the opposite end of the room, his brows knit together tightly in concentration.

I ignored him in favor of looking absolutely anywhere else, not far gone enough into insanity yet–despite the fate's best efforts–to get jealous of stone and mortar.

When he started kneading it, massaging it like dough with his large calloused hands, though, I had to say something. "Alaric, what are you doing?"

A small click sounded, and the last thing I expected to see was some sort of cupboard that definitely had not been there before with a barely dressed, slightly shaken looking Eva being pulled out of it and into the room.

Her silver and black hair was braided back out of her face and her big eyes were so wide and frantic, I saw her pupils constrict as they hit the light. "How the–"

"If yer gonnae sneak around the castle, at least be fuckin' quiet about it, Angel," Alaric growled as she struggled to shake his grip off her arm. *What the fuck?* How did he know she was in there? Where even *was* there?

She visibly relaxed at the sound of his rough timbre. "Fates, Alaric, you scared me. I thought it was Charles or Desmond, or worse... Elikai." She shuddered, and just hearing my twins' name on her lips brought my simmering rage to the surface, all sense of the calm I was trying to project pushed aside.

After shaking off Alaric's grasp and brushing the dust from her dusky pink nightgown, she met my eyes and smiled.

I smiled back and was surprised to find it felt like a genuine, dimpled one, despite the anger she'd just unknowingly unleashed.

"Aye. Thank the fates it wasnae them, but it easily fuckin' coulda been, an' you'd be in a whole fuckin' lot of hot water right now if it had," Alaric hissed, pacing and running a hand through his dirty blonde locks several times before pausing to turn to her. "Just what do yeh think you were doin' in there?"

Her smile turned into a pout as she folded her arms, unintentionally pressing her breasts together. I watched on as Alaric fought between lecturing her and the sudden onslaught of dickstraction.

We'd both experienced what her body could do to a male now, and no amount of stress or the need to unravel a riddle could make my eyes wander from the sight of her in front of me.

'I fucked Angel' wasn't the first thing I had expected Alaric to tell me when he returned from his fake mission to hunt down the thrakos we'd pinned the death of my father on. It sounded like a confession, as though he had expected me to be pissed off about it. But more than anything, all I felt was jealousy. Not of him fucking her, but of me not being there.

Taking in a lungful of the dusty air that carried their alluring scents, I massaged my temples. I could feel another headache setting in, but I couldn't muster the energy to say anything to diffuse their back and forth that was only adding to it.

Eva argued her case like a queen, while Alaric, in full over-protective alpha male fashion, told her of all the ways she would have been tortured if they had found her spying. None of which sounded much like a good time.

How had Eva even found the room? Was I the only one that didn't know there were concealed doorways in the walls of the home I had grown up in? She had hardly been living here any time at all and was already more familiar with the castle than I was.

I hadn't needed the reminder today that I had been walking around with my eyes closed for the past twenty-five fucking years, but it would be good to know if my brother knew about them. Hopefully not if I was to stand any chance of finding where he'd hidden the sword.

My mind was back on the prophecy by the time Eva and Alaric–finished with their battle of wills–came over to stand with me near the crackling fire.

"Look, I accidentally stumbled across this room a while ago when I was first brought here. So when Elikai left his chambers this morning in a *disturbingly* chipper mood, I followed him in the hope he might lead me to where he was hiding the sword," she huffed.

"Or at least something that we could use against him in order to get it back." She sunk down into the chair with a sigh, causing the material of her nightgown to bunch around her smooth thighs. "When I saw he'd gone into the throne room… I knew that would be the perfect place to look in and find out what was putting an extra spring in his step. Especially just hours before the *funeral…*" She let the word hang heavy in the air.

None of us were particularly upset over the funeral service happening later today, but we weren't exactly looking forward to it either.

I looked toward the secret room. Perhaps I could just stay in there today instead and shirk my responsibilities?

Annoyingly, one of them had already righted it because the entrance was nowhere to be found. Even knowing where the doorway was, it blended in so well with the wall that I'd fucking lost it already.

Eventually, Alaric cleared his throat to ask, "How much did yeh hear, Angel?"

She dropped her gaze, fidgeting her hands in her lap sheepishly as she confessed, "Everything."

I watched her for a moment, taking her in. It felt like an age since the kiss we'd shared. A kiss that had been so potent I'd left to speak to my brother with no real thought aside from feeling like I would move mountains to have her, like nothing and nobody could stand in my way.

It hadn't gone to plan, not that there had been a fucking plan. My brother had succeeded in finally showing me his true face in the most unfathomable way, and I'd been caught up in his twisted games ever since.

Suddenly, Eva shot up from her seat, breaking me from my memories of that fate's cursed day. "I need to write it down… the prophecy I mean… I'm already struggling to remember the words and–"

Reaching into my pocket, I pulled out the folded paper, holding it up between two fingers. "You mean *this* prophecy, Princess?" I asked, and her eyes widened.

I'd stashed it mere moments before Elikai had snatched the file from my hands. I might have been ignorant of his intent before, but I was no fool now. Knowing I needed to remain sharp at all times, I was steering clear of the mind-clouding booze. Now more so than ever.

The temptation to give into the lure of drowning in a bottle of whiskey at the Crooked Claw was high. It would be nice to relax, even just for a few hours, but it wasn't an option. I could no longer allow my brother to have the upper hand.

Eva was on her feet, making for the scrap of paper. "You took it?" She beamed, and I nodded, handing it over.

She unfolded it hurriedly and narrowed her eyes as she pored over the words. The prophecy itself was written with perfect penmanship, but the notes scrawled into the margins told a whole other story of the madness behind the scribbles trying to decipher it.

There were areas with thick lines slashed through them, obviously they were theories that had been disregarded, and others were barely legible in untidy scrawl.

Alaric stood with us now, muttering some notes under his breath that must have been my father's attempts at decoding.

"I can't put my fingers on why exactly, but it's familiar..." Eva muttered, and Alaric's eyes shot up to meet hers.

"Yeh ken the prophecy?" he asked, a little too eagerly than was normal for him.

"I think so," she said, her voice softer than it had been, as if she was trying to remember why it was so familiar to her.

Closing her eyes, she hummed a gentle tune, gradually getting louder and more confident with it until she froze entirely, letting out a small gasp and looking between the two of us.

"I think maybe my mum knew about it... she sang these words to me. Or at least something similar. It was a nighttime lullaby to soothe me to sleep, though it has been thirty or so years since I last heard it..." she trailed off.

Her stare was a thousand miles away and as I thought over what she'd said, I realized how little I still knew about her. It was probably for the best. The more I knew, the more I liked, and with the direction my life was currently taking, I had a feeling my days were numbered in the castle. Or just numbered, period. At the very least, she was better off staying away from me. I couldn't offer her the future she deserved.

Alaric had been eying her warily, like she was a puzzle he was trying to solve on his own. "The prophecy isnae what we need to discuss righ' now, anyway."

I rolled my eyes, already knowing where he was going with this.

When the advisors spoke of the bargain my father had made to overthrow his predecessor and then the subsequent predicament he had been in to sire an heir, I'd not missed the irony of how fate had served him a taste of his own medicine in the end. Only, arguably, what my brother had done was worse, or at least more unsettling in its deviousness.

Unlike our father, Elikai hadn't had to make any deals or alliances. He hadn't even gotten his hands dirty to achieve his goal. He'd seen an opportunity and ran with it. Now I was held over a barrel like a fucking pawn, and I hated it.

If I didn't do what he said, if I didn't support his claim to the throne, he would pin our father's murder on me, and I'd be locked in the dungeons, waiting to be executed for treason. If I went along with it and spent my immortality as his dutiful puppet, I'd likely regret not taking the execution while I'd had the chance.

"Alaric's right," Eva sighed. "Kane, do you realize what this means? That you have every right to stake a claim on the throne..."

She was so close now I could feel her breath. She took my hand in hers, pressing the paper into my palm and looking at me with pleading eyes.

I didn't know what to say. I had felt the allure Elikai had layered on his words, not that it had worked on me. My mental shields were up around him all the time to stop him from doing exactly that.

Even if we found the sword and my hands were no longer tied, it wasn't a position I'd ever wanted. I'd always thought Elikai would be much better at ruling the realm than me, and I'd grown up assuming he was the foregone conclusion for our father's throne.

He'd been the golden boy from birth, training for this role his entire life. He had been invited to royal meetings from a young age, while I'd been little more than a shadow darkening the castle's hallways, neither welcome nor wanted.

Elikai had always acted the part of a prince, the way he spoke, the way he dressed, the way he was with the fae in the city, winning their adoration with a lifetime's worth of false charm.

I realized now though, that either way, the realm would be fucked. Our father had no intention of making either of us heir apparent. His disdain for me had always been obvious, so it was expected that Elikai would step into his shoes. The question was why create this illusion if he had no plans of ever giving up the crown in the first place?

Problem was, I didn't even know the secrets of the castle I'd grown up in, so how could they expect me to know anything about the places and politics beyond its walls? Elikai might be a cruel, unhinged king, but I'd be no better at ruling it blind.

It dawned on me as I looked between Alaric and Eva that I cared more for these two fae than all the others.

I refused to be like my father, caring nothing for anyone, not me, not even Elikai, and least of all his realm. He'd just wanted the power of being the monarch all to himself, and to do that, he'd needed to keep up appearances.

What kind of father willingly let his son go into dangerous situations, knowing he wasn't even properly trained? Knowingly putting his heir apparent's immortality at risk, like with the kraken or the rebels in the Vale?

It didn't matter that Elikai talked a big game. Alaric would have reported back that he had dropped out of his training years ago. Yet he let him run head first into situations that could cause his death.

The *one* living being I thought my father cared about... he didn't.

As for the realm, his subjects, those who diligently followed his rule to the letter–

whether through fear or respect, it didn't matter–he'd left them with no one fit to reign in his stead. All because of his egotistical fantasy of being king forever.

The realization was a punch to the gut.

I met Eva's eye and told her truthfully, "Of course I know what it means, Princess. In the same way, I know what you want me to say, but I can't."

"You heard the prophecy. The line about 'twin heirs' is obviously about you and Elikai. One will bring horror and one will bring honor… That's *you*, Kane! *You* will bring honor! I just know it."

A selfish part of me *really* liked the way she looked at me as she spoke with so much conviction, like I was actually worth something, but I couldn't let her think I was some savior.

"You couldn't possibly know that for sure. I promise you, I'm not meant to be the king, never have been."

The hold she still had on my hand tightened. "I've *seen* the horrors your brother is capable of. Believe me. But I have also seen you show great honor, Kane. I saw with my own eyes how you dealt with the spider shifters of Rangaran–"

"How?" I interrupted, thinking back to that day in the throne room and quickly answering my own question with a glance at where the hidden doorway had been. "You know what? It doesn't matter. You also will have seen the way Elikai reacted to the prophecy, heard the threat he made as he left that room. You know as well as I that he won't think twice about resurfacing that blade the moment I make any kind of move against him, and I fucking guarantee you it won't be to hand it over, shake my hand and bid me good luck in our little competition. This isn't just sibling rivalry, Princess. It would be war."

I watched as the hope dwindled from her face, and it pained me to know I'd caused it, but it didn't change a thing. She knew the monster my brother was. She'd called him as much the very first day I'd met her. Deep down, she probably only thought it was a good idea for me to reach for the crown because I was the lesser of two evils, not because I was remotely worthy of it.

I didn't know how to rule a kingdom. I knew how to fight, fuck, and drink liquor. End of list.

I turned to Alaric to back me up, but was met by a look of utter disappointment, which was almost worse than Eva's despair.

"Not you as well," I moaned in exasperation. "It's not happening. Besides, we haven't even buried the last asshole that sat on the throne yet, so maybe we should get to that," I sniped.

Today was really not the fucking day for having this shit dumped on me.

"Fine," Alaric said. "For now, let's just stay focused on findin' the sword. We're runnin' outtae places to look, so we should be close."

"Yes, maybe we should talk about it again once we have the sword," Eva agreed, clearly not yet fully appreciating how much I would not change my stance on this.

I had no problem fighting my brother. Fuck, I would welcome it with open arms, bare fists, and a shit-eating grin on my face, but it didn't mean I wanted to be king afterwards. He'd spent *years* winning the hearts of the fae, and I'd just nodded my head to them on the streets of Ezerat when en route to the tavern.

"Where's next to search?" Eva asked. "It's not in Elikai's chambers, of that I'm certain."

"Yeh need to be careful, Angel. Leave it to us."

If looks could kill, Alaric would be a goner, but I nodded my agreement. Any irritation I'd been feeling toward her suddenly swapped for worry.

She'd fulfilled her part, turning Elikai's rooms upside down whenever his back was turned, but it was too risky for her. Fates, if Elikai ever grew suspicious of her... A full body shudder ran through me. It wasn't worth thinking about.

"I want to help–"

Alaric cut her off. "The funeral starts soon," he said, changing the subject.

"Yeah. We need to get out of here. Thalia will no doubt be looking for you to get ready," I said.

Eva expelled her exasperation in a huff. "Fine," she said, pushing her way through Alaric and me, heading for the exit.

Several paces from the door, she abruptly stopped, turning back to us.

"Kane," she called, her voice softer now than mere moments before. "Your father... he, he was a bastard, no offense, but he was still the only parent you had," she said earnestly, her eyes glazing slightly as she turned and looked up at me. "My parents' death was... well, let's just say I know what it's like when you're dealing with grief at the same time as trying to survive. Battling every day to keep putting one foot in front of the other and not trip up. I don't have siblings, but I have a best friend, who... might be lost to me... and I guess after what your brother did, I've been thinking that maybe you feel you lost him too in that room with your father..."

She gulped, closing her eyes for a moment as she took a deep breath in.

"I never know what to say before funerals, but I just want you to know that you will be okay and I'm here for you."

Rubbing the back of my neck, I forced myself to meet her eyes as I spoke through the hardness that was suddenly in my throat. "Thanks, Princess," was all I managed, but she'd hit the nail on the head.

Though my grief over my father's death wasn't all-consuming–I only had to remind myself of the countless years of abuse at his hands to shake off any sadness I might have felt–it *had* felt like I'd lost the only family I'd had at that moment in his suite.

I hadn't told either of them, and maybe I never would, but in the days since my father's death, I'd started thinking of them as my family. Or perhaps I'd seen them like that for a while. Alaric especially.

They may not be my family by blood, but by choice. And unlike the way my biological family had always treated me, I knew without a doubt that there was nothing I wouldn't do to keep them safe. I'd always protect them, whatever the cost.

CHAPTER 7

Axel

I kicked back on my scarcely cushioned horizontal leaning post, tired of waiting around as a small fire crackled away in the hearth.

It was always more fun with at least two fae, but here I was an hour in, growing increasingly bored with playing 'extreme catch' on my own. Tossing my pretty little dagger into the air over and over, catching it perfectly by the hilt every time.

Wouldn't want to lose a finger or gut myself like a fish by accident. I was trying to kill time, not myself.

The funeral was set to start soon, and no one would notice my absence at the ceremony, so I planned to make the most of it by going down into the catacombs while everyone was busy paying their final respects to their shithead king. I'd been waiting for the castle halls to clear, but it was taking *forever*.

Putting the dagger down, I shifted in my too short, sorry excuse for a bed, knees bent to keep my feet from dangling off the end.

My room here was alright, or it would be if I were a foot shorter and slept in the fetal position, but it was a place to sleep and the other soldiers who shared the rooms surrounding mine weren't too annoying.

My room at the castle had been Alaric's once, but he'd let me take it once he started living up on the Princes' floor in one of Nekane's guest suites. It wasn't like Alaric would let just *anyone* have his room, even if it meant it sat empty otherwise. He liked to be a bastard whenever he could get away with it. Not that many knew that.

The rest of the horde hadn't been impressed that someone as seemingly fresh faced and new as I was had been given the general's room, but who really gave a fuck if they were pissed off? Definitely not me. And certainly not Alaric, who'd just glowered at any of them that'd tried to raise an objection.

Besides, it wasn't *that much* better than the rest–though probably larger, and private, with a bedside table to keep shit in–it still had the same uncomfortable single bed and dull decor, but at least it afforded me some privacy being tucked away from the majority of the horde, who all had roomies to deal with.

Everyone knew Alaric had trained me personally, and assumed he looked at me as his protégé. They just didn't know, and never would, how strong our bond truly was.

The truth of who I was, who we were.

Alaric was practically a brother to me and, unlike those twins, I'd die for him without question. The twins proved that being a rich, stuck up, spoiled prick meant you lost out on the more basic things in life, like morals and the ability to be a remotely decent fae.

Ok, maybe that was a little unfair.

Nekane seemed actually halfway decent from what I saw of him. He actually seemed to care more about what the horde soldiers thought of him than he did his own father or the high fae elite, which was weird for a prince.

Alaric spoke pretty fucking highly of him, too. But that might also be because Alaric had a massive influence on his life, like he did mine.

I had known Alaric my entire life. He was always a presence even before I'd been living in the castle. Still, having him around didn't stop me from missing Aunt Rose any less, and the charming home she kept and, most of all, her cooking.

His mum took me in as a babe and raised me as her own. I fucking hated the thought of how lonely my adopted mother had become since I'd taken a position within the horde, working for Alaric. Moving into the castle had been inevitable. Fates, Rose had even been the one to suggest it, but I liked to keep an eye on her, and from here I couldn't do a very good job of that.

When I visited on my days off, I never missed that faraway look she got when she thought no one was looking. She was lonelier than she let on. Not that the stubborn old luna would admit it.

She'd probably insist I move back in with her actually if she knew about my penchant for playing extreme catch. Or I'd get another speech about how I was unnaturally immature for an immortal of my age.

I just didn't like to take life too seriously. That was Alaric's job, and he was serious enough for the both of us.

Nothing seemed to shake him. But in all the years I had known him, the day he'd recounted what had happened between the King and princes was the first time I'd smelled actual fear on him, and that scared me. After all, what could unsettle that big bastard?

If it hadn't been for what I am, I wouldn't have caught it. The scent of it was partially masked by the sheer fucking rage he'd been emanating toward that little cunt, Prince Elikai. Add to it the fact he hadn't showered off Lady Evangelia's scent, it really wasn't easy to detect. But being the hybrid mutt I am, it was hard to keep shit like that from me, and he knew it.

The corridor outside had finally fallen quiet, and no more distant footsteps or low voices could be heard. I swung my legs off the cramped bed and stood, deciding I'd waited long enough. Stretching out my tense muscles, I left the room.

As expected, the hallways were empty, aside from the rows of creepy portraits and gleaming suits of armor that lined almost the entire route from my room to the entrance of the secret passageways to the catacombs.

It made a nice change not having to be stealthy and stick to the shadows, and I mentally thanked Augustus Regis for doing me a solid for the first time in his disgusting life. Or death. Whatever.

I made my way down the rocky, uneven paths of the catacombs, torch in one hand while my fingers traced the damp, rough walls with the other, heading for the portal.

Alaric needed to be present for the funeral and had been busier than Aunt Rose on All Fates Morning lately, so I was doing this on my own again, but it was no biggie.

Despite all the risks and extra work it had put on him, taking on the burden of the cover-up hadn't even been a question for Alaric. He was always going to support Nekane, regardless of whether he liked the prince or not, which I was pretty sure he did. Like a lot.

I saw the way they were together, especially recently. If Alaric weren't one for sticking to the rules the vast majority of the time, I was sure they would be banging already. Maybe they were? He'd told me of some crazy shit that went down between the three of them in the training halls the one day… and then he'd thoroughly fucked Lady Evangelia on her wedding day no less, so there was that…

Regardless, there were bigger reasons that he needed to make sure Nekane didn't end up going down as the King killer, so his efforts were necessary.

The bitch of it was, it left me to investigate this portal on my own. Alaric had spent the better part of a year making sure I was familiar with the maze that was the catacombs, so I didn't get lost down here. Between that and all that had happened recently, we hadn't had time to track down a witch trustworthy or powerful enough to tackle the stupid barrier.

The glow of it was intense as ever as I reached the cavern it was concealed in and perched on my usual rock, facing the ruins carved into the five pillars. As tall as three males, I had to bend my head backwards to see all the way to the top.

I struggled to concentrate on what was in front of me, the itch to satiate my never quite satisfied thirst to hunt, putting me on edge. Alaric was a damn sight older than me, and I couldn't control it like he did. Though his control was insane, despite how much practice he had over it.

Despite having a lot in common, we certainly weren't the same. I'd never met anyone like me. I wasn't even exactly sure *what* I was, really. Not for sure.

I watched yet another rodent making its way to the edge of the dome's purple hue and fought the urge to sink my fangs into it.

Whaaat? It was going to be dead soon anyway if it continued its path toward that lethal spell covering the area.

Just as I decided to give in to the urge to hunt the embarrassingly tempting snack, so I could get to work and focus, I heard a faint echo of voices coming from a passageway off to the left-hand side of the vast chamber.

I shot over to a darkened alcove toward the muffled sounds in a blur. Closing my eyes, I listened intently, but couldn't make out who or what it was. No one was ever down here. Most didn't even know these catacombs existed, and they definitely didn't know there was a portal to some unknown realm.

So who the fuck is it?

I needed to check it out, but Alaric would have my balls for taking a route I'd never explored. These tunnels were vast, and it would be far too easy to get lost down here.

Think Axel, think.

I remained in the shadows and turned toward where I'd seen the rat. I silently squatted into a crouch and once I had the little blood bag, I mean rodent, fixed in my sights again, I lept and snapped its tiny neck before it knew what was happening.

Sorry, mate. Needs must win, and I really needed something to mark my path.

Using a sharp canine, I pierced his skin through the rank fur and clenched my jaw as the metallic smell almost overwhelmed me. I wiped the traces of blood from my teeth with a sleeve, unable to trust myself not to drain the poor fucker if his blood hit my tongue. He was no use to me drained.

Inching my way into the passage, I held the rat out to my side, letting the crimson liquid slowly drip to the ground, leaving the perfect trail for me to find my way back to where I was supposed to be.

As I crept my way further into the expansive and unknown part of the catacombs, I felt a breeze washing over my face, like I was nearing an exit.

Hearing movement up ahead, I froze and moved flush to the wall to avoid being seen.

Up ahead, Prince Elikai's cuntish cronies were leaving a chamber and heading towards the source of the soft breeze. *What the fuck are they doing down here?*

I waited impatiently for them to disappear while my mind struggled to come up with a plausible reason they would even be down here. Elikai had to have something to do with it. Obviously. They were nothing if not his most loyal followers, hovering around him like moths to a flame or, more accurately, flies to shit.

I moved toward the carved stone archway they'd left, curiosity getting the better of me as I swallowed my laugh, picturing those idiots sprouting little wings, fluttering around a poo shaped Elikai. I'd have to think more about it later, at a less unknown and dangerous time, but maybe I'd draw it and post it under one of their doors in the near future.

I startled as an unfamiliar female voice called out, "Axel, is that you, dear?"

Dropping into a fighting stance, my dagger drawn and in my now vermin free hand, my eyes darted around, but no one was there that I could determine.

The voice had come from inside the chamber, and unless whoever it was could see through thick stone walls, how the fuck did she know someone was here? And how the fuck had she known *I* was that someone?

Her tone had been warm and grandmotherly, almost like she was going to finish with, 'I baked you a cake', and invite you in for tea.

I slunk closer and, with my back still against the wall, craned my neck around the archway to see inside, sniffing the air for any traces of a clue to who was in the room.

The small cave was decorated like a shrine to the Regis princes. Though from the portrait on the wall, I'd say specifically Elikai.

Items of furniture came into view, a bed and table, like someone was living in there. I couldn't imagine Nekane hiding some witch in the catacombs. I don't think he even knew about these tunnels.

Every surface was piled high with what smelled like items of Prince Elikai's clothing, and I fought a gag at the eau de pompous. There was the scent of something else, but it was hard to be sure given the reek. Maybe a witch?

Then I saw her. Sitting in an armchair across the room was a petite female, obviously waiting for me. Judging by the crow's feet that appeared with her smile when she saw me, I'd say she had several hundred years on my not quite eighty.

Her warm voice and friendly smile gave off a motherly vibe, and it was impossible for me to not feel warm and fuzzy.

At ease in her presence, I lowered my dagger and tried to make myself seem smaller as I entered, not wanting to scare the female. It was instinctual. A part of me didn't want to intimidate her. I knew my size made me look like a scary asshole, regardless of how Rose always swore I was more of a teddy bear.

Fates, I'd only recently visited her, but I missed her and her warm hugs already.

"Who are you?" I asked tentatively, taking in all the details of the room and the female within it, committing them to memory. "What the fuck is this place?"

"It's a long story, but trust me when I say you are the reason I allowed myself to be brought here, Axel, blood of my blood. We have much to discuss."

I cocked my head to the side, eyeing her warily as I took in the female's odd words. *Blood of my blood.* Not possible. I didn't have any relatives. Not blood related anyway. It was just me, Aunt Rose and Alaric, the three mutineers.

Backing away slightly, I shook my head. "You've mistaken me for someone else, witchy-witch," I told her. The warmth I had felt fading away with her cryptic words.

My senses were on high alert to her every movement now, my dagger raised, ready to use.

Why couldn't she have just said she'd baked me some sponge cakey goodness? I didn't want to kill the little old dear, but if she was a threat, I'd eliminate her.

The only thing I'd be adding to Alaric's already full plate would be eggs. Fuck you very much.

"Axel, please," she said, "I know it's you. I have been watching you all your life–"

"You're lying. I have never met you," I told her firmly. I breathed in again, more deeply this time, to fully take in her scent and noticed that it was somehow… familiar. *But, how?* The hairs on the back of my neck raised in awareness. Usually my gut instincts were on point, but I felt uneasy all the same.

"We met all too briefly, when you were a babe," she said, as though she was recalling a fond memory and my brow furrowed. "I have seen you more times than I can count."

Goodbye, motherly vibes. Hello, stalker vibes.

I could feel the desperation coming from her for me to hear her out though, so I gestured for her to continue.

"I know you don't understand and you have no reason to trust me, but please, let me explain. There is much to know and little time to tell you."

"You said we met when I was a babe? Expand." I demanded before I could stop myself, my thoughts racing in a war between ending this now and wanting to know more, as I tried to make sense of the situation.

"Yes, though it was so much more brief than I had ever hoped. Rose was in a much better position to raise you than I..."

At the drop of Rose's name, I darted forward, grabbing her by the hair and exposing her neck, pressing my blade hard enough for her to feel the warning.

"Who are you? And how the *fuck* do you know that name?" I hissed through gritted teeth, a snarl pulling at my upper lip as my protective instincts kicked into overdrive.

The witch flinched, but she didn't use her magic to defend herself.

A pang of guilt sparked through me, making me glance away, only to be met by the fucking portrait of Elikunt staring at me.

Why isn't she using her magic on me?

Perhaps I should hear her out? Maybe we *had* met? No, I couldn't confuse her familiar scent with loyalty. She was just some stranger, a nutter living in a cave dedicated to an even bigger nutter. And I was right to be pissed that she seemed to know things about me and my chosen family that she had no right knowing.

"I know the name because I am the one who sent you to her, Axel. To Ezerat..." When my grip on the blade didn't falter, she continued. "I know you have no reason to trust me, so perhaps it would help to see for yourself?" she suggested, and I released my hold to take a few steps back.

Warily eyeing the hand she was holding out for me to take, I realized that she wanted to share her memories with me.

"You're a seer?" I hedged, my probing gaze cutting between her eyes and her outstretched palm.

Only seer witches could *show* you their visions or memories, and only when they chose to. Alaric said it would exhaust them and leave them vulnerable, so why would she be willing to drain herself if it wasn't important?

She nodded. "Not just any seer, the most powerful seer in the realm. Well, since losing my sister, Thaelias, your grandmother, all those centuries ago."

At the word 'grandmother', I strode forward, grabbing her hand. A magical current immediately jolted through me, connecting us as it spread up my arm with a tingling sensation.

Fuck, I'd acted on impulse, but now wasn't the time for regrets. I'd gone with my gut and would have to deal with the consequences.

I felt another push of energy from the witch and my eyes rolled back into my head as nausea threatened to overwhelm me.

I'd never met a seer, not to my knowledge anyway, and it was just fucking typical of me to go jumping into a vision with one literally minutes after finding her living in a shrine to a lunatic.

Classic me.

Alaric was going to be so fucking pissed when he found out.

CHAPTER 8

Elikai

Where is that petulant female of mine?

It was at *least* ten minutes ago now that she'd *insisted* on me going ahead of her to join the procession, while she 'took a minute' to compose herself in the bathing chambers.

Being the gracious and understanding fiancé I was and not wanting her to embarrass us both, I'd allowed her the requested time alone. I would not have her shedding tears like an unattractive sniveling troll in front of my new subjects and humiliating me at the service. I would not allow pathetic female tears at a funeral to usurp this moment from me.

I might have known it wasn't a one minute job. She'd likely cried off all her makeup and was having the servant reapply it. I'd made it very clear to them both that dark makeup was essential to match the dress I'd had made for her to wear today. It truly was the perfect mourning gown, but she needed to walk at my side looking beautifully grief stricken, not out of control.

I fought not to tap my foot impatiently, it wouldn't do for my subjects to think her tardiness was frustrating me. Every set of eyes that landed on me, and there were many, would find a composed heir to the throne. The perfect prince, ready to step into his role as King. And my queen needed to compliment that.

Everyone was here now, all except my pretty little pet. I was keen to get the show on the road and out of the way, and all I needed to do was nod my head toward the officiant and everyone here would obey with haste. They'd begin the walk down the mountain to the soaring bell towers that were the Temple of the Fates the moment I ordered it. So why was my pet so ill mannered?

In hindsight, I should have just told her to suck it up. Threatened her somehow. Promised her more tears if she didn't compose herself. Perhaps a lesson in how to control her emotions under immense stress or pain would work. Conditioning could be fun…

Biting back my grin at the idea, I looked around at Ezerat's most elite. They'd come to bid farewell to their former king, and I saw more than one soiling their handkerchiefs as they sniffled, dabbing their tear-filled eyes, then their nose, and then back to their eyes again. *Disgusting.*

Perhaps I should be relieved that my pet had been smart enough to know better than to lose control of herself in public like they were. Yes, getting it out of the way in private was for the best, but now she was just taking liberties, and frankly, that had to stop. There would still be a lesson for her to learn.

Hurry up, pretty pet, I thought to myself over and over, as more and more high fae fought to catch my eye to give me a sympathetic look. The impulse to roll my eyes was strong, but thankfully, acting was one of my many talents.

I had perfected my sad smile and small nod over the last few days, but today, I added a quick 'look away' to the routine, as though seeing their sadness made my own all the more unbearable.

Truthfully, I didn't care for the funeral. It was little more than an inconvenience after the news I'd received this morning. What I *really* wanted to do was get back to my late father's office and continue my research.

Between leaving the throne room and now, I'd ransacked the entire space in search of his will, but alas, had discovered that the advisors were, in fact, correct. There wasn't one to be found.

I'd been about ready to murder the insolent fools, but amidst the papers and chaos, I'd uncovered… other things. Exciting things. Notebooks on experiments he'd partaken in. Weapons, spells, potions he and some insane warlock had invented. Some of which I could hardly wait to test out and put to use.

First though, I needed to meet with my dearest estranged uncle. King Vandenburg of the Mount Mortum Kingdom. While he hadn't been in Ezerat in a very long time, talk of his ruthless, evil nature was prevalent in the rumors that often spread throughout the castle.

If only I'd known he was of my blood, I might have done something to convince father to invite him to visit, though he clearly hadn't wanted him anywhere near Dezrothian soil. With good reason: King Vandenburg was a predator through and through.

Graves and Sloane were on their way right now, heading for the coast to sail to Mount Mortum, still in their funeral finery. There was no time to change, let alone pack. The first boat to leave the dock since my father banned it so many years ago. Just one of many changes to come. Reconnecting with my long-lost uncle was more important than obeying the rules of the mourning period.

They had strict instructions not to read the contents of the envelope, just to hand deliver it directly to the king himself. An invitation to Dezrothia and a promise of bloodshed as the entertainment of choice during his stay.

Not that he'd likely need the added encouragement to visit me, but we needed to bond quickly and naturally, and I'd thought up a genius way to ensure it.

I could hardly wait.

The way he ruled intrigued me, and I barely knew the half of it yet. The brief passages I'd skimmed this morning while reading my father's journals spoke volumes of his fear of him, and that excited me more than the lack of a will worried me. After all, my brother wasn't exactly in a position to step on my toes.

He didn't know it yet, but King Vandenburg and I would be great friends. He would become, for a time, my most powerful ally, and unlike my father, I would ensure that the power and control remained firmly in my hands. The deals made with him would give me the upperhand and he would never even know it was happening until it was too late.

"Elikai," Kane sneered through gritted teeth as he took his place next to me at the front of the procession, just behind the horse-drawn hearse carrying the coffin. "Where's Evangelia?" he asked, glancing around with a confused look on his otherwise attractive face.

With a deep sigh and a thoughtful expression, I reached out to give his shoulder a gentle squeeze, keeping my hand there just long enough for all to see this tender moment between the grieving princes.

Then, oh so quietly, I answered his question. "I do believe that it is none of your business where my female is."

Shrugging me off in a less than friendly manner, I saw the fool's eyes travel to the top of the castle steps, where something had clearly caught his eye. My curiosity peaked at his softened expression, and I followed his gaze.

My pretty pet's breath fogged in the chilled air as she cleared the castle doors, looking exactly as I'd envisioned in her gown. The skirt was made up of layer upon layer of the finest black tulle, puffing out around her shapely hips like a bell until it hit the ice frosted floor. It truly was a work of art.

The fitted bodice was made of real bone, pulling her waist in tightly before it met the skirt, which was covered with lace and beads, perfectly hiding where the two different materials met.

Her arms were covered with more of the delicate tulle, creating long flowing sleeves that trailed to the ground and–

My perusal was interrupted when the oaf of a horde general blocked my view of her. He was holding out his doubtlessly calloused hand, offering to help escort her down the steps, and my blood boiled at the thought of him touching my things.

I relaxed a little as I weighed up my options and considered the alternative; her slipping on the ice and humiliating me by toppling down the steps. I decided to bite my tongue and stay put.

Closing my eyes, I focused my exceptional hearing in their direction. "General Alaric," I heard her say, taking the hand he offered without so much as a flinch.

"Lady Evangelia," he greeted with a slight bow of his head.

Her silver hair was curled and pinned atop her head with a black veil of matching lace to cover most of her face, but I didn't miss how her cheeks flushed a deep pink. Obviously, she couldn't handle the cold crispness of the courtyard with just lace to cover her arms.

I wouldn't allow for her to ruin the aesthetics of the gown by covering it up with a coat; she would have to live with the cold during the service. Just another lesson for her to learn.

As the commoner assisted her in navigating the deep steps, he said something that I didn't catch and she... *giggled*. Giggled! What could he possibly have said that was so funny she'd *laugh* during a funeral?

Perhaps it was the chaotic female emotions. I'd heard funerals could have that effect on the emotionally weaker fae.

They eventually reached the bottom, and with a bow, he finally released his paw from my pet. "Thank you," she said, then dropped her voice to mutter something so quietly, even I couldn't hear it.

How strange. I would have to find out exactly what that was all about later.

I had plans for this evening with my pet and once I'd enacted them, she'd be putty in my hands. And if she wasn't, well, I was particularly gifted with the power of allure. Even high fae didn't stand a chance against it. So one way or another, tonight she would be more than happy to do and say *exactly* as I desired.

"Evangelia," Kane said with a nod, then mumbled, "Nice dress."

"Of course it is, *I* had it made specifically for her," I told him, loud enough for those around us to hear. Reaching an arm around her, I pulled her to me so she was flush against my side. "Don't we look the perfect picture of a grief-stricken couple, Nekane?" I muttered for only their ears.

I didn't miss his nostrils flare in anger as he turned away, his focus now on the black stallions attached to the hearse in front.

Tightening my grip with a squeeze, I murmured against her lobe, "The dress truly is perfect. But there is something missing. Hmmm." Inhaling deeply into her neck, I waited a few moments to ensure I had her full, undivided attention.

"What's missing?" she eventually asked, still frozen at my side.

"Pretty pet," I purred, nipping at her lobe. "Do you remember the look on your face when your parents' heads were sliced off?"

She stiffened in my grip and audibly gulped, loud enough to rival the ward alarms.

"Well, perhaps, try for a more toned-down version of that?" I suggested.

CHAPTER 9
Evangelia

The perfectly in sync march of the horde soldiers who flanked either side of the procession and the clip clop of horse hooves were the only sounds now. The eerie, chilled air surrounded us as we made the short journey to the temple.

Elikai's cruel words played on a loop in my mind as we approached our destination, and I began to think about all of the fae who deserved a burial like this one, but instead barely had a marker over their final resting place. All thanks to the king we were all supposed to be mourning.

Casting my mind back to my life in the Vale always sent a sharp bolt of grief directly through my heart.

I knew that no matter how hard I tried, there was nothing that I could do about what had happened when I'd last been there or what might have happened since. So instead, I tried desperately to stow thoughts of the place and the fae I associated with it away into a tightly locked box in my mind.

Problem was, it was beginning to overspill with memories and dark thoughts I refused to face, or even think about, these days. And I tried to ignore that too.

My chest felt heavy with homesickness as I considered what today would have been like in the Vale. News surely would have reached the Rebel Alliance by now. The story of the King's demise culminating in celebrations filled with whoops and joy.

I just hoped they were prepared for Elikai, *if* he became King. *Don't go there, Eva. Think of something else, anything else.*

The team of four stallions in front of the carriage looked like shadows, blacker than the heart of the completely still male they now pulled.

As they came to a slow stop at the driver's command, Kane, Elikai and I remained behind the carriage as the attendees made their way inside the temple, offering their condolences as they passed and then filtering to the awaiting seats.

My gaze drifted from the crowd of fae, and I spotted Alaric as he was briefing several of the horde soldiers. I couldn't hear what he was saying, but I assumed by his hand gestures that it was about where they were to be stationed during the service.

I felt a flush heat my cheeks at the memory of what he'd said to me as he'd led me down the castle steps not long ago. Of his willingness to subject this black atrocity of a gown to the same treatment he'd given the white one on the day I was to have been married to Elikai.

I was immediately thankful for the gaudy lace covering most of my face to hide my blush.

Realizing I was staring at, or rather admiring, Alaric's form, I glanced away and found my gaze landing on the carriage once more. It was gleaming black and had four thin wheels; the two at the back where the casket sat were larger than those at the front that supported the bench for the driver to sit.

It was made almost entirely of glass, allowing the casket to be viewed from any angle, and my eyes met with Kane's from where he stood on the other side of it.

With Alaric busy, he was alone, and I wanted to reach out to him, wrap my arms around him, provide comfort to him while seeking comfort of my own from him.

But his father was a wedge between us even in death.

We continued our individual perusals of the carriage in silence. The ornately decorated casket itself was made of dark mahogany with lavish metalwork and embellishments, and I wondered how many fae were burned or injured in the short amount of time they'd had to make it in. All of them unlikely to have been given any thanks for their incredible talent and skill.

Laying atop the lid was a solitary red rose, with matching bouquets and wreaths surrounding its base. They reminded me of the wild rose fields that grew on the edge of the Vale and thus, in turn, of those who hadn't lived to see the death of the male who'd made their lives a misery. He'd likely been responsible for taking away their immortality, even if he hadn't been the one personally holding the weapon that killed them.

Drawing in a deep breath, I started counting back from ten in a vain attempt to put a stop to thoughts of home or the party they would be having, unaware of the shit storm that was brewing within the castle walls.

My pulse slowly calmed, and I shifted my gaze up to the tall temple. It was built into the side of the mountain below the castle, and like most things in Ezerat, was large and opulent.

Its imposing stone walls flanked with a steepled bell tower on either side before they disappeared into the rocks' surface. The large windows surrounding the entrance were all colorful mosaics.

I had no doubt I'd be able to better appreciate them from inside, when the winter sun beamed through their intricate, colorful panes.

As much as I missed the Vale, I had to admit that Ezerat was truly breathtaking in its beauty. It was just a shame its residents were made up of self-absorbed, snooty snakes who likely didn't appreciate it, or worse, even notice it. Too wrapped up in their own self importance or getting a leg up in society.

An impatient tug at my arm from Elikai told me it was time to get this funeral out of the way. Kane rounded the carriage to join us, and with a final swallow of the cool, fresh air, we made our way inside.

All eyes were on us the moment we passed through the heavy doors, and I focused solely on putting one foot in front of the other, ignoring the murmurs coming from the gathered fae as the three of us made our way to the seats awaiting us at the front of the temple.

STILL FACING THE DAIS, I could feel the faces of the Three Fates etched into the stained glass, boring a hole into the back of my skull. After the sermon had been given, and songs that I didn't know the words to had been sung, we were instructed to take part in two minutes of silence to remember the late King, to 'reflect on his bravery, his love for his fae, his dedication to making Dezrothia the greatest Kingdom in all the realms.'

I used the quiet time to consider the words of the prophecy instead.

When twin heirs are born, the raven shall mourn.

Tilting my chin toward Kane, I thought of his jet black hair that he'd inherited from his dad and the way it had always reminded me of the ravens Nix's mother had kept close at camp.

Fates I missed my best friend and his never ending supply of hope and optimism. I sent a silent prayer to the fates that he was okay and out there somewhere, safely hidden in the forest and still smiling that cheeky grin of his.

His mum's ravens had given me the creeps at first. You always hear stories of how they symbolize a bad omen or impending loss, but witches have a special connection with the bird and treat them like well-trained pets.

They could use them to send messages to other witches of their bloodline or coven, no matter what distance separated them.

Perhaps Nix had finally managed to get a message to his mum after the battle, and reconnected with her. Of course, he'd not heard back for the best part of a year using that method last I saw, and I was still unsure of his fate...

Focus on the prophecy, Eva.

Kane's mother had died in childbirth, so I'd initially assumed it was referring to their father mourning her death. After the counselor's revelations this morning, I struggled to believe that he'd mourn her at all, knowing what I did now about the circumstances of their union.

Perhaps that wasn't entirely fair. Fae entered arranged marriages all the time, and some grew to care for their other half almost as you would a true mate.

Augustus Regis just didn't strike me as the type to fall in love with anyone other than himself though, so I had a feeling that if the raven the prophecy referred to *was* him, then perhaps he mourned the end of a life where he could relax in the belief the prophecy may not actually have any truth to it.

The birth of twins would have been the first real evidence he'd had that the prophecy should be taken seriously.

From the coming of age, the brave can change.

I wasn't so sure about the next line. Kane and Elikai had come of age the day my camp had been attacked, but if it was referring to that day, then who was the brave? What could they change?

Movement drew my attention to the front of the temple, where the casket was now slowly being lowered into the crypt, its backdrop the same plain jagged rock of the mountain's interior. The walls on either side were much the same, gently lit with sconces and dotted with a handful of doors leading to who knew where.

The service had been shorter than I'd expected, largely due to the fact that I'd assumed Elikai would have taken the opportunity to put on a performance at the pulpit to garner sympathy from those gathered that he could exploit later.

Whenever we'd lost a loved one in the Vale, their closest family or friends would say a few words. Apparently not in Ezerat, as neither son offered any words for their late father, and if the guests thought it odd, no one made it known.

Kane's face had barely moved throughout the various blessings and prayers, like a stone statue, he'd just watched on with his jaw tight, but otherwise, giving off no inkling as to what he was feeling.

Elikai had possibly been too caught up with the news of the prophecy and the will, or lack thereof, to have prepared anything to say, but still, it had surprised me that he hadn't taken advantage of the opportunity.

Perhaps he'd tried and just couldn't think of a single nice thing to say without vomiting? I knew I couldn't. Unlike his twin, he *had* made a point of looking heartbroken, letting out little sobs and sniffles at times, to ensure the audience behind him continued to believe his show of grief.

The casket disappeared from view, and I sat up straighter to better see the elite of Ezerat as they began to file out. There was an impatience about them, like they were all keen to be the first out and on their way up to the castle for the feast. Probably so they could snag themselves a seat closest to Elikai.

They're more than welcome to take mine.

"Immediate family and closest advisors, please make your way through the archway to my left for the final portion of the service," the High Archon instructed.

As I shuffled across the space and approached the archway, I realized it revealed a small antechamber with a tight, barely lit stairwell.

The small group began to make its way down in single file. I followed behind Elikai, but just a few steps in, we were in pitch darkness, and it felt like the walls were narrowing further as it descended.

The confined space was becoming stifling and panic crept its way into my chest, making it difficult to breathe. Placing both palms flat against the rough, damp walls, I paused for a second, trying to calm myself.

Suddenly, the reassuring weight of a warm, familiar hand trailed down my spine and landed on my waist with a firm but gentle squeeze. I didn't need his overwhelmingly delicious scent of apple and cinnamon to know it was Kane. I just leaned into his touch for a moment, and it was like the walls were gradually beginning to fall away.

Slowly releasing one hand from the wall, I reached behind my back and our fingers interlaced. I peered over my shoulder in his direction, and though I couldn't see much more than his silhouette, the claustrophobia of the spiral staircase slipped away almost entirely, knowing that he was beside me.

We couldn't say anything, not with Elikai and the royal advisors all crammed into the stairwell too, but I knew in my gut, or perhaps even my soul, that we didn't need words to communicate. We understood each other.

It was his father's funeral, yet he sought to comfort me, and I wouldn't forget it.

His touch was all too brief as we soon made it to the bottom. The floor leveled out and someone handed out torches to light our dark path. The moment he let go, I missed his warmth as the clammy cold air of the stone corridor engulfed me.

We walked past several alcoves, each housing a stone tomb with an engraved plaque identifying the name of the royal laid to rest there, most of whom were from the Dyvrad bloodline.

A sense of foreboding came over me as I made my way past the epitaphs, but it was quashed when Elikai shoved his torch into my spare hand. "Hold this, and stay close so I can see, pretty girl."

As we neared the end of the vault, I noticed that where the most recent King Dyvrad should be, there was only an effigy in his place. *Weird.*

I felt an almost overwhelming desire to take a closer look, but the plaque that read King Augustus Regis was upon us and everyone was coming to a halt around it.

The High Archon arrived and confirmed all that was left to do was seal it with the thick stone slab.

A few final words later and a warlock whom I didn't recognize, but who was wearing similar clothing to the High Archon, lifted his hands to cast in the direction of the slab. *"Leibheis–"*

"Stop." Kane said, raising a palm to the warlock and cutting off the levitation spell.

Elikai frowned at his brother, who nodded toward the slab. Then, as one, the princes stepped forward in perfect synchronicity. It was the first time I'd ever seen them act remotely like the twins they were, moving in unison like a single being.

Kane handed his torch to the warlock, muttering a quick thanks, and took his position at one end of the slab, while Elikai crouched down at the other end.

Like it weighed nothing, the two of them lifted the thick stone with their bare hands and high fae strength, before setting it down perfectly in place to seal their father's tomb once and for all.

I couldn't help but wonder for a moment what their relationship could have been if the late King hadn't treated them so differently. Would it have changed anything? Or had they just been born so different from each other?

One will bring horror. One will bring honor.

Alas, it wasn't worth brooding over. Knowing what I did about both males meant I knew they had stepped up to take the weight of the slab for two very different reasons. Kane, as a show of respect for the male who'd sired him, despite the way he had been treated over the long years. Elikai, so he didn't look weak, and for a story to tell his cronies and followers later.

Kane was wiping his hands on his trousers, while Elikai pulled a handkerchief from his breast pocket to wipe the dust away as he returned to my side.

Taking his torch from my hand, only to replace it with the now dirty hanky, I bit my lip as he said patronizingly, "There, there, pretty girl. It's over now."

His words haunted me as we walked back past the many Dyvrad tombs, ascended the tight staircase and were out into the fresh air again at last. I glanced back at Kane, who was walking behind us, reunited with Alaric. He hadn't been invited down to the crypt, but had, unsurprisingly, been waiting at the temple's entrance when we emerged.

Elikai took my arm in his and began talking about the hideous gown he'd had made for me, but I couldn't even pretend to concentrate.

It's over now, he'd said in the crypt, and fates how I wished that were true.

Yes, King Augustus Regis' reign of terror may well be over, but his Lores of ruin were still in place and something far, far worse was just on the horizon: the reign of King Elikai Regis.

No, that couldn't happen. Fae had suffered for centuries. We'd find the sword and Kane would take the throne. It wasn't a choice; it was what had to happen. Nothing would stop me from helping in any and every way I could.

I couldn't bring myself to consider what the alternative would be.

CHAPTER 10

Elikai

Finally, the service was over, and the most boring hours of my life were behind me.

I was very much looking forward to getting back to my new office to make plans for my uncle's visit, but first, I had a few small matters to attend to.

The feast awaiting me at the castle would be the perfect opportunity to plant a few carefully placed seeds regarding my plans for the realm upon the Mount Mortum's arrival.

I wouldn't have time to plan it all by myself, or even spread the word, but I knew exactly who the most influential folk in Ezerat were, as well as those who wanted to be, and I would use them to my advantage.

I had plans for those who would be best placed to start trickling out rumors in the city, telling of a *very* exciting event that was to happen soon and thus, securing their invitations. But first, I had a job for my pretty pet. I was still frustrated at the audacity of her keeping me waiting and prolonging the funeral, but I'd have my revenge for that later.

"Pretty girl, I will be rather busy over the coming weeks preparing for a special guest to visit ahead of my coronation, and I simply will not have the time to entertain you. Particularly during the long days."

As expected, she looked rather saddened at the thought. "Okay..."

"Worry not, our nights together will more than make up for it," I told her, and she sucked in a breath, losing her footing briefly before quickly blaming it on the ice, so clearly an attempt to cover up her excitement over what I'd implied, it was almost laughable.

Regardless of her vow to abstain before marriage, I could tell she was struggling to control herself around me. Why else would she have insisted on sleeping like a peasant on the couch all this time? I knew she was putting this distance between us because I was just too irresistible for her to trust herself to keep her silly vow.

Aware that I needed to calm her naughty thoughts down, I brought the conversation back to business. There were other things we had to discuss before our sex life.

"I still intend to marry you, but the crown is, of course, at the top of my priorities, and so you understand that a needy female would be rather bothersome while I am dealing with such important matters, correct?"

"Sure. No rush," she said, glancing back, not for the first time, to where my brother and the horde general lingered several paces behind us.

Clearly, they had nothing interesting going on in their own lives and needed to listen in on my private conversation with rapt attention. Good thing I'd be giving them something worth listening to, even if my pet was worried about what they might think.

Linking my arm in hers, I steered us toward the castle steps. "You may think that now, but I know in a few days' time you will start trying to gain my attention, and frankly, it would be most unattractive. So I have made plans for you to keep your pretty little head occupied."

"Honestly, it's fine," she said, still trying to put on a brave face.

Holding a finger to her lips, I silenced her. "Sh, sh, sh, I will tell you when I'm finished, and it's your turn to talk. Initially, I'd intended for Graves and Sloane to bring an array of fae specialists to the castle to ensure you are trained to the highest standards to be my wife and the Queen of Dez–"

"Initially? So that plan has changed?"

"Will you *just* be quiet and listen? Graves and Sloane are unexpectedly busy dealing with something else now, not that it's any of your business, but plans have had to change all the same. While they are dealing with other pressing matters, I actually have an important task for you."

"You do?"

"Yes. It involves the library and books, which I understand you are rather fond of."

"I am…"

"Well then, you are going to love the task I have for you. I need you to do some research for me. Graves and Sloane would have been my first choice naturally, but you will suffice. I am planning an event of sorts, one I have no doubt will be as superb as it is shocking. I will keep the finer details a surprise, but in order to make it unlike anything Dezrothia has seen before, I need detailed information on its residents."

Her brow peaked in interest, her mind finally out of the gutter after my little hint at what's to come in our relationship, and I was pleased to see her listening so intently at last, awaiting my instructions.

"Not just the High Fae and witches and the stronger, more palatable species of shifters that you may assume I'm interested in. I already know plenty about them. I need you to focus on the creatures who dwell far and wide. The less important ones. Lesser shifters, trolls, elves. All of them. And spare no detail, no matter how grotesque."

"Why?"

"What do you mean, why?" I scoffed. How dare she challenge me?

"Why do you need to know about them? They don't cause you any trouble, they stay well out of your way, so why?"

"Word of advice, pet, more listening, less talking. And zero asking questions. That goes for our marriage, too. The sooner you learn that, the more enjoyable your life will be. I will give you a species each morning, and you will spend your day researching it extensively. Following that, you will return to our chambers, hand over your notes and tell me everything you have learned over dinner–"

"But–"

My hand was still close to her face, and I ran it along her jawline, telling her exactly what I expected of her. "After dinner, you will change into something skimpy, preferably lacey and revealing, but never purple. Then, you will climb into my bed and you will prove to me that I was right in choosing you over all the others."

"No! Y-you said you'd wait until–"

"Enough," I snapped, grasping her chin. "From this evening forth, you will be sleeping *in my bed*. No arguments. And that includes anytime you are in bed with me. I will not have you sleeping in a chair like some commoner. It is outrageous. I have just been too busy to do anything about it and honestly thought you'd be weaker willed in upholding your vow of chastity around a male as fine as myself, but alas, it ends now–"

"But–"

"I have told you countless times that I have every intention of marrying you, so I will not hear any more of your absurd beliefs about saving yourself for your husband. *I will be your husband*. The rest is semantics–"

"I–"

"I told you I need a wife. I told you I want an heir. *Many* heirs. We will deal with your virginity tonight. Then in the morning, you will begin your research. You will do it thoroughly and dutifully until I know everything there is to know about every foul beast living in my realm–"

"But I–"

"Stop with all the buts. Just nod if you understand," I growled, allure seeping into my words. Annoyed that she would question me and my plans. Stupid girl.

A commotion from behind her caught my eye, but my pretty pet had finally decided to show me some obedience and tugged me to face her as she nodded her understanding a little too keenly. Thank the fates, she was finally learning her place.

"Good. I have been more than patient with you, particularly where your virginity is concerned. If I have to force you, it will only hurt more. *Especially* the first time."

I picked up my pace, leaving everyone in my wake to hurry to keep up behind me as I entered the castle to my waiting admirers without so much as a backward glance.

The feast was due to get underway, and it couldn't possibly start without me.

CHAPTER 11
Nekane

"Let. Me. Go," I growled, trying to force my way out of Alaric's firm hold.

His strong arms held me in an impenetrable embrace as they crossed over my chest, locking my arms in place and rendering them damned near useless.

"Not until yeh calm the fuck down, Kane. You're a fuckin liability as yeh are."

Ignoring his words, I continued to struggle against him. When Eva had retreated into the castle just moments ago, I'd been hot on her heels, but as she'd disappeared into the restroom, Alaric had basically fucking tackled me into this quiet alcove and out of sight of the public before I knew what had hit me.

"I'll fucking kill him, Alaric. And you are the last fucking fae I'd expect to get in my way."

"Yer too emotional righ' now."

"Yeah? Well, perhaps you're not emotional enough. I thought you actually gave a fuck about her."

His hold let up a fraction, and I twisted to break free, but he'd known it was coming and his palms flew out, grabbing onto my shoulders and slamming my back against the wall so we were now face to face.

His silver eyes were on fire, blazing so hot they reminded me of molten mercury as he leaned in close.

I could feel the warmth of his breath against my neck and the rumble of his chest practically touching mine when he spoke in a low growl. "Yeh think I dinnae want to rip his arms from his body every time he touches her? Yeh think I dinnae want to cut his tongue from his mouth every time he opens it to blackmail yeh, or threaten her? 'Course I fuckin' do, but it wouldnae help anythin'."

"Him being dead would fucking help everything, Alaric," I said, shoving against him, but he was as immovable as a thousand year old tree clinging to the earth with its thick, deeply embedded roots. "How can you not see that? I've never been more fucking sure of anything in my life."

"Now isnae the time. The fates' can be fuckin' cunts, an' it doesnae take a seer to have worked out that yer brother making disgusting threats isnae the worst thing that female has lived through. She's a survivor. His threats willnae come to pass. She willnae let it fuckin' happen."

"Surviving isn't the same as living, Alaric. I want to see her happy."

"I want a lot o' things, Kane, but it doesnae mean I can just throw a fuckin' fit and get them."

He was right, but I was struggling to care about what was right and what was wrong. All I could think about was Eva going back to those fucking chambers tonight... him forcing himself between her thighs.

"Listen, if she wants our help, *I'll* deal with it, but righ' now, all yeh should be worryin' about is getting that fuckin' sword back."

"He's going to hurt her, he's going to–"

"She can handle him. I've gone toe to toe with her enough times to ken that. Yeh will do her more damage if yeh go after Elikai with murder on yer mind. Do yeh ken how many guards are on duty today? Enough to stop the fight before it's even started."

"I don't need long–"

"Fuck, Kane. Listen to yerself! Yeh attack him, and the guards will stop it. If he catches wind you have feelings for his female, guess what happens next? He plants that fuckin' sword of yours and yeh'll be executed by the time the night's out–if yer lucky. How the fuck will that make her happy, eh?"

"Fine," I sighed. "I won't kill the bastard... not today, anyway. But I still want to talk to her. You heard him, he's planning on taking her *virginity* tonight."

He released his grip, and I rolled out my neck and shoulders. He was still eyeing me warily, wisely not trusting that I wouldn't bolt off after my twin if given half a chance.

Fates how I wanted to, but he'd made a good point, and I'd be a fool not to listen. He'd always been better at seeing the bigger picture than I was. But still, I'd expected his desire to protect his Angel to be stronger.

"Aside from the fact she's not a fucking virgin, *I* can't, and *won't,* let him do as he threatened. So I need to know she has a plan. And if she doesn't, I'll do whatever it takes, offer whatever aid I need to, to help her come up with one. You can either come with me or you can go join the farce of a feast to celebrate the life of a lunatic."

I left our private corner to head for the restroom Eva had disappeared into and prayed to the fates that she'd still be in there. I didn't turn back to check if Alaric had followed. The exasperated groan he let out gave away that he was going to make sure I wasn't going to do something stupid.

I entered the restroom without knocking and was relieved to see that my disagreement with Alaric hadn't meant I'd missed her.

"I'll guard the door," Alaric mumbled. I fucking hated arguing with him, so said a quick thanks over my shoulder before the door clicked shut at my back.

A glance around told me that she was alone, so I moved up behind her.

"Princess," I said, making my presence known. She stood with her hands flat on the countertop, her head bowed to the sink and a tenseness to her shoulders that I wanted nothing more than to massage out.

Keeping her eyes closed, she took a deep breath. “What are you doing in here?”

I placed a hand on her waist, and she flinched as she spun around, the voluminous skirt of the dress getting in the way. Quickly breaking contact, I stepped back.

Why had she cringed? Did I remind her too much of her tormentor? *We do share a face.*

“It’s me, Princess, I’m sorry. I didn’t mean to startle you.”

My heart was breaking at the thought that I looked too much like him for her to see past it. The idea that whenever she saw me, she was reminded of his evil threat to rape her. Of his plan to impregnate her, whether she liked it or not.

“I know it’s you, Kane. You didn’t startle me, it’s this dress. It’s been digging into my ribs and hips all day, and as quickly as I can heal, it just bruises me again and again and the aches remain.”

I opened my mouth to speak, but she held a finger up to my lips, hushing me.

“Before you try to apologize, don’t. You didn’t make me wear it, and you didn't know.”

Dropping her hand, she gave me a small smile, but it didn’t light up her eyes the way I longed to see. I traced my hands down her arms, releasing a small amount of my own healing magic to bolster her own, and she shivered under my touch.

I couldn’t stop the dress from breaking the wounds open again, and I certainly couldn’t heal any of the mental scars she was now carrying, but I could give her this.

My magic would filter through her systems, finding where it was needed, and speeding up the healing process. Hopefully bringing her the comfort I so desperately wanted to give her.

The tension in her posture relaxed slightly as she let me do this small thing for her, but her beautiful face was plagued with an emotion I could not read.

Was it defeat? I sure fucking hoped not. Perhaps it was a regret I was seeing? She was struggling to keep eye contact, her eyes looking anywhere but at my face, and it was like a knife through the chest.

“You know I won’t let him do what he threatened, right? That I will do what I have to, to stop him?” I told her. Refusing to even say the word rape, because I would not allow it. It made my stomach churn that this was the position that we were in and we even had to have this conversation.

“Look, if that’s why you came in here, you may as well leave because I don’t want to talk about it, OK?” she said, and I could see her shield slam into place as her emerald eyes hardened.

“I promise you, just trust me, Princess. I’d die before I–”

“Kane, I’m not talking about it. It's your father’s funeral, your brother was just acting out. He has made threats like this before, and I’ve always found a way out. I just needed a minute to think and to be alone. It’s already been a long day.”

“That it has,” I agreed, rubbing the back of my tense neck, and we fell into a brief silence.

"How are you doing after the service?" she eventually asked. "It was pretty intense in the temple."

It was an obvious change of subject, but I went with it. "He might have been my biological father, but he was never a dad to me. I'd be lying if I said I'll miss him, Princess," I told her honestly.

I didn't mention how it had felt like a huge weight had been lifted off me when Elikai and I had sealed the tomb. Like closing a really long and shitty chapter of my life.

The conversation I'd overheard between Eva and Elikai outside had riled far more emotions in me than saying goodbye to the only parent I'd ever known, which spoke to how little I actually cared about the conniving bastard.

"I'm sorry you were given such an awful father, and brother for that matter, Kane. But you must remember, you are not them, you are so much better than them. Please promise me you'll remember that?"

Her eyes were glistening with unshed tears as they finally met mine.

"Why does that sound like a goodbye, Princess?"

"Well, it wasn't supposed to. But listen, there's something I need to tell you about the sword. Before the funeral, I spoke to Thalia about it–"

"You told your handmaid?!"

"Sh, just listen, please. She's become a really good friend to me, and I trust her. I want you to know that she can be trusted. Besides, I didn't tell her *exactly* what the sword was or why I needed to find it, just to keep an eye out. She knows this place and Elikai's movements better than anyone, after all, and she was happy to help. Her and Westly will be careful, and–"

"Westly, too? My butler?"

"They would never breathe a word. Fates, they know secrets of mine that I haven't even had a chance to share with you and Alaric..."

"You talk to Thalia *and* Westly?"

"Yes, they are good fae. Loyal to those they feel are good and moral. Should you ever need them, they'll be there. Promise you'll remember that?"

"This is *really* sounding like a goodbye, Prin–"

"Kane, yer needed in the dining hall. They are waitin' for yeh so they can start," Alaric mumbled as he came through the door.

"Fuck," I cursed. "Ok, I'm coming," I said, cupping her face in my palms. "Princess, this conversation isn't over. Alaric and I finally have the chance to search the top floor tonight, while everyone is preoccupied by the wake and feast. You'll come meet us if you can?"

"The King's chambers?"

"Yes–" I confirmed.

"Only if yeh have an opportunity to leave safely without Elikai noticing, Angel," Alaric interjected.

"Ok, I'll try," she said, but I wasn't so sure I believed her.

With no choice but to leave her for now, I dropped a chaste kiss on her lips and headed off to the dining hall with an uneasy feeling in the pit of my stomach that I could neither put my finger on nor shake.

CHAPTER 12

Axel

My nostrils were overwhelmed with the acrid scent of blood and burned flesh coating the air.

Pausing to allow the nausea to pass, I tried to will my sight past the bushes encroaching on the scene before me.

Trees blocked much of my vision, but there was no denying that a battle had recently taken place here or, perhaps more accurately, a massacre.

Bodies littered the floor, blood pooling around them. Fires consumed the area, as tents and carriages burned furiously, providing the only light in the otherwise pitch darkness of the forest.

A pained sob to my left stole my attention, and I moved involuntarily, the vision zeroing in on where the sound had come from to focus on two bodies lying on the forest floor.

The male, a thrakos in his shifted form, was eerily still as he remained prone. Blood pooled around him as his glassy eyes stared vacantly at the female a few feet from his side.

No one could lose that much blood and survive, not even a thrakos.

Grief painted the female's cheeks as she lay clutching his lifeless hand with a strength that should have been impossible from someone who looked so close to death herself. She whimpered as she clung to him tightly, their hands cradling her protruding belly as she lay on her back.

Tears tracked down her face as her fading gaze focused on the night sky.

My instincts were screaming at me to help her, but I was a puppet whose strings were being held at the whims of the vision. It was like I was brought here, able to watch, but unable to intervene without a physical form. Frustration drove at me as I watched helplessly, hating not being able to do any more than observe as an ethereal presence.

"Alita!" a voice roared in the dark. Another large thrakos came into view, sliding to his knees on the blood-soaked ground, crouching beside the crying female as his wings tucked away into his shoulder blades like they had never been there.

He leaned over her, his face obscured. He was huge, probably the biggest male I had ever seen, maybe even bigger than Alaric. His back was broad with thick muscle as he stooped over her. "I came as quick as I could. Fuck… what happened?" he rushed out.

"B-Braxton… i-it was a s-slaughter. R-Rainer… he… he…" Her teeth chattered uncontrollably as she spoke before she descended into sobs and her hand tightened on the thrakos' hand, her knuckles white.

"Shh, sh, sh… I got yeh, lass. It'll be alrigh'. I'll get yeh an' the babe help. There's another rebel camp no' too far," he grunted, but the female, Alita, shook her head.

"I'm d-dying B-Braxton, I-I know it. I won't s-survive this, not with R-Rainer already g-g-gone, but h-he can," she said, finally letting go of the males' hand and trying desperately to lift her wet crimson blouse to uncover her baby bump. "P-please take the b-babe. C-cut him f-from me. T-take him to my Aunt E-Edelin. She w-will know what t-to do…" She sobbed, her limbs jerking in the throes of her oncoming death, and turned her head to face the unmoving male, Rainer, she'd called him. My heart broke for the strangers. "I-It's too late for us. S-Save our son, p-please…"

"Alita, lassie, jus' hold on," Braxton murmured as he frantically looked her over, but it was obvious that her injuries were fatal.

"S-Save my son…" she whispered, a gurgle cutting her off as she hacked up more blood.

Braxton yelled out a curse again, but was quick to pull a sharp blade from his belt, clearly aware that time was of the essence as he moved it to her swollen stomach. "I'm so sorry, lassie…" he breathed before slicing into her flesh. "I wish I coulda done more for yeh and yer mate."

Her scream pierced the air as the vision blurred for a few moments, like ripples in the water distorting its reflection of the world. When it eventually cleared, all that was left was an echo as Braxton stood with the blood covered babe. I held my breath, the poor thing looked so fragile in his large arms. I had expected a cry of life, but instead there was nothing. Was he too late?

"Yeh deserved better, both o' yeh," he told them, reaching down with his free hand to gently swipe two fingers down their faces, closing their eyes one at a time. "The usurper King'll pay for this," he vowed before turning to walk away, the babe finally letting out a wail that betrayed its small size.

The scene spun, knocking the breath from my lungs, and I found myself standing in a different forest clearing, only it was daylight now. Braxton still carried the now swaddled infant as he strode with purpose to a female who was racing towards him from the tree line on the other side.

It was Edelin, a slightly younger version than the one who now stood in the cavern with me, though not by much. "Braxton," she called as she neared, her arms outstretched to embrace the thrakos and the babe in his arms.

"I'm sorry, I couldnae save 'em. Just the bairn." He offered the crying newborn to the witch, and she took him in her arms, checking him over as best as she could without exposing him to the elements by fully unwrapping the makeshift blanket. They hurried toward the cover of trees in the direction Edelin had appeared from.

The vision skipped again to another camp, only this one looked to be in one piece. A fire pit burned in the center of several tents as rebels rushed around and grabbed supplies to tend to the baby.

"The baby can't stay here," Edelin sobbed. "As much as it kills me to say… even if we could keep him safe, without a mother to nurse him, we can't hope to feed him without regular village trips. Trips that will endanger his life further."

Braxton didn't respond, just continued his relentless pacing, his hands knotted in his dirty blonde hair.

"Send him to Rose…" she said pleadingly, and he froze. "She will be able to give him the care he needs… I've seen *it. I just didn't know what it all meant at the time. But she will take him. You know it."*

Braxton nodded, and a tear fell from Edelin's eye as the babe cooed. The vision moved to follow her gaze as she stared down at… me.

Fuck.

I sucked in a breath and was suddenly back in the cavern. The contact with Edelin had broken, and the vision evaporated with it.

"You're… I'm… My parents… Fuck." I started, but my mouth was too dry, my throat too tight, and my head too jumbled to form a sentence.

For all the answers that the vision had provided, it had only left me with more questions. I had always wanted to find my family, and now, as I stared down at Edelin, I found myself speechless for the first time in my life.

"Your mother, Alita, was my niece. When we lost my sister and her mate, I'd fallen into a vision and been given insight into life under the new ruler. I'd barely come out of it in time to get us and our coven out of the town we lived in. There were so many possible outcomes, the majority of which included hybrids being chased down and slaughtered relentlessly, and myself captured to be the King's personal seer. I could have dealt with that fate for myself, but your mother needed me. She had just lost her parents, and as you have probably worked out by now, she was a hybrid. Half wolf, half witch. The only way I could save her from Augustus Regis was to flee to the Fading Vale," she explained, tears dancing in her eyes and threatening to paint rivers down her cheeks as she recounted her past and the losses she had endured.

Rose had never told me of my heritage. I'd asked her about it plenty of times as a boy, but she had always skirted around it, changed the subject or said something vague like 'Your parents loved you very much'.

Eventually, I had gotten over the fact I would never know my parents and stopped asking, accepting Aunt Rose as the only parental figure in my life. But to experience my mother's last moments and see that her last wish was to save me.

To see what she had put herself through in her final moments to make sure I lived. It was overwhelming, and try as I might, I couldn't calm the emotions rampaging through me.

"It worked for a time. For many, many years, we managed to remain hidden in the Fading Vale. We met others like us, hybrids or fae too powerful for the King's liking. We were exiles, and formed an uneasy alliance, eventually living together as a big family, but we were constantly on the move. The thrakos soon joined us, which is how your parents came to meet, but when we received a prophecy that told of a chance for change, we decided it wasn't safe to live together as one. If the King's horde found us and we lost, then the knowledge of the prophecy would die with us. We couldn't allow that to happen."

She paused, as if needing a moment to collect herself before digging further into her memories and continuing the story of what had happened to my parents.

"So we separated, creating multiple smaller camps. Each needed a witch to be able to send messages by raven between camps with updates on the movements of the King's hordes or new findings about the prophecy. That sort of thing."

"That's why I wasn't with Alita that night. Witches were quite rare in the Fading Vale. Full-blooded witches like myself weren't hunted, so we could live in Ezerat or the surrounding towns in relative peace. There weren't many hybrids with witch blood strong enough in our camp, so we had no choice but to part ways. Alita and Rainer were the leaders of the camp you saw in the vision... They were ambushed, and, well, you saw what happened," she said as she sagged down into her armchair, exhaustion tugging at her features.

She looked tired, and I remembered what Alaric had said about witches draining themselves when they shared memories.

"Thank you," I told her earnestly, as I crouched in front of her chair to hold her hand gently. "I have questions, so many fucking questions, but you must be exhausted, and I need time to process. It's... a lot."

I gulped, unable to fathom what life would have been like for them. Back then, they were still learning to live and survive under the new rule of the tyrant king, with no way to conceal having mixed blood. I surmised that we were only able to do so now thanks to the witch in front of me and, perhaps, my mother as well.

She nodded her understanding, patting my hand that grasped hers. "That's fair, Axel. I have seen some terrible things in my time, but the vision I showed you... It was the hardest thing I have ever witnessed..."

She leaned forward to take both my hands in hers, but this time no visions occurred and we remained in the cavern.

"Please know that if I could have done anything to change your parent's fate–if I had seen it sooner–I would have found a way to warn them. Sometimes visions come hundreds of years before they happen, but other times they come too late. It only takes one being to have a slight change to their plan for everything to suddenly be turned upside down," she said wistfully, her voice thick with emotion.

"I want to know more about my parents... my grandmother... you..." I said, pulling back and absently rubbing my arms to fight off a sudden chill in my bones.

"Of course. I will tell you as much as I can while I'm here."

"Why are you here? I mean, you said you let yourself be taken so you would be here to meet me, but why was it so important that I know? I have spent nearly eight decades not knowing."

"There are several reasons I need to be here. Some are more clear to me than others. I want to help you with the portal. But I also need your help with something in return, if you are willing. It involves saving Alaric from a fate worse than death–"

"Tell me what I need to do."

The words left my mouth before I had time to fully register them.

When it came to Alaric, there was nothing I wouldn't do for him, and from the tired smile Edelin gave me, she understood that all too well.

CHAPTER 13
Nekane

The low hum of conversation and somber music filled the dining hall along with the funeral guests all dressed in colorless finery fit for the funeral of a king.

It was the perfect backdrop for their slow movements and pensive expressions as they lined up to pay their respects to me and my brother.

My brother was perched in our father's old seat, soaking in the fae flocking around him. It was obvious he felt at home in that chair and had no intention of giving it up. It wouldn't even cross his mind that I'd attempt to stand in his way. Why would it?

Elikai may not be fit to rule, but there was no denying he'd been a better chess player than I. He knew how to maneuver the board with strategy, always several moves ahead of anyone else. He would soon learn that sometimes you had to take a step back in order to take better steps forward.

There was no denying the realm didn't need another Regis with a crown on his head; more power would not suit him, and my ass certainly wasn't made for sitting on a throne. But until I removed the sword he kept hung over my head from the equation, my hands were tied. There was no chance to make any moves to get in his way.

His blackmail was the only leverage he had to stop me. I'd just have to bide my time and navigate this chessboard in silence, making sure not to speak out of turn until I had the sword in my hands and was ready to say 'checkmate'.

I wasn't sure what I'd do when I got there, but at least at the end of this particular game, the King and the Pawn would go back into the same box. I would remove his power over me and, in turn, my inability to speak out.

I watched Eva make her way through the room, weaving between the mourners as she made her way toward us. The smug look on Elikai's face as he patted the chair next to him for her to take a seat made my stomach roll. Unlike me, she did not have the buffer of the mourning period to get out of her situation.

I couldn't watch anymore. I needed to get out of here and search my father's floor while Eva had the safety of a room full of guests to keep Elikai's attention from her and prevent him from making good on his threat.

He'll never make good on those threats.

The line of supposed mourners grew longer by the minute, and Elikai was clearly basking in their attention, feeding his ego and his belief that he was the most important fae in the room.

I'd had enough of mingling with guests within five minutes of being here. It hadn't taken long before it became a chore to listen to the same old spiel over and over.

"He was a good male..."

"He will be missed..."

"How are you and your brother coping?"

"You must be devastated that he died so suddenly..."

"Will you be renewing your father's attempt to eradicate the thrakos?"

Even worse were the countless offers to 'take my mind off' my father's passing. I was embarrassed to admit to myself that not so long ago, I would have likely taken some of them up on it. But now, it only made me feel physically sick.

Eva was sitting to Elikai's left, sandwiched between the line of adoring fans and the table itself. Looking bored, she absently jabbed her knife into the table's surface like it had done something to piss her off. Or maybe she was picturing Elikai's face there.

She didn't even seem to have noticed she was doing it. The way her stare glazed over, it was as though she was oblivious to what was going on around her, her mind entirely elsewhere.

Alaric caught my eye across the crowded room and a subtle tilt of his harsh, yet handsome, face told me it was time for us to go. He slipped from the dining hall, and I followed a few moments later.

The hallways were empty. Everyone was suitably distracted in the room we'd just left.

We made it to our destination without encountering anyone who would question what we were doing or where we were going.

Alaric opened the door that led into the main chambers and ushered us in to begin our search.

As soon as the door was closed, I immediately loosened the collar of the shirt that felt like it had been choking me.

Last time I'd been in this room, the scent of blood and death had been overwhelming. Thank the fates the stench was gone now, but as I took in my surroundings, memories I had been working on burying reared their ugly head.

Cracking my knuckles, I crossed the space to search around the bed first, knowing that Alaric would rather remain close to the door to settle his paranoia that someone could walk in at any moment and catch us.

"You alrigh' Kane?" Alaric asked from behind me. I nodded distractedly, knowing if I spoke, he'd hear the lie. "I'll search near the door an' make sure no one finds us here, yeh can search the bathing chamber."

We set to work, searching every drawer, nook, and cranny. Checking behind artwork on the walls, under the mattress, behind pieces of furniture.

Nothing.

We checked his office next, which looked to have been turned upside down already. Still, we checked everywhere, twice over. I could feel myself growing more desperate as we ran out of places to look, and more disappointed each time I stumbled upon what looked to be the perfect hiding place, only to find it empty.

Suddenly, there was a strong hand at my back, soothing up to my shoulder.

Alaric.

He turned me to face him, then placed his hand at the nape of my neck. "Close yer eyes, Kane," he said, and I did. "Take a deep breath in, an' count back from ten. It'll help," he murmured quietly enough that we didn't miss the click of the door to the office opening.

"It really does work," Eva said quietly from the doorway. "An old mentor taught me the same trick."

She closed the door behind her quietly. I was both relieved to see her and nervous about what would happen should she be caught here with us.

She made her way across the space. Reaching out her hands, she grasped my face. Alaric was frowning, confusion lining his deep brow as he watched her. Perhaps he too had thought her words earlier had been a goodbye.

"You didn't think I'd let you have all the fun without me, did you?" she asked.

"I wasn't sure you'd be able to get out of there. How *did* you get away?" I asked.

"I told a few fae around me that I had eaten something that didn't agree with me and needed to get to a restroom. They looked mortified on my behalf, and, thank the fates, they practically fell over themselves to make space for me to leave."

Alaric shook his head at the ridiculousness of the Ezerat elite. "Well played, Princess," I said and she offered me a small smile.

"Well, we've tried the bed chamber suite and this office. Let's stick together an' try the solar room," Alaric said.

"That's the place where we had that dinner with your father, right?" Eva asked me.

I nodded my confirmation.

WE SPLIT up around the solar room, but there weren't many places to look. It was fairly minimalistic, with just a few side cupboards, a single couch, and the large rectangular table we'd eaten at stretched before me in the center.

Eva pushed closed a set of cupboard doors with a huff, then moved to check the drawers below. Alaric was running his fingers along the walls for secret nooks and checking behind the few paintings on the flat parts of the walls before they curved around the large windows framed with deep purple curtains.

It was a beautiful space, and the way the setting sun lit up through the three stained glass windows made the colors dance across the room.

Eva growled her frustration when her dress got in the way as she crouched down, looking in the bottom row of drawers. I moved to the opposite side of the room to upturn the cushions on the couch.

After a few minutes of fruitless searching, I leaned on the hardwood table, my head hung low in frustration, ready to admit defeat in yet another room.

Running my hand over the table as I pushed myself back up with a sigh, I felt a seam running through the table.

I ran my fingers across it, following the barely visible groove spanning the width of the tabletop.

I crouched, trying to figure out what it was. Had it needed a repair at some point? Why would a solid wood table top be separated into two pieces?

The polished surface on other tables in the castle ran smooth and solid. I had only ever seen this table dressed up for dinner, always adorned with a beautiful linen or silk cover protecting the wood, so I hadn't noticed it before.

I dropped to my knees to look underneath and found a brass catch on its underside, perfectly in line with the split. I loosened it and made my way over to the matching one on the other side.

I saw Eva and Alaric's feet making their way over. "Grab either end of the table and get ready to pull it," I told them as I reached the second catch and unlatched it like I had the first. "Either this table extends or there's a hidden compartment. Or both."

Their feet moved into position. Alaric, ever the protector, unsurprisingly took the end closest to the door. "Ready?" Eva asked.

"Aye," Alaric confirmed, and together, they pulled their respective ends of the table.

I quickly got to my feet to join Eva. Eventually, after some tug of war, both ends of the table began to pull away from one another.

Slowly, it parted in the center, revealing a shallow compartment. As we continued to pull open the table, the glint of rubies was unmistakable.

There, in the middle of the table, lay my black sword. Still marred with my father's blood, though it was dry now.

Check fucking mate, brother.

My heart thumped in my chest like a drum. We'd found it.

We'd finally fucking found it.

Eva ran at me, a beaming smile spreading across her lips before she jumped into my arms, kissing me hard.

I returned her kiss, pulling her in tight to me. My hand found her hair and lost in the moment, I sunk my fingers in possessively as relief settled into my bones.

"WHAT IN FATE'S NAME DO YOU THINK YOU ARE DOING!?" Elikai's furious voice boomed, and we jerked apart.

My twin was racing towards us. Alaric was at my side in a flash. My brother closed the distance, showing no sign of slowing as he neared.

Alaric pulled Eva out of the way so I could focus solely on Elikai's attack.

I didn't even get the chance to drop into a fighting stance or brace myself before his shoulder met my sternum with all of his might.

I was flying through the air with the momentum of the blow.

He was furious, absolutely seething, as jealousy rolled off of him in waves. For the first time in our lives, I'd won. I had found my sword, and his female had chosen me.

And he fucking hated it.

I felt a hard, cold impact across the full width of my shoulders, then the sound of shattering glass.

Elikai had stopped himself dead and was now staring at me with a maniacal smile plastered across his face.

I watched as Eva and Alaric raced toward me, only to stop dead in their tracks, too.

I was still moving backwards rapidly, the distance between us growing even quicker.

My body felt weightless as I continued to move through the air, the frame of the window I'd crashed through passing my peripheral vision, the curtains now blowing gently in the breeze. I watched as Eva retreated back into the room and out of sight.

I felt myself tilt, and my breath left my chest. Reaching out in sheer panic, I tried to grab rapidly at anything to stop the momentum, but there was only the vastness of the sky surrounding me.

The deafening roar of the air rushed past as I fell through air and away from the castle.

Time had no bearing as my eyes zeroed in on where I had been just moments ago. Or was it minutes?

I could still feel the imprint from Eva's kiss on my lips as shadows flew around my vision and terror enveloped every muscle.

Complete helplessness suffocated me as I realized this was my end.

Immortal or not, no one could survive a fall from even a quarter of this height.

I had no choice but to accept what was happening as my fate.

I really hadn't thought death would be like this. I thought there would be darkness, then a bright light of the fates embrace.

Instead of bracing for the impact that would surely hit at any moment, I closed my eyes and allowed memories to consume my mind, but they were clouded with my fears and regrets.

The knowledge that I would never again experience what Eva, Alaric, and I had barely even had a chance to start. How I would never find out what it would have been like to love them, to see if we could have found true happiness together. No matter how unconventional and against the Lore, I hadn't fought hard enough for us when I'd had the chance.

I'd always assumed fae were granted the small mercy of passing out before hitting the bottom of a fall as great as this. I had no idea how I was still conscious.

Instead, I just felt overwhelming nausea, my stomach lurching. I wasn't sure if it was because every part of me was accelerating at such a rapid rate or if it was the thought of how I would never know what would become of Alaric and Eva in that room with my brother, the killer of kin, once I was gone…

I held onto the hope that they'd find a way to save each other as I opened my eyes and stared up at the window that was rapidly looking smaller as I fell farther and farther away from it.

Only it wasn't empty anymore.

There was no mistaking the silver hair blowing around Eva's face high above me.

I desperately tried to focus, needing her beauty to be the last thing I saw.

Then I realized she was *standing* inside the frame, on the sill, crouched between the broken panes.

What the fuck was she doing? What was happening up there? I wanted to yell at her to get down, but the wind choked me as I attempted to open my mouth.

Then she jumped.

Fuck no.

No, no, no.

The distinct scent of a powerful shifter hit my nostrils at the same moment the blare of the castle wards began to war with the wind whistling in my eardrums.

Torn shreds of her black dress danced in the sky as she began transforming before my eyes. She was diving towards me at a speed so incredible her form was little more than a blur.

A really fucking big blur.

My heart stopped as my brain finally caught up with the truth of what my eyes were seeing.

Eva wasn't high fae at all.

Not even fucking close.

CHAPTER 14
Evangelia

From the moment I heard Elikai's furious voice, everything went to shit.

Kane and I broke apart, and I immediately found my eyes landing on the sword next to us, its blade dull with dried blood. I tried to grab it, but before I could even reach a hand out, Alaric had pulled me out of the way of my fiancé's rampage.

His strong arm banded around my waist, leaving me helpless to watch as Elikai rammed his shoulder into Kane.

Horror washed through me as I watched him be lifted off his feet from the sheer power of the tackle, his body sailing through the air as I fought against Alaric's hold, desperate to do something, anything.

I could feel myself yelling, screaming for Alaric to let me go. He eventually did when the deafening shattering of glass reached my ears before my eyes had even caught up to the reality of what had caused it.

"Kane!" I screamed, but there was nothing he could do. Nothing any of us could do but watch as he tumbled through the glass and then air, nothing between him and the ground but a sheer drop.

Alaric's steely eyes widened in utter disbelief. The nightmarish scene playing out in their silver reflection.

All I could think was that Kane was going to die if I didn't do something and do it *now*!

I raced toward the window, Alaric hot on my heels. We were at the highest peak of the castle, built into a mountain, and there was no way that he would survive the fall.

Could I even get to him in time to save him? The distance was vast, but I doubted it would take long to get to him when falling at speed.

My hands clasped together, feeling for my rings as I reached the frame. Alaric would deal with Elikai and leave Kane to me. I turned to tell him as much, but he wasn't next to me as I'd thought.

"Stop," a voice called, and my brain felt like it was being filled with cotton wool. Alaric was frozen in motion. The voice spoke again, *"Come to me, whore."*

It was Elikai.

Only different. His words had a sing-song tone and were all-consuming.

Unable to help myself, I stopped tugging at my rings and obediently made my way over to him as instructed.

"Elikai!" a gruff voice strained out, and I dazedly looked at the source to see Alaric, his veins bulging like he was fighting against restraints; only no one was holding him.

"Shh, dog, I told you to stay," Elikai's voice spat in Alaric's direction. *"Get on your knees, pretty pet,"* he said to me.

I was powerless to stop my own movements, panic gripping at my heart as I complied with his orders. Allure. *Fight the allure, Eva.*

"Stop… this… Elikai," I gritted out, but still I couldn't move away from him.

Alaric growled, but his knees began to shake, then somehow he managed to force himself to take a single step forward. Elikai's attention was forced to focus on the immediate threat of a very powerful and very fucking angry shifter trying to break free of his compulsion.

How fucking wrong he was about who was the biggest threat in the room. If only I could just…

Alaric broke free first. He tackled Elikai, ramming him against the wall with a roar.

"Run!" he shouted.

Fuck that. It was now or never.

Fates, please don't let me be too late.

Climbing up onto the window ledge, I saw Kane's form still falling through the air. He looked so small, so far away now. Apprehension danced through me. What if this didn't work? What if my beast had been suppressed for so long that she was broken? Or she refused the shift?

I guess I'd find out.

I tugged the two rings from my fingers in quick succession, not caring where they fell.

Then I dove out the window after Kane. Whether I was following him to my death or his salvation, I wasn't sure.

CHAPTER 15
Alaric

"Run," I hissed at Angel as red bled into my vision.

My fists pounded into Elikai's stomach quicker than he could react. I wanted to hurt him. I needed his blood.

I heard his ribs crack under every blow, but it didn't matter how hard my punches landed, it wouldn't be enough, nothing would be enough to relieve my grief, my fury, and the sheer fucking rage I felt over being rooted to the spot, helpless to save Kane. But I could give Angel time to get out of this room and start running, never to look back.

A crunch of glass underfoot had my head spinning in the opposite direction, toward the window, just in time to see Angel climbing onto its ledge. A glinting of metal caught my eye as she discarded her jewelry and then–

This had to be Elikai's compulsion. He was making me see things that just couldn't be real. But I knew full well that wasn't how *allure* worked.

She'd jumped right out of the window before my fucking eyes.

No sooner than she had lept, the castle wards were blaring. I released my hold on Elikai and bolted for the window.

"Look what you've done now!" Elikai spat, and I heard the scrape of metal on wood as he lifted Nekane's sword before darting to the window just a few paces behind me.

Fuck, he was fast, and we reached it at the same time, only to see shreds of black lace and tulle littering the air, and below the torn pieces of her dress was a massive fucking–

"It's... It's a–" Elikai started, one hand covering his mouth as though he was going to be sick as he stared wide eyed, but I was distracted by movement near the door.

Axel filled the frame, antique vase in hand, before launching it with all his might upon entering the room. The vase flew so fast it was little more than a blur, a testament to the power he'd put behind it, finding its target with force as it smashed into a thousand tiny pieces off the back of the prince's head with a loud crack.

Elikai dropped unconscious to the floor in a heap, and before I could get back to the window, Axel was grabbing my arm, tugging hard, pulling me toward the door instead.

"Get off," I growled.

"No. Alaric, you have to listen to me."

"Kane an' Angel–"

"Nekane and Evangelia will be fine, I promise you. But if you don't come with me right now, *you* won't be."

"Get the fuck off of me!" I roared, shaking him off violently. He had no idea what had gone down. How dare he think to come in here and start forcing his will on me too.

Whatever he had to say could wait. I needed to get back to that fates-damned window and find out what the fuck was happening. I needed to be sure that my eyes weren't fucking with me and that the incredible beast falling from the sky had truly been my Angel.

And if it was, could she actually fucking get to Kane in time to save him before he fell to his death?

I'd thought his fate was sealed. Fuck, the thought of seeing his lifeless body on the ground at the bottom of the mountain far below made my stomach roll, but it only fueled me as I lunged toward the window again.

Axel was still desperately trying to pull me in the opposite direction. "If you don't believe me that they will be just fucking fine, maybe you will believe the word of Edelin Sybilline?!" he yelled, and I stilled at the name.

No, there was no fucking way that witch would come anywhere near this castle.

"Alaric, just fucking listen to me. I know you know her. I know that she's my great aunt. *Think* Alaric, How would I fucking know that? How could I possibly know that information? You certainly never fucking told me. Rose didn't either. Edelin is here, in this castle, and she's going to help me with the portal–"

"I dinnae ken who you've been talkin' to, but it's no'–*Oof*!" Axel was done talking, done trying to make me listen and instead grabbed me around the waist as though to fucking carry me out of here over his shoulder.

We fell as I tried to push him off, but I was close enough to reach out and grab the windowsill. As I did, my hand slipped on something cold and hard, making my fingers lose their purchase and I clattered to the floor.

I watched the small object fall as Axel's weight landed on top of me with full force. Rolling, I shoved him off, but as I turned, the light caught the metal object. Angel's ring. The one that looked like two wings that didn't quite reach in the middle. It lay discarded on the floor and suddenly my brain was catching up with what I'd fucking seen.

That nagging feeling I'd always had that she had been hiding something big from me assaulted my mind and everything suddenly made a lot more fuckin' sense. And the evidence of how she'd managed to keep this massive fucking secret was staring back at me.

"Alaric," Axel panted. "We don't have time for this shit."

I quickly sprung to my feet, looked out the window, and found I was too late. They were gone; nowhere to be seen.

"The witch told yeh they would be fine? Edelin told yeh they would live?" I hollered over the ward alarms.

"Yes, I swear it," he promised, a pleading look in his genuinely worried eyes. I knew Axel would never lie to me, so he clearly, truly *believed* that they would be okay.

"Where's Edelin? Take me to her righ' now."

"What the fuck do you think I've been trying to do? Come on. She's in the catacombs," he confirmed. I glanced at Elikai, who was still out like a light, but would be waking up soon, his body's healing ability working rapidly.

I bent to pick up the ring, then the sword, then jogged after Axel. We had a witch to meet, and she'd better have answers.

"How long has Edelin been here?" I asked as we made our way to the hidden entrance of the catacombs. The hallways were empty, so we made it in record time. I grabbed a torch from the stone wall before picking up the pace and all out sprinting towards the cavern that held the portal.

"I found her down here earlier today, but let's just say we have covered a lot of ground while everyone was tied up at the funeral."

"Clearly."

"I don't know everything, but Edelin has *seen* this all happen with a hundred different outcomes, all ending with you dead, sometimes worse. Everything you have sacrificed, every taint you have subjected your heart to for hundreds of years, would have been for naught. Unless we hurry up and you just listen to what she tells you to do," he said, knowing that I wasn't the kind of male to blindly follow orders without the proper thought and planning.

I didn't say anything, just followed as he raced straight past the portal and deeper into the labyrinth of tunnels until he reached what looked to be… sleeping quarters?

Stepping inside, there was no denying the face staring across at me, even if it was one I hadn't seen for what? Two hundred years? More?

"What the fuck are yeh thinkin' being here? Do yeh ken what would happen if Prince Elikai or one of his followers…" I trailed off, seeing the prince's belongings filling the space. What the fuck? Was she his captive?

"Good to see you too, Alaric. You've grown into the image of your father," she said, her voice shaking as her eyes pooled.

Closing the gap between us, she wrapped her arms around me in a tight hug. I surprised myself as I hugged her back, ignoring the comments about my dad. Was it really only a few weeks ago I'd been asking the fates for a sign that the time had come…

Fuck, if the prophecy being uncovered wasn't a clear enough sign, then seeing Edelin here would do it.

Axel cleared his throat. "As much as I want in on this hug fest, and really, truly I do, are you forgetting that small matter of life or death you mentioned, Aunty Ede?" Axel asked her jokingly, like he hadn't *just* met her. But that was Axel.

Elderly females just had a way of speaking to his protector instincts. His biggest weakness was my mother, Rose, followed closely by Melina at the Crooked Claw.

Then add to that Edelin being his only blood relative, and I hoped she realized she'd have a job convincing him to let her out of his sight now. Family was everything to Axel.

Pulling out of her embrace, she didn't waste another second before getting down to business. "Axel, dear, could you grab the supplies you packed for Alaric, please?" she asked, and he nodded, moving over to the bed and pulling a huge bag from its depths.

"Supplies?" I asked, knowing it would be pointless arguing with a seer. Especially one as powerful as her.

"Yes, Axel has spent the last couple of hours collecting essentials to help the three of you on your trip."

"Aye, that trip I didnae ken I was goin' on?" I asked, and Axel snickered before thrusting the bag into my chest. "By 'the three o' you', yeh mean…"

"You, Prince Nekane, and Evangelia of course," she said, and the way she listed our names together so freely had me feeling uncomfortable for some reason.

"If I'm leaving this castle, you pair are comin' with."

"I told you he would say that," Axel muttered under his breath to Edelin, placing a friendly hand on her shoulder like they had known each other all their lives.

"We will be with you, in a sense, well Axel will, just not the way you have in mind," she said, causing memories of her uncanny and mysterious ways to assault me.

Fucking seers.

"This is the best part," Axel said, rubbing his hands together gleefully. His excitement was obvious. I rolled my eyes, knowing if he was reacting like that, then I would likely prefer to shit in my hands and clap than go along with whatever their plan was.

"Axel and I are needed here, for now, at least. I need to help Axel with the portal, and he needs to be your eyes in the castle. But there is a way…"

"Dinnae fuckin' say what I think yer gonna say," I snapped. Surely she wasn't about to fucking suggest what I thought she was, was she?

"The battle bond!" Axel blurted, a shit-eating grin spreading across his face.

Before I could argue, Edelin jumped in. "You know if it wasn't important, I would never suggest it, but you have to trust me, Alaric. The battle bond will allow you to communicate with each other, regardless of the distance between you. And I know there is no one you trust more than your adopted little brother."

I just looked between the two of them, Edelin's pleading eyes and Axel's best puppy dogs, desperately trying to think of another way.

Any. Other. Way.

"Alaric, there really isn't time to question it like I know you want to. Elikai will wake soon, and you really don't want to be here when he does," Edelin said.

For fates fuckin' sake.

We hadn't seen each other for centuries, yet still she knew me too well. "Do it," I said, holding out my hand to Axel, who was now standing opposite me.

Edelin moved to stand between us and began chanting under her breath, calling on the old magic few witches were strong enough to wield effectively. *Ceangal Catha.* Battle bond.

With a nod to Axel, he clasped his palm tightly around mine, then Edelin hovered her hand above our joined ones.

As her chants got louder, I felt the magical energy starting to pulse as the bond began to form.

The air around us felt thicker than it had moments ago, charged with an ancient power, but she continued to chant.

She grew shaky on her feet; her face paling as she continued to cast the spell. A splitting agony pounded in my skull, and I had to close my eyes to bear it, so painful it felt like my body would shut down at any moment just to make it stop.

Edelin continued, exhaustion evident as her chants turned into pants, and I squinted to check on her condition. Axel was wincing, but refused to take his eyes off of the witch, his jaw clenched and nostrils flaring through the pain as the bond snapped into place.

I tightened my grip on his hand, and he squeezed back reassuringly. It felt like I was being suffocated.

Just as panic threatened to choke me, Edelin finally dropped her hands and sagged backwards.

She let out a sharp gasp and the current in the air evaporated immediately, like it had never been there.

I didn't know much about the battle bond, so wasn't sure how it was supposed to feel exactly, but as I stared across at Axel, I found I needed to know that he was alright.

Before I'd really even finished the thought, an odd sense of knowing flooded me, and just like that, I knew he was okay and that he wasn't in pain anymore.

My headache dulled, and Axel's features relaxed. Knowing this must have exhausted her, he held out an elbow for his great aunt to take and began to guide her toward the armchair.

"Did it work?" I asked.

Axel shrugged, but Edelin nodded. "Yes. But there isn't time to test it now. You must go. All being well, Axel will fill you in on the details later, but for now, there is only time for him to show you the exit."

I nodded reluctantly. "Look after each other. If anythin' happens to him because I left, I'll come after yeh, witch. Allies or no'," I warned her.

It had been too long since I'd known Edelin well enough to trust her completely, not where Axel's safety was concerned, anyway. But I could feel that for whatever reason, Axel trusted her intentions explicitly. And even though he was a pain in my ass ninety percent of the time, I'd taught him myself and trusted his instincts.

"He's my blood, Alaric. I will protect him with my life," she said earnestly. "Take care out there, and mark my words: if you hurt the young thrakos hybrid you meet on your travels, I will send a thousand ravens to pluck out your eyes."

Damned seers and their cryptic bullshit.

Now, just to find Angel and Kane, get some answers, and then make a plan.

Because there was no fucking way we were coming back to the castle.

CHAPTER 16
Evangelia

I made it.

It was close, so fucking close. There hadn't been a second to spare, but it didn't matter. I'd caught him in time.

Now I just had to hold on to him while I found a safe place to attempt a landing.

My wings spread out behind me, throbbing from lack of use as my gaze finally landed on an open space beneath me that might actually be large enough to accommodate my shifted form.

I wasn't used to shifting, let alone flying any sort of distance, but I still hadn't been prepared for this kind of exhaustion so quickly.

I shuddered at the thought of how Kane might be dealing with all of this, clasped firmly in my large claws. He was conscious and shouting my name, but I was absolutely not ready to face him yet.

I knew I needed to land, my body unable to keep this up much longer. As I flew further from the castle, I felt more and more of a pull to go back for Alaric. He'd been winning when I'd left him, and he'd have wanted me to save Kane over himself. There hadn't been time to help them both, and now it was too dangerous to go back anywhere near that awful place.

I'd acted without thinking. Once I was on the windowsill and saw Kane falling, I knew I needed to save him. Consequences be damned. But now it was time to face the music, and fates, I didn't want to.

I'd lied to him. Lied to everyone. About so much. It wasn't without good reason, but in doing so, I'd let him break so many Lores unknowingly. The words 'I am high fae' had never passed my lips, but that didn't make it any better. A lie by omission was still very much a lie.

He'd never questioned that I was a high fae, not once. Had never given me any indication that he was onto me the way I sometimes wondered if Alaric was. And I'd just carried on lying to him the whole time.

I extended my wings, banking awkwardly to slowly begin circling my way down to the ground.

Once I figured I was close enough, I extended the claws holding Kane and gently dropped him down with an *oof*, before circling back and landing a little way away on shaky legs.

The ground shook under my feet, but I hadn't fallen on my face, so I was taking it as a win.

It wasn't graceful, far from it, but it had worked.

I took some steadying breaths, but my beast wanted to revel in being free for the first time in decades. I needed to shift back, but honestly, I had no idea how to handle her. It wasn't like I could shift in the Fading Vale. How the heck do you hide a–

"Dragon!? You're. A. Fucking. Dragon?" Kane's disbelieving cry rang through the silence, thoroughly breaking through my thoughts.

He stood behind my massive form, but I had no intention of turning to face him. Not yet. I didn't think I could stand to see him look at me in any other way than how he had been these past few weeks. What would he think of me now?

Overall, since our arrival at the castle and the king's death, we hadn't been able to spend much time together. The idea that he would despise me, that we would never get the chance to know each other properly, it broke my heart. And that was barely together in the first place.

"But- But dragons are extinct…" he said shakily, mostly to himself.

Ignoring him, I curled into myself, busying my mind by watching the way the bright light of the moon glinted off of my silver scales.

I thought back to being a small child and realized I was unable to remember a time ever having seen myself in the light in this form before. On the few occasions I'd shifted, I'd been so young, and it had always been in the pitch of night with the tree canopy blocking the glittering stars and moonlight so that my scales had looked as black as the shadows around me.

"This isn't possible. Unless… Did I die falling out of that fucking window and this is what the other side looks like?"

Sighing, I pushed my snout further into my side to hide from him, and continued the perusal of my shifted form that I hadn't seen in so long, I'd forgotten what it looked like. The movement caught in the moon's luminescence, and my armored skin shimmered beautifully in its reflection.

I followed the opalescent glow on the skin of my wing all the way to the tip, where a wicked-looking onyx talon capped it off.

Kane's voice was still breathless when he said a little while later, "Eva… I think… We really need to talk."

Was he horrified by me? By what we did together?

Fates, I can't stand to find out.

I was proud to be a dragon, and had always resented having to pretend to be something else. I just had never been in the situation before where someone had found out, not like this anyway.

I moved my tail to curl around me in an attempt at making myself appear smaller. But all I achieved was showing off the lethal jet black spikes running along the length of my back.

Where the spikes cast shadows over my scales, the silver turned into a dark iron, and I quickly became fascinated with moving it back and forth, watching as they changed colors.

As I imagined how insane I must look to Kane right now, I snorted a surprising, albeit odd, laugh, sending a plume of smoke from my nostrils.

I startled as I watched it drift away in the breeze. Shit… I could *breathe fire,* couldn't I? How did I do that again?

Consumed in the moment of finally seeing myself, like really truly seeing all of myself, I ignored Kane's now incessant attempts at talking to me and focused on trying to get a flicker of flame to ignite.

I was exhausted, but I set my sights on a patch of grass just ahead of me nonetheless, and breathed.

Nothing.

Well, that was disappointing. I frowned, or at least the dragon equivalent of a frown, trying to work out how the heck I'd managed it the first time.

Still getting used to my dragon form, I could sense a gentle touch moving from my hindquarters to mid-tail, and I flicked it gently. Not wanting to break my concentration, but wanting to warn away what I assumed was an insect or wayward leaf.

Okay, Eva, you can do this. It's just new. You are not a broken dragon. You are a badass dragon.

I mean, it wasn't as if I'd had much practice at this. Fates, my parents never even *told* me, let alone *taught me* how to do this!

My thoughts began to darken with the reminder that my parents would never get a chance to teach me. My grief for their loss was still strong. But then I remembered, I wasn't alone in this.

I closed my eyes and turned my thoughts inward. I'd ignored her voice for most of my life, suppressing her inside me, letting the rings I always wore do their job. My inner dragon. I needed to trust her, trust that she would guide me.

I felt for her inside of me, and a rumble of contentment rose from our chest as she damn near whooped at finally being released. To feel the wind on her scales, *our* scales even, to feel grass under our feet, to feel something, *someone* touching us–

Wait, what? Touching?

My eyes shot open to find Kane standing right in front of me. He quickly moved his hand away from me and folded his arms across his broad chest. Was that a scowl or a frown? He seemed tense. Oh fates, he hated me.

Shit shit shit.

I pushed up, feeling too heavy for mere earth to hold me, and turned half a circle to face away from him, not ready for his rejection. My heart couldn't take it. It was still fragile from thinking he was about to die. I just couldn't do this yet.

He'd been raised by the male who had hunted my race so tirelessly that he'd driven us to extinction. Or at least he thought he had. Just because I'd seen Kane show mercy to other races, like the spider folk, didn't mean he wouldn't detest me based on whatever nonsense had been drummed into him since birth.

"Eva, if this is some kind of attempt at hiding from me, it's really not working. Besides, you don't need to," he said, taking off his tattered shirt. His voice was much gentler now than when he'd yelled 'dragon'.

I shifted my snout further away from him, hoping he would take the hint and leave me be.

Of course, it didn't deter him in the least. He ran around my flank and before long, he was in my line of sight again.

"Massive fucking dragon or not, we have to talk," he said, standing there topless and holding his shirt to me in a peace offering. "And we can't talk while you are like this. Please shift back?"

He was right. We couldn't talk while I was like this, and the longer I stayed like this, the higher the chances someone would see me. Though I suppose it was a bit late for that. It was delusional to think that nobody had seen us flying across the darkening skies of Ezerat before landing in this clearing.

Where even is this clearing?

My heart thundered harder as I thought of the implications of being spotted. The adrenaline must have helped facilitate my shift back somehow, because without knowing how I'd done it, I found myself knelt on the ground back in my fae form, naked as the day I was born.

I stood on trembling legs, my arms trying to cover my exposed flesh. I was so not at all ready to face this. Not ready to open up and tell him the truth about everything. Not ready to lose my kind prince.

"Princess? Are you okay?"

"Go away, Kane. Please. Just leave," I said, fear and adrenaline drumming in my blood.

The mask I usually wore must have burned away with my shift, because I was struggling to keep it together. Or maybe it was my worry for Alaric. Or the soul-crushing pain I'd felt when Kane had been falling and I wasn't sure if I could save him. Maybe it was a mixture of everything.

"Eva, I can't do that. You have to know that, right?" he said.

Of course, he couldn't. He was a prince, for fates sake. He had a duty to fulfill. He couldn't leave me alive.

My dragon rattled the cage she had been pushed back into, trying to communicate something to me, only this time she didn't have any locks to stop her from taking over. My lack of control was dangerous.

"Kane, I can't control her. Go away before I hurt you. I can't trust myself." I hugged myself tighter, backing away.

"Please, Eva–"

"Kane, no. Please go, there is nothing else to say."

"There is so much to say," he said. He sat on the cold grass beneath him and patted the ground next to him. "How about we just start from the beginning and go from there?"

I met his eyes. The way he looked at me. It wasn't the same as before, but it wasn't completely hate filled either. He held up his tattered shirt for me again, and with a small, half smile, I took it this time. After shrugging into it, I kneeled down across from him.

It dawned on me that I was back to where I had been all those weeks ago after the attack on my camp. Alone and with nothing to lose.

With that realization, I took a deep, shaky breath and began to tell him my story. No more secrets, no more half truths. Just the whole truth this time. The good, the bad and the ugly.

I told him about my two rings, one that concealed my shifter scent and the other that kept my dragon subdued.

I told him how I'd spent my entire life running with my parents, and how they had made me swear to never breathe a word of what I am to anyone outside of our camp's inner circle.

I explained how, as a result, I had never learned to control my dragon because there was nowhere safe we could go to train, to let her be free without the constant danger of being spotted and hunted down.

I barely stopped for breath as I told him about how I had lived in the Fading Vale with the Rebel Alliance alongside hybrids and thrakos my entire life. I was honest about how most of my closest friends and allies were the very beings that he had been taught his entire life were evil.

I told him the truth of what had happened in the Vale the day Elikai had taken me. I told him how his twin brother had commanded Sloane and Graves to kill my parents, and that he'd demanded that I come with him as some sort of prize.

Then I moved on to my best friend, Nix. How I had no idea if he'd survived, and that his unknown fate was eating me up inside. I admitted to the slither of hope I held that he'd managed to escape and was out there somewhere looking for me. How he was the closest thing to family I had left, and I wasn't even sure if he was alive.

My breath stuttered a little as I began my final confession. I shakily confided how I had planned on murdering his father myself, believing that had been the fates purpose for me being in the castle.

Once my secrets were divulged, I realized my breath was coming hard. To save myself from looking at Kane to find disgust or horror on his face, I spotted a flower in the grass that I plucked and started counting its petals.

I waited in silence for him to finally say something.

His feet came into view under my nose, and I jerked my head up to see him walking towards where I was kneeling, my virtual nakedness doing nothing to alleviate how vulnerable I was feeling.

My breath quickened, panic clawing its way through my chest at not knowing how he was going to react. I pushed my hands out, a vain attempt at stopping him from getting too close to me, as my tears threatened to fall.

"That's what you meant, the day you arrived at the castle and we shared our first dance... You told me you weren't the villain I thought you were."

I nodded.

He reached down for my hand and pulled me up to stand. Placing my hands to lie on his shoulders, he enveloped me into his warm embrace, and I looked up at him with bated breath.

"You're safe with me, Princess. I swear it," he murmured as he kissed the crown of my head.

My heart stuttered as I tried to comprehend what was happening. He *wasn't* rejecting me? "But I'm a shifter. We... You can't..." I sniffled into his bare chest.

He pulled back and cupped my face in his hands, forcing me to meet his intense blue eyes. "I don't care, Eva. Shifter, high fae or a fucking troll. It is *you* that I want," he told me, wiping a tear that had pooled in my eye before it had a chance to fall.

He tilted my chin with his hand and closed the remaining distance between us with what could only be described as an earth shattering kiss.

"*Kane,*" I murmured against his lips. Ignoring me, he trailed more kisses across my jaw. "You really don't care?" I asked quietly, still struggling to believe that he hadn't been brainwashed by his upbringing.

Banding an arm around my waist, he pulled me flush against him. Unlike that night on the dance floor, there was very little material between us this time.

I felt his hardening length hidden beneath the leather of his pants pressing against my hip, and heat crept up my face. He trailed one hand up my spine and curled his fingers into the silver hair at the nape of my neck, forcing me to look up at him.

"Princess, I might be a good for nothing waste of air, or so I have spent my life being told, but do you really think so little of me?" he asked. Before I could answer, he carried on, "Fuck, have I not been clear about how I feel for Alaric? A *shifter.* If my words aren't doing a good enough job of convincing you that things like that don't matter to me," he paused, and using his other hand, he reached for one of mine, then started trailing them down between our bodies to land on his rigid cock straining against his pants. "Then maybe *this* is proof enough of how much I still fucking want you. Even now, after listening to every last fucking word you just told me."

I didn't know what to say, so I kissed him again. Pouring my feelings into him, I tried to communicate everything his words had meant to me through our locked lips.

"Fuck, Eva," he said, breaking the kiss too soon. "Alaric would cut my balls off if he knew we were out in the open like this."

"*Shit,*" I hissed, internally chastising myself for getting caught up in this moment when I should know better.

I had literally *just* told him how I'd spent my life evading detection, and yet here I was, ignoring everything I had been taught.

Kane began to button the few buttons that were still hanging on by a thread on the ruined shirt that was swamping me. It wasn't ideal, but it offered much more modesty than without. Even with the back that was slashed open from what must have been either the window or my claws. Maybe both.

We were sitting ducks, practically asking to be found if we stayed out here in the open.

"We can't be too far outside of Ezerat. I can steal some clothes from the nearest town," I muttered as I watched his nimble fingers loop the final button.

He tsked. "You really are my little rebel, aren't you, Princess?"

"Sorry, I–"

"Fuck, don't apologize. Fates, it's *hot*. I'm just worried you'll go to all that trouble stealing them, and I'll be helpless but to rip them off."

Butterflies filled my stomach. "I dare you," I challenged, biting down on my lip and his bright blue eyes sparkled, making my dragon purr. "Just as soon as we find somewhere safe and come up with a plan to help Alaric."

CHAPTER 17

Alaric

I was running all-out on large black paws, my wolf enjoying being pushed to his limits under the moon, when a sudden wave of nausea hit me like a twenty-pound mace.

The pain went as quickly as it came, but I felt off, dizzy, like something was scratching at my mind and sending me off balance.

I knew I needed to stop, but I'd barely crossed the border of Ezerat yet. Passing through the busy and heavily built up towns, I was far too exposed and the risk of being seen was too great to stop now. I hadn't planned to slow down until I reached the more tree-rich areas further out, closer to the villages. But fuck, something wasn't right.

I spotted an open brick built barn, half filled with hay. It wasn't ideal, but it would do. I hadn't even made it inside when Axel's voice thundered into my mind, as though he was talking directly into my ear. *"Think my words, think my words."*

I yelped, dropping the heavy pack I'd been carrying in my jaws.

"Fates, this isn't working. I just look like an idiot. Edelin said to think my words, so here I am, thinking, thinking, thinking."

"Fucking idiot," I muttered aloud.

"Alaric, hellloooooo, Alaric, Alaric, Alaric. Anyone there?"

"Axel! Enough!" I thought back.

"Holy fucking shit, it worked! Hey boss!"

I hadn't been looking forward to using the battle bond for the first time, and I definitely wouldn't have gone through with it had it been anyone else and under any other circumstances.

I'd never known anyone who'd forged such a bond; they existed only in rumors.

Created a millenia ago for soldiers to communicate at war, the battle bond had never taken off, and for good reason. For starters, there was the obvious issue of needing to trust the fae you were bonded to explicitly.

Then there was the fact that the spell was beyond difficult. Not many knew how to do it, and even if they did, they tended to keep that knowledge to themselves, unwilling to risk their own immortality attempting to bond others.

Legend was that the witch who'd first attempted it had barely survived the first bonding and then actually died during the second attempt. Her body completely shutting down, never to rise again. Why you'd try a second after the first nearly finished you off, I had no clue. There really was no cure for stupid.

"Is Edelin okay?" I thought through the bond.

Aside from the dizziness when Axel had first attempted to open the link, this wasn't too bad. I could sense his mood almost like an aura, but I couldn't hear his wayward thoughts, only those that he was trying to communicate. Thank the fates.

"Wow, this is so weird!"

"Axel." I warned.

"Ha, who knew you could growl even in your thoughts? Anyway, yeah, she's in her cave sleeping it off. I watched her for a bit to make sure she was breathing okay and then snuck back up to the horde quarters to see what kind of commotion you'd stirred."

"And?"

"The princeling woke up, unfortunately. But the good news is he doesn't seem to know it was me who vased him in the head. Word in the barracks is that he basically begged to break the mourning period so he could hunt you all down with the weight of the horde behind him. So far, he hasn't gotten anywhere with the advisors on it, but I'll keep you posted."

"What's he tellin' everyone? That we are traitors to the crown?"

"Aye. That Nekane killed the king with the help of you and his fiancé. That he confronted you all, and then you fled."

"Anythin' 'bout a dragon?"

"Yeah. How did you guess? I figured he'd imagined that part. You know, on account of the whole getting vased thing."

"Edelin didn't tell you how Angel and Kane got away?"

"Not yet, but we've had a lot to talk about."

"She's a fucking dragon." Even as I thought the words, they felt strange, like it was something that was just too far-fetched to be true.

"Edelin? That's not very nice–"

"Evangelia."

"Fuck off! That. Is. Epic!"

"Aye." It was pretty fucking epic, but that didn't mean I'd be letting her get away without an interrogation.

"Oh, before I forget, Edelin said to tell you that Prince Nekane and Lady Evangelia are heading for the Beguiling Broom Bed and Breakfast."

"Which is where?"

"Hazelbrook."

"The brownie village," I clarified.

It was one of the closest villages to the towns that circled the city. I'd visited plenty of times to collect their taxes, but never stayed for more than however long it took to take their hard earned coin and move onto the next.

"That's the one. Be careful with those bastards. It's like you've always told me, never piss off a brownie."

"Aye." They were a friendly and helpful race. Or they were, right up until you angered them and they would change entirely. Grow several inches in height and width, and sprout nasty fucking jagged teeth.

"Didn't one bite you once?" Yes, the fucker had stung for days, even after it looked to have fully healed.

"Aye, it did. This pack yeh gave me, what's in it?"

Hazelbrook was around a two day run from the city, and I didn't intend to come out of my wolf form when I slept, so wouldn't be able to check it until I'd found them.

"Mostly just supplies and some essentials for life on the run. Leathers, a few capes, Edelin said clothes to help blend in, so I grabbed some training gear for each of you, it's dark and casual so it should work. There's some camping gear too. Stuff to hunt and cook with. Oh, and a tent. It should *sleep three... at a squeeze."*

"Weapons?"

"Those twin daggers of Lady Evangelia's, and a few others. Nothing major. There wasn't much room after the essentials were added. But you've got Nekane's sword already, so all in it will be enough to defend yourselves should you need to."

"Thanks, brother." I thought, surprising myself.

I never called him brother. We weren't even related, but the word had come out of my thoughts, no less.

"Any time, boss. Check in when you find them, yeah?"

"Will do."

"Good luck."

Suddenly, everything around me was back in focus. The dizziness completely dissipated and I could no longer feel Axel in any way, not even his mood.

Picking up the huge pack in my jaws, I nodded to the moon to check it had my back, and then I ran.

And ran. And ran. And ran.

IT WAS dark as I pulled leather pants and a dark hooded jerkin from the top compartment of the bag to cover my nakedness.

I hadn't been able to sleep when I'd stopped to rest not far from the towers of Crystal Peak, near one of the many witch towns along the way. I'd given up quickly and continued on my journey, traveling through the following day and arriving at the edge of Hazelbrook in record time.

I knew there was an inn to the south of the village, so I stuck to the woods where I could and headed that way. I couldn't imagine the brownies would have more than one guest house, so I was counting on it being the Beguiling Broom.

And thank the fates, it was.

As I left the cover of the trees and walked the dark cobbled pathway, lit only by the near full waxing moon overhead, I was torn between eagerness to see them both safe and a strong desire to beat their arses for being fools enough to be staying in such a public fucking place.

Small town or not, mourning period or not, word would get out that the three of us were on the run and then it would spread across the realm like thrakos fire.

If someone recognised them...

It wasn't worth thinking about.

Over the course of his reign, Regis had pretty much left the brownies alone. Forgetting their existence until it was tax collection time. They served no real purpose and were no threat to him, and so they were left alone.

They lived simple lives with no real luxury, most of their coin being saved to pay their annual taxes. Compared to other races in the realm, they had it easy.

As I entered the Beguiling Broom, my eyes immediately darted around the dimly lit room to the tables that surrounded the bar.

Hopefully Angel's upbringing in the Vale and the lessons I'd spent years drilling into Kane would have at least taught them enough to not be total fucking eejits and sit out in the open to be gawked at.

Last time I'd seen Angel, she'd been shifting into a massive fucking dragon to save Kane from falling to his death. And as relieved as I was that she had wings and could save him from that unthinkable fate, the drive to question her was no less strong.

I'd had plenty of time to think about her during the run here. To mull over all that she shared with me, intentionally or not, over our time together. Now that I knew what she truly was, I had formed a pretty clear picture of what her truth might be, but there was still a whole lot that was unknown and I had every intention of making her spill everything.

It was fairly quiet inside, not too many patrons around, and I eventually spotted them at the table closest to the backdoor, right by some stairs, furthest from the bar and main thoroughfare.

The moment I spotted them, the burdensome feeling of concern that I had carried with me for days lifted. I hadn't realized it was so heavy. They were here, and they were safe. Maybe we'd survive this shit show we were in after all.

They were already looking my way, their faces half concealed by tattered cloaks they must have acquired from somewhere, or someone, along the way. The fact they had seen me before I'd seen them meant their senses were on high alert.

Good, another point for them.

As we made eye contact, Kane moved to stand. I sliced my head to the side once to signal him to keep his arse firmly planted where he was, not wanting to bring any unwanted attention our way, but Angel's grip on his arm stopped him at the same time.

"Fuck, it's good to see you," Kane said as I reached them. I took the empty chair next to him and dropped the bag on the floor, keeping it nice and close.

"It's really you, but how?" Angel breathed opposite me, her calf softly caressing my leg under the table as if she needed the contact to be certain I wasn't a figment of her imagination.

As much as I wanted to return the gesture, I couldn't let her think all was okay. Not yet anyway. I needed to get the whole truth out of her first.

Instead, I raised a brow, giving her a look that said *'What the fuck do you think you're doing, dragon?'*

She quickly broke the contact and began nibbling on her bottom lip.

Like I was going to ignore the fact that the last time we'd been in each other's company, her lies had unraveled faster than she'd jumped out of that fucking solar room window.

"Are we okay?" she asked, her walls snapping into place.

"We all have our secrets, Angel, some bigger than others. We'll talk about yours later, when there are less ears in the room."

As if proving my point, the server came over just then with two bowls brimming with hot stew. Eva nodded her agreement to me, but her attention quickly shifted to the food.

My stomach growled as I tried to remember the last time I'd eaten since being separated from them two days ago.

"We'll have one more bowl for our friend, please," Kane told the brownie, clearly having heard my stomach and knowing I could use a good meal as much as they did.

With a nod, the scrawny wee male disappeared back into the kitchens and Kane drew his attention back to me. "Thank the fates you're okay, Alaric. But how did you manage to get out of the castle? How did you find us?"

He didn't wait for me to answer before picking up his spoon and beginning to devour his meal as if it was his last. Or first in days.

Angel did the same.

"Axel burst in jus' as Angel decided to go for a dive outtae the window after yeh," I said.

The server returned just then, placing a bowl of stew down with his hair covered hand on the table. He followed it with a loaf of seeded bread for us to share.

When I was sure he was far enough away, I continued. "Axel had some… help from someone at the castle. He got me out through the catacombs. A bag was already packed for me an' I took the opportunity to get outtae there quickly before Elikai had the chance to slap me in chains and throw me in the dungeons," I explained, knocking the bag at my side with my foot.

I needed to go through it properly to see what we had and start making a plan based on the supplies in hand.

"The catacombs? I thought they were all sealed off?" Kane asked, ripping himself a piece of bread.

I glanced around subtly before answering, all too aware my back was to the rest of the room. "Nah, I found a collapsed entrance several decades ago. Axel was helping me with somethin' down there, I'll explain more later, but the short of it is, he found another exit that takes you out onto the side of the mountain," I explained, purposely leaving out the finer details until we had more privacy.

"You said Axel had help. Was it Thalia or her uncle? Are they okay?" Angel asked, worry etched in her pinched brow.

I was surprised again by how much she clearly cared for the witch and warlock, but banked it for the list of questions I intended to ask her later.

"Nah, another witch, a seer. Axel found her livin' doon there. Elikai's been hidin' her away."

"A seer witch?" Eva gasped, her spoon clattering in the bowl as she leaned forward on her elbows. "Do you know who it was? Or how long she'd been there? Did they give you a name?"

"Calm doon. Aye, I ken the name," I told them. "But no' here."

They glanced around the room and nodded their agreement that it could wait.

We went back to quickly finishing our stew in a comfortable silence. I took the opportunity to soak up their presence. I breathed in deeply, taking in their delicious scents that never failed to ground me. Angel's was different, stronger and definitely a powerful shifter, but no less mouth watering.

"We have a room upstairs, so let's head up and have a proper conversation. *Out* of earshot." Kane said, wiping his mouth on the cloak's sleeve. Not very princelike, but then, he never really was.

I nodded, grabbed the weighty satchel from the floor as I stood and followed as we made our way up the stairs.

I DROPPED the bag in an alcove near the door as we entered, and immediately made my way to stand by the curtained window, while Kane and Eva shrugged out of their heavy cloaks.

I peered out to ensure that no one was outside lurking or looking for us, then drew it tightly shut.

Angel climbed up onto the bed to sit cross-legged, and Kane headed into the bathing chamber that was joined to the small space. "Before you tell us all the reasons that we need to leave soon, I'm taking a shower. Fates know when I'll get the chance again. Besides, I'm sure you have questions about the whole dragon thing."

"Aye," I certainly did.

Angel had kept her shoes on, no doubt ready to run at a second's notice. I wasn't sure if it was because of her upbringing or if it was doubt that I would accept her now that I knew what she had been hiding.

Glancing around the small space, I noted it was sparse but clean, and there was only one bed in the room. While I wasn't exactly jealous at the thought of the two of them sharing a bed, something tugged at my gut as I wondered just how much time they had had to spend in each other's arms in my absence after Angel's secret came out.

If there had been an issue between them, if Kane had been an asshole about her being a shifter, it had clearly been worked out. But I doubted he'd have stayed mad at her for long, if at all.

She was looking up at me from the bed now, worry etched into her features as she nibbled that fucking lip again.

"So, yer a dragon." I stated, cutting the bullshit as I faced her.

She nodded. "The one and only," she said with a sad smile as she stared at her hands that fidgeted in her lap.

Guilt racked through me at the knowledge it was, at least partially, my fault she was the last of her kind. Guilt wasn't new to me, but I had gotten damn fucking good at pretending not to feel it over the last few hundred years.

"Are yeh a hybrid? Yer parent's dragon and something else? High fae?" I asked, needing to know for sure whether her camp was the one I now suspected it to have been.

I'd been too distracted by Elikai's stunt that day in the Fading Vale, and then allowed myself to be blinded by the bloodlust during the fight.

Those I saw hadn't been familiar, so I'd been doing a pretty good job at convincing myself it was some random camp of rebels.

Until Angel had grown wings, that is.

She nodded and straightened, pulling her shoulders back slightly as she drew in a steady breath.

"My parents were full-blooded dragons, as far as I know. Though I don't know much about my family beyond them; they were all long dead before my time and my parents rarely spoke of the past. I am pretty sure they were dragons too though. So yeah, I'm a full-blooded dragon."

"*Kur an' Levina...*" I sighed to myself, pressing my fingers into my eyes as my worst fears came true.

How could I ever look at myself in the mirror again? How could I expect Angel to ever see me as anything less than the monster I'd become? How the fuck could I have been so fucking stupid not to realize?

"*What* did you just say?" Angel asked in disbelief, her face turning white.

I should have kept my fucking mouth shut, but it was too late.

"How do you know those names, Alaric?" she asked shakily.

"It doesnae matter how I ken those names. Are they yer parents?" I snapped, defensively, but it wasn't her I was angry with–it was myself.

"They *were* my parents. Before you took Elikai out for his birthday slaughter party and, well, I already told you the rest. How do you know them?!"

"It's my job to ken the names of powerful creatures that could've been a threat to the King. Even if he did think them dead. Tha' hunt... it was last minute. I tried, but fuck, I didnae realize whose camp it was OK? Jus' drop it."

"Not good enough, Wolf," Angel growled, getting to her feet and crossing the small amount of distance between us. "Like it would have mattered or made any difference whose camp it was–"

"It would've mattered to me. But yer right, it wouldnae've made a fuckin' difference. Regis pointed, and I attacked. It's been that way for centuries. If I didnae, I wouldnae be the general now, would I? No' that any o' it fuckin' matters anymore. He's dead, an' they are dead. I did what I could, but it wasnae enough, an' there isnae a fuckin' thing I can do about it."

Angel cleared the remaining space between us in a flash, ready to attack and take out her grief and frustration on me. "Oh, I can believe that. But I call bullshit on the reason you know my parents' names."

"Believe what yeh want."

Her hand lashed out in what would have been a harsh slap had it not been too obvious.

I caught her by the wrist before she made contact. She growled, and I could have sworn I saw her green eyes turn slitted for a second.

A knee came up to hit where it would really fucking hurt. I really didn't want to fight her, not like this, so I pushed it away.

The rumbling in her chest grew in volume as her frustration intensified. She knew I wasn't going to take the bait. I wouldn't fight her over this.

She ripped her wrist away, stumbling a few steps back. "Yeh done? Ready to answer my questions now, Angel?" I asked, leaning against the wall, hoping that she would just stop.

Of course, the fates laughed at me instead.

She launched herself at me, and I realized I needed to stop this now before it got out of hand. As she leaped, I stepped out of the way. Her face was a gnat bollocks hair away from slamming into the wall when I hooked an arm around her chest, turned with the momentum and pulled her to me.

Securing her with one arm wrapped across her chest, I brought my other up to her hair, wrapping it around my fist to control her head and stop her from throwing it back to break my nose.

The fury radiating from her was intense as she gritted her teeth and tried to twist and kick aimlessly to struggle free. Her breath was coming in short pants. "I might have secrets, Alaric, but so do you," she seethed. I could feel her heart beating faster and faster against my forearm. "I want the truth this time, how do you know my par–"

Before she could finish the question, I tugged her hair, making her head turn to the side to face me. Green flames danced in her eyes, but they were fae, not slitted. I closed my mouth around hers and our lips locked as our tongues tangled in a duel for dominance.

My cock twitched to life, straining against my leather pants, and she leaned into it, returning my kiss with every ounce of the anger she held.

Tightening my hold on her hair, I released my grip around her chest to slide my hand down her body, lightly trailing her hips and the top of her thigh before cupping her.

When she gasped into my mouth, I couldn't resist giving her pussy teasing strokes through her trousers. "Calm down, Angel." I said against her lips. "I won't fight yeh. No' tonight. No' when I just found yeh."

Kane entered from the bathing chamber just in time to hear a moan pull from her throat. He had just a small towel wrapped around his waist, and his cock began to demand attention underneath it.

Breaking the kiss, I moved my attention to her throat, guiding her head with her hair to look at Kane while I began kissing and nipping her neck.

I watched Kane, standing there in nothing but a towel, his physique on display, skin still damp from his shower. Too good looking for his own good. He stood watching me hold her in my grasp the entire time. A wicked grin tugged at his lips. And fuck, I liked that he could see what I was doing to her.

I liked the idea of him joining me to pleasure her even more, though.

She was *ours*, and we were finally alone, the three of us. If her moans and grinding hips against my palm were anything to go by, she too was greedy for more.

"Angel," I growled into the crook of her neck, keeping my eyes locked with Kane's. "Since learning yer a shifter, has the high fae prince yer sharin' this room with kept his hands to himself?"

I needed to be sure that he was still as desperate for her now as he had been when he'd believed her to be high fae like him.

"Not entirely," she whispered. "We kissed, after he found out what I am."

"Good. Kane, lose the towel. Angel, on the bed. Now." I ordered, releasing my hold on her completely.

Unsurprisingly, Kane didn't miss a beat, letting the towel fall to the floor at his feet. Angel kicked her shoes off, then climbed up on the bed, her eyes darting between Kane and me standing on either side.

I joined her and began peeling her pants down her toned legs, discarding them on the floor until she was just in her underwear.

She lay back on her elbows, and I moved into position. Planting an arm on either side of her body to support me as I dipped my head and kissed her lips, then her neck. I trailed kisses over her collarbone and planted one on either breast. Her nipples were covered, but I was too impatient to give them the attention I was sure they deserved, anyway.

I continued to make my way down, glancing at Kane occasionally to find his eyes were still locked on what I was doing.

After kissing my way across her thigh, I licked my lips. Eager to taste her pussy for the first time. Dipping my head low once more, I ran my nose up the damp material, reveling in the scent of her arousal.

Pulling her panties to the side, I kept my eyes on Kane as I dragged my tongue through her folds and groaned.

Fuck, she was so wet already.

I pushed her thighs further apart to let me have full access as I ripped the material off her flesh. I watched him as I sucked her clit into my mouth, enjoying the way he bit his own lip.

"Tell me, Princess," Kane said. "Does that feel as good as it looks?" he asked her as he stepped forward to set a knee on the side of the bed, his hard cock pulsing between his muscular thighs.

She must have nodded in answer, because Kane tutted in disapproval. "Alaric can't see you with your thighs wrapped around his head, Eva. Tell him how good he makes you feel, or he'll have to stop."

I let out a growl, not ready to stop feasting on her wetness. Instead, I thrust two fingers into her tight cunt, softly biting her clit to bring her a step closer to the edge.

Kane was fully on the bed now, crawling closer to her head. "Come on Princess, I know you can, or have you already forgotten about that night in the library?" he pushed.

"*So good,*" she panted. "His mouth feels so fucking good."

Kane gripped her chin, pushing his thumb into her mouth, watching intently as I fucked her harder with my fingers.

I was done suppressing my urges when it came to these two. Kane had almost died. We were fucking wanted criminals. What was breaking one more fucking Lore?

My free hand wrapped around her hips to pull her sweet pussy closer to me and my desperate mouth. I renewed the vigor I devoured her with, curling my fingers as I sucked and nipped at her tender flesh.

"Such a good girl, holding still for Alaric. How close are you, Princess? Does he have you teetering yet?"

I glanced up to see her nodding, then she nipped at the digit still in her mouth.

"You see that, Alaric? She's close. Do you think she deserves to come yet?"

"No' yet," I growled into her glistening sex, then forced myself to pull away for a moment. There was something missing. "I want to feel how soaked you get with him in yer mouth. Angel, do me a favor an' suck his cock."

Kane smirked at me devilishly. He knew the game I was playing. He'd seen it many times, but never with a female we both wanted so carnally. Never with a female we could share.

Kane kneeled to give her better access, and she shifted to free up a hand. Curling her fingers around the base, she opened wide for him and then closed her lips around him.

I smirked as I saw her teasing him, knowing it wouldn't take long for him to force himself down her throat. He may be high fae and she may be a dragon, but he was the one who turned into an animal in the bedroom.

He groaned as she started bobbing along his shaft, his fist in her hair, encouraging her to take him deeper.

Kane met my gaze, and with a nod, I went back to work on her delicious cunt. She was drenched, her enjoyment of sucking Kane's thick cock evident. And I was going to make her scream as he fucked her naughty mouth.

Her walls quivered around my fingers as my tongue moved quicker across her clit. Her legs tried to tighten around me, and the muffled sounds coming from her told me she was close.

She was squirming under my ministrations, trying to rock her hips in time with the thrusts of my fingers as I added a third digit.

A final crook of my fingers and suck of her clit had her screaming around Kane's shaft.

As she rode out her orgasm, I released my own throbbing length from my leathers and lined myself up to fuck her through the remnants of her high.

The sensation of her wet cunt clenching and fluttering around me as it adjusted to the intrusion mid climax was like nothing I had ever experienced.

My hips found their rhythm as I watched Kane grip the back of her head to fuck her throat. Meanwhile, his eyes were very much locked on me and the way I was fucking our girl, his thrusts perfectly matching my own.

I reached down to circle her swollen clit when her noises reduced in volume again, not willing to let her completely leave that peak of pleasure.

She panted as Kane let her pull away from his cock so she could use her hand as she licked and nipped her way along the length. Kane gripped the back of the bed, his knuckles turning white.

"I need to come again," Angel breathed.

He pulled away from her teasing mouth to dip down to take her lips in a ferocious kiss as I continued my relentless torture on her dripping cunt. I could feel how close she was again, but I was determined to drag this out as long as I could. I knew the second she came around my cock, I would follow right after her.

"*Please…*" she begged.

Fates, I could listen to her beg for eternity.

Kane trailed his hand down to where mine had been, his fingers spreading around my cock as it thrust into her wetness. "Fuck, so needy isn't she?" he asked, locking eyes with me as he started to tease her clit, swirling small gentle circles and brushing my swollen cock as it moved in and out of her.

"Kane, Alaric… Fuck… Please…" she panted, her nails scored their way down Kane's chest.

"You want to come on Alaric's cock? You want to scream for him?" he growled.

"Please…" she moaned. "Please, it hurts… Let me come."

Fuck, how were we to say no to that?

I picked up the pace of my thrusts as Kane worked her quicker. Soon she was calling our names in ecstasy, shivering on the bed.

"*Fuuuck.*" I groaned as I came. Ecstasy flooded my veins as I followed her to that orgasmic bliss.

Eventually, my hips slowed before I pulled away completely.

"I didnae tell yeh to stop suckin' Kane, now did I?" I whispered to her as I leaned forward.

She shook her head sheepishly, desire still sparkling in her eyes.

Fates, our dragon is insatiable.

"I was hungry for some dessert," Kane said, sitting up with a smirk and licking his lips.

"You pair, switch," I said, wanting to see my sweet Angel ride Kane's cock now. "Take off yer shirt and face me. I want to see you ride him. Hard."

I moved back a little, allowing them to swap positions. My come was dripping from her, and there was something about it that made this even better.

She straddled his hips, and he held her waist as she sank down onto him with a gasp. Kane groaned at the feeling of her completely seated on him. I would never get bored of hearing that sound.

Eva moaned as he thrust fully inside her. I leaned forward, taking her mouth roughly, kissing her senseless as I allowed Kane to fuck her from below.

I trailed kisses down her jaw, over her throat, and to her tits. Every bounce made them draw my eye, and I took a taught nipple in my mouth. I bit down hard, enjoying the gasp of surprise before she groaned at the dueling sensations of pain and pleasure.

I gave her other breast the same attention before moving on, down her lithe body, to her pussy. I dragged my tongue up Kane's cock as it plunged into her before sucking her clit into my mouth, lapping up the mess we were making of her pussy. Tasting her and me mingled with the newly added flavor of Kane. Shit, this was addictive.

"Fuck yes, Princess. Tell me, how does it feel to have me fucking this pussy while Alaric cleans up the mess?" Kane ground out.

Angel's hands found their way into my hair as she panted. "Oh fates... So good, so fucking good."

Fuck, they tasted good together.

Kane's movements became jerky as he found his release. Eva panted and her grip on my hair tightened.

If this was my last task in this realm, I would ruin this pair for anyone else.

Her body grew taut as she arched, a silent scream trapped in her throat as she came.

"Fuck," I groaned as I sat up on the bed. Angel's hands were still buried in my locks as she pulled me up to her mouth, tasting the three of us on my tongue.

Kane sat up behind her, hands moving to her nipples to send zaps of pleasure through her to prolong the rapture as he gently kissed her neck.

Eventually, I let her mouth go and Kane rolled her onto her side on the bed.

"Fates... that was... Wow." She muttered.

We settled on the bed, exhaustion pulling at me as the stress of finding the two of them finally left my shoulders and I felt myself relax.

I guess my questions could wait until morning.

CHAPTER 18

Nekane

A small chalkboard was propped up on the bar, listing the various options available for breakfast at the Beguiling Broom. I skimmed through and smiled when I saw today's special circled at the bottom: eggs four ways.

Perfect.

We hadn't exactly had the luxury of time to plan or think about making sure we had any coin available for our trip when we'd gone through the top-floor window of the castle, so I'd used the thin gold bracelet I'd been wearing as payment for the room.

The brownie at the reception desk had refused at first. I'd assumed she was questioning whether it was real gold and worth the cost of the room–which it was, multiple times over, I imagine–but that hadn't been what she was quibbling about.

She'd said it was too much to accept, which surprised me. Thankfully though, after some great bartering from Eva, we reached an agreement that she'd include dinner, breakfast and her silence should anyone ask if she'd seen two fae with our description.

It was a different brownie behind the bar now, so I had to hope that his colleague had filled him in when I said, "I'll take the eggs four ways, please. Three times."

He nodded, scribbled it down, and headed for the kitchen. So I took that as a yes and took a seat at a table behind the bar.

It wasn't visible through any of the tavern windows and I was already dressed in some training leathers and a black cloak with the hood up, so the risk of being recognised was low.

I'd left Eva and Alaric in our room to talk. He had questions about her, understandably, and being as I'd already heard her truth, I offered to grab breakfast and leave them to it.

I wasn't sure where we were headed today. None of us knew. All we knew was that we had to leave, and that we had to put as much distance between us and Ezerat as possible. It was going to be a long day with a lot of ground to cover, and to get the best start, we needed full stomachs.

"Eggs four ways, three times," the brownie said, placing a large tray carrying three very full plates down on the table in front of me.

"Thank you," I said. "This looks delicious. Am I okay to take it up?" I asked, unused to the etiquette at places like this, and he nodded once before walking off to return to his position behind the empty bar.

I carried the tray up to our room and tapped the door with my elbow awkwardly. "Open up," I said.

I heard Alaric's boots approaching from the other side of the door before he swung it open a second later. "Eggs four ways," I said, holding the tray out to him.

His eyes lit up as he took in its contents. "I knew I kept yeh around for a reason," he said, snatching it eagerly and heading back inside.

They were both already dressed and ready to go, so we ate quickly, perched on the edges of the bed with the plates on our laps.

I saw Alaric eyeing our food when he'd finished, as if to see if there were any leftovers going, but we'd both wolfed ours down too and fates near licked them clean.

"Ready?" Eva asked.

"Aye," Alaric said, grabbing the bag off the floor and heading for the door.

NO SOONER HAD my feet hit the cobblestone street when Alaric froze.

Following his gaze, my eyes narrowed on a scrap of paper nailed to the building opposite. It definitely hadn't been there when Eva and I had arrived. And judging by the speed in which Alaric was crossing the space to rip it down, it hadn't been there last night when he'd joined us either.

His silver eyes skimmed its contents quickly, then he held the piece of parchment out to us to take a closer look.

Staring back at me was my own face with the words 'WANTED' spelled out in thick, bold lettering above it. Eva cursed as she came to the same conclusion as me.

We were fucked.

"It must've been put there during the night," Alaric said, frustration obvious in his tone. Whether it was frustration at the situation or at himself, for letting his guard down while giving into his desires with Eva and I, I wasn't sure. Probably both.

"This must be Elikai's plan to work around the mourning period rules," Eva muttered as she read.

Below the portrait of my face were the words:

'Nekane Regis: Wanted for regicide'

Below that were two smaller portraits, side by side. The one on the left was Alaric. His scar was so pronounced in the drawing it was the first feature you saw. He looked dangerous, deadly, almost evil.

'Alaric Durand: Wanted for aiding and abetting a criminal, and treason to the crown.'

To his right was Eva. The artist had captured her perfectly, including the onyx streak that ran through her silver hair. It read;

*'Evangelia *Unknown*: Wanted for concealment of species and treason to the crown.'*

"The first time he gets my name right, and it's on a fucking wanted poster," she gritted.

"What's your family name?" I asked.

"Malion."

"Evangelia Malion," I repeated, trying the name on my tongue.

Worse than the mugshots and crimes listed was what was written along the bottom. A clear loophole my brother had found to account for his hands being tied when it came to sending the horde after us during mourning.

'Reward for any and all information. More gold coin than you can carry.'

We were fucked. Truly and royally fucked.

Even the most unlikely folk would be looking for us now, chasing the reward. It wouldn't matter how they felt about the King I was accused of killing or whether they cared that Eva had concealed her race; they would hunt us anyway to get the gold.

Balling the parchment in his fist, Alaric pocketed it. "Let's go," he said.

Paranoia set in as we walked quickly toward the cover of trees in the distance. I swear I could feel eyes on my back, but every time I glanced over my shoulder to check, the area was empty.

There was no doubt in my mind that for every poster we found, there would be another thousand hammered onto trees, buildings and sign posts across Dezrothia.

Fates, they'd probably been scattered into the wind to land at the feet of those not looking up to see them.

We made it into the wooded area and I relaxed a fraction, but not one second later, Eva's squeak of alarm had both Alaric and me spinning in her direction.

Eva was frozen still aside from her eyes, which darted back and forth between us. One large hand held her left arm tightly, and another held a sharp blade to her throat. At her back was a male, wearing a cloak with its hood up, hiding his identity completely aside from his mouth and stubble.

How fucking dare he.

Alaric was growling low in his throat, but the only movement he made came from the clenching of his jaw. I balled my fists, needing an outlet. Tearing his head from his shoulders would do it.

"Well, well, lookie what we have 'ere," he drawled, his chin on Eva's shoulder.

He was tall, thickly built, and soon to be dead. I didn't need to take my eyes off Eva to know that Alaric's sharp stare was fixed on her and the stranger, too. And how fucking dangerously close to piercing our female's skin his blade was.

Eva's initially startled expression morphed into anger. Fury danced in her emerald depths, mirroring what she saw in our eyes looking back at her. Only hers didn't share the element of sheer fucking terror that I knew ours would hold glimpses of.

"Any an' all information doesnae give yeh the righ' to be puttin' yer hands on your future King's fiancé, does it?" Alaric warned.

"Just let the female go and we will let you live to tell the tale." I said.

"Ha! Nice try," the male spat. "But no, I don't think I will be letting her go. Not until I've delivered her to that future King you think to threaten me with." The cocky asshole pressed his blade even firmer against her flesh. "A hand delivery would warrant a much tidier bounty than a simple sighting, wouldn't you agree, beautiful?" he whispered in her ear.

I was likely faster than the male in a race, but this wasn't that. There was no fucking chance I'd get her out of his hold before he could react. He'd only need to move an inch to slit her throat wide open. Any more pressure as it was, and he'd be piercing her skin.

I couldn't strike unless I knew I'd win. I wouldn't risk Eva like that just so I could murder the bastard. I knew, without having to look, that Alaric would be thinking the same.

I needed to distract him with words, more conversation, an offer of something far more valuable than his weight in gold. Perhaps a trade? Me for her.

I opened my mouth to speak, but saw Eva shuffle her feet a little. Was she widening her stance? It was subtle enough for him to mistake her movement as discomfort from the way he held her, but I knew her better than that.

Our girl wasn't planning on submitting to this bastard. And she certainly wasn't planning on hanging around to let us figure out a way to save her.

No, she was going to save herself.

The palm of her right hand landed on the male's fist that clenched the knife. Before he could react, she'd ducked down, twisting under his arm, keeping a firm hold on his fist the entire time as she brought it down and turned so both her and his arm ended up behind him.

The hood fell away from his face, his mouth twisted into a snarl that he didn't get a chance to let us fully appreciate before Alaric was in front of him, his back to me.

A sickening crack wrenched the air, then Alaric's hand hung at his side, dropping the male's heart to the ground with a wet thud.

Eva ran to my side, and the male collapsed to the ground in a heap. Red blood covered Alaric's fingers, hand and wrist as he remained facing away from us, his shoulders rising and falling as he took deep breaths, like the adrenaline was leaving him slowly.

"What the *fuck?!*" I demanded and Alaric finally whirled to face us.

"Better him than us," he said, as though he hadn't just ripped a male's heart from his fucking chest with his bare hand.

"H-how the *fuck?*" I asked, looking between the dead male, his heart, and Alaric's hand.

"I'm a wolf. I have claws," he shrugged.

"Sharp enough to slice through a fucking rib cage?" I said, incredulous.

"We cannae stay here. We need to hide the body an' get gone."

Eva didn't miss a beat as she leapt into action, following Alaric's lead as they removed his cloak, laid it flat, then lifted the body and organ on top of it and wrapped it up tightly.

I watched slack jawed as Alaric lifted the male over his shoulder. Eva grabbed the backpack he'd been given by Axel, then followed closely at his flank, scanning the horizon for any more lurkers.

"Kane, come on. We can't be here. It's too dangerous," she called over her shoulder. Her eyes never fully met mine, constantly scanning to ensure that no one else had seen our crime.

Fates, what is fucking happening? It didn't make sense. Yes, the male needed to die. I certainly wouldn't be mourning his loss. But the way he'd died, it just didn't make sense.

"Seriously, come on," she said again.

"Lesson in survival, Kane, it's you or them." Alaric grunted as he readjusted the body on his shoulder. "Dinnae give them the benefit of the doubt, and dinnae try to talk them round. Coin does all the talking and righ' now, the enemy we're facing has infinite resources. It's kill or be takin' back to the castle to *be* killed."

"That's not what–" I started, but Alaric wasn't done.

"Think about it Kane. Yer wanted for killin' the king. These fae dinnae give a fuck whether yeh did it or no', only that the reward is more gold than they could ever spend. Yeh can bet yer arse they are gonnae come for us, hard and fast. So we need to be harder and faster."

"He's right, Kane. It's kill or be killed."

I glanced at Alaric's crimson hand again, holding the body steady on his shoulder. I hadn't actually seen him strike, not with the way he was standing. I'd seen him partially shift between one blink and the next many times. So maybe with wolf claws, enough force and momentum, and the perfect angle, it was possible to tear a heart clean out?

"OK, I get it," I said, deciding to drop it and just let them think I was being precious or squeamish over taking a life.

I followed and eventually we made our way to a stony embankment next to a narrow, but fast-flowing river.

Alaric worked soundlessly and efficiently, grasping loose stones and rock, tying them to the stranger's cloak using shreds of the fabric itself.

Once he seemed to be happy with a job well done, he hefted the body into the water and proceeded to wash the blood that coated him away. Pink briefly tinged the water, and I waited with anticipation on my breath for the body to resurface, but it never did.

"I ken life was shite to yeh in the castle, Kane. But out here, when most o' the realm wants yeh dead, it's gonnae be way fuckin' worse. Brutal. We cannae risk being tracked, an' if that means we need to do some questionable shite, so be it. I won't watch either of you die, and in the last few days, you've both come too fucking close."

His freshly washed hand came down to land on my shoulder, his way of showing comfort, I guessed.

Welcome to the life of a fugitive.

But then, what had I fucking expected? That it would be exactly like palace life, but just outdoors with flowers and shit?

THERE WAS a weird awkwardness between the three of us. One I wasn't used to. I didn't like it much and was ready to break it before it got any worse.

"What's in this thing? It weighs a fuckton." I grumbled, hefting the bag up on my shoulder to relieve the pressure it was creating, an annoying kind of pain.

I caught Eva staring at me as I did so; her gaze lingering on my arms as they flexed with the movement, giving away that she liked what she saw.

I smirked at her, and she turned from me, red staining her cheeks. I'd caught her staring a few times now, and was enjoying the way she blushed every time.

"Fuck if I ken what's in there," Alaric replied. "Like I said last night, Axel packed it. I was plannin' to go through it at the inn, but... Angel can be very distractin' when she's angry."

His face was caught up in a smile as he glanced Eva's way. Fate's help me, I couldn't get enough of these two. They could say jump, and I'd ask how high, regardless of my recent near death experience involving a window and great heights.

I'd been doing quite well to not think about it, but even so, it spent more time haunting me than I'd like. I had woken in a cold sweat reliving those moments the first night when it was just Eva and me, only to realize I was on a cold hard ground.

Eva smiled back, glanced sheepishly between Alaric and I, then fixed her sights on me. "Kane, is it safe to stop and talk here?" She asked, and I paused to listen hard to our surroundings, finding that there wasn't much around us except for some wildlife.

"We're alone, Princess," I confirmed. "At least for as far as my ears can reach, so you're pretty safe to talk away."

"I know you won't like it, but hear me out." She cleared her throat. "I think we should join up with one of the rebel alliance camps."

Her voice was hushed and unsure, lacking her usual confidence and rightly so. Was she completely fucking insane?

I scoffed.

"Listen, I know one of the leaders, he's a thrakos male. If there were any survivors from the attack on my camp, they would have headed to his."

"What's the thrakos' name?" Alaric asked, completely skipping over the fact that we would be walking straight into enemy territory. A different enemy, but enemy all the same. They would kill me and Alaric on the spot. Who knew what they might do to Eva?

"Braxton," she said.

The name wasn't one I recognised, but Alaric flinched as if it burned him.

She continued anyway. "The last time he visited my camp, he told us he would be heading southwest next to a site he'd made a base of several times before. I think I could find it."

"Not to point out the obvious, but are you aware who my dad was? Who *I* am? They will execute me on the spot and then send my head in a pretty package back to the castle the moment they recognize me."

This plan was insane. There was no way we were going to–

"Then let's head southwest," Alaric said, ignoring my reservations so completely it was like he hadn't even heard me. "On one condition. When we get there, you let me do the talkin'."

"OK," Eva agreed slowly, a frown knitting her brows.

"Wait. How exactly do you think that's going to go?" I asked. "'Hi Rebels and sworn enemies of the crown, we come in peace, please don't kill–oh no, too late, we're already dead," I deadpanned.

I realized they weren't listening to a word I'd said when Eva said. "So you agree, Alaric? That we should head southwest and try to join up with the rebels?"

"I didnae say I agreed, Angel. We're a couple day's walk from the Vale righ' now, with no better option as it stands," he reasoned. "Let's just head that way an' find somewhere safe to camp for the night. We can go through that bag, see what supplies we have, an' what we might need to acquire before we are too far from civilization."

"The rebels won't be bribed by a reward. We will be safest with them," Eva said. "But we need to travel fast."

"Aye, I'll be in wolf form. Kane, you will be able to keep up using your high fae speed. Angel, you can ride me if you want…"

"Now there's an offer," I muttered.

"Yeh ken what I meant."

"Oh, so you *can* hear me?"

"Aye. It's no' like she can fly there. We're tryin' to stay *under* the radar, an' nothin' about a dragon takin' to the Dezrothian skies is inconspicuous. So, Angel. Do yeh want to run or ride?"

She contemplated the options. "Both," she eventually said. "I'll run for now, but if I start slowing us down, I'll take you up on your offer. It could be fun. I've never ridden a wolf before, so–"

"Now, now, I thought you were done lying to us, Eva," I teased.

Confusion washed over her beautiful face. I closed the space between us until she was pressed flat against the tree. Curling a hand behind her neck, I tilted her head to face Alaric, forcing her to watch as he was stripping off, half naked and getting ready to shift.

I brushed my lips against the sensitive skin below her ear and whispered. "I've seen you riding a wolf with my own eyes, Princess. And what a beautiful fucking job you did of it too."

I didn't need to see her face to know she would be turning a similar color to Alaric's hand earlier when he'd ripped out the still beating heart of the male threatening to harm her.

CHAPTER 19

Evangelia

We made it to a flat patch of bare ground, ringed by a thicket of trees and bushes, just on the edge of a clearing.

Looking around the space and at each other, we silently agreed this was a good place to set up camp for the night.

The sun was due to disappear soon, and we needed to get settled. Alaric wasted no time pulling the tent out of the bag. Laying it out flat, we began pitching it, needing to get it up before true darkness fell.

Sure, we could all see pretty well in the dark, but having it done would just make things easier.

We'd crossed a lot of distance today, and thankfully, without adding any further to our body count.

Alaric led the way and navigated us expertly, keeping to the sheltered areas, all while ensuring we stayed on course for the direction of the rebel camp I'd told him about.

I'd also managed to keep up for the most part, or so I'd thought; only having to take him up on his offer of carrying me for the last couple of hours. I'd tripped on a fallen branch, and as I'd gone to stand and catch up to them, my ankle gave out beneath me. Kane had healed it easily with his gift, but Alaric insisted I rest it for a while.

Once I was atop his fur coated back, holding onto the necklace around his thick neck like reigns, the icy wind racing through my hair, I'd quickly realized they hadn't been running at full speed before. Not even close. They'd obviously had to slow themselves down so I could keep up. Why hadn't they just said something?

"I'm kind of embarrassed how useless I am at this," Kane said, rubbing the back of his neck as he looked down on the–now almost erect–little tent before us.

When I say 'little', I mean it was probably issued for a lone soldier to sleep in. Definitely not three fae. And definitely not when two of them were over six feet tall and stacked with muscles on top of muscles.

It would be snug for sure.

"Good job Angel knows her way around a tent or I'd be doin' it on my own with as much use as yeh are," Alaric teased Kane, going over the pegs with a final hammer, while I tied the lace around the two poles which crossed over the top, pulling the tent into a firmer shape.

It was nice to see a slightly more playful side to Alaric. His smiles, on the rare occasions he offered them, were mesmerizing. I'd noticed they were definitely easier to pull from him now that we were away from the castle.

Kane rolled his eyes. "You'd have managed," he said, crossing his arms and taking a few steps back to look at the finished product. "I'm pretty sure an armless dwarf could have handled a tent of that size on his own."

"Oh really? But not a high fae Prince, eh?" Alaric countered.

"Where's the rest of it?" Kane asked.

"Seriously," I said. "Are you sure Axel intended for all three of us to sleep in that?"

"Aye, Angel. Axel thinks he's a funny bastard. I disagree."

"It's growing on me," Kane said, sitting on the cold ground, using the tent to shelter one side somewhat from the elements. Alaric and I followed suit.

Alaric pulled out three sleep sacks along with several items of clothing and tossed them inside the tent, while Kane reached for a pouch from a side pocket.

"What the fuck." Alaric cursed, snatching his hand out from the bottom of the now virtually empty bag.

As it emerged, I saw a slimy substance coating his fingers.

Kane looked up from the pouch he'd been sifting through with a glint in his eyes. He saw Alaric's digits and snickered.

"How much lube did Axel pack?" he laughed. "I just found three bottles of the stuff from Rhalynn's R-Rated Remedies in here. Love that shop, by the way. Oh! There's a note too..."

He held it up to us, and we both leaned in closer, squinting to work out what in fate's name it was meant to say.

It wasn't actually words, more of a picture. More accurately, a doodle.

From what I could tell, it was a really badly hand-drawn sketch of a shallow box...

Or wait, was it a sandwich?

Yes, a sandwich. Only, he'd drawn a stick figure on each of the two crusts.

Where the filling should be was another stick figure, a female judging by the triangle depicting a dress and the two squiggles of hair sprouting out of the circle that vaguely resembled a winking face.

I gasped, a hand flying to my mouth to stifle the laughter bubbling from my chest as I realized what Axel had drawn and proceeded to slip into a pouch filled with lube. Inside a bag he'd been told to pack with items for emergencies by a powerful seer witch, no less.

What kind of emergency involves needing so much lube?

I made eye contact with Kane, who was biting down hard on his bottom lip, trying to fight an all-out laughing fit as he waited to see Alaric's reaction.

"I'll kill him. I fuckin' told yeh the wee fucker thinks he's funny," he growled, wiping his fingers clean on the slightly damp grass.

Pulling the bag closer, I eyed the last of its contents, preparing to clean out the exploded bottle of lube.

But it wasn't lube in the bag.

I snorted, recognizing what the culprit to Alaric's sticky situation truly was.

"Um Alaric, if it makes you feel any better, *that* isn't lube." I said, eyeing the ground where he'd been wiping his hand. "It seems Axel packed you some snacks. Only why someone would pack eggs at the bottom of a bag, and without a box, I'm not sure?"

Alaric let out a trail of curses, some I'd never even heard before. Kane lost it, bursting out laughing and sending me with him.

When he finally gained control of himself again, he was looking at the sketch. "This sandwich is making me all sorts of hungry," he said, meeting my eyes with a wink.

"Oh, really?" I said, the memory of last night still fresh in my mind. As it had been for most of the journey.

"Aye, me too," Alaric said, surprising me. Any irritation at his friend had completely disappeared from his tone.

I straightened, my lips parting slightly as the air seemed to thicken and warm around us.

"Oh, yeah–" I started, but before I could finish, Kane had tossed the bag out of my hands and was pulling me onto his lap.

Smiling, I glanced over to Alaric and was met with an animalistic glare in his eyes. I could have sworn he actually licked his lips as Kane started nuzzling my neck.

"Fuck, Princess. I'm glad you didn't die today," Kane said.

"Me too," I agreed.

"If you ever fancy practicing that move on me, I'd happily oblige. But on the condition you are naked–"

"In the tent." Alaric growled, readjusting his leathers. "Now. I'll be back in a minute. Kane, make sure she's good and needy by the time I get back. I just gotta check the perimeter before you pair distract me, an' get us killed."

Kane stood with me in his arms, and I let out a little squeal as he fates near flung me into the tent, as eager as I to do good on Alaric's orders.

CHAPTER 20

Nixen

The edges of my vision flickered as I blinked back the fog swarming in my mind.

Where was I?

The disjointed haze receded to the point where I could see clearly enough to meet the glassy stare of Ambrose, lying chest down on a bed of blood-soaked dirt, completely still. I realized he was, in fact, looking through me, off into the abyss.

Shit, our camp was under attack.

The last thing I remembered before darkness had engulfed me was fighting a warlock. Then a bear shifter had come at me out of nowhere and then… nothing.

I tried to sit up, but was assaulted by a wave of nausea. If only the pounding in my head would stop, I could get back to the fight.

I tried again, this time rolling over first to attempt to get to my hands and knees, but everything hurt. My stomach heaved and before I could stop it, I was vomiting into a pool of my own blood.

I emptied the contents of my stomach, and then sat back on my heels and checked for serious injuries. My hand landed on a sticky clump of hair at the back of my head, but it seemed my body had already closed any open wounds and the blood was old.

How long had I been out?

I eventually staggered to my feet, taking in the scene around me. The air was thick with the smell of death, and only now did I realize how eerily quiet it was. I'd missed the battle. I was too late. I'd fucking lay useless on the ground while my friends had fought for their lives.

I stumbled with every second step, some sort of damage to my leg that hadn't quite healed yet, sending pain through my system. But I had to find her.

"Eva?" I called, but there was no one still breathing to hear me. "Eva?!"

I trudged around the camp that bore little resemblance to my home anymore, searching for survivors.

All I found were cold, broken bodies.

Ambrose, dead. Innis, dead. Cyrus, dead.

I spotted two bodies laying side by side, and as I got closer, I vomited again. Only this time, it had nothing to do with the drumming in my skull.

Kur and Lavina.

I shook my head, ignoring the pain and dizziness, as I refused to believe it was real. Because if I didn't, it would mean that Eva's parents had actually been… brutally executed.

I tried to blink away what I was seeing. They were family to me. They had acted like parents to me in the year since my mum had vanished.

I searched the immediate area more thoroughly, trying to shut out the bodies littering the forest floor. I knew Eva better than I knew myself, and she would never have done as she was told and stayed hidden. She would have gone to find her parents, to fight at their sides and defend our camp.

I circled every inch of the battleground for hours, wincing through the pain as my body continued to knit itself back together. I called out her name over and over, but it just floated away in the wind, unanswered.

Eventually my legs gave out, and I sank to my knees, slamming my hands to the ground in frustration, and shifted into the very thing the King hated most.

Flames burst from my fingers and licked the ground as my wings wrapped around me in an embrace, as if to shield my heart from all the loss, all the pain, grief, and despair rushing through me.

Bolting upright in my sleep sack, my breaths were coming in short, sharp pants as I frantically looked around the tent, fully expecting to be back in that fate's cursed camp, surrounded by death.

"It wis jus' a dream, lad," Braxton called from the tent's entrance, his palms raised to show he wasn't a threat. "Ah got yeh. Winnae be long now 'til we can reunite yeh with yer friend," he assured me calmly. As he did every time this happened.

I wasn't sure what was worse, the insomnia, or the nightmares that plagued me on the rare occasion that sleep took me. It was always the same dream, and I'd always wake up at the same point.

Surrounded by death and unable to find Eva.

Three days I'd remained at that camp, searching, waiting, but she was gone.

On the second day, once my body had healed sufficiently, I'd shifted into my thrakos form and dug a mass grave, using only my claws. Whenever they became too broken and bloodied to continue, I'd just wait for them to grow back and start again.

I knew it wasn't my fault that they had died, that there was nothing I could have done differently, or so Braxton was trying to convince me. But the guilt of being the sole survivor had been eating me from the inside out, and it had only gotten worse in the weeks since.

Once the grave was ready, I'd painstakingly collected every being, every limb, every last piece of my friends and given them a burial of sorts. Something that I still hadn't been able to fully wash away, despite the many baths.

I'd been shoveling dirt to seal the grave with my hands when Braxton had found me.

Word had reached his camp from a rebel spy located on the edge of the city that our camp was to be attacked. But it hadn't reached him in time. He and a small group of rebels had come to help, but all that awaited them was me and destruction.

Why me? One of two questions that haunted my every waking hour. Why had I been the one to survive? And where the fuck was Eva?

Thankfully, the latter Braxton could help with. She wasn't dead, but likely wished she was. She had been taken by one of the princes. The relief of knowing she was alive was short-lived as the dark thoughts descended. What if the prince found out she was a dragon? What if he forced her to do things she didn't want to? So many what if's... so little by way of answers.

Even now, weeks into our journey to save her, I was no closer to seeing her with my own eyes.

I'd wanted to run straight for the castle to save her the moment he had told me the news, but he'd talked me down. Braxton had lived through a lot and was a natural born leader; if you ignored the fact, he wasn't actually born at all.

"Mornin'" Braxton said in the same gruff voice I'd grown to find comforting. He was never far away and was always there to try to help me get back to reality after a nightmare.

Climbing out of the tent, I took in the just-risen sun as it shone its first rays. What I wouldn't give to watch the sunrise with Eva, just like this, admiring its beauty and chatting about everything and nothing like we did around the campfire.

I reminded myself for the thousandth time that she was alive and not all was lost. That it was still a possibility. She was the only piece of family that hadn't left me, and I needed her to know how sorry I was for abandoning her that day the horde had come for our camp.

My mum was still nowhere to be found, and Braxton hadn't heard any news on her whereabouts through the rebel network. As much as I'd always held onto hope that she was safe out there, I now realized how delusional and immature I'd been.

Braxton handed me a mug of tea and some bread, for which I nodded a thank you. He lingered for a moment, checking I was okay, then carried on with packing up our things.

I breathed more freely as I watched the pinks and oranges bleed across the sky, slowly chasing the darkness away.

I was sure that once I was reunited with Eva again that she would do the same for me; chase the darkness that had been consuming my mind away with her light.

Finishing the somewhat stale loaf, I washed it down with the tea and helped with packing up camp. We didn't have much; a few sleep rolls, a couple of tattered tents and enough supplies to keep us going on our journey.

Braxton and I had been walking for two days, heading toward the village we'd been told that Prince Elikai and his bride had been spotted in. We were so close now, maybe another day's walk at most.

Setting out, we stuck to the woodland wherever possible, as we always did, and I sent a silent prayer to the fates that today would be the day that I would find her.

SHOOTING OUT AN ARM, Braxton halted me mid step. Successfully grabbing my attention, I looked over to find a finger slammed to his lips to silence me.

Unable to ask what the fuck was wrong with him, I listened, nothing. He sniffed the air, and I looked around to see what I was missing. Smoke. A fire? Or more likely, an encampment somewhere in the distance.

Braxton nudged his head to signal we'd be following the scent, and as we grew closer, I heard voices.

Looking in the direction of the faint sound, I could just make out a solitary tent, pitched near the protection of some trees.

Suddenly, a cry pierced the stillness. A sound I had no problem picking up. I would know that voice anywhere. Could it really be?

Eva.

"Is it real?" I asked Braxton, ready to dart away the moment he confirmed this wasn't just another dream, or my mind playing tricks on me.

He grabbed me by the scruff of my collar and yanked back before he nodded his confirmation. "Yer bein' too hasty youngin'," he growled low, his eyes trained on the small encampment, but his energy very much focused on holding me in place.

"It was her, wasn't it? It's Eva. I need to get over there. I need to save her." I turned on him. Anger quickly replaced my elation, and I could feel it burning in my veins. How dare he stop me from going to her!

She needed help. Fates only knew what had been done to her. What was currently being done to her? My breaths started to come hard, suffocating me as the anger turned to panic.

"Braxton, just tell me you heard it too, and this wasn't my head fucking with me again..."

"It's no' in yer head lad, it's real, but do yeh really think that a fuckin' prince'll be unguarded? We cannae just rush in, think before yeh act, eh? What use are yeh to her dead?" Braxton scolded. And fuck, I didn't want to listen, but it made him no less right.

I counted back from ten, the way he'd taught me, and my breathing came easier.

He released me and silently started to strip. Discarding his shirt, he brought his thrakos out to play. I wasted no time following suit, my beast settling over me and giving my eyes a much needed boost to be able to find potential threats well before they'd find me.

Aside from the two figures next to the pitched tent, it was suspiciously quiet. But I was certain one was Eva.

The male had her up in his arms like she was his plaything to do with as he wished. It had to be that fucking Prince Elikai. So where were the guards? Strategically placed in the trees? Ready to attack in the event of an ambush?

I couldn't smell more than two individuals, maybe three at most. Was it a spell to lower the guard of anyone who thought to approach? Wouldn't put it past the high fae bastard.

On his command, Braxton and I darted forward, using our thrakos speed to our advantage. I saw the male throw Eva into his tent. *Not my best fucking friend, you asshole! Never again. Not now that I've found her.*

I crossed the remaining distance before he'd fully gotten through the tent's entrance. Ripping him off of her, I caught a glimpse of Eva's familiar wide eyes and I felt more alive than I had in weeks... or had it been months? I turned my attention to her captor.

Prince fucking Elikai.

Of course, he was built every inch the perfect future King; strong build, disgustingly good looking and an aura about him that screamed, 'I'm a pompous cunt'.

I attacked, and unsurprisingly, the bastard could fight. He had clearly been trained well, likely better than I had been. But I had fire and wings on my side.

I grappled with the Prince, aware Braxton was pulling Eva out of harm's way, though he seemed to be struggling to get her to stay there. The prince needed my full focus though right now, the asshole was going to die, only then I could see what was going on with Eva.

Her yell tore through the air, and then a bellow from Elikai soon followed, but I couldn't register their words. All I knew was that this male needed to be put down. Then I'd have my best friend back. She would no doubt have her own trauma to deal with, as did I, but we could help each other find ourselves again.

"Stop!" Eva's voice cried out, but when a ball of fire shot past out of nowhere, narrowly missing me, I maneuvered to shield Braxton and Eva with my wings. My eyes darted in the direction of the fire, and then I saw him.

In the shadows, another thrakos.

His lethal black wings were wide, and he had more fire building at his fingertips, ready to throw it our way. *A fucking traitor to our species.* There was no other explanation.

"Stand down!" he shouted.

Yeah. Fuck that.

If he thought I was going to take commands from an enemy, he had another thing coming. Forming a ball of my own fire between both hands, I spread my wings as wide as they would go.

Must keep Eva safe.

The prince had stopped fighting. He was stock-still and gawking at the traitorous horde soldier that had come to his rescue. The unknown thrakos launched forward, landing mere feet in front of me and driving me back. Away from the princeling.

He was protecting Elikai with his wing shield the same way I was protecting Eva, and fire now ignited across their entire span. It didn't make sense, a thrakos still in the crown's pocket? It couldn't be right. It was unheard of, but there was no denying what I was seeing. *Unless this isn't real...*

"I said stand down! Yeh've got the wrong prince yeh fuckin' fool. An' I have a feeling you're the young thrakos hybrid I'm no' allowed to kill. So dinnae fuckin' make me," he said.

Braxton had loosened his grip on Eva and was cutting in front of me. He moved, going toe to toe with the horde's thrakos, tucking his wings away as if in some sort of surrender.

What's wrong with him? The male was fucking huge.

"Do as he says and stand down, Nix," Braxton commanded, without looking at me. He was focused solely on the large thrakos in front of him.

There was a wobble to his voice, one that I'd never heard before. Some sort of emotion he was struggling to talk past. What in the fates was going on here?

"Nix, Braxton–" Eva's familiar voice said warily. She appeared from behind my protective barrier, and I finally allowed myself to look at her properly, dropping my wings to fold at my back.

Please don't be a dream, please don't be a dream, please don't be a fucking dream, I chanted to myself, not sure I could handle waking up from this one.

I'd finally found her.

Thank you, fates!

Then she pushed past both me and Braxton, walking *away* from us and toward the soldier. Her hand outstretched, landing on his leathery wing, and she trailed her fingers over it in what looked a lot like a fucking caress, albeit a tentative one.

"Alaric?" she whispered.

Who the *fuck* was Alaric?

CHAPTER 21

Nekane

"Aye, Angel."

It was Alaric's voice coming from in front of the thrakos–whose wings were blocking me from seeing what the fuck was happening–only it couldn't possibly be Alaric. Could it?

Using my enhanced speed, I rounded the beast in my way, moving in protectively beside Eva. I was there so quickly, she barely had a chance to register me at her side before her hair settled from the breeze my swift appearance had created.

She looked between me and the apparent stranger in confusion. The stranger, who, until now, had been the only constant in my life.

I took a moment to process what I was seeing. Alaric's silver eyes staring back at me, the same scar running down the beast's face, his dirty blonde hair trailing across his broad shoulders, but shooting past them were immense wings.

They had to be wider than he was tall, their intimidating size casting a vast shadow over the area surrounding us. They were lethal looking, capped with dangerous talons at the end of each of the three points.

They vaguely reminded me of Eva's when I'd seen her in dragon form, but where hers were obviously draconian, his looked to be a mix of a few different species.

Reptilian like a dragon, leathery like a bat, and larger than any winged shifter I had seen, aside from Eva. *Thrakos wings.*

Combined with that, were vicious claws extending from his fingers, dark as night, and sharper than a blade. Fangs protruded from his gums that looked just as lethal as the rest of him.

I'd always thought of the thrakos as both my father's greatest achievement and biggest regret. Whatever he'd used in their creation, he'd made them far too deadly than he was meant to, but that wasn't the only reason why he'd hunted them.

They could reproduce, something he'd been too arrogant to account for. They could create cross breeds that a high fae king could never hope to control through fear, which was the way he had maintained control over everyone else.

Though somehow my father controlled Alaric for centuries…

"H-How?" Eva asked, doing a better job than I was at finding the words, but the catch in her voice told me she was no less surprised.

This had to be a trick, a lie, something that meant what I was seeing wasn't true. It couldn't be true.

Only. Constant. In. My. Life.

"I never said yeh were the only one with secrets, Angel."

He was being purposely vague, but fuck that, I was so fucking over those I let in lying to me.

Yes, I'd managed to get on board with Eva being a dragon pretty quickly, but I'd always had a feeling she was hiding something. I barely knew her, just knew that she was mine and our connection was instant. We hadn't spent years knowing each other.

Alaric, on the other hand, owed me a fucking explanation. How was this even possible? A thrakos?

A. Fucking. Thrakos.

Alaric.

I had never seen a thrakos in the flesh before today. I had only ever heard stories of their brutality, yet I'd been sleeping with one in the room next to mine, a room I'd given to him no less. We had spent years as drinking buddies. Fates, I had shared a female with him, shared *Eva* with him.

I clenched my fists tightly as I waited for him to start explaining himself, but it was the younger thrakos I'd been fighting that spoke first.

"Braxton, care to start explaining why I can't kill this traitorous prick?" he asked the older male, who was now standing shirtless in his fae form.

The older male, Braxton, clasped palms with Alaric, who pulled him in and clapped him on the back, like they were old friends.

They *looked* similar.

They broke apart and Alaric focused on the fool who'd called him a prick. Fangs descended from his gums again, only they were shorter and sharper than the canines in his wolf form.

"Insult me again an' I'll forget the promise I made to yer mum, kid," Alaric growled.

The moment he finished his threat, his attention was back to flicking between Eva and I.

"He's no' a traitor, Nix. Far from it," Braxton told the young one. "An' what do yeh mean, Alaric? What promise yeh made Edelin? Have yeh seen her this past year, son?" Braxton asked.

Son?

Son!

No. No, no, no.

That couldn't be right. Alaric's father was… who the fuck *was* Alaric's father? More to the point, *what* the fuck was Alaric's father?

I'd never asked. And he'd only ever spoken of his mother on rare occasions, always keeping it brief...

"Aye. I saw her with my own eyes a few days ago. She let herself get taken by Elikai, but she's safe. For now, at least. Axel is keeping an eye on her."

Braxton sighed in relief, while Eva and the younger male, who I was now sure was the friend she'd spoken about, met eyes.

"She's alive?" he asked her disbelievingly. Eva nodded her confirmation as though to say it was true and his word was to be trusted. "Who's this Axel?"

"I'll tell yeh later, lad, but he's a good male, and more than capable from what I've heard. Yer ma's a powerful female, and when you add Axel to the mix, they are a force. Trust me," Braxton said. Nix didn't look happy about it, but he didn't push him further.

So Axel's in on this, too?

And what had Braxton meant when he'd said Alaric was no traitor?

As I looked around the strange group, I didn't want to admit to myself the conclusion I was drawing.

But it was the only thing that made sense.

If these were rebels, and Alaric wasn't a traitor, it had to mean...

"This is ma son, Alaric," Braxton said.

Eva's hand shot to her mouth as she gasped at my side.

"He's a hybrid, like yeh are lad. Only his ma's a wolf shifter. I havnae seen him since–"

"Too fuckin' long," Alaric remarked, cutting him off before he could finish.

Nix's brow furrowed in Alaric's direction. "I know you from somewhere," he said.

Eva's eyes widened in panic. Was I the only one here who wasn't either related to someone or long lost fucking friends with them?

"You were there that day at the rebel camp. You fucking killed my friends! Eva, get away from him. He was with them when Kur and Lavina–"

"She kens. She was there and there's no one that can hate me for that disaster more than myself," Alaric growled.

"Yeh tried, son. It's no' your fault the message didn't get to us in time."

What message? Fates, what was happening?

Pawing a hand through his hair, Alaric glanced at me with guilt in his eyes. "It was Elikai's birthday massacre, and the King dinnae give me the luxury of time to properly plan–"

"Who the fuck are you?" I snapped. I'd heard enough, and yet, I needed more answers.

"Kane," he sighed.

"Who. The. Fuck. Are. You?" I repeated.

"Kane, yeh have to understand, this has nothin' to do with you an' I–"

"It has fucking *everything* to do with you and I. You fucking used me to get close to my father!"

He glanced toward his father and then let his gaze fall to the ground. "It's complicated–"

"Enough bullshit. Fucking admit it!" I yelled, closing the space between us and shoving him in the chest.

I needed him to admit it, but I was fucking petrified that I was right at the same time.

"I dinnae use yeh to get close to yer father. I was already close to him. I'd been living under his roof for centuries before yeh were even conceived. I'd made my way to the top of his ranks long before yer time. I didnae need yeh for–"

"Why?" Eva cut in.

"It's a long story."

I scoffed. "Then you better get started."

Alaric let out a long breath before he spoke. "I was sent to infiltrate the King's horde."

"When?" Eva asked.

"Shortly after the prophecy was first told by Edelin," Alaric admitted.

"You *knew* about the prophecy?" Eva asked, incredulous. "Why didn't you say something?"

"I couldnae say anything. I spent the best part of three fucking centuries doing unthinkable things for a male I loathed, waitin' for that fucking prophecy to come to pass. I couldnae risk everything by tellin' yeh. There was too much at stake. I was gonnae tell yeh once we reached the Vale."

Eva looked shocked. She was staring at him open-mouthed, like she wasn't sure what to say or do next, and she hadn't been betrayed by Alaric the way I had. It was a lot to learn in a short period, and she was clearly struggling to process exactly what was going on.

I, on the other hand, was angry.

No, I was more than angry. I was fucking furious.

Hurt.

I thought I knew him. I thought he cared about me in the same way we cared about Eva. How fucking wrong I'd been. He'd acted like the prophecy was news to him, like he was hearing for the first time along with us.

How many more lies have I blindly fallen for over the years?

I shuddered at the thought, but thankfully the hurt was quickly being swallowed entirely by the anger.

"The prophecy that speaks of twin heirs being born?! You're trying to tell me that your betrayal had nothing to do with me? Do you think I'm a fucking idiot?"

"Kane, calm down," Eva said gently, placing a hand on my arm that I quickly shook off. "It's Alaric, and he cares about you. Just hear him out."

How can she take his side in this?

"He lied to us," I said, calmer this time, but not by much. I could barely recognize my own hard, icy voice. I looked at Alaric again. "For over twenty years, you've been at my side and not once had you thought to tell me?"

Of all the fae in the realm, he was the one I'd trusted more than any. The one I could count on.

Yet it had all been a lie.

"He was under orders lad, yer father wasnae the only one he answered to," Braxton said, and I glared at him.

"Oh, OK then, that makes everything better," I seethed, sarcasm dripping from every word.

"Calm down, lad. We only attacked today, because we thought yeh were Elikai. Alaric speaks highly of yeh in his letters, and there'd be no reason for him to lie to us about that. Just take a deep breath and count back from ten, refocus yerself before yeh do somethin' irrational."

I was instantly transported back to my father's chambers when we'd been looking for that fucking sword.

Close yer eyes, Kane. Take a deep breath an' count back from ten, it'll help, Alaric had said before Eva joined us.

It truly does work. An old mentor taught me the same trick, she'd added.

"*You*. You're Eva's old mentor. And Alaric's father," I started as more dots connected.

Then a more recent memory hit me. The way Alaric's fist had gone through Eva's assailant like butter. A wolf couldn't do that. A thrakos though...

All he needed to have done was shift his hand for the briefest moment.

The more I put it together, the more alone I felt. An outsider. I truly had no one. Not a single fae I could trust.

I didn't belong in the castle. But I didn't belong with them either.

I didn't belong anywhere anymore.

"Kane, let me explain. Please" Alaric pleaded.

Fuck that.

I wasn't going to fall for any more of his lies. My heart was tearing to pieces. I needed to get away from him, from all of them.

I was no use to him now, so why would he even keep me around? Elikai was probably already secretly starting preparations for his coronation to happen as soon as the mourning period was over.

I didn't need to hear Alaric's excuses to have figured out that everything he'd ever said to me was for the rebels' gain. My guess? They wanted a puppet they could control on the throne after my father ruined their lives, but I was a dead male walking now and couldn't be their pawn.

Alaric's teachings suddenly made sense. Why he had tortured me with all those lessons. He was molding me into the perfect marionette.

I turned to Eva. "You know these males? Braxton and Nix?" I asked, and she nodded. "You trust them?" She nodded carefully again.

That was all I needed to know for now.

Before anyone could try to stop me, I sprinted for the trees, not stopping until I was sure I was alone and far enough away to not have to listen to any more of their lies and schemes.

I rested back against a tree and slowly let my knees give way as I slid down to the ground.

Knotting my fingers in my hair, I tried to calm down enough, so I didn't lash out and do something I could never take back.

My chest hurt and my breaths were coming too fast. I needed to think straight.

Alaric's, or rather Braxton's, words rattled around my mind again.

Reluctantly, I took a deep breath and began counting back.

By the time I made it to three, I was no longer shaking, and breathing was easier.

And fuck, I hated that it worked.

CHAPTER 22

Evangelia

"You mean to tell me that *you,* someone who has spent your entire life hiding what you are, are saying you had no idea he was a hybrid?" Nix asked from my side.

We were slowly walking toward the trickling sound of a stream coming from inside the woods. While Braxton set up their tents for the night, Alaric had gone off in an attempt to find Kane.

I'd wanted to go with him, but this was Alaric's storm to calm. He needed to do this alone.

That left me and my best friend to have some much needed time together, while we still did our part by collecting water to boil.

It was instant nostalgia, and I found I kept pinching myself to make sure Nix truly was back in my life.

I nodded. "Seriously. I'm still struggling to believe it, and I saw him in his thrakos form with my own eyes! I mean, he lived in the castle for *hundreds* of years, he was the King's general for fates sake. I was there for what? A couple of months? And was *petrified,* every single day that someone would find out I wasn't high fae like they'd assumed."

"So that's how you got away with it? I had wondered a time or five hundred. But fuck, yeah. That male has big balls, I'll give him that." His tone was half-joking, but I knew he was just trying to break the awkward tension between us.

"I can't believe I missed it. He and Braxton look so similar, but I just didn't connect the dots until they were right in front of me. I knew Alaric was hiding something, he knew too much about the rebels not to, but he would just say he was old or it was his job to know these things."

I linked my arm with Nix's, needing to reassure myself again he was really alive and here.

I cleared my throat. "Nix, can you imagine the things he must have had to do to stay in the King's trusted circle?"

I shuddered at the thought of the toll it would take on someone to be a rebel spy for centuries. Killing your allies to save face. It was unthinkable.

Nix shook his head, a pensive expression on his face. "You'd think we would have been told that we had allies in the castle," he said. "Fuck, I don't know what you've been through, but I'm sure it would have been helpful to have known there was someone you could turn to while being held a captive there."

"Probably. I was definitely drawn to him, even though his position meant I should have stayed well out of his way. I guess the fates had great fun watching me learn he could be trusted the hard way." I snarked.

Nix's brow raised in interest, and I knew he was thinking about my relationship with the horde general, so I continued before he got any ideas about prying further.

"I get the feeling that there is so much more we don't know, so much our parents sheltered us from," I sighed.

The rebels were meant to be our people, yet there was so much Nix and I were blind to. I'd come of age the better part of a decade ago. So why hadn't they filled us in? We'd never done anything to make them think we couldn't be trusted; we were rebels born and raised.

He cringed. "Maybe they didn't want to burden us with all the politics. They'd stayed hidden for a long time. Perhaps they thought it could wait," he shrugged, staring off into the trees ahead.

We continued in silence for a moment before I felt him shudder at whatever was plaguing his mind. Then, swallowing hard, he rubbed the back of his neck with his free hand.

"Eva, I'm so sorry, about your parents," he said, his voice cracking with emotion and I felt a lump form in my throat at his words.

I wasn't sure if I was ready to open that wound.

"Fuck, I'm sorry about everything. I shouldn't have raced off and left you like that–"

"No." I said, cutting him off. "Don't talk like that. There was nothing you could have done. It was a slaughter that none of us were ready for."

"Well, I truly am sorry about your mum and dad," he said. "They were good fae."

"The best," I agreed. I squeezed his arm tighter, resting my cheek on his bicep as we walked. "Fates, I missed you so much, Nix."

"You too. I'm not even sure if this is all real or if it's just another dream and I'm going to wake up in that nightmare camp again at any minute," he said, causing the lump in my throat to thicken, almost choking me.

As we reached the stream, I let go of my hold on his arm to sit on the ground and patted the spot next to me for him to join.

I could feel his eyes burning into me, but the moment I looked up, his gaze would dart anywhere else.

He looked so different, so tired.

"So much has happened since we were in Dorgoil, I don't even know where to start." I told him truthfully as he joined me on the embankment.

The discomfort of the leaves and bark beneath us was so familiar, I could almost pretend that we were back at our old camp. But that wasn't reality. So much had happened, I could barely recognize the male who I used to know better than myself.

"I buried them. Your parents, our friends, everyone... I buried them together," he murmured. "It wasn't much, and they deserved better, but I couldn't just leave them to rot without being honored..."

I reached out to take his hand in mine, blinking back the tears pooling in my eyes.

"I spent so much time alone in the castle, Nix. With just my thoughts for company. My mind would torment me with images of my parents still lying there now. So thank you. Thank you so, so much for doing that," I choked out. "I thought about you every day, even though it hurt and I tried not to. I didn't know if you were alive, and I had no way of finding out who had made it out of there. If anyone had at all."

"Just me," he confirmed. The truth was like a blunt spear to the chest. "I'd been knocked unconscious. They must have thought I was dead, or dying, so didn't bother finishing me off. When I woke up, it was too late."

"Shit, I'm so sorry, Nix. Honestly, I can't even imagine what that must have been like," I told him, trying to blink back the tears pooling in my ears.

He just nodded, keeping his gaze on the ground. He was hurting, and I didn't know how to make him better. I'd been a captive and suffered at the hands of Elikai, but he'd been left behind, completely alone and surrounded by death.

My heart hurt for him more than I could ever express, but I was at a loss on how to help him.

I shuffled closer, resting my head on his chest and after a few seconds, he placed an arm around my shoulders and hugged me tightly to him.

We just sat in silence, comforting each other in the only way we could right now. At least without having to relive the tales of what had happened since that day that our boring existence had been turned upside down.

"I was so fucking scared I'd lost you forever, Eva. I think I might have lost myself somewhere along the way to finding you," he eventually said, obliterating my heart into a thousand fragments.

His words were filled with so much pain. So much I honestly had no doubt that he meant every last syllable of them.

I had been too much of a coward to face the possibility that he'd been killed, that I hadn't really given much thought to how surviving it would have been for him.

"You found me, Nix. I'm in one piece, and it's thanks to you. It was the hope you always gave me so freely that kept me pushing on. The hope you had that everything happens for a greater reason and that the path I'd been put on would serve a purpose. Even if it was hard at times to work out what it was exactly."

He tsked.

I pulled away slightly, needing him to see the truth of what I was saying in my eyes.

His usually shaggy, brown hair was partly pulled back in a top-knot, keeping it out of his face. His normal stubble had grown into a beard, completely changing his features from baby faced to a grown male.

More than anything, he looked drained, like I'd stolen all of his hope and taken it to Ezerat with me that day on the back of Elikai's horse.

It took more than a bad night's sleep to make an immortal look so fatigued.

"When did you last feed?" I asked, thinking more about his thrakos side more than his witch blood.

"A while ago," he said.

Knowing what he needed more than anything, I immediately began to roll up the sleeve of my blouse, and held my wrist out to him.

He shied away. *But why?* I'd always fed him, making sure the blood lust from his thrakos side never took over.

"Drink," I insisted, waving my wrist in his direction.

"I'm not sure that's a good idea," he said.

There wasn't much I could do to help him right now, but this was something. A good place to start. I wasn't going to take no for an answer.

"Nix, just do it. No offense, but you look like shit, and it would make me feel better knowing you weren't starving, not when you have a perfectly decent source sitting right here."

"I don't want to hurt you. Like I said, it's been a while."

"You're my best friend, and I trust you."

Hesitantly, he took my wrist, dipping his head as he raised it to his lips. "Tell me if I'm taking too much," he said around his fangs that had already descended from his gums.

"Nix, we have done this a hundred times. Just stop talking and–"

The short, sharp sting made me wince slightly as he punctured my skin. Then he was drinking deeply. I closed my eyes for a moment, trying to remember the first time he'd fed from me, but the memory was fuzzy.

It was just so normal for us, for all thrakos in the Fading Vale, to be fed by willing rebels. The only one I'd ever known who chose to satiate the bloodlust by feeding from rabbits and rodents was Braxton.

I gasped as I remembered why my mum had said he did that, and Nix quickly pulled away.

"Are you okay? Did I take too much? I'm sorry."

Worry etched his features, and I couldn't stand to see him like this.

I shook my head. "No, it's not that. Carry on. Honestly. I was just remembering when Braxton visited that time and we saw him hunting for rabbits to feed from. I'd asked my mum why he didn't just feed from a fae and she'd said it was in respect for his true mate. Do you think that's Alaric's mum?"

Apparently done feeding, he dropped my hand and wiped his mouth with the back of his hand, not that there was a single drop of blood that had missed his mouth.

"He never told me much about his mate, only that he had one, and it was complicated. If Alaric is their son, maybe she left with him when he infiltrated the castle."

"Shit." I said, unable to find any meaningful words for how awful that would have been.

For all of them.

We fell into a companionable silence for a while, contemplating it. Eventually, I was the one to break it. "How did you find Braxton?"

"He found me. He and a few others from his camp heard about what had happened and came to help. He's a good male. I don't think I'd have lived through the guilt if it weren't for him," he said.

He was back to avoiding my eyes, but at least he didn't look so pale now. Far from his usual self, but a step closer to it. Hopefully, a few more feedings would sort him out, on the outside at least.

"I'm glad he was there for you when I couldn't be," I said. "We have so much to talk about, but we need to get back before they start to worry. I should really talk to Alaric, too, and see if he found Kane. Fates, I hope he caught up to him."

"You mean Prince Nekane?"

"He prefers Kane, but yeah, him."

He furrowed his brow. Now wasn't the time to explain my complicated relationship with the prince and the general.

"It's a long story, but they are good males. I trust them with my life. I think you'll like them once you get to know them. It's not like they can go to the castle anytime soon, so they are rebels now, just like us."

"Hmmm, maybe," he grunted noncommittally. "Let's just fill the canteens and head back."

CHAPTER 23

Alaric

Finally able to call on my thrakos abilities without fear of imminent death, I raced through the trees that Kane had disappeared into, enjoying the sensation of being in this form despite the situation that brought me here.

It didn't take long to acclimatize, and soon I was traveling at a speed I knew could rival Kane's own. Hunting him with the wind in my wings and desperation in my chest to fix this mess, I followed him by scent alone.

It called to me in the air, sweet apples and sharp cinnamon, easily distinguishable against even the strongest wildflowers or citrusy cedar surrounding me.

I hadn't wanted him to find out like this. Not at all. When I'd been running the perimeter and picked up the familiar scent of two thrakos, the need to protect Kane and Angel had been all-consuming.

Kane was skilled, strong and fierce, but he'd never faced a thrakos. Well, not in thrakos form. I'd taught him what I could, but my hands had been tied when it came to teaching him more than that.

My wolf wouldn't be a guaranteed win against two of them, not if they were trained anyway, and being a thrakos in this kingdom meant making sure you could defend yourself and your own.

It was a life revolving around survival, which begged the question whether they had a life at all? It hadn't felt like it when I'd lived in the Vale. I had my wolf, Edelin's boy, Nix, was part witch, and Axel had... options, but for those like Braxton, without another form to hide behind, it was become the weapon or be run through with one.

So yeah, no fucking thrakos went through life untrained, and therefore the odds weren't in my wolf's favor.

In that moment, I'd turned to my other beast. My stronger, more deadly, bloodthirsty form and I hadn't paused to consider how he'd react, finally knowing my biggest secret.

I wasn't ashamed of being thrakos, and I needed Kane to know that. I'd kept it from him because it had been impossible for him to know the whole truth of what I was, without needing to know the full story.

It would have run the very serious risk of altering the prophecy and destroying everything I'd committed my existence to. Everything my friends and family had committed their lives to. Not to mention the danger he would be in knowing the truth.

Before Kane and Angel, I'd spent hundreds of years with one goal, one purpose, one destiny. And I had not once wavered. But they made me desire things I'd never thought were remotely possible, not until recently. Until them.

I'd grown to care for Kane over the years. I was protective of him, but I'd always managed to keep the end-game in mind. *Prepare him for the day his father's throne will 'lay bare'.*

After the prophecy had been given all those years ago, it had taken longer than we'd hoped for Edelin and Alita to perfect the scent blocking charm, so I'd used that time to train tirelessly with my da'.

The shift suppressing charm; the one I now knew Eva had used came much, much later. So at the time it was essential to the mission that I had absolute control of my thrakos side and shifting.

When my ma' and I had moved to the capital, leaving my da' in the Vale to help run the Rebel Alliance, we'd had no way of knowing what the timeframe for the prophecy would be. We just knew that our salvation could be heard in its words.

I'd wasted no time joining the horde, then worked my way through the ranks, needing to be in the King's inner circle the day twin heirs were born.

By some miracle, and some close calls that resulted in a darkness on my soul I'd never be able to remove, I'd evaded detection the entire time.

Over torturous centuries, I'd learned to keep up the ruse. Eventually, finding a way to live with myself after carrying out the king's dirty work. I'd just had to convince myself that I didn't have a heart.

Someone without a heart could commit atrocities without guilt or remorse, right?

Apparently not entirely, but it had worked pretty well for a really fucking long time.

When Kane and Elikai had been born, the King had reacted in a way that I'd never predicted, never even understood, until recently. I'd been certain that he would deal with the birth of his 'undoing' the way he dealt with everything else: murder.

When he hadn't, I'd come to the conclusion that perhaps even the foulest of creatures were capable of love, however the fucked up way they showed it.

He'd been a complete bastard to Kane, true. Scorned him, beat him, blamed him for his wife's death virtually every time they were in each other's presence, but the cunt hadn't killed him. He'd always been careful not to go too far.

After hearing the advisors speak of the deal Augustus had made before he knew of the prophecies' existence, I'd realized it wasn't love at all, but that he'd been well and truly over a fucking barrel. There was only so long he could put off fulfilling his bargain to produce an heir with the Mount Mortum royal after all.

Since the revelations that day in the throne room with Kane, Elikai and the advisors, I hadn't had as much free time or head space as I'd have liked to think about the past, but there were some things that had struck me immediately as making more sense now I knew more of the truth.

Like Queen Kahina's behavior while she'd been expecting the twins.

There was never a moment she was alone with the King. She'd been off her food at mealtimes, which I'd assumed was the pregnancy, but could that have been because she didn't trust that the food hadn't been tampered with on the King's orders?

She'd slept separately from Augustus too, among other things, which made me think that perhaps she knew of his predicament with the prophecy.

Perhaps she warned her uncle that if harm came to her or the babes, it would have been her husband's doing. She was a smart female. Maybe she'd even made sure Augustus knew that she knew to stop him from getting any ideas.

Regardless of what if's, it was quite the predicament he'd have found himself in.

It hadn't mattered which path he took where his children and the prophecy were concerned, he'd ultimately lose power, which is the only thing he ever cared about. Break his bargain with the Mount Mortum King and he'd bring war to his doorstep. One Dezrothia could not win; not with the way he ran it. Or uphold his bargain, and live with knowing that his children were prophesied to be his undoing.

Nevertheless, it was now clear he wasn't a monster who secretly loved his son deep down, not even close. Just a monster.

He thought he'd found a loophole, outsmarted the prophecy, but the fates worked in mysterious ways and he'd played right into their hands, anyway. He'd thought he was being clever by not naming an heir, but prophecies were not easy to understand. The moment the princes were born, the prophecy came into play, irrespective of what he did.

In a fucked up way, I was glad for the King's abhorrent treatment of Kane; it was what had made him the better male. It didn't take long before it was obvious which twin I was to help and which was as evil as his father.

Smelling the air deeply, Kane's intoxicating scent became almost overwhelming.

I'd found him. Sitting at the base of a tree, head bowed, while his elbows rested on his bent knees.

I had no fucking clue what to say when his head snapped up as I neared. He glared at me with his piercing blues, like I was a stranger.

I met his eyes. A lot had changed between Kane and me, in a way I definitely hadn't planned. Yes, we had built a relationship as drinking pals, becoming closer still those nights we'd used that room above the Crooked Claw.

But it was in the weeks since he came of age and his scent had changed that I'd become addicted to him. Desiring him but being unable to do fuck all about it.

Through Angel, we'd had some forbidden, stolen moments, but it wasn't enough. It would never be enough. And now he fucking hated me.

"Come to convince me to take part in your rebel scheme?" he growled coldly.

"It's no' like that, Kane and yeh ken it." I said, rubbing the back of my neck.

"What is it like, then?" he spat. "Because from what I heard, you have played me like a fucking puppet."

"For fuck's sake, Kane. You can't truly believe that. Our relationship was one of the only real things I had in that fuckin' castle."

I didn't have the ability of allure like the high fae, but I didn't need it to push the truth into my words.

"Ha. You expect me to believe that? You were the closest thing I had to a fucking friend, and I was just a means to an end for you wasn't I? Here I was thinking we respected each other, treated each other as equals, but you just saw me as a spoiled brat of a prince didn't you?" he accused me, getting to his feet.

I choked out a laugh of my own. "Equals? You're a fuckin' high fae prince. We have never been equals and we never will be as long as Dezrothia is ruled by a prejudiced fucking King! At first, yeah, o' course I thought yeh were a brat. Yeh were five fucking years old when I started training yeh and yer brother. What else was I to think? I'd planned to watch yeh from a distance, never get too close, but yer cunt of a father decided to make me yer tutor."

He looked taken aback for a moment, hearing me speak so candidly at long last about his father, but he wasn't done yet.

"I bet that was fucking perfect for you and your rebel friends, wasn't it? What about all the time we spend together now? I guess that's just you doing your duty too, huh?"

"Yeh are more than a fucking duty t–"

"Just fuck off, Alaric!" he cut over me and moved to walk away.

No. Fucking. Chance.

Launching myself at him quicker than he knew I could move, I grabbed his throat, pinning him against the tree.

He didn't get to just walk away.

My hand flexed, contemplating squeezing tighter as my teeth ground together. I wasn't just in his space; I was his entire fucking surroundings, the air he breathed and all he could see.

As I looked him in the eyes, I saw his pupils dilate.

In a move I'd taught him myself, he escaped my grip, giving himself just enough space to take a swing for my jaw. We had sparred and fought too many times to count over the years, his skills only getting better as time moved on, but this was the first time that he'd swung for me with the intensity that belayed his desire to hurt me more than I had hurt him.

He may have high fae strength, but I was part fucking thrakos, and I could finally show him what that meant.

Catching his fist in my left hand, I used my right to catch his throat once more, no gentle hold this time as rage bled into my vision.

Rage that he'd found out this way, rage that we might never get past this, rage that he no longer trusted or believed a word I fucking said.

"Fuck you," he gritted out, his voice strained as he forced the words out around my tightening hold.

My beast was close to the surface, clawing at its cage, and my wolf was goading it on as the red closed in.

My eyes zeroed in on the thundering pulse below my thumb. Closing what little space there was between us, I pulled him forward, angling my head so I could speak directly into his ear.

"You'd like that, wouldn't yeh," I growled low, my teeth grazing the sensitive flesh of his neck. "For me to fuck yeh…" It was bold and assumptive, but no less true.

I sucked in a lungful of his scent and my fangs elongated of their own accord, forcing me to back up slightly so I didn't accidently pierce his skin.

I felt a hand tentatively glide up my thigh, landing on my cock. The fire in his eyes told me he liked what he found as it strained against my leathers.

My beast was desperate to slake its thirst, and the challenge in Kane's smirk did nothing to deter it. "Kane…" I groaned as my hips pressed into his hand.

"I should have fucking known you weren't full wolf," he said. "Shifter claws don't slide through flesh and bone like yours did so easily–"

"Yeh thinks that's fuckin' easy for me?" My fangs were on full display and his eyes widened. "Yeh have no i-fucking-dea of the shite I have to live with on my conscience."

"Oh yeah, that's right… because you didn't fucking tell me! Maybe you'll tell me this, Alaric; have you ever thought about sinking those fangs into me? Or was that not part of your duties?"

His snarl came out as pure seduction as he moved his hand, nimbly stroking the hard length through my breeches. It was a mind fuck as the bloodlust bled into carnal lust.

"Dinnae fucking tempt me," I rumbled, leaning fully into his body now, his back pressed up against the thick tree trunk by my entire body weight.

He groaned in response, biting down on his bottom lip with his pearly white teeth and making my own fangs ache in jealousy.

His hand tightened on my cock, his desire without a fucking word needing to pass through his fuckable lips. If this was some kind of game, I didn't have the mind to figure it out as my desire to dominate him in the best way engulfed me.

"You smell so fuckin' good. I doubt I'd be able to stop at just a bite," I warned, but it came out as more of a purr than a threat as I nuzzled my nose into his throat.

He was silent for several moments, letting my words hang in the air, all the while continuing his teasing with his hand like he was doing it unconsciously.

Mind. Fuck.

"Then don't stop, " he eventually said.

With my hand still on his throat, I tilted his face and covered his mouth with my own.

Fuck. I had wanted this since the day I'd walked into that training hall after Elikai's birthday hunt. His scent had become the most tempting poison to me. Trying to play the good general, I'd not been able to give myself over to it fully. Between the confusion over what had changed, the fucking Lores stopping me and my mission, I had never acted on it.

Fuck the Lores. I thought as I deepened the kiss. *Fuck the fates. Fuck my duties. And fuck denying myself what I want.*

Kane was a lot of things, but submissive he was not, and he fought me with his tongue as he kissed me back with an intense passion. His grip on my cock broke as he brought his hands up to fist in my hair with urgency.

Pressing into him to close the space where his hand had been between our bodies, I growled as I felt the hardness of his own cock now straining against mine as he rutted his hips against me, desperate to find friction.

It was me who broke the kiss.

Greedy for more of him. I loosened my hand from around his throat, "On yer fuckin' knees." I demanded, and to my surprise, he dropped.

His hands made short work of sliding the leathers down my thighs to release me. I throbbed at the anticipation of fucking his mouth. *A prince on his knees just for me.*

Not just any prince. *My prince.*

With one hand on my thigh, his other curled around my length before I felt his tongue slide from base to tip. Another growl escaped my chest.

"Tell me, what do you want me to do next, Alaric?" he had the bollocks to taunt me, even when on his knees. my rigid cock pulsing in his hand.

He would learn soon enough exactly who was in control here.

Laying my palm on the top of his head, I grabbed a fistful of his raven hair and watched as pain briefly flickered across his face when I yanked his head back harder than necessary. This battle for dominance was new, but I was so fucking here for it.

"My cock should be so far down yer throat that talkin' becomes a problem."

I relaxed my grip on his hair. Without a word of argument, he opened his mouth and swallowed me, bobbing to fit the whole fucking thing down his throat. The moment he hit the base, his chin resting on my balls, my wings burst from my back.

He peered up in surprise, his mouth stretched around my cock. I expected to see alarm in his eyes, but to my own surprise, flames of desire danced within them instead as he took in my dark, leathery wings.

He moved a hand to my arse, his fingers digging in as the other cupped my balls, fondling them gently. A total fucking contrast to the way he was sucking me eagerly and I would be damned if I let myself come already, no matter how fucking close I was.

The bastard quickened his pace, sliding along my length and making sure to go from base to head with every mouthful. He didn't break eye contact as he watched me watching him move with skill, and those blue eyes held me captive.

He was seeing me, truly seeing me, thrakos side and all, and he still wanted me.

His tongue swirled at my tip before breaking away altogether and I growled involuntarily, a rattle deep in my chest. I wasn't ready for his mouth to leave me. It felt so fucking good, I could have drowned in the sensation.

"Kane..." I groaned. "*More.*" For fucks' sake, I was reduced to single fucking syllables, but who gave a fuck if it meant he got back to it quicker.

With a dimpled smile, he stroked my cock in his fist and dipped down, running his tongue from tip to base before sucking one of my balls into his mouth, pulling a feral noise from me.

My fist in his hair flexed as I leaned forward heavily on the tree, steadying myself with my other as my claws sunk into the bark and I looked down at him.

The hand that had been kneading my arse had moved to his pants, and he was stroking himself while toying with me.

Watching my cock disappear into his perfect mouth over and over reminded me of how Angel had worked his, and the memory was doing all kinds of shit to me; triggering thoughts and ideas for things I hadn't even realized I wanted until now.

I pictured Angel joining us, the three of us joined as one as we fucked, a fantasy I'd had time and again. Except this time, she wasn't the one in the middle, it was Kane.

Fucking her as I fucked him.

The thought had me on the brink and I had no doubt that if I were to come down his throat right now, that he would swallow every last drop.

Not yet.

I yanked him to his feet, spinning him around and pressing into his back as he was forced into the tree. "Did yeh enjoy suckin' my cock, Kane?"

The groan that tumbled from his mouth at my words was sinful and in this moment, not even the fates would stand a chance at denying me him.

I reached around to his straining cock, teasing the hard ridge. "Feels like yeh did." He pressed into my hand, seeking that delicious friction that I refused to give him.

Bringing my wings around us, the lethal tips penetrated the bark, keeping him captive and at my mercy. Not that he was putting up a fight.

I pressed my straining cock into his back as I brought my free hand to his throat once more, the other still between his legs.

"Yeh think I used yeh, Kane? Yeh think I dinnae care a damn about yeh? How fuckin' wrong yeh are," I told him. "Yeh ken what I want? I want to fuck yeh so fuckin' good an' hard that yer ruined for every other fae aside from our female. And I think yeh want that too..."

Fuck, I want that so badly.

I needed him to say yes, but he took his sweet time to respond.

Eventually, he tilted his head enough to look at me. "Fight me, use me, fuck me. Just don't fucking lie to me," he said.

It wasn't the simple yes I'd hoped for; it was better. It was Kane, and it was raw and real. I kissed him hard, taking the years of frustration out on his mouth that I'd had to lie to him to begin with. He returned the kiss with a desperation of his own.

"No more lies," I promised.

Slowly, I brought my hand from his neck to his mouth. He knew exactly what I wanted as he opened for me. His tongue lashed my fingers as I stroked him.

Fuck, he felt good in my hands, so fucking good.

His trousers dropped to the ground with a thud and I removed my fingers from the heat of his mouth, bringing them to his hole.

Fates forgive me, we both knew this wasn't going to be enough, but there was no way I was breaking this moment to race back to the tent to get lube. We needed this, Kane and I, here and now.

Smearing the saliva around, I pushed my middle finger in, up to the first knuckle.

He clenched at the intrusion before arching his back into me to make it easier. I worked him, feeling the muscles relax as I coaxed a second, then third, finger inside.

Fates, the moans that spilled from his lips were a sinful tune to my ears. He was usually a talkative male in bed, but this was different. Having him at my mercy, words failing him, this was exactly how I wanted him.

If he had enough words to try and take control, then I was failing as a lover. I wanted him incoherent, ruined, lost to lust.

The groan that left his throat as I reclaimed my fingers had me ready to explode. His cock was pulsing in my hand, and he was close already. I lined the head of my swollen cock to him, pushing forward slowly. So fucking tight, but fuck he felt good.

"Alaric." Kane gasped as I took measured thrusts, working to seat myself entirely inside him. *So fucking perfect.*

He thrust back on me, his hips moving in time with my hand on his cock as he tried to take control. I laughed hoarsely as he moved, my hips meeting his as we gradually found a delicious rhythm.

My hips picked up pace as we moved together. My hand found its way around his neck again, tilting his head to groan in his ear. "Fuck you feel so good..."

The red haze was creeping back into my vision as I registered how close to his thudding pulse I was.

Just a little taste.

The thought sent a euphoric buzz through my veins. My lips trailed his neck as I kissed and nibbled up to his ear.

"So good," he agreed breathlessly, bracing a hand out in front of him so he could reach up and knot his fingers in my hair, holding me to him with the other. My fangs grazed his flesh, and he groaned, pushing me tighter into the crook of his neck. It was almost too much.

He clenched around my cock, incoherent words tumbling from his mouth as his own shaft pulsed in my hand. He was on the verge of coming too, and I was warring with myself, unable to decide whether I should let him or deny him.

A fang scraped his sensitive flesh.

"Bite me," he said. "Please Alaric, just fucking do it," he begged, pushing back so my cock was seated deeply inside him.

My teeth sank through his delectable flesh as my beast took charge, my arm sliding up his chest to hold him tight to me and collaring his neck again.

Kane gasped, his blood coated my mouth in a burst of flavor, my wings spreading wide in ecstasy. I sucked greedily while thrusting harder into him, over and over as my hands tightened on both his throat and his throbbing cock.

"Fuck... *yes*... like that," he moaned.

Reluctantly, I released my fangs from his throat, fucking him harder. Just as his thick length started twitching violently, on the brink of ecstasy, I bit down again, more savagely this time, before ripping my mouth from him quickly and he exploded, my hand milking his cock as my thrusts became frenzied, chasing my own end.

I licked up the mess at his neck, wanting every last damned drop I could get of his addictive blood before his body healed the wound.

His grip tightened in my hair. *Shit, this was too good.* My hands shifted to his hips, and with one final thrust, I emptied myself into him. Pleasure bursting through my body, heat sizzling through my veins. I never wanted the sensation to end.

"Mine." I groaned as it began to ebb.

I dropped my head to rest it on his shoulder, fighting to catch my breath, still filling him to the hilt. The red haze that had been teasing me was gone, and I felt not even a hint of the itch that I could usually feel even after feeding it.

Fates, that was more incredible than I could have imagined.

Slowly, I withdrew from Kane. He turned to face me as we fought to draw a steady breath. "Fuck, Alaric… that was..."

"Aye, it was," I agreed, grasping his face, pulling him in for another heart stopping kiss, which he returned tenfold as I let my thrakos side retreat.

"It most definitely was." Angel's whispered voice floated over to us.

CHAPTER 24
Nekane

Eva's gaze explored Alaric and I in turn. She stood on the forest's edge, her eyes wide as they traveled from top to bottom, taking in everything.

Fascinated by the scene in front of her, she unconsciously sucked in her bottom lip and caressed her clavicle, her other arm hanging loosely down at her side.

"Enjoy the show, Princess?" I asked.

She arched her back against the tree across from us, but stood straighter at my words. Her green eyes blinked hard, breaking the trance she was in.

"Yeah. Um. What? I mean no. Well yes, but… uh, I'm sorry." She said, turning to leave as though she was suddenly desperate to be anywhere but here. "I'll wait back at camp. I just wanted to check. I didn't mean to–"

Alaric arched his brow in confusion as he redressed at a leisurely pace. I had an inkling as to what was going on with her, or at least I thought so. The only other option was that she didn't like what she saw, and if that were the case… Well fuck, that wasn't an option, not even worth thinking about.

The only thing that made sense, that explained why she'd go from looking like she was about to slide her hand down into her undoubtedly wet panties, to suddenly praying the ground would swallow her whole while she squirmed, was that she felt she was interrupting something.

She'd walked in on Alaric and I, sharing a moment, a private moment, as intimate as it gets. It must have been confusing for her. Did she feel like she shouldn't be here? Like a third wheel? I had a lot more experience than she did when it came to voyeurism, but I think even *I'd* feel a little awkward in her shoes.

She didn't need to feel that way, none of us did. She was part of this. Part of us. One third of what we have was her. This thing between the three of us, this… relationship? Whatever it was, we needed to talk about it and avoid moments like this happening.

I didn't feel the need to put a label on what we had. Fuck that. I wouldn't even know where to begin putting it into a category, and I hated that everything had to be put into a fucking box all the time.

Why did everyone have to be one thing or another to please society and fae they didn't even know, let alone care about? But even so, we needed to be honest with each other if we had any hope of knowing where we stood and moving forward.

Without hesitation, I knew I was all in. The walls of the castle had been our prison for too long, and without them, we were finally getting to taste the forbidden fruit, and it was fucking delicious.

I hated the thought of what they'd had to hide. The secrets, the lies, concealing their true natures… I fucking hated it. And for all that I hated it, I wouldn't let it come between us even more. There could be no more keeping secrets from each other. Fates, I was still fucking angry at Alaric. He'd betrayed me, and unintentionally or not, it didn't change the fact that he had lived a lifetime of lies and I had been the center of them since my birth. Of course, none of that was magically forgotten because he'd fucked me.

Pressed up against that tree, it felt like all our problems had become miniscule compared to the vastness of the connection that had grown between us these last few months, building to the point of bursting at the seam until it exploded in the best fucking way.

But I wanted to understand him on every level, learn everything there was to know about him, not just how to pleasure him, but how to make him… happy.

No more lies, no more secrets. Just the truth. Without that, we had no chance of making whatever this was, work.

We needed to figure out how we were going to make this work, but we had a bigger problem that we'd have to deal with, too. This was Dezrothia, and here, it was a massive fucking no for our species to even be friends, never mind being lovers.

A high fae, a dragon and wolf-thrakos hybrid… It sounded like the start of a terrible joke, one that ended with all of us being killed. If only we hadn't been born to this realm, maybe who we were and what we had would be accepted.

"What are yeh apologizin' for, Angel?" Alaric asked.

"I just…um… uh…" she fumbled, looking everywhere but at us.

"Unless it's for not getting here sooner, so you could take center stage, then you have nothing to apologize for." I told her firmly.

Yanking up my trousers, I righted my clothes as I stalked toward her, crossing the space between us and her in just a few short strides.

Taking Eva's hand, I walked backwards, leading her back over to where Alaric stood. I smiled at him, the two of us had needed that moment together, it was a breakthrough for us. The same way we'd both had our time alone with Eva, but I never wanted her to feel like she needed an invitation.

Alaric didn't return my smile. Instead, he sniffed the air, as though he'd suddenly sensed a threat.

"What is it?" I asked, concerned.

His gaze fell between me and Eva, where our hands were linked. "Why do I smell your blood, Angel?" he asked darkly, his fangs on display even though he wasn't fully shifted. The male had remarkable control for someone who'd been hiding that part of himself for so long.

"My blood?" Eva asked.

He took her hand from mine, holding her wrist upward in his grip. I tried to get a better look at whatever injury had him reacting so strangely, but couldn't see anything to have caused this sudden change in him.

In yet another display of incredible control over his thrakos form, he held out an index finger and the single digit transformed; its nail elongating into a sharp black claw.

I frowned as he traced it down the fabric of her sleeve, and his jaw clenched so hard I heard his teeth grind as the material fell away.

On her otherwise smooth, fair skin, there were two faint marks on her wrist where her flesh had been punctured and was in the process of healing. A bite mark.

"Which one was it?" I snapped, wondering how Alaric would feel about me killing his father so soon after they'd been reunited, then realizing I didn't care.

I might not be a prince anymore in the Kingdom's eyes, but she was my Princess, and no one fucking hurt her.

"Nix." Alaric answered for her. "My da' would never feed from a fae that wasnae his true mate."

"Where is Nix now, Eva?" I demanded.

"Oh, stop it. Both of you. Like I'd tell you when you're acting like it's a crime to feed my best friend," she said, trying to tug her arm back.

"It is to me." Alaric growled, gripping her chin to look him in the eye. "You're *mine.*"

Eva's eyes widened as she looked at me, as though she wanted me to tell him he was being ridiculous.

I wasn't well versed in thrakos etiquette and was livid that someone would lay a finger on her. I felt a soul deep need to protect Eva, but Alaric was murderous, and I had a feeling it had everything to do with some code the thrakos had when it came to their need for blood to survive.

"I'm *yours*? Are you trying to claim me as your source, or your female, Alaric?" Eva demanded.

"Both." Alaric said flatly. "And there is no *tryin'* about it, you will never feed that male, or any other, again."

The tone he used left no room for argument, but there was a glint in his silver eyes that was almost daring her to do just that.

"I have been his source for as long as I can remember," Eva said, crossing her arms over her chest. "How *dare* you tell me–"

"He can find a new source." Alaric cut over her. "Or do as my da' does, feed off animal blood instead," he finished matter-of-factly.

Eva's nostrils flared, and I wasn't certain she wouldn't go full dragon on him at any moment. Shelving my own frustration at the situation for now, I said. "Princess, I believe what Alaric is saying is that he would very much like it if you were *his* source from now on… exclusively."

She shook her head softly. "Why can't he feed from *you?*" she said stubbornly. "I didn't see you complaining just now when he had his fangs in your neck."

Despite her tone, her cheeks pinkened at the memory of what she'd seen.

"I plan to," Alaric said.

I bit the inside of my cheek to conceal my own surprise at his bold claim. Eva wasn't wrong about what she'd said. I'd enjoyed his bite, it had been the perfect spark of pain that added even more intensity to the pleasure he'd been giving oh so skillfully.

"Good, because my friend needs me now more than ever. He's in rough shape, fates only knows the extent of what he has been through. He barely looks like himself and it kills me. I don't know how else to help him right now...."

"It's okay, Princess–"

"No! It's not okay, Kane! The least I can do is help make his body strong, even if I don't know how to make his mind strong. He's a shadow of who he was just a couple months ago... he's trying to hide it, but I *know* him. Better than anyone, and he's not okay, and now you want to stop me from helping him?!"

Alaric's sharp features softened a little at her words. "Angel, I'm sorry, but I dinnae intend to share you *or* Kane with another thrakos," he said. "If yeh dinnae want to be my source, either of yeh, I'll deal with that. Fates, I've fed from animals and scraps on the battlefield for a long fuckin' time. I can slake the bloodlust that way if need be. But bein' someone else's source... seein' these marks on yeh, made by another thrakos... that I cannae deal with."

"Why?" Eva and I asked together.

"It's like he's claiming yeh, not just as his source, but his female."

I bristled. "That's a solid fucking no, Princess," I interrupted before I could stop myself. "We'll find someone else for your friend, another strong fae. One with nice tasty blood or whatever it is that a thrakos looks for in a blood supply."

"When a thrakos finds his true mate, the thought of feedin' from another fae is sickening. It feels like cheatin'. I've never known a true mate bond go three ways, so I dinnae ken why picturin' his fangs sinking into yeh while he tastes yer blood on his lips feels like torture, but that's how it is for me... with both of yeh." Alaric explained.

He looked uncomfortable admitting it, but it was just more clarification for me that we needed to work out what the fuck this was between us.

"Like a true mate bond?" I questioned. Is that what this was? Is that why I felt so connected to both of them?

Alaric nodded stiffly.

She sighed, pinching the bridge of her nose. "Even if it was that, which is highly unlikely given the rarity and the fact there are three of us, I really don't see the issue. He's my friend, nothing more. It's not sexual or anything."

They were mules on a narrow track, and we were just going to go around in circles, both of them feeling so strongly about this.

"The issue, Princess, is that we care about you. A lot. And though we share well with each other, we are greedy bastards and won't share well with others. We are going to a rebel camp, aren't we? He won't need to feed again before we get there, right?" They both shook their heads, confirming we had time. "We need to find him someone else, Princess. If you decide to carry on feeding him yourself, you can't blame us if he wakes up dead."

I was joking with the last bit, sort of.

She sighed, her anger dissipating a little with the air in her lungs. Eventually, she mused, "How do you wake up dead?" My lips twitched.

"No one knows," I said, pulling her into my chest, wrapping my arms around her protectively and placing a soft kiss on her head. "Those who've experienced it aren't big into sharing either." I told her, trying my best to fight my grin and remain as deadpan as possible.

I watched Alaric over Eva's shoulder shake his head in exasperation.

"This complicates things," she sighed into my chest.

"You mean it wasn't complicated before, Princess?" The relationship between us was anything but straight-forward. Even if it felt right.

I desperately wanted to ask the questions that had been playing on my mind. *What are the three of us? Are we in a relationship? Are we going to hide it? Will we embrace what we have and kill anyone who tries to kill us for it?*

In the same way Alaric needed to claim his source, I needed to know they were serious about what we had. I was so used to being fucked over by the fae that were supposed to care about me that I needed to hear it from them that this wasn't just a temporary thing. That this was more than just a bit of fun with a time limit. I needed to hear the words from them to have any hope of believing that my heart was in safe hands.

Fates, we were being hunted, had our faces on wanted posters up and down the realm, yet I wanted nothing more than to climb up on Eva's scales and fly through the skies yelling that they were mine for all to hear. I knew that would never be an option for us, but the least we could do was be open with each other.

"Fine, I won't feed Nix," Eva said eventually. "But what do I tell him if he asks?"

"Leave that to me." Alaric said, then from one blink to the next, he was gone. Darting back through the trees, leaving Eva and I staring in his wake.

Fuck me, that male was a force. Unapologetically dominant, as handsome as he was fierce, and one with whom Nix most definitely should not fuck.

"What do you think he is going to do?" Eva asked, worry etched in her features.

"You agreed not to let him drink from you again, so he probably won't kill him, if that helps," I said, and she gulped nervously.

Cupping her cheeks in my hands, I kissed her on the forehead before resting my chin on the top of her head.

"That wasn't quite as reassuring as you might have thought it was, Kane. We really should get going after him."

"OK, but first. I have a question, and I want an honest answer."

"OK..."

"Why did you freak out after catching Alaric and I?" I asked, suddenly needing to know for certain that it wasn't because she was uncomfortable with *what* we were doing.

I tilted her head up, so she had to look me in the eyes when she answered. I needed the truth. Even if I couldn't handle it. I needed to know. Fates, if she hadn't liked seeing me and Alaric together like that it would ruin everything.

"I… I guess I felt bad for gawking at the two of you when you were… um, enjoying alone time with each other."

I raised a brow. "Gawking?"

A flush covered her cheeks. "Yes, I would definitely call it gawking."

A full dimpled smile spread across my face. I kissed her, firm but brief, enjoying the little gasp of surprise that escaped her.

"I'm glad you gawked," I told her, looking directly into her emerald eyes, wanting her to see the truth of my words. "Now, let's go find our male before he kills your best friend."

CHAPTER 25
Nixen

I poked at the fire in front of me, pointedly ignoring Braxton, who was staring so hard in my direction I wouldn't have been surprised if he was about to give me a detailed description of what my internal organs looked like.

I grew more and more anxious by the minute, waiting for Eva to return. She left what felt like an age ago, insisting she should go and find her new friends without me.

It had, of course, crossed my mind that one of them was more than a friend to her, but I didn't like the idea of it any less the more I thought about it. Instead, I banished those hateful thoughts and found myself quickly spiraling down a dangerous road of even darker thoughts instead.

Only they weren't just intrusive thoughts, these were real life memories. It felt like flashbacks of my darkest day followed me around every corner these days. No matter how fast I tried to outrun them, they were always there. Like part of my shadow, always close, visible night and day.

As I gazed into the warm glow of the campfire, head in my hands, I reminded myself for the hundredth time since Eva had gone into the forest that all was not lost, not anymore. I'd found her. She was alive and in one piece.

Sometime later, Braxton pulled me out of the trance the flames had locked me in. "Yer lookin' well, kid."

I narrowed my eyes at him. Was he being sarcastic? He wasn't the type to give random compliments, so what was his deal? "Thanks?" I said, my tone uncertain.

I picked up a small twig and began twirling it around between my fingers. Either he had bad news or… Oh.

I relaxed a little as I caught on; I'd fed. Ever vigilant, he clearly noticed I wasn't as pale as I had been since returning from my all too brief catch-up with Eva.

Her blood was like a magic elixir, and with it pumping through my veins again at long last, I had to admit, I felt a lot stronger than I had in months. In body at least, even if not entirely of mind.

Eva had fed me since the very first day bloodlust had reared its ugly head. By the time I'd been born, the rebels knew well and good that the thrakos' curse, the bloodlust gene, passed down to their hybrid young.

Feeding from a source in the Fading Vale had become part of daily life, and everyone in a position to offer up a vein was happy to do so. Naturally, because Eva and I were together all the time, I'd grown accustomed to solely feeding from her.

The idea of feeding from another had felt like giving up somehow. Like it was admitting to myself that I may never find her. Eva had been my source for so long, I couldn't fathom feeding from another. So I'd kept the edge off the bloodlust by snacking on small animals here and there.

It wasn't until I felt that first drop of her blood on my tongue earlier that I'd remembered how superior fae blood was. Especially one as powerful as Eva.

She'd only fed me to begin with, but as she got older, in her later teenage years, she'd often fed thrakos who'd visited our camp too. Decanting her blood at first into a cup or vial for them to drink from, but she'd soon grown tired of that long process, realizing that with her body's ability to heal so quickly, it was much easier to just allow them to feed directly from her wrist.

Initially, her parents had been protective. They were leaders in the rebel alliance, and there really wasn't much they wouldn't do when it came to helping others, particularly those who found themselves wandering the Fading Vale. Still, they'd struggled with the idea of their little girl feeding the huge males, most of whom they'd only met that day.

It was Eva in the end who had told them to 'chill', and they had, to an extent. *'As long as it's in the presence of Nixen, and from the wrist, not the neck, we'll allow it, Evangelia."* Aunt Lavina had said. I could hear her voice so clearly in my head, a painful lump formed in my throat that had nothing to do with thoughts of feeding.

"She gave yeh blood, didn't she?" Braxton stated, and I didn't miss the accusatory tone that underlined his otherwise harmless words.

"Yes. What of it?" I said, a little too defensively.

I focused back on the flames, hoping to end the conversation. It was all I could do to stop myself from going to find her. She may know those males, but I didn't. Trusting that she was safe in a forest with them wasn't something that came to me easily. It went against everything I'd promised myself during these months without her. I swore I'd never let her out of my sights again once I'd found her.

Before today, the last time I'd seen her, I'd left her alone in a forest not too different from the one behind me.

"Yeh better be careful is all, kid." Braxton said. A clear warning.

"Why?"

"They might no' be happy with yeh for it."

He turned his attention to the sky above as though that was that. He'd said what he needed to say and was done with the conversation. Usually, I kind of liked that about him, but what did he mean *'they might not be happy'*? Who were *they*? The prince and his bodyguard?

I tried to reconcile that the massive male I had fought was *Braxton's son*. I mean, there had been rumors going around the camp that Braxton had taken me to following the attack on my home, but the warrior at the forefront of them had never been named.

He'd seemed like more of a myth. Countless stories were told around the campfire regularly, tales of bravery, songs of hope. I'd thought them little more than fables to take our minds off the sorry state of bullshit that was our lives, but to see him, to go toe to toe with the male, I could understand why he had such a reputation. As much as I hated it.

I looked at Braxton, registering his sharp jawline, straight nose with a prominent bridge and long hair, a tone of blonde so dirty it perfectly matched the glares he offered free of charge. Glares, his son mimicked perfectly.

It was a little unnerving, how much they truly looked alike. How had Eva not noticed? I guess she hadn't spent *that* much time with Braxton, or gotten too close, never having fed him when he'd visited. He'd always had a purpose for showing up and was usually busy in meetings with our parents or hosting training sessions for the entire camp to help sharpen our fighting skills.

Though we'd enjoyed the training, Eva and I hadn't bothered with attending the meetings, not that we'd been invited. I regretted that now.

But how had the resemblance between the two males gone unnoticed over the centuries Alaric must have been in the castle? Surely someone had to have been alive while the thrakos were there. Even briefly. Perhaps they were all wilfully ignorant? Had chosen to turn a blind eye to what was right in front of them? More likely, they didn't care to look too closely at a thrakos's face, seeing them only as soldiers who were created to defend until death.

It didn't matter really, it's not like I was about to ask him, or pop over to the castle to investigate with the horde veterans.

The only time I'd been keen to pay that castle and its residents a visit was to save Eva, and Braxton had put a stop to that. Fighting every idea I had with logic and sound advice; it was tiresome, but no less necessary.

I cleared my throat. "You mean Alaric wouldn't be happy?"

"Aye."

"Wait. You think he has some kind of claim on her?" I scoffed.

He raised an eyebrow, giving me a glassy stare, then nodded once in confirmation at the absurd idea.

"How? She clearly didn't even know he was part thrakos until today, so how could he think to claim her as his source?"

He shrugged his huge shoulders. "Call it a hunch," he eventually said, propping his head on his fist.

I sighed. "Whatever. I'm going to go find her." I told him, throwing the branch I'd been twiddling into the flames.

He opened his mouth as though to object, or perhaps criticize, but stopped short when his eyes landed on something behind me, toward the forest.

I looked over my shoulder just in time to see Alaric crossing the clearing toward our camp. I rolled my eyes and went to stand. Speak of the bastard and so he shall appear…

In the mere moments it took me to stand, he was toe to toe with me. What *now?* "Like fuck yeh are goin' to find her," he said. "Yer staying righ' here until I've made a few things crystal fuckin' clear to yeh, understood?"

For all his personality faults, there was apparently nothing wrong with his hearing, unfortunately. And wow, he was *not* a happy hybrid.

Once again, I was reminded that Braxton had an annoying habit of being right about everything all the fucking time. *Tiresome.*

I stood my ground. "Look, clearly you are used to throwing your weight around and getting what you want but–" my words dried up in my throat as he shoved me backward with such force I flew through the air, over the fire and landed on my ass several feet back from where I'd been just moments before.

I wasn't a small male, far from it. Not that you'd have thought it with the way I flailed through the air. He'd attacked so quickly, I hadn't even managed to unleash my wings to soften my landing.

Slamming my palms down on the ground at my sides, I called on my mother's side for a change. He'd expect me to shift into my thrakos form. It was a thrakos hybrid's strongest weapon, after all. But I needed the element of surprise if I was to stand a chance against him.

"*Terrae motus,*" I whispered under my breath, calling the element of earth to me and feeling the power seeping into my veins.

The ground beneath Alaric's feet began to shake, and it wasn't long before a crack was appearing between his legs.

"Nix, enough," Braxton said, trying to keep his balance on the log he was perched on. "Stop."

"Put your son on a leash and I will," I gritted back.

Braxton sighed deeply. Alaric shifted, his wings moving in slow, measured swoops to levitate just above the widening fissure. "Dinnae get cocky with me, yeh wee shite," he fumed.

I looked up to see fire balling in his sky facing palms, licking at his wings.

"What's your fucking problem?" I demanded, releasing my connection to the earth so I could scramble to my feet.

"Angel's blood. Consider it off your fuckin' menu."

"I don't know any *Angel's,* but if you are talking about my best friend, *Evangelia,* well, *she's* a free female and can do whatever the fuck she wants. If that means offering me her blood, then you're just going to have to deal with it."

I tried to sound as cocky as possible and not in the least bit intimidated by him.

It didn't work.

What the fuck was wrong with me? Alaric was a big bastard. The horde general had intimidation down to a fine art. He'd spent years perfecting his craft, working for the king in a fancy castle lined with pretentious shit. But I had never been one to let that sort of thing worry me, not since…

I glanced at Braxton like he was an anchor capable of keeping me in the here and now. *Why are the memories still haunting me?*

Braxton was usually quick to notice when I was on the edge, could more often than not tell when I'd been triggered before the panic attack hit, but apparently stargazing was his new favorite thing.

He was so consumed by it, in fact, it was as though he was somehow oblivious to the shit storm brewing right next to him. *Deep breath, Nix. Count back from ten.*

Blood pounded in my ears. My hands began to shake and tingle. *Not now. Not in front of him. Not when Eva could get back here at any moment...*

That did it. Thank the fates. My heart was no longer thudding so violently in my chest. The desperate desire to retreat was losing its desperation.

"She *is* a taken female," Alaric said. "*My* female. An' if I catch so much of a fang out within ten feet of her–"

"Let me guess, you'll kill me?" I finished for him, back to feigning confidence I no longer had.

The male before me was exactly what I imagined a horde general to be like, and I could see why he assumed I wouldn't question his demands to stop feeding Eva. I doubt anyone questioned him, ever.

Maybe that was what it was like for him in the castle, fae following his orders without question. But we weren't in the castle, and Eva was my best friend. It didn't matter that I'd barely pulled myself from the brink of a panic attack. I would die before I let this male, or any other, come between Eva and I.

If that meant wearing a mask of confidence, I'd fucking wear it with every ounce of power her blood had gifted me.

With no more than a thought, Alaric doused the flames in his palms. His hands balling into fists at his sides. When he released them a second later, they weren't fae, nor thrakos, they were shifter. Wolf.

"There are worse things than death, kid." He stated, as though I couldn't possibly fathom such a thing.

Images of death flashed into my mind involuntarily. Breathing was hard once more. Really fucking hard. Suddenly I was back home, alone, wishing I hadn't woken up that day. Wishing I'd remained completely still on the ground with them all, so I could have left this life blissfully unaware of how completely we'd lost that battle.

I scrunched my eyes tightly, willing away the memories. And let rage take their place this time.

"Believe me. I know." I gritted out.

How fucking *dare* he make assumptions about me. He had no idea what I'd lived through, what these long weeks had been like, what kept me awake at night.

I desperately reminded myself this was about Eva. Not what happened to us that day. We were family, and she was all I had now. If he had truly claimed her, and she even remotely felt the same about him, she wouldn't want us fighting.

But he wanted to control my relationship with her.

No fucking way.

"If you think for a second that I'm going to cower to your demands when it comes to her, you are more of a fool than I first gave you credit for," I seethed. "Like I'm going to just take your word for it that she's yours–"

"Alaric. Nix." Eva's voice rang out, interrupting my tirade. "Stop this right now."

She was walking toward us, radiating that kind of scary calm it seemed only females could muster. The kind of calm that says everything while saying nothing at all. It was obvious that we needed to be very fucking careful when deciding our next moves because fates forbid that it wouldn't be in line with what she wanted it to be.

Fates, she was beautiful when she was angry. She looked like the warrior I'd always known her to be. The princeling was standing behind her, snickering too comfortably as he murmured something over her shoulder. At least *he* looked significantly less hostile than he was earlier.

As they stalked toward us, I caught something unusual on their scents. No, it was *his* scent. It was...

I looked between Alaric in front of me and the prince not far behind him now, my eyes wide.

Well, wasn't that an interesting fucking development...

Made all the more confusing by Alaric claiming Eva as his own.

I tried to work it out, watching in fascination as Eva came to a standstill next to Alaric and started berating him, clearly unfazed by their difference in height and weight.

"Put your fucking claws away this instant," she ordered him.

He glowered down at her. I wanted to put myself between them, but she stood her ground. *That's Eva for you.* I thought, proudly. Nothing would stop her chewing your ass out if you pissed her off.

Despite the fucked up situation, I was relieved that whatever trauma she'd experienced as a captive hadn't ripped that out of her. If anything, she was even more fierce now.

"You said yeh wouldnae let him drink from yeh, Angel. I'm just makin' sure *he* kens that."

Wait. *What?*

"You said that?" I snapped. She looked across the fire to me and swallowed. "Eva, why didn't you say that earlier, if that's *really* how you feel?"

She continued to stare at me, at a loss for words. I fucking hated it. She was never at a loss for words around me.

Eventually, her features softened. "Nix, I'm sorry. I didn't realize he'd be such an asshole about it."

The asshole in question moved to stand behind her, his large palm on her shoulder. The prince was at her other side.

"Can we just talk?" she asked. "Alone," she added, as though for the males crowding her.

"No." Alaric growled.

Eva tensed.

The Prince noticed. "Alaric, drop it," Nekane told him.

Something passed between them that I didn't understand, but eventually Alaric nodded slightly. It was a small movement, but I hadn't imagined it.

I looked around the temporary camp. They had one tent between them, the size of just one of mine and Braxton's, and ours weren't big or luxurious by any stretch.

I looked back between the three of them.

The memory of Eva's cry earlier chose that moment to play back in my brain. Only this time it wasn't a cry at all, but more of a squeal, the type of sound one made when excited or running away from someone in a game of tag. I'd heard her make a similar sound myself a hundred times.

Alaric hadn't been present when Braxton and I had found her with the prince. What had she and the prince been doing that had caused her to let out a playful shriek like that?

Eva was talking low with Alaric, much more quietly now. I listened in.

"I'm not sorry Angel, yer mine. An' Kane's. I cannae stand the thought o' yeh having another male's mouth on yeh."

My toes curled, and I stepped back, suddenly feeling like I needed more space between me and them.

There was no way. I'd misheard.

Yer mine. And Kane's...

I looked over to Braxton, who'd finally torn his gaze away from the stars and was now staring at his son with something unreadable in his expression.

My skin felt like it was suddenly too tight. My mind replayed everything that I'd seen and heard today in agonizing detail.

Eva blanched, her eyes shooting to me. In fact, everyone's eyes had now shot to me.

"Calm down, kid," Braxton said, approaching me, his palms outstretched.

It was only when I saw the orange and red of flames dancing in his eye's reflection that I realized they were coming from me.

Flames I hadn't even known I'd summoned ran around my arms and were growing, engulfing my entire body. I tried to breathe deeply, but it wasn't working.

"Nix, please, calm down." Eva said, trying to step toward me, only to be stopped by the prince's arm, forming a barrier in front of her body. "I can explain."

"What the fuck happened to you when you were gone?" I demanded.

"It's complicated," she said, her voice soft. "I'll explain everything, from the beginning. Just calm down. Please, Nix. We are all on the same side here. Just calm down." She pleaded, trying to push past the prince's arm. "I'm a dragon, Kane. Fire doesn't fucking scare me. Let me go to him," she snapped at him, her voice calm but stern.

Rage, panic, and shame warred for my undivided attention. I knew I needed to ignore them, calm down, but I couldn't get past Alaric's words.

Yer mine. And Kane's.

Eva was approaching me, looking like a stranger wearing the face of someone I once knew. What had these males done to my best friend for them to think they both had a claim to her?

"Axel." Alaric muttered, as though to himself.

The name was familiar. Why was the name familiar? My mum. He was the male protecting my mum.

"What about him? Don't tell me he's involved in whatever the fuck this is, too?" I demanded.

Eva ignored me, turning to Alaric. "Is he okay? Edelin?"

"What's going on, son?" Braxton asked, looking around for threats.

The flames had distinguished themselves at some point. Likely at the mention of my mum.

"Shh." Alaric hissed, and everyone did.

CHAPTER 26
Evangelia

We all watched as Alaric silently communicated with Axel. I quietly told Braxton and Nix that it was the battle bond. That was all Braxton needed to know, but Nix wasn't familiar with it.

My best friend was already on the edge of some kind of breakdown thanks to me, and he'd heard enough to have worked out somewhat what was going on between Alaric, Kane and I.

Add to that worry for his mum, and it wasn't surprising that he looked like he was breaking from the inside out right now.

I took Nix by the arm and moved a few paces away so I could explain without causing too much of a distraction for Alaric. I mouthed to Kane to stay with Alaric, and Braxton followed Nix and I.

I told Nix what my limited knowledge of the battle bond allowed, and Braxton filled in the gaps. We spoke in hushed whispers, but the moment we were done, Nix asked loudly. "Ask him if my mum's okay."

"She's alright, kid." Alaric said, any viciousness that had underlined his tone during their previous encounter was gone. He said no more as his eyes glazed a little once again, which I took as meaning he was back in Axel's head.

Nix visibly relaxed next to me. I truly hadn't wanted him to find out about my bizarre love life like this. Fates, I didn't even know where to start. How could I expect him to understand when I didn't quite understand it myself?

Part of me was furious with Alaric. He hadn't even tasted my blood. Why was he so possessive of it? Why couldn't he just understand that my relationship with Nix was *very* different to my relationship with him? Nix had never been possessive like that when he'd witnessed me feed countless others. I shuddered at the thought of that kind of information getting back to Alaric.

"Are you okay?" Nix asked quietly, concern for me heavy in his voice.

"Yes." I told him, linking my arm with his. Kane noticed, but didn't say anything. "And I will explain everything to you, I swear. Now isn't the time, but please know, they are good males. They would never hurt me or do anything I didn't want them to do."

I was a little embarrassed saying it in front of Braxton, but I knew it was important for Nix to hear. He was like a brother to me, and I couldn't blame him for being protective. I'd be the same whenever he got a girlfriend. Let alone two. Fates, I almost laughed at the thought.

I could understand why Braxton looked like he'd just found out his son was pregnant. And why Nix looked like his brain was going to explode into a million glass fragments. What he had always known of me had changed so drastically and so suddenly, I could appreciate it was hard to reconcile.

But was what we were doing so wrong? Was it so wrong for the three of us to be together that we would have to hide it from the realm and be embarrassed by it? It didn't feel wrong to me.

Nix squeezed my hand. As though, right now, that was the only way he could trust himself to acknowledge what I'd told him.

We fell into an uncomfortable silence, watching Alaric, who eventually said. "King Vandenburg is on his way to the castle. An' Elikai is workin' on some event to take place durin' his visit. Most likely his coronation."

I frowned. "He mentioned something like that to me on the day of the funeral... an event of some kind. I'm not so sure it is his coronation." I said, unable to stop myself from interrupting as the memory hit.

"What did he say?" Kane asked.

"Not that much; he wanted it to be a surprise. Just that he had plans for an event unlike anything Dezrothia had ever seen. He was excited. I think he used the words 'superb and shocking' to describe it. It was unnerving."

"Well, he's keepin' the details close to his chest. Axel's going to keep an ear out between spendin' time in the catacombs and workin' on gettin' the portal working with Edelin," Alaric said.

"Aye. I received word in a letter from yer ma' some time ago that yeh'd found the old portal. What of it?" Braxton asked.

"It's barricaded with a strong magical force field. I had no luck with it while I was there, but Axel was workin' on it for me. I figured it would be a useful escape route should we ever need one, but Edelin says it's the reason she is there with Axel. To help him open it."

"What does Elikai want with my mum?" Nix asked.

"Her visions," Alaric said. "A seer is very useful when yer ruling over a kingdom. The ability to stay several steps ahead... It's invaluable. Axel said she's givin' him enough to no' question her loyalty, but nothin' of much importance. Nothin' to affect our cause."

"And King Vandenburg? Why's he visiting?" I asked Alaric.

"Elikai must've invited him after finding out he's his uncle. I assumed he was comin' to attend the coronation, though it's early still, and with what he told yeh at the funeral, fuck knows."

"How long left for the mournin'?" Braxton asked.

"Three weeks and three days," Kane answered quickly.

"We need to get back to my camp. The rebels have been gatherin' others and the ravens were sent to deliver messages to the leaders of each camp calling a meetin'. They should be arriving soon, if no' already. We were hopin' to return with Evangelia, learn what she had to tell us from her time in the castle, an' decide what to do from there. They'll be pleased to see yeh, son." Braxton said.

The male in question gave a small nod. "Let's get some rest, set out at sunset," Alaric said. "That'll give us a few hours' sleep. If we travel through the night, we can stick to the shadows."

"Aye," Braxton agreed. "We should reach the alliance within a day or so, as long as we move fast and eat as we go." Everyone nodded their agreement. "Nix, come help me hunt, we'll need some food for the journey," Braxton added, pulling him out of my grip and dragging him off.

He looked back at me over his shoulder, and I gave him a reassuring smile. The sooner he realized that Kane and Alaric weren't a threat, the better it would be for all of us.

It was just the three of us now, and as awful as it was, I was actually relieved Braxton had taken Nix out hunting. Did that make me a terrible friend? I hoped not.

"We need to talk," Kane said, cutting the silence with a knife.

"I really don't want to argue anymore," I said, done with conflict for the day.

"Not argue, Princess. We need to talk. Openly. About the three of us. If we don't, it will be over before it's even started at this rate. I don't give a fuck if no one else understands, but I sure as shit would like the three of us too."

"Aye," Alaric grunted.

I nodded, then pushed my way inside the small tent. I don't know why, but having this conversation out in the open made me feel vulnerable.

Kane followed closely behind me, quickly making himself comfortable. He lay back against his elbows, his legs out straight in front of him. I shuffled around on my knees, too tall to stand upright. He nodded for me to sit between his thighs, and I did, enjoying the closeness.

Alaric was rustling around with something outside. The fire, I assumed. I relaxed back into Kane's lap. He made a show of blowing my hair out of his face, lifting a hand to brush it to the side before placing a gentle kiss on the crook of my neck.

It sent tingles directly south, his soft lips and warm breath brushing against the sensitive flesh, and my thighs clenched of their own accord.

Alaric joined us, zipping up the tent behind him before filling what little space was left next to Kane and I. It was snug, but I loved it, relishing in the closeness between us despite all the obstacles that seemed to have kept falling in our path all day.

"So," Kane said, a nervousness in his voice that was unusual for him. "I like this," he nodded his head to gesture at the three of us squished into the tent.

"Axel could've found a bigger one if he'd wanted to," Alaric said, but his tone was light.

"Not that." Kane said. "Well, kind of that. What I mean is, I like this, the three of us. Together. And I think it's about time we all admitted it out loud."

I could feel his heart rate picking up speed against my back, and realized that he really was nervous about what we'd say.

So I decided to put him out of his misery. "I like it too. And I realized tonight that I don't want to hide it. I don't want to creep around, ashamed or embarrassed. I should have told Nix as soon as I'd sat down to talk with him earlier. Perhaps if I'd just told him, then the drama wouldn't have happened."

"It wasnae yer fault, Angel," Alaric said. "I shouldnae have been such a prick to him. I just lost it when I pictured his fangs in yer skin…" he cleared his throat, "I like this too, whatever the fuck it is, an' I dinnae want to fuck it up by acting like an arsehole."

Alaric's version of an apology. I hadn't expected those words to come out of that male's mouth. It couldn't have been easy for him.

Butterflies fluttered around inside my stomach that they were as serious about us as I was.

An idea came to me. "Would it make you feel better to mask his bite with yours?" I asked tentatively.

"What're yeh askin', Angel?"

"I don't know if it would help or not, but what if you fed from me? Staked your claim or whatever it is that you seem so set on."

I was trying to clear the air. I didn't want to make him feel like I hadn't taken his claim seriously. Despite the way I'd argued it.

"Or you could bite her thigh, that would be kind of hot," Kane said from behind me. I didn't need to see his face to know he would be grinning that cheeky smirk of his.

Alaric moved with the grace of one much smaller than his huge, muscular self. Silently pulling my leathers down my legs and discarding them, taking the suggestion to heart, apparently.

Anticipation made me giddy as a growl rose in Alaric's throat. I felt Kane harden at my lower back, and his arms tightened around me. Alaric looked me in the eye, and I nodded, confirming my permission.

His fangs snapped out, and I waited eagerly for his mouth to close around my thigh. But it didn't. He surprised me by sitting back slightly and taking my wrist in his hand. He trailed his fangs up my wrist, the material already shredded and out of the way from his claw earlier.

He bit down when he reached the place Nix had fed from earlier, as though he had memorized the exact spot.

The sensation was nothing like what it had been with Nix. It was like a lightning bolt that led directly to my core, making me desperate for more than just his fangs.

He took just a few pulls of blood from my wrist before he released my arm, letting it fall to land on Kane's leg, and then his mouth was on my thigh, his lips seeking out the perfect spot.

I panted as he settled and his teeth pierced the femoral artery, just below the apex of my thighs. I let out a gasp, leaning my head back onto Kane's shoulder.

He kissed my neck, and I turned my head to meet his lips. Alaric growled again, the sound so erotic it made our tiny tent feel too big, like I needed our bodies to be even closer than they already were.

"Good talk." Kane said roughly, half sarcasm and half ready to give over to the desire completely. Any thoughts of having a serious talk were almost forgotten, but the intimacy of the moment spoke volumes of our feelings as far as I was concerned.

I chuckled softly. "Consider me yours, both of you." I told them, sliding my fingers into Alaric's hair as I kissed Kane. "On one condition."

"What's that, Princess?" Kane asked between kisses that made my dragon purr.

Alaric released his fangs from my thigh, licking every last drop of my blood from his lips as though it would be a crime to waste a single drop.

"If I'm yours, then you are *mine*." The words came out of *my* mouth, but I had a feeling my fire breathing other half was just as much behind the statement as I was.

"Always, Angel."

"Your wish is my command, Princess."

He reached for Alaric, pulling him in. He kissed Alaric deeply, and I was reminded of the mesmerizing way I'd found them both earlier, Alaric fucking Kane against that tree like his life depended on it.

Then Kane kissed me, and as though he knew what I'd been thinking about, he said. "Why don't you tell Alaric what you told me earlier?"

"What did I tell you earlier? I tell you lots of things… these days." I knew what he was talking about, but I still felt shy about interrupting their moment together.

"Oh you know, Princess. Tell him about how watching his cock fucking my ass earlier had made you wish you could paint yourself in bark and have swapped places with the tree–"

A flush flooded my cheeks. "I-I'm not sure that's exactly what I said–"

"OK, fine. But admit it, you were *thinking* it."

"It could be arranged." Alaric said low, his eyes hooded with desire over the memory with Kane and new memories we could make. *So long as we survive Elikai.*

"OK, fine." I admitted.

"Fine what, Princess? I want to hear you say it."

"It was the hottest thing I have ever seen, OK?"

"And?" he pushed.

"And yes, I might have pictured myself in the place of the tree."

I was fully aware of how ridiculous the words were as they came out, but they made my males happy, which I found made me happy.

Now just to survive this war as the three most wanted fae in the whole of Dezrothia.

CHAPTER 27

Nekane

From the constant hum of insects, to the never ending rustling of wind through the leaves, it was a wonder how anyone could concentrate while navigating the Fading Vale.

Everything looked the same too, from the trees to the unrelenting, lingering fog. Even my high fae eyesight was struggling to pick up whatever markers Braxton was using to find this seemingly elusive camp.

Alaric walked at the front with his father, talking in a low whisper. I'd noticed that when they spoke privately together, their accents became thicker. I struggled to understand a word of it so had given up trying.

I was at the back, behind Eva and Nix. The never-ending forest didn't phase her; she danced over upturned roots without even needing to look out for them. Nix was less nimble on his feet and had tripped a time or two, much to my amusement, but she'd caught him, chastising him in a friendly way, almost like one would a child.

Like the males up front, they too had spent the journey 'catching up'. Where Alaric and Braxton seemed to be all business with one another, Eva and Nix were talking about anything and everything.

Their conversation started off shaky, sticking to safe subjects like reminiscing on the time when so-and-so did this or what's-his-face did that. As the hours went on, they grew more and more animated in their discussion, until eventually they'd become comfortable enough to discuss what they had, so far, done their best to avoid. I could only assume they both desperately did and didn't want to talk about it, but needed to nonetheless.

The months since they'd been apart.

Nix had seen some horrible shit. I'd give him that. It was a wonder the male could function around the darkness that had him in a chokehold. Hearing Eva recount her tale had been just as heart-wrenching. I'd failed her, failed to see what had been under my nose and then failed to do fuck all about it.

No female in their right mind would have chosen Elikai. I knew that now. Had he not tried to kill me, had Eva not followed, she'd still be in that castle, married to a monster.

Ice trickled down my spine at the memory of the conversation I'd overheard after my father's funeral and I thanked that fates she'd been brave enough to reawaken her sleeping dragon. It had been crazy and risky, yet she'd done it anyway–for me.

I watched the four fae ahead of me and realized they were at home here. Not only that, they were completely in sync with one another. Each pair managed to hold a conversation, all the while keeping up a good pace, remaining vigilant, keeping a close and consistent eye on their surroundings, glancing for threats in unison, and ensuring all directions were accounted for.

It was ridiculous, and I'd never admit it aloud, but I was jealous. Me, a prince, raised in a castle with every and any luxury at his fingertips, jealous of rebels who literally didn't have a pot to piss in.

If it hadn't been for the conversation Alaric, Eva and I had last night in that blessedly small tent, I'd probably have struggled to stop myself from interrupting their conversations.

Not to be rude, there was just so much I wanted to know. I craved to know everything about Alaric and Eva; the wolf, the dragon and the thrakos, too. What little there was to know about me, they already did. But they were far more interesting.

I distracted myself by trying to gain my bearings. It was still pointless. Everything looked no different than it had an hour ago. Well, until it didn't.

Almost as if its purpose was to protect the camp's inhabitants from those who wished them harm, the fog seemed to lift from one step to the next. Like we had crossed an invisible border. Could a witch do that? Summon fog for miles? It would explain why they had mostly eluded the hunt for centuries.

The trees suddenly gave way to a clearing. It was much larger than I'd expected, with torn up tents, handcrafted wagons that were as basic as they were charming, and fire pits scattered around in measured intervals.

Unease crept over me as Braxton marched us through the camp, the silence from our little group surrounded by an unnerving choir of low, indistinguishable murmurs.

It was impossible not to notice the stares directed our way, or more accurately, my way.

The few children I spotted were being gently pushed behind adults in an attempt to hide them from my view. Was it that obvious that I wasn't some rebel from another camp? Was it possible that they knew what I looked like? I had no clue whether they would know my face this far out. Unless it was from a wanted poster? We'd passed plenty getting here that Braxton and Nixen claimed hadn't been there just a day before.

I scrubbed my hand over the stubble now coating my jaw after several days on the run. Perhaps they were always this wary of strangers? I tried for a smile, but it was met by petrified eyes, making me wonder if my smile had been too toothy, too forced. Or maybe it had come out like how you'd imagine the smile of a maniac after he'd just bathed in the blood of his victims. I dropped the smile immediately.

Braxton led the way, nodding occasionally to those closest to us. With all of them dressed the same, it was hard to tell who was in charge, who were the leaders Braxton was expecting. Well-worn leathers, linen shirts, and an array of weapons tucked into belts. Even the young ones.

If her blank expression was anything to go by, Eva didn't seem to know too many here, either. Then again, I doubted there was an annual rebel alliance party where they all got to mingle, feast like pigs, get drunk and forget about the whole 'get found and die' predicament.

I shuddered, knowing that the male who'd sired me was responsible for it all.

Unlike Eva, Nix seemed to know everyone. Handing out reassuring smiles to the growing crowd. Even waving to a few of the children poking their head out around their parents' legs. I listened closely and realized I wasn't the only subject of the murmurs, Alaric was too.

Either he didn't care or was schooling his reactions. It was odd, and seemed impossible, but they knew who he was, or at least that he was Braxton's son.

"Who are they with Braxton and Nix?"

"Is that him?*"*

"Is he back?"

"Is that… Braxton's *boy?"*

"Did Nix find his friend? I assumed she'd be dead…"

"A high fae? That can't be good."

"Is that the Prince?"

It was disconcerting. I had spent most of my life with fae whispering about me. It was inevitable being royalty, but this was different. I was the monster to this community. Guilty by association for the family I'd been born into.

Alaric's hand sliding up my spine to grasp my shoulder jolted me out of my thoughts. It was warm, comforting and exactly what I didn't know I'd needed.

I'd missed him on the hike here. I looked at him to find his eyes already staring at me. A small smirk pulled at his mouth, reassuring me that these were his people and everything was going to be okay.

A small hand slipped into mine next, Eva. A bright smile on her face. So what if everyone else hated me? At that moment, I had nothing to worry about because I had the only two fae that would ever matter to me at my side.

I'd had my feelings hurt worse. And surely the desire to make all of these strangers like me would fade… right?

"Come on, I'll get yeh somewhere to rest. It's been a long trek to get here." Braxton grunted as we neared the largest tent.

It seemed to be a congregation area, probably where they strategized and devised tactics. It didn't seem to be any one fae in particular's home.

"We have a tent, dinnae worry over that." Alaric said, surprising the shit out of me. Braxton nodded, trying to hide his own surprise.

We ducked inside. There were many already gathered, clearly coming in through the rear entrance, which was just a loose flap of material. Their attention was firmly on us as we entered, their hands resting on the hilts of their swords as I came in last.

Yeah, they definitely have an idea of who I am.

I wasn't entirely sure if the tall male with shaggy dark locks and more than a decade's worth of hair coating his jaw, was going to let Braxton formally introduce me before he decided I was too much of a risk to live another moment.

Eva had fallen into place in front of me, Alaric at my flank, with his hand back on my shoulder and an expression on his face that said, touch him and feel my wrath.

It would be hot. These two fae, as intelligent and powerful as they were beautiful, protecting me with their bodies. If only it wasn't for the fact that I could protect myself just fine. Or perhaps they were protecting the rebels from me, knowing I wouldn't go down without a fight if they tried anything.

The tension and hostility in the tent was palpable. I was glad I couldn't read minds, because whatever they were thinking was most certainly not friendly. To these fae, I was the lowest of the low.

Fates, I couldn't even blame them. They didn't know me, they only knew I had done nothing to ease their suffering, and now, here I was, needing protection. I was imposing on them. Using them. Relying on their kindness to defend me from my brother's machinations. Well, fuck. I'd hate me, too.

Still, the desire to make them like me hadn't faded, at least not yet.

Allure might make them relax a little, like that male from Rangaran. The spider shifter who'd been convinced I was going to order his death, or perhaps do it with my own bare hands. No, Allure wasn't a good idea. Someone would notice.

And it was just... wrong somehow. My least favorite of all the high fae abilities I possessed. A last resort that I rarely used unless I had no other choice.

"Braxton, mind explaining what the fuck you are doing bringing the *Prince of Dezrothia* to our home?" A female snarled. She was short, with red hair pulled back in a braid, and her knuckles tight on the dagger at her hip. Her dark eyes narrowed on me, challenging me to step out of line so she could put her blade to use on my throat.

Alaric cleared his. "This is Prince Nekane. Not to be confused with his twin, the nasty piece of work, Prince Elikai. Nekane is gonnae help us," he said and I was surprised to see Braxton nod his agreement. I wasn't sure what I'd done to earn his trust, but I had a feeling it had everything to do with the male whose hand was squeezing my shoulder as he spoke.

"And who the fuck are you?" someone snapped from the back of the tent.

Alaric's palm squeezed tighter still. He was close enough that I could hear his jaw tighten.

"Talk to my son like that again an' yeh'll be on washing up duties for the next year. With one hand less than you have now, and absent o' that tongue so it cannae get yeh into trouble anymore, Erix." I couldn't see the male in question, but his audible gulp as he registered the threat was deafening.

"Nekane's no' like his brother. Alaric has talked o' the prince in his letters for years. Yeh all know well an' good he speaks highly o' him..." Braxton said to the rest of the fae and I tried to hide my shudder at the reminder of Alaric's betrayal.

"No disrespect, sir," a younger male that couldn't have even been my age said from the right. I tensed, waiting for whatever disrespectful shit was about to spill from him. No one started like that when they had anything nice to say. "Why are we to believe the word of someone who hasn't been around for three hundred years?"

A female piped up next to him. "And who has *actively* slaughtered our people?"

Alaric bristled behind me, the emotion on his face was unreadable to most, but I knew it had hurt him.

"If you can't take his word, then take mine." Eva said, stepping toward the fae with conviction. "My name is Evangelia Malion. I was born and raised in the Fading Vale, in a camp just like this one run by my parents, Lavina And Kur Malion." A few gasps rang out around the space. "Several of you knew them. You have likely heard already, but for those who need reminding, my camp was attacked, wiped out entirely aside from myself and Nixen Sybilline, son of the great and powerful seer, Edelin Sybilline. After witnessing my parents' murder before my eyes, I was taken against my will by Prince Elikai. A male that, I can assure you, could not be more different than the prince standing before you now. I have spent months in the company of these two males, and I give my word that they mean you no harm. Fates, they *saved* me in more ways than they know."

My heart simultaneously swelled and stung at her words as murmurs broke out. They clearly knew exactly who she was, but the distrust in the air was still intense. I really couldn't blame them.

"How can you be sure this prince doesn't have you under his *allure*? Everyone knows that the high fae use it indiscriminately. *Especially* a fucking royal!" the young male spat.

"I would never!" I seethed before I could stop myself.

Fuck. I could practically feel the blade at my throat. We should have never come here. At least, *I* should never have come. They would never trust me. And with good reason.

My teeth gnashed together as I held my tongue. Words wouldn't get through to them. Nothing I could say would get through to them. They would only think I was using compulsion. I needed to show them I wasn't who they thought I was, but I couldn't very well do that dead.

Alaric spoke up next. "Are yeh so weak that yeh cannae feel when a fae is usin' their gifts?" he accused, his muscular arms folded against his chest. He looked at the rebels filling the tent, staring each of them down until they dropped their gaze one by one. He was an alpha. Just like his father. He sneered as they eventually all looked away. "That's what I thought..." he spat.

"Nekane is to be treated like any other new member o' the alliance. Here he isnae yer enemy, and he isnae a prince. Any problems, yeh ken what to do." Braxton told them, effectively shutting down that conversation.

It went against everything in me to allow them to speak on my behalf. But I knew that whatever I said would only make things worse. They needed to get to know me as a male, see that I wasn't who they thought I was, and then make their decisions.

If anything, they'd be disappointed once they realized I was a sorry excuse for a prince and more of a horde soldier who'd never seen a day's battle. I almost looked forward to disappointing them, if only to show them how different Elikai and I truly were.

"Now that's over with, it's good to be home and see so many new faces have joined us while I was gone." Braxton said while surveying the crowd, giving a nod to some he recognized. He clapped his palms together. "Righ', now everyone can fuck off an' get back to whatever yeh were doin'. Alliance leaders, stay."

As the majority filed out, a smooth, round slab of wood was carried in and placed on top of four tree stumps, spaced out in a square. More tree stumps were rolled in and spread out around the outside of the makeshift table. Our chairs, I assumed.

I followed Alaric's lead, taking a seat next to him. Eva looked hesitant, unsure whether she was meant to stay for the meeting. Nix too. Braxton nodded to the spaces on either side of Alaric and I and they sat too.

I would never have picked the leaders out of the crowd. I'd assumed they would all be older fae, or perhaps those with the best, sharpest swords. Nicer clothing. But that wasn't the case. I could scent the witches, warlocks, shifters and thrakos among those that stayed. Young and old. We sat uncomfortably around the table, until someone broke the ice.

It was an older fae, a witch. "Good to see you, Alaric. Fates, it has been a long time.""

"Aye. Good to see yeh, Iona. The years have been kind to yeh," he said, and she smiled widely.

"I see you haven't lost that charm, Ric."

Ric? Who the fuck was this female, and even more importantly, who the fuck got to call Alaric *Ric* and live to fight another day?

I quirked a brow and met eyes with Eva next to me. She was visibly biting her tongue, annoyed at how friendly this female seemed to be with our male.

"I haven't been called that in a long time, Iona."

She giggled. "I can call you General Alaric if you'd prefer?" she flirted.

Eva huffed, a small cloud of smoke coming from her nostrils. No sooner had it happened than she was turning crimson, covering her nose with her hand as though pretending she had a sneeze threatening to come out, and she was doing her best to hold it in.

Her dragon had given away her anger at the female's obvious flirtation, and it was adorable. Jealousy looked good on her.

I placed a hand on her thigh under the table, just above her knee. That sweet spot that everyone claimed was supposed to give you a quarter of an orgasm when squeezed, but could also make you squirm and jump like a pig who'd had their tail pulled.

I was tempted to squeeze. And as though she'd heard my thoughts, she met my eyes, her own green ones widening. *Don't you dare.* I could almost hear her screaming it at me. Willing the thought from her mind and into my own.

Alaric and Iona were still talking, but my distraction had worked. Eva's possessive anger and subsequent embarrassment faded, and she appeared to relax a little for the first time since we'd arrived. I felt her fingers slide over mine and we both waited quietly for Braxton to finish whatever he was doing and start the meeting.

Braxton took his seat and cleared his throat. "Thank yeh for traveling here and sorry I wasnae here to greet yeh. There is much to update yeh on. Yer all aware that the usurper King is dead, but his heir is soon to be runnin' riot. He has Edelin. And Alita and Rainer's boy, Axel…"

While Braxton updated the rebel leaders on the shit show up at the castle, I looked around the table at the rebel leaders that had joined us. I had never felt like more of an outsider in my entire life, and I'd never really fit in in the first place.

Not at the castle, and certainly not here. I'd expected it, had felt it on the trek through the forest, watching Alaric and Braxton, Eva and Nix. What I hadn't expected was to feel… ashamed.

Ashamed that these fae had to hide. Ashamed that I'd never really thought about anyone outside of Ezerat. Outside of the castle and the Crooked Claw, even. Ashamed by the mess the Kingdom was in. How vulnerable it was right now. But more than anything, I was ashamed to be related to these evil fae that they spoke about so disparagingly. With so much hate. Hate they deserved. Hatred my father had started, and I had no doubt my brother would only add to it.

Eventually, they agreed to regroup tomorrow. We needed to rest after having hiked all night. I wasn't sure how easily sleep would come, surrounded by fae who despised me, but I was ready to get out of this tent.

It had been clear that the leaders weren't comfortable sharing information with me present, and as we left, the side eyes or long looks followed my every step.

I drew a long, deep breath and pretended not to notice as we took our bag and followed Alaric to a private patch on the edge of the camp to pitch our tent. It was our little safe space and I already much preferred it to my room in the castle.

Alaric and Eva pitched the tent, while I stood awkwardly, not even bothering to pretend to help, knowing it would be a dead giveaway that I wasn't experienced with the camp life and not wanting to expose myself any further.

The whispering picked up with every minute. I was used to fae muttering about me behind my back and had managed to somewhat easily tune out in places like the Crooked Claw.

This was different, though.

There was an obvious hostility in the air that hadn't been there back in Ezerat.

And I fucking hated it.

CHAPTER 28

Axel

"King Vandenburg's arrived," I told Edelin as soon as I entered her cave in the catacombs.

"Which means it's now or never," she said. "He won't want his uncle knowing he has a seer down here. It's the perfect time to throw everything at that barrier without worrying he could surprise us with a visit."

"Have you seen it?" I asked. "Us succeeding, I mean?"

"I have seen us succeed, and I have seen us fail. What I don't know is how we got to any of those outcomes. Visions are fickle things, and the fates don't like to make things too easy."

"Of course they don't. Where would they get their kicks from if they did?" I asked, but she knew it was rhetorical. "Let's go."

The route from Edelin's quarters, if you could call them that, to the portal was second nature to us by now. We met up every day, at least once. Sometimes in the early evenings when everyone was in the dining hall, other times in the dead of night while the castle was sleeping.

Elikai was pretty predictable, visiting mostly in the mornings straight from breakfast, but Edelin had warned repeatedly that we mustn't get too complacent. Ensuring I always checked and then checked again that I was never followed when I came to find her.

I still wasn't used to her always seeming to know exactly when I'd turn up to get her so we could work on opening the portal together. I say together loosely, I had barely tapped into my warlock heritage, but I was learning. Most of the time, I'd taken opportunities to visit the catacombs as and when they became available. We didn't plan times, it just wasn't possible given the circumstances, yet she was always ready and waiting the moment I stepped into her cavern.

Then again, what else did she have to be doing?

We'd bonded over the last week or so, and fast. She'd told me about her son, Nixen or Nix as apparently most called him, and how she missed him. And she'd told me of the thrakos male who'd sired him. They weren't true mates, but it had still hurt her when he'd been killed.

I'd never fully appreciated how much of a solid Alaric had done for me by keeping me off the list of horde soldiers to go on the hunts. But after hearing Edelin's stories of how they had spent their lives running and being needlessly slaughtered, I realized I would never have been able to focus on the bigger picture if I'd been in Alaric's shoes.

The toll of having to kill innocents to keep up the act to be able to remain in the king's favor and inner circle would have been too much. I knew why he'd had to do it, but fuck, it was cruel for the rebels to burden him with that when they sent him here. Especially by his own father.

Since seeing my own parents' fate in the vision Edelin had shared, I'd wondered whether my dad would have asked the same of me if he hadn't been killed. I guess I would never know.

We arrived at the portal. Its purple hue lit the entire vast cavern as usual. It always gave off a faint buzz, like an electric pulse.

"I am going to use the spell we tried last time, only if you see me… struggling, I need you to not interfere," Edelin explained as she looked at the portal with her usual quizzical glare.

"Fine," I reluctantly agreed. "I could have sworn I saw it tear slightly. You must have been close."

Edelin nodded, rolling up the sleeves of her tattered cloak. "Make sure you stand well back, Axel. I mean it." She ordered as she raised her palms to the air in the direction of her target.

I fucking hated being useless, but I'd only recently started to learn how to wield magic like a warlock and I had so much to learn that I'd only be more of a hindrance and get in her way.

Or, as she repeatedly told me, worry her.

She began to chant. So quietly to begin with it was almost inaudible. The purple dome barely wavered under her assault. She became progressively louder and more aggressive in her words, and I'd be lying if I wasn't worried someone would hear her from all the way up in the castle.

I sent a silent prayer to the fates that she wouldn't be heard. This was important. I didn't know why, but if Edelin said it was, then it had to be.

She was hissing the words now through gritted teeth and the purple was rippling in the spot where her hands were just inches away. She'd said that unlike attack and defensive spells where often bright lights flashed with a witch or warlock's spells, this was more subtle and much more tricky.

I didn't fully understand it, but it was like she was trying to force her way in, only she couldn't just slam all of her power into one hit, or she'd risk the spell rebounding off the barrier.

She had to slowly but surely break down its strength until it couldn't hold her off any more and began to crack. She had likened it to trying to wedge a knife into stone. It could be done, but it would be damned hard and took a lot of time and power to chip away.

To begin with, she'd tried spells that would just undo whatever spell the previous witch or warlock, or, perhaps, various witches and warlocks had put in place. But with thousands of possible combinations, she'd quickly realized that wasn't the answer.

Her arms were shaking now, sweat beaded on her forehead from the effort of the spell, and her brows pinched together as she continued her chant. I watched on, chewing my knuckle in a desperate bid to stop myself interfering. She was close to exhausting herself, and I fucking hated it. It went against every instinct I had to see her in pain and suffering while I did fuck all.

I wanted to get her out of the castle desperately, but she was adamant that it was her fate to be here with me. And she was a stubborn female.

The portal's prison seemed to be finding that out, too. I noticed a slight tear appear in a direct line with her palms. We were close. So close I could almost taste success in the damp air around us, despite the worry for her wellbeing.

Her knees began to shake, like they were struggling to support her. I wanted to call out to her, tell her to stop, but at the same time I didn't want to distract her, so I just bit down harder on my knuckle. Fuck, she was so close this time. I began cheering nervously in my head. *Come on, Edelin. So close. You've got this.*

But she didn't have it. She was about to go down like a sack of shit.

I didn't want her to have to put herself through this again, so I strode towards the portal, stopping at her side and raised my own palms. Angling down slightly with the hope that I could direct whatever magic I had at the same spot she'd weakened considerably. I had no idea if that's how it worked, but it made sense to me and I couldn't very well ask her right now.

Repeating her words, I began to chant with her. Over and over again, until our words and movements were perfectly in sync.

Suddenly, there was a great flash of purple, and I was momentarily stunned. As my eyes readjusted to the room, I expected to find the barrier gone, but was met with the last thing I had predicted to see.

Wide, bright, scared eyes met mine through the tear in the portal's shield. I couldn't make out the colour from here, but what I could make out was that there was most definitely a petite female on her hands and knees inside the shield, who most definitely hadn't fucking been there before.

"Axel! Listen... I can't... hold it much longer. Get her out of there. Go now. Quickly!" she cried over my chants, her eyes fixed to the female frozen in front of her while she started up her own again immediately.

Alaric had always told me never to go running into situations blindly, but the old bastard had also taught me the devastating effects of reacting even a millisecond too slowly–

Before I'd finished the thought, I was diving through the tear toward the female. Her eyes widened further, but she didn't speak, or even open her mouth. She was frozen, petrified to the spot.

As I crouched, placing one arm around her back and the other arm around the bend in her knees, I realized I wasn't even sure where I was supposed to be taking her? Back through the portal? Back to Edelin?

"Quick–" my aunt ground out.

I spun with the female in my arms and darted back through the rip we had created. Just as I passed through the barrier, I felt the sizzle of it closing back up.

Terror squeezing my chest, I dropped the female down and moved to Edelin to pull her away from the portal before it regenerated fully. Having seen what happened when anything got too close to it, I couldn't let her suffer the same fate. Her breathing came out in heavy, shallow pants and I knew she'd exhausted herself with the spell she'd cast.

I lifted a weak and tired Edelin into my arms and took in the new female for a moment. Her auburn hair was pulled back from her face in a messy updo, and she wore some thin metal frame that wrapped around her face. Hooking over her ears and balancing on the bridge of her nose.

They held two glass circles which covered her eyes that I could now see were a rich hazel, the amber and brown warring in them as various emotions surged through her.

I took a subtle sniff. She smelt good, really fucking good, but not fae. Not a fae from here anyway, not that the strange face accessory hadn't already clued me in. *What is she?*

"Can you walk?" I asked her.

She took the metal and glass contraption off her face and began to rub her eyes with the back of her free palm.

"Can. You. Walk?" I repeated slowly. She blinked at me. Several times. Long lashed and fast, but made no attempt to answer me.

Fuck it. Placing Edelin carefully over one shoulder, I crossed the space and lifted the female over the other.

"Please don't kill me," she rushed out in a strange accent I'd never heard before.

"I'm a fucking teddy bear, darlin. Don't give me a reason to, and we'll be good."

Fates, Alaric was going to lose his shit.

But first, I needed to get Edelin tucked up in bed. Then I'd question the unknown female. And then I'd tell him.

CHAPTER 29

Alaric

It's good to be back, I thought as I stood watching the 'warriors' of the encampment train, arms crossed, the forest floor under my feet, and a judgmental frown on my face.

It wasn't that my da' hadn't done a decent job, given the time he could give them, but he was constantly traveling from camp to camp, and so during his absences, he'd left others in charge of the training. And by 'others', I meant complete fucking eejits, apparently.

I'd checked in with Axel a time or two since we arrived a week ago. He and Edelin seemed to be making some headway. Slowly, but surely, they seemed to be weakening the portal's seemingly impenetrable barrier.

Who knew how many fae had been trapped when Augustus closed the portal? The coward was so scared of outsiders getting in and threatening his rule, he likely hadn't given a second's thought to how many of his own fae he'd locked out. Away from their families with no way of getting home.

I wanted to get the portal open for the rebels. I wasn't sure where it led. There was little to nothing by way of literature about the portals of Dezrothia in any library I'd found, but anywhere would be better than here.

Opening the portal was plan B. If plan A didn't work, then at least the rebels could escape and start new lives if we lost the inevitable war that was on the horizon.

I wasn't sure what Edelin's motivations were for getting the portal working, but from what Axel had said, the stubborn old witch was showing no signs of giving up on it.

Her son, Nixen, had inherited that stubbornness. In the days since we'd arrived here, Angel had tried, to no avail, to close the bridge between him, Kane and I. We knew he meant a lot to her, so we were open to playing nicely with him. Nixen, on the other hand, trusted us naught, and had even less intention of doing so in the future.

Fucking stubborn bastard was upsetting Angel. He just couldn't see it through his own problems that clouded his every move.

I watched more eagerly now as Kane landed a heavy blow on the thrakos hybrid he was up against. He'd been in the training circle for hours, fighting anyone who had the balls to challenge him, as he had been every day since we arrived.

Sweat glistened across his brow, though he showed no signs of tiring. His opponent, on the other hand, was panting as he dropped, then proceeded to lay sprawled on the ground, either afraid to get to his feet or genuinely unable to thanks to the sheer exhaustion of going up against someone who'd spent most of his life in the training ring, fighting far superior warriors.

Kane offered a hand to him to stand. The male slapped it away and struggled to his feet on his own, far less than graceful.

I was surprised Kane had even offered a hand. There were surely only so many times they could ignore it, bat it away or–on one occasion–actually spit at it.

Kane's head shook slightly, raven hair falling into his eyes as he tried to hide the frustration that had been building within him since we arrived. It didn't take a genius to see he was trying with them, really fucking trying, yet they didn't give him an inch.

They still treated him with the disdain they had on the first day we'd arrived, an outsider who couldn't even be trusted enough to help them up off their sorry defeated arses after a fight.

I stood, releasing my wings, and made my way over to the high fae. It was good to be able to do that. I had spent far too long hiding them.

"Good job." I told him. Plenty loud enough for all to hear. "You had enough for today?" I asked.

"Nah. One more round."

"How about someone a little more to your level this time, eh?" I asked, making it clear to the others that they could learn a thing, or fifty, from Kane if only they could get over their scorn for him.

He rolled his eyes at me, not impressed by me calling the others out like that. "Who do you have in mind?" he asked.

"Me."

As expected, there were several gasps from the crowd surrounding the training ring. We'd not trained together since arriving here, but they all knew of my reputation.

I noticed a few fae out of the corner of my eye race off, presumably to get others to come watch Kane get his arse kicked. They'd watched him for a week and still had no fucking idea of what this male was capable of. They'd witnessed him kick the arses of some of their best young fighters, yet still chose to underestimate him. Every. Fucking. Time.

He chuckled, giving me one of his dimpled smiles that did all sorts of fucking things to me. Things that weren't appropriate in the present moment or company.

"I'm not sure, Alaric. Wouldn't want to embarrass you in front of your–"

Going for the element of surprise, I shifted. Bursting out of my leathers and landing on black fur-covered paws. The only warning was the howl I let out as I lept at him.

The rapidly growing crowd cheered as my paws slammed onto his bare chest, forcing him to land hard on his back.

He was ready for it though, having fought me in my wolf form many times; he used the momentum of the fall to throw me off, rolling back, landing on his feet and whipping around to face me just in time for me to attack again.

We fell into the comfortable battle dance easily. It was like being back in the training halls at the castle, alternating between who had the upper hand. Pushing each other to our limits. Holding nothing back. Playing on each other's weaknesses because we knew them all too well.

Angel's scent reached me before I spotted her. She was at the edge of the circle, a smirk tugging at her lips, watching with an open-mouthed Nixen.

Kane and I grappled under the stare of what felt like a thousand eyes and the three fates themselves, and I couldn't hide my toothy grin of pride as he held his own. I just hoped the rebels were taking it for the lesson it was. Learning from us so they could do better next time. Learning that Kane was not a male deserving of their sneers.

After some time, I had Kane pinned again, well fucking aware he'd find a way out of it any moment, when a familiar niggle scratched at my mind.

Shifting back to fae form immediately, I hissed under my breath, *"Not now, Axel."*

Most males would use the distraction to gain the upper hand. Especially under the scrutiny he was receiving. But Kane wasn't that male.

"The bond?" he asked.

"Aye." I told him, while Axel's voice floated through my mind.

"Hey Alaric old buddy ol' pal. Now a good time?"

"No." I thought back, offering Kane a hand up. Which he took without any hesitation.

"Cool, cool, cool. But you're going to want to hear this."

"Fine. One second." I clapped Kane on the shoulder to thank him for a good session. He smiled, but I didn't miss the way his eyes dropped down to my now very naked fae form.

He grabbed a towel from the floor. "Here," he said, handing it over so I could have this conversation with Axel without being completely exposed.

The rebels tripped over themselves to make a gap, letting us out of the circle. Eva, Nixen and Braxton followed. As well as Iona and a handful of the other leaders too. More had arrived now, bringing with them a group of five to ten rebels each. The camp was getting crowded.

I glanced over my shoulder. Everyone who hadn't been invited to follow looked pretty fucking confused by the sudden end to the fight. They'd find out soon enough; word would spread about the bond Axel and I had formed, if it hadn't already.

"OK, I'm here," I thought through the bond.

"Busy day, boss?"

"Training again. The rebels have a lot o' work to do if they wannae face the horde and live to tell the tale one day."

"Well, you're not gonna like what I have to tell you, so I may as well be quick. Just spit it out nice and fast. Get to the point. Make no bones about–"

"Axel." I growled.

"Elikai's uncle arrived today with eight of his Mount Mortum's."

"Any idea why he's been invited yet?"

"Not yet."

"OK, well, keep me posted."

"That wasn't the bad news. We managed to make a hole in the barrier."

"And that's a bad thing, why?"

"It was temporary. The barrier regenerated."

"For fuck's sake." I sighed. Kane handed me a flask of water he'd been drinking from and I took it with a nod of thanks.

"That's not the bad news either."

"It's no'?"

"Nope. It gets much, much worse."

"Axel," I growled again.

"Someone came through it."

I stopped in my tracks, fates near choking on the mouthful of water I'd just swigged. *"What do yeh mean, someone came through?"*

"I mean, when me and Edelin managed to force a split in the barrier, a female came through it."

"Are you fucking serious?"

"On Rose's life."

Fuck.

"Then yeh need to find out where she came from an' then send her right fucking back there."

"This can't be good," I heard Angel say to the others. "He looks pissed."

"Edelin is burnt out. It's not as easy as just sending her back, boss. Little Red's not very chatty right now either, too fucking petrified of me to talk without stuttering and shit.

"Little Red?"

"She won't tell me her name, so I gave her a temporary one."

"Are yeh with her now?"

"Aye."

"Ask her where she came from."

"I have, she won't tell me."

"Ask her again. Tell her you need to ken so yeh can send her home."

"OK, one sec."

The sensation of him being in my mind vanished for a few moments and I used them to fill in the others on Axel's news, but before I could answer any questions, he was back.

"The mortal realm."

"A human?"

"Aye."

So that's where it leads. It wasn't ideal, but it was better than running from Dezrothia only to find yourself in a place like Mount Mortum.

"Righ'. Get that portal open as soon as yeh can and send her back. A human doesnae stand a chance in Dezrothia. From what I ken about them, which isnae much, they are weak things, so fragile it's like they want to die*."*

"Fuck. OK, Edelin hasn't come around yet. She collapsed again right after Little Red appeared and has been out longer than usual."

"She breathin'?"

"Oh, aye, boss. She's breathing, just drained. It really took it out of her this time."

"OK, keep me posted."

"Will do. How's things there?"

"No one's actively tried to murder Kane in his sleep yet, but some of them clearly want to. And I'm no' convinced that they wouldnae have already tried if it wasnae for him sharing a tent with me an' Angel."

"Damn. I always thought he was alright. I should have come with you, they'd love me."

"Why the fuck would that change anything, or remotely fuckin' help the situation?"

"Well, cause I give off cool vibes. They would have seen me being friends with him and–oh fuck balls."

"What?"

"Gotta go. Little Red's making a run for it. All I did was tell her I needed to enter my mind palace to talk to my brother from another fae mother."

"For fate's sake, Axel. Fine, but–"

Before I could finish the thought, he'd left my head, leaving me standing next to our little tent. Several fae around me all looking very keen to ask their questions and get some answers.

"The female who came through the portal is from the mortal realm."

"Fates, save her!" Iona gasped from behind the hand she'd thrown over her mouth at the news.

"No, Axel and Edelin will *save her*." Eva snapped.

She really didn't like Iona for some reason. She blushed as though embarrassed she'd snapped, and coughing, she corrected herself.

"I mean, Axel and Edelin can send her back, right?" she asked.

"Edelin exhausted herself opening the barrier. She likely won't be strong enough to reopen it for a few days yet," I said.

"She's pushing herself too much," her son mused. "Why is she so set on opening this thing?"

"She's strong, Nix," Braxton said. "But she's too stubborn to let the portal get the better o' her. She'll rest for a few days an' then she'll be good to send the human back."

"I want to get her out of there," Nixen said. "It's too dangerous. If someone finds the human, they'll know she's the only witch in the castle powerful enough to have let her through the portal. Then they'll know she's been trying to open it and then–"

Eva gave his arm a squeeze. "It's okay. She's a seer. She'll know if she's about to get caught and will make sure that fate doesn't come to pass. She's done it a thousand times. She will manage a few days hiding a human female."

I chose not to mention that a seer was about as useful as tits on a boar hog when unconscious. The last thing we needed was him racing fangs first into another rescue mission.

"Any news on Elikai?" Kane asked.

"Yer uncle arrived today. Axel doesnae ken much yet, though. I'll check in with him later to see if he's found out more, but the human made a run for it so he might have his hands full. We know Ezerat still has a couple weeks left of its mourning period before he can make any real moves, like crown himself," I said.

"Two weeks and three days," Kane mused. "I'm surprised he's even honoring it."

"The minute it's over, he'll have a crown on his head and will be waging a full scale war to find us, so we have to use this time wisely, get all the rebels capable of swinging a sword, properly trained."

Everyone nodded their agreement. Everyone except Kane, who said quietly, "He'll get bored of waiting."

Braxton spoke next. "Either way. We need to be ready when they come. I want every wakin' hour spent training. That includes you, Evangelia."

"I have been training. With Nix," she said.

"I don't think those twin daggers are the weapon he had in mind," Iona said.

"Are yeh ready to let yer dragon out to play, Angel?" I asked.

Her audible gulp was answer enough.

CHAPTER 30
Evangelia

By morning, the camp had undergone a complete makeover.

Tents for sleeping in were all taken down and had been re-erected in the tight spaces between the trees lining the clearing. Three tents remained in the main part of camp, lined up in a neat row along the eastern stretch. The largest one in the middle housed the round table that the leaders gathered around for their meetings. The ones on either side held weapons and food.

Who needed an entire castle when you could make a perfectly functioning weapons room, war room and kitchen along one stretch of soil, eh?

The corners of the camp were now a dedicated space for combat training. Stones and logs had been placed out in large circles, creating four fighting rings where thrakos, shifters, witches, warlocks and hybrids could hone their skills. And in the center of the clearing, where I now stood waiting for Braxton, lay a huge expanse of… nothing.

Though all being well, that would change soon.

I wiped my clammy palms on my leathers as Braxton appeared out of the meeting tent. I hadn't gotten much rest last night, too nervous for my own training that was starting today to be able to sleep.

Shifting into my dragon form shouldn't make me feel this uncomfortable, but it did. Nothing about it felt natural to me. A lifetime of being told to hide oneself could do that to one's psyche.

"Ready, Evangelia?" Braxton asked as he neared.

"As ready as I'll ever be," I told him.

It wasn't a lie; I didn't think I'd ever be ready for this. It hadn't been a choice when I'd shifted last time. Kane's life had depended on me pulling it off, so I'd not had any chance to overthink it before I was already hurtling through the air.

"Go on then."

"What? Here? Now?" I glanced around at the training rings, and all eyes were on me. Even those mid-dual had paused to watch. This must be how Kane feels all the time with the eyes and whispers.

"Aye."

I gulped. "Right. OK. Um. You might want to stand back," I said.

"Where'd yeh want me? How much space do yeh need? Sadly, I didnae get to see yer parents in their dragon forms, so yeh'll be the first."

"Well, I'm not entirely sure." I admitted. "Over there should be okay," I gestured to the nearest tree at the edge of the clearing.

He jogged to where I'd pointed without another word, and leaned back against the bark, his arms folded across his chest. Looking far too relaxed.

I hadn't lied when I'd told him yesterday that I had no idea how to control my other half. It was dangerous for everyone. Yet they all just stared at me, making no move to hide and take shelter in case this went terribly wrong.

A surprise sneeze was all it would take to fry anyone unfortunate enough to be in my path. Fates, I could wipe out an entire training ring and all its spectators before they even had a chance to say 'bless you'.

Everyone watched me expectantly. *Come on Eva, you got this.*

I spotted Kane in my peripheral vision. He was giving me a double thumbs up, mouthing what looked like '*You can do this, Princess*'.

Alaric was at his side. They'd left the tent while I was sleeping this morning, not wanting to wake me after a night of tossing and turning, knowing I'd be needing a lot of energy today. By the looks of it, they'd already gone a few rounds in the ring, both shirtless and glistening with sweat.

My dragon purred.

I held onto her, using that tether to connect, letting her take control instead of squashing her back down like I always did when she stirred.

The shift was fast, yet I felt every moment of it, unused to the sensations.

Thank the fates for the camp's renovation. From snout to tail, I almost filled the entire space they'd cleared for me. But not quite. I could swing my tail, probably turn an entire rotation if I wanted to, and hopefully avoid accidentally taking out any of the fae training in the corners of camp in the process.

I shook my wings out first, the daylight that managed to penetrate the tree canopy reflecting off my silver scales. Then my neck, which felt... amazing. Like that first stretch you do in the morning after a night of sleeping on top of cold hard earth, twigs and thick tree roots.

My huge green slitted eyes landed on my males, drawn to them like a pile of gold.

I hadn't been as close to them as I would have liked since we arrived here. We were watched constantly and none of us had wanted to give the camp even more reason to be gossiping about us behind our backs.

Alaric was... smiling. Beaming more accurately. His ethereal eyes were wide as he stared at me, looking more silver than usual with my form in their reflection. He took in every inch of my silver scales and wide wings. My dragon was definitely enjoying his attention and so I let her preen.

Just don't sneeze if you don't want to accidentally turn him to ash, I warned her.

Kane winked. He was the only one here to have ever seen me this closely. But this time, I wasn't crippled by the fear of his rejection, and I allowed myself to relax a little under his stare.

Nix had been very young when I was little enough to shift on occasion at our old camp, but my beast had grown so quickly that I'd soon had to wear the shift suppressing ring at all times and he'd not seen her since. I wasn't sure if he'd even remember.

Do not sneeze, do not sneeze.

Of all the things the fae around me might assume to be on my mind right now, I doubted that fear of sneezing would make the list. I snorted at the ludicrousness, and a plume of smoke escaped my nostrils.

Shit, shit, shit.

Don't laugh either.

No laughing. No sneezing. No nothing. Just…

Braxton hadn't told me what to do after I'd shifted.

Was I supposed to fly? Attempt to breathe some fire into the sky? Do a fucking tap dance?

I turned to face him, my tail swishing around my body and landing near Kane and Alaric. I wasn't sure how exactly to ask Braxton what he wanted, but hopefully having a giant dragon staring him down would trigger him to say something. Right?

Wrong. He just stood and stared. Like he'd just found the answer to all of his problems looking down a giant snout at him. He'd soon learn I was beyond useless at being a dragon. But he deserved to enjoy the delusion of having one up on those who hunted him for once.

The fact of the matter was, I was much more likely to kill my allies on the way to battle with a poorly timed coughing fit than be of any actual help.

I felt a light, tickling sensation at my tail, but unlike last time, I knew exactly what it was. I looked over to Kane and Alaric once more.

Ok maybe not *exactly* what it was.

Alaric was stroking the scales along my tail. Kane, on the other hand, was trying to… climb on me. Did he have a death wish?

I concentrated harder than ever on the movement this time. Focusing specifically on the very end of my tail. As he placed his palms on the ridge between two lethal spikes, preparing to jump. I flicked my tail up and over, narrowly skimming the top of his head so it was behind him now, and before he had time to turn, with a teeny tiny whipping action, I spanked his ass.

Or that's what I'd intended to do.

With the way he moved through the air, I wondered whether high fae did, in fact, have the gift of flight. I fought the laugh that bubbled up in my chest, fear of flames bursting forth enough to dampen my mirth.

I opened my mouth to apologize, but quickly snapped it shut. The last thing he needed as he tried to make a dignified landing was a swift toasting.

I heard a deep rumbling sound, and realized it was Alaric, laughing harder than I had ever seen the male laugh. I didn't know he had it in him. It quickly became my favorite sound in all the realms.

Kane had landed perfectly, thank the fates. And broke down into a fit of his own laughter. My dragon wanted to join in. But I couldn't trust her not to accidentally hurt someone. I'd never forgive myself.

"OK, that's enough. Shift back," Braxton said.

I nodded. Or at least what felt like a nod. Then focused on the shift.

Come on, shift back, shift back.

"Evangelia, shift." Braxton said after several minutes of trying and nothing happening.

I was trying, fates, I was trying really hard. So many fae were watching me. I'd wager that there wasn't a soul in the camp right now who wasn't watching my every move. *Come on, Eva.*

"Give her a minute." It was Nix's voice. He was joining Braxton by the tree. "Take your time, Eva. You've got this," he said.

He understood more than anyone here my experience with my dragon. Or the lack of it. He knew my parents had spent most of my life teaching me how to hide her, not how to control her once she came out to say hello.

Not knowing what else to do, I took a deep breath and counted back from ten. I'd gotten to two by the time the shift happened. Again, it was fast. But no sooner had I changed back to my fae form than Alaric was wrapping my naked body in a black cloak.

"Thank you," I said.

"I promise yeh it's for selfish reasons, Angel." He whispered as he closed it at the front. "The treasure under this cloak is too dazzling for any ol' eyes."

Butterflies danced in my stomach, but before I could unscramble my brain enough to think up a good response, Braxton and Nix approached.

"Good work." Braxton said.

"But I didn't really do anything," I told him. "It wasn't until I shifted that I remembered you hadn't actually said what you had planned for my training."

"For now, we just work on yer shift. It needs to be second nature, like Alaric between his wolf, thrakos, and fae forms."

"Right. OK, I'll work on it." I promised, feeling a wave of exhaustion come over me. It seemed simpler than what I'd assumed he was going to try to get me to do, so I wasn't about to argue.

"OK. Again." Braxton said.

"What, now?"

"Aye."

Everyone moved back to their positions and waited expectantly.

Looked like I'd be sleeping like the dead tonight. That's if I didn't *actually* die of exhaustion first.

I DOVE under the surface of the clear water. The heat from the natural spring had relaxed the tense, exhausted muscles in my shoulders. It had been a day, to say the least.

I'd managed seven shifts before Braxton had called an end to our training session. *Seven shifts!*

After the third, I'd felt the stares from my camp mates dissipate, thanks mostly to Braxton telling them they had training of their own to be getting on with. After that, the shifts had become easier to navigate.

I wasn't sure if it was because I was getting used to it by then or if it had been some kind of stage fright. Even so, they became no less exhausting as I grew more familiar with the transition of each shift. By the end of it, I'd been shaking. Barely able to hold myself upright in my fae form, let alone as my dragon.

I finally surfaced, feeling the balmy air on my face. I took a calming breath and just enjoyed the feeling of the water around my naked body. I had missed the natural spring baths that we were afforded living here in the Vale in the time that I had been away.

Sure, a rose scented bath or steamy shower was great and all, but nothing beat nature. The sensation of the contrast from the cold air in your hair, and the warm water hugging your skin, was just too hard to beat.

I turned at the sound of splashing behind me. Watching as Alaric's impressive form entered the water.

He smirked at me as he made his way over, and I made no attempt to hide my admiration for him. It had been too long since we'd been intimate, either of us. I bit my lip at the thought. Fates, we'd barely had a moment to ourselves since reaching the rebel camp.

My eyes fell over Alaric's large shoulders at the sight of Kane stepping into the water behind him. He wasted no time ditching his towel and getting comfortable. Reclining back against some rocks, arms resting along the moss covered edge, his eyes looked bluer than ever as he relaxed in the warm liquid.

"Hey, Princess," he said, looking up at the canopy above us, letting me greedily take him in. How had I gotten so lucky to have both of these incredible males? I could pinch myself.

Seizing the moment, I swam over to Kane. Sliding my hands up his thighs as I steadied my feet on the rocks below. His deep blue eyes bore into my own. He'd had it the worst since we'd arrived here. We'd expected it, but I would have thought by now that at least some of the rebels would have warmed to him. How wrong I was.

It was clear it was taking a toll on him, despite his dimpled smiles and cheeky winks he offered whenever we made eye contact across the training ring or camp fire.

I could almost see the tension and stress falling away from him in waves as he enjoyed this stolen moment with just Alaric and I. He didn't need to worry about anyone stabbing him in the back in this pool. He didn't need to pretend he hadn't heard the obvious insults being muttered every time he passed a group gossiping about him and his family by birth.

All he needed to do at this moment was relax. And I had the perfect idea to help him do just that.

Glancing over my shoulder at Alaric with a devious smile, I signaled for him to join us. Turning my attention back to Kane, I ran my hands from his thighs to his chest, leaning in. A smile tugged at his lips as he wrapped my hair in his fist and dragged me to his mouth.

He devoured me like I was the air he needed to breathe, so deeply, it left my lungs feeling empty. I would have gladly given him my last breath, and I kissed him back like I was.

Alaric's lips brushed my shoulder, working their way down my spine in kisses far more gentle than I wanted. I knew what this male was capable of.

A groan left me as I enjoyed the sensations of having both of them touching me. But right now, I wanted to make this about Kane.

Pulling away from Kane's lips, my hands ran down his chest, slowly sliding lower and lower until they were under the water, brushing the delicious V between his hips and landing on his already hard cock.

He moaned as I grasped his length, moving in strong, sure strokes. As he bit down on his lip, Alaric pushed me further onto Kane's lap, caging me between them, as he leaned over me so he could steal a kiss of his own.

I was sure dragon fire danced in my irises as I watched my males lose themselves in the taste of each other.

Fuck, it was so good to see them enjoying one another the way I enjoyed them. So different from the way they were in front of others. Only I was lucky enough to witness this.

Dipping my head between their bodies, making sure not to get in the way of their locked lips, I licked and nipped my way down Kane's chest, reveling in the vibrations of the noises he made as Alaric and I focused our entire attention on him.

A shiver raked my spine as Alaric's hands grasped my waist. Then slid down to my inner thighs. The memory of his teeth sinking in a week ago sent liquid heat through my entire being. His hands spread my legs around Kane's hips and he parted my pussy, his fingers finding my clit with ease as he teased me.

I panted, my forehead resting on hard muscle as pleasure set my blood ablaze. They were both solid, as I was crowded between them.

Alaric broke from Kane's lips, moving to kiss my neck, while Kane joined him, nuzzling and kissing the other side. Alaric's hand slid from my clit to Kane's throbbing cock as he guided me down. My mouth opened with a moan of pleasure as our bodies met and he filled me.

The delicious feeling of being stretched around him had me moving my hips, slowly at first, gradually growing more and more desperate.

"Fuck, Princess," he groaned against my neck.

Alaric's hands were cupping my breasts from behind me, his fingers teasing my nipples as the cold wind blew gently against them, making them even more sensitive to his touch.

He dropped one hand into the water. "Are you ready, Angel?" Alaric asked, and before I could clarify what for, I felt his finger slide from where I was joined with Kane, up between my cheeks and over my ass where it hovered.

It was like being struck by a bolt of lightning. So intimate, so sensitive, and so fucking welcome that I wanted him to do it again.

I leant my head back against him, and he brought his lips down to meet mine. *"So ready,"* I breathed.

Alaric pressed a thick finger inside me. It was intense. Entirely different from the feeling of Kane's cock as he thrust in and out, but no less arousing. He moved his finger, and I felt so full already I wasn't sure what he planned to do was even possible.

Another finger joined the first, then a third. It wasn't completely painless, yet I found myself hungry for more of it.

He removed his fingers, and took my hand, pulling it around my back and to his thick, hard cock. "Can you handle us both?" he purred.

Probably not, but I was more than ready to try and prove myself wrong.

Kane stopped his thrusts. "Hold my shoulders, Eva." He ordered. "And don't be shy to dig those talons in if you need to."

I did as he said, then his hands moved onto my cheeks, spreading them apart, his cock still fully seated inside my pussy.

Alaric took his time, lining himself up with my hole. His first thrust had me sinking my nails into the muscles of Kane's shoulders. *Fuck, it hurt.*

"That's it, Princess. Good girl."

His praise spurred me on. "OK. More." I said.

Alaric pushed his cock in another inch. Then another. My breath caught every time, until eventually, I was fuller than I'd even known feasible.

"Ready?" Kane asked, and I nodded.

After a few moments, his cock began to move again, using his grip on my ass to ensure every thrust forced his length deeper and deeper inside me. Alaric slowly eased in and out, picking up his rhythm until he was matching Kane's.

I'd never felt so close to my males, and I was relishing every moment. Kane's moans of pleasure. Alaric's almost undecipherable strings of curses that rumbled from his throat. My own pants and gasps as they drove me closer and closer to orgasm.

It was euphoric.

But it was all becoming too much as our bodies moved against each other in the water like crashing waves in a rough sea. My body was already in rapture when Kane dropped his hold on one cheek and began to tease my clit, faster and faster as my hips moved.

The sensation was a bliss I didn't know how to handle. Kane must have known I was ready to explode around him when he whispered, "Come for us, Princess."

At that exact moment, Alaric bit down on my neck, his fangs piercing the skin. It was hard and sharp and breathtaking.

I cried out, my orgasm hitting me so hard I forgot how to breathe, forgot how to talk. All I knew was the males inside me, filling my pussy, my ass. Fucking me so perfectly, it was like we were three puzzle pieces made to fit together exactly like this.

I rocked between them, faster and faster, grinding my hips to meet every one of their desperate thrusts. *"Fuckkk,"* Kane cried out, throwing his head back as he climaxed.

Minutes later, or perhaps it was just a few seconds, Alaric found his release on a roar, slamming into my ass with hard jerks of his hips. Time lost all meaning when you were sandwiched between two hulking males, riding the highs of a pleasure you didn't even know existed in this realm, or any other.

We were all panting when Alaric eventually pulled out. I slid off Kane and floated over to the side of the pool, crossing my arms over the edge to hold myself up and placing my chin in the nook between them. Unable to move, unable to think, unable to speak, just trying to get my breath back.

That… that was… there are no words.

Kane reached out and took my hand, pulling me through the water back to him, clearly not ready to break contact.

His face was soft in the afterglow of what we'd done together, but his eyes were bright, like he'd just had some great epiphany, "Fuck, I think I love y–"

Alaric stumbled, water dove out of his way in a crash, splashing Kane and I across the face. His large palms barely came down on the moss covered edge of the pool in time to catch himself.

It was frightening how three little words could hold the power of a thousand when put together in that specific order. The power to bring even a male like Alaric to his knees…

Holy shit. I hadn't expected those words either. There were fae I loved, my parents… Nix… but I'd never been *in* love.

Was there one specific, divine moment when you realized you were in love? Or was it a series of lots of little things? Stolen moments, shared glances, selfless acts of kindness. A constant and all-consuming desire for one another, mixed with friendship and mutual respect.

I didn't think I'd find that sort of connection with one heart, but I realized now I had found it with two. The words were on the tip of my tongue when I spotted the glazed look in Alaric's eyes.

Oh no.

No no no.

Kane saw it, too. His silver eyes weren't glazed with emotion. It was the exact look he got when Axel pulled on the battle bond and sprang into his head.

Not now. *Why* now?

He'd checked in only earlier today. What could be so important that he needed to speak to Alaric again so soon? Had he heard what Kane had been confessing before he stumbled? Had I read it completely wrong, and he had just been taken off guard when Axel's voice jumped into his mind?

I squeezed Kane's hand under the warm water as Alaric's eyes came back into focus; their metallic hue now as sharp as the tip of a steel blade.

"Yer brother sent fifty soldiers out under the cover of darkness tonight, armed with wax sealed envelopes. One for every town and village in Dezrothia."

Kane squeezed my hand back.

We both knew the moment was gone.

Stolen by his own fucking brother's impatience, lost thanks to his blatant disregard of the Kingdom's mourning period. But not forgotten, not by me.

Alaric continued, oblivious to the strange tension in the suddenly frigid air. "Axel was in the catacombs when the soldiers were selected to go. He didnae manage to get his hands on one of the letters so doesnae ken what they say. Apparently, the soldiers who were selected were given strict instructions no' to open them. Or so he's told."

Kane was looking to the skies as though silently cursing the fates. He must have felt the weight of my stare, because he quickly met it. He shook his head. The message was clear: *now's not the time, Princess.*

To Alaric, he said, "Braxton and the others will want to hear this. We need to come up with a plan to get one of those letters, and soon."

"Aye." Alaric agreed, already climbing out of the pool. Kane and I followed.

The crisp night hit my skin, causing lazy heat trails to drift into the air as I quickly dressed into a loose cotton dress. *Fates, Axel.* You'd think spending so much time with a powerful seer would have helped with his less than ideal timing, but apparently he hadn't inherited his aunt's gifts.

It wasn't his fault, though. He was just the messenger. A war was brewing, we could all feel it, even if we were blind to know when or where or how it would happen. Those letters could hold the information that we desperately needed about Elikai's next move.

CHAPTER 31

Nekane

Just minutes ago, nothing had existed but them.

Now we were in some camp version of a war room, discussing all the fucked up ways my brother's mind might work and attempting to guess what his letters might say.

Fates, why must you hate me so? Can't a male make declarations of love undisturbed these days?

Clearly, the mate bond wasn't meant to be split three ways or it would have happened by now; so why couldn't the Fates have just gifted me with five more fucking seconds before Alaric had been pulled away into Axel's mind?

I hadn't even had a chance to finish my sentence, let alone tell them that they didn't need to say it back, or explain that I'd just needed to say it for my own selfish reasons of not wanting to die without ever having told them I loved them.

The realization had hit me and my lips were moving of their own accord. Now Alaric was completely oblivious that anything had changed. Eva didn't know where to look, how to act or what to say to me, and we had proof that Elikai wasn't going to wait for the mourning period to end before he started making his moves. It was a whole fucking mess, but fuck it. I'd said what I said, and I wouldn't take it back.

Time waited for no fae living out here in the Fading Vale, and we happened to be the three at the top of the most wanted list. I was just thankful to be at the very peak of it. It was the only power I was sure I had when it came to being face to face with Elikai again.

We all knew it wasn't a case of if, but when my brother's army found us, and from what I'd seen, the rebels didn't stand a chance against them. I was surprised they even allowed us to stay here, knowing the added risks we brought them.

Braxton and Alaric led the meeting. It wasn't just the various camp leaders present.

When word had quickly spread we had important information from inside the castle, half the camp had gathered in and around the large tent.

I wondered how often this happened here. How many times they'd received a lead, and gotten their hopes up that it would bring them one step closer to their salvation? Only to realize they still couldn't do anything about their situation, short of waging a war they couldn't possibly win.

As the message was delivered and discussion began, there was no debate about whether or not we needed to see what potential answers the letters held. There was, however, plenty of debate over everything else.

Which village to visit? Apparently, it needed to be one Alaric was familiar with. It needed to be close enough to Ezerat for the letter to have already arrived and the soldier delivering it to be well on his way to the next village or back to the castle by the time we did. But then it needed to be close enough to the Vale that we could stick to the forests when traveling and get the information back as quickly as possible.

But it also had to be far enough away from any other rebel camps, so if something went wrong, if we got caught, it wouldn't put the camp at risk of being found in any searches after.

Someone suggested that it could be a trap. That Axel might have been discovered as a spy and been fed purposely misleading information to bring us out of hiding. I didn't think so. The battle bond was too subtle a way of communicating. It wasn't like Axel had been leaving the castle to send letters of his own, or hunting down witches, asking if they could whisper to a raven.

Even if someone caught him with that strange, glassy-eyed look, he'd die before he told them anything about the bond he'd made with Alaric. That I was sure of.

I just hoped that the letter wouldn't turn out to be only an ego trip from Elikai. Nothing more than an announcement that he was to be king. I wouldn't be surprised if it simply held the offer of an increased reward for our heads. My brother must be growing more and more furious with every day that passed, and we weren't captured and brought to him. Cursing the Lores of Dezrothia that he had to honor a millennia old ritual of a mourning period after the passing of a monarch. No war while his society weep.

Or at least he knew he had to *appear* to be honoring it. Elikai was nothing if not one to keep up appearances.

We really needed that letter to be something of value about his plans. For it to give some indication of his future whereabouts, the date of his coronation, something, anything, to give us a purpose. To give the rebels hope.

Hope.

Eva's words from the first day I met her floated into my mind. *Hope, Nekane, is for children. I used to have it…*

My gaze fell on Nix. It must break Eva every time she looked into her best friend's eyes and saw that the hope she'd once known she would find in them, the hope she'd held on to herself, had well and truly been extinguished.

Despite his best efforts at feigning otherwise, it took no more than a look at Nix to see he'd lost the hope he'd once held so tightly to. I should probably make an effort to break down a few of his walls. After all, while I'd spent year after year drinking myself into a stupor and fucking my way through Ezerat's high fae, he'd been the male who'd held my female through the hard times.

I pulled my thoughts out of the past to hear them discussing my uncle now. Whether he would still be in Dezrothia or if he'd returned to Mount Mortum. What my brother might have wanted with him.

"Wait," Eva said. "Elikai had asked me to research all the species of fae in Dezrothia. I had no idea why, other than that he'd said it was somehow linked to the event he was planning, but perhaps those letters will hold the answer?"

She must be exhausted, but she didn't show it as she answered everyone's questions as best she could with the limited insight my brother had given her.

Part of me wanted to tell them they were wasting their time trying to work Elikai out. I was his twin. He had blackmailed me and then tried to kill me. I wouldn't put anything past him at this point. He was as unpredictable as he was cruel.

To give Eva a break from the questions, I interjected, offering what I hoped was a possible solution. "Would Hazelbrook work? It's got to be about halfway between here and Ezerat."

Eva gave me a small smile of thanks as everyone began discussing the pros and cons of Hazelbrook.

Eventually, Braxton announced the plan. "Then it's decided. Hazelbrook is around two, maybe three, days northeast from here, if travelin' at a good pace, only stoppin' for essential breaks an' a brief sleep. It's around two days from the capital too. If a small group of us leave two days from now, we should arrive a good day or so clear of the letter bein' delivered. Addin' the extra day isn't ideal, but assuming each soldier has one, maximum two, stops to make each, an' that they will likely need to stay the night at one of their stops to rest, it's the safest option. We dinnae ken if this letter holds anythin' of value, so we aren't takin' any unnecessary risks."

Alaric nodded. "Aye. A team of six will work. Any volunteers to come with me?"

"I will." I said automatically and saw several hands shoot up.

Alaric didn't look at me when he said, "Ideally, wolves. We can travel as a pack, stick to the shadows, an' run most of the journey. No need to carry heavy packs an' tents, either."

Four hands went down, leaving just Alaric and two others. I recognised them as the young male and female who'd questioned Alaric's word the day we'd arrived. I knew them now to be Miles and Raine.

They were half wolf, and had been at the training ring every day, either spectating or fighting. They usually went up against each other, but a couple of days ago, I'd heard Raine telling Miles he could beat me, egging him on. I'd welcome the challenge and invited him into the ring.

It hadn't gone well for him. It wasn't that he was weak or lacked the grit and determination needed, he just hadn't grown up with a fully equipped training facility or with the best tutor in the realm at his beck and call.

Alaric nodded, then looked around as if hoping there were a couple more wolves with their hands up that he just wasn't seeing. There weren't.

"I will go." I said again, more forcefully this time. "I might not be a wolf, but I'm fast, and we've trained together long enough for you to know full well that I am capable of having your back if shit goes sideways. I can do without a tent for a few days. It's mostly forest anyway, so there will be shelter."

In my mind, everyone else faded into the background as I spoke. I wasn't taking no for an answer. I stared him down, my jaw set, waiting for him to agree.

I could practically hear his mind whirring, trying to come up with a good excuse for me not to. But why? There was no way I would let him go without me, and he knew it.

"That's four." He nodded, eventually conceding. "Two more?"

I could sense the inner turmoil rolling off Eva in waves. She wanted to volunteer, but I knew her well enough to know she wouldn't. Not because she was scared to, but because she wouldn't want to slow anyone down. Her fae form couldn't keep up with wolves or a high fae, and she couldn't very well fly there.

Nix looked torn too. There was no way Alaric would let him go, though. He'd want him to stay with Eva. He didn't have to like him to know he was the best male to have her back should she need it while we were gone.

Braxton too. Though it felt like forever ago, he and Eva had only started their training sessions together this morning, and Alaric was unlikely to trust anyone else with that task.

Iona raised her hand next. "I'll go. I'm no wolf, but my fur's almost as dark as Alaric's and I'm as fast."

Braxton and Alaric nodded, then a slim male with yellow blonde hair tied back in a knot and small, too-close-together eyes stepped out of the crowd, maneuvering his way to the table.

"I'll go," he said. "I'm not a wolf either, but I'm still a shifter hybrid. I'll be able to keep up and I won't stand out in the shadows."

"Jarrah." Braxton announced, obviously familiar with the male. "Yeh, that works. Righ', we have two days. Alaric, Nekane, Iona, Raine, Miles and Jarrah, I want you training together from sunrise 'til sunset. Learn to work together and make a plan with each other's strengths in mind."

"Me an' Kane have both been to Hazelbrook, so between us we should be able to map it out so yeh aren't goin' in blind. Most likely, the letter will be delivered to the mayor. His house and office are in the center of the village, which makes things more difficult, but not impossible." Alaric said.

It was late now, and it had been a long day for everyone. Eva was leaning against me as though she was too exhausted to stand on her own. I couldn't imagine how she must be feeling after shifting to and from her dragon form, over and over. Then Alaric and I had gone and tired her out pretty fucking well in the pool, too. She needed to get some rest.

"Ready for bed, Princess?" I asked quietly.

"I'm fine," she said through a yawn and I smirked.

"Come on."

I took her hand and led her through the crowd and away from the tent. Alaric would join us as soon as they'd all finished pretending to be seers and trying to predict every possible thing that could go wrong.

Maybe Edelin would wake up soon and could tell us exactly what we needed to do to walk in, grab the letter, and walk back out entirely unscathed. I doubted it worked like that, but it would be nice.

Maybe I could attempt to speak to a witch or warlock tomorrow between training. It would be good to find out if there were any scryers here. They'd likely be all of a sudden too busy to help me, but it was worth a go. Maybe I could kill two birds with one stone and see if Nix would be willing to try a quick scry.

Eva and I crossed the clearing in silence, heading for our tent. There was something uncomfortable hanging between us. Was it what I'd said in the water earlier or something else? "What's up?" I asked.

"I don't know. I feel uneasy about this plan. I just, I don't like the idea of you and Alaric leaving."

"Would it make you feel better to know that we'll be running extra fast so we can hurry up and get back to you?" I asked, only half joking.

She let out a soft, humorless giggle. "A little," she lied.

"Don't worry about us, Princess," I said, scooping her up. She let out a little gasp and clung on tightly around my neck as I carried her the last several meters to our little home. "Mmmm. Have I ever told you that you smell like campfires and vanilla?" I asked, changing the subject.

"I do?"

"You do to me," I said. "Also, have I told you that you were amazing today?"

"Ha. For what? For managing to take far too long to do something that should be second nature?"

"I was actually talking about managing to take Alaric and I at the same time." I dipped my head to whisper against her ear, "I know from firsthand experience that he's a big male."

She laughed, and though she was so tired she could probably pass out at any moment, it was loud and real.

"I could say the same thing about you," she teased.

"That I'm amazing in bed or have a huge cock?" I joked.

She chuckled again, and I wanted to bottle the sound. "Can I say both?"

"I mean, you can. But any more compliments like that and I might change my mind about taking you back to the tent for *just* snuggles and sleep."

"It's tempting. But snuggles and sleep sounds too good."

I kissed her on the forehead. "You truly were amazing today, Princess. Your dragon is the most stunning thing I have ever seen."

"I'll tell her you said that."

"I'll tell her myself, just as soon as you've had a good night's rest, so you have the energy to bring her out to see me again tomorrow."

EVA WAS fast asleep by the time Alaric snuck into bed last night, careful not to wake her. We hadn't spoken, he'd just undressed about as quietly as a giant could when squeezed into a pixie sized tent. He'd slid into his spot for the night behind me, thrown a heavy arm over me and Eva where we spooned, and no more than a few minutes later, I must have passed the fuck out.

The three of us squeezed up tight like sardines. Snuggles and sleep. I decided it was definitely my happy place.

I woke to the feel of Alaric's cock hard against my ass. His soft snores told me he was still asleep. I kissed Eva gently on the head and rolled over as carefully as possible to do the same to Alaric, planning to sneak out and get to the training ring nice and early.

"Mornin'" Alaric's sleep-thick voice grumbled before I'd even leaned in. So much for not waking him up. Fates, he sounded so sexy in the morning.

Perhaps the training ring could wait five minutes. There was suddenly something else I really needed to do first.

Closing the small gap between us, I kissed him. "Good morning," I said against his mouth.

As his soft, warm lips parted, allowing room for my tongue, I carefully reached for a corner of the blanket we all shared, and scrunched it in my fist.

As I pulled my own mouth away, I stuffed the balled up corner of the blanket into his mouth. "That should keep you quiet."

He spat it out. "Why do I need a blan–"

I slid my hand down to his cock, and it jerked at my touch. Alaric sucked in a stuttered breath of surprise. I loved the feeling of knowing he was both bewildered and at my mercy.

"Because I'm going to take care of this." I said. The training ring could definitely wait. This wouldn't take long. I could already feel Alaric's cock throbbing under my touch.

Releasing his length, I began slithering down under the blanket, stopping when I reached his knees. Slowly, I trailed soft kisses against the sensitive flesh of his thighs, making my way up until I found the perfect position and wrapped my fingers around his shaft.

"Mmmm," I breathed, my lips parted and just barely pressed against his head. Close enough that I knew he'd feel every vibration.

"Kane." he growled low.

I licked my lips, then lowered my mouth to the tip. The salty pearl of arousal excited my taste buds as his hips jolted ever so slightly. I'd never get enough of his taste. I started teasing him, circling my tongue around the head, my hand stroking up and down his length in slow movements.

As much fun as tormenting him was for me, I found myself wanting to please him as much as I enjoyed teasing him.

I licked up the length of his shaft and when I reached the peak, I took him in my mouth. Unable to stop myself from moaning as his length neared the back of my throat.

His impatient hand found my head, his fingers knotting in my hair. I allowed it as he steered me to take his cock further. He groaned, tightening his grip.

"Morning," Eva said sleepily. I could hear her rolling over, and felt the blanket pulling over me as she sat up, about to give away my position. This morning was about to get even better. "Where's Kane?"

"He woke up hungry," Alaric said tightly.

The blanket was ripped away, but Alaric's hand didn't loosen as he continued to guide me up and down his length.

"Hmmm," Eva breathed. Her voice was pure seduction in the morning too. "Is that right?"

Fates, it was times like this where I wished I had two mouths.

"Morning, Princess," I mumbled around Alaric's cock. The hiss that came from the male as the vibrations in my throat did all sorts of delicious things to his cock made me chuckle. Causing him to hiss again.

I managed to pry my mouth away, much to Alaric's resistance. I licked my lips again, continuing to stroke his cock with my hand. "Princess, care to keep him quiet for me?"

"How exactly do you suggest I do that, Kane?" she asked.

"With your mouth?" I suggested helpfully.

"Or yer cunt," Alaric growled. Impatiently pulling a pink cheeked Eva into position over his face. Her knees resting against his shoulders.

Fuck, his dirty words spoke straight to my own horny heart.

I went back to work on his cock. Taking him all the way to the back of my throat without any resistance. His hands were busy now. I watched eagerly as he pulled Eva's panties to the side. Watching his tongue flick out and run the length of her pussy was almost my own undoing. She'd still be sore from yesterday had it not been for a night of her body healing itself. Instead, she was glistening wet and ready.

It was a shame we had places to be this morning and fae who would be coming to find us soon if we didn't make this quick.

I found a rhythm and Alaric matched my pace with his mouth on Eva's pussy. His tongue greedily licking and sucking on her clit while she tried desperately not to cry out. I sped up, sucking him harder and faster.

Alaric pushed a thick finger inside her and I watched as her thighs clenched tight around his head. He added another finger and began sliding them in and out in time with every dip of my head.

Eva's legs were shaking as she moved her hips, fighting for more friction. Her back arched, and she threw her head back as she rode out her silent orgasm. Alaric didn't stop, his tongue lapping up her mess as his thrusts slowed.

With my free hand, I fondled Alaric's balls as I pleasured his cock. I took him as far down my throat as I could, and when I couldn't go any further, I let go and ran my finger over his tight hole.

His entire body tensed as he came. His arousal filled my mouth, and I swallowed as I continued to suck, slower now.

I meticulously licked up and down his shaft, making sure not to miss a drop. He tasted of male and salty and I couldn't get enough. I might have been raised a prince with a butler to clean up after me, but *this* particular mess I was more than happy to clean up by myself.

Once I was satisfied, I sat back on my knees. "Well fuck, my breakfast was egg-cellent. What about yours?"

Eva let out a sigh, fates near falling off Alaric, who groaned at my pun, to lie next to him with an easy smile spread across her face. "I'm fried."

"I'm eggs-bene-dicked, nice to meet you," I told her. "You look more scrambled than fried to me."

"Thanks, I think?"

"If you need some toast for it, I heard there's a big scary dragon who roams this camp during the day who could help you out."

"Big and scary?"

"Oh yes. The biggest, scariest dragon *I've* ever seen. If you see her, tell her I said hey, yeah? I kind of have a crush on her. I was going to tell myself, but you and Alaric made me run late."

Eva chuckled. Alaric rolled his eyes.

It was fun while it lasted. But we were all well aware it was a stolen moment and now it was time to get back to reality. No matter how much that reality sucked.

CHAPTER 32

Alaric

Even after the delay from the morning wake up, Nix was the only one to have beaten Kane and I to the training ring. Waking up to that was something I could definitely get used to, even if it meant being the last ones to arrive.

Since arriving at camp, Nix had found a female who was all too happy to be his blood source, and he was looking pretty fucking good for it. He was a big male, not as big as Braxton or I, probably closer to Kane's build, and he was much improved physically.

Despite regaining his strength, his big, brown eyes held darkness in their depths. He hid it well enough, but it was never more present than it was around Eva.

I didn't much like the male. And he despised both Kane and I. Whenever Eva wasn't with either of us, or training with Braxton, she was with him. Which both pissed me off and reassured me she was safe at the same time.

I nodded to him as I neared.

"Where's everyone else?" Kane asked.

Nixen gestured behind us. I turned to see Raine, Miles, Jarrah, Iona, and a few others leaving the weapons tent, their arms full. This should be interesting.

"Prince Nekane." Raine called over.

"Call me Kane," he corrected stiffly. He was still cautious around everyone, and they seemed to enjoy his discomfort. "What's up?"

"Did you mean to leave this fancy sword in the weapons tent?" she asked, and Kane winced slightly as she waved the sword around that triggered memories he'd been trying to get rid of when he'd put it there.

"Yeah," he said. "You can have it if you want?"

"Seriously?" Miles said, eyes bugged.

"What's the catch?" Raine asked.

"No catch, have it," Kane confirmed, surprising every set of ears listening in.

"Oh. Well, thanks, I guess," Raine said, confusion knitting her brows. It was obvious that she hadn't expected such easy generosity from him. As if she'd expected him to ask her for her weight in gold or her firstborn or a favor in return.

They reached the edge of the training ring and dropped their weapons into a pile on the ground. Everyone bent down to take the weapon of their choice, all except Raine, who clung to the onyx and ruby royal sword like she didn't plan on letting it go even to sleep.

Kane bent to pick up a random long sword, weighing it in his palm. I didn't miss the way most of the fae stepped backwards, instinctively putting more space between him and themselves. Everyone except Nixen. I sighed. Clearly, the rebels still didn't trust he wouldn't turn the sword on them.

I pointed to Nixen and Iona. Their power was well matched, despite Iona being a few hundred years his senior. Nixen was obviously a powerful warlock, just based on his heritage being a Sybilline, but he didn't seem as confident fighting in that form as he was in his thrakos form. Still, they would make a good pair to spar with each other.

"Nixen, I want yeh to fight Iona without using yer thrakos side. If we get spotted, we dinnae want it to be obvious we are rebels. Same goes for the rest of yeh with thrakos blood."

He nodded, and they stepped into the ring. I watched the match closely, analyzing their strengths and weaknesses. I needed to know what I was going to be working with.

Iona muttered spell after spell, bright balls of energy making their way to Nixen, who blocked and countered with spells of his own.

After some time, Iona looked tired. Nixen seemed to note it and slowed down his attacks. Rookie mistake. Because then she shifted.

A huge ball of dark brown fur barrelled towards him far faster than such a stocky bear should have been able to move. Nix dropped into a fighting stance, all magic forgotten as he opted to fight her bear form with bare knuckles in his fae form.

She swiped at him with long, curved claws which he managed to duck and avoid, sometimes by little more than a hair's breadth.

I eventually called time. They'd both held their own well and Nixen had managed to avoid shifting into his thrakos form, which was one of the main purposes of the exercise today. They still had work to do, though. Tomorrow they would be learning how to fight *with* each other, but first, they needed to fight *against* each other to learn from one another.

Next up was Raine, a wolf-thrakos hybrid like myself. She usually trained with Miles, another wolf-thrakos hybrid, but today we were mixing things up.

I signaled Jarrah to get in the circle. I didn't know the male, aside from that my da' had said he was new here and came from another camp up north in the Vale. He didn't look much of a fighter, more gangly than anything, as he shuffled his way into the ring.

Raine shifted into her wolf immediately, while Jarrah was fighting in fae form. It took a minute for me to work out exactly what he was. When Raine lunged for him, he threw a spell that hit her in the chest, sending her barreling across the dirt floor. She'd barely landed when he shifted.

Fuck, I was not expecting a spider.

He scuttled on top of her while she was sprawled on the ground and scurried around her in strange, fast circles. I couldn't see what was happening. He was so huge that he blocked my view of Raine below him completely.

"That's enough now, Jarrah." Iona called, and he darted away from Raine immediately, then shifted back to his fae form.

We didn't have spider shifters in the horde, so I was unsure what exactly I'd just fucking witnessed.

My eyes widened as I saw Raine. She was almost completely cocooned in a silk web. Only her large, gray wolf snout and face had escaped being trapped in the thick entanglement.

Fates, death by spider would be a shit way to go. Especially for an immortal. Wound tightly enough, you would slowly waste away over the course of years. I shuddered.

Raine shifted back to her fae form, which was much smaller than the giant gray wolf that Jarrah had wrapped up a little too snug and warm for comfort. She crawled out of the nest of webbing, not in the least bit bothered by her nakedness, but very, very bothered by what the spider shifter had done.

"Jarrah!" she growled as she stalked over and began jabbing him in the chest with her finger. "You could see I was down, that spell hit me right in the chest! I was knocked out for fates sake! I did *not* need to wake up to your creepy, crawly ass rubbing up all over me!"

"You didn't? I figured you'd enjoy it." Jarrah shot back. Miles frowned.

Raine growled, then turned to Miles, who I assumed was her boyfriend, or at least her fuck buddy. "Ugh! I'm itching all over. Is it still on me? It's on me, isn't it? Get it off!"

I could see Kane fighting a laugh. These fae already hated him enough, he didn't need to give them an excuse to dislike him any further. I shot a glare at him and he brought himself under control, but he was clearly itching for a fight himself.

Miles was up next, but I'd already seen him fight Kane and lose. So I paired him up against an older male who was a warlock-wolf hybrid that had been spectating. He wasn't happy about it, but if he didn't have the balls to volunteer himself for the mission, meaning I had to agree to Kane coming, he could at least make himself useful here instead.

Miles won the round, much to Raine's excitement if the kisses she plastered him with were anything to go by. Then the scent of food wafted over and I called lunch.

Kane and I found Eva talking with Braxton near the space we'd claimed for eating our meals. Nix joined us moments later, though we'd not spoken two words to each other since our initial brief, non-conversation earlier.

"How's it going?" Eva asked.

"Alright," Nix said.

At the same time as Kane said, "Brilliant."

"Brilliant?" I questioned, quirking a brow at his enthusiasm.

"Well, they obviously have a long way to go, but their skills are so diverse. Imagine if they trained to fight together, back to back, instead of against one another, they could be an unstoppable force."

I hadn't told him that was my plan for tomorrow, and the fact he'd drawn the conclusion on his own gave me a pang of pride.

"Wha' makes yeh say that?" Braxton asked, and I knew a lot of eyes would also be on the high fae prince, keen for his answer.

"Well, just imagine it. What a battlefield would look like if there were hybrids in the horde," Kane said as though he could see it clear as day in his mind, and it was a sight to behold. "A warlock-spider hybrid, fighting back to back with a thrakos-wolf hybrid. Magic, fire, wings, teeth, claws. Webs to trap your enemy, wings to escape them. A high fae or regular shifter, witch or warlock wouldn't stand a chance. Well, except maybe you, Princess," he told Eva with a wink.

You could hear a pin drop around camp as everyone looked at Kane, slack jawed.

"Aye. Imagine," Braxton said.

Oblivious, Kane turned to Eva. "Hungry?" he asked.

Eva's stomach rumbled right on cue and she covered her belly with her palm as though that would help. "Sure," she beamed up at him. "I missed breakfast, so I'm starving."

I smirked at the reminder of her sitting on my face that morning... Fuck, I loved waking up like that.

"Dinnae look so surprised," I told Braxton a few moments later, along with the many more sets of ears I knew would be listening in. The only one I didn't want to earwig had just walked off across the clearing, talking animatedly with a silver-haired temptress who I knew first hand could hold that male's undivided attention.

"He's nothin' like his father. Even less like his brother. The sooner everyone here realizes that, the better."

"Aye. He didnae even fuckin' realize how much weight his words held. Like the hope we felt when we'd heard the prophecy for the first time." Braxton said, looking at the male in question as he walked away.

He was right. For someone I knew to be so clever, Kane could be so fucking clueless when it came to certain things.

"I'm sure by nightfall, every sorry soul in this camp will have heard. But even then, he won't understand what the big deal is or why everyone's talkin' about it," I said.

Braxton nodded. "A prince speaking of imagining hybrids fighting in the horde... As their kin, not their enemy. It's a big deal alrigh'."

It was. It hadn't happened since before our time, since Augustus stole the crown.

I tore my gaze away from Kane and instead watched the others as they watched him. I'd wager there wasn't a male or female in this clearing who didn't live in fear of their immortality being both far too long and not long enough.

To spend months, decades, centuries on end even, living a monotonous, usually nomadic, existence. Waiting for an attack you knew was coming, but didn't know when it would arrive until it was on your doorstep. Suddenly, the immortality you hadn't thought you wanted is ripped away from you before you've even lived a day of it.

I fuckin' hated that I'd seen the look in their eyes myself as they took their last breath and realized it was over for them.

To exist is not to live. I'd seen it happen too many times.

On a lot of occasions, I'd been able to get word out to the camps that a hunt was coming their way, but not every time. Failing once would have been many times, but I'd been forced to be one of the monsters breaking down their invisible doors, setting fire to their tents more times than I wanted to admit to myself.

I had blood on my hands that would never wash off thanks to my centuries under cover. Centuries that would be for naught if Kane didn't start to think about his future soon.

Kane's comment today, as insignificant as it seemed to him, held the weight of a thousand possibilities for the fae here. If the King, who'd driven everyone to the Fading Vale, had had a glimmer of his son's way of thinking, well, they wouldn't be here at all.

They'd have lives. Jobs that paid them well, a solid roof over their heads where they could raise their children on promises of keeping them safe without it being a promise they knew they'd inevitably break.

Lunch time was drawing to an end, and fae were getting back to whatever task they'd been assigned. Still, my father and I stared at the prince, who didn't look anything like a prince, didn't talk like a prince, or act like a prince. He didn't look down his nose at anyone like they'd assumed he would.

"The sooner everyone else starts to see the king Kane could be, the sooner he might start to see it himself," I mused.

"Trust takes time, kid. Let's just hope we have enough of it."

"Aye. Let's hope," I agreed. "Have yeh had much thought on the prophecy since I told yeh about Kane's mother's parentage?"

I recited the words in my head that I'd committed to memory hundreds of years before and knew Braxton would be doing the same.

Pretending to Kane and Eva that day that I was also hearing it for the first time was one of the biggest lies I'd ever told either of them. The truth was, there was barely a night I got into bed in that cursed castle and didn't think about them.

When twin heirs are born, the raven shall mourn.

From the coming of age, the brave can change.

Those impure shall grow, to rise with the low.

The throne will lay bare, for the true rightful heir.

One will bring horror, one will bring honor.

The chance to transcend, before one will ascend.

To bring forth this feat, much bloodshed and deceit.

With the blood of the last, restore what has passed.

An odd feeling came over me, causing goose bumps to appear on my arms and the hairs to stand up on end.

I was standing in the very same clearing, almost the very same spot, where Edelin had been gifted the prophecy from the three fates. The camp had moved a hundred times since, but they'd ended up right back here.

The centuries since she'd jolted out of that vision had somehow gone by both tortuously slowly and within the blink of an eye. My life had come full circle, and though I knew we still had a long way to go, we were closer now than we'd ever been to living out this prophecy and finding a better life.

It was partly why I hadn't wanted Kane to come to Hazelbrook to retrieve the letter. He was too important in all of this to take any unnecessary risks.

In the short time since escaping the castle, I'd gotten a taste of what that better life might look like. I'd likely fuck it up, but at least it would at last be *my* life to fuck up. Free of this duty that pressed down heavily on my shoulders and haunted me in my moments of weakness.

I found my eyes landing on the two fae across the clearing, eating together and laughing at who knew what stupid fucking jokes. *Who cared, so long as they were laughing.*

"Alaric, m'boy?" my da' said, bringing my attention back to what we'd been discussing. The prophecy.

"Yeah?"

"I said, I've thought about it a lot, and discussed it with the other leaders. We ken the twin heirs are Elikai and Nekane, we ken that Augustus mourned, even if not for the reasons we'd originally thought. We're no' sure what their comin' of age has changed though. Maybe yeh can help with that?"

I nodded. I had thought about that line a lot since returning from Elikai's birthday hunt, and I kept coming back to the same conclusion. That it might be about me. Or at least my relationship with Kane. Something had changed between us the moment I'd seen him again after that hunt, and had it not been for that change, we wouldn't be here now.

"Yeah, I have an idea," I said. "But what of the next line?"

"Look around yeh, lad. *Those impure shall grow to rise with the low*. Our numbers are growin', we've not had this many rebels in one place since the prophecy was given. An' yeh dinnae get much lower by Dezrothia's standards than a prince whose face appears on every wanted poster in the realm."

"True enough. But I'm no' so sure. Our numbers would need to grow a hundredfold to come even close to standin' a chance against the horde. Fates, we could do with gettin' a good chunk of them on our side," I scoffed. "The villagers and townsfolk, too. Augustus always overlooked them–"

"Son, I think yer on to somethin'." Braxton said, cutting me off. "*Rise with the low.* What if 'low' is talkin' about lesser fae? Those Augustus looked down upon an' Elikai will likely overlook, too?"

"Unless he hasnae overlooked them," I mused. "What if that's the reason he's sendin' out those letters? To grow his army. The difference between Elikai an' his father, is that Elikai won't stop at Dezrothia, an' the army he has right now isnae enough to conquer realms. What if he hasnae overlooked them, but sees them as disposable soldiers?"

Braxton sighed, lifting one shoulder and then letting it drop. "Let's hope no'. Everytime I think about this fates damned prophecy, I end up thinkin' I have all the answers, only to be proven wrong."

"Aye. All I ken for certain is that Elikai is destined to bring horror, an' I've spent enough time around that male to ken that power winnae suit him. He's as clever as he is cunnin' that cunt. An' he's twice the threat Augustus ever was."

"Then we'd better get back to work. Evangelia's shift is improvin' already. At this rate, by tomorrow she'll be shiftin' at will like any other shifter does. Then the real work starts."

"An' how exactly do yeh plan to teach her to fly and breathe fire with accuracy good enough for the battlefield? The moment she takes to the skies, it'll be like puttin' a flag up an' announcing the camp's location."

"I dinnae plan for her to take to the skies at all, m'boy. I plan for her to master partial shifting." He paused, as though to let that sink in. It wasn't. "She could fight on fae legs but with steel scales for protection, dragon fire to attack an' wings to retreat."

He said it so matter-of-factly, like it wasn't something that neither of us even knew would be possible for a dragon. But fates, if she could...

"WHO'S NEXT?" I asked as soon as everyone had returned to the ring side from lunch.

"Me," Kane said, predictably.

"Against?" I asked.

"Him," he said, pointing to Nixen. This *would* be interesting.

"But Nix has already been in once–" Raine started.

"It's fine. I've been looking forward to this, princeling," Nixen said, cutting her off and shrugging off his shirt.

Clearly, he meant business and had no intention of losing. This fight had been long overdue, ever since they met and first went toe to toe, but they'd be fools to let personal feelings get in the way, they never helped in a fight.

Kane chuckled, "Show me what you've got then, Nix. No holding back."

Apparently, he didn't plan on it. He launched himself at Kane before he'd fully entered the ring, but Kane dodged it easily. Nixen's growl of frustration told me he likely knew he'd played too obvious of a move, letting his personal feelings for Kane cloud his decisions right from the gate.

Nixen turned on him, fist first in another attack, this time connecting with Kane's jaw, drawing blood.

Kane smiled. "Come on, you can do better than that," he goaded, causing anger to bubble in Nixen's veins while that delicious crimson dripped down his lip.

Pulling back, Nixen drew the sword from his hip and swung it at Kane. But he moved out of its path easily before it had come close to landing, thanks to his high fae gift.

Kane drew his own sword and fell into a lazy fighting stance. Nixen gritted his teeth and swung his sword once again, but Kane easily parried it. He batted away every one of Nixen's blows without breaking a sweat.

It wasn't that Nixen was weak, or a particularly bad warrior, but he was fighting with his heart rather than his head. And it was making him sloppy.

"Come on, Nix," Kane taunted, continuing to block each strike as he spoke. "I've seen you training with Eva. I know you can do better than this."

"Of course I can. I've lived in this terrain for my entire life. What have you had? Cushy training rooms and dummies to play with?" he spat. "What would a high fae prince know about fighting outside of the safety of a ring anyway, huh? Real-life problems, real battle, real trauma, you don't know the first thing about any of that!"

I'm not sure what Nixen had expected to achieve from his outburst, but it sure as shit wasn't for Kane to discard his sword and look at him with complete exasperation.

"You use the words *high fae* and *prince* like they are a weapon, Nix," he said, dodging the next blow seemingly unconsciously. "You say it like they should mean something significant." Another strike missed when Kane ducked again. "But they are just fucking labels that make you believe I am someone and something that I'm not. Someone I have never *been*!"

Kane moved in another blur of speed so he was at his back now, too fast for Nixen, who'd already lifted his sword in the air to strike at the male who was no longer in front of him. Kane grabbed his wrist, squeezed the perfect pressure point, and caught the sword by the hilt before it clattered to the ground.

He discarded it next to his own as Nixen whipped around to face him, his fists clenched tightly, itching for his pound of flesh.

Kane continued, "How many times have you heard me say anything that would indicate I think I am better than you because I am high fae? Because I was born a prince? Just fucking stop a second and think about it, Nix. Really fucking think about it." He dodged a punch to the jaw. "Guess what? You don't fucking know me! You just assume to, like everyone else who's been whispering behind my back for days. I know damn well that my race doesn't make me any better or worse than you!"

The fire burning in Kane's eyes told me of his complete conviction in what he was saying to everyone around us, Nixen included. He'd bottled it up since arriving here, and finally, he was ready to do something about it.

They say pride comes before a fall, but his pride had taken a beating since setting foot in the Vale, and even still, there was no self-importance in his tone, nothing conceited in his words. He was finally holding a mirror up to the camp and showing them who it really was that looked like a judgemental fool.

And he wasn't even done.

"Just because I'm high fae, doesn't mean I'm going to go around murdering those who are different to me, or maliciously manipulate fae to do what I say with allure just because I can. In the same way that you don't burn down all these fucking trees with your thrakos fire, just because you can. It's not my race that determines the male I am or the male I want to be, it's those I choose to have around me. And shocker, it certainly isn't my brother, and it was *never* my father! Do you think Alaric or Eva are such poor judges of character? Do you think they would let me into their lives if I was all of those things? Or is it only convenient to you when it demonizes me?"

His chest was heaving harder than when he'd been fighting, but so was Nixen's when he said, "What have you ever done from your cozy castle to help any of us in the Vale, eh? What *exactly* do you think you have done since arriving here to change our minds about you? You certainly haven't shown any signs of wanting to take the throne, to change the Lores." He argued.

Kane paled. "You're right. I did nothing. But there is no one more ashamed of themselves for that than I am," he admitted. "I spent too long wrapped up in my own problems to even see what was happening out here. But believe me when I say no one should live their lives in fear of being hunted down like fucking animals. It makes me sick to my stomach."

"Then what are you going to do about it?" Nixen questioned.

Kane looked around, trying to meet the eyes of everyone that had gathered as he thought about his answer.

"Honestly, I don't know," he said. "But I want to help you in your fight for freedom, and right now, the only way I know how is to start by making sure you all know how to fight. You're strong, capable, and powerful. But the horde and castle guards are no joke. Alaric has trained them for long enough that they are formidable. Fates, learn from him if you don't want to learn from me. He's the best there is, but either way, you need to believe that I am on your side."

Everyone held their breath, waiting to see what Nixen would say or do next, including the dragon watching from the center of the camp.

Eventually, Nixen bent down, picked up the two swords, and held one out to the high fae prince.

"Okay. Let's have at it then, *Kane*," he said, and I could have sworn I heard the dragon purr her happiness at the unlikely alliance that was finally beginning to form.

CHAPTER 33
Evangelia

There wasn't a soul in the camp who hadn't put whatever they'd been doing aside to listen in on Kane and Nix's rather heated discussion during their training session after lunch, myself included.

I was so proud of Kane for transcending opinions of himself, and though perhaps not everyone would have understood my best friend's gesture afterwards for what it was, seeing him hand over a weapon capable of killing him to Kane after he'd said his peace, symbolized that he was ready to start over.

That he was finally acknowledging they were on the same team and that he wasn't just willing, but *wanted* to work with him and learn from him.

I was on my last shift for the day now and my dragon preened as she enjoyed the wind blowing across our scales. It made me want to take off into the skies. I cast my mind back to the last time I'd done it.

It really was such a free feeling to glide through the air, and I realized it was something I desperately wanted to experience again, only without the crippling worry over Kane clutched in my talons.

"Yer doing great," Braxton's rough baritone cut through my thoughts. I gave him a toothy grin before transforming into my fae form.

"Thanks," I said. He threw a thick cloak over, which I caught and quickly wrapped around my nakedness before I continued, "It's definitely getting easier. I am feeling more at peace with her now, my dragon, I mean." I smiled as I felt her purring in contentment.

I'd spent years ignoring and denying her, when really she was a huge part of me. It took me training to control her to realize that I didn't need to control *her* at all. She was me, and I was her. We were one being and once I understood that; it became easier to tap into changing my form.

"Once yeh are feeling confident with shiftin', we will work on yer other gifts. Like using yer dragon fire," he said.

"We will?" I asked. "How? Where?" I was bone tired, but his words gave me a spark of energy. For once I was more excited than nervous to tap into my other 'gifts', as he'd called them.

"I have an idea, but it can wait," he nodded to something behind me. Turning around, I saw Kane, Alaric, Nix and a couple of members of the group they'd been training with heading our way. Raine and Miles.

They were training just as hard and were no doubt as tired as I was, but you'd never tell with the way they all seemed to be enjoying easy conversation and laughing together.

"Hey," I said, waving. "How was training today? Feeling prepared for Hazelbrook?" I asked as they reached us.

"It was really good, yeah. Well, once the males sorted their shit out. Kane gave me this too, which is pretty fucking epic." Raine said, holding up the sword that had given me many sleepless nights back in the castle when I shared quarters with Elikai. "How about you?" she finished.

I shouldn't have been caught off guard or surprised that she'd been the one to answer–I'd not had a chance to properly talk to the female yet but from what I had seen, she didn't struggle with confidence–but still I was.

She was slight in her fae form, a force in her wolf form and one of the few thrakos females I'd met. She wore her long dark hair in a tight braid that snaked over her shoulder and had a look in her almost black eyes that said she wasn't afraid to speak her mind and wouldn't lose sleep if she hurt your feelings in the process. I liked her.

"Good, thanks," I said. "I'm not as scared to sneeze as I was yesterday, so that's something."

"What do you have against sneezing? I heard that if you do four in a row during sex, it's meant to trigger an explosive orgasm."

Braxton choked, Nix and I laughed, Miles looked like he wanted the ground to swallow him, and Kane seemed suddenly very interested in finding out more.

"I dinnae think it was explosive orgasms she was afraid of," Alaric mumbled, and Kane gave me a look that said *challenge accepted.*

"Ha, no, definitely not. More that I'd accidentally burn someone to a crisp," I clarified.

"Oh, right. Well, I don't recommend that," Raine said. "Anyway, we were just talking about having dinner around the campfire together tonight, so Alaric and Kane can talk us through the layout of the village. You should join us."

It was a nice idea. We hadn't been invited to strategize with the other rebels often, and certainly not to socialize, but I'd kind of been looking forward to being sandwiched in between my males in our tiny tent at the earliest opportunity.

Still, this was more important; they needed to be as prepared as possible before they entered Hazelbrook. Not to mention that Kane had clearly made a lot of headway today with the rebels and this was a great chance for them to get to know him better, outside of the training ring.

"Sure," I said. "Sounds good."

WE SAT on wooden stumps circling the firepit and I helped myself to a bowl of the bubbling stew and some bread before the hungry warriors around me devoured it all.

Raine sat opposite me, still carrying Kane's sword, and I wondered whether she liked it so much because it was so valuable or because she knew it had killed Augustus Regis. Or maybe she just liked the feeling that came with carrying sharp, pointy things capable of slaying her enemies?

I found my hands wandering to Mayhem and Chaos that sat at my hips and realized I could definitely relate to the latter.

I had so much to thank Axel for when I saw him. Not just helping Alaric get out of the castle, going through with the battle bond to be our eyes and ears in the castle, protecting Nix's mum or the tiny tent and the copious amounts of lube he'd packed. But he'd reunited me with my twin daggers and though I was learning to fight as a dragon, which didn't require daggers, carrying my blades again felt like carrying my parents with me. My protectors.

Whether he knew how much they meant to me or not, I'd be forever grateful that they'd not ended up lost in the castle somewhere, never to be wielded by me again.

I sat between Kane and Nix, only I didn't feel like I was torn between them. They weren't deep in any meaningful conversation together or putting the realms to rights or anything, but just the fact they were comfortable socializing together was huge progress.

Nix had brought Camille, the female he'd been using as his source with him. There was a rosy flush to her face as they watched the large fire beyond their bowls. She was definitely his type. And not just in the blood sense.

He was more and more himself by the day, though there were definitely parts of him that would never be the same again. It broke my heart, but the only thing he hated more than me asking him if he was okay, was me looking at him with pity in my eyes, so I tried to just act like we used to.

Once everyone finished eating, we stacked our bowls to one side, and Alaric pulled out a large sheet of parchment.

He'd mapped out the brownie village to the best of his knowledge and was talking through the route they would take in and out.

Everyone listened closely as he went through plan A and then plan B, but once he'd finished and was answering questions the group had, I noticed Kane talking quietly with a little boy who'd joined us. Raine's brother. He couldn't have been more than eight.

"–big sister said you killed the evil King with the sword you gave her, so why doesn't that make you the King now?" the boy asked Kane.

If the combination of natural childhood innocence and curiosity, mixed with the seriousness of the subject matter, was surprising to Kane, he didn't show it. Such was life growing up in the Vale: you learnt about the ugliness of the circle of life pretty early on.

"It doesn't exactly work like that," Kane whispered back.

"Why not? The evil King took the throne from the good King by killing him. My mama said no one even asked to see a body before they accepted his claim and new Lores," the boy said.

"It wasn't usurping this time. Not exactly. It's complicated. Besides, I have a twin brother who has spent his life wanting to be King someday, and the realm believes him to be the heir. He's not a very nice male..."

"Raine said he's a nasty piece of shit, like your dad."

"OK, looks like we're calling a spade a spade then..." Kane muttered to himself before saying to the boy. "He is. They both were."

"But *you're* not," the boy said confidently, and I didn't miss the way Kane's eyes widened in surprise. "And you're an heir too, right?"

"Yeah," Kane said.

"So you could be King if you wanted to be?"

"If I challenged my brother and won, yeah. But I've never wanted to be. I hadn't even thought about it until recently," Kane said honestly.

He was speaking so quietly, that if he hadn't been right next to me, I'd have struggled to hear. Alaric was at his other side and must have finished his mapping meeting, because he met my eyes and gave a small nod. We were both listening in with bated breath.

"But you've thought about it now?" the boy asked.

"Yeah."

"And?"

"I don't want to be King. There are fae out there who'd do a much better job of it than me, and I'd probably hate every minute of it."

"But?"

"Can you keep a secret?" Kane asked, and the boy leaned in close, nodding his head. "If the only alternative is Elikai, I'd do it."

The boy dove at him, wrapping his arms around Kane's middle and hugged him tightly. Kane looked to me as if to say *Help!* And I just smiled.

"Da'," Alaric said, standing from his stool. "Can I have a word? *Alone*."

"Aye, son." Braxton said, getting to his feet too. "An' Blaze, yer mum will be lookin' for yer, it's time yeh should be in bed."

"I'm ready for bed too," I said through a yawn.

"We'll meet you back at the tent, Alaric," Kane said and Alaric nodded.

Raine walked over to her little brother to pry him away from Kane. Lifting him into her arms, she said, "I'm not sure what that was about, Blazey boy. But if you want him to give you a fancy weapon too, I'm pretty sure he only had the one."

Kane chuckled, then held out a hand to help me stand, which I took with no objections. "Night all," I said, and we walked back in contented silence.

Today was a good day, I thought as I climbed into my tent for snuggles and sleep.

CHAPTER 34
Nekane

I woke from a deep sleep feeling refreshed for the first time in what felt like forever, my beautiful princess cocooned in my arms. The only thing missing was the hulking male who I could usually feel at my back.

I'd slept like the dead, and hadn't even felt him leave. He was probably just eager to get to the training ring early again. We were set to leave for Hazelbrook tomorrow, and he was sensible enough to know he didn't need the distraction of an impromptu BJ breakfast again, like yesterday.

His loss. I sucked at those in the best way.

Eva stirred shortly after me so we washed, dressed and made our way over to the main part of camp to grab something to eat and a canteen of water each before training.

"There yeh are," Braxton said as I stuffed some stale, nutty, buttered loaf in my mouth. It wasn't great, but I'd take it over Kraken entrails any day. I shuddered at the memory of the foul feast my father had put on to celebrate wiping out their entire race.

As much as I hated it, there was nothing I could do about the Kraken's now. It was too late, so I blocked those thoughts and focused on Braxton. "Morning," I said.

"Alaric wanted me to let yeh know he's gone on a hunt this mornin' to get some meat, so yeh dinnae have to worry about finding food while yeh travel."

"Oh. When did he go?" Eva asked, her surprise was evident in her tone.

"Yeh just missed him. He's asked yeh to head up trainin' this mornin', Nekane. Said he wants yeh all fighting back-to-back today, an' that he'll leave it for yeh to decide which combinations of skills to pair up."

It was strange that Alaric hadn't mentioned he was going to hunt. From what I had seen since being here, it was usually the wolves who went, so it made sense. And they were never gone too long before returning with the goods, so they must stick pretty close to camp.

But still, why not wake Eva and I to let us know?

It didn't feel right for him not being here, but any irritation I might have over it eased a little as I set my mind to the task he'd left for me. I found I was actually quite looking forward to seeing what happened in practice. My mind was racing with thoughts of whose gifts would be more complementary to each other when wielded in unison.

"Sounds good," I said.

He nodded. "I'll come over with yeh to make sure yeh get no arguments from the others, though yeh seem to be doin' a pretty good job yerself of winnin' them over." I chose to ignore his comment, but he turned his gaze to Eva, anyway, "You good to carry on with yer trainin' without me for a bit?" he asked.

"Sure. Do you just want me to keep working on shifting between forms?" she asked.

"Aye. But today I want to see if yeh can do it in stages. Like this." He held out a hand, and we both watched as he shifted each fae-like nail into a long black claw one by one.

A partial shift. It was incredible to watch, so slowly and so close up, albeit a little creepy. It was something most shifters could do, but I understood it took a deep understanding and connection with both or all forms to master.

"So you want me to partially shift?" Eva asked, and Braxton nodded. "I'm not even sure that's possible for my kind, but OK, I'll try it." Then to me she said, "I'll see you at lunch, Kane."

"Good luck, Princess," I said. "You've got this."

I walked with Braxton to the ring, where everyone was already gathered, looking much more eager today than they had been yesterday morning. It was refreshing, and I even got a wave from Raine and a nod from Nix. Progress.

Raine's little brother, Blaze, had come to spectate too. "Hey, kiddo," I said, ruffling his hair, as we joined the group and I stood next to him.

"Morning Prince Kane," he beamed.

"Just Kane." I chastised gently, but he just rolled his eyes at me.

I had no idea why I'd decided to admit to him something I'd not even wanted to admit to myself, let alone out loud last night. Maybe I just hadn't been able to deal with the idea of letting him down as he'd questioned me.

To him, it was so obvious that I should want to be king, like it was a black and white decision. But that didn't mean I wanted it for myself. What I'd experienced in the last couple of weeks had taught me that I wanted to dedicate my life to defending the realm against evil, not run the entire fucking thing.

My family had proven they didn't deal well when given power. What if I didn't either? What if it was in our blood? The thought of becoming like them repulsed and scared the shit out of me.

Not only was I made up of half of my father, but my mother was a princess of Mount Mortum, a kingdom revered by my father for its cruelty. I couldn't help but question if that was why Elikai was capable of being even worse than our father? What if I had it in me too and power triggered it?

Still, I hadn't lied to Blaze, I *would* do whatever I could to stop my brother from taking the throne and as the only one who could take his place as heir afterward, I knew I had to do it.

Fates, if I was lucky, maybe I'd be usurped before the power inevitably tainted or changed me. And if I died in the fight for the throne that I knew was inevitable, I had no doubt my last prayer to the fates would be that Elikai himself be usurped. Ideally by someone like Braxton or Alaric or Eva. Someone who cared about all races without prejudice.

Before any of that, we needed to be successful in this mission, and Alaric had left me in charge this morning, so it was time to get to work.

"Iona, Raine," I said. "I want you to pair up today. Before we start, spend some time coming up with a strategy to incorporate the use of all of your gifts to take on your opponents. Witch magic, bear claws, thrakos fire, wolf intelligence. Use them all in any and every way you can. Surprise us."

Raine nodded, and I could almost hear the cogs in her brain working as she immediately began to strategize. Iona, however, gave Braxton the side eye.

"Great choice, Kane. They'll make a strong pairin'," Braxton said, nodding his approval and subtly quashing any argument Iona may have thought to make.

It was good Eva wasn't here. She already had a short fuse when it came to her males and that particular bear shifter.

"Jarrah and Miles. You will be a team. You have similar skills to the females, but where they have the brute of a bear, you have the speed and secrets of the spider. Silk webs and venom at your disposal."

They nodded and moved to stand next to each other.

"That leaves me and Nix. You good with that?" I asked the male, more a courtesy than a question, and he nodded. "Good. Let's break off into our three groups for a few hours and focus on working together. We can come up with some moves that could be useful in battle, but wouldn't be possible had it not been for you mixing your abilities. Then when Alaric's back, we can put the theory to real life practice and go up against each other in our teams. Winners stay on."

"YOU HAVE THAT SHIELD SUSSED NOW," I said to Nix as we walked toward where Eva waited.

Nix and I had been working pretty well together. Our game plan for taking on the others later would be for him to be our defense, to protect us from behind with his thrakos wings and from the front with a magic shield, while I would be on the attack, long sword in hand.

"Just need you to not get under my feet now," he said, half joking.

It was beyond strange. At first, we'd begun to practice moving together. It was definitely hard to get used to putting all your trust into the fae at your back, relying on them to read your next move and do their part in unison. To allow them to become your shadow.

But over the hours, we had gotten pretty good, pretty fast. I hadn't been able to watch much of what the others were doing, but they seemed as focused as Nix and I.

As Braxton came over and called lunch, I knew I wasn't the only one looking forward to showing Alaric what we'd been working on.

"Hey, Princess. No Alaric yet?" I asked.

"No. He should be back by now though. Hunts never take this long. I asked Braxton, but he wasn't concerned," she said. "I see you have a fan down there at the training ring," she added with a chuckle. "Blaze isn't it?"

"Oh him, yeah," I said, rubbing the back of my neck. "I have no idea why."

"I think I might," she said.

At the same time as Nix said, "I do."

Apparently, my conversation with the kid hadn't been entirely private. Either that, or there was something else going on that I wasn't privy to.

"Look, I heard what you said to him last night, that you'd challenge your brother for the throne. It was no small thing, Kane," she said.

I sighed. "And you Nix, you heard too?"

"Me and everyone else that sat around the fire," Nix confirmed.

An uncomfortable feeling suddenly came over me, like a wave of dread.

Everyone else that sat around the fire…

"Wait. You don't think…" I trailed off.

"What?" Eva asked.

"Why isn't Alaric back yet? From what I've seen, hunts don't usually take this long." I said, thinking aloud and not waiting for an answer. "You said Braxton wasn't concerned when you asked him… What are the chances Alaric heard what I'd said to Blaze and decided to do something really fucking stupid?"

Eva sucked in a breath as she followed my trail of thought.

"Like what?" Nix asked, but before I had a chance to answer, he'd caught on. "He went off to talk to Braxton right after your conversation with Blaze... I'd assumed at the time it was to do with you finally deciding you were prepared to go for the crown because of the timing of it, but Braxton was present, he would have heard the conversation himself, so why go off to talk about it?"

"For fate's sake," I muttered, running a hand through my hair, fully connecting the dots and coming to a conclusion that I didn't like one bit.

"There's Braxton." Eva snapped. "Let's go have a chat about where his son really is."

He saw us coming, and took a deep breath, as though he realized his ruse was up and was mustering the strength to deal with us.

"Braxton, where's Alaric?" Eva questioned.

"The truth this time," I said before he came up with some more bullshit about a hunt.

He cleared his throat, gave Eva and I an apologetic look and finally said, "About eight hours run from here, headin' to Hazelbrook."

"Fuck," I hissed. "What is he thinking?! Hold on. You knew? And you let him go?"

"I agreed with his reasons." Braxton said, folding his arms over his chest.

"Who's he with?" Nix asked.

"No one," I said, through a strained voice, glaring at Braxton.

I was as mad at myself as I was at him for covering for Alaric all morning. I should have worked it out sooner. He'd never have left the camp to go on a hunt without telling us. But he would definitely leave without a word if it was to do something he knew full well we'd never agree to, yet planned to do anyway.

"Aye. He left alone during the night. Told me to buy him time this mornin', so yeh didnae get any ideas about going after him or catchin' up when yeh found out. Said it would be much less risky if he went alone. He realized it wasnae worth the risk of you goin', when we dinnae ken if the letter even holds anythin' of importance or value," he explained.

"So what? He just decided to put added risk on his own safety to save us risking ours? Why?" I seethed.

Meeting me dead in the eyes with his red ones, he said. "He sees yeh as his King, Nekane. Has for years. All he needed was for you to admit yeh saw yerself that way too. Last nigh', yeh did."

"Holy fucking shit, Eva!" Nix gasped.

My eyes shot to the female in question who'd not breathed a word since Braxton had come clean.

Her eyes glowed green, but in place of her pupils were black slits. Her wrists and forearms were coated in silver scales, like mirror fragments, but I had no doubt they were as impenetrable as her scales in dragon form.

Where she clenched her fists at her sides, blood dripped to the ground as though the nails digging into her palms had morphed into talons. My jaw fates near hit the floor at the ethereal beauty of her.

"Eva, calm down," Nix said. "Braxton was only doing what Alaric told him to do."

"Nah. Dinnae calm down. Hold on to that rage or whatever emotion is causing the partial shift, memorize it, remember the anger or pain or fear that triggered it and hold on to it. This is perfect."

"*She's* perfect," I breathed and her slitted eyes moved to me. "*Stunning.*"

"We need to go after Alaric," she gritted out. I wasn't sure whether it was Eva or the dragon speaking, or perhaps both?

"We can't," I told her. "Alaric knew what he was doing. If we were to go after him now, we'd have no hope of catching up. He knows we have no choice but to wait here for his return."

"What if something happens to him? What if he's captured and we have no way of even knowing?" Her fists were still clenched tightly at her side, and her breaths were coming too quickly. "I can't… I can't do nothing!"

"Yeh won't be doin' nothin'. He will be back in three days, four at most. Use that time to perfect yer partial shift, so yeh can kick his arse when he gets back if yeh have to. An' Kane, he wants yeh to focus yer energy on trainin' the rebels to fight back to back. When he gets back with that letter, he wants to see not just yer little group fighting in pairs and teams, but every rebel here willin' to pick up a sword. He wants yeh to start building yer army."

For fuck's sake, Alaric. I sighed.

He'd played this perfectly; we were at his mercy and helpless to do anything to help him. But he could help himself, I reminded myself.

He was the best warrior and strategist in the realm. He just needed to sneak into Hazelbrook and get a letter. If he wasn't confident he could do it alone, he wouldn't have gone. I had to believe that.

I took Eva in a hug and kissed her forehead. She released the heavy breath she'd been holding and with it, her partial shift dropped.

"We can kill him once he gets home, Princess," I promised.

CHAPTER 35

Alaric

Act first and ask the fates for forgiveness later.

My mantra circled my mind every time I thought about Kane and Angel back at camp. So for almost two days now, I had thought of little else other than those nine words. I knew what I needed to do, focus on putting one paw in front of the other until I had the letter and could get back to them.

I had no doubt that they would be furious with me for making the decision to do this alone, but the moment I heard Kane admit to that young male that he would be willing to challenge his brother for the throne, it had no longer been a choice.

Sending him on a potential suicide mission with potentially no gain, after he'd finally admitted aloud what I'd been waiting to hear for what felt like a fucking age, wasn't something I was willing to do.

I'd told my da' that I planned to go alone and needed him to cover for me while I put as much distance between me and them as possible. It was the only way I knew for certain they wouldn't come after me.

"Be safe, son," was all he'd said when I'd finished telling him of my new plan, and I knew he would take care of the rest. We may be too alike in some ways, but in this he understood why I had to. Especially after he too had heard the words Kane had spoken.

The last time I'd been heading for Hazelbrook, it was to find Kane and Angel. This time I was running away from them, and it went against all my instincts, but I was doing it for them. For everyone. No matter how fucking wrong it felt. My duty hadn't ended as I'd left the castle grounds after all. I just wasn't the general to the pretender king anymore.

When I'd returned from my private talk with Braxton, Kane and Angel had been fast asleep, so I was careful not to disturb them as I climbed in.

I lay awake for a few painfully long hours before carefully sneaking back out in the wee hours. I found the clothes and supplies that Braxton had promised to leave for me so that I could leave swiftly. I secured the satchel to my back and shifted into my wolf.

I'd run fast and hard up to this point, sticking to the shadows as much as I could to allow my dark fur to conceal me. Thankfully, the fates had been on my side and I hadn't encountered any trouble.

It was close to sundown now, and the dull lights of Hazelbrook finally came into view. I was ahead of schedule by several hours. If we'd traveled as a group, the full two days would have been necessary, but I'd made it in just over a day and a half by skipping sleep and going alone.

I shifted into fae form and shook off the satchel from my mid-section, using the movement to stretch out my tired muscles. I dressed in black from head to boot and covered most of my face with the low hanging hood of the cloak.

This wasn't a mission you could plan perfectly. There were too many unknowns for that kind of luxury. After all, I was looking for an envelope or piece of parchment that was fuck knows where, and couldn't even ask for someone to point me in the right direction, but I was here now and I didn't plan to leave empty-handed.

I took several deep glugs of water from my canteen, dropped it into the satchel, and took out a dagger. Slinging the ropes of my bag over one shoulder, I carefully made my way toward civilization.

Reaching the end of the forest, I lingered in the dark depths of the trees and waited to check that no one was around or heading this way. Deciding it was safe, I crossed the cobblestones and dipped into a narrow alley between two buildings, melting into the protection of the shadows it offered.

Assuming it had already been delivered, the letter was likely in the mayor's office or home. Possibly the village hall. But with the sun still slowly moving down in the sky, neither of those places was easy to reach unnoticed.

I moved deeper into the alleyway and waited for complete darkness to cover the brownie village. To my annoyance, the shuffling footsteps and whispers of conversation from the adjoining street only seemed to grow louder and more frequent the longer I waited. I listened to the voices, but none of what was being said was helpful.

Impatiently, I continued into the alley until I reached a brick wall. A dead end. My eyes landed on an old metal ladder screwed into the stonework that I hoped would lead to the roof of the buildings I was sandwiched between.

Though I could hear plenty, I was basically blind to what was going on around me while in the alley, but if I could get to the top of the building, I would have a pretty good vantage point of the village.

The sky was as dark as it was likely going to get now, the midnight blue splashed across the sky with the occasional black cloud drifting lazily past the moon. Holding the dagger between my teeth, I climbed up, careful to tread evenly to remain as silent as possible and praying to the fates that it could hold a male of my size when it had obviously been made for the much smaller brownies.

It creaked and groaned beneath my weight, but thankfully held out while I climbed up onto the flat roof. Dropping down low, I crawled my way to the edge and was pleased to find the building I was on top of was higher than most of the others surrounding it.

It looked out over the village square, to the bustling center of Hazelbrook. There were several street vendors dotted around the space, packing away their wares in the light of the candle lanterns illuminating the area. A shoemaker, a blacksmith and a winemaker, among others.

In the center was a noticeboard, with two pieces of parchment pinned to it.

I couldn't make out the words this far away with just my fae vision, so I closed my eyes for a moment and when I opened them, I was looking through those of my wolf.

One of the brownies sniffed the air as though their senses were warning them of a threat nearby. But after a brief look around, he chose to ignore it and carried on about his business packing away.

The notices were clearer now, but still not as clear as they would be to my thrakos eyes. The threat of a shifter was much easier to ignore though than that of a thrakos.

Squinting, I saw that one notice was unsurprisingly the WANTED poster, obvious by the triangle of three portraits. But I still couldn't make out the words on the other bulletin.

Yes, I'd lectured the team we'd put together for this mission on not shifting into their thrakos forms, but they weren't here and didn't need to know I wasn't opposed to breaking my own rules sometimes.

Between one blink and the next, I looked at the notice through thrakos eyes.

A few of the brownies below bristled, and began to look around more frantically as they sensed the threat that I could be, catching one another's wide eyes.

I quickly read the contents of the bulletin.

We, Molrad and Ornus, cordially invite you to join us on the twelfth day of the third month at Hazelbrook Hall as we exchange vows and celebrate the start of our lives together. Come one, come all, and be a part of this grand celebration.

A wedding. Good for them… fucking useless for me. I shifted my eyes back quickly, but it didn't seem to help ease the nerves of the brownies in the square.

"What was that?" I heard the shoemaker brownie say.

"You felt it too?" the blacksmith asked him.

"I'd say it's to do with that horde soldier who arrived earlier," a female passerby said, suddenly grabbing my undivided attention. The two brownies waved the female over to join them and my eyes narrowed as I recognized her as the receptionist from the Beguiling Broom.

"Come for taxes during mourning?" the shoemaker snarked. "Are they that desperate to take our coin?"

"Perhaps," she shrugged. "He checked into the B&B this evening and sent me to arrange a meeting with the mayor for early tomorrow morning. I'm just on my way back from the mayor's house now. He wasn't happy to be disturbed."

Fucking perfect.

They continued to gossip, but I had what I needed, so tuned out of their conversation and shuffled back toward the ladder. The Beguiling Broom was on the southern edge of the village, and I wasted no time dropping down into the alley and moving quickly back to the forest from where I'd come.

Finally, a fucking lead I could work with. Maybe the fates were on my side.

I LAY in wait behind a row of high bushes outside the Beguiling Broom, watching the receptionist make her way up the dark street at a painfully slow speed.

As she finally neared my position, I rolled the pine cone I'd found on the way here and had since been holding directly into her path.

"Where did you come from?" she asked the fucking cone, bending to pick it up, exactly as I'd hoped.

Before she stood straight again, I was behind her. My right palm plastered across her mouth as my left reached around her waist. I picked her up and sprinted for the cover of the bushes again, holding her close to my chest.

She was already shifting in my grip, becoming larger as she angered, and I knew I was seconds away from her razor jaws chowing down on my hand.

"I dinnae want to hurt yeh, lass," I growled low, but she writhed and wriggled, forcing me to tighten my grip to a suffocating level. I'd been bitten by a brownie before and had no plans to relive that experience. "I dinnae want to hurt yeh," I repeated.

She continued to kick and twist in my arms, but eventually I felt her commitment to escape me ebb a little.

"If I remove my hand, do yeh swear to the fates yeh winnae scream?" I asked, and she nodded several times before going still. "Good." I kept my grip strong around her body, but carefully removed my palm from her mouth. "The horde soldier staying here. Which room is he in?" I asked.

She was breathing heavily, clearly petrified, but thankfully seemed willing to talk to save herself. "Room f-f-five," she stuttered.

"Ground floor?"

"Y-yes."

"Front or back o' the building?" I asked.

"A-At the end of the corridor, o-over t-there," she nodded to the last window on the right that peeked out behind the bush where we were concealed.

"Does the horde soldier have dinner reservations in yer tavern tonight?" I asked, and she nodded.

Fuck, she was trembling, but a solid plan was finally coming together in my head and I couldn't let her go until I had the information I needed.

"What time?" I demanded.

"H-He's probably eating now. P-please don't h-h-hurt me," she begged.

"I winnae hurt yeh so long as yeh cooperate. Soon, I'm gonnae let yeh go and yer goin' to walk in like nothin' happened. Yer goin' to check the soldier is in there eatin', then walk to one o' the tavern window's visible from here and nod once if he's in there. Understood?"

"Y-Yes," she agreed, but it was too quick, too easy.

I let the silence hang for a few minutes. I needed to know she wasn't just giving me lip service, only to walk inside and give up my position to the horde soldier at her first opportunity.

To do that, I needed her scared of the consequences, to fear me more than she feared the soldier.

When she couldn't bear the silence any longer, she said, "I-I swear it to the fates."

"Good. And then yer goin' to forget we ever had this conversation, yeah?"

She gulped. "Y-yes."

I released my grip and righted the hood of my cloak to ensure my face was fully covered, but she didn't turn to look at me anyway. She took a few deep, shaky breaths to calm herself enough to shrink back down to her usual size and then walked on stiff legs toward the entrance of the B&B.

She paused at the doorway, stood a little straighter, her shoulders visibly pulling back, then went inside.

Several minutes went by with her out of sight, far longer than she needed to do as I'd ordered. Just as I was about to start making a plan B, she appeared silhouetted in the middle tavern window, nodded once as instructed, and then disappeared once more.

There was every chance she was bullshitting me and I could be walking into a trap, but I didn't have much choice. I needed to get the letter and get the fuck out of Hazelbrook and back to Kane and Angel in the Vale.

The street was empty, so I didn't waste any more time on thoughts about all the ways this could be an ambush, and instead moved quickly.

Between one heartbeat and the next, I was at the window to what was apparently room five. I tested the sill, checking if I could lift the window to enter. Unfortunately, it didn't budge.

Fuck. I shifted my hand to my thrakos claws and etched a rough circle into the glass. Pushing firmly at the top, the bottom of the circle popped out, and I wriggled it free, cringing as the glass screeched a little as I removed it.

I placed it down against the building, carefully hiding it in the long weeds. Then reaching inside, I lifted the latch and wiggled the window high enough for me to fit through.

The scent of a warlock was very present, leading me to believe the brownie hadn't lied about this being the room assigned to the horde soldier.

There were plenty of warlocks in the horde, and nothing in the room made it particularly obvious which one it was, but I had no doubt that he'd recognize me the moment he saw me, so I needed to search the place fast so that couldn't happen.

The room looked much the same as the one I'd shared with Kane and Angel, though the bed was still perfectly made. The space was sparse, aside from a horde issued backpack which sat on the desk table below the mirror.

I crossed the space, opened the bag and turned to empty its contents out onto the bed behind with a shake.

I smirked as a crisp envelope looked back at me, with the royal wax seal still perfectly intact, as it lay amongst the other items. Along with a small bag of gold coin and a few items of clothing. I picked up a garment at random and brought it to my nose. It would be helpful to know which soldier was in the building in case it was someone I may be able to trust.

As I inhaled, there was a faint clink of metal touching metal from the doorway. The room's occupier was back and sliding their key into the lock chamber. *Fuck.*

Dropping the garment, I swiped the envelope and bag of coin from the bed and dropped them into my satchel, tightening the strings as I crossed back to the window.

The key turned as I fastened the bag around my waist, and I shifted into my wolf just in time and dove through the open window. I didn't pause to look back as I sprinted for the forest on all fours, but just as the trees around me began to thicken, a familiar dizziness hit me.

"Guess what, guess what, guess what, boss!" came Axel's voice through the bond.

"Can it wait?" I thought back. *"Now is not a good fucking time."*

I could still function with Axel in my head, but it was harder. My vision wasn't as sharp, my senses were distracted, and I just couldn't focus the way I needed in order to navigate threats and obstructions simultaneously.

"When is it ever a good time? Literally never, apparently. Besides, I have good news. You really want to hear this!" he thought excitedly.

"Make it quick, then get the fuck outta my head."

"We sent the human back! And this time, this time, the shield around the portal came down for good!"

As much as good news was always welcomed, I desperately needed my mind to myself right now. There was no way the horde warlock would have found a hole in his open window and his bag upturned with the letter and coin missing, and not given chase.

I needed to run faster than I'd ever run, lose any tail I might have. But right now, I was moving at a fast jog at best, easily slow enough for a warlock to keep pace with.

"That's good, Axel. Fill me in later, yeah?"

"Did you hear that? Is someone down here?" Axel thought, and I could sense a sudden nervousness in his aura.

"Who yeh talking to?" I demanded.

"Edelin. Fuck, I think there's someone down here. No. Fuck. Graves and Slo–" I howled as pain tore through my skull.

I tripped and rolled, coming to a stop only when I crashed into a tree. My ribs took the brunt of it, but that pain was overshadowed by the ripping and tearing taking place in my brain.

The howl became a whine as I pawed at my ears frantically, which felt like a river of hot wax was being poured through them.

I couldn't feel him.

I couldn't fucking feel Axel.

His voice was gone, his aura utterly and completely absent. Where his presence had been was just… empty, non-existent outside of the thudding misery and burning throb that had taken its place.

I whimpered as the pain eventually began to ebb. It had been exactly like the agony of the battle bond being forged, only somehow, I knew in my gut this was it being ripped away. But that meant…

"Axel, brother, talk to me. Now is a good time. Anytime is a good time. Just fucking answer me." I thought desperately through the ache in my mind, but my calls only landed in a hollow vastness that was once my connection with the male I looked at and loved like a brother.

He couldn't be dead. No. There was no way he could be dead.

Fuck that. I refused to believe in a reality where that was the case. The realm needed more males like Axel, but he was the only one I cared about. It had to be something else…

Graves and Sloane had clearly found him, found them both, and the link had severed…

Maybe he was unconscious? Maybe Edelin had removed the bond when they realized they'd been caught? Fuck. I didn't know enough about the ancient magic to know if those were even possibilities.

I needed to go to the castle. I needed to find them, see for myself what the fuck was happening.

I forced myself to stand on four paws, then launched into a run with everything I had, but was caught mid leap as another sharp yelp left my lips, and an entirely new agony cut into me.

I whirled around, only to find my right side wouldn't cooperate. *What the fuck.* Something sharp and strong was wrapped around my hind leg, holding on with a grip like a bear trap.

"Long time no see, General," came a familiar voice as its owner stepped out from behind a wide trunk, a vine whip wrapped around his clenched fist.

Jarid.

He tugged the vine, hard and fast, forcing a howl to tear from my chest. His bald head shone under the moon and the disturbing smile across his lips told me he was enjoying this.

Cunt.

He'd been in the horde for centuries, was capable and did a decent job at everything I'd ever tasked him with. Everything apart from winning the respect of his peers.

I knew it; he knew it, everyone fucking knew it. And the glint in his eyes now told of the rush he was feeling finally holding some power over another soldier. His General of centuries, no less.

I growled, showing him my teeth that would soon be tearing through his skin and gnawing on bone. He pulled the vine again, and it sliced further into my skin. I couldn't see the extent of the injury, but I could smell the blood and I was pretty fucking sure it had sliced through fur and muscles and was wrapped around the bone.

"Before I drag you back to the castle, I have some questions for you, Alaric. Shift back. Now." he demanded, as though talking to someone that wasn't about to murder him as soon as the stifling pain receded enough that I could bring myself to pull my leg free.

I needed to get to the castle and find Axel and Edelin, but I wasn't about to let Jarid drag me there as his prisoner. I didn't have time for his inferiority complex and bullshit, but I also couldn't risk pissing him off any further and risk him doing damage to my leg that would completely incapacitate me more than I already was.

"Shift," he demanded again with another pull of the vine whip.

The sheer magnitude of pain that shot through my entire being told me that the injury might be worse than I'd predicted.

Raising his free palm, he muttered *'Atharrachadh'*. Change.

I clenched my jaw so tightly as the transformation back to my fae form was forced upon me that I was surprised my teeth didn't crack under the pressure.

I refused to give Jarid any more pleasure by hearing me cry out in pain inflicted by his hand. My wolf's reaction to pain was instinctual, something I couldn't control, but in my fae form, I'd fucking die before I let him see the full extent of the agony he held me in.

I glanced down at my leg and was greeted by exposed bone tearing out through the skin that should have been covering it. My leg wasn't just being shredded into by the whip like I'd thought. He'd timed his attack perfectly as I'd sprung off the ground to run, and the bone had snapped against the whips' sudden resistance to my wolf's movement.

I needed to set the break before my body began to heal. Any injury inflicted in my wolf form would remain in my fae and thrakos forms, too.

Though constant pain controlling my body was making it hard to think straight, I remembered the weapon I had at my disposal that Jarid would not have accounted for. I wasn't just part wolf. I was a hybrid fucking thrakos. And he'd soon fucking learn who really held the power here.

Holding my breath, I shifted into my thrakos form. Using Jarid's disbelief to my advantage, I raked a claw to tear through the vine, removing the control he'd had over me. I knew I couldn't bear any weight on my leg, not for a long fucking while yet. At least until it had been set and healed sufficiently, but I could fly to some degree. Not like a dragon, but I was willing to put that particular gift to the test to get the fuck away from here.

Getting to the castle wasn't a possibility, not in this condition, not when I needed to stay under the cover of the trees in the forest to have any hope of traveling in thrakos form without being spotted.

I'd have to go back to the camp, have the bone set properly, get Kane to heal me, and then I could go after Axel and Edelin. I wasn't sure what Axel's fate would be, whether they'd kill or question him. I sent a prayer to the fates that it was the latter, because he was smart enough to keep himself alive.

He'd give them pieces of non-information to string them along enough to keep him breathing. Or so I had to believe. I couldn't allow myself to think of the alternative.

As for Edelin, she was too valuable to Elikai for him to allow her to be executed. Yes, I was certain they wouldn't kill her. But they could make her life very fucking uncomfortable.

Now free of the vine, I willed the thrakos flames to burst from my body to keep Jarid back as I used my arms and good leg to stand.

Suppressing a wince, I tried to ignore just how much it fucking hurt and focused instead on how I would make the cunt wish he'd left me in my wolf form.

Jarid's eyes widened with unspoken fear in the face of the fire engulfing my body. I quickly turned my back on him, swinging a leathery wing wide enough so that a deadly sharp tip skimmed his neck far too quickly for him to have any hope of reacting.

He cried out, and the sound gave me a boost of much needed energy. It wouldn't kill him, unfortunately, but it would make breathing really fucking difficult for a while as all of his energy went into healing it.

I glanced over my shoulder to be sure I'd aimed true, and smiled as I saw blood spurting from the wound, his hands grabbing at his very open throat.

I was sure he would hope it killed him, failure wasn't an option in the horde. Not when Augustus was in charge, and I doubted his maniac of a son was any different. A better male might have made sure it was fatal, but not me. Not today.

Every moment counted, so I flapped my wings in slow measured strokes, enough to lift a few inches off the earth to take my weight off my broken and bloodied leg. It still hurt like fuck as it hung useless, but it was fixable.

Extinguishing the flames, I took a deep breath, sent a silent prayer to the fates that I'd make it back and see Kane and Angel again, then flew and flew and flew.

CHAPTER 36

Evangelia

Day one without Alaric had been filled with anger.

On Braxton's advice, I'd held onto the emotion and used it to channel my partial shift. It didn't matter that my rage had helped immensely, making quick progress with my training, and it didn't make up for the reason why I was filled with so much anger in the first place.

Just when I had become content in the knowledge that the three of us weren't going to lie to each other anymore, Alaric leaving had felt like a lie and a betrayal.

I knew when I saw him again that he'd argue he hadn't lied, and I'd argue that omitting the truth was the same thing. We'd go back and forth. And then I'd kill him for the worry he'd put us through, just like Kane had promised I could.

I wouldn't really kill him, but I was more than open to hurting him a little. A slap around the head with my dragon's tail would work. It would either knock some sense into him, so he never pulled a stunt like this again. Or it would give him a headache to match the one I'd not been able to ward off since discovering he'd left.

Whether the constant dull throb was due to lack of sleep or constant intrusive thoughts over his safety, I wasn't sure, but I guessed it was likely both contributing to it.

Kane had held onto me tighter than ever that first night, and I was glad for it. Our tiny tent felt too large without Alaric in it. The space where he should have laid was filled with unspoken questions and worries that I knew both Kane and I wanted to ask each other, but couldn't bring ourselves to.

Day two without Alaric had been filled with worry.

We knew, all being well, that he'd be due to arrive at Hazelbrook at some point that night. And with that knowledge, I'd discovered something that I hadn't fully appreciated before. That the anxiety you felt from not knowing what was happening, being utterly blind to it and having no choice but to draw your own conclusions, was in fact far, far worse than the stress of actually being there and seeing it with your own eyes.

I guess, in reality, it would depend on what it was you were seeing. But the things I was imagining would wake even the most hardened folk in a pool of sweat in the middle of the night.

I couldn't know if he arrived safely. We wouldn't know if something had gone wrong.

It wasn't that I didn't think he was perfectly capable of the task he was doing in Hazelbrook. There was arguably no one more capable than the male himself for it. I had full faith in his abilities. I just didn't trust anything or anyone that might be around him.

The mind was an incredible yet impressionable thing, and given the opportunity, was capable of morphing into a very effective, personal torture device. It could happen as quickly as between one thought and the next and knock the feet out from under you.

This was a mental battle. So unlike what I had imagined torture at the hands of an enemy. Now the torturer was your own mind, your own too vivid and wild imagination, and it knew no bounds for the ugly and terrifying things it could subject you to.

And there were no instructions on how to make it stop. Only a deep, dark void that was far too easy to fall into.

One moment I could be watching Kane training the rebels, admiring the way they were all learning to not only respect the male they'd once scorned, but to genuinely like him, and maybe even care for him. I'd feel such pride in my chest. Then in the next moment, I'd think about how Alaric would feel pride too, if he were there to see it, and suddenly my mind was back to why he wasn't there and where he might be. Alone. What he might be feeling, what he might be dealing with.

And that's when my mind's torture would hit with something so awful I couldn't believe I'd managed to think it up in the first place.

Day three without Alaric had been filled with anticipation.

Kane and I had discussed all the different ways we would make Alaric pay for the previous two days of turmoil and torment, just as soon as we saw he was okay. And the anticipation was because we knew that moment could be very soon.

I'd managed a partial shift at will that day, finally managing to get my wings to pop out from my spine. Kane had said that he'd never seen a creature as beautiful, and I'd thanked him by accidentally melting his favored long sword not ten minutes later with my dragon fire.

In the same way that Kane had thrown himself into turning the rebels into warriors, I'd thrown myself into learning my dragon and our gifts. When I transformed fully into my partially shifted form, we truly felt like one being.

I walked on two legs, but I could fly with the silver wings of my stunning beast. Not that I'd been able to practice it too much. We were restricted by the height of the canopy and the circumference of the camp, but I'd managed it a time or two in the space we had to fly laps enjoying the feeling of being able to do so much.

Kane said my green orbs glowed, dimmed only by the jet black slit running down their center. It pleased me to discover that the rest of my facial features remained unaltered. I'd been worried my nose would grow into a great long snout or my teeth would become too big for my mouth. Not that there was anything wrong with that, fates, Alaric made a very handsome wolf after all.

Fuck, Alaric...

He was never far away from my thoughts and his name never failed to make my stomach sink.

I was currently still working on breathing fire, hence Kane's melted sword. But I now knew that unlike the way a thrakos' flames could engulf their body, or be balled between their palms to wield, my flames came only from my throat.

Kane had joked about how I was never to take him down my throat ever again, and I'd told him if that's what he really wanted, I was sure Alaric wouldn't mind double the attention.

Later that night in bed he'd whispered that he took it back, that he was just joking and that a life without the feel of my lips around his shaft was no life at all. He hadn't dropped it, teasing and tickling me until I'd agreed that blowjobs were no longer off the table for him.

It was silly, but I loved him for being a source of comedic relief when I didn't even know I needed it so desperately. He was as worried for Alaric as I was, and was just as angry, but he hadn't let a day pass by without making me smile or laugh over one thing or another. He had made it his personal mission to ensure I was still happy, as if he saw the dark clouds in my mind.

When I laughed, sneezed, or huffed and puffed, little black plumes of sooty smoke would escape my nostrils, but thankfully they didn't seem to be harmful to anyone around us. Braxton called it my irritation indicator, as it only seemed to happen when I was annoyed or angry now.

Overall, they had made a lot of progress in a short space of time, and I was really starting to see the makings of a small army inside our camp.

Though we still had a long way before we would be fit to take on the horde.

Day four without Alaric had been filled with a mixture of hope and nerves.

The day had started with a lot of reassuring words being shared around camp that Alaric could be back at any moment, holding the letter high above his head and waving it around. Kane and I had shared a look of our own that said *Alaric would sooner die than do any such thing*. But still, the hope was there.

As the hours had passed though, and the sun had done its round in the sky, the nerves had slowly been creeping their way in. By nightfall, dread had reared its ugly head again and swallowed whatever hope I had left almost entirely.

That led to today.

Day five without Alaric was shaping up to be the worst of them all so far.

From the moment Kane and I awoke from a terrible night's sleep, to find Alaric's side of the tent still empty, dread had come back with a vengeance, and moved over a little to make room for crushing fear.

With every passing minute, it felt like a dark cloud was creeping its way through camp, poisoning everyone with fears for what might have happened to Alaric.

Well, that's how it felt to me, anyway.

Like an inescapable mist that would surely suffocate you, gripping you by the throat as it forced its way into your mind.

Five days was too long.

We all knew it. Even Braxton, who'd been unshakable, was nervous. He'd proven as much when he'd called a meeting this morning to discuss our 'options'. He'd made out like he had faith in the fates that Alaric would return, but had added that there was no harm in coming up with a Plan B, just in case. That if he wasn't back by the end of the week, we would need to be prepared to send fae after him.

It was exactly the sort of thing that Alaric would have said, and I wondered whether Alaric had any idea how much he and his dad were alike.

"Yer no' concentrating, Evangelia," Braxton said from his usual position propped against a tree.

"Are you surprised?" I snapped, my fuse shorter than ever. There wasn't space in my head right now to focus on training. "It's been five days, Braxton. Five days since your son left this camp on his own. A male whose face appears on wanted posters up and down the realm. Anything could have happened to him in five days!"

"Yeh think I dinnae ken that?" Braxton hissed back. "Yeh think I'm no' as worried as you are?"

"Then why did you let him go?!" I yelled.

I instantly regretted my cruel words the moment they'd fallen from my mouth and hit Braxton like a bucket of ice cold water.

"I'm sorry. I didn't mean that. It's not your fault, I'm just... I'm just so fucking worried about him, but I feel helpless to do anything. I could leave here this afternoon and spend months looking for him, to no avail. He could be anywhere. What if he's hurt? What if he needs us and we aren't even out there looking for him?"

"He'll be back, Evangelia. Yeh need to have faith in him. I've had centuries practice at it, so yeh can take my word for i–"

"Braxton!" Nix's voice called from the northern treeline of camp, cutting Braxton off abruptly and making us both drop into a fighting stance on instinct, ready for anything. "Eva! Come quick!"

CHAPTER 37
Nekane

"Prince Kane!" Blaze's little voice called as he appeared from around the knees of a couple of fae in the crowd watching Nix and I as we gave a demonstration on different ways to combine your gifts to disarm an opponent without them seeing it coming.

"I told you it's just Kane, remember? What's up, Blaze?" I asked, looking down at the kid who'd managed to wrap me around his little finger this past week.

"Over there!" He pointed to the tree lined boundary of the camp closest to the training circle we were in.

I followed the line of his outstretched arm with my gaze. *"Alaric?"* I breathed, shaking my head as I saw a male who looked very similar to *my* Alaric stumbling through the trees. His wings hung low and sweat poured from his hair, down over his exhausted face that was set in a permanent wince.

"He's hurt." Nix said, cocking his head as I felt his palm land on my arm.

No sooner had the words left his lips when the male I'd always seen as an unbreakable warrior collapsed in a heap to the ground with a hard thud and grunt of pain.

"Get Eva and Braxton now," I ordered Nix, concern knotting my stomach as my heart beat faster. With a nod, he was running full speed toward the center of camp where they'd been training, calling their names.

I forced my way through the group surrounding the circle, who all now had their backs to me, gaping open-mouthed at the place where Alaric had fallen.

"Alaric," I gasped as I made it to his side and fell to my knees. His eyes were screwed tightly shut, but he was breathing. I quickly scanned his body for injuries. "Fuck, your leg!" I hollered as I took in the thick dry blood coating the misshapen shape of what was once his right leg. "What happened? Alaric, talk to me. *Please*."

Any elation I might have felt seeing him alive was set aside as worry for the male I loved held me in a chokehold.

"We need to get him to the medical tent!" I called to anyone who would listen as I looked up. "You," I pointed to a strong looking fae at the front of the rapidly growing crowd. "Help me carry him. Grab his other side and mind his leg."

"We don't have a medical tent," the pale male pointed out as he crouched at Alaric's other side.

"The one where everyone meets then, with the table, we can lie him down on that, it'll be easier for me to heal him."

The fae nodded, and on the count of three, we picked him up as carefully as we could. He hissed and then went heavy like dead weight. Everyone moved out of the way as we carried him to the stretch of communal tents and I saw several fae scrambling to make space on the table and add some extra logs beneath the round top to reinforce it.

Whispers of his return were quickly spreading throughout the camp and I could see fae running toward us in my peripheral vision from every angle, ready to help in any way they could as we lay Alaric down.

He was in and out of consciousness, and I'd never been more grateful for my ability to heal the pain away that had his face set in a deep frown, lips peeling back as he tried to force himself to stay awake through the agony and exhaustion.

Placing my hands on either side of his head, I sent a gentle trickle of my power into him. His face visibly relaxed a little, and he opened his eyes to find my face directly above him.

"I'm going to make you better, Alaric." I told him, placing a kiss on his salty forehead and pushing a little more of my gift into him as they connected with his skin. "Just try to relax."

"*Kane,*" he breathed. "I made it," he said, as though he couldn't quite believe it.

My stomach sank at how close he must have been to not making it here for him to sound so disbelieving that he had. "Of course you did," I told him. "Now be quiet while I help you. There will be time to talk later," I promised.

"Where is he?!" Eva roared as she pushed her way to the table and I watched any anger she had over the male leaving us all those days ago bleed out of her as she took in Alaric's condition. A hand flew up to cover her mouth. "What happened?" she asked, her fierce green eyes darting over his body to take in the wounds that were mostly closed.

"Fuck, son." Braxton said, appearing at Eva's side, cracking his knuckles as though he was preparing to either put his son back together with his bare hands or strangle those responsible for hurting him.

"Eva, I need one of your daggers," I said, holding my hand out. Relieved for something to do, she unsheathed Mayhem from her hip and handed the sharp blade over. I thanked her and turned my attention back to Alaric. "Hold still," I told him, then carefully sliced the leather of his trousers around the wound to get a better view of the break.

I sucked in a sharp breath as I saw that the bone must have pierced his skin at some point, before his flesh had healed over the open fracture. I handed the blade back to Eva, and she used it to cut the satchel that was still secured around his side so he was not laying on it awkwardly.

"Alaric, I need to re-break the bone to set it properly," I cautioned him.

"Do it," he gritted. "I need to get to the castle, so just do what yeh need to do." I arched a brow at him and he sighed, "I'll tell yeh everythin' just as soon as yer done."

I nodded and ripped a few strips of leather from his ruined trousers with my hands. Twisting them together, I wedged it in his mouth and told him to bite down.

Taking a steadying breath, I pulled his leg as straight as it would go to see how best to do this. I'd reset my own broken bones plenty of times thanks to dear daddykins when he'd been alive, but nothing that had obviously already been healing for days. And definitely nothing as severe as this.

"Is anyone here medically trained?" I asked no one in particular, just in case there was someone more qualified to do this.

Alaric growled impatiently. "Just fuckin' do it Ka–ARHHH FUCK!" he roared as I placed my hands on either side of the lump of bone and snapped.

The skin tore open again, blood free flowing, and I flooded the area with wave after wave of healing magic, directing it at the break as I manipulated the leg. Lining up the ends of the bone together, I made sure they were properly aligned before forcing my power into the area and watching as it began to fuse together where I held it in place. All the while, Alaric squeezed his eyes tightly shut and breathed deeply through the agony I was sure he was feeling.

Eva held one of Alaric's hands in hers, while his other was clenched so tightly his knuckles were white. The fist made repeated contact with the solid wooden table in response to the pain and discomfort he was in as I worked to fix him up.

The groans he was trying to suppress sent guilt bouncing around my mind, but there was no other way for me to do this. Maybe a more skilled healer could have done this more painlessly, but I was the best he had. I could make up for it later.

I felt myself becoming light-headed as I continued to throw every ounce of healing magic I had into his wound, but it was working, so I pushed through it. He was looking better with every minute that passed. I would use every ounce of my magic if I had to.

"Kane, enough," Alaric eventually snapped when I started to sway. He tried to roll over as though he thought to stand, but Eva stopped him with a firm hand on his chest and a warning glare in her eyes.

"You can talk from there," she said. "So, what happened to you?"

"Jarid." He spat the name as though it was poison on his tongue.

"The warlock, Jarid? Soldier of the horde?" I asked. Finally, content knowing that he was no longer on death's doorstep, I released my hold on his leg where I'd been pushing my power into him, letting my weight lean heavily on the table through my hands as exhaustion swept over me.

I pictured the dark-skinned bald-headed male who'd been in the training halls almost as often as Alaric and I.

It was odd, but if Jarid hadn't been there so regularly, I probably wouldn't have noticed him. I wasn't sure why, but I couldn't remember any specifics about the male, nothing particularly notable anyway. Some fae in the training ring stood out without even really trying to, like Axel or Krista, but others just didn't. He was one of those.

"Aye, the cunt found me at a bad time, caught me with a vine to stop me from gettin' away. I didnae realize the extent of the damage he'd done until he forced me back into fae form," he recounted with obvious hatred for the male in his tone.

"Caught you at a bad time?" Nix asked, his arms crossed over his chest and the tension in his muscles visible. "So this Jarid was the horde soldier delivering the letter?"

"Aye. I got the letter too easily, shoulda known the fates wouldnae let me get away without throwing some trouble my way," Alaric said.

"You got the letter?" Eva asked, wide-eyed for a moment before frowning. "Or did he take it when he did that to your leg?"

"Nah. I got the letter," he confirmed, nodding to the satchel she'd cut off of him.

"Was it worth it?" I asked. "Whatever the letter said, was it worth it? Worth this?" I gestured to his bloody leg, but he'd know that wasn't the only thing I was referring to.

He'd left Eva and me without a fucking word, and then come back to us half dead. I needed him to know that he wasn't allowed to pull that shit on us ever again.

"The fuck if I ken," he said, choosing to ignore the deeper meaning with so many fae around to listen in to our personal issues. "Didnae exactly get a chance to stop an' read the thing."

Eva had his satchel open already and pulled out an envelope with an unbroken royal seal holding it shut. Breaking the wax, she slid the folded parchment from its sleeve and cleared her throat. All eyes were on her, waiting with bated breath to hear what my brother was up to.

It was silent, as though even the bugs and the birds were listening in. You could hear a pin drop in the clearing.

"Fae of Dezrothia,

As the mourning of our beloved late King, Augustus Regis, comes to a close, I trust you have taken this time to properly reflect on his efforts during his reign, as have many here in the castle these past weeks.

I, Prince Elikai Regis, write to assure you that I am soon to be coronated at the Temple of the Fates, where I will devote my life to the service of this realm and the fae therein, so that our Kingdom can take comfort in knowing that Dezrothia is in safe hands with a strong and fierce leader at its head.

First, to commemorate the occasion, I would like to personally invite the most skilled warriors our land has to offer to compete for the opportunity of a lifetime in the Coronation Games, which will take place at the castle. Whomever is victorious at the end of a series of trials, shall be appointed the most honorable role of General to my entire horde army. Furthermore, the entire town or village of the winner will be invited to live here in Ezerat city, never to want for anything again.

The crown looks forward to welcoming warriors who wish to enter within one week of receiving this letter.

A representative of the crown will greet you at the gates.

Your Royal Highness,

Prince Elikai Regis, crowned Prince of Dezrothia."

"Coronation games? What the fuck is he playing at?" I thought aloud, and suddenly there was muttering breaking out amongst the rebels, coming from every direction.

"Shit," Eva whispered. "That must be it..."

"What yeh thinkin' Angel?" Alaric asked, looking like a different male to the one who'd arrived here not long ago, though it was still hard to hear him over the chatter going on around us now.

"Everyone quiet!" Braxton growled, pinching the bridge of his nose like this was giving him a headache. They fell into silence immediately, and he gestured to Eva to continue.

"Remember I'd told you that before we left the castle, Elikai was determined to set me tasks to do research on the species of Dezrothia? He wanted to know about the 'lesser' fae. Said he would give me a species a day to research in the library and I was to tell him all about it that night before moving on. I think... I think it was in preparation for this."

"It's smoke an' mirrors. That's no' how the General is selected." Alaric grunted, the only one of us with first-hand experience. "It has to go to the most capable of the senior members of the horde, there's a ceremony for it. An' knowing that wee cunt, there is no way he would let anyone other than high fae lead his armies. He fuckin' hated that I was shifter and in the role."

"He's right," I said, stroking the stubble on my jaw. "My brother never cared for fae outside of the high fae. And even with them, it was questionable."

"But even so, the reward he is offering will be tempting to the masses. He is exploiting those who have nothing, which is over two-thirds of Dezrothia, with a promise of being something, giving them everything they think they want and need to be happy," Eva said. "But it'll be a slaughter for his own amusement."

"An' King Vandenburg's. I'll bet this has somethin' to do with showin' off to his uncle."

"Is my uncle at the castle at the moment? Maybe ask Axel." I suggested, and he winced.

"Yes!" Eva agreed. "Have you heard from Axel much while you were gone?" she asked.

Alaric paled. "I cannae," he said.

"Why?" Braxton asked, frowning deeply.

"Yeh ken I said that Jarid found me at a bad time? I was leaving Hazelbrook after getting the letter from Jarid's room at the Beguiling Broom, an' Axel jumped into my head. Was excited to tell me that he an' Edelin had sent the human back to the mortal realm an' managed to take down the barrier to the portal for good."

"That's great news," Eva said, smiling.

Alaric shook his head sharply. "I was an asshole to him, told him it was a bad time, that I needed to concentrate on gettin' away from Hazelbrook. I knew the horde soldier wouldnae be far behind me. Then it felt like somethin' went digging in my head with a hot scalpel an' yanked out the battle bond. I fell an' went into a tree from the shock of the pain of it. It was crippling, but once the pain went away, I couldnae feel Axel. I still cannae feel Axel. The last thing I heard him say before he vanished was somethin' about Graves an' Sloane." There was a lack of emotion behind the words, but that only told me how much they were hurting him to say.

"Shit!" Eva gasped. "You don't think Elikai's cronies found them do you?"

"Theres no' many reasons for a fuckin' battle bond to suddenly disappear," Alaric said.

"You don't mean–" Eva cut herself off, a hand going to her mouth.

"Death or magic." Braxton confirmed, a hand running through his blonde hair.

"Wait, what does that mean for my mum?" Nix snapped, alarm in his eyes. "If the male with her might be dead, then... What about my mum?"

"I dinnae ken, Nixen," Alaric admitted with a sigh. "I doubt Elikai would let them do anythin' to yer ma', she's too valuable."

"Maybe she removed the bond when Graves and Sloane found them?" Eva suggested.

"But why would she?" I mused. "What would that do to help them? It's not like it's easy to detect. It would be their only way to tell us they were in trouble, so it makes no sense to cut that connection."

Nix looked like he was about to throw up, and I instantly regretted voicing my thoughts aloud before thinking about what they meant for Axel and Edelin.

"It's all guesswork. We dinnae fuckin' know. We cannae fuckin' know." Alaric groaned as he tried to stand up again.

I pushed him back down onto the table as he glared at me, but he barely had the strength to fight the matter right now.

"We need to get my mum out of there. Axel too, if he is still alive." Nix said, and he looked about ready to storm the castle on his own to save her.

I nodded my agreement. "I'll come too." I said. We couldn't leave our allies there, knowing they were in imminent danger.

"Me too." Eva said, a challenge in her eyes that said just try to stop me. To both mine and Eva's surprise, Alaric didn't argue with us.

"When our own are in need, we will answer the call." Iona said from the opening of the tent. Clearly, she had been listening to most of the conversation and it looked as though the majority of the group I had been training with were as well, as I spotted them peering over her shoulders from behind her.

I sighed in relief, nodding at the group in thanks. "There are just eight days left before the mourning period is over. We need to get there and get them out as soon as we can."

"We will help." Miles said, moving into the cramped space as we shuffled to let the extra bodies in, but the tent wasn't designed to hold this many fae. "You haven't been training us for nothing."

"There aren't enough of us for a full scale attack. Even if the entire alliance bands together an' heads for the castle, we dinnae stand a chance against the horde with our numbers," Braxton said. "This needs to be a rescue, not a war."

"Agreed." Iona said. "We take the original group meant to join Alaric in Hazelbrook.

"And me," Eva snapped.

"And the dragon," Iona confirmed.

"I'll be joinin' too. Noah can take charge while we are gone." Braxton said, then looked at Alaric. "How long until yeh are fully healed?"

"A good sleep an' I'll be ready," he said.

I looked him up and down. "I can heal you some more after a bit of rest, too." I said, feeling the effects of using all my magic so quickly.

"We leave first thing tomorrow." Braxton said, pushing past everyone to leave the tent. Everyone followed except Eva and Alaric, who was still looking worse for wear.

"You sure a night will be enough?" I asked him. I had never seen him so injured in my life.

"It'll have to be. I cannae no' go and get Axel. I cannae tell if he's dead or alive, but I need to go. It'll take us days to get there, an' I can use that time to heal more if I need to." He gruffed with a wince as he put weight on the previously broken leg.

Stubborn bastard.

"KANE!" Blaze called as he ran toward me the moment I poked my head out of my tent, causing a wave of déjà vu to roll over me before he crashed into my legs. "I had a bad dream last night, and you were in it!" he said, tugging at the hem of the tunic I was still in the middle of lacing up. "I don't think you should go today."

Though I'd slept infinitely better having the other third of my soul back in our snug tent last night, I wasn't ready to meet his energy levels so early.

I stifled a yawn and tried to blink the sleep out of my eyes as I said, "Good morning to you too, Blaze."

"Kane, out of the way." Eva grumbled from behind me.

"Sorry, Princess." I said as I ushered Blaze over with me so we weren't blocking her way as she crawled out of the tent herself.

She was a hangry dragon in the mornings, though I was sure she too had managed to catch up on some much needed sleep last night.

We'd made Alaric lie in the middle of us and not allowed a single word of complaint to leave his lips. He'd rolled his eyes as though we were being ridiculous, but I was pretty sure he loved every minute of us fussing over him.

I turned my attention back to Blaze as Eva stretched. His big eyes were glazed with worry as he looked up at me expectantly. "It was just a bad dream, kiddo," I told him. "Let's go get some breakfast and you can tell me all about it."

It surprised me that he was even awake this early, and I hoped he hadn't been up all night worrying about his dream and waiting to warn me.

Eva placed a hand on his tightly coiled shoulder and squeezed. "I won't let anything happen to him, Blaze," she told him, meeting my stare with a wink.

Blaze relaxed a little at her words, and the three of us walked over to meet everyone. Alaric, Nix, Braxton, and Iona sat around the embers of last night's fire, eating their breakfast. Crowded around a tray set up with several large bowls of steaming, honey covered porridge, Raine, Miles and Jarrah helped themselves before joining the group.

Morning hunger silenced the air as everyone took a moment to nourish their body before the long day ahead.

Based on the look of the male, it was obvious Nix hadn't gotten much rest. Eva noticed immediately too, took a bowl of breakfast and went over to sit in the free space next to him. He'd need comfort and reassurances over his mums wellbeing, and she was the best to give them to him.

I took a bowl for me and handed one to Blaze, then sat down to Alaric's right side, balancing the bowl on my knee so I could place a hand on his leg. I subtly pushed some more healing magic into him and he flinched a little at the spark on contact, but didn't complain.

The difference in how he looked today compared to when he'd been falling back into camp yesterday were day and night, but still, I wanted to be as sure as I could be that he was at least ready for this rescue, even if not fully back to his prime physical shape.

His body absorbed the magic eagerly, healing away the injuries that weren't visible on the outside. The break had been a bad one, and that was before the fact that it had healed itself completely wrong and had needed to be rebroken. It was a miracle that he'd managed to make the journey back from Hazelbrook at all.

Blaze took the seat next to me and started to push the porridge around his bowl. "So what happened in this dream?" I asked him.

"You're not still worrying about that, are you, Blazey boy?" Raine asked her little brother. "I've told you already, it was just a nightmare. It didn't mean anything."

Ignoring his sister, he took a deep breath. "In my dream last night, you were captured by your evil brother. It was definitely him. He looked just like you, only he wore fancier clothes, and he laughed with this horrible cackle when he cut your head off in front of this big crowd who all cheered. It was horrible. I haven't been able to get the sound of his laugh out of my head since I woke up in the middle of the night. What if it was a warning?"

"It's not a warning, Blaze, it was just a bad dream," I assured him. "You've seen me in the training ring, and I can look after myself. Fates, if you don't trust my abilities, look at your sister and the others, and how well they've been fighting this last week. Besides, you heard Eva, she won't let anything happen to me and no one would dare try to get in the way of a huge fire-breathing dragon protecting what's theirs."

"So you think I'm being stupid for worrying, too?" he asked, casting a quick glance his big sister's way.

"No, not at all. I had loads of horrible dreams like that while Alaric was at Hazelbrook. But none of those came true." I squeezed Alaric's knee gently and his eyes shot daggers at me, but he was healed enough for me to know it hadn't hurt him. "See, he's fine and my bad dreams were just my imagination playing tricks on me."

"Promise me you won't let him capture you?" he asked, his big eyes silently pleading with me.

"I swear it." I told him, having no intentions of getting anywhere near my brother. "Now either eat up or get back to your tent for some more sleep before you have to get on with your chores."

"Ugh. I hate chores." He whined, piling his spoon with porridge and finally taking a bite.

The tension in the camp grew as more and more fae appeared from their tents.

News had spread last night to anyone who hadn't been present at the war tent when Eva had read the contents of my brother's letter and I could understand everyone's worry.

The species Elikai had invited to take part in his 'Coronation Games' was more than a little concerning, and of course had sparked more than just Blaze's imagination to run wild over what my brother might have in store.

Add to that the news that the battle bond had been severed between Alaric and Axel meant we'd lost our eyes and ears in the castle, and it was no surprise that unease was high.

It was no secret that we were leaving the camp this morning with the plan to rescue Axel and Edelin. Though Axel had been raised in Ezerat, many here knew Edelin personally or at least were aware she was one of the founders of the rebel alliance and so there were many whispers from those nervous for her safety. No one was more worried for her than her son, though.

I sent a silent prayer to the fates that we found them alive and could reunite Nix with his mum and Alaric with his brother by bond, then finished my cool porridge and joined the others in packing and armoring up.

I was going to be ready for everything, especially after Blaze's dream.

THE INCREASINGLY THINNING forest told me how close we were to the city, yet a plan had still not been decided upon. The weather had been against us for the journey so far, the thick clouds and unrelenting rain were heavily impacting the group's morale.

Despite it all, there were some positives. Alaric's leg had fully healed, correctly now, and the rain did a good job of covering our tracks more effectively as the torrents of water washed away any evidence. We were all alive.

We'd attempted to come up with a plan for what we'd do once we arrived in Ezerat, and so far the only thing everyone had agreed on was that we'd head to the Crooked Claw and go from there. None of us wanted to spend more time in that castle than was absolutely necessary, but we needed to gather intel on Axel and Edelin before we could go racing in blind.

"Let's stop here for the night," Braxton said. "We're running out o' trees to take cover between an' we're close enough to the capital now to make this our final stop before finishin' the hike tomorrow."

Alaric looked like he wanted to argue, but before he could voice his protest, Eva placed a soft hand on his arm and met his eyes. Without speaking a word, she conveyed what I was thinking as well: be reasonable, or if you can't manage that, be smart.

He knew we couldn't go much further today. Besides, we would be no use to Axel and Edelin if we were sleep deprived and hungry. We needed to be sharp for the last and most dangerous leg of the journey.

We set up camp in a miserable silence, spreading the tents out to make the most of the trees in order to camouflage us into the environment. Eva and Alaric set to work on our tent, and I borrowed Alaric's axe to go in search of some wood to burn despite its sodden state.

It wasn't long until I noticed a thick branch hanging low from a tree not far from where Braxton was pitching his tent and so took the axe to it, breaking it down into smaller pieces and setting them down in the slightly more open space that the tents roughly circled.

Jarrah cast a flame onto the wet wood we'd collected, which would burn despite the constant water pouring and I held up my palms to the heat, grateful for the warmth, not realizing until now my fingers and toes were completely numb.

Finished with pitching the tents, the others slowly joined us. Eva came over and huddled into my side, shivers wracking her body as the fire heated her again. Despite dragon fire running through her veins, even she was feeling the bitter chill prickling the air.

"Hey, Princess." I said, wrapping an arm around her to cocoon her into me.

Alaric sat on her other side, but as was usual on this hike, his eyes were far off, looking through the flames before us. He had that glazed look on his face he would have when he spoke with Axel, but I knew the truth was that he was searching for that connection again. Reaching for anything to reassure him that Axel was somehow okay.

Raine was holding onto Miles on the other side of the fire, the hybrids deep in conversation with each other. It made me smile to see that they found so much comfort and love in each other. Everyone deserved to find it, no matter their circumstances.

Iona and Braxton were further from the group, murmuring out of earshot of everyone else, frowns marring their faces. Whatever they were discussing wasn't good, and I couldn't help but think it was to do with Alaric.

Braxton seemed unusually worried for him, which made me concerned that there was more to the severing of a battle bond than just losing the link and being unable to communicate.

Whether it was worry for Axel as his friend, or the deeper connection the battle bond had created taking its toll on him, I hated seeing the male so tormented. Seeing him like this just made me all the more determined to find Axel.

Nix had spent the majority of the journey lost to his own thoughts too, despite my best efforts to try to reassure him that it wouldn't be my brother's style to kill a seer as powerful as Edelin. He'd keep her alive so he could use her, of that I was certain.

Jarrah took a seat on his own, staring into the flames. He'd started to keep to himself more with each passing night, turning into the biggest loner in the camp, rarely socializing with anyone, even at mealtimes.

Whenever I tried to engage him, the conversation quickly ran dry and I couldn't find much to talk about with him. I wasn't sure if all spider shifters were that way when they got stressed or perhaps trying to deal with nerves; it wasn't like I'd met many.

Kumo, the mayor of Rangaran, was the only spider I'd interacted with, and though he'd struggled to put a sentence together during our meeting that day that felt like forever ago, that entire situation had been completely different to the circumstances in which I'd met Jarrah.

Kumo had been pleading for his life, convinced I was going to take it from him for falling short on his taxes. I'd never given Jarrah a reason not to trust me, but perhaps he just couldn't find it in himself to trust a high fae period. Only that didn't explain the way he was with the others as we neared our destination.

I'd thought I was making some headway with him last night when I'd decided to tell him about Kumo, hoping it would spark some common ground and distract him from whatever was going on in his head. He seemed interested at first, but it hadn't taken long for him to shift into his spider form and scuttle away into his tent for the night, much as he was doing now.

"We are going to get an early night too," Raine said, her hands linked with Miles' as she pulled him to his feet. "Night."

"Night," Miles grumbled, and they disappeared through the trees to the tent they shared.

I squeezed Eva a little tighter in my arms. "Ready for bed, Princess?" I asked her.

"Mmhmm," she said. "My feet are aching so much from all the hiking."

"Want a foot rub?" I asked against her ear.

"You'd actually rub my feet?"

"Come on, I'll prove it." I said.

"You coming, Alaric?" I asked as we made our way back to the tent. I was glad for the secluded area we had set up in. It afforded us an illusion of privacy, despite the fact that everyone here had sensitive hearing and could listen to every word we shared if they wanted to.

We got to the grand entrance of our little home and I saw Alaric hadn't followed, which was odd. Perhaps he'd decided to sit up with his dad to talk about one thing or another instead? It wasn't that I minded. Fates, they had centuries of catching up to do, but I hoped he didn't leave us waiting too long. I had plans for the three of us tonight, and not just the fun kind.

"I'll do that," I told Eva as she bent to take off her shoes. "Sit there." I gestured to the center of the tent. "Your feet this way." She gave me a skeptical look, but did as she was told. "Good girl." I said, and she giggled. If it hadn't been so dark, I'd say her cheeks had definitely gone a little pink.

I knelt down and made a show of slowly removing her boots and socks, then kicked off my own and climbed into the tent, crawling up her body so I was leaning over her, taking my weight with my hands and knees.

"You're not really rubbing my feet, right?" she asked.

"When are you going to learn, Princess? So long as my hands are on you, I don't care what part of this perfect body I'm rubbing." I bent down and trailed a line of kisses from her mouth, along her jaw and into the crook of her neck. Then paused there. "Though my preference is further north than your feet."

"Is that right? How about you start on my shoulders instead then while we wait for Alaric?"

"Your wish is my command." I said, rolling our bodies so that I was now underneath her.

I maneuvered her body so she was sitting between my legs, my cock against her back. *Fuck, hurry up, Alaric.*

Now that I was certain he was no longer in any immediate danger and his injuries had healed, a bit of the anger I'd bottled up during the five days he'd been gone had begun to simmer under the surface again. I tried to ignore it, particularly when I could see him struggling with his worry for Axel, but we still hadn't talked about what he'd done. I'd been focused on healing him, but with every day that passed, the tension in the air only grew.

"I'm going to talk to Alaric tonight," I told Eva as I massaged her tense shoulders. "Just as soon as he gets here."

"Good idea." She exhaled, and I felt her relax a little more under my touch. "We need to say something. If we don't, he might think he can pull something like that again, you know? Because we went too easy on him this time?"

"Yeah. I was about ready to murder him that first day, and the feeling hasn't really gone away." I admitted.

"Exactly. It was just put on pause when we'd seen him so badly injured. But he's better now, and there's no reason for us to bite our tongue anymore." She agreed, sitting up and turning to face me. She sat back on her knees between my thighs. "Fuck, Kane. He could have died."

"I know, Princess. That's why we need to make him sweat a little to make sure he doesn't pull anything like that again. Are you up for it?"

She willed her eyes to transform with the slits of her dragon. "How's this? Think he'll know he's in trouble?"

"Hmm, maybe some scales too." I said, smirking a little.

She removed her shirt and concentrated a little harder this time until scales crept up her arms and over her shoulders. "Now?"

"Perfect. He might welcome the distraction of our wrath, take his mind off Axel. Two birds, one stone. Now kiss me before we tear him a new one."

"Tear who a new one?" Alaric's gruff voice asked from just outside the tent, and before I could answer, Eva shot out, putting her shirt back on as she went toe to toe with him.

"You owe us an apology," I heard her say. "You left us in the middle of the night. No note, no warning, no goodbye and now you expect us to just be okay with it?"

"No I–" he started as I crawled out and stood next to Eva, my arms folded across my chest.

"I'm not done. Then you turn up at camp FIVE DAYS later with a shattered leg and barely conscious! What in the ever loving fates were you thinking? Did you consider what it would do to us if you'd not come back?"

"I was thinkin' that I couldnae risk anyone else. I knew what needed to be done, so I did it. I'm sorry for leaving yeh, but it was safer this way." He said, his hands out in placating surrender to our feisty female.

A growl rumbled from her chest, and with it, a plume of smoke escaped her nostrils. I noticed in this faded light that her scales looked black.

"Safer for who? For you? Doesn't look that way considering Kane fates near passed out from having to heal you."

"I knew you'd be pissed off, but I didnae mean to worry yeh so much. I'm sorry for that. But dinnae yeh get it? If yeh didnae mean so much to me, I wouldnae have done it."

"Oh, so it's our fault?" I said, arching a brow. "Tell me Princess, would you say that sorry excuse of an apology makes up for the sleepless nights you had? For breaking the promise he made to us to not lie? Do you feel better now?"

"Not even a little bit." She said, and I snorted. Fuck, she was hot when she was angry like this, even if I knew she was putting it on.

"You have a lot of making up to do." I told him. "You can't just leave us without speaking to us first, understood?" I asked, as though our roles had reversed and I was the horde general.

"Aye. I get it. I fucked up and I plan to make it up to yeh."

"How?" Eva asked.

"By trustin' yeh can look after yourselves. That I dinnae need to protect yeh. I mean, just fuckin' look at yeh Angel," he said, gesturing to her partially shifted form. "Yer a force of nature to have made the progress yeh have in such a short time. And Kane, yeh made me so fuckin' proud stepping up and trainin' yer army. Winnin' their respect despite them havin' no intention of given' it."

"*My* army?"

"Aye. They're the start of what is to be yer army. Yer my fucking king Kane, and Angel my queen. The stupid shite I do is cus I'm fuckin' petrified of somethin' happenin' to yeh. I cannae guarantee I won't do more stupid shite in the future. Yer to important to the realm. But more than that, yer too important to me."

The two of us just gaped at him. Being king was a huge responsibility, one I likely would never be fully ready for and didn't much look forward to. But being *his* king… Alaric didn't do it often, but when he spoke from his heart, you felt it in every essence of your being. It was as close to an 'I love you' as I imagine the male before us might get.

I looked at Eva and mouthed the three little words that she'd heard me say once before, then crossed the space between Alaric and I so we were toe to toe.

"I love you, too." I told him, then reached up to fist my hands in his hair and pulled him down so his mouth met mine as I sealed my declaration with a kiss that could shake realms.

He returned it, but I pulled back as I felt his tongue dip inside my mouth. "Inside. Both of you."

"Yes, sir." Eva said as she disappeared into our safe space. The wicked smirk on Alaric's face told me he had every intention of following us inside this time.

Shucking off the tunic I had on, I crawled in behind Eva, admiring her ass as it waved in front of me. I placed a palm on her lower back and she took the hint to lie on her stomach.

"Now roll over," I told her, spanking her delectable derriere and drawing a wanton gasp from her as she arched a brow at me over her shoulder. She did as she was told by rolling over onto her back, but then, reaching up, she sank a hand in my hair and pulled me down for a kiss. "I love you, Princess," I breathed against her mouth.

"I love you too," she moaned back and our tongues collided desperately.

I'm the luckiest male in the realm.

I felt Alaric move behind me, purring as he placed kisses up my bare spine, his stubble prickling my sensitive flesh. Fates to be sandwiched between these two. This was my home, these two fucking fae. It didn't matter where we were, so long as I had them with me, I would be whole.

I pulled the leathers down and off Eva's legs as she unbuttoned the loose shirt she wore. I needed to feel every perfect curve of her body in the flesh. As though Alaric could read my thoughts, I felt him pull back for a moment before his bare chest pressed against my back.

Removing Eva's panties next, I leaned down, backing up into Alaric so I could begin my feast on her pussy. Alaric's palm landed in my hair as my tongue slid through her folds.

"Fuck, I'll never be bored of your taste, Princess." I said, then cupped my mouth over her clit and flicked my tongue over her sensitive bud, pulling a moan from her lips.

Alaric tugged at my hair, forcing me to sit up. "Angel, swap places with me," he growled.

They swapped positions so Alaric lay down in the middle of the tent on his back, his feet poking out through the door and his body beautifully naked.

I licked my lips as I took in the sight of his thick length, a bead of his delicious seed glistening at its head.

"Kane, come here," he demanded, moving the pillow next to his head out of the way to make room. I crawled over him, enjoying the feeling as my balls brushed over his shaft as I went.

I knelt in the space he'd made for me, and he lifted his head so my right thigh could slide in to be his new pillow. Alaric's tongue licked out, running up my shaft from the base to the tip, and then his warm mouth was closing around my cock.

My abs tensed at the sensation and my fingers laced in his thick hair so I could guide his head. He growled deep and low, "*Fuuuuck, Alaric.*" I cursed.

His left arm was hooked around my thigh and he fisted the muscles there roughly to keep me in place. *Like I have any intention of moving.*

Eva's eyes were hooded as she watched Alaric take my cock to the back of his throat, over and over and over.

I reached out my free hand for her to hold on to, and she climbed up to straddle Alaric's waist, but I wasn't ready to watch her ride his cock yet. No, first I wanted her to take her time to watch her males the way she'd wanted to the day Alaric had fucked me in that forest.

"Does watching Alaric deepthroat my cock like a good male make you wet, Princess?" I asked, forcing my cock to the back of his throat. Her hand dipped between the apex of her thighs and she nodded, not taking her eyes off where his mouth joined my length. "You know I like you to use your words, Princess."

"So wet," she whispered, her delicate fingers sliding between her folds.

Alaric growled, the vibrations nearly sending me over the edge, and I looked down to see his mercurial eyes watching her touch herself while he continued to take me deep in his throat, right to the base.

Fuck, he sucked me like he was desperate to get a taste of my come and if he carried on much longer, he would.

Not yet.

“Play with your clit, Eva. I want to see you make yourself come.” Her hips began to thrust as her fingers moved against her most sensitive ball of nerves faster and faster. “Fuck, Princess. You look so fucking sexy right now.”

She started to pant, little moans slipping from her mouth until she closed her eyes and the orgasm took her. She continued to move her hips, her fingers still teasing her clit as though she needed more.

"Open your eyes.” I ordered, and she did, meeting my eyes as she bit down on her lower lip hard. “How about you show Alaric how fucking soaked you just made yourself?”

She reached behind her back and Alaric tensed as she grasped his cock, pumping his shaft a few times before lifting herself up and sliding down on him.

Alaric paused as we both watched as she placed her hands on his lower abdomen and raised her hips to sink down again. Alaric growled again, and combined with the noises tumbling from Eva’s lips, I wanted to bottle the sound in the tent so that I could listen to them over and over again.

Eva began to rock her hips and Alaric swallowed my length again, causing heat to tingle down my thighs and up my spine as we both moaned.

His grip loosened on my thigh, and I felt him trying to free his arm. I lifted myself up a fraction and sucked in a sharp breath as a thick finger sunk into my hole. “Fuuuck, I’m not going to last much longer,” I moaned.

Eva’s eyes were locked on us. One hand on Alaric's abdomen to support her, the other playing with her clit. I leaned forward slightly, grabbed the back of her head and pulled her in for a deep kiss, which she returned with vigor.

Alaric's cock slammed into her at the same pace as he swallowed me down, and now that I was tilting forward, his fingers started a delicious pace in my ass.

Fuck, I’m the luckiest damned bastard in all *the fucking realms.*

I could feel my climax building to a crescendo as Eva gasped into my mouth, hurtling toward her own orgasm, and I drove my hips into an erratic pace between Alaric's mouth and his thick fingers as they plunged in and out of my ass.

Eva pulled away from my mouth, a prolonged groan leaving her lips as her hand stilled on her pussy. Watching the pleasure wash over her, her body shivering as it consumed her, her hips still rolling over the cock still firmly seated inside her, I groaned. The pleasure becoming too much as I came hard. I was pulled even closer to Alaric's face, his arm banding around my hips to keep me in his mouth as he groaned himself, swallowing my cum down his throat.

I slumped back, struggling to catch my breath. Fates, every time felt like the first with them. Every time I felt more complete.

"I could watch you two for the rest of time," Eva whispered as she slid off her perch. The satisfied smile she gave us filled my heart with happiness. "Who knew being kidnapped would lead me to the two males I love, eh?" she said, as we moved so she could lie down between us. "I didn't think I'd find one male who'd steal my heart, growing up where I did, but I found two. And thank the fates I will never have to choose."

She dropped a gentle kiss on Alaric's lips and turned to kiss mine.

And there it was, filling my chest was the feeling that had so long been absent. The feeling of finally belonging.

I would fight the fates themselves to keep them both.

CHAPTER 38

Alaric

Despite Kane and Angel being the best kind of distraction last night, Axel was still on my mind from the moment I opened my eyes this morning, and I had no doubt he would remain there all day.

Not knowing whether I'd make it back to the camp in the Fading Vale after my run in with Jarid had given me way too much time in my own head. One thing I'd discovered was that guilt had become my friend.

Whether it was since my last conversation with Axel or if I'd started to realize it sooner than that, when I'd crept out of bed and left Kane and Angel without a word, I wasn't certain. Either way, I'd spent too long trying to ignore guilt, shut it out, banish it from my often dark existence.

I hadn't had the energy or mind to quash it on my way back from Hazelbrook and in the week or so since, I'd had to let it in, and found that actually, guilt wasn't my enemy anymore.

It was what had given me the resolve I needed to get back to the camp during the times that the pain in my leg and exhaustion in my wings had brought me to the brink of consciousness and left me vulnerable to attack.

It was what allowed me to have Kane and Angel on this insane rescue mission at my side instead of hidden away safely, like I wanted them to be. And as a result, I had last night with them, a night I wouldn't forget for the rest of my immortal life.

I had no fucking clue what I'd done to deserve their love. Fuck, I adored those beautiful bastards and had every intention of proving it to them, even if pretty words weren't my thing.

Guilt was also what drove me closer and closer to the castle every day since we left the vale. Fuck, even when I'd been moving in the opposite direction and at a painstakingly slow speed, it gave me the grit and determination to find my adopted brother and the centuries old witch ally, and ignore the intrusive thoughts that I might be too late. Because I couldn't let myself give up.

Although I'd decided to turn my insurmountable guilt into my friend, that didn't mean to say it was a particularly good friend.

Far fucking from it.

It was also what made me feel like an asshole whenever I looked at Kane and Angel, knowing I'd caused them more worry and hurt than I ever intended to. All to save myself from dealing with the same thing if anyone else had come to the brownie village.

It was what made me question if I'd done the wrong thing by not telling the two fae that held my heart in a vice-like grip that I was leaving in those wee hours of the morning, despite me being convinced what I'd done was the right thing.

Guilt was an incessant throbbing in my heart, telling me I should apologize for being a cunt to Axel the moment I saw him again, even though I knew I wouldn't stop being a cunt to him after the apology.

I'd always been so hard on him that I'd never told the kid that I actually found him pretty fucking funny sometimes. Not as funny as he found himself, but he definitely wasn't the pain in my arse I made a point of telling him he was.

It was the guilt I felt over my last conversation with him and the many, many conversations before that had stopped me from accepting death was the reason for the bond being severed.

Guilt was a mind fuck. And it often came as a package deal with shame, an emotion I wasn't ready to deal with. It was something that would dig up my past and throw it in my face.

Shame also felt like admitting defeat and I wouldn't be giving up until I'd seen Axel again.

Maybe guilt was more of a companion than a friend. Perhaps an ally, regardless it was ever present, suffocating and heavy in my chest. But no less essential to let in.

"Ready?" Braxton asked, pulling me from my thoughts. I looked over to see he'd already packed up and had his backpack on.

Today was a big day for him. I hadn't seen my mum in far too long, but it was barely a blink of time compared to how long it had been since Braxton had. Tonight, that would change.

A few nights ago around the fire, Iona had asked Braxton if he would be bringing Rose to the Crooked Claw with us, knowing that she lived in Ezerat. My da' had choked on his broth and then seemed to be battling a sudden bout of muteness.

I'd answered for him, telling Iona that I planned to bring her to the Crooked Claw once I'd spoken with the landlady Mel and sorted them out rooms for the night. I'd hoped that they'd drop the subject, but Miles had asked why Braxton wasn't going to get her.

My da' eventually found his voice to tell the young hybrid that he couldn't because he didn't know where she lived and that had triggered Raine into asking how and why he didn't know where his true mate lived.

I already knew why he didn't know the address, even after so many years of her living there, but it didn't make it any less fucking heartbreaking to hear him tell the others. I hadn't fully understood his reasoning until recently, but now that I had Angel and Kane in my life, I wasn't sure where my da' had found the strength.

The strain in his voice was hard to listen to as he'd kept his gaze on the ground and explained that he'd vowed to never ask or try to find out the address of the home my ma' and I had found to live in Ezerat. And how it was because he knew he couldn't trust himself to stay away if he did. He explained that it would have put us, me and my ma', in danger if he ever attempted to see us in the city, and that he knew seeing us once or twice would never be enough.

So he'd stayed away completely.

Over the centuries, whenever he'd found the pull to find us too unbearable to ignore, he'd either move his camp or go to visit another of the leaders' camps to distract himself, give himself a purpose that would keep him from tracking down his true mate and child.

To have to work for and follow the orders of the male who was causing my parents that kind of pain and heart shattering longing had been more than challenging, but whenever I felt sorry for myself for the bad shit I'd done or for having to nod along with his cruel plans, I'd just remember all that my parents had sacrificed and I'd suck it up.

"Son? Ready?" he asked again.

"Aye, almost." I said, kicking up some loose wet soil to try to put the campfire out, to no avail. *Fucking stupid magic flames.*

"Jarrah, put this fire out, would yeh?" Braxton called over to the male who was standing talking with Kane. The spider had actually come to Braxton with an idea this morning, one that was actually pretty good and might fucking work.

In the last few days, we'd already discussed that the chances were high Axel and Edelin would be being held in the section of the catacombs that housed the castle dungeons. Trouble was, it was such a long and winding maze to get to when entered from the mountain side, that I'd deemed it a near impossible feat when we'd been brainstorming ideas for how we'd go about getting them out of there.

That left entering the way I knew, through the castle itself, but that was a suicide mission.

I'd been struggling to think of a better way to go about getting into the dungeons and coming up short until this morning when Braxton had shared Jarrah's idea with us at breakfast.

As he'd spoken, morale had been boosted, and we'd all listened in with keen interest. Jarrah had suggested enlisting the spider's help. He said we could use Kane's sort of alliance with Kumo, their mayor, to ask the spider folk of Rangaran to use their gifts of being able to blend seamlessly into the shadows and move soundlessly, to map out a route with their silk web inside the catacombs for us to follow.

They likely couldn't unlock the dungeon cells in their spider form and shifting would trigger the wards, but they could make our job a fuck load easier by giving us the most direct route and path to follow.

Kane had agreed instantly, and I'd bitten my tongue when I'd wanted to argue against it. So despite wanting to keep him with the protection of the group, I'd agreed when he said he would continue North to Rangaran once we made it to Ezerat.

Jarrah had volunteered to go with him, given that he was half spider, and had hinted that any more than just the two of them could likely spook the reclusive village in the mountains.

Rangaran was only a couple of hours north from Ezerat and the Crooked Claw and it was as good of a plan as we'd had, so we agreed that while Kane and Jarrah went to speak with Kumo, the rest of us would go to the Crooked Claw to speak with Mel and Bill; the lion shifters who'd run the place for forever.

In all the nights I'd spent in their tavern, I'd never opened up to them about my true identity, it wasn't a risk that I could take, but I'd heard the way they spoke of Augustus Regis and his discrimination enough to know that they were our best chance of an alliance and a place to shelter while gathering information on Edelin and Axel and waiting for Kane and Jarrah to return with news from Rangaran.

I saw Angel and Nixen coming to join Braxton and I by the fire. "If we leave soon, we should be at the Crooked Claw before it closes," I heard her tell her best friend. "We are long overdue for an ale together in a tavern."

Guilt twisted in my gut like a blade at the reminder that it had been, at least in part, my fault they hadn't managed to the last time they'd tried in Dorgoil.

Usually I'd try to ignore it, try to quash the emotion entirely, but this time, I decided that I'd embrace it. I'd use the feeling I despised so much to light a fire in my stomach to right the wrongs I'd done. I'd get them safely to the Crooked Claw and talk Mel into an alliance that would mean they got to have that ale together and then, all being well, the guilt would hopefully ease.

The rest of the group joined us, bags packed and on their backs, weapons attached to their hips. *"Cur às,"* Jarrah muttered, extinguishing his magically burning flames and with that, we were on our way.

"THIS IS WHERE WE SPLIT UP." I said as we finally reached the border to Ezerat city, the wattle-and-daub homes of the villages and uneven cobblestone trails of the towns long behind us, and with it it seemed, the depressing weather too.

The late afternoon sun bathed the city streets ahead in its warm light, beginning to cast shadows between the buildings we'd soon be navigating. The Crooked Claw wasn't far from here, but there was something else I needed to do first.

I pointed to the castle up ahead and explained that Rangaran was in the mountains just beyond, and off to the right. I told them to go around the outside of the city and only cut across once they were sure they'd passed the castle.

Kane nodded his understanding. "Jarrah is going to shift so we can both run there. Shouldn't take us more than a couple hours each way. We'll be back by midnight," he said.

Eva hugged him tightly. "Stay safe," she said.

"Always, Princess," he said, bending to kiss her.

Part of me wanted to hug him, but that felt like too much of a goodbye, and this wasn't that. "I dinnae need to ask yeh if yeh ken the way to the Crooked Claw," I said instead.

"Ha, no. Ask Mel to save me some of my favorite stew. We'll be back before you know it," he said, then surprised me as he grabbed the scruff of my tunic and pulled me forward for a kiss. It wasn't deep or long, more of a peck on the lips, and I made a mental note to show him what a proper kiss felt like just as soon as he returned.

I ignored the obvious shock plastered across Iona's face from Kane's public display of affection toward Angel and I.

Jarrah shifted, and then they raced away. I sent a silent prayer to the fates that Kumo remembered the just and fair way Kane had dealt with his sentencing and offered to help.

Angel hugged herself around the waist as she watched him leave, but soon enough, they'd be out of sight.

"He'll be fine," Nixen said to her. "Don't tell him I said this, but the male knows how to look after himself. The spiders wouldn't stand a chance, or anyone else, for that matter, who tried to get in his way."

"I'm totally telling him you said that," Eva said, trying to put on a brave face when I knew firsthand how she was really feeling. Like a piece of her just left with him.

"Tell him then," Nixen said with a shrug. "But don't be mad if I accidentally let it slip what happened in Pinefall with the pixies."

Angel sucked in a breath. "Oh, you wouldn't dare!" she said, swatting him with the back of her hand playfully. I made another mental note to find out one day about the pixies in Pinefall, but for now I nodded to Nixen in thanks for distracting my female from her worry for Kane, even if it was only briefly.

I knew the male had enough on his mind worrying over his ma', so it was good of him to dig deep and try to shelve his own problems to make his best friend feel better.

It was time for me to do the same with my da'.

"Braxton," I said to the male at my side as the others passed around a canteen of water. "It's your turn to go now, too." I said, shrugging off my heavy backpack. I reached into the side pocket and pulled a crumpled piece of parchment free. "This is for you," I said, holding it out to him.

He frowned. "What's this?" he asked, taking it from me. I waited for him to unfold it and see for himself. I didn't want this to get weird or anything by explaining what his plans were for the next few hours while I took care of things at the Crooked Claw.

He memorized the map I'd drawn in silence. It started from the exact spot we stood now, and would take him to the home Axel and I had both grown up in but no longer shared with its lone she-wolf occupant.

He folded it and tucked it into his pocket. "Thanks, son," was all he said, but the emotion in his voice hung heavy in the air around us.

"She'll get yeh to the tavern," I said. "Yeh should go. I'll tell the others."

He nodded, pulled the hood of his cloak down to cover his face, and then was gone, too.

CHAPTER 39

Evangelia

Through the stacks of stained water crates and greasy looking puddles, Alaric led us in silence down a tight alley running behind the Crooked Claw.

We reached a wooden gate, and he paused to listen. My hands gripped Mayhem and Chaos a little tighter as we waited in silence, anticipating his next instruction. His hood covered most of his face aside from his prominent scar, stubbled jawline and skilled mouth.

He turned and pressed a finger to his lips in a shushing gesture to us, while the thumb of his other hand carefully pressed down on the gate's metal latch.

It lifted free, and he began to gently push the gate open. I didn't need to see his face to know his eyes would be darting around for threats as more and more of the courtyard beyond came into view.

The gate opened with a creak that only got louder the more careful Alaric tried to be, until it was halfway open and he stepped through it, holding it in place with his foot as he ushered us through then closed it much quicker this time behind us.

The courtyard was more of a storage area, where three large barrels stood, filling most of the space. Broken glass covered the ground at their base from various clear and green bottles of liquor, and a lone cockroach scuttled across the slabs near Iona's feet.

Alaric pointed to the barrels and made a circling gesture with his hand that said he wanted us to wait behind them. Nix and I silently moved into place behind the middle barrel, our backs to the wood and our necks craning around either side to keep an eye on Alaric.

He glided over to the solid wood door, which must be the back entrance that led inside the Crooked Claw, and he tested the handle. I heard a faint click and watched as he tried to push the door, to no avail.

With his hand still firmly on the handle, his elbow came back as he pulled and a beam of light poured through the crack, growing wider the more he opened the door.

The perfect silence was broken as the door flew open and an almighty roar filled the air. Alaric flew backwards, landing with a crunch on the broken glass on his back with the paws of a huge lioness pinning down his shoulders. I drew my twin blades and began to inch my way around the barrel, not taking my eyes off my male and the assailant on his chest with claws as sharp as her teeth.

He kicked the beast off with a hard shove of his legs, rolled out of her clutches and was on his feet again in a flash, his palms raised in a calm down gesture but his feet planted and ready to fight should he need to.

"Calm to fuck down, Mel, it's me," he said to the lioness mere feet away, ripping his hood down to uncover his face.

Mel released a low growl before shifting back to her fae form. A male came running out of the now wide-open door, a fluffy robe in hand that he quickly shrugged over her naked form like their plan when they sensed intruders was for her to attack them and him to be on standby with clothing should it be friend not foe. I recognised him as Bill, her husband.

"What in fates name are you doing here, Alaric?" Melina hissed.

"I'll explain, but no' here. Are the rooms upstairs free?" he asked quietly.

"Rooms? How many does one male on the run need?" Bill asked, obviously more than aware of Alaric's recent fall out with the crown.

"There are five of us now, but another four will be joinin', so as many as yeh have, we'll take."

Mel growled. "Let me see these friends of yours first."

"Swear it to the fates yeh won't attack them, an' yeh can meet them," he said.

She growled again, her frustration obvious. "Fine, I swear to the fates I won't attack them, so long as they don't try anything with us or our patrons."

He nodded his agreement, then turned to look at the barrels and nodded for us to join him. I sheathed my twin blades, but kept my hands hovering over their hilts under my cloak.

She looked everyone up and down like they were big slabs of raw meat and then, when her stare landed on me, she paused, narrowing her eyes.

"For fuck's sake, Alaric. You better have a real good reason for being here," she said, her head whipping back to him.

"I do, but first, the rooms. Are they free?" Alaric asked.

"They will be. Wait here, give me a few minutes to kick the *paying* guests out and then you can head up there. You know the way."

My stomach knotted as I was transported back to the day I'd visited the Crooked Claw with Kane and Alaric, while Elikai had been off slaughtering an innocent Kraken. I'd known our plan was to come here, but I hadn't accounted for the odd jealousy I felt over the nights Kane and Alaric had shared those rooms with random females.

"Yeh ken I'll pay yeh well, Mel." Alaric said, and I remembered the bag of coin I'd found in his satchel that he'd later told me he'd taken from Jarid. *My clever, cunning bastard.*

At the promise of gold, Melina and Bill headed back inside, leaving the door slightly ajar, and we waited.

"Are you sure we can trust them?" Iona eventually asked when she was sure they were out of earshot.

"She really didn't look happy to see you," Miles added.

"That's just Melina," Alaric said. "She's a bitch and absolutely savage, but she's made of good stuff."

"Hmm, sounds like it," Nix said with a skeptical look. "Maybe don't let her hear you say that."

"She'd be alrigh' with it," Alaric shrugged.

"Fates, I think I might be in love with her." Raine said, throwing a faux apologetic look in Miles' direction. "Sorry babe." Miles gave her a look that said he was going to remind her why she was with him, making Raine smirk wickedly like that was her plan all along.

"I remember now why I like her." I said, thinking back to the last time I'd seen her and how she'd nearly managed to make Graves and Sloane piss themselves in fear with a mere grin that had somehow perfectly screamed danger when they were being assholes and calling me Elikai's virgin whore or something to that effect.

If only they knew what that frigid whore was doing last night, with Elikai's brother and the horde general no less.

THE DIVINE SCENT coming from the cauldron of stew cooking in the fireplace was making me salivate as Melina and Bill listened intently to what Alaric had to tell them.

He'd started earlier with the truth about himself, the Fading Vale, and his history with the rebel alliance. Thank the fates, they hadn't freaked out and gone running for the castle guards. They'd actually said they wished they'd have known sooner.

Melina had asked where Kane was shortly after that, her concern for the wanted prince apparent in her features. Alaric explained he was on his way to Rangaran and was one of the four who'd be joining us later and she'd visibly relaxed at the news he was alive and well.

Not long after that, she'd called a break and started to cook the stew that was now bubbling away. Bill had excused himself to put fresh bedding on the beds in the rooms we'd be staying in tonight and the moment they'd left the room, Raine and Miles had beamed as they realized they would be sleeping in an actual, real bed, potentially for the first time in their lives. Even Iona had cracked a smile.

The fact that over half the fae left in the room had spent their entire lives sleeping on the hard ground in tents reminded me of how far we still had to go when it came to the unfairness of Dezrothia and the way in which it was run. I wasn't sure exactly when I'd decided it was my burden to bear, but at least now I knew I wasn't alone in what would be the inevitable war to save our realm from its cruel leadership.

Nix didn't seem to care about the sleeping arrangements, he just wanted to get to the castle, and I couldn't blame him. From where we were gathered around a table in the upstairs of the Crooked Claw, you could see the castle at the top of the mountain, though it looked much smaller than it was up close. Nix had barely taken his eyes off the window at the front, the one that faced the castle directly, since we'd arrived.

When Melina returned with the cauldron stuffed full of delicious ingredients, Bill hadn't been far behind. He dropped a pile of room keys on the small table near the door, and while waiting for the stew to cook, we took our seats. Alaric finally asked what I knew he'd been desperate to ask the moment we'd arrived. "Have you heard any news of Axel? He's a big male, wolf shifter and soldier in the horde. I used to come in here with him."

"We know who Axel is, dear. And we know he disappeared. We have our sources who keep us updated on what's happening up in the castle. Plus, there's always plenty of gossip going on downstairs, especially when the drinks are flowing. No one really knows what's happened to him, though. Just that he stopped showing up in the horde quarters a week or so ago. He's not been in here for a drink in a long while."

"*Fuck*," Alaric gritted, closing his eyes. He tilted his head back and took several deep breaths. He'd been holding onto the hope that they'd have some proper answers for him, but they obviously didn't know any more than we did.

"It's okay," I said softly, reaching out and squeezing his hand that rested on the tabletop. "The spiders will help. They'll search the catacombs and find them. Then we can get them out of that awful castle for good."

"Aye," he said, letting out a long breath. "I hope yer right, Angel."

We fell into silence then until Melina could bear it no longer and eventually asked, "Who's hungry then?"

She stood and grabbed the ladle hanging from a small hook wedged into the brickwork around the fireplace where the cauldron hung. Bill disappeared briefly and returned with several bowls.

As Alaric took his bowl, he muttered something to the male that I didn't catch. Bill nodded, placed the stack down on the table and rushed off again.

"Save some for Kane," I said to Melina. "Please. It's his favorite."

"Of course m'dear," Mel said, doing her best sweet old kitty cat impression that I knew was just an act, but still, I had no doubt she'd save him more than he could hope to eat in one sitting.

"Ale anyone?" Bill asked, appearing in the doorway, this time with a tray full of overflowing tankards in his hands.

Nix tore his eyes away from the window to meet mine and we shared a quick smile. We both signaled that we wanted one and Bill handed them out. We drank ale and ate the delicious meal in silence, until eventually, Braxton arrived.

The first thing I noticed was the smile on his face, the second was the necklace he wore around his neck and I absently stroked my fingers where my rings had always sat. The necklace was exactly like Alaric's, so I'd bet he'd worn it to block his thrakos scent on his way here.

I hadn't actually thought about how he planned to get in here, but I doubted Rose made a habit of entering the tavern via the alley in which we'd used.

Rose must have kept spares at her home in case Alaric or Axel ever lost or damaged their own. They were rare, but it made sense that she'd had been gifted with several, given the danger her son was putting himself in when he'd moved into the castle.

The female herself, the one I'd been most looking forward to meeting, appeared from behind Braxton.

Alaric was on his feet immediately, crossing the room and taking his mum in a tight hug. She was shorter than I'd expected. Dressed plainly as though she didn't want to draw attention, but her bright silver eyes made her anything but plain.

They were the same ones her son had inherited and I could easily get lost in. Alaric planted a gentle kiss on her head, then stepped back and just stared at the couple who'd made him for several long seconds, as though committing it to memory. *When was the last time he'd seen his parents together like this?*

"Fuck, it's good to see yeh ma'," he eventually said.

"It's good to see you, too. I just wish the circumstances were better. I've missed you. And Ax–"

The sound of footsteps thundering up the stairs cut her off. Braxton pulled her out of the way of the door and shoved her behind his back protectively.

"Draw yer weapons." Alaric ordered quietly, and we were all on our feet, weapons in hands. I saw the others move to stand in pairs like Kane had taught them. I hadn't been very involved in their training, too busy with my own, so instead I moved with Alaric toward the door.

A high fae female panting for breath crossed the threshold into the room, clearly in a rush, her large eyes wide. Alaric hadn't moved immediately, as I'd expected him to. Instead, he took in the undeniably beautiful female, long strawberry blonde hair, perfect celestial nose and wearing the sort of extravagant dress that Elikai would have had made for me.

Unlike Alaric, I didn't hesitate to do what needed to be done. The female was an unknown threat, and the high fae weren't known for being trustworthy.

I moved fast and before she had even registered my existence, I held Chaos to her throat and the sharp tip of Mayhem at her back. Silver scales quickly coated my arms and shoulders at my will, making more than one fae in the room gasp in surprise and I had a strong feeling my eyes were slits and glowing green too.

"Alaric," she gasped. "You're here."

"Crystal." He mumbled, moving to stand next to me as he stared down at the female. "What are yeh doin' here?"

"Nekane."

I growled. "He's neither here, nor interested," I said into her ear. Had she seriously raced in here like that because she thought he was doing whatever the fuck they used to do in these rooms? I wasn't sure how I knew, but I was certain this female and Kane had a history. A cloud of smoke escaped my nose.

"You must be Evangelia," she said. "I suppose I have you to thank for Elikai turning his sights on me. Oh wait, no, he's a fucking evil monster," she spat, her throat bobbing against the sharp blade still pressed there. "Whatever you plan to do with those little blades of yours, you should know, death doesn't scare me. Not anymore."

My grip didn't waver, but her words sent ice down my spine. Surely she didn't mean what I thought she had?

Could Elikai be subjecting this female to what he'd threatened me with? She was high fae, and stunningly beautiful. And if my gut feeling about her having a history with Kane had any truth to it, then I could imagine Elikai feeling like he was getting some sort of sick revenge against his twin in choosing her specifically.

"Evangelia, let her go," Alaric said sharply. *Since when did he call me Evangelia?* "Da' shut the door an' guard it. An' you Nixen. The rest of yeh, watch the windows but make sure yer no' visible. Crystal, start explaining what the fuck yer doin' here an' what Nekane has to do with it before I tell Evangelia to have at it."

He sent out the orders in quick concession, and everyone moved into action without hesitation.

"I came to speak to Melina, to see if she'd seen *you*. One of the wait staff told me she and Bill were upstairs in a private meeting, so I raced up here to see if it could be you she was meeting with," Crystal explained, rubbing her throat where my blade had been.

"Why were you looking for Alaric?" I demanded, my hackles still up. Especially after Alaric insisted on using my name. Clearly, this wasn't someone to relax around in his book. Or in the very least he didn't fully trust her.

She didn't look at me when she answered, her eyes were focused on Alaric alone. "Because I knew that if Nekane was in Ezerat, that *you* would be, too. You were always here together, so it's the only place I could think to look–"

"What the fuck do yeh mean Nekane is in Ezerat?" Alaric growled, cutting her off.

"It's a long story. But since *she* left with you and Nekane, Elikai decided I was his new plaything. I've been living in the castle, and earlier tonight I saw a group of the horde leading some yellow-haired male up the castle steps. He was dragging something behind him. Something big. As they passed me, I saw it was a male, unconscious and cocooned in some kind of silk bag. I heard one of the soldiers say they were taking him directly to Elikai."

"Who, Crystal? Takin' who to Elikai?" Alaric asked, leaning over the table.

"It was Nekane!" she cried, tears welling in her eyes. "Elikai plans to execute him tonight! He's spreading the word as we speak, waiting for some sort of venom to wear off that the male who'd captured him had poisoned him with so he can *publicly* execute him at the castle in a few hours' time," she sobbed. "I don't know who the other male is–"

"Jarrah." Braxton growled as Alaric's palms slammed down on the table so hard it split and splintered, collapsing in on itself. The fragile bowls, dirty cutlery and tankards of ale clattered and smashed to the floor with it.

I couldn't breathe, couldn't speak, as her words sunk in.

"Why should we believe you?" Raine asked from across the room.

"I have no loyalty to Elikai. If I could kill him myself, I would. The things that disgusting male has done to me..." she trailed off, and I saw Nix was clenching and unclenching his fists as he saw the pain in her eyes.

"And what loyalty do you have to Kane?" Raine probed.

"Nekane and I used to be involved. Nothing serious, but we had an understanding. He was always good to me, unlike most males around here." She said, and I believed her. *He is a good male,* my *male.*

Alaric was practically vibrating as he tried to remain level-headed enough to think up a way to save not just the male he saw as a brother, but also the male he'd fallen in love with and saw as Dezrothia's future king and savior.

My own mind raced too, but I was coming up with a whole load of nothing.

"Is Kane being held in the dungeons?" I asked Crystal, my voice strained.

"No. He's in his old chambers. I saw Graves and Sloane heading there with thick chains. I assume they plan to keep him there until the execution."

"Fuck!" Alaric cursed, his hands now in his dirty blonde hair as he paced the room.

"So Jarrah betrayed us?" Nix said. "Heard Kane had a history with Rangaran, made up some bullshit story about enlisting their help, all to get him away from us?"

"Aye. Sounds that way. Greedy fucking cunt won't get a chance to enjoy his reward. I'll fucking murder him for this." Braxton seethed, holding Rose close to him.

"We have to save them all." Rose said with confidence none of us could muster.

"Yer not goin' fuckin' anyway." Braxton growled. He'd just gotten his true mate back in his life, I couldn't blame him for wanting to protect her.

"Axel is as much a son to me as Alaric is. Edelin was my closest friend for the longest time and Nekane is apparently going to be our salvation. If you don't want me to go, fine, but we need to come up with a way to save them all." Rose said, shrugging out of Braxton's arms and walking to the head of the table. Or what was left of it.

"What can we do?" Melina asked.

"We need to split up. Half of us go to the dungeons in the catacombs and the others to save the Prince." Braxton said, joining Alaric in his pacing.

"The catacombs?" Crystal asked. "Where they are holding that soldier and the seer witch?"

Alaric's eyes landed on the female. "They are being held prisoner there? Alive?"

"I haven't seen them, but I spend half my time bored and the other half wishing I was bored, so I hear things. Just over a week ago, Elikai was called to the catacombs to deal with two traitors. I'd thought it might be you and Kane, so it got my attention. He's moved up to the top floor where the late King stayed, and so I was with him in the suite when Graves and Sloane came to get him. He left the suite we were in immediately and I watched him as he went into his office and came out with two thick metal cuffs big enough to go around your thigh or neck. He held them with a gloved hand and the magic coming from them made me feel uneasy."

"The bond," Braxton said, stopping mid stride. "Could whatever those magical objects are, be something to do with why yeh cannae feel Axel anymore?"

"Maybe," Alaric said. "What happened next, Crystal?"

"Well, I don't really know, but late that night, Elikai gathered witches and warlocks, and he led them down to the catacombs individually. He was at it for hours. One of them was my maid, so I asked what was going on the next day and she said she'd been ordered to ward the entire area to stop anyone from getting in. If you plan to go inside, you'll need a strong ward magic user to get past them."

All eyes shot to Nix. "What the fuck would I have warded fae away from? My tent? I know some spells, but I'm no 'strong ward magic user'."

"The maid. Is her name Thalia?" I asked Crystal, a plan coming together in my mind.

"Yes," she confirmed.

"Would you go back to the castle and give Thalia a message from me?" I asked.

She paled at the idea of going back to the castle, but nodded.

"Tell her Eve sent you and that I wouldn't be asking if it wasn't desperate. Tell her that I need her and her uncle, Westly, to meet a group of fae at the entrance to the catacombs from the side of the mountain. Alaric, can you draw a map? To the place you escaped out of."

"Aye." Alaric said. Bill left the room again and came back with several sheets of parchment and a pencil a few moments later. He handed them to Alaric, who began to draw.

"Will you do that?" I asked Crystal. "Please."

She gulped, then nodded. "Yes. I swear it to the fates," she promised.

"Thank you." I said sincerely, and Alaric handed her a slip of parchment, which she folded and tucked into the top of her corseted dress.

"Okay," I thought aloud. "Now draw another one for Nix. He can take Raine, Miles, and Iona to the catacombs to find his mum and Axel. When Thalia and Westly arrive, tell her who you are, Nix. I told her plenty about you when I lived there, so she'll know who you are and to trust you. Help her and Westly take down the wards and keep them at bay while you search. Raine and Miles, shift into your wolves before you go in there, so it doesn't trigger the shifter wards. Find them by scent if you have to."

I paused and realized I was out of breath. Every set of eyes was watching me like I'd grown two heads.

When Nix, Raine, Miles, and Iona nodded their agreement to the plan that was building in my brain, I took a deep breath and carried on.

"Braxton, Alaric and I will go to the castle. Crystal, do you know where the execution is taking place?"

"The balcony," she said. "I'll go now. Thalia usually draws my bath around this time, so I should catch her alone. Good luck." She said, then turned on her heel to leave.

"Crystal." Alaric said just before she disappeared from view. "Thanks. I'll repay this debt and get yeh away from that cunt, I swear it to the fates."

She nodded, a sad smile twitching at her lips, then she was gone.

"Evangelia's plan is as good of a plan as I could think of," Braxton said.

"Shit. The streets are getting busier," Iona called from her window, which looked out directly to the main stretch of Ezerat high street. "I'd say that the female was telling the truth. They are all heading toward the castle."

"Sick bastards." Rose muttered, cracking her knuckles.

"Ma', do yeh have anymore of those necklaces? Alaric asked, pointing to the one around Braxton's neck.

"At home I do. Two. Maybe three. I'll bring them all. Won't be long." Braxton tried to stop her, but the glare she gave him was enough to bring the most alpha male to his knees. When all this was over, I'd try it on Alaric and Kane. Braxton cursed but didn't try to stop her again, just kissed her quickly and then she left.

"Melina, Bill, do yeah have anythin' for the three of us to wear that might help us blend in?" Alaric asked, gesturing to himself, me and Braxton. "The necklaces will block our scents, but we cannae risk being recognized. There isnae a soul in this city who wouldnae recognize me an' Evangelia."

"Yes, come with us, we'll find something," Melina said, and we did.

CHAPTER 40
Nixen

Iona, Raine, Miles and I left the Crooked Claw the way we'd arrived, down the alleyway, armed with our weapons, as well as other equipment we might need like rope and ice picks. Forest floor was a terrain I was used to, but rock and sheer cliff faces would be new.

According to Alaric's very vague map, there was no way of completely avoiding the busy streets in the city to reach the part of the mountain we needed to find to start our climb, but he'd provided a route that should be mostly quiet residential paths or dark alleys.

We had to get to some kind of cave where we'd be meeting Eva's witch and warlock allies. Raine and Miles chose to make the short trek on four legs in wolf form. Iona had gone with her fae form, given that a huge bear would be much more likely to draw attention. And despite my panic for my mum's safety, and my excitement to see her again at long last, I kept my thrakos side firmly suppressed.

There had only been one scent blocking necklace to spare for our group when Rose had returned, and my best friend had insisted I wore it. With Raine and Miles as wolves, their thrakos scent would be somewhat masked. Iona didn't have any thrakos blood to hide, and the hybrid scent she gave off was easier to ignore. So they'd all agreed I would be the one to wear it.

It wouldn't stop me from shifting should I need to, but it would help if we ran into anyone before we got up to the side of the mountain.

I led the group as we carefully made our way down the first of several alleyways, listening intently to my surroundings and taking occasional deep breaths to check no one was nearby.

I caught a familiar scent just as a low growl vibrated from one of the wolves behind me, and quickly turned to see why that particular scent was in the air, when it definitely shouldn't have been.

"Rose?" I said, seeing the dark-haired female hurrying to join our group. "What the fuck are you doing here?"

"I raised Axel as my own. If you think anyone could stop me from being here to help save him, you're sorely mistaken," she said.

"But Braxton said–" I started.

"What Braxton doesn't know won't hurt him. He's on his way to save the prince, and by the time he's back, I'll be at the Crooked Claw with my boy like I'd never left," she insisted.

"Fuck. You're going to get the rest of us killed," I cursed, turning to continue my way along the alley. We were nearing the end and would soon have to cross a street to get to the next.

"You underestimate me, boy. Based on who your mother is, I'm shocked you'd think a female on a mission to save her child would be a hindrance," she growled, misunderstanding what I'd meant.

"I meant your mate will murder us, not that we couldn't use your skills," I told her.

She was instantly at my side, plucking the map from my hand. Giving it a quick once over, she pocketed it, apparently not needing it. "I also happen to know this fate's cursed city better than any of you. Follow me, I will get us there undetected."

She did, pretty fucking successfully too. Despite having to wait for longer than I'd have liked to at the busier areas, needing to be sure they were clear before we could slip back into the shadows, we made it to the spot that I was sure matched Alaric's map relatively quickly.

We all looked up at the jagged cliff face, squinting to find the mouth of a cave somewhere around halfway up.

"There," Iona said, and I moved closer to her, following the line of her outstretched arm and pointed finger until my eyes landed on a darker spot on the already virtually pitch black rock.

"I see it too," Rose said, absently fussing Raine's thick neck of fur. She patted the other she-wolf on the flank and said, "Chop chop, you can lead the way now."

Raine nudged her head to coax Miles to go with her and they started to navigate a route up for us to follow. We only had four ice picks, so I handed mine to Rose and opted to shift my hands and use my thrakos talons. We began making slow but sure progress toward the entrance, following the nimble wolves up the treacherously narrow path. There was no denying it was an exhausting climb, but with every step, every stumble, and every heart stopping slip, I could feel in my gut that I was getting closer and closer to my mum.

As we neared, I saw the silhouettes of two dark figures making their way down the rocks. Thalia and Westly. It had to be. Raine sniffed the air at the same time as I did and nodded. I understood it to mean that she'd confirmed they were magic folk and so we continued on.

"That Crystal was a pretty little thing," Rose mused quietly behind me and I wasn't sure whether the comment was meant for herself or me. "Would be a shame if that vile prince damaged her heart and mind beyond repair."

Not sure whether she was expecting an answer, I just nodded my agreement. The look in Crystal's eyes when she'd told Eva she wasn't afraid of death spoke directly to the dark spots on my soul. I'd been there. Still often went there. Especially since Alaric had told us that she'd been caught trying to open that stupid portal.

Aside from learning it went to the mortal realm, I couldn't understand why she was so set on staying in what I'd been told was little more than a dank cavern. I knew better than to not trust my mum's process, but I just couldn't understand why it had been so important.

We needed to make Dezrothia a better place to live. Not look for somewhere else to go that was probably just as shitty.

Rose said no more about Crystal and so I looked up to see that Miles and Raine had made it to the wider platform of stone that led into the cave. I tilted my head further and saw that Eva's friends had about as far left to go as me, so I picked up my pace, knowing I needed to beat them there so they didn't spook when they found two huge wolves waiting for them.

I slammed my clawed hand into the ledge and pulled myself up, pulling it free from the rock just in time to see the witch holding out a hand and helping the older warlock down to meet us.

They were heavily cloaked from head to toe and stood at a similar height. I trusted that Eva knew what she was doing by bringing these two in and so I let go of the transformation in my hands, held one out to them and said, "I'm Nixen Sybilline."

The warlock pushed the cloak down to uncover his face, then grasped my palm with his. "I can feel your family's magic," he said, before releasing my hand. "We were in a coven together once."

"Eve told us Edelin had a son, but she wasn't sure of your fate. I'm glad she found you," the witch said, reaching out her own hand which I shook. "I'm Thalia."

"We found each other," I said. "I assume you spoke to Crystal or you wouldn't be here?"

Thalia nodded. "Yes, she said Eve needed us to meet here. We assume you want help with the wards blocking the entrance."

"If you can, my mum, Edelin, is inside. And Axel."

"I never met your mum, but Axel's a good male." Thalia said.

"I've not met him, but I've heard. Kind of hard to get your head around having a cousin you never knew existed, especially one who is almost three times your age, but stranger things have happened."

"They certainly have," Westly said, now standing near the cave mouth. His hand was raised to cup his ear, and he bent forward, almost as though he was listening to some invisible, soundless barrier. "Ready, Thalia?" he asked.

She wiped her palms down her cloak and then shook out her wrists. "Ready," she said, getting into position next to Westly. They each held up their outside palm and joined hands in the middle. "You might want to stand back. We only cast two of the spells warding this place and have no way of knowing what other enchantments are protecting it from intruders."

The wolves backed up and Iona, Rose, and I joined them. The witch and warlock began to chant, and I used the time to discuss the plan.

"Alaric said there is a fork almost immediately at the entrance, so Raine and I will go one way, while Iona and Miles go the other. Rose, you should wait out here with Thalia and Westly. If we aren't out in one hour, then we are either lost or dead, so you will need to get word back to the others."

Rose's nostrils flared a little at the thought of being a lookout and messenger, but eventually, she agreed. "Fine."

"Almost there," Westly gritted from behind me and I stretched out my slightly sore muscles from the hike, ready to get this underway.

"Everyone clear on what to do?" I asked.

Iona agreed, and the wolves nodded. I arched a brow at Rose, the only one to not have answered. "Crystal. Clear," she said through clenched teeth. "Now go save my boy and friend."

We had no way of knowing how the other team were getting on in saving Kane, but when I sent a silent prayer to the fates that I'd be seeing my mum really soon, I sent one for Kane too.

Thalia was sweating and panted as she said, "We don't know if the wards will start to attempt to repair themselves, so we will hold it."

"I hate to rush you, especially when we can't be of any help with directions inside the labyrinth, but if you could try to be quick, that would probably be best," Westly said.

Translation: get out before we pass out from exhaustion.

I nodded. "Thank you."

We entered the cave in our pairs, and hadn't walked far before we were faced with a fork in the cave, like Alaric had said.

Raine moved forward, sniffing the ground and pacing back and forth between the two directions. She looked over at Miles, who joined her in sniffing. It seemed they came to an agreement that they couldn't tell which way we needed to go.

"I guess we'll take the right and you two go left?" Iona said.

"Let's do it." I replied, there wasn't much choice in the matter.

I'm coming for you, mum.

CHAPTER 41

Evangelia

We were swept along with the masses as everyone moved in tandem to the castle. Though it was a good sign that we weren't too late with so many still heading for the castle, fear still strangled my heart as I forced myself to think about how we would get Kane out of this.

I refused to let myself think about the alternative because I couldn't live if it came true. Kane *would* live. He didn't have a choice. I'd save him even if it killed me.

Thankfully, the night was cold, so most of the high fae around us wore cloaks with their hoods up. I peeked out from under mine and saw several children up ahead of me, causing my breath to stutter.

No child should ever see death, but for them to actually look *excited* made my stomach sink. No one was born with an appetite to witness such an atrocity as an execution. No, their parents were to blame. The thought of them seeing something so gruesome, so *evil,* with their innocent eyes just gave me another reason to do everything in my power to stop this from happening. If not for myself, then to preserve the innocence of those so young.

The closer we got to the castle, the more animated the crowd became, their chatter picking up in volume with every step as they neared the gates.

There was a lot of jostling, pushing and shoving as fae tried to get into the courtyard as though they wanted to make sure they got a good view. If I didn't know what was really about to take place, I would have thought it was for some kind of celebration.

Come to think of it, they hadn't been anywhere near this excited when I'd watched fae turning up from my window in Elikai's room on the morning he and I were meant to be wed.

We reached the gates that opened into the courtyard, and the balcony came into full view.

It had been fucking decorated, much like on my wedding day. As I gaped up at the disgusting sight, I felt a hard shove in my side and was forced from Alaric's side and back into the bottle-neck, trying to push their way in.

I stretched up on tiptoes, desperately trying to locate him, but he was nowhere to be seen.

Shit, shit, shit!

I was being pushed and pulled in every direction apart from the one in which I needed to go, further and further from where I'd last seen Alaric. As I was forced away from the castle, I had no choice but to focus my strength on calming my dragon. I might have much better control of her now, but there was only so much she'd take of being shoved and trodden on before our temper was shot.

My gaze darted around desperately. I needed to get out of here. But Kane needed me more. My eyes landed on one of the towers that lined the stretch up to the gates and a memory surfaced from my time on the inside of the castle, when I'd been to one looking out from the other side of that balcony.

The tower was the perfect place to look down over the courtyard, and at its tallest point was probably twice the height of the balcony.

The seeds of a plan began to sew themselves in my frantic mind, but as tempting as it might be, I knew I couldn't just shift right here and fly up to the tower's roof without causing a scene.

The balcony was empty, aside from the flags, silks, and ribbons hanging from it. I had time to do this the less stupid way.

Ignoring the grumbles and confused faces as I went, I pushed through the throng of the crowd and away from the castle's courtyard, heading for the tower with the most direct line of sight to the balcony.

The courtyard must have been filled to capacity because I noticed that the fae around me were coming to a stand-still, moaning about how they wouldn't be able to see very well so far back, but still I shouldered through.

Finally, the circular stone tower was within touching distance and I reached out for the handle of the wooden gate that would lead inside. The bolts at the top and bottom were already unlocked and so I glanced over my shoulder to make sure everyone's eyes were firmly fixed on the courtyard ahead and not me, then darted inside.

The circular space was small, only large enough to house the staircase that looked to spiral all the way up to the top. Taking a few deep breaths, I sprinted up the winding stone steps as silently as possible and only slowed when I saw a narrow slab platform at the top with a horde soldier looking out of the glassless window, on guard and watching for trouble in the crowd.

Shame on him for not thinking to look down.

I held my breath as I shifted my right arm, hoping the wards didn't extend this far from the castle gates.

Nothing.

Letting out a silent sigh of relief when there was no wailing to be heard, I crept up behind the male.

When I was sure I was close enough, I lept onto his back, my impenetrable scaled arm wrapping around his neck and cutting off his air supply. My other hand came down over his mouth and I put every ounce of my strength into squeezing his neck as tightly as possible. His lips were trying desperately to move under my palm, but the hold I had around his throat stopped any words from slipping out.

He began to stagger, and I twisted my body, hearing a sharp snap from his neck as I landed on my feet and he fell in a heap. I kicked him down the steps for good measure. If the snapping of his neck didn't keep him down, the fall surely would.

Righting my hood back in place to cover my face, I dropped the partial shift, and I peered out of the window. I scanned the crowd below, my heart pounding as I struggled to find Alaric and Braxton amongst the masses.

You would have thought two hulking males would have been easy to spot, but not so much when they were going out of their way to blend in.

As I attempted to search row by row, a deafening cheer went up, making the hair on my arms stand on end as it rumbled through the crowd. My attention flew to the balcony on instinct.

My throat closed up when I saw Elikai, dressed as if he was already king, minus the crown, with Graves and Sloane trailing behind him.

Between Elikai's lackeys was a dark-haired male, his hair falling forward to cover his face as they dragged him by the arms out onto the balcony before the crowd.

Kane.

A knot balled in my throat, tears threatening to sting my eyes as I stared helplessly at the male I loved so deeply in the hands of the enemy. All because he put his trust in the wrong fae.

We all had.

Jarrah, the fucking traitor, stepped onto the balcony next, his beady eyes down as they should be. I wanted to incinerate him to a pile of ashes for what he'd done.

Fates, I wanted to burn them all, aside from Kane. But there was no way I could do it without taking him down with them.

Last to slither onto the balcony was a male I didn't know. Judging by the crown on his head, the staff in his hand, and the nasty smirk on his face as he waved patronizingly to the crowd, I'd say it was the twins' great uncle, King Vandenburg of Mount Mortum.

He had the same piercing blue eyes as Kane, only they held the coldness that I'd always found in Elikai's on the occasions he forced me to look at him.

Elikai cleared his throat, a sign he was about to start some long speech. Likely about how he'd heroically tracked down the most wanted fae in Dezrothia.

I took the opportunity to scan the crowd once more. I tuned out his voice, not caring what he had to say. So long as he was talking, he wasn't slaughtering.

I went back to searching row by row, but movement near the front drew my eye. Braxton was red faced, veins straining as he held Alaric at bay, like he planned to leap up onto the balcony or scale a wall. Furious wasn't strong enough a word for the look on his face as he turned on his father, trying to shove the male off of him.

Though most were transfixed on the fae on the balcony, they were drawing the attention of several fae in their immediate vicinity. I watched as Braxton grabbed Alaric's shoulders, pulled him close and said something in his ear that somewhat calmed him down enough for him to drop his hold on him.

"...while we have all mourned my father's passing, this spider shifter risked his life to find the king killer and bring him to the castle to face the justice he deserves!" Elikai's voice drawled, and the crowd cheered wildly. "To honor his just acts of bravery, he will be granted an immediate place in the coronation games!"

Jarrah's eyes bugged. The reward Elikai had planned for him had obviously come as a surprise. He gulped, the blood leaving his face but bowed stiffly to the fae below who roared and whistled their excitement.

I almost wanted to throw my arm up and volunteer to face him in the games myself. It would be the perfect punishment for what he'd done.

Kane said something that I couldn't make out, but it made Elikai turn and grasp his chin as he said something back, then threw his head back and laughed maniacally. Every pair of eyes in the courtyard watched the brothers exchange, adrenaline fueling some of them to shout out to just murder him already.

I gasped as Kane was thrown forward, and Elikai pulled his sword from the sheath on his hip, holding it up for the crowd. They roared their approval, and panic squeezed my chest as I looked around frantically for a solution.

I looked to Alaric and Braxton and was shocked when I found them both staring at the tower, directly at me.

I felt as if we were locked in place by the fates, time freezing as Alaric stared at me so hard it was like he was trying to send a message through the air directly to my brain.

Then Alaric whipped around to face the balcony, cupped his hands around his mouth and shouted loud enough for the entire city to hear. "He's innocent! You cannae do this!"

He wasn't an idiot. No, he was creating a distraction. For me. To do something. But what?

Kane was close to the edge of the balcony and though he couldn't move to look, he'd know exactly whose voice it was.

"Well, well, well," Elikai said, lowering his sword. "I'd know that common accent anywhere. If it isn't the traitorous former General. Come to save the criminal he helped to cover up our late king's murder. Seize him!" He called, and I saw several horde soldiers appear from every alcove and corner of the courtyard, heading directly for Alaric. "Now all we need is Evangelia and we can execute them all! Come out, come out, wherever you are..." he taunted, looking around the crowd.

King Vandenburg smiled, but it was wiped from his face when a deep rumble shook the ground, causing violent tremors and the fae in the crowd to cry out in panic.

An explosion of some kind rocked the mountain the castle was built on and Elikai and his supporters rushed to the edge of the balcony in an attempt to get a look at what was going on. I couldn't see anything from where I stood, but the sound had clearly come from that one side specifically.

Make the most of the distraction, Eva.

Seizing the opportunity amidst the chaos, I jumped onto the sill and launched myself into the air, my wings tearing from my back, scales coating my arms, neck, and shoulders as I opened my mouth wide and roared at the top of my lungs.

Elikai was smiling like the explosion wasn't news to him and everything was going perfectly to plan, but it was wiped from his face at the wail of my wrath.

I shot toward Kane, sparing a quick glance down to Alaric and Braxton and nearly falling out of the sky when I saw Braxton on the ground, Alaric cradling him protectively with one arm. His sword out drawn in his other, fighting off the soldiers one by one as they reach him.

I'll come back for them.

Elikai was moving toward Kane, his sword high in the air, and I tucked up into a ball, somersaulting into my landing, my back to Elikai, silver wings wide and acting as a shield between Kane and our enemies.

Elikai's sword slammed into my left wing and I tensed, but it ricocheted off with a loud ringing noise as the metal blade clashed with my steely scales.

"He's *mine*!" I hissed over my shoulder at Elikai and watched the shock on his face morph into horror as he took in my partially shifted form. My chest swelled with satisfaction, but this was far from over yet.

"You!" He sneered.

"My, my," King Vandenburg said, stroking the tuft of hair that was shaped into a point on his chin. "I thought the dragons of Dezrothia were all gone but it doesn't take a genius to see what line you're bred from," he spat, stepping up next to Elikai and sneering like the words were poison on his tongue.

The look he gave me sent a harsh shiver down my spine and through my entire being.

I didn't have the luxury of time to process what he meant about my heritage as another tremor shook the castle and threatened to knock me off balance.

Kane was leaning heavily on the balustrade for support. Jarrah's venom hadn't fully worn off and the battle taking place inside his body as it fought the toxic poison would be exhausting him.

"Eva, get out of here," he croaked.

I shook my head sharply. "You need to jump." I told him, glancing over the balustrade, down at Alaric, to find he was hurt. Bleeding from several places, but still holding the guards off despite desperately protecting an unconscious Braxton.

"Jump. NOW!" I snapped from gritted teeth, and he hooked a leg over the balustrade.

"Stop right there." Elikai demanded, stepping around my wings with his uncle in tow.

His allure took a hold of me, rooting me to the spot and leaving me utterly powerless to block or stop him.

Kane was frozen too, and I wasn't sure whether it was his fear for me, or the strength of his brother's allure that was the cause.

You failed, Eva.

We were going to die, and at the hand of the male I loathed more than any other being.

I couldn't allow it. I couldn't give him the pleasure of being responsible for the deaths of all three of the final dragons of Dezrothia. Truly driving my kind to extinction.

I couldn't give him the satisfaction of killing his brother.

Vandenburg was moving towards me, a large bronze cuff in his hands, similar to what Crystal had described. Elikai was moving toward Kane with his sword high once more. I couldn't fucking move. Rendered completely useless.

Kane's fists were white as he gripped the balustrade, like he was digging deep for strength that his body no longer had to offer him.

His eyes met Elikai's. "No brother. *We are leaving, and none of you will stop us,*" he gritted out. Only the intense power behind every word was unmistakable, as all-consuming as it was petrifying.

Elikai and King Vandenburg stopped immediately, rooted in place.

I was no longer held by Elikai's allure, which could only mean one thing. Kane's allure was stronger.

Even in the condition he was in, the gift he so rarely used was stronger than his twin.

Dangerous male. *And mine.*

"JUMP!" I screamed. And he did.

I nose dived off the balustrade and shifted into my dragon in all of her glory this time, losing Mayhem and Chaos in the process. My heart plummeted with the fall as I mourned their loss. They were such a huge part of my past, but right now, I needed to save my future.

We were only a few stories high, so everything had to happen fast.

I swooped under Kane so he landed on my back and I felt his hand wrap around the spike on the bottom of the back of my neck. *Thank the fates he didn't land on one.*

Fae were screaming, falling over themselves as they raced for the gates. Whether it was the explosions rocking the castle or seeing a real life dragon in the flesh, I wasn't sure, but the courtyard was rapidly clearing as fae rushed away terrified, leaving space for me to land close to Alaric and Braxton.

The ground shook again, this time under the weight of my dragon form, and I heard Kane call down to Alaric. "What's wrong with your dad?"

His voice no longer held that power I'd heard moments before. He needed to rest, to heal and to do that, I needed to get them.

"No' a fuckin' clue," Alaric answered, panic creeping into his voice. "He dropped like a fuckin' stone an' I cannae wake him."

There wasn't much that could make a fae drop without warning, even less a thrakos, and none of it was good.

Alaric hooked his battered and bloodied arms under Braxton's knees and shoulders, then lifted him with more effort than I knew it would take had he not been drained from fighting for both of their lives.

I heard shouting behind me, and craned my neck to see several members of the horde, who hadn't been clever enough to run for the hills, racing toward us. Alaric stiffened, as though deciding whether to drop his dad and reach for his sword.

Certain that everyone I cared about wasn't in the line of danger, I acted on the adrenaline pumping through my beast. I sucked in a deep breath and exhaled with a roar.

Flames poured from my lips, eviscerating every last one of them to piles of ash on the ground where their feet had last stepped. *Fuck!*

Turning back to Alaric, I ignored the look of shock on his face as I crouched as low as was possible in this form so he could climb on my back.

Kane was shuffling around up there, either helping or making room, probably both.

"I've got him," Kane said. There was more moving around, and then I heard the words I'd been waiting for. "Fucking fly, Princess. Fly."

CHAPTER 42

Axel

The ringing in my ears is what pulled me back into consciousness. I blinked through the dust and rubble that was settling around me and pushed myself up.

My head was pounding where I was sure half the cave wall had come down on it. My neck would have likely broken if it weren't for the bronze cuff clasped tightly around it, though it completely sapped my energy.

I looked around for Edelin, worry filling me as I couldn't see her and the ringing meant that even if she was calling for me, I couldn't hear a fucking thing. Stumbling as I moved, I called out for her, desperate to find her and get out of this place before it collapsed.

"...xel! Ov... re." I moved to where I could hear fragments of sound, praying to the fates it was Edelin.

"Aunty Ede?" I called back, noticing my hearing was getting better as the ringing began to fade away.

"Hurry, over here!" I heard, and I moved as quickly as I could make my body move to where I found her trapped under several large boulders. I began to roll and lift as many of the rocks as I could away, cursing the cuff preventing me from being able to sift or even muster the strength to move the heavier ones.

"Just hold on, I got you." I promised her, then froze when I saw a red pool of blood oozing out across the dust. With my thrakos side suppressed, the bloodlust didn't consume me, but concern did. She was bleeding under there and I couldn't get her out quick enough.

"Listen to me Axel–"

"Tell me later," I dismissed, using every muscle in my body to lift the boulder crushing her legs. "I'm almost done. Just a few more and–"

"Axel!" she snapped at me, surprising me enough to give me pause. I don't think I had ever heard her shout like that before.

"What?"

"I haven't been completely truthful with my reason for being here. The portal's important, but it's not the reason I allowed myself to be captured." She took a few stuttered breaths, and I frowned, trying to work out what the fuck she was talking about. "There's no time to explain everything now, but one of the wards guarding this place caused the explosion when it was broken. I've seen it happen a thousand times, but it's what I've seen only once that is what drove me to leave my son in the Fading Vale to make sure we were in this very place when the wards were taken down. The rocks that fell behind me should have created a hole to another room. I need you to stop trying to save me and get in there to rescue the fae that are trapped inside."

"Have you lost your fucking mind? I'm not leaving you!" I seethed.

"My son is on his way, he will get me out, I promise. Just go. *Please.* This is more important than me or you or any portal." Her voice sounded too weak, but the tears in her eyes told me how much this meant to her.

"You promise me, swear that you will be okay."

"I swear it."

"Fuck. Fine, I'll go and check, but I am coming straight back here to get you." I vowed.

She nodded, a smile spreading across her face, causing a tear to trickle down her cheek. "You won't be rid of me yet."

"Mum! Edelin!" a distant voice echoed from a nearby chamber. "Raine, stay close!"

"That's your cue to go, Axel. Nix will get me out. Feel for a gap in the rubble back there and it will lead you to where you need to be. Save them."

I nodded and moved to the area Edelin indicated, but before I crawled through the gap, I yelled. "She's here! Edelin's here and she's injured!" *That ought to do it.*

"Raine, over there! Start digging!" was the last thing I heard before blindly following Edelin's insane plan and crawling through a tight gap that used to be a solid rock wall separating our cell from whatever the fuck this room was.

I clambered to my feet to find myself in some kind of laboratory. It hadn't been damaged by the explosion, but it was clearly old, and thick with dust from the floors to every surface.

My eyes darted between hundreds of specimen jars, each filled with sights so gruesome I found myself rubbing my eyes because surely they were deceiving me. Perhaps the ceiling of a dungeon falling on my head had fucked something up inside my skull more than I'd realized?

I blinked, but the scene in front of me didn't change. Some of the glass jars were small, with an organ here and there, others were much bigger, larger than most fae, with hulking shapes floating inside them, filling them almost entirely. A sense of foreboding crashed into me like a wave.

I equal parts wanted to take a closer look, and work out what the fuck these... *creatures* were, but at the same time, I wanted to burn my eyeballs so I never had to look at them again. My gut told me I didn't want to know what the *things* were.

The subtle movement of metal, maybe a chain, moving against stone tore my attention from the glass jar atrocities as I scanned the large space. There were cages carved into the stone running the length of the far wall and I moved closer to them. Wrapping my fingers around two stone bars, I looked inside to see the skeletal remains of at least one fae.

A wheeze came from one of the cages a little further down, and I silently made my way down the row. I wouldn't lie, I was fucking petrified of what I might find.

I startled as a frail finger poked out from a cage, and began to tap as though that was all he or she could do to call for help. I felt sick as I saw the finger was little more than a skeleton wrapped in thick skin, no muscle or fat in between.

Get a fucking hold of yourself, Axel.

I took a deep breath and forced myself to put one foot in front of the other until I was face to face with the most sickly looking pair of fae I had ever seen.

Arguably harder to look at than whatever the fuck was in the jars behind me.

They were old and frail looking, but to the point where I had no doubt that a strong wind would end them.

The male was dressed in soiled rags and his auburn hair, though coated in a layer of dust and cobwebs, was peppered with white and well past his shoulders. He had cuffs on his wrists, not dissimilar to that which I had around my neck, but there was a lot of old dry blood crusted around his.

I heaved, "Fuck, sorry." I said to the male before I could stop myself.

He was cradling a female, her silver gray hair long and unkempt, matted in several places yet still fell past her hips. She too had cuffs around her wrists, painted with old blood.

Whoever had kept them here clearly hadn't liked them very much. Or even put any amount of effort into keeping them alive. No, they were just wasting away, cursed by their own immortality.

Who the fuck could do this to another fae?! Let alone two.

The male tried to hide the female behind himself as I approached. So I slowed, holding my hands up to show that I didn't have a weapon, then pointed to my neck to show I was a prisoner too, with a shiny cuff just like them.

"I'm here to get you out of here," I told them. "Do you think you can shuffle back a bit so I can try to break these bars?" My voice was as friendly and soothing as I could make it sound without verging on coming across as a lunatic.

They looked at each other and then winced as they dragged themselves to the back of the cage. I grabbed two stone bars and pulled them apart with everything I had, but it wasn't even close to being enough. "Fuck."

I paced the room, looking for something that could help, but aside from the jars, there wasn't really anything that could be used as a weapon against the cage.

"OK, I'm going to have to try brute force. Try to shield yourselves."

I ran at the wall of the cage, jumped to grab the bars of one a couple rows above and used the momentum of my swing to kick through the bars.

Dropping down, I saw that three of the bars had broken, it didn't leave them much of a gap to crawl out of, but let's be honest, there wasn't a lot to them. It would be enough.

"Sorry about that. Can you walk?" I asked gently, trying to avoid scaring them any further. The female peaked over the male's shoulder, staring at me with wide terrified eyes.

"Are we dead?" she whispered.

I looked them up and down. "Unfortunately not. I'm Axel and a seer called Edelin sent me in here. You can thank her when I get you out, 'cause I certainly won't be thanking her for subjecting me to this shit." I gestured to the jars behind me. "So can you walk? We need to get out of here before the catacombs collapse and we get stuck with whatever the fuck that is." I pointed to the largest of the jars. "We really don't have long."

"Edelin?" The male muttered as though testing the word on his very dry lips. He shared a glance with the female and finally nodded to me. "We will follow you."

"Great, my only rule is no souvenirs be taken from this room." I said, trying to lighten the mood and instantly regretting it as I realized they likely knew exactly what had happened in this lab to have made such unnatural creatures grow.

Perhaps this is where my sire was made.

The thought was meant to be lighthearted, in the way my dark humor was in the privacy of my own thoughts, but it hit me harder than the ceiling of my cell had.

"They were Augustus' experiments. His attempts at creating his monsters. The *thrakos* he'd called them," the male said in disgust, triggering a chill that shivered down my spine.

Probably a good job I can't shift right now.

I bent to move some of the rubble around the small gap I'd crawled through to make it easier for them when another rumble rocked the catacombs. Realizing there really was no time to waste, I ushered them through the gap, then offered them a quick apology as I bent forward and scooped them up, hoisting their bony forms over my shoulders.

Edelin was gone, thank the fates, and the path from our dungeon had been cleared enough for me to get through while carrying the fae.

I was drained, but I ran as quickly as I could in the direction I hoped would lead outside.

We'd woken up in the dungeons with the cuffs around our necks after Elikai's cronies had found us and knocked us out instantly with some strange darts.

Another of Augustus' experiments?

With several walls down, there weren't as many twists and turns to navigate and it wasn't long before a breeze swept over me and I saw Thalia, Elikai's maid and Lady Evangelia's friend, with wind blowing through her hair.

I'd fucking made it.

A tall male I didn't recognise, yet seemed familiar, was supporting Edelin and helping her take the final few steps out of the labyrinth and I almost whooped my relief. He had mousy brown hair just like her, and I knew he must be Nixen. *Hello, cousin.*

Crossing the threshold between the dank caves and the great outdoors, several sets of eyes fell on me and the two skeletons I held in a not very dignified position. "Do any of you fancy giving me a hand?" I asked the bunch of strangers before me.

"Axel?" Nix asked Edelin, and she nodded, smiling at me.

Nix carefully steadied his mum so she could stand on her own, with just a little bit of help from the jagged mouth of the cave. Then he stood in front of me, ready to steady the two fae as I carefully crouched down onto one knee and bent forward. I stayed there as he gently helped them to get their balance.

Someone gasped, and I looked across to see Westly at my side, staring wide-eyed at the fae like he'd seen a ghost. His mouth opened and closed around words that appeared to be putting up a fight against being unscrambled into audible sentences.

Then he dropped down next to me, mimicking my position.

Was he trying to be funny?

Fucking strange male.

Unlike Westly, the roar of a dragon had me jumping to my feet. I watched in spell bound awe as Lady Evangelia appeared like the badass and beautiful dragon she was; her scales shimmering in the moonlight as she soared onto land.

She dug her talons into the mountainside and some rubble fell under the impact of her weight, but she'd landed with far more grace than I'd have thought a beast of her size could manage. Her huge eyes searched us, landing on the two strangers, and she sniffed the air.

The vision of her made me regret not being alive when her kin would have sauntered through Dezrothian skies, wings wide in all their majestic might.

My eyes landed on the fae she carried on her back. "Alaric," I breathed, my lips curling until I realized I was beaming at the male I wasn't sure I'd ever see again. He smiled back, but it didn't make his scar crinkle. I wasn't surprised to see that Kane was there too, but the other male–

"What's wrong with Braxton?" Nix asked, clearly alarmed as he looked at the male I realized was being held onto tightly by Alaric.

"I dinnae ken," Alaric answered, worry etched in his tone. "He jus' collapsed."

"When?" Edelin asked, looking more confused than I'd seen the seer ever look before, her forehead wrinkled. Whatever had happened to the male, she hadn't foreseen it coming.

"When the explosion went off, I thought he lost his balance, but he didnae get back up," Alaric explained.

I moved closer to the dragon to get a better look.

Braxton, why do I know that name?

"Braxton's the male who cut me from my mum's womb, isn't he?" I asked Edelin and she nodded. "And that's also your dad's name?" I directed to Alaric, and he nodded carefully.

"True mates," Nix whispered, then cursed, looking around frantically. "Where's Rose?" he snapped.

"Back at the Crooked Claw where we left her. Who are we waitin' for?" He looked around the group, doing a quick head count, pausing as he frowned for a moment at the sickly fae who Westly was likely making feel rather uncomfortable at this point with his odd behavior. "Iona an' Miles?" Alaric eventually said.

Nix gulped. "And Rose," he muttered.

I was behind him before he finished speaking, grabbing his shoulder and whirling him around to face me. "What the fuck do you mean, *'and Rose'?"*

He stepped back out of my grip. "She followed us, caught up with us in the alley, and insisted on saving *you,"* Nix said, then turned his attention back to Alaric. "When we got here, she agreed to wait outside."

"Well, she didn't," Thalia said. "She went in straight after you."

Alaric and I growled in unison.

"I'm so sorry, I didn't know or we'd have tried to stop her.' Thalia said with a nod to Westly, who wasn't following any of what was happening around him.

My stomach dropped out of my arse as reality hit me.

Fuck. No, no, no.

Please fates, don't let her be inside that fucking death trap of a labyrinth.

I turned to look inside the catacombs, then back at Alaric, then at the catacombs again.

It wasn't a decision at all.

I ran inside.

CHAPTER 43

Nekane

The fog in my brain from Jarrah's venom hadn't fully cleared when I heard Alaric roar, "Axel!" at the top of his lungs.

His palm landed heavily at the top of my arm, shaking me to get my attention.

As I turned to face where he was sitting behind me on Eva's back, the fear in his silver eyes somehow cut through the haze briefly. But my body was struggling to muster the energy I needed to meet his urgency.

I felt like I was moving in slow motion, but it was nothing compared to the powerlessness I'd felt when the huge spider had jumped on my back, sunk in its fangs, and rendered me instantly paralyzed with his poison.

As I dropped to the ground and lay there helpless to do anything about him wrapping me in his strong yet soft and sticky webs, his betrayal hadn't been what consumed my thoughts the most. Neither had it been Alaric or Eva.

No. I was suddenly back in the castle, facing my father's wrath. For showing mercy to none other than a spider. One I had no doubt had nothing to do with Jarrah's traitorous scheme, but still, a spider no less.

"You had one job while I was gone. One easy fucking job fell to you to deal with. All you had to do was sentence the cretin mayor to death. What did you do instead? You fucking helped it!?" My father had seethed with such fury that I'd felt his spittle hitting my face.

So much had changed since that day we'd fought over me disappointing him so thoroughly. I was no longer turning a blind eye to evil like his. I was trying to do something about it, to fight against it.

I had allies, friends and two fae I loved deeply, depending on me getting to Rangaran and creating an alliance.

I'd needed their help the way they'd needed mine when I'd been called to the throne room as the only royal available to deal out their sentence while my brother and father were away slaughtering the last kraken.

But Jarrah had fucked it all up with his greed for a reward. Or perhaps he thought he'd receive acceptance. That my brother would be so thankful he'd forget he was a hybrid and welcome him into Ezerat with open arms and a nice safe place to live. Whatever his motivations, he'd clearly never met Elikai if he thought handing me over would make his life better somehow.

The memory of that specific run in with my father had continued to torture me as I lay prone for Jarrah to do with as he pleased, paralyzed, just like I had been shortly after my father had called Eva a 'sympathizer bitch', and then used his grotesque ring to pierce my skin and poison me too.

If only he'd known just how sympathetic Eva truly was when it came to those my father had wronged. She'd planned to kill him herself for those wrongs, for fates sake, instead of running from my brother and the castle at her earliest opportunity.

As Jarrah had proceeded to drag me to the castle, my healing magic had warred desperately inside my body against the toxic liquid flooding my veins. It was an agony impossible to ignore, but I tried to fill my thoughts with the good in my life instead of my father.

But everything kept coming back to that singular day.

Of how it was then that I'd had the realization that Eva was everything. *She was the sun. She was a queen. She was mine,* I'd thought. And of how Alaric was a thousand times the fighter, the protector, the male my father would ever be.

For me, there was no feeling more vulnerable than being paralyzed. I was a fae who relied on my body and its speed and strength. I'd worked hard on honing it into a weapon. Not having that, it took me back to the boy I'd once been.

Hiding in alcoves when I heard my father's footsteps turn down the castle corridor I'd been exploring, knowing if he saw me I'd spark a rage inside him and be powerless to do anything except curl up in a ball, scrunch my eyes tightly shut and wait for him to tire or grow bored.

Unlike the hydra venom my father had used on me by lacing his thorn like spiked ring, I knew that spider venom didn't have the ability to kill, only to disable while the spider smothered its victim in their silk.

As we'd drawn nearer to the castle gates, I almost regretted that it couldn't kill me, because that meant I'd die at my brother's hand instead, which was so much worse. Either way, I truly thought I was going to die before the day was through.

My father's words had reared their ugly head again as I'd heard Elikai unsheathe his sword above my exposed neck out on that balcony.

"You are good for nothing, a total fucking waste of space! Why don't you just die already?!" he'd said, and though death had been terrifyingly close a few times, his wish had yet to be granted.

For that, I had Eva and Alaric and Braxton, and likely everyone else stood before us now to thank.

"Kane, here," Alaric said, somehow managing to sound frantic while being careful as he pushed his dad's unconscious form toward me. Reaching for my hand, he set it down on Braxton's chest for support. "Hold on to him," he said.

I tightened my fist on instinct, gripping onto his dad's clothing to make sure he stayed balanced on Eva's back.

I knew Alaric was going to do something stupid even before he moved to climb down off of our stunning dragon's body, but I was also very aware that I had no hope of doing a fucking thing about it while I was still so weakened from the venom.

I was hardly in any fit state to support myself, let alone Braxton too, all the while clinging onto a giant spike that protruded from the base of Eva's neck.

Still, I had to attempt to stop him from racing inside the catacombs after Axel and his mother, Rose.

"Alaric, wait." I slurred, watching the space between us grow larger with every step he took toward the mouth of the cave and away from Eva and I.

He paused to glance over his shoulder in our direction. "I love yeh both, but I cannae just wait out here to discover the fates of my ma' and brother. I'll never forgive myself if they die and I dinnae do anythin'."

The frail male and female were staring our way too, only their gaze was firmly planted on the huge dragon specifically. So much so, I doubted they'd even noticed anyone else around them, bar their savior who had just run back into the caves they had exited.

Not even my former butler on his knees at their backs, head bowed and Thalia crouched beside him as they whispered, seemed to draw their attention the way the dragon did. Then again, everyone believed them to be extinct.

"It's not just yourself you'll be killing if you go in there, Alaric," a wise sounding female tried to caution him. She was standing close to Nix. It had to be his mum, Edelin. The seer. But her words had come too late. Alaric had already continued his race for the catacombs entrance and crossed the threshold, fading from sight.

I had so many questions but so little vitality left in me to voice them all as I clung to Eva, Braxton and my own consciousness with the last drops of energy I had. Questions like, what the fuck was Alaric thinking? What could I say to make him turn back? Who the fuck were those skin-and-bones fae staring at my female and what had my uncle meant when he'd said it didn't take a genius to work out what line she was bred from. What had the seer meant when she'd said it wasn't just himself that Alaric would be killing if he entered those caves?

"What do you mean by that?" I managed to ask her as I tried to shake the fog clouding my mind that was only thickening.

She scoffed. "Surely you've worked it out for yourselves by now?"

Eva let out an impatient snarl as she directed her attention to the witch. She was tense beneath me, her deep breaths much more shallow than they'd been even as we'd flown from the castle to these mountains below, in search of the cause of the explosion.

I didn't need to see her large slitted eyes to know they'd be narrowed on the seer.

"Enlighten us," I gritted as dizziness made my head feel like it wasn't properly attached to my neck. It felt like a spinning top when it began to wobble before dropping completely.

She laughed, but it was humorless. "You truly have no idea, do you? Don't tell me you've been waiting for a bolt of lightning to strike the ground between the three of you while you admit your feelings for one another? Or perhaps for the three fates themselves to appear in the clouds and write it on the moon for you?"

"You mean to say..." I trailed off, gripping onto Eva tighter as my eyes then shot toward where I'd last seen Alaric. The male whose scent called to me as strongly as the female beneath me had from the moment I'd met her. One no more or less than the other, because both were more potent and consuming and instinctual than anything else I'd ever known.

"The three of you are true mates," she said, exasperated.

And I knew immediately that there was no way it wasn't true. Because even at full strength, with a poison free body and mind, I wouldn't be challenging her on it. There was no need to, because I felt their truth deep in my bones. My head, my heart and my soul somehow just knew...

"He dies. You two die too," Edelin continued. " I've seen it happen to my sister and her true mate. I'm seeing it happen to Braxton right now as Rose hangs onto life by a thread. And I'll see it again with the three of you if Alaric doesn't get out of those catacombs immediately."

As I processed her words and what they meant for us, I realized that not only was my body moving in slow motion, but time itself seemed to stand still as my eyes darted from Braxton, who was barely breathing, to Raine, who looked sick with worry for her lover, Miles. To Nix, who had paled as he took in his best friend, like he was about to lose her all over again, only for good this time. Then to the malnourished male and female who looked wide-eyed at Eva the way my uncle had. Only now, tears pooled now in their previously dry, sunken sockets as they clung to each other as tightly as they could, as if the fates had answered their prayers, then ripped it all away again.

My own gaze settled on the cave entrance. I was so lightheaded and shaky, and it took me a moment to realize that the rocks themselves had actually begun to shake, too.

Time caught up at the sound of a thundering crash, then a thick cloud of dust rolled out of the cave mouth in a plume of smoke and debris, like a tidal wave crashing on the shore.

The cave was falling in on itself and we could do nothing but watch uselessly as Alaric, Axel, Rose, Miles and Iona became its victims, eaten alive, swallowed whole by its fatal depths.

Eva's head reared back, causing me to cling onto her and Braxton tighter.

A roar that I was certain could knock the stars out of the sky itself left her lungs. Dragon fire erupted from her throat in its wake in a river of orange and red and blue.

"*Alaric!*" I cried out.

The name tore from my chest and echoed around the mountain.

A cacophony of shouting rang out from the others, so much fucking pain in the sounds that it felt like a hundred daggers piercing my heart.

There was crying and screaming too, though it sounded far away. Too far away, considering I knew they were right in front of me.

A raspy bellow rattled from Eva.
It was the last thing I heard before blackness engulfed me.
And then there was nothing.

PART THREE
Wisdom of Fates

CHAPTER 1
Evangelia

When I was twelve years old, I fell through a frozen lake in the Vale. One moment I'd been joking around with Nix, egging him on to join me in my reckless game. The next, every ounce of air I had was stolen from my lungs.

As I swam for the surface, my head met with a solid wall of ice. I vividly remember seeing dry land through the glass roof sealing me in with the frigid water. Safety and freedom were right there, if only I could just get to shore. But no matter how hard I pounded my fists against the barrier, my next breath remained out of reach.

As my heart rate slowed, the panic accelerated, until I was certain it was the end.

Frozen in fear. No air in my lungs. Trapped. Unable to find a way out.

That's how I feel now.

Only this time, it wasn't my life I feared for.

Like me, Alaric had been reckless. Where thick ice had once held me captive, the walls and ceilings of the catacombs' collapse were his prison. He'd known the dangers when he shot through the cave entrance, just as I'd known the risks of playing on the ice. But again, like me, he thought he could find a way out—would find a way out—even if the worst happened.

Nix had been there to save me that day. But Alaric… He was the one supposed to be doing the saving.

The debris cloud dissipated, slowly revealing the cave's entrance.

At the same time, the reassuring grip on the spike at the top of my spine vanished.

Kane.

My tightly coiled muscles strained as I moved to see what was going on. Why hadn't he climbed down? Why wasn't he saying anything? He'd seen Alaric go inside the labyrinth as well as I had. He'd heard the explosion. He'd seen the wave of smoke as it poured from the catacombs. Why wasn't he doing something? Panic set in and I twisted and turned my body, but there were no sensations of him moving on my back, just a dead weight.

"Eva, please. Stop!" A male voice gritted out from my flank as I thrashed more violently. Familiar, but not Kane. "You have to calm down."

How could I calm down when Alaric had gone and taken Kane with him?

A roar tore from my throat, ripping from my chest, and echoing around the mountain. The ground shook, and I was faintly aware of the rocks slipping free beneath my claws as I watched Nix dash between my front legs. My best friend jerked back into my eyeline, his lips moving, but whatever sounds he made were drowned out by my deep pants and growls.

As he continued his frantic dance of racing toward me, only to retreat again, large boulders came loose under the pressure of my weight. Tumbling down the mountainside, like a cascade of giant stone raindrops.

If you don't heed his warning and calm the fuck down, he'll join them.

"Be still!" Nix said, projecting his voice loud enough this time to be heard from the castle. "We need to get Kane and Braxton down from your back."

I tensed, face snapping to my friend, but found the slumped silhouette of my mate in my moonlit shadow. Behind him; Braxton's unconscious body lay flush against my scales, too. Nix was trying to get to them, to help them, and I was the one stopping him. I had to get my dragon under control.

We are one and the same being.

If I was calm, she would be too.

The sight of Kane's still form on my back, a male usually so strong and full of life, only added fuel to the already blazing fire inside me. *Get it together, Eva.* Closing my eyes, I focused only on my breathing, ignoring the chaos around me as I counted back from ten.

Ten... nine... eight...

Thalia's voice drifted to my ears, drawing closer and closer until I felt her at my flank. She was talking to Nix, who was on my other side now, his palm stroking my scales. If she was surprised by the sight of my dragon, she hid it well in her firm tone. I listened to their exchange as they discussed how to help those balancing on my back, all while maintaining a calmness I admired.

Seven... Six... Five...

My muscles loosened a little as it occurred to me that Kane had to be alright. If he wasn't, I would be dead, too.

Flattening my body to the ground, I crouched down as low as I was able while clinging to the earth with just my talons.

Four... Three... Two...

My eyes opened. Alaric was okay. He was still breathing. We were true mates, if I was alive. He was too.

He could be trapped, though. Pinned beneath the debris of the collapse. How long did he have left? Not long enough for me to waste any more time. With my underbelly pressed to the rocks beneath me, I held still as a statue, giving my friends an invitation to climb up my massive form.

Nix called out instructions from above, while Thalia moved to stand at the end of my snout, not in the least concerned for her safety.

With the lift of her palms, she muttered a spell, and a weight lifted from my back. Nix lowered Braxton safely to the stony ground below as Thalia kept her focus on Kane. *Holding him in place to keep him from falling?*

As Kane's body was laid down before me, a mournful whimper left my chest. Nix was being so gentle with him. If Kane weren't in such a fragile state, my heart would have swelled at the unlikely bond the two had built.

Not long ago, I couldn't have imagined my friend treating my male with such care.

One.

With Braxton and Kane no longer on my back, I partially shifted to my fae form. It was easier than expected, likely thanks to the adrenaline still pumping through my veins. Silver scales covered my body in armor, though they appeared almost black in the darkness. I crouched by Kane's side, willing away the wings at my back, stopping them from dragging uncomfortably against the hard ground. Wiping the beads of sweat from Kane's forehead, his skin burned as hot as dragon fire. At least he was breathing, albeit shallowly.

"What's wrong with him? It can't be tied to Alaric, or I'd be sick too." I murmured, trying to keep my voice steady. "Why isn't he healing?"

Edelin joined me. "Poison," she mused.

"Spider venom." I confirmed. "But he's high fae, his body heals quicker than most."

Edelin winced. "Spider venom is among the most potent poisons in Dezrothia. He needs to rest. Every ounce of energy his body has left is being used to fight it and heal."

My chest tightened. I assumed he bested his brother because he'd healed. That he'd managed such a feat, still suffering the effects…

"You need to help him." I demanded. "Please, Edelin, please help him to heal."

She shook her head, and my fists clenched.

"She can't." Nix said, crouching next to me, a hand laid on my shoulder. "It's the collar around her neck. It is blocking her magic."

"Then *you* heal him," I said to Nix, then turned my gaze to Thalia. "Or *you*."

Her eyes widened as my dragon made herself known in both my voice and fiery glare. I looked to Westly next, whose eyes were flitting between Kane, who'd been his master for more than two decades, and the two strangers before him. The frail pair walked toward me, and I moved on instinct to guard Kane. At their penetrating stare, I remembered the way they'd gawked at me in dragon form. Like they were analyzing me down to my very soul. It was disconcerting.

They shuffled closer, clinging to each other as they hobbled. I sniffed the air. Something even more disturbing laced in their scents, beneath the weakness and grime, something familiar to me. *Home.* Had they lived in the Vale too? The female opened her mouth to speak. "*Blood…*" Her voice was so hoarse, it almost hurt to hear. Not as much as it was hurting her though, if the pinch in her brow was anything to go by.

Westly unclipped the canteen of water from his waist and held it out. She took it with a grateful nod of her head, and I watched as she winced every time her throat bobbed in delicate swallows. Clearing her throat, she said. "You need blood… to open the cuff. Augustus Regis' blood." She took one more measured sip from the canteen and passed it back to the male. "Augustus used it to create the seal on these cuffs. His blood is the only way to remove them."

How do they not know? "He's dead–"

"There has to be another way," Thalia cut over, looking to Westly.

"Edelin..." he said, emotion so thick it made his voice break. How long had it been since they'd been in a coven together? Since they'd last been face to face? "Perhaps it doesn't need to be Augustus's blood," he continued, and I frowned. "What about the blood of his *line?*"

My eyes fell on my mate's face. It was relaxed, as though he was merely in a deep sleep. It was too easy to forget he's blood related to such evil, to the late king.

Edelin's eyes narrowed on the male as she thought over his words before at last nodding. "Hmm. That *could* work," she said.

"How much is needed?" I asked, turning my gaze to the ancient fae couple.

"Not much. Maybe a drop or two," the female rasped.

The male at her side spoke next. "You won't find a Regis willing to part with their blood, not even to save a high fae like this male." He gestured to Kane.

A loud rumble from the catacombs entrance drew everyone's attention. I gulped, watching the rise and fall of Kane's ribs, waiting for either of our hearts to stop beating. Neither did. But we were running out of time. Kane wasn't the only one who needed saving before we could flee.

Not looking at the male who'd scorned Kane's bloodline, I muttered, "Good thing this high fae is Prince Nekane Regis then."

The male gasped, but I ignored it. Cradling Kane's hand in my own, Edelin didn't miss a beat as she held her hand out to Nix. Unsheathing a dagger, he placed the blade's hilt in her palm.

Edelin pressed the sharp blade against Kane's finger, and I sucked in a breath. "Be careful," I said.

"He won't feel a thing, dear," she assured, then dragged the blade across the skin of his fingertip, allowing the crimson to well up.

The stare of the fae couple was like a lead weight bearing down on me. They were too broken to be much of a threat right now. And if they tried anything, I trusted Nix and Raine to deal with it.

Ignoring them, I focused on my mate. "He can't afford to lose much blood, not if he is still fighting off the poison," I said, locking eyes with her across his body. She looked like she wanted to say something. Instead, she nodded as she gathered the red liquid on the dagger's edge.

"I know, Evangelia," she said, firm but not unkind. Fates, I'd missed my best friend's mother. She was like an aunt to me.

"Nixen," she said. "I need you to find where the cuff joins together. Look for markings or something to indicate where it opens."

As he moved the hair covering the back of her neck to the side, I glanced at Raine. She was watching the unknowns among us, ready to pounce should they attempt any attack.

"Here," he said, shifting the collar a little so a faint line in the metal could be seen. With a steady hand, she gave him the blade.

Nix smeared the bloodied edge across the joint. The collar illuminated slightly, a golden glow so faint I couldn't be certain I hadn't imagined it, then snapped open, falling into Edelin's lap.

The seer inhaled deeply as though taking her first breath and I let out the air I'd been holding.

"Thank the fates," I whispered. "Now please, help him."

Her small smile and nod reminded me of the old times, and I knew she could do this. "I'm going to need some room, Evangelia," she said, and I shuffled backward. "Nixen, you can help boost my power."

"I can help too." Westley offered, his gaze firmly on his former charge.

Edelin smiled wider than she had in years, pleased to be using magic with her centuries-old friend once again. The two males placed a hand on her forearm and shoulder. Thalia joined them too, and the moment Edelin pressed her fingers against Kane's temples, they began to chant as one. Kane was in safe hands. I squeezed his leg gently before getting to my feet, and finally let myself look around the group properly for the first time since transforming back onto two legs.

Raine paced outside the entrance to the catacombs. While Braxton lay motionless on the cold ground, his chest scarcely moving. Though no one had voiced it, we all knew the only way to save him was to save his mate. It was the only plausible explanation for why a fae like him would drop like a stone without obvious ailment or injury.

The old couple were looking from me to Kane, then back to me. Deep emotion evident in their eyes. I had no doubt they'd been prisoners of King Regis, for far longer than most of us here had been alive if their condition was anything to go by. They were strangers to me. I shouldn't care what they thought, but I couldn't shake the urge to make them understand Kane was nothing like their torturer.

"He's not like his father," I said.

Their eyes went wide, but I dropped my gaze to Edelin before they could answer. "Is it working? Whatever you're doing, is it helping?"

She paused her chants. "He will be fine, Evangelia. Now do what you know you need to do."

She didn't need to say the words for me to understand.

My other mate needed me now.

Raine's large wolf eyes met mine as I joined her. Though she looked ready to take on the entire realm, her worry over the fate of those trapped inside swam in their depths.

Miles is in that death trap, too.

"Together?" I asked.

Unable to speak in her wolf form, she dipped her dark shaggy head, and I took it as the affirmation it was intended to be.

As one, we entered the catacombs.

WE PAUSED ONCE we made it to a fork in the tunnel. With a shrug of my shoulders, my wings released, ready to protect us from the falling rocks and rubble. The left-hand side had completely caved in, so Raine sniffed her way down the right. Her hackles raised, like she'd caught a scent, and she followed it without a backward glance.

Propelling myself to go after her, I kept close, but the dust was thick and the light minimal; any more than a few paces between us and I'd lose sight of her. She stopped abruptly, her nose twitching in the air. Whatever she'd scented was causing her stress. I opened my mouth to ask what was troubling her, but before the words came out, she took off.

Fuck. "We need to stick together," I called, sprinting after her. "Raine!"

She skidded to a halt, clawing at the ground with fervor as she tried to fight her way through the rocks blocking the way. Primal growls turned into loud barks between pushing her snout into the cracks, trying to force her way through. Crouching at her side, I went to work with her, clearing the area she was so determined to break through.

"Eva! Raine!" The echoing sound of my best friend's voice yelled out from behind us.

"Over here," I called back to Nix, and seconds later, he was looming over us.

Raine and I continued to move rocks under the protection of my wings, and I tried to position one to cover my best friend too, though he quickly brought his own out to shield himself. As a jagged spike shot up my nail, I hissed at the pain but didn't stop, shoving the rocks aside one by one.

"Horde soldiers are marching on us from above and below," Nix said.

"How long do we have?"

"Not long enough to stick around. We need to get out of Ezerat, now."

Those climbing down from the top would be dangerously close. But they'd have to move slower than those coming up from the base, where the ground was a little less treacherous.

"How's Kane?"

"Still unconscious, but my mum said he's fought off most of the venom."

Thank the fates. "Then help us," I told him. "I don't know what she's found, but the sooner we clear the path, the sooner we'll know and can leave."

We worked together in silence, until eventually a large boulder shifted, just enough for us to pry it away from the rest. Several smaller rocks tumbled down as we moved it and a haunting whimper had me whirling to see what was wrong. My eyes landed on a paw. Not Raine's paw. Not even that of a wolf. It was a bear. The same shade as Ilona's.

"No... Please, no," I whispered, but my throat was so tight it was barely audible.

Ilona. She'd been so close to the exit. So fucking close. I didn't know her well, but she was always one to follow the rules. That she'd broken them by shifting into her bear form, told of how desperate she'd been. She'd almost made it. If Ilona was here, where was Miles? And Rose and Axel. My mate.

Alaric.

The only thing keeping me from losing all hope was knowing Alaric had to be alive, because I was still standing.

So long as I'm breathing, he is too.

Grief was heavy in the dust filled air around us as we worked together to clear the stones pinning Ilona. When a rancid metallic scent became overwhelming, bile filled my throat. Blood was pooling around her. She'd been completely crushed. No fae could survive what her body had endured. Nix fell to his knees, pulling her massive bear head onto his lap as he checked for a pulse through thick, matted fur.

We all knew it was futile, but I didn't stop him. Hope sparked in my heart as he was silent for several beats, only to be dashed with the shake of his head. *Hope, Nekane, is for children.* The words I'd once said to my mate flashed through my mind, breaking my heart further.

A howl tore from Raine, echoing the pain I felt. Turning to comfort her, I saw the other wolf.

Miles.

Just as motionless as Iona. Just as broken. Just as dead. The fearless she-wolf let out mournful yips, like she was begging him to wake up. To come back to her. To be okay. Tears fogged my eyes as she howled, long and low and filled with heartbreak. She couldn't bring him back, no matter how much she nuzzled him. This wasn't one of their cute games. He was truly gone.

I reached out a hand but stopped shy of touching her. "I am so sorry, Raine."

My throat closed. There were no more words of comfort coming. What was there to say?

She collapsed; her muzzle pressed into the belly of the wolf who'd held her heart. It didn't matter their pairing hadn't been written by the fates. You don't have to be true mates to love someone with your entire being.

Nix cleared his throat. His face was hard and detached, as though he couldn't let himself feel their deaths. "The horde will be here soon."

"What about Alaric? And Rose? What about Axel? He's your family!" I pleaded, but I knew we had to go. I'd failed. Failed to find my mate. Failed to save Ilona and Miles.

I had to trust the others. I had to trust my mate to find a way back to me. No one knew the catacombs as well as Alaric and Axel. And no one would fight harder to aid their escape than Rose would. She was a mother protecting her children. She'd die before giving up.

Raine's bark drew my attention as she got to her unsteady feet. I joined her, but she didn't stop to wait for me. Lifting her snout in the air, she let out another roar of grief, this one fiercer, ringing of vengeance and hate. Then took off, darting back the way we had come, leaving Nix and I in her dust. Red flames engulfed her fur. But it didn't burn away. I blinked, dumbfounded, as her thrakos side ignited with the anger of her wolf.

Nix's hand landed on my shoulder, stopping me from going after her. "She needs some time, Eva," he said. "Help me with Ilona and Miles. They deserve to be buried back home."

Home. To the Vale. But why didn't the Vale feel like home anymore?

Shaking off the thought, failure filled me with bitterness as we worked silently.

The only thoughts I allowed myself to give credence to were all the ways I would make Elikai pay.

CHAPTER 2
Alaric

Stopping dead at a cavern born of my nightmares, a sudden deafening silence engulfed the moonless depths.

The constant roar of plummeting rubble just a few tunnels ago, I could deal with.

The heavy lashes against my wings as ceilings caved in around me, I could deal with.

Fates, I'd take walking into them screaming or fucking crying over this…

This eerie quiet of hopelessness.

Rose lying unconscious, her chest flattened under the weight of stone. A fate that would have instantly killed a fae who hadn't come of age and attained their immortality yet.

Fuck, it could kill an immortal.

Veins bulged in Axel's battered arms as he fought to lift the giant boulder pinning her down. Crushing her into the dust-covered ground as though it wanted to be certain to finish the job and slice her completely in two. Despite the sweat cascading down his face, Axel's efforts were futile… feeble even. The vision of a desperate male fast running out of hope, a sight I neither recognized from him nor wanted to see ever-a-fucking-gain.

My throat was tight. "Is she…?"

"Alaric, what the fuck are you doing in here?" Axel said, his voice strained as he looked up, face contorted with the worry he tried to conceal as anger.

The thick cuff I'd seen him wearing remained clamped around his throat, fucking with him somehow. Despite that, he didn't release his hands from where they gripped the underside of the giant stone.

"Is she dead?" I asked, my jaw set rigid. Caging in the overwhelming emotions hitting me over the condition of my family.

"I don't know," he admitted. "Help me lift this boulder off her? I can't fucking move it." Without so much as a nod, I moved to stand opposite him.

Squatting down, I shoved my fingers under the bulk, not bothering to be gentle. Gentle wouldn't save her, just like a little scratch wouldn't kill her. Fuck, she wouldn't even notice it next to her other list of injuries. She probably couldn't feel much of anything, and I couldn't decide if that was good or bad.

Together, we strained, but Axel's side wasn't moving. The cuff was weakening him, but we couldn't afford to fail. We had to save our ma'. As my side lifted, I forced my arms farther beneath it, straightened my legs, and threw the boulder aside. As it hit the ground, a cloud of debris and dust swept through the catacombs. Followed by the ominous rumble of collapsing rocks. *Fuck.*

Blinded by the dust, I reached out to Axel. Instinctively, we clasped each other's forearms, creating a bridge over Rose's body. Locking shoulders, we ducked our heads low, teeth gritted as the debris assaulted us. I willed my strength into Axel, hoping to bolster his efforts. Time lost all meaning as our bodies endured the shower of sharp rocks.

At some point, the shaking of the walls subsided, and everything became still once more. I needn't have bothered opening my eyes, it was almost impossible to see anything with the cavern so completely engulfed in the dust clouds cloak of darkness.

"Yeh alright?" I asked.

"Never better."

Sarcastic arsehole. Usually, I'd tell him it was the lowest form of wit, but right now I was too happy he was alive and had found his sense of humor to be an arsehole right back to him. I needed a plan to get us out of here, but with no way to see what lay ahead, we had no choice but to wait it out. Assess the situation once the dust settled.

Blinking it out of my eyes, things started to come back into focus. I crouched down beside ma', checked for a pulse and my breaths came a little easier. The thuds were slow and weak, but there. She was alive, and we'd managed to shield her from the waist up, protecting her head and heart. But her legs were crushed, likely broken in several places.

Relief washed over me, knowing that she'd heal, but the danger remained.

"Thank you, brother," Axel said, then cleared his throat. "Don't suppose you have any idea how we're going to get her out of this place?" he asked, his voice steadier than I'd expected.

"Well, we cannae get out the way we came. I barely outran the collapsing fuckin' ceilings to get here." He winced, but I pretended not to notice. "We'll find another way."

"Through the castle?"

"Nah, that's just askin' for trouble. We'll head that way," I said, pointing behind him. "Find another tunnel then try to circle back. Some must have remained intact, or we'd have been fuckin' buried already. Can yeh carry ma' while I start moving this shit?" I asked, gesturing to the rubble.

His nod was firm, but I didn't miss the way his legs shook as he bent to pick Rose up carefully. It was either carry the female or move a thousand rocks, so I didn't have much choice but to watch him struggle. He didn't complain, just stood tight-lipped with her in his arms while I concentrated my efforts on moving stone after stone; careful not to disturb the larger ones, which seemed to be stopping the precarious roof of our cavern from collapsing.

"Alaric!" Axel called out, making my heart skip several beats. I hated the sensation of being so on edge but couldn't stop myself from jumping back from whatever threat he was warning me of.

Thank the fates I did, because a thick blade of rock fell from the ceiling, smashing into the ground where I stood not a second before.

My hands were shaking. I needed to get it together and show Axel we weren't royally fucked. I clenched my fists to cover the weakness, but the male wasn't easily fooled.

"Calm down, Alaric. We'll find a way out of here."

"It's no' that," I confessed. "That fuckin' seers got my nerves shot," I muttered, irritated to still be shaken by the close call. I tried to ignore it and resumed shifting the rubble, but Axel was like a mutt with a bone.

"How so?" he asked, his curiosity tinged with concern.

"Just somethin' she said as I came in after yeh," I said.

"What did she say?"

I didn't want to worry him, or even talk about it, period. That would mean trying to unravel her cryptic bullshit and I didn't have the energy for that right now.

A warning of my own death wasn't anything I wasn't unused to, but warning of the death of others, of the brave males and females who'd come on this mission with me, was harder to take. Especially when I was meant to be in these catacombs with them on the mission, but chose to go to the castle to save Kane from execution instead.

"Alaric, talk to me."

Crouching to lift the next rock, I took a deep breath and repeated Edelin's parting words. "She said, it's not just me I'd be killin' coming in here."

"Fuck," he let out an exasperated sigh. "Why is it always so morbid with her? I mean, she can't help it, but… Wait. You don't think she means–"

"That we 're goin' to die in here?" I asked, tossing the rock and moving on to the next. "Aye. One wrong move and I might jus' kill everyone who's still in here. If I pick the wrong boulder, the wrong tunnel, the wrong anythin', the whole place could cave in."

The weight of her warning wasn't lost on me, but what other chance would Axel and Rose have had if I'd remained out there? Waiting for Braxton to die with them.

What if they hadn't found each other? How would Axel live with himself knowing she came in here to find him in the first place?

Axel started to tut in the annoying way he did when his mind whirled, doubtlessly thinking over all the ways I could be the harbinger of his death. Of his adoptive mother's death. Of the death of the rebels who'd stormed in here under my command.

AFTER CLEARING THE FIRST PILE, we made our way along the tunnel with caution, but before long, we hit another block. My hands were cracked and cut, and as quickly as they began to heal, the wounds would be reopened. But we were alive, so a few flesh wounds I could deal with.

Axel must have been desperate to bring up Edelin's warning. Somehow he had managed to keep his mouth shut—until now.

"So... You're sure Edelin meant the fae in here? What about Kane and Evangelia?"

I shook my head, dismissing the idea. "Nah. They're safe. Angel's still a dragon and Kane, though he's still weak, is recovering. If a threat came, she could take to the skies," I said. "I wouldnae have left them if I thought they were in imminent danger."

"Like you are," Axel said, brows pinched.

I scoffed. "Aye. But someone had to save yer stupid arse."

"No, Alaric. You're not getting it," he snapped. The seriousness in his voice caught me off guard. He clearly had every intention of being heard out.

A sense of dread sunk into the pit of my stomach. *Fine.* "What the fuck am I not gettin'?" I bit back.

"Maybe Edelin wasn't talking about you bringing about *our* deaths. What if she was trying to tell you something else? Something... deeper."

He glanced down at Rose, my ma' still hanging heavy in his arms.

"Your da', Braxton, he was fine? Right up until Aunt Rose wasn't?"

My brow furrowed, unsure what he meant. "Yeah, cause they are true mates."

Axel nodded, "Exactly."

"Exactly what?"

"If one is about to cross over to the other side, so would the other. Fates forbid it, but if Aunt Rose had died, she'd have brought about the death of Braxton."

"Aye..."

My eyes went wide, nostrils flared. *Fuck. No.*

I finally stopped what I was doing and turned to him properly. "What yer thinking is not possible."

"But what if it is? What if Kane, Eva, and you are true mates? You've said it yourself—seers talk in riddles. What if she was telling you that you *are* true mates, and coming in here, getting yourself killed, would kill them?"

My head was shaking, but the denial didn't stop my heart from skipping several beats as the possibility began to sink in. True mates were rare among the fae. The bond was unbreakable. A connection that ran soul deep. It was something I had never found myself worthy of.

What was left of the tunnel walls seemed suddenly narrower as it sank in. *What if they* are *my true mates?*

"We'll figure it out later, I guess," he shrugged, as if he could see into my mind. Could feel how conflicted I was. "Right now, we need to focus on getting out of here alive and keeping Aunt Rose safe, right?"

My nod was hesitant. "Right."

We pressed on in silence, pushing aside rubble and debris. Axel's arms were full, but he kicked the smaller stuff out of the way. It didn't help much, but it made him feel slightly less powerless under the control of the collar and not anywhere close to his full strength.

Together we inched our way through the gloom with the revelation of the true mate bond adding another layer to the sense of urgency of getting out alive. I couldn't help but dread what other truths awaited us around each corner. Time alluded us in the endless tunnels. The lack of light only added to our disorientation; every step we took was met with new challenges and thick dust filled the air, making it hard to breathe.

"Are you okay?" Axel asked, cutting through the uncomfortable tension.

"Aye. Fine," I replied, hardly recognizing my own exhausted voice. "Just knackered. And worryin' about ma'."

Axel nodded in understanding. "We'll get through this. We have to."

We pushed forward. Every inch gained felt like a small victory, but the catacombs seemed to conspire against us. Crumbling walls, unstable ceilings, and narrow passageways forced us to slow down and navigate with caution. My thoughts kept returning to Edelin's warning. If Kane, Eva, and I were true mates, what did that mean for us? Was our bond strong enough to overcome the obstacles we faced? And what about the prophecy that foretold upheaval?

I couldn't shake the feeling that our destinies were entwined with forces beyond our control. I had to protect my loved ones, not only from the physical dangers around us, but from the unpredictable future that lay ahead.

"All good?" I threw over my shoulder at some point, pulling myself from my thoughts.

"Aye, still breathing." He murmured, shifting as he cradled ma's limp form.

"Yeh ken, it's probably a good thing she's unconscious. She'd kick yer arse if she knew yeh looked at her like she was about to break."

Axel glared in my direction. "If you tell her anything of the sort, I'll deny it."

As I let out a surprised chuckle, we stumbled upon a glimmer of hope—a narrow crevice in the wall with light shining through from beyond.

Doubling down my efforts, relief washed over me as the blockage crumbled away, blinding me with natural light.

Axel released a shivering breath, then tightened his grip on Rose. "I swear to the fates, if I never have to step foot inside this place again, it'd be too soon."

"Fuckin' right," I said, pushing through the narrow space myself, before turning to support Axel as he traversed the unsteady stones.

We squeezed through the tight space, emerging onto the side of the mountain. We'd gained height from where we'd entered, but the dimly lit sky had never been a more welcome sight.

"Alaric, look," Axel said, pointing toward a plateau below.

A glint of silver caught my eye. *Angel.*

Then a battle cry met my ears. The horde were racing down the mountain, and we'd just stepped out, straight into their path.

"I'll take her," I said, quickly slumping my ma's body over my shoulder.

Fighting them wasn't an option. Sacrificing ourselves wouldn't slow them down by more than a few seconds, but me dying would kill Eva and Kane, and Eva dying would mean the survivors had no way out. We had to run, but Axel wouldn't be able to outrun them like this, either. He was too weak, his abilities too compromised. Bending low, I shoved my shoulder into his gut at the same time my free arm closed around the back of his knees. "What the fuck are y–"

Before he could finish, he was on my other shoulder and I was racing down the mountain to my mates. My true mates.

CHAPTER 3

Nixen

Arrows flew overhead. The horde below so close now, we were within their sights. Their sole focus and single-minded target, Eva.

I held onto the hope that we were in the air before they noticed the giant hole in their plan of taking down the dragon first; her impenetrable metal-like scales protecting us in the interim. As arrows splintered and fell uselessly to the ground, the witch female, Thalia, and I helped a semi-conscious Braxton up onto Eva's back. After settling him beside my mum, we went back for Kane.

The loud twang of another round of arrows being released had me covering my head as we ducked for shelter, behind the silver-scaled wing shielding her mate. One of her mates. If only the other would hurry the fuck up and join us. I had no doubt he would be tearing through stone and rubble until his fingers were worn down to stumps to get through those tunnels and back to her. To get Rose back to Braxton, too.

The memory of my own nails, broken and bleeding, came to the forefront of my mind, but now wasn't the time to face past trauma. Shaking it off, my eyes met with Thalia's just as an arrow whistled past her ear, drawing blood. "Get down!" I shouted, and she did, mirroring how I shielded my head with my arms.

Fates, that was close. Any closer and I'd be covered in her brains right now.

Fuck, we needed to take to the skies, but before Eva had shifted, she'd been adamant we wait for Alaric, Axel and Rose. I'd agreed to her plan, but it had been a lie. I hated to lie to her, but no fucking chance was I risking any of us being captured by the horde. Not today. Not ever again.

I'd just gotten the only fae I loved in this realm back. I wasn't about to risk losing them again. Even if Axel was family. I didn't know him, and you couldn't miss those you didn't know.

"You pair!" I called to the fae Axel had carried out of the catacombs, slumped over his shoulders. "If you're coming with us, climb on." They shared a glance but didn't move. “Now!” I yelled. If I wasn’t even waiting for our allies, I wasn’t about to wait for strangers.

“Help them,” Thalia said to the warlock I now knew to be her uncle. The two fae shared another look, silently deciding to fight another day, and the female took Westly’s outstretched palm. The male refused the help, but followed closely behind the female, who I had to assume was his mate.

Since we’d agreed to let them use the blood on my dagger to remove their cuffs, they’d been gradually looking a little better. Still completely starved and frail, but not quite as fragile. They climbed up Eva’s back with surprising grace and I turned to do a quick head count. Braxton, my mum and our two deceased comrades were in place on Eva’s back. Westly and the elderly couple were soon to join them. Kane lay at my feet, his eyelids flickering. Thalia was on his other side, ready to help me lift him.

And Raine was nowhere to be seen.

According to the others, she’d found her way out of the catacombs and bolted toward the woodland at the base of the other side of the mountain, fur still on fire, and howling her grief to the moon. I sent a silent prayer to the fates for her on the off chance they’d listen to my plea. I liked the female. Just not enough to wait.

“Ready?” I asked the witch.

“Ready.”

I took Kane’s arm, pulled him upright and stooped to drape it across my shoulders.

“Now.”

As I squatted down preparing to lift him, Thalia muttered a spell, using her magic to take some of his weight. It would make it easier to navigate the arrows while simultaneously trying to climb a dragon. Hefting him over my shoulder, I used Eva’s tail as a step and peered down the mountain for a split second, just a glance to see the soldier's progress.

Shit. The shifters were too close. They’d be biting at Eva’s heels the moment we took to the skies and that’s if we got moving in the next minute. If it hadn’t been for their heavy armor, the high fae would already be upon us.

Those tailing behind a little were the witches and warlocks, but it wouldn’t be long before they were in casting distance. Then we’d be completely outnumbered and utterly fucked. The soldiers closing in from above suddenly began to yell out, their cries growing louder with every passing second. I couldn’t see them, not from this angle, but they must be able to see us. A dragon was hard to miss.

Thalia helped as I lay Kane down, then took her seat behind him, holding him in place between her knees with her thighs. Ilona and Miles were on either side of her and she reached an arm across each of their bodies without hesitation and didn’t wince over the blood-matted fur. Fates, it hurt so much to see them like that, but I couldn’t afford to let grief in. It would freeze me, suffocate me, render me useless, and I needed my mind sharp now more than ever.

“Let’s go.” I said, sitting to straddle the place where Eva’s tail joined her back. With any luck, she hadn’t noticed Alaric didn't make it in time.

Yeah right. The growl that rumbled from her chest vibrated under us like thunder born of the fates before leaving her throat. I felt the heat of her flames, heard the yelps of the shifters who'd gotten too close, before I saw the dragon fire itself.

Holding Kane's ankles under my arms, I used my heels to cling on. "Eva, fucking fly!"

The prince stirred at his mate's name. I watched as he reached out a hand which landed on Ilona's hind leg. Then, knotting his fingers in the fur, he turned as though to roll over, keeping his grip on the bear.

It was as though in his dream fucked mind, he thought he was in a cozy bed in the castle and one of his fur blankets had fallen off. I shuddered. *Fuck no.*

"Kane." I said, shaking his leg. "Wake the fuck up."

When he tried to roll over onto his side again, not only did Thalia and I stop him, but the 'blanket' didn't glide the way he was expecting.

He tugged once, then his eyes flew open, thankfully meeting mine and not the blood-soaked foot of Ilona's bear form.

"Morning, sleepyhead," I said, trying to pretend like everything hadn't gone to shit while he was out. "Hold on tight."

"Where the–" His eyes went wide as he tried to release poor Ilona's fur, but his hand came away a second later than it should have, getting stuck to some of the bloody fur. "No! Is that?" He shook his head, desperate for me to tell him it wasn't what he'd assumed. "What the fuck happened?"

Swallowing hard, I nodded once. "She's gone." I admonished. "And we are about to be too if your mate doesn't move soon."

"No," Kane said, glancing around, only to find Miles just behind him on the other side. "We have to save them. I can help them."

He pushed his way to sit up, his legs hanging on either side of Eva's spine as he grabbed onto Ilona's body and started trying to push his healing magic into her. He reached for Miles next, repeating the same.

"It's no use Kane, it's too late for them. We will give them a proper burial fit for warriors. But to do that, we need to get the fuck out of here."

Ignoring me, he continued his efforts, trying to pour his healing magic into them.

"Your nose is bleeding, Nekane. Please, just take my word for it. There is nothing you can do for them. Your strength is better served healing yourself. You nearly died and I swear to the fates, if you die and take my best friend with you, I'll come to the other side just to kill you again myself."

Eva let rip another roar of fire and the screams were of fae males and females too this time, not just the barks and howls of shifters.

Fuck, fuck, fuck. "Eva, GO!"

"Alaric." Kane said, his eyes distant.

"Charge!" someone called from close by. Down the mountain? Or was it from above? It was too close to tell.

"There's no time. We tried. We have to go." Desperation to save us all from a slaughter like the one on my camp had me kicking my heels into my best friend's sides like she was a stubborn horse refusing to move. She could kill me for it later.

"Alaric!" Kane said, louder this time.

His eyes weren't distant at all, but were sharp as blades, looking just behind me.

"Rose." Hearing Braxton's deep timbre surprised me, and I glanced up at the pile of fae squeezed onto Eva's back, to find he was supporting himself too now.

"Make room for another three." Kane said, and my head flew around, looking over my shoulder.

Alaric was charging down the mountainside, two fae over his shoulders, one much larger than the other. And a small army at his back.

But they'd made it. They'd fucking made it.

"There's no room," Thalia said.

"Then we make room," Braxton shot back.

"We can't leave Ilona and Miles," I said, just in case the thought had crossed anyone's mind to make more room by leaving them behind.

I'd give them an honorable burial befitting their bravery. I'd been the one to lead them to their deaths. The least I could do was help them find peace on the other side and keep them from the hordes' hands.

As we tried to shuffle up closer together, someone cleared their throat. "We'll find our own way," the ancient female said.

I stared at her, dumbfounded by the ridiculous suggestion, but the male nodded too. Agreeing with her that they'd forfeit their place. He helped her to stand with an ease that floored me and managed to climb their way down Eva's back quickly. Behind them, Alaric had made it to where the mouth of the cave used to be and then hopped down as though the drop was no more than a small step.

"Put me down now, you fucking asshole," Axel said as Alaric made it to Eva's tail.

Just then, she curled her tail around Alaric's waist and lifted all three of them onto her back. Then swung her neck around and let out another breath of flames, turning the soldiers closing in from behind to ash.

"Wait." Kane said, "We can't go without them." He was looking at the soon-to-be-dead fae couple. Even with their cuffs removed, as my mum's had been, they were no match for even one horde soldier, let alone an army of them.

"Go." The male said, his tone leaving no room for argument. Fates, his voice held a power far greater than his appearance led you to assume. "We'll follow."

As soon as the orders left his mouth, Eva's wings began to move, flapping up and down in slow strokes as she straightened, preparing to fly. We all clung on tightly, those helping the injured or supporting the dead adjusting their grip to make sure no one would fall when we took flight.

Arrows flew alongside spells from the witches and warlocks as Eva jumped into the sky; unable to do anything helpful, I squeezed my eyes closed tight and prayed to the fates we'd make it to the Vale.

As we gained height, I began to relax a little, believing we might actually make it out of this alive. But then guilt set in. We'd just left those two strangers. What if we could have made room? Eva was a massive–

"DRAGONS!" Kane called, his eyes wide on something behind me.

I glanced back to see not one, but two fucking dragons, taking to the sky, one golden and even bigger than Eva. The other silver, like the moon… just like… Eva.

I turned back to the others. Surely I was seeing things? Because after her parents died, Eva was the only remaining dragon in Dezrothia. Right?

My mum was smiling, her eyes bright with a sense of accomplishment. What had she done? What has she *seen?*

"It's really them," Westly said, breaking the silence we'd all fallen into as we fixated on the dragons behind us.

Eva let out a roar into the sky, and the dragons returned it with a call of their own as though communicating.

They were gaining on us fast, and soon enough, they'd be flying at Eva's flank. They might be weak, but Eva was carrying more weight than she'd ever carried, and flying in full dragon form wasn't something she had much practice at.

"Who?" a voice asked. It didn't matter, we all had the same question.

Westly was too mesmerized to answer, so I turned to my mum. "Care to enlighten us?"

Her smile turned into a grin, making her look younger than I ever remembered her looking.

"Before Augustus, Dezrothia was ruled by dragons."

"Aye. But Eva is the only one left. Augustus killed the rest after he usurped King Dyvrad. He made sure no heir or dragon could take the throne again," Alaric said.

"He clearly kept hold of two," I said.

"Not just any two," Westly murmured. "The greatest two dragons who ever lived."

Alaric was shaking his head as he said, "The old king and queen of Dezrothia."

Axel's hand flew to cover his mouth. "Are you telling me… Are you seriously telling me I fucking retched in the old king's face and then threw him and his *queen* over my shoulders like fucking rag dolls?"

"I think so," I said.

"Why me?" Axel moaned.

"You saved them," my mum said.

"Like that's going to stop him from murdering me. I dry heaved! In. His. Fucking. Face."

"Wait. Dragons ruled Dezrothia?!" I asked, not appreciating how friendly he and my mum seemed to be. "What does this mean?" Why didn't I know? Did Eva know?

It wasn't a conscious decision, but I found I was looking at Kane as I spoke; who was paler than he had been when filled with spider venom.

"I don't know," my mum said. She mustn't have seen farther ahead than the rest of us without her gifts.

"What do yeh mean, yeh dinnae ken?" Braxton snapped. "How long have yeh known the old king and queen were even alive?"

"Since the day I left my Nixen in the Vale," my mum admitted. "I only had one vision of them, but it was enough to know there was a possibility."

"I knew it," I mumbled, but it was to myself. Maybe to Eva too. I'd always told her the only reason my mum would have left was because she'd had a vision that gave her no other choice. What could be more important than one about the cruel king's predecessors being alive?

"That's why yeh let yerself be taken by Elikai?" Alaric stated.

My mum nodded. "That, and other things, but yes, mostly that, dear."

"I need a drink," Kane said, at last remembering how to speak.

"Aye," Alaric agreed. "Get us to a safe place to land, Angel," he said, patting her scales affectionately. "Somewhere remote an' far enough away tha' the horde won't catch up with us too soon," he turned his silver eyes on my mum, "We have a lot to talk about."

CHAPTER 4

Axel

It wasn't until the sun rose that Lady Evangelia decided we were far enough from Ezerat to risk landing and began her descent. She'd flown for hours and the miserable fuckers on her back weren't exactly the best company. Myself being the most miserable of all, and two of our passengers were dead.

Not funny, Axel.

Had it not been for the tight collar choking me, I was pretty sure my stomach would have come out of my mouth when we suddenly dropped through the clouds, far quicker than I'd been prepared for. Picking a clearing in an area as desolate as the conversation, it wasn't long before Lady Evangelia landed. With all the grace of a thrakos, giving over to bloodlust–

Blood.

I licked my lips. I couldn't remember the last time I fed. I'd hoped the collar around my neck would block the need to. Fates, it blocked everything else, but my gums ached where my fangs sat—covered in cobwebs.

I'd never experienced all out bloodlust before, not fully, not to the point of my mind blanking out my actions, and had no intention of starting now.

After a not-so-subtle glance around the group, I couldn't imagine feeding from any of them. Though it didn't need to be sexual, it was intimate, the act of drinking blood. But the company I was currently keeping was either family, claimed by family, or strangers. In some cases, a mix of both family and stranger.

I looked to Nixen; perhaps he was starving too? There was no way Alaric would have let him feed from Nekane or Lady Evangelia during their mission from the Fading Vale to Ezerat. Braxton wouldn't have been the source either, being thrakos himself. So, unless his source had been one of the deceased or that female I'd heard him with inside the catacombs, the chances were he'd need to feed soon as well.

We would have to wait for now. Hopefully, we'd be heading to a rebel camp in the

Fading Vale, and he could point me toward a willing source soon enough. I had a feeling he would be cool like that. That's if he could even look at me after seeing Alaric shoulder carrying me down the mountain like the virgin this fucking collar made me feel.

That's not what you're really embarrassed about though, is it, Axel?

I sighed. No. I wasn't against throwing someone over a shoulder to get out of a sticky situation. I'd been both a giver and receiver of it in just the last day, double teaming it with the ancient royals. When needs must, and all that. Perhaps the old king and queen were of the same opinion?

I sighed again and found my eyes falling on the gold and silver dragons flying in a perfect arrowhead, not breaking form even as we descended. So majestic, despite their obvious malnourishment. *Fates, you really didn't make a good first impression.* I shivered. I would apologize just as soon as they were in fae form again.

Pulling my stare away before they caught me, I turned my attention to Alaric's father. These sorts of mishaps would never happen to someone like Braxton. No way. I'd never even spoken to the male and I could just tell. Aside from exchanging a few words with Alaric, he'd spent the last several hours watching Rose like if he blinked, she might disappear. Or as though the force of his stare alone could make her heal quicker. Kane was healing her as best he could, but had to stop whenever he became too lightheaded, so the process was slow and painful for all involved.

The awkward silence we currently sat in had fallen when Alaric announced he was done with trying to get more information out of Edelin about the dragons, and had yet to be broken. Personally, I found Edelin's elusiveness kind of endearing. Though that might have less to do with Aunt Ede herself and everything to do with how insane it made Alaric when trying to deal with her.

He had spent centuries trying to work out a prophecy, only to find out he didn't have all the facts about the potential players involved. Not even close. I could understand his frustration, but my aunt still insisted she only saw one vision with them in, and that the future was a 'fickle thing'. Even without her collar on.

Without her collar on…

"Aunt Ede," I said as her son helped her down, sparing a moment to shoot daggers my way at the use of her nickname. I ignored it. We'd have plenty of bonding time later. "How did you get your jewelry off?"

"Oh. Nekane, dear."

I gave Nixen a look that clearly said, 'do you want to tell her she's lost it or shall I?' but he just looked back at me blankly, like *I* was the one a sandwich short of a picnic. "Ax-el." I said slowly.

"I know who you are, Axel dear. I meant the metal cuff, Nekane can remove it," she said.

"I can?" Kane asked as he stepped down too, a confused expression on his alarmingly pallid face.

"Yes," Edelin said. "They were your father's making," she added, as if that clarified anything. "You were unconscious when you removed mine, and the dragons used the remaining drops of your blood from Nixen's dagger."

Kane turned his blue eyes on Nixen. "You stabbed me?" he asked, but his tone lacked any real conviction. Fates, he didn't sound pissed at all.

"It was barely a paper cut," Nixen said, shrugging.

"Whatever." Kane sighed, too exhausted to press further. "Just tell me what I need to do?"

Nixen talked him through it and the relief that came with the collar's release was like climaxing, only without the mess. "Thank you," I said seriously.

I shifted into my wolf, quickly followed by my thrakos form, and rolled my shoulders several times, stretching out my wings before concealing them away. Then, using what feeble magic I could wield accurately, I called upon my warlock side to make a fire from the hard ground, just like Edelin had taught me during our time in the catacombs together.

Fuck, it was good to be back. And away from the castle, where I'd had to suppress everything that made me, me. There was one final thing to test, though. I closed my eyes and pushed out the thought, *"Knock knock."*

"Hello, Axel." Alaric thought back, squashing my hilarious joke before it had really started. Classic Alaric.

"There he is!"

He rolled his eyes and turned his attention back to Lady Evangelia, who remained with her underbelly to the ground, even after her back was empty. It wasn't until the gold and silver dragons shifted that she allowed herself to do the same. Alaric wrapped her in his shirt, and Nekane helped her up. While the castle witch and warlock, Thalia and Westly, attended to the gold and silver dragons.

"Yeh okay, Angel?" Alaric asked.

She nodded weakly. "So tired," she said. "You?"

"All good," Alaric said.

"Do you need to feed?" she asked, concern etched in her brow. "I don't remember the last time you did?"

Nekane was shaking his head. "He can drink from me," he said. "You just focus on conserving your energy for the next leg back to the Vale."

My fangs throbbed just listening.

"I'm good," Alaric said, and my eyes went wide. How could he refuse such an offer?! "Just worry about yerself. I'm no' the one with another day or two of flying. Or emptying my entire well of magic healing someone."

True, but seriously, he wasn't going to even take a drop?

"What about you, Nix?" Lady Evangelia asked next. "Or you, Axel?"

Alaric growled, but I ran my tongue across my teeth anyway, wiping the cobwebs away in readiness.

"It doesn't have to be me," Evangelia said. "Nor Kane. I'm sure someone else would be happy to help. Westly's pretty busy," she nodded toward the dragons where Westly was fussing like a mother hen, while Thalia tried to keep up with his demands on what she needed to do to help. "But I'm sure Thalia would be happy to assist if you asked."

Yes! I wanted to shout, but I was unfamiliar with the rebel's protocol when it came to such things, so I decided to wait for Nixen to take the lead. When he said yes, it would set the precedent for me to do the same.

Nixen shook his head. "Thanks, but I'm okay." *So not cool, cousin mine.* "The thought of drinking blood doesn't feel very appetizing right now. I'd rather get some food, water and sleep. In that order."

What was wrong with these fae?!

I'd been so looking forward to meeting my baby cousin. Figured we'd be thick as thieves in no time at all. It hadn't crossed my mind he might be a blood-blocking asshole.

It's just the thirst talking. Right, he's probably not an asshole. He just doesn't want to take what little energy anyone else had left.

"Axel?" Lady Evangelia pressed.

If I agreed now, I'd be the asshole, so instead I said, "No, thanks."

Nixen frowned. "Then why are you nodding?"

"I'm not," but I absolutely was. "I was just thinking about this other thing I need to do."

"Righ'. Well, we cannae stay here long," Alaric said, combing his fingers through messy hair. "There's no water source here, so the chances of finding food worth the energy hunting would take are slim." He glanced at the fire I'd made. "And we have barely a fire." *Wow, thanks, brother.* Just announce to my new friends I have a small cock, why don't you?

"I'll find something to wrap our dead so they are ready for burial as soon as we reach the Vale," Braxton said. "Evangelia, try to get a few hours of sleep. We leave at sundown."

"I'll let the others know," I said, keen to get the apology out of the way so we could start bonding. They looked like they could use a hug. And a bath. Shame about the lack of lake or stream, the hug would have to wait, less I end up gagging all over them. Again.

Their expressions were unreadable as I crossed the space between us. I wasn't sure whether I was supposed to bow, so went with a more casual wave instead.

"Hey, I'm Axel," I said. "The guy from the catacombs–"

"We remember," the male said.

"Of course you do," I sighed, humiliation making my face burn despite the chill which had been whipping against it during the entire flight here. "About that, I'm so sorry, truly. I wasn't gagging at you. It was the stuff in the jars." The male arched a brow at my attempted deception. "Okay, fine, you got me, that's a lie. It was mostly the stuff in the jars, only a little bit was you. Maybe half and half, max. Who could say for sure? Not me. But based on my gag reflex being totally okay now, I'd say it was the jars."

Fuck, I was rambling.

"I meant we remember you as the male who saved us from centuries of imprisonment," the not-so-late, late king said.

I rubbed the back of my neck. "Oh yeah, that too. Maybe just forget about all the other stuff, yeah?"

"It's forgotten," the female said, and I took a deep breath.

It was possibly the worst thing I could have done as the scent clinging to them filled my nose and transported me back to that horrific place. The laboratory of Regis's experiments. The jars of–

My empty stomach convulsed and before I could make a quick getaway, I was bent over, vomiting bile at their feet.

Why me?

CHAPTER 5
Evangelia

After flying for two full days with only a brief rest in between, I still struggled to believe the two dragons flying at my flank were real.

No matter how unbelievable though, it wasn't a question of if I needed to fear them, but how *much* I should fear them. Would I win if they turned on us? Could they be trusted? Were they friends, foes, allies?

Distant relatives?

Now wasn't the time to think too deeply about that. Or to contemplate what the news of their identity meant for us. Especially Kane. Neither was it the time to embrace these past days for the unfathomable miracle they'd been; soaring free with others like me, in the flight I didn't know I'd dreamed of until it was happening.

No. Right now, all I allowed myself to think about was those on my back, my established allies, and true mates, all counting on me to get them to safety. To a place they could feel protected while they healed. Not only the living, but the dead too. They deserved to be honored with a proper burial. And their families deserved to say goodbye.

"Find somewhere remote," Alaric had told me, but Braxton's camp was drawing me to it. So much so that I hadn't consciously decided to land there until I circled the trees above it. My sights on the clearing that doubled as my training area.

I watched and waited, my wings throbbing with every stroke, as rebels stepped into the space in their tens; craning their necks at the spectacle in the sky.

Raine's brother, Blaze, was the first to spot us. "They're back!" he called, and his mother rushed to his side. My stomach twisted. We'd have to tell him the sister he idolized as much as he did Kane was missing. That her daughter was out there somewhere, all alone. New faces were smiling up at us. More rebels had congregated here during our absence, ready to fight the right fight. Willing to die to make a better life for others, just like Ilona and Miles had.

It just made sense to land here. It was familiar. We knew all the routes in and out, and where the closest villages were for supplies. The unmated thrakos could feed too. More than all of that, this place wasn't just a camp or training ground; it had become a sanctuary, a testament to our struggle, where the seeds of rebellion had been sown and nurtured.

It was where Kane had started to see himself as worthy of the throne, and where he'd won over the fae who'd despised him. That may all change, depending on what the Dyvrad's would have to say once they shifted from gold and silver dragon to king and queen. It would never be for nothing, though.

Finding a new camp now would be counterproductive, right? We were stronger in numbers. Sending word of a new location to these brave fae who'd been waiting for us would take too long. War was no longer just a mere possibility, it was here. And Elikai knew we weren't going to hide and make his path to rule easy.

"What's she doin'?" I heard Alaric ask the others as I began my descent.

"Looks like we're landing here," Kane said.

"Aye," Braxton agreed. "It's a risk, but at least we have numbers here. An' a medical tent."

Thank you, Braxton.

Alaric growled his disapproval but didn't try to convince me why this was a bad idea. There had to be a reason I was missing, something Alaric had thought about that I hadn't. Fates, it had been an intense few days. I couldn't remember when or even where the last place I slept was.

Yes, Alaric had centuries of experience being the horde general, and I should probably listen to him and keep going. Search for somewhere deeper in the Vale that was farther from Ezerat. But I had a gut feeling driving me, telling me this was where we needed to be. Besides, Alaric did what he wanted, when he wanted, half of the time, and didn't ask permission. Just forgiveness. It was my turn to take a leaf from his book.

It helped that I had a very good excuse for not asking permission—in this form, my words came out as growls and roars, or deadly flames.

Swooping in to land, the other dragons remained in the clouds, continuing to circle. Their wings looked tired, their heads heavy, but there wasn't room for three fully grown dragons to land at once here. Fates, the clearing barely had room for me.

My own exhaustion made itself known again as I lowered us down faster than I meant to, as I had yesterday morning. Though Braxton's guidance and my daily training had carved every inch of this ground into my memory, I was relieved to see the fae race for the tree line, giving me more space.

As my talons ground down into the earth, my body followed. As far as anyone else needed to know, I was just laying as flat as possible to aid those on my back. Now I just had to hold still and remain in this form long enough for the others to disembark. The idea of moving was as unwelcome as torture for my exhausted muscles anyway, so I closed my eyes and silently listened to the chaos around me.

The moment the last weight left my back, the scent of apples and cinnamon became thicker in the air. "You can shift back now," Kane said, stroking the end of my snout.

My lids shot open and my eyes crossed as I tried to focus on him while standing so close.

"Better make room for those two. You know, before they fall out of the sky and half the camp goes splat," he said, holding a piece of fabric between two hands.

Convinced, I shifted back, naked, and shivering on the ground. Kane made quick work of wrapping the fabric around me as he helped me to stand. Before I could mutter a thank you, his lips were pressed against mine. He kissed me in the middle of the clearing like no one was watching and I melted against him, enjoying his taste, his warmth, his love.

Too soon, he broke away. "Fuck, I didn't want to do that."

"Kiss me?"

He shook his head. "Stop kissing you. But we need to move," he said, taking my hand in his. "You did good, princess."

My eyes dropped to the ground as I shook my head. "I killed so many of the horde back there."

"This is war. It was kill or be killed then, and it will be kill or be killed again later," he said, gently lifting my chin and meeting my eyes with the piercing blue of his own. "They were soldiers. They understood the risk to their immortality that comes with that role. Besides, if we didn't find making that decision hard on our soul, we'd be either dead or fighting for the other side. I hate it, but none of us get the luxury of coming away from this with clean hands."

"They were acting under orders," I said. "They didn't have any other option."

"Yeh didnae either, Angel," Alaric said, as he joined us and placed a soft peck on my lips.

Together, we made our way to stand with the others. As I walked, I fashioned the cloth into a dress, wrapping it around my body and tucking it in so it would hold.

We looked around the group; Rose was being helped to the medical tent by Braxton and Axel, with Edelin in tow, but Ilona and Miles' bodies were nowhere to be seen. Likely already returned to their nearest and dearest to mourn privately and prepare them for burial. Braxton had done his best to wrap them with what he could find during our quick break. To preserve their bodies and dignity when they no longer could themselves. Their families would be able to honor them properly now.

Alaric's palm landed on my waist, pulling me close. "You good?" he asked both Kane and me.

We shared a glance, and both of us nodded as we looked back to Alaric.

Life for an immortal was far too long to be holding grudges. But for an immortal amid war? It was far too short. Especially when it came to those you loved.

A gust of wind swept Alaric's thick hair across his scarred face, and we turned just in time to see the golden dragon come into land. Alaric's hand remained around my waist, squeezing me tighter, while Kane crossed his arms over his chest and watched the dragon wearily. Though he looked relaxed to everyone else, we knew better. He was ready for anything.

King Dyvrad's landing was as majestic as I was sure he once was, before he'd been King Regis's captive for centuries. He gracefully shifted to his fae form the moment his claws met the earth, and Westly was at his side a blink later with a cloak as he helped him move toward us and out of the way. By the time the female dragon followed suit, aided by Thalia, several fae were returning with more clothing to wrap them in.

Whispers turned into loud chatter as the rebels buzzed like a hive. Like the rest of us, they thought I was the last of my kind. Unless you were over three hundred and fifty years old, chances were you hadn't seen one, never mind three, dragons in your lifetime.

Those newest to the camp were frozen in awe, like they were witnessing a shift in the tides of fate happening before them.

Were three dragons enough to win a war?

No.

But the identity of two of them could change the odds. I just wasn't sure yet whether that would be for the better.

As though reading my thoughts, Alaric said, "Time to find out what we're dealin' with."

ROSE HAD REGAINED consciousness at some point during the flight, but was barely able to talk, let alone stand on her own. Braxton, however, appeared to be back to exactly as he'd been in the crowd while watching Kane's almost execution. While canteens of water and bowls of hot broth were passed around, the rebel leader returned from the medical tent and led us to the war tent.

A feeling of déjà vu came over me. It was exactly like when we'd arrived here with Kane for the first time. Only it wasn't the Regis Prince being called into question. After all, he'd long since proven his loyalty to the rebels, as far as I was concerned.

Now it was his father's predecessors. The much loved King and Queen of Dezrothia. If the little information my mother had given me as a child was true, they were strong and feared, but not by their own kingdom.

To the fae of this realm, they were said to be fair and just in their treatment. They could live where they wanted, love who they desired, and do as they liked to a certain degree. I'd never had reason to question whether my mother had told me the truth, but it was more than a little odd that she'd never thought to mention they were dragons, too.

The three of us dipped inside the tent. Alaric steered us to stand with his dad, and Nix was already at Braxton's side. When Axel returned from getting Rose settled, he stood beside Alaric and whispered something in his ear, likely an update on his mum. Nix looked solemn as we shared a look, smiling to acknowledge we were glad each other had survived the trials of the last few days, while Axel had a bounce underfoot, just like Nix used to. It was easy to believe they were related.

"Lady Evangelia," Axel said with a dip of his head. A thousand expressions crossed the male's face as he took in his surroundings, like he couldn't settle on just one. It made him hard to read, and so different to Alaric, despite how close they were. "Sorry, I wasn't very chatty when we stopped yesterday. Kinda hard to talk around the giant boot I'd managed to shove in my mouth." I frowned, and he shook his head. "It's a long story. That was quite the ride, any chance I get to do it again?"

"Glad you had fun," I said quietly, elbowing both my mates, who growled, knowing this wasn't the time or place for a chat. Not with Axel. I wouldn't put it past him to decide now was the perfect time to say something entirely inappropriate, like, 'Did you make good use of the lube I packed?'

Alaric's expression was as unmoving as it was fierce. As were Braxton's and Kane's. Rightly so. We'd be fools to all react to the former king and queen as Westly had. All bent knee and doting admirer.

For one, what would they think of the thrakos here? They'd come after their time and were the creation of King Regis. What if they sought to destroy them solely because of his involvement in their coming to be?

Plus, who knew what hundreds of years trapped inside the catacombs might do to a fae's psyche? They'd likely not only lost their marbles but had them stomped all over until they shattered into tiny fragments. How did someone even begin putting themselves back together after that?

The fabric of the tent swung wide and Westly stepped inside. "Announcing King Drayke and Queen Vyara Dyvrad," he called, welcoming them through with his head bent low. Holding onto each other tightly, but with heads high, they entered to a chorus of gasps from the rebels gathered around. Blaze's eyes shot to Kane as he tried to puzzle out what that meant for his favorite royal.

Thalia was close behind them, but once she'd crossed the threshold, she nudged her uncle as though telling him to stand straight. He was among the few who'd lived during their reign, and his reaction to their presence was understandable, if not a little embarrassing, for his niece.

King Drayke and Queen Vyara's gazes landed on me and stayed there. Soon, everyone followed suit, and I wanted the ground to open under my feet and swallow me whole. Did they know I was the only one of their kind left?

"How are yeh both alive?" Braxton asked, his voice demanding of their attention.

Ignoring him entirely, the couple stopped in front of me. "What is your name?" Vyara asked.

I looked around, as though someone might be standing just behind me and that's who their question was truly posed for. Of course, no such luck.

Alaric nodded, encouraging me to answer. "Evangelia. My name is Evangelia Malion."

"Daughter of?" the king pushed, his voice thick with emotion.

"Daughter of dragons, the late Kur and Lavina Malion."

The king swallowed hard, and a tear swelled in the female's eyes. Fates, they were so familiar.

"Malion was your father's name?" the king asked. I nodded, confirming what he already seemed to know.

"Do yeh ken what Lavina's name was before she took Malion?" Alaric asked hesitantly, not taking his calculating eyes off the dragon king.

"No," I said.

At the same time as Queen Vyara said, "Dyvrad."

The word hung in the air as everyone held their breath, but in my mind, I was already back on the balcony with Kane, Elikai, and their uncle.

'I thought the dragons of Dezrothia were all gone, but it doesn't take a genius to work out what line you are from.'

Silver scales swam across my vision next, taking one memory's place and filling it with another. Queen Vyara moving through the sky, glinting with scales so similar to those which coated my own skin.

Her desperate eyes, so similar to my mother's, pooled with unshed tears. Too similar to have belonged to anyone but her own mother...

Alaric choked, "Yer a–"

"–Princess," Kane murmured.

The pet name he so often called me should have been comforting, but the way he said it now... It was like it had taken on a whole new layer of meaning.

My mouth dropped to the floor as I stared, dumbfounded, between the king and queen.

"Lavina was your *daughter?*" someone said from the crowd. It was a rebel alliance leader. Though I couldn't remember his name, I recognized him from visiting my old camp. He knew my parents, yet this was news to him, too.

The king nodded. "Princess Lavina Dyvrad, *true and rightful* heir to Dezrothia."

Impossible. My head was shaking. My mother's parents were...

Think Eva, think.

She never spoke of her parents.

"Is it true?" I asked the queen, as though if she were the one to say it, I'd all of a sudden be able to believe it.

Queen Vyara nodded. "She was our only child. When rumors began to circulate in Ezerat that Augustus was planning an attack from the inside, we ordered her to flee."

"Kur was sent to protect her," the king added. "To keep her hidden at all costs."

"They hid well. Were leaders of the rebel alliance," Braxton said, breaking the uncomfortable silence that had befallen the entire camp. "Sadly died no' long ago."

"H-how?" Vyara asked.

"Killed at the orders of Elikai Regis," Nix spat.

Kane winced, and their eyes moved to him as one. Despite how malnourished they were, their stares carried the weight of a thousand battles, hard fought and hundreds of years of pent-up hatred.

Pulling out of Alaric's hold, I took an instinctual step in front of Kane. "As I told you before, he is not like his father, or brother, for that matter."

They shared a concerned look, but must have decided to trust me because they didn't question him or where his loyalty lay.

"We have missed much." King Drayke said.

"Aye." Alaric agreed. "How long were yeh in those catacombs?" he asked.

"Since the day Augustus stole the crown from my head," the king confirmed.

"You will know better than us how much time has passed," the queen said, lifting her pitch at the end as though the statement were more a question.

"Almost four hundred years," Westly said.

"Fuck," Axel said, visibly shuddering. It truly was unfathomable.

Alaric and Braxton seemed to have a silent conversation, broken only when Alaric asked, "Can we trust yeh mean no harm to any of the rebels here?"

"Thrakos, hybrid, Regis or otherwise?" I added.

"Yes, we owe you our lives, granddaughter mine." Queen Vyara said, making a tingle spread across my skin and a chill run down my spine.

"An' you?" Braxton asked the king.

"You have my word."

Braxton's shoulders sagged an inch. "Then we shall eat and rest. When the sun next rises, we'll talk."

With that, he left before they could answer, heading in the direction of the medical tent.

As Alaric, Kane, and I moved to leave too, Vyara placed a palm on my arm. "Can we talk?" she asked.

Fates, I wanted to. I had so many questions, but… "Later," I promised. Then turned my back and left them both in the capable care of Westly and Thalia.

My limbs shook, my brain ready to explode. The invisible box in my mind, where I locked away everything I didn't want to deal with, was already full. No space for long-lost grandparents or thoughts of what they meant for our future.

For *my* future.

And I had no desire to open it for long enough to relive my parents' lives or deaths, despite how much they deserved to know. Right now, I wanted to be just Evangelia Malion, and the only fae she wanted or needed were her general and her prince. But the fates had other ideas for me as Axel caught up to us, followed closely by Nix.

"Where are you going?" my best friend asked.

"My da's right. We all need some food and somewhere to sleep," Alaric answered for me, pushing a hand through his hair.

"You're not going to talk about what just happened?" Nix shot back.

"Right?" Axel said.

Alaric shook his head once.

"I can't believe it," Nix said, rubbing the back of his neck.

"Nor me." Axel agreed, clamping a firm hand on Nix's shoulder, like they were already at that stage in their very new relationship. "It's unbelievable. King D and Queen V. You couldn't make this shit up," he said with a wink.

Nix was stunned still, Kane barked a laugh that seemed to surprise him, and Alaric's face relaxed a little as he told his adopted brother to, "Shut the fuck up," and gave him an affectionate shove.

My lips pulled into a smile and a laugh escaped my throat, in spite of everything we'd been through, it dawned on me Axel wasn't just inappropriate, or unable to read a situation, he was a genius.

And exactly the sort of fae we needed at a time like this.

CHAPTER 6
Nekane

We were long past ready for some downtime, but I had something to do first, before I could find some peace with my favorite fae.

Alaric and Axel went to commandeer a few tents and check on Rose, while Eva and Nix filled me in on what had happened between me leaving with the traitorous spider, and when I woke up on her back. I was there and awake for some of it, but things had been hazy.

They confirmed that most of what I'd hoped I'd imagined did, in fact, happen. But thank the fates, the one thing I was desperate to be true, was. We were true mates. The three of us. Though it didn't change my love for them, which was as fierce and willingly given as ever, it changed just about everything else.

The thing that scared me the most—our lives were all connected now.

We had to be more cautious and careful than ever. We were one stupid move in battle or a dangerous rescue attempt away from being each other's demise. The three of us would have to wait to talk about the true mate bond later. It wasn't a conversation we needed Nix to be in on, though as the best friend of Eva, I'm sure he had plenty he wanted to say.

As he and Eva made it to the end of their retelling, it was clear she didn't want to talk about the rest of it just yet. Specifically, the news of her mother, and now her, being heir to the Dezrothian throne. We didn't push it. I was having a hard enough time wrapping my head around it myself. I couldn't imagine how she would be feeling.

Once I had all the information, I left Eva talking with Nix and made my way to find Blaze and his mother. We owed them some answers about Raine's whereabouts, even if we weren't sure where she was exactly. It didn't take long to find them; crossing the clearing in the direction of the medical tent. Likely ready to demand Braxton start talking.

They'd have learned Miles' fate and knew Raine was never far from the wolf hybrid's shadow. They would have come to their own conclusion, assumed she hadn't made it, or we'd left her for dead. I couldn't let them spend the evening without knowing the truth while we all slept and regained much needed strength.

"Blaze," I called, and he grabbed his mother's sleeve, stopping her.

Turning to me, he asked, "Did you kill him?" He was talking about Elikai. Truthfully, I hadn't even come close. Even if I hadn't been drugged full of spider venom, killing my twin would be… difficult. Not just physically. "Do I call you King Nekane now?"

I chuckled but shook my head. "Sorry, kid."

He sighed. "What happened?"

"To Raine," his mother added.

Taking a deep breath, I nodded toward the trees lining the clearing. "Come on, let's talk."

I lost track of how many circuits of the camp we did as they walked with me in silence, and I told them everything that had happened from the moment we reached Ezerat. Both the parts I'd been present for and those Eva and Nix had just finished filling me in on. They'd been with Raine when she'd found Miles, and I recounted how her wolf had lit up with thrakos fire and ran without a backward glance.

"What was she thinking? Separating from everyone like that?" her mother asked.

"She was hurting and filled with anger at the unfairness of everything. I can only assume she needed some space." I rubbed the back of my neck. "I'm sorry we couldn't wait for her."

"That isn't your fault," she said.

"She'll be back," Blaze said with confidence.

I offered him a smile. "If anyone can, it's her. She knows how to find this camp and is skilled at tracking. And if she comes into any trouble on the way, well, I feel sorry for her attackers."

"Exactly. Don't worry mum, she'll find her way back when she's ready."

The female nodded. "Thank you, Nekane, for coming to tell us. I'd assumed she was–"

"Well, she isn't," I cut over. "And don't thank me. I'm sorry it's not better news, but at least you know now."

"Go get some sleep," she said, subtly bowing her head as she stepped away.

"Yeah. you look like shit, Prince Nekane." Blaze added, then threw his arms around me, before darting off after his mother.

"Thanks." I called after him, then headed back to where I'd left Eva and Nix.

Several tents had appeared, all in various states of being put up. "Need a hand?" I offered.

Alaric and Eva paused only to raise their brows, knowing tents were not exactly my skill set and when neither of them said anything, Nix answered, "Yours is erect." He gestured to the larger one in the middle.

Axel smirked. "I know you're talking about the tents, but did you have to look at his cock when you said that?" he asked.

It was bullshit. Nix had done nothing of the sort, but if Axel's plan had been solely to piss off Alaric, it worked.

Maybe he wasn't too happy with the male for running into the catacombs after him, either. Get in line.

Alaric growled, turning more than a few heads our way, including the king and queen, who were several tents down, waiting for Westly to stop fussing with it so they could sleep.

Nix's eyes flew wide. "I didn't–"

Axel took a subtle step in front of Nix. "Calm down, brother," he said to Alaric, his palms raised. "I was just messing with him. That's what we do Nix and I–"

"No, we don't." Nix said, frowning.

"But we will." Axel assured him.

"No. We won't."

"Try telling that to the all-powerful seer who foresaw it," Axel said.

"My mum told you we'd have some weird bromance relationship, or that I'd be looking at the prince's cock?" Nix asked, crossing his arms over his chest.

Nothing good ever happened when fae were over tired. Except maybe this conversation.

"Ew no. Edelin doesn't use words like cock. Penis? Maybe. But cock, dick, shaft, schlong, member–"

"Axel, enough," Alaric snapped.

"Look. As flattered as I am Nix, my male here hasn't had his eggs yet today, so his sense of humor is lacking," I said, enjoying watching Nix squirm a little too much as he tried to work out what Axel's game was.

He didn't have one. The male was just a one off. No one understood him, and the only one who could control him was Alaric.

"The only fae looking at the prince's cock are me and the princess. Understood?" Alaric said.

Eva paled at the use of the title. She'd worn the same title before, for different reasons, but this was her birthright now.

"Now fuck off to yer tents and get some sleep."

He didn't have to ask twice.

Eva and Alaric, already shoeless, climbed inside, while I unlaced my boots that had seen better days. It was apparent our new tent was bigger than the last, so naturally I should hate it. But for the first time in… I wasn't actually sure how long I had Alaric and Eva to myself, and nothing could wipe the smile from my face.

As I bent to step inside, Alaric grabbed the scruff of my shirt and pulled me to him so I was looking directly into his eyes. His mouth slammed against mine in a possessive kiss, sucking my bottom lip between his fangs before he released his hold.

"Where did that come from?" I asked, ready to open a vein and let him have at it.

He just shook his head.

"You know Axel and Nix have no interest in Kane as a lover, right?" Eva asked.

Raking his hands through his messy hair, he said, "I didnae ken."

"You didn't know what?" she pressed.

"About the bond. I didnae work it out until it was too late. *Fuck*. I could have killed yeh both. I'm so fuckin' sorry."

"Would knowing have changed anything?" I asked.

"Yeh. No. Fuck. Ah dinnae ken," he said, his accent getting thicker and sexier while his guard crumbled to dust.

Eva untucked the fabric where it held her makeshift dress in place and let it fall as she crawled into his lap. Placing a hand on his scarred cheek, she said, "It's okay. Well, it's not, it was reckless. But this bond, as incredible as it is, it's going to take some getting used to."

I squeezed his leg. "She's right. And short of the three of us running away to some remote cave and never stepping foot in harm's way again, there are going to be times we are all in the same position as you were last night. It's just something we need to learn to navigate."

"Fuck, I dinnae ken what I did to deserve this. To deserve the two of yeh."

"We love you too," Eva said, sliding her hand up his face until her fingers fisted his hair. Bringing his mouth to hers, she kissed him the way I'd needed to kiss her earlier in the middle of the clearing.

"Get over here, Kane," she said against Alaric's lips, reaching a hand out behind her and pulling me in.

Tearing my tattered shirt in two as I went, she tugged it down my arms as she moved her lips to mine. She was kneeling in front of me now, ripping open my leathers with impatient fingers. Holding the back of her head, our lips locked while our tongues explored the heat of each other's mouths.

Alaric shuffled around, closing the tent door tight, before he too stripped down. The need to be close to them, to feel every inch of them skin against skin, was stronger than the need to breathe. Over Eva's shoulder, Alaric was on his knees, stroking his cock in slow pulls, his silver eyes sharp as he watched us. When Eva and I parted, I was hard as stone and panting for more of them.

"Eva, lie back and put your thigh on his shoulder," I instructed, shoving my leathers the rest of the way down and kicking them off.

She lay back and Alaric crawled up her body on hands and knees before lifting her thigh and hooking it over his shoulder, exposing her naked pussy. A breathy moan escaped her swollen lips as Alaric's thick stubble grazed her sensitive inner thigh. While he licked his way slowly to her entrance, I trailed kisses down from her neck to her pert breasts.

Meeting eyes with Alaric, his mouth closed over her clit the same moment I took a nipple into my mouth. Eva's fingernails dug into the material of the ground sheet beneath us so hard I heard a rip. A fresh wave of arousal permeated the air when Alaric growled his approval of her losing control against her slick heat.

As I turned my attention to her other nipple, I asked, "How does she taste?"

He released her clit, and I groaned as I watched his tongue enter her. Her back arched, and he slowly licked his way back up to her sensitive bud of nerves.

Swallowing, he said, "Like creamy fuckin' vanilla."

"So perfect," I said, fates near salivating.

"So ours," he corrected.

The muscles in her thigh clenched as she desperately sought out that delicious warmth of his mouth against her again.

"Bite me," she begged, and Alaric obliged.

Turning his face into her thigh, I caught a flash of fangs before they sunk into her flesh. At the same time, I nipped her nipple, then quickly sealed my mouth over hers.

"Fuck," she cried out, but I swallowed the sound.

Only Alaric and I got to hear the sweet sound of our female's orgasm.

Swinging a leg over Alaric's head, I straddled her torso, supporting my weight with my knees. Prying her hands away from the torn material, lifting them above her head to find the armor of her scales covering her skin from elbow to fingertip, where lethal claws had formed.

I smirked. It was so fucking satisfying to see her so thoroughly undone. Staring at my hard length on her chest, she licked her lips as she lifted her head to taste me, but I didn't want to come in her mouth. Not today.

"Feeding time's over," I said to Alaric. It was our turn now.

He released his fangs and straightened behind me, then grabbed my waist and forced me back, so my cock was almost touching her drenched pussy.

Taking my shaft in his hand, he purred, "Ready, Angel?"

"Always," she breathed.

Lining my cock up with her entrance, his other hand found my ass. He stroked my length with several delicious pulls, before guiding me inside her and moving his hand away to circle her clit with his thumb. The hand on my ass lowered to cup my balls. Then he was dropping his head lower once more, until I felt the wetness of his mouth take the place of his hand.

Pinning Eva's arms above her head with one hand, I rocked my hips, pushing my cock deeper inside her with every thrust.

She took all of me like the good dragon she was, and I drew back again when Alaric let my balls drop. Spreading my cheeks with strong hands, I shivered as he slid his tongue between them. My thrusts became quicker, more and more urgent, as Alaric drove my hips with his hands on my ass, controlling our rhythm and the pleasure that came with it. Eva's hips rocked with mine as she chased the pleasure I was offering.

As the need to come rolled over me, his tongue entered my hole, forcing my climax to leave me on a long groan. *"Fuuuuck."*

Eva's walls clenched around me, and I closed my mouth over hers again as another orgasm rocked her. I kissed her deeply, then whispered into her mouth, "Fuck me."

The words weren't for her, but the male at my back. The pressure on my ass was answer enough that he'd heard me loud and clear. And he wasn't wasting any time. The pain was brief as he slowly pushed his cock into my ass, inch by glorious fucking inch.

My lips remained on Eva's mouth, showing her with the ferocity of my kiss just how good it felt to be fucked by Alaric while sinking in and out of her tight pussy. I was a male amidst a storm of pleasure. Every nerve in my body was struck by lightning.

My cock hardened all over again as my hips flexed with Alaric, enjoying the way he took his time with me. Eva's breathy sighs encouraged me as I rocked into her. Her pussy clenching and fluttering around me as she watched us. Alaric's hold on me tightened as his hips slammed into me, over and over and over, until my thighs were shaking. My lips found Eva's neck, kissing, licking, and biting my way across her flesh.

Biting down on Eva's lip, I rode out the ecstasy exploding within me as I came hard again. With one final slam, Alaric's cum filled me as he found his release with a choked roar.

All I could see were stars as we lay there in complete fucking bliss.

We were alive, and I couldn't think of a better way to remind each other of that.

We'd faced my brother and his horde and were still here, able to fight another day. And with any luck, we'd delayed his coronation by leaving a mess in our wake for him to deal with first.

CHAPTER 7
Elikai

Nekane's execution had been a disaster, but only in so much as he was still breathing. Everything else that had happened in the days since was nothing short of blessings from the fates, and ultimately led to the expedition of the incredible event I'd long waited for, finally taking place.

Thanks to the very public attack by my brother's rebel friends, whispers had run wild through the city that my coronation couldn't come soon enough. That the only reason the rebels and enemies of the crown had the audacity to enter Ezerat, let alone the castle grounds, was because of the uncertainty that came with not having a king on the throne.

Naturally, I did right by my fae and answered their call. The fact that I'd been the one to start the whispers was irrelevant. Yesterday morning, as the city stores had opened their doors for a fruitful day of business, Graves and Sloane, clad in long red coats with fine gold trim, took to the streets of Ezerat, bell in hand, and finally announced my coronation. By the afternoon, every residence occupied by fae of worth had received the invitation on gold leaf pressed parchment. And by sundown, the city folk were making the finishing touches to their best outfits in readiness for today.

Now, as high society watched my every breath, along with the three fates themselves—shining rays of sun on me from their stained-glass depictions like a spotlight—I was finally basking in the day I'd been born ready to live. Committing every moment of it to memory, in all its perfection and glory

From my grand entrance, adorned from head to toe in the finest vestments, to taking a seat on the throne, which hugged my glutes more perfectly than any pretender who'd sat in it before me. And all the parts in between; the oath, the disrobing and anointing, the hollers of the fae rejoicing. It was everything and more.

At the High Archon's request, I stood before the brimming temple of guests and allowed my muscles to feel every last grain of material as the imperial cloak of

Dezrothia, woven of silk and gold, was placed carefully upon my shoulders. My audience gasped through their sobs of happy tears, and I pretended not to notice the High Archon gesturing for me to sit once more, allowing my audience to experience the moment with me thoroughly.

The High Archon's eyelid began to twitch, and eventually, I sat back down. He cleared his throat and moved onto the next stage. Paying respects to the late king. Like anyone cared? This was about moving forward. He'd had his moment in the obscenely long mourning period. It was time to focus on the new king, and I was willing to wager that there wouldn't be a fae in the temple who didn't agree wholeheartedly.

I bit my tongue and allowed my father his final moment. After all, it was part of the order of ceremony, and I wasn't about to do anything to risk this day not being executed by the book. My uncle sat proudly in the front row and the moment Augustus was mentioned, his eyes glazed over. Fates, he was in my good graces today. Usually, I just suffered his presence and used it to my advantage whenever the opportunity arose.

Even here, inside the Temple of the Fates, where I assumed nothing could tear my mind from my special day, it wasn't long into the spiel about how wonderful of a ruler my father had been, before my thoughts wandered back to this morning. Specifically, learning of my special surprise being shipped in from Mount Mortum at this very moment.

As castle maids had fastened the belt of my golden supertunica, the last thing I'd expected was to be interrupted. Not even by Vandenburg, who carried an heir of superiority that was rather irritating at best, but utterly insufferable on any normal day.

Alas, allowing him to come in had led to the blood red cherry on the cake. The way my dear uncle had been bursting with wicked glee from the moment he entered my chambers, I'd known it was going to be wonderful news he brought with him.

I wasn't disappointed.

For as a token of respect and support of my reign, he had pushed the boat out, so to speak, in preparing the most exquisite gift. Or gifts to be accurate. 'A pair' he'd called them. They'd arrive soon enough, and I couldn't wait to see if they were as deathly beautiful in the flesh as they'd been in his description.

It wasn't until the High Archon lifted the crown from its velvet cushion that I forced my face to relax into a more stoic expression and all thought of my uncle's gifts vanished. At last, all that was left was the crowning itself, and it would be official. I would be king and there wasn't a fae in Dezrothia who could overrule me. I'd have the final say in every decision and the ultimate power and control of my land and the fae I let live on it.

The High Archon lowered his arms above my head. Despite trying it on multiple times already, I was taken aback by the neck-breaking weight of the crown as it pressed down on my raven hair. Even more so when he let go. I didn't need to see it for myself to know that the beams of light coming in through the large tapestry of windows would be reflecting off the jewels beautifully. The blue ones complimenting my eyes, the red reminding me of the blood spilled to get here, and the green, my favorite of all, signifying my brother's jealousy that it wasn't him sitting here.

The High Archon spoke loudly as he said, "All in the Temple of Fates, and the realm of Dezrothia, it is time to say together–"

Every fae in the room joined in as he continued. "I swear that I will pay true allegiance to His Majesty, King Elikai Regis, and to his heirs and successors, according to Lore. So help me, Fates."

The corners of my mouth ached by the time I left the temple and climbed inside the carriage waiting in front of the doors. As soon as I was settled comfortably, we embarked on the coronation procession, where the lower class fae would lay roses before me. And in return, they'd receive a glimpse of my face. More handsome than ever, framed by the golden crown and royal vestments. There would be a feast awaiting the elite at the castle, which I'd, of course, attend. But first I had one quick piece of business to take care of.

I was finally king, and there was no better way to remind myself of that than by visiting the cells that held the contestants for the upcoming Coronation Games. There truly was no more fitting way to let them know that it was almost time.

Upon receiving my invitation, entrants had arrived at the castle gates from towns and villages far and wide. Expecting to be welcomed into my home for the duration of their participation in the games. *Idiots*. Like I'd allow them to set so much as a nine-toed foot within my courtyard.

Instead, they'd been bound, blindfolded, and taken to the true location of my games. The best kept secret in Dezrothia, and it would remain that way until the arena was complete and ready for its big reveal.

CHAPTER 8

Axel

The only downside to life in a rebel camp thus far was the paranoia that came with being deep inside the Fading Vale.

The paranoia wasn't from the fae around me being unknown; I could deal with them and was already making fast friends. It was the sounds coming from the forest itself, creeping me the fuck out. It was hard to stop your imagination from running wild, wondering what was behind every crunch and rustle, knowing the tent walls were so thin.

Though I should have slept like the dead, exhausted from too much time spent collared inside the mountain beneath the castle, I woke with every slight disturbance in the leaves and creak from the trees. With every new sound, my mind spiraled into more and more fantastical reasons for the cause of the noise. Some were more unrealistic than others.

At first, when my friends, old and new, had retired to their tents, life as a rebel had been great. And it stayed that way for a couple of hours. With a long sword on loan, and a female to make moan, what more could a male ask for?

It had been the perfect two birds, one stone situation.

I'd met the female on my way to the weapons tent, and by the time we fell through my tent door, we'd been as naked as I'd felt without a dagger tucked under my pillow and a heavy, bladed piece of steel to cuddle during the night. Both of which I now had.

Things had quickly shifted from awesome to amazing around the time she tilted her neck and asked if she could be my blood source. In that instant, 'rebel life' had 'soldier spy in the horde life' well and truly beat. Really, though, pretending to be a wolf shifter at the castle, with no witch or thrakos blood, and only rabbits and rats on the menu, there wasn't much to be beat. But a fae blood source, willing to be my very own faucet, was one of my greatest fantasies.

I wasn't about to live a monogamous life, especially not when it came to fucking or feeding around here. But even two rounds with the shifter witch sharing my sleep sack hadn't been enough to distract me from the anxiety of being surrounded by the endless forest. Blind to whatever lurked beyond the thin material of the shelter.

The problem now, as I lay awake white knuckling the sword I'd snagged from the weapons tent, was that the blood I could smell did not belong to her. I wasn't a wasteful male. I'd been sure to clean up every last drop from where my fangs had pierced her soft skin.

This wasn't another figment of my imagination, either. Unlike the many sounds I had almost convinced myself that I'd somewhat exaggerated in my head, this was fresh blood. And I knew blood.

My thrakos side thought of little else. It beat against its cage trying to get to the source, a good indicator I wasn't imagining the scent. As a muffled, but no less real, thud echoed from behind my tent, I bolted upright.

"Alaric! Boss!" I yelled in my mind, hoping Alaric would be awake.

"Get out of my head, Axel. I'm yet to sleep and was jus' noddin' off." I snorted at that, of course he had his attention elsewhere.

"Your mates' been keeping you up? No judgment from me. I have a female here, too. Who needs sleep, right? Then again, she's pretty exhausted after two rounds. Wait, does that make us even–"

"What the fuck do you want, Axel?" Thank fuck, he was finally listening to me.

Sweat beaded on my forehead as I silently slipped out of the sleep sack, doing my best to not disturb the female deep in a slumber I envied. How I longed to be able to sleep so deeply that these smells and sounds didn't have me on such high alert. Perhaps she was just used to it? Desensitized or some shit.

My boots caught on the material of my sleep sack, and I fought the growl climbing my throat while tugging at it hard. Moving without making a sound was something Alaric had drilled into me, something he'd taught me long before I ever joined the horde.

I sniffed the air again. *"I can smell blood. Fresh blood."* Though it wasn't any stronger, thankfully.

"Then don't be such a messy eater," Alaric said.

"No, not hers, boss. I think something went down, hard, behind the tent line." There had been no more sounds since that first thud. But I wasn't going to just brush it off.

"Yer imagining things. Go to sleep, or fuck. Whatever, but get out of my head," Alaric said. *"An' dinnae ever compare yerself going two rounds to me having two mates, again. Ever. Jus' get that idea outta yer head."*

"Okay, but last time you were an asshole to me I almost died. Remember that?"

He sighed in my head. Maybe I shouldn't give him such a hard time. *"Axel, I don't smell any–wait."*

"What? What is happening?"

"Fuck, aye, that's blood." My heart pounded in my chest. Fuck, I was beginning to hope that I was wrong, or that Alaric was going to tell me it was Kane or Evangelia.

The female, whose name I'd forgotten to get, opened her eyes just as I freed my foot from the suffocating bedding.

"I don't think I can handle another round just yet, Axel," she rumbled, her voice low and seductive enough to contradict the words.

Holding a finger to her lips, I mouthed for her to stay quiet. Then shifted into my thrakos form, keeping my wings tucked tight at my back as I moved carefully to the opening and drew it wide enough to see out.

"What do we do, boss?" I asked, the scent of blood grew stronger under my more acute thrakos senses, and the unmistakable snap of twigs under boot met my ears like the blow of a warning horn.

We fight. Came Alaric's simple reply.

"Stay here, and don't make a sound," I whispered, glimpsing a flash of panic across her features.

No time to reassure her, I needed to move. Sword in hand, I crept out of the tent and the chill of the night air pricked my skin. Listening to the faint footsteps, I froze in place to sniff the air. Something wasn't right, but apparently only Alaric and I had noticed. I didn't see any other heads peeking out of tents.

Out here, the blood I'd smelled from inside the tent was still quite distant, but a new, stronger scent, similar to that given off by a wounded shifter, was suddenly overwhelming and much closer. Too close. Whatever was bleeding was doing so not far away from the tent I was crouched behind.

Unmoving, I waited as the footsteps drew nearer. *"That's right, come to daddy."*

"Axel, what the fuck?" Alaric snarled into my mind. Whoops.

The location I chose for my tent was deliberate; at the far end of the row, closer to the forest's edge than the rest. It made sense whoever was out there would target us either first, or last, depending on where they entered the camp from. It had been a gamble, but I sent a silent prayer to the fates that it was the former.

Crunch.

The moment a horde issued boot stepped into my peripheral, I moved. Standing quickly, I straightened my arm skyward, keeping the tip of the blade facing the ground. Using my body's momentum, I twisted, tightened my grip on the hilt and pushed enough power into the pommel that when it made contact with the soldier's neck, the break was instant.

The body rag-dolled to the ground, and I caught it, laying it down gently to avoid alerting any of his companions. Once he was prone, I gripped the hilt of my blade with two hands and helped him on his way to the fates' embrace. Skewering his heart and giving an extra twist of my arms for good measure.

"Boss, it's the horde. Just took one out."

As I pulled the blade back out, his back hit the dirt and blood bubbled up from his mouth.

One down. But they never traveled alone.

"Fuck. It's a fuckin' ambush."

Replaying my movements in reverse, I unsheathed the sword and was once again crouched down in front of the tent.

"W-what's happening?" the female stuttered the moment I poked my head back inside.

"What's your name?" She must have told me, but let's be honest, I was too distracted to commit it to memory. Which had to be a complement to her seduction skills, right?

"M-Marnie," she said, a little put out amid her fear. "Is this some kind of kink? Role play? Blood play? Please tell me it's a kink and we aren't under attack."

"There's a time for kinks, love. Sadly, this is not one of those times. Can you fight?"

She shook her head but said, "I can try."

"That's a firm no then," I confirmed, running the bloodied blade along the entrance of the tent, fraying the fabric so it looked to the horde like the targets inside had already been dealt with.

"What are you doing?" she asked.

"Time to play dead, or be dead. You choose. Just know, it would be an awful waste if you go with the latter. Especially now I know you're open to a bit of kink. Blood play sounds good, if you're game?"

As I spoke, I ran two fingers down the flat of the blade, sending the soldier's blood in a spray across Marnie's face and the sleep sack beyond.

In hindsight, the timing was terrible. "What, *now?*" she spat, incredulous.

"Ew, no." I shook my head, taking more blood and coating her slender throat. She had some learning to do if she thought blood play would involve some recently deceased horde soldier. Lessons I'd be willing to teach under any other circumstance. "Sorry, love, was just staging the scene. Now lie the fuck down and don't move. Understood?"

Her nod was the only confirmation I had time for before I was spinning to stand.

Back outside, I asked Alaric, *"Time to alert the camp?"*

"Aye. Go for it."

Cupping a hand around my mouth, I yelled, "AMBUSHHH!" then fell into a fighting stance, sword raised and ready.

The warning cut through the night like a clarion call to arms. Alaric was already out of his tent, battle-ax in hand, snapping instructions to Kane and Lady Evangelia, who were still inside their tent.

Knowing their element of surprise had been blown, the horde soldiers entered the camp in a tidal wave of bodies from every direction.

I swallowed. We were surrounded, but suddenly the camp erupted with rebels who moved in surprisingly organized chaos. Between the clangs of the clashing of steel and pained cries filling the air, fae split into groups.

Some headed for the weapons tent, coming away with armfuls of blades to hand out while others covered them. Some in fae form, others in their thrakos or shifter forms.

I let my wings out wide and free, no longer needing to hide them at all costs. It felt fucking fantastic.

The witches and warlocks collected the smaller rebel children, both defending and shielding them with spells. While the rebels who didn't have a specific role split up too. Some ran headlong into battle, where the rest split themselves between guarding the king and queen's tent and, surprisingly, most popular of all, Alaric's tent, protecting their newfound dragon princess.

Goosebumps rolled down my arms as I caught whose name most of them whispered.

Prince Nekane.

It wasn't just Evangelia they were protecting. They were flocking to Nekane too, despite them having other royal options now. The rebels wanted to defend the Regis Prince they'd once hated. They were willing to lay down their lives to ensure he didn't lose his…

And it was a fucking beautiful thing.

He had earned their respect despite his bloodline. But fates—a smile pulled at my lips—he would *not* be happy about their sacrifice. Lady Evangelia, neither. Luckily, that sounded like an Alaric problem.

As I took off for the clearing at the camps center, where most of the horde were heading, I caught Alaric telling his mates to "Stay."

"Good luck with that, brother."

He growled back at me. Fuck, I needed to remember to control my thoughts. But he didn't really think they would hide, did he? He should have learned by now that he couldn't control them any more than he could control the fates. I'd observed them enough, both individually and together, during their time at the castle to have worked that out.

Alas, the poor bastard was more easily deluded when it came to matters of the heart.

A soldier stepped in my way, and our swords met. As sparks flew, a pang of guilt for making Marnie play dead hit me. Once she was over the initial shock, maybe she'd have jumped into action like everyone else? As much as I wanted to turn toward my tent to see if the ruse was working, I knew if I did, I might lose my head.

Once I'd put Marnie from my mind, it didn't take long to best the soldier. My sword cut through his neck and I relished in the spray of blood that erupted. With two of the horde dealt with, I went looking for the next. Scanning the many battles taking place to work out where I could best serve.

A glimpse of silver caught my eye; Lady Evangelia had joined the fight. Badass dragon scales coated her exposed flesh, which was already flecked with blood. She was lethal with those daggers, slicing through every one of the horde members who came up against her.

Kane wasn't far away from her, his muscles bulging as he parried the blows coming his way. If I wasn't so busy swinging my own sword, I might have laughed at how quickly and thoroughly they'd disobeyed Alaric's orders to stay put.

Nix was at the prince's back, working with the high fae like an impenetrable shadow. Switching positions when necessary, depending on whose strengths and gifts were better suited to deal with their attackers.

But as swiftly as we dealt with our enemy, rebels I hadn't met yet, and now never would, fell. Faster and in greater numbers, despite our best efforts. How the fuck had the horde found us? And so soon after arriving.

I'd been told of how resident witches had spells cast in the forest surrounding camp to turn fae around, cloaking us and preventing any unwanted folk from finding us. Only someone who knew exactly where the camp was could find it.

Or lead someone to it.

A blade sunk into my bicep, forcing my arm to dip from the sudden sharp pain. As the soldier swung back to strike again and the metal hit, his sword slid away despite barely being able to raise my own arm. Exploiting my weakness, he attacked again and again, quicker than I could recover.

Then two more turned their attention our way, trying to overwhelm and beat me down.

Fuck. This.

Spreading my wings wider, the claws at their tips came out to play. I swiped at the female who'd sunk her blade into my arm first, my talons raking down her face, slicing through an eye and blinding her as blood poured from the wound.

I fanned my wings in, creating a gust of wind, pushing the other two back and giving myself a moment to breathe.

My arm began to tingle as it healed, the open wound stitching itself back together, and I readied my weapon again. The next swing I made sliced through a torso and I grimaced as the body crumpled to the ground in two parts.

Spinning, I moved onto the second, but beyond their shoulder, caught sight of a group of fae with terror glowing in their wide eyes.

They huddled near the tent where the king and queen were staying, as if they hoped to protect them, but knew the only aid they could offer was the self-sacrifice kind. Slowing the horde, they had no hope of beating.

Unable to reach them, I sent a silent prayer to the fates for their survival, vented my frustration on the soldier, and moved onto the next opponent. The horde was relentless, but we defended our camp with everything we had. Several rebels had paired up now, fighting like Nekane and Nix. While Alaric joined forces with his 'Angel'.

Braxton's voice met my ears as he barked out orders. I turned to find the male single handedly trying to stop the enemy from entering the medical tent…

Aunt Rose.

Her mate fought in thrakos form, his wings bleeding as he killed fiercely, but he was outnumbered. So very outnumbered. When he lurched to stop a sly fae getting past him, I saw what he was covering behind his wing.

Not a what, a who.

Edelin. Her eyes turned to white orbs as they rolled back into her head.

The tunnel she had into the future was an incredible gift most of the time, but it didn't close just because she was in mortal danger in the present. Fighting my way across the clearing in a constant dance of battle, I focused entirely on reaching the medical tent until Braxton and I were fighting side by side.

"She's too exposed out here," I called to the rebel leader.

"Aye. Get her inside with Rose," he snarled, gutting a wolf mid-pounce.

With a nod, I did as ordered and made quick work of picking Edelin up and disappearing into the medical tent.

Then froze when I saw Aunt Rose; sitting up in bed, trying to push her blankets off.

"That's a hard no, ma'," I said. "Stay here. You'll only distract Braxton if you go out there in your condition."

"I'm fine," she snapped as I placed Edelin down carefully on a spare bed opposite her.

Stubborn female.

With only the sounds to go by, anxiety over what was happening on the battlefield made me impatient to get back out there.

"Sure you are," I said. "But look, Edelin's vulnerable. If you have to protect someone, protect her. She needs you more than Braxton does right now. Agreed?"

Her jaw was set, but at her sharp nod, I bolted to rejoin the fray.

As I moved the material aside with the back of my palm, a hand reached through the gap, fisting tight on my shoulder before ripping me out of the tent. The male was large, and too close for me to swing my sword. With my free arm, I grabbed his wrist to pry it away, needing to get a little more distance between us. Simultaneously, the most intense pressure pushed against my abdomen.

The hold on my shoulder built to a bone crushing brace as he pulled me closer still. But I didn't have the strength to shake his grip, despite being bigger in both height and muscle.

A sudden fire lit up inside me. Not the type fueled by anger or determination to escape the unwanted hold and slay my attacker. No. It wasn't like that at all. It was like an actual fire was blazing inside me, lancing my veins, causing a pain like nothing I'd ever experienced.

A cough erupted from my throat, and with it, a metallic taste. Then a crimson spatter covered my assailant's face.

Fuck.

As the soldier's long blade slid free from my stomach, I choked on the pain and crumpled to the ground.

A deafening howl vibrated in the air above me, followed by the silhouette of a she-wolf, flying over my head in a perfect arc, despite the sky spinning sporadically above the trees. My vision became dotted with black, fading in and out as the wolf tore into the soldier in a frenzy.

With every break of consciousness, I could have sworn the enemy was missing an additional limb. But as blood bubbled up my throat, air could no longer reach my lungs. And all that was left to do was smile at my adopted mother and watch her messy revenge kill.

I took the gory image with me all the way to the other side, where the fates should be, but only empty nothingness lived.

CHAPTER 9
Nekane

Amid the chaos of battle, Alaric's voice cut through the clashing of steel, "Kane!"

I turned, but it wasn't Alaric who my eyes landed on. It was Axel. Folding to the ground, clutching his stomach where crimson began to spill from a vicious wound that marred his abdomen. A white wolf appeared from the depths of the medical tent, and before all four paws were on the ground, it was tearing into Axel's assailant.

"Kane!" Alaric called again with an urgent desperation. "Get over there. Yeh have to heal him!"

Leaving Eva's side, Alaric followed my path to the tent. Nix joined us as we fought our way across the bloody swamp that transformed the clearing we had briefly called home. My stomach was in knots as we moved closer toward his brother, but the same adrenaline that had my heart pounding in my throat was what kept me focused.

I had to get to him. Had to save him. Had to help.

We couldn't lose Axel. It wasn't just how formidable he was when faced with the physical acts of war, but the emotional toll we knew it would take on the camp. He'd be a source of morale for everyone with his positive attitude and penchant for making everyone laugh. Dark humor was the soldier's second language, and I had no doubt it would be our crutch and coping mechanism in the coming weeks and months.

Not to mention my own desire to protect the male I love from the immeasurable pain that would come with losing a piece of his family. As we reached the tent, Nix blocked a spell from a warlock aimed straight for us with his own magic. With a growl, he went after the soldier, using his thrakos wings to slash any who tried to cross his path.

Rose, whose white fur was now completely red as it soaked up blood, released the piece of the soldier she had mauled and turned her attention to Axel instead. The way she clamped her jaw around his ankle to drag him inside the tent was a far contrast to the way she'd been ripping into horde flesh moments before. Her canine face was contorted with worry as she looked up at Alaric with a gentle whine. When her silver eyes met mine, they were sharp and carried a threat that told me if I didn't heal him fast, I'd be the next to feel her wrath.

"You get his legs," I said to Alaric as I returned my sword to its sheath. "On three." I bent to wrap my arms under his shoulders and said, "Three."

We carried him to a bed, still warm from where Rose must have been resting before shifting. Edelin was in the bed opposite, her eyes white and rolling, breathing steadily but otherwise completely still. Stuck in a vision, perfect timing from the fates as usual.

Rose shifted back to her fae form. "Save him," she ground out, not bothering to cover up.

Closing my eyes, I shut out the sounds of death and destruction beyond the canvas walls. With the safety of having Alaric at my back, I focused only on channeling my healing magic. It poured from me, and when my eyes opened again, the air around us shimmered with a faint, silvery green light as I pushed my energy into Axel's body.

"How did they find us?" Rose demanded of Alaric, even as her voice trembled with concern.

"Jarrah," he spat.

"The rebel who turned traitor?" Rose asked. "Braxton filled me in when I woke up. But if you both knew he'd give up the camp's location, why let the dragon bring us here?"

Though her desire for needing someone to blame stemmed from her worry over Axel, the thinly veiled accusation that this was somehow Eva's fault made my nostrils flare. A rumble echoed from Alaric's chest.

"If we hadn't returned here, the horde would have ambushed the camp anyway," I said, trying to keep my magic steady. "There would be no battle taking place out there right now, because it would have been little more than a slaughter."

"Aye," Alaric agreed. "Without a leader, without the warriors we brought back here, they wouldnae stand a chance, and yeh ken it, ma'."

Rose sagged with a sad nod.

"Angel was right to bring us here. I knew the risks of Jarrah knowin' our location. If anythin' it's on me and da' for knowin' the risk an' thinkin' the move could wait a couple of days."

"Don't you dare blame yourself," I snapped. "This is on Elikai." As I snarled his name, hatred toward my brother filled me.

Rose sighed. "I'm sorry. I didn't mean to accuse, I just..." she turned her attention to me, "Please heal him, Prince Nekane."

"Kane, just Kane." I muttered.

Taking a few deep, steadying breaths, I tried to focus my energy back on Axel's wound. The only thing that was going to tempt my hands away from pushing healing magic into saving him was the thought of Jarrah being just outside this tent and the desire to wrap them around that traitor's neck instead, not letting go until they met in the middle.

"Do you think he's here?" I gritted, despite already knowing the answer.

"Jarrah?" Alaric shrugged, then ran a hand through his tangled hair. "I havnae seen him, but he doesnae need to be here to have told them exactly where to find us."

Elikai had said Jarrah was to take part in his games, so the probability of him being here so I could tear him limb from limb was non-existent.

I found Alaric and his mother's gazes flicking between Axel and the tent's doorway. The hypnotic silver color they shared swam with a desperation for him to survive. Combined with our shared need to join the fight and finish this before more were injured and further lives lost.

Glancing down at Axel's wound, relief washed over me to find it was no longer the gaping, bloody maw it had been moments ago. Granted, it was far from perfect, the previously smooth skin marred with an angry red blemish, but he was stable. There was little I could do for his blood loss, but his own healing would take care of the rest.

He'd live.

Alaric and I shared a look, and Rose whispered her thanks as she grasped Axel's hand and brushed a gentle kiss to his knuckles.

"Stay with him," Alaric said to his mother, though she didn't look to have plans of being anywhere but at Axel's bedside. Then to me he asked, "Yeh good to carry on or yeh need some rest?"

"I'm good," I said.

Though the wound was severe, Axel was powerful and his body called upon the gifts of all his forms to help heal as soon as he was able. Thank the fates, I'd help get him there without sapping my energy too severely along the way.

Alaric and I stepped over broken bodies, some of our comrades, some of my brother's fallen soldiers, and guilt knotted in the pit of my stomach as I brandished my sword once more. The feeling soon vanished when a hyena shifter darted toward us. Alaric, as his stunning black wolf, intercepted the shifter. As he barreled into the hyena's side, they tumbled, snarled, and fought.

I scanned the area, trying to pick up on clues of what had happened in the minutes that passed while I was in the medical tent. The first thing that stuck out to me was how horribly outnumbered we still were. The horde was converging on us, dominating our numbers. Second, Eva was nowhere to be seen. My heart thumped painfully as my eyes jumped from fae to fae, searching her out. She obviously wasn't dead, but what if they'd taken her?

I swallowed the bile threatening my throat and tried to focus my senses more sharply on my surroundings, searching for her sweet and smoky scent, and the sounds she made when fighting hard in the training ring.

She was here, and the faint sounds of her voice were coming from the direction of our tent. I managed one step in that direction before a blinding burst of light illuminated the battlefield.

Quickly followed by searing heat.

A shockwave rippled through the air, knocking both friend and foe to the ground. I tried to shield my eyes from the burning brightness, but the sight before me was something impossible to look away from.

The Dyvrad royals formed a line, Eva in the center. Her arms draped over her grandparent's shoulders on either side as she struggled to stand by herself. Apart from some minor nicks and scratches, she didn't appear physically injured. With the lack of blood, I could only assume a spell had broken through and struck her. She looked dazed, her eyes slightly unfocused, but her protectors, the old king and queen, her grandparents... they looked furious on her behalf as they unleashed their immense magical powers on the camp.

Vyara and Drayke's eyes glowed from the light of their flames, which poured like a waterfall from their mouths. They stood in their partially shifted forms, the same one Eva had been mastering, while they spewed fire. I couldn't move, not even to blink, as I watched the ancient dragons driving the horde's forces back. While Thalia and Westly stood at their flanks, creating a barrier of protection around any who weren't wearing horde armor.

The fire stopped and Drayke's voice echoed with authority as he addressed them as one, "Drop your weapons!" His words carried a weight that demanded obedience, and metal dropped to the ground from every direction.

"Leave now, or die." Vyara commanded with equal dominance.

"We can't let them live!?" someone called out, panicked mutterings agreeing with the anonymous voice.

"They have rebel blood on their hands!" another snapped.

"They came here to kill innocent fae in their sleep. Why should we let them live?!"

The weight of countless stares bore into me. So intense I was aware of it before managing to tear my eyes away from the dragons and see the rebels for myself. A few seconds passed, but Braxton said nothing, and when I met Alaric's eyes, he just lifted a brow as though he too was waiting for my order.

The horde soldiers were paralyzed, weapons at their feet. All color drained from the features of those who weren't too coated in blood to see skin. Even if they didn't know who these fae were, they knew to fear them. To respect their authority as they would a king, queen, or horde general.

I cleared my throat. "Leave or die," I said, echoing the dragon queen's words.

Silence.

More staring.

I took a deep breath. "Yes, these soldiers have killed our own here today. Just as we have killed many of theirs," I announced, gesturing around the clearing. "But they did so under orders they are trained to follow, not question."

I slid my sword into its sheath and stepped forward. "They will have to carry that innocent rebel blood on their hands for the rest of their lives," I continued. "But if we kill them like this, we are no more than the savages they have been brainwashed to believe we are."

"Aye," Braxton said. "Leave or die," he agreed.

"Leave or die," Alaric echoed, followed by several others, Nix included.

"M-more will come," a horde soldier said.

"Of that I have no doubt," I agreed. "Are you in charge of this group?" I asked.

He swallowed, then nodded.

"How did you find us so quickly?"

"We were already in the Vale looking for camps when a raven delivered a message of your location. We must have been the closest, but more *will* come."

"What will you tell Elikai when you return?" I asked.

Several flinched at my casual use of his name. "That the rebels refused to pledge their allegiance to their crown, so we killed them all. That no one of interest to the crown was here."

"Good. Now take your dead and leave," I hissed. "But remember the kindness bestowed to you today by hybrids and thrakos alike."

I waited as his group rushed from the clearing, most without pausing to collect their fallen.

Today was not the day my brother would win. But now we had work to do.

IN THE WAKE OF BATTLE, I found myself sitting at a table inside the brimming war tent, forcing down the most unpalatable broth I'd ever tasted. I wasn't alone. We all seemed to share the same thoughts, although we kept them to ourselves. When the bowls of the not-quite-lukewarm, savory liquid were handed out, we took them greedily with thanks, needing the energy to repair our tired and aching bodies. I drank deeply, directly from the bowl, but instantly regretted it when my eye began to twitch at both the taste and texture. It was a struggle to swallow for several seconds, but when I did, a glance around the table revealed every face contorted in similar grimaces, despite their best efforts to hide them.

Marnie, the fae who'd filled the bowl, announced, "We have seconds for everyone."

Suddenly, everyone was very interested in their bowl, or spoon, or a random spot on the table. King and Queen Dyvrad excused themselves on account of their bodies not being used to so much food. As I tried to think of an excuse of my own, I didn't notice until too late that Marnie had moved to my side. "More, Prince Nekane?" she asked, leaning over my shoulder. Holding out my bowl, I forced a dimpled smile of gratitude and spotted Alaric in my peripheral do a full body shudder, but neither of us attempted to save my taste buds from further torture.

If it wasn't for the *why* of the broth being so foul, it might have been funny.

Aside from a few guards dotted around the perimeter, the camp's cooks had been the only rebels awake when the horde had struck in the early hours. Untrained in combat, they hadn't stood a chance when the soldiers had snuck up on them. It had been determined in the immediate aftermath, as Braxton and Alaric walked the battleground and beyond, searching for survivors too injured to get themselves to the medical tent, that they were likely already dead before Axel alerted the rest of the camp.

While the injured rested, and bodies were being prepared for burial, everyone remaining wanted to help in some way. Feeding the exhausted warriors had been a task several had jumped at. As much as I appreciated their efforts and initiative, I wished they hadn't let it cool before someone decided to add all the raw eggs. *Eggs should never be an afterthought.*

The strategy meeting we were in was arguably worse than the broth, though. With me, a Regis Prince, the old dragon king and queen, an ex-horde general and several rebel leaders giving our thoughts simultaneously, we were going around in circles and my patience was wearing thin.

Too many cooks in every scenario…

Frustrated with our lack of progress an hour in, and possibly to avoid more spoiled broth, Alaric spoke above us all. "One thing yeh can all agree on is that we cannae stay here," he stated. "It doesnae matter whether we trust the horde soldiers' word, more *will* come. It only takes one to break and tell Elikai the truth of how their hunt ended, an' they'll be back with reinforcements."

"Not to sound cold or insensitive, but we could use some reinforcements ourselves, too," I said. "We can't go up against Elikai and the horde as we are. We need allies."

Drayke Dyvrad nodded, "Then we leave now. Move camps and find allies in villages along the way."

Braxton arched a brow. "Ever tried movin' a camp like this? It will take a few days to pack up, plus we'll need to send some fae on a supply run if we're to go deeper into the Vale. I ken we need allies, but there are few villages we are welcome in, less who'd keep quiet about our presence, and fewer still who'd be willin' to join our side."

Was that seriously our plan? Go deeper into the Vale and just… hide?

"The injured need some time to rest," I said instead. "As do most of us here. I'll continue to do what I can to help with the healing, as will the witches and warlocks, but there is only so much we can do."

"How long do you think we need?" Vyara asked no one in particular, steepling her fingers.

Braxton shrugged. "Three days might be enough."

The former queen sighed, then placed a hand over her mates and squeezed. "I must admit, you all know much more about this than we do. Too long has passed, and so much has changed since we were in the war room making plans like these."

It was hard to imagine what the castle war room would have been like then. Very different to the discussions during my father's reign, no doubt.

"It is true, your majesty," Westly said sadly. "Dezrothia is not the great place it once was."

"Clearly," Drayke said, clearing his throat of the slimy meal.

"Those who died here tonight were fighting to change that," I said.

"We want to help change that too," Vyara said.

"Yeh want yer throne back, yeh mean," Braxton said, triggering several eyes to go as round as the yolks bobbing in the broth.

Vyara squeezed Drayke's hand again, but shook off the comment. "Right now, we share one goal, which is to help this realm thrive. If that involves Dyvrad's reclaiming the throne, so be it."

Her eyes met mine, expecting me to challenge her on it. As though she fully expected me to insist the throne was mine. That they couldn't come back from the dead and pull it out from under me. I neither thought nor said any of those things. Instead, I asked, "Why did my father keep you in the catacombs? What purpose did keeping you alive serve him?" If we were to discuss our next moves with them, we should know more about their story.

I'd racked my brains for any information my father might have let slip over the years about his predecessors, but came up blank every time. He'd buried or burned everything that so much as resembled dragons, along with many other subjects he'd deemed unsavory. The only remaining hint had been some faint carvings on the throne, but unless you had some inkling about the history and were looking for them, it was easy to overlook or mistake for something else. Some other winged creatures like the thrakos. They had been his greatest invention, after all. Until they weren't.

"I've been wonderin' that myself," said Alaric. "Regis only kept fae alive if they served a purpose."

Pushing my broth aside, I leaned forward, placing my elbows on the table in what was probably a very un-prince-like gesture, but I didn't care. We'd saved them from a fate far worse than death, regardless of their former station in society, they owed us answers. If not for the war effort, then for Eva. Even if she was recovering in the medical tent herself, she'd appreciate any information they offered.

The war tent fell into complete silence as the old king took a glug of water, then shared a look with Vyara, who gave him an encouraging nod. "Where to start?" he mused to her.

"The day the realm thought we died is as good a place as any, my flame."

He dipped his head. "The day the realm thought we died, we'd been traveling with a small horde of draconian guards from the castle, set to join the bulk of our forces several hours ahead at Kelpie Cove."

When he looked up, I saw vulnerability in his eyes, which made my stomach knot.

Taking a deep breath, he continued. "Word had reached us that hundreds of Mount Mortum boats were headed for our coast, starting an all-out war. It wasn't something we could ignore, despite how inconceivable it might have been," he explained. "We had heard the rumors that Augustus had his sights on our throne and planned to act on it soon, but we had to defend our realm. We couldn't very well ignore such a threat based on the possibility of it being a ruse."

I frowned. "Why did you send them ahead?" I asked. "If you intended to fight alongside your soldiers and not lead the war from the safety of the castle, why leave yourself so exposed by traveling separately?"

Vyara's eyes closed as though she was reliving a painful, centuries old memory. "Though our relationship with King Vandenburg was anything but friendly, it wasn't like him to charge on Dezrothia, especially knowing his army was so much weaker than ours. So when the warning of the Mount Mortum attack on Kelpie Cove reached us, we decided it was time to send our daughter away, in case it was the trap we'd been warned of. She was to lay low, and conceal her identity until the time was right to reclaim her rightful place on the throne."

With the blood of the last, restore what has passed.

Only Lavina hadn't been the last. Eva was. Her veins flowed with the blood of the last king and queen. Was it her fate to restore the realm to its former glory? I'd never stand in the way of her fate, but it begged the question. Where did that leave me? What was my fate? My purpose in all of this?

"So yeh made preparations for Lavina to go with Kur, said yer goodbyes and set off for Kelpie Cove?" Alaric prompted, eager for more of their story.

Drayke gave a slow nod. "Yes, we were suspicious that all may not be as it seemed in Kelpie Cove, but we hadn't expected Augustus to ambush us enroute."

His eyes glazed as a memory seemed to take his attention, his face scrunching into something akin to sadness or deep regret. Like he wished he could have prevented it from ever happening, if he had just listened to the secrets being whispered. He swallowed and his words were quieter when he spoke again. "We spent centuries thinking he must have had a spy we weren't aware of, someone close to us. Someone who'd told him we planned to send Lavina away that morning and therefore would be accompanied by just a small group of guards."

"We believed he must have gone looking for her, or found her first," Vyara added, her voice strained. "They used to be close. Never more than friends, despite him proposing marriage."

"He loved her?" I whispered as my heart plummeted in my chest.

I hadn't meant the thought to be voiced; it wasn't meant for anyone other than myself. It just slipped out while my mind reeled. Nevertheless, they heard it.

Drayke scoffed, shaking his head. "He loved the *idea* of her, of what she could offer him," he said. "As my mate said, they were close, back when he was just an innocent child. After she rejected him in her teenage years, he never spoke to her again, and it broke her heart that he had tried to use her for her crown. By the time your father reached adulthood, she no longer recognized him as the boy she'd once known. He'd become poisoned by his narcissism and solely driven by his desire for power."

Sounds about right.

"Even if our Lavina had been interested in a male like him, we'd never have allowed it," Vyara said with guilt marring her brow. "We couldn't have. She was our only heir, and her husband would be a prince consort. Someone like him would not have been content with the title of prince. He'd want to sit on the throne himself. For a fae to do that, they must understand that power does not belong to the crown. It belongs to the fae of the land, and they must do right by them first and foremost."

Despite knowing I was nothing like the male they spoke of, I couldn't help feeling guilty, or perhaps somehow responsible, in part for the way my father ruined so many lives. To go from a king and queen who understood they worked for society, society did not work for them, to a dictatorship made worse by personal bias and prejudice.

"Like father, like son," Nix muttered, before his eyes, filled with regret, darted to me. "Not y–"

"It's true," Alaric cut over him. "*Elikai* is no better suited for the throne than his sire was. Kane, thank the fates, is no' like either of them."

"So our granddaughter seems to agree," Vyara said. "Perhaps we shall continue?"

"Yes, please do," I said, desperate to move on as heat creeped up my neck.

Drayke cleared his throat. "It turned out the Mount Mortums were already in Dezrothia, assisted by Augustus and his supporters, of course. So when we were ambushed, they came at us with the force of an entire army. We should have died with our guard. Instead, the supposed usurper took us to the catacombs. We've remained there ever since."

"Yes, I… We…" Vyara choked out.

"I think that is enough for tonight." I offered, seeing how difficult it was for them to continue.

"Aye, we can take it from here. We ken what needs to be done to move," Braxton agreed.

With a nod of thanks, they took their leave, Westly and Thalia close behind.

Unfortunately, there wasn't much help I could offer to rally a rebel camp to move. So I muttered quietly to Alaric that I was going to check on Eva. I was sitting on her bed when he joined us a few short minutes later. His gaze immediately landed on the faint glow of magic from our joined hands, where I sent more healing into our mate. Stepping up behind me, he placed a hand on my shoulders and kneaded his thumbs into the tight spots in my neck, relieving some of the stress and tension. "That's enough for one day, Kane," he said.

Eva gave him a bright smile. "I tried to tell him I was fine, he wouldn't hear it," she said.

Alaric rolled his eyes. "How are yeh?"

"Much better." Eva said, then glanced across to the bed next to hers. "Plus, I've been in good company. Axel's made it his mission to save me from boredom."

"He's sleepin'?" Alaric asked, frowning at where Axel lay on his back with a gauze across his bare stomach and eyes closed.

Eva raised a brow. "Pretending to sleep more like it," she said. "He was explaining the rules of extreme catch to me before Kane walked in here. Not a bit tired." She dropped her voice, despite knowing he would still hear every word. "I think this might be his way of giving us some privacy."

"If yeh ever play that game with my Angel, yeh won't be tossin' a dagger in the air, it'll be yer scrotum. Understood?" Alaric said.

"I can't hear you," Axel mumbled. "I'm asleep."

"Yer tired?" Alaric asked, but he wasn't looking at his adopted brother. His gaze had fallen on the half full bowl of broth beside his bed and his smirk pulled at his scar.

Picking it up, he tipped the remains that Axel obviously couldn't stomach into Eva's near empty one. "Then perhaps yeh missed lunch an' need some energy," he suggested.

A smirk tugged at my lips. "You must be starving," I agreed.

"Good job Marnie has enough for seconds, eh?" Alaric taunted.

"I can go get her?" I offered.

"Stop," Eva said, but her voice lacked any real conviction. "Don't be cruel."

"You mean gruel?" I corrected.

Axel shot up, wincing a little as he clung onto his stomach. "No, please," he begged. "Can't you just shove another long sword through my stomach or something instead, boss? Please. Anything but another bowl of that."

I barked a laugh and watched relief wash over Alaric's features. Despite being pale, he was healing well. And thank the fates, hadn't lost his sense of humor.

CHAPTER 10

Evangelia

Three short days had passed since the horde soldier's ambush, and we were leaving the camp forever. So much had happened in such a small amount of time, but we were as ready as we could be to go our separate ways and do our part, taking the next steps to win the war against Elikai.

Kane and Nix had taken me from my grandparents and straight to the medical tent as soon as the horde soldiers had fled. Where they worked together to speed up my healing after I had been pummeled by a barrage of spells from the horde's witches and warlocks. My scales were effective in deflecting a few spells, three at most. But dozens of spells landing one after the other? Apparently not so much.

Blaze had come to visit me in the tent, or maybe he'd just been there because that's where Kane was spending a lot of time. Either way, he'd sat with me and told me what he saw. After cursing out the adults, who, unlike him, had all reached immortality, he'd peeked through a gap in the opening of the tent to watch the battle. He'd wanted to take up a weapon to help, of course, but the warriors protecting the tent had kept pushing him back into safety.

The assault of spells had hit me in the back, and I'd dropped like a sack of potatoes. It wasn't long after that my grandparents had appeared in their partially shifted forms, scooping me up between them and letting a stream of white hot flames leave their mouths. Fates, it was still so strange thinking of Drayke and Vyara that way. A few days with the knowledge and it felt no more real. *How do I have grandparents?*

Thalia had visited me in my sickbed, too. Though she was no longer my handmaid, our friendship was still strong, and she panicked when she saw me fall in the midst of the battle. She'd been the reason my grandparents knew I'd needed help, when she'd begged her uncle to tell them I'd been hit. Thankfully, Westly had moved quickly, and it hadn't taken long after my fall for them to come to my rescue. Drayke and Vyara had commanded the fae surrounding their tent to get out of their way, their wings forcing them to move. And I wasn't surprised to hear that none had dared question them.

Thalia and Westly's magic had healed me enough to regain consciousness, but I'd had barely enough strength to stay upright without my grandparents' support. How they'd managed to find the energy to carry me while unleashing their power on the horde, I had no idea. They'd been nowhere near full strength, but they grew stronger by the hour without the cuffs weakening them.

We hadn't won, but with Kane's support, my grandparents had ended the battle early and planted a seed in the heads of those soldiers. One I had a feeling would continue to grow during their journey home. Our side of this war had shown the soldiers mercy, and because of that, we'd come away as the victors as far as I was concerned, despite our tragic losses. We hadn't forced them to bend the knee and change allegiance, instead we'd shown that the rebels were more than just savages who needed to be put down for no reason other than our existence. We still had many to grieve, and almost all who'd fought were injured to varying degrees.

Axel was among some of the more seriously hurt, and we'd ended up being neighbors in the medical tent. His wound was far worse than mine, yet he'd still made it his duty to keep me entertained. I appreciated it more than he knew and was glad to see him make a full recovery over the days that followed.

While we were on bed rest, Alaric and Braxton had gathered in the war tent with Kane, the Dyvrads and the surviving rebel leaders to discuss what our strategy should be. We had to move to a new camp as soon as possible, but before that could happen, a lot needed to be done. They'd instructed the witches and warlocks to reinforce our protections, then separated the camp in two; day watch and night watch. The only time everyone had been awake at the same time in the days since the ambush was for the funeral.

We'd buried our fallen, Ilona and Miles included, keeping with our traditions. And with the honor they deserved for defending our fae, our home, our beliefs and our cause so valiantly. Though the burial had been devastating, we were all very aware there would be many more before the war was done.

Mistakes made in war were paid for with casualties. Being the one to make the call to come back here, without properly considering the traitor who knew the camp better than most of us, I shouldered a lot of responsibility for the deaths that night.

Axel had stopped me from letting the guilt weave itself too deeply around my heart. And the following night, back in the relative privacy of our tent, Kane and Alaric had made me see that there hadn't been a better alternative.

Had we not been here, the horde would still have attacked, and the outcome would have, without a doubt, been even more difficult to live with. It was better this way. Even if it didn't feel like that right now.

Thank the fates no more soldiers marched upon our camp as we packed to leave.

When two fae volunteered to do the supply run yesterday, Nix and I had shared a look, and later reminisced on some of our best memories together during our own rare supply runs. As well as those memories which still haunt us.

Vyara and Drayke had transformed from the frail, emaciated fae they'd been when they were pulled from the catacombs. Practically unrecognizable, yet more familiar to me than ever. They looked centuries younger, their faces no longer gaunt, skin no longer stretched taut over bones. They appeared as I imagined they would have centuries ago, maybe no longer in their prime, but just as healthy.

The resemblance between my mother and grandmother was unnerving. The same nose, their eyes, and especially the silver hair that I had inherited. It brought tears to my eyes that my mum never knew, and never would know, her mother had been alive all these years. Would it have made a difference? Would she have fought harder against Augustus Regis? Faced him head on rather than hiding?

A mixture of emotions churned within me—gratitude for their survival, awe at their resilience, and a deep-seated yearning to have my mother alive, so she, too, could get to know them all over again with me. My grandparents sat across the campfire from me now. Vyara exuded an air of regal elegance. Her glowing hair, like a waterfall of moonlight, cascaded down past her shoulders to rest at her hips. A stark contrast to her dark and intense eyes that held within them the wisdom of ages. She sat straight and stood tall; a symbol of strength forged through trials. Beside her, Drayke emanated a sense of quiet power. Salt and pepper hair framed his face and blue eyes, as pale as the vast sky above, seemed to always be watching.

Westly was nearby, as always, the ever-dutiful warlock taking his self-appointed role seriously. No one asked him to attend to the old king and queen, but I guessed some habits were harder to break than others. At least Kane had convinced him to not bow every time he walked by. He had all but renounced his titles.

Alaric was passing out the weapons, while Kane was with Blaze and his mum. He'd woken up this morning, determined to find a way to lead Raine back to her family should she eventually return to this area and find it deserted. Though Blaze looked to Kane as his idol, Kane had taken on more of a big brother role in Raine's absence. When he wasn't attending meetings in the war tent, of course.

Alaric caught my attention, and I knew it was time to go. He had a large bag on his back, weapons hanging from his waist and further baggage at his feet for Kane and me to carry. Rather than travel south to find safety in the deeper depths of the Vale with the rest of the camp, we had a mission of our own. One which Braxton had determined he, Rose, my grandparents, and Westly would be joining us on.

It became clear during the meetings inside the war tent that keeping my grandparents' existence a secret did little to help our cause. Especially given three dragons had taken to the skies over Ezerat in front of an army of horde soldiers. It had actually been Vyara's suggestion to spread the word by first visiting villages and showing them they were alive. They hoped to gain allies, and the plan was for them to open up and tell their story.

Once they had their attention, they'd make it known they would be reclaiming what was theirs and asking the villagers to pick a side for the war that would soon be upon us. Though it wasn't our only strategy, it was one we depended on most.

We'd spent countless hours together over the last few days planning a route to visit as many villages as we could. Finding villages with plenty of fae who'd lived during the Dyvrad reign was the priority when mapping. If no one in the village recognized them, convincing them to side against Elikai and join our rebellion would be impossible.

Of course, the rebel leaders had tried to recruit too many times to count during their centuries of hiding, all to no avail. But they hadn't had the aid of a dragon king and queen then. Their presence alone came as a beacon of hope and promise for a better future.

"Ready to tell your story again?" I asked. "And again, and again, and again."

"Yes," they said together, smiling warmly.

"Then let's do this," I said, getting to my feet. "I'm certain that with your help we can convince every villager we encounter to be on the right side of Dezrothian history."

After all, remaining neutral toward the injustices the current Lores brought down on Dezrothia was no longer an option.

CHAPTER 11
Nixen

Not for the first time, I cursed Eva's grandfather for putting me in a group with Axel.

Before the camp had been ready to move south, Drayke Dyvrad had, quite rightly, pointed out more went into winning a war than battles and bloodshed.

Shortly after, I'd been assigned to what my *distant* relative liked to call 'Operation Raid Route.'

Now, two days after leaving Braxton's camp, I was balls deep in freezing pond water, questioning how Axel had convinced not just me, but the other four members of our team, to strip down and climb in too.

After a very long hike, with very little sleep, he'd slowly worn me down. Then, based solely on the false hope he would stop going on about it, I'd agreed.

Already regretting it.

"You know what, Nixy Nix?" Axel asked as he got straight to work on step one of his camouflage plan. "It literally feels even better than I imagined. Go on. Get your hands in there and start slathering."

I raked my nails into the pond's edge and scooped two fistfuls of the gooey clay-mud mix. Pushing down the sickening feeling that stirred in my stomach at the sight of my fingers covered in mud, I began to smear it into my skin.

"That's it. Don't be shy," Axel encouraged, using two hands to massage it into his recently heeled abs, while Shauna, a lioness elven hybrid, helped with his back.

The female had some serious skill with a bow. Why she hadn't just turned it on Axel when he'd first mentioned this ridiculous idea, I'd never know.

The more time we spent together, the more I questioned how we were even related at all.

Sure, once upon a time, it might have been easier to believe. But as I watched him climb out and announce, "Time to duff up," I found myself shaking my head and considering renouncing the name Sybilline altogether.

Thalia, the witch on our team, pulled herself up to sit on the edge and finished coating her legs. "Need an extra pair of hands, Nixen?" she asked.

Shaking my head, I sighed, "Go on then."

Though I'd never say it out loud, especially to Axel, I had to admit to myself it wasn't entirely terrible—nimble fingers kneading the gloop into the tight muscles along my shoulder blades.

Then I watched Axel and the rest of our group rolling around the forest floor in duff, debris and leaf litter and hung my head. I was wrong. No amount of massages from Thalia would make this okay.

Before we'd gone our separate ways, Alaric had shared everything he knew of the trade routes. While Kane had buried his face in his hands for knowing nothing of the pathways which fed supplies to the castle he'd grown up in.

I hadn't known Kane when he lived there, and was glad of it. I couldn't imagine the male I knew being so… detached. So caught up in his own pity party that he'd been blind to what was happening around him. The male he spoke of on the few occasions he shared stories of his past just wasn't a male I recognized.

With everyone on board with the old king's plan, there'd been no shortage of rebels keen to help. Alaric had broken down the volunteers into small groups of five or six, making sure we had at least one witch per team able to send messages back via raven.

He drew each group a map and sent us on our way. Between us, we could cover all the main roads leading in and out of the city, and it wouldn't be long before Ezerat was feeling the pinch on their resources.

Despite Axel over complicating things with this particular part, our job was simple. Hide along the most well-trodden trade route and wait for fae to come bringing goods. Then intercept and convince them to turn around. Ideally allowing us to keep some of what they carted to take back to our new camp.

The way in which we did that would be determined by them. With words or by force, it didn't matter, so long as the city ended up short on supplies.

The pond Axel had found wasn't far from the path we were to guard, with the road just visible through the trees. According to Alaric, the closest villages were a few hours' walk away from our spot, and so the villagers weren't due to start filtering it down until late morning and into the afternoon. Though it wasn't much after sunrise right now, I was keen to find a good position and get into it.

Thalia and I joined the others, and when she lay down in the underbrush, I took a deep breath, and muttered, "Fuck it," and joined her.

Two rolls from front to back was all it took to be plastered in the stuff. As I got to my feet, I expected it to itch, but somehow it didn't. Part of me wished it did, just so I had a good reason to wash it straight off, without undermining Axel.

Bryon, brother of Ilona and a huge bear shifter warlock hybrid, was patching in some sparse areas on Axel's body when my second cousin suddenly stood straighter. All signs of the laid back, playful, pain-in-my-ass male vanished.

"Did you hear that?" he whispered, his brow furrowed.

On Axel's lead, those with thrakos blood, myself included, shifted. Now wasn't the time to mention it to the male, but as I scanned the area for the threat, I couldn't unsee the obvious floor in Axel's camo plan.

We looked like fucking tree trunks with reptilian wings sprouting from our backs—standing out far more now than they ever usually would.

Moving into position now, while battling the crunch of leaves hanging off our every limb, would be far from ideal. Especially for those wingless folk who couldn't use them to hover and glide closer toward the path.

With a finger pressed against his lips, Axel tucked his wings away and gestured for the rest of us to remain here while he moved with the stealth of a well-trained soldier to get a closer look at the trade route.

Vanishing my wings too, I tried to ignore the rancid earthy smell assaulting my senses and did my best impression of a tree. Watching Axel from the corner of my eye, he mouthed the word *'Horde'*, and I swallowed.

We waited with closed lips as the stomp of heavy boots grew louder and louder. The veins in my neck throbbed as I fought back the desire to attack with the knowledge we couldn't win. Not with six of us and what sounded like an entire army of them.

As they marched by, my eyes went wide. The flashes of figures visible through the thick tree line were changing shape and size. Not by a few inches here and there. No. These weren't horde. Not all of them.

The stench of swamp grew stronger. It wasn't coming from us. It was coming from the behemoth trolls being escorted by the horde, toward Ezerat.

My eyes darted around our small group. The rebels weren't the only ones recruiting. Elikai was too. And if what we were witnessing was as it seemed, he'd soon have an entire village of trolls at his disposal.

We remained frozen in place for longer than necessary after the final clomps echoed away into the distance.

Eventually, Axel broke the silence. "So there's good news and bad news."

My shoulders sunk as I released the breath I'd been holding. "The horde have enrolled trolls," I said, stating the obvious.

Axel pinched his nose. "So it seems. They didn't look like prisoners, and I can't think of any other reason Elikai would want them. Maybe for his weird coronation games?"

I shook my head. "I don't think so. There were too many of them."

"I agree." Thalia said, wrapping her arms around herself.

"We need to get a message out to the others," Bryon said. "Warn them to steer clear of the troll villages with the dragon king and queen."

"On it," Thalia replied, her eyes moving to the sky before chanting the call to summon a raven.

"So, what's the good news?" I asked. "Don't say the fucking camo–"

"The fucking camo worked!"

CHAPTER 12
Elikai

"It's perfect," I breathed, watching the final drop of one hundred witches' cloaking spells. But that wasn't a strong enough word to describe it. It was awe-inspiring. Designed by yours truly, it was a living entity that seemed to breathe with every beat of my heart. Meticulously crafted by hundreds of fae with back-breaking speed, for one very important purpose; the Coronation Games.

A surge of excitement coursed through my veins as I marveled at the genius of the arena's design. An elegant oval amphitheater, enclosed by inescapable walls of hard-ened metal. So strong it would laugh in the face of any who thought to bring it down. Not even dragon fire could hope to melt the towering gates. Tiered benches rose from the pit of nightmares, all the way up to the clouds. I sat in the royal box on my custom throne of red velvet with pillows hugging my back and glutes, cushioning the fierce frame molded of the same hardened steel as the walls trapping us in here. The box was built halfway up, and naturally, as becoming of the king, provided the best, most central view of the trials.

Not a single death would escape my attention from here.

"Your gifts should be approaching Dezrothian waters soon," my uncle said from the far less impressive throne at my side. "They will fit perfectly on those platforms you've got on the wings." He gestured to the large, empty circles halfway up the seating area, one on each side.

I nodded. "Yes, I had them designed as a last-minute addition using the dimensions you gave. They will be the perfect base, wouldn't you agree?"

"It's all perfect," he said. "You must share your blueprints, Elikai. I know just the place in Mount Mortum to build a replica."

I scoffed, making a mental note to burn the blueprints at my earliest opportunity. "Of course. But first, we must welcome my guests." I clapped twice and the soldiers guarding the gates, the only way in or out, separated into two groups to heave them open.

As the hundreds of Ezerat elite presented their invitations and began to fill the seats, I turned my gaze to the wintry sky above, its serene beauty a reminder the fates themselves were watching over me. This was destined to be the grandest celebration of a new king they had ever witnessed.

My restless companion at my other side began to fidget her leg as equally excited guests flooded in. She was a stark contrast to her predecessor—more compliant, more suitable. Unlike the filthy dragon deceiver, my new pet showed promise. Yes, the restless leg syndrome was irritating enough for me to consider a swift amputation, but it spoke of her eagerness to get the show started. It helped that she was beautiful too; a reflection of the refined tastes that governed my desires.

While my uncle bored me with topics such as trade routes and his ideas for Dezrothia's future, I did as I always do, nodded along, feigning interest where I had none. When it came to King Vandenburg, I took a firm stance of keeping your friends close and enemies closer. Of course, I had no intention of implementing any of his suggestions, and even if I did, it would only be because I'd already thought of them.

Though his cruelty was inspiring, I had much grander plans than him. Building an army large enough that I could set my sights on his kingdom being near the top of my list.

He wasn't even aware half my horde was already missing. While I was preparing to be crowned, I'd broken them down into smaller squadrons and sent them to every corner of Dezrothia. Their instructions were simple: grow your numbers tenfold before returning to Ezerat, or come bearing gifts. My brother, his dragon whore, the former general, or a leader in the rebel alliance, would suffice.

As the stadium filled and anticipation built in the air, the crowd's murmurs grew louder. It was almost time to orchestrate the wicked spectacle that had me laying wide awake all night practically vibrating with anticipation. Especially with the news of a very exciting surprise entrant still singing in my ears.

As the final fae took his place, I stood, and the crowd went wild, a deafening roar of hands clapping, feet stomping, and wolves whistling. Raising a finger in the air, I signaled for silence. Eyes penetrated me from all directions. Pure power burned within me, like I held the strings to control fate itself.

"Welcome to the Coronation Games!" I called. "It is wonderful to see you all again, so soon after my coronation. Though the celebration at the Temple of the Fates couldn't have been more perfect, my rise to rule was not without its complications. During my late father's reign, traitors lurked in our midst, some even living under his roof! Commanding the horde! That ended with this crown being placed on my head."

The crowd cheered again.

"You fine fae know as well as I that for Dezrothia to be greater than ever before, not only do we need a fair ruler at the top, but a fierce army led by the strongest general at their head! That is why I have searched far and wide, seeking out the most superior warriors in our realm to take part in this most honorable showdown. A life-changing competition of strength, agility, and cunning. Who's ready to join me in finding the best general to run my horde?"

The standing ovation was expected, but I didn't have the inclination to enjoy it. It was time to welcome the participants.

"Without further ado, stepping into their father's shoes, it brings me great pleasure to introduce my newly appointed Royal Advisors, Graves Eelhorn, and Sloane Alred."

I gestured down to the sand covered pit, where Graves and Sloane stood at its center. As they raised their arms, a warlock dropped the final concealment charm, and twenty cages were revealed in a semi-circle along the far side of the oval fighting pit. I squeezed my pretty pet's leg a little too hard, struggling to contain my excitement. My eyes scanned the crates. Some I already knew about, but most I'd wanted to keep a surprise.

As Graves and Sloane took turns to announce each competitor, the bars would drop, and the fae revealed themself to the crowd. The elite took note of each name, species and region, likely preparing to rate them so they could place early bets on the winner. One by one, they surfaced. Their diverse forms and expressions both repulsed and intrigued me. Some were bursting with excitement; others had a nervous energy. My favorite was the look of terror that left their faces drained of color.

In turn, they paraded around the oval stage once, showcasing a variety of armors and costumes. Very few were empty-handed, most having decided to carry whatever weapons they believed would best serve them in the battles to come. They'd been permitted to bring with them whatever they liked, so long as it fit in their crate. Some had stacks of food, water or medical supplies, others mostly weapons and armor.

As the introductions continued, I observed each participant with a critical eye. Representatives of Kelpie Cove, Cloverae, Rangaran and Pinefall had finished their loop of the oval and taken their places back in front of their crates.

"Jarrah of the Fading Vale. Spider shifter, warlock half-breed," the announcer proclaimed, and the audience gasped, catching my attention. My favorite magical arachnid. His yellow hair was brighter in the daylight, but his eyes were just as beady as I remembered. The crowd wasn't sure how to respond when hearing his status as a half-breed confirmed. A true abomination in the eyes of all.

Time flew by as name after name was called, and before I knew it, we were on the second to last reveal; a troll from Bouldercliff who stirred up quite the reaction from the crowd as she swung her club to wave.

My grin was all teeth as the last participant, and the reason for my sleepless night, was finally upon us. Excitement brought me to my feet. "Thank you, Graves and Sloane, sterling job, but because of the nature of this last beast, I shall take it from here."

They bowed low and walked quickly across the sand to escape the pit and creatures at their backs.

"Our final entrant signed up at the eleventh hour and joins us fresh from the Fading Vale. As she wishes to keep her true name to herself, she will be known as Anon."

The entire audience held their breath. Even Crystal stopped bouncing her knee and froze, completely still in her chair.

"Step out and greet your fans, Anon," I taunted.

Bound by a magic-blocking collar and held in check by five of the strongest members of my horde in case she tried any funny business, she stepped out of her crate. The crowd remained in utter silence as they watched the petite female with hair as deep red as fresh blood.

"Don't be fooled by her appearance," I said. "Though she may look like a malnourished waif, Anon is a half-breed of the most deadly kind." I paused. "Part wolf... Part *thrakos*."

Crystal gasped at my side, obviously too paralyzed with fear to join the rest of the fae as they jumped to their feet and cheered their applause. The only sound that left my pretty pet's mouth was a prayer to the fates, begging them for rain.

Nothing would stop the Coronation Games, especially not a bit of rain.

CHAPTER 13

Alaric

Four days and as many villages later, we had managed to convince exactly zero fae to ally with us. As if morale wasn't low enough, it was made worse by the news that the horde had secured an entire herd of trolls to join their fold. Like they needed any more fucking power on their side.

As we approached village five, Ulana Hill, I cast my mind back, trying to remember the specifics of the wrongs Augustus had done to the elves. Of the poverty the proud fae had been forced to live in under his reign.

Though he hadn't shown hatred and aggression toward the elves like he had others, he'd basically abandoned them, much like the brownies and all the others. Providing no resources when they'd asked, and only remembering they resided in his realm when it was time to collect taxes. As far as allies went, the elves weren't exactly going to make the horde run scared, but after being rejected at every turn we'd made so far, we were desperate for a win. If that came from the elves pledging allegiance to the rebels, I'd take it and fucking smile.

As the steady creak of the turning water mill at the foot of the hill reached our ears, our group tentatively discussed a change of approach, given how badly all previous meetings with village mayors had gone up to this point. I kept my mouth shut, knowing it wasn't a decision for me to make, given my presence here being part of the problem.

Before a decision was made, the village came into view, and those debating fell into silence. Just focusing on getting there and then dealing with whatever reception we received once it was upon us. We were too close now to be able to do much else; they would already know we were here.

The smell of rain and mud was heavy in the air, and my boots squelched with every step as I dug my toes into the hill. Spring would be here soon, but would it bring a warmer life with the warmer weather? It certainly didn't fucking feel like it now.

Despite its name's suggestion, Ulana Hill was actually made up of several rolling, grassy mountains. But the steepest, and the one we climbed now, was the one I was most familiar with. It held the community buildings, such as the leaking temple and quaint town hall. As well as a rundown market which wound through the middle, where the elves would swap wares and food. Coin rarely exchanged hands between the sharp-eared fae, and the little coin they made to pay their taxes likely came from illegal deals they struck with the nearby villages.

Once we reached the dirt track dotted with market stalls, I pointed out a barely standing building to Drayke and Vyara, the town hall, then held back and let them take the lead. With any luck, we'd find the mayor there.

Over the last several days, I'd learned the hard way that my presence was proving to be more of a burden than anyone else here, Kane included. And not for the reasons I'd assumed when setting out on the alliance seeking mission. Given my history with tax runs between villages when running the horde, as well as being featured on every wanted poster nailed to trees and notice boards, I knew being recognized as the former horde general would inspire a fair amount of resistance.

How wrong I was about what the villager's biggest problem with me would be.

Though those things certainly didn't help, the biggest issue was the fact I no longer wore the necklace which concealed my thrakos nature. And let's just say, undoing hundreds of years of brainwashing and fear instilled in the fae of Dezrothia was proving to be the hardest task of all. Even with a much-loved king and queen in tow to distract them, so far we were four for four on alliance rejections, and four for four on their reasoning being that they would not fight with thrakos at their backs.

Or *"breathing down our necks and salivating over our blood,"* as the dryads of Cloverae had so delicately put it.

I'd be a liar to say I hadn't been considering the possibility of my da' and I leaving the group to head to the new rebel camp. See if we could be of more use there than we were currently. But we couldn't forge an alliance based on false truths. It would make us no better than those we sought to remove.

Pretending as if there wouldn't be thrakos in our army, no matter how tempting right now, would be both wrong and stupid. Fates, we were some of the most formidable warriors in the ranks, it's not like we would agree to stay in the Vale and let the others fight when the time came just so elves or gnomes, forest fae or pixies, could join the alliance. Not because they weren't skilled and valuable in their own right, it was just a plain fact that they were no match or substitution for a thrakos on the battlefield.

I recognized Findis, the elven mayor, the moment he stepped outside. He had a lithe form, with sharp pointed ears and high cheekbones, made only more pronounced by the way his mouth always looked to be sucking something sour. Mailia, his wife, was tall, blonde, and at his side a moment later. Though Findis was in charge of the elves by title, Mailia was very much the one who held all the power by whispering in his ear. Making her the one who actually needed to be convinced.

The last time they'd seen me, I'd been with Elikai, who had mocked their run-down village and thrown a fit at how meager their bag of coin was. They shouldn't hold much loyalty to him as their next king. But they also wouldn't have any loyalty or pleasant memories where I was concerned, either.

Unlike the mayor in Cloverae yesterday, both Findis and Mailia had been alive during the dragon's reign. And based on the way their eyes just went wide upon landing on Drayke and Vyara, they knew exactly who the fae were that walked into their village, uninvited.

"Findis..." Mailia gasped. "Do my eyes deceive me?"

I hung back while Drayke and Vyara continued to cross the space between the dirt track high street and where the elves froze, just outside the town hall doors—if you could even call them that. The two rectangular pieces of splintered wood swung limply, opening the place up to the elements with every gust of wind.

"I-I," Findis stuttered. "I don't think so, dear."

"Findis?" Vyara said, then dipped her head in a slight bow to his wife. "Mailia?" They both nodded stiffly. "It's a pleasure to see you. My name is Vyara Dyvrad. This is my husband, the allegedly deceased King of Dezrothia, Drayke Dyvrad."

Their jaws hit the floor, and as they stood dumbfounded, other elves began to appear and fall into place behind them. Some gawking openly, others frowning with obvious confusion.

"H-how?" Mailia managed.

"It is a long story, but if there is perhaps somewhere dry we can sit with you, we will gladly share it," Vyara said, her voice kind and soft.

Mailia and Findis nodded in tandem, then moved to lead the way, just as one of the more confused elves poked his head out from behind them, flaring his nostrils. I held my breath, like that would stop him from being able to sense the naturally intimidating aura a thrakos gave.

It was less the scent than the feeling itself that fae had in our presence, which made them shy away. Or so I'd been told. Though the scent was always the dead giveaway. Without my necklace, it was only a matter of time before the mayor or his wife caught it, too. Just as soon as they remembered how to breathe.

As more elves joined, it became easy to tell who recognized the old king and queen and who were too young to have known them. The former appeared to have seen a spirit from the other side, and the latter's eyes darted around our small group before landing on my da' or I.

"Are they... *thrakos?*" a young male asked Findis quietly, tugging at his worn sleeve.

"No, son," Findis said. "They are *dragons*. Though how they are here... How they are alive–"

"Not them," the young elf interrupted. He thrust a finger out toward my da' first, then moved it to point to me. "*Them*."

Findis frowned, but Mailia sniffed the air, and all the color left her face. "Get the children inside," she muttered out of the corner of her mouth to some of the elders. Turning back to Drayke and Vyara, she said, "What in fates' name are you doing associating with *them?*"

"And what did we ever do during your reign to deserve you bringing those bloodthirsty creatures to our homes? Where our children sleep!" Findis seethed. "You realize what they are? What they *do?*"

Guilt washed over Vyara's face, and her eyebrows knitted as she looked between the gathered elves. It hurt more than I'd expected. Not because of who she'd once been, but because of who she was now. Angel's grandma'.

I rolled my eyes and my da' gave a fang free, half smile. Though without it reaching his eyes, he looked more threatening than ever.

Here we fucking go, again.

WE SET up camp for the night somewhere between Ulana Hill, Swamphollow, and the new rebel camp which Axel had named 'Camp Camille', despite him not having been there yet. Whenever we'd checked in over the last few days via the Battle Bond, that's how he referred to it. I eventually asked and quickly regretted it.

Camille was Nix's source, and though I didn't know for sure, I didn't think there was anything romantic between them. Though, admittedly, I'm not the best at observing that sort of thing. I'd sooner be able to tell someone was about to stab another in the back than confess their love. But if there was anything going on outside of keeping bloodlust at bay, they were good at hiding it, and Nix clearly had no problem being away from her.

Nix had refused her offer to join their group of bandits and Axel thought he was an idiot for it. So in the days since, he'd been trying to get a reaction out of Angel's best friend by telling him things like how much he was looking forward to joining back up with everyone at Camp Camille so he could stick her with his flagpole instead.

We'd caught up earlier today, just as my group were leaving the elves with yet another hard pass to our proposal weighing heavily on our mood. Before I'd finished telling him of the elves' objections, Axel had cut over me and thought through the bond, "Ugh, if you don't cheer up soon Nixy Nix, I'm going to pitch my teepee so damn hard inside Camp Camille, she will be all like, Nix? Nix who? My inn is full–"

I'd cut him short, and he'd gone silent to repeat it to Nix out loud as intended, before slipping back inside my head a few moments later to receive the rest of the day's debrief. Though Axel was having more fun than us, enjoying the freedom of the forest and several successful interceptions along the trade routes, my group was feeling the pressure and nerves of building an army. What if we couldn't find a single village to join us?

The only way we'd win this was if we had the upper hand in numbers and the element of surprise when the time came to seize the castle. The horde was composed of some of the strongest fae, and now had an entire herd of trolls on their side, too. Plus an endless supply of weapons, food and armor at their disposal. Though, perhaps not so endless if all the bandit groups were as successful as Axel and Nix's with their trade route missions.

The battle would be bloody regardless of how many alliances we forged, but aside from the dragons torching the entire city of Ezerat, with the numbers we had now, we'd be slaughtered in seconds.

And then there was the very real, and very worrying, possibility that Elikai could have invented some lethal weapon to take down dragons. It would have been his first priority after learning of what Angel was, and even more important once his horde reported back that there were two more flying around Ezerat with her the night he tried to execute Kane.

My ma' boiled up some hearty rabbit soup over the campfire, while the rest of us pitched the tents. Our limbs were heavy under the weight of our failure to get yet another camp to hear us out.

No matter how much Angel or my ma' had tried to convince the elves that me and Braxton weren't dangerous, that none of the thrakos we associated with were dangerous when they fed frequently, they wouldn't hear it. They'd gone as far as to insinuate they just had Braxton and I 'well trained'.

The fucking elves… A species of fae who'd had every reason to want to align with us had banished us from Ulana Hill because they feared what they'd been taught to despise. Taught to be terrified of, despite never having actually experienced any terror at the hand of a thrakos.

Fuck, it was infuriating.

We gathered around the fire when my ma' announced the food was ready. The Dyvrad's pushed soup around their bowls, and the rest of us forced it down our throats, despite it tasting just fine. It had been decided earlier that if tomorrow's village, Swamphollow, gave us the same reception upon seeing thrakos, that our next move would be to head to the new rebel camp.

Swamphollow was the closest village to it, and though I fucking hated giving up, I had to agree we needed a new tactic. Likely, a new group was needed. The dragon king and queen would remain the main driving force. The overall reaction to them being alive and wanting vengeance had been overwhelmingly positive. But if we were to be successful getting allies before the war came to us, it was looking more likely that Braxton and I would no longer join the village visits.

If I had to stay at Camp Camille without Kane and Angel, I'd despise every moment. But everyone would have to make sacrifices at some point over the coming trials, and we were no exception.

"Alaric?" Kane said, pulling me back to the here and now. "Me and Eva are going to collect some firewood," he nodded toward the deeper forest and… winked. "You coming?"

Standing to join my mate, I dropped my voice low and asked, "Is that a question or statement?"

"Whatever you want it to be," he replied and walked away, his hand at the small of Angel's back as he led her away. She glanced over her shoulder, lust smoldering in her eyes as she crooked her finger to follow.

I didn't need to be told twice. My feet moved swiftly to catch up with them.

We walked a few hundred meters away from camp, ensuring we were totally alone. Angel pulled Kane into her as he crowded her into a nearby tree. "I seem to recall you wishing you were a tree once," he murmured to her as he pulled from her lips. I grinned at the memory. Fuck, it had been too long.

"I did, didn't I?" she agreed, her arms resting along his shoulders. I swiftly moved in behind Kane. The feeling of his warmth bleeding through his shirt to me.

"Somethin' like this, wasn't it?" I hummed as I took in their mingled scents. She swallowed hard, nodding slightly.

"I think it was actually like this," Kane said, as he reached back to grasp my hair and pulled me in for a kiss. Groaning, I lost myself to it. Fuck, this male could kiss me like that any time.

"Yeah..." I broke away to see her watching us with rapt attention. "Definitely like that," she agreed.

Kane turned his attention back to Angel, pulling her closer as he devoured her like he had me just moments before. The way she whimpered into him made my cock ache for them both. I would be forever fucked for them. They held my heart. There was no fucking question about it.

My hands landed on the rough bark of the tree, pressing my hard cock into Kane. His resounding groan sent a throb through my cock as it begged for attention. Angel's eyes popped open, her hand reaching to me, beckoning me closer. Kane moved his lips to her throat, and I took advantage, swallowing whatever words she was about to say.

Our clothes were soon discarded, the need for us to have our skin pressed against each other too much to resist. Kane had Angel pressed against the tree, her luscious legs wrapped around him. While I was enjoying the flavor of Kane's skin. The desire for that ache in my gums, the one that drove me to slide my fangs into his flesh, was near desperate.

Sliding my hand up Angel's thigh, I dipped my hand around to her soaked cunt. I groaned at the sensation of her clenching against my fingers as two dipped inside. The breathy moan that left her had my head spinning, needing to fuck them. Rocking against Kane's ass, desiring friction, I picked up the pace of my fingers.

Angel's thighs flexed as she tried to take her own pleasure for herself, and I added a third finger. Kane's cock rocked against her clit, sending her closer to the orgasm she was chasing. But before she could reach her precipice, I withdrew my fingers. I had plans of my own.

Her whimper at the loss tugged at me, but as Kane shifted before me, I smirked. The groan that echoed as her head hit the tree told me all I needed to know. His slow thrusts were nothing more than to tease.

My wet fingers found his hole, using her natural lubrication to make it easier for me to fuck him. Working my way, one finger at a time. As I worked him, he worked Angel into a frenzy. Hearing her incoherent as she was fucked made my beast preen.

Sliding my cock forward, I thrust into Kane. His groan as he pushed back onto me while he withdrew from Angel I could listen to for eternity. It was sinfully delicious. She opened her eyes to see me looming over him, her ankle sliding down my side as she beckoned me closer.

Taking her mouth in a ferocious kiss, my claws sank into the wood. *Fuck*. Her whimpering into my mouth as Kane groaned was hypnotic. All I could focus on was them, the feeling of Kane clenching as he moved on my cock pressing back as I thrust into him, Angel's hips flexing as she took more pleasure.

Pulling from her lips, I lifted her leg so it rested on Kane's shoulder. His moan told me how much he appreciated the change. He ground his hips into our female, drawing hushed whimpers from her.

Snapping my hips forward, I drove him into her. His head dropped onto her collarbone as she gasped. Seeing them so lost in the pleasure made me throb with the need to possess them completely.

I angled my hips up to hit that spot that would send Kane into a frenzy. He started cursing, his hips moving frantically as he fucked Angel, his hand working her clit. I moved to keep pace with him, eager to make him come. Unable to resist, I let my teeth sink into his throat, enjoying the sound he made at the prick of pain. A splash of his blood landed on my tongue and I licked up his throat and he jerked, coming hard.

Gripping his hips, I watched as Angel eyed the bite mark on his neck, her own teeth biting her lip so hard I wondered if she would break the skin. My teeth grazed Kane's shoulder, the way his ass clenched on my cock made my balls tighten. I never wanted to leave this bliss. They felt too good to ever be tired of.

Angel moaned, long and low as Kane's hips stilled, but his hand continued to move. His face was buried in her throat as he stilled. Panting, I felt the lightning shoot down my spine as I came, Kane gasping as he felt the splash of my cum.

"Fuck," Angel said, her shoulders rising and falling with each heavy breath.

"Again, princess?" Kane said, a sinful smirk tugging at his lips while his eyes traveled up and down her naked form. Angel playfully shoved at him, though she didn't say no.

Pulling back, I let him help her down. Her legs shook as he settled her on to her feet.

Once steady, her hands dug into my hair, and she pulled me in for a deep kiss.

Her teeth captured my lower lip. "Bite me too," she murmured. "Please."

How could I say no when she begged so beautifully? Nuzzling her jaw and kissing my way to her throat, I reveled in her moans, which turned to a gasp as I took a bite. It wasn't enough to break the flesh, but I was enjoying teasing her so much more.

I felt her open her mouth against my ear, no doubt to tell me that wasn't what she meant. Before she could let the words fly, my teeth slid into her flesh the way she desired, yet I still didn't take a drop. Seeing them both with my mark on their necks filled me with pride. Everyone would know they belonged to me, mate or not.

"We should really gather that wood now," Kane laughed as he threw his tunic back on.

"Before they send a search party for us," Angel laughed in agreement as she searched for her second boot.

"Yeh ken they wouldnae be looking for us just yet," I said, pulling my pants back on.

Angel just raised an eyebrow at me, "Still, let's not give them reason to come looking, yeah?"

CHAPTER 14

Evangelia

Anxiety began to stir in my chest the moment I opened my eyes and gradually grew into utter dread over breakfast in the new rebel camp. I was all too aware that we had to update the camp's members about our failures, but the thought of sitting through a meeting in the war tent, reliving the rejections of the past week… I shook my head. I just couldn't face it today.

The only good thing to come out of the last seven days was a stolen moment with my mates in the forest. Everything else, it had just been setback after setback. And we had no magic answer on how to turn the tables in our favor to overcome the villager's objections and deeply ingrained fears.

"Everythin' alright, Angel?" Alaric asked, sensing my mood.

I nodded as I dragged my tired ass across the clearing. Neither of my mates seemed to believe me if the doubtful looks on their faces told me anything.

"Why don't you skip this one?" Kane suggested. "You already know what happened. You lived and breathed every depressing minute of it, and you don't need to be there if you don't want to be."

Was it really that simple? Just don't go. What if everyone decided they too wanted to put war talk on pause for a day? No. It wasn't right. This wasn't something you could just say 'not today' about.

"It's okay," I lied, trying to hide the defeat in my voice. "I want to be there."

"Angel," Alaric said, stopping in front of me and reaching out to hold me in place by the tops of my arms. "Yeh dinnae need to lie to us."

"Seriously, no one is going to judge you for skipping one meeting, if that's what you are worried about," Kane said.

Was that what I was truly worried about? Maybe. Fates, I couldn't think straight today. "You really don't think anyone would mind?" I asked, pleading with my eyes that they would say yes.

Alaric and Kane shook their heads. "Nah. Dinnae worry about that. And anythin' yeh need to ken, we can catch yeh up on after."

The sigh that left me was confirmation enough for my males that I needed to take a minute for myself. Some time to shake off this mood and find some glimmer of hope that all was not lost in our search for allies.

"Okay," I relented. "Thank you." My anxiety eased, and the relief I felt was instant. Ignoring the voice in the back of my mind still telling me I was hiding from my problems, I stretched up onto my tiptoes and kissed them both in turn. After a quick goodbye, I turned, heading back for the tent.

I hadn't had a chance to explore the new camp yet, having only arrived late yesterday. But now, in the foggy daylight, it quickly became the most beautiful part of the Vale I'd ever seen.

The place that had been chosen for the new camp was huge, made up of several clearings circled by trees so high they seemed to touch the sky. It was breathtaking, with scatterings of bushes sprouting up out of the damp grass—each flowering with violet roses. They'd bloomed early, and I breathed deeply, letting their sweet scent relax me. The toe of my boot scuffed a fallen stem, and I bent to pick up the beautiful purple flower, twirling the stem between two fingers, careful to avoid the sharp thorns.

As I continued toward the tent, my eyes took in the layout and setup of the new camp. There was so much more room for any fae that might be joining us, though that felt more like a fool's hope now. I paused just in front of the fabric opening as a glitter of light caught my eye. A pool of water shimmered from just beyond the trees protecting our tent from the elements, catching my gaze and holding it. I skirted the tent to take a closer look.

Fates, it wasn't a pool or pond. It was a vast lake, glistening and silent and still. Peaceful.

It hadn't been visible in the darkness that covered the camp when we arrived last night, and I'd been so exhausted when we'd left the tent this morning that I'd missed it. Now, it drew me to it like a moth to a lantern's flame. It wasn't far from the main camp, only a few meters on the other side of the tree line, yet it promised the quiet headspace I was craving. *You can just make up for the much-needed break by gathering some wood on your way back,* I told myself.

I was at the edge of the lake before I'd even finished convincing myself I shouldn't feel guilty for taking five minutes to rest. When was the last time I just stopped? And a moment later, my pants were rolled up, my boots were off and I was perched on the edge, soaking my aching feet in the bliss of its cold depths. I pulled a petal from the rose and tried to relax, dropping it into the water and watched, waiting for it to embark on its journey over the lake. Wondering how far away it would float until it disappeared from sight.

Only the water was so still, it just lay there, floating on the surface. Going nowhere fast.

Like the rebels, a voice whispered in my head.

I let out a sigh. As lovely as this new camp was, we were still hiding. We were still waiting to make our stand against Elikai and his supporters. We weren't going backwards, but we certainly weren't going forwards either. Just staying in the same place. The same life of just about getting by and surviving.

I pulled another petal free, and it did the same. Again and again, petals spread out on the water as they pushed each other out of the way as I tore them from the stem. Then there was one petal left, small and lonely. It had been hidden until I had pulled it apart. Would that be the rebel alliance? Slowly dwindling until there were none of us left. Or just one fae with a dream and hope that there was still a chance.

The only way out of this life was to take control of the realm and rewrite the Lores. And the only way to do that was to stop Elikai. We all knew it, despite wishing it wouldn't come to that. I wondered if Kane hated his brother as deeply as Alaric and I did. He was still Elikai's brother by blood. His *twin*. Did that matter anymore?

How could we hope to change anything with the current size of our army? No matter how brave, strong, or formidable, we simply didn't have the numbers.

The familiar sound of feet crunching over the forest floor drew my attention, and I tossed what remained of the rose into the lake. It sank slowly into the water, resting on the muddy bottom.

"Evangelia?" my grandmother's soft voice called. I pushed to my feet. "What are you doing here alone, Little Flame?" she asked, moving to stand beside me.

I shrugged, not wanting to say anything that might make her feel any worse about how things had gone down during the village visits this past week. It was all I could think about. The full house of failures had been hard on everyone. Not just our small group, but the entire rebel camp who had been waiting, filled with bubbling hope and anticipation for our return, with plentiful allies in tow.

Braxton and Alaric had managed, just barely, to remain calm as they listened to truly awful things being said about their race—offensive at best, damn right cruel at worst. Kane, Rose and I hadn't found it so easy to control our emotions though, and at times, we'd argued with the villagers against their prejudiced beliefs on our mates' behalf.

As my grandparents had been the ones to do most of the speaking, acting as the rebels' spokesfae to convince the villagers to join forces, they'd taken the failures particularly hard.

They'd opened up more than any king or queen would normally, yet it had been thrown back in their faces every time. Not only had their character and motivations been questioned, but their entire story was met with skepticism. Perhaps the bone shaking chill that came with hearing about their lives in Augustus's captivity was too tragic for most to fathom. The fae of the Fading Vale found themselves unable to sympathize with a tale that was impossible to believe.

"Little flame?" she asked, her concern thick in her tone. I didn't hate the pet name. Logically, I knew they were my grandparents and in my mind, I referred to them as such. But in my heart… it wasn't quite there yet. If I'd known them since childhood, it would be easier, Kane had pointed out, and suggested I just call them by their first names.

Aware of how rude I was for keeping my back to not just a royal but also my grandmother, I turned my body to face her, but kept my eyes down. Hovering over a spot of dirt on her boots. Scared that if I met her eyes, she'd mistake the disappointment shining back in mine for being directed in any way toward her or Drayke.

"I just needed some space to think," I said.

"Mind if I join you?" she asked, and I nodded, then sat back down, dangling my toes in the frigid water and patting the ground next to me.

"Of course," I said. "What are *you* doing alone? Where's Drayke?"

"He's with the other males in the war tent," she said. "I'd been wanting to catch you alone, so I left him to it and came looking."

"Are they any further ahead with coming up with another way of getting the villages on our side?"

She shook her head sadly.

"I wish there was something more I could do, something I could say that might make the villagers see that the thrakos aren't the dangerous monsters they were brainwashed into believing they are," I said. "But it's like nothing will be good enough, nothing will ever get through to them."

"What makes you so sure?" Vyara asked.

I raised a brow. "Because I said everything I could think of to convince them while we were there. If you have any ideas, I'd love to hear them. Surely you'd have used them while you were there, though?"

"No, what I meant was, what makes you so sure they aren't dangerous?" she asked.

My brows dropped into a deep frown. "Because I know them," I said, a little too defensively, but something about the way she'd asked, or perhaps just that she would question such a thing at all, had my back up. "By now, so should you, surely?"

The sides of her mouth dipped as she lifted her shoulders, not committing to an answer.

"How many have tried to attack you?" I questioned, a frown pinching my brow. "How many have gone after your blood?"

"It might not be their fault, but they *do* suffer with bloodlust. They are the creation of an evil male–"

"–and so are lots of fae," I cut over her.

"Like Nekane?" she muttered.

My nostrils flared, and I skimmed a hand over the ground beside me, feeling for anything to distract my hands from clenching into fists.

I grabbed a pebble and began fiddling it around my fingers, my eyes glued to the tiny stone as I snapped, "Whatever you are skirting around saying, Vyara, just say it."

She took a deep breath. "The thrakos are abominations, Evangelia. I'm sorry, but they should never have been created. There is no place for them on Dezrothian soil."

My mouth hung loose as I tried not to lose my temper too viciously. Every time I tried to form words to respond, I'd stop myself just before spitting them at her.

Eventually, taking a deep calming breath, I settled on, "My best friend in the entire realm, one who has been with me since I was born, is part thrakos. Not to mention my *mate* is as well."

She placed a gentle hand on my knee, and I flinched away from it. "Which is exactly why you don't see it. You are blinded by love."

"I see perfectly," I spat, throwing the pebble into the water, watching as it splashed and created ripples. Pushing to my feet once more, her hand dropped from where it rested. "Just as I can see you are no better than those villagers when it comes to your prejudiced views. Fates, I only wish you could have told me a week ago that's how you truly felt. It might have saved us all a lot of walking and sleepless nights."

"Please, calm down, Little Flame. I assure you, I have very good reason to dislike them," she said, joining me to stand.

"What possible reason could be enough to justify such disdain for an entire race?"

Her lips pressed together, a war dancing in her eyes like she debated the words to say. "You asked if a thrakos has ever attacked me or gone after my blood..." she said, trailing off.

"What? A thrakos here, has?" I said, shaking my head. Not possible. "If that's true, show me who it was and I can assure you, we will deal with them."

"Not here," she said. "The thrakos here have been... civilized."

I sighed, "I need a moment... I need to think."

My brain was reliving every interaction my grandparents had with any fae with thrakos blood, and they didn't appear to treat them any differently than everyone else. Had they been working hard to hide it? Had Braxton been right that first day they had entered our old camp of rebels and accused them of just wanting their throne back?

Would they lie to their only living relative to get it?

I turned to pace, possibly even leave, as my mind raced, but Vyara's hand landed on my arm, stopping me. "Please, don't go."

"If I don't, I will say something that I regret."

"Please, Evangelia. Just let me finish. I didn't mean to offend or upset you."

"Really?" I snapped, incredulous. "Because it feels like you are going out of your way to do just that. To throw the hospitality of every damned fae in this camp back in their face."

"I just needed to know you were certain about the thrakos. That you didn't share any of my views. I realize now you are as loyal to them as any fae. And at least certain enough about them being good fae to turn on your own blood to defend them, which is enough for me."

"Again, whatever it is that you are trying to say, just say it," I said through gritted teeth, patience wearing thin.

"What if I told you there was another way?" she quickly asked, her eyes glassy with unshed tears.

"It's out of the question," Drayke's deep voice sounded from nearby. *How long has he been here? How long has he been listening in?*

"Drayke, we have to tell her..." Vyara said, her eyes pleading.

"Tell me what?" I asked, my eyes darting between the other two dragons. "What's out of the question?"

He shook his head once. Sharp and sure. "It's. Out. Of. The. Question," he gritted, defiantly.

"Tell me anyway," I shot back. "I can decide for myself if it's out of the question."

"The villagers fear the thrakos because of the bloodlust," Vyara said, and Drayke hung his head.

"I know," I said. "But we have plenty of fae in the alliance that are willing to make sure it's always sated."

Drayke arched a brow. "Evangelia, you can't surely think that's a good enough argument to win over the fae who have been taught to fear them for hundreds of years?"

"I–" I paused, unsure of what I planned to say to that. Did I expect them to take our word for it?

"What if one day no one wants to feed them anymore? What then? Blood sharing is not something that would have been fathomable when I was king. What's to say that times don't change and fae are no longer willing to be blood bags for them?"

"It's not like that..." Wow, my argument was feeble, but I didn't want to admit he had a point. That would be like admitting defeat, and we didn't have any other options after this one.

Except...

My eyes met with Vyara's. "What did you mean when you said you needed to know I was certain the thrakos were good fae? You said something about another way..."

Drayke and Vyara shared a glance, and then she nodded slowly. "There is."

"But that doesn't mean it's an option," Drayke growled.

Vyara shrugged, her attention on her mate. "I guess that's her choice. We made our choice to keep this to ourselves and try all other options."

He scoffed. "Look how far that got us."

"Exactly," Vyara said. "We have wasted a week already. It's time to tell her the truth, and then she can do with the information as she sees fit."

Drayke closed his eyes and shook his head. "It's not safe for her."

"She has not one, but *two,* formidable warrior mates to look out for her," Vyara argued.

"I can decide for *myself*. Please, tell me." I said, anticipation building in my chest of having a way to reassure the villagers the thrakos were no threat to them.

Drayke glanced around, making sure we were alone, then gestured to the bank of the lake. I frowned but followed their lead, taking a seat and looking out across the still water.

And then listened intently as they finally came clean, telling me *everything*.

CHAPTER 15

Nekane

"There's a way to convince the villagers to join our side," Eva said as we approached, her voice barely a whisper. She didn't face us, her eyes remaining focused on some purple petals gently bobbing in the water in front of her.

I shared a look with Alaric, but his expression gave nothing away. "What? How?" I asked, moving to her side and crouching down.

Her shoulders slumped, and I glanced across the surface of the lake. Fates, she'd really done a number on the poor rose—shredding its petals from the stem and scattering them on the water.

"You're not going to like it," she whispered, still not looking at us, her hands wringing together.

"How no'?" Alaric asked before I could. I glanced at him and his brow was furrowed.

How bad could it be? "We've been discussing our options in the war tent all morning. Long story short, we are out of them," I admitted, ready to hear whatever plan she had with an open mind. "Whatever you think we can do, trust me, we're all ears."

"Aye. We were jus' comin' to fill yeh in," Alaric said. "I winnae lie to yeh, Angel. We are pretty fuckin' desperate. If yer grandparents cannae convince the next villages–"

"We are fucked," I finished.

"I was sitting here all out of options too, but then Vyara and Drayke came by," she said. "When they left, I began playing it all around in my head, trying to work out how to word it to you. But then that got me thinking, why and how you hadn't worked it out yourself?" She finally pulled her eyes from the water and they narrowed on Alaric. Only Alaric.

"Just tell us," I said, confused why she was looking at him like he was guilty of murdering an entire village of ancient fae and children. "As long as it doesn't involve you sacrificing yourself in some weird ritual, I'm sure we can get on board."

She took a deep breath and turned her attention back to the lake. "My grandparents saw a lot of Augustus's experiments with creating the thrakos. His failures, but also his successes."

She paused, and Alaric and I waited like statues, barely moving to breathe as we waited for her revelation, whatever it was.

"He had perfected the thrakos creation, or so he thought, with the help of a warlock. But it wasn't long before the bloodlust reared its head. Rather than see it as another failed attempt, Augustus decided it could be his way to control them. But in order to do that, he needed a way to fix it. So if one of them came after him, he had a bargaining chip to play. Something he could use to ensure they did his bidding without question."

"The cure," I gasped, suddenly remembering the night my father had attacked and then paralyzed me with the poisoned ring. "He told me once he knew how to fix the bloodlust, but he was dead before I ever found out. Tell me they know what it is, and the cure didn't die with the bastard?"

She nodded slowly. "My grandparents said it was a fluke how he found it, but he found it no less."

"Then why didn't they tell us before? We have wasted an entire week. Elikai could be king by now for all we know," I said, hoping she had the answers.

Ignoring my question, she went on. "One of the thrakos he was holding escaped his cage one night and attacked my grandmother. She thought she was finally going to die, and after a decade of captivity and watching the sick acts Augustus committed against the fae he captured to experiment on and the fae he created, she welcomed death."

"But?" I hedged.

"But she didn't die. The thrakos drank from her and was sated. He stopped drinking before draining her completely."

"Aye, that's how it tends to go," Alaric said, like there was nothing new happening here. Almost like he was bored with the story. "We feed, and the bloodlust is sated for a while."

"No." She lifted her eyes to meet Alaric's and shook her head. "His bloodlust was sated… Forever."

"Not possible," I breathed, but Alaric held up a hand to stop me, then gestured for Eva to continue.

"He tried the blood of every species in Dezrothia, as well as another dragon he'd been holding. Only two fae in the realm had the blood that could cure the bloodlust forever."

"Drayke and Vyara's?" I asked.

She nodded. "More specifically, he determined it was the blood of a *mated* dragon."

"So they are going to feed the thrakos in the camp their blood? Cure them so we can tell the villages they no longer crave blood?" I said, thinking aloud.

Her eyes dropped to the ground near my feet, and she shook her head. It was the smallest movement, but no less clear. They didn't intend to do that at all.

Alaric had been worryingly quiet while Eva spoke, and she was hesitant when she looked up at him. "Well, Alaric, what do you think?" she asked, finally finished with recounting what the old dragon king and queen had told her. She seemed to be wanting a specific answer from him, but I was still confused.

"That Kane's right, it's no' possible," he said, then without another word, he stalked away, leaving us watching as he left.

"Has he gone to convince them to share their blood?" I asked, watching Alaric's back as he strode away.

"I don't think so," she said, sounding deflated. "He's been lying to us."

"Lying to us? He had no way of knowing–"

"*I'm* a mated dragon, Kane," she reminded me. "He has drunk from me. Several times. I think he's been feeling the effects of the cure and not told us."

"Why would he do that? Alaric?" I whirled around and called after him, but he ignored me and kept walking, eventually disappearing from view. "Why would he..." Then it hit me. "Because–"

She nodded. "It doesn't matter that my grandparents are too proud or scared or whatever bullshit personal reason they have to not offer their blood to the thrakos. I will do it. I will give my blood to every thrakos and thrakos hybrid until I have none left to give, if that's what it takes."

No, you won't, I thought, but out loud said, "And Alaric knows that." I cursed. "He almost killed Nix for feeding from you."

She nodded. "I know. But Alaric has also suffered more than most thrakos with the bloodlust. Surely, he can get past his alpha-overprotective stuff and look at the bigger picture?"

It was true, not having a source in Ezerat, he'd barely gotten by living off animals. He knew better than Eva or I what it was like to live with the constant thirst for blood. Then there were the blackouts when he'd given over to it. And the guilt he still suffered as a result.

"True," I conceded. "But you also know how he gets when it comes to our blood. It's not just him being greedy and wanting us to himself. It makes him murderous. Fuck, I can't stand the idea of it myself. But even if he managed to put his feelings and instincts to one side, you do realize this would make you one of three cures in the realm. You will be a target the moment others find out."

"Kane, if there is even the slightest chance of gaining the trust of villagers so they will ally with us, and I have a way to help bring it about... You know it doesn't matter how much of a target I am, or how much Alaric doesn't want me to, I'm going to do it, anyway. I have to."

I sighed, then pulled her in for a hug, resting my chin on her hair. "I know, princess," I said. "And it's not like they'd have to drink from the vein. But fuck, it doesn't mean I like it."

"I know," she sighed into my chest. "I understand that."

We remained there in silence as my mind began to spin. "How do we even know if it's actually going to work? Alaric has still been using us as his source. He'd have said something if your blood had cured his bloodlust. Maybe it's only your grandparents who will be able to do it and we need to focus on convincing them?"

"Maybe," she said, but it wasn't very convincing. I thought over the times since Alaric first tasted Eva's blood. He'd bitten her several times, but– "When Alaric has bitten you recently, has he actually taken blood?" she asked.

I cast my mind back to the times he'd bitten me. It wasn't even long ago when we took that moment in the forest. He definitely bit me. How could I forget how fucking good it felt? But I couldn't remember if he pulled from the vein. Eva moved out of my embrace, and I let my arms fall. Her brow knit tightly together as she cast her mind back, too.

"I couldn't be sure," I eventually said. "Say he hasn't been drinking, why cover it up by biting? Why wouldn't he just tell us that something was going on with him? That he no longer needed it."

She shrugged. "He didn't want to worry us?"

"I wouldn't be surprised," I said. "That sounds like something he'd do. He really fucking likes seeing his mark on us. Or maybe it's just a habit? Hundreds of years of doing something would be a hard one to break, even without bloodlust driving him, the habit would be too deeply ingrained–"

"–Nix!" Eva said, cutting over me.

I glanced around to the edge of camp, expecting to see him and Axel arriving. Perhaps Axel could talk him around, he was a thrakos after all. But neither Nix nor Axel had appeared. "He's not here."

"No, I know. But Nix has drank from me."

"Yes, but that was a while ago. Didn't you say it has to be a mated dragon's blood?" I asked.

"Yes. But when did the true mate bond actually click into place? Not much is known about them. What if it has been there since we met?"

"I did feel drawn to you from the first time I laid eyes on you in Elikai's chambers," I admitted. "And Alaric too, ever since he returned from that hunt."

"I didn't even particularly like the smell of cinnamon or apples before I met you. But when you walked in on me in my towel," she blushed, "even though I stupidly mistook you for *him*, the scent was impossible to ignore."

"That's how I smell to you?"

"Yes, and Alaric…"

"Leather and cedarwood," I said.

"Yes," she breathed.

I'd told her once before how she smelt to me, but we'd never really talked about the true mate bond or the signs we missed before Edelin confirmed it. The draw toward your true mate's scent was one of the few known things, yet we'd missed it. It wouldn't have been impossible to have missed Alaric's change in feeding habits if we missed something so large.

"But as I said, Nix isn't here. It's not like we can ask him to confirm," I said.

"Maybe not him, but his source is," she said. "Remember, she offered to go with them to the trade route and he refused?"

"Fuck, of course. It was Camille, wasn't it? His source?"

"Yes," Eva confirmed. "I could go talk to her?"

"Princess, it's not safe for you to just tell her. There's nothing to say she would keep it to herself. The thrakos here may be our friends, but imagine being tortured by something you hated your entire life to suddenly find there's a cure. You would want to know about it, right?"

"Yeah, I know," she said. "I will just have to try to make it sound natural. Ask if she's missing him or something and go from there? Try to work out when the last time he fed was. If he hasn't fed for a while and then refused for her to join him, that means something, right?"

"I don't like this," I admitted. "But it's so much bigger than the three of us." I sighed. "You do that, and I will try to talk to Alaric. Try to make him see."

"I think he already knows," she said.

I nodded. *That's why he left.*

CHAPTER 16

Evangelia

Camille was helping Marnie with preparations for tonight's dinner when I found her.

"Hi," I said, waving awkwardly. It suddenly dawned on me how little chance I'd had to get to know the other rebels. Especially the females close to my age. My questions for her likely wouldn't be any more suspicious than me just randomly striking up a conversation in the first place.

The females shared a look of confusion at my intrusion, but Marnie said, "Hey Evangelia. Or do we call you *Princess* Evangelia?"

I snorted a laugh. "Please don't. Evangelia is fine. Or Eve," I added as I thought about my conversation with Thalia while at the castle. Fates, that felt like a lifetime ago. I'd barely had a chance to speak to her since she and Westly had joined the alliance. What with the ambush and then being separated when I'd been visiting the villages and she'd left with Nix and Axel.

There will be plenty of time for catching up once the war is won.

My priority right now was figuring out whether what my grandparents told me was true or not. Was it any mated dragon's blood? Or was it specifically *their* mated dragon's blood?

Kane had left to find Alaric, a promise between us he would talk to him and help him see. Despite how much I loved the male, he was as stubborn as they came. And the most protective fae I'd ever met when it came to his mates and those he considered family.

My chances were probably higher getting some answers from a virtual stranger than Kane asking our mate.

He'd come around with time, I was sure of that. But how much time did we have? Not long enough for alpha-male tantrums. Not when the stakes were so high.

"Can I help?" I asked, looking at the giant cooking pots, wonky vegetables and wood carved utensils.

"Sure," Camille said. "You peel, I'll chop," she said, pushing the carrots down the bench toward me.

"Do you have a blade that hasn't been covered in blood?" I asked, my cheeks heating as I gestured to the new twin daggers that sat at my waist.

"Here," she said, handing me a makeshift peeler.

We all got to work and Marnie began deboning a fish, which Camille said some of their friends had caught on the lake the day before. But it was hard to watch. The poor fish... It was less of a deboning and more a butchering. But she was trying, so who was I to judge?

"So," I started, weirdly nervous and completely out of practice at this sort of thing. Even before meeting my mates, the only fae my age I'd hung out with was Nix. Our time together usually consisted of training to better defend ourselves and camp, or watching others do the same.

"You know Axel, right?" Marnie said, like she'd burst if she didn't ask.

"Yes, though he's closer to my mate."

"Which one?" Camille asked with a wink and my cheeks flushed again. I wasn't embarrassed. I was the luckiest female in the realm to be blessed by the fates with my two males. It just wasn't something I was used to talking about. Especially not like this.

"Alaric," I said. "The bigger one," I added stupidly.

"Oh, we know who Alaric is," Marnie said. "Nekane too. They seem like good males."

"The best." *Apart from right now; when one of them is being a stubborn ass, standing in the way of knowing for sure if I have the potential salvation of all thrakos running through my veins,* I finished in my head.

"So, Axel..." Marnie said. "Do you know when he will be back?"

I shook my head, "Sorry, I don't. He's been checking in with Alaric and says they have managed to stop a lot of supplies and cargo from reaching Ezerat, though."

Marnie huffed. "That's good," she said, though her face told a very different story. So *someone* had a pretty big thing for Alaric's little brother then, good to know.

"I'm guessing you met him at the old camp?" I asked.

She nodded. "Met him? We did a lot more than *meet*," she nudged Camille, "if you know what I mean."

Oh, I knew *exactly* what she meant.

The same way I knew Axel was not the kind of male looking to settle down any time soon. Unless he found a mate, of course. He was a free spirit who'd spent his life in chains. He would break plenty of hearts before settling for one.

"Nice," I said, not knowing how else to answer. Now just to steer the conversation to Nix...

Keeping my eyes down on the carrot in my hand, I cleared my throat.

"He saved me, you know," Marnie said. "The night of the ambush. He's so brave."

"The bravest," Camille added. *Poor Nix*. Apparently, both these females were pretty hot for his big cousin.

But it was a perfect way to steer the conversation. "I thought you and Nixen Sybilline had a thing?" I hedged as casually as I could muster.

"I *was* his source," Camille said.

"*Was*. As in, not anymore?" I asked.

She shrugged. "I think he's met someone else," she said, her eyes down and lips pouting.

"He has? I haven't seen him with anyone. Who is it?" I asked.

She shrugged again. "I don't know. Marnie and I have been trying to work it out. All I know is that we had a good time while it lasted, but…"

"But what?" I asked, a little too eagerly. "He broke things off?"

"Not really. I don't know," Camille sighed. "Things just fizzled out. He didn't break up with me, but I offered to go with his team, you know, being his source and everything. And he said he didn't need one."

"As in, he didn't need another one? Like he already had one?" I asked, seeing hurt flash across her face and realizing too late I was being too direct for 'girl talk'. But this was important. "Do you think it's one of the other fae in their group?"

I tried to picture the group and work out if any were Nix's type.

"I don't know," Camille said sadly. "I guess? But things had started to cool off between us before he'd even met Shauna. And the witch, what's her name?"

"Thalia?"

"Yes, that's it. Well, she's been around even less time than Shauna, so…"

So… he hadn't fed from Camille for some time, then? And it didn't sound likely that he was getting his thirst quenched elsewhere either.

"I'm so sorry," I said. "I've known him all my life and I would never have said he was *that* guy. He has been through a lot lately. Maybe he's just not in a good place for a relationship right now?"

Fates, I felt so lame. Were these words even coming out of my mouth? My friendship with Thalia had been much easier than this. And she'd been my handmaid in a castle I was being held at against my will.

I peeled the rest of the carrots as quickly as I could while Camille and Marnie continued to gossip and talk about all things sex. It was enlightening to hear them discussing what it was like being with the other thrakos. Heat filled my cheeks as they discussed who their favorites were, smirking when they noticed my reaction.

That triggered them to ask me about my love life. Clearly, they wanted to know how our relationship worked. I tried to give them vague answers, but it didn't satisfy their curiosity.

I just had to finish peeling the carrots, then excuse myself and find Kane. Before I spilled too much information and it became camp gossip.

HALF AN HOUR and a million questions later, I finally managed to get away from the two females. Our task of preparing the food for dinner had been abandoned as they turned their attention to me. They had been a little *too* interested in my love life. Was this how female relationships worked? They seemed to expect me to just tell them every sordid detail.

I placated them with small details here and there, but some of the questions they asked made me blush just thinking about them. Why they needed to know what we did and how we did it, I didn't think I would ever understand.

As I'd excused myself, they said they could use an extra pair of hands making breakfast tomorrow and said we could continue our conversation then. I had smiled at them tightly, neither accepting nor declining, but as I walked away, I realized I hadn't hated their company.

Right now, I had to confront Alaric. And let my mates know that Nix hadn't fed from Camille in quite some time. So when I reached the tent and pulled the flap back, I smiled at the sight before me. Kane stretched out in our tent, his hands cushioning his head as he relaxed. His pants slung low on his hips, his shirt already discarded.

I bit my lip while I appreciated the view. He really was a gorgeous male—dark hair, bronze skin and hard muscles that I all of a sudden wanted to trace my tongue over.

"Alaric will hopefully join us soon," he said. "Just needs a bit more time to clear his head, but he promised he'll talk."

"That's good, I guess," I said. "Talking with Camille and Marnie was... interesting. Nix hasn't fed from Camille recently, and as far as Marnie and Camille know, there isn't anyone else parading around as his new source instead."

He raised his eyebrows. "So we talk to Alaric first, then share what we know with the others?" he suggested.

"Mmhmm," I confirmed, before my tongue flicked out to lick my lips. I wasn't sure if it was all the sex talk earlier with the females, but as I watched him, all I could think about was how much I needed to mark my territory. To kiss and lick and taste him. To have him inside me, and then do the same with Alaric later.

My mouth watered as thoughts of what I wanted to do to him flashed through my head, and he looked up. His eyes darkened as if he could read my mind or sense my desire to claim him right here and now.

"Are you planning on coming over here and putting that tongue to good use, princess?" he said. Fates, he was insatiable. And his dirty mouth...

"Mmhmm," I confirmed, only this time it came out as a purr. Crawling over to him, I straddled his legs, pressing a hard kiss against his lips before dipping to place a softer one on his chest.

His arms closed around me, his fingers trailing my spine before landing on my thighs.

I put my tongue to work right away, giving in to the desire driving me. Slowly kissing across his torso, my mouth traveled across to a nipple and I bit down, giving it a light tug.

He groaned, his eyes closing as he let me do what I wanted. I gave the other side the same treatment before moving down his body, licking, kissing, and nipping as I went.

I traced his abs, grazing my teeth over the swell of muscle and trailing my tongue along the crevices. The salty taste of his skin was divine, but I wanted more. *Needed more.*

I tucked my fingers into the waist of his pants, tugging them down slightly as I licked up that V that pointed straight at what I really wanted—smirking when I noticed he was already hard. Fates, would his thirst for me never fail to send a thrill straight to my core?

He lifted his hips for me as I tugged his pants down and off. Still, he didn't open those eyes, but that small smile had turned into a full-blown smirk. He was waiting to see what I would do.

Pushing his thighs wider, I settled between them. Returning my attention to his cock, I watched as it flexed, demanding attention. I ghosted my lips along it, enjoying the slow torture as he lifted his hips again, seeking friction. I ran my tongue lightly back down, amused when he huffed out an impatient sigh.

Grasping his length, I lightly dragged my hand up the smooth skin, loving the way he drew in a tight breath. Bringing my hand back down, I gave his head a lick, enjoying the salty precum that beaded there.

Deciding that I had tortured him, and myself, enough, I leaned over and swallowed as much of him as I could. Dragging my lips up to his head, my tongue danced along the underside of his cock. I dipped back down, hollowing my cheeks as I tried to seat him as far back into my throat as possible.

His hips jerked up to meet my mouth as a hand tangled in my hair. "Princess," he muttered, "Are you trying to kill me?"

As if I could answer with his fist in my hair, and cock stretching my mouth. Instead, I moved back up before letting him push me back down. Taking a deep breath, I swallowed around him as he hit my throat. My eyes watered, a tear leaking down my cheek as he kept me there. Finally, he let up enough to allow me to pull back and breathe again.

Replacing my mouth with my hand, I fixed my eyes on my mate, who was propped on an elbow as he stared at me. His blue eyes filled with desire. It sent a throb down to my pussy and I squeezed my thighs together, desperate for friction.

"Well?" he asked, and I took a second to realize he wanted an answer.

"Wouldn't it be a good way to go? Though I don't think I could ever have enough of you to let you go." I whispered, my hand moving at a leisurely pace. "An immortal life would never be enough time for me to have you and Alaric."

The sinful grin that stretched across his face sent heat coursing through my body. I swallowed him down again, my free hand stretching up his torso, feeling every inch of skin. His hand held onto mine as he controlled my pace. His eyes never moved from my face as he used me and fucked my mouth.

A chill hit my legs, and before I could move to look who had entered, a hot body leaned over mine. "Here I was thinkin' yeh were waitin' for me, Angel." I groaned at the gravel in his voice, the vibrations making Kane curse as I kept moving.

"This is our idea of waiting for you," Kane muttered, eyes sharp as he watched.

Alaric chuckled, a free hand gliding down my side to land on my ass. My back arched as I enjoyed the warmth of his hand, gasping as it came down hard.

I moaned as he soothed it, his fingers tracing the seam of my pants to between my thighs. I spread my legs further in invitation for him to continue his exploration, the gentle grazing not what I needed, or wanted.

"I figured yeh'd be wantin' to talk," he whispered in my ear, and a shiver ran down my back. "But I cannae imagine talkin' around Kane's cock would be easy. An' I dinnae want yeh to stop."

His hand traced my spine under the loose top I wore, sending goose bumps across my flesh as I whimpered for more. His knuckles brushed back down, with it a tearing sound and the cloth pooled around my elbows as it fell away. The sheer thought that he had ripped it from my body sent a fresh wave of slick arousal between my thighs.

"How about a truce for now?" Alaric suggested.

I nodded as best I could, but Kane answered for us both, "Fuck now, talk later," he mumbled on a groan.

Alaric moved away once more, and Kane's eyes followed him. I couldn't see what he was doing, but the rustling of clothes and the pulsing of Kane's cock told me that he was stripping.

My breath caught in my chest as I waited in anticipation of what he would do. Not being able to see him sent a thrill through me as I felt his hands on my waist again.

Lips pressed to my skin, making me arch even further at the unexpected sensation. The graze of his stubble stroked me as he moved from the middle of my back to my ass, where I felt teeth through the leather.

It was gone as fast as I had felt it, rough hands tugging the last of my clothing off. I squeaked in surprise at being handled so deliciously roughly.

Kane watched as I was moved by our male, slowing my movements to accommodate him. His hand flexed in my hair, gathering as much of it in a single hand as he could. Not once did he let my mouth come free from his cock. I shivered in anticipation, and it heightened with every touch I couldn't see.

I gasped as I felt Alaric's warm tongue on my pussy, my thighs trembling as he pulled away from that all too brief sensation.

"Tastes like someone is enjoying herself," Alaric said from behind. I could basically hear the grin plastered on his face as he spoke. "Do yeh enjoy suckin' his cock?" He asked, and I nodded, moaning when Kane thrust his hips up.

Sighing in relief as he returned his mouth to me, the steady rhythm I had fallen into stuttered to a halt as I struggled to focus on anything but Alaric's tongue. I could feel my heartbeat in my clit as he paid special attention to it.

He sucked hard, and I trembled as my moans were muffled. My pussy clenched as it begged to be filled and pleasure bordered on pain.

Spreading my thighs as far as I could get them, I pushed my ass in the air and tried to ride his face. His palms held my thighs and his fingers dug into my rear as he held me still.

I whimpered again, prevented from satisfying myself. I ached with need. I wanted him to fill me up so badly. Yet I couldn't voice it as Kane thrust into my mouth in time with the strokes of Alaric's tongue.

Just as I was about to come, his mouth left me cold. I was about to pull away to beg him to fuck me, but Kane's hand tightened and pain spread on my scalp, yet it only made me want to beg for more.

"Look at me," Kane whispered. "Good girl."

My chest heaved with anticipation as I tried to get my heart under control from the denied orgasm.

Fingers slid into my pussy and I nearly sobbed in relief before they were withdrawn after only a few pumps. I tensed slightly as they probed my other hole, waiting to see what he would do.

They left, and I relaxed again, only to groan as Alaric's cock slid inside me and I clenched around him. Pushing back, I took his length and moaned as he filled me.

Slowly rocking, I moved my body to swallow Kane as I fucked myself on Alaric. Fuck, it felt so good. They let me take what I wanted from them for a few minutes, enjoying it before they decided that they wanted to give me more.

Kane's eyes flicked above me, probably to Alaric. Something passed between them because I was shoved harshly down on Kane's cock as Alaric snapped his hips into me. I gagged around Kane as my body fought to breathe, taken off guard by the sudden movement.

They fucked me like that, and I finally managed to figure out breathing around Kane as they continued thrusting into me. Those probing fingers returned to my ass, but I relaxed into them this time, groaning as one pushed past the ring of muscles there.

"Fuck, look at her, filled by us completely," Kane groaned, and I watched him as I balanced myself on my elbows to let him thrust up into my mouth.

The flex of his muscles, the sapphire fire in his eyes and the way his mouth was slightly open as he flicked his eyes between me and Alaric drove me wild with need.

"Her cunt is so fuckin' good. So fuckin' wet." Alaric groaned, his cock never missing a beat as his fingers moved too. My thighs shook from the force he rammed into me, lurching me forward and keeping my rhythm as I sucked Kane down.

"Her throat is so tight. She's swallowing my cock like it's her favorite snack," Kane said, his hand flexing as he adjusted his grip.

Fuck, their words drenched me again, my body desperate to be owned by them.

My breath came in quick pants, a maelstrom of sensations overwhelming me until it felt like every nerve ending was on fire.

Alaric bit down on my shoulder and a tide of fire ripped through me as I came hard, screaming around Kane. *"Mine,"* Alaric growled as he released his teeth and roared his own release.

I clamped down and held him in place as I milked his cock for every last drop. Kane held me still, his hand a vice in my hair, as he chased his end, moaning as he came, and I swallowed everything he had to give me.

He released me and I slumped to the side as much as I could, while maintaining my vice grip around Alaric. I rested my cheek on Kane's thigh and smiled sleepily. But now was not the time for a nap. Especially as I knew this time that Alaric *hadn't taken any blood.*

"So you're ready to talk?" I eventually asked, rolling over to look at the male who'd just staked his claim with a bite. Had he done that to reassure himself that I was his when it came to thrakos and their fangs? More importantly, did that mean he was ready to come clean about his own bloodlust?

And if my veins did, in fact, hold such a cure, could he handle what that meant? Could he cope with me feeding hundreds of thrakos the antidote to their curse?

He shook his head, and I turned my back to him. Cursing myself for getting lost in the moment. Had he been ready to talk about it when he got here? But after what we just did, reaffirmed to himself why he was possessive of his mates? Perhaps I had to keep sex off the table? Give him time and space to get his head around it?

But time wasn't something we had a lot of.

CHAPTER 17

Axel

My team and I had this bandit business nailed. Though we hadn't managed to gain any allies—not even the team on *Operation Village Schmooze* were managing that from what Alaric had told me—the fae we had encountered had handed over their goods to us and rushed back to their villagers with barely a drop of blood being spilled.

On a negative note, Nixen had poisoned our team against the camouflage, and though I'd never say it to his face, we hadn't actually needed it. At least, not once we had our hiding spots dug out. Perfectly concealed and scattered along the dirt track, any unfortunate souls crossing our path were completely surrounded before they had any inkling we were even there.

His negotiation skills left something to be desired, but luckily, he had me. Together, we had this awesome good fae, bad fae, thing going on. It worked like a dream every time.

Over a week in and we now had two carts stacked and strapped, ready to pull back to Camp Camille. It would be easier to travel with our heavy cargo under the cloak of darkness, so it had been decided that there was no harm in spending one final day here.

"Shh," Nixy Nix hissed from his spot furthest south of our line. "Someone's coming."

I passed the message along to Thalia, who in turn told Shauna, and so on, reaching Bryon, who lay in wait furthest north. The team fell into silence without question over Nix's claim. We'd done this enough times to know the drill.

A small group of dwarves, pushing a barrow of shiny metal objects, came into view soon enough. *Dwarven forged weapons for the castle?*

We had a process for dealing with fae we encountered who were heavily armed, such as species with an affinity for forging metal, like the dwarves. Only, as I squinted, looking more closely at the group rather than the weapons themselves, I realized we couldn't go in all swords swinging.

It didn't matter that we rarely actually used the swords we swung on the fae, I didn't have it in me to scare children out of being able to sleep at night for the rest of their long immortal lives. I couldn't, in good conscience, attack a family such as those about to breach our ambush zone.

So instead, I stood and stepped out, my weapon hanging loosely at my hip rather than in my hands above my head. The dwarves hissed, pushing the children behind them. Their eyes glanced between the weapons in their barrow and me.

"Easy there," I said. "I'm not going to hurt you or the children."

"What do you want?" the older male dwarf asked.

"The barrow, and your alliance in the upcoming war against Prince Elikai when he takes the throne," I said, trying my luck.

"*When*?" the dwarven male scoffed. "He was crowned a week ago."

He was?

Fuck.

"I meant once he has found a new general in his games, to lead the horde against the rebel alliance," I hedged, hoping the recovery worked *and* gave us information on the games.

The family shuddered. "They aren't games. Children play games. What he is doing at that arena..." he trailed off, shivering again.

"So you agree, the male is sick and not capable of ruling Dezrothia?" I asked. I could practically feel Nix's eyes penetrating my back. *I've got this, cousin.*

"Who's asking?" the female who I deduced to be the mother of the children asked, her tone untrusting.

"We work for the dragon king and queen. The Dyvrad's."

The male and female frowned. "Truly?" the female asked. "We had heard they were alive but didn't hope to believe it."

"They are both alive and as savage as any dragon I have ever seen," I said, embellishing a little. Though they'd had longer to heal and regenerate to their former glory now than when I last saw them, so it very well could be true.

"If that is so, what have they sent you here to do?" the male asked. "What do they want with my family?"

"They would like to form an alliance. Those weapons and your allegiance in exchange for fair treatment, peace, and freedom once Elikai is usurped." Fuck, Alaric would not be happy he'd already been coronated.

"As his father usurped King Dyvrad before him," the dwarven male mused.

I nodded and gave them a moment to discuss my proposition.

Eventually, the female cleared her throat. "We accept, though we can only speak for our family. We cannot speak for the rest of our village."

"Perfect," I said, smiling as warmly as I could without looking psychotic. That was easy. *Too easy?* The thought niggled at me, but I pushed it aside. "Then you'd better meet my friends," I said. My team stepped out with their weapons lowered and palms raised. "We plan to head to Camp Cam–the rebel camp at sunset. Care to join us for something to eat first?"

"So long as we are not on the menu," a little boy said, stepping out from behind his father.

"I don't know what you've heard about thrakos, kid, but we'd sooner eat our sword carrying arm than children."

"Or any fae, for that matter," Nix interjected, stepping closer to check out the weapons we'd just bagged for the rebels. "Just to clarify, we don't eat fae. Children or grown."

OVER A WARM MEAL, the female, Greta, told us how they had been supposed to be traveling to the capital with their finely crafted wares.

Nix engaged her more than me, my eyes on the two children, running around with little wooden swords they too carried at their tiny waists. Strange emotion tugged at me as I watched them, and I fucking hated that they would be caught up in this war. That they would likely see things that they never should.

Their pure, innocent laughter was like the finest music played in the castle ballroom I'd stood guard at for countless events. And when they began playing pretend that one was an evil bandit and the other a good soldier, even Nix lost interest in the political talk with the parents and turned his attention to them instead.

What even was good and evil now? The rebels were evil in many fae's eyes, and Elikai good, certainly if you asked the elite of Ezerat. In my opinion, there were too many shades of gray to say which side anyone fell on.

Eventually the children's play was stopped to eat something on account of having a long journey ahead, and as silence fell, Nix went back to gathering as much information as he could about the horde, the new king, and the games.

They didn't know much, not the nitty gritty anyway, just rumors they'd heard over the recent weeks. The dwarves hadn't put forward a champion to take part in the games, so though that was the topic I was most interested in learning more about so I could feed back to Alaric, there wasn't much information we hadn't already surmised.

Having put it off for long enough, I decided now was as good as any time to update Alaric. *"Boss, got something to tell you,"* I murmured in my mind.

"Axel?" he replied a few moments later.

I took a deep breath, muttered a quick *'fuck it'* to myself and told him, *"Elikai is king."*

AS THE SUN began to rise, I started looking for places to rest up for the day. We'd covered a fair amount of ground on our trek to Camp Camille, considering we now had kids in tow. We'd begun to forge a bond with the dwarves, our conversation, both easy and informative.

So naturally, that's when shit went sideways, fast.

A high-pitched squeal rang out, sharp and sudden and tearing my eardrums to shreds. A horrible sound that I immediately knew would forever haunt my dreams.

Jerking around, I found a male holding the child Garrid, a hand covering his little mouth to stop his cries and the other holding a blade. It wasn't to his neck, but it was close enough for me to decide I would castrate the bastard at the first chance I got.

I narrowed my eyes and tried to take everything in at once. I had to make a plan that would guarantee the dwarf family and my team's safety, and I had to act before any rebel died at the hands of a horde soldier. I shared a look with Nix, who was pulling the barrow. With a slight nod and a jerk of his arms, it tipped, sending weapons sprawling out across the ground with several loud clangs. A distraction? *Thanks cousin.*

The soldier behind the kid looked at the weapons with wide eyes, but I was already moving. By the time he opened his mouth, as though to call for back-up, my hand came around his mouth in a hard silencing slap. My free hand grabbed the dagger I kept in my boot and I stabbed into his upper arm so brutally that his hand could no longer hold his own weapon and it dropped to the forest floor with a thud.

Garrid, who barely reached the soldier's waist, twisted out of his hold, and raced back for his parents. His mother wrapped him in a tight hug, before desperately looking over him for injuries, while his father stepped in front of them protectively. Shoving the other child gently behind him.

From where I stood now, I noticed the group of horde soldiers sat around a campfire, just visible through the trees but there was no denying they had heard Garrid's scream by the way their ears perked up and heads looked around, brows furrowed.

We had to get the family out of here before they came looking for the source.

I did a quick head count. There were nine of them and nine of us. Two of those being children. And another two being more used to making weapons than wielding them.

Fuck.

We had to get out of here. We couldn't risk a fight that we weren't certain we would win. Not with children on our team. Nix had the same thought, only he was several steps ahead of me. And about to enter the horde's eye line as he crept through the trees surrounding their overnight camp.

What the fuck are you doing, Nixen?

"Go," I whispered to Shauna. "Take the family and the cargo. All of you get out of here. Nix and I will catch up.

The soldier in my arms must have passed out from the pain or blood loss, but as I dragged him with me, he suddenly came to and was thrashing like a selkie in the sea.

"Stop moving or I'll slit your throat," I told him. He fell still, and I thanked the fates he had the self-preservation to do this the easy way. I needed him alive if I was to barter his life for Nix.

They hadn't seen him yet, but I had no doubt he was planning to make himself known any moment. To play the role of the distraction to allow our team to get away. Me included. *Families don't leave one another, Nixy Nix.*

I moved as silently as possible while carrying a full-grown male in a backward bear hug and headed in the direction of Nix and the soldiers.

I paused as the murmur of their voices caught my senses. I couldn't make out the words, but they all sat back down around the fire, obviously deciding not to follow up on the young boy's scream. Idiots. Alaric would have killed them with his bare fists for doing that when he was in charge.

I shouldn't complain though, having them at ease would help my plan.

I crept closer until I could hear every word. They were talking about the games. About a redheaded thrakos, who was savaging her way through every contestant. About how Elikai had offered the horde soldiers to put themselves forward for the final rounds with the hope of defeating the freak. And how none of the males in this circle had fancied it.

"Well, how about another mongrel to beat her?" Nix said casually. Stepping out from his concealed spot behind a tree.

What the fuck are you doing?!

"I'm a witch *and* thrakos mix," he continued as the soldiers got to their feet, but remained rooted to the spot as they puzzled over what the foolish hybrid was thinking, walking into their space like a sacrificial lamb offering himself up to the slaughter.

"Anon is a thrakos and wolf mix," a soldier said. "You'd lose. And we'd end up with not just a mongrel in charge, but a female too." With that, the soldiers laughed and Nix's wings released from his back, his fists clenched.

He'd told me about his friend, the thrakos wolf hybrid who was missing. I couldn't say for certain she was a redhead. But her name was Raine, not Anon. Though from what Nix had said of the female, she wasn't the type to bend over for anyone, let alone the horde if they'd caught her and threw her into the games. It wasn't at all implausible that Anon was the name given to her when she refused to willingly give her own.

With my plan to blame the little boy scream on the male in my arms and barter should Nix be seen officially off the table. I ran my blade across his neck and helped him drop to the floor to die quietly. It wasn't as satisfying as castration, but it was a lot less screamy.

After wiping my blade clean on the dead soldier, I skirted around the circle and stepped out onto the opposite side of the campfire to Nix, who let out a low growl upon seeing me.

They might not believe he could beat Raine, if that's who they spoke of, but they wouldn't dismiss me so quickly. They would have known my reputation for being second only to Alaric in the horde. And likely knew of my hybrid status too after my time in the castle dungeon.

"Nixy!" I called across the space. "Who are your new friends?"

All heads swiveled around in my direction. I recognized one immediately by name. Sterling. He'd lived just a few rooms down from me at the castle and we had trained together often. Judging by the wide eyes and panicked gazes, I'd say they all recognized me to some degree.

"Axel?" Sterling said, his eyes widening further still as I sauntered over and placed a hand on his shoulder. He flinched, but didn't move to attack, so I kept my hand there, squeezing his shoulder a little too hard to be friendly.

"What are you doing here?"

"I heard you were thinking about taking Nixy here to the games," I said, like that was answer enough. "I bet Elikai would pay handsomely for someone able to knock that Anon bitch off the top spot? Am I right?"

"Axel," Nix gritted in some kind of warning. But Alaric had always taught me to read a situation and work at always being several steps ahead. Though, several steps ahead of where we were now was likely chained and dragged to the location of games, Nix having insisted on having himself captured so he can get close to Raine and go all hero on her ass. Perhaps we could walk there together nicely with my ex-colleagues if we went willingly?

Either way, I had to give my battle bonded brother a heads up. *"Sorry Alaric!"* I called out in my mind, hoping he was listening.

"What stupid shite are yeh doing now?" he growled back almost instantly. *"I dinnae need any more bad news. Fuck. If yeh have pushed Nixen too far with yer Camp Camille bollocks–"*

"Be right back," I cut over him. It was time to multitask like a pro.

Alaric's string of curses bounced around my brain as I spoke, "Did you tell them that we are a package deal, Nixy Nix?" A quick scan of faces and there was definitely interest there.

Even if they didn't want coin from Elikai, they'd likely do anything to be in his good graces. Two new entrants to his games, both savage hybrid thrakos, would get them lots of evil points with their new king.

"Nothing stupid, boss," I said, forgetting where exactly I'd left things with Alaric. *"Got a lead on Raine."*

"Yeh saw her?" he sighed, prematurely relieved.

"Not exactly. Long story. No time. I'll check in when I can. And tell Lady Evangelia her bestie is with me," I said. *"We are a package deal."*

"Who? You an' Nixen?" Alaric asked, confusion evident even in his thoughts. *"What kind of weird shite are yeh–"*

Fuck. *"One sec."*

"We are a package deal," I corrected out loud. Then in my head, *"Anyway, nothing to worry about, boss. We've thought this through and decided it's a lead we need to chase. Well, I say 'we' in the loosest form of the word. I barely know the female, but Nix is pretty keen on her. So I guess I'm off to chase tail with Nix."*

"Axel, what are yeh no' tellin' me?" Alaric growled.

"Please hold," I said, focusing on the horde soldiers once again.

"Package deal? Like we'd enter into any deal with you. We know exactly who and what you are, *Axel*," he spat. The initial shock and interest had somehow morphed into something akin to hatred in its purest form, with plenty of small penis problem aggression splashed in. Fuck. *Think fast, Axel.*

"Where is your traitorous boss?" One of the males hissed, hatred bleeding into his words. I recognized him too. We had joined the horde around the same time but fuck if I could remember his name.

"Listen, I have a lot going on right now. Far too much to start pointing fingers over who is or isn't a traitor or filthy hybrid, or whatever petty bullshit you had in mind. As fun as it sounds." I feigned a yawn. "Nix and I have some steam to burn off, and we heard the games are the place to do that. Especially if we don't want some unknown female running the ship. Tell me I'm wrong?"

No one did.

"So, are you going to hand us over to Elikai, or should we find another group to do it?" Nix asked, and I was oddly relieved we were on the same page, despite the death trap we'd be entering. Fuck, it would have been a mess if I'd read the entire thing wrong and he'd been planning to enter a fight against nine horde soldiers, that we couldn't be sure we would be the victors of. Then again, these nine were more like six.

"Don't move," a soldier said. "Either of you."

Sterling slipped out of my hold and moved to join the others as they huddled. I mouthed to Nix, "We could just kill them now?" while their backs were to us. Seriously, had they listened to a word Alaric had taught them? Or somehow forgotten it all in the short time he'd been gone?

Nix shook his head and mouthed back something that looked like "No" and then something, something, "Raine."

"Axel?" Alaric snapped as the horde began to discuss the pros and cons of taking us to the arena, as they called it. *"I needed to talk to yeh today, anyway."*

"Fire away," I thought back.

"It's about bloodlust. If there was a cure, would yeh be interested?"

Would I be interested? Fuck, what kind of question was that? *"Was Augustus evil? Fuck, I'd kill for it. Why?"*

"No reason."

"Nah, I'm going to need more info." The horde had split into two groups, four heading toward Nix and five toward me. *"Just one sec."* I told Alaric.

"We will take you," Sterling said, confirming my suspicion. But any hope that we could go with them willingly and with dignity vanished as I watched him pull out a recognizable cuff from his pack.

"Uh boss, if you feel any kind of pain… it's nothing to get all worried about," I thought quickly to Alaric.

"Axel? What's happening?"

"If you can't reach me, don't worry, I'll just be unconscious."

I tried to sound chipper about it, but fates, how could I forget how awful it felt to wear one of those things?

"Axel–"

"About to run headlong into a tree, boss! Brace yourself."

Nix was collared first, sagging to his knees under the weight of having all his strength and magic sapped away in an instant. A feeling that still haunted me.

"Now, come on. We can talk about this…" I said, my hands raised and palms forward. "We'll come quietly."

The sadistic smile on the cunt's face told me we were absolutely not going to talk about this.

His face twisted into an ugly grin, stretching wider as he stepped forward.

Every instinct in my body wanted to fight him, but this wasn't a rescue mission to save myself. I had no choice but to go with it unless I wanted Nix to go with them alone.

"Bangggg–" I yelled in my head for Alaric's benefit just as it snapped into place.

He wouldn't buy it, and it would do nothing to save him the pain, but what other choice did I have than try to at least make him believe it wasn't the same severing of the battle bond we'd experienced before. He'd done enough saving me over the decades. He was needed exactly where he was.

I dropped to my knees, my head feeling like it would split open as white-hot fire burned the connection I shared with Alaric away.

The pain receded quickly enough, thank the fates, leaving an emptiness where the connection to Alaric usually was, once again.

I wasn't given any time to recover or mourn it, though. They packed up their camp, tossed some water from a canteen over the fire, and set off for the capital. Dragging us behind them with ropes, they decided to turn into leashes.

I might be part wolf, and open to a bit of kink, but fuck's sake. Nix had some explaining to do.

CHAPTER 18

Alaric

"Alaric?" a concerned voice whispered from somewhere in the back of my mind. I released a heavy breath as the pain finally ebbed, giving my mind a moment to catch up with what the fuck was happening.

Axel was waist deep in some shit, of that I had no doubt. There was no fucking chance him running into a tree had caused the sudden blistering headache that would have brought me to my knees had I not already been lying in my sleep sack.

I was several day's walk away from the trade route he was stalking, never mind the fact I was already neck deep in my own bullshit right now. I was more aware than any he was not the fool he liked to present himself to be, and I tried to remember that as I forced myself to remain within the tent walls with Kane. But it didn't mean every part of me didn't want to go after my little brother and find out what he was hiding.

For now, I had little choice but to leave him to it, to trust he knew what he was doing. Just like I now knew what needed to be done, no matter how much I despised it. I'd put this off long enough. I was being a selfish prick, and if I didn't get it together soon, my mates would never forgive me for it. Fates, they'd been more patient with me than I deserved.

The news Axel had given yesterday evening, that Elikai was now king, only narrowed down my already nonexistent time frame to get my head around Angel being one third of the most desirable blood source in Dezrothia, and telling the thrakos to 'have at it'.

I shivered, suddenly chilled to the bone. *Fuck*. It didn't matter how many times Angel and Kane tried to convince me otherwise, I couldn't shake the image of what could end up happening. All I envisioned was Angel surrounded by thrakos, being robbed of every ounce of blood in her system. And when I finally managed to tear them off her, all that remained of her was a drained corpse.

At least you'd die with her.

Like that's any consolation.

The fact I was part thrakos myself only added to my desire to wrap Angel up in wool and swim across the Dezrothian waters with her over my shoulder until we reached some other kingdom. One where thrakos didn't exist.

What she wanted to offer them was huge. So big, I couldn't stop playing scenarios around in my head of how they might react. It was impossible to settle on one. It was too unprecedented to be predictable. I knew what it was like to be a victim of the bloodlust's spell. Just like I now knew what it was like to no longer feel that pull, even if I hadn't understood what was happening to me until Angel's grandparents had told her of the cure.

The moment I'd caught on, I'd panicked. And knew I had to get out of there. I knew my female well enough to know she would not share the same view as her grandparents—that their blood was too precious and powerful to share. That a Dyvrad was not a blood slave to a creature born from an evil male's experiments.

No, I knew she would want to help. I wanted to help too, but using my female as a crimson fountain for thrakos in order to do that? The Fates truly fucking hated me.

"Alaric, talk to me," Kane said. "What happened?"

I kept my eyes fixed on the tent roof and shook my head. "Nothin'," I lied, pushing worry for Axel to the back of my mind, because what was one more arsehole move against those I loved? "But this morning's meeting can wait," I said, knowing I had to get this conversation out of the way now before any more bad news came crashing down on me.

"This meeting is about as important as they get," Kane said, shifting onto his side to stare at me. True enough. Braxton was going to break the news to the rest of the camp that Elikai was king. We needed to be there to show we were still strong and determined to win this war. Even now, knowing Elikai had the power of the crown behind him.

"It can wait for this," I gritted, knowing the news would be less of a blow if good news shortly followed. "Unless yeh dinnae want our female to feed the thrakos? It willnae take much to convince me to change my mind again."

Kane sat bolt upright in bed. "Are you saying you're on board?" he asked, blinking the shock out of his features.

I sighed and rolled over, turning my back to him. "I'll never be happy about it, but I cannae live with knowin' I stood in the way of our best chance o' making alliances. Or the two of yeh knowing it was my fault."

Kane's palm landed on my bicep and he squeezed, then pulled me around to face him. "I hate it too, you know," he admitted, capturing my eyes with his so I couldn't look away again even if I wanted to. "But this is bigger than us. Not to mention, it's what Eva wants. We will be there the entire time to make sure she's okay. That will always be my main concern, that she's okay, you know?" He said it like he was still trying to convince himself, not just me. "My personal feelings about it will just have to be put on pause. Can you do that too?"

I cursed under my breath. "We'll see. But before we make this common knowledge, we need to talk. To set out some ground rules," I swallowed. "I cannae watch them drink from the vein."

Not because I was asserting my dominance or any of that bullshite, but because I genuinely couldn't guarantee I wouldn't kill some of our strongest warriors the moment their fangs broke her skin.

"She's helping Marnie and Camille with breakfast again. Said she'd meet us after in the war tent."

"Aye," I said, having heard her leave while Axel had been in my head. I hated that she was distancing herself from us. Not us, *me*. Kane had done fuck all wrong.

As though sensing my thoughts, Kane said. "She just misses Nix and Thalia. And apparently, those females are the next best thing when she needs a rant."

"About me?" I asked. Of course it was about me, but the pinch in my gut at the thought of her being so angry at me she'd avoid me to go and confide in others hurt more than Axel's 'running into a tree' bollocks.

"Well, I don't see any other alphahole having a tantrum about his female wanting to save an entire race from a curse." He paused to glance around, making his point, and his eyes fell back on me. "A curse you know better than any they have no control over, yet an entire realm hates them for it, anyway. So yeah, I'd say it's about you."

"I ken I fucked up," I admitted, then dropped my voice so low Kane had to lean forward to hear. "But I didnae lie to her. To either of yeh. I didnae ken her blood was the cure for *all* the thrakos. Not that she'll believe me."

"She's torn. Regardless of if she thinks you knew and kept it to yourself, she knows how hard it will be for you. Just like she also knows it's something she has to do. She's just trying to give you space to come to the conclusion on your own."

"Yeh don't think she's told them, do yeh?" I asked. "Marnie an' Camille?" I didn't know the females well, but knew they weren't thrakos hybrids. Camille had been Nix's source, and I was pretty sure Marnie wanted to be Axel's.

As soon as the question left my lips, I wanted to take it back. Angel was too smart to tell a soul outside of the few who knew. I hadn't even told my da'. There was no way she'd have told them.

Kane shook his head. "Fuck, no. She's giving you space. Though, I think she might actually quite like listening to their mundane woes, to be honest."

I didn't blame her for needing an outlet, or to just not be talking about the war every waking hour. Not when she had a potential answer to the allies' problem. We were going around in circles, trying to figure it out. Several meetings a day and we were no further forward.

It was eating her up. I saw it every time we met in the war tent and she had to bite her tongue.

Fates, I saw it every time I looked at her.

Not only had I been a cunt for reacting the way I had, her grandparents were being stubborn, too. I'd noticed her avoiding them around camp almost as much as me in the couple of days since she spoke to them at the lake.

Before I could talk myself out of it, I sat up in bed and grabbed for a shirt scrunched up at the foot of my sleep sack. It wasn't too late to fix this. Not yet. Even if I had to have Kane or my da' knock me unconscious for the entire time she was curing our camps' thrakos, I wouldn't stand in her way any longer.

"I'll get her, shall I?" Kane asked, shrugging on some clothes. At my nod, he disappeared from the tent.

NO SOONER HAD I stepped outside, Kane returned with Angel.

"Kane tells me you're ready to talk about this?" she said, straight to the point, not giving me any leeway to skirt around it.

From the moment I'd found out about Elikai being king and told them, I'd known my time to sort my head out was about to run out. "Aye," I said, then nodded toward the trees and lake beyond. "No' here. It's more private over there."

Angel didn't wait, just kept walking, and I followed. If I'd been in wolf form, my tail would be firmly between my legs.

We reached the edge of the lake, and she crossed her arms. "Why didn't you say anything?" Angel demanded. "Why keep it to yourself that your appetite had changed?"

"It's no' that simple," I said. "Before drinking from you two, I hadn't had a fae source for centuries. I'd lived off weak animal blood or the blood I managed to get on hunts. I was used to feeling like I was starving for blood all the time. Having two fae as strong as yeh to drink from whenever I wanted... I wasnae used to it. My body wasnae used to it. I figured I was just more sated than I'd ever been before."

"Makes sense," Kane said, turning to Angel with a shrug.

"You had to have worked it out at some point," Angel said, not in the least bit ready yet to let me off the hook.

"I didnae ken about the cure. I swear it to the fates." Hating the feeling of being under my mate's scrutiny, I started to pace. "At first, I guess I was biting yeh out of habit and well, because..." I rubbed the back of my neck, then cleared my throat. "I like it. And I really fuckin' like the way yeh both react to it."

Heat filled Angel's cheeks, much to her annoyance, no doubt. "At first? So what happened later? When you realized our blood wasn't wearing off?"

I shrugged. "I started to notice I didnae need to drink, but thought it was somethin' to do with my thrakos side, not the blood I'd drank. I'd considered that my wolf might just be more dominant, or that it was to do with us being mates somehow. Fuck, I even considered that the rebel diet of so much raw meat had something to do with it."

I crossed the space between us and took Angel's hands in mine.

"Listen, I'm sorry I didnae say anythin'. I didnae want to worry yeh. We have a war to fight and enough problems to fill a graveyard. I'd concealed my thrakos side, pushing it down and suppressing it for as long as possible and only letting it come out when I had to feed, that noticing something like the bloodlust being cured... Fuck, I didn't even consider it. Until–"

"Until I told you what my grandparents said, and rather than talking about it, you stormed off."

"I knew yeh would already have made yer mind up that if such a cure existed, yeh'd stop at nothin' to feed every thrakos, born and created, until they were all cured. With no consideration over yer own safety. Or the target that yeh'd have on yer back."

"My safety is linked to the safety of my mates. Of course I'd consider the risks and make sure we came up with a plan that worked for all of us first. I'm not a selfish female."

"Aye," I said, releasing her hands and letting them drop. "But I *am* a selfish male."

"You put your entire life on hold to be a spy in the castle," Kane said. "How can you seriously think you are selfish?"

I shook my head. "I'm selfish when it comes to my mates and their safety. I'm selfish when it comes to thinking about another fae's lips on yer flesh."

"Then we can just fill vials. There are plenty in the medical tent to get us started," Kane said. "We could come up with some kind of rotation so Eva can fill them as soon as they are empty and refilled ones can be passed around."

"Yeh'd do that?" I asked Angel.

She nodded. "It would be quicker to feed from the vein," I fought the growl creeping up my throat, "and a lot less mess too, but if it's filling vials or making my mates uncomfortable, I choose vials."

She relaxed a fraction, and I pulled her into my arms, needing her warm body close after too long of only getting coldness from her. "Did I ever tell yeh how fucking incredible yeh are?" I asked against her hair.

"Just promise me you won't keep anything from me again, no matter how big or small," she said.

"So long as yeh promise not to give me the cold shoulder again. Fuck, I'd rather yeh punch my teeth from my mouth than give me the silent treatment."

She pulled away and glanced toward Kane. "Those vials, you know where they are?"

Kane nodded. "You want to do this now?"

"The rebels could do with some good news after this morning's meeting."

Truer words had never been spoken. And thank the fates, I wouldnae have to watch any other thrakos feeding from my female. Not directly, anyway.

CHAPTER 19

Nekane

Eva sat at the edge of the water, Alaric crouched beside her with several vials scattered around them. The bag I was clutching with white knuckles held many more, ready to be filled with the precious cure.

Leaning against a tree not far away, I grimaced every time she sliced the dagger across her palm. It was taking six or seven slices just to get enough for one vial. Her curses cut the air much like the blade, only their echoes lingered longer than her blood would.

Alaric growled low in his throat, the only warning before ripping the blade from her hand and launching it into the water—for the second time since she'd started. It landed with a *plop* and I reached for the dagger in my boot, knowing Eva was protective of her new twin blades and Alaric had already lost both of his to the depths.

"Alaric, I know this is hard for you to watch. But would you rather they bite me?" Eva scolded. He growled again, only this time there wasn't a blade to throw, otherwise, he absolutely would have.

My nostrils flared at the thought of another male's mouth anywhere near her body. Murder felt like a lesser crime. For Alaric and I, this was supposed to be the easier option, but I was beginning to doubt it.

I didn't want to release the dagger from my grip as she took it, knowing what she was going to use it for, but Eva smiled and fucking thanked me as she pried it from my hand. She continued on, my jaw clenching and teeth grinding hard as I watched her. Over and over. Refusing to give up or admit to the discomfort and pain that doing it our way was causing her.

"Fuck, Angel," Alaric bit out. "Stop. Please, just fuckin' stop. I cannae watch this."

"Then look away," she said, squeezing her fist tightly over the vial, only to get a few drops out before the wound healed.

One hour crept into two, and she had just five vials to show for it. It would take weeks at this rate. Time not only did we not have, but time I couldn't stand the thought of her continued suffering. She might not admit it, but that's what it was.

"Can I help?" I asked, pushing up from the tree and approaching the water's edge. She didn't turn, just shook her head.

I reached out for the crimson filled glass she was filling. Once the blood clinging to the sides of the vial settled, there would be barely a mouthful inside. My eyes dropped to the dagger that she was about to run across her palm. You could barely see skin below where the thick blood had already dried. I held my breath, and she scored her flesh once more. The blood welled to the surface, and I held out the vial as she clenched her fist so tightly her hand shook, encouraging just a few small drops to slide inside.

She looked up and met my eyes, forcing another smile. "Maybe I should switch hands again?" she suggested. "Or maybe you could keep the wound open with the dagger?"

"Or, maybe, just stop altogether," I countered.

"And do what? Choose our five favorite thrakos and give only them the cure?" she let out a sarcastic laugh. "Not happening, Kane. It's all or nothing, and nothing isn't an option. So–"

"What if we give them to the strongest?" Alaric suggested.

"And have just them to take to war with us? Have you lost your mind?" she snapped.

"Hear me out, Angel," he said. "We get the strongest five thrakos in camp, tell them about the cure, and offer them the vials. Once they are cured, we head into camp an' the thrakos take turns…" he trailed off.

"Take turns what?" Eva pressed. "Waiting for the vials to fill?"

His head sank into his hands, massaging his temples, and eventually shook his head. "No. While they take turns drinkin' the cure directly from yer wrist."

"You're serious?" she asked, and I watched her shoulder sink in relief. She discarded the vial she'd hardly filled a millimeter and moved to crouch next to Alaric, an arm around his shoulders. He didn't say anything, just nodded his head. Eva's eyes lifted to meet mine, like she was waiting for permission.

Fates, I couldn't stand the thought of watching males do something so intimate with her. Especially not when every time I'd witnessed Alaric feed from her, it had either been during sex or leading up to it.

But fuck. I hated the thought of watching her decant blood into these vials even more.

"If you're comfortable doing that, and it won't cause you any discomfort, like–" I gestured between the knife, her hand and the spilled vial, "–this shit, then I won't get in your way or try stopping you."

She sighed, but her brows quickly lowered into a frown. "Why specifically does it need to be the strongest ones we give the vials to?"

"Because you will be a target?" I guessed. "To help us protect you from the thrakos once word gets out that their salvation runs through your veins?"

Alaric shook his head and sat up straight, meeting her eyes for the first time since the first slash she'd made across her palm. "No, to stop me from killin' any of them when they bite yer wrist."

ALARIC ARRIVED BACK at the lake just a few minutes later, with Braxton and a few other rebel alliance leaders in tow. One I knew to be full-blooded thrakos and the other a hybrid thrakos witch.

"What's all this?" Braxton said, looking at the bloodied glass and dagger at Eva's feet.

"For you," she said, holding out a vial to him. "Should you wish to take it."

Alaric kept his voice barely above a whisper as he explained to the five thrakos about Eva's blood, of what had happened to himself since drinking it, and what we assumed had happened to Nix too.

They listened in silence, their expressions incredulous. Alaric finished, surprising me, having left out the background of how Eva's grandparents also had the cure flowing through them.

Without a word, they popped the corks and drank, keeping their heads back and vials bottom end in the air for several seconds, making sure they tasted every drop.

"Now what?" I asked. Would they just know? Alaric certainly hadn't.

"Kane," Alaric said, guilt flashing through his eyes. "I would do this myself, but it willnae work."

"It's fine. Whatever you need, it's done," I said, stepping forward.

He picked up Eva's discarded blade, then took my hand, raising my palm and making a small cut. "Da', come here," he said, looking at his father.

Braxton joined him, already sniffing the air. I found I was holding my breath, desperate for whatever Alaric had planned to work. Desperate for Eva's efforts to not be for naught.

"Closer," Alaric ordered his father, lifting my hand to his nose. Braxton took a deep inhale, and I saw his tongue move across his top row of teeth under his lip.

"Nothin'," Braxton said, but I didn't release my breath, still unsure.

"Nothing. As in, it worked? You have no desire to drink?" Eva asked.

The cut on my hand had already healed, but Alaric's mouth came down over it anyway, licking across to either clean away the blood or mark his territory after his father had gotten so close. Probably both.

"My fangs didn't even flinch," Braxton confirmed. "Can Archer and Remy try?" He asked, gesturing to two of the others waiting on the side, and I nodded.

We repeated the same process twice more. Then for good measure Braxton tried again several minutes later, followed by Gideon and Wyll. "We can't keep this to ourselves," Braxton said.

"Yeh think I dinnae ken that, da'?" Alaric growled.

"How long does it take to fill a vial?" Archer asked, one hand rubbing his chin.

"Too long," I said, looking at Eva.

"My mates and I have agreed it's best to feed any who want to be cured of bloodlust directly from the wrist," she said.

The thrakos' eyes went wide. "Yer sure?"

"Positive," Eva said.

"An' you?" Wyll asked, eyeing Alaric and I.

"It's no' our choice to make," Alaric said. "But we winnae try stopping her."

'Maybe yeh shouldnae be there to witness it, son?" Braxton suggested. "Nor yeh, Nekane."

"I have to be," Alaric said. "For as long as it's safe, anyway."

"Same," Eva looked at me as if to say, 'you don't have to', but I shook my head. "I need to heal her. She has a lot to get through and only so much energy to keep healing herself and replenishing blood."

Braxton nodded. "How do yeh want this to work, Evangelia?"

"We'll head over to the main part of camp, and the thrakos can form a line from the fire pit in the center? Maybe tell them then and any who don't want it can leave. Everyone else waits their turn, or they will have my males to deal with."

"Us too," Archer said, nodding to the other three. "Thank you, Evangelia Dyvrad. You must tell us how we can repay you."

"Just make sure my males don't kill anyone and we can call it even?"

"That's not enough, but I'm not sure what is," Remy said. "But it's a start, I guess. And something we can absolutely do." He glanced at Alaric, who looked just about ready to commit murder already and we hadn't even started. "Something we can absolutely *try* to do," Remy corrected.

Eva chuckled, then got to her feet and led the way.

She sat herself down by the crackling flames, but Alaric swiftly lifted and placed her on his lap, his arms crossing over her waist. I covered her back, watching over her shoulder and ready to heal her. Archer, Remy, Gideon, and Wyll closed in on either side of me and Braxton cupped his hands around his mouth and shouted for any with thrakos blood to come to the clearing and make a single line in front of the fire which Eva sat behind.

Our female was buzzing with emotions, none of which were fear. Excitement and adrenaline, yes, but not fear. Fates, I couldn't be more proud. Or more petrified.

The Dyvrad's joined us around the fire as Braxton explained everything, and I didn't miss the way their eyes scanned constantly. Ready to take on any who threatened their granddaughter. Eva was well protected, nothing would happen to her.

When Braxton gave the cue for any to leave, should they not wish to take the cure, no one did. And shortly after, they began to step forward, one by one. Only one, in all the hundreds of thrakos who joined the line, made a run at Eva. Calling something about the blood running out and him not missing his chance.

Eva's grandparents stayed the entire time, looking like they were about to drown in their guilt, moved as one, covering their bodies in scales and opening their wings wide, forming a solid barrier stronger than any metal in front of Eva. Braxton grabbed him by the scruff and marched him to the end of the line, then set two newly cured thrakos to guard him.

Alaric kept his arms around Eva's waist the entire time. I left my hand on the back of her neck in a comforting gesture, focusing my mind on pushing healing magic into her, while Alaric provided the background music, by way of a constant low growl vibrating from his chest. A hum to warn any who thought to step out or over the line with our female that their life would be ended swiftly should they try it.

For the most part, it worked, though I was pretty sure he had just as little control over doing it as he'd had over Eva insisting she wanted to remain here until every thrakos in camp had taken their turn.

The final thrakos finished drinking, bowing low in thanks before backing away. Before he'd turned his back, Alaric moved for the first time since we'd begun, lifting Eva with him and marching toward our tent.

"What are you doing?" she snapped, though there was no anger in her voice.

I followed, but when he reached the tent, he didn't stop, continuing on through the trees toward the lake. Pausing only to kick the vial, which would have been her sixth, had she finished filling it. It rolled over the edge and into the water, just as Alaric finally answered.

"Washing their fuckin' stench off yeh," he growled. She had a single moment to plug her nose with her hand before he jumped into the lake, fully clothed, clad in weapons.

Though she was doubtlessly exhausted, she'd just accomplished more in one day than an entire village of kings and queens could hope to achieve in their entire immortal lifetime. Nothing could piss her off right now. Not even Alaric plunging her into a lake full of icy water, if the playful squeak she let out was anything to go by.

"Yer mine, Angel," he growled into her mouth, and I smirked. I knew he needed this. He needed to assert his claim over her.

"Forever and always," she muttered before kissing him thoroughly.

CHAPTER 20

Axel

It took a few days of walking with my body aching the whole damn way, to adjust to the lack of magic in my system and the silence in my head. But we finally made it to the capital. I just couldn't settle on whether that was a good or bad thing. I guess it would depend on whether we survived it.

We reached a part in Ezerat where the entire area was bustling, even now, in the dead of night. The soldiers eventually stopped, and my stomach turned as I lifted my head to find the arena where Elikai was holding his games.

I swallowed. Though I was no small male, the imposing structure ahead was so vast, it made me feel tiny. Which in turn made me feel vulnerable, something I despised. A lesson I'd learned the first time I'd worn one of these fates cursed things around my neck.

Never show it, Axel. Think it, feel it, just don't fucking let them see it.

I'd known they were bringing us here, the cuff around my neck cut off my power not my ears, I'd heard them talking about it. But what now? Were they going to execute us as a warm-up act in tomorrow's games? Enroll us?

"What's the plan now, chaps?" I asked, barely concealing the nerves from my voice.

Silence.

They soon started moving again, dragging Nix and I along with them. We shared a look; Nix's filled with guilt, and mine a false hope that we'd get out of this alive.

We reached thick metal gates, as tall as the trolls guarding them. As though expecting us, they were immediately pried open from the inside. No knock required.

We stepped into a vast stadium; tiered seats curving around three sides, all facing a stage. I could smell the blood that had been spilled, it lingered and no amount of brushing it away seemed to have helped. I sniffed the air again and multiple species' scents all hit me at once, despite my lack of wolf or thrakos senses working right now.

Instead of being taken to Elikai or led out onto the dark, empty pit-like stage, we were ushered behind it. The cuff around my neck suppressed the gag, and I shuddered at the sight of a vast wall lined with cages as flashbacks of the catacombs descended on me. *Fates, no.*

The male responsible was truly as psychotic as his father. Only somehow less subtle about it. Regardless, he had no place sitting on the throne. I wanted Kane to be the one to lead the realm, but if the dragon king and queen were what it took, then I'd worship at their feet gladly if they stopped Elikai.

Only a handful of cages were closed tight. *Occupied by contestants?* The rest hung open, though only just a little. I tried to memorize them, counting how many were left, until a high fae moved in on one side, a shifter on the other. They took hold of my shoulders and pushed me toward a cage, slamming the door shut in my wake.

The ceiling and walls were of solid, but unknown, construction, and the only view was of the pit, seen through the thick bars that made up the door. A warlock appeared, blocking the view and muttering a spell. I scrambled to my hands and knees, launching myself toward the bars. But the warlock had fallen silent, his spell complete by the time I made contact. Just as quickly as I wrapped my fists around them, I was catapulted backwards.

I gulped slowly as my hand landed in something slimy. It was too dark to see anything properly in my basic fae form, so I sniffed the air again. More blood, harder to decipher with the stage so close, but this was mostly one species, one I wasn't familiar with.

As I pushed myself to sit upright, my neck craning slightly thanks to the low ceiling, something hard dug into my ass. I pulled it free, only to drop it immediately. It hit the bars of the door but thank the fates it didn't have the same reaction as I did upon contact with the warlock's spell. *Good to know.*

I squinted at the object. A bone? Likely a deer, it had been sucked clean of every last scrap of meat. Something I'd done plenty when hunting for blood in the castle woods with Alaric.

As quickly as it crossed my mind that it might have belonged to the previous occupant of this cage, I dismissed the rancid thought. There were no minibeasts scurrying around or crawling up my leg, and the games hadn't been taking place long enough for that level of decomposition.

The stench became overwhelming, and I was almost glad my keener senses were saved from experiencing it. I lay on my back and extended my legs into the air, ignoring the list of nightmares beneath me that the poor bastard to have occupied this cell before had left behind. I couldn't straighten my knees, not even close, so I tried to brute force my way out with several kicks.

Nada.

I tried again, and again, getting more and more frustrated, ignoring the sound of the guards' laughter as they watched from outside.

But it was fucking useless.

The guards moved on to taunt Nix, who was in the cage to my left. I pictured the row from where I'd stood on the outside; every cage to my right was open, aside from one at the far end, which wasn't. The one to the left of Nix was one of the few where the door had been locked tightly shut.

I stared out of the cage, my arms clenched tightly around my knees, and fought the urge to rock. Like a fucking babe needing comfort. *Snap out of it, Axel.*

"Why any fae would voluntarily enter into these games is a fucking mystery to me," I called out to Nix, a poor attempt to get the guards' attention away from him.

Before he could answer, if that's even what he intended to do, he'd been pretty fucking sheepish the entire journey to get here, a round-faced guard filled my view with his bulbous nose and lips with stringy saliva clinging to the corners.

"*You* volunteered, you stupid mutt," he said.

"You're right," I said, holding my hands up, feigning my innocence, not wanting to argue and risk him remaining there long enough for more spit to gather. "My mistake."

The asshole guard didn't need to know I had only volunteered because of the stupid shit Nix had pulled. And I wasn't about to tell him. Just like he would never find out Nix was my baby cousin and already had my loyalty based solely on the blood running through his veins.

A group of horde soldiers were led in and I sat forward, trying to get a better view. Some were walking tall, others on shaky legs. Five in total. *More volunteers?*

They were told to pick a cage and after assessing which was the cleanest—a luxury Nix and I weren't afforded—I heard the doors swing shut and the warlock go to work with his sealing spell.

So Elikai was prolonging these games, hoping that one of the soldiers could kill either Anon, or Nix or I after we'd killed her? *Not going to happen.*

If Anon truly was Raine, a thrakos wolf hybrid, and she was allowed to fight without her cuff on, that would mean Nix and I could as well. I sent a silent prayer to the fates that the guards had enjoyed whatever meal they ate before arriving here, because it would be their last.

One of the horde soldiers called out from behind their cages, begging them to let him out on account of a change of heart. It distracted the guards enough for Nix to call out, "Raine!"

"She won't talk to you," a voice hissed from my left. It had to be the occupied cage beside Nix.

"Jarrah," Nix growled, clearly recognizing the voice. The name was one I had heard a lot about, none of which being good. The prize for his traitorous actions had been a ticket to the coronation games. But how was such a cowardly fae even still alive?

"The one and only," he confirmed, his voice a low whisper I had to strain to hear over the argument ensuing between the guards. And their soon-to-be dead ex colleague several cages to my right, who was, in fact, not allowed to change his mind.

"Anon," Nix hissed. "Is that Raine?"

"Who else? The female is a psychopath," Jarrah muttered back. "She won't talk to you, though. Crazy bitch hasn't said a word since she got here."

"To you," I said.

"Who's that you came in with?" Jarrah asked Nix, and I instantly hated him talking about me.

"None of your business," Nix spat.

"Whatever. About Anon, I assumed she was holding a grudge at first, because of the whole Kane thing, but apparently she just doesn't want to talk to anyone. I'm pretty sure it's because she knows every contestant here is a threat."

I tutted several times.

"Or she sees you as the traitorous piece of shit you are," Nix said. "The kind of male to betray the alliance and our entire cause for some gold."

"Or, as it turns out, a ticket to this stadium of horrors," I added.

"Ugh," Jarrah complained. "She needs to get over it. It's not like he died, did he?"

"No thanks to you," Nix muttered.

"She should have just agreed to work with me from the start when we were caged next to each other. We could have been out of here by now. Such a stubborn female," he sneered.

Whether the female in question could hear, I wasn't sure, but a large part of me hoped she had. Just so she could make his death that much more painful.

Nix barked out an unhinged laugh. "Are you *truly* blaming her for not wanting to help you?"

"I know you told me a lot about this guy, but you failed to mention how fucking funny he is. Traitorous cunt aside," I said to Nix.

"You would have done the same," Jarrah growled. "Given the same opportunity, you would have taken it too."

"So you're not a traitor, you're an opportunist?" I asked, not letting my anger show in my voice.

"Exactly!" he said, loud enough to get the guards' attention.

"Shut up, mutts!" one of them called, then went back to dealing with the now sobbing soldier volunteer.

I dropped my voice a little more when I spoke again, "Seriously, Nix, where have you been hiding this guy?" I snarked, then to Jarrah I said, "You really believe *that* was a good opportunity?

I sighed. Jarrah was fast becoming too exhausting to talk to. I'd rather paint a face onto the deer leg bone with a bit of this gloopy blood and strike up a conversation with it, than continue one with him. But the more he said, the less bad I'd feel killing him, if Raine or Nix didn't beat me to it, that is.

Nix, who'd been too silent, spoke up again. "Say we forgot that you almost got Kane executed. Did it not cross your mind she wouldn't want to talk to anyone because she knows that she will ultimately be forced to fight against and murder them?" he asked.

"Right, 'cause *she* could murder *me*. I've fought and beaten her before, and I'll do it again," Jarrah said.

I frowned. Surely these were death matches? Winner stays on? If he'd fought her and won, why wasn't she dead?

"Please don't tell me you are talking about that time in training with Kane?" Nix asked, sounding exasperated.

"Yeah, so you do remember. I wrapped her up in my web and–" the laugh that burst from my chest cut him off, and nearly knocked me out as the back of my head hit the cage ceiling.

To my surprise, Nix joined in. Then again, it was fucking hilarious that someone would think a round in the training ring and a death match were remotely close to the same thing. Especially against a she-wolf cornered. Of course Nix would laugh. It was impossible not to.

"What's funny about the truth?" Jarrah snapped, but the guards were already walking in our direction, some kind of weapon I'd never seen before in hand.

"When you fought her in the Vale, she wasn't the fae she is now," Nix murmured, like he didn't care whether the guards heard him. "Back then she had Miles, she had family, she had a home. Now? She's grieving, broken and desperate. She's lost hope, which is one of the darkest places to be on its own. Add to that, all she has known since getting here is kill or be killed. I just hope she is put against you in that pit before I am. She deserves to be the one to end you after the bullshit you just spouted."

Nix hadn't just been speaking about Raine. No, he was speaking from experience. He'd seen some fucking horrors, drowned in the darkness, and was still sinking by the sounds of it. Despite him seeming to be getting better by the day, before the soldiers had collared us.

Either way, I was so fucking proud that he'd come up for air long enough to spit those fucking words at Jarrah.

Before I could tell him as much, the guard thrust the long stick toward me and the collar around my neck tightened. Or maybe it just felt tighter because every muscle in my body was suddenly spasming.

Whatever dark magic the weapon held shook me to my bones, right up until my brain decided to take a time out.

CHAPTER 21
Evangelia

"It's done," Kane said as soon as we entered the war tent. Aside from feeling a little light-headed, and leaning against Alaric in case my shaking legs gave out, it had gone well. Really well.

Even the cold dip Alaric had forced on me, and the too fleeting moment in our tent just now as we'd pulled on clean clothes and my mates reminded me exactly who I belonged to, had been perfect.

"Thank you, Evangelia," Braxton said, his voice more sincere than I'd ever heard it, and unless I was mistaken, his eyes glistened with tightly held back emotion.

The smile I gave him was one of the most genuine to have ever pulled at my lips. "It was my pleasure," I said. "I'm just glad I could help."

I glanced toward my grandparents, both wearing the same guilt-ridden expression they'd worn all day. I wanted to be mad at them for being so stubborn and not letting the thrakos drink from them. Fates, my mates were pissed enough for the three of us. But how could I expect them to give something as precious as their own blood when their instincts were screaming at them not to?

With a front row-seat to every failed attempt Augustus made during his grotesque experiments, they likely didn't know where to draw a line between what the thrakos had been like then, to the thrakos now. They'd been viciously attacked by a thrakos, and at their most vulnerable time, it was something most of us, myself included, had never experienced. Not only that, they had witnessed their very creation by an evil king whose madness had taken everything and everyone they loved from them.

With time, Drayke and Vyara would learn as well as I that the thrakos were just like any other fae. They had their strengths, weaknesses and fears. Only now, they had one less weakness to worry about, and I was proud to have been able to help. A fate I would not have known I could fulfill had it not been for them telling me it was possible.

Drayke cleared his throat. "Though the thrakos have all received a dose of the cure, what is to say the fae of Dezrothia will simply take our word for it and believe us?"

It was a good question, and one I was embarrassed not to have thought about sooner. The thrakos didn't look any different. Fates, I hadn't even noticed my mate was cured. He'd barely been figuring it out for himself.

"I will offer a blood promise," Braxton said, and several fae in the tent gasped, understandably so. A blood promise wasn't just some empty words of reassurance. If the fae giving the blood promise broke their word, they'd lose their immortality.

"I'll do it too," Alaric said. "We can cover more villages if we split. But yeh have my word, I will swear to their mayor an' every villager who needs it that I have no desire or thirst for blood. They will ken the consequences of breakin' such an oath."

"How certain are you that you are truly cured and no longer a threat?" Vyara asked matter-of-factly, and my nostrils flared that she would still question them.

"I'd bet my life on it and by default my mates' lives," Alaric said.

"And you Evangelia?" my grandmother asked. "Would you swear it on your life, and by default, the lives of your mates?"

I pushed my shoulders back and forced myself to straighten. "Yes. In fact, I would offer a blood promise myself."

Vyara smiled down at me, then turned to Drayke and nodded once.

The old king stepped forward. "Then it is decided."

"What is?" I asked.

"Vyara and I will be the ones to offer a blood promise to the villagers," he announced, and the tent fell into such a silence that even the air stopped breathing. "It is the least we can do after being unable to help our granddaughter today."

"We will leave tomorrow at first light," Vyara added. "Separately." I frowned. My grandparents were rarely away from each other's side, could she really mean they would split up? "We will need two teams if we are to make up for last week. I will visit the six villages that refused us before, and Drayke will venture far and wide to as many others as possible with whatever time we have."

"Thank you," I said, as sincerely as Braxton had thanked me.

"It is the least we can do," Drayke said.

"I truly am sorry we couldn't help you today," Vyara added softly. "I wanted to. Fates, I did. I just–"

"That's okay," I said. "I'm fine. It was fine. It's really okay."

"And thanks to you, so too is every thrakos in this camp," she added. "I'm so very proud of you, little flame."

No sooner had my grandparents excused themselves and retired to their tent for the night, when another almost equally ancient fae appeared through the war tent's fabric door. This one more familiar, carrying a look in her all-knowing eyes as she flitted them between me and my mates. As if that wasn't warning enough that we wouldn't like whatever she'd *seen* that triggered her to arrive here so late, the worry became personal when she headed directly toward the three of us.

"Edelin," Braxton said with a nod, but she continued to pass him until she stood at Alaric's side.

She propped an arm on his shoulder before finally turning her attention back to Braxton. There was obviously something she had to tell him, or perhaps all three of us, and I found myself sending a silent prayer to the fates that she didn't plan to give whatever message she had by way of riddles. Even those first few days of training with Braxton weren't a scratch on how drained I felt right now.

"We're just about to discuss the logistics o' the next few days. Drayke and Vyara have offered to share a blood promise with the villagers, so they'll set off at sunrise tomorrow." He raised a brow. "Unless yeh have anythin' yeh'd like to tell us first?"

Straightening, she gave Alaric's shoulder a squeeze and murmured so quietly I could barely hear, despite sitting right next to them.

"I have a message for you and your mates. It's very interesting indeed." She tapped his shoulder a few times, like she might pet a filly. "But it can wait," she finished, before moving to join Braxton.

A low growl rumbled from deep inside his chest. "Fuckin' seers," he mumbled. Then to me he muttered. "Why mention it if she has no intention of givin' me the fuckin' message yet?"

"What was that all about?" Kane asked from Alaric's other side, leaning forward, his voice hushed.

"Fuck if I know," Alaric grumbled.

Edelin cracked her knuckles, then stretched her arms above her head, a satisfying pop sounding before she held out her hands. "I only intend to relive this once, so make sure you are touching me directly."

Braxton and Alaric shared a concerned look, but soon enough, Braxton took her left hand in his and Alaric stood from his stool to join him, crossing the room and taking her right. Kane and I joined them. Kane slid his hand onto Edelin's wrist, and I quickly followed, doing the same on her other side. Several more of the alliance leaders followed suit and suddenly my eyes were rolling and I was no longer inside the war tent. I was on a sandy beach.

Atop the choppy water ahead stood two huge ships, their sails flying high and proud as they entered Dezrothian waters, heading for the shore. Though I couldn't see the faces of those sailing our way, the insignia on the mainmast was one I knew well, thanks to Kane's uncle. Mount Mortum.

Vessels flying that banner could mean nothing good for Dezrothia.

Had Edelin brought us to the past? To the day my grandparents were dethroned? To the future? Or perhaps most worrying of all, the present?

The vision swirled, and I was surrounded by dozens of sea fae fighting on the beach in a gruesome, messy battle. Their enemy, all wearing the Mount Mortum armor I'd seen King Vandenburg's guards wear, and the weapons they wielded looked precise and deadly. The foreign fae continued their slaughter until all who opposed them folded in a heap on the sand.

Vandenburg's guards searched the shore for those still breathing, swiftly exterminating any of those unfortunate enough to have survived the initial attack. A steady stream of fae disembarked the ships, piling onto the Dezrothian shore and gathering on the bloodied sands in the hundreds before separating like automatons as they split off into rank.

My ears were ringing with the harsh whistling of the wind. I couldn't work out what was being said, but soon, two groups headed back for the ships. I held my breath as they unloaded two giant crates mounted on wheels, and with their cargo in tow, the soldiers peeled away, marching ahead.

To their king in Ezerat?

As the vision faded away, I quickly cast my mind back to what I knew of my grandparents' usurping. They had told of hundreds of ships, where in the vision, there were only two, albeit both filled with hundreds of the mountain realm warriors. My gut told me this battle hadn't happened yet, but that didn't mean we'd have time to stop it.

"How long do we have?" Braxton growled as he jerked his hand away from Edelin like it burned him.

"I don't know," she confessed. "It may already have happened. It could be happening now. But if there is any chance to stop it, we must ensure that it is," she said. Unspoken sadness swam in her eyes for the Dezrothian lives taken so callously, and I didn't envy her for her gift.

"We cannae send soldiers to Kelpie cove *and* move the camp farther south," Braxton said, rubbing the scruff on his chin.

"True," Edelin said. "But perhaps a warning delivered by your fiercest three will suffice?"

The witch's eyes locked on Alaric's, as though he should be able to read her thoughts and fill in all the gaps.

"I'll go," Jeremiah said, and Alaric and Braxton nodded their approval.

Obviously a veteran rebel with his chin held high and his back straight, shoulders strong, looking every bit that he could handle whatever was thrown at him. I nodded in agreement, along with my male and his father.

Edelin shook her head. "I don't see Kelpie Cove in your path, dear."

"If yeh have a trio in mind, witch, jus' say it," Alaric snapped.

"I think you know, Alaric," she said.

"Angel is drained," he argued. "Did it skip yer attention that every thrakos, full-blooded male an' hybrids alike, fed from her today?"

Edelin rolled her eyes. "She will be back to her full strength by morning."

"You want to send the three dragons?" Remy asked. "But what about the hunt for allies?"

Braxton shook his head, "The old dragon king and queen are too essential to be present at the villages," he said. "They cannae go."

Kane's spine straightened. "If Eva's going, you can try to stop me from joining, but I promise it won't end well," he gritted.

"Dinnae worry. She means for you an' I to join Angel anyway," Alaric said to Kane.

Edelin smiled. "Excellent idea," she said, spinning on her heel and marching out of the tent.

Alaric was hot on her heels, and Kane and I followed him out.

As the crisp outside air filled my lungs, I hung my head back, looking toward the sky beyond the trees. *Fates help us.*

"That's yer message? That the three of us go to Kelpie Cove to give the sea folk a warnin'?" Alaric asked.

Edelin nodded, but a smile pulled at her lips. "I find when visiting the coast, caves make for a wonderful place to rest, don't you?"

Alaric frowned, but Edelin was already walking away, crossing the clearing toward her own tent.

"Fuckin' seers an' their cryptic bullshit," Alaric mumbled, loud enough for her to hear.

"I find it is easier to agree with witches, especially when a seer is involved," she replied without so much as a glance back, like she wasn't referring to herself in third person. "You'd do well to do the same."

THE NEXT MORNING, as Kane disassembled our tent, I went to find my grandparents. We were all leaving camp today, going our separate ways to do our next part in the war effort. Whether we would get to meet again would be a luxury only the fates could decide. I found them sitting around the campfire, bowls of thick porridge warming their hands.

I cleared my throat. "Looks like we're leaving soon," I said, my voice thick with emotion. "So I guess this is goodbye, for now?"

Their eyes met mine, and Drayke stood, placing a strong hand on my shoulder. "May the strength of a Dyvrad, and the wisdom of fates, guide you true and keep you safe, Evangelia," he said.

The fire crackled away at my back, but its warmth couldn't drive away the chill from my bones. I hadn't expected this goodbye to be a hard one, but I knew more of their story now. They'd told me piece by tragic piece over the last week, and they no longer felt like the strangers they'd once been. Fates, we'd even had our first falling out and managed to come back from it.

Drayke let his hand drop and Vyara crossed the space between us next. She wrapped her arms tight around me. She smelled like cedar embers after the flames died down. Like my mum. Like home. I hugged her back, and she dropped her voice low, "Stay safe, little flame," she said, then in my ear, whispered, "Look after your mates, as I know they will look after you."

We hadn't spoken of my relationship with Kane and Alaric, and though it had been approved by the fates, it was still nice to have her blessing, which was what her words felt like as they sunk in. It was a weight I hadn't known I was carrying until it lifted with her quiet words.

CHAPTER 22

Nekane

After days of walking, the trees finally fell away, disappearing to a great expanse of nothingness on either side. For the first time in my life, I stepped on the soft sand of the Dezrothian coast and I found myself enraptured by the waves. Like a team of horses charging under the moon and crashing on the beach, retreating and then charging back, relentless in their pursuit of the shore.

"So, this is Kelpie Cove when it *isn't* plagued with blood and death?" I eventually asked Alaric, who stood several paces ahead, casting a large shadow across the other-wise moonlit ground.

"Aye."

"It's so… peaceful," Eva breathed, swaying side to side slightly, testing how the sand moved beneath her worn boots, like she was rocking to music only she could hear.

Alaric turned back toward us, shaking his head. "Nah," he said. "We might have beaten the Mount Mortum ships here, but Kelpie Cove is far from peaceful."

"Let me guess, my father had a hand in that?" I asked, adding yet another wrong I would one day have to right, to the already too-long mental tally. Even if I didn't take the throne, which was looking more likely, now the Dyvrad's were back, and despite us not speaking about it formally yet, it was still a responsibility I needed to bear.

Alaric pulled a face, as though unsure how to answer. He eventually settled on, "The selkies are their biggest problem."

My brows dropped into a deep frown. Had my father really not done them some horrific injustice?

"Though, the selkies wouldnae be tryin' to claim the kelpie's land had yer father not fucked with theirs," he finished.

I breathed out a sigh. "Of course he did," I muttered.

Eva's stomach rumbled, and she tried to cover it with her hand, looking up at us apologetically.

We hadn't paused to eat since leaving our last rest stop at sunrise, and it was the dead of night now. It was no wonder her body was demanding she did something about that. With any luck, we all could soon.

While Alaric knelt down to feel around inside his large pack for something, Eva reached into her pocket and grabbed a handful of nuts. Then tossed them into her mouth for several chews, before washing them down with a glug of water from her canteen.

"Want some?" she asked, and I nodded. It wasn't much, but it still beat the broth.

I did the same and in the eerie silence, my mind went to Edelin's vision of the battle. I hadn't been expecting to find such beauty here, but even the most awe-inspiring places could be ruined by war.

Not just in appearance, but memory, too.

"Where is everyone?" Eva asked when neither kelpie nor selkie showed, despite several minutes having passed since we'd been standing on their beach.

Alaric shrugged. "It's the middle o' the night, most will be sleepin'. They will have a few night guards standin' by, though. Watchin' us from the trees and sea."

Squinting toward the Dezrothian waters, the only movement was the natural rhythm of the ocean. Alaric's keen eyes focused on the trees lining the sand, but if anyone was out there watching, they were doing a good job of hiding themselves.

Eva tucked the canteen away and swung her bag onto her back once more. "Let's go find one then, I guess," she said.

We set off up the beach and it didn't take long before a horse-like creature trotted out of the forest, making their presence known.

"Here we go," Alaric muttered under his breath. "They can be… difficult to deal with. Just dinnae let them tempt yeh to climb on their back."

"Why?" Eva asked. "I mean, I don't plan on it but, why?" she added.

"Kelpies have several gifts, but the most deadly to fae like us is the ability to trap you," I said, recalling reading about them in the library. "Think of their magic as an invisible saddle you can't escape from."

"Aye," Alaric confirmed. "No' bein' able to dismount, they'll drag their prey into the water, drownin' them. It's partly why the selkies best them so often. Selkies cannae be drowned."

Eva swallowed, "Noted."

As the creature came closer, I took in its dark body, almost black, but the moonlight highlighted the deep green it truly was. Its mane and tail had strands of seaweed knotted in it, as though it had just rose from the depths of the sea.

Patchy scales glinted through the coarse hair covering muscular legs, and if memory served, the hind two would change to a powerful tail once in the water. Ensuring the kelpie could propel itself, and any victims, into the depths.

Lips peeled back in warning, revealing a set of sharp teeth that would meet no resistance ripping its victim to pieces.

"Hey you there, why the long face?" A voice said, loud and crisp and... only inside my skull.

"Alaric. Eva," I breathed, uncertain at the sudden intrusion. "Please tell me you heard that too?"

"Aye." Alaric confirmed, while Eva nodded, her eyes wide in alarm at the kelpie. The voice was unmistakably male, and far more friendly than I'd expected.

"I could ask yeh the same thing, kelpie" Alaric said.

"Me?" the kelpie asked, lifting a foreleg and angling its hoof to point at itself while looking around, feigning confusion. *"I'm fine. Never been better. You three, though? No offense, you look like someone just skinned you, scaled deep, and ran off with your mane."*

"What?" Eva asked.

"Miserable," he clarified. *"You look miserable, mare. But worry not. I know just how to cheer you up."*

Eva raised a brow.

"How about a nice ride up and down the shore?"

"No offense taken," Alaric said, canting his head to the side. "But we'll skip the ride."

The kelpie backed up several steps, and despite me never having seen a horse look offended before, it was somehow apparent on his face. He huffed a neigh, then back inside our heads said, *"Fine. But the offer is always available to you. Though while you're here, how about putting those nimble fingers of yours to good use and getting this fates awful seaweed out of my locks? You wouldn't* believe *how itchy it gets."*

Eva and I shared a quick glance with Alaric. Sure, we'd expected him to try to trick us onto his back and into the water, but subtle about it, he was not. Alaric shook his head once, then clenched a large, calloused hand into a fist as he fought off the same sudden wave of compulsion trying to wrap itself around me. Though nimble wasn't a word anyone would ever use to describe Alaric, the kelpie hadn't seemed to notice. Then again, Alaric's fingers would have a better chance at fishing seaweed out than hooves.

"We dinnae have time for yer tricks," he said. "Where's Maximos?"

"Who's asking?" The kelpie replied, his equine eyes suddenly suspicious and narrowed.

"The fae who's just walked for three days to deliver him a message," Alaric said.

"What message? I will give it."

"A warnin' from a seer who witnessed the demise of your entire herd."

The kelpie rolled his eyes. *"Ugh. It's the selkies isn't it?"*

He swung his head to look down toward the water, making his matted mane swish to one side.

"I know their slippery ways. They might have Maximos fooled, but I *know. I've been on to them and their tricks for years."*

Alaric shook his head. "It's the–"

"It's always about the selkies with you two-legged folk," the kelpie whined over him and if I wasn't mistaken... pouting? *"Selkie this, selkie that. Well guess what, this is* Kelpie *Cove, not* Selkie *Cove. You know what? You tell those slimy seal freaks we know what they're up*

to and we're not going to stand for it. They think they can move our net and we wouldn't notice?"

A sarcastic laugh vibrated my brain.

"It's no' the–" Alaric started.

"–Like we haven't given them enough! They are just take, take, take. More, more, more. An extra centimeter here, an inch there. It's not like we haven't already given them a section of our waters after the king demanded it, not theirs, ours!"

As the kelpie ranted, seemingly oblivious to who we were and the price on our heads, an idea formed in the back of my mind. Somewhere deep where his tirade hadn't reached. I couldn't guarantee it would work, or even that it wasn't a terrible idea, but it was worth a try.

Alaric let out a low growl of impatience, but I rested a hand on his arm, giving him a look that said I'd take it from here. Clearing my throat, I said, "You're saying the selkies are moving the sea net to make your territory smaller?"

"Of course they are! You can't fool my eyes. They always move it, then grumble and threaten us when I move it back," he snorted.

"Well, that simply won't do," I said, raising my chin almost as high as my voice. "Not in my realm."

Eva and Alaric's eyes flashed with something I never wanted to see again, but I kept my focus on the male before us. I could explain later that hearing such pretentious words leave my lips repulsed me just as much as it clearly did them.

"That's what I keep telling Maximos!" The kelpie agreed, missing the sudden change in my tone and not understanding what I meant by my words.

"If Maximos refuses to do what is just, I will go myself. Order them to stop their nonsense," I said.

"What makes you think they will listen to you?" the kelpie asked, tilting his head and making a strand of seaweed break away and land in the sand as the wet hair unstuck itself from his neck.

"You don't know who I am?" I asked, incredulous. "What is your name?"

"Sherbet."

Interesting name. "Well Sherbet, it seems you are telling me you don't recognize the face of *your king*." I spat.

The expression on Eva's face told me exactly how close I was to matching Elikai's voice perfectly.

"K-King?" the kelpie stuttered. *"You ar–Oh, your majesty, you have to forgive me!"*

He closed the space between us and fell into a horse's bow, his front legs folding under him as his nose nearly touched the sand. Making himself sneeze and sending a cloud of sand around his face and more seaweed flying from his mane.

"I'm so stupid sometimes. Stupid, stupid, stupid. It's just... When you got me talking about the selkies... I just... They get under my scales, you know? Like the Kraken did to you last time you were here. With the late king. So sorry for your loss, by the way. Us kelpies understand loss."

"That's right, it made quite the centerpiece in my dining hall," I said. "And thank you," I quickly added, remembering his condolences.

Alaric shivered at my words, thinking back to that awful dinner. But even worse was the way Eva closed her eyes, as though she couldn't bear to look at me. I had to end this before I forever reminded her of *him*.

"Let's not reminisce on the past," I said. "You have suffered long enough dealing with the selkies. I will rid you of your woes with them, on one condition."

"Anything!" the kelpie said, straightening to stand.

I raised a brow at Alaric. It was time for him to take over so I could shake off the facade and stop making my mates so repulsed and uncomfortable.

"Get us an audience with Maximos at sunrise," Alaric said.

The kelpie's head snapped around to look at him, but Alaric's gaze was far away. Like something in the distance was distracting him.

A threat? Most likely.

My hand skimmed the sword at my hip on instinct.

"Done," Sherbet said. *"Do you need somewhere to rest? Some food? Shelter?"*

"Nah. We've a place to stay," Alaric said, shaking his head.

I raised a brow at Alaric, *we did?* I wondered. Eva, finally able to look at me again the moment I dropped the pretense, gave me a look that said she was just as confused as I.

Neither of us would question him in front of the kelpie, though. If Alaric didn't want to take him up on the offer of somewhere to stay, it would be for good reason.

CHAPTER 23

Alaric

"Fuckin' seers'," I mumbled when the kelpie eventually left, disappearing beyond the tree line, leaving my mates and I alone. When Kane had been impersonating Elikai, like Angel, I'd wanted to look anywhere but directly at him. It was uncanny how accurately he'd mimicked his twin, unsettling and not something I wished him to do again.

The idea itself, though, it was as brilliant as it was dangerous, as obvious as it was shocking. It was risky, and could bite us in the arse, but our goal was to get an audience with the kelpie stallion, Maximos, and Kane's deal would get us there.

"–Alaric?" Kane said with impatience in his tone.

I pulled my eyes from the cave that seemed to call for my attention despite its plain appearance; its mouth pitch dark and tucked in the towering cliff walls of the cove.

"Mind explaining why we are waiting until sunrise to meet with this Maximos?" he asked.

"And why are you cursing Edelin?" Eva added. "Again."

Even now, without looking directly at it, the cave entrance beckoned to me. An invitation to uncover the mysteries it held within. Made only more fascinating the moment I'd remembered Edelin's cryptic bullshit.

Running a hand through my matted hair, I said, "I think the witch wants us to visit that cave over there."

"Why?" Kane asked, his blue eyes never leaving the almost swirling darkness.

"No fuckin' idea. But yeh ken what she's like," I shrugged. "I reckon it's better to check it out sooner than later. I didnae want to risk no' havin' a chance after givin' our message to Maximos. There's no guarantee he will believe us, especially if he's seen the wanted posters."

"So you're saying you don't think Sherbet's a… sure bet?" Kane asked, his lips lifting at the edges.

"How long have you been waiting to say that?" Angel asked, rolling her eyes, but the tension in her shoulders loosened. I loved how he could do that for our female.

Kane shrugged. "Since he said it."

"How very un-Elikai of you," Angel said. "Seriously though, being the leader of the creatures here, Maximos is likely fully aware of the realms most wanted," she added, and we both nodded our agreement.

"What makes you think Edelin wants us to see a random cave so badly?" Kane asked. "Surely stopping the attack on Dezrothia would be a higher priority, no?"

I couldn't blame him for struggling to understand the point of a delay, especially given the stakes that brought us here. I was the one to suggest it and was just as torn between going with my head, or the strange gut feeling.

"She said when she visits the coast, she always likes to find a good cave to rest in." I winced at how ridiculous it sounded out loud.

"It's probably nothin', yeh can just ignore me. We can jus' find the kelpie. Take him up on his offer."

But I still couldn't shake the pull. Or the odd sense of knowing we had to go. There was something to the witch's words, besides her just being a bit mad.

Angel's shoulders sagged. "Except, we do have to go," she sighed. "She wouldn't have said something like that if she didn't mean anything by it. She's the reason I have a famil–"

"We're yer family," I growled.

"I mean blood relatives," she said, placing a hand on my arm. "It's thanks to her I am no longer the only dragon in Dezrothia. It's thanks to her prophecy the rebel leaders held onto hope and didn't give up for hundreds of years. You included. She never says anything without meaning."

"Eva's right," Kane agreed, "We shouldn't ignore it."

"Aye, alright. Let's get this outtae the way," I said, rolling my shoulders.

Relief lifted a weight from them as we headed for the cave, which either held all the answers, or absolutely fuck all.

"YOU'RE SURE THIS IS IT?" Angel whispered as she peered inside the glowing cavern.

"She wasnae exactly specific, but..." I tried to think of the words without sounding like I had lost my mind. "It feels like it is. It feels right."

"I feel it too," Kane said.

"Yeh do?"

Kane nodded. "Like a powerful source is calling me inside."

"Mm-hm," Angel mused. "But I can't decide which way I should run. Toward it, or as far from it as possible."

I nodded and took the first step as though my leg was being controlled by an invisible rope. Angel and Kane followed. Whether because they trusted I knew what I was doing, or because they were experiencing the same pull, I wasn't sure.

It was cool, yet comfortable, unlike the frigid air outside. The moonlight at our backs hit blue, luminescent crystals which lit our path. They cast an ethereal light that danced across our skin, giving the otherwise dull cave an otherworldly feel. My eyes squinted as I tried to make out details in the dim, unsure if it was shadows or something more moving in the distance. When something I was certain wasn't just the light playing tricks flashed in front of me, I forced my legs to pause in place.

I held out an arm to keep Kane and Angel back, but they'd already stopped.

The caves' echoing silence yielded to a warning growl. And a shadowy figure made itself known, drifting into a spotlight that wasn't there a blink before. As the thing approached, I watched its threatening stalk wearily and pulled my blade from my back, readying it in my palms, its heavy weight a necessary reassurance.

Then two more appeared at either side, standing much like the three of us were. The shadow creatures were twisted and indistinct, as though they weren't really there at all, while being everywhere at the same time.

I swung my blade at the one opposite me, expecting a clash of steel against whatever the fuck their smokey weapon was to reverberate up my arms. Instead, it was like swinging a sword through mud, as though the air itself was resisting my movements.

Sweat beaded across my skin as the three spawned more and more shadow creatures until they swarmed us. No sooner had I cut one down, another took its place. Awareness slithered up my spine, sending goosebumps up my arms. I called my wolf sight to me, hoping it would help discern the difference between what was shadows, and what might be potential foes.

There wasn't time to contemplate what the attackers were, magic or otherwise, I had to push on. To fight. To protect.

But it was never-fuckin-ending. The more I cut down, the more appeared–

My attention drew away at the sound of a scream.

Not any scream.

Angel.

But that couldn't be right, because Angel had been right beside me, and the cry for help was far more distant. I spun, swinging my sword in a circle to give myself some breathing room. Where were Kane and Angel? I couldn't see either of them.

Fuck.

When did they leave? Where had they gone?

I searched for a tunnel, an opening, an exit.

They've left me. They've finally worked out that I'm not worthy of them. Two royals…

My mind was fuzzy, like the intrusive thoughts were put there by something else. Like they weren't my own.

Before I could shake them, or convince myself they weren't true, a blade sliced down my face. Its path, reminiscent of the one which scarred it all those centuries ago —when my father trained me to fight, preparing me to join the horde.

The shadows took on forms as more memories surged forward, replicating what happened at some of the worst times in my long existence. I fell into them, or perhaps was pulled, because they weren't a place I went willingly. I'd spent centuries burying them, locking them away to never be seen again.

First the blade my da' cut me with. Forever marring my face as a young lad.

Working in the horde, being sent on hunting parties.

Killing my friends and allies to gain trust in the castle.

Fighting my beast, hunting for blood on desperate nights, waking in the mornings covered in sticky crimson, fearing for what I had done.

Gaining the notice of the king after being the sole survivor of a 'thrakos' attack that had killed the previous general and being awarded his position.

Seeing my mother with Axel for the first time. Her telling me she would be taking care of him. Tasking me with teaching him how to control his beast.

The king sending me out with word to the villages he had twin sons born. And how his queen died in the process.

They kept coming, making it hard to breathe. Reminding me I was alone, that I would carry the burdens of my life alone.

I will forever be alone.

I couldn't stop it. The lid had been peeled off, and the memories just kept coming. I was drowning in them. Centuries of guilt and regret, overwhelming me.

Those experiences taught me to lock away my heart, and later convince myself I didn't have one at all. Only someone without a heart can commit atrocities without guilt or remorse. I'd told myself the lie more times than I could count until it became true. Until I locked my heart down and the actions I had to take didn't plague me.

They'd made me hate myself, what I was, and what I would become.

All so I might aid a fucking prophecy to come to pass.

"Why?" Kane had demanded not so long ago when he found out my multitude of sins.

"Because I had no fuckin' choice." I'd said to him. Like that was a good enough excuse.

It was what I told myself to survive what I had to do. To continue on the path I had been put on. I didn't have a choice if I was to survive. It was my fate.

Though my actions probably cemented me as an evil bastard in the thoughts of many fae. I wasn't. Not really. But they shaped me. They shaped me to be the male I was right fucking now. A male who was capable of helping us with this fates-forsaken war.

A male worthy of love.

Worthy of my two mates.

The memories I'd created with Kane and Angel began to creep in, a breath of fresh air after being suffocated by my sins. They chased them away, not completely but pushed them back. They couldn't replace the pain, but they softened the blow immeasurably.

Enough to breathe. Enough to see. Enough to know that even in the darkness, I was not alone.

I would escape this cloud of misery because I had to. I would find the fae whom I loved so deeply it scared me. It wasn't a choice.

My self-loathing had no place between the three of us.

Dezrothia was the realm I was fighting for. But Angel and Kane? They were *who* I fought for. They were my motivation now.

My blade felt suddenly light in my hand, and I lifted it, slicing through the air. It cut through as if it weighed nothing. Each swing hit its mark, slicing through the shadows and dispelling them back to wherever the fuck they came from.

I glimpsed a way out as the cluster of shadow-foe finally thinned. The exit I was certain hadn't existed before called to me louder than even the cave itself had. It was like the fates were truly calling me to it.

The closer I got, and the fewer enemies I faced, the brighter the crystals on the walls seemed to glow. Their light was leading me on the right path. Back to them. Because we were stronger together. Because *I* was stronger when I believed that.

I just had to rid myself of these shadows.

The exit seemed to be a shimmering beacon of hope as I drew nearer. The fight roared on, the smoke continuing to press in. But as I began to understand these were *my* demons, manifesting in a way I could physically combat them, my strength against them increased.

As the last shadow figures exploded into wisps, I sprinted to the exit. My breathing labored as the desire to get to my mates drove my feet faster.

The end of the tunnel opened into a massive, cavernous room. As I skidded to a halt, the two fae my mind obsessed over and wanted more than life itself, lay motionless on the cold hard stone.

Angel's scream still echoed in the chamber, a fragile thread that linked me to her. Males were circling her utterly drained body. An arm lying at an awkward angle, obviously broken from them holding her down as they drank. Raspy breaths sounded from under the snarls of the shadowy males that took turns making sure not a drop remained in her veins. A rumble pushed up my throat as a roar pushed out of me.

Kane was motionless, an arm stretched out to reach her. Though he was just shy of making contact. His face angled away from me, but the pit in my stomach told me his blue eyes would be unseeing. They had drained him fucking dry and now they'd done nearly the same to my female.

My mates were dying. I was running on borrowed time.

Seeing them like that broke something inside me. They were mine to love, mine to protect, mine to drink from. No other would *ever* taste them.

I charged. A primal ferocity guiding my actions as I carved a path through the writhing tide of shadows. Every swing, slice, and cut I made was a defiance against what was happening. I needed to close the distance between us, but for every stretch of ground I fought through, my mates kept getting farther and farther away. Like something in the very essence of the cave didn't want us together.

Well. Fuck. That.

It sent wave after wave to block my path, but nothing was going to stop me now. If I needed to be an unstoppable force to pull them back to me, then that's exactly what I'd fucking be.

"Alaric!" Angel's voice tore through the cavern. Its anguish and urgency shredded my heart, knowing I wasn't getting to her quickly enough. It firmed my resolve. *I will reunite with my mates.*

The onslaught of the shadows increased, as if they sensed the desperation leaking from me. Each movement, every swing, and every enemy killed reminded me time was short and precious. It wasn't something I could waste as it trickled through our fingers like sand.

As the seconds slipped by, I spent another calculating the quickest way to outwit the darkness. But the harder I tried, the more futile my efforts were. I was being forced to give up.

Giving up is not in my nature.

"Is this the fate you wish for?" A chilling voice whispered through my mind. It's cruel words, a seduction that slowly emerged from the heart of the darkness.

They sowed seeds of doubt in my mind. But I couldn't dwell on the meaning. If I lost focus, I would fall, too. And take everyone straight to the fates' embrace.

Adrenaline surged in my veins as I doubled my efforts. Every arc and swing of my great sword was a defiance against the malevolence of the voice. My assailants pressed on, unyielding in their insistence to prevent me from reaching my goal.

Yet, in the viciousness of battle, a moment of clarity hit me. My mates were my beacon of hope, and the thrakos no longer lusted for blood. The enemies dissolved in a mist of black, returning to wherever they came from. My breaths came ragged, sweat trickling down my face, my arms trembling as the adrenaline rushed from me, leaving exhaustion in its wake.

I moved as fast as I was capable of on such weak legs. Working to get back to them, only to find them no longer prone on the floor. I had to get my breathing under control. Closing my eyes, I listened to the world around me, listened for clues to where they were.

A faint thread pulled me again, a connection I was certain was them. I allowed my instincts to guide me, pulling me along another tunnel surrounded by those blue glowing crystals. I moved forward, not caring what my destination was as long as I reunited with Angel and Kane.

I would find them, and I would never let them go again. I was worthy of them and the happiness they brought me.

A gust of wind whipped past my face, cold against the sweat that still coated my brow. My footsteps were a drumbeat, echoing as I moved with a singular purpose and urgency propelling me forward. A new archway appeared ahead, its radiant light so blinding it burned to look at it directly. As I neared the glow, frigid air washed over me, and everything changed.

I was on my knees in the grass, my hands covered in blood. Sweat dripped into my eyes. Not just sweat, but tears, too. My gaze lifted from the broken body slumped over my lap, and found thousands more unmoving bodies, of all shapes, sizes, and races.

One after another after another.

For as far as my keen senses could reach.

CHAPTER 24

Nekane

My heart pounded with the inherent knowledge this was no ordinary place. There were mysteries here that wanted to be solved. Though I had a feeling no single fae could hope to unravel them all.

I followed the wall, letting it lead me deeper into the cave, willing it to show me its secrets. My footsteps echoed as I took each careful step, tugged forward, as though someone had tied a rope around my middle and was pulling me toward whatever lay ahead.

Eventually, the narrow stone walls opened into a large, cavernous space. In the center sat a pedestal, gilded in gold and encrusted with every precious gem I'd ever seen, and some I hadn't. I took measured steps forward, letting the strange stirring in my gut lead me. Laying on it was a roughly bound leather book; aged and well-worn. It looked like it had been loved over several fae lifetimes. It seemed out of place on such a beautiful plinth, yet ancient enough to be the most deserving at the same time.

The tome gave off a crackling energy, like a thunder and lightning storm hummed around it. I slowly reached for it, my hands trembling with awe as I brushed the soft leather of the cover. Pages rustled as it flew open and started searching for a chapter of its own accord. I watched in fascination as foreign symbols and markings danced across the parchment, a long-forgotten script not seen by the fae in millennia.

A language of kings and queens long departed from this world.

The grimoire beckoned me to read it, promising power beyond my wildest dreams. Tantalizing secrets that offered to unlock untold potential. The ability to change fate itself. Yet, for all its allure, the words on the pages remained elusive, like fragments of a dream that slipped away upon waking.

The temptation to take the book, to use it to win against my power-hungry brother, consumed me. My hands reached out as whispers told of how I would understand its pages if I just claimed it. Took it for myself. It was intoxicating. It was all I wanted, everything I needed. Promises of the chance to secure lasting peace for our realm, the respect of the fae, and to lead a fair reign after the horrors of my father and brother before me. To share a peaceful life with my true mates.

My mates…

I snatched my hands back and glanced around the room properly for the first time.

They weren't here.

How had I not known? Where had they gone? Were they looking for me when I wandered off deeper into the network of tunnels? Or had I fallen behind when this book called to me?

"It could be yours. It could change everything."

I spun around, finding a dark figure waiting for me just beyond the pedestal.

My heart skipped a beat, torn between desire and apprehension. Could I trust myself with such potent knowledge? Could anyone? Was I strong enough to resist the siren call of the grimoire's power? The ancient words seemed to weave a spell, each sentence chanting guarantees of dominion and triumph.

Yet, intermingled with the allure, a cautionary thread emerged. The memory of those who succumbed to the same temptations whispered through the shadows, a haunting reminder of the darkness that unchecked power might unleash. The grimoire's promise contrasted sharply with the images of destruction it conjured, setting the stage for a moral battle within my heart.

Apprehension filled my chest as the whispering from the book became more insistent.

"Take it. You know you want to."

Its gentle caress to my mind was an insistent press. What would Eva and Alaric do?

"What do you *want to do, Nekane?"*

Shaking my head, I spied an exit. Had they left that way when the words slithered through my mind?

The pages continued to unravel a tantalizing tapestry of secret knowledge, each unread sentence beckoning me closer to the precipice of a life-altering decision. I knew instinctively the book's words promised mastery over the elements, a chance to ensure lasting peace in our realm. Yet, in the same way, I knew it was… cheating.

My head fogged. The thought of wielding such power was intoxicating, a vision of victory that bloomed like a mirage in the desert of my uncertainties.

"It's so easy. Just pick it up."

The insidious whisper cooed in the recesses of my mind, but so did a reminder of the price that came with such power.

As though aware of my internal battle, the shadows conjured images of those who'd faltered, their ambitions morphing into obsessions that consumed them. Like it was something *I* should want for myself. Only, I shuddered at the thought of joining their ranks, of becoming a puppet manipulated by an insatiable desire for power.

Eva and Alaric's faces flashed before my mind's eye. My resolve hardened. I refused to be swayed by the grimoire's siren song, its promises now tempered by the warnings that danced at the edges of my consciousness. The absence of my mates only solidified my drive to make the right choice, to resist the seductive pull of power's embrace.

With my palms to my forehead and every ounce of willpower within me, I closed my eyes and took several deep breaths, and found myself counting back from ten. With every passing second, I focused on centering myself amidst the chaos of emotions swirling inside my mind.

When my mind cleared, I crossed my arms over my chest. Then, pushing my shoulders back, I shook my head. "I don't want your book," I said, my tone firm and decisive. "The knowledge it offers may be powerful, but the risk is too great." Of that, I was certain. "The price of such power is not one I'm willing to pay. I will not jeopardize this realm or my very soul for it."

As my declaration echoed through the cavern, the mysterious figure chuckled darkly and retreated through a concealed passage. Without hesitation, I followed, my heart racing with a sense of purpose.

Footfalls that were not my own echoed through the passage. I turned toward the sound. Emerging from the shadows was a figure cloaked in mystery, an enigma that seemed to carry the weight of ages on its shoulders.

A shiver ran down my spine as I met the gaze of the stranger. In their presence, emotions swirled like autumn leaves caught in a gust of wind. Who was this mysterious being? And what role did they play in my journey?

Their footsteps led me into a beautifully decorated chamber. In the center was a large four-poster bed, surrounded by several fae. Their faces were all grief stricken as they looked at something on the bed.

I took measured steps as I walked around, not wanting to disturb them. My breath caught in my throat as I took in a female. She was pale, sweat beaded on her skin as she took shallow breaths. My eyes fell to the bed, and a strangled gasp left me. Crimson stained the sheets. A small babe lay next to her, though her stomach was still rounded. I swallowed hard, realizing who this was.

Queen Kahina

My mother

Her eyes focused on me, a small smile pulling her lips as she paled impossibly further.

"My boys. My beautiful boys," she whispered, before her eyes fell closed and a clamor of fae shouting and moving filled my ears.

I was witnessing my birth. Why were they showing me this?

"You could save her. The book has the power to save her."

Visions of me growing up with my mother swirled in my mind, showing a life that could have been. No longer abused by my father, my mother favored me. She was there my whole life, protecting me. It was her that taught me to be a good male. Taught me how to rule. Taught me love.

Emotion choked me, tears pricking my eyes. It was everything I could have ever hoped to have had.

But it wasn't real.

Nothing could bring her back. Not without rewriting the fates' will.

The shadowy figure that had led me there appeared again, the scene of my mother disappearing. Its head tilted unnaturally.

"Are you sure? You just need to read the grimoire."

"Never been more sure of anything," I said.

As the footsteps came to a halt, a palpable silence settled between us—a hush laden with unspoken questions and veiled revelations. Their form was obscured by smoke and shadow, their features hidden from view, yet their very presence seemed to carry a weight of cosmic importance.

"Who are you?" I asked.

The stranger's lips curved, a faint smile that held a glint of amusement in their eyes. *"You can think of me as a guide. A messenger through the currents of fate,"* they replied, their voice a melodic whisper that brushed against my consciousness. Their words carried an air of both ancient wisdom and intrigue.

"Fate? You mean to say it was the fates who brought me to this cavern? Why?"

To test me?

The figure's shrug was accompanied by a soft rustling of its cloak. The cavern's secrets, the grimoire's allure—it all seemed intertwined with a greater design, one that required my active participation.

My concern for Eva and Alaric resurfaced, and the stranger seemed to sense my unspoken worry. Their gaze held a depth of understanding that surpassed mere words. *"Your companions are safe,"* they said. *"Paths intertwine, yet each holds its unique journey. Trust in the bonds that unite you."*

Trust. The word resonated within me, a reminder of the unbreakable bond we shared. Eva and Alaric were more than companions; they were pillars of strength in times of uncertainty.

"What is that book? Why do you want me to take it?"

"Perhaps the book is *a test,"* the voice said, as though reading my earlier thought.

I wanted to ask whether I'd passed, but as quickly as the question popped into my mind, I found it didn't matter. *If the alternative is losing myself to the madness of power, I'd rather fail.*

A strange sense of gratitude and understanding was exchanged in our gazes with the thought, and I was filled with a renewed sense of purpose. The path ahead may be uncertain, but it was mine to tread.

The narrow passage wound deeper, the air growing colder. But with each step, I carried with me the knowledge that true strength was not found in the allure of power, but in the choices we make in its presence.

The walls crumbled around me, and in their place, a thick metal door stood alone, attached to nothing and seemingly leading to nowhere. I swung it wide, and on the other side… my stomach plummeted. I wasn't sure what it was called, or even if it had a name, but there was no mistaking it for what it was.

The place I'd hoped to not see for a very, very long time.

"This is it?" I demanded of the vast nothingness around me. There was no pain, no sadness, no joy. Just utter emptiness.

"It could be," the voice echoed inside my mind. *"Though one must remember, fate is not a rigid path; it is the choices one makes that shape one's destiny."*

CHAPTER 25

Evangelia

With only my racing heartbeat for company, I sped along the winding tunnels of the cave, not stopping for breath despite my lungs screaming at me. Every turn I took forced me deeper into its belly as I became more and more lost.

I couldn't remember how long we had been separated, or even when or how or why my mates weren't here. All I knew was the need to run, lest the shadows at my heels consume me. I took a sharp left, and suddenly, the walls were no longer jagged rock, but row upon row of trees, just like those found in the Fading Vale.

This I knew. This I was comfortable with. This I had done before.

Navigating crisscrossing tree roots. Ducking under broken branches. Swerving around hanging moss as it brushed against my cheeks.

Running from a faceless threat.

Forever running, only slowing once we put enough distance between our friends and foes. Not stopping until we found somewhere new to call home. Albeit briefly.

Only that wasn't right.

That wasn't my life anymore. We didn't run. We fought.

A quick glance over my shoulder confirmed the shadows hadn't relented. But they never would. So instead, I stopped dead, whirling around to face them, and lifted my chin in challenge. "I'm done running," I gritted.

The shadows morphed together into a giant male. And I knew instinctively the bulges at his shoulders and sword at his waist were horde issued uniform, despite the silhouette holding no real details.

I braced myself, ready for his attack. Ready for pain. Ready to fight him until one of us lost. But an attack never came. Instead, he swung his head back and cackled. The eerie laugh stretched on and on, growing louder and louder until it reached an unbearable crescendo.

My hands flew up to protect my ears from the ringing bellows, but it did nothing to shield them from the noise. My legs buckled, and I fell to my knees, closing my eyes and gritting my teeth. I had no idea how much time passed but when the ear-splitting shrieks became more distant, I opened my eyes to find I was curled up tightly in a ball on the floor.

The trees around me were no more. Below me was neither a stone path, nor the forest underbrush, but a rich red carpet. A chilling sense of déjà vu swept over me. I was in the castle throne room. But the foreboding familiarity wasn't from recognizing the throne or decor, but from the scene itself.

From the fae in the room with me. To the papers rustling in the hands of the royal advisors and the sneer in Elikai's voice as he chastised Kane for arriving late. The last time the prophecy had been read, I'd watched while concealed inside a secret nook, spying. Now, I was front and center, under the direct scrutiny of all eyes in the room.

My hands fidgeted, grabbing for the rings at my fingers. But they were gone. My body began to tremble as fear enveloped me. Every instinct demanded I hide myself somehow, somewhere. *Blend in*. Escape before they discovered I wasn't high fae at all.

Before they found out I was irrevocably in love with two of the males in the room, neither of whom were my fiancé.

No, Eva. That's not right. I shook my head. *This isn't real.*

My secrets were already out. They knew that not only one dragon, but three existed in Dezrothia. And the fates had blessed my relationship with the *former* general and the *once-upon-a-time* uninterested prince.

I forced myself to ignore the stares and look around the space. Unlike before, where the brothers had sat across from each other, a third chair sat at the table. Not just any chair. A throne. With dragons carved into the hand rests, and a deep red velvet back adorned with golden studs.

Augustus Regis's throne.

No. My grandfather's throne.

My throne.

The princes watched my every step as I moved slowly to take my rightful place.

Elikai seethed, hurling abuse I found I could easily ignore. He could call me what he liked, I was proud of who I'd become. I was proud to be a dragon and would never let another fae make me feel like I had something to hide, make me feel less than.

What I couldn't ignore; what broke my heart and made it bleed, was when I heard Kane joining in with his brother's taunts.

"What do you think you are doing, *princess*?" he sneered, his tone laced with venom as he spat the last word.

"I-I'm a Dyvrad–"

Kane's palms slammed down on the table, making it explode beneath his fury. "The throne belongs to the Regis line!" he bellowed.

Though I could see it was *Kane* talking, that it was *Kane* throwing his weight around, my head and what was left of my heart demanded it wasn't him. That it had to be Elikai. That the brothers weren't one and the same. Not even close to being as identical on the inside as they might look to some on the outside.

My stomach churned, and my mouth filled with saliva.

Why was Kane acting so strange? Did he hate me now that he knew royal blood flowed in my veins?

"Never," I growled at the shadow lurking behind the throne. "The crown will never–could never–come between us."

The shadow fizzled into smoke, which swirled around me, filling my lungs and eyes until I could neither see nor breathe. As quickly as it came, it was gone. And I found myself alone in the castle grounds, my twin daggers in my palms.

A stranger's voice penetrated my mind. *"You wield Mayhem and Chaos, is that what you sow? Or will you serve Victory and Justice?"*

More faceless figures emerged from the air, their forms flickering like ghostly apparitions before settling on one I knew by the aura he emanated alone. *Elikai.*

His expression twisted into a sneer that held malice and a hint of amusement. *He's not here*. Just like he hadn't been in the throne room. This was just another vision. A manifestation conjured by the fates themselves?

"Hello, whore. Did you seriously think you could win?" he said, then spat at my feet.

"This isn't about winning, Elikai," I said, pushing my shoulders back. "This is about the fae of this realm. The fae you have hurt and murdered. But the hunt will come to you. And when it does, just know, you deserve nothing more than death!"

The shadows jeered around me as the Elikai apparition started to laugh, eerily similar to the shadow giant's cackle.

"You think you have the power to end me?" he seethed. "No, pretty pet, you don't have the strength to do it."

He finished speaking, and a gust of wind sent leaves spinning around me. As they dropped to the floor, I found myself wearing an extravagant gown, relaxing on the velvet cushion of the throne.

How? I hadn't moved or changed. But here I was. Whatever this nightmare was, it had to be a test of some kind. From who, I wasn't sure.

An invisible shove forced me to lean forward, and without moving my mouth, I asked the shadow figures for a weapon.

A sword appeared in my hand, and Elikai was on his knees before me, his hands tied in his lap with magic blocking cuffs, and his mouth covered, stopping him from using his allure.

Slice his head from his neck for his insolence to his queen.

The thought was not mine, yet it somehow was. It was my voice, but cruel and cold.

But I couldn't.

I *wouldn't.*

No matter how much I wanted to, I couldn't kill my mate's brother out of pure vengeance. Not like this. On a battlefield, yes. In a dual where it was my life, or his? Absolutely. My life was tied to others I cared about too much to let die. But an execution while he was defenseless? The memory of the last time I saw my parents' faces flashed across my mind. I shook my head.

I will not lower myself to his level.

Unlike in the throne room, here I somehow sensed the weight of my mates' support. Their invisible presence was a steady anchor in the storm of emotions, even if they weren't physically with me. I clenched my sword-free fists and met Elikai's gaze. "You deserve justice," I said. "But not like this. The fates will determine what becomes of you, not my anger or vengeance."

As if in response, Elikai sunk into the shadows and the faceless figures rippled, their forms shifting as if in acknowledgment of my words.

"You coward," Elikai's voice snarled in the wind.

"No," I said. "Unlike your twin, you are your father's son. You kill indiscriminately and are driven by power and prejudice. One day soon, you will be tried and your punishment will fit the crime. And I have no doubt you will quiver and beg in the face of justice. For it is you, Elikai, who is the coward."

Suddenly, the oppressive atmosphere lifted, and I was back in the heart of the cavern, standing amidst the blue glow of the crystal stones. As I retraced my steps through the darkness, no longer running scared or trying to hide, a sense of relief washed over me, lifting an intense weight from my back.

I didn't know where I was, where my mates were, or much of anything. The only thing I knew for sure was the fates had challenged me. Tested my resolve. And I had emerged victorious.

With that thought, the corridor opened up into a grand hall, bathed in a gentle, ethereal light. Row upon row of fae stood before me, their expressions ranging from awe to reverence as they howled and whooped. I needed neither of those things, though seeing such joy on their faces gave me a feeling I wished I could bottle. The only fae I needed right now were on the dais at the other end of the room.

Their eyes found mine, and I smiled.

Alaric wore a full set of ceremonial armor. His hair was drawn back from his face and held in a leather strap, showing off his scar with pride. Kane was in full royal regalia, a stunning black-on-black suit, with a sword at his hip and his dimpled smile lighting up his eyes.

The celebrations taking place around me while I crossed the room were as surreal as they were welcome. And I knew in that moment that the sight would forever be what I held onto whenever hope felt like it was escaping us in the war ahead.

As I climbed the steps, Alaric and Kane each took a step to the side, making space for me in the middle. I took my position, and then, as though all three of us were compelled by the same allure, our hands clasped together.

Upon contact, everything fell away.

Almost everything. Blinking several times to adjust to the much darker space, I found myself sitting in front of a fire in an otherwise sparse cavern.

I sighed to see my males were still beside me. Alaric on his hands and knees, fighting to regain control of his breaths as they came too fast, but otherwise he was in one piece. Kane sat up straight, glancing between me and Alaric, his own palms and the fire. No, he wasn't looking at the flames, but *through* them.

On the other side were three figures whose mere presence shook me to my core. I blinked. They were still there. I blinked again, then rubbed my eyes with the back of my palms. And my jaw hit the floor.

Three strangers to me, yet their identity was undeniable, despite us never having met. There wasn't a fae in Dezrothia who could mistake these beings for anything other than who they were.

"Is it truly you?" I whispered, squinting through the red and orange flickers.

The figures nodded in a strange synchronicity that made gooseflesh prickle up my arms, and a shiver down my spine. One a young child, innocence incarnate. The one in the middle was a young fae who appeared to have just come into their immortality. And the last an old fae, their face wrinkled as it told tales of their many, many years.

"Welcome to the realm of the Three Fates," one of them said in an androgynous voice. "Our congratulations to you all."

My eyes went wide before shooting to Kane and Alaric. I'm not sure what I expected them to say or do, I just needed them to give me some kind of sign that I wasn't imagining our deities' presence before us. My gut knew it was real though, in the same way I'd known the visions before weren't.

"Evangelia Dyvrad, Nekane Regis and Alaric Durand, you each passed our tests, proving you are worthy," the one opposite Kane said, the old fae.

"Worthy?" I asked. "Of what?" Then I remembered myself and quickly shut my mouth tight.

I wasn't sure what the common courtesy was when it came to speaking with the fates, or if there even was such a thing, given how incredibly *un*common it was. The only fae I knew to have any kind of close connection with them was Edelin, and she'd never really explained how close of a connection it was.

"Worthy of our help," one answered.

"With the war?" Alaric asked as he tried to sit up, but his arms shook under his own weight. His head sagged as though too heavy for his neck. Concern knitted my brow. What had happened to him?

Together, the fates let out a soft laugh, but there was no humor in it.

So that's a no to helping us with the war then?

As though invisible hands were guiding me, my head twisted toward the fire pit and my eyes locked onto it. "Look into the flames one last time, brave fae," the young fate said, and the flickers danced and twisted, until they morphed into some kind of memories. More visions? Glimpses into the future?

I squinted to focus as several scenes flashed before me. From battle and blood, to celebrations and joy, to a vast, eerie nothingness. Death.

The celebration was the only one which was familiar. Exactly as it had played out before I'd somehow landed here. I watched as it repeated on a loop. They were three very specific, though very different, scenarios playing out.

A voice spoke from behind the flames, and I couldn't move my eyes from the fire to look at the source, even if I'd wanted to. "These are but three of the thousands of possible outcomes of your war and revolution."

"You each experienced a glimpse of a potential future here this day," another of the fates said.

Alaric cursed as Kane sighed. Though I couldn't move, I could see the glow of the fire reflecting off their faces from my peripheral vision and desperately wanted to know what they were thinking.

"None the same future as the other," added the third, and Kane and Alaric let out the breath they must have been holding, neither willing to let it go first. Their shoulders visibly relaxed as they continue to stare dead ahead. I frowned.

I'd seen the fae of Dezrothia free and celebrating with my mates and I, at what seemed to be an important, but joyous occasion. Of all the visions the fates subjected me to before now, that one had been the most real.

Then again, that was likely only because it was the only scenario I desperately wanted to be real. Yet it was an illusion, a pipe dream, no more possible than the other horrifying sights in the fire. Just one in thousands of possible endings. But it was possible. And there was no doubt in my mind that it would be worth risking our lives in order to live and breathe it for real.

My stomach twisted as it dawned on me why my mates were so shaken. Had Kane and Alaric lived through us being defeated? Had they passed their tests, only to experience death and tragedy at the end?

As much as I didn't want it to be true, I knew the answer.

But what did all of this mean? Why would the fates test us, only to show us all different ways in which the dice may fall at the end of the war?

CHAPTER 26

Alaric

"You think to question us, Evangelia Dyvrad?" one of the figures snapped at my female, despite her not doing anything of the fucking sort.

I growled and the compulsion to stare into the contrasting futures presented in the flames fell away. Though my physical exhaustion was slowly fading, I couldn't shake the uncomfortable feeling stirring in the pit of my stomach.

With my head no longer feeling like it was made of lead, I got a proper look at them—the three fates in the flesh, appearing as the three stages of immortality,

Her eyes were wide and though her mouth was moving, she was struggling to find or form words under their scrutiny. "I-I didn't question–" she stuttered.

"You don't need to speak for us to hear you."

Fucking, great.

It shouldn't be a surprise that our inner thoughts weren't safe in their presence, but the knowledge made it no easier to control where your thoughts went. Besides, Angel wasn't the only one mentally questioning their motives since entering this cavern.

Fae weren't supposed to question the fates. Fuck, most fae didn't question any who were higher than them in society or rank, so living deities were obviously a hard fucking no.

But of course we had questions. Like why had they decided to show themselves to us now, of all times? Why had they tested us or needed us to prove our worth? Had we not proven ourselves by surviving all the shite they'd put us through already? Not just in the lives we'd lived together, but separately and alone.

If they wanted our unquestioning respect and loyalty, maybe they shouldn't have given Kane a father who would beat him black and blue? Or had Angel witness the cold-blooded murder of her parents. Or let me do the despicable shite I spent most of my life hating myself for, just so I could live long enough to help with a prophecy *they* had given.

My nails dug into my palms as I clenched my fists. I couldn't count how many times I'd cursed them inside my mind over my lifetime. Fuck, I'd said it out loud enough times too. They deserved to hear every stray thought we'd thrown their way.

But would they hold them against us now?

I shook my head. Fuck it. It didn't matter. If they'd wanted us to only think happy thoughts where they were concerned, maybe they shouldn't have been such fucking cunts to us so often over the years.

Three pairs of eyes landed on me, but I fought the desire to back track or apologize. They *had* been cunts, and they knew it. Everything since entering this cave had been a mindfuck, and I was running out of fucks to give.

"F-Forgive me," Angel said, and I wanted to steal the words before the fates heard them. "I don't mean to question you. I just don't understand."

"Then we shall enlighten you," the one opposite me said.

My head was shaking. Did we want to be enlightened? By *them*?! Would I even be able to handle what they had to say when what they'd shown me so far had been filled with so much pain and trauma?

As though she could read minds too, Eva's hand landed on mine and squeezed. With her skin against mine, I took a deep breath, and unclenched my fist on the exhale. Ready as I'd ever be for whatever un-stomachable shit sandwich they were preparing to feed us.

"Without our help, one of those futures will never come to be," the figure nearest to me, the child, explained.

What. "Why?" I snapped, leaning forward so much my hair was dangerously close to the flames.

The three fates tilted their heads as they looked at me. "Because, Alaric Durand, you won't make it to the final battle. None of you will."

Kane, who'd been worryingly quiet and still, swallowed. "Because death will come for us first?" he asked no one in particular, his eyes far away. Lost somehow or somewhere in his own head. Just another thing to hate the fates for.

Of the three of us, he was usually the one to snap us out of getting too caught up in the shit storm of our own minds. The one who didn't let us dwell for too long on our problems before lightening the mood. The one who was determined to keep fighting, keep moving forward, keep following our dream of a better life, whatever form that took.

Kane cleared his throat and brought his eyes up to meet the fates. "That nothingness... That's what awaits us?"

The fates nodded, and his shoulders slumped.

"How does it happen?" I asked. "If yeh can jus' tell us how, we can–"

"You think it's so easy to manipulate fate?" the child asked.

The one in the middle laughed. It was an eerie sound, with no joy or lilt.

The first one continued, "As we speak, your kelpie friend and his stallion are discussing a wanted poster with your faces on it. By the time you find the way out of this cave, they will have it surrounded. You will die the moment you step outside."

"Then we will be ready for it," I said, already glancing around for potential weapons.

All three of them laughed, and the sound made me bristle.

"We know little is easy where fate is concerned," Angel said. "But we've survived ambushes before. We can do it again." She looked between Kane and I, "Together."

"You think we underestimate you." More an observation than a question. I wasn't even sure which one had spoken; my mind was already reeling, strategizing our escape and what form might be best to take to fight the sea folk.

Thrakos, I settled on. Though I couldn't fly like Angel, my wings could still help get me back to shore should the kelpies somehow get the better of me and drag me out to sea.

Silence fell in the cavern. Were they waiting for me to answer?

I looked at Angel and she just shrugged, not knowing how to respond. Kane appeared to still be struggling to come to terms with whatever he'd *seen*. His usually bronze skin looked unnaturally pale.

Did I think they underestimated us? Abso-fucking-lutely if they thought we were no match for the kelpies. The one we'd spoken to earlier couldn't even get some seaweed out of his mane. I'd like to see him try to untangle an ax. Then again, I had no idea how large their herd was. I'd only ever met with small groups when visiting during horde business.

I cleared my throat. "Yeh said you'd help us?" I asked.

"We shall," the first fate said. "But not with your war."

"Then yeh'll help us evade the kelpies?" I asked.

"Not evade. Edelin Sybilline sent you here for another reason, too. Not just to meet with us, but to stop Mount Mortum's landing here."

"We can't very well stop that slaughter if we're busy dealing with our own," Angel mused.

I nodded. We needed whatever help they were willing to give. "How do yeh–" I paused, not sure how to word it, "*Foresee* our meetin' with the sea folk goin' down? With yer help, I mean."

"The meeting will take place tomorrow morning, but only Nekane Regis shall attend–"

"–No," I snapped.

"Alaric," Angel said, looking at me with pleading eyes. "Just hear them out. *Please*."

Closing my eyes, I took a few deep breaths. Despite my centuries-old anger at our deities, I wasn't going to refuse their help, even if that help involved doing something that went against every instinct within me. Aid from them didn't come often enough for me to question it. I needed to get my head straight and fast, so I didn't fuck this up for all of us.

"Why does Kane need to go alone?" I asked, my tone less murderous.

"Maximos isn't sure whether he believes the young kelpie messenger you met with. Sherbet has somewhat of a reputation and isn't in Maximos's inner circle. As with all communities, trust must be earned. The kelpies are no different and the risk that the intel is incorrect poses a great threat. After all, if you truly were who you pretended to be, Maximos would be going after the new king."

"Elikai is king?" Kane asked. "The coronation games are over?"

"Your brother has extended his games until an acceptable victor is found to lead the horde."

I frowned. An *acceptable* victor?

Angel laughed. "Of course, he has no intention of allowing a true winner to be found fairly. He plans to continue the games until one of a race he can stomach wins."

"We can neither confirm nor deny," the old fate said. "Elikai Regis' fate is complicated, and as we have already said, we will not help you with the war directly."

Kane sat up straighter. "So you are suggesting I go alone tomorrow, and pretend to be Elikai?" he asked, and they nodded as one. "I can do that," he said with a firm nod. "I'd rather go alone, anyway. My brother isn't a male I wish my mates to be reminded of, any more than they already have to be, thanks to us sharing a face."

"True mates cannot be swayed away from those they have bonded with over such menial nonsense," the oldest one said. Then reached inside the robe, swamping its form, and pulled out a large shell. Far too big to have been tucked inside a pocket.

Holding it out between wrinkled fingers and thumbs with nails so long they'd begun to twist and warp, the cloaked figure gave no explanation as to what to do with it, just said, "Keep this safe."

Fuckin' seers and fuckin' fates.

Kane took it with two hands and muttered, "Thanks," though what he was thanking them for, he was clearly as clueless as me.

"We shall grant you a second and final favor," the young one said, like the giant shell truly was their first. "A sanctuary of sorts to spend the rest of the night."

"Thank you," I said, actually really fucking grateful for that boon. "Do yeh ken where our bags and weapons are?"

"They are already waiting for you," the middle fate said, then waved a hand in the air and a fluorescent blue crystal, just like the ones I'd followed when arriving here, appeared, hovering in place.

"This crystal will guide you there," the ancient fate said. "You will know you've arrived when you reach a wall with a loose boulder. Remove the stone to reveal the first truly safe place any of you have ever slept."

"Thank you," Angel said.

The fates nodded slowly. "You have our word that you will be safe until morning. And you will know when it's time to leave."

CHAPTER 27

Nekane

"What just happened is impossible," I insisted as we followed the path lit for us by the blue crystal's glow. "Right?"

"The three of us being true mates had seemed impossible not long ago," Eva shrugged. "I'm pretty sure anything is in the realm of possibility at this point."

"Aye," Alaric agreed. "Even the realm of the three fuckin' fates."

The crystal's glow died out as we came to a dead end.

"Looks like we made it," Eva said, and my eyes briefly scanned the wall for a loose rock, but I was still having a hard time believing any of this.

My mind just kept taking me back to the end of my test from the fates. I'd never feared dying, not until my life was tied to my mates. I'd always assumed when we died, we just carry on, in spirit form, only able to communicate with others who'd also passed on. I figured I'd be able to get to know the mother I'd never had the chance to meet, while watching over those I loved and left behind.

But the reality of what had waited for me on the other side of that door–

Alaric slammed his palms against the wall, startling me out of my thoughts. He lifted a knee to kick out, and exactly as the fates had promised, the boulder subjected to Alaric's boot came away, leaving the rest of the wall otherwise in one piece.

I heard a splash, like it rolled into water, and frowned. Alaric's shoulder rose, then dropped. "Fuck it," he muttered. "Let's see where they plan for us to spend the night." He crouched down to lead the way through the gap the boulder had concealed, and Eva followed closely behind him.

I took a second to shake myself, turning the shell over in my hands, knowing I needed to get back to living in the here and now, wherever and whenever this was. The fates had given us a blessing of peace for one night. I didn't want to just exist with my mind elsewhere, I wanted to live it and enjoy it to its fullest.

"Kane?" Eva beckoned. "You're going to want to see this."

"Coming," I said, then tucked the clamshell under one arm and dropped down to crawl through the hole. The sharp rocks dug into my knees, but any discomfort was quickly forgotten as I looked up. My breath caught and my eyes tried to take in all the beauty before me at once, but it seemed impossible.

An expanse of crystal-clear water reflected an ethereal glow, allowing you to see all the way down to the smooth, rocky bed beneath. Surrounding the lagoon, rugged walls rose up, revealing intricate formations and textured surfaces, before reaching the stalactites covering the ceiling. Hanging like nature's chandeliers and only adding to the mystique of the surroundings.

On the other side of the huge pool lay three sleeping bags. Strategically placed on a flat section of the uneven floor, offering a cozy refuge within this otherworldly haven, where the tranquil ambiance was heightened by the subtle echoes of water droplets and the distant murmur of what I could only guess was an underground stream.

When I eventually pulled my eyes away from the entrancing beauty of it, I turned to my mates. The smiles lighting up their faces, so genuine and relaxed, compelled my lips to move.

"I love you both so fucking much," I murmured, bending slightly to place the shell down. I'd said it several times before, but it had never felt so brutally honest. Yes, the fates' vision had me shaken, but if anything in this realm could fight the emptiness of the other side from echoing right down to my bones, it was them.

As though understanding my internal struggle, Alaric's strong arms wrapped around me and his lips pressed down on my head in a firm kiss. I ran my hands up his spine, trailing my fingers over where his wings joined his shoulder blades. Even tucked away, it was still a sensitive spot.

Lust burned within me as Eva's eyes lifted to mine from behind Alaric, and I found a pool of heat simmering in them. Relaxing into Alaric's embrace, I ran my fingers back and forth over the tender skin and he let out a groan for me.

My gaze remained fixed on Eva and I watched, entranced, as she slowly stripped off her clothes. She stepped out of them, and her delicate curves descended into the pale cyan depths of the lagoon beside us. She sank into the steaming water and sighed as tension ran from her.

Stepping back, careful to dodge the shell, my fingers found the clasp of Alaric's leathers, yanking it with urgency as I wanted them both naked. With his help, we made quick work of pulling them down his thighs, releasing his cock. He threw his tunic off as I dropped to my knees.

His cock grew hard before my eyes, and I licked my lips. Any thoughts of death were fully vanquished. A splash from the pool grabbed my attention, and I saw Eva dive below the water from the corner of my eye. She didn't surface until she reached the pool's edge next to where I kneeled, that intense fire still ablaze in her gaze.

"What are you thinking?" I asked her.

"That we know we have tonight. That for the first time in my life, I have the word of the fates themselves that we will survive until morning." She was leaning her arms on the rocks now, laying her head down on them while she held my eyes.

"And how exactly do you wish to spend tonight with such a gift?" I asked.

Green flames danced in her gaze. "To start with…" she nibbled her lip, hesitating as a blush creeped onto her cheeks.

"Say it, Angel," Alaric cooed.

She took a deep breath. "I want to watch…"

When she trailed off again, I coaxed, "Watch what?"

"I want to watch as you take Alaric into your mouth."

My lips pulled into a smirk at one side. "You mean you want to watch as one of your males makes the other come undone?" I asked, lifting a brow.

"Shatter like fuckin' glass more like," Alaric murmured. It wasn't a challenge, more an observation of the last time we did this, but I decided to take it as one.

"Yes," she breathed, and I shuffled forward.

What our female wants, our female gets. It just so happened to be exactly what I was salivating for.

With one hand on his ass, my other curled around his shaft, I began to work his cock with my fist the way he liked. When the tip beaded with a pearl of precum, I let out a soft, slow breath against it.

Alaric's hand landed on the back of my head and he twisted my hair in his fingers, impatient for me to use my mouth. *That makes three of us.* I gave him my most wicked grin before letting him guide me.

As my mouth hovered over his head, our female's right arm dipped below the water, slowly tracing her skin as she went. Resisting his pull, I stopped short of taking him into my mouth.

Missing the movement that had given me pause, Alaric snarled. I tutted at his impatience, making sure my lips brushed his tip with every word even though they weren't aimed at him. They were for our female. "As I can't see *exactly* what your fingers are doing under the water, Eva, I'll set the pace," I said. "If I suck him slow, I want you to circle your clit nice and slow for me. When I speed up, you speed up. Are we clear on the rules?"

"Mmmhm."

"That's my good mate."

In the next breath, my lips were parting and Alaric, done with waiting, thrust into my waiting mouth.

"Uh-uh," I mumbled around him, knowing the vibrations from my throat would be wreaking havoc with his control. But like I'd told our female, I was setting the pace here. My game, my rules.

His cock was sliding between my lips in the next heartbeat, the salty taste of his precum landing on my tongue as I slowly went deeper. A growl of desire escaped me and Alaric's hips thrust forward, sending a jolt of pleasure through us both.

I gripped his firm ass harder, fingers digging into the muscle as he pushed his hips forward, grabbing my hair and forcing me to take him to the back of my throat. He didn't know how to let go of control, so I would need to take it from him.

"*Kane,*" he groaned, spurring me to move faster.

Sucking, licking, and worshiping every glorious fucking inch of his cock, all the while knowing with every dip of my head, Eva would be playing with herself, circling her clit faster while her pussy grew wetter and wetter. Fuck, the thought had my own cock throbbing harder, aching to be buried deep in her tight pussy with Alaric in my mouth... or better yet, my ass.

I peered up at Alaric through hooded eyes and saw his head was back, his chin high. His chest moved, panting in time with my practiced movements. Was he too close to his climax to bear watching Eva or I? Or just giving himself over to the sensations of my warm mouth against his throbbing shaft as I took him back into my throat. Taking another inch, I started to gag around him, my throat tensing and squeezing him tightly.

The hand on his ass shifted to caress his balls, stroking the sensitive skin and back to his hole. His back arched as a growl left his lips, his hips trying to move quicker under my attention. Eva's breaths were coming in pants as she watched Alaric fuck my mouth, the muscles in his thick thighs bunching as he fought the need to come down my eager throat.

Eva cried out, and I tried to slow my pace, wanting to draw out this moment, give Alaric a second to breathe while we enjoyed Eva's moans in the bliss of her orgasm, but he thrust in harder, hitting the back of my throat deeper. I coughed a laugh at his impatience, and he came instantly, like the vibration along his shaft severed the invisible thread he'd been holding onto.

I swallowed every drop before licking my lips as I moved to stand. "How was that, Princess?" I asked, watching Alaric's chest rise and fall, feeling pretty fucking pleased with myself.

"Just when I think I've seen the hottest thing I'll ever witness, you two prove me wrong," Eva eventually answered, her face blushed and breaths coming quickly.

I laughed at her naivety. "That was just the start, princess," I said, stripping my clothes.

Alaric nodded and lowered himself down into the heated water. With a playful look in her eyes, Eva gave him a wink and then dove under, disappearing for a few seconds and coming up for breath halfway across the pool. After a quick glance our way, she swam as though her life depended on it, heading for the far side where the sleep sacks lay.

Alaric and I shared a look. "I think our female wants chasin' down," he said, his voice filled with a promise to make her pay by withholding orgasms when he caught her.

My lips rose into a shit-eating grin. "Whoever catches her, decides her fate for the rest of the evening," I said, then using the side to spring from, I dove.

Water filled my ears, distorting the sounds around me, but the low growl which Alaric let rip from deep in his chest was unmistakable as he accepted the challenge.

Fates help Eva if he caught her first. Has no one ever taught her not to run from a hungry wolf?

Opening my eyes as I swam below the surface, I found her closer than I'd expected. The momentum from my dive meant I was closing the gap between my female and I fast. I used my speed as I kicked and before long, she was within reaching distance.

I stretched out my arm, but as my fingers grazed her calf, she quickly moved it away and changed direction, forcing me to follow. As I kicked faster, something grabbed onto my ankle and stopped me dead. *Alaric*. As I started to turn, intent on kicking free from his grip, Eva somersaulted under the water, then twisted out of it just as her feet met the bottom and pushed up. And up. Until she was out of the water completely.

Alaric's grip on my ankle vanished and as I turned onto my back to face him, he copied Eva's move. Flipping under the water and using the pool's floor to kick off and spring into the air.

My chest burned as my lungs begged for breath. As I came up and took a deep breath of air, I wiped the water from my eyes. I found Eva, her wings wide, flitting around the ceiling of the cavern, with Alaric using his own wings to give chase, though he could fly much higher than a few feet above the ground.

Unfortunately for Alaric, thrakos weren't strong fliers. No matter how much time they spent honing the ability, their wings weren't built for flight the way a dragon's were. Eva clearly knew that too as she hovered in wait, just out of reach. Only to lower herself down and then dart to the other side of the cavern the moment Alaric began to close in on her.

"That's cheating," I called, wishing in that moment I had wings to summon too.

"And you using your speed to catch me wasn't?" Eva called back, lowering down again with the biggest smile splitting her face. Just as Alaric neared her, she zipped away, giving him the slip again.

Her laugh bounced off the walls as Alaric cursed, "Angel, get yer arse down here," he ordered. "Don't yeh want me to fuck that pretty cunt? Yeh'll feel better than yeh've ever felt if yeh just let yerself be caught. I'll make yeh come so hard for me, don't yeh want that?"

I fucking wanted that.

Apparently our naughty little dragon princess did too, because Eva banished her wings and let herself fall back into the water, like an angel shot out of the sky. Alaric did the same, with far less grace thanks to the way flying exerted him so much, but he still managed to swim to her side, throw her over his shoulder and spank her naked ass with a loud, wet *slap*.

This was what it meant to be alive. Here with my true mates, enjoying each other and not worrying if someone is about to slit our throats while we sleep.

Her half gasp, half giggle as his palm came down on her now red cheek again was instantly one of my favorite sounds, so different from the vast silence of the other side. "Please tell me this is real and not the fates fucking with me," I muttered as I watched Alaric's hand soothe the red of her ass before dipping to her soaking pussy and soothing the pain with teases of pleasure.

Alaric whirled, his silver eyes swirling. He released Eva down from his shoulder, strode to where I stood and yanked me against his chest. "Yeh didnae die today, Kane," he growled and kissed me hard before I could reply, crushing me back until I was against the jagged stone wall of the pool. "It was jus' a vision, one possibility in a thousand fates."

I moaned into his mouth as I gripped my legs around his thighs, pulling him flush against me, breathlessly kissing him back as his cock, already getting hard again, ground into mine that was still demanding attention.

"Tell me yeh ken that," he demanded, tugging my lower lip between his teeth before pulling away. "Tell me yeh ken this is real and yer alive. Yer with me, an' Angel."

Was he saying this for my benefit, or his? Probably both. If Eva had seen the only happy ending to this war, it meant Alaric had seen the version which ended in a massacre of the rebels.

I swallowed. "If this is what it's like to be dead, I'd welcome it."

His growl was feral as he pushed his hips forward, grinding his cock against mine and causing that delicious friction he knew drove me fucking wild.

"I've never felt so alive," I said, flexing my thighs. "Anyway, you caught our mate first…"

He shook his head but let the subject drop. This night wasn't going to last forever, and we had to make it count. "Angel," he growled, holding a hand out to where she stood watching us. Eva's eyes were hooded as she took his outstretched arm and let him pull her through the water. "Yeh touched yerself with these fingers, didn't yeh?" he asked, glancing at the hand he held.

She nodded, biting down on her lip.

Lifting the hand to his lips, he took two fingers into his mouth, sucking the digits with a moan as he pulled them free, like her juices were the most delicious thing to his taste buds. He wasn't wrong, though as far as I was concerned, the taste of his cum was tied with hers.

Hooking an arm around Eva, he scooped her up, so she was sandwiched between us, balancing where my legs linked around his waist. She faced me, her clenched thighs tucked up either side of my waist to support herself, and her breasts in my direct line of sight, hard nipples begging for my mouth's attention.

Alaric's head dipped around her shoulder and she let her head hang back, exposing her neck. He kissed her, slow and sweet, until she began to moan for more. Unable to stand his teasing any longer either, I took a pert nipple between my teeth, then closed my mouth around the areola and began flicking my tongue against the peak. Her hips ground against my abs and I knew it wasn't just the water of the lagoon making her slick pussy so wet.

"I'm going to bite you now," Alaric breathed against her ear, and she nodded. As fangs descended from his gums, I released my leg hold on Alaric, planting my feet on the pool's floor, and tucked one hand under Eva's ass to support her while the other slid over her thigh.

Alaric punctured her skin with his teeth at the same moment I pushed two fingers inside her heat. She gasped and rocked against my hand as I circled her clit, teasing the swollen bundle of nerves as I moved slowly. She rolled her hips, trying to ride my hand as Alaric released his mouth from her. Every time her walls began to tighten around me, I would stop, letting that pleasure drift away. She was in a frenzy, begging to be filled more thoroughly, demanding that we let her come. I had every intention of obliging, and then some.

Alaric and I shared a look, communicating without words. Tonight we were going to destroy our female together. In the best possible way. But apparently, I would be the one who would be dictating what happened.

I nodded, understanding what he wanted, then inserted another finger inside our perfect female. "Alaric's going to fuck you now," I said, mimicking the way he'd announced his plans to feed. "And just as you think you can't come again, I'm going to join him. And when I do, I want to feel Alaric's cock against mine. I want to know every time he slides in and out, and just how deeply his cock fills you as we stretch your pussy together."

A moan fell from her lips as she hung onto my every word, Alaric holding her steady as I worked her with my fingers. Punctuating every syllable with a hard thrust. Her lips found mine, and she panted against my mouth. "Then what are you waiting for?" she purred, an attempt to make me lose control and give her what she wanted.

Alaric and I chuckled. "Easy now, Princess," I said. "All in good time. We want you to feel the burn of us stretching this perfect pussy around us. Feel every single movement that we make. We don't want to rip you in two, so you will have to trust me and do exactly as I say." She swallowed at that, tilting her face as she nodded.

"Aye," Alaric agreed, and under the warm water, his hand clamped around my wrist. With a quick tug, my fingers left Eva's pussy, her whimper of discontentment echoing around us. Alaric's shaft brushed against my knuckles as he lined up to her entrance. I wrapped my fingers around the throbbing girth, stopping him from thrusting up into her. After several long, hard strokes, I guided him to ease inside her. "Yer cunt is so fuckin' perfect, Angel," he groaned as he felt her walls wrap around him. "But yer not ready for us both. Not yet."

She gasped as she adjusted to his size, and I kissed her harder, swallowing the sound as our tongues dueled in her mouth. Alaric pushed deeper and her thighs tightened against my ribs as every muscle in her body clenched.

Releasing her mouth, I went to work on her nipples. Biting just hard enough for her to whimper at the sting and then sucking and teasing her with light licks of my tongue. She gripped my hair tight, a bite of pain that drove me to continue the torture that she so enjoyed.

The scent of Eva and Alaric's arousal combined with my own filled the towering cavern as moans echoed around the vast space. I basked in it, letting it all fill my senses as sweat, sex, and cries of pleasure enveloped me.

"Do it," Eva groaned, her words a plea and a demand at once as she begged for me to fill her too. She rocked on Alaric faster, moans tumbling from her lips as I teased her clit over and over, but never enough for her to come.

"No' yet," Alaric growled as he drove into her again and again. Her breasts bounced, making her nipple tug against my teeth as she rode Alaric like a fucking queen battling to assert her dominance.

And this female was absolutely every inch our queen, and dominance over us wasn't something she needed more of. She already had us exactly where she wanted us. Worshiping her body, in awe of her beauty, inside and out, and ready to let her fly over that sweet edge of oblivion.

She was so close. So fucking close.

My fingers found her clit again, and I circled it. Faster and faster in time with Alaric as he quickened his hips, driving into her with more ferocity, making waves crash in the water around us.

"Come for me," I groaned. "I need you so fucking wet." As I spoke, my breath tickled the flesh I gave torturous attention to. I could taste the salty sweat of her skin against my tongue as she moved with unparalleled passion, chasing the orgasm she'd been denied so many times already.

She cried out as she found her release, then moaned softly as I slowed the movement of my thumb but continued to devour her nipples. Two hard, aching points which I cherished between my lips like I couldn't get enough. I would never get enough. Even if we had hundreds of immortal years together, it'd never be enough. I would forever crave them, forever be an addict of what they gave me, of the way having them like this made me feel.

As Eva arched her back, my cock strained with impatience. Alaric's hips slowed to a stop, but his cock remained firmly planted inside her as he kissed and nipped her neck.

"She's almost ready," Alaric said, and I finally pulled away from her breasts to smile up at him.

My cock was pressed up against my stomach, trapped between mine and Eva's bodies. "Loosen your grip," I told her and she did, her thighs trembling after holding on so tightly from her delayed orgasm.

Alaric hooked her thighs over his arms, opening her to me. She hung her arms loosely around my neck, damp hair falling into her face as she looked down the line of our bodies like she was contemplating how I would fit too. We might have both fucked her before, but never like this.

I tucked the hair back behind her ear with my free hand and watched the water from my skin trickle down her cheek. She was so beautiful. Cupping my hand around the back of her head, I tilted her face up to meet my eyes. "You're sure you can handle us both?" I asked.

She didn't answer right away, and though I held my breath, I was glad she was giving it proper thought. No way would this be entirely painless, not to begin with at least, not while her body adjusted to fit us both.

"I want this," she finally said. "Please."

"We'll go slow at first," I promised, then released her face and ran my hand over her thigh, dipping it below the surface to where Alaric's cock filled her.

I started by adding just one finger. Fuck, she was so tight, so full already.

Alaric began to move slowly, rocking his hips, as I followed his movement with my finger. When Eva's moans grew more impatient, I added a second, letting her adjust again before a third.

She ground her hips, making us move quicker and leaning into her ear, I whispered, "I'm going to fuck you now, Princess."

Eva nodded, and I palmed my shaft as Alaric watched hungrily. Leaning back into Alaric's chest, Eva pulled herself up a little, using her arms around my neck.

I removed my fingers and Alaric pulled his cock out until just the head remained. Unable to wait a moment longer, I pressed my own in. Eva groaned, a shuddering breath between her teeth. She lowered herself down a little as Alaric and I pressed in a little further. The delicious friction from being sheathed so fucking tightly between her slick walls and Alaric's girth had me questioning how long I could make this last.

It was everything I had wanted this to be, and we had only just begun.

As we rocked another inch into her, she let out a sharp hiss.

We stopped immediately. "Yeh okay, Angel?" Alaric asked before I had a chance.

Eva took several deep breaths instead of answering. Eventually, she nodded and moved her hips again, lifting until only our heads were at her entrance. Then began to lower herself to take more.

I shook my head, stopping her. "Words, Eva," I insisted.

As desperate as I might be to do this, I needed to know she was alright throughout every step. I had to be sure we weren't pushing her too far or too fast.

"Yes," she said, lifting and rolling her hips, stretching herself until she held us both at her mercy, making Alaric and I shudder at the ecstasy of filling her so completely.

"*Fuck,*" Alaric ground out.

I swear I could feel every ridge, every vein, and every clench of muscles like this.

"Such a good mate," I praised when I realized that we were both fully seated. I paused to marvel at her, though I knew that if we didn't move soon, it would be too much.

Alaric gripped her jaw, pulling her neck back to kiss her deeply. The way she clenched around us and Alaric jerked, pulled a groan from my chest. Fuck, they felt amazing.

"Take it slow, Angel. Yeh control it, tell us, show us, whatever yeh want."

I nodded. "This is all you," I agreed.

With her nails digging into my skin, she lifted herself up once more. Then dropping down and sheathing our cocks farther inside her heat. Doing it again and again with every rise and fall.

Her eyes fell closed as she tortured us so sweetly. Alaric and I remained still, waiting for her to tell us when we could move.

Gasps of discomfort turned into groans of pleasure, and she picked up the speed of her hips as she became more used to the new intrusion.

"Okay," she said. "I'm ready for you to show me what you've got."

"Are you sure?" I asked, desperate to move. "You can take all the time you need."

"Do I need to beg?" Fates, she was incredible. "Fuck me, Kane. Fuck me with Alaric." She groaned between every demand as she ground her hips. "Ruin me. Whatever. Just fucking move."

I shared a look with Alaric and together we found a rhythm. Sinking in and out with slow, measured movements. I wasn't sure what she was expecting, but we didn't pick up the pace, just gradually thrusting deeper, taking it slow and savoring every moment.

"Oh, *fuck*, yes…" she panted as her grip on me became punishing. Her abdomen quivered with every breath.

"You are doing so good, Princess," I told her. "Look at you. Taking us both in your pussy. You're a fucking vision."

She whimpered at my words, her thighs trying to widen to take us even deeper. She clamped down, and I groaned as Alaric's cock slid against mine.

"Such a good mate," Alaric mumbled into her hair. "Lettin' us own yer body like this."

"More. Please. I want to come with you both inside me," she moaned.

Hotter words had never been spoken. I smirked at Alaric, who adjusted Eva on his forearms to hold her open for us. Alaric held still as I pulled my hips back slowly, teasing her with the movement, then slammed back in. I remained deep inside her and my hand found her clit, drawing gentle circles around it while Alaric withdrew. He thrust inside her, whispering a string of curses at the intense pleasure as she cried out her own.

The assault on my senses was too much. Alaric's hard shaft. Eva's tight pussy suffocating us in the most delicious way. Her swollen clit beneath my fingers. Warm water splashing against my flesh. Echoes of pleasure bounding around the cavern.

We built an alternating rhythm as we fucked her, making sure she was always filled with at least one of our cocks. Every time she clenched down or her walls fluttered, I slowed down and lifted my fingers from where I stroked her clit.

When she came, I knew we'd be forced over the edge with her, but I wasn't ready to let this end.

"Please," she begged. "I need to come so bad it hurts."

We lost our rhythm and became lost to the pleasure as she writhed. Her nails dug into my shoulder at the same time she took a handful of Alaric's hair. Her words became incoherent mumbles as we fucked her, our thrusts getting more frantic.

Just when I thought she couldn't take any more, she proved me wrong.

Just when I thought I couldn't feel any better with my mates, they proved me wrong.

Just when I thought I couldn't love them anymore, they proved me fucking wrong.

Sweat beaded on my forehead, mixed with the tidal waves of the pool we stood in. I tried to hold my orgasm back, but the lightning shooting down my spine told me I couldn't hold out much longer.

My thumb pressed down on Eva's clit, making tight, fast circles as I came. I pulled her in to kiss her hard, my hand fisting in her hair. My other hand moved frantically as I built Eva's pleasure, her body quivering as she tightened on us. She tried to keep rolling her hips, but she was locked in place as we kissed. Forced to take what we gave her, she began to curse our names against my lips.

"Fuck, fuck, fuck, fuck," Eva screamed, her orgasm crashing into her, and her whole body shaking with the intensity of it. I groaned as she strangled my cock, her pussy clenching against us as we continued to thrust into her. Alaric grunted, and it was the most feral sound I'd ever heard leave his throat, and Eva and I gasped as his hot come coated us.

Crushing Eva between our sweat slick bodies, I pulled Alaric in and kissed him like he had the only oxygen in the vast cavern and I was yearning for breath. Another orgasm washed over me hard and fast. My lips tearing from Alaric's, I leaned back against the wall and relied on its support to keep me from drowning as I gasped for more of that precious air.

I watched as my mates kissed just as desperately. Tonight we would take full advantage of the safety the fates' had granted us.

And I couldn't fucking wait.

CHAPTER 28
Alaric

By the time my mates began to stir, I'd lost count of how many lengths I'd swam of the lagoon. Just enjoying the weightlessness of gliding through the warm water; making the most of this moment before we were back to the realities of war.

Last night had been bittersweet; the most incredible, yet almost regrettable, night of my life. Not because I regretted a moment of how we'd spent the time, but because I now knew what it felt like to be the smuggest fucking fae in Dezrothia. And therefore knew exactly what we'd be missing the moment this bubble of safety inevitably burst and we were back to our reality of being rebels fighting for such freedom.

"Mornin'," I said, as Kane stretched out like a werecat, while Angel covered her mouth with her hand to stifle a long yawn. "How did yeh sleep?"

Angel sighed. "Surprisingly well, actually."

"Like the dead," Kane agreed.

"How long have you been up?" Angel asked, rolling over onto her stomach and propping her chin up with her hands.

Fates, she was a vision. The untamed silver strands sticking out in every direction only added to how lost I was for the female. I wasn't the only one to appreciate the wild look. Kane lay out on his side next to her, and ran a hand through her wayward hair until his fingers got caught in a knot, then pulled her in for a kiss.

"Well-fucked hair's a good look on you, Princess," he murmured before kissing her again.

"Aye," I agreed once I reached a shallower part of the lagoon. I stood and ran my hands through my hair, ringing out the water as I waded my way to the pool's edge.

"Alaric's gone and got his all wet," Angel pouted, like I'd committed a crime.

"What's wrong with tha'?" I asked.

"Nothing," she said, biting her lip. "I'm just trying to decide if I prefer it like this, or your unruly waves. What do you think, Kane?"

"Asking me to pick is like asking Alaric to choose between hard-boiled and scrambled," he said. "The answer is always both, just depends on what mood you're in at the time. Hot and steamy or wild and messy. Both are equally delicious."

I nodded my agreement to the egg comment, though I wasn't convinced he was talking about eggs at all, then pushed myself up onto the edge and climbed out.

"Okay, ignore everything I just said. I take it all back. The answer is, *that,*" Kane said, tilting his head my way.

"Umm-humm," Angel purred in agreement, her eyes traveling up and down my naked form.

"*That?*" I asked, quirking a brow.

"Yes. That. As in, *that* right there is my favorite look on you," he said, then gave me a wink that spoke directly to my cock.

A smirk pulled at my lips as I wrung my hair out some more, not hating the way they watched me.

"What's with the early morning swim, anyway?" he eventually asked. "Couldn't sleep?" I shook my head. After staying up late to make the most of our time here together, I'd slept little, but I'd slept well. Perhaps better than ever before.

Before I could answer, Angel's eyes went wide, focused on something on the other side of the cavern. "Is that the shell the fates gave you?" she asked Kane.

I followed her gaze to find a blue crystal, just like the one that had led us here, glowing as it hovered above a rock. I squinted at the large shell balanced on the jagged peak, lit up by the crystal's radiance above.

Kane and Angel scrambled to their feet and were at my side by the time I reached it. Scratched into the rock were the faint words, *'A peace offering from Nekane Regis to Maximos III, Stallion of Kelpie Cove.'*

"I left it over there," Kane said, pointing to where we'd entered the lagoon.

"It wasnae here or there when I woke up," I said.

"It only just appeared," Angel said. "I literally watched it come from out of nowhere."

"*The fates,*" Kane muttered. "So this really is how they plan for me to get an audience with Maximos?" he asked, doubt evident in his tone. "A clamshell."

I shrugged. "Apparently, but I dinnae ken why a clam would have the power to make them hear yeh out. Unless yeh talk into it or somethin'?"

"Is that a thing?" Angel asked, but I was pretty sure it wasn't. If talking into a clam was enough to get an entire species on one's side, I'd have seen Augustus using them. I shook my head. "I guess it would be stupid to ask if either of you have ever heard of clams being important to the Kelpies?"

Kane shrugged.

"No' that I've heard," I said.

"I guess we will find out soon enough," Kane said, glancing to where our bags of clothes lay back over by the sleep sacks.

"This showing up here means it's time to go, doesn't it?" Angel sighed. We all knew our time here would be coming to an end sooner than we would like, but that didn't mean I was ready to feel the bubble of bliss pop so suddenly.

"Yes," Kane said, reaching down to pick the shell up.

"Does it open?" Angel asked, leaning over for a closer look. "I was meaning to try last night but… you know," she blushed.

Kane turned the thing over in his hands. "With enough force on the crack between the shells, probably. But I have a feeling handing it over broken would be less of a peace offering and more of an insult and invitation to attack."

He was right. It was bad enough that the fates had insisted he go down to the beach on his own. We weren't about to do anything to further jeopardize his safety.

The three of us headed back to our bags to get dressed and settle on a plan. As Angel plaited her hair to keep it off her face, the solid rock wall near the floating blue crystal suddenly crumbled. Swallowing the glow until it disappeared and a small archway was revealed.

Daylight poured in, and I shielded my eyes with an arm. Visible on the other side of the new hole in the rock wall was an unobstructed view of the shoreline of Kelpie Cove.

We were significantly further down the cliffs from where we'd entered yesterday, and looking directly over the beach where Kane was set to venture soon. Alone.

Fuck, I hated this plan.

ANGEL and I watched from the cliff as Kane made his way down to the beach. Empty-handed, with no weapons in sight.

"How long would it take yeh to fly down there, Angel?" I asked, knowing it was a stupid fucking question, but I was too worried for Kane's safety not to ask it.

"Not long," she said, peering over the edge.

We both knew there was fuck all we could do about it if they ambushed him. Even if a portal appeared to take us directly to the beach, we wouldn't get there fast enough to save him from the brunt of their attack.

Kane reached the forest at the base of the mountains, disappearing from view, and I stopped breathing, clenching my jaw tightly as time seemed to slow.

"He will be okay, Alaric," Angel said, sensing my agitation.

"What if it's a setup? The fates leading him to go down there without back-up," I said. "What if this is some kind of trap? Or another test? What proof do we have the fuckin' fates dinnae want him dead?"

Fuck, if they wanted the three of us out of the way, there was no better way of doing it. Split us up, kill one and they'd kill us all.

"Alaric, I know the fates haven't always been kind but–"

"When have they *ever* been kind to our plight?" I cut over her.

"–we have to trust them to at least be just right now," she finished anyway, placing a hand on my arm. "We passed their tests, and they said they'd help us. They made good on their word last night."

True. "I'd just feel better bein' down there," I said.

"So would I. But just because he's weaponless, doesn't mean he's defenseless. You trained him yourself."

"Aye. I ken that," I said. She was right, the male could look after himself. I trusted that much. I just didn't trust any of the rest of this entire fucking situation. "I jus' feel fuckin' useless up here."

"Look, there he is," Angel said, pointing toward the row of trees lining the sand and I sighed in relief.

It was short-lived, though. Now it was time for what was probably the most dangerous part of the entire plan. We watched in silence as he strode forward with confidence, despite all the unknowns. Like where the kelpies would even meet him, for starters. With no clear instructions from the fates, we'd decided it was best for us to keep hold of the 'peace offering' up here, as a bargaining tool. With every minute that passed, I was questioning the decision more and more.

As Kane stopped still, halfway between the trees and the sea, a disturbance in the water drew my attention. As one, an entire herd of kelpie emerged from the water, transforming into their horse-like forms as they moved through the waves crashing onto the beach. They exchanged a few glances, then walked slowly toward where Kane was waiting.

"At least they didn't charge," Angel whispered. "That's a good start."

"Aye, but look at their formation," I said. "They are spreading themselves wide so they can surround him."

They drew closer, their circle closing in and Kane held up his hands, palms out, to show he meant them no harm. Lips moved as words were exchanged, but the wind was blowing the wrong direction for their voices to have any chance of reaching us, and I couldn't hear any of what they were saying.

A problem I hadn't accounted for.

"Shift," I told Angel. "To yer dragon form."

"Not yet," she said with a shake to her voice that betrayed her nerves. "The last thing I want to do is spook them. We just have to wait for his signal."

Before Kane had left for the beach, we'd decided on three signals. The first, a simple point in our direction, telling us it was time to show off our 'giant cockle' as Kane had called it. The second, a nod to indicate they would welcome Angel and I down to the beach to join him and bring the ridiculous gift, and they would hear us out in exchange. The third, the one I didn't want to see, had him lowering one hand to his hip, where his sword would ordinarily sit. If he did that, we'd move in. The message was loud and clear: things were getting hostile or about to go sideways.

"Somethings wrong," I said. "Why hasn't he so much as glanced this way yet?"

"Give him time," she gritted out, her eyes never leaving him.

They already had him surrounded and outnumbered by at least thirty. While I watched the group of kelpies, Angel watched Kane, ready to leap and shift without hesitation if they suddenly attacked. They had no weapons or gifts at their disposal that would be a match for Angel in dragon form if she took to the skies. She could kill them all with one breath. She'd only do it if Kane was well out of the range of fire, and there was absolutely no other choice. We were here to *save* them from a slaughter after all, not to be their demise.

Despite breathing fire seeming to most to be arguably an incredible, unstoppable gift and a great fatal weapon to have in your arsenal, carrying out mass executions wasn't something any fae should or could have forever on their conscience.

The last thing we needed was to survive this war and then lose Angel anyway, when the guilt became too much to bear. Kane and I knew we had to protect her from the guilt that would slowly kill her, and the only way we knew how was by never asking her to commit such atrocities.

I knew firsthand what it was like to feel like a monster, and I never wanted that for her. If there was no other way, she would do what she had to, however she saw fit. But she'd trained hard in her partially shifted form and had plenty of other options first.

"There's the signal," Angel said. "Hold it up."

Clasping the clam with two hands, I held it above my head and shook it to make sure I got their attention. "Fates, please don't fuck us over," I whispered.

I could have sworn the air around me gasped. A heartbeat later, the entire herd buckled at the knees, their front legs dropping as they hit the sand and didn't attempt to get up.

What in fates' name is so special about this scallop?

"There's the nod," Angel said. She pulled her dress off, threw it at me, and leapt from the cliff, shifting into the most majestic sight I'd ever seen. I clung to the clam with one hand and picked up her dress from the ground near my feet.

I kept an eye on Kane as I waited for Angel to get into position on the cliff face. The kelpie folk wouldn't have seen a dragon for hundreds of years, the younger ones only having heard stories of the magnificent creatures, yet they remained with their noses in the sand, barely noticing the beast.

The long grassy mounds scattered between rocks blown flat in the gust as she flapped her wings in slow strokes, before planting her talons into the rocky earth just out of sight below where I stood. Angel let out a soft grunt, her signal to me it was time to move, and I ran to the edge. Before I reached it, I jumped, landing on her back. With my free hand, I slapped her side twice, letting her know it was time to fly.

She pushed off the cliff, causing several boulders to slide down the mountainside as she sprung into the air. There wasn't much distance to cover, but we needed to land *behind* Kane and we were approaching from the front right now. Angel circled wide so the vast sea was beneath us and I saw the mouth of the cave we'd entered last night. The fates were right, we wouldn't have stood a chance.

What must be over one hundred kelpies guarded it. Rows of them lined up on either side of the mouth, while others scattered above and below. Sherbet was there, closest to the black hole, seaweed still firmly matted in his mane. But was Maximos one of them? Or was he down on the beach with Kane?

I guess we'll find out soon enough.

I clutched onto the clam as Angel swooped round, getting into position to land behind Kane. It was rare to see her like this during the daylight. Her scales gleaming mirrors that reflected the sun's rays. The sight took my breath away every time.

Kane was watching us, an unreadable expression on his face. What had been said in their exchange? Had the kelpie stallion been friendly? Probably not, but Kane clearly felt comfortable enough to turn his back on the herd to watch us land.

I dug my knees in tighter and wrapped my free hand around a spike protruding from the neck of her spine, preparing to descend. But the sand covered ground wasn't getting any closer. Angel suddenly began to flap her wings harder. We were rising higher and higher until we were close to reaching the clouds, Kane and the kelpies shrinking to the size of miniature toy figurines below.

"Angel, what are yeh–"

My throat bobbed when I saw the reason for her sudden change of plan. While I'd been distracted with the kelpie army surrounding the cave, Angel must have been looking out over the sea.

There, in the distance, where the deep blue waves met the horizon, great masts rose from the water. All flying flags I knew would be adorned with the image of three black mountains with crimson creeks zigzagging down them, until they reached the red sea at their base.

Is this why the fates had split us up?

So Eva would be in the skies at this very moment. Cannons and arrows couldn't reach her here, not even close. So did that mean the fates had simply wanted her to witness the ships' approach? Exactly as in Edelin's vision, the pair of Mount Mortum ships entered Dezrothian Waters. Only we had failed to do our part and give the kelpies enough warning for them to have any hope of being prepared for the mountain savages' attack.

Angel landed and morphed into her partially shifted form, with scales covering most of her body. Though her wings jutted from her back, she walked on two feet in her fae form as she stormed across the sand. She ignored the dress I held out, jaw set and focused only on closing the space between where we'd landed and where Kane stood within the circle of still bowed horse creatures.

She crossed a gap between two kelpies and low rumbles left their chests. With no better ideas, I held the clam in the air with one hand and made calming gestures with the other, still holding the dress I'd had ready for Angel.

They didn't move to attack, just pivoted on the spot, so their head end faced the clam.

"Kane," she said, reaching his side. "We're too late."

Did they blame me for it? Maybe not aloud, but deep down, would Kane and Angel know this was my fault? After all, I'd been the one to delay this meeting by suggesting we visit what turned out to be the Realm of the Three Fates.

As much as I didn't want to be the reason any kelpie died here today, I still couldn't bring myself to regret last night. Yes, I was a selfish asshole where my mates were concerned, but even if it meant fighting ten times harder today to help the kelpie, I wouldn't change a second of the time we'd had together.

"They're here?" he asked, not missing a beat.

"Almost. That's why I flew higher. I saw something but couldn't be certain."

"But now you are?" he asked. "Certain?" Angel nodded, then finally took the dress from my hand with a quick thanks and slipped it on.

The kelpies' low rumblings grew louder and louder until Kane said, "Alaric, hand over Maximos's grandfather."

I frowned, but he just nodded in encouragement.

"His grandfather is a clam?" Eva asked tentatively, as certain as me that she must have misheard.

Kane shook his head once. "*Inside* the clam."

The words sunk in and my eyes went wide as I fought the desire to throw the fucking thing into the sea. Angel's gaze darted between the peace offering in my hand and the kelpies bent low, perfectly pointing their heads my way.

"This is Maximos III," Kane said, gesturing to the kelpie directly in front of him. He was the only one who'd lifted his nose from the ground, though he still kept his front legs bent and rear end in the air. "In your hand is Maximos I, this herd's founder. And they would very much like him back."

CHAPTER 29

Evangelia

"Have yeh told them about Edelin's vision?" Alaric asked Kane under his breath, trying not to react to the news of what he was holding.

I knew him well enough to have a pretty good idea of what he'd be thinking. *The fuckin' fates gave us the founder's burnt fuckin' remains and didn't think to fuckin' mention it?!* Or something to that effect.

If Axel ever heard about this… If he caught wind that his adopted brother had stood shaking someone's ashes above his head, with just two shells stopping the charred bones of the dead kelpie king from showering down in a cloud, Alaric would never hear the end of it.

If we survived this, I'd be sure to tell him. There really was no better way to thank Axel for keeping me sane during our unnecessarily extended stay in the medical tent.

Kane nodded, but it was Maximos who spoke. Maximos III should I say; I'm not sure Alaric would survive the shock if it were Maximos, the grandfather. *"We appreciate the warning, but I'm afraid we do not have the fight in us to face them."*

"Why?" Alaric asked, confusion knitting his brows. Frustrated that they would roll over and admit defeat so easily.

"We have suffered so much loss of late. The most recent just yesterday. That's why Sherbet was buying time. Why he would not just bring you to me. We were burying our strongest soldier."

Sherbet had been passionate about his frustrations with the selkies, so why wasn't his leader showing even an ounce of that passion in the face of the threat Kane had warned them of?

"You should have seen what they did to him," he continued. *"I've never seen scratches like it. No wolf or bear could slice down to bone with one scratch the way that thing tore him up."*

"Thing?" Alaric asked.

"I don't know what it was. Everyone's talking about her though."

"Who?" Alaric pressed.

"Anon. The favorite to win the Coronation games. She tore poor Colt to pieces."

Being in the Vale, we had little intel on the games, but from what Maximos was saying about his best soldier's demise, those competing were as bloodthirsty as Elikai himself. Unable to do a thing about them until we had grown our numbers, the only thing making it a little easier was knowing the fae who were entering had, at the very least, some idea of what they were applying for.

"I'm so sorry for your loss," I said. "Truly. I would not wish for an enemy to fight in those games. But what do you plan to do about your cove, if not fight?"

The Mount Mortum ships were coming to this beach, whether the kelpies liked it or not. *Why* they would come here, and in such force, was a mystery. One we'd spoken about during the journey to Kelpie Cove, and we only assumed it had everything to do with Elikai's new relationship with his uncle.

We'd gone around in circles debating their ultimate goal and decided it wasn't worth wasting any more time trying to puzzle it out. We just had to stop them from achieving it and get back to helping the rebels prepare for the battle on Dezrothia's horizon.

The stallion looked at me for the first time since I'd landed on their shore and I found so much grief and fear in his eyes, it hurt my heart. *"Help us,"* he begged. *"Please."*

Did he know who he was begging for aid from? Had Kane shared his true identity with the kelpie? Or did he assume the entire horde would join us here soon to fight for them? How sorely mistaken they were about Elikai's motivations for running this realm, if that were the case.

Still, in that moment, as I stared down at the kneeling leader, I knew it didn't matter to this poor male which of the Regis brothers had walked onto his land uninvited. He didn't care, because he'd lost all hope and that was an awful place to be.

Alaric stepped forward and placed the clam-shaped urn down gently in the sand in front of Maximos III. Like the victory of having this lost treasure back might give them the strength and fight they needed for what was approaching the shoreline.

"Thank you," the stallion said into our minds. *"You don't know how much this means to us. The selkies took him from our trove not long after the late king took away their land, forcing them here. It was the beginning of a long feud, one which still plagues us daily. I don't know how you got him back, but we are forever in your debt."*

"As I told you, Maximos, we came all the way from the Fading Vale to warn you," Kane said, his tone gentle but firm. The voice of a true leader. "But we cannot help you further if you are not willing to help yourselves. If you want to repay us, then fight."

"We have families. We can't just lay down our lives against evil like you rebels can," he said, successfully managing to pull a low growl from Alaric's chest.

"It's because yeh have fuckin' families that yeh should!" he snapped.

Kane had obviously told them more than we'd planned to. Not only that, he wasn't Elikai Regis, but that we were part of a larger alliance too. I understood his decision to go off script, given that the loose plan we'd managed to put together hadn't accounted for the presumed-to-be fearsome kelpie leader being so broken.

The kelpie looked down at the ground under the weight of Alaric's anger, and remained that way, silent for several seconds. Eventually, he lifted his eyes to me.

"You're a dragon. Can't you just set the ships ablaze? End this quickly so you can get back to your rebellion?"

I tried to answer, to tell him exactly how many levels of wrong that would be, but the words lodged in my throat. What he suggested was barbaric, yes, but he wasn't thinking clearly, he was speaking out of pure desperation. Out of fear for the imminent deaths of his entire herd.

"No," Alaric and Kane said together, and I relaxed a fraction that they agreed we weren't that desperate yet. Not even close.

"Why?" came a different voice, yet still spoken directly into my thoughts. A glance around showed a mare to the right of Maximos, who had lifted her head.

"You honestly don't know why?" I asked.

She shook her mane.

I took a moment to find the right words, but Kane stepped in to save me from having to. "We have no way of knowing whether those ships hold children and other innocents. Even if the deck contains only soldiers, it's impossible to be certain who's inside the cabins. It's not a risk worth even considering, not to mention a grotesque burden to put on my mate."

"Aye. We might be rebels, but we are no' savages," Alaric added. "We will still have to live with ourselves after this war is won."

"You truly believe you can win?" Maximos asked. Though his eyes were fixed on the clamshell before him, there was no mistaking it was his voice.

My mates and I shared a look. We couldn't lie and make out like it would be an easy win, but this herd needed motivation, and giving them a glimmer of hope might go a long way.

I closed my eyes and thought back to the vision the fates had shown me at the end of my test. Of my mates on the dais, of the fae of so many species smiling. Relaxed and carefree as we celebrated. I tried to remember whether any kelpie had been there, but drew a blank.

Opening my eyes, I addressed the herd. "Yes. I truly believe we can win. But we aren't asking you to join us in the war, just in this fight. Will you please help us help you?"

Silence fell on the beach, broken only by the crashing waves. I caught Alaric glancing out to sea several times, but the ships weren't visible from down here just yet.

Eventually Maximos stood, and I held my breath, praying to the fates that between us we'd gotten through to him. *"We appreciate you coming here, and for returning our founders' ashes,"* he said. *"But I'm sorry, we just can't."*

My stomach sank. I wanted to tell him that I wasn't angry, just disappointed, but I wasn't his mother. And it wouldn't make a difference.

Alaric cursed his frustration. "We shouldnae have come here," he said. "We have our own fight to win."

"Look at the bigger picture, Alaric," Kane pointed out. "This fight is inevitable, it's not a question of if, but when."

"Yeh think I dinnae ken that we either deal with them now, or we meet them on another battlefield?" he asked. "At least the latter we would have greater numbers than only three willing to pick up a weapon and a herd set on doin' fuck all." *Despite it being their territory in immediate danger,* I finished for him in my head, because it was the former horde general now taking the reins where the kelpies were concerned.

I rubbed my temples and Kane's fingers steepled as they pressed to his lips. There had to be another option that didn't involve my mates and I dying, this herd and their cowardly leader or me having to massacre hundreds, perhaps thousands, of foreign fae.

Kane cleared his throat. "Would the selkies help?" he asked.

Maximos scoffed. *"The selkies do not care about Kelpie Cove–"*

"That makes two of yeh," Alaric muttered, and went back to his pacing in the sand.

Maximos ignored him and continued. *"–they only care about playing games with us and stealing our land whenever our backs are turned."*

"So we're on our own," I said. "But that doesn't mean we are out of options."

"Yer no' doin' that, Angel," Alaric said.

I shook my head. "No, I won't. But the Mount Mortums don't know that."

"What are you thinking, Princess?"

ADRENALINE, fear, and apprehension raced through me in the most unnerving mixture as I shot back into the sky. Though the air would be icily cold for Alaric and Kane on my back, the chill just made me feel more awake.

With my senses heightened, I could better focus on the ships up ahead. Watching intently as they traveled much faster than I'd first thought they were moving upon seeing them earlier.

My males held onto me, their thighs clutching on tightly. When I'd told them my idea, there hadn't been time to work out the details, so they were discussing them now. The big question was how best to deal with the Mount Mortum fleet once we were within negotiating distance.

Kane stopped mid-sentence. "What's that?" he asked Alaric. Unable to see which direction he was pointing; I scanned the wider area around the ships.

Shit. Off to the right, a pod of seal-like creatures raced through the ocean toward the fleet. "Wait. Aren't they, *selkies?*"

"Aye. But what the fuck are they doin'?" Alaric seethed. "They are no match for the archers on board, let alone the cannons."

No sooner had Alaric spoken, the fates laughed in his face. Cannon muzzles poked out of several portholes dotted along the hull. I waited for the selkies to retreat, but they didn't seem to notice them or they didn't care if they did.

Swimming as fast as their fins would take them toward the side of the leading ship, their heads bobbing in and out of the water so quickly it was a wonder they didn't impale themselves on their own spears. Their hind flippers flashed above the surface every other second as they continued closing in, getting closer and closer to their target with every dread filled second that we watched uselessly, too far away to do anything to help.

Kane cursed. "Why aren't they retreating? They need to dive down and get as deep as they can before the cannons are fired!"

Both he and Alaric went silent, doubtlessly willing the selkies to save themselves before it was too late. I did the same as I watched with bated breath.

Kane cursed again. "I can't decide if they are really brave or–"

"Really fuckin' stupid?" Alaric finished. "I dinnae ken, but I'd have them at my back over the kelpies."

Me too.

But shit, *for the love of the fates, dive down! Dive down now!*

I wanted to scream at them to notice the cannons, to demand they get deep enough that the balls fired would lose their power against the water's resistance. But they were utterly determined and set on their course, heading for the ship.

My eyes darted between the selkie pod and the cannons poking out of the portholes. And my stomach plummeted as the muzzles were suddenly tilted more downward than before, pointing toward the water. Based on the angle, they'd land exactly where the selkies were about to reach. *Fates, please let them notice them in time!*

Plumes of smoke shot from the muzzles, immediately followed by several loud booms in quick concession as cannonballs blasted toward the selkies, wreaking havoc in the water surrounding them. Dark red ink-like pools clouded the sea on that side of the ship. The poor creatures hadn't stood a chance. Not with them swimming so close to the surface as they hit.

"So much for the selkies not being interested in helping," Kane said. "They just lost half their pod trying to divert the ships. Eva, are you seeing this?"

I released a snort of smoke from my nose to confirm and flapped my wings faster. Desperate to get close enough to scan the bloodied water for any signs of life.

The crimson water bubbled, and several survivors sprung up. A second later, they all disappeared back under, too deep for us to see them.

Another round of cannon fire thundered out from the ship, but my eyes didn't leave the spot where the creatures had vanished. Eventually, fae-like heads and upper bodies reappeared once more. Though they'd gone down empty-handed, they came back up, clutching at least two fallen friends in their arms. Some thrashing in agony, others heartbreakingly still.

They began to flee, and I didn't blame them. They were hideously outnumbered in every sense. But then they did something that not even Edelin could have foreseen. For every selkie soldier who left the area beside the ship, more of their pod suddenly emerged to take their place. With replacement soldiers now ready to put their lives on the line this time, they continued their plan for the ship's assault.

One group held back, watching the cannons, while the others darted forward to the ship and started striking true with their spears against the hull. After causing what I could only imagine would be a great amount of damage to the ship's structure, the selkies spread themselves out so each of their heads protruded from the water directly below a cannon's muzzle. Shocking me once again.

"Fuck," Alaric cursed. "Are they gonnae–"

He trailed off as the selkies moved in perfect synchronicity, using their strong tails vertically in the water to push themselves high enough out for them to reach their arms up to the portholes, and grip on with their fingers. They began to pull themselves up, as though they planned to use the portholes to climb aboard. But as soon as they got close to succeeding, the cannons would fire, and they'd drop back into the sea.

The second ship caught up and began moving in, so tightly toward the lead ship that the selkies in the water were trapped, and forced to dive down, retreating again. We were close enough now to see the Mount Mortum crew clearly, meaning any moment now their attention would switch from the selkies' desperate attack, to the much larger threat heading their way through the clouds. Their cannon's would be useless so long as I remained high enough above the water, it was the arrows that could prove more deadly. Not against my scales, but to the males on my back.

Deep voices shouted as a commotion broke out on the deck. Two warriors dragged a selkie across it by the tail, leaving a thick trail of blood in her wake. Another warrior bent and grabbed a fist full of her hair and... *shit shit shit. No.*

Like a coward, I wanted to close my eyes, so I didn't have to watch them beat her for a second longer. Some used fists, others various weapons, one even reached for a broken arrow and–

I shivered.

"Fucking savage cunts," Alaric gritted.

As the seconds ticked by, I found myself praying to the fates to put her out of her misery sooner than later. And as though they'd heard my desperate plea, the poor selkie finally fell still.

"We have to stop this," Kane said. "Now."

"Angel," Alaric called. "Get us within shouting distance of th–"

The hiss of an arrow cut through Alaric's words. I swerved and rolled just in time to dodge it going straight through my eye, and heard it clank against my scales as Kane yelled, "Alaric!"

As I straightened, I felt the absence of his weight from my back as strongly as my fae form would have felt an arrow pierce through my heart. Panic threatened, but I tried to remain calm, not make any more sudden movements. My eyes darted around the air below me, fully expecting to see my male free falling through it. If only I could see where he'd fallen, I could swoop down and catch him.

"Got him!" Kane called. I listened intently as he heaved, as though pulling him back up. "That was close," he eventually said, and I felt Alaric's legs hugging my back once more.

"Aye. That'll teach me not to hold on," he said.

The only thing I didn't like about being in this form was the inability to communicate. I wanted so badly to explain about the arrow but could only speak in snorts and smoke and fire.

"Angel," Alaric said. "Get us within shouting distance. We need to end this."

When I didn't immediately speed up, Kane added. "We're *both* holding on now."

Soaring across the vast open ocean, I closed the distance between us and the ships as quickly as my wings would take us. The archers let loose tens of arrows at a time, which I dodged until I determined the maximum height they seemed to reach, and then rose just above and ignored them as they ricocheted off my underbelly. Soon we were close enough to hear one of the Mount Mortum warriors call, "Stop wasting arrows on the dragon, you idiots."

So he'd finally notice they were achieving little more than snapping in two against my skin? Hopefully, that would help the next part of my plan. I wasn't sure who was going to do the talking until I heard Alaric's deep timbre call, "Turn yer ships around or burn with them."

The male who'd called for the archers to put down their bows raised a brow. "Says who?"

"Says the male with the fuckin' dragon," Alaric called back.

"We were invited to Dezrothia," he said. "You can ask your king."

"I'd rather watch your ships burn. Now turn the fuck around, or–"

I tilted my chin and roared a cascade of flames at the various masts, moving my head from one side to the other in one fell swoop. Disintegrating the Mount Mortum flags so the ashy remains drifted slowly down on the heads of the warriors aboard.

Several scrambled to douse what remained of the wooden masts before the fire spread to the deck, and would eventually engulf the ships if they didn't act fast. That wasn't our intention, but we had to make them believe it was.

"Okay, okay, enough!" the male snapped.

Alaric and Kane laughed. "It's like yeh think that's yer call to make," Alaric said, and I didn't need to see him to know he'd be arching a brow so his scar stretched and crinkled across his features. The menacing look was a favorite of mine and Kane's, but it never failed to instill great fear in most everyone else.

"We have families on board," the warrior said. A last-ditch attempt to appeal to Alaric's softer side?

"Good job I havnae bothered to feed my dragon in days, then, isn't it?"

"You sick bastard."

"Yer no' one to talk," Alaric said. "I doubt the sea beast behind yeh did tha' to herself."

"She deserved it," the warrior cried. "She had no business climbing aboard my ship."

And just like that, he'd walked straight into Alaric's trap.

"Jus' like yeh have no business sailing on my king and queen's sea," he said. "A quick toasting by dragon fire is a far more peaceful death than what she endured at yer hands." *Shit*, hearing him speak like that set off something feral within me. "Turn back for Mount Mortum now, or don't. Either way, the dragon will start spewin' flames by the time I've counted back from ten."

The ship with the damage wouldn't get far before sinking. But they'd still have the other one, which looked mostly undamaged and still watertight. Nothing would be stopping them from piling onto that one later.

Not our problem.

Alaric made it to nine before the ships' engines fired up. I glanced around the still red-tinged water and couldn't find any sign of the selkies aside from the wooden debris they'd broken off spearing the hull, which now bobbed peacefully in the waves.

By "Seven", they were desperately trying to turn around.

And as Alaric yelled "Five," the warriors were turned around, beginning their long mastless trawl home.

"They'll be back," Kane said quietly.

"Aye. But we've bought some time."

As I waited for the ships to crawl a little farther away, movement at one of the portholes of the damaged one caught my eye.

Two figures dropped down into the sea and I squinted to find severely injured selkies fighting against the churning waters. Desperately trying to help one another escape despite their broken bodies.

"We can go now, Angel," Alaric said.

No, we can't, I wanted to argue. We couldn't just leave them.

I growled, trying to get my males' attention to show them something wasn't right. That something else needed to be done before we could turn back for shore.

"Angel?" Alaric called, "Everythin' okay?"

I let out a cloud of smoke, hoping to draw their attention to it so they'd see the selkies beyond as it dissipated.

"Wait," Kane said. "Look."

Please fates, let him be pointing out the selkies. I couldn't save them on my own unless I wanted to risk hurting them further with my talons. Or worse, they're tails slipping out.

Alaric cursed when he finally saw the selkies as they dipped below the lapping waves, reemerging for a moment before sinking once more.

"Angel, I need yeh to get as low as yeh can. I'll dive in to get them. Kane, stay on Angel's back to help pull them up. Clear?"

"Yes," Kane said, and I let out a grunt of acknowledgement.

Diving downward, I didn't pull back and straighten until my nose touched the water. My underside skimmed the surface, and Kane and Alaric sprang into action. I twisted my neck around just in time to see Alaric, wings wide, holding a selkie under each arm.

Kane slapped my back twice, and I began to flap my wings, struggling with the water so close.

"Fuck. Come on Angel," Alaric encouraged.

"She's got this," Kane said. But I wasn't sure I did.

Every foot of height I gained felt like ten miles of flight, but I focused on pushing every scrap of power and energy I had into my wings and eventually, the water was no longer an obstacle and all I could feel was the wind around us.

My heart thudded as I waited for Alaric or Kane's instruction on where to land. I'd made the decision myself before and would never forgive myself for the ambush that had taken place shortly after. I wasn't about to risk anything. Not when we were so close to being done with our mission to Kelpie Cove.

"Looks like we have a tail," Kane said. I looked down and in my shadow on the water swam what remained of the pod of selkies.

"Head back to the beach," Alaric said. "I have an idea."

CHAPTER 30

Nekane

I spent the short flight back to land pushing healing magic into the selkies. One hand placed gently on the forehead of the female in my lap, and the other, reaching back to the slightly less injured one with purple hair Alaric was holding.

What they'd tried to do out there, not many fae in this realm would be brave or daring enough to attempt. I respected the shit out of their efforts, no matter how futile. Perhaps more so for that very reason.

It was impossible to know how many of their pod they had lost in that first cannon blast, but I had no intention of adding another two to that figure.

By the time we approached the shoreline, their wounds had healed, and it was time to see if they were well enough to talk.

"My name's Nekane," I said, keeping my eyes forward and chin up, looking out toward the group of kelpies on the beach, so as not to make the female uncomfortable. I was already having to hold her pretty tightly to stop her from falling. It couldn't be helped, but that didn't mean I had to make her feel any more vulnerable than she doubtlessly was already feeling.

"These are my mates, Alaric and Evangelia," I continued, pride seeping through my voice. "We aren't going to hurt you, but I have some questions about what just happened out there. Are you well enough to talk?"

"We know who you are. Though I assumed Evangelia was high fae from her picture," the selkie in my arms said, her eyes wide as she tried to take in the dragon she rode upon. I quirked a brow at the high fae comment. We had that in common. "We heard you are not like the Regis' we met before you, but fates, you look so much like *him*."

Ouch. My stomach twisted. How was I supposed to respond to that?

"Where exactly did yeh hear that?" Alaric asked, saving me from having to address the fault in my facade that I could do nothing about.

"It's a long story," the female in his arms said.

"We can make time," I said. "But perhaps you'd be more comfortable in your other form?" I suggested, not much wanting to hold a fae who wasn't my mate like this for any longer than I had to in order to heal her.

The female nodded, then wriggled in my lap until her tail shed and two legs appeared, transforming from her partial seal form to that of a fae as the wind took the old rubbery skin away. Selkies were said to be known for their beauty more than any other attributes, both the females and males of their kind. But after seeing them in action, I wondered whether that was what they wanted to be known for. Or if it grated on them.

Once the selkie were straddling Eva's neck, facing Alaric and I while holding on tightly to a spike each, I asked, "Eva, could you circle round again?"

The kelpie herd would have noticed us given how close we'd been to landing, but I figured it wouldn't hurt to make them sweat a little. And while we eventually needed to join back up with the rebels at the new camp, the longer we were gone, the more villagers they would win over.

Tilting her body, Eva arched out widely, then headed back out toward the sea. She flew slowly, so the wind didn't whip too loudly in our ears, saving us from shouting. "Thanks," I said to Eva, then to the selkies, "Let's hear it then."

"What, everything? Now?" the one with deep blue hair asked, looking down at the water far below. "*Here*?" I nodded, and she swallowed. Then, pulling her eyes from the drop below, she began. "Like everyone in Dezrothia, we received an invitation to take part in the Coronation Games. And like everyone, we put forward a fighter from our pod."

"Why?" I asked.

"Honestly? We were just happy to have been included."

We'd heard little about my brother's wicked contest before today. Learning about the kelpies' tribute and how he'd been brutally murdered by some other savage contestant had made me sick to my stomach.

Alaric was right when he'd said it was for the best that we didn't know many of the details. It's not like we could go marching in there and tell Elikai to call them off.

"What happened?" I asked, unable to help myself, even knowing the answer would keep me awake.

"Despite putting forward our best, without the might of our pod working with her, Rinn was no match for the land fae. She was killed in the first match." She choked, like the grief was too thick in her throat to get any more words out.

Her friend took over. "We should never have let her go, but we were desperate for a new beginning and thought a new king might mean a fresh start. We wanted to impress him with Rinn's abilities. Prove that our kind were a race to be taken seriously," she paused, contemplating her next words. "Let's just say we thought the Coronation Games would be a fair test. We thought the male running them would be different."

"Yeh thought?" Alaric asked. "As in, you dinnae think that anymore?"

"No," the blue-haired female said with a shiver. "We were naïve, when we truly shouldn't have been. We've spent centuries committing crimes against other sea folk under the orders of the late king, and we should have been more weary."

"But we know better now. And we were desperate, Safi. The fates will forgive us," the purple-haired selkie said, consoling her friend. Then cleared her throat. "Please try to understand, Nekane, we no longer recognized ourselves after what your late father made us do. Despite being to blame for their extinction, we feel the guilt and mourn the hydra and kraken every day. King Regis took everything from us and then made us work for every scrap of sea and land we gained back. It's why we've been assholes to the kelpie, so long as we were warring, your father left us alone. But those games... I'm sorry... I can't."

Eva let out a sad sigh and Alaric cursed. "I can't imagine," I said. "And I'm sorry."

"It's not your fault. You aren't the male we heard laughing from his throne as we sat outside the arena praying to the fates for Rinn to be okay," the purple-haired selkie said.

"But how did yeh come to know of Nekane?" Alaric pressed.

"It was because of Emily, actually," Safi said. "She's better to explain."

Emily, the one with purple hair, squirmed a little. "Well, when we'd accompanied Rinn to the arena, I was tired of walking and bored, so I counted the posters with your faces on them. You know, to break up the monotony of trees. The ocean is much more interesting. It wasn't until after we collected Rinn's body that I started to think about the contents of the posters. About the fae behind the faces. The more I thought about it, the more I questioned who the real criminals were."

Safi nodded. "Emily spoke about the three of you to our entire pod at Rinn's funeral. You can imagine her surprise when last night another friend of ours saw you arrive at Kelpie Cove."

"Still, that doesnae explain why yeh were willin' to die out there today," Alaric mused, almost to himself. Like he had such little faith in the fae outside of the rebel alliance, he just couldn't make it make sense.

"We know we can't take back what we did to the sea folk of the Dezrothian coves during Augustus Regis' reign," Safi said. "But we want to try to make things right. If not in the eyes of all, then in that of our kin. Of our children."

"Once we were aware of you being here, we knew something had to be amiss, especially after hearing the kelpies talking of a warning you wanted to give them," Emily continued. "They wanted to kill you, you know? We tried to find you, to warn you, but there was no way of getting into the cave without having to go through the kelpie herd guarding it."

It checked out, but Alaric apparently needed some more convincing. "So, how did yeh find out about Mount Mortum?" he asked. "We didnae get a chance to give our full warning until this mornin'. You'd have already been well on yer way to the ships by then."

"Our job for centuries has been to stop fae leaving Dezrothian waters. The habit of watching the borders didn't die with the king," Safi said. "A pod out at sea saw the ships bearing the flag with the bleeding mountains. The last time we saw a fleet of ships flying those flags, King Dyvrad died." At the name, the great muscles in Eva's back tensed under our thighs. "We knew we couldn't let them reach land, so we tried to turn them around. When that didn't work, we tried to sink them. And I guess you know the rest…" she looked down sadly, trailing off.

Alaric nodded. He tapped Eva's flank twice and said, "Land as near to the water as yeh can, Angel. The kelpies can meet us there for the debrief on how, between us and the selkies, they get to live to fight another day."

"Or not, as it were," I said.

Eva circled the beach once, over the heads of the kelpies. By the time she landed on the beach face, just shy of the swash, the kelpies were already cantering down to meet us.

Though I'd not seen them while Alaric and I had been speaking to Emily and Safi, it wasn't long before a small pod of selkies arrived too. Able to travel through water almost as fast as Eva could in the sky.

They stopped at the point where breaking waves rolled up onto the sand, and shortly after, Alaric and I—more used to traveling by dragon—helped the two selkies down to join their comrades. Though from the way Emily and Safi had spoken, they were more friends than anything else. The selkies clearly were loyal to their kind and had a close connection with one another.

As the kelpies reached us, Eva shifted back to her fae form, and I handed her a dress.

Maximos and his herd neighed their displeasure at seeing their nemeses being so bold-faced as they encroached on their land. But before he could say anything in protest and piss us off any more, I spoke before he got the chance.

"The Mount Mortums ships have turned around. Thanks to the brave efforts of our friends here–" I said, gesturing to the long line of selkies in various stages of shedding their seal skin and revealing two fae legs.

Several kelpies suddenly found something very interesting in the sand to stare at rather than having to face the grieving and injured creatures who'd risked everything to help their realm.

"–they will soon be one ship down. And reliant on just their engines, thanks to Evangelia Dyvrad burning their masts, making sailing impossible."

At the use of Eva's true last name, several murmurs broke out among the selkie herd. How many had lived during her grandparent's reign? More importantly, would they be loyal to the old dragon king and queen if they knew they'd actually lived?

"The selkies helped?" Maximos asked, raising his eyes to look at their foe who'd stepped up today.

"Aye," Alaric confirmed. "Yeh owe them a great debt. They lost a lot o' brave friends out there."

Maximos was silent for several long seconds. *"Thank you,"* he eventually said. *"As the land fae said, we owe you greatly for laying down your lives to defend our cove."*

"We were cowards," a familiar voice said. Sherbet.

"No, Sherbet. It is I who was the coward. I made the decision. It's on me." Maximos confessed, and I found my annoyance at the male softening. It can't have been easy to

admit in front of his herd. Even harder in front of the selkies. *"Will you accept our thanks by payment with our land? Name your price. Tell us how much you need."*

"We don't want to take your territory from you," Safi said, walking over the swash and onto the dry sand toward Maximos. "We want to share it. Live here in harmony like we used to. The selkie, kelpie, and any other sea folk who wish to join us."

Maximos III's jaw hit the sand harder than he'd dropped it when Alaric waved the clamshell holding his grandfather's ashes. *"You want an* alliance?" he hedged.

Safi glanced over to her friends paddling in the water. Then walked over to Sherbet and every kelpie on the beach held their breath. Sherbet included.

"We do," she said. "Very much so." She reached out with nimble fingers and removed the seaweed knotting his mane.

His large horse's head nuzzled against her hand in thanks, and she smiled, stroking his cheek.

"Then we accept," Maximos said, and the kelpie all neighed their excitement at the long overdue truce.

Alaric unsheathed his sword, and it was mine and Eva's turn to hold our breath. *What in fates' name was he doing?*

He cleared his throat and said, "May the past remain in the past." He used the point to draw a line in the sand. "When the rebels win this war, and yer truce is no longer as necessary, jus' remember this moment," he said. "May this alliance outlive the war."

I smiled. "Where's Melina with the drinks when you need her?"

CHAPTER 31

Alaric

A bark of a laugh left my lips at the thought of our favorite tavern and its fierce, lioness landlady, Melina. The reminder of the Crooked Claw, and my old life in Ezerat, brought with it more memories. Most of which included my not-so-little brother, who I'd been busy trying not to worry about.

"It'll be a long time before we can get back to the Crooked Claw," I said as guilt settled in over Axel's unknown status. I'd tried to check in with him over the last few days, keen to tell him about the bloodlust cure and see how he was getting on with his lead on Raine. But there was nothing.

It was like the bond had been severed, only he must have done it himself this time, because there was no fucking way he was still unconscious from *'running into a tree'*, which was the story I'd been trying to convince myself wasn't utter bullshite.

I shook the thoughts away. "We need to get back to the Vale, see what army lies in wait," I said.

"Well, you can count us in," Emily said with a dip of her head. "We may not be the strongest fighters on land, but we have the numbers to make a difference."

"And the bravery," Angel said, a kind smile tugging at her lips as the selkie blushed.

"Us too," Maximos said. *"Whatever and whenever you need, we will be ready."* I arched a brow. They hadn't exactly proven to be reliable. *"I swear it this time."*

"Thank you," Kane said, choosing to give the kelpie the benefit of the doubt. "When the day comes, we will send word. If the Mount Mortums return, find a witch and send a raven if you can."

The sea folk bowed their heads as we backed away. But after just a handful of strides across the sand, a niggling tugging at the back of my brain had me turning back.

"I ken it's hard to talk about, but what *exactly* happened to yer fallen warriors?" I asked. "The ones yeh said were in Elikai's games."

Maximos lowered his head, sadness radiating from him. *"It was awful. Like a beast had mauled him. Scales torn apart by claws as sharp and strong as razors. He was so excited for the chance to gain the king's respect...*" he trailed off and I couldn't bring myself to push him further.

It was beyond sickening and while I hadn't seen any of the brutality with my own eyes, I could imagine it. And I fucking hated that I knew what I pictured wouldn't do Elikai's barbarity justice, despite having witnessed some of the worst acts of cruelty to shake this realm over the last two centuries.

Safi sniffed, angling her head back and looking toward the sky as if praying to the fates to undo what had happened to her friend. "Rinn's body was much the same," was all she managed before she dropped her face. Tears had filled her eyes and began to fall.

Somehow, it was harder to hear the selkie speak of their friends' fate in those games, knowing the horrific losses they'd just suffered and that what had happened to Rinn seemed to affect them far worse.

As much as I didn't *want* to know, I suddenly *needed* to know how Elikai was running this so-called competition. If for no other reason than so I could convince my da' and the others back at the camp that we could no longer turn a blind eye.

Maximos was shaking his large head. "*Sounds like they fell against the same warrior.*"

Emily nodded. "I imagine so. You could hear the crowd's reaction to her from outside. When we were handed her body, the gouges were as deep as they were vicious," she added, swallowing a lump in her throat. "I pray to the fates it was a fast death, but that doesn't make it any easier to bear. She was blindsided. She fell for the invitation and entered herself willingly, thinking she could be our salvation."

Safi swallowed hard. "They call her, Anon," she breathed the name, like voicing it might set a curse down upon her entire species.

"That's the one. Apparently, she's a half-breed, and far more deadly than any other fae in the games."

"So far..." Emily said.

"So far?" Angel asked.

She nodded, then pushed her purple hair back from her face. "Horde soldiers are entering now. As well as anyone else stupid or strong enough to think they can beat her."

"He's sacrificing the Dezrothian army for entertainment now, too?" Kane spat, disgust mixed with utter disbelief plastered across his face.

Maximos nodded. *"We haven't sent any more kelpie candidates. It's a death sentence. She's literally tearing apart the competition while the so-called elite cheer and place bets."*

"Yer sure she's a hybrid?" I asked.

"She's definitely a shifter of some kind. Could be bear and wolf, probably mixed with something else too? Dragon?" Maximos suggested, looking at Angel, but the chances of there being another dragon out there that we weren't aware of was slim. A thrakos though...

Emily shook her head. "She's like you," she murmured, tilting her head toward me and my stomach knotted. "Thrakos and wolf. Or so I heard."

"Yeh ken what I am?" I asked, knowing my thrakos side had not been mentioned on the wanted posters.

A sinking sensation began to settle in the pit of my stomach as I waited for her to answer. It was all lining up far too well with the nagging feeling that was quickly becoming a full-blown theory, especially given what Axel had told me last time we communicated. But it was what he hadn't told me that had driven me to turn back and ask the kelpie and selkie to relive their fallen comrades' deaths.

"I told you I've been looking into you. And, well, rumors and gossip travel faster by sea than land," she confirmed. My centuries kept secret had become fucking gossip, yet that was quickly turning into the least of my worries.

"Alaric, you don't think it could be...?" Kane asked in a hushed voice. I nodded, then shook my head once. If my theory was correct, and Kane was coming to the same conclusion, our new allies didn't need to hear us admit that this mysterious Anon might actually be a friend of ours.

I felt around inside my brain for the connection I had with Axel once again. *"Axel, yeh there?"* I thought.

Nothing but silence greeted me once again.

The kelpies were right that the wounds described were unlikely to be made by a shifter alone, but it could easily be a thrakos. And messy too, if the attack occurred while under bloodlust.

"Did any of yeh go to the games, yerself?" I asked, desperately wanting my theory to be wrong, and hoping a better physical description of Anon would help with that.

"As in, inside the arena?" Safi asked, and I nodded. "No," she said. "The king wouldn't allow sea fae like us to watch his games from *inside* the arena. We just heard rumors from outside and during our travels." The bitterness in her voice was thick and left no room to mistake what she thought about Elikai.

"Thanks. That helps us more than yeh ken," I said, nodding to Kane and Angel that I was done with my questioning and ready to get off this beach.

"We will be in touch when the time comes," Kane said. "Be ready. It could be a year from now, perhaps a month or as little as a week. Either way, be ready."

Safi shared a look with Maximos and said, "We will be."

THOUGHTS TUMBLED around my mind as we crossed the beach and continued to distract me as we headed deeper into the forest. Even the changing scenery faded into the background as I remained lost in my own head. The theory I desperately wanted to dismiss consumed me so thoroughly, I didn't even notice Kane and Angel trying to talk to me until a hand grabbed my shoulder and spun me around. Pleased to have gotten my attention, Kane released his grip, but the way he stared at me didn't change. They were worried about me.

"What is going on with you?" Angel asked, her arms folding over her chest. "We have been trying to talk to you for hours."

Hours? I used to lose time like that easily, willing away the days while waiting for the prophecy to come into play. Guilt washed over me, but I wasn't sure whether it was guilt at ignoring my mates, or guilt that I'd not followed up on what was happening with the games. Or for waiting this long to let myself think deeply about Axel and his lead on Raine.

"Sorry, it's just… somethin' Axel said when I last spoke to him."

"When *did* you last speak to him?" Angel asked, a frown weighing down her brows.

"Too long ago," I admitted.

Anger flashed over Angel's features. "How long?"

"Before yeh fed the thrakos yer blood," I admitted, keeping my eyes down.

"Why has it been so long?" Kane asked, confusion tightening his brow.

"He's gone silent on me, jus' after tellin' me he an' Nix had a lead."

"On Raine?" Kane guessed. I wasn't the only one to piece together that the injuries Anon was causing matched what Raine was capable of. Kane had spent a lot of time training with her and had witnessed it firsthand.

"Aye. After what the seafolk said, I cannae help but wonder, what if this Anon is Raine? What if *that* is the lead he found on her?"

"So he told you that he and Nix were following a lead on Raine and then went silent?" Kane asked.

I nodded. Even if it wasn't her, the coronation games needed to be brought to an end, and if not by us, then who? From what the selkies had said, those watching the games weren't about to put a stop to their *entertainment*.

Angel opened her mouth, ready to tell me exactly what she thought about me keeping it to myself, especially when it concerned her best friend. But Kane's eyes went wide as he focused on something behind me, and his arm reached out into the air as he pointed to the sky. I turned to follow his gaze, but all I could see was something black, small and fast, flying in our direction. Kane's vision was better than mine, though.

As I tensed, my nails shifted into claws, ready to defend us. I let my eyes change too, and could make out wings beating on either side of its body and something strapped to its talon.

"Is that a raven?" Angel said, stepping closer toward it as she squinted up at the sky.

The bird appeared larger and larger as it neared, its wingspan the size of a child as it began to glide in its descent, then fluttered to a halt to land on Kane's outstretched arm, claws gripping around his wrist.

Angel reached into her pocket for a handful of nuts and held them up, palm flat. It pecked away at them as Kane removed the note and handed it over to me to read. It was splotchy, like the fae who penned it had been crying as they did, making it hard to decipher. Some words I had to guess to fill the gaps, but I read it aloud as best I could.

I hope this message finds you safe and well.

At the time of writing this, we are one week from spring. What's left of my group and I just returned to the new camp, bringing with us a dwarven family we met on the trade route who agreed to join the alliance.

I spoke with Edelin to make sure she had received our last raven, and she told me it arrived with them shortly after you left for Kelpie Cove.

My message is not one of good news, I'm afraid. We encountered a group of horde soldiers as we embarked on our journey from our allocated trade route to the new camp. A soldier had one of the children, and to save them, Nixen and Axel distracted the soldiers and ordered us to go on without them.

We aren't certain of their fate, and I am so sorry I can't tell you more, but we haven't heard from them since.

I know they are very dear friends of yours.

Lia.

I cursed as my concerns over Axel and Angel's lifelong best friend increased a thousandfold.

Angel gasped as all the color drained from her face instantly. "Speak to Axel," she demanded. "Right now. Ask him what's going on and where they are? Whatever reason he has for going quiet on you–"

"It isnae like that. He's not just gone silent because he's ignoring me," I said. "I've not been able to feel him in my head since he told me about his lead on Raine. It's like the bond is being blocked again."

"Fuck, why didn't you tell us any of this?" Kane asked, pinching his brow like a headache was coming on.

"We've had other things to worry about, things that wouldn't or couldn't wait. Axel hadn't sounded like he was in a life or death situation when the link disconnected," I told them, kicking myself internally for not letting myself accept sooner just how much trouble he could be in.

Fuck, what if they'd killed him? What if he'd known his death was coming and the entire conversation had just been his way of making sure I kept my head in the game?

"That isn't something small. What if it was severed because he was captured? Like last time, in the dungeons," Angel said.

"He didnae mention the horde was there," I said, running a hand through my hair. "Said he was chasing a lead on Raine and was his usual annoyin' fuckin' self, albeit maybe weirder than normal. But how was I supposed to guess?" I began to pace, kicking up dirt under my boots.

"Still, you should have told us," Kane said.

"I was busy trying to get my head around lettin' our female feed an entire camp of thrakos without being allowed to kill any of them for it. An' we've been on a fuckin' wild goose chase thanks to seers and the fuckin' fates themselves ever since. I couldnae have put any of that shite on pause to look for my brother an' yeh ken it."

"You're right," Kane said. "But you don't have to bottle that stuff up."

I sighed. "I ken, and I'm tryin' to learn not to, but it isnae going to happen overnight," I admitted. I'd spent centuries keeping secrets and locking down my personal bullshit. "It's still new to me this whole sharing shite freely, an' that's no because I dinnae trust yeh. I trust yeh with my life."

"Because you have to," Kane snarked.

"I wouldnae change it for the fuckin' realm, world, or universe," I snapped.

He sighed, "I know, I know. I didn't mean that, it's just..." Kane trailed off, searching for the right words.

"Old habits die hard," Angel finished instead. "Regardless, what are we going to do now? We could go and see if we can pick up his trail on the trade route he was covering?" she suggested. "You could track him from there?"

Despite my head being elsewhere during our walk, a glance to where the sun would be setting in the next few hours confirmed we were on track and heading south. If we continued, we would reach the new rebel camp in a few days, and the old camp a day or so sooner. But my gut told me we didn't have that kind of time if we wanted to do something to stop the games.

West would take us back to Kelpie Cove. If we headed north, we would be approaching Ezerat soon enough. Southeast and we'd be at the trade route in less than a day, but I wasn't convinced that wouldn't be a waste of time too.

"The trade route their group was on was the busiest," I said. "There will've been too many fae crossing it since. Not to mention the weather we've had. The rain will have washed away most o' the scents."

"Didn't Thalia say they were already heading to the new camp when they encountered the horde, anyway?" Kane asked. "They could have been anywhere."

"Aye. If they captured them instead of killin' them, there's only two places that the horde would take them, and we all ken it," I said, glancing north.

"The castle dungeons or the arena," Angel clarified.

"Fuck," Kane cursed. "Those games need to be stopped before my brother sacrifices half the realm to them."

"He needs stopping all together," Angel gritted. "But what do we do now? We can't not help them. And I refuse to believe they are dead. Axel and Nix are survivors."

"We find a witch and send a message back," Kane said, rubbing his jaw in thought. "We need to tell the camp Alaric lost contact with Axel. That the bond is broken again. That we have allies and the games are far worse than we imagined."

"Any ideas where we will find a witch willing to spell a raven?" Angel asked, hope absent from her voice.

"Crystal Towers isnae far from here. Half a day's march Northeast. Less if we ran it," I said, thinking over what and who I knew in the witch town whose inhabitants had chosen not to live in Ezerat and form part of the most elite society. I'd always respected them for it, though had no clue where their allegiance would currently lie.

"Know anyone there who would be willing to help us?" Kane asked.

"Nah," I admitted, coming up short.

"Then we find someone *un*willing to cooperate and ensure their silence," Angel said, fire lighting up her sexy, serious eyes.

That I could get on-fucking-board with.

THE TOWN of witches loomed over us, its namesake central tower reaching high into the air. Its peak hidden by clouds where birds blacker than the night's sky flew in crazed circles just below.

A masterpiece of craft; dark stone making the multitude of small colored windows all that much brighter, especially as darkness enveloped the land, making the glow of lights within even more fluorescent.

Small houses, each built from the same dark stone, spiraled out from the tower. Laid out in a specific pattern, for what, I wasn't certain.

The central tower would be a bustling hub of activity, as it always was. Even at this late hour, it would be wise to avoid it, and I'd told Kane and Angel as much before shifting into my wolf and setting off.

It had been light when we left Kelpie Cove, so Angel flying us to Crystal Towers hadn't been an option. Instead, I'd made the journey in wolf form, with Angel on my back. While Kane had run next to me, easily able to keep up.

"Where do you suggest we start?" Angel whispered as she slid from my back.

We'd usually figured out at least a vague plan before turning up in a town or village uninvited, but traveling in wolf form meant we hadn't been able to discuss any kind of plan enroute.

Gawking up at the imposing tower, Kane shrugged.

"Despite what I said before," Angel began. "I've thought about it, and I'd really rather not force someone's hand. It would make us no better than *him.*"

I nodded my agreement. I'd done a lot of thinking of my own during the journey here. We were closer to Ezerat now than we had been since leaving the catacombs, having stuck to villages surrounding the Vale when hunting for allies. The closer we drew to the castle, the more I thought about the coronation games, and the more I knew it was time to end them.

Though I had been the one to suggest ignorance would be bliss when it came to that particular problem. That our focus needed to be on building an army and interfering with the trade routes instead. It was past the time to do what we should have done weeks ago, yet weren't in any position to.

I couldn't be certain we were much more ready now; that would depend on what happened when my letters were received. For now, I could only hope my mates agreed with me that what I planned to write was the right thing to do.

Shifting back, I pulled on the clothes from the pack that Kane carried. "I stopped here because these stones–" I gestured to the line of large, evenly spaced boulders circling the hub "–alert the witches whenever a fae not from their coven crosses. When we pass, there'll be no going back. They'll ken we're here."

Concern knit their brows, but I crouched down beside the closest stone anyway and waved them over, pointing out the faint, almost invisible glyphs etched into the surface.

"Careful no' to touch them," I warned.

Unless you knew to look, you would miss them completely. I only knew about them thanks to having visited on horde business so many times. At first glance, they were just stones marking the line of the edge of the town. But when you looked closer, you could see their true purpose.

Augustus had liked witches more than most other races. Not in the way he'd regarded high fae, but they were second or third in his hierarchy. However, he didn't like the fact these particular witches had decided to live outside of Ezerat as one cohesive large coven, under the control of a High Priestess that they looked upon as their queen. Though they'd never told him as much. Still, he didn't hunt or stop them. They were too valuable to him, so instead he sent the horde here regularly to keep an eye and remind them whose cock was the biggest.

Whenever we crossed boulders that circled the town's hub, it wasn't long before the witches came to see what we wanted. No matter how stealthy or careful we were to stick to the shadows.

"Are there any witches who live outside of this warded area?" Kane asked.

I shook my head. Not that I was aware of. "No, they like to stick together. Rare to find a lone witch. Our best bet is to draw them out," I explained. "We'll trigger the glyphs and wait for them to come to us. If there are too many, we can pull back. Whenever I've triggered them before, they've sent three at most to come and see us, which we can handle between the three of us."

"And what then?" Angel asked. "I doubt they will be happy to send a raven for us just because we got the jump on them."

"Whatever it takes to convince them," Kane said. "Refusing isn't an option we can accept."

"Aye. When they come, get behind them and cover their mouths to stop them from using their magic. Nothin' too vicious. We can question them on their allegiance, and go from there," I finished, purposely leaving out what we'd have to do next if they refused to help. Because that would depend on the reception they gave us.

But now I knew at least that Angel and Kane had spent our silent journey with the same thought as me bouncing around their heads. It was time to put an end to the games, and in order to do that, we needed help.

"I think we should split up," Kane suggested, glancing around the giant stones, his mind ticking as he studied at each large boulder in turn.

The concern on Angel's face at the thought of being separated, when surrounded by a town-sized coven, pretty much mirrored my own feelings on it. It wasn't something I was comfortable with either, but I gestured for him to continue.

"We will trigger this one. Then separate and take a stone each, the next three closest, and wait behind them. That way we have some protection against their spells should they attack us straight away, but can also have their flank the moment they cross outside the warded border should they take a closer look at the glyph which was triggered."

"Alright, but I'll set the ward off. We dinnae need to each trigger it, one intruder's presence will be enough," I said, but when they didn't move, I continued. "This way they will be jus' expecting one fae, not three." With a nod of understanding they both took a stone, Kane crouched behind one to the right of where we stood, and Angel moved a bit further away, crouching behind one a few over to the left.

Taking a steadying breath, I reached out and skimmed my hand through where the ward line should have been. As easy as it would have been to touch the glyph itself, that would probably send too many alarms through the central spire to be useful. I wanted them to suspect someone had come into the village, not someone trying to get their attention.

Crouching low to the ground, I hid behind the boulder to the right of Angel. Avoiding touching the damned thing, lest I give away our position, I waited for anything. My breath was shallow as I waited, scanning the cobbled street for any sign of a fae coming this way.

There was no wailing alarm, but I hadn't expected one. The witches would know, they always did. They liked to have the upper hand against anyone entering their territory.

"Alaric Durand," a low voice whispered from behind us, forcing me to tear my eyes away from the tower just as a door flew open, revealing a group of fuck knew how many witches piling out onto the lawns leading our way.

My eyes landed on the one who'd called my name. She was short and cloaked in not only shadows from a tree beside her, but the long black coat she wore with the hood pulled down low, covering her eyes and hiding her identity.

"Who the fuck are yeh?" I hissed under my breath, "Angel, Kane, eyes forward. Tell me how many there are and how long we have."

"Too many." The cloaked witch said, her head tilting. "But I can help you."

"At least a dozen," Kane whispered, ignoring the witch at his back despite it going against all of his training. "More are coming. They must know it's you."

Fuck.

"How?" I asked the witch. "How did yeh ken it was me?"

"Isn't it obvious?" she asked, clicking her tongue.

"Answer me," I growled.

"You've triggered them before. We know you. The *wards* know you," she said. "Now, do you want my help or not? It won't cost you much."

"What the fuck are yeh talkin' about?" I snapped. How long had she been stalking us? How much had she heard? How had she beat the other witches here and why would she want to go against them to help us?

So many unanswered questions, and zero fucking time.

"Alaric, we don't have time for this," Angel gritted, mimicking my thoughts. "What do you want us to do?"

"Oh, so *she* must be the dragon," the witch said, sounding far too interested.

"The wards," I growled, changing the subject back. "Start talkin'." I didn't care too much about the finer details, but I needed to know if she could be trusted and I didn't have long for her to prove it.

"It's a long story and looks like your time is about to run out," the female crooned. "Decide. Do you accept or decline my offer to help?"

"If we are going to engage, now's the time," Kane urged as though he'd tuned out the witch's taunts in the face of the bigger threat.

I risked a quick glance back over my shoulder as several colorful flashes erupted from the fast approaching witches' palms, smashing into the rock beside which I'd triggered the wards. We were about to have no choice but to engage in what would doubtlessly be a messy fight. "What's yer price?" I asked.

"Alaric," Kane gritted. "We need to move or act. What's your call?"

"Yer price, witch. Name it."

"Tick…tock…tick…tock," she said slowly, ignoring my question and a string of curses from Angel snapped my attention her way.

The boulder she crouched behind wouldn't withstand much more, and my female was fatally close to being exposed to the brutality of the coven's wrath. Her scales danced up her neck as she tried to make herself smaller.

My eyes darted between my mates and the cloaked witch. Angel's head was moving quickly, nodding her encouragement for me to take the deal with desperation. She could fight them, but we needed the witches' help. Slaughtering them wouldn't endear them to us.

I looked at Kane again. "Do it," he urged as spells battered the rock at his back.

Fuck. Fine. "I accept," I snapped. No sooner had the two words left my mouth I regretted them. The binding spell washed over me, tying me in to the deal.

An open-ended deal was a fool's business, especially with a witch, and I never took myself as a fool. But what choice did I have? We needed a witch and fleeing Crystal Towers, or killing them, would get us one willing to help.

The cloaked female stepped forward, a smirk tugging at her lips. They were familiar all of a sudden. She raised an elegant hand in the air, and I knew beyond any doubt that something wasn't right.

I'd expected her to cloak us and lead us to somewhere safe so we could talk. So we could send our messages and learn what she wanted in return. Instead, pulling the hood down from her head, she revealed her presence to the witches. And her face to me.

Dark hair blew in the wind as she approached us, and I knew exactly who she was. I held my breath, dread sinking into the pit of my stomach. *Taylah.* But why would the High Priestess of Crystal Towers go against her coven and force me into a deal?

She wanted something, something big. Something I would have to refuse. And I couldn't break the magic bargain. It wasn't a blood oath, it was worse. I'd be a slave to the coven. Theirs to do with as they saw fit. If that included killing me, they could. But they wouldn't.

What have I done?

"You made that too easy, Alaric. But to answer one of your many questions, the wards remember all those who cross them. So we know who comes into our territory at all times, especially horde members. Current or otherwise," she said, smirking as she looked down at where I crouched on the ground near her fucking feet. "Not that we needed it. I could hear your thoughts from one town over. You really should be more careful," she said, her tone condescending.

My thrakos claws descended, shredding the grass and sinking easily into the soft earth.

Taylah was one of the most powerful witches in all of Dezrothia. Her gift, though not as rare as Edelin's, was something that had always made me uneasy around her, yet had somehow slipped my fucking mind. If I disliked seers knowing my business, I fucking despised telepaths playing inside my head.

"Alaric," Kane warned from low in his throat. My head whipped around to him and I focused on his piercing blue eyes and the way they looked navy in this light. "Calm down," he mouthed, and I tried, but fuck, I hated that the witch had played me so well. She had me over a barrel without a way out by doing whatever the fuck she wanted.

My mates will hate me for this.

The thought was as sudden as it was irrational. I stared back at Kane, finding he wasn't angry. Nor did he look let down or disappointed, despite the feeling crawling all over my skin that he was. No. That thought wasn't my own. Seeds of doubt were being forced into my mind. The witch didn't know the connection I experienced with my mates was deeper than that. He was trying to tell me, without words, that we would deal with whatever the witches had tricked us into. Together.

"Get the fuck out of my head, witch," I hissed, baring my teeth.

We were outnumbered, an entire town against the three of us. If I couldn't talk our way out of this, it could spell disaster. Angel might have to burn Crystal Towers and its residents to ashes, consequences be damned. It wasn't an option I even wanted to consider.

Taylah laughed. "You'd stop your dragon from giving you a way out of this?" she asked. "To save her from what? A little guilt."

"Don't compare him to your own low standards," Angel spat, her voice much closer now than it should have been. She'd crept over to my side and as her hand came down over mine gently and my claw retracted. I took a deep, calming breath of her scent. The smoky campfire mixed with vanilla soothing any lingering doubt.

"Perhaps you aren't the male I thought you were," Taylah mused as she tilted her head to the side. "Not that it matters. Now, about our deal, I will uphold my end and have your messages delivered."

"And in return?" Kane asked, standing slowly as he moved toward where Angel and I were still crouched.

"Oh hello, princeling," Taylah said, looking him up and down slowly. "Isn't he just a handsome thing?" she cooed, looking out over the lawn of witches.

I wasn't sure if the growl that reverberated through the air came from me or Angel, but it didn't make Taylah so much as flinch. If anything, it encouraged her, given the way she giggled as murmurs of agreement came from her coven.

"And in return?" Kane said, slowly repeating himself and ignoring the kind of attention that he used to enjoy in his former life. There was an undertone of allure creeping into his words, but he'd have to use more than a subtle suggestion to manipulate this witch's mind. Her entire existence and place in her coven was thanks to her mind's abilities. Though I suspected he was reminding her that he could use it but was choosing not to.

"Well, that really depends on how much you will owe us once you are done here, doesn't it?" she said happily. "You can hardly expect me to be able to determine such a thing when I don't know the extent of what brings you here."

"She's a telepath," I told my mates. "She ken's exactly why we are here and what we want. A fuckin' strong one too, given she's in charge 'round here."

"Though it's always nice to hear, flattery won't get you out of our deal, Alaric," she said. "And on that note, I better take you to the library." She walked straight past us and continued up the path to the tower. When my mates and I didn't immediately follow, she turned back to eye us, "Come on, those letters aren't going to write themselves."

WE FOUND the library on the top floor of the tower. It was a circular space with several windows and not much else. Perhaps they'd given up on reading in here, given how impossible it would be to relax with a book when an entire flock of ravens insisted on circling the windows. Some whizzed by, while others landed on the sills, pecking at the colored glass with their beaks or squawking sporadically.

"This is your library?" Kane asked, turning in a slow circle. "But where are the books?"

Taylah muttered something beneath her breath as she waved a hand and whatever concealment spell she used to hide this place dropped, revealing the library in all its... mess.

Grimoires were piled in great stacks, some as high as the ceiling, others just two or three tall. There was no organization or rhyme nor reason as to why the books were placed the way they were. The smile on Taylah's face as she dismissed the witches who'd followed us up here spoke of how perfect the space was to her.

It was unsettling that she was confident enough to stay alone with us, and I knew it had everything to do with that stupid deal she had forced me into. But what had driven her to do it in the first place? Yes, I needed to get the letters sent, but fuck, I had to know her motives before I let her uphold her end, tying me in completely to do the same.

"The seer," she said, pulling the question from my mind without me having to ask or even form it. "We don't have one and I understand you do."

"Yeh've lost yer damn mind, Taylah," I said. "I cannae give yeh the Sybilline witch."

"Then break the deal," she smiled. "We will have you instead."

"What?" Angel growled.

At the same time, Kane snapped, "No."

I shook my head. "She's no' getting me or the seer."

"You want to test that theory?" she asked. "I believe it's been quite the day of theory spirals for you already."

"How do yeh think I'm goin' to convince the most powerful seer to come and join yer coven?"

"You tell her, and she decides whether she'd rather sacrifice you or herself," Taylah said. "We are easy either way."

My mates stood straighter, ready to attack, but thankfully didn't make a move to gut the witch, not yet, despite how badly I knew they'd want to. Instead, they just stepped in closer to either side of me.

Fucking seer would be the death of me. I'd cursed Edelin more times than I could count, but I'd always liked her deep down. And she was one of the fae I respected most in this realm. Despite her cryptic way of doing things.

"Well," Taylah pushed. "Are you going to agree to uphold your end if I do mine? Or are the letters not that important after all?"

"Yer price is too high and yeh ken it," I said. "A few ravens to spell? It's fuckin' child's play to yeh. And yeh want the most powerful seer in Dezrothia in return?"

"A few ravens delivering letters to *start a war against our king,*" she corrected. "Perhaps my price isn't high enough? Trust me, you should agree to my terms while I'm feeling so generous that this is all I'll ask for."

I find it is easier to agree with witches, especially when a seer is involved.

The words drifted through my mind as I remembered where I'd heard them. The last words Edelin had spoken to me before we'd left for Kelpie Cove.

You'd do well to do the same.

She'd known this was coming. Of course she fucking had. And she wanted me to agree, otherwise she would never have told me.

Clever fucking seer and her cryptically brilliant bullshit.

I pushed my shoulders back and fought the smile that twitched my lips. "I agree."

"What?!" Angel gasped. "Alaric! No–"

"–It's fine," I cut over her protests. I would explain just as soon as the ravens left this tower with our letters. There wasn't time now; we needed to get out of this place sooner rather than later. Before any more witchy bullshite was thrown at us.

My mates would understand why I'd made the call. No, not just understand, they'd agree that it was the right call to make. Because with every ounce of my being that didn't trust Taylah, it was the exact opposite with Edelin. I trusted that witch implicitly. Angel and Kane did, too.

She was old, ancient even. And she'd been playing her cryptic seer fuckery for a very long time. Angel had said it herself; Edelin never said anything that didn't have meaning.

Taylah smiled. "Then we have a deal." She gestured to the writing table and surprised me when she didn't follow my mates and I over. Then again, she could just listen to our thoughts to get all the information she needed. Opening a window, she selected a bird to fuss over instead.

I reached for several pieces of parchment, my thoughts turning to what message to send. "If we're to stop those games, we need to call in every alliance, favor, and friendship we've ever made," I said.

Angel swallowed hard. "It's really time, isn't it?" she said, like she'd dreamed of this since the day she was born in the Fading Vale.

"Aye."

"Agreed," Kane said. "If we leave the games to end on Elikai's terms, then he will be able to prepare for us. Even turn the tables in his favor. There's no way he would just let us live our lives otherwise. We will lose any element of surprise we might be able to gain if we don't." There was no excitement in his voice at the prospect, some sadness, but mostly it was matter of fact.

"It certainly feels like now or never," Angel said, reaching for a quill. "Once he focuses his attention on hunting us, our numbers will only go down and down. And fewer and fewer fae will join the cause, which is hard enough to convince them. There's no fighting him on his terms."

"Aye," I agreed, reaching for a quill of my own. There was no way of knowing how Angel's grandparent's search for allies had been going the second time around, but we had more now than we'd had at any point in my existence. Even if just the sea folk, the Dyvrad's, Camp Camille rebels and some dwarfs that Axel and Nix's team had won over, showed up, we had a better chance of winning than we'd ever had before.

"I'll write to the sea folk," Angel said. "Though I'm not sure how well received it will be so soon. They've barely had a day to work things out with each other."

I shook my head. "They'll come," I told her.

"I'll finally try to call in that favor with Rangaran," Kane added.

"Good idea," I said. "I'll write to my da'."

"When? And where?" Angel asked.

I glanced over my shoulder to where Taylah stood in the doorway, very interested in her long, dark nails. Fuck it. There was no way of keeping it from her. And so long as I held up my end with whatever she wanted from me, she had no reason to betray us to Elikai or the horde.

As I thought it, she glanced up, met my eyes with the darkness of hers and smirked.

"The first day of spring," I said. One week from now. It was long enough for us to get there and start making plans. As well as greet any to arrive early. *Fates, please let there be allies to greet.* "At the place we wrapped Miles and Ilona's bodies."

Vast and desolate enough to risk camping for a few nights as our allies arrived. Close enough to the city that we'd only have half a day's march before reaching Ezerat. The selkies could direct us to the arena from there. Aside from our camp of rebels, the selkies were the only other alliance I was confident would be a sure bet. And they happened to know exactly where Elikai was holding his sick fucking games.

I drew maps to send with the letters going to Rangaran and Kelpie Cove and a third, as I remembered some old friends in Ezerat. I asked Kane to write one more letter addressed to the Crooked Claw once he was done with Kumo's; they might not be able to get out of the city easily, but they'd murder me for not inviting them.

I could rely on Braxton, the Dyvrad's, Westly and Thalia to direct Camp Camille and any other new allies from the Fading Vale.

All that was left was my own letter. I dipped the quill into the ink bottle and began.

Da',

It's time...

CHAPTER 32
Nixen

"The moment you've all been waiting for," Elikai announced from his dais. "Guards! Bring out Jarrah and Anon!"

"Does this mean all the horde candidates are dead?" Axel asked through the cage wall adjoining our cells.

"I guess so," I murmured back, craning my neck to get a better look toward the other end of the pit where Raine's cage opened.

Seeing her now was no easier than the first time they'd let her out and escorted her onto the stage. Not that I'd expected it to be. It hadn't been any more bearable when they had done the same several times in between that first shocking day and now.

Jarrah looked so bad I almost felt sorry for him. But Raine… She was virtually unrecognizable.

The guards led them to the oval from either side and Jarrah didn't waste a second trying to get into her head, telling her how she should just roll over and prepare to go into the fates' embrace.

The crowd didn't react to his drivel, rather they fell into an eerie silence, noticing at the same time as I that they were both weaponless. They would have to rely solely on their physical strength and the might of their hybrid forms. Perhaps they hadn't been allowed to use them?

Let the best fae win. Just fates, please let it be Raine.

"Come on, Raine," I muttered. "You've got this." My face was as close to the cage door as I could get without triggering the warlock's spell. I knew she'd heard me, she was right outside on the edge of the pit, yet she didn't so much as glance my way.

No sooner were the collars removed and Raine shifted into her wolf form, her hackles raised. Tearing forward in a surge of speed, she pounced before Jarrah was done with his taunts. If he'd planned on psyching her out, it hadn't worked.

Rather than use his magic, he transformed into his spider form, scuttling out of the way just in time for Raine to crash down hard into the pit floor.

As the she-wolf shook off the impact, Jarrah scurried on top of her, just like he had in the Vale. Weaving his webs somehow faster despite him doubtlessly feeling as shit as he looked, having survived weeks' worth of fights to the death.

The crowd, who'd been chanting "Anon! Anon! Anon!" at the tops of their lungs, fell into silence. When Raine shifted again, into her thrakos form, and her wings sliced through the webs easily, they resumed chanting her false name.

Since arriving here, I'd been trying to work out whether the spectators cheered her name because they truly wanted her to win, or because they'd bet so much coin on her victories at this point that they feared what would happen to their fortune should she lose.

When Raine gathered a ball of fire between her hands, and the crowd breathed a sigh of relief at her having the upper hand once again, I determined it to be the latter.

Some of the fights had been too hard to watch, so I'd watched the so-called *'elite'* of Ezerat instead. I couldn't believe there was a time that a different version of me had wanted nothing more than to be like them. All I cared about now was waiting out my time until I was let out of this fates' forsaken cage to fight. The moment my collar was off, only death would stop me from getting Raine and Axel out of this arena.

With the cuff blocking their bond, Axel couldn't even send word for help. Our friends and allies had no idea where we were, or that Raine was here too.

Axel spoke to me through the cage wall every night and fantasized about ways we might get out of this, each becoming more and more unrealistic as his need for blood increased. The scraps of leftovers they shoved through our cage doors weren't enough to give us the energy we needed to be at full strength for whenever Elikai decided it was time to announce our first fight, nor was it so lacking, we'd starve.

Axel had let his rot and was using it to lure rats in. He'd discovered the warlock's spell on the bars only affected the fae, so he'd spent hours and hours sitting completely still, waiting and waiting until some rodent came sniffing, walking right into his trap.

He thought I was doing the same because that's what I'd told him. The truth was, the bloodlust had somehow not hit me yet. Maybe my thrakos nature was getting all it needed by feeding off my guilt.

I'd never forgive myself for getting Axel into this with me. But when I'd heard the guards talking that day in the forest about the thrakos-wolf female, I'd seen a chance to make it up to Raine by coming to help her. After all, I'd been the one to let her go, insisting she needed space to mourn Miles. I'd been the one to want to leave the catacombs on Eva's back and not wait for her to return first.

Jarrah and Raine continued to fight, like two tornados amid a storm. Switching forms and abilities between one heartbeat and the next, never pausing for breath. Sweat and blood dripped down Raine's face, but she didn't wipe or even blink it away, focused completely on her target and the desire to hurt, maim, kill.

She was beautifully savage, but in a way that shattered my heart. She was a tough female. Fuck, she was one of the toughest fae I knew. And I could only pray to the fates that she wouldn't remember every gory detail of her time here. That the bloodlust blackouts would save her from those memories.

Raine made a swift slash with her thrakos claws. Jarrah, who had shifted into his fae form, managed to dodge most of the damage by quickly pulling back. She was aiming for his throat, her eyes focused hard on the thrum of his pulse.

She struck out again, and a line of blood appeared across Jarrah's jaw. But it was barely a scratch.

Jarrah muttered a spell that struck true. She yelped. It was an agonized noise and the first sound to have crossed her lips in all the days of trying to talk to her.

"Raine!" I called, her name ripping from me. My cheek brushed one of the bars, and I was jolted backward as the jolt of lightning shot through me. Cursing at the pain, I scrambled forward on hands and knees just in time to see her on the ground. She shifted again, but so had Jarrah.

The giant spider jumped into the air, and I heard a rib crack as he came crashing down on her fur. Raine thrashed uselessly below him as he wrapped her in his wire-like web. Scurrying around her so quickly, my eyes could barely keep track of him.

White silken strings wrapped around her head, torso, and front legs. Only her hind legs were free to kick out, which they did with a desperation she hadn't had during any of the other fights I'd witnessed. Not once this week. She'd been put against horde soldier after horde soldier, even a troll, and hadn't writhed about the pit floor like her life depended on it.

Axel called out from his cage, reassuring her she could come back from this, but I wasn't sure. Jarrah had done this to Raine before using this very tactic. The more she moved, the faster she emptied her lungs, working too hard to catch a breath. And the sooner she'd suffocate.

Once she was completely covered and fell still, Jarrah shifted back to his fae form. "I gave you the chance to work together," he said. "I told you that you couldn't beat me. Now look at you! You brought this upon yourself!"

I felt the heat against my face before I saw what was causing it. Flames burst through the webs, rendering them to ash. Raine was up on all fours in an instant, thrakos flames engulfing her wolf form as she flew toward Jarrah, her jaw open.

She clamped her teeth over his shoulder, biting down so hard the scream that left his lips was inaudible.

Axel cheered, and the crowd sat forward, while I held my breath.

Raine unlocked her jaw and Jarrah fell backward. His mouth was moving, but none of what he was saying made sense.

A thrakos burst free from the wolf, and took the few steps it took to be at his side, looking down over him. The crazed pleas turned into begging as the wound on his shoulder began to knit back together.

He could still use his mouth. He could send curses and spells at her, but fear had paralyzed his brain from thinking clearly. His eyes were wide as he pleaded for her to spare him. Promised that they could work together for the rest of the games. Even told her that Axel and I had come to put her down, not save her.

"End this, Raine," I said, done with listening to his shit.

To my astonishment, her head turned my way, eyes locking with mine. She didn't say a word, just nodded once, then turned back to him.

She ran her tongue across her lips, but rather than satisfy the craving to swallow it down, she spat it at him. Red splattered across his face as she narrowed her eyes on him, deciding how exactly to finish this. Would she make it hurt? Make it painless? The Raine I knew wasn't cruel, but it was impossible to know how much of that female was still inside her.

If they ever wrote a book about these games, it would be titled *'Raine of Terror'*. Elikai wouldn't even be featured on the cover. No. The twisted tale would be wrapped in a painting of this image right now. She stood over Jarrah's petrified body, her thrakos wings on full display, his blood smeared across her lips and a vast nothingness in her eyes.

She dropped down into a crouch beside him and cleared her throat. "This is for what you did to my king." She stretched out a clawed hand and hovered it above his chest. Tilting her chin, she looked toward Elikai, sitting on his throne among the crowd. Crystal was at his side, her fist clenched tightly, as though willing Raine to hurry up and murder the traitorous bastard. "*Nekane* Regis," she finished, then plunged her nails through Jarrah's ribs and tore out his heart.

It was a quicker and easier death than he deserved, but the look on Elikai's face, and the fact it had been witnessed by the entire arena, made up for that. Fury was too gentle a word.

Axel cheered and hollered with the crowd, though for very different reasons. Raine had just enough time to look my way and mouth, "It's done," before the horde were upon her, wrestling her to the ground beside where Jarrah's heart lay, forcing the collar back around her neck.

She didn't fight them, just kept her eyes on me until they dragged her out of my line of sight and back to her cage.

CHAPTER 33

Evangelia

Shortly after Taylah's raven's took to the skies, I shifted and followed, flying with my mates on my back for the first stretch of our journey from Crystal Towers.

As we'd only packed enough supplies for our mission to Kelpie Cove, and had no intention of asking the witches for anything more than what we'd agreed to, Alaric made the call for me to land a few hours before sunrise; a day's walk short of the barren lands where we'd find the meeting point.

I'd dropped through thick clouds, gliding low enough to see a little better in the darkness cloaking Dezrothia and eventually spotted a patch of land with several lakes and streams zigzagging through it.

As soon as we'd landed, we filled our canteens from a freshwater spring, drank deeply, and refilled them to the brim.

Alaric shifted, traveling in wolf form so he could hunt for food, while Kane and I hiked, but with no deer or even rabbit in sight, we stopped at a lake flush with salmon. While he dove for fish, Kane pitched the tent, and I assembled sticks, dry leaves and some larger logs, then set them ablaze with a quick breath of flame. With our stomachs full for the first time in days, we slept at the side of the moonlit lake through the daylight hours. Then continued on at sun set, heading a little further south toward our destination.

As we walked on through thick trees, I couldn't help but wonder where we would be a week from now. Whether the letters had reached the intended recipients. And what Edelin had planned for the deal Alaric had made with Taylah, because surely her intention when she'd hinted for him to agree wasn't to actually join their coven, right?

We reached the clearing two nights after leaving the witches and though I knew even those closest to the location would not have reached it before us, my stomach still sank when we arrived at a great expanse of nothing and no one.

While Alaric had been keeping us busy, already in full horde general mode, Kane had been keeping us in good spirits, as he was now, attempting to debone his first fish. Though I didn't think he was being intentionally funny with it.

Times like this, watching him struggle with something that I'd grown up doing, I was reminded of where he'd been and how far he'd come. While he'd gone from royal to rebel, even more difficult to get my head around was that I had somehow done the opposite. Going from Evangelia Malion of the Fading Vale to Princess Evangelia Dyvrad.

My grandparents hadn't actually said whether they truly intended to reclaim the castle. For now, it was just the story they were going with when trying to build alliances. It gave us the best chance at eradicating the bigger, more immediate problem. *Elikai*. We'll deal with the politics later.

The thought of being the heir of Dezrothia was an impossible one to get my head around. I couldn't even think about the responsibility that would come with it. It just wasn't fathomable. I'd barely recognized myself in the tailored gowns Elikai had insisted I wore.

And while killing time during long treks with only my own thoughts to entertain myself, I'd often tried to picture my mother in a princess' gown and tiara, but just... couldn't. She always seemed so at home in rough spun tunics and leather pants. To think of her any other way was near impossible. There were so many mundane questions I wanted to ask my grandparents about her life back then, but the time had never felt right.

What bedchamber had been hers in the castle? Was it a room I'd been inside of? Had she known about the secret spy hole hidden in the wall that looked out to the throne room? And so many more questions that felt equally pointless when compared to the bigger picture of what we faced now, yet felt important to me. Especially if I was ever to understand who my mother had truly been and why she'd kept so much from me.

My father too. His life and their story of how he'd gone from her guardian to her mate was something that had died with them. Just another tragedy Augustus and Elikai were responsible for.

"We might just have to eat this one with a few bones in it," Kane said, pulling me back to the here and now as he poked the sad-looking salmon with the point of his knife.

"I'd help, but it sounds like a job for nimble fingered land fae," the familiar voice said directly into my mind.

"Sherbet?" I gasped, shooting up from where I was crouched beside Kane. My eyes scanned the trees lining the clearing as I turned full circle, searching for its owner.

Kane leaped up too, sending the poor butchered fish flying. It flopped down and landed in the duff, just as Alaric stepped out from the trees to the eastern side, holding stacks of freshly chopped wood under one arm and over the opposite shoulder, his ax tucked through the belt at the waist of his tunic.

"Over here!" came another familiar voice, this one female. Our eyes darted westward as we turned as one, where Emily was waving. I smiled so widely my cheeks strained as I waved back.

"Is she… *riding* Sherbet?" Kane asked.

"Aye," Alaric said as he reached us, dropping the firewood in a pile beside our tent. "Comin'?"

"Absolutely," I said, still beaming. I couldn't decide what had me smiling more, the fact they'd shown up, or that they had worked together, having the kelpie carry the selkie on their backs, to make sure they got here quickly.

Safi and Maximos appeared from the tree line as we began to make our way across the clearing. And by the time we made it halfway, hundreds of sea folk pairs had stepped out of the thick forest and entered the clearing.

"You came," Kane said as Emily, Safi and a pink-haired friend of theirs climbed down from their kelpies. The rest of the sea folk unit held back a little, forming row upon row of lines across the grass.

"Of course we did!" Safi said.

"Did we ever give you any reason to doubt us?" Maximos asked, but his tone was light and my mates and I, along with the selkie trio, snorted a laugh, while Sherbet hung his head dramatically, lifting a hoof as though to hide the blush from his fur covered scales.

"Yeh had us worried for a minute there back at Kelpie Cove," Alaric said. "But we knew yeh'd come."

"A weak moment," Maximos explained. *"One that will not happen again. Though we expected a bit more time to pass before hearing from you."*

"Things changed," Alaric said. "Yeh helped us realize we cannae ignore what Elikai is doin' to fae like yer friends in those so-called games. We dinnae have the time to wait any longer."

"It's scary to think what else he's capable of. He needs to be stopped before we find out," Safi said. "And sorry to be the bearer of bad news, but you should probably know… the Mount Mortums ships came back. Both of them intact, like we'd never almost destroyed one of them. We were already gathered on the beach planning our attack when your raven arrived."

"Fuck," Alaric said. "Any idea why they're so set on gettin' here?"

"To deliver Elikai's coronation gift," Emily said. "Though we have no idea what kind of extravagant present takes two entire ships to transport. We had spies listening to the warriors out on deck, even a few trying to get inside the ship, but none spoke of exactly what it is."

"We made the decision to let them deliver it, so we could come straight here," Maximos said. *"Otherwise, we likely wouldn't have made it here at all."*

"I'd have done the same," Alaric said, stroking his chin in deep thought while Maximos neighed his delight at the former horde general's approval.

"Definitely the right call," I agreed. "As I explained in the letter, it's time we put an end to such cruelty in Dezrothia, and to do that we need an army to rival theirs." I cleared my throat as too much emotion seeped its way in, threatening to choke me. "You are brave fae to stand with us. It won't be forgotten when we win."

I wasn't sure I had the authority to make such promises, but I would make sure I did good on my word. Just as they had theirs by showing up here.

"Where's the rest of the army?" Sherbet asked, his large head looking up, down and around the clearing.

"On their way," Kane said. "I believe you were the closest. Most are traveling from the southern part of the Vale."

"We look forward to meeting them," Emily said. "What can we do to help you prepare for their arrival?" she asked, looking directly at me. Her gray eyes reminded me of a stormy sea.

I reached out for Alaric's hand and linked his fingers with mine. "I'm sure Alaric here can think of a few things," I said, smiling up at my mate, before giving Kane a quick wink.

They'd soon wish they never asked.

WE WORKED LATE into the evening building shelters for the kelpie and selkie to sleep under, picking a large patch of the forest at the west end of the clearing.

Being sea fae, whose homes were built into caves around the cove, I didn't imagine they had tents or supplies for sleeping rough like rebels did. Plus, they'd left their land in a hurry.

With so many mouths to feed while we waited for more allies to follow suit, this morning Alaric left with a small group of kelpie and selkie in search of a lake. With the experts in fishing on his team, far more naturally talented at it than Kane or I, they planned to fill several bags with fresh catches to bring back and bury in the cool soil to keep fresh for the few days we would be here.

The rest of us continued to build shelters and forage, preparing as best we could in anticipation of more mouths to feed and bodies in need of a place to rest after days of marching.

I'd chosen to join those foraging, but it was slim pickings. Nothing edible seemed to grow within miles of our base. Nothing that wouldn't kill you, that is.

We only had four days left until the first day of spring, which was when we'd told our allies we planned to attack the arena. That gave us less than three days before having to leave this meeting spot.

With every hour that passed without new faces showing up, it became harder and harder to stop the nerves from creeping in. Doubts rearing their ugly heads as I wondered if anyone would come at all.

Though I'm sure I wasn't the only one wondering how feasible a full scale attack against Elikai would be with just our sea fae friends, Alaric didn't seem worried. Certain more would show up soon, the male was wired for this sort of thing and didn't seem stressed in the least. Whether that was just a front he put on for our benefit or years of working in the horde, I wasn't sure, but it was working, and I decided that I'd only allow myself to panic if he did.

As I walked back to my tent with sore fingers stained with berry juice, movement around the tree line on the southern end of the clearing gave me pause. Kane was off to the west, still building shelters, and Alaric hadn't yet returned from his fishing trip.

I held my breath, waiting to see who stepped out.

A large male, unmistakably Alaric's father, appeared. "Braxton!" I called. Before my brain had a chance to catch up with my feet, I was racing across the grass. By the time I reached him, Rose was at his side and I barreled into her as she pulled me into a hug, her nose nuzzling into my hair like a she-wolf might to her cub.

"We got yer message," Braxton said, snatching me into his chest and clapping me on the back. The large male crushing me in the tightest hug.

As I stepped back, more familiar faces of the rest of the rebel alliance came into view. Edelin caught my eye, giving me a knowing wink before looking very interested in a solitary berry by her boot.

Camille and Marnie were red faced, among a larger group of fae with sweat drenched foreheads, struggling with a huge wooden barrel. Though it was corked on its side and strapped using vines, I recognized it instantly as the one which collected and stored the camp's rainwater.

I smiled. "You remembered this place well, then?" I asked Alaric's parents, tilting my head to the water supply they'd dragged all the way here.

"Not so much me," Rose joked, and I shivered at the memory of her condition last time they'd been here, "but my mate is nothing if not thorough when it comes to the rebel alliance's needs."

I nodded. "He's spent long enough running the show. I would probably have been more surprised if he *hadn't* thought of it."

"Where are Alaric and Kane?" Marnie asked.

"Kane's over there somewhere, building shelters with the seafolk–"

As I pointed west, Braxton asked, "Seafolk?"

"Long story short is that the kelpies and selkies have set aside their differences and joined forces with us. They are good fae, and will be excited to meet you."

"As we are to meet them," Rose said. "I've never met either species of fae before."

"Where are Vyara and Drayke?" I asked.

"They'll be here," Braxton said.

Rose rolled her eyes. "Why are males always so..." she trailed off.

"Awful?" Camille muttered.

"Infuriating?" Marnie whispered back.

"Vague?" I offered.

"Exactly. Why are they always so to the point?" she asked. "When we received your raven, they sent word to the villages they struck alliances with, giving a meeting point from where they would gather and guide them here."

"So they did it?" I asked, my jaw hurting as I tried to stop the smile from spreading across my face prematurely. "They convinced the villages?"

"Not all of them," Braxton said. "But enough."

"And Alaric?" Rose asked, ever the protective mother. "Is he with Kane?"

I shook my head. "He's fishing, but he should be back soon," I assured her. "Anything I can help carry?"

"We're good," Braxton said. "Lead the way."

ONCE THE REBELS had set up and Alaric returned with enough fish to feed a village, we spent the evening around the fire, smoking salmon and learning everything there was to know about the arena from the selkies.

They told us about the fae guarding it, composed of a mass of trolls and horde soldiers, and the pathways and routes to reach it. How far it was from the castle and how lively the area was day and night. We discussed how the oval-shaped stadium would be best ambushed by circling it first, and Braxton and Alaric began to talk the selkies and kelpies through the bones of a plan.

With every passing hour, the plan got more detailed, more strategic, more like something that could actually give us a good chance of winning this. Not without more allies showing up soon, though. Tomorrow morning would mark just two full days left to gather an army, brief and arm them, and give them the remaining time to fill their stomachs and rest. The last thing we needed was to have an army of rebels capable of going against the horde, only to march them into battle already half dead on their feet.

This would likely be our first and last chance. We couldn't mess it up for the sake of not treating our soldiers right and skipping the basics like making sure they had the energy needed to be on top form and effective on the battlefield.

YESTERDAY HAD BEEN ROUGH, with exactly zero new faces joining us. We'd worked hard all day, physically and mentally, and then sat up late into the evening. Just waiting. And waiting some more. I was nauseous with how many times my eyes had scanned the tree line and found nothing.

We talked about Axel, Nix and Raine a lot, theorizing mostly, but when talking about them got too difficult, we moved onto getting to know the selkies and kelpies better. Learning their strengths and weaknesses so we knew how best to utilize them in the impending fight. In the end we'd had to call it a night, retiring to our beds with the hope that more would come soon.

As I opened my eyes, my first thought was exactly that. "Do you really think the others will get here in time?" I asked my mates. I'd promised myself not to crack first, and I hadn't. I still had hope. It just slipped out and I couldn't very well swallow the words back down.

"Aye," Alaric said, like it was inevitable. "We have all of today an' dinnae need to leave until mid-mornin' tomorrow."

"See, *loads* of time, Eva," Kane chuckled, giving me a dimpled smile. I gave him a playful nudge just as his stomach rumbled, signaling it was time to prepare some more salmon.

As we climbed out of the tent, my heart skipped a beat. Thalia was walking across the clearing, heading toward our row of tents. Shauna and Bryon flanked both her sides, while an impossible-to-count number of brightly colored pixies flew above their heads.

"Eve," she said as soon as we'd caught up to them. "It's so good to see your face."

"Yours too," I said, squeezing her into a quick, tight hug. "How are you? You look well. How was the trade route mission? Do you know anything more about Nix and Axel? Fates, sorry," I said, stepping back several paces. "It just feels like forever since I saw you, Lia." I cut myself off, unprepared for all the things I'd wanted to talk to Thalia about over the past weeks to come tumbling out at once.

I took a breath and looked at the pixies. Then I instantly regretted it. My cheeks burned as I recognized Dana. Nix would be devastated. He was missing the opportunity to tell the story of what happened the one and only time I ever visited the pixie village of Pinefall. It didn't matter how much older or wiser you got. Embarrassing yourself as thoroughly as I had during that supply run with my parents; it never became less traumatic when confronted with the memory.

"This is Dana, the mayor of Pinefall." Thalia said. "Dana, these are the fae I told you about. Meet Evangelia, Nekane and Alaric."

"We've met once," I blurted. Fates, I was out of control this morning. It had to be the backlash hitting me from yesterday's low.

"Yes, I remember you well," she said in her high-pitched squeak of a voice, causing another wave of blood to rush to my face. "I'm sorry about your parents."

With her words, my childhood memory of Pinefall faded into the background of my mind, and suddenly, I was flustered no more. "Thank you," I said, giving her a small smile. "I miss them."

Alaric cleared his throat. "Good to see the three of yeh, too," he said to Thalia, Bryon, and Shauna. "An' thank yeh for joining us," he told Dana, tilting his head toward the pixies hovering in the air behind their leader.

"You're welcome," Dana said, her chin high and arms crossing over her vivacious, barely covered breasts.

When she didn't say anything else, an uncomfortable silence fell and I could almost hear Alaric's brain ticking. Working on overdrive as he tried to puzzle out what role he would assign the pixies in this war.

We were all likely thinking the same, and it wasn't out of disrespect or unappreciation. The pixies were less than half a foot tall, with a neon complexion to match their brightly rainbow-colored wings which fluttered at a rate so fast you'd get dizzy if you tried to watch them too closely. And no one really knew anything about their magic, if they had any at all.

"Um," Thalia started, her eyes panicked. "When we told the pixies about the trolls joining forces with Elikai, they were keen to join the alliance," she explained, and I could have hugged her again for breaking the tension that choked the air.

"You don't get along with the trolls?" Kane asked. "Did something happen?"

"Did something happen?" Dana scoffed. "Only every time they use our village as a shortcut, swinging those clubs around. I swear, they pretend they can't even see us. Just swing, swing, swing, no regard for the lives of my brothers and sisters!"

"I'm sorry you have to deal with that," Kane said. "Hopefully, things will change when the war is won. We are glad you decided to join us, though. Even if the trolls were your primary motivation, we appreciate having you here all the same."

Fates, he'd make an excellent fucking king.

NO SOONER HAD Thalia's group been introduced to everyone and briefed, Vyara arrived. We exchanged a warm greeting, and she quickly got to introducing the small army-sized group of fae who accompanied her. Findis, Mailia, and the elves from Ulana Hill stepped forward first, apologizing profusely to Alaric and Braxton for their treatment toward the thrakos.

Erato and the dryads of Cloverae were introduced next, apologizing for not being able to shake anyone's hands on account of them being full of wood carved weapons. Those at the back dragged sacks filled to the seams, too. Daggers, bows, and lethally sharp arrows.

Eventually she introduced Nazgritt and Nirrank, the goblin couple from Swamphollow, who wasted no time requesting that Alaric put them on the front line in the upcoming fight. Insisting they didn't want to miss a thing.

Drayke arrived just after the sunset with the gnomes of Dorgoil and dwarves of Kalgulir. Thalia knew one of them, a female who I could only assume was part of the dwarven family they'd met. She told Thalia of how her husband had stayed home with the children and it wasn't long until the two were wandering off up the field together, catching up.

Before heading to a meeting in the temporary war tent Braxton was setting up, Kane, Alaric, and I took a moment to ourselves. And it was probably the most bizarre and surreal moment of my life. Looking out across the clearing, hand in hand with my mates. Love and pride bursting in my heart, while a fear like I'd never felt and couldn't explain, chilled me to the bone.

I SAT between Alaric's strong legs beside the large fire pit, just enjoying the dance of the flames before me as they bathed me in their warmth. My head rested against a strong thigh as his hands combed through my hair, sending tingles down my spine.

"No' a bad turnout," he mused shortly after finishing the final strategy meeting for tomorrow's march to the city.

"No' bad at all," Braxton agreed. I wanted to bash their heads together. This was more than '*not bad*'. The first day of spring would arrive tomorrow, and in just a few short days, we'd built an army like the rebel alliance had never seen. "Any no' show up?"

"Rangaran an' a few friends in Ezerat," Alaric said. "I doubt Mel and Bill will come, no' with how busy the selkies say the city is. It'd be too suspicious to leave the tavern at a time when business is bound to be boomin'."

Kane nodded. "I'm not holding my breath for Kumo. Rangaran would have been here by now if they were coming," he said.

"Aye. But there's still time. The dryads an' seafolk might be headin' for the castle at first sun, but the rest of us dinnae need to make our move for the arena 'til mid mornin'."

Kane nodded just as Vyara stifled a yawn. "We'll see you in the morning," she said, then took Drayke's hand and led the way back to their tent.

Rose pushed herself up to stand, and Braxton followed, excusing themselves for the night before leaving the circle around the fire too.

Though I needed a good night's sleep tonight more than ever before, I was wide awake and the thought of lying there staring at the dark tent roof for hours, trying to force sleep to come, would be not just pointless but unbearable. Instead, I patted the ground on either side of me and my mates slid down from the tree stumps they'd been using as stools.

Alaric rested back on his elbows and I draped an arm around his waist, curling myself around his huge body. Kane propped himself up on his side next to me and used his free hand to trace soft circles and squiggles on my thigh.

We lay there like that for a while, just listening to our new allies and old friends chat and mingle and get to know each other. Having been made to live so separately for so long, there wasn't a quiet moment and it was beyond incredible to experience and listen to.

At some point, Kane started tracing words, and I'd try to guess them. Some sweet, some that made me blush and I wouldn't repeat out loud. It had turned into a game. He would give me messages to whisper to Alaric, some that he would want me to do. It was almost perfect.

The steady up and down of Alaric's heavy breathing under my head relaxed me, my eyes growing heavy. As if I needed any more reasons to love him, when I began to yawn through my answers, Kane wrote, *Bed?*

CHAPTER 34

Nekane

The first day of spring arrived, and we woke to a sea of arriving spiders. But before I could find which one was Kumo and thank him for answering our call, a thundering roar echoed around the clearing. A roar I knew instinctively to have come from Alaric.

As my eyes scanned the hundreds of fae filling the clearing, my stomach knotted. The sound replayed over and over in my brain with every passing second of searching the vast crowd. There was no quiver of fear or gasp of pain in it. No. It had been a growl, a warning.

Eva's hand wrapped around my wrist. "Over there!" she hissed, her jaw set and eyes sharp. Ready to burn realms to get to him.

We pushed through the tsunami of fae rallying north toward where our mate stood, his back to us, wide shoulders hiding the recipient of his wrath from view. Edelin was at his side first. "What the fuck are yeh doin' here, witch?" he snapped, but the question wasn't aimed at the seer, who he shielded with his form.

No sooner had Taylah stepped around Edelin and into our line of vision did Eva's wings snap out, scales tumbling down over her body like a wave of falling leaves. She sprung into the air, and I used a burst of speed to propel myself forward.

I stopped dead at Alaric's flank, Eva landing in front of Edelin, just as the High Priestess of Crystal Towers coven said, "Not the reception my coven and I expected after deciding we'd come and help you in your war." She crossed her arms, looking down at her long nails where they strummed against her velvet sleeve, "I'll let it slide, given you never have been very eloquent."

"If you wanted to join the alliance, why not tell us while we were in your tower?" I asked, my eyes narrowing on her.

As Taylah considered her answer, Eva remained in her partially shifted form, her wings wide in front protecting Edelin, while Alaric's fangs were bared.

"She wasn't certain then, but she is telling the truth about helping. She knows there is no bargain if Alaric or I are dead," Edelin explained, laying a gentle hand on a silver wing as she moved around Eva, her eyes on Taylah. "And you really don't want that, do you? It's taken you how many centuries to get this close to getting me to join you? Three? Five? More? It's impossible to be sure, what with all the potential timelines pickling my brain. Now, are you going to drop the cloaking spell, or shall I do it for you, dear?"

Taylah huffed and rolled her eyes, then dropped the spell, revealing her entire coven of witches. Some were immediately next to her, while others were dotted between trees. "A handy trick for concealing an army enroute to incite an ambush, wouldn't you agree?" she said, looking too pleased with herself.

I really didn't like the witch, but I had to admit, she was good at proving a point to get her own way.

Alaric cursed. He *hated* the female, that much was obvious. But he was also one of the ones in charge of leading our army of misfits and outcasts to a battle where the odds were stacked against us. Not so much in the way of numbers, but in every other way that counted. Weapons, armor, training, experience, and brawn, to name a few.

Alaric sighed. "Split up. Spread yerselves evenly between each group of rebels. They will brief yeh from there," he ordered. "But witch, I swear to the fates, if yeh or any of yer coven betray us–"

"–We won't," she said, cutting him off. "Unless Edelin here wants to just come with us now and save us the trouble?" she turned her gaze on the seer, who just shook her head once. "That's what I thought. So it seems we will fight with you, and when all is said and done, you *will* give us the seer. Do we have a deal?"

"No more deals, dear," Edelin said. "When the war is over, I will come with you to Crystal Towers willingly, and any hold you have over Alaric will be broken." She held out a hand and Taylah smiled victoriously as she took it. They shook once and a flash of bright magic sparked where their palms met.

So much for no more deals, Edelin. What was the witch up to?

"What's going on here?" Drayke's booming voice called as the crowd parted for him and Vyara.

Taylah's toothy grin turned into a look of utter disbelief as she blinked and stuttered, "My king."

She dropped to the ground like someone had just taken a sword to the back of her knees, much like Westly did with every new encounter he had with Eva's grandparents. I imagined it would become annoying pretty quickly, but neither the old dragon king nor queen seemed to mind, or even notice.

"Taylah," Drayke greeted. "It has been a long time. Based on the stir you've made, I assumed time has not changed you."

"How are you alive?" she whispered in disbelief.

We had no way of knowing how far and wide word had spread of the late king and queen coming back from the supposed dead, but apparently not as far as the reclusive witch coven.

"That's a story for another day," Vyara said. "You're here to fight with us, yes?"

She nodded.

"Alaric?" Vyara said. "I imagine you have a plan for where the witches will best serve? The spiders too."

"Aye. The first wave of warriors will be leaving shortly. The spiders can join them." He turned to the witch leader, "Taylah, come with me so we can ready yer witches."

THE ENTIRE CLEARING became the war tent for the final briefing. With the help of our friends, family and allies, we all had a role to play and a purpose to fulfill.

The first wave of rebels would leave soon, accompanied by a group of Taylah's witches, to cloak as many as they could. They were to head straight for the castle, where they would lie low and wait for word to seize control from Elikai's horde. Only making their presence known should the horde inside learn of our attack on the arena and try to send reinforcements.

Centuries of being kept from joining forces had weakened the fae fighting with us, and our plan was to give the horde a taste of what that was like. The rest of us would march directly for the arena, splitting as we neared to surround it. The selkies believed there was only one way in and out, so the Dyvrad's would circle around to the opposite side of the towering oval and wait for the signal to fly in from above with troops on their backs.

The army was clad in tunics spun from the spider's silk and armor welded by the goblins. Each was given a weapon of their choice, from expertly whittled bows and arrows gifted by the dryads, to great, long swords of Kalgulir steel from the dwarves.

They were as ready as they'd ever be and all with full stomachs thanks to the sea folk's fishing and gnome's harvest.

No one was entirely sure what role the pixies would play, but they had chosen to join the front line which Alaric, Eva and I would lead, heading for the doors and remaining cloaked by the witches for as long as they could hold the spell. So long as they could get us somewhere in the close vicinity without being seen, they'd have helped us immeasurably.

Alaric had tried to reach Axel several times a day when he wasn't tirelessly planning the attack, but their connection remained silent. Still, he'd worked with an unwavering focus that every fae here admired and respected, and I'd heard many tell him as much. As I watched him step forward to address his rebel army for the final time, my heart hurt with pride for the male I loved.

"For centuries we've been forced apart," he called, his voice so loud it traveled all the way to those at the back. "Many of yeh have been hunted, while others, forced into poverty. But not one of yeh have had free will. No' even close. No matter what cards yeh were dealt when the Lores were made, freedom wasnae one of them. Every fae yeh can see around yeh on this field has been told where they can live, who they can trade with, and worse of all–"

He gestured for Eva and I to come to his side. Once there, he slid his hand into mine and linked our fingers, while doing the same with Eva on his other side.

"–who they can love. But that ends today, for this marks the beginning o' spring. Where fresh flowers bloom under yer feet, so does hope for a better life. Separated we were strong, together we are stronger, united we will be unstoppable!"

The rebels went wild, whooping their agreement at the tops of their lungs to ring out across the desolate lands. I watched with awe, trying to take in and memorize every face. Braxton whistled, Rose beamed, and Eva's grandparents cast her a kind smile.

"That was quite the way to finally say 'I love you'," I said, grinning at my male before tugging him down for a heart stopping kiss while the army continued to cheer and chant and stamp their feet.

He pulled his lips from mine. "Yeh ken how much I love yeh, Kane," he said. Releasing Eva's hand and moving his palm to rest on the back of her braided hair. Bending slightly, he kissed her deeply, too. "Yeh too, Angel."

"Separated, we are strong," I said.

"Together, we are stronger," Eva added.

"United, we are unstoppable," Alaric finished.

CHAPTER 35

Axel

The sound of trolls grunting mixed with overly excited clapping woke me, feeling dazed and more than a little confused.

My stomach tightened at the prospect of finally being allowed out after three torturous days of building anticipation; ever since Raine had killed Jarrah and Elikai had put the games on pause. He'd announced the next round would be the final one of his coronation celebration and search for the horde general. I'd rather bend over and have the guards take turns spanking my ass with their evil magic sticks than win that title. Not that Elikai would truly allow a mut like any of the three of us to hold such a position.

Though Raine had remained silent, Nix and I had killed countless hours trying to work out how the final round would go down. The chances were slim that he'd pit the three of us in a fight to the death. We'd determined he'd either have the both of us against Raine, then make us fight each other. Or bring us out to fight her one by one, and the winner stays on.

The latter was more likely. But if that was his plan, the fact I'd somehow slept through the announcement didn't give me much hope that I'd be the first out and forced to go against her. I wouldn't fight her, obviously, but I'd been making sure I said plenty of vile things about her for the guards to hear and feed back to King Elikunt.

I didn't know the version of Raine before she'd become Anon and famous among Ezerat's elite, but she had clearly changed at some point during the transition from the female Nix had described. The last thing I wanted was for Nix to go against her first and end up getting himself killed for being too soft as he tried to get her to remember him.

Though I didn't want Nix to be the one to test my theory, I was pretty sure she knew exactly who he was, and that she wasn't as crazy as the crowd and guards liked to say. The way she'd looked at Nix before pledging her allegiance to *her* king, was not the way one looked at a stranger. The hate in her voice toward Elikai as she'd spat her truth for all to hear was admirable and medal worthy, though slightly insane. She was pretty much my hero at this point, and when all three of us got out of this, I'd be sure to tell her.

Wait. How *had* I slept through not just the announcement, but the arrival of the clapping crowds, too? The guards hadn't poked me with their spelled zappy probes since the arena had temporarily closed. I almost missed the guaranteed restful sleep that came shortly after they thrust one of those inside my cage.

I'd told them as much whenever they'd neared the bars. Had literally pleaded with them to give me another quick poke and had gone as far as to ask if they could lube it up with some extra spicy spells. No luck.

It was darker than normal, so on instinct, I attempted to shift to call on my sharper thrakos sight, but it wasn't there. My hand reached up around my neck to the collar, still shut tight.

It occurred to me there was no cheering, and the clap wasn't the sound of a crowd's applause. No, the noise was being made by just one set of hands, the claps sporadic. Forcing myself to sit upright, I dragged my body a short distance to the cage door and found it was the middle of the night. The games hadn't started yet. I glanced around as my mind tried to piece everything I was seeing together.

Two pairs of trolls each carried some kind of giant catapults. Slowly making their way up the steps and toward the empty platforms on the wings of the tiered arena seating. Of course, the clapping came from Elikai, who was standing at the bottom of the steps, his back facing me. His uncle was at his side, barking instructions to the Mount Mortums, whom I didn't recognize as King Vandenburg's usual guards, following the troll's slow progress as they lugged the giant, solid oak structures up and up.

"Are you seeing this?" I whispered.

"Yes," Nix replied so quietly there was no way Elikai or King Vandenburg would hear. "Presents for the new king from Mount Mortum, shipped in earlier tonight."

"Are they catapults?" I asked, squinting through the darkness to try to make them out more clearly. "Perhaps his uncle just delivered us a way out of here..." I mused, not even a little bit joking.

"I don't know. It's definitely some kind of weapon, though," Nix said. "I guess we'll find out in the morning."

"I guess we will."

THE REST of the night and the following morning ticked by slowly. Once I was awake in this place, getting back to sleep was no easy task. My body didn't care that I'd only had a few hours of tossing and turning; sleep would not come until exhaustion won me over once more. Or I'd been zapped out of consciousness.

Thanks to all the noise from Elikai's near death traps, no rats had wandered into my cage either, so my fangs ached and my thrakos side allowed me to think of little else but blood.

What I'd initially thought were catapults turned out to require some sort of sharp, arrow shaped stake that was at least as large as a troll arm. They were testing the various angles and trajectories all morning, only stopping when high fae began to fill the seats. More so than ever, they were buzzing like an arena full of those spelled dick-shaped toys they were so fond of buying from Rhalynn's R-Rated Remedies.

Thus far, Elikai had kept mine and Nix's identities a secret. Though the fae in the audience could see our cages were occupied, he'd not given them any answers as to who we were—yet. This afternoon, that would change. I could feel it.

"Welcome, welcome, welcome back for the final round in the Coronation Games!" Elikai began as soon as the final few guests took their seats. "Just as many of you noticed the two new entrants who joined us several days ago, you will have spotted on your way in today that the arena has undergone some slight changes itself since your last visit. My coronation gifts from King Vandenburg and the Mount Mortums have at last arrived, and just in time for this most exciting day of the entire contest. Let's show our appreciation with a round of applause!"

Elikai didn't join in as heads whipped around and gasps spread through the audience as they looked between our cages, and the unsightly new toys Elikai should never have been given control of. Then again, he had an entire realm under his control. What were these new inventions being shipped in from afar going to add to his playground of horrors?

Before the fae had managed more than five claps each, Elikai was silencing them. "Enough. On to the entertainment! Anon will go against one of our new excited friends here," he gestured toward Nix and I. "Both of them so desperate for the chance to prove themselves worthy after watching the firm fan-favorite stamp out the spider, they could not decide who went first and had to toss a coin to make the decision for them."

We did fucking *what* now? When?

"Who will it be?" Elikai asked the crowd, rubbing his palms together. "Will Mutt be the one to finally slay Anon? Or perhaps Viper can manage the seemingly impossible feat?"

"Which one do you suppose I am?" I muttered to Nix.

"Does it matter?"

"No," I said, as Elikai had the crowd start to count back from ten. "Viper. I'm totally Viper."

I braced myself, sending a silent prayer that it was me up first. Nix had been through enough.

"Release Mutt!" Elikai finally called, and my cage door swung open.

Fucking thank you, fates.

"Good luck," Nix said as several guards appeared at either side of my cell. "You know what to do."

Heaving a sigh, I did as the guards instructed, and soon enough, I stood inside the pit, facing Raine, her sharp eyes watching my every movement.

She'd been dressed in armor for today, a far cry from the rags I'd grown used to seeing her in. The emblem Alaric had worn on his armor emblazoned on her chest, and

I snorted a sarcastic laugh. He'd seriously marked her as the Horde fucking General?! Was there nothing Elikai wouldn't do for a reaction or shock value?

"No funny business until the king announces the start of the match, understood?" the unmistakable drawl of Sloane's voice asked from behind me, so close I could feel his foul breath as he spoke.

I was too busy preparing myself for the rush of strength and power and magic to hit to answer him.

"Oi," he hissed. "If you step so much as a rat's bollock hair out of line, Mutt, then you see them?" he pointed toward the giant crossbow type mechanisms around the arena, and I nodded. "They will take aim and be coming at you before you even hear them being fired. Get it now?"

"Loud and clear," I said.

"Don't kill her," Nix whispered as I waited for Sloane to remove my collar. His hands fumbled about my neck and as the joint clicked open, I rolled my neck and stretched out my muscles quickly, then gave Nix a big, toothy smile.

I was fucking back!

"Alaric? Brother? You there?" I asked.

"Axel! Fuck. Yer alive!"

"Yeah, for now. But listen, I'm in the arena. The pit, to be specific. They just removed my collar so I can fight Raine. She's here by the way, but they call her–"

"Anon," he finished for me, reminding me why I fucking looked up to this male more than any other. He'd worked it out. Or at least that Raine was in the games.

"Yep, exactly," I thought back.

Sloane and the guards that had surrounded me raced toward the sideline, while Graves and his army of protection did the same.

"Tell me everything," Alaric said.

"Did you miss the part where I'm about to fight Raine?" I snarked, swinging my hips side to side as I continued to feign limbering up. *"Who, by the way, is about as close to giving herself over to the bloodlust to the point of no return, as I have ever seen or heard of a thrakos being."*

"Fuck," Alaric cursed.

"Who wants to see who the winner will fight?" Elikai called, and the crowd cheered again as several more guards moved in to block Nix's cage, while the warlock took his sweet time joining them. "Let the Viper out of his cage!"

After a string of curses, Alaric asked, *"An' yeh? How are yeh holding up against it, Axel?"*

"I drained a rat a few days ago, so pretty much every fae in the audience looks like a delicious meal to me right now."

He cursed again. *"We are on our way to you as we speak,"* he said. *"Can yeh buy some time?"*

"No. Alaric don't come here. They have enough trolls, horde and Mount Mortum soldiers here to populate a new realm."

"We have an army of our own," he said.

"The rebels won't stand a chance," I insisted.

"We do. And we dinnae need long. Just buy a bit more time, please, Axel."

"How close are you?"

"Close enough I can see the trolls guarding the doors."

"Please, turn around. Me and Nix have a plan. He's already out of his cage, which is a bonus we hadn't planned for. All I need to do is get through to Raine, then I'll play dead, and they'll remove Nix's collar so he can fight her next–"

"–There's too many 'what if's' in that plan," he said, cutting me off before the best part. His tone wasn't scolding, more warning me we needed a plan B should plan A not work. *"Just focus on gettin' through to her. Kane says to talk to her about Blaze, her kid brother."*

"Got it," I said. *"Please tell me you've got someone with you willing to open a vein?"* Since the collar had come off, the bloodlust was becoming more intense with every passing second.

"Better than that, brother. We have a cure for the bloodlust," he said, almost exactly like he just said, 'We have a cure for the bloodlust.' But that was impossible. He couldn't have said that, right?

Only that was *exactly* what he'd said. I swayed on the spot as his words sunk in. A cure? No. How? Wait, he'd asked about a cure last we communicated, but I hadn't even considered it since, figuring it was entirely a hypothetical question. A dream that it was nice to fantasize about, but it remained just that, a fantasy.

I glanced at Nix's cage, only to find it empty. And then to Raine, who was charging directly toward me.

I'd missed Elikai's announcement to begin the fight.

Fuck. *"This is the final round,"* I said. *"Raine's heading toward me now and she doesn't look like she plans to pull her punches. I don't know how much time I can buy."*

I sidestepped just in time to avoid the impact of her attack, but she quickly whirled back around. I held my hands up, palms forward. "Raine," I said. "Stop. You gotta–"

She swiped her clawed nails across my palms and I whipped them back toward my body, fully expecting to find no fingers there. The blood dripping from the slices made it look worse than it was, but it was no more than a flesh wound. Had she done that by mistake or had she intentionally not severed through to the bone?

Alaric was still talking in my head, his voice becoming more urgent with every second I didn't reply.

"I'm here, brother," I muttered in my mind, then to Raine I whispered. "We can't kill each other–"

She shifted into her wolf form, and thankfully the fire didn't ignite her fur. She pounced, and I shifted too, bursting out of my skin and shaking off the remnants of my tattered clothes. I had no fucking clue how she was willing her thrakos flames to cover her, but my wolf was bigger. It would be easier to counter her blows and defend her attacks without having to hurt her too badly back.

We fought like that for several minutes. She would use her smaller size to try and sneak under my defenses, darting close and snapping at my throat and stomach. Luckily I'd trained for this in the horde, Alaric often pitting the largest shifters against smaller ones. Keeping my belly close to the ground, I was primed and ready for anything she would try to come at me with.

She nipped viciously at one of my back paws, like she was trying to herd me to where she wanted me. I didn't know what she was trying to do, but I couldn't fall into her trap. I needed this to play out for as long as possible.

Restless chatter came from the crowd as I did nothing more than defend myself against her, despite having so many opportunities to attack. Unlike me, she showed no signs that this would be a friendly fight. She wanted my blood. She wanted me *dead*.

When she launched at me again, I shifted into my thrakos form and twisted so my wing caught her mid leap, the momentum sending her rolling across the pit. She got back up a heartbeat later, teeth bared.

"Don't do this," I said. "Blaze needs you. The rebels need you. Your name is Raine. Anon is a puppet in Elikai's show. Raine is a warrior who fights for the true and rightful heir."

I just kept talking to her as she stalked me around the pit, hoping that at some point, something would worm its way into her mind and burn away the lock she put on her memories.

Nix joined in from where he fought against the guard's hold at the side of the pit, recounting experiences that the two of them had shared. Spraying sprinkles of Raine onto the seeds I was planting, with the hope they'd grow until she remembered who she was.

She growled, then launched at me again. I used her momentum to throw her past me, but she'd just spring back up and start again. She would tumble a few times but never remained off her feet for long, coming back with a fresh wave of determination guiding her next onslaught of attacks.

"Okay Raine, I get it," I said, quickly running out of both patience and time. "It's been a shit show in here, I get it. Life has been one giant pile of shit lately, and it probably wasn't fucking great before that. But we have friends." I nudged my head toward the arena's doors. "We have *friends*."

I couldn't tell her Alaric had an army of rebels outside the building, but I was trying to tell her help was on the way in the only way I could think of without revealing it to a single soldier or fae in the arena. But fates, she wasn't getting it. She didn't *want* to get it. She didn't want to let the pain back in.

"Are you really going to let the bloodlust win?" I asked, knowing she could hear me, even if she didn't want to absorb what I was saying. "You realize I'm thrakos too? That my blood would taste about as nice as shoe polish to your tongue?"

Though that gave her pause as she shifted from paw to paw, contemplating her options, it wasn't long before a vicious snarl came. Deciding her wolf wasn't enough, as she jumped at me, her thrakos burst free from her fur. A sharp swiping of claws aimed at my face and snapping teeth hurtling toward my neck as she wrapped her arms and legs around me.

"Alaric. Brother. Boss. Please. Hurry," I thought as her canines tore into my skin.

CHAPTER 36
Evangelia

Despite the selkies' detailed descriptions of the outside of the arena, none of what they'd said could have prepared me for the sheer size of it. To even see the open top roof, I had to crane my head all the way back as far as my neck would allow.

Alaric decided we would be the ones to lead the march, so we reached it first. It wouldn't be long before the next wave of troops joined us, led by Braxton and Rose, shortly followed by a third. Then we'd attack.

My grandparents had traveled with us most of the way, but once the imposing structure came into view, they'd split off to approach from the other side. They had an entire village of elves and dwarves in tow, along with multiple witches, including Thalia, Westly, Edelin, and Taylah. She'd refused to let the seer out of her sight, her single-sighted determination to have Edelin be a part of her coven driving her.

We found a place to gather with our own team of witches, goblins, pixies, rebel hybrids and thrakos, under the protection of several witches cloaking spells. As close as we could get to our target without having droves of pedestrians to dodge.

I squeezed Alaric's hand in mine, but when he loosened where he'd usually squeeze back, I frowned, before finding he'd checked out on us mentally. Just like he did whenever–

"It's Axel, isn't it?" I asked the moment his eyes came back into focus several long seconds later.

Rather than answer, he let out a barrage of curses and scoffed, "If yeh want to make the fates laugh, tell them yer fuckin' plans." Like he had by planning every last detail of this battle? Whatever Axel said, it had changed things. But how? Why?

"He's inside the arena, isn't he?" Kane asked, and I inhaled sharply at the implication.

"Aye. Nix too," Alaric confirmed, but his eyes quickly glazed once more.

If the witches' silencing spells dropped right now, we needn't have worried, barely taking a breath while we waited for Alaric to tell us more.

Feeling both useless and sick to my stomach, I glanced up at the arena again. Quickly focusing my mind on thinking about the swiftest possible way to get them out of there, rather than about all the horrific things that could be happening to them right at this moment.

Alaric sucked in a breath. "Axel's fightin' Raine. He's tryin' to buy us some time, but she's given over to the bloodlust. Nix is out of his cage but unlike the others, he's wearin' a magic blockin' collar," he quickly burst out. "Angel, how many vials of yer blood do yeh have?"

"Three," I confirmed, thanking the fates for the hindsight to have prepared some. A small win when everything else was quickly crashing down.

"Empty one," Alaric ordered, instantly stamping out my little victory. Though, so long as Nix was already cured, two vials would work. "Fill it with Kane's blood instead and tie something 'round it so we ken which is which. Yeh can fly the vials to wherever they are once we're inside and have a visual. Get the collar off Nix as soon as possible. Then get the cures to Axel and Raine."

We nodded and did as he instructed with the vials while he began to vent. Thinking aloud about how this changed everything. How there wouldn't be time to wait for the rest of our troops to join us. How we'd been so close, but the fates, yet again, had decided to fuck with him.

Despite so many of us helping in whatever way we could, my mate had taken on the bulk of responsibility for the battle. He'd instructed in great detail the plan for what every group of rebels he'd scattered across Ezerat needed to do today, and exactly where the sun would be in the sky to mark the time they needed to do it by.

He'd done it all without showing so much as one flicker of weakness or doubt, both in the plan working and in his abilities to orchestrate it. Where most fae would shy away or not know where to start, he'd taken the lead and everyone respected and relied on his word. But even with a seer in his ranks, the one thing he couldn't predict was what the future would hold.

For the first time in the days since declaring we were going to war, Alaric needed someone else to step up for a minute. To deal with the immediate problem so he could figure out the rest. Like how to get his brother, Nix, and Raine out before it was too late, while simultaneously working out how the change would affect every other rebel in this city and the timeline they were working on.

I took a steadying breath and clutched the vials tightly in my hand. The one with a strip of fabric, torn from the hem of my tunic, tied around it, held Kane's blood. I'd chosen not to wear armor anyway, as my scales would protect me in my partially shifted and full dragon forms. Instead, I'd just accepted the tunic for the journey here and would shift soon enough.

"I'll fly over," I said, tilting my chin and looking toward the top of the arena. "I'll give the vials to Axel. He and Raine can take the cure and then unlock Nix's collar. At least then the three of them have a fighting chance to save themselves while they wait for the rest of you to get inside."

Rather than immediately argue against me putting myself in even more danger than we already were, Alaric fell deep into thought, then his eyes glazed.

Telling Axel the new plan? Hopefully.

The moment they were sharp again, they met mine. "Okay," was all he said, then turning his attention to the pixie mayor he barked out, "Dana? Yeh said yeh dislike the trolls?"

"Dislike? I hate them," she squeaked.

"Think yeh can distract them while we get through that door?" he asked.

"Try stopping us," she smirked, suddenly looking vicious.

"When Angel takes to the skies, yeh move. Do whatever it takes to distract them. Witches, hold the cloaking spell for as long as yeh can as we charge toward the doors, but if yeh need to fight, then fight. Dinnae leave yerselves exposed tryin' to hold the spell. The horde and Elikai will ken we are here the moment they see the dragon flying overhead. An' remember, more rebels will be here soon, so make sure yeh ken friend from foe."

"There will be horde hidden everywhere," Kane added. "They'll be coming from every direction as soon as they see Eva. Pair up and fight back-to-back if you can. Better to have an ally than the enemy there. Don't be afraid to use everything in your arsenal."

"Aye," Alaric agreed. "An' Angel? Get in, get out. Dinnae take any risks. Dinnae land or dive down too low."

"I won't," I said, stretching up to brush a kiss across his scarred cheek. "I've got this."

"That you have, princess," Kane said, planting a kiss on my forehead.

"So do you," I told him earnestly, wishing there was another way for my high fae prince to end this, knowing as well as he that there probably wasn't. The moment he set foot inside, everything and everyone would fade away, aside from his one true target.

Pulling him in for a hug, I tucked my twin daggers into the back of his weapons belt. "I won't be needing these," I whispered. "They might not be the original daggers, but they are still more than capable of causing Mayhem and Chaos."

He chuckled. "Thanks," he said with a ghost of a smile. "Good luck."

I slipped away, jogging down the narrow alley between distasteful souvenir shops, and even more grotesque buildings with signs announcing them as betting shops, and with the odds proudly on display out front.

After checking no one was looking my way, I shifted partially, using my smaller wings to get me up onto the roof. No longer under the protection of the witches' charms, I carefully peered over the edge and saw only the trolls circling the arena and a few groups of civilians. The cloak was holding out well.

With no time to waste, I stripped off my torn tunic, wrapped it around the vials as a makeshift bag, and shifted into my dragon form. I tried to ignore the trolls' grunts of alarm as I carefully pinched my talons around the fabric holding the blood. Then sprung into the air, flapping my wings with everything I had.

Tiny pixies swarmed around the trolls' boulder-sized heads, stopping them from being able to call out for back-up. Stabbing needle-sized blades up their nostrils, in their ears or just slashing blindly, the pixies were a force of uncaged fury.

Despite the trolls not being able to communicate what was happening, the commotion still caught the attention of horde soldiers, who began to race toward the arena from every direction. The cloaking spell suddenly dropped, and I caught a glimpse of the rebel army's appearance just before I was gliding over the lip of the arena.

A HUFF of smoke threatened to leave my nose as my eyes immediately found Elikai. Perched on the edge of his throne, dead center in the crowd of hundreds of the high fae elite. He wore an excessively extravagant crown, covered in so many jewels that if the sun hit it at the wrong angle, it would blind a fae.

Crystal sat at his side. Her spine ramrod straight while her knees and body twisted slightly to face away from Elikai. Like her subconscious couldn't hide its repulsion. The way she fidgeted betrayed her anxiety too, and I felt a punch of guilt in my gut that we hadn't been able to help her the way she had us.

On Elikai's other side sat his uncle, his face relaxed and in complete comfort as he crooked a leg over one knee and lounged back, enjoying the show.

Every fae in the arena looked on as Axel, bleeding badly, tried to fight off Raine. She looked vastly different to the female I knew. Thankfully, she had no obvious wounds or blood.

Nix struggled against Sloane and Graves as they locked his arms up behind his back and pushed against his shoulders to keep him pinned to his knees. The moment my shadow rippled across the floor of the fighting ring, my best friend's eyes flew up to meet mine. Immediately followed by Axel's, and then Raine's too.

As hundreds of more pairs of eyes shot up, complete chaos erupted, and everything played out in slow motion. A chorus of screams pierced my ears. Elikai roared. Trolls, horde, and the Mount Mortums all jumped into action.

Tucking my wings tight to my sides, I dove down. Twisting as I picked up speed, I hurtled directly toward Nix on the far side of the stage. Once my talons were almost above where Axel stood, I released the vials.

My heart sank when two of them came immediately free of the tunic's protection, sliding out and barreling end over end toward the ground.

Axel shifted into his wolf form and lunged into the air. Every muscle in his legs coiled as he sprang forward, catching them carefully between his teeth just as the third came loose and began to tumble awkwardly toward the pit. Sloane's arm flew out, snatching it out of the air and smashing it across the back of Nix's head.

His collar thudded to the ground as he yelled out in pain. They viciously wrestled to gain control over him, but his strength was no longer suppressed and he was close to tearing free of their grip. The sight of Graves unveiling a dagger and aiming it directly at Nix's back had me seeing red.

A roar ripped from my chest as my anger and hatred for the fae who'd murdered my parents enveloped me. They'd taken enough, they didn't get to take my best friend from me too. When I should have pulled out of my dive, I leaned into it instead. Graves and Sloane's eyes went wide, their mouths too as they screamed in fear.

They released Nix just as I extended my jaw. Graves grabbed Sloane, trying to use him as a shield. Nix covered his head with his arms, tucking it under tightly as he shrank down as close to the ground as possible.

While Elikai's friends struggled between themselves, they missed my mouth opening wider and wider. And then it was too late for them to do a thing about it as my jaw curved over them and my teeth were sinking into the flesh of their necks.

My wing desperately shot out, working to propel me upwards.

"Eva, go!" Nix yelled. "Get out of here! It's not safe for you!"

With a jerk of my head, I felt the snap of Graves and Sloane's spines and their bodies went completely limp. Unlocking my jaw, I spat them out at the crowd. *A fitting death*, I thought, yet far kinder than they deserved.

Once I'd built up enough height again, I hovered in place; making large, slow flaps of my wings to keep me there. I waited as I watched Axel pop open a vial, sniff it quickly, and then dart towards Raine.

No longer holding himself back, he gripped her face harshly and forced the cure down her throat. He held the vial there after it was empty to ensure that she got as much as she could. Raine stumbled on the spot, then stared up at me, dazed.

Elikai continued to scream for my imminent death while the hundreds of civilians stampeded down the steps, climbing over the tiered seats too, as they raced for the one and only exit out of there.

Battle cries rang out from the other side of the doors, and my eyes widened when I realized a bottleneck of horde soldiers, Mount Mortums and civilians was growing rapidly.

Axel joined in with Nix, shouting up at me to go. That it wasn't safe. But I was the safest fae here? They were right about me needing to leave, though. I had to get back down on the ground and warn the others of the blockage of panicked civilian bodies on this side of the doors.

Just as Elikai yelled, "Fire!" I flapped my wings, soaring skyward.

I hissed as white-hot pain seared my side. Something had lodged its way between my scales and I fought to breathe around the pain, but no breaths would come.

"Again!" Elikai ordered, and just as I noticed a giant crossbow being loaded, another blast of agony hit me, shooting across my flank this time.

Ice spread out from the wounds, making me shiver with every slow drag of my wings.

I tried desperately to move my body, to turn toward the direction of the rebels I'd arrived with. I had to warn them.

I was on the other side of the towering stadium walls when the lip of it smashed into my side.

I flew blindly for what felt like an agonizing amount of time, before eventually realizing I wasn't flying anymore.

I was falling.

CHAPTER 37

Nixen

"EVA!" I cried as the second huge stake sunk into her flank. Thick droplets of blood rained down on the arena, and I uselessly watched every excruciating second of her suffering.

My heart was locked in a vise, being wound tighter and tighter with every frantic flap of her wings. She fought against what had to be the most debilitating pain, desperately trying to gain enough height to scale the roof.

The warlock responsible for keeping me caged appeared in front of me, pulling my gaze away from my best friend as he muttered a spell. I swiftly blocked it with one of my own, then shifted into my thrakos form. I formed a ball of fire and sent it soaring toward his gut. As he fell, Raine was on him. Claws out and ready to plunge into his chest.

I looked up just as Eva reached the roof line. My heart shattered as her huge form fell, crashing down onto the lip and folding over it. Then disappearing from sight completely as she tumbled over the back of the arena.

"Nixen! We need to disable the crossbows!" Axel called as he ran toward me, a thrashing Raine now slung over his shoulder, her red hand dripping with the warlock's blood. "Alaric said the Dyvrad's will be flying in from the rear soon with rebel troops."

He set Raine on her feet, quickly turning to intercept the two guards charging toward us.

My palms came down on her shoulders, holding her there, before she started taking out any and all who crossed her path. Pulling her in front of me so she had to meet my eyes, I snapped, "Raine? Are you in there?"

Making quick work of the guards' deaths, Axel was back just as Raine's face formed into a deep frown. His breaths came quickly as he said, "No bloodlust anymore, just pissed. There's a cure. That's what Evangelia dropped in. Vials of her own blood. Kane's too, though that stupid cunt of Elikai's took good care of that for you."

Cure to the bloodlust? I had so many answers, and yet a thousand new questions at once. None of which could be asked or answered if I didn't get my head straight and fast. There would be time later. If we survived.

"Raine?" I snapped again, shaking her shoulders like it might help her suddenly remember me. "Can you fight?"

"What the fuck do you think I've been doing since I got here?" she spat, then her eyes dropped to the floor as shame crept up her face. She shook her head. "Sorry, Nix. You didn't deserve that."

I sighed in relief at the use of my name. "Don't apologize, I'm just relieved you know who the fuck I am," I said. "You had me worried you were lost to us. That you'd checked out."

"It got close," she admitted. "Especially with my thrakos thirst consuming my mind. But no, I promised myself I wouldn't let them break me. I've spent every day since being captured reminding myself of that."

Tugging her forward, I surprised myself by planting a quick kiss on her forehead before releasing my grip. "Stay here with Axel and make the guards pay, yeah? When the route clears, take out the other crossbow."

She glanced at Axel, who had already turned his attention back to the horde climbing into the pit.

"He's like us, okay?" I said. "One of the rebel alliance. He's my family and I trust him. You can too."

She nodded once, and that was all the confirmation I needed to move my focus to the crossbow.

I took off running toward the closest one. My focus on destroying the huge wooden contraption which sat on a platform at the left wing of the stadium seating. I refused to let my mind go to Eva. I had to believe she'd survive. Somehow, someway, she'd survive. If she was dead, Alaric would be, too. And Axel would know if his brother-by-bond had died. He loved that male and his mother more than any other fae in this realm. He'd have said something.

The only thing in my power to do right now, was make sure her grandparents could join the battle, bringing with them their reinforcements, and not suffer the same fate.

The aisles were completely jammed, so in my thrakos form, I used my wings to balance myself as I climbed over the empty seats. All while keeping half an eye on the horde giving chase close behind, moving just as quickly from either side.

Not even half of the way toward my target, the soldiers following me increased in numbers, their swords raised. Though I missed the reassurance of a weighted weapon in my hand, I didn't need one. Not now that I had my wings, claws, thrakos fire, and magic all working again. So long as I remained focused on only the task at hand, wielding the gifts I was born with could cause enough damage.

Don't think about Eva. Do not think about Eva.

I just had to make it to the crossbow before engaging. The moment a fight broke out, they wouldn't stop coming, and I couldn't afford to be slowed down like that.

Halfway up and I passed Sloane's broken body, hanging limp where Eva had flung him from her jaws. Folded at the hips over two of the arena seats, his arms hanging loose and head barely attached. With a massive pool of blood collecting below.

The Mount Mortum troops surrounding the crossbow finished reloading the deadly machine. And scrambled to point it in my direction.

Fuck.

Rather than give in to the panic, I suppressed it down to the place where all my dark and unwanted thoughts lived, and pulled my magic from my mother's side around me. It created a gust under my thrakos wings, propelling me up into the air, much higher than the few feet my wings alone allowed me to fly.

I glanced at the pit, where Axel was still fighting his way across the stage with Raine at his back. They had a circle of fallen soldiers around them, including a troll and bloody organs piling up. His eyes searched the arena while he simultaneously took on soldier after soldier with precise, quick movements.

The crossbow fired, gunning for the horde who chased me and narrowly missing the bottleneck at the door where the so-called 'elite' had formed an impassable crowd.

The foreign warriors cursed their frustration at missing me, not caring in the least that they'd almost just hit hundreds of innocents, and had killed several horde soldiers fighting on their side.

They looked up at me with fury burning in their eyes as I came down to land on the platform with them. But just before I was in reaching distance, the huge stadium doors started to give way.

Helped by the crossbow's hit? Probably.

"Aim for the doors!" Elikai ordered, and a second later, another stake fired from the opposite crossbow.

I caught a flash of Axel breaking away from the pit, but forced myself to peel my eyes away. I used the Mount Mortum warriors' momentary distraction to gather a ball of fire between my hands. Blasting it down on the wooden weapon.

The crossbow burst into flames, sending the warriors to scatter back, away from the blaze. I didn't pause for breath as I set to work slashing with my wings and claws. While the crossbow burned, they came at me in a blur of pure, unadulterated aggression.

Panting hard, I tried to steer the fight so I could maintain a good view of both the doors and the second crossbow on the opposite side of the arena, where the soldiers were definitely getting faster at loading.

The doors came down, and I stared wide eyed as not just a camp worth of rebels, but a fucking army of them, surged forward. Goblins, witches, hybrid shifters, thrakos, and more races of all different shapes and sizes.

I scanned the crowd of fae down at the entrance, all in various stages of terrified, injured, or dead. Just as many were trying to race inside the arena as were trying to get out. I cursed out loud as an army of rebels were revealed on the other side, desperately fighting their way through, while trying to decipher civilians from warriors.

My eyes landed on the royal box halfway between me and the other crossbow.

Crystal, the high fae with strawberry blonde hair who'd been a big part of the reason we'd managed to stop Kane's execution, was being grabbed roughly by the so-called king. He pulled her body in front of his own, then began slowly moving toward the tightly packed aisle.

All I could think about as his eyes—so similar to Kane's—met mine, was how strange it was to hate someone so viscerally, on such a deep, personal level, when they had no idea who you even were. Baring my fangs, I hissed, desperate to fall the last of my attackers and shake the horde from my ass so I could turn my wrath to him. To *Elikai*.

He just looked back at me with distaste tugging at his lip and a blankness in his eyes. To him, I was nothing. No one. But to me, he was so much more than that. A fact I fucking despised.

"Reload!" he called out.

He was the one responsible for the field of death I'd woken up in after he'd hunted my camp and murdered my friends.

He was the male who'd captured my best friend and almost succeeded in forcing her hand in marriage.

His very breaths were the difference between a hopeful future and a helpless one.

And with everyone surging toward the exit, my path to him was virtually clear.

CHAPTER 38

Axel

"Be still my beating heart," I cooed down to the somehow still thundering organ in my hand that I'd just torn from a troll.

As though it heard me, the pumps slowed to a stop, and I tossed it onto my pile just as the troll fell backward, taking out two of the Mount Mortum warriors on its way down.

"You good?" I called over my shoulder.

"For now," Raine grunted "You?"

"Perfect," I lied. The truth was, I was petrified that at any moment, a headache would hit, signaling Evangelia had died from her deep wounds or the subsequent fall, taking Alaric, and Kane, with her.

We'd been edging our way across the pit at a painstakingly slow speed, back-to-back in thrakos form, our wings slitting throats while our claws extracted hearts left and right.

"I'm not saying it's a competition or anything, but my pile's bigger than yours," I said, trying to keep her talking, so I knew she was still with me and hadn't reverted to Anon.

"Take that back right now or I'll be adding yours to it next," she hissed, confirming it was Raine. Or at least the version I was quickly getting to know.

"Keep talking dirty, love. My attackers won't be able to put up a decent fight," I told her.

"Oh yeah? Let me guess, distracted by the giant bulge in your pants?" she snarked back just as I heard another soldier drop at her hand.

"How did you gu–What the fuck?" I cursed as a stake left a ballista, firing toward the doors.

Did the bastards seriously not give a shit that the fae taking the brunt of the hits were those invited to watch a show? Albeit a show where other innocent fae were brutalized and killed. Not the other way around. Fuck. They were still civilians, no matter how disgusting they were as fae.

I really didn't want to leave Raine down here alone to go after the crossbow on the right platform, but the cunts firing them were leaving me no choice. "Cover me?" I asked.

"On it," she said, then grunted before a familiar thud sounded—another foolish soldier who thought to take her on taught a lesson in why that wasn't a good idea.

The path to the crossbow I needed to destroy was blocked by a sea of fae, easily over one hundred deep. Rather than head straight for it, I climbed up onto the cages to see if there was a better route.

I glanced up at Nix just as he reached the lethal weapon and torched the thing in thrakos fire. Then dropped into battle with the large group of Mount Mortums who'd been guarding and controlling it. I sent a prayer to the fates that he'd seen the river of horde snapping at his heels too.

As I straightened, the doors finally gave way and a wave of rebels charged forward, weapons in the air and instantly colliding with the mass of bodies, desperately trying to get out.

"Alaric?" I thought down the bond. *"Are you on your way inside yet?"* He'd been worryingly quiet since I'd told him what had happened to Evangelia.

"Nah. Fuckin' troll cunts slowing me down," he said. *"Kane should be in. An' the Dyvrad's will be flying in any minute. Are the crossbows disabled?"*

"One down, one to go. They're firing them at the door. Watch out and warn the others."

"Braxton an' Rose are leading the troops at the door," he said, and I felt suddenly nauseous.

Sprinting over the cages, I didn't stop until I stood on the one that had held Raine, nearest the arena's entrance.

Mount Mortums, horde soldiers, rebels, and bystanders clashed, making it impossible to discern friend from foe, soldier from civilian. I could barely see the broken bodies on the ground who'd passed on to the fates with so many fae climbing over them to get out.

Kane's face was the first one I recognized. He'd plastered himself against the wall on the far side and was making progress, almost past the worst of the bottleneck. Though his eyes were trained on the royal box in the middle of the arena's seating, from his position, he could be at the other crossbow far quicker than me.

"Kane!" I called out. "Kane!" I tried again, cupping my hands around my mouth. His eyes snapped to me as he frowned and mouthed my name. "You have to take out the crossbow!" I shouted, pointing to where it sat up on its platform.

He didn't answer, but his head jerked to the deadly weapon. His eyes flicked between the crossbow directly in his path though still in the distance, and his twin, who was pulling a female away from the throne and toward the crowded aisle.

He paused, looking between the two targets before he tore his eyes back to me. I could feel the conflict he was faced with, but he nodded anyway. Then continued pushing forward, using his incredible strength and speed to force his way free of the worst of the gridlock of frantic bodies.

I scanned the crowd near the door again, my eyes darting wildly until they finally landed on the face I was truly searching for. Rose.

Alive. Breathing. Fighting hard.

Braxton was directly in front of her, battling the enemy like the warrior he was created to be. He was fierce, but Aunt Rose? Fuck. She reminded me exactly why I feared ever getting on her bad side. Fighting in her fae form, but with wolf claws to tear her way through any who dared get in her way.

But for all her viciousness, all I could think was how I couldn't wait for this to be over so we could go back to the house she'd raised me in to have a bowl of her stew again. She'd be so disgusted when I told her all about what the guards had been feeding me that she'd shove seconds and thirds in front of me, insisting I needed to eat every last bite to make up for it. And fuck if I couldn't wait.

Braxton could join us, too. Or maybe we'd all move into the castle? Kane was a good guy, he wouldn't mind Alaric's family having a few of the guest suites. Maybe even a whole wing. Or two.

If the Dyvrad's claimed the throne… talking my way into moving into the castle would be a little more tricky. We hadn't spent as much time together, and I'd like to be able to properly apologize for our bad start.

But I *had* gotten them out of that grotesque lab. That was a pretty fucking big deal. If they could get past the undignified way I'd gone about things, then maybe…

I was getting way ahead of myself.

None of that would happen if the fae didn't clear the doors. Elikai would keep ordering for them to fire into the crowd blindly; killing everyone in its path. My friends and family included.

"Reload!" Elikai shouted, as if on cue.

"Out of the way of the door!" I yelled from where I stood on the cage, looking down on the herd.

Though some fae called out for help in response, Braxton and Rose didn't so much as glance up.

"Rose! Braxton!" I cried, but they remained focused on selecting the enemy from the innocent while fighting their way further inside.

"Fire!" Elikai called far sooner than I'd expected, sending panic of the most potent kind to rock me, binding my limbs as my eyes went wide with horror.

"Fucking move!" I bellowed. "Rose! Braxton! Out the way of the doors! Everyone fucking out!" But it was useless, utterly pointless. If they could get out, they would have. That was the entire fucking problem.

Rose finally looked up at me, and I held her eyes with my panicked stare. "Go back outside!" I called. "Get out now!" I cried out so loud my throat strained around the words.

I pointed wildly in the direction of the crossbow, up ahead on its firing platform, yelling for her to see it, to run, to turn around, to get moving before it was too late.

She frowned but shook her head. Fuck! She was too small. Even stretching up on her toes, she wouldn't be able to spy what I was frantically trying to make her see. Not with the hive of huge warriors, trolls included, swarming inside the bottleneck with her. She looked so fucking tiny in there.

I watched as Braxton's eyes followed where my finger was pointing. They went wide, and I sighed in relief as he didn't miss a beat, grabbing for Rose's wrist.

Braxton held onto Rose as he pushed back through the throng the way they'd come, while his other hand remained clasped around his weapon, threatening anyone, innocent or horde or otherwise, to get out of his way.

The crossbow fired.

It hit the tightly packed flock at such speed, and with so much force, it was impossible to see how many or who it took out. Where Rose and Braxton had been just a blink before, was a crater sized hole in the crowd.

My breath caught in my chest, and I waited. But nothing moved. No fae moved.

And I knew. I somehow knew with every fiber of my being that my adopted mother and her mate had taken the brunt of the hit.

My limbs moved too slowly, suddenly weighing ten times what they had just seconds before, as I jumped down from the cages.

Fae barreled into me, but I picked them up blindly, tossing them aside. Body after body was thrown out of my path as I forced my way closer and closer to where I'd last seen her.

To where the giant stake had been launched. To where it was embedded into the ground.

My heart stopped beating as I found her. My breath caught in my throat, and a wave of ice ran down my spine, leaving me paralyzed.

"No," I breathed, refusing to believe it. My eyes had to be deceiving me. But no matter how many times I blinked it away, I was drowned with a certainty I refused to accept.

She lay so still on the ground, the woman who'd raised and molded me into the male I was today.

I fell to my knees and my wings wrapped around me in a warm hug, like the ones she would give so willingly.

I'd never feel one of them again.

I'd never be warm again.

I'd never feel again.

No matter how many times I shook my head in denial, pain gripped me like a vice, my heart beating once more only so it could pound painfully in my throat. I forced myself to look at the large hole carved through her chest and a sob escaped my own. The exact size and circular shape of the crossbow bolt.

It was a clean shot, a quick death. And not at all fucking fair.

She didn't get to leave me. She didn't get to leave Alaric. She'd just got her mate back…

Braxton's hand was still clinging to her wrist, where he lay unmoving at her side. Protecting and holding onto her even as they crossed on to the fates. A matching hole in his chest.

I tensed my muscles as fae knocked into me, refusing to move and let them charge over their bodies like they were discarded trash on the floor.

"Again!" Elikai called, and the invisible walls I'd mentally put up around me came crashing down. Rose and Braxton, both really good fucking fae who deserved so much more time together. Gone.

All I knew was rage. What was left of my heart called for vengeance.

Forcing myself up off the ground, I stood over their rigid forms protectively as I twisted to face the onslaught of fae trying to escape.

It was time to clear the way for the rebels.

By whatever means necessary.

CHAPTER 39

Nekane

Blood and scrapes flecked my cheeks and hands as I continued climbing the aisle toward the crossbow. For every step forward, it was several steps back as more and more horde recognized and came charging at me.

Adjusting the grip on my sword, I hit one of the males in the throat with the pommel. He doubled over and I brought the full weight of the Kalgulir steel down onto the back of his head. He collapsed, blood pooling around him, but I didn't wait to see if he got back up. The flap of dragon wings growing louder with every second drove me onto the next.

I gripped his wrist and pulled him forward, slamming an elbow into his shoulder. Disarmed, I threw him to the floor and looked up to face whoever made themselves my next target just as the Dyvrad's appeared. Soaring above the arena, breathing fire into the air and clueless about the dragon penetrating crossbow below their underbellies.

"Dragons!" my uncle called from not far up ahead, where he stood on the platform loading another stake. Were these the 'gifts' the selkies had heard his warriors speaking of?

"Aim high!" my brother ordered, and I swallowed my disgust at what was happening around me. I risked a quick glance his way, needing to know exactly where he was at all times.

Up to this point, he'd been focusing his hideous weapon on the entrance, where Axel now stood. Moving like a tornado, sending fae flying out of the doors like debris. A whirlwind of barely contained violence and rage as he made gaps for the rebels to swarm through.

With every glance I spared to take in what was happening in the battle, more of our allies came into view.

Goblins climbed the deserted stadium seats, engaging in fights to the death against every soldier Elikai sent down after them.

Rebel witches fell into intense duels with the horde's magic users, while simultaneously blocking their attacks against other species who had no gifts or defenses in their arsenal to counter the magic.

I refused to give in to the fear threatening to paralyze me over my mates' current wellbeing. Instead, I'd been wearing a false front ever since Alaric and I had folded over with sudden nausea and Axel had explained via the bond what had happened to Eva.

Alaric ordered me to carry on inside with his parents while he dealt with the trolls and I hadn't questioned it; knowing this wouldn't end until we'd dealt with Elikai. Ignoring the vise around my heart and sensation of my chest slowly caving in as I tried to send my mates to the back of my mind, I pushed forward. Keeping in the forefront that if they received a fatal injury, I'd go down with them.

Despite having a single-minded focus when first forcing my way inside the arena, my sights were now set on the second, and only, crossbow in play. Thanks to Nix turning the other into the ash he fought beside now, sending gusts of dust around him with every slash of his wings.

Using the distraction of the dragons setting fire to the skies overhead, I surged forward, not stopping for breath until I reached the platform.

"Fire!" Elikai called, and the bolt shot upward. The Dyvrad's danced and twisted out of the way while the rebels on their backs held on with what I knew would be a white knuckled grip.

Drayke roared as the bolt flew past him, nicking the edge of his wing. While Vyara immediately dropped lower, scanning the arena.

"Here!" I yelled, desperate to get her attention, but those guarding the crossbow chose that moment to set themselves upon me.

A horde soldier ran at me with his sword held over his head like a club. I parried it, but the strength of the attack sent reverberations up my arm. He knocked me off balance, and before I could return the blow, another was on me.

He came at me with fast, furious strikes, pushing me back. Vyara circled around and out of my line of sight as I engaged the soldier. His attacks were relentless, showing no signs of tiring.

With the machine within lunging distance now, I had no clue how to disable it. I didn't have thrakos flames like Nix. Short of my enemies taking a time out and waiting for me to pull it apart piece by piece–

"Reload!" my brother called from halfway between his throne and the aisle, struggling with Crystal, who desperately tried to pull out of his hold while he gave his demands blindly. Not caring about the repercussions or innocent lives being lost with each and every one of them.

His order to reload sparked an idea, and my eyes quickly glanced at the pile of huge wooden stakes they were feeding into the crossbow one by one.

Goblins grunted loudly as they suddenly scattered toward the aisle. Then deadly talons caught my eye as Vyara dug them into the seats to land.

Fae jumped down from her back, splitting in every direction, several darting to help Nix, who was bleeding and red faced, in desperate need of relief from his never-ending stream of attackers. Many of the others rushed toward Raine, who stood in the center of what could only be described as a horde graveyard.

Vyara shifted to her partial form, silver scales so similar to Eva's covering her body in almost impenetrable armor. Drayke landed behind her the moment she reached the aisle. He remained frozen for several seconds for the fae to clamber down from his back and swung his head round to watch Vyara racing toward me.

My own assailants froze in the face of the golden dragon's snout and jaws so close to them. So much larger and more terrifying than when they were in the sky. I didn't have the same fear though, so I called on a burst of speed to dodge around them, ducking and darting until the pile of stakes was in front of me.

My uncle lunged at me, but with one hard kick, the stack collapsed. Sharp wooden missiles tumbled down from the platform, rolling and falling behind the arena seats. As I threw up my sword to meet my uncles, an all too familiar roar sounded, chilling me to my bones.

I defended blow after blow, stepping strategically around him until his back was facing the arena entrance instead. Over his shoulder, I looked where the sound had come from, toward the crowd near the doors which Axel had single-handedly cleared.

My eyes landed on the male who'd made the realm tremble with his roar.

Alaric.

Bleeding from a deep gash across his jaw, like someone had tried and failed to slice his head from his shoulders. He looked down at the bodies, which I only now realized Axel had been using his own form to shield. To protect and preserve.

The grief and utter devastation on their faces could only mean one thing.

Braxton and Rose were gone.

With a fresh surge of fury swimming through my veins, I threw all my weight behind the next blow aimed at my uncle. His arms shook with the force it took to block it, but block it, he did.

Vyara approached from behind Vandenburg, quickly followed by Drayke. As fae fell over themselves to get out of the old dragon king and queen's way, I caught sight of Elikai, walking backward up the aisle, ordering a flock of horde to go with him.

That's when I spotted Nix making his way across the stands toward my brother. Stumbling around the seats, panting with exhaustion, yet determined to reach him. *Fuck.*

Elikai had let Crystal go, and I watched her walking quickly toward Nix, stopping short of reaching him to stand beside the throne. *What the fuck is she doing?*

"Destroy the crossbow," I shouted to Eva's grandparents. "Incinerate the fucking thing. It took down Eva."

"No!" my uncle yelled, throwing himself at me, sword first, yet again.

"We know about Evangelia," Drayke said, ignoring the king of the mountain warriors, before sucking in a deep breath of air and releasing it on the crossbow, lighting it up like a dry campfire.

"She landed not far from where we were waiting. We defended her while she was being healed, but had to leave her with the others to come and help in here," Vyara said, worry filling her eyes.

Drayke's head shot up toward my twin, whose eyes were now on Nix as a group of Mount Mortums rushed him, blocking his path. On his orders, no doubt. Crystal remained standing still beside the throne, like she was frozen in fear.

"Leave your uncle to us," Drayke said. "Go!"

And so, turning my back on them and running up the aisle for my brother, I did exactly that.

CHAPTER 40

Evangelia

With ice burning through my veins and agony screaming in my mind, I trembled with every failed attempt to shift to my fae form. I focused what little strength I had into peeling my eyes open instead. But any more than a crack, and it was like something was splitting my skull in two.

I could hear voices. Familiar voices I should be able to put faces to, but couldn't. Like the female speaking now, telling me to "Breathe, dear."

Like breathing wasn't the most painful thing of all. My lungs fought against opening even for the shallowest of breaths.

"Nothing's working," another female voice said from somewhere near the white-hot searing sensation at my flank. "My healing spells aren't strong enough," she sobbed. "*I'm* not strong enough. We need Kane."

"No," the first voice asked. "Where's Taylah?"

Fates, what was happening? I knew these females. My gut told me I trusted them. Why would they need to bring the High Priestess of Crystal Towers to me when I couldn't move, let alone defend myself?

"She's helping the Dyvrads hold off the horde," a male answered.

Dyvrads? Why were my grandparents not in the arena?

"Westly, be a dear and get her. The dragons need her less than we do," she replied. "Thalia, preserve your strength until Taylah gets here."

"She's dying, Edelin. I can't let her die. I won't. What if Taylah refuses to help? I've seen the way she looks at Eve. It's not friendly."

"She *will* help," the first voice insisted, the one belonging to my best friend's mother. Edelin wouldn't hurt me, if she was bringing Taylah here, it was because she'd foreseen that was what needed to be done to save me. And in turn, my males.

"What if the dragons can't hold the horde off alone? What then? Just tell me what I need to do, Edelin, and it's done," Thalia said. "I can't just sit here watching her bleed out. Fates, look how slow her breaths are coming."

"That's enough," Edelin said. "I only have time to fix one broken fae today. And you're not it, so you're going to have to hold it together."

"Like I told you when she fell out of the sky, you're wasting your time," Taylah's distinctive voice said. "You have two more dragons there. Not just any old dragons, either. Just send *them* in and forget about this one."

Fell out of the sky… Shit. The crossbow. That explained why my grandparents were here instead of the arena, but where exactly was *here*?

I tried to open my eyes again and saw the gold scales of Drayke's dragon forming a blockade in the distance, and the towering wall of the arena beside us.

Fates, I'd tried to save Alaric's plan from failing, and only destroyed it further.

I needed to get back in there. The rebels might need me. They needed the old dragon king and queen, and the witches and elves who formed part of their group, too.

First, I needed to live. My mates depended on it.

"I'm not going to ask you to help heal her, Taylah," Edelin said. "I need you to reach inside her mind and force her to shift."

"You realize the only reason she's not done it herself is because her mind isn't capable of pushing through *that* kind of pain, right? No one's mind is." Taylah explained, and bone-chilling fear wrapped itself around me.

"Yes, but we are more likely to be able to heal a small fae body than a dragon," Edelin said. "And I'd rather everyone *not* die in the process of trying to heal her, which is what will happen if she doesn't shift. Now, wipe that smile off your face, Taylah, and force the shift."

"Fine," she said. "But I'm not helping with anything else."

"We'll see," Edelin said. "Thalia, once Evangelia is in her fae form, place a hand on each wound. Westly, cover Thalia's hands with yours and push your magic into her. I'll be the last to place my hands and will lead the chant of the healing spell. Ready Taylah?"

The coven leader didn't give me any warning that she was in fact ready, though I wasn't sure that would have made any difference as she started her agonizing assault on my mind.

The blinding, searing pain was like two hot daggers freshly removed from a kiln and then stabbed through my skull, penetrating my brain. It was unlike any pain I'd ever felt, or even imagined, was possible. Though that wasn't what the witches had described, it was the closest thing I could think of that might be remotely on a par with the agony that Taylah was subjecting me to.

The pain peaked and heightened, forcing me to quiver intensely, until I lay in my fae form, naked on the ground. All I knew was pain as cold hands landed on my now burning skin. My breath was forced in and out of my lungs like razor blades.

Agony.

Everything was agony.

With every excruciating second that passed, the witches' chants grew louder and my mind sharper, until I could hear the warning roars of dragons, the battle cries of the horde, and the clangs of weapons ricocheting off one another.

As the pain level became easier to manage, I regained control of my breathing. Opening my eyes, I found my body lying in the center of a dragon sized crater in the ground. I tried to rise to my knees, but their hands pushed me down. My cheek and stomach were being forced into the cold dirt.

The chants turned into urgent whispering, which was broken by Taylah's voice as she screeched, "Stop! That's enough. You're killing yourselves!"

I attempted to twist my head around to see what Taylah was seeing, but my body wouldn't allow it.

"Edelin, release her now!" Taylah demanded. I pried an eye open and watched helplessly as Taylah joined the witches, slamming her hands over Edelin's and joining in the healing chant. Using the pauses between lines to curse the seer.

My strength was coming back quickly, and my muscles no longer ached. The pain of the wounds faded to that of an older injury or a fresh bruise. Whatever they were doing, it was working. And it was seriously potent magic.

As I craned my neck around, Taylah's sharp nails scratched my bare flesh and she frantically pulled Edelin's hands off of me.

"Don't you fucking dare die!" Taylah screamed, scrambling to touch Edelin's too-still form and yelling the healing chants with a vicious sharpness lacing each syllable.

My eyes landed on Thalia and Westly as they too hunched over on the ground. Thalia trembled like she sat in the epicenter of an earthquake. Westly's eyes rolled back in his head as his niece crawled to him, reaching out a hand and whispering more healing chants. "Westly," Thalia sobbed. "Wake up. Please."

"I'm okay," he muttered quietly as his eyes stopped rolling, but slid closed. "I'm okay. Just give me a minute..."

I dragged myself over to the female who was like an aunt to me in every sense of the word, just not by blood. "What happened?" I asked Taylah, my voice rough.

"You!" Taylah spat. "You happened. You got yourself shot, and the stupid, stupid witch... Ugh." Her hands went to her head, nails gripping her hair. "She knew. She fucking knew."

"Knew what?" I asked as my eyes scanned Edelin's unmoving form and a sob choked me.

"That's why she allowed the deal to happen! That wretched witch."

"Evangelia..." Nix's mother's weak voice murmured.

"Edelin," I breathed, taking her small hand in mine. "How? *Why?*"

Tears filled my eyes, blurring her face before I quickly blinked them away. She gave me a small smile, but a cough ripped from her throat, snatching it away. Her breath gurgled as she tried to fight for air.

"Do not blame yourself for this, dear," she said. "Promise me."

"Edelin, no, please. You can't–"

"I knew it was my time," she croaked. "The fates need me now."

"Nix needs you! I need you. Fates, we all need you, Edelin. Why? Why would you do this to yourself?"

"You are important, Evangelia Dyvrad."

"So are you!" I screamed through the lump lodged in my throat.

She tried to shake her head, but was too weak and instead broke into another fit of coughs. "Only the blood of the last…can restore what has passed…"

"No," I begged as my tears fell, landing on her face. "No, please. Don't go. Taylah, heal her! Thalia, Westly? Anybody, *please*."

Her breath rattled, and she fell utterly still.

I held my breath. Waiting, watching, needing her chest to rise again. I wasn't sure how much time passed as I sat like that. Begging her to live, pleading with the fates to let her stay. But every second felt like a century.

And her chest didn't rise again.

"Eve?" Thalia whispered. "Your grandmother's asking if you're okay? If they can go and join the battle in the arena?"

Fates. The arena. The battle. The war that still hadn't been won.

Nix would be in there. I'd have to tell him what happened. Maybe not right now, but once the battle was over, I'd tell him all of it. That it was my fault. That I'd taken his mother's immortality to keep my own.

Do not blame yourself for this, dear.

But how could I not? I hadn't accepted the promise she'd wanted me to make. I hadn't even thanked her. Would never get the chance, either. All I could do now was thank her by helping to end this and win the war. Prove that her sacrifice had been worth the fae she'd made it for.

I took a deep, slow breath. "Yes," I told Thalia. "Tell them that I'm okay, that I will see them in there as soon as I'm able."

"Eve, you can't. You almost died. You need to rest and let your body heal."

"I promise I'll rest, Lia," I told her. "Just as soon as Elikai is dead and the war is won."

Breathing was difficult as I summoned scales to my flesh. Rippling across my body, they came to a stop where my neck met my jawline. Bending my knees and hissing at the painful pull of my recently closed wounds, I forced myself to spring into the air, pushing my wings wide the moment my feet left the ground.

Either my body was heavier than the last time I did this, weighed down by sadness, or my wings were suddenly weaker, because my movements were completely off as I flew up and over the edge of the arena once more.

I swallowed as I saw the chunk taken out of it, the bent and warped metal around the lip where the walls curved over. My stomach knotted as a spark of the memory of my dragon form slamming into it flashed before my eyes. Nervousness filled my stomach, threatening to stop me from flying over for innate fear of the crossbow's stakes, but I forced it away. Edelin hadn't sacrificed herself for me to become a cowering shadow of my former self.

The first thing I saw were the blazing fires where the crossbows once stood and my shoulders relaxed a fraction. But then, as my eyes darted around the scene before me, what they landed on had me almost falling from the sky. More death and destruction than I could ever have prepared for.

I refused to let the tears threatening my eyes fall as I lowered myself down. Instead, I forced myself to take in every detail, to look everywhere, to feel everything.

Alaric and Axel fought back to back like they were one being. Bodies piled up around them, but still more attackers came.

They moved in a strange way, like they were intentionally making an impenetrable circle around the two still bodies between them.

My clawed hand shot to cover my mouth as I gasped. But there was nothing I could do to stop the tear which escaped, trickling down my cheek as sorrow surrounded my chest.

Fates, so much death. So many friends had fallen.

A bright stream of dragon fire to the right of the arena forced me to peel my eyes away from the heartbreaking sight. My grandparents wore the same form as me, and though I could only see the backs of their heads, I had the perfect vantage point to watch King Vandenburg's face as it melted off his skull.

They didn't stop when he turned into a pile of ash at their feet. No, they had too much anger to take out on the male who'd helped Augustus Regis take their throne and imprison them for centuries to be able to stop so soon. It wasn't until a hole formed in the arena's wall that they sucked in a breath, extinguishing their flames.

I flew toward them as I continued to lower myself down.

I'd searched out where among the battles I could be most useful, and where better than at my grandparents' side, just in time for when the Mount Mortum army would come charging for revenge.

CHAPTER 41

Alaric

Blinding rage, that's all I could feel.

Loss was part of any battle. Death was part of life. I knew that. But fuck, it hurt.

Upon seeing my ma' and da's broken forms, I was hit with an overwhelming wave of emotions that I was neither prepared for nor capable of dealing with. The weight of sadness coming from the organ in my chest was unbearable, crushing my ribs with the unfairness of it.

As quickly as their love had rekindled, their lives had ended. I hadn't even had the chance to get used to seeing them together, after spending most of my existence apart, and already their immortality had been taken away.

Which fucking enraged me.

All around Axel and I, bodies fell on top of bodies already piled several high. Our shared grief exploded from us in the only way we knew how. On the enemy. Violently.

As a hyena shifter collapsed onto his warlock comrade, I breathed heavily, taking in the sight around me, needing to know whether we were winning or losing this thing. I would not let their sacrifice be in vain. I would not allow this battle to end in more loss for the rebels. My da' had spent his entire existence helping and preparing for the day this fight came. I would not let his life's work be without victory.

My female, in all her stunning silver glory, dropped steadily into the arena and my heart skipped a beat. Though I would not be breathing now had she not survived the shots and her fall. When Axel had explained what had happened, I'd expected her injuries to be of the life-altering kind. Instead, her darting gaze was sharp, her jaw set and wings wide, like an angel coming down from the skies for vengeance.

Whatever and whoever had healed her, I would forever be in their debt.

Flames danced in the reflection of her eyes and I followed her gaze to the stream of fire engulfing Vandenburg; only recognizable from the red crown melting at a slightly slower rate than his flesh, leaving a pile of ashy bones.

By the time Drayke and Vyara stopped, I was already reaching for Axel, pulling him with me. They'd just killed a king on foreign soil, in front of a small army of Mount Mortums. And we were too far away to help.

With a backward glance at my ma', Axel forced his feet to move away from her and we took off running toward the aisle. Before we reached it, mountain fae in every direction dropped their weapons simultaneously. Then surged toward the dragons with a scary calm gait that could only come with deep-rooted fury.

"Fuck, do you think they plan to rip them apart with their bare hands?" Axel asked directly into my head.

Angel was already with her grandparents, but Axel and I had barely left the doors behind us, let alone reached the busy aisle we'd need to climb to help them. I glanced at my fingers wrapped around the ax's hilt and shrugged. *"Good job we have claws too,"* I thought back as desperation to reach my mate drove my heavy limbs to move faster and faster.

As I started up the aisle, my eyes found my male. Not a moment too soon to see him lunge for his brother. Elikai barked orders to the horde to attack, and I frowned as they stepped aside. At the first clang of swords, the twin princes were locked in a duel to the death.

I kept half an eye on the group of soldiers who'd just committed treason before their king's eyes. *"That group of horde, do yeh ken them?"* I asked Axel.

He frowned, squinting up at them. *"The male at the front, he was in the group who ambushed the rebel camp."*

"Fuck. Yer right." Kane had let them live that day, and this was their way of telling him they had not forgotten his kindness. Perhaps not all of the horde were beyond redemption. Fates, whatever they'd done, I'd probably done worse.

Elikai retreated further up the aisle and across the seats with every opening, making Kane arch and twist and stumble as he tried not to lose his footing. The way their bodies moved was so similar; so perfectly matched in height, weight, and posture. But they looked nothing alike.

Kane had clearly fought hard just to reach his brother. Where Elikai looked on the outside to be a well put together monarch, Kane was every inch the rebel warrior. Sweat damp hair, dried blood smearing his cheeks, chest rising and falling too quickly as his lungs fought for air.

Elikai parried a blow and retreated further from Kane, moving closer to his throne in the center of the arena's seats, where Crystal stood like a statue as she watched the brothers. They exchanged words back and forth, though I couldn't hear any of what was being said.

The fight wouldn't end until one of them died. Kane knew that.

Elikai had taken away his brother's choice when he'd proven himself irredeemable. Too dangerous to society to be allowed to live. Though Kane had conceded to the only course of action remaining, that wouldn't be making this fight any easier for him.

The fact his opponent wore the same face as him only made it impossible to forget it was his brother he was trying to kill.

A soldier clad in horde armor shoved into me as he ran down the aisle. Stopping dead, I turned, just as he did the same. My nostrils flared, and a growl rumbled up my throat. "Jarid," I spat. "Where the fuck do yeh think yer going?"

Upon meeting his eyes, I was transported back to the woods surrounding Hazelbrook. It was the first time my bond with Axel had been severed. And the male I'd once trained to be a soldier took the opportunity of me being down to snap the bone of my leg with a vine.

He mouthed my name and turned to run, but I'd already unsheathed a thrakos claw and sliced through the weapons belt fastened around my tunic. Dropping into a crouch, I whipped the belt out so it wrapped around his leg. With one fast tug, he was next to me.

Grabbing his leg, I dug my claws in so tightly, his bone would have shown had there not been so much blood pouring from the savage wound. Jarid's scream was so high pitched it was inaudible and Axel watched on as I broke both legs with my bare hands, followed by his arms, and stood.

"We can go now," I told Axel.

"Wasn't he the soldier who–"

"Aye," I said, not having time to go into the whole sordid story. The Mount Mortums pursuit of the old dragon king and queen was almost complete as they ignored every fae in their path, both enemy and ally. The Dyvrad's were their target, much as Jarid had been mine, and everyone else in the arena seemed to have faded away.

"Fucking. Cunt," Axel said, then leaned over Jarid's silently screaming form, and relieved him of his heart. "Sorry, I just needed to check whether you actually had one. Turns out you do... Well, you did."

Launching the heart at the stage where Raine fought, her hand snapped out, catching it without even having looked up.

"Put that in my pile!" Axel called. She just rolled her eyes and reached for the next attacker. *"Still Raine. Okay,* now *we can go, boss."*

I cursed as the mountain fae surrounded the dragons, hiding Angel from view.

Elikai was slumped onto his throne, Kane's sword trained directly on his heart.

"Fuck, what's Nixen doing?" Axel snapped.

I'd seen Nix earlier, trying to make his way to Elikai, but a group of Mount Mortums had got in his way. With them no longer blocking his path, he came barreling toward the brothers. The thrakos witch hybrid could barely stand, clutching an arm around his waist so tightly it was like he was trying to stop his innards from falling out.

Fuck.

I pushed and shoved my way through the fighting horde and rebels until the Mount Mortums at the back of the crowd were within touching distance. I reached out a hand, intent on turning the male around to face me so he could at least see the face of the fae who was about to kill him. But my hand slipped through the air as he, and every other mountain warrior, dropped to the ground.

Knee bent, head dipped, and body angled toward Drayke and Vyara. Angel's eyes went wide, but her expression quickly changed to confusion when the warrior closest to the grandparents called, “The mountain has fallen!”

I braced myself, claws out and ready for anything.

“Where one crumbled, two more have risen in its place!” the warrior continued. “To you, your highnesses, we pledge–”

Followed by a chorus of deep voices, hollering in perfect unison, “–My sword, my life, my honor.”

CHAPTER 42

Nekane

Again and again, my sword slammed against his, forcing him backward until he was almost at his throne, where Crystal stood, watching my brother and I. Through every swipe and slash of our swords, she hadn't torn her eyes away once.

"Crystal. Go," I said through gritted teeth. Her eyebrows pinched together as her eyes locked on me, but still, she didn't move.

Elikai's face reddened and my muscles bulged with effort at the relentless clanging of steel hitting steel. My arms ached, threatening to go numb from the constant clashes they endured.

His eyes flashed wide on something behind me, but I resisted the temptation to look. There were only three fae I was concerned with right now. My mates and my brother. I'd know if the worst happened to either of the former, which meant I had no reason to take my eyes off the latter.

Pushing my body beyond its limits, I used the momentary distraction for everything it was worth, knowing I wouldn't get another. Forcing his blade down, I tucked it tightly into my side, wrapping my arm over and around it. I hissed as it sliced through my armor, cutting into my waist, but I ignored the pain, squeezing it even tighter to my body as I snaked my forearm and wrist up and under, reaching for the cross guard.

The moment my fingers closed around it, I twisted, throwing the weight of my entire body into it. The blade's edge cut deeper into my side. It was quickly growing damp as blood swelled from the wound, but I bit down on my teeth until it tore free from his grip.

Tossing the sword aside, it came clattering down several feet away, and I finally had his attention. As his gaze darted to his weaponless hand, I leaned back, pulled my knee up high and brought my boot down, hard into his chest.

He stumbled back, the seat of his throne digging into the back of his knees until he fell, slumped into the deep seat of the ridiculous chair. His crown toppled to the floor at my feet. By the time his eyes met mine, the tip of my sword was pointed straight at his heart. Still, Crystal didn't move.

"I bet that throne is a lot less comfortable now," I spat, adding a little more pressure to my blade and watching it slide through the ribbon which held together the imperial cloak of Dezrothia he wore as a robe. It fell open, revealing the chainmail armor beneath. It was strong, and would put up a fight, but it wouldn't stop Kalgulir steel. Before I could strike, something, no, someone, shoved me off balance.

I whirled to find my attacker and cursed when I saw… Nix.

"What the fuck did you do to him?" I snapped, turning back to my brother to find Crystal now on his lap. Her eyes widened with fear as he whispered something in her ear.

The hum of his power filled the air.

Allure.

Fucking coward.

She sat rigid, her brows pinching like she was desperately fighting every movement, and it physically pained her.

"I'm sorry," Nix gritted as he ran at me again, claws bared and body half broken, but Elikai's allure was forcing him to ignore the pain that just moving must have been causing him.

"Nix, please, stop. You can fight this," I said, my palms raised in mercy.

"Oh, the puppet has a name," my brother said, his lips turned up in an ugly grin. *"Nix. Crystal. Kill Nekane Regis."*

Crystal leaped off Elikai's lap, stooped to pick up the discarded weapon, and turned it on me.

Fuck.

"Stop," I said, hating myself for turning the gift I despised so much on *any* fae, much less my friends, but having no other option.

"Kill him, now!" Elikai demanded.

"You don't want to kill me," I ordered, and they both stopped. *"Go. Now. Go as far as you need to until you can't hear mine or my brother's voices any longer."*

"No," Elikai snapped. *"Kill him!"*

"Go!" I growled over him.

Holding my breath, I watched as they warred between the two orders.

Nix grabbed Crystal's wrist, and she dropped the sword. I kicked it aside and slammed my fists into Elikai's shoulders, while one closed around my sword's hilt, shoving him back down. My friends tore away, hurdling the seats as fast as their bodies would allow to put as much space between us and them as possible.

A slow smile spread across my twin's face as his eyes once again fell on whatever he was alluding to happening behind me. A laugh bubbled up in his throat. His attention was focused on where I knew the crossbow to be, but I'd watched Drayke incinerate it with my own eyes. There was no way it was working and trained on my back.

"At least I only wanted *one* throne," he sneered.

At my frown, he tipped his head toward whatever had him so distracted and entertained.

With my sword back pressed against his chest, I followed his eyeline to see our uncle's soldiers bending the knee to Vyara and Drayke. At their feet was a pile of cinders. The former king of Mount Mortum.

The pledge of the mountain warriors' allegiance echoed around the walls.

A smile tugged at my lips as my eyes scanned the arena and found that without Mount Mortum support, there weren't many defending the crown.

The tides had turned in our favor.

"Why are you smiling?! You just handed them a throne," my brother seethed. "They used you, brother. I saw you fighting them. That was your throne to take. *So take it!*"

But his allure didn't affect me. Nor did his manipulations. Nothing could wipe the smile from my lips as I looked down at him, my blade to his chest, his crown on the ground, and the velvet of his throne at his back, as something else dawned on me.

Something I'd worried I'd desire when the possibility came as close as it was now.

The intensity of the feeling washed over me as I realized I had no desire to be king. No lust for the power that came with the throne. Though Elikai had obviously designed the one beneath him now, like it was some significant symbol of his authority, to me, it was little more than an ugly chair.

"Go! Take *your* castle!" I called to the dragon king and queen, my eyes not leaving my brother as I spoke. "Reclaim your home!"

"NO!" Elikai bellowed. "You are a traitor to the name Regis! An embarrassment to our blood!"

"I don't fucking *want* the Regis name," I growled. "I'm embarrassed we even share the same blood."

Two huge dragons flew up and out of the arena, on their way to take back the castle that should have never belonged to my family in the first place.

I put more pressure on the blade at his chest. "I wish it didn't have to happen like this, brother."

He laughed maniacally. The sound sent a chill down my spine. "First, father. Now, me. You truly are the killer of kings, Nekane. Perhaps you do deserve your birth name. Perhaps you are more Regis than you care to admit."

I shook my head, refusing to let his words fester. "You've left me no choice, Kai," I told him through the lump forming in my throat. "I didn't want it to come to this."

"Then don't let it," he said. "I can change. Just like you did."

His words gave me pause, only the smallest fraction of a second, but long enough for his hand to clamp around my blade and shove it aside.

He kicked out, sending me stumbling backward. I let him take the sword, my free hand already reaching behind me. Elikai lifted the blade in the air just as I unsheathed one of Eva's daggers from my back.

He lunged for me, but I didn't flinch or pause or even think. One hand came down on his shoulder, pulling him in close. The other steered the dagger, driving it straight through his heart. His body twitched as blood soaked my hand.

Time stood still as I waited for him to stop convulsing. Dead weight slumped down on me and my knees gave out. I fell to the floor, my brother's utterly still body slumped over my thighs.

My mates were at my side before I heard them coming. Alaric's arm came around my shoulder and his mouth pressed against my hair. Angel knelt before me, soft hands cupping my jaw and lifting my head to meet her eyes.

"Kane," she gasped. "It's over. You did it."

CHAPTER 43

Evangelia

Three days. It took us seventy-two grueling and fatigue-filled hours to move the bodies of those who had embraced the fates in the battle.

On the evening following our victory, Drayke and Vyara had charged me with the preparations for the burials. With the adrenaline that came with war still coursing through me, making my limbs tremble in its wake, I'd asked for direction for the task. Pulling it off alone and without guidance was daunting, and I felt unsure how to best manage it.

They'd just given me apologetic looks and told me they trusted me to decide on how to best honor the dead. Seeing how stressed they were, I'd left them to it. Taking on the responsibility of two realms had never been part of the plan. Their plates were overflowing with Mount Mortum matters alone; the kingdom no one had expected to fall. The least I could do was help them by taking on planning how to honor the fallen.

With my mind still reeling from the victory and too many losses to count, I left Augustus' former chambers that my grandparents had taken up residence in and stepped out onto the balcony. Perhaps the fresh air would give me the breathing room I needed to think straight.

The only experience I had with the fall of a monarch and the following mourning period was when Kane's father had died. Was it the same after a war? I stared out over the fuzzy, flowering lawns of the rear grounds aimlessly, unsure how much time passed before the idea took root. Perhaps the seed had been planted as soon as I'd stepped out, and the time spent with the view had helped it grow.

I'd gone straight to our chambers to meet with my mates. Kane had lived in these alone for years and this is where the three of us would be staying for the foreseeable future. I trusted my mates' judgment and knew they'd be honest if the idea was too ridiculous. Even as it formed in my mind, it had been verging on ludicrous.

"It's perfect," Kane had said once I explained, and then pulled me in to place a gentle kiss on my head.

Alaric had remained deep in thought, his silver eyes sharp as he considered it. "What do yeh need us to do to make it happen?" he finally asked, and relief flooded me.

It didn't take him long to order the horde that had not seen battle to set about making my vision happen. There wasn't a selkie, kelpie, dryad, or spider who had refused his request. Later, joined by the rest of the remaining rebel army, once they'd seen what they were doing and insisted they wanted to help, too. Those who Alaric had agreed were fit enough to lend their aid, anyway. He'd personally assessed each warrior, sending those who needed medical attention to the infirmary wing of the castle to be healed by high fae volunteers.

Every fae had worked together and spent the past three days collecting and carrying the dead to the castle—rebel, horde and Mount Mortum alike. Then laid them with care onto the lawns of grass I had spent hours watching before the plan had formed.

We'd opened the grounds to anyone who wished to come and identify their loved ones. And they'd remain that way, forever open to the fae of Ezerat and Dezrothia. Giving them not only a place to say goodbye, but to revisit whenever they wished to be closer to them.

With everything having happened so quickly after I dropped the vials into the arena, the first the horde soldiers who'd been off duty knew of the rebel attack was when the castle's former king and queen had landed in the courtyard and ordered them to, "Kneel, leave or die."

Emily and Safi had walked me through, in great detail, what had happened next. How the spiders had come out of the shadows from where they'd hidden and swarmed the castle. Climbing the walls, squeezing through windows, and scurrying across parapets to the curved towers. Snipping down the flags and banners with their poison-filled fangs.

Though none had chosen to die, some had pledged their allegiance to the dragon royals there and then, while the rest had chosen to leave. Those soldiers came barreling toward the arena instead, but stopped dead in their tracks when they saw Kane, carrying his brother's body from the arena to the castle.

At seeing their king dead, they had dropped to their knees, muttering about allegiances. Kane had soon set them right. Letting them know he was not the one they should pledge themselves to.

I couldn't blame them for their confusion. Usurpers, historically, had *always* taken the throne for themselves. To kill the reigning monarch and *not* sit on their throne was... unheard of. They had paled as they pieced together that the ones who had demanded they kneel were the ones they should have pledged to.

We'd fallen into silence after that. The only sound was our footsteps on the cobblestones as we carried our friends to their final resting place at the castle. While Kane had held his brother, Alaric carried the body of his father and Axel, his adopted mother, Rose.

Nix had walked a little behind us with Raine, a silent support, while he cradled his mother. Though for a few moments, we hadn't been sure he could. Not because he didn't want to, but because he had discovered a note when he had lifted her.

As soon as the battle was won and the horde had laid down their weapons, I'd left Alaric with Kane to find Nix and told him everything as I'd taken him to his mother's body. Though his heart had shattered into a thousand shards, he had repeated over and over how he didn't blame me. I'd spent the days since coming to terms with not blaming myself.

As Nix had lifted Edelin into his arms, a scrunched-up scrap of parchment had fallen from a pocket, and I had read aloud for him.

Nixen, my dear boy.

Leaving you will never be easy, but this time hurts the most, for I know we won't see each other again for the longest time.

I'm so sorry I couldn't always be there. My favorite days will forever be the ones I spent with you, and my most cherished memories, those of when we were together.

Rest easy with the knowledge I will never truly be gone. I may be with the fates now, but I will never stop watching over you.

I have one favor to ask of you, and I hate to ask this, dear, but please release my body to the High Priestess to be laid to rest at Crystal Towers, such was our deal.

I love you and I am proud of you, son.

The words sliced through the grief lodged in my throat, making my voice break a little more with every line I read. Nixen had listened to each word with his eyes closed, as though picturing his mother saying them directly to him.

Thalia and Westly had sobbed and held each other. The sacrifice Edelin had made even sparked some emotion in Taylah that I hadn't thought she was capable of. Or at least, it had triggered her conscience. Her voice sounded choked when she'd muttered, "Forget the deal," before gathering her coven to leave. We hadn't seen or heard from her since.

Though we'd all put our immortality on the line and fought with everything we had, I struggled to imagine the warring emotions Kane must have felt during the hours between the battle ending and us falling into bed that night. What he'd done, not just physically, but mentally, was no small thing.

He'd marched into that battle knowing that remaining on the throne wasn't an option for his brother, just as well as he'd known he'd never step down peacefully. Which left him with only one option. Though he had grown resentful of his twin, I don't think he could have ever truly hated him. Strong dislike and anger? Yes, but there wasn't a doubt in my mind that driving that dagger through Elikai's heart would have killed a part of him.

The first chance Alaric and I got at a private moment to see how Kane was doing wasn't until we'd found somewhere for everyone to rest for the night, and our bodies had insisted we go to bed, too.

As we'd entered Kane's old chambers, Alaric had reached for him, placing his hands around the back of his head and resting his forehead down against Kane's before whispering the words that, hopefully, lifted the weight on his heart. "I'm so fuckin' proud of yeh, Kane."

"Why?" he'd muttered, his eyes searching like he'd truly needed the answer. "What makes me different from them?" My chest had tightened. It was like looking into the past, seeing the version of Kane I'd first met.

Alaric hadn't missed a beat, though. "That couldnae be further from the truth. Yer nothin' like them."

He'd pulled out of Alaric's hold and shrugged off my hand as he began to pace. "They were both usurpers, and now so am I. That's how the realm will see me. That is who I am." A laugh escaped him, but there was no amusement in the sound. He was defeated. "I don't even want a crown or throne, and I've still ended up just like them," he'd scoffed. "Maybe blood wins out in the end and I can't change it."

"Maybe you *are* like them," I'd told him, hurrying to finish my sentence when his eyes had widened in horror. "But not in the way you are thinking. When you set your mind and heart on something, you refuse to stop until you achieve it. But Kane, where you differ completely is in all the places that count. Like how you did what you did for unselfish reasons. Not to take the crown and throne for your own self-centered desires, but to stop the greed of another. That is something your father and brother could never comprehend."

"Aye," Alaric had agreed, just as desperate as me to help our male realize his worth at such a hard, vulnerable time. "An' yeh didnae enjoy doing what yeh had to do to get there. Another distinct difference between yeh. It boosted their ego to take what they wanted. It has done the opposite for yeh."

After a night's rest and some more reminding that he had done the right thing, Kane gradually began to come to terms with the death of Elikai. Just last night in bed, he'd admitted that he had already mourned the version he wanted to keep alive in his memories. The ones of him before the madness of power set in. The ones before Elikai had shoved him out of the window or tried to frame him for murdering their father.

I was so proud of my mates, our friends, and the rebel army. Not just for the bravery they'd shown on the battlefield, but the honor they'd shown after the battle. Embracing change and working together.

Our victory and all that had happened in the days since had led me here, looking down over what remained of the arena, hovering in my partially shifted form. The funeral would begin shortly, but there was something I had to do first.

A niggling had been in the back of my mind since my mates and I had finished with the preparations for the burials, like I was missing something. It wasn't until waking this morning that I'd worked it out.

Sucking in a lungful of air, I let my dragon fire free and relished in its blistering heat as it engulfed the arena. My intention to destroy the place was not for Dezrothia to forget the battle that had happened here; the entire thought process behind how the burial would happen today was to make sure we'd *always* remember how and why so many had lost their lives.

The barbaric event the arena had been built for in the first place was what I wanted to rid from the Dezrothian landscape. Where fae of every race had been sent to their deaths, so needlessly and pointlessly. Murdered in brutal ways by other fae who had no desire to kill them in the first place.

So no, this wouldn't stand as a monument to where we'd fought for freedom. The building itself was not what was significant to Dezrothia's history. It was those who'd fought to be on the right side of it, both the survivors and those who'd passed onto the fates, that we must always remember.

And the graveyard we'd spent three days creating would make sure no one ever forgot them.

Especially those in power.

CHAPTER 44

Nekane

To anyone else, the way Alaric leaned against the doors to the castle would be the picture of relaxation. But that couldn't be farther from the truth. I could see it in the way his hands twitched on his arms where they folded, the way he shifted to feel the comforting weight of his sword at his side.

Alaric would never be relaxed so long as he couldn't see both Angel and me, not after the events of the past half year. Though perhaps his stress would lessen with time as Dezrothia became a peaceful realm.

I sat on the steps as we waited for our mate, enjoying the spring sun as it beamed down on us. Neither too warm like the summer, nor crisp as the winter. I kept my chin tilted as I watched for our dragon princess; we had a message for her from her grandparents. One that they were eager for us to give her before the service this afternoon.

Beyond the gates, Ezerat was bustling, busier than I'd ever seen it. With fae from not just the city, but every town and village piling into the castle grounds; blankets tucked under arms, ready to be laid out over the dewy grass once they found their preferred spot to watch the proceedings and pay their respects.

Bill and Melina were handing out refreshments 'on the house' from the temporary stall they'd set up at the entrance to the castle grounds. It had appeared two nights ago after the apologetic tavern landlords had tracked down Alaric and offered to put up as many of the rebel army as the Crooked Claw could house. Even the fae not staying with them had been offered to enjoy cold drinks and warm bowls of broth courtesy of the lion shifters. Alaric had explained that the castle could foot the bill, but they'd refused, insisting it was the least they could do after not being able to get out of the city to answer his call to war.

A shadow cast across the ground and Eva landed with the grace of a dancer, despite how fast I knew she'd have been moving through the sky to get back here. "Is it done?" Alaric asked, finally pushing himself upright and letting his arms drop.

As she nodded, he moved toward the steps, but paused as she raised an eyebrow. "Were you about to come looking for me?" she accused, a small smile tugging at her lips.

"No, we just wanted to catch you as soon as you got back," I said. Alaric held out a hand, and I took it, pulling myself up.

"Why?" she asked, worry making her bite down on her bottom lip. "Not that I mind. But what's happened?"

"Nothin'. Yer grandparents want to meet with us before the funeral," Alaric explained.

"They hate it, don't they?" she frowned, referring to the order of service she had put together and left with them this morning. Just before she had left to destroy what remained of the arena. Hopefully, the betting and gift shops too.

"I doubt that, princess. They probably want to tell you how proud of you they are. I know we are."

"Aye, yeh've nothin' to worry 'bout. But let's no' leave them waitin' any longer."

We crossed the hallway, Eva's hand in Alaric's while my arm draped over her shoulder. "They're in the throne room," I said when she went to steer us toward the sweeping staircase.

"Oh, an' Thalia said that yer dress for today is ready, too," Alaric said as he knocked on the door with two thundering booms.

"I told her she didn't need to worry about that," Eva sighed as we waited. "I asked her what she wanted to be, what she wanted to do, now things would be changing, but she insisted being my handmaid was her calling."

"Ever think she might like taking care of yeh?" Alaric asked. "That she sees it as an honor?"

Eva sighed again. "I just feel bad telling her what to do. She's my friend first, you know?"

"Yes, but you are the princess of Dezrothia. As Alaric said, serving a fae like you is an honor for Thalia and her family. Have you not seen how her face lights up every time you say thank you or praise her for something she's done? Besides, if not Thalia, who else?"

"I guess–" she started but was cut off as the doors opened. Eva curtsied while Alaric and I tipped our heads in a quick bow before they waved us inside to join them. "You wanted to see us?" Eva asked. "If it's about the funeral, perhaps I could explain and you'll understand–"

The dragon royals smiled at her and shook their heads. "The service will be perfect," Vyara said. "As is the entire idea for the burials. Something we'd never have come up with ourselves yet is so fitting it's a wonder it's never been done before."

A bright blush covered Eva's cheeks. "Just how many wars has Dezrothia had?" she asked, changing the subject.

"Several," Drayke said. "Though, I'm not surprised you don't know that, given all the records our ancestors collected for millennia are missing."

"My father destroyed it all long before my time," I said. "I'm sorry."

"Never apologize on that male's behalf again, Nekane," Drayke ordered. "Do you understand? What he did bears no reflection on you."

Swallowing hard, I nodded. "Thank you," I said, surprised by how much the words meant to hear. From a male with his experience with my bloodline, not just Regis, but Vandenburg too.

"Take a seat," Vyara said, gesturing to the solid table that had been set down on the dais, just behind the mahogany throne. Eva and I pulled out a chair, but when Alaric remained standing behind us, brow creased, she pressed, "Alaric, please, sit with us." Taking the seat on the other side of Eva, he pressed steepled fingers to his lips.

"We don't have much time. The service starts soon and none of you are ready. But I'm afraid this can't wait," Drayke said, placing his elbows on the table and clasping his hands tightly.

"Well, that doesn't sound good," she said, her voice shaking slightly as she fought to conceal her worry. "What's happened?"

In the last three days, we'd quickly learned we were so used to losses and things going wrong, making us constantly on edge that a storm must be brewing, about to turn the realm upside down once more.

"The Mount Mortums will be returning home tomorrow. Some have gone ahead to prepare the boats already," Drayke said.

"Yeh want us to see they get safe passage?" Alaric guessed, but Vyara shook her head, causing his frown to deepen.

"We can see to it ourselves, as we will be going with them," she said.

"For how long?" I asked, but when neither of them answered, I felt compelled to continue, "You can't leave Dezrothia without their king and queen at such an unsettled, unprecedented time."

Rather than lash out at me for questioning their authority and decision, Vyara and Drayke shared a knowing smile. "That's what we want to speak with you about. Well, with Evangelia specifically, but we knew she'd want you both here."

"You want us to run things while you're away?" Eva asked.

Vyara reached her arms across the table and took her granddaughter's hands between hers. "Not just while we are away, little flame." Eva's eyes went wide. "We cannot rule over two realms. Not effectively anyway. And both Mount Mortum and Dezrothia will need committed rulers for the changes which need to be made to make them great for the citizens residing within."

"You're abdicating?" I breathed.

Drayke nodded. "We have watched you closely since the day we met. There are no other fae more capable and qualified to serve Dezrothia than you. Not even us. Not anymore."

"As our heir, you are next in line to the throne," Vyara said, squeezing Eva's hands tightly.

"B-but what you're saying, that would make *me* Queen," Eva said, pulling her hands back and free of her grandmother's grip as she shook her head.

"If you were to accept, then yes. And we both truly hope that you do." Vyara said, searching Eva's eyes. "We believe in you. We could not hope to have the insights the three of you would have for the needs of the fae."

"Like your mother, you would make a fine Queen, Evangelia," Drayke added. "And your mates," his eyes flicked from me to Alaric before landing on Eva once more. "They would make excellent advisors, or another role perhaps? Prince Consort and Hand of the Queen have quite the ring to it. That is, if you are open to suggestions."

"It would still be your choice, Evangelia," Vyara said. "But we have seen what Alaric is capable of. We witnessed the respect earned as you commanded and led the army." She turned her stare to Alaric. "We hear you were general for a long time. It is only right that you are recognized for your efforts."

"And Nekane, you have made it clear as a summer day that you do not wish to bear a crown. Even though you have every quality of a fae deserving of it. You fight for the fae that don't have a voice. Even now, when you fear that they will be left without guidance, you defend them by questioning us. You would be more than an asset to Dezrothia, and you could do that as an advisor and Prince Consort to our granddaughter," Drayke said.

I was stunned silent. We all were for several long minutes, all eyes finally landing on Eva as she fidgeted with her fingers and her face twisted into a frown.

"We know this will be sudden, and a shock," Drayke eventually said. "But we have given this a lot of thought."

"Fates, the representation between you will give you a better understanding than we could ever have. Two different kinds of shifter, a thrakos hybrid and high fae. Then to consider what you all have lived through over the years, and your time in the Fading Vale..." Vyara drifted off.

There was a passion behind their words. Hope too. They truly believed that Eva would be the right fae to lead Dezrothia, with the support of myself and Alaric.

"Little flame?" Vyara asked, as the silence began to stretch again.

"Can... Can I have a moment with my mates?" Eva finally asked.

"Of course, take all the time you need. We need to finalize some things." Drayke said, standing and holding out a hand for his mate to take. They left us still sitting at the table, but as soon as the door clicked shut once more, Eva burst out of her chair to pace.

"Queen?" she seethed. "I don't know the first thing about being a queen."

"Perhaps that's exactly what would make you so great," I said truthfully.

"You *agree*? I thought you didn't want anything to do with the throne?!" she exclaimed, pausing in her steps.

"I don't want to be *king*. But I *am* mated to a princess. I have made my peace that I will be close to the throne whether I like it or not," I admitted. When I realized who Drayke and Vyara were, and who that made Eva, I made my peace that the fates had wanted me to remain close to the throne. Even if it wasn't mine to take.

"You would be happy with that? To be a prince consort?" She asked, a flash of something flickering through her green eyes.

"I have seen you as *my* queen for a while. It wouldn't be too much for me to think of you as a queen in the eyes of all of Dezrothia too," I said, then found my lips pulling up into a proud smile as I imagined it.

"And you?" she asked, rounding on Alaric, "You would be happy as the Hand of the Queen?"

"I agree with everythin' yer grandparents said," he said, a grin tugging at his face too.

"You do?"

"Aye. There is no fae I would rather serve."

She fell silent once more and I could practically hear her mind churning. "What's on your mind, princess?"

"What Alaric said before an entire army followed us on what should have been a suicide mission," she admitted.

"What about it?" he asked.

"Alone, it would not be a consideration. But together..."

"We are stronger," I said.

She sighed. "But I've never believed in one fae having jurisdiction over an entire realm."

"That's how it's always been," Alaric said.

"But what if it wasn't? What if a council was formed? With a seat for every race of fae. Is that possible?"

"Not without yeh as our queen," he said.

"Kane?" she asked, her eyes almost pleading with me.

"If your wish is to form a council, unite the realm and become unstoppable, we will help you make that happen."

The longest silence so far fell. But as her grandparents had said, with every second that passed, we were getting closer and closer to the service starting.

"So, what do you think?" I pressed.

She took a deep breath and collapsed back into her chair. I waited, counting from ten as I suspected she would be doing herself. Clearing her throat, she spoke again. "Would you both be truly happy? Living here, in this castle as my Prince Consort and Hand of the Queen?"

"As long as it is with both of yeh, I dinnae care where we end up," Alaric said, and I nodded.

"Then, I say *yes,*" she whispered, as if she couldn't believe that she was actually saying it.

Before she could change her mind, Alaric was on a knee, and I followed suit. Our heads bowed before her, as we acknowledged her as our queen.

Together we pledged, "I swear that I will pay true allegiance to Her Majesty, Queen Evangelia Dyvrad, and to her heirs and successors, according to Lore. So help me, fates."

CHAPTER 45

Alaric

While Thalia helped Angel with her dress on the other side of the castle walls, I found myself once more walking among the rows of individually dug graves housing the fallen just outside.

Axel and I had spent this morning watching the sun rise from the side of my parents' grave; the first we'd dug after Angel had determined the castle grounds would be the burial site. While she'd helped Kane dig Elikai's final resting place, my adopted brother had suggested Braxton and Rose be laid to rest side by side without a wall of earth between them. I'd agreed without a heartbeat of hesitation. After spending most of their lives apart, the least we could do was make sure they would be forever together in death.

It wasn't my parents grave that called to me now, though. The one I was drawn to this time belonged to the singular fae I had cursed more than any other. The seer who had made it her life's work to fuck with me. Looking down at her still form, I lifted a hand to rest on my chest and tilted my head in thanks. For all her cryptic ways, which had driven me insane, the female had been right. About everything.

The truth was, Edelin Sybilline's sole focus wasn't really just to get under my skin, though I was sure she'd enjoyed doing it along the way. But no, she'd done so much more than that. From the moment she'd predicted the princes' birth, all the way to her getting me out of the bargain I'd struck with Taylah.

The words of the prophecy that left her lips all those years ago would forever be burnt into my brain. Mulling over them was a habit I wasn't sure I'd ever break. Like muscle memory from so many years of doing it over and over.

Where my mind used to spin, sending me in infuriating circles, now I at last had my answers. As she'd foretold, Nekane and Elikai Regis had been born, and with it their father had known his rule was in jeopardy. Rather than trust the fates to do right for

Dezrothia, he'd tried to manipulate and plot and scheme his way to never have to mourn the loss of his crown.

Though not even a year had passed since the princes' had reached twenty-five and come of age, so much had changed. But it had taken bravery and courage from countless fae to get to this point. *Just as the prophecy had claimed.*

Though we were only at the beginning, with much yet to do, I'd certainly never forget the lessons I'd learned while the riddle had played out. Like the need to forgive myself and not hate the male looking back at me in the mirror. I was sure every other fae would remember and hold on to their own lessons, too.

Though once it had seemed unthinkable, with the Lores keeping races separated, Edelin had predicted that those the King looked down upon would rise together. And though there were times as recent as within the last few weeks that had seemed impossible, we'd grown an army and been victorious.

We'd all shared different experiences under the Regis' rules, but what brought us together was the same desire for freedom and drive for a better life, even if that better life was as simple as having the choice of where you wanted to live and who you wanted to live with.

Once again, the throne lay bare, but now, there was no doubt in my mind, and soon enough, the minds of society too, who the true and rightful heir worthy of sitting in it was.

Though she hadn't known of her grandparents' wishes for her when she'd come to Kane and me with her idea for this service and burial, the way she'd honored the warriors, both allies and enemies alike, would tell the fae of the realm exactly what kind of female would soon wear the crown.

One of compassion, vision and respect of others.

One who was willing to embrace change, as she had forever changed the view from every window at the back of the castle. Meetings in the war room would now always be set against the backdrop of what can happen should violence be the first and last resort.

The final duel between the princes had been the tale of two fae, both seeming to be equal in strength, appearance, and determination. But where one had been fighting for good, and to bring honor back to Dezrothia, the other had fought to continue his reign of horror.

Kane had risen above his upbringing and transcended from the male he'd once been, a drunk who walked the castle halls in fear of his father's next attack and so broken inside he was blind to how broken everything was around him.

Becoming the male he was now had been a journey that fae would write stories about and I was so fucking proud of him it hurt, but I couldn't think of a better male for young fae across Dezrothia to read about and look up to.

He may not ascend to the throne, but somewhere along the path of self-discovery, he'd ascended his father and brother and there was no other fae more perfect for the role he'd been given of Prince Consort. He'd support, guide, and love his queen with passion, integrity, and heart. And in turn, Angel and I would love him with equal vigor.

I looked up, across the sea of graves that held the still bodies of those who'd helped us bring forth this feat. There had been too much blood spilled, sacrifices that Angel had ensured would never be forgotten.

Her vision for the castle grounds would forever act as a constant warning of the consequences of becoming a corrupt, deceitful, power-crazed ruler. And a daily reminder of why she would never change from the rebel girl of the Fading Vale, who'd grown up hunted by those more powerful, just because they could.

She would grow, but never change. And Kane and I would help should the pressure and responsibility ever become too much.

With the blood of the last King and Queen running through her veins, I did not doubt that my Angel, of the purest heart and bravest soul, would restore Dezrothia to what it had once been.

I would do whatever she needed me to do to help her along the way, knowing whatever orders that came from her wouldn't leave me unable to sleep at night.

I'd committed unspeakable acts against fae so as not to break my cover, crimes that went against the essence of my moral compass. Which for decades I'd tried to forget, thinking that was how I had to deal with them. But now, given the chance, I wouldn't vanish those pages from the book of my life.

Yes, I was ready to turn to the next fresh page and start filling it with new chapters, but I would never forget that part two would not have been possible without part one.

The months ahead would not be easy. I'd spend every day of the quiet that came with the tradition of the mourning period sharing with her everything I'd learned of our realm over the last few centuries. The good, the bad, and the stuff that would never stop hurting to think about.

By day, Kane and I would bear whatever burdens our female needed us to so she could grow into the ruler she wanted to be. And by night, we'd show our queen how much we worshiped her in the privacy of our chambers.

Not just while she found her footing and learned to carry the weight of responsibility she couldn't have guessed was in her future, but for the rest of our immortal lives.

I looked up at the balcony and saw movement behind the drapes. It was time for me to take my position up there with them.

I tried to picture what the living would see when we walked out. Kane at her left, me at her right.

Regardless of how breathtaking I knew she'd look in the black mourning gown befitting a queen, I hoped they'd see a strong female who knew her own mind. And two perfectly imperfect males at her sides, ready to take on realms to defend theirs.

Willing to take on the burden of writing the wrongs of those who'd come before us.

CHAPTER 46

Evangelia

The service was a beautiful afternoon of reflection, paying respects, and ultimately sending off those we'd lost to the fates. Though we were honoring the dead, we ensured it was a celebration of their life.

Once Alaric, Kane and I had joined my grandparents on the balcony, it wasn't long before the High Archon had begun to lead the service and blessings for every fae that lost their lives.

For as far as the eye could see, fae covered the castle gardens, flanking a wide strip up the middle where the dead would be forever laid to rest. A small, engraved plaque at the head of each, ensuring every brave soul's name would be permanently marked on the grounds of the castle. A reminder of what could happen when those with power wielded it with the wrong intentions in their hearts.

Once the High Archon fell silent, the dryads and gnomes had stood, calling on their earth magic for the final part, the burial itself. Soil had filled the graves, quickly covered by the rapid growing of fresh grass. The flowers came next, mesmerizing us all as they sprouted as one before our eyes, under the guidance of the fae's skilled manipulations of nature.

Gasps came from every direction as each and every grave was marked with a single rose. Green for the horde soldiers, red for the Mount Mortums, and violet for the rebels. The cemetery was filled with color, the beautiful scent from the roses filling the air. I tried to commit every word, every face, every moment to memory, but it had been so overwhelming, it was hard to focus on it all at once.

After all was said and done, when I tried to recall the smaller details, it was just a blur. But I would have years to walk among the eternally blooming flowers and think back on this day. I sighed in relief as I watched the mourners mingle between the rose-marked graves, reading the plaques, and giving thanks for their sacrifices.

It filled my heart with warmth as I watched fae from all walks of life mingling together. It was a stark contrast to Augustus' funeral, where only the elite had been invited. But with so many fae in attendance today, not even the grand castle was large enough to hold a wake for such an event.

While there would be smaller wakes and celebrations of life in Ezerat, and even back in the villages scattered through Dezrothia, Thalia had suggested we hold our own smaller gathering in the solar room. A private farewell to our own nearest and dearest that we'd lost and missed terribly.

The last time I had been inside the solar room, I had been jumping out of a window after Kane. Revealing my secret that I hadn't been high fae, not even close. It still surprised me that nobody had questioned what I was. They'd just assumed or taken Elikai at his word.

The room was back to a pristine state, the regal purple drapes framing the now clear glass windows. Though they were no longer the stained glass of their former glory, the clear, curved windows framed the newly rose-covered field below beautifully. Providing the perfect view of the fae still walking through and paying their respects. Something I hoped would continue for a long time.

Both Kane and Alaric had insisted I sat at the head of the table, taking their respective seats to my left and right. I would forever be the luckiest female in all the realms to have the love and loyalty of these incredible males. How I had earned the favor from the fates to be deserving of them, I would never know, but I would silently thank them every day of the rest of my immortal life.

Nix and Raine arrived first. I raised an eyebrow at Nix, seeing them together. They bowed to me, and I was suddenly on my feet, hurrying to them.

"I'm not queen yet, stop that!" I said. "And even if I were, in private, my family will never have to bow to me," I told them. Ever since I had broken the news that I would be the next queen of Dezrothia, they had started doing this to me. They'd been hardly surprised that Vyara and Drayke were abdicating to leave for Mount Mortum.

No date had been set for my coronation, but it would need to be soon after the mourning period ended. Dezrothia deserved stability, so my mates had suggested it be held in three months' time, on my thirty-fourth birthday.

Nix laughed before pulling me in for a tight hug. I relaxed into it, wrapping my arms around him. I pulled away and tugged Raine in for a hug, before gesturing for them to take a seat.

As I retook my place between my mates, I asked, "Where's Axel?"

"On his way," Alaric grumbled.

"Everything okay?" Kane asked, frowning.

"Aye. Somethin' about Camille and Marnie having somethin' to show him. I dinnae ask for more details."

"Probably for the best, knowing him," Nix said.

I thought about the care package he'd packed for the three of us when we'd fled the castle. The copious amounts of lube and accompanying sketch in particular. "Definitely for the best," I agreed, rolling my eyes but not fighting the chuckle that escaped my lips.

Nix leaned in to Raine and whispered something in her ear. I gaped as she giggled and batted his arm playfully. Catching my quirked brow, my best friend waved me off as if telling me not to bother asking, as he wouldn't tell me anyway. I smiled, glad they had each other. Raine was battling darkness and Nix knew about that better than most. Their darkness was matched, but they pulled the light from each other too, which gave me hope they would be good for each other. Heal together.

I sighed happily as I watched them. The first order I would need to make would be revoking the Lores that Augustus Regis had implemented. Allowing everyone to love whomever they wanted.

As I reached for Kane's and Alaric's hands, Axel burst into the room. I gave them a quick squeeze, butterflies fluttering in my stomach as they returned it. Would I ever lose the thrill of enjoying their attention? I truly hoped not.

Axel collapsed into a chair next to Alaric before I could stand to greet him.

Alaric clapped him on the back in greeting. "Nice o' yeh to join us," he said, giving him a look that told me he knew exactly why he was late. Thalia came in next, and immediately gestured to the wine, to which Axel eagerly held up his goblet, making her beam.

As Thalia poured, Axel launched into a very long and excessively detailed apology about why he was late. Not even pausing for breath as he turned to his bond brother, punched his arm and stated, "Now I understand why you are so happy with two mates, Alaric. I totally understand you three on a–" he made air quotes with his hands, "–'deeper level' now." He winked at me and a flush rushed over my cheeks, but the embarrassment was short-lived and he yelped.

Wine overflowed his goblet, gushing down his arm and onto the table. Thalia gasped, only now noticing, and grabbed at the tablecloth more flustered than I'd ever seen her. Trying desperately to mop up with it.

"How are we even related?" Nix murmured, shaking his head as Axel drained half the goblet in one swallow.

"Yer done, Axel. We dinnae need to ken anymore," Alaric said, choosing not to use the battle bond, and there were a few sighs of relief that we would never hear the 'climax' of the story.

"Oh, come on," Kane half moaned, half laughed. "You can't stop him *there*. He was just getting to the best bit." He gave Axel a wink, and I narrowed my eyes at my mate for encouraging him.

I cleared my throat. "Well, I'm sorry to pull you away from what I'm sure was a very… *fulfilling* experience, Axel. Truly, I am," I said just as the clack of Vyara's heels across the flagstone floor announced the arrival of my grandparents.

"Well, I guess if anyone would understand, it's you, my Queen," he replied with a glance between my mates and I, followed by an over pronounced, dramatic wink in my direction. I stared at him, open-mouthed, as my grandparents walked into the chaos that was the solar room.

"Understand what?" my grandfather asked.

Axel sucked in a breath, ready to launch into his story all over again, but Alaric's growl stopped him before another word could tumble from his lips.

That's when it occurred to me, in this most unbelievable time in my life, when there had never been more uncertainty, the only thing I could be certain of was that I was looking forward to the next thirty-four seconds as much as I looked forward to the next thirty-four years.

My cheeks heated as my eyes shot between my mates, both completely unhelpful as Kane gave me a look full of unspoken promises for later, while Alaric's large hand squeezed my inner thigh beneath the table.

Fates, they were insatiable.

Better make that thirty-four lifetimes.

THE END

Epilogue

Three Months Later: Coronation Day

"How are yeh feelin'?" Alaric asked, but I wasn't sure I had the words to answer him.

I just took a deep breath and stared back at my reflection. It felt like a lifetime ago since I last stood in this very room, looking into this very mirror. Last time, I'd been petrified, wrapped in a lavish gown of white and gold, about to be forced down the aisle to marry Kane's brother.

Now, I was just as terrified, for very different reasons. Though much more comfortable at least, in my partially shifted form; silver scales rolling down my neck and arms, disappearing at my chest where my gown shimmered. Matching my scales so beautifully, it was impossible to see where the fabric stopped and my dragon skin began.

"Like I have no idea where the last three months have gone," I eventually said as I looked up at him through the mirror and took in his appearance. Dressed in full ceremonial armor, its black plate molded to his body in all the right ways, while silver studding created swirls of intricate patterns across his shoulders. In the center of his chest sat a fierce dragon head. The symbol of my bloodline.

"You've got this," Kane said as he moved in close enough to push the stray strands of silver curls back over my shoulder, then planted a gentle kiss to my collarbone. "Look how far we've come in such a small amount of time."

"Aye," Alaric agreed. "The fact yer fae adore an' respect yeh already shows how much yer hard work is noticed and appreciated."

"*Our* hard work," I corrected. They knew as well as I that we ruled Dezrothia as a unit. I never made a decision without running it past them, making sure that I never let the power go to my head. Soon that number would be growing once the formalities of the coronation were out of the way and we could move onto realizing my dream of forming a council.

"There isn't a single home in Dezrothia that hasn't responded to either accept your invitation to be present today, or sent good luck wishes and gifts in their steed," Kane said. "Even Taylah said she is looking forward to it."

"That one doesn't shock me as much as you would think," I admitted. The witch had become one of our closest allies since falling in love with one of the thrakos who had left Ezerat with her coven to go back to Crystal Towers. She'd even gone as far as to offer the aid of her entire coven to help rebuild villages which had been in the worst states of rack and ruin thanks to being denied the tools and materials they'd so desperately needed for such a long time.

A knock sounded at the door, and Kane crossed the room to open it. His outfit was the same as Alaric's in color, but where Alaric wore armor, Kane wore a black tailored suit. Free of any excessive embellishments upon his own request, aside from the dragon head pinned to his breast pocket, where a lilac handkerchief poked out.

"Thalia," Kane greeted.

"It is almost time," came the familiar, kind voice of my handmaid. "How is she?"

"She hasn't thrown up all over the dress yet," Kane said. "So that's something."

I chuckled. "I'm fine, Lia. And the dress is beautiful. You really do have an eye for this sort of thing."

"Mmhmm," Alaric purred, looking me up and down like he was deciding how best to rip it from my flesh later.

Kane gave him a smile that told me he was counting down the hours too, and I felt a blush creep up my face.

Though it had crossed my mind that they might suddenly start treating me like a fragile female made of glass, being their queen had somehow made my males even more feral behind closed doors. Both with me and each other. A fact I loved and looked forward to every night. A reminder that although we served Dezrothia, we belonged to each other in every other way.

Thalia beamed, the smile lighting up her entire face. "I'm glad you like it," she said. "It's certainly very you. The other thing we discussed, did you–"

I quickly shook my head, cutting her off. Her eyes widened, realizing I hadn't gotten around to speaking with my mates about that little detail just yet.

"Oh, okay. Do you need help with the dress down the stairs and getting into the carriage?" she asked.

"No, you've done more than enough. Alaric and Kane will make sure I don't fall flat on my face. Go get yourself ready and stop worrying about me. I'll see you down there."

The moment Kane closed the door behind Thalia, my mates whirled on me. "What other thing yeh discussed?" Alaric asked.

Stepping down from the stool, I turned to face my handsome males and took a deep breath as I fought the sudden onslaught of nerves.

"Marry me," I asked, though it came out as more of a statement. "Today, once the ceremony has finished and I can rewrite the Lores, will you marry me?"

Kane crossed the room first, stealing the air I'd been holding in my lungs with a deep kiss. "Yes," he murmured against my mouth. "Of course, yes."

No sooner had he ended the kiss and Alaric was pulling me into his arms and kissing me with equal passion. "Aye, Angel. I will marry yeh today, one thousand years from now, or any day in between."

I relaxed into him. "Thank the fates," I sighed as the butterflies settled. "I kind of already spoke with the High Archon and had the Lores drafted. Just as soon as the ceremony ends and I sign the parchment, we can be legally wed."

Kane smiled widely. "So it would have been rather embarrassing if we'd have said no?" he joked and I swatted his arm.

"The fates have already decided you are mine and I am yours," I said with a light laugh. "But this... getting married, it feels more like it is our choice, you know? Not to mention, it shows our society that love is love, no matter the shape or form that it comes in. And besides, we will be even more busy soon, once the council meetings start. I don't know when we will get another chance. So yeah, I figured why not now? We are all dressed up, have a venue, and the High Archon's schedule is clear for the coronation."

Fates, I was rambling.

"Angel," Alaric said. "It'll be perfect."

"Let's go and get married, then," Kane said, dimples spreading across his face as he smiled from ear to ear. "And get you crowned, of course, my queen," he added, taking my hand and pushing a leg out behind him, bending low in a bow as he kissed my hand.

While my mates gathered the trail of my gown in their arms, I glanced out the window at the roses and plaques and silently prayed that I would make those who'd fallen in the war proud today.

Then, with one final 'thank you' whispered to the fates themselves, we were moving. Descending the stairs, on our way to my coronation ceremony.

THE CEREMONY TOOK place in the temple of the fates and was filled with enough formalities that I was convinced at least one thing would go wrong, but it never did.

Entering the room had been the hardest part, but the happy, relaxed faces of the fae around me, and their calls of well wishes and support, helped enormously. I moved slowly, my mates at my flank, as I followed the High Archon through the aisle to the center of the temple.

He directed me to kneel before the fates depicted in the stained glass, and once I did as instructed, the ceremony had begun. I focused only on following the High Archon's lead the entire time and found it helped keep the nerves held at bay. Before long, I was repeating the coronation oath to the congregation of fae around me.

"I swear to give my life to the service of the realm, guided by the wisdom of fates. In their light, I shall lead with honor, justice, and compassion, ensuring the prosperity and unity of Dezrothia for all its inhabitants." As my last words echoed from me, a crown was placed on my head.

The crown was as perfect as the ceremony itself. An exact replica of the one my grandmother had worn. Forged in the bleeding mountains of Mount Mortum and brought with them for their short stay before they'd return to their new home tomorrow.

A staff was handed to me at some point, gilded in gold with twining dragons around its length. At the top, a solitary gemstone was set in place. It was heavy, and nearly as tall as I was, but I held it steady as the High Archon proclaimed me Queen of Dezrothia.

The cheers that erupted felt like they shook the mountain that the temple was built into. They continued as I walked back up the aisle, my mates joining me once more as we left to greet the fae, as was tradition.

Eventually, we returned to the temple, leaving the fae to continue to celebrate in the bunting adorned streets, while we prepared to take our vows to each other.

The wedding was a much smaller affair and exactly as I'd hoped it would be. With only the High Archon, my grandparents, and our closest friends joining us. Usually, the monarch getting married would be a huge affair in itself, but this wasn't for the fae of the realm. This was for *us*.

As soon as we arrived back at our chambers, Kane swung the door wide, stripping his jacket off, and Alaric hooked his arm under my legs, swooping me up to cross the threshold.

Alaric's mouth was against mine in the next instant, and his claw dragged through the strings of the corset at my back in one quick, clean rip.

My dress fell to my feet, and I shifted back to my full fae form, disappearing the scales just as Kane's hands tucked behind my thighs. I jumped into his arms, wrapping my legs around his waist and kissed him deeply as he walked us to our giant bed.

His lips didn't leave mine until we were falling onto the soft mattress. At the rustle of clothes, I looked up to find Alaric's naked form at the foot of the bed. His cock already hard and throbbing between his thighs.

His palm came down on Kane's shoulder, and he rolled away from me to fall into a kiss with our mate. Kane was stripped quickly, Alaric's impatient hands tearing his clothes from his taut body. As fabric was thrown about the room, he revealed our male and a growl of satisfaction rumbled in the air.

Shimmying back on the bed to prop myself on the pillows, I reached up to grab my crown. But Kane's rough voice quickly stopped me. "Leave it on," he ordered. "These too," he added, tapping my heeled shoes as his hand smoothed its way up my leg.

Grabbing me behind the knees, he pulled me into the middle of the bed. His eyes remained locked on mine as his head dipped down and tongue darted out. My nails dug into the silk sheets as he licked from my entrance to my clit.

I shuddered in utter bliss as he wrapped his arms around my hips and pulled me closer as he devoured me. Alaric's mouth descended on my breasts, nipping and licking his way over them. Lifting me with ease, he slid in behind me and his cock throbbed at my back.

Kane growled into my pussy, his hands spreading me wider and I leaned fully into Alaric's chest. Just as I felt the familiar warmth of an orgasm building, Kane pulled away and kissed up my torso. He kissed me with vigor and I moaned as I could taste myself on him.

Alaric shifted behind me, reaching for something, as Kane continued to devour my mouth. "I love yeh both so fuckin' much," Kane murmured against my ear as his fingers dipped inside my pussy, before sliding between my cheeks and pushing into my other hole.

I groaned at the intrusion, realizing what Alaric had been reaching for. Arching my hips, I rested my head on Alaric's shoulder as he guided his slick cock into my ass. As I sank down, taking him inch by inch, his hand reached around to Kane's cock, which was demanding attention too.

He guided him to my soaked pussy, teasing my clit with his head before pressing into my entrance. I moaned at the bliss of him pushing into me. "So fucking much," Kane groaned, thrusting his thick shaft deeper inside.

They moved and I rolled my hips, my breaths coming in pants as the pleasure built. Their mouths met over my shoulder in a frantic kiss as they pressed their cocks deeper still and I clenched my thighs.

Then joined their kiss. Hot, messy, and unapologetically us.

"Ready to be worshiped, our queen?" Kane groaned, his hips flexing into me as he pressed me back firmer on to Alaric.

"By you two?" I purred. "Always."

I would forever adore these males.

Forever and always.

Need more from these authors?

MJ Colgan's debut solo work, Daughter of a Demon Prince, is a dark paranormal romance series of interconnected standalones. Join the first of seven perfectly imperfect women as she navigates her sin, her sisters and her shot at love.

Want to find out more about these strong FMC's taking center stage in the Daughter of a Demon Prince series? Join MJ's newsletter and follow her social media to never miss out on a new release, update, ARC or giveaway opportunity:

AC Lawlor is working on a spicy demon omegaverse story but doesn't have any dates to give yet. Be sure not to miss a thing by following her on social media here:

Milton Keynes UK
Ingram Content Group UK Ltd.
UKHW010705220524
443011UK00016B/210/J

9 781399 981101